(2ⁿᵈ edition)

AHISTORY

AN UNAUTHORISED HISTORY OF THE
DOCTOR WHO UNIVERSE

LANCE PARKIN

with additional material by
LARS PEARSON

mad norwegian **press**

Des Moines, IA

Coming Soon from Mad Norwegian Press...

About Time 3: The Unauthorized Guide to Doctor Who (Seasons 7 to 11) [Second Edition]

Fluid Links: The Unauthorized Guide to the Doctor Who Eighth Doctor Adventures
[a successor to Mad Norwegian's *I, Who* guidebook series]

Also Available from Mad Norwegian Press...

THE ABOUT TIME SERIES
by Lawrence Miles and Tat Wood

About Time 1: The Unauthorized Guide to Doctor Who (Seasons 1 to 3)
About Time 2: The Unauthorized Guide to Doctor Who (Seasons 4 to 6)
About Time 4: The Unauthorized Guide to Doctor Who (Seasons 12 to 17)
About Time 5: The Unauthorized Guide to Doctor Who (Seasons 18 to 21)
About Time 6: The Unauthorized Guide to Doctor Who (Seasons 22 to 26,
the TV Movie)

OTHER SCI-FI REFERENCE GUIDES
Doctor Who: The Completely Unofficial Encyclopedia by Chris Howarth and Steve Lyons

Redeemed: The Unauthorized Guide to Angel by Lars Pearson and Christa Dickson

Dusted: The Unauthorized Guide to Buffy the Vampire Slayer
by Lawrence Miles, Lars Pearson and Christa Dickson

FACTION PARADOX NOVELS
Stand-alone novel series based on characters and concepts
created by Lawrence Miles

Faction Paradox: The Book of the War [#0] by Lawrence Miles, et. al.
Faction Paradox: This Town Will Never Let Us Go [#1] by Lawrence Miles
Faction Paradox: Of the City of the Saved... [#2] by Philip Purser-Hallard
Faction Paradox: Warlords of Utopia [#3] by Lance Parkin
Faction Paradox: Warring States [#4] by Mags L. Halliday
Faction Paradox: Erasing Sherlock [#5] by Kelly Hale
Dead Romance [related novel] by Lawrence Miles

Copyright © 2007 Mad Norwegian Press.
www.madnorwegian.com

Cover & interior design by Christa Dickson.
www.christadickson.com

ISBN: 0-9759446-6-5
Printed in the United States of America.
First Edition: November 2007.

**mad
norwegian
press**

mad norwegian press | des moines

TABLE OF CONTENTS

The following *only* catalogs main story entries for each adventure; some stories occur in muliple time zones, and hence have more than one page number listed. For a complete listing of *all* story references, consult the Index.

Some stories proved undatable and lack main entries; for a list of these, consult the None of the Above section (page 414-415).

TABLE OF CONTENTS

TABLE OF CONTENTS

TABLE OF CONTENTS

TABLE OF CONTENTS

Footnote Features

ACKNOWLEDGEMENTS

A great many people have been involved with this book. This is the fourth version. The first - *The Doctor Who Chronology* - was produced by Seventh Door Fanzines. It covered the television series. The second - *A History of the Universe* - was published by Virgin in 1996, and covered the television series plus the New and Missing Adventures up to *Happy Endings* and *The Sands of Time* respectively. It proved very popular. Nearly ten years on, the third version was published by Mad Norwegian Press, and covered roughly twice as many stories as the Virgin edition. This is an update of that, and also incorporates the *DWM* comic strip for the first time.

Thanks first and foremost to my editors - Mark Jones, Rebecca Levene and Simon Winstone, and for this latest version, Lars Pearson.

Thanks to the many other people who have offered information, comments, help, material, corrections or just said nice things. In alphabetical order, these are: Ben Aaronovitch, Nadir Ahmed, Keith Ansell, John Binns, Jon Blum, David Brunt, Graeme Burk, Andy Campbell, Andrew Cartmel, Shaun Chmara, Mark Clapham, Finn Clark (big, big thanks for his comics expertise), Paul Cornell, Alex Dante, Jeremy Daw, Martin Day, Zoltan Dery, Jonathan Evans, Michael Evans, Simon Forward, Martin Foster, Gary Gillatt, Donald and Patricia Gillikin, Craig Hinton, David Howe, Edward Hutchinson, Alison Jacobs, William Keith, Andy Lane, Paul Lee, Steve Maggs, Daniel O'Mahony, Steven Manfred, April McKenna, Iain McLaughlin, Adrian Middleton, Lawrence Miles, Steve Mollmann, Kate Orman, David Owen, David Pitcher, Andrew Pixley, Marc Platt, Jon Preddle, Justin Richards, Gareth Roberts, Trevor Ruppe, Gary Russell, Jim Smith, Robert Smith?, Shannon Sullivan, Richard Thacker, Lynne Thomas, Michael Thomas, Steve Traylen, Stephen James Walker, Peter Ware, Martin Wiggins, Gareth Wigmore, Guy Wigmore and Alex Wilcock. I'm genuinely sorry if I missed anyone.

Thanks most of all to the innumerable people involved with the production of *Doctor Who*, in any and every form ... past, present and future.

A special, and sad, note this time. The *Doctor Who* writer and critic Craig Hinton died late in 2006. Craig was an early enthusiast for this project, and his *Doctor Who Magazine* review of the original fan version helped bring it to the attention of Virgin, who would go on to publish it. He wrote *The Crystal Bucephalus*, his first novel, specifically to fill a large gap in the future history of the Whoniverse that the original version of this book identified for him, and he was keen to see each new edition. As befits the man who coined the term "fanwank" to describe excessive continuity, a healthy proportion of the entries in this book refer to his novels - including the very first and the very last.

One of my first notes for this edition reads "check with Craig that it's not the same Millennium War", and I only wish I could.

This book seeks to place every event referred to in *Doctor Who* into a consistent timeline. Yet this is "*a*" history of the *Doctor Who* universe, not the "definitive" or "official" version.

Doctor Who has had hundreds of creators, all pulling in slightly different directions, all with their own vision of what *Doctor Who* was about. Without that diversity, the *Doctor Who* universe would no doubt be more internally consistent, but it would also be a much smaller and less interesting place. Nowadays, fans are part of the creative process. Ultimately, we control the heritage of the show that we love. I hope people will enjoy this book, and I know that they will challenge it.

A total adherence to continuity has always been rather less important to the successive *Doctor Who* production teams than the main order of business: writing exciting stories, telling good jokes and scaring small children with big monsters. This, as most people will tell you, is just how it should be.

Much of *Doctor Who* was created using a method known as "making it up as they went along". The series gloried in its invention and throwaway lines. When the TV series was first in production, no-one was keeping the sort of detailed notes that would prevent canonical "mistakes", and even the same writer could contradict their earlier work. It's doubtful the writer of *The Mysterious Planet* had a single passing thought about how the story fit in with *The Sun Makers* ... even though they were both authored by Robert Holmes.

Now, with dozens of new books, audios, comic strips, short stories and a new TV series, not to mention spin-offs, it is almost certainly impossible to keep track of every new *Doctor Who* story, let alone put them all in a coherent - never mind consistent - framework. References can contradict other references in the same story, let alone ones in stories written forty years later for a different medium by someone who wasn't even born the year the original writer died.

It is, in any case, impossible to come up with a consistent view of history according to *Doctor Who*. Strictly speaking, the Brigadier retires three years before the first UNIT story is set. The Daleks and Atlantis are both utterly destroyed, once and for all, several times that we know about. Characters "remember" scenes, or sometimes entire stories, that they weren't present to witness, and show remarkable lack of knowledge of real world events or events in *Doctor Who* that happened after the story first came out.

"Continuity" has always been flexible, even on the fundamentals of the show's mythology - *The Dalek Invasion of Earth*, *The War Games*, *Genesis of the Daleks* and *The Deadly Assassin* all shamelessly threw out the show's established history in the name of a good story. Their versions of events (the Daleks are galactic conquerors; the Doctor is a Time Lord who stole his TARDIS and fled his home planet; the Daleks were created by the Kaled scientist, Davros; Gallifreyan society is far from perfect and Time Lords are limited to twelve regenerations) are now taken to be the "truth". The previous versions (the Daleks are confined to one city; the Doctor invented the "ship" and his granddaughter named it before their exile; the Daleks are descendants of the squat humanoid Dals, mutated by radiation; the Time Lords are godlike and immortal) have quietly been forgotten.

However, I don't want to write a book so vague that it becomes useless. I have to make firm decisions about where stories are placed, so I show my working. Each story has a paragraph explaining why I placed it where I did.

In some cases, this is simply a matter of reporting an exact date spoken by one of the characters in the story (*Black Orchid*, for example). In others, no firm date is given. I attempt to look at internal evidence given on screen, then evidence from the production team at the time (from the script, say, or from contemporary publicity material), then I branch out to cross-referencing it with other stories, noting where other people who've come up with *Doctor Who* chronologies have placed it. What I'm attempting to do is accurately list all the evidence given for dating the stories and other references in as an objective way as possible, then weigh it to reach a conclusion.

For a good example of this process at its most complicated, look for *The Seeds of Death* or *The Wheel in Space*. You may not agree with the date I've assigned them, it might make your blood boil, but you'll see how I've reached it.

This book is one attempt, then, to *retroactively* create a consistent framework for the history of the *Doctor Who* universe. It is essentially a game, not a scientific endeavour to discover "the right answer".

All games have to follow a consistent set of rules, and anyone attempting to fit all the pieces of information we are given has to lay some groundwork and prioritise the information. If a line of dialogue from a story broadcast in 1983 flatly contradicts what was said in one from 1968, which is "right"? Some people would suggest that the newer story "got it wrong", that the later production team didn't pay enough attention to what came before. Others might argue that the new information "corrects" what we were told before. In practice, most fans are inconsistent, choosing the facts that best support their arguments or preferences. *The Discontinuity Guide* has some very healthy advice regarding continuity: "Take what you want and ignore what you don't. Future continuity cops will just have to adapt to your version".

BASIC PRINCIPLES

For the purposes of this book I work from the following assumptions:

• Every *Doctor Who* story takes place in the same universe, unless explicitly stated otherwise. The same individual fought the Daleks with Jo on Spiridon, Beep the Meep with Sharon, the Ice Warriors with Benny in London, became Zagreus in the Antiverse, blew up Gallifrey to prevent Faction Paradox taking over the universe and saved Rose from the Autons.

For legal, marketing or artistic reasons, it should be noted that some of the people making *Doctor Who* have occasionally stated that they don't feel this to be the case. However there are innumerable cross references (say, Romana being president of Gallifrey in both the books and the audios) and in-jokes that suggest very strongly that, for example, the eighth Doctor of the books is the same individual as the eighth Doctor of the Big Finish audios - or at the very least they've both got almost-identical histories.

• The universe has one, true "established history". Nothing (short of a being with godlike powers) can significantly change the course of history with any degree of permanency within that universe. The Mars attacked by the Fendahl is the Mars of the Ice Warriors.

• I have noted where each date I have assigned comes from. Usually it is from dialogue (in which case I quote it), but often it comes from behind-the-scenes sources such as scripts, publicity material and the like. It is up to the individual reader whether a date from a BBC Press release or draft script is as "valid" as one given on screen.

• In many cases, no date was ever given for a story. In such instances, I pick a year and explain my reasons. Often I will assign a date that is consistent with information given in other stories. (So, I suggest that the Cyber War mentioned in *Revenge Of The Cybermen* must take place after *The Tomb of the Cybermen*, and probably after *Earthshock* because of what is said in those other stories.) These dates are marked as arbitrary and the reasoning behind them is explained in the footnotes.

• Where a date isn't established on screen I have also included the dates suggested by others who have compiled timelines or listed dates given in the series. Several similar works to this have been attempted, and I have listed the most relevant in the Bibliography at the end of this section.

• I have assumed that historical events take place at the same time and for the same reasons as they did in "real history", unless specifically contradicted by the television series. I assume that the Doctor is telling the truth about meeting historical figures, and that his historical analysis is correct. (It has, however, been established that the Doctor is fallible and / or an incorrigible name-dropper.). When there's a reference to "science", "scientists", "history" or "historians", unless stated otherwise it means scholars and academics from the real world, not the *Doctor Who* universe (they are usually invoked when *Doctor Who's* version of science or events strays a distance from ours).

• Information given is taken literally and at face value, unless it's explicitly said that the person giving it is lying or mistaken. Clearly, if an expert like the Doctor is talking about something he knows a great deal about, we can probably trust the information more than some bystander's vague remark.

• My version of Earth's future history is generally one of steady progress, and as such I tend to lump together stories featuring similar themes and concepts - say, intergalactic travel, isolated colonies, humanoid robots and so on. If the technology, transportation or weaponry seen in story A is more advanced than in story B, then I suggest that story A is set in the future of story B. I also assume that throughout the centuries humans age at the same rate, so their life spans don't alter too dramatically, etc. A "lifetime" in the year 4000 is still about 100 years.

• All dates, again unless specifically stated otherwise, work from our Gregorian calendar, and all are "AD". It is assumed that the system of leap years will remain the same in the future. For convenience, all documents use our system of dating, even those of alien civilisations. The "present" of the narrative is now, so if an event happened "two hundred years ago" it happened in the early nineteenth century. On a number of occasions we are told that a specific date takes place on the wrong day: in *The War Machines*, 16th July, 1966, is a Monday, but it really occurred on a Saturday.

• I assume that a "year" is an Earth year of 365 days, even when an alien is speaking, unless this is specifically contradicted. This also applies to terms such as "Space Year" (*Genesis of the Daleks*), "light year" (which is used as a unit of time in *The Savages* and possibly *Terror of the Autons*) and "cycle" (e.g. *Zamper*).

• If an event is said to take place "fifty years ago" I take it to mean exactly fifty years ago, unless a more precise date is given elsewhere or it refers to a known historical event. If an event occurs in the distant past or the far future, I tend to round up: *Image of the Fendahl* is set in about 1977, the Fifth Planet was destroyed "twelve million years" before. I say this happened in "12,000,000 BC", not "11,998,023 BC". When an event takes place an undefined number of "centuries", "millennia" or "millions of years" before or after a story, I arbitrarily set a date.

• A "generation" is assumed to be twenty-five years, as per the Doctor's definition in *Four to Doomsday*. A "couple" of years is always two years, a "few" is less than "several" which is less than "many", with "some" taken to be an arbitrary or unknown number. A "billion" is generally the American and modern British unit (a thousand million) rather than the old British definition (a million million).

• Characters are in their native time zone unless explicitly stated otherwise. Usually, when a *Doctor Who* monster or villain has a time machine, it's central to the plot. On television, the Cybermen only explicitly have time travel in *Attack of the Cybermen*, for example, and they've stolen the time machine in question. It clearly can't be "taken for granted" that they can go back in history. The Sontarans have a (primitive) time machine in *The Time Warrior*, and are clearly operating on a scale that means they can defy the Time Lords in *Invasion of Time* and *The Two Doctors*, but there's no evidence they routinely travel in time. The only one of the Doctor's (non-Time Lord) foes with a mastery of time travel are the Daleks - they develop time travel in *The Chase*, and definitely use it in *The Daleks' Master Plan*, *The Evil of the Daleks*, *Day of the Daleks*, *Resurrection of the Daleks*, *Remembrance of the Daleks*, *Dalek*, *Army of Ghosts*, *Doomsday*, *Daleks in Manhattan* and *Evolution of the Daleks*. Even so, in the remaining stories, I've resisted assuming that the Daleks are time travellers.

• Sometimes, stories occur with the sort of impact that means it seems odd that they weren't mentioned in an earlier story. For instance, no-one from *The Power of the Daleks* and *The Moonbase* (both shown in 1966) recalls the Daleks and Cybermen fighting in *Doomsday* (shown in 2006). For that matter, when the Doctor and his companions refer to their past adventures on TV, they rarely mention the events of the Missing Adventures, Past Doctor novels, comic strips or Big Finish audios. (There are exceptions, however, usually when a writer picks up a throwaway line in a TV episode.) In *Doctor Who* itself, this may point to some deep truth about the nature of time - that events don't become part of the "Web of Time" until we see the Doctor as part of them ... or it may be simply that it was impossible for the people making *Doctor Who* in the sixties to know about stories authored by their successors - many of whom hadn't even been born then.

• And, in a related note, few people making *The Tenth Planet* (in 1966, depicting the distant space year 1986) would have imagined anyone in the early twenty-first century worrying how to reconcile the quasi-futuristic world they imagined with the historical reality. Whenever the UNIT stories are set, it was "the twentieth century", and that's history now. Some of the early New Adventures took place in a "near future" setting, which is now the present day for the tenth Doctor, Rose and Martha. I've therefore accepted the dates given, rather than said that - for example - as we still haven't put a man on Mars, *The Ambassadors of Death* is still set in our future. There's clearly a sensible reason why the "present day" stories made now look like our present day, not *The Tenth Planet: The Next Generation*. The in-story explanation / fudge would seem to be that most *Doctor Who* stories take place in isolated locations, and that there are agencies like UNIT, C-19 and Torchwood tasked with keeping alien incursions covered up.

• There are still errors of omission, as when a later story fails to acknowledge an earlier one (often in other media) that seems relevant. No-one in *The Christmas Invasion*, for example, notes that it's odd Britain is making a big deal about sending an unmanned probe to Mars, when there were manned UK missions there in the seventies (in *The Ambassadors of Death*) and the nineties (*The Dying Days*). As with Sarah in *School Reunion* remembering *The Hand of Fear* but not *The Five Doctors*, there's got to be an appeal to clarity in storytelling. With so many *Doctor Who* stories in existence, it's almost impossible to tell a new one that doesn't explictly contradict an earlier story, let alone implicitly. The reason no-one, say, remarks that the second Doctor looks like Salamander except in *The Enemy of the World* is the same reason that no-one ever says Rose looks like the girl who married Chris Evans - it gets in the way of the story, and doesn't help it along.

THE STORIES

This book restricts itself to events described in the BBC television series *Doctor Who*, the original full-length fiction and the audio plays. This is not an attempt to enter the debate about which *Doctor Who* stories are "canon", it is simply an attempt to limit the length and scale of this book. There are two types of information in this book, and these are distinguished by different typefaces.

1) The Television Series. Included are the episodes and on-screen credits of the BBC television series *Doctor Who* as first broadcast, the spin-off *K9 and Company* episode, *Torchwood* and *The Sarah Jane Adventures*; and extended or unbroadcast versions that have since been commercially released or broadcast anywhere in the world - there are few cases of "extended" material

contradicting the original story.

Priority is given to sources closest to the finished product or the production team of the time the story was made. In descending order of authority are the following: the programme as broadcast; the *Radio Times* and other contemporary BBC publicity material (which was often written by the producer or script editor); the camera script; the novelisation of a story by the original author or an author working closely from the camera script; contemporary interviews with members of the production team; televised trailers; rehearsal and draft scripts; novelisations by people other than the original author; storylines and writers' guides (which often contradict on-screen information); interviews with members of the production team after the story was broadcast; and finally any other material, such as fan speculation.

Scenes cut from broadcast were considered if they were incorporated back into a story at a later time (as with those in *The Curse of Fenric* VHS and DVD). I have not included information from unreleased material that exists (for example, the extended footage from *Invasion of the Dinosaurs* or *Kinda*), is in release but was kept separate from the story (for instance, the extra scenes on the *Vengeance on Varos* and *Ghost Light* DVDs) or that no longer exists (such as with *Terror of the Autons*, *Terror of the Zygons* and *The Hand of Fear*). Neither does the first version of *An Unearthly Child* to be filmed (the so-called "pilot episode") count, nor "In character" appearances by the Doctor on other programmes (e.g.: on *Animal Magic*, *Children in Need*, *Blue Peter* etc.).

2. The books, audios and webcasts. This present volume encompasses the New and Missing Adventures published by Virgin, the BBC's Eighth Doctor Adventures, the BBC's Past Doctor Adventures, the BBC's New Series Adventures (up through *Wooden Heart*), the first three *Torchwood* novels, all of the Telos novellas and a number of one-off novels: *Harry Sullivan's War*, *Turlough and the Earthlink Dilemma* and *Who Killed Kennedy*.

The audios covered include *The Pescatons*, *Slipback*, *The Paradise of Death* and *The Ghosts of N-Space*, as well as the Big Finish *Doctor Who* range (that is, specifically, the ones with the Doctor in) up to *Frozen Time* (BF #98).

The BBC webcasts *Real Time, Shada, Death Comes to Time,* and *Scream of the Shalka* (the last two somewhat controversially) are included.

A handful of stories were available in another form - *Shakedown* and *Downtime* were originally direct-to-video spin-offs, some Big Finish stories like *Minuet in Hell* and *The Mutant Phase* are (often radically different) adaptations of stories made by Audio Visuals. This book deals with the "official" versions, as opposed to the fan-produced ones.

This volume covers two stories that appear in two different versions, because they were told in two media that fall within the scope of the book and were adapted for different Doctors: *Shada* and *Human Nature*. I've dealt with them on a case by case basis. *Doctor Who* fans have long had different versions of the same story in different media - the first Dalek story, for example, was televised, extensively altered for the novelisation, changed again for the movie version and adapted into a comic strip.

I haven't included in-character appearances in non-fiction books (e.g: the *Doctor Who Discovers…* and *Doctor Who Quiz Book Of* series). I was tempted.

3. The comic strip that has been running in *Doctor Who Weekly / Monthly / Magazine* since 1979 (up through "Warkeeper's Crown", DWM #378-380), along with all original backup strips from that publication, and the ones from the various Specials and Yearbooks. Note that this doesn't include the comic strips in, or that first appeared in, any other publication.

With a book like this, drawing a line between what should and shouldn't be included is never as simple as it might appear. Including every comic strip would include ones from the Annuals, for example. This book doesn't include the text stories that *Doctor Who Magazine* has included at various points during its run.

In the end, there's a relatively straightforward distinction between the *DWM* comic strip and other comic strips: while it's the work of many writers, artists and editors, it also has a strong internal continuity and sense of identity. This book, in all previous editions, has confined itself to "long form" *Doctor Who* and there's a case to be made that the *DWM* strip represents one "ongoing story" that's run for over a quarter of a century. The *Doctor Who Magazine* strip has now run for longer than the original TV series, and most fans must have encountered it at some point.

That said, this book also excludes *DWM* strips that are clearly parodies that aren't meant to be considered within the continuity of the strip. This is for the same reason charity spoofs like *Dimensions in Time* aren't included. For the record, the affected strips are "Follow that TARDIS!", "The Last Word" and "TV Action".

DWM has reprinted a number of strips from other publications over the years. I have tended to include these. The main beneficiary of this is *The Daleks* strip from the sixties comic *TV Century 21* (and *DWM*'s sequel to it from issues #249-254).

It's certainly arguable that the *DWM* strip exists in a separate continuity, with its own companions, internal continuity, vision of Gallifrey and even an ethos that made it feel quite unlike the TV eras of its Doctors. This certainly seemed to be the case early on. However, this distinction has broken down over the years - the comic strip companion Frobisher has appeared in a book (*Mission: Impractical*) and an audio (*The Holy Terror*), and for a number of years the strip and the New Adventures novels were quite elaborately linked. In the new TV series, we've met someone serving kronkburgers (in *The Long Game*, first mentioned in *Iron Legion*) and the Doctor even quoted Abslom Daak in *Bad Wolf*.

The strip tends to "track" the ongoing story (the television series in the seventies and eighties, the New Adventures in the early nineties) - so the Doctor regenerates, without explanation within the strip and on occasion during a story arc. Companions from the television series and books come and go. Costume changes and similar details (like the design of the console room) do the same. It's broadly possible to work out when the strip is set in the Doctor's own life. So, the first *Doctor Who Weekly* strips with the fourth Doctor mention he's dropped off Romana, and he changes from his Season 17 to Season 18 costume - so it slots in neatly between the two seasons. There are places where this process throws up some anomalies, which I've noted.

On the whole, the television series takes priority over what is said in the other media, and where a detail or reference in one of the books appears to contradict what was established on television, I have noted as much and attempted to rationalise the "mistake" away.

The NA/MAs built up a broadly consistent "future history" of the universe. This was, in part, based on the "History of Mankind" in Jean-Marc Lofficier's *The Terrestrial Index*, which mixes information from the series with facts from the novelisations and the author's own speculation. Many authors, though, have contradicted or ignored Lofficier's version of events. For the purposes of this book, *The Terrestrial Index* itself is non-canonical, and I've noted, but ultimately ignored, whenever a New Adventure recounts information solely using Lofficier as reference.

Useful information appears in writers' guides, discussion documents and the authors' original submissions and storylines. Where possible, I have referred to this material.

Despite this volume's efforts to be inclusive whenever possible, there are also some significant omissions:

The book *doesn't* cover short stories, whether they first appeared in annuals, *Doctor Who Magazine*, the *Decalog* and *Short Trips* anthologies or any of the innumerable other places they have cropped up. It also doesn't include proposed stories that were never made. These primarily include the trio of sixth Doctor stories abandoned after the Season Twenty-Two hiatus - namely, *The Nightmare Fair*, *Mission to Magnus* and *The Ultimate Evil*, all of which were later novelised. The unmade *The Masters of Luxor*, published as a scriptbook, was excluded for the same reasons - as was *Campaign*, a Past Doctor novel that was commissioned but never released by the BBC (it was later privately published).

Since the last edition of this book there has been a proliferation of spin-off series that have featured characters from *Doctor Who*. These include:

• Bernice Summerfield (books, short stories and audios from Virgin, then Big Finish. Featuring the Doctor's companion who was first seen in *Love and War*).

• Big Finish spin-off series (*Dalek Empire*, *UNIT*, *Gallifrey*, *Sarah Jane Smith*, the *Unbound* stories etc).

• Faction Paradox (books, audios and a comic, featuring characters and concepts seen in the EDA *Alien Bodies* etc.).

• Iris Wildthyme (books, audios and short stories. A character seen in the original fiction of Paul Magrs, and who first appeared in *Doctor Who* in the *Short Trips* story "Old Flames" and the EDA *The Scarlet Empress*).

• Kaldor City (audios, spun off from *The Robots of Death* and the PDA *Corpse Marker*).

• Miranda (comic, from the character seen in the EDA *Father Time*).

• Time Hunter (novellas, featuring characters from the Telos novella *The Cabinet of Light*).

I have included information from these when it sheds light on an otherwise unclear aspect of *Doctor Who* continuity. The Benny audio *The Plague Herds of Excelis*, for instance, is helpful in dating the "Excelis Trilogy" in the *Doctor Who* audios.

KEY
The following abbreviations are used in the text:

BF - The Big Finish audio adventures.
DWM - *Doctor Who Magazine* (also known for a time as *Doctor Who Monthly*)
DWW - *Doctor Who Weekly* (as the magazine was initially called until issue #44)
EDA - Eighth Doctor Adventures (the ongoing novels published by the BBC)
MA - Missing Adventures (the past Doctor novels published by Virgin)
NA - New Adventures (the ongoing novels published by Virgin, chiefly featuring the seventh Doctor)
NSA - New Series Adventures (featuring the Christopher Eccleston Doctor, and then the David Tennant one)
PDA - Past Doctor Adventure (the past Doctor novels published by the BBC)
SJA - *The Sarah Jane Adventures*
TEL - Telos novellas

TV - The TV series
TW - *Torchwood*

In the text of the book, the following marker appears to indicate when the action of specific stories take place:

c 2005 - THE REPETITION OF THE CLICHE ->

The title is exactly as it appeared on screen or on the cover. For the Hartnell stories without an overall title given on screen, I have generally used the titles that appear on the BBC's product.

The letter before the date, the "code", indicates how accurately we know the date. If there is no code, then that date is precisely established in the story itself (e.g. *The Daleks' Master Plan* is set in the year 4000 exactly).

"**c**" means that the story is set circa that year (e.g. *The Dalek Invasion of Earth* is set "c 2167")

"**?**" indicates a guess, and my reasons are given in the footnotes (e.g. we don't know what year *Destiny of the Daleks* is set in, but it must be "centuries" after *The Daleks' Master Plan,* so I set it in "? 4600").

"**&**" means that the story is dated relative another story that we lack a date for (e.g.: we know that *Resurrection of the Daleks* is set "ninety years" after *Destiny of the Daleks*, so I set *Resurrection of the Daleks* in "& 4690"). If one story moves, the linked one also has to.

"**u**" means that the story featured UNIT. There is, to put it mildly, some discussion about exactly when the UNIT stories are set. For the purposes of this guidebook, see the introduction to the UNIT Section.

"**=**" indicates action that takes place in a parallel universe or a divergent timestream. Often, the Doctor succeeds in restoring the correct timeline - those cases are indicated by brackets - "(=)". As this information technically isn't part of history, it's set apart by boxes with dashed lines.

"**@**" is a story set during the eighth Doctor's period on Earth between the books *The Ancestor Cell* and *Escape Velocity*. During this period he was without a working TARDIS or his memories.

"**w**" refers to an event that took place during the future War timeline in the eighth Doctor books. Events in *The Ancestor Cell* annulled this timeline, but remnants of it "still happened" in the real *Doctor Who* timeline, just as *Day of the Daleks* "still happened" even though the future it depicted was averted.

I've attempted to weed out references that just aren't very telling, relevant or interesting. Clearly, there's a balance to be had, as half the fun of a book like this is in listing trivia and strange juxtapositions, but a timeline could easily go to absurd extremes. If a novel set in 1980 said that a minor character was sixty-five, lived in a turn-of-the-century terraced house and bought the Beatles album *Rubber Soul* when it first came out, then it could generate entries for c 1900, 1915 and 1965. I would only list these if they were relevant to the story or made for particularly interesting reading.

I haven't listed birthdates of characters, except the Doctor's companions or other major recurring figures, again unless it represents an important story point.

Before our universe, others existed with different physical laws. The universe immediately prior to our own had its own Time Lords, and as their universe reached the point of collapse, they shunted themselves into a parallel universe and discovered that they now possessed almost infinite power.[1]

Rassilon speculated that the beings Raag, Nah and Rok had created and destroyed many universes.[2] **The Disciples of the Light rose up against the Beast and chained him in the Pit, before the creation of the universe. It was theorised that the Beast would go on to inspire archetypes of evil on many planets, including Earth, Draconia, Skaro (where it was rendered as the Kaled god of war), Damos, Veltino and Vel Consadine.[3] Abaddon, a creature that apparently hailed from the same race as the Beast, was imprisoned beneath the Cardiff Rift.[4]**

The third Doctor once almost accidentally sent the TARDIS into the void before the universe started.[5]

The Dawn of Time

The universe was created in a huge explosion known as the Big Bang. As this was the very first thing to happen, scientists sometimes refer to it as "Event One".

"Among the adherents of Scientific Mythology [q.v.] the element (Hydrogen) is widely believed to be the basic constituent out of which the Galaxy was first formed [see EVENT ONE] and evidence in support of this hypothesis includes its supposed appearance in spectroscopic analysis of massive star bodies."[6]

The Time Lords of Gallifrey monitored the Big Bang, and precisely determined the date of Event One.[7] **The Doctor claimed to have been an eye-witness at the origins of the universe.[8]**

"The dawn of time. The beginning of all beginnings. Two forces only: Good and Evil. Then chaos. Time is born: matter, space. The universe cries out like a newborn. The forces *shatter* as the Universe explodes outwards. Only echoes remain, and yet somehow, *somehow* the evil force survives. An intelligence. Pure *evil*."

The evil force retained its sentience and spread its influence throughout time and space. It became the entity that the Vikings would call Fenric.[9]

One ship managed to travel to the dawn of creation, albeit by accident. Terminus was a vast spaceship built by an infinitely advanced, ancient race capable of time travel. The ship developed a fault, and the pilot was forced to eject some of its unstable fuel into the void before making a time jump. The explosion that resulted was the Big Bang. Terminus was thrown billions of years into the future, where it came to settle in the exact centre of the universe.[10] The universe was created when the time-travelling starship *Vipod Mor* arrived at this point and exploded.[11]

The Urbankan Monarch believed that if his ship could travel faster than light, it would move backwards in time to the Big Bang and beyond. Monarch believed that he was God and that he would meet himself at the Creation of the Universe.[12]

TIMELESS[13] -> The eighth Doctor piloted the TARDIS back to before the Big Bang, hoping to avoid a myriad of parallel realities by entering the correct history from the

---

1 *All-Consuming Fire, Millennial Rites, The Taking of Planet 5.*
2 *Divided Loyalties.* These are the Gods of Ragnarok seen in *The Greatest Show in the Galaxy.*
3 *The Satan Pit*
4 *TW: End of Days.* The Doctor, Rose and Jack's discussion about the Rift in *Boom Town* seems to indicate that it pre-dates events surrounding it in *The Unquiet Dead.* References to the "darkness" might mean that Abaddon is trapped in the Void seen in *Army of Ghosts* and *Doomsday,* with the Rift merely providing access. Alternatively, Abaddon's presence might be what weakens space-time in the Cardiff area, facilitating the creation of the Rift in the first place.

In *End of Days,* Bilis almost seems to imply that Abaddon is the "son" of the Beast - the point is unclear,

however, especially as "Abaddon" is also given as an alias of the Beast itself in *The Impossible Planet.*
5 *Island of Death*
6 This appears on the console screen in *Castrovalva.*
7 *Transit.*
THE AGE OF THE UNIVERSE: The date of the creation of the universe is not clearly established on screen, although we are told it took place "billions of years" before *Terminus.* Modern scientific consensus is that the universe is about fifteen billion years old, and books that address the issue, like *Timewyrm: Apocalypse* and *Falls the Shadow,* concur with this date. In *Transit,* the seventh Doctor drunkenly celebrates the universe's 13,500,020,012th birthday (meaning the Big Bang took place in 13,500,017,903 BC). *The Infinity Doctors* establishes that the Time Lords refer to the end of the uni-

very start. Chloe, a small girl from a devastated planet, arrived onhand with Jamais, her time travelling dog. Jamais aided the overstrained TARDIS in reaching London, 2003. The Doctor's party again visited this era when Sabbath and Kalicum, an agent of the Council of Eight, attempted to seed an intelligence gestated within a heap of diamonds into the start of history. The Doctor failed, and the intelligence became part of the fabric of the universe.

The diamonds allowed the Council of Eight to map out events throughout the whole of history.[14]

Insect-like "forces of chaos" fed on the debris of the big bang, just as they would feed on the collapse of the universe.[15] Eleven physical dimensions existed at first, quickly collapsing down to the five dimensions familiar to us. The other dimensions came to exist only at the subatomic level.[16] Beings named the Quoth evolved inside atoms and were the size of quarks.[17] The Sidhe came to exist in all eleven dimensions.[18] The remaining six dimensions became the Six-Fold Realm, and each of the six Guardians represented one such dimension.[19]

As the universe was formed, an eight-dimensional "radiating blackness" infused space and time. Eventually, the Unity of the Scourge evolved in this darkness.[20] **The Weeping Angels, also sometimes called "the Lonely Assassins" were as old as the universe or very nearly. They were quite nice where they hailed from, but developed into quantum-locked hunters who turned to stone if seen.**[21]

The first few chaotic microseconds of the universe saw extreme temperatures and the forging of bizarre elements that would be unable to exist later. This was the Leptonic Era, and one of the bizarre elements created was Helium 2. The Rani would later attempt to recreate this on Lakertya.[22]

Time and Space as we understand them began as these bizarre elements reacted with each other and cooled.

The Shadow, an agent of the Black Guardian, claimed to have been waiting since eternity began in the hopes of obtaining the Key to Time.[23] The Master attempted to kill the newly-regenerated fifth Doctor by sending him backwards in time to a Hydrogen Inrush early in the universe's history.[24] Matter coalesced, elements formed.[25]

"The Dark Time, the Time of Chaos"

The Time Lords from the pre-universe entered our universe, and discovered that they had undreamt-of powers. They became known as the Great Old Ones: Hastur the Unspeakable became Fenric; Yog-Sothoth, also known as the Intelligence, began billennia of conquests; The Lloigor, or Animus, dominated Vortis; Shub-Niggurath conquered Polymos and colonised it with her offspring, the Nestene Consciousness; Dagon was worshipped by the Sea Devils. Other Great Old Ones included Cthulhu, Nyarlathotep, the Gods of Ragnarok; Gog, Magog, Malefescent, and Tor-Gasukk. Across the universe, the earliest civilisations wor-

---

verse as Event Two.
8 The Doctor reads the book *The Origins of the Universe* in *Destiny of the Daleks*, and remarks that the author "got it wrong on the first line. Why didn't he ask someone who saw it happen?".
9 *The Curse of Fenric*
10 *Terminus*
11 *Slipback*. This is a clear continuity clash with *Terminus*, and a discrepancy made all the more obvious as *Slipback* was broadcast within two years of *Terminus* and was written by its script editor, Eric Saward. If we wanted to reconcile the two accounts, we could speculate that the *Vipod Mor* explosion was the spark that ignited the fuel jettisoned in *Terminus*.
12 *Four to Doomsday*. Monarch never achieves this goal.
13 Dating *Timeless* (EDA #65) - This occurs at the universe's start.
14 *Sometime Never*
15 "Hunger from the Ends of Time"
16 In *An Unearthly Child*, Susan defines the fifth dimension as "space".
17 *The Death of Art*
18 *Autumn Mist*

19 *The Quantum Archangel*
20 *The Shadow of the Scourge*
21 *Blink*
22 *Time and the Rani*
23 *The Armageddon Factor*. It's possible this is just hyperbole on the Shadow's part.
24 *Castrovalva*.
  EVENT ONE: The term "Event One" is first used in *Castrovalva* to mean the creation of "the Galaxy", but in *Terminus* the Doctor talks of "the biggest explosion in history: Event One", which he confirms is "the Big Bang" which "created the universe". There are a number of stories where the writers definitely confuse the term "galaxy" and "universe", and a number of others where they seem to. Rather than rule which is which, this book will list what was said in the stories, noting the more egregious examples, rather than ignoring them or trying to rationalise them away.
25 *The Curse of Fenric*

shipped the Great Old Ones.[26] Not even the Time Lords knew much about them.[27]

Six almost-omnipotent beings, **the Guardians, existed from the beginning of time. They were the White Guardian of Order and the Black Guardian of Chaos**, the Red Guardian of Justice, the Crystal Guardian of Thought and Dreams; the twins, the Azure Guardians of Mortality and Imagination; and the Gold Guardian of Life. They formed the upper pantheon of the Great Old Ones.[28]

The Guardians created The Key to Time to maintain the balance between Order and Chaos. It was composed of six segments that were scattered throughout time and space to prevent it falling into the wrong hands.[29] Each segment of the Key to Time represented a particular Guardian.[30]

Shug-Niggurath was pregnant, and died giving birth to the Nestene Consciousness on the planet Polymos, causing the whole planet to absorb the Consciousness. The Nestene Consciousness went on to colonise many planets, including Cramodar, Plovak 6 and the Reverent Pentiarchs of Loorn.[31]

The Chronovores existed outside the space-time continuum, consuming flaws in its structure. They weren't constrained by the laws of physics.[32]

The first of our universe's native entities - such as the Mandragora Helix, the Eternals and the grey man's race - **sprang into being.**[33] The Mandragora Helix was old even when this universe was born.[34] The Time Lords would come to worship some of the more powerful Eternals, such as Death, Pain, Vain Beauty, Life and Time. Certain Time Lords entered a mysterious arrangement to serve as the "champion" of one or more of these Eternals.[35]

Over the first few billion years, the first stars were born. Planets and galaxies formed.[36]

? "The Life Bringer"[37] -> The fourth Doctor freed Prometheus, a member of a hyper-advanced race resembling the Greek Gods. From their vast city, they were co-ordinating the re-engineering of the lifeless galaxy, moving black holes and stars. Prometheus had been imprisoned for releasing the "life spores" before Zeus was satisfied that they would grow into "perfect peaceful loving creatures". The Doctor helped Prometheus escape with a sample of imperfect life spores, and Prometheus headed for another planet to spread them once more.

On many worlds, sugars, proteins and amino acids combined to become primordial soup, "the most precious substance in the Universe, from which all life springs".[38] Hundreds of millions of years later, the first civilisations began to rise and fall.

Jelloids from the binary quasars of Bendalos were the longest-lived race in the universe, and many think they were the first living creatures.[39]

Thirty thousand million light years from our Solar System, the first civilisation came into being. The beings were humanoid, and developed for ten thousand years before wiping themselves out in a bacteriological war. The grey man and his race saw all this, and he constructed the Cathedral, a machine "designed to alter the structure of reality". The grey man's race had been extremely dualistic, but Cathedral formed ambiguities and chaotic forces that ran throughout the universe, breaking down certainty. Its interface with physical reality was the Metahedron, a device that moved from world to world every eighty thousand years, remaining hidden.[40]

What remains of the ancient races suggests awesome power - many had great psychic ability and matter-transmutation powers that were almost indistinguish-

---

26 *All-Consuming Fire, Millennial Rites, Business Unusual, The Quantum Archangel, Divided Loyalties.*
27 *White Darkness*

THE GREAT OLD ONES: Novels such as *All-Consuming Fire, Millennial Rites Business Unusual, Divided Loyalties* and *The Quantum Archangel* state that many of the godlike beings seen in *Doctor Who* have a common origin. These Great Old Ones are also referred to in *The Infinite Quest*.

The Great Old Ones were a pantheon of ancient, incomprehensible forces created by horror writer H P Lovecraft, and adopted by the novels for this purpose. Perhaps the most well-known of Lovecraft's creations, Cthulhu, had already made an appearance in *White Darkness*. *The Taking of Planet 5* uses Lovecraft's characters, but has them as fictional characters brought to life by Time Lord technology.

Other *Doctor Who* entities explicitly referred to in the books as Great Old Ones include - but aren't limited to - Fenric (*The Curse of Fenric*), the Intelligence (*The

Abominable Snowmen, The Web of Fear, Millennial Rites and *Downtime*), the Animus (*The Web Planet, Twilight of the Gods*), the Nestene Consciousness (*Spearhead from Space, Terror of the Autons, Business Unusual, Synthespians™* and *Rose*) and the Gods of Ragnarok (*The Greatest Show in the Galaxy, Divided Loyalties*). Gog and Magog - or at least beings with the same name - appeared in "The Iron Legion" comic strip.

The Doctor claims at the end of *Ghost Light* that Light is "an evil older than time itself". From the context, this appears to mean that Light arrived on Earth before human history started, not that he existed before the universe's creation, but he might also be a Great Old One. The Great Old Ones in the audio story *The Roof of the World* don't seem to be connected to this grouping.
28 The White and Black Guardians are first referred to in *The Ribos Operation. Divided Loyalties* says there are six Guardians, adding Justice, Crystal and unnamed twins to the two from the television series. *Divided Loyalties* also states that the Guardian of Dreams is the

able from magic. All considered it their right to intervene in the development of whole planets - and to destroy such worlds if they failed to match up to their expectations. Immortal beings such as Light and the Daemons of Damos were worshipped as gods by more primitive races. The legends and race memories of many planets still contain traces of these ancient civilisations. Horns have been a symbol of power on Earth since man began, and beings of light have been worshipped.

? "Voyage to the Edge of the Universe"[41] ->
Commander Azal launched a mission from Damos that reached the edge of the universe. There he merged with a version of himself from another universe, gaining infinite power... but couldn't decide which universe was his to return to. Nearby, beings faced the same dilemma... one had waited for ten thousand years, another for twenty five thousand years, another seventy three years.

Nothing lasts forever, though, and these great races gradually disappeared from the universe.[42]

New societies sprang up to replace them, and soon the universe was teeming with life. In the late twentieth century, the Institute of Space Studies at Baltimore estimated that there were over five hundred planets capable of supporting life in Earth's section of the galaxy alone.[43]

The Dark Times and the First of the Time Lords

"There was a time when the universe was so much smaller than it is now. Darker, older time of chaos. Creatures like the Racnoss, the Nestenes and the Great Vampires rampaged through the void."

The *Infinite*, a spaceship that could grant your heart's desire, came from this time. It was later lost to legend, and used to be inhabited by one of the Great Old Ones.[44]

The first humanoid civilisation in the universe evolved on the planet Gallifrey, and mastered the principles of transmat technology while the universe was half its present size. They became the first race to master Time. Some legends said the Time Lords existed far in the past; there was some evidence that they lived in the present, and some say they come from the future.[45]

See the section on Gallifreyan History for more detail.

Celestial Toymaker. *The Quantum Archangel* assigns them their colours and adds the Gold Guardian (counting the twin Azure Guardians as one entity). *Divided Loyalties* says they are members of the Great Old Ones.
29 *The Ribos Operation*
30 *Divided Loyalties*
31 *Synthespians*™
32 Chronovores first appear in *The Time Monster; The Quantum Archangel* and *No Future* clarifies their role.
33 *The Masque of the Mandragora, Enlightenment, Falls the Shadow.*
34 "The Mark of Mandragora"
35 The Time Lords' gods were mentioned or seen in a number of New Adventures such as *No Future, Set Piece* and *Human Nature.* The seventh Doctor was often referred to as "Time's Champion". Mortimus (the Meddling Monk) is "Death's Champion" in *No Future*, and the Master is hinted as the same in the audio *Master. Vampire Science* has the eighth Doctor as "Life's Champion", and in *The Dying Days* he declares himself to be "the Champion of Life and Time".
36 The prologue to *Timewyrm: Apocalypse* is a brief history of the formation of the universe, and it follows the modern scientific consensus.
37 Dating "The Life Bringer" (*DWM* #49-50) - The Doctor puts it best: "As I still don't know whereabout in time we are, I suppose I'll never be able to puzzle it out ... if that was Earth I found him on ... or if that's Earth he's

heading toward." The story is set either in the distant past before life as we know it began, or the distant future after it died out. A character called Prometheus appeared in *The Quantum Archangel* - he was a Chronovore, a race first seen in *The Time Monster*, so it would seem to be a different individual.
38 Primordial soup appears in *City of Death* and *Ghost Light*; the quotation comes from the latter story.
39 *The One Doctor*
40 *Falls the Shadow*
41 Dating "Voyage to the Edge of the Universe" (*DWM* #49) - The story occurs before the Daemons become extinct, seemingly at the height of their empire. The rocket is nuclear-powered, which doesn't sound terribly advanced, although it does get them to the end of the universe. This can't be the same Commander Azal as in *The Daemons*, for obvious reasons.
42 *The Daemons.* Light appears in *Ghost Light.*
43 *Spearhead from Space*
44 *The Infinite Quest*
45 "WHEN THE UNIVERSE WAS HALF ITS PRESENT SIZE": The phrase, uttered by a Time Lord in *Genesis of the Daleks*, has no clear scientific meaning and should probably be considered a figure of speech, the Time Lord equivalent of "as old as the hills". Then again, the universe at various points is referred to as having edges, a centre and corners, which suggests a discernable "size".

As the Gallifreyans were the first sentient race to evolve, they established a morphic field for humanoids, making it more probable that races evolving later would also be bipedal and binocular. Non-humanoid races only evolved in environments that would be hostile to humanoids.[46] Rassilon ensured that only humanoid lifeforms survived on many planets, primarily to prevent the Divergents from existing. He used biogenic molecules to restructure the dominant species of sixty-nine thousand worlds.[47]

Evolution on Gallifrey, as on many other worlds, had been accelerated by the mysterious Constructors of Destiny.[48]

A civilisation devoted entirely to war developed the Raston Warrior Robot, then vanished without trace.[49]

The Time Lords explored space and time, making contact with many worlds and becoming legends on many others. Rassilon's experiments created holes in the fabric of space and time, which unleashed monsters from another universe, including the Yssgaroth.[50]

The Time Lords unwittingly loosed the vampires on the universe. Until the Time Lords hunted them, vampires fed off mindless animals to service their needs. They later resorted to feeding off other beings.[51] **Seventeen known worlds, including Earth, have stories of vampires.[52]**

The vampires enslaved whole worlds until the Time Lords defeated them.[53] **The vampires were immune to energy weapons, but Rassilon constructed fleets of bowships that fired mighty bolts of steel and staked the beings through the heart. The Vampire Army was defeated, and only its leader, the Great Vampire, survived by escaping through a CVE into the pocket universe of E-Space.[54]**

The origins of the Time Lords are obscure, but in the distant past they fought the Eternal War against the Great Old Ones and other invaders from outside our universe, beating them back and imposing Order. Science and Order supplanted Magic and Chaos as the Time Lords mapped, and so defined, the universe.[55]

The Carrionites lived at the "dawn of the universe", and discovered a means of manipulating reality - using words as science - that resembled magic. The Eternals found the right word to banish the Carrionites "into deep darkness", and nobody thereafter knew if they were real or imagined.[56]

46 *Lucifer Rising*

47 *Zagreus*

48 *The Quantum Archangel*

49 The robot is seen in *The Five Doctors*, and according to *The Eight Doctors* it comes from a time when "the Time Lords were young". *Alien Bodies* mentions a Raston Dancing Robot, and Qixotl claims that the ancient legend is just the manufacturer's marketing ploy.

50 *The Pit*

51 According to a highly suspect account from the vampire Tepesh, part of a historical simulation in *Zagreus*.

52 *State of Decay*. Vampires appear in that story, *Blood Harvest*, *Goth Opera*, *The Eight Doctors*, *Vampire Science*, *Death Comes to Time*, *Project: Twilight* and *Project: Lazarus*. Some also appear as a part of the holographic record in *Zagreus*.

53 *Project: Twilight*

54 *State of Decay*

55 *Cat's Cradle: Time's Crucible*

56 *The Shakespeare Code*. Eternals were seen in *Enlightenment*.

57 "The Tides of Time"

58 *So Vile a Sin*

THE ETERNAL WAR: On screen, we learn that the Time Lords fought campaigns against the Great Vampires (*State of Decay*), that they destroyed the Fendahl (*Image of Fendahl*), that they protected other races from invaders (*The Hand of Fear*), that they maintained a prison planet that contained alien species (*Shada*) and that they destroyed huon particles and the Racnoss (*The Runaway Bride*). In the New Adventures, particularly *Cat's Cradle: Time's Crucible*, *The Pit* and

Christmas on a Rational Planet, this was the Eternal War in which the forces of rationality and science defeated the forces of superstition and magic.

59 *The Pit*

60 *Sky Pirates!, The Infinity Doctors*.

THE THREE TIME WARS: This is not the Last Great Time War between the Time Lords and the Daleks that's the backdrop to the 2005 television series. In the *Doctor Who Annual 2006*, Russell T Davies states, "There had been two Time Wars before this - the skirmish between the Halldons and the Eternals, and then the brutal slaughter of the Omnicraven Uprising, and on both occasions, the Doctor's people had stepped in to settle the matter." Although they don't mention those specific incidents, the books concur that there were indeed two previous Time Wars - one in the ancient past (which, to avoid confusion, we might term the Ancient Time War, although it's not a term used in the stories themselves) and the War against the Enemy in the eighth Doctor's future (which has become known in the *Faction Paradox* range as the War in Heaven).

61 *Sky Pirates!*

62 *Heart of TARDIS*

62 *Sky Pirates!, The Infinity Doctors, Heart of TARDIS*.

63 *The Gallifrey Chronicles*

64 *The Crystal Bucephalus*

65 *The Time Warrior, Horror of Fang Rock*

66 THE PROGRESS OF THE SONTARAN-RUTAN WAR: We hear a number of status reports from the battlefront of the Sontaran-Rutan War over the course of the series. Both sides have periods of success and failure, but implicitly, the Sontarans visit Earth far earlier and far more often than the Rutans. Earth is some way from

The vast bio-mechanical complex known as the Event Synthesizer began operating.

"Since the dawn of time, the synthesizer has produced the ordered vibrations of the cosmos... creating events in a logical, harmonious sequence to flow into the main time-stream."

It was built by the people of Althrace, who were known to Rassilon, to simulate the effects of a white hole.[57] The last form of magic to survive was psionics.[58]

During this war, the great Gallifreyan general Kopyion Liall a Mahajetsu was believed to have died. He actually survived, and vigilantly watched in secret for signs of the Yssgaroth's return. He would deal with the threat of such an incursion in 2400.[59]

This war may or may not be the same conflict as the Time War, in which Time Lords from a generation after Rassilon fought against other races developing time travel. The conflict lasted thirty thousand years. The Time Lords wiped out many races during this time.[60]

One such race was the Charon, who were capable of warping space, and whom the Time Lords destroyed before they ever existed. One Charon survived this and created its own clockwork mini-universe. Another unnamed race used Reality Bombs to disrupt the control systems of time machines. A few of these weapons sur-

vived hidden for billions of years.[61]

The Doctor witnessed the horrors of the Time War. At one point, the Time Lords were themselves attacked by an unnamed race in retaliation for something they hadn't yet done.[61]

The Time War ended with all threats to Gallifrey contained, or so completely destroyed that no evidence remained to suggest they even existed. Time Lords were encoded with genetic memories of their ancient enemies and were compelled to destroy any survivors. The Time Lords were ashamed of the Time War, to the point that they deny it ever happened.[62]

Mr Saldaamir, who would become a friend of the Doctor's father, was the last survivor of the Time War.[63] There was a Celestial War in which the Ooolatrii captured at least one primitive TARDIS.[64]

The Sontarans and Rutans were involved in "eternal war".[65] The origins of the conflict between them was lost in the mists of time and was the subject of much propaganda. Much later, the Rutans blamed the war on the Sontarans for attacking the Constellation of Zyt, which the Sontarans claimed was retaliation for a Rutan attack on Holfactur, which the Rutans said had been the base for attacks on the Purple Areas of Rutan Space, which in turn was revenge for an attack on Mancastovon. The war quickly escalated, and it would rage, ebb and flow across the entire galaxy for many millions of years.[66]

---

the front lines (but close enough to strike the enemy using their most powerful emplaced weapons), with the Sontarans between us and the Rutans. According to "Pureblood", when Earth becomes a spacefaring power, its territory borders the Sontaran Empire, but it's in neither human nor Sontaran interests to pick a fight with each other.

It's also worth noting that in *The Time Warrior*, Linx states "there is not a galaxy in the Universe which our space fleets have not subjugated", and Styre talks about invading "Earth's Galaxy" in *The Sontaran Experiment*. Sontarans and Rutans are both prone to boasting but, even so, a war fought across one galaxy is already incomprehensibly vast, and I suspect the writers - as happens on occasion elsewhere in the TV series - are confusing "solar system" with "galaxy".

We never hear about either the Sontarans and Rutans coming into conflict with other space powers. From this, we might infer that Skaro, Draconia, Telos and Ice Warrior territory are all located on one side of Earth, the Sontarans and (a little further away) the Rutans lie in the other.

In Ancient Egypt ("The Gods Walk Among Us"), Earth is a suitable place for the Sontarans to "outflank" the Rutans (given both sides' use of rhetoric, this might suggest that the Rutans are making a major advance).

In the Middle Ages (*The Time Warrior*), Earth is of no

strategic importance, but the Sontarans send a reconnaissance mission there. The Sontarans and Rutans both have fighter squadrons. Then in the seventeenth century ("Dragon's Claw"), the war is being fought close enough to Earth for a Sontaran ship to crash there.

By the early twentieth century, the Rutans are losing the war. They had previously dominated the Mutter's Spiral (our galaxy), but now were beaten back to the fringes. Earth is of strategic importance. In the late twentieth century (*The Two Doctors*), Earth is "conveniently situated" for the Sontarans' attack on the Rutan-held Madillon Cluster.

As humans spread into space, they encountered the Sontarans and found themselves caught in the crossfire ("Conflict of Interests", *Lords of the Storm*). Humanity and the Sontarans sign a non-aggression pact in 2420.

In Benny's time, the Rutans made great advances, and even managed to devastate the Sontaran homeworld. Following the Doctor's intervention, the Sontarans survive to serve as a buffer between humanity and the Rutans ("Pureblood").

There is a demilitarised zone between the later Earth Empire and the Sontarans. The Sontarans lose a war to the Federation in the sixty-third century, and their Empire soon lies in ruins.

Then in the far future (*The Sontaran Experiment*), a Sontaran invasion fleet is poised to invade Earth (the

Around the time the war started, the Sontarans became a clone race. Their greatest warrior, Sontar, had defeated the Isari. He was the model for all future Sontarans. To increase efficiency, the Sontaran body was simplified. All non-clones soon died. The leader of the Sontarans, always called General Sontar, had the memories of all previous General Sontars.[67] The "pureblood" Sontarans were originally less squat, with long hair and five fingers.[68]

The Time Lords colonised planets such as Dronid and Trion. Sharing their secrets with lesser races, though, led to disaster. Evolution on Klist was reversed, and the civilisation on Plastrodus 14 went insane.[69] **Eventually the Time Lords recognised the dangers of intervention when their attempts to help the Minyans resulted in the destruction of Minyos.**[70]

The Time Lords interfered on Micen Island, resulting in chemical and biological warfare and the destruction of the entire civilisation. The Time Lords built the Temple of the Fourth on the ruins, and codified the Oath of the Faction. They scattered in repentance for what they had done.[71]

The Time Lords remained content to observe, but monitored the universe and tried to prevent other, less principled races from discovering the secrets of time travel.[72] **They occasionally sent out ambassadors and official observers.**[73] **They also attempted to enforce bans on dangerous technology.**[74]

For more information on the history of the Doctor's people, see the Gallifrey section at the end of this book.

The Ancient Past

Xaos was the oldest planet in the known galaxy.[75] **Before life evolved on other planets, the Exxilon civilisation was already old.**[76] Other races such as the Raab of Odonoto Ceti, a race on Benelisa and the Cthalctose of 16 Alpha Leonis One evolved.[77]

= **THE NOWHERE PLACE**[78] -> More than fifty billion years ago, a dominant life-form evolved on Earth and would come to develop space travel in future. However, a mishap occurred during the race's first attempt to journey out of the solar system. A mis-setting of the spaceship's coordinates - when paradoxically combined with the energy of a nuclear missile strike in 2197 - resulted in the engines getting caught in their own time warp. This created the hyper-spatial equivalent of a Mobius Strip, and ripped the entire race out of space and time. They were consigned to the realm known as "Time's End": a point at which all cosmic laws were invalidated.

Other dominant species would evolve on Earth, but the original race - consumed with madness and jealousy, and using the insane logic of Time's End to its advantage - continually subverted each race's bid for space travel. Each new race was erased from history, made to suffer continuously in the matter-crushing forces of Time's End. Billions of Earth-born species were snared in this fashion.

The original race tried to similarly capture humanity, but the sixth Doctor ventured into Time's End and reprogrammed the original race's spaceship coordinates into a linear fashion. The nuclear strike from 2197 destroyed the vessel rather than creating the Mobius Strip, which obliterated the original species. Time's End was either nullified or at least moved. The dominance of humanity and its time-stream was assured.

c 6,000,000,000 BC - ETERNITY WEEPS[79] -> Jason Kane used a Time Ring to reach 16 Alpha Leonis One, the home of the Cthalctose, from Earth in the year 2003. He met the Astronomer Royal, who had detected a black hole in their solar system and provided force field technology.

story says "Earth's galaxy", but see above), which is of tactical importance. The Doctor says there's a "buffer zone" between human and Sontaran territory.

The war ended three hundred thousand years before the end of humanity, resulting in the greatest demobilisation in universal history. Far, far in the future, the two races apparently merge.

67 *The Infinity Doctors*. The war has lasted as long as the Time Lord civilisation.

68 "Pureblood". The Doctor's assertion that the Sontaran / Rutan war started "ten centuries" before can't be right, as it would mean it started in the 1500s - in other words, after *The Time Warrior*. Other stories place the start of the war far back in Earth's prehistory.

69 *The Quantum Archangel*

70 *Underworld*

71 *Death Comes to Time*
72 *The War Games*
73 *The Two Doctors, The Empire of Glass*
74 *Carnival of Monsters, The Empire of Glass*
75 "Warrior's Story". It's unclear if this means it's home to the first known civilisation or physically the oldest planet.
76 *Death to the Daleks*
77 *Frontier Worlds, The Taint, Eternity Weeps.*
78 Dating *The Nowhere Place* (BF #84) - The Doctor dates a tool of the original species - a mysterious door in 2197 - as being "more than fifty billion years old". This is a scientific absurdity, given that the universe is no more than fifteen billion years old.
79 Dating *Eternity Weeps* (NA #58) - It is "six billion years ago" (p3).

Jason was placed in a stasis field and watched the Cthalctose civilisation develop for five hundred years. The Cthalctose attempted to contain the black hole, but eventually could no longer power the force fields.

Unable to save themselves, they built a device - "the Museum" - that could convert another world to resemble their own. This entailed using a terraforming virus that would generate sulphuric acid, which was present in the seas on their homeworld. The Cthalctose launched the Museum out of their solar system, and the forces of the black hole destroyed 16 Alpha Leonis One. Jason Kane's stasis field failed and he returned to 2003.

? - "Time Witch"[80] -> Before the Earth was formed, Brimo was imprisoned in an eternity capsule for attempting to dominate the planet Nefrin. She watched civilisations rise and fall, and when Nefrin's sun went nova, the capsule fell into the resulting black hole. Once there, she entered a realm where her thoughts became reality.

Later, the TARDIS was torn apart and the fourth Doctor and Sharon were pulled into a dimensional rift to Brimo's domain. The presence of the TARDIS started draining Brimo's abilities, and the Doctor fought a battle of wits with her, finally trapping her by getting her to imagine the eternity capsule. Restoring the TARDIS aged the Doctor and - more noticeably - Sharon by four years.

As Earth's solar system formed from dust, the Tractite named Kitig arrived through time via a time tree. As Kitig intended, this destroyed the time tree at the cost of his own life.[81]

Earth formed billions of years ago.[82] **The Time Lords "got rid" of huon particles, which were capable of unravelling atomic structure.**[83]

4,600,000,000 BC - THE RUNAWAY BRIDE[84] **-> The Time Lords and the "fledgling empires" all but eradicated the Racnoss - spider-like monsters who were born starving, and devoured entire planets. Four point six billion years ago, as the tenth Doctor and Donna**

witnessed, **Earth formed around one of the last of the Racnoss ships. Without the huon particles needed to revive the Racnoss within, the creatures would sleep until the twenty-first century. The Empress of the Racnoss also survived, and retreated to the edge of the universe to hibernate.**

While the Earth was still forming, the Time Lords were in negotiations with the Tranmetgurans, trying to organise a planetary government and end the war that was ravaging the planet. The Hoothi - a fungoid group-mind that lived off dead matter and farmed entire sentient species - attacked Tranmetgura, introducing their dead soldiers into the battle. War broke out, and two thirds of the population were killed. The Hoothi harvested the dead, taking them aboard their silent gas dirigibles. When the Time Lords sent an ambassador to the Hoothi worlds, the Hoothi used him as a host and attempted to conquer Gallifrey. The Time Lords launched a counter-attack, forcing the Hoothi to flee into hyperspace. The Hoothi vanished from the universe.[85]

A plague wiped out Curcurbites - machines that were fuelled by the blood of their enemies. The last of them fell into the magma of primeval Earth.[86]

The universe passed the point when it would naturally collapse. It was sustained by the people of Logopolis, who opened CVEs into other universes.[87]

Three billion years ago, carvings were made of the Great Old Ones on the planet Veltroch.[88]

c 3,000,000,000 BC - VENUSIAN LULLABY[89] **->** The Venusians were an advanced race, surprisingly so since all metals were poisonous to them with the exception of gold, platinum and titanium. Their cities were crude, with the buildings in cities such as Cracdhalltar and Bikugih resembling soap-bubbles made from mud and crude stone, but the civilisation lasted for three million years.

By measuring the day, which got steadily longer, the Venusians calculated that their planet was dying. For tens of thousands of years, most of the Venusians were resigned

---

80 Dating "Time Witch" (*DWW* #35-38) - Brimo was imprisoned "at a time before the Earth was formed" according to the opening caption. She says she was imprisoned for "millions of years", but even that might be an underestimate - the Doctor's encounter with her could well take place at any time in this timeline. Her situation inside the black hole is very like Omega's in *The Three Doctors* (and *The Infinity Doctors*), although there's no indication she's trapped there.
81 *Genocide* (p279).
82 *Inferno*
83 "Billions of years" before *The Runaway Bride*.
84 Dating *The Runaway Bride* (X3.0) - The Doctor and

Donna witness the Earth's formation.
85 *Love and War*
86 "Tooth and Claw" (*DWM*). The Curcurbites know of the Time Lords.
87 *Logopolis*. It's unclear when this happened, but there have been "aeons of constraint", and an aeon is a billion years.
88 *White Darkness*
89 Dating *Venusian Lullaby* (MA #3) - The Doctor tells Ian and Barbara that they have travelled back "oh, about three billion years I should think".
90 *Interference*

to their fate. Most of the Venusian animal species had become extinct: the shanghorn, the klak-kluk and the pat-tifangs. To conserve resources, Death Inspectors killed Venusians who had outlived their useful lives. Anti-Acceptancer factions such as the Rocketeers, the Below the Sun Believers, the Magnetologists, the Water-breathers, the Volcano People and the Cave-Makers believed that they could escape their fate, but the majority saw them as cranks.

The first Doctor, Ian and Barbara visited Venus at this time, just as the Sou(ou)shi arrived to offer the Venusians a place within their spacecraft. The Sou(ou)shi were vampires, and merely wanted to consume the entire Venusian race as they did the Aveletians and the Signortiyu. The Venusians discovered this with the Doctor's help and destroyed the Sou(ou)shi craft. The debris from the ship entered the Venusian atmosphere, blocking some of the sun's rays and lowering the planet's temperature. This prolonged the Venusians' existence for another one hundred generations. The consciousness of the Sou(ou)shi survived and travelled to primeval Earth.

w - Time Lords from the future launched an unmanned warship to destroy Earth, the original homeworld of the Enemy. The ship travelled at sublight speeds, and three billion years would elapse before it arrived there in 1996.[90]

The Nestene, a race of pure energy, began their conquests a billion years ago.[91] Around this time, the last seas dried up on Androzani Minor in the Sirius system.[92] The Scarlet System became home to the Pallushi - a mighty civilisation that would last a billion years until it fell into a black hole.[93]

The TARDIS was possessed by an elemental alien around 1983 and travelled back five hundred million years. Here the alien revelled in the forces of primeval Earth. The TARDIS returned, but the alien was free.[94]

The Great Provider began its intergalactic conquests four hundred million years ago.[95]

Life On Earth

c 400,000,000 BC - CITY OF DEATH[96] -> Four hundred million years ago, an advanced race - the callous Jagaroth - wiped themselves out in a huge war. The last of the Jagaroth limped to primeval Earth in an advanced spaceship. The pilot of the ship, Scaroth, attempted to take his vessel to power three - warp thrust - too close to the Earth's surface and the spacecraft detonated over what would later become the Atlantic Ocean.

Scaroth was splintered into twelve fragments and materialised at various points in human history. He would influence humanity's development for tens of thousands of years. This culminated in the building of a time machine in 1979, which he used to return to the past in an attempt to prevent his ship exploding. The fourth Doctor, Romana and their ally Duggan prevented Scaroth from changing history.

Earth at this time was a barren volcanic world, but it had already produced Primordial Soup, and the antimatter explosion acted as a catalyst. Life on Earth began.

The explosion of the Jagaroth ship left a radiation trace that the Euterpians detected many millions of years later.[97]

Life evolved much as palaeontologists and geologists think that it did.

Earth was home to a species of malignant wraiths that resided in the "lost lands". It was said that they hailed from the dawn of time, but these creatures - who resembled evil fairies - had their origins in humanity's

---

91 "A thousand million years" before *Spearhead from Space*. This date is confirmed in "Plastic Millennium".
92 "A billion years" before *The Caves of Androzani*.
93 *The Impossible Planet*
94 "The Stockbridge Horror"
95 "4x10(2d8) yrs" ago, according to *The Gallifrey Chronicles*.
96 Dating *City of Death* (17.2) - Scaroth and the Doctor both state that the Jagaroth ship came to Earth "four hundred million years ago". Contemporary science has a number of estimates of when life on Earth started, but all are far, far earlier than that. *The Terrestrial Index* takes that as a cue to set this story three and a half billion years ago.

SCAROTH OF THE JAGAROTH: In *City of Death*, we actually *see* Scarlioni, Tancredi and four other Scaroth splinters: an Egyptian, a Neanderthal (the one some

fans think looks like Jesus - the DVD commentary notes that Julian Glover thought the same), a Roman and a Celt (although most reference books, including the earlier versions of this one, describe him as a Crusader), in that order, in the flashback at the start of Part Three.

Further examination of this story can account for all twelve Scaroth splinters, assuming that none of them live for more than a century, and that they acquire Scarlioni's antiques while they are new. One Scaroth version (presumably the Neanderthal that we see) demonstrates "the true use of fire"; a second gives mankind the wheel; a third "caused the pyramids to be built" (we see this one both as a "human" Egyptian Pharoah and as a Jagaroth on an ancient Egyptian scroll); a fourth caused "the heavens to be mapped"; the fifth is an ancient Greek; the sixth is the Roman that we see (a Senator, or possibly even an Emperor); the sev-

children. They came to reside backwards and forwards in time, and would develop into creatures who were invisible to detection, and took to murdering people in their sleep. They had control of the elements, and were especially protective of their own: children named the Chosen Ones.[98]

Werewolves were among the oldest races on Earth. The werewolf Stubbe claimed to have been around at the Earth's creation.[99]

Around two hundred and sixty million years ago, the Permians - skeletal, lizard-hipped carnivores, bound together by a bio-electric field - were top of the food chain on Earth. They had a degree of intelligence, and the ability to mentally guide other creatures. They consumed electrical energy from living things, and were so efficient as predators that they wiped out 96% of life on Earth. With food becoming scarce, the Permians fed off each other. The last few of them went dormant and became fossils.[100]

In the 1970s, Dr Quinn discovered a colony of reptile people living below Wenley Moor in Derbyshire. They were the remnants of an advanced lost civilisation, and had spent many million years in hibernation. Quinn mistakenly believed that they came from the Silurian Period, and had a globe showing the Earth as it was before the great continental drift, two hundred million years ago.[101]

c 200,000,000 BC - "Time Bomb"[102] -> The Time Cannon of the Hedrons sent the sixth Doctor, Frobisher and TARDIS from the year 2850 far into the past of Earth. This was the destination for all the genetic impurities of that world - including many dead bodies that went on to influence genetic development on Earth.

The seventh Doctor watched the first Lungfish walk on a Devonian beach.[103]

The Age of the Dinosaurs

One hundred and sixty five million years ago, dinosaurs started to emerge on Earth.[104] In a different galaxy from Earth, which had become known as Home Galaxy, a number of advanced races made contact and reengineered themselves so that they could interbreed. They developed advanced artificial intelligence technology. The People and Also People constructed the Worldsphere, a Dyson sphere that completely enclosed the star Whynot, with a surface area six hundred million times larger than that of Earth. The regulating intelligence of the Worldsphere became known as God.[105]

An unnamed race created the Omnethoth, a sentient weapon that could control and alter its physical state, to conquer the universe. The Omnethoth wiped out its creators, seeded the universe with colonisation clouds and then went dormant.[106]

While dinosaurs walked the Earth, the Millennium War was fought across the galaxy. The Constructors of Destiny had created the Mind of Bophemeral - the ultimate computer and the most massive object ever built - from black holes, blue dwarfs and strange matter. Bophemeral, though, went insane within instants and destroyed the Constructors. A thousand races, including the Time Lords, Daemons, Euterpians, Exxilons, Faction Paradox, Greld, Grey Hegemony, Kastrians, Maskmakers of the Pageant, Ministers of Grace, Nimon, Omnethoth, Osirians, People of the Worldsphere, Uxariens, Rutans and Sontarans fought the Mind of Bophemeral and its drones. Kastria and Xeraphas were devastated in the war, but Bophemeral was defeated. The Time Lords and People time-looped Bophemeral and the Guardians intervened, using the Key to Time to erase all knowledge of this War.[107]

---

enth is the Celt that we see; the eighth gives mankind the printing press (presumably, this accounts for why Scarlioni has more than one Gutenberg Bible); the ninth is Captain Tancredi; the tenth is an Elizabethan nobleman (who obtains the first draft of *Hamlet*); the eleventh lives at the time of Louis XV (and is presumably the splinter who purchases the Gainsborough that's just been sold at the start of the story - he's named as Cardinal Scarlath in *Christmas on a Rational Planet*), and the twelfth is Carlos Scarlioni.
97 *Invasion of the Cat People*
98 *TW: Small Worlds*. Jack says the fairies are "from the dawn of time" - it's possible that he's speaking metaphorically, although in truth the fairies reside "backwards in time" and might pre-date humanity, even though they hail from it. Mention of the "lost lands" might suggest that they held more of a foothold

on Earth until Scaroth's spaceship sparked humanity's birth. It might be far simpler, however, to assume that their development coincides with that of mankind.
99 *Loups-Garoux*
100 *The Land of the Dead*
101 *Doctor Who and the Silurians*
CONTINENTAL DRIFT: According to scientists, continental drift is a continuing process. In *Doctor Who*, there's evidence that it was a single event. The Doctor talks of "the great continental drift, two hundred million years ago" in *Doctor Who and the Silurians*. In the broadcast version of *Earthshock*, the Earth of sixty-five million years ago looks like it does today. Continental drift was a reality according to *Invasion of the Cat-People*. In *The Ark*, the Earth of ten million years hence also looks exactly like contemporary Earth, although we saw the continents devastated in *The Parting of the*

c 150,000,000 BC - THE HAND OF FEAR[108] -> On Kastria, the scientist Eldrad built spacial barriers to keep out the solar winds that ravaged the planet. He also devised a crystalline silicon form for his race, and built machines to replenish the earth and the atmosphere. Once this was done, he threatened to usurp King Rokon.

The Kastrians did not share Eldrad's dreams of galactic conquest, and so Eldrad destroyed the barriers. The Kastrians sentenced Eldrad to death. As killing a silicon lifeform was almost impossible, they constructed an Obliteration Module and sent it out into space, beyond all solar systems. The Module was detonated early at nineteen spans, while there was still a one-in-three-million chance that Eldrad might survive. The Kastrians elected to destroy themselves and their race banks rather than lead a subterranean existence. Eldrad's hand eventually reached Earth in the Jurassic Period, where it became buried in a stratum of Blackstone Dolomite.

> = **150,000,000 BC - "Time Bomb"** [109] -> The sixth Doctor and Frobisher returned to the distant past from 2850 to discover that the Hedrons were disposing of bodies in this era, too. History might never be restored.

The Vardon-Kosnax War was meant to run fifty years, but disruption to history meant that it lasted three hundred.[110]

140,000,000 BC - TIME-FLIGHT[111] -> The planet Xeraphas was the home of the Xeraphin, a legendary race with immense mental powers. It was rendered uninhabitable when it was caught in the Vardon-Kosnax War. The surviving Xeraphin came to Earth, hoping to colonise the planet, but they suffered from radiation sickness. They abandoned their physical forms, and became a psychic gestalt of bioplasmic energy until they were able to regenerate. The Master became trapped on Earth five hundred years after this and attempted to harness the power of the Xeraphin Consciousness.

Building a Time Contour Generator, the Master kidnapped a Concorde from the nineteen-eighties, and used the passengers as slaves in an attempt to penetrate the Xeraphin citadel. He was defeated when the fifth Doctor followed him back through time and broke the slaves' conditioning.

About one hundred and thirty million years ago, the Plesiosaurus became extinct. Before this, the owner of a miniscope had kidnapped an example of the species.

Ways, and *The End of the World* acknowledges that technology was used to arrest continental drift.

102 Dating "Time Bomb" (*DWM* #114-116) - "Earthdate 200 Million Years BC", according to the caption.

103 *Transit*. This may be a dream sequence or an allegory.

104 In *Earthshock*, the Doctor states that the dinosaurs existed for "a hundred million years or so" and died out "sixty five million years ago", which is in tune with scientific consensus.

105 *The Also People*. No date is given, but the People fight in the Millennium War in *The Quantum Archangel*.

106 "Millions of years" before *The Fall of Yquatine*. The Omnethoth also fight in the Millennium War according to *The Quantum Archangel*.

107 *The Quantum Archangel*. The Millenium Wars (consistently misspelled with one "n") were a feature of the early *Doctor Who Weekly/Monthly* comic strips, but this would appear to be a different conflict.

108 Dating *The Hand of Fear* (14.2) - The Doctor identifies the rock in which Eldrad's hand was discovered, and twice tells Eldrad that he has been away from Kastria for "a hundred and fifty million years".

109 Dating "Time Bomb" (*DWM* #114-116) - The caption reads "Earthdate 150 Million BC".

110 *Neverland*. The war is referred to as over by *Time-Flight*. The Vardons are probably not the Vardans seen in *The Invasion of Time*. A Kosnax appears in *Cold Fusion*.

111 Dating *Time-Flight* (19.7) - The Doctor informs the flight crew of the second Concorde that they have landed at Heathrow "one hundred and forty million years ago". He states, correctly, that this is the "Jurassic" era, but then suggests that they "can't be far off from the Pleistocene era", which actually took place a mere 1,800,000 -10,000 years ago. *The Seeds of Doom* gives a more accurate date for the Pleistocene.

112 *Carnival of Monsters*. The Doctor states that the Pleisosaurus "has been extinct for one hundred and thirty million years". The miniscope presumably captures its specimens in a time scoop like those seen in *Invasion of the Dinosaurs* and *The Five Doctors*. Vorg's Scope contains both a Plesiosaurus and humans from 1926, specimens taken from eras over a hundred and thirty million years apart.

113 *Doctor Who and the Silurians, The Happiness Patrol*.

114 *Invasion of the Dinosaurs*. Whitaker tries to take Earth back to a "Golden Age," but there's no indication that this is the age of the dinosaurs, which would hardly be an Earthly paradise for humans. He uses dinosaurs to scare people out of London.

115 *The Mark of the Rani, Time and the Rani*

116 "Cuckoo"

117 *Made of Steel*. The two dinosaurs they see are the Apatosaurus and Tyrannosaurus, creatures of the Upper Cretaceous.

118 Dating "A Glitch in Time" (*DWM* #179) - It's "the

Miniscopes were built from molecular-bonded disillium by the Eternity Perpetual Company, and would literally last forever - as a result, the company went bankrupt. Concerned that many miniscopes contained sentient specimens, the Doctor successfully lobbied the High Council of the Time Lords and had miniscopes banned. Many years later, though, the Lurman showman Vorg travelled the Acteon Group with one of the few surviving miniscopes, which he had won at the Great Wallarian Exhibition in a game of chance.[112]

The Doctor visited Earth at the time of the dinosaurs. He reckoned the Cretaceous Era was "a very good time for dinosaurs".[113] Professor Whitaker kidnapped various dinosaurs using his Timescoop.[114] The Rani visited this period and collected Tyrannosaur embryos, one of which almost killed her later. She also expressed an interest in reviving the era with a Time Manipulator.[115] Millions of years ago, a Surcoth explorer was lost on Earth. His body eventually fossilised and was discovered in 1855.[116] The tenth Doctor and Martha visited the Cretaceous, and a Tyrannosaurus chased them.[117]

= c 100,000,000 BC - "A Glitch in Time"[118] -> The seventh Doctor and Ace arrived at a nexus point in Earth's history, the Cretaceous, and immediately met a team of time-travelling dinosaur hunters. Despite the Doctor's objections, they were convinced they were part of history so couldn't change it. They shot an early mammal... and a team of reptilian time-travelling hunters materialised to hunt apes. The two parties fighting inside the nexus cancelled each other out, and both returned to their respective futures.

= The paleontologist George Williamson tested his newfound time travel abilities by observing dinosaurs first-hand. Williamson's mere presence encouraged some saurian lizards to start walking upright and gain an evolutionary advantage, creating a parallel timeline. A dimensional doorway from this timeline would open in Siberia, 1894, and some advanced

---

saurians went through it. The timeline was erased due to the Doctor and Williamson's actions in 1894.[119]

c 65,000,000 BC - EARTHSHOCK[120] -> Sixty five million years ago, the dinosaurs became extinct when the anti-matter engines of a space freighter that had spiralled back through time from 2526 exploded in Earth's atmosphere.

A hundred thousand years before the Silurians, the Earth had been ruled by "gargantuan entities".[121]

The Age of the Reptile People

On Earth, some reptiles had evolved into intelligent bipeds. There were two distinct species: the land-based Silurians, who built a great civilisation in areas of extreme heat; and their amphibious cousins, the Sea Devils.[122]

Silurian civilisation started as scattered clans, which were eventually united by Panun E'Ni of the Southern Clan, whose deeds were recorded in the Hall of Heroes. Panun E'Ni was deposed by Tun W'lzz, who freed the enslaved tribes to create a united Silurian civilisation.[123]

Silurians had advanced psychic powers, which seemed to be concentrated through their third "eye". They had telekinetic and hypnotic abilities, could project lethal blasts of energy and establish invisible force fields. Much of their equipment was operated by mental commands, although the Silurians were also known to use an almost-musical summoning device. Much of Silurian technology appears to have been organic. The Silurians domesticated dinosaurs, using a tyrannosaur species as watchdogs. They constructed the Disperser, a device capable of dispersing the Van Allen Belts.[124]

They used brontosaurs to lift heavy loads, and dilophosaurs as mounts. They communicated using a sophisticated language that was a combination of telepathy, speech and gesture. They had Gravitron technology which allowed a sophisticated degree of weather control.

Cretaceous", so between 145 and 65 million years ago.
119 "Several million years" before *Time Zero*.
120 Dating *Earthshock* (19.6) - The Doctor dates the extinction of the dinosaurs, and confirms that the freighter has travelled to that era, back "sixty five million years". In the original TV version, the pattern of prehistoric Earth's continents are those of modern-day Earth. A correction was attempted for the DVD release, where an effects option allows the viewer to see an updated special effect. However, the correction itself is historically awry, as it features the super-continent Pangea, when the proper configuration should be somewhere

between Pangea and the present day.
121 *All Consuming Fire*
122 *Doctor Who and the Silurians, The Sea Devils*. See the "When Did the Silurians Rule the Earth?" sidebar.
123 *The Scales of Injustice*
124 *Doctor Who and the Silurians*

They travelled in vast airships.[125]

Their science was more advanced than human technology of the late twenty-first century, with particle suppressers and advanced genetic engineering. They also created creatures such as the Myrka, a ferocious armoured sea monster. Silurian Law prevented all but defensive wars, but the Sea Devils had elite army units and hand-held weaponry, and the Silurians built submarine battlecruisers.[126]

The Silurians lived in vast crystalline cities with imposing architecture.[127] One estimate is that their technology was three or four hundred years more advanced than Earth in the twentieth century. A provision of Silurian law was to execute members of different castes who mated. Strict laws also prevented experiments into genetic engineering and nuclear fission.[128]

Turtles existed at the time of the Sea Devils much as they do in our time. Sea Devils didn't eat meat.[129] The Silurians worshipped the Great Old Ones, with the Sea Devils venerating Dagon in particular.[130] They also worshipped a lizard "devil god", Urmungstandra.[131]

The Prime Serpent was a Silurian deity.[132]

= The Silurian scientist Mortakk performed illegal genetic experiments. He was tried and executed before the great hibernation.[133]

The Silurians saw apes as pests who raided their crops, and developed a virus to cull them.[134] Silurians also ate the apes, using Myrkas to hunt them.[135] Apes were caged and tortured.[136]

A rogue planetoid was detected by Silurian scientists, who calculated that as it passed by Earth, it would cause extensive natural disasters. The Silurians built hibernation shelters deep underground to survive the catastrophe.[137]

? - "Twilight of the Silurians"[138] -> Apes in the wild were beginning to organise into packs and attack vulnerable Silurians. One ape, Kin, had emerged as a leader and was captured. Many Silurians viewed the threat of the approaching Moon as a scare story, but new calculations reveal they were merely five days from disaster. Led by Kin, the apes escaped by rebelling against their captors.

The Silurians' preparations took twelve years. Silurian hybrids were sent to Shelter 429.[139]

? - BLOODTIDE[140] -> The surface of the Earth became a freezing wasteland. The Silurian scientist Tulok genetically augmented some of the apes to improve their flavour, and as a side-effect they also become sentient. As the Silurian Triad entered hibernation, Tulok was banished to the surface for the crime of illicit experimentation. He was rescued by his friend Sh'vak. They headed to the hibernation chambers, sabotaging the controls so that most of the species would not revive when planned.

The Silurians retired to their vast subterranean hibernation chambers, but the rogue planetoid settled into orbit around Earth, becoming the Moon. After the Moon's arrival, the Van Allen Belt developed, filtering out much of the sun's radiation and cooling the Earth. The climate quickly stabilised at a lower temperature than the reptile people had predicted, and so they failed to revive as planned. The apes slowly began to evolve a greater degree of intelligence. Before long, the only trace remaining of the reptile people were the race memories of these first hominids, the ancestors of mankind.[141]

The planetoid was the moon containing the Museum of the Cthalctose. The gravitational forces wrecked havoc on Earth, destroying many Silurian shelters. Race memories of this event survived in human mythology as a great flood.[142]

125 *Blood Heat*
126 *Warriors of the Deep*
127 *Blood Heat, The Scales of Injustice, Bloodtide*
128 *The Scales of Injustice*
129 "The Devil of the Deep"
130 *All-Consuming Fire*
131 *The Crystal Bucephalus*, named in *The Taking of Planet 5*. The name was spelled Urgmundasatra in the Benny New Adventure *Twilight of the Gods*.
132 "Final Genesis"
133 "Final Genesis". This is set in a parallel universe, and it's unclear if Mortakk also lived in ours.
134 *Doctor Who and the Silurians*
135 *Bloodtide*
136 *The Scales of Injustice*
137 *Doctor Who and the Silurians*

138 Dating "Twilight of the Silurians" (*DWW* #21-22) - It's "millions of years before history began". There's a note to the effect that the Silurians are also known as Eocenes.
139 *The Scales of Injustice*
140 Dating *Bloodtide* (BF #22) - It's set at the time the Silurians are going into hibernation, "over a million years ago", and "ten years" after Earth's surface has become uninhabitable. In *Doctor Who and the Silurians* and *The Scales of Injustice*, it's stated that the Silurians don't revive because Earth's climate stabilises below the levels the Silurians set. In *Bloodtide*, Tulok claims he prevented the reactivation, and the Doctor in Part Three finds evidence of his sabotage.
141 *Doctor Who and the Silurians*
142 "Twenty million years, give or take" before *Eternity*

WHEN DID THE SILURIANS RULE THE EARTH?:
There are a number of contradictory accounts in the TV series, the books and the audios of when the Silurian civilisation existed, and it is impossible to reconcile them with each other, let alone against established scientific fact.

A lot of the dating references are very vague: *Doctor Who and the Silurians* says the Silurians "ruled the planet millions of years ago". *The Scales of Injustice* states the Silurians existed "millions of years" and "a few million years" ago, but also uses the term "millennia". *Bloodtide* says it was "many hundreds of thousands of years ago" and "over a million years ago". *Eternity Weeps* features the Silurians and shows the arrival of the Moon in Earth orbit. However, it's inconsistent with its dating, stating that this happened both "twenty million" (p127) and "200 million" (p117) years ago.

Ironically, the one thing we can safely rule out is that the Silurians are from the actual Silurian Era, around 438 to 408 million years ago. Life on Earth's surface was limited to the first plants, and the dominant species were coral reefs. The first jawed fishes evolved during this era. If nothing else, in terms of *Doctor Who* continuity (according to *City of Death*), this is before life on Earth starts. It's Dr. Quinn who coins the name "Silurian" in *Doctor Who and the Silurians*. Despite the name being scientifically inaccurate, everyone at Wenley Moor - including the Doctor - uses it. We don't learn what the reptile people call themselves, but the Doctor calls them "Silurians" to their face and they don't correct him. The on-screen credits also use the term.

In *The Sea Devils*, when Jo calls the reptile people "Silurians", the Doctor replies, "That's a complete misnomer. The chap that discovered them must have got the period wrong. Properly speaking, they should have been called the Eocenes". Yet the Doctor never uses the "correct" term in practice. The novelisation of *Doctor Who and the Silurians* (called *The Cave Monsters* on its first release) called them "reptile people", and the word "Silurian" only appears as a UNIT password. The description "sea devil" is coined by Clark, the terrified sea fort worker in *The Sea Devils*, and the term appears in the on-screen credits for all six episodes. Captain Hart refers to them as "Sea Devils" as though that's their name. For the rest of the story the humans tend to call them "creatures" while the Doctor and Master refer to them as "the people".

By *Warriors of the Deep* and *Blood Heat*, however, the reptiles have adopted the inaccurate human terms for their people. *Bloodtide* starts with a flashback where Silurians refer to themselves by that name in their own era. In *Love and War*, we learn that the Silurians of the future "liked to be called Earth Reptiles now", and that term is also used in a number of other novels. The designation 'homo reptilia' that crops up in a number of places is scientifically illiterate. In *Blood Heat* the Doctor uses the term "psionsauropodomorpha".

In *Doctor Who and the Silurians*, Quinn has a globe of the Earth showing the continents forming one huge land mass, the implication being that it's the world the Silurians would have known. *The Scales of Injustice* follows this cue. Scientists call this supercontinent Pangaea, and date it to 250 to 200 million years ago. Again, this seems too early, as it predates the time of the dinosaurs.

That said, while most fans have assumed - and the novels, audios and comic strips have often stated - that the Silurians come from the same time as the dinosaurs (around 165 to 65 million years ago, according to both science and the Doctor in *Earthshock*), there is no evidence on screen that the Silurians were contemporaries of any known dinosaur species. In *Doctor Who and the Silurians*, the Silurians have a 'guard dog' that's a mutant, five-fingered species of tyrannosaur that the Doctor can't identify, and in *Warriors of the Deep* we see the lumbering Myrka. Likewise, while it seems obvious to cite the extinction of the dinosaurs and the fall of Silurian civilisation as owing to the same events, it's not a connection that's ever made on screen. Indeed, we know from *Earthshock* that the dinosaurs were wiped out in completely different circumstances than the catastrophe that made the Silurians enter hibernation.

The key plot point with the Silurians' story is not that they existed at the time of the dinosaurs, it's that as their civilisation thrived, the apes who were humanity's ancestors were mere pests. The Sea Devil leader in *The Sea Devils* says "my people ruled the Earth when man was only an ape". *Bloodtide* says the Silurians ruled "while humanity was still in its infancy", and goes on to specify that the apes at the time were Australopithecus. The earliest evidence for that genus is around four million years ago - which ties in with the date for the earliest humans in *Image of the Fendahl*. Although *Doctor Who* continuity has established humanity dates back millions of years more than scientists would accept, it doesn't seem to stretch anything like as far as the Eocene, 55 to 38 million years ago.

We don't know how long Silurian civilisation stood. One solution to the dating problem might be to say that it lasted for tens of millions or even hundreds of millions of years, from before the time of the dinosaurs (and surviving their extinction somehow) through to the time of the apemen. However, all accounts have the reptile people as a technologically-advanced, innovative, stable and centrally-controlled civilisation. At the time of their going into hibernation, they were merely "centuries" in advance of the human race in the twentieth century. This would seem to point to a civilisation lasting thousands of years rather than millions.

We have to conclude that the Silurians and apelike human ancestors were contemporaries, and that Silurian civilisation ended long after the time of the dinosaurs. There are more than sixty million years to fit the Silurians in, then, including the Eocene period that the Doctor favours in *The Sea Devils*. It seems most likely, though, that the Silurians flourished for a few millennia at some point in the last five to ten million years.

The Birth of the Cybermen

There have been a number of accounts of the origins of the Cybermen.[143]

Millions of years ago, a twin planet to Earth - Mondas - was home to a race identical to humanity (indeed, Mondas was an old name for Earth). Mondas started to drift out to the edge of space.[144]

It soon became clear that the Mondasian race was becoming more sickly. Their life spans were shortening dramatically and they could only survive by replacing diseased organs and wasted limbs with metal and plastic substitutes. A new race was born.[145]

"Mondas had a propulsion unit, a tribute to Cyber-engineering - though why they should want to push a planet through space, I have no idea." [146]

Mondas had been created by the Constructors of Destiny to research collective intelligence.[147]

? - "The Cybermen"[148] **->** On Earth's twin planet of Mondas, the Silurians created monsters: the all-devouring Titan R'lyeh and the giant Golgoth, the distillation of the greatest reptilian bloodstock. The Silurians eventually imprisoned them.

Mondas spun away from the sun, but was still habitable. The Silurians became tyrants, the unquestioned rulers of the world and augmented the apes to make cybernetic servants. Eventually, the reptiles were driven into hibernation by worsening conditions.

After a thousand years, and the Millennium Winter, the Cybermen had evolved from the augmented apes. They destroyed their former masters and set out to conquer the planet, but soon discovered - when they accidentally

released R'lyeh - that they were not the only surviving creations of the lizard kings. A lost Cyber-mission returned as phantoms, then the Cybermen fought necromantic Sea Devils and their deity, Golgoth. He created a son for himself, then destroyed himself and the Cybermen in a battle lasting forty days and nights.

The Cyber-civilisation fell.

Mondas and Marinus were the same planet.[149]

? - THE KEYS OF MARINUS[150] **->** The people of the planet Marinus built the Conscience - a machine that originally served as an impartial judge but eventually became capable of radiating a force that eliminated crime, fear and violence for seven centuries. Yartek, the Voord leader, learned how to resist the Conscience, and thus his followers robbed and cheated without any resistance. The scientist Arbitan deactivated the Conscience, hiding the five micro-keys needed to operate it around the planet; this prevented the Voord from using the device to control the population.

The first Doctor, Susan, Ian and Barbara arrived on Arbitan's island. A year earlier, Arbitan had sent his daughter Sabetha to collect the micro-keys, but she never returned. The Doctor and his companions recovered all the keys on Arbitan's behalf, but returned to find that Yartek had killed Arbitan and taken control of the Conscience. Ian tricked Yartek by giving him a facsimile of one of the keys, but once it was inserted into the Conscience, the duplicate broke under the strain. The Conscience exploded, killing Yartek.

? - "The Cybermen"[151] **->** Three thousand years after the fall of their civilisation, the Cybermen were legends to the humans that ruled Mondas. Once again, the planet's

---

Weeps, according to Benny.

143 See "The Creation of the Cybermen" sidebar, p35.

144 *The Tenth Planet*

145 *The Tenth Planet*, and elaborated in *Spare Parts*.

146 According to the sixth Doctor in *Attack of the Cybermen*. The implication seems to be that Mondas left the solar system deliberately and under its own power. However, *Spare Parts* shows the propulsion unit coming into operation at the far end of Mondas' journey ... and the fifth Doctor learning why.

147 *The Quantum Archangel*

148 Dating "The Cybermen" - "The Cybermen" strip ran from *DWM* #215 to 238, and covered the early history of Mondas. It places the creation of the Cybermen in the Age of the Reptile People, which may or may not support the date for the creation of the Cybermen less than five million years ago given in "The World Shapers" (see "When Did the Silurians Rule the Earth?").

149 "The World Shapers"

150 Dating *The Keys of Marinus* (1.5) - There is no way of dating this story in relation to Earth's history, but taking the comic strips into account, it has to happen before "The World Shapers". As it's set on Mondas, the only place it can fit is after the first fall of the Cyberman civilisation seen in "The Cybermen".

There's confusion within the chronology of the story - Arbitan seems to state that Yartek is thirteen hundred years old (as the Conscience was built two thousand years ago, and Yartek broke its conditioning after seven centuries). Arbitan has been working to upgrade the Conscience to defeat the Voord, and he and his followers have hidden the micro-keys around the planet, but there's no indication of how long Arbitan's been at work. Arbitan is mortal and feeling the effects of old age, and there's nothing to suggest anyone on Marinus has anything other than a normal human lifespan.

151 Dating "The Cybermen" - It's "three thousand years" after the previous strip.

THE CREATION OF THE CYBERMEN: The origin of the Cybermen (in our universe, at least) has never been depicted on television, but the broad facts were established in *The Tenth Planet*, with additional information in *Attack of the Cybermen*.

DWM has offered two distinct origins, Big Finish a third. (The creator of the Cybermen, Gerry Davies, pitched his own origin story for television in the eighties, and this was reprinted in Virgin's *Cybermen* book.)

The three origin stories that were made might seem to contradict each other, but none of them contradict what we learn on TV. They can, with a little imaginative licence, all be reconciled with each other.

"The World Shapers" appears to diverge the furthest from the television account, roping in the planet Marinus and making the Cybermen the descendants of the Voord from "The Keys of Marinus", but the story doesn't contradict anything like as much as it seems. The Voord are human underneath their wetsuits, and they become Cybermen to survive global environmental collapse. It would mean Marinus is Earth's twin planet - which is a stretch, but not an enormous one. (We know from "The Keys of Marinus" that it's a planet where humans, wolves, chickens, grapes and pomegranates can all be found). The issue of Marinus / Mondas leaving the solar system isn't addressed, but neither is it ruled out.

The *Cybermen* strip in *DWM* takes fan speculation that links the Cybermen and Silurians, and is more consciously mythological in tone.

Spare Parts has, perhaps, the most orthodox interpretation of what we're told in *The Tenth Planet* - the civilisation on Mondas is roughly the equivalent of the mid-twentieth century, with a sickly population surviving in subterranean cities. Mondas travels into interstellar space, and as it does so, the population need to take existing medical technology to extremes to survive. Note that for a third time, an established *Doctor Who* race is part of the Cyberman recipe, as here the fifth Doctor's physiology provides the template for the future Cybermen.

These stories can be placed in order. The *DWM Cybermen* strip comes first - it's the only one that depicts Mondas leaving its original orbit. Not only that, it establishes that there's a period of three thousand years when Mondas settled into a new orbit where the Cyber-civilisation has collapsed and an advanced, fragmented human civilisation dominates. This is an ideal place to fit "The Keys of Marinus" and "The World Shapers" - all it needs is for (some of) the humans on Mondas now to think of their planet as 'Marinus'.

Again, this seems like a stretch - and, of course, it isn't what any of the writers intended or planned. But there *are* elements of Marinus technology in "The Keys of Marinus" that look remarkably like remnants or precursors of Cyber-technology: the Conscience itself is based around the idea of negative emotions being eliminated to create an ordered society and is built with 'micro circuits'; the Troughton era Cybermen had hypnotic and sleep-inducing technology much like that of the city of Morphoton; in episode three, Darrius' experiments, like those of the Voord in "The World Shapers", have increased the 'tempo' of nature; there's a group of soldiers frozen in ice; the Voord and Cybermen are the only two monsters the Doctor's ever met who were human once, have handles on their heads and wear wetsuits.

So... Mondas settled into its new orbit and became known as Marinus. Within a thousand years, the Conscience of Marinus was built and soon came to control the population. For seven hundred years, the planet knew total peace. Then Yartek learned how to resist the Conscience's influence - it's hard not to picture the second Doctor breaking Cyber-hypnosis in *The Wheel in Space* and *The Invasion*. The Voord's physical appearance might mean they've found some remnants of the legendary Cyber civilisation. They haven't abandoned emotions in favour of logic and the good of society, though - ironically, it's rather the opposite. If Yartek is part-Cyberman, it might explain why he apparently lives at least thirteen hundred years. Neither is it a paradox that Yartek manages to resist the Conscience - yes, the Conscience should have quelled his urge to break the conditioning if his intent was purely malicious, but it could have been an accident or motivated by... well, the fairly uncontroversial belief that having free will is a good thing. (The Doctor says as much at the end of "The Keys of Marinus" itself, and in many other stories.)

"The World Shapers" sees the Voord consciously evolving into Cybermen to survive sudden environmental collapse. We have to speculate to join the dots, but it's not a wild thing to do. The surface of Mondas is, once again, uninhabitable for humans. The *DWM Cybermen* strip explicitly states it also leaves its new orbit. The Voord understand the problem and are ready for it - they now achieve their aim, and take control of the planet (presumably there are at least some other survivors), and build subterranean cities (or merely extend them - their base is already underground in "The World Shapers"). Perhaps the most highly-evolved Voord - the ones who had become the Cybermen at the end of "The World Shapers" - became the Committee from *Spare Parts*.

Spare Parts itself is set later - how much later isn't specified - when the people of Mondas are used to their sickly, subterranean life. Without the Worldshaper, while they know their destiny, the early Cybermen have had to learn the science of cybernetics gradually - until the fifth Doctor comes along, at any rate.

orbit decayed. All life on the planet was extinguished, except for the reborn Cybermen.

? - "The World Shapers" [152] **->** The sixth Doctor, Peri and Frobisher landed on a deserted area of the ocean on Marinus. They discovered a TARDIS and its dying pilot, who whispered "Planet 14" before dying, his regenerations exhausted. His TARDIS was an ostentatious new model that told the Doctor they had been sent by the High Council to investigate temporal disturbances.

Time had sped up on Marinus. The new TARDIS returned to Gallifrey, the Doctor and his companions to their Ship. The Doctor remembered hearing about Planet 14 in his second incarnation, but not the context. The travellers headed to the eighteenth century to meet up with Jamie McCrimmon - his companion at the time - to see if he remembered. As they left, a Worldshaper ship arrived at Marinus - Worldshapers reformed uninhabited planets, but were banned years before after the Yxia planetary system collapsed.

The Doctor's TARDIS arrived back from the eighteenth century a week later than it left... but the planet was a now rocky desert. The Voord captured the Worldshaper and used it to rapid-evolve themselves and sculpt time. They were becoming the Cybermen. The Doctor and Jamie sneaked into the Voord base and met the future Cyber Controller. Jamie sacrificed himself, aging to death to destroy the Worldshaper. Time accelerated so that geological processes occurred in front of the Doctor's eyes. The effect died down, and the Doctor emerged from the TARDIS to find a group of Time Lords present.

Marinus had become Mondas. The Doctor lobbied for the Cybermen to be prevented from coming into being, but the Time Lords told him things were in hand. After he had gone, they noted that in five million years, the Cybermen will have evolved into peaceful beings.

A sect from Mondas, the Faction, believed in total conversion into cyborgs. They were at odds with the mainstream, who viewed the technology as a last resort. The Faction left Mondas for Planet 14. [153]

? - SPARE PARTS [154] **->** The fifth Doctor and Nyssa arrived on Mondas when it was at the furthest point in its journey away from the Sun, on the edge of the Cherrybowl Nebula, "a crucible of unstable energy". Civilisation sur-

---

152 Dating "The World Shapers" (*DWM* #127-129) - The story is set no more than five million years in the past, as the Time Lords calculate that the Cybermen will become a force for peace in that time, and they haven't even by our far future.

The Doctor mentions the Fishmen of Kandalinga, from the first *Doctor Who Annual,* and the TARDIS initially lands on a platform very like the one seen in the illustrations from that story. However, as the name suggests, that story was set on the planet Kandalinga, not Marinus.

WHEN WERE THE CYBERMEN CREATED?: It's unclear when Mondas leaves the solar system. In *The Tenth Planet,* the Doctor says it was "millions of years" ago. The Cyberman Krang says it was "aeons", and an aeon is a billion years. But the Mondasians were "exactly like" humans when Mondas started to drift away. As the land masses of the "twin" planets of Earth and Mondas are identical, it seems logical that life evolved in the same way and at the same rate on both worlds (we have to gloss over the fact that aliens such as the Daemons and Scaroth accelerated human development on Earth, but presumably not on Mondas).

"The World Shapers" sets the origins of the Cybermen within five million years of the present day - the Time Lords, at least, believe the Cybermen will be a force for good five million years after their creation. David Banks, in both his *Cybermen* book and his novel *Iceberg,* dated Mondas' departure to 10,000 BC. *The Terrestrial Index* concurred. Banks suggested that the "edge of space" was the Oort Cloud surrounding the Solar System. The audio *Spare Parts* contradicts that, saying that Mondas reaches the Cherrybowl Nebula, and states that Mondas left orbit because of the Moon's arrival. *Real Time* says Mondas left "millennia" ago. In a story outline for a proposed sixth Doctor story, *Genesis of the Cybermen,* Gerry Davis set the date of the Cybermen's creation at "several hundred years BC". *Timelink* notes that as the Fendahl planet was the "fifth" twelve million years ago, Mondas must have already left its orbit by that point.

Over the years, a number of fans - including myself in the first two versions of this timeline - have speculated that the Mondasians and the Silurians were contemporaries, linking the disaster that put the Silurians into hibernation with the one that threw Mondas out of its orbit. There's little to either support or contradict this in the stories themselves. The Cyberman design seems to echo the Silurian third eye at the top of the head, but the Cybermen clearly aren't cyborg Silurians. Not only are we told in *The Tenth Planet* that the Cybermen "were exactly like you [humans] once", the same story shows them with human hands, not reptilian ones. The *Cybermen* strip in *DWM,* though, ingeniously solves that problem by depicting the Cybermen as descendents of apes augmented by the Silurians.

In the Virgin edition of this book, I suggested that Mondas was subject to time dilation, explaining why the Cybermen weren't more advanced. *Timelink* and *The Death of Art* reached the same conclusion. However, the continents on Mondas are exactly like those on Earth, so this theory doesn't account for the

vived under the surface of the planet. Mondas was rife with diseases like TB, and "heartboxes" were common for cardiovascular problems. Mondas was ruled by a bionic group mind, the Committee, who were building Cybermen capable of working on the desolate surface of Mondas. The Cybermen were engineering a propulsion system to deflect Mondas away from the Nebula.

A scan of a tertiary lobe in the Doctor's brain suggested solutions to various organ rejection problems that had plagued the planet's Cyber-program, and the Cyber-templates were augmented with this new design. The Doctor realised he could do little to prevent history from unfurling as planned.

During the Miocene Era, around twenty five million years ago, the rocks on which Atlantis would later be built were formed.[155]

The Origins of Man

It's unclear when humanity evolved, and it depends on one's definition of humanity. Some estimates have men walking the Earth six million years ago. The scientific consensus in the 1970s was about four million.[156]

The evolution of mankind received a boost when the Fendahl skull arrived on Earth twelve million years ago. On a nameless planet in our solar system that no longer exists, evolution went up a blind alley. Natural selection turned back on itself, and a creature - the Fendahl - evolved which prospered by absorbing the energy wavelengths of life itself. It consumed all life, including that of its own kind.

The Time Lords decided to destroy the entire planet, and hid the fact from posterity. But when the Time Lords acted it was too late, as the Fendahl had already reached Earth, probably taking in Mars on its way through. The Fendahl was buried, not killed. The energy amassed by the Fendahl was stored in a fossilised skull, and dissipated slowly as a biological transmutation field. Any appropriate life form that came within the field was altered so it ultimately evolved into something suitable for the Fendahl to use. The skull did not create man, but it may have affected his evolution. This would explain the dark side of man's nature.[157]

The Doctor visited Mars before it became a dead world.[158]

---

identical continental drift, assuming such a thing affected the ancient Earth in the *Doctor Who* universe.
153 "Ten thousand years" before the novel *Iceberg*, which uses the same dating system as David Banks' other book, *Cybermen*. This schism is the given explanation for the difference in appearance - and apparent lack of contact - between the Cybermen from *The Tenth Planet* and *The Invasion*.
154 Dating *Spare Parts* (BF #34) - There is no dating evidence in the story itself. It takes place when Mondas is at its farthest point from Earth and the implication is that the return journey to Earth will be much faster than the outward one, as it will be powered. *Spare Parts* could, then, take place a matter of decades before *The Tenth Planet* (and further evidence for this might be the Mondasian society of *Spare Parts* resembles Earth's in the mid-twentieth century).

That said, while it's never quite stated, Mondas seems to have left the Solar System within the lifetimes of the older characters, not the "millions of years" the Doctor spoke of in *The Tenth Planet*. There's no indication that Mondas immediately set course for a return to the solar system. We know that the Cybermen didn't attend the Armageddon Convention (*Revenge of the Cybermen*) and that the Convention was signed in 1609 (*The Empire of Glass*), so that they were a force to be reckoned with by the seventeenth century.

I would therefore speculate that the Cybermen piloted Mondas around the galaxy for a long time (certainly millennia) before finally returning to their native solar system.

155 *The Underwater Menace*
156 When asked in *Autumn Mist* when humanity evolved, the Doctor says "the accepted figure's about half a million years, though its really nearer six". It's only one suggestion that human origins in the *Doctor Who* universe stretch further than conventional scientific wisdom would have you think. According to *Image of the Fendahl*, the Fendahl skull arrived on Earth twelve million years ago, just as the first humanoid bipeds evolved - this is eight million years before Dr. Fendelman had believed.
157 *Image of the Fendahl*
158 *The Creed of the Kromon*
LIFE ON MARS: The Fendahl couldn't have wiped out all life on Mars, as the Ice Warriors come from Mars and lived there at least from the time of the Ice Age on Earth (*The Ice Warriors*) until the twenty-first century (*The Seeds of Death*) and apparently far further into the future (*The Curse of Peladon*). It should be noted that in *Image of the Fendahl*, the Doctor only speculates that the Fendahl attacked Mars.

As it happens, *Image of the Fendahl* is not the only occasion that the show seemingly ignores the existence of the Ice Warrior civilisation on the Red Planet. *The Ambassadors of Death* has manned missions to Mars that don't encounter the Ice Warriors (yet they *do* meet another alien race there - one that's not from Mars itself). *Pyramids of Mars*, as the name suggests, has the Doctor and Sarah visiting a pyramid on Mars and never mentioning the Ice Warriors. We never see UNIT encounter the Ice Warriors, although *Castrovalva* has

c 12,000,000 BC - THE TAKING OF PLANET 5[159] -> A Celestis outcast became concerned that the Celestis base of Mictlan might attract the Swimmers - beings large enough to crush the universe. The outcast hoped to destroy Mictlan before this occurred.

Using a Fictional Generator, the outcast brought the Elder Things from HP Lovecraft's work to life in Antarctica. This attracted Time Lord shock troops from the future, who slaughtered the Elder Things and subsequently readied a fleet of War-TARDISes. They intended to break the time-loop around Planet Five, hoping to use the Fendahl trapped within against the Time Lords' future Enemy.

A wounded TARDIS created a time fissure that would later be exploited by Professor Fendelman. The time-loop was breached, but this actually released the hyper-evolved Fendahl Predator: a Memovore, capable of consuming conceptual thought. The Memovore consumed Mictlan, and thus destroyed the Celestis, before the eighth Doctor banished it to the outer voids.

By now, the planets Delphon and Tersurus had developed their unique forms of communication.

The first true human became aware of herself and immediately developed a sense of self-doubt. The Scourge had established themselves in our universe.[160] The owl evolved on Earth around this time.[161]

Ten million years ago, a derelict primitive TARDIS from the war against the Vampires began orbiting the planet Clytemnestra. Human colonists from the Earth Empire of the thirtieth century would mistake it for a moon, and name it Cassandra.[162]

Five million years ago on Earth, the climate of Antarctica was tropical.[163] Millions of years ago, an advanced civilization on Betrushia built an organic catalyz-er to test species for survival traits. The catalyzer exceeded its design and threatened all life it encountered, causing the inhabitants to build an artificial ring system that constrained the creature to Betrushia.[164] The people of Kirbili wiped themselves out millions of years ago.[165]

Millions of years ago, the neighbouring worlds of Janus Prime and Menda - respectively inhabited by giant spiders and a race of humanoids - ended a war. They agreed to build a doomsday device as a deterrent against further hostilities, and constructed a device that, if needed, would move a moon of Janus Prime and a moon of Menda into parallel orbit around the Janus System's sun. A hyperspace link between the two moons would then turn the sun into a black hole. The spiders later wiped out the Menda humanoids anyway, but not before the Mendans seeded Janus Prime with isotope decay bombs. This made the spiders devolve into savagery, leaving the doomsday device untouched until 2211.[166]

By the time of the Pliocene on Earth, the Martian civilisation equivalent of the Industrial Revolution had already taken place.[167]

Around 3,639,878 BC, a group of Tractites arrived from the future using a time tree. They established a colony on Earth, which threatened to wipe out humanity and give rise to a future where the Tractites controlled the planet. The eighth Doctor, aided by Jo Grant and Samantha Jones, arrived through time to try and prevent this. Jo obliterated the Tractites and their colony with a laser cannon, which prevented the aberrant future. The Doctor's Tractite ally Kitig stayed in this period to carve messages in rock for Jo and Sam to find 1.07 million years hence. At the end of his life, Kitig travelled back in time to destroy the time tree.[168]

Three million years ago, civilisation had started on Veltroch.[169]

---

the newly-regenerated fifth Doctor mimic his previous selves, and refer to an adventure with the Brigadier and the Ice Warriors. In *The Christmas Invasion*, UNIT knows that there are Martians, and that they don't look like the Sycorax.

Humanity hasn't got as far as Mars by *The Seeds of Death*, explaining why they don't know about the Martians. It's harder to explain why Zoe, who is from a time when the solar system has been explored, is unaware of them.

Some fans (as well as sources like the FASA roleplaying game) have concluded that the Ice Warrior civilisation was subterranean - a view that's practically taken for granted in the books and audios, even though there's no evidence for it on screen. The books and audios have made further attempts to explain why the Ice Warriors are not well-known to future humanity. In particular, *Transit* featured a genocidal war fought in the late twenty-first century between Earth and Mars.

Its vision of most Martians leaving the planet - with a few left behind as an underclass to the human colonists - is depicted in later stories such as *GodEngine* and *Fear Itself*.

Benny Summerfield is an expert on Martian history, but most accounts have her believing that the Martian civilisation is a dead one (or at the very least, that there are no Ice Warriors on Mars itself).

The Dying Days attempted to reconcile some of the UNIT-era accounts by depicting a Martian culture influenced by the Osirians, who are disturbed by a British space mission (and there's a fleeting reference to the aliens from *The Ambassadors of Death*). As it's set in 1997, it would explain why UNIT know what Martians look like in *The Christmas Invasion*, and some fans have interpreted the line in the TV episode as a reference to the book.

159 Dating *The Taking of Planet 5* (EDA #28) - It is "about 12 million years ago" (p71). The Elder Things

2,579,868 BC - GENOCIDE[170] **->** Captain Jacob Hynes, a genocidal UNIT member, arrived through time with a virus intended eliminate all mammalian life on Earth. Jo Grant and Sam Jones prevented him from releasing a deadly prion, and some primitive humans killed Hynes. A message from the eighth Doctor's Tractite ally, Kitig, enabled Jo and Sam to find the buried TARDIS and locate the eighth Doctor 1.07 million years in the past.

? 2,500,000 BC - FROZEN TIME[171] **->** The Martians gave one of their number, Arakssor, a life sentence because he wanted to lead his people to war. Arakssor and about twenty of his followers were branded as war criminals and frozen in Antarctica, with a group of Martians assigned to watch over them. The seventh Doctor arrived at this time, but the guards were betrayed and Arakssor's warriors broke free. A firefight led to everyone involved being covered in ice - the Doctor fell into freezing water and went comatose. Sediment congealed around him in the centuries to follow, and he would remain frozen until 2012.

A humanoid race sent probes out into the galaxy to build transference pylons, capable of teleporting people between solar systems at the speed of light. Ninety nine percent of the probe ships failed, but the remaining one percent allowed the Slow Empire to be established.[172]

The Ulanti were a race that developed a technique called "bio-harmonics", wherein they transformed their entire planet into a musical instrument and produced a natural melody using the biological rhythms of their ecosystem. The Ulanti homeworld was an unspoilt wilderness, and the music produced was incredibly sublime. Nonetheless, the Ulanti died out two million years ago. Some of their musical work survived in ancient alien scripts that wound up in the archives of the planet Nocture, and caused calamity there circa 2800.[173]

A million years ago, the Mastons of Centimminus Virgo became extinct.[174] The Hoothi made the first moves in their plan to conquer Gallifrey. They enslaved the Heavenites, keeping them as a slave race and turning their planet into a beautiful garden world.[175] The Tralsammavarians died out.[176] The planet Wrouth was an enormous diamond with a monetary value in excess of the number of molecules in the universe. For a million years the planet had been defended by war asteroids. In that time, it attracted a number of attackers, including the Daleks (driven away by the Doctor and Captain Nekro) and the Gantacs.[177]

The Ice Warriors of Mars had space travel a million years ago.[178] Around the same time, diamonds were formed in the remnants of a Jovian planet in the Caledonian Reef.[179] **The earliest splinter of Scaroth gave mankind the secret of fire in his efforts to accelerate human development.**[180]

The Thal civilisation had begun half a million years ago on Skaro, and writings survive from this time.[181] A quarter of a million years ago, the Monks of Felsecar began collecting objects and information.[182] **Two hundred thou-**

---

aren't the same as the Great Old Ones seen in Lovecraft's work, so there's no direct clash with this story and the appearance of the Great Old Ones elsewhere in the *Doctor Who* novels.

Delphon was mentioned in *Spearhead from Space*, Tersurus got a mention in *The Deadly Assassin* but didn't appear until the Comic Relief sketch *The Curse of Fatal Death*. According to *Alien Bodies*, the Raston robots are built on Tersurus.

160 *The Shadow of the Scourge*
161 *Just War*
162 *So Vile a Sin*
163 *The Seeds of Doom*
164 *St. Anthony's Fire*
165 *The Quantum Archangel*
166 *The Janus Conjunction*
167 *The Dying Days*
168 *Genocide*. It's 1.07 million years before 2,569,868 BC.
169 *The Dark Path*
170 Dating *Genocide* (EDA #4) - The precise date is given (p260).
171 Dating *Frozen Time* (BF #98) - The Doctor, upon his revival, says he was frozen "millions of years" ago. There

is no evidence that Arakssor's imprisonment bears any relation to Varga's mission (*The Ice Warriors*), and it could substantially pre-date it.
172 "Millions of years" before *The Slow Empire*. The Empire lasts "two million years" once it has been set up.
173 *Nocturne*
174 *Slipback*
175 *Love and War*
176 *A Device of Death*
177 "A million years" before "Invaders from Gantac".
178 *The Dying Days*. They would send an expedition to Earth, as seen in *The Ice Warriors*. Its loss presumably convinced them to use their scarce resources another way, and put them off conquering our planet.
179 *Synthespians*™
180 *City of Death*. The earliest known use of fire was around 700,000 BC. Supporting this, the "second splinter" of Scaroth seen on screen is presented (somewhat confusingly) as a Neanderthal.
181 Measured from the time of *The Daleks*, which I place around 2263. The Doctor says that the Thal records "must go back nearly a half a million years".
182 *Love and War*

sand years ago, homo sapiens - "the most vicious species of all" - began killing one another.[183] As man evolved, the alien entity that the TARDIS dropped off on primeval Earth was summoned. It took human form and existed "on the edge of fear", always seeking the TARDIS.[184] The Lobri were created in the collective unconscious of primitive mankind. They were xenophobia incarnate, living symbols of our fear of the alien.[185]

The planet Hitchemus was 7/8ths covered by ocean, and the shifting climate there threw the genetics of the indigenous species of tigers into flux. A generation of tigers was born hyper-intelligent and built a weather control system. However, the tigers' progeny lacked the increased intelligence of their parents - presumably as a survival mechanism to prevent the tigers from over-developing their limited resources. Before passing on, the intelligent tigers built a hidden storehouse to preserve something of their developments. Intelligent tigers would sporadically be born in future, with multiple generations of instinctive tigers in-between.[186]

The First Ice Age

A Martian ship crashed on Earth, and became encased at the foot of an ice mountain.[187] Ice Warrior spaceship designs changed little after this time.[188]

One hundred thousand years ago on Earth, the First Ice Age began. By this time, two rival groups of intelligent primates had developed: Neanderthals and homo sapiens.[189] Another group, the Titanthropes became an evolutionary dead end. They possessed more intelligence than Neanderthals, but their innate hostility made them kill themselves off before the emergence of Homo-sapiens.[190]

The being named Light surveyed life on Earth for several centuries during the Ice Age. Ichthyosaurs were included in Light's catalogue, as were the Neanderthals. Around this time, the Doctor visited a Neanderthal tribe and acquired the fang of a cave bear.[191]

The Daemon Azal wiped out the Neanderthals. Race memories of beings with horns and their science survived in human rituals. Light had preserved a single specimen - Nimrod - and a few individual examples of the race survived for tens of thousands of years.[192]

c 100,000 BC - AN UNEARTHLY CHILD[193] **-> The first Doctor, Ian, Barbara and Susan met a prehistoric tribe which was struggling to survive "the great cold", and was in the throes of a leadership struggle between Kal and Za. Ian made fire, and the leadership dispute was settled in Za's favour when Kal was exposed as a murderer.**

c 100,000 BC - THE EIGHT DOCTORS[193] **->** The eighth Doctor observed his earlier self.

The Cold, a form of intelligence, evolved in the Siberian ice. It became dormant as the planet warmed, but would emerge in the savage winter of 1963.[194]

The box entity that the sixth Doctor flung into a space-time tear in 1965 fell into "the distant past", and arrived on a desolate asteroid. It would remain there so long, it came to forget the Doctor entirely. At some point in the ages to follow, a spaceship crashed on the asteroid and the box entity merged with a young boy to become The Wishing Beast. It would subsist off hapless travellers for three hundred years until the Doctor and Mel defeated it.[195]

The Galyari evolved as an intelligent lizard race that was descended from avians. They sought to overrun the homeworld of the Cuscaru, but the Doctor came into possession of the Galyari's Srushkubr, the "memory egg" deposited on

---

183 *The War Games*
184 "The Stockbridge Horror"
185 "Ground Zero"
186 "Hundreds of thousands of years" before *The Year of Intelligent Tigers*.
187 *The Ice Warriors*. Arden states that the Ice Warrior Varga comes from ice dating from "prehistoric times, before the first Ice Age". Arden's team have discovered the remains of mastodons and fossils in the ice before this time. In *Legacy*, the Doctor states that Varga "crashed on Earth millions of years ago".
188 According to Benny in *The Dying Days*.
189 *An Unearthly Child, Ghost Light*
    THE FIRST ICE AGE: According to *Doctor Who*, the Ice Age was a single event around one hundred thousand years ago. In reality there were waves of ice ages that lasted for hundreds of thousands of years as the ice advanced and retreated. We may now be living in an interglacial period. *An Unearthly Child* seems to take place at the end of the Ice Age: the caveman Za speaks of "the great cold" - although this might simply mean a particularly harsh winter. Similarly, the butler Nimrod talks of "ice floods" and "mammoths" in *Ghost Light*, and he's one of the last generation of Neanderthals. In *The Daemons*, the Doctor says that Azal arrived on Earth "to help Homo Sapiens take out Neanderthal man", and Miss Hawthorne immediately states that this was "one hundred thousand years" ago.
190 *Last of the Titans*
191 *Ghost Light*
192 *The Daemons, Ghost Light*. Science tells us that the Ichthyosaurs actually died out at the time of the dinosaurs. In *Timewyrm: Genesys*, Enkidu is one of the last Neanderthals. In reality, Neanderthals only evolved

every colony world. He destroyed it when General Voshkar of the Galyari refused to withdraw. This released a dose of neural energy that would taint the descendants of the Galyari present for generations. The Galyari left the planet, and their race later became nomads aboard a fleet of ships named the Clutch.[196]

The Doctor's role in this affair made the Galyari regard him as "the Sandman," a legendary killer of Galyari children. The threat of the Sandman's return helped to keep the Galyari's aggression in check.[197]

Scaroth, the Fendahl and the Daemons all continued to influence human development until the late twentieth century.[198] At some point mankind will become embroiled in a conflict with the Leannain Sidhe, an energy-based race dimensionally out of phase with humanity, existing in all eleven dimensions rather than the "visible" four but sharing the same planet. A truce between the two races will eventually be reached.[199]

The Gubbage Cones were the dominant empire in the galaxy.[200] The Master had a Vortex Cloak stolen from the ruins of the Gubbage Cone Throneworld on the edge of the Great Attractor.[201]

about one hundred thousand years ago and survived for about sixty thousand years, until the Cro-Magnon Period.

193 Dating *An Unearthly Child* (1.1) and *The Eight Doctors* (EDA #1) - Ian confirms in *The Sensorites* that the story is set "in prehistoric times". (*An Unearthly Child* itself never explicitly states that it's set on Earth, rather than another primitive planet.) Now that we know that the production team called the first televised story *100,000 BC* at the time it was made (the title appears on a press release dated 1st November, 1963), dating the story has become a lot less problematic. Anthony Coburn's original synopsis of the story also gives the date as "100,000 BC".

The first edition of *The Making of Doctor Who* placed the story in "33,000 BC" (which is more historically accurate), but the second edition corrected this to "100,000 BC". *The Programme Guide* said "500,000 BC", *The Terrestrial Index* settled on "c100,000 BC". *The Doctor Who File* suggested "200,000 BC". *The TARDIS Special*

claimed a date of "50,000 BC", *The Discontinuity Guide* "500,000 BC - 30,000 BC". *Timelink* says 100,000 BC.

194 *Time and Relative*

195 *The Vanity Box.* Events on the asteroid take place in *The Wishing Beast.*

196 *Dreamtime*

197 More than a hundred thousand years before *The Sandman.*

198 *City of Death, Image of the Fendahl, The Daemons.*

199 *Autumn Mist*

200 "Seventy thousand years" before *The Crystal Bucephalus* (p34). The fungoids on Mechonous in *The Chase* were named "Gubbage Cones" in the script but not on screen.

201 *The Quantum Archangel*

Antiquity

The ozone layer of Urbanka collapsed around 55,500 BC. The Monarch of the planet stored the memories of his population, some three billion, on computer chips which could be housed in android bodies. Monarch built a vast spacecraft and set out for Earth. The ship doubled its speed on each round trip, and the Urbankans landed and kidnapped human specimens.[1]

Cave paintings on one Mediterranean island date from the Cro-Magnon period, forty thousand years ago, demonstrating that a primitive human culture had developed by this time.[2] Around 35,500 BC, the Urbankans kidnapped the Australian Aborigine Kurkurtji and other members of his race.[3] An Onihr captain took command of a vast Onihr ship thirty thousand years ago. In the twenty-first century, the same Onihr captain would seek to acquire time-travel technology on Earth.[4]

29,185 BC (24th May) - ONLY HUMAN[5] **->** The ninth Doctor and Rose arrived from the twenty-first century, on the trail of a "dirty rip" time engine. They quickly discovered a group of researchers from the far future who were monitoring the local Neanderthal tribe. Rose accidentally married the prince of the caveman tribe, Tillun, while the Doctor discovered that Chantal - one of the time travellers - had engineered fearsome Hy-Bractor creatures. She planned to release them, changing history to wipe out the inferior homo sapiens. The Doctor defeated her.

The Neanderthals died out around twenty eight thousand years ago.[6]

The T'Zun began space conquests around 23,000 BC. They defeated the fungoid Darkings of Yuggoth, but their genetic structure became corrupted and they mutated into three subspecies.[7] The energy fields of the dormant Permians influenced the early Inuit legends.[8]

Two Krynoid pods landed in Antarctica in the Late

---

1 *Four to Doomsday*

MONARCH'S JOURNEY: There is a great deal of confusion about the dates of Monarch's visits to Earth, as recorded in *Four to Doomsday*. The story is set in 1981. The Greek named Bigon says he was abducted "one hundred generations ago [c.500 BC], and this is confirmed by Monarch's aide Enlightenment - she goes on to say that the visit to ancient Greece was the last time the Urbankans had visited Earth. Bigon says that the ship last left Urbanka "1250 years ago", that the initial journey to Earth took "20,000 years" and that "Monarch has doubled the speed of the ship on every subsequent visit."

This is complicated, but the maths do work. The speed only doubles every time the ship arrives at *Earth*, perhaps because of some kind of slingshot effect. Monarch's ship left Urbanka for the first time in 55,519 BC, it arrived at Earth twenty thousand years later (35,519 BC), the speed doubled so the ship arrived back at Urbanka ten thousand years later (25,519 BC), it returned to Earth (15,519 BC), the speed doubled and the ship travelled back to Urbanka (arriving 10,519 BC). Monarch returned to Earth (in 5519 BC), the speed doubled once again and the ship arrived back at Urbanka (in 3019 BC). The ship made its final visit to Earth around 519 BC, and now the trip back to Urbanka only took 1250 years. The ship left Urbanka (731 AD) and reached Earth in 1981.

However, this solution leaves a number of historical problems - see the individual entries.

2 Peri has just turned down an opportunity to visit the caves with her mother at the beginning of *Planet of Fire*. Although filmed on Lanzarote and named as such in the story, the island in *Planet of Fire* shouldn't be

Lanzarote, as it was nowhere near any ancient Greek trading routes.

3 *Four to Doomsday*. Bigon states that Kurkurtji was taken "thirty thousand years" ago. Examples of Australian Aboriginal art that are at least twenty five thousand years old survive.

4 *Trading Futures*

5 Dating *Only Human* (NSA #5) - The Doctor and Jack calculate the precise date.

6 According to the Doctor in *Only Human*, which doesn't take into account the two survivors he met in *Ghost Light* and *Timewyrm: Genesys*.

7 "Twenty five thousand years" before *First Frontier*. Yuggoth is another reference to H P Lovecraft (it's his name for the planet Pluto).

8 "Twenty five thousand years" before *The Land of the Dead*.

9 *The Seeds of Doom*

10 "Eighteen thousand years" before *The Spectre of Lanyon Moor*.

11 *Four to Doomsday*. Bigon claims that Villagra is a "Mayan". Although the Doctor boasts of his historical knowledge, he then suggests that the Mayans flourished "eight thousand years ago", but the civilisation really dated from c.300 AD - c.900 AD. The Urbankans, though, don't visit Earth after 500 BC. It would appear that Villagra must come from an ancient, unknown pre-Mayan civilisation.

12 "A dozen millennia" before *The King of Terror*.

13 Martin says he's fourteen thousand years old in *The Tomorrow Windows* (p256).

14 "Eleven thousand years" before Nyssa's time, according to *Cold Fusion*.

Pleistocene Period, twenty to thirty thousand years ago. They remained dormant in the Antarctic permafrost until the twentieth century.[9] Around 16,000 BC, Sancreda, a scout of the Tregannon - an alien race with great mental powers - was marooned on Neolithic Earth.[10]

Around 15,000 BC, the Urbankans returned to Earth. They kidnapped the princess Villagra.[11] Circa 13,000 BC, the Canavitchi of the Pleiades begin conquering neighbouring star systems, building an empire that would eventually stretch over seven galaxies.[12]

The being named Martin was born on Frantige Two, a dull planet and home to a species with an extraordinarily long lifespan. He would live fourteen thousand years into the twenty-first century.[13]

Circa 9000 BC, Traken outgrew its dependency on robots.[14] Around 8000 BC, the Euterpian civilisation died out.[15] Around the same time, the Jex from Cassiopeia started their conquests. They would eventually dominate several galaxies, including a planet in the Rifta system where the Doctor encountered them.[16]

The wolf-like Valethske had worshipped the insectile Khorlthochloi as gods, but the Khorlthochloi believed the Valethske were becoming too dominant. They destroyed the Valethske warfleets, and released a plague that devastated the race. The Valethske swore vengeance for this affront.

The Khorlthochloi later found a means of abandoning their physical bodies for a higher plane of existence. A threat to their new forms made the Khorlthochloi try to reunite with their bodies, but this proved impossible, as the bodies had become too independent. The threat killed off the Khorlthochloi's minds, but their bodies lived on as sedate herds of giant beetles.[17]

About ten thousand years ago, the inhabitants of a dying planet encoded everything about their world - including genetic information on its plant life, animal life and inhabitants - onto a crystal. This was dispatched via a slow-traveling spaceship to another solar system, in the hope that the pre-programmed crystal would rebuild their civiliza-

tion and preserve its history. When word of this endeavour spread, half the races in the universe coveted the crystal and its transport was obliterated. The Doctor acquired the crystal itself, but the item's magnetic fields ruled out the possibility of it undergoing time travel. He therefore deposited the crystal for safekeeping in Earth's past, where various royalty guarded it for millennia. The fifth and seventh Doctors arranged to retrieve the crystal in the 1960s - the same period that the spaceship had been due to arrive at its destination.[18]

Around ten thousand years ago, humanity developed the wheel - with a helping hand from Scaroth.[19] **Around the same time, in the Prion planetary system, the Zolfa-Thurans developed a powerful weapon. When the Dodecahedron, a power-source, was aligned with the giant Screens of Zolfa-Thura, an energy beam - "a power many magnitudes greater than any intelligence has ever controlled" - was formed. The beam was capable of obliterating any point in the galaxy.**

Zolfa-Thura fell into bloody civil war, and everything on the planet's surface except the Screens was devastated. The Dodecahedron was taken to Zolfa-Thura's sister-planet, Tigella, where the Deons worshipped it.[20]

Around 6000 BC, the humanoid Thains, arch-enemies of the Kleptons, died out.[21] Circa 5900 BC, the inhabitants of Proxima 2 created the Centraliser, which linked them telepathically.[22] **Around 5500 BC, the Urbankans visited Earth for the third time. The Urbankans kidnapped the mandarin Lin Futu, along with a number of dancers.**[23]

The Mogor, a warlike race, lived on Mekrom.[24]

Seven thousand years ago in the Nile delta, the Egyptian civilisation was flourishing. A variety of extra-terrestrials visited Egypt around this time, and they were seen as gods: Khnum was either one of the Daemons or a race memory of them, and Scaroth posed as an Egyptian god and Pharaoh around this time, building the earliest Pyramids.[25]

---

15 "Ten thousand years" before *Invasion of the Cat-People*.

16 "Ten thousand years" before *King of Terror*.

17 "Many thousands of years" before *Superior Beings*.

18 *The Veiled Leopard*

19 *City of Death*. Scaroth says that he "turned the first wheel". Archaeologists think that mankind discovered the wheel around 8000 BC.

20 "Ten thousand years" before *Meglos*.

21 "Ten thousand years" before *Placebo Effect*.

22 "Eight thousand years" before *The Face-Eater*.

23 *Four to Doomsday*. There is no "Futu dynasty" in recorded Chinese history. The Doctor has heard of it, however, and claims it flourished "four thousand years

ago". The date does not tie in with the details of Monarch's journey as described in the rest of the story. Archaeologists have discovered a piece of tortoiseshell with a character from the Chinese alphabet on it that is seven thousand years old, so it seems that an early Chinese civilisation was established by that time, and the timescale does tie in with the dates established by Bigon.

24 "Six thousand years" before "Echoes of the Mogor".

25 *The Daemons, City of Death*

The Osirians

By 5000 BC, the highly-advanced Osirian race had influenced the cultures of many planets, including Earth, Mars, Youkali (the scene of a devastating battle between the Osirians and Sutekh) and Exxilon.[26]

Osirian technology depended on magnetic monopoles, and the Osirians set about building a power relay system on Earth. The Sphinx was carved from living rock, built to serve as a dispersal point. The Osirians then left instructions on how to build pyramids to serve as receptacles for their power. They either constructed similar pyramids and a Sphinx on Mars, or found a religiously fanatical group to do it for them.

The face of the Sphinx originally had perfect alignment with the path of the sun, but this became imperfect as the angle of the Earth altered over time. Also, sand would periodically cover the Sphinx and fog the reception. The Sphinx was equipped with a mental pulse that would influence individuals to dig it out.[27]

The Osirians fought a war in our solar system. Sutekh, also known as the Typhonian Beast, and his sister Nephthys captured Osiris and sent him into space in a capsule without life support. **Sutekh destroyed his homeworld of Phaester Osiris and left a trail of destruction across half the galaxy. Sutekh became known by many names, including Set, Sadok and Satan.**[28] Sutekh and Nephthys tracked the body of Osiris to Egypt and totally destroyed it.

Osiris' sister-wife Isis looked for her lost husband, and the remains of his mind endowed themselves in the mind of her spacecraft pilot. This psi-child became Osiris' son Horus. **Along with seven hundred and forty of his fellow Osirians, Horus located Sutekh on Earth, trapping** and sealing him in a pyramid. Nephthys was imprisoned in a human body and mummified. Her mind was fragmented, the evil side placed in a canopic jar. **The Pyramid of Mars was built to house the Eye of Horus, and the Osirians set up a beacon there to broadcast a warning message. The Egyptians worshipped Horus and the other Osirians. Even Sutekh was worshipped by many on Earth, and the Cult of Sutekh survived for many thousands of years.** The influence of the Osirians brought on the unification of the Egyptian kingdoms, and the local humans were genetically enhanced, becoming taller and with increased mental capacity.[29]

The original face of the Sphinx on Earth was that of Horus.[30]

Around 3600 BC, a Sontaran ship landed in Ancient Egypt. Its pilot was worshipped as the Toad-God Sontar and set the natives to work building an ion cannon emplacement. The Sontaran planned outflank the Rutans with it, even knowing that the Rutan counterstrike would destroy the planet. A priest learned of these plans, and had Sontar entombed.[31]

Around 3500 BC, the Trakenite living god Kwundaar re-engineered Traken's sun to become a vast computer - the Source - which regulated the climate, provided energy, stored information and destroyed all who were evil. With the Source performing such duties, the people of Traken had no further need for a god and exiled Kwundaar from their star system.[32]

On Earth, the classical Greek Gods were long-lived beings with psionic abilities. They had forgotten their origins. Some of them believed they were aliens, although Hermes came to suspect they were an early mutation of humanity. Zeus, Poseidon and Hades were the oldest of the

---

26 *Pyramids of Mars. Return of the Living Dad, GodEngine* and *The Quantum Archangel* contain the further references.

27 All according to the Doctor in *The Sands of Time* (p233-235), who says the Sphinx was built "between eight and ten thousand years ago" (p234).

28 THE DEVIL'S IN THE DETAIL: Both *Pyramids of Mars* and *The Satan Pit* feature a god-like being - Sutekh and the Beast, respectively - who is said to be the inspiration for the Biblical Satan. The two of them even sound the same (purely because Gabriel Woolf portayed Sutekh and voiced the Beast). *The Daemons* also features a devil-like being, but no-one in the story quite says that he's Satan - it's just that the Daemons have inspired myths of powerful horned beings. Finally, the *Torchwood* episode *End of Days* has another creature (named Abaddon) that's apparently of the same race as the Beast in *The Satan Pit*.

The Beast and Sutekh do not appear to be the same being - not if the Beast truly was imprisoned before the universe began, and only released in Earth's future - but the two beings' stories do contain parallels. Much of human mythology in the *Doctor Who* universe seems to be a mish-mash of dimly-remembered ancient encounters with alien races. It therefore seems possible - and forgivable - that people have elided legends of the Beast and Sutekh, although the extent of this isn't clear.

29 *Pyramids of Mars*, with additional detail from the novel *The Sands of Time*. Egyptian mythology can't decide on Horus' exact relationship to Set; *The Sands of Time* (p142, 158) solves this by making Horus a "psi-child" of Osiris, which simultaneously makes him Sutekh's brother and nephew. The Cult of Sutekh also appears in the New Adventure *Set Piece*. In the scripts for *Pyramids of Mars*, the name Osirians is also sometimes spelt (and is always pronounced) "Osirans".

30 *The Sands of Time* (p235).

gods, although they were not yet five thousand years old.[33]

The TARDIS came to be represented in some Egyptian hieroglyphs.[34]

c 2700 BC - TIMEWYRM: GENESYS[35] -> By the third millennium before Christ, man had developed irrigation, and the human race had developed from hunters into city-dwellers. In the Middle East, walled cities were built and a warrior aristocracy developed. The earliest human literature was written at this time, and commerce had begun between cities. The deeds of one warrior-king - and his contact with extra-terrestrials - soon became legend.

Gilgamesh refused the advances of the alien Ishtar, who had crashed near Uruk. Ishtar went on to the temple of Kish, taking the form of a metal snake woman, and had a vast temple built. The seventh Doctor, Ace and Gilgamesh travelled to the mountains of Mashu and contacted Unapishtim, a member of Ishtar's race, leading him to his prey. Ishtar infiltrated the TARDIS computer, and the Doctor ejected her into the Vortex ... inadvertently turning her into the Timewyrm, a creature foretold to herald the end of the universe. The Timewyrm became capable of independent travel through space-time.

Around 2650 BC, Zoser was one of the first Egyptian Kings.[36]

c 2650 BC - THE DALEKS' MASTER PLAN[37] -> The first Doctor was pursued to the time of the construction of the Great Pyramids by both the Daleks in their time machine, and the Monk in his TARDIS. The Doctor made his escape during a pitched battle between the Daleks and Egyptian soldiers.

Around 2350 BC, the inhabitants of Uxarieus had used genetic engineering to become a psychic super-race powerful enough to come to the attention of the Time Lords. They built a Doomsday Weapon, a device capable of making stars go supernova. The Crab Nebula was formed as a result of testing the device. Soon, though, radiation began leaking from the weapon's power source. It poisoned the soil and the race began to degenerate into primitives.[38]

Around four thousand three hundred years ago, the Chinese were making the first astronomical measurements with Scaroth's help.[39] Over four thousand years ago, an elemental "burning" entity was worshipped by various cultures on Earth. It was known as Agni the fire god in India, and Huallallo to the Peruvians.[40] **Four thousand years ago, the Futu dynasty was flourishing in China.**[41]

The space explorer Moriah conquered Krontep and built a civilisation there. He left the planet shortly after his wife Petruska killed herself. Their descendants, which would come to include King Yrcanos, would rule the planet for millennia.[42]

The Chronovore Prometheus and the Eternal named Elektra broke an ancient covenant to sire the Chronovore Kronos. The Guardians spared the half-breed's life, but sealed him in a trident-shaped crystal prison and threw it into the Time Vortex. The crystal came to simultaneously exist on many worlds.[43]

Five hundred and thirty seven years before the fall of Atlantis, the priests of that land captured the god Kronos. At this time, a young man called Dalios was king. Kronos transformed a man, one of the king's friends, into a fearsome man-beast - the Minotaur. After this, the King forbid the use of the Crystal of Kronos, for fear of destroying the city.[44]

---

31 "The Gods Walk Among Us". The archaeologists estimate that the tomb is "5500" years old in 1926, so it was built around 3574 BC.

32 "2523 years" before *Primeval*.

33 *Deadly Reunion*. It's suggested the "gods" were the product of the Daemons' experiments.

34 Egyptian hieroglyphs were in use from 3200 BC to 400 AD. The TARDIS would not be represented as a phone box icon under such a language system - nonetheless, the Ship is plainly seen in some hieroglyphs in *Love & Monsters*.

35 Dating *Timewyrm: Genesys* (NA #1) - The Doctor says the TARDIS is heading for "Mesopotamia, 2700 BC".

36 "City of Devils"

37 Dating *The Daleks' Master Plan* (3.4) - The three time machines land at the base of a "Great Pyramid" that has nearly been completed. This might well be the Great Pyramid of King Khufu, built around 2650 BC. *The Terrestrial Index* pins the date at "2620 BC" whereas *The*

Discontinuity Guide offers a wider range of "2613 BC - 2494 BC". *Timelink* says 2635 BC.

38 *Colony in Space*. The date isn't given, but this is when the Crab Nebula was formed. It was first visible on Earth from 1054.

39 *City of Death*. Scaroth says that he caused "the heavens to be mapped", and mankind's first star maps were made in China around 2300 BC.

40 "Over four thousand years" before *The Burning*. The entity is drawn to Earth as the result of events in Siberia, 1894, in *Time Zero*.

41 According to the Doctor in *Four to Doomsday*.

42 Unspecified "thousands of years" before *Bad Therapy*.

43 *The Quantum Archangel*

44 *The Time Monster*

c 2000 BC - FALLEN GODS[45] -> The Titans had evolved at the bottom of the sea. Most left to live in the Vortex, but some remained on Earth as humanity amused them. Humans bound these Titans using special crystals. The Titans could manipulate time, and were compelled to grant the people on the island of Thera four harvests a year. They ended a war between Athens and Thera by stealing life energy from the Athenians - which was taken to be a plague - and using it to extend the lifespan of the elite on Thera.

Fiery demon bulls attacked Thera, and King Rhadamanthys believed that Athens was seeking revenge. However, the Titans themselves were causing the attacks, hoping the king would free them to repel the "invaders". Rhadamanthys was killed, and his son Deucalion succeeded him. Deucalion felt the Titans' abilities had been used unwisely, and ordered their crystals scattered far and wide, curtailing their power.

The blessings the Titans had bestowed on Thera were stolen from the future. In the times to come, the island would experience barrenness and a volcanic eruption.

Around 2000 BC, in the fourth year of the Twelfth Dynasty, Kephri the beetle god was one of the 740 gods that captured Sutekh. It was given an area of Egypt as a reward, but wanted the whole of Africa. Horus had it sealed in a casket, where it would wait, plotting revenge for four thousand years. The Doctor witnessed at least some of these events.[46]

c 2000 BC - "The Power of Thoueris" [47] -> The eighth Doctor easily defeated the "third rate" Osirian - the hippo-like Thoueris - while on holiday in ancient Egypt. Thoueris was devoured by crocodiles.

c 2000 BC - THE SANDS OF TIME[48] -> Tomb robbers entered the pyramid of Nephthys, breaking the canopic jar that contained her evil intellect. The Egyptian priests sought a pure vessel to contain it and chose the fifth Doctor's companion Nyssa, sealing her in a sarcophagus until the 1920s.

At around the same time, Cessair of Diplos, a criminal accused of murder and stealing the Great Seal of Diplos, arrived on Earth. She posed as a succession of powerful women over the millennia, while her ship remained in hyperspace above Boscombe Moor in Damnonium, England. Around this time, a stone circle named the Nine Travellers was set up. Subsequent attempts to survey the circle proved hazardous.[49]

In 1936 BC, the Emperor Rovan Cartovall of the planet Centros became bored with his imperial life. He disappeared without a trace, and took the immense palace treasury with him. His younger brother Athren succeeded him to the throne. The mystery of Rovan and his missing treasure became legendary.[50]

An alien race - possibly as an experiment, possibly as part of a battle - released two viruses, Fear and Loathing, into Jupiter's atmosphere. They would remain there for millennia, and grapple with each other for supremacy.[51]

---

45 Dating *Fallen Gods* (TEL #10) - It's "the Bronze Age" (p91). This is a retelling of the creation of the Atlantis as related in *The Time Monster*.

46 "The Curse of the Scarab". The casket is "four thousand" years old. The fourth year of the twelfth dynasty would be around 1988 BC. *Pyramids of Mars* placed the imprisonment of Sutekh "seven thousand" years ago, but this dating does coincide with the dating given for events of *The Sands of Time*, perhaps suggesting that the Osirians maintained some sort of presence in ancient Egypt for millennia.

47 Dating "The Power of Thoueris" (*DWM* #333) - No date is given, and this is clearly not the height of Osirian power, so I've placed it at the same time as events of the backstory for "The Curse of the Scarab".

48 Dating *The Sands of Time* (MA #22) - The date is given (p57).

49 *The Stones of Blood*. *The Terrestrial Index* dated Cessair's arrival on Earth at "3000 BC", but this contradicts the Doctor and Megara, both of whom claim that only "four thousand" years have elapsed since Cessair came to Earth.

50 "Five thousand years" before *The Ultimate Treasure*.

51 "Thousands of years" (p236) before *Fear Itself*.

52 *Deadly Reunion* (p115). The first part of the book takes place in 1944, and Persephone says she is three thousand, seven hundred and two years old.

53 "Several millennia" before "Invaders from Gantac". The Daleks do not appear to have been created until after this point, so the ones referred to here must be time travellers.

54 Dating *The Time Monster* (9.5) - The traditional date for the fall of Atlantis is around 1500 BC, and the Doctor states on returning to the twentieth century at the end of this story that it was "three thousand five hundred years ago".

The Terrestrial Index and *The Discontinuity Guide* both suggested the traditional date of 1500 BC, the FASA Role-playing game claimed 10,000 BC. *The TARDIS Logs* included the presumed misprint of 1520 AD. *Timelink* goes for 1529 BC.

55 *The Underwater Menace*

56 *The Underwater Menace, The Daemons*

THE FALL OF ATLANTIS: We hear of / witness the destruction of Atlantis in three stories: *The Underwater Menace*, *The Daemons* and *The Time Monster*. In *The*

In 1758 BC, the "goddess" Demeter gave birth to Persephone, the future beloved of Hades. The Greek gods passed into legend, and some attempted to live quiet existences among mankind.[52] The seventh Doctor helped the people of Wrouth defeat the Daleks "in '38".[53]

The Fall of Atlantis

c 1500 BC - THE TIME MONSTER[54] **->** The Master arrived in Atlantis, claiming to be the emissary of the gods. King Dalios didn't believe the stranger, who seduced his wife, Queen Galleia. The Master and the Queen plotted to steal the Crystal of Kronos. King Dalios died of a broken heart, and the Master seized power, proclaiming himself King. Queen Galleia, filled with remorse, ordered his arrest. The Master released Kronos the Chronovore, and Atlantis was destroyed.

Some Atlanteans survived beneath the ocean, off the Azores.[55] The Daemons would later claim to have destroyed Atlantis.[56]

The Ikkaban Period of Yemayan history was in progress around 1500 BC.[57]

The Great Sphinx was now buried up to its neck by sand. It mentally influenced the young Thutmose, who was on a hunting trip, to dig it out.[58]

Erimem ush Imteperem, "Daughter of Light", was born to the Pharoah and one of his sixty concubines, Rubak.[59] When Erimem was a child, her father the Pharoah -

Amenhotep II - trapped the Great Old Ones in a pyramid in the Himalayas.[60]

Erimem's father, Ahmenhotep II, defeated a rival king and came to possess the alien crystal that the Doctor had deposited on Earth many millennia previous. Ahmenhotep II also claimed one thousand slaves and the rival king's sister as a wife, but he prized the crystal most of all. The crystal was regarded as a diamond; it had many names, but became known as "the Veiled Leopard" because it almost seemed to glow, and possessed odd spots that looked like leopard markings.

When her father died, Erimem ordered priests to place the diamond inside Ahmenhotep's bandages as he was prepared for burial. The Leopard was later separated from his body - possibly owing to graverobbing - and become known as one of the world's most famous jewels.[61]

c 1400 BC - THE EYE OF THE SCORPION[62] **->** Erimem's father had died, and her three half-brothers had died in mysterious circumstances. She was now ruler of Egypt. A starship containing prisoners crashed near Thebes, and a stasis box containing a dangerous gestalt energy being broke open. It began possessing local mercenaries. The fifth Doctor and Peri joined forces with Erimem to defeat it. Following this, Erimem joined the Doctor on his travels.

The face of the Sphinx was damaged, and Peri whimsically issued orders that it be reconstructed with Elvis' features, confident that Napoleon's troops would damage it in the late eighteenth century.

Underwater Menace, the island in question is in the Atlantic, and in *The Time Monster*, "Atlantis" is another name for the Minoan civilisation in the Mediterranean. In *The Daemons*, Azal warns the Master that "My race destroys its failures. Remember Atlantis!". *The Terrestrial Index* attempts to explain this by suggesting that the Daemons supplied the Minoan civilisation with the Kronos Crystal. This might be true, but there is no hint of it on screen.

57 *SLEEPY* (p102).

58 As theorised by the Doctor in *The Sands of Time* (p234). Thutmose ruled Egypt as Menkheperura Thutmose IV from 1400-1390 BC and was actually a prince, but the need to have Erimem on the throne in this era rules against his having such a lineage in the *Doctor Who* universe. Historically, Thutmose was the son of Amenhotep II, whom *The Roof of the World* also names as Erimem's father. However, Thutmose and Erimem explicitly can't be siblings, as she would never have ascended to the throne in *The Eye of the Scorpion* if one of her brothers had been alive. Some Egyptologists believe that Thutmose's restoration of the Sphinx sealed his right to become Pharoah, which suggests in *Doctor Who* terms that he wasn't a blood-

heir but ascended after Erimem on the merit of his works.

59 *The Eye of the Scorpion*. Erimem is "seventeen" when she joins the Doctor.

60 *The Roof of the World*

61 *The Veiled Leopard*

62 Dating *The Eye of Scorpion* (BF #24) - The Doctor estimates the date as "about 1400 BC" from hieroglyphics. This story has the Doctor and Peri visiting a chamber *under* the Sphinx, which suggests that if the statue was previously buried up to its neck, Thutmose had, at the very least, enacted much of its restoration by this time. Writer Iain McLaughlin had privately decided that Fayum would get renamed and become the historical Thutmose, but nothing was ever scripted to substantiate this. That being the case, it's probable - until proven otherwise - that Fayum and Thutmose were separate individuals, that Fayum had a very short rule, was succeeded by Thutmose and - like Erimem - was lost to history.

Peri's claim that Napoleon's troops damaged the Sphinx's face (historically, they arrived in Egypt in 1798) owes to an urban legend that they used it for target practice. The Doctor doesn't correct Peri on this point,

1366 BC - SET PIECE[63] -> Fleeing from the Ants, Ace spent some time in Egypt during the rule of Pharaoh Akhenaten. She served as a bodyguard to Lord Sedjet, but escaped through a time rift.

The Monk helped build Stonehenge using anti-gravity lifts.[64] The Ragman had been born at the other end of the universe as a psionic force. It had travelled on Earth in a stone, drawn to the power inherent in Earth's ley lines. The rock containing the Ragman was incorporated into the stone circle at Cirbury, and the creature was dormant.[65]

Classical History

The Doctor claimed to have met Theseus.[66] The Rani was present at the Trojan War, extracting a chemical from human brains.[67]

c 1184 BC - THE MYTH MAKERS[68] -> Captured by the Greeks outside Troy, the first Doctor was given two days to come up with a scheme to end the ten-year siege. He rejected the idea of using catapults to propel the Greeks over the walls of Troy - if only after Agamemnon insisted that the Doctor would be the first to try such a contrivance - and came up with the idea of using a wooden horse containing Greek troops.

Vicki left the Doctor's company and re-named herself Cressida. Katarina, the prophetess Cassandra's handmaiden, joined the Doctor on his travels.

Vicki and Troilus married, but the Trojans came to believe that she was cursed or possessed. While Prince Aeneas and the main party traveled onward, Vicki and Troilus settled in Carthage. They had two children - "two young heroes", as Vicki called them.[69]

1164 BC - FROSTFIRE[70] -> Vicki wept alone one day, and came to discover the Cinder - all that remained of the phoenix she had encountered in 1814 AD - amongst her tears. She contained the Cinder in an oil lamp, and kept it beneath the Temple of Astarte. It amused her to call the Cinder "Frosty", and to visit it and share memories of the Doctor.

Knowing that the phoenix would devour Earth if it hatched again, Vicki cared for the Cinder - and thereby set up a loop that would end its cycle of rebirth. The Cinder would remain in Carthage until the nearby city of Tunis arose, then become part of Captain McClavity's Collection of Curiosities in the nineteenth century - and then travel back with Vicki again to ancient Troy.

At this time, Troilus was supervising the building of a new quinquereme.[71]

The Sorshans let the hostile Lom past their planetary defence shield, then reactivated it and released a biological toxin - deliberately killing themselves and their planet to prevent the Lom from spreading.[72] The Doctor was given a copy of the *I Ching* by Wen Wang.[73]

Thousands of years ago, the Exxilons were "the supreme beings of the universe... Exxilon had grown old before life began on other planets". Archaeologist Bernice Summerfield once wrote, "There are half a dozen worlds where the native languages develop up to a point, and then are suddenly replaced by one of the Exxilon ones."

Worlds visited by the Exxilons include Yemaya and Earth, where they helped to build temples in Peru. The Doctor visited one of these temples at some point after this date, and examined the carvings there.

On their home planet, the Exxilons created one of the Seven Hundred Wonders of the Universe: their City, a vast complex designed to last for all eternity. It

---

but there's otherwise no evidence that Napoleon's troops perpetrate the crime in the *Doctor Who* universe. In the real world, at least, erosion is the far more likely culprit.
63 Dating *Set Piece* (NA #35) - The date is given as "1366 BCE".
64 *The Time Meddler*. The earliest parts of Stonehenge were built around 2800 BC, but the final building activity occurred between 1600-1400 BC.
65 *Rags* (p160).
66 *The Horns of Nimon*
67 *The Mark of the Rani*
68 Dating *The Myth Makers* (3.3) - The traditional date for the fall of Troy is 1184 BC, although this date is not given on screen. The Doctor mentions being at the fall of Troy in *The Unquiet Dead*.
69 *Frostfire*

70 Dating *Frostfire* (BF *The Companion Chronicles* #1) - The audio booklet concurs on a dating of 1184 BC for *The Myth Makers*, and the back cover dates the story to 1164 BC, something that is reiterated within the story.
71 *Frostfire*. A quinquereme is an oar-powered warship, and was developed from the earlier trireme. It was in use from fourth century BC to the first century AD.
72 "Three thousand years" before "The Grief".
73 *Timewyrm Revelation* (p14). Wang was the last king of the Shang Dynasty.
74 *Death to the Daleks*. The Peruvian temples influenced by the Exxilons are around three thousand years old, so the collapse of Exxilon civilisation must be after that. In *SLEEPY*, Benny detects Exxilon influence in the Yemayan pyramid, dating from around "1500 BCE".
75 *Mawdryn Undead*. The ship has been in orbit for "three thousand years" according to the Doctor.

was given a brain to protect, repair and maintain itself, and thus it no longer needed the Exxilons, who were driven from the City and degenerated into primitives.

The City needed power, and began to absorb electrical energy directly from the planet's atmosphere. The City also set an intelligence test that granted access to those who might have some knowledge to offer it. Over the centuries, a few Exxilons attempted the test, but none returned.[74]

At around the same time, Mawdryn and seven of his companions stole a metamorphic symbiosis generator from the Time Lords, hoping to become immortal. Instead they became horrific undying mutations, and the Elders exiled them from their home planet. Their ship entered a warp ellipse. It would reach an inhabited planet every seventy years, allowing one of the crew to transmat down to seek help.[75]

c 1000 BC - PRIMEVAL[76] **->** Kwundaar launched a bid to reconquer Traken. He engineered an illness for Nyssa, knowing the fifth Doctor would seek out Shayla, the greatest physician in Trakenite history. As Kwundaar expected, Shayla was unable to help and the Doctor approached Kwundaar himself. He implanted a psychic command in the Doctor's mind, thus getting the Doctor to deactivate Traken's defences. Kwundaar's forces consequently invaded the planet, but the Doctor tricked Kwundaar and harnessed the Source's power for himself. The Doctor thus became the first Keeper of Traken. He reactivated the defences, which destroyed Kwundaar, then abdicated and allowed Shayla to become the second Keeper.

On the planet Avalon, a technologically advanced race created a system that focused solar energy to deflect the abnormally large number of asteroids in their system away from their planet. They also built thought-operated nanobots that allowed them to affect matter and energy. This discovery prolonged the race's existence but made

their lives futile. They drained the machines of energy, but it was too late. Their civilisation fell, and the natives regressed to being reptilian cephlies, lacking all ingenuity.[77]

The Doctor met the Queen of Sheba.[78]

Evidence found by Professor Horner in the twentieth century suggested that pagan rituals took place at Devil's Hump at around 800 BC.[79]

Around 600 BC, a Nimon scout arrived on Earth and was killed by his own sword by Mithras, who was later worshipped throughout the known world as a result of his deed.[80]

The Doctor was present when Pythagoras discovered the connection between mathematics and the physical world.[81] Around 500 BC, the Doctor met Sun Tzu at least twice and discussed the *Art of War*.[82] The Doctor replaced Sun Tzu as the Chinese emperor's military advisor but wasn't terribly effective, as he kept holding conflict resolution seminars rather than fighting.[83]

Ancient Greece

The Daemons and Scaroth both influenced ancient Greek civilisation.[84] **The Athenian philosopher Bigon lived in Greece around two thousand five hundred years ago. In Bigon's fifty-sixth year, the Urbankans kidnapped him. For the first time in their visits to Earth, the Urbankans encountered resistance.**[85]

The Doctor visited Athens and saw the Parthenon being built.[86] **The Eternals kidnapped a trireme of Athenian sailors from the time of Pericles.**[87]

The Doctor wrote many of the Greek Classics.[88] **He met Alexander the Great**[89] **and Pyrrho**[90]**, possibly on the same visit.** The Doctor met Praxiteles, who sculpted the Venus de Milo.[91]

The first lighthouse was built at Alexandria, the fire of its lamp provided by Astrolabus. Within a year, starships began to land. "The city had become a crossroads in time. Past and future had conjoined - sorcery and science now

---

76 Dating *Primeval* (BF #26) - It is "three thousand years" before Nyssa's time.
77 "Thousands of years" before *The Sorcerer's Apprentice*.
78 *Other Lives.* The Queen was a contemporary of King Solomon, who lived circa 970-928 BC
79 *The Daemons*
80 *Seasons of Fear*
81 *Option Lock.* Pythagoras lived 580-500 BC.
82 The fourth Doctor namedrops Sun Tzu in *The Shadow of Weng-Chiang*, and the seventh Doctor and Ace refer to meeting him in *The Shadow of the Scourge*.
83 *Set Piece*, during the "Fourth Century BCE".
84 *The Daemons, City of Death*
85 "One hundred generations" before *Four to*

Doomsday.
86 *The Spectre of Lanyon Moor.* This would be around 440 BC.
87 *Enlightenment.* Pericles died, age 70, in 429 BC.
88 *Cat's Cradle: Witch Mark*
89 *Robot.* Alexander lived 356-323 BC.
90 *The Keys of Marinus.* Pyrrho lived c.360-270 BC.
91 *Omega.* This would have been around 350 BC.

walked hand in hand." The aliens wanted Astrolabus' charts, and stole them. Alexandria fell, destroyed by a sea monster.

> "It was then that Voyager came ... from the realms of old time, from the dawn of myth ... the very spirit of legend."

Astrolabus attempted to navigate the timelines, but the disturbances were too great.[92]

The Doctor visited one of the Seven Wonders of the Ancient World, the Pharos lighthouse.[93] **The Great Wall of China was built around 300 BC.**[94] **At the time the Ch'in dynasty ruled in China, the Eternals kidnapped a crew of Chinese sailors.**[95] The first Doctor and Susan met Archimedes, and **the Doctor acquired Archimedes' business card.**[96] The third Doctor visited Athens and spent time with Archimedes.[97] The Doctor taught the playwright Eratosthenes at least some of his craft.[98]

On the planet Skaro, the Thals and the Kaleds went to war. During the first century of the conflict, chemical weapons were used, and monstrous mutations developed in the Thal and Kaled gene pool. To keep their races pure, all Mutos were cast out into the wastelands that now covered the planet. As the war continued, resources became more scarce for the foot soldiers - plastic and rifles gave way to animal skins and clubs, but both sides developed ever-more potent missiles. The war would last for a thousand years until there were only two cities left, protected by thick domes.[99]

In 210 BC, an alien intelligence imprinted the minds of Qin Shi Huang, the First Emperor of China, and two of his generals into a stone engram. They would remain dormant until 1865 AD.[100] The Jex brutally subjugated the Canavitchi, and killed two-thirds of them. The Jex's resources became strained, and the Canavitchi successfully revolted. They swore to eradicate their former masters.[101]

Two thousand years ago, Varan Tak from the Anthropology Unit on Oskerion was marooned in the asteroid belt when his spacecraft was damaged. He began collecting specimens from Earth.[102]

The Star Abacus of Beta Phoenii 9 was destroyed by the Paragon Virus in 87 BC.[103]

Ancient Rome

The Doctor met Julius Caesar.[104] The eighth Doctor, Fitz and Trix defeated Thorgan of the Sulumians. He had been planning to prevent the signing of the Treaty of Brundusium.[105] **At the height of the Roman Empire, the War Lords lifted a Roman battlefield.**[106] The Celestial Toymaker abducted a Roman legionary.[107] The Doctor, Jamie and Victoria attended a gladiator fight in ancient Rome, and Victoria was appalled by the violence.[108]

One of the splinters of Scaroth was a man of influence in Ancient Rome.[109] **The Doctor visited Rome, met Hannibal and Cleopatra, and was very impressed by the swordsmanship of her bodyguard.**[110] The captain of Cleopatra's guard was a "friend of a friend" to Ace, and taught her the art of sword fighting.[111] **The Doctor men-**

---

92 "Voyager"
93 *Horror of Fang Rock, Logopolis*
94 *Marco Polo*
95 *Enlightenment*
96 *City at World's End, The Two Doctors*. Archimedes lived c.287-212 BC.
97 *Island of Death*
98 *Eye of Heaven* (p181). Eratosthenes lived c.276-194 BC.
99 "A thousand years" before *Genesis of the Daleks*.
100 "Two thousand years" before *The Eleventh Tiger*. Historically, Huang ruled under the name "First Emperor" from 221-210 BC, and died in that year.
101 "Two thousand years" before *The King of Terror*.
102 "The Collector"
103 *The Quantum Archangel*
104 *Empire of Death*
105 *The Gallifrey Chronicles*
106 *The War Games*
107 "The Greatest Gamble"
108 *The Colony of Lies*
109 *City of Death*. He's listed as "Roman Emperor" in the script, but it's possible he's a senator or other Roman of

rank.
110 The Doctor has already visited Rome on his travels before *The Romans*. He mentions Hannibal (247-182 BC, he crossed the Alps in 219 BC) in *Robot*, and Cleopatra (68-30 BC) in *The Masque of Mandragora*.
111 *The Settling*
112 *The Girl in the Fireplace*
113 *Loups-Garoux*
114 Dating *State of Change* (MA #5) - The Doctor thinks that it is "the year 10 BC, approximately" (p41). Cleopatra died around 15 BC (p45). Terra Nova is part of the universe's timeline by the end of the story, yet despite its evident prosperity and technological advantage over humanity on the proper Earth, it's never heard of again.
115 *Matrix*. The Wandering Jew was a shoemaker or tradesman who mocked Jesus on his way to the Crucifixion, and was reportedly condemned to walk the Earth until the Second Coming of Christ. There is little Biblical evidence for this, but records of the legend go back to the thirteenth century.
116 *The Slow Empire*
117 *Human Nature*

tioned meeting Cleopatra once to Rose and Mickey.[112] According to the Doctor, Cleopatra herself had "the grace of a carpet flea".[113]

10 BC - STATE OF CHANGE[114] -> After watching Cleopatra's barge on the Nile in 41 BC, the sixth Doctor and Peri had decided to travel a little way into the future to follow the history of Rome. The Rani compelled a Vortex entity, Iam, to copy the Doctor's TARDIS console, but this also duplicated a section of the Earth around 32 BC, creating a flat disc-shaped world. The TARDIS console was duplicated and came to rest on the copied Earth, where it was regarded as an Oracle.

With information from this Oracle, the Roman Empire made great advancements. The battle of Actium went against Octavian and Agrippa because they faced opponents with steamships. Electric lighting, airships and explosives were developed. The culmination of this technology was "Ultimus", the Roman Empire's atomic bomb programme. Capable of kiloton yields, Ultimus could destroy any known city. Cleopatra's three children - Cleopatra Selene, Alexander and Ptolemy - ruled as a triumvirate.

The Doctor defeated the Rani's plans, and convinced Iam to relocate Terra Nova into the real universe. It settled into an unoccupied sector of space.

Joseph Liebermann, who would encounter the Doctor in 1888, claimed to be the Wandering Jew of legend.[115]

The Doctor visited the court of Caligula.[116] The Iceni, a Celtic tribe led by Boudicca, razed many Roman-occupied British towns to the ground.[117] **Roundstone Wood in England always "stayed wild", and in ancient times it was considered bad luck to collect wood there. The Romans in Britain stayed clear of it.**[118]

Iris claimed that Salome did the fan dance with the Doctor's scarf.[119]

64 AD - THE RESCUE[120] -> **The TARDIS landed on the side of a hill and toppled from it.**

64 AD - BYZANTIUM![121] -> The TARDIS had materialised just outside Byzantium. The Romans mistook Ian for a contemporary Briton and granted him some respect as a citizen of the Empire. Ian helped the Roman General Gaius Calaphilus and his political opponent, city praefectus Thalius Maximus, to settle their differences. Calaphilus and Maximus united efforts to purge corruption from the city, instigating a period of reform.

The first Doctor met the scribes Reuben, Rayhab and Amos, and helped them to translate the Gospel of Mark into Greek, producing a version that complemented the writings of Matthew the tax-gatherer.

Returning to the TARDIS, the travellers discovered that the Roman Germanicus Vinicius has found the TARDIS and taken it to his villa near Rome. They followed it there...

64 AD (June / July) - THE ROMANS[122] -> **The first Doctor, Ian, Barbara and Vicki spent nearly a month at a deserted villa just outside Rome. Becoming bored by the lack of adventure, the Doctor and Vicki travelled to the capital. Captured by slave traders, Ian and Barbara were sold at auction. Ian's ship was wrecked, and he ended up as a gladiator in Rome. Barbara became the servant of the Emperor Nero's wife, Poppea, and the object of the Emperor's attentions. The Doctor, meanwhile, was posing as the musician Maximus Pettulian (despite a complete lack of musical ability). When the Doctor accidentally set fire to Nero's plans to rebuild Rome, the Emperor was inspired. As Rome began to burn, the four time travellers returned to the TARDIS.**

A Dalek arrived in Roman Britain from the Time War, with orders to imprint the population with the Dalek Factor. Its capsule malfunctioned, and it was only able to release a tiny amount of the Factor before being buried.[123]

79 AD - THE FIRES OF VULCAN[124] -> The seventh Doctor and Mel arrived in Pompeii, just as Mount Vesuvius became active. The TARDIS was trapped in the rubble of a collapsed building, preventing their escape. The Doctor managed to antagonise the gladiator Murranus by beating him in a dice game. The Doctor and Mel escaped to the TARDIS just as the volcano erupted, destroying Pompeii and the surrounding area.

> = Temporal distortion resulted in an alternate history where Vesuvius took much longer to erupt, and the city's populace evacuated in their boats.[125]

---

118 *TW: Small Worlds*
119 *The Blue Angel.* Salome lived in the first century AD.
120 Dating *The Rescue* (2.3) - This happens right at the end of the story, as a literal cliffhanger. The date is established in *The Romans*, but *Byzantium!* establishes that the TARDIS crew have another adventure first ...
121 Dating *Byzantium!* (PDA #44) - This story takes place immediately before *The Romans*.

122 Dating *The Romans* (2.4) - The story culminates in the Great Fire of Rome. The TARDIS crew have spent "a month" at the villa.
123 Archaeologists date the site to "about 70 AD" in *I am a Dalek* (p24).
124 Dating *The Fires of Vulcan* (BF #12) - The story ends with the eruption of Vesuvius.
125 *The Algebra of Ice* (p15).

The tenth Doctor and Martha had some "unlucky business" at Mount Vesuvius.[126] Valnaxi refugees hid themselves and some of their works of art in a warren on Earth, to prevent destruction by their enemy, the Wurms.[127]

120 - THE STONE ROSE[128] **->** The tenth Doctor and Rose arrived in Rome, hoping to explain how a statue of Rose from the second century ended up in the British Museum in the twenty-first. They discovered a GENIE from the year 2375 and captured it, preventing the damage its reality-altering powers could cause.

Jack Harkness attempted to sell tickets to horse racing in second century Rome to the Cephalids, but they didn't understand the concept.[129] On a visit to Condercum, the Doctor debated military ethics with a group of Romans fighting the Caledonians.[130] A group of third-century Romans was kidnapped by Varan Tak.[131] The Romans drove the Celts from their lands. Gallifreyan intervention allowed King Constantine to pass into the parallel world of Avalon. Even while sleeping, Constantine ruled Avalon for two thousand years.[132]

A Roman legionary fell through the Rift to arrive in twenty-first century Cardiff.[133] Around 200 AD, the Doctor defeated a silicon-based life form called the Ogre of Hyfor Three - its foot ended up in the British Museum.[134]

The Demon Melanicus was a native of Althrace, a member of the race of Kalichura. He sought to conquer the advanced culture, generating legends of gods and demons. His armies were defeated and Melancius fled to third century Earth, where he came in a dream to the tyrant king Catavolcus. Melanicus bestowed great power on him and the secrets of time travel.[135]

c 275 - "The Futurists"[136] **->** Valente and Secundus, two Roman soldiers fighting in Wales, saw a strange green fire in the sky. Valente was enveloped in the energy. Shortly afterwards, the tenth Doctor and Rose arrived from 1925

and defeated the alien Hajor, who were attempting to master Time.

The Doctor challenged Fenric to solve a chess puzzle. When Fenric failed, the Doctor imprisoned him in a flask, banishing him to the Shadow Dimensions.[137] **By the end of the third century, the Old Silk Road to and from Cathay had been opened.**[138] **The Cult of Demnos had apparently died out by the fourth century.** [139]

> = In a potential timeline, the Daleks used time machines to invade Roman Britain in 305.[140]

= 305 - SEASONS OF FEAR[141] **->** The Roman Decurion Gralae worshipped Mithras, and had made contact with the Nimon, who posed as his god. They granted Gralae eternal life in return for his making sacrifices to them.

The eighth Doctor met Gralae at this time. Between now and his next meeting with the Doctor - seven hundred and fifty years later - Gralae would become known as Grayle, and spend eighty years repenting with monks. He married twelve times, all his wives dying of old age while he stayed young.

The Doctor sent some Nimon from 1806 to here, and rallied the Roman troops to wipe them out. He then rewrote history by buying out Gralae's commission before he met the Nimon.

A time warp briefly sent a Roman soldier to the late twentieth century.[142]

325 (May) - THE COUNCIL OF NICAEA[143] **->** In Nicaea, the Roman Emperor Constantine held a conference so that bishops could settle issues of dispute within the Christian Church. Among other concerns, the assembled council sought to decide the matter of Christ's divin-

---

126 *Made of Steel.* It's not specified that this was during the famous historical eruption.
127 "Two thousand years" before *The Art of Destruction*.
128 Dating *The Stone Rose* (NSA #7) - The date is given.
129 *Only Human*
130 *Ghost Ship*
131 "The Collector"
132 *The Shadows of Avalon*
133 *The Stone Rose*
134 *TW: End of Days*
135 "The Tides of Time"
136 Dating "The Futurists" (*DWM* #372-374) - It is "the late third century".
137 "Seventeen centuries" before *The Curse of Fenric*. The novelisation likens this contest to an ancient

Arabian tale that takes place in "the White City".
138 "A thousand years" before *Marco Polo*.
139 *The Masque of Mandragora*
140 *The Time of the Daleks*
141 Dating *Seasons of Fear* (BF #30) - The date is given.
142 "The Tides of Time"
143 Dating *The Council of Nicaea* (BF #71) - The year is given. The Doctor says the TARDIS has landed "a few days before the council is set to begin," but Athanasius more accurately says it is "the night before the council starts". Historically, the Council opened on 20th May.
144 *Eye of Heaven* (p181).
145 *Timewyrm: Apocalypse*
146 *Time and the Rani*. Hypatia of Alexandria, a neo-Platonic philosopher and mathematician, lived circa

---

ity. The deacon Athanasius believed Christ was divine, but the presbyter Arius held that Christ was subordinate to God. Erimem found Arius to be honorable and aided his cause, threatening to derail history. Tensions mounted, but the Doctor encouraged Constantine to defuse the situation with his oratory skills. In accordance with history, the Council adopted Athanaisus' views.

The Doctor was ejected from the staff at the Library of Alexandria after he misshelved the Dead Sea Scrolls.[144] The Doctor saved two Aristophanes plays from the destruction of the Great Library of Alexandria.[145] **The Rani kidnapped Hypatia to become part of her Time Brain.**[146]

In 375, Mongol hordes swept into central Europe ... and were wiped out by Nazi tanks.[147] The Doctor suggested that the joke "What's the most ruthless thing in the bakery... Attila the Bun!" was much funnier if you had known the man.[148]

In 514 AD, warfare broke out on the planet Q'ell. The Recruiter, a device created to destroy the Ceracai race, extended the war as part of its programming. The conflict would last until the twentieth century, and cause at least 2,846,014,032 casualties.[149] In the seventh century, Lord Roche's TARDIS crashed in England and died on impact. One of the Furies trapped within eventually starved to death, but the other survived until the Ship was discovered in 1999.[150]

The Doctor caught a huge salmon in Fleet and shared it with the Venerable Bede (who "adored fish").[151] Bede made the Doctor Dean of Westminster Abbey.[152] The *Necronomicon* was written by Abdul Al-Hazred, a mad poet of Sanaa, in Damascus around 730.[153] **Around this period, Monarch left Urbanka for the last time.**[154] **The Rani visited Earth during the so-called "Dark Ages".**[155]

The Galactic Heritage Foundation emerged as an organization to halt alien property development on planets with indigenous populations. In the eighth century, the third princess Tabetha of Cerrenis Minor spent a weekend in Lewisham. Despite her finding it all a bit gauche, Earth was accorded a low-level ranking of Grade 4, which put it under the Foundation's protection.

With planets under such development bans selling for cheap, the Frantige Two native named Martin "purchased a hundred or so worlds for next to nothing". Among his acquisitions, he bought the planet Earth for a few thousand Arcturan ultra-pods from a Navarino time-share salesman going through a messy divorce. The Navarino threw in the rest of Earth's solar system for free.[156]

The Doctor defeated the Tzun at Mimosa II in 733.[157]

> = "Sideways in time" on an Earth where the truth about King Arthur was closer to the myths of our world, a future incarnation of the Doctor was known as Merlin. During the eighth century, Arthur and Morgaine fought against one another, despite their childhood together at Selladon. The Doctor, who regenerated at least once during this time, cast down Morgaine at Badon with his mighty arts.
>
> Eventually, though, Morgaine was victorious and Arthur was killed. The Doctor placed Arthur's body and Excalibur in a semi-organic spaceship, and transferred it to the bottom of Lake Vortigern in our dimension. Morgaine imprisoned the Doctor forever in the Ice Caves, and went on to become Empress of the solar system.[158]

Godric, a swordsman in the age when Arthur ruled, found the Holy Grail in a freshwater spring. A wood dryad seduced Godric into her tree, where he slept until 1936. The Doctor once claimed to have taught Lancelot how to use a sword at King Arthur's court.[159]

370-415 AD.
THE RANI'S TIME BRAINS: The Rani kidnaps eleven geniuses before we see her plans nearing fruition in *Time and The Rani*. In the televised version only three of these are named: Hypatia, Pasteur and Einstein. The rehearsal script and the novelisation both mention three more: Darwin, Za Panato and Ari Centos. The novelisation also states that the Danish physicist Niels Bohr is kidnapped.
147 "The Tides of Time". The date is given - this is the opening battle of the Millenium (sic) wars. See the main entry (c 1983) for more.
148 *Memory Lane*
149 *Toy Soldiers* (p208). The novel takes place in 1919, and the war on Q'ell has been going on for "fourteen hundred and five years" by that point.
150 *The Suns of Caresh*

151 *The Talons of Weng-Chiang*. Bede lived c.673-735, although he never went to London, only leaving Jarrow once to visit Canterbury.
152 *Companion Piece*. This is a neat trick on Bede's part, as he died in 735 and the building of Westminster Abbey didn't start until 1050.
153 *The Banquo Legacy*. It was attributed to the Silurians in *White Darkness* (p89).
154 *Four to Doomsday*
155 *The Mark of the Rani*
156 *The Tomorrow Windows*
157 "Twelve hundred and twenty four Terran years" before *First Frontier*.
158 *Battlefield*. The archaeologist Warmsley thinks that Excalibur's scabbard dates "from the eighth century".
159 *Wolfsbane*

The Birth of the Daleks

Fifty years before the end of the war between the Thals and the Kaleds on Skaro, the Kaleds set up an Elite group, based in a secret bunker below the Wasteland. It was run by chief scientist Davros, the greatest mind Skaro had ever seen[160]

Details of Davros' early life are given in the Big Finish series I, Davros.

& 760 - DAVROS[161] **->** Although he continued to develop weapons - one of which sunk the entire Thal Navy in a day - Davros had come to realise the war was futile. Prolonging the war with the Thals and using increasingly deadly weapons would mean that soon Skaro would become a dead planet. He believed that no other world could support life, and it was impossible to end the fighting, as both races would inevitably compete to exploit the same ecological niche. Logically, the Kaled race could not possibly survive.

One of his research students, Shan, came up with what she called "The Dalek Solution", a plan to reengineer the Kaled race to survive the pollution on Skaro. Fearing that Shan would become a more brilliant scientist than him, Davros framed her for treason and had her hanged.

Davros was greatly injured, and the only survivor, when the Thals shelled his laboratory. He was given a poison injector to kill himself, as none of the Kaleds could bring themselves to put Davros out of his misery. At that moment, Davros realised how weak the Kaleds were and how true power was being able to grant life and death.[162]

Davros was crippled, but survived by designing a life support system for himself. He created energy weapons, artificial hearts and a new material that reinforced the Kaled Dome.[163]

? 760 - GENESIS OF THE DALEKS[164] **->** Davros succeeded in selectively breeding an intelligent creature that could survive in the radiation-soaked, environmentally desolate world of Skaro. Using the Mark III Travel Machines, the Daleks could survive in virtually any environment, even the dead planet.

The Time Lords foresaw a time when the Daleks had become the supreme power in the universe. They sent the fourth Doctor, Sarah and Harry to the time of the Daleks' creation, and gave the Doctor three options: avert the Daleks' creation; affect their genetic development so they might evolve in a less aggressive fashion; discover some inherent weakness that could be used against them.

The Doctor failed to achieve any of these objectives, but reckoned he set Dalek development back a thousand years. He reasoned that the existence of the Daleks would serve to unite races against them.

The Doctor's interference on Skaro spared thousands of worlds from enduring the Dalek wars. The Time Lords calmed the resulting time disruption.[165] **At some point, at least a thousand years later, the Daleks developed space travel and began their galactic conquests.**[166]

c 800 - "Doctor Conqueror"[167] **->** The seventh Doctor invented the game of conkers.

The Catholic Church founded the Library of St John the Beheaded in the St Giles Rookery, a notorious area of Holborn, London. The library contained unique, suppressed and pagan texts, including information on "alter-

---

160 *Genesis of the Daleks*
161 Dating *Davros* (BF #48) - The story fills in details of Davros' life around the time he first started to develop the Daleks, and fits just before *Genesis of the Daleks*.
162 *Davros*, drawing on sources such as the novelisations of *Genesis of the Daleks* and *Remembrance of the Daleks*. The circumstances of how Davros came to be in his life support system are never given on screen - it's described as "an accident", which doesn't directly support the idea it was in a Thal attack.
163 *Genesis of the Daleks*. There's no indication how old Davros was when he was crippled, or how much time passed between the accident and *Genesis of the Daleks*.
164 Dating *Genesis of the Daleks* (12.4) - The date of the Daleks' creation is never stated on television. *The Dalek Invasion of Earth*, *The Daleks' Master Plan* and *Genesis of the Daleks* all have the Doctor talk of "millions of years" of Dalek evolution and history. *Destiny of the Daleks*,

however, suggests a much shorter timeframe of "thousands of years", and Davros has only been "dead for centuries". The Daleks seem to have interstellar travel at least two hundred years before *The Power of the Daleks* (so by 1820), although *War of the Daleks* suggests those were time-travelling Daleks from the far future.
My dating of this story is derived from the *TV Century 21* comic strip (for full details, see the dating notes on "Genesis of Evil" [1763]).
165 *A Device of Death*
166 *The Dalek Invasion of Earth*, and most subsequent Dalek stories. Again, taking what the Doctor says at face value, the Daleks are set back a thousand years by the Doctor in *Genesis of the Daleks*.
167 Dating "Doctor Conkeror" (*DWM* #162) - No date is given, but it's set at the time of the Vikings.

ARE THERE TWO DALEK HISTORIES?: There are a number of discrepancies between the accounts of the Daleks' origins in *The Daleks* and *Genesis of the Daleks*. In the first story, the original Daleks (or Dals) were humanoid, and it is implied they only mutated after the Neutronic War. This version was also depicted in the *TV Century 21* comic strip, where the Dalek casings are built by a scientist called Yarvelling and a mutated Dalek crawls into a casing to survive. Whereas in *Genesis of the Daleks*, we see Davros deliberately accelerate the mutations that have begun to affect the Kaled race (a process the Doctor calls "genetic engineering" in *Dalek*).

Fans have attempted to reconcile these accounts in a number of ways. Perhaps the most common nowadays is to completely dismiss the version in *The Daleks*, and declare the Thal version of events to be a garbled version of the true history seen in *Genesis of the Daleks*. This would mean that the Doctor's comment that the Thal records are accurate is wrong - which isn't too difficult to justify. The idea that Skaro's civilisation lost knowledge following a nuclear war and that the two races would have subjective, propaganda-driven history is tempting... but it *doesn't* explain why both the Thals and the Daleks in *The Daleks* believe in exactly the same version of events, especially as they've had no contact with each other for some time. It's also suggesting that Skaro's historians are so incompetent that they can't tell the difference between a war that lasted a thousand years with one that lasted a day.

Another possible explanation is that the Doctor changes history in *Genesis of the Daleks* - before then, history was the version in *The Daleks*, afterwards it's the *Genesis* version. This is tempting, because altering history *was* the Doctor's mission, after all, and he says at the end that he's set the Daleks back "a thousand years". *The Discontinuity Guide* suggested that in their appearances after *Genesis of the Daleks*, the Daleks are nowhere near as unified a force as they had been before. Morever, Davros - who previously wasn't even mentioned - plays a major part in Dalek politics. *The Discontinuity Guide* credits all of this to the Doctor changing history, looking closely at the evidence, though, the Doctor hasn't actually made much of a difference. The Daleks are an extremely feared, powerful and unified force in the first of the post-*Genesis* stories (*Destiny of the Daleks*), and it's their defeat to the Movellans after that story which weakens them. In other words, no alteration of the timeline need be invoked to explain the change in the status quo. Perhaps the clincher is that *The Dalek Invasion of Earth* still happens in the post-*Genesis* stories - Susan remembers it in *The Five Doctors* (indeed, she's been snatched from its aftermath), and *Remembrance of the Daleks* contains references both to the Daleks invading Earth in "the twenty-second century" and to events on Spiridon (*Planet of the Daleks*). That's before factoring in the dozens of references to pre-*Genesis of the Daleks*

stories in the novels, audios and comic strips featuring later Doctors.

All told, it looks like the Doctor setting the Daleks back a thousand years in *Genesis of the Daleks* is part of the timeline we know, not a divergence from it - again, they still invade Earth in 2157, not 3157. With that in mind, it's interesting to note that the sixties strip has the Daleks developing space travel very soon after they take to their mechanical casings, but that this happens a thousand years after the end of the Thousand Years War (which we would later see ending in *Genesis of the Daleks*). If the Doctor hadn't been there, the Daleks would have developed space travel very soon after *Genesis of the Daleks*, and so the Doctor - as part of the original timeline - *has* set them back a thousand years.

There's a second problem: We have to reconcile the fact that *The Daleks* shows a group of Daleks confined to their city on Skaro and wiped out at the end, while all the other stories have them as galactic conquerors. Nothing in any *Doctor Who* story, in any medium, accounts for this.

The FASA roleplaying game and *About Time* both explain the discrepancy by theorising that soon after *Genesis of the Daleks*, there's a schism between Daleks who want to stay on Skaro to exterminate the Thals and those who want to conquer other planets. The FASA game names them the "exterminator" and "expansionist" factions, and states that the exterminator Daleks never leave Skaro, eventually wither on the vine and end up confined to their city - finally dying out in *The Daleks*. (In this scenario, spacefaring Daleks later recolonise their home planet.)

In *About Time*'s version, the "exterminator" Daleks do venture beyond Skaro, but only on limited sorties - like the invasion of Earth - and they're not galactic conquerors. There's nothing on screen to suggest an early divergence in Dalek history, and only a line in *Alien Bodies* (p138) supports it. *If* this was the case, it seems the spacefaring "expansionist" Daleks completely broke contact with the Daleks on Skaro. Adding speculation to speculation, we might infer this schism was because the Daleks on Skaro continued to mutate - indeed, perhaps they become the humanoid Dals mentioned in *The Daleks*, a different race altogether. Given what we know of Dalek history, it seems unlikely that this was an amicable arrangement, so there could have been a Dalek civil war of some kind.

While we're speculating, we might wonder if the Thals joined the Dals in their efforts to rid the planet of Daleks. Following this, the Dals and Thals lived together in (relative) peace on Skaro for a long time - until the Neutronic War, which I place in 1763. The spacefaring Daleks eventually return to Skaro - somewhere between *The Daleks* (?2263) and *Planet of the Daleks* (2540).

continued on Page 57...

native zoology and phantasmagorical anthropology".[168]

The imprisoned Fenric still had influence over the Earth and the ability to manipulate the timelines. He summoned the Ancient One from half a million years in the future. Over the centuries, the Haemovore followed the flask containing Fenric. It was stolen from Constantinople; Viking pirates took it to Northumbria. Slowly the Ancient One followed it to Maiden's Bay.

By the tenth century, a 9-letter Viking alphabet was in use, although the later Vikings used a 16-letter version. Carvings in the earlier alphabet claimed that the Vikings were cursed, and they buried the flask in a burial site under St Jude's church.[169]

Merlin banished the Demon Melanicus from our universe. Melanicus waited a thousand years for an opportunity to escape the black, formless void.[170] Viking legends referred to the Timewyrm as Hel.[171] The Doctor, Ace and Bernice were at an Angle settlement when the Vikings attacked it.[172] The Doctor met the Anglo-Saxon king Alfred the Great and his cook Ethelburg, "a dab hand at bear rissoles".[173] The Doctor became known as Shango the thunder god of the Yoruba tribe when he demonstrated static electricity.[174]

A thousand years ago, a new Keeper of Traken was inaugurated. The Union of Traken in Mettula Orionsis had enjoyed many thousands of years of peace before this time.[175]

c 1001 - EXCELIS DAWNS[176] -> By this time, numerous civilizations had come and gone on the planet Artaris. The populace was mostly relegated to communities living on mountainsides for defensive purposes. A nunnery emerged on Excelis, the highest mountain on the planet.

The fifth Doctor landed on Artaris and met the warlord Grayvorn, who was on a quest for "the Relic", a powerful

artefact and purported gateway to the afterlife. The Doctor also met the time traveller Iris Wildthyme, who couldn't remember how she ended up there. Grayvorn discovered the Relic, which was mysteriously shaped like Iris' handbag, but he soon went missing. The Relic's energies inadvertently made Grayvorn immortal.

The Doctor saved Aethelred the Unready from what would have been a fatal fever.[177] An amoral Time Lord used a twenty-fourth century flood controller to turn back the tide for Canute, giving him great influence. The Doctor set history back on course.[178] The Doctor met the eleventh century ruler of Ghana, King Tenkamenin, and they talked of philosophy.[179]

Around one thousand years ago, Martin instigated a get-rich-quick scheme that entailed the washed-up actor Prubert Gatridge going to planets that Martin owned and posing as a god. This was intended to seed "selfish memes" - philosophical concepts that would lead each world's populace to destroy themselves. Each genocide would lift the Galactic Heritage Foundation's development ban, allowing Martin to sell the worlds at fantastic profit.[180]

During the building of the Cathedral of St Sophia, a casket fell from the sky. It was believed to contain an angel and was placed in the catacombs.[181] In 1033, Clancy's Comet was mistaken for the Star of the West, sent to commemorate the millennium of the crucifixion.[182] **A monastery was established on the site of Forgill Castle in the eleventh century.[183]**

= During his time in the Godwins' court, Grayle was once bishop of all Cornwall. The Doctor defeated Grayle's plan to stockpile plutonium for the Nimon, and rewrote history to prevent Gralae from making contact with the Nimon in 305 AD.[184]

168 The Library of St John the Beheaded was mentioned in *Theatre of War*, and made its first appearance in the following NA, *All-Consuming Fire*. In that book we learn much about the library, including the fact that it has been established for a "thousand years" (p15). The library still exists at the time of *Millennial Rites*. In *The Empire of Glass*, Irving Braxiatel acquires manuscripts for the library (p245).
169 *The Curse of Fenric*. The Ancient Haemovore arrived in "ninth-century Constantinople" according to the Doctor. Ace says the inscriptions are "a thousand years old".
170 Melanicus has waited for "a thousand years" before "The Tides of Time". It's tempting to link the void he was in with "Hell", the gap between the worlds in *Doomsday*. Merlin here is the Merlin from our universe, a recurring character in the *DWM* strip, not the future Doctor who will pose as Merlin in a parallel universe according to *Battlefield*.

171 *Timewyrm: Revelation*
172 *Sky Pirates!*
173 *The Ghosts of N-Space*
174 *Transit* (p204).
175 *The Keeper of Traken*
176 Dating *Excelis Dawns* (BF *Excelis* series #1) - The story takes place a thousand years before *Excelis Rising*. See the dating of *Excelis Decays* (2301) for dating notes on the Excelis saga.
177 *Seasons of Fear*. The meeting is also mentioned in *The Tomorrow Windows*. Aethelred was king of England, and lived from circa 978 to 23rd April, 1016.
178 *Invaders from Mars*
179 *Transit*
180 *The Tomorrow Windows*
181 *Bunker Soldiers*
182 *The Ghosts of N-Space*
183 *Terror of the Zygons*
184 *Seasons of Fear*. The date is given, and it is exactly

...continued from Page 55

It might be straightforward, then: the "expansionist" Daleks are the ones with slats in their mid-section, the "exterminators" are the ones with bands (as seen in the first two TV stories, *The Space Museum* and the *TV Century 21* strip). However, the Daleks in *The Chase* are based on Skaro and are out to avenge the defeat in *The Dalek Invasion of Earth*, so that would also seem to be the "exterminator" faction (unless the first order of business when the "expansionists" return to Skaro is to go after the man who twice inflicted crushing defeats - and so wiped out - the "exterminators").

Alternatively, it could be that the Doctor changes history in *The Daleks* - his first encounter with them might affect Dalek development. We know from *The Evil of the Daleks* and *Dalek* that the Daleks can be altered by contact with aliens, particularly time-travelling ones. Their first contact with the Doctor in *The Daleks* might have been the catalyst that set any Daleks that survived on course to conquer the universe and challenge the Time Lords' supremacy. Again, though, there's no evidence from the series that this is the case - and every Dalek on Skaro appears dead at the end of *The Daleks*.

Ironically, the *one* thing fans seem to agree on is that the Doctor is simply wrong in *The Dalek Invasion of Earth* when he said *The Daleks* was set "a million years" in the future. At the time, it was the television series' own attempt (and in only the second Dalek story!) to explain the discrepancies in Dalek history, but virtually nobody credits the Doctor's statement now.

So ... reconciling the account given in *The Daleks* and *TV Century 21* with *Genesis of the Daleks* may not be as difficult as it appears, but merely needs a little *speculation* to smooth things over. The Thousand Years War ends in *Genesis of the Daleks* with the Kaleds wiped out and the first Daleks buried underground. These Daleks either leave Skaro to become galactic conquerors or they simply die out. For the purposes of this chronology, I'm going to assume the Doctor set the Daleks back a thousand years, so no Daleks leave Skaro at this time. Six hundred years later (according to *The Dalek Outer Space Book*), the Daleks evolved ... meaning the blue-skinned humanoid Daleks (or "Dals"). We could speculate that the Dals are mutated Kaled survivors, or perhaps Dalek mutants who've escaped from the buried bunker.

A thousand years after *Genesis of the Daleks*, Yarvelling builds a "metal casing" that looks like Davros' Mark III travel machine - even though it's not exactly the same design (the mid section and colour scheme is different, matching the ones from *The Daleks* and *The Dalek Invasion of Earth*), it's too similar to be a coincidence. Perhaps Yarvelling has based it on a design from history that he knows will scare the Thals, although it seems more likely he's got access to ancient records of Davros' work, or maybe he's even managed to excavate an old Dalek casing from the Kaled bunker. The Dals also develop the Neutron bomb, which goes off (deliberately according to *The Daleks*, accidentally according to the *TV Century 21* strip) and all but wipes out life on Skaro. A mutated Dal - the creature predicted by Davros' experiments, perhaps even a thousand-year-old survivor of those experiments - crawls into one of the casings, and becomes the sort of Dalek we're familiar with.

Very quickly, these Daleks develop a thirst for galactic conquest, the early days of which are recounted in the *TV Century 21* strip. At some point, apparently soon after *The Dalek Invasion of Earth*, there's a split - one group of Daleks completely abandons Skaro to become fearsome conquerors elsewhere in the universe, another group becomes confined to their city and dies off in *The Daleks*. Eventually spacefaring Daleks return to Skaro and reoccupy their planet, sharing it with the Thals, at least for a while (as seems to be the case in *Planet of the Daleks* - although, ominously, there are no Thals seen on Skaro in later TV stories).

Edward the Confessor's reign was one of the Doctor's favourite times and places.[184]

1066 (Late Summer) - THE TIME MEDDLER[185] **->** Landing on a beach in Northumbria, the first Doctor learnt that the Monk, a renegade from his own people, was planning to destroy a Viking invasion with futuristic weapons. Harold's army would then be fresh for the Battle of Hastings, and after defeating the Norman invasion, Harold would usher in a new period of peace for Europe. The Monk had arrived several weeks ago and occupied a monastery overlooking the coast. The Doctor foiled the Monk's plans, and removed the dimensional control from the Monk's TARDIS.

It "took a bit of time" to fix, but the Monk resumed his travels.[186]

Two bright green children were seen in Wulpit in Suffolk, and viewed with suspicion by an angry mob. These were actually alien Lampreys.[187]

Joanna Harris, a future geneticist and vampire, was born.[188] The order of the Knights Templar was founded in 1128.[189] The Canavitchi claimed responsibility for founding the Knights Templar.[190] The Doctor rode with the templars in Palestine. Elsewhere, the Templars recovered the Imagineum, a mirror like device built by an ancient race of alchemists. It had fallen to Earth in a spacecraft, and could create a dark duplicate of anyone who looked into it.[191]

The Doctor saw the completion of Durham Cathedral in 1133. Sir Brian de Fillis built Marsham Castle in Yorkshire in the twelfth century. The knight went mad, believing his wife was haunting him.[192]

During the twelfth century, the Convent of the Little Sisters of St Gudula was founded with Vivien Fay pos-ing as the Mother Superior.[193] In the same century, the Doctor saw the King of France, Phillippe Auguste, lay the first stone of the Louvre.[194] Around 1168, the Aztecs left their original home of Aztlan and became nomads. They took a holy relic, the Xiuhcoatl, with them.[195]

The other end of the Time Corridor formed by the timelash was in 1179 AD.[196] The Borad was disgorged from the timelash and quickly killed by operatives of the Celestis, the investigators One and Two.[197]

In 1190, Stefan, a Crusader, lost a bet with the Toymaker that Barbarossa could swim the Bosporus. Barbarossa drowned, and Stefan became the Toymaker's most loyal servant.[198]

c 1190 - THE CRUSADE[199] **->** The first Doctor saved Richard the Lionheart from an ambush, and became embroiled in court politics. Richard planned to marry his sister Joanna to the brother of Saladin, the Saracen ruler, but Joanna refused. The Doctor was mistaken for a sorcerer and the TARDIS crew narrowly escaped.

Whitaker's Time Scoop accidentally kidnapped a peasant from the Middle Ages.[200] **Scaroth possibly posed as a Crusader.**[201] **Around 1205, a man was boiled in oil for the entertainment of King John.**[202]

The Doctor delivered Genghis Khan.[203] **The Doctor claimed to have heard Genghis Khan speak.**[204] **The Master implied that the Doctor *was* Genghis Khan.**[205] **The hordes of Genghis Khan couldn't break down the TARDIS doors.**[206]

In the early thirteenth century, a Khameirian spaceship was rounding Rigellis III when a Yogloth Slayer ship attacked and damaged it. The Khameirian vessel crashed to Earth and destroyed the chapel at Abbots Siolfor, home of a secret society led by Matthew Siolfor. The Khamerians

---

750 years after the Doctor and Charley met Decurion Gralae.
185 Dating *The Time Meddler* (2.9) - The story takes place shortly before the Battle of Hastings (14th October, 1066), the Doctor judging it to be "late summer". The Doctor discovers a horned Viking helmet, although the Vikings never wore such helmets.
186 *The Daleks' Master Plan*
187 *Spiral Scratch*. This was in "the twelfth century".
188 *Vampire Science*. Joanna says she was born before the end of the 1st millennium, but also on the day William the Conqueror died, which was in 1087.
189 *Sanctuary*
190 "End Game" (*DWM*)
191 *The King of Terror*
192 *Nightshade*
193 *The Stones of Blood*
194 *The Church and the Crown*
195 *The Left-Handed Hummingbird*

196 *Timelash*
197 *The Taking of Planet 5*
198 *Divided Loyalties*. Stefan was created for the unmade story *The Nightmare Fair*.
This is slightly at odds with established history. Frederick Barbarossa was made Holy Roman Emperor in 1155, and died in 1190 after being thrown from his horse into the Saleph River in Cilicia (part of modern-day Turkey), whereupon his heavy armour made him drown in hip-deep water. As if that weren't enough, one chronicler claimed the shock additionally made Barbarossa have a heart attack.
199 Dating *The Crusade* (2.6) - A document written for Donald Tosh and John Wiles in April / May 1965 (apparently by Denis Spooner), "The History of Doctor Who", stated that the story is set between the Second and Third crusades, with the Third crusade starting when Richard's plan fails.
Richard is already in Palestine at the start of the story,

put their life essences into what would later be called "the Philosopher's Stone." They mentally enthralled six of the brotherhood to work toward restoring them to health. The descendants of the society would spread throughout the world, influenced by the Khamerians.[207]

The sunburst icon became known as a sigil of extraterrestrial power from the thirteenth century.[208]

1215 (4th - 5th March) - THE KING'S DEMONS[209] ->

The Master attempted to pervert the course of constitutional progress on Earth by trying to prevent the signing of Magna Carta. On 3rd March, 1215, an android controlled by the Master, Kamelion, arrived at Fitzwilliam Castle posing as the King. He was accompanied by the Master, who was disguised as the French swordsman Sir Giles Estram. The Fitzwilliams had served the King for many years before this, giving him their entire fortune to help the war against the abhorrent Saracens, but the King now demanded even more of them. "King John" began to challenge the loyalty of even the King's most devoted subjects, but the fifth Doctor exposed the Master's plan.

Around 1225, the Doctor defeated Thorgan of the Sulumians, who was attempting to kill the mathematician Fibonacci before he wrote the *Liber quadratorum* (*The Book of Squares*), a text on Diophantine equations.[210]

1240 - BUNKER SOLDIERS[211] ->
The first Doctor landed in Kiev, and was asked to help in repelling the Mongols. The Doctor knew that history recorded the sacking of the city and refused, but the governor of the city, Dmitri, imprisoned him. Dmitri sought supernatural aid, uncovering a casket under the Church of St Sophia. This held an alien soldier, who emerged and started a killing spree. Tragically, he infected Dmitri with a virus that drove him mad, leading to Dmitri refusing the Mongols' offer of sparing the city in return for an honourable surrender. The Mongols ransacked Kiev, but the Doctor discovered a way to deactivate the soldier.

1242 - SANCTUARY[212] ->
The seventh Doctor and Benny made an emergency landing in the Pyrenees. The Doctor discovered a plot to recover the skull of Jesus Christ from the heretical Cathare sect, even as Benny fell for the knight Guy de Carnac. The Church forced an attack on the Roc of the Cathares sanctuary and set it afire, but the Doctor found the skull was a fake. The Doctor and Benny escaped the destruction - it's possible that Guy de Carnac did also.

Marco Polo was born in Venice in 1252. When he was twelve, English crusaders occupied the African port of Accra. In 1271, Marco Polo left Venice to explore China.[213]

The arachnid Xaranti destroyed Zygor, the homeworld of the Zygons.[214] The Zygons retaliated and destroyed the Xaranti homeworld in Tau Ceti. The Xaranti consequently became nomadic.[215] **A Zygon spacecraft crashed in Loch Ness. While awaiting a rescue party, they fed on the milk of the Skarasen, an armoured cyborg creature that was often mistaken for the locals as a "monster".**[216]

---

indicating a date of around 1190. Ian claims in *The Space Museum* that *The Crusade* took place in the "thirteenth century", but this seems to be an error on his part. The *Radio Times* and *The Making of Doctor Who* both set the story in the "twelfth century". The *Programme Guide* gives a date of "1190", *The Terrestrial Index* picks "1192".

200 *Invasion of the Dinosaurs*

201 *City of Death.* Most fans have interpreted the last of the four Scaroths we see as a Crusader, although the DVD says it's a "Celt". Although Julian Glover plays both Richard the Lionheart in *The Crusade* and Scaroth in *City of Death*, I don't think Scaroth posed as King Richard.

202 "Ten years" before *The King's Demons*.

203 *Tragedy Day*

204 *The Daemons.* Genghis Khan was probably born in 1167, and died in 1227.

205 *Doctor Who - The Movie*

206 *Rose*

207 *Option Lock*

208 "End Game" (*DWM*)

209 Dating *The King's Demons* (20.6) - The TARDIS read-ings say it is "March the fourth, twelve hundred and fif-teen".

210 *The Gallifrey Chronicles*

211 Dating *Bunker Soldiers* (PDA #39) - The Doctor says "we are in Kiev in 1240" (p16).

212 Dating *Sanctuary* (NA #37) - Benny "persuaded someone to tell her that the year was 1242".

213 *Marco Polo.* Barbara states that Marco Polo was born in "1252", although actually it was two years later.

214 *The Bodysnatchers*

215 "Several centuries" before *Deep Blue*.

216 *Terror of the Zygons.* The Zygon leader Broton tells Harry that they crashed "centuries ago by your timescale". While disguised as the Duke, Broton later tells the Doctor that there have been sightings of the Loch Ness Monster "since the Middle Ages", the implication being that the Zygons and Skarasen have been on Earth since then.

In *Timelash*, we're made to believe that the Borad has been similarly swimming around Loch Ness from 1179 onwards, but the Borad's death in *The Taking of Planet 5* suggests he doesn't actually contribute to the Loch Ness sightings. The *Programme Guide* claimed that the

During the Middle Ages, Stangmoor was a fortress.[217] A medieval knight was kidnapped by the Master using TOM-TIT.[218] The Middle Ages was the native time of Justin, a knight who would help the fifth Doctor fight Melanicus - and would later be canonised.[219]

The Doctor was based for a time around 1268 at Ercildoune in Scotland. He cured a crippled stable hand called Tommy. Two years later, the Queen of the Charrl contacted Tommy from the far future, promising him immortality in return for his stealing the Doctor's TARDIS. Tommy came to be known as the wizard Jared Khan.[220]

In 1270, a mysterious doctor who tended King Alexander sent his stable boy Tom away. The legends of Kebiria claimed that the Caliph at Giltat was visited by mysterious demons, the "Al Harwaz", who promised him anything he wanted - gold, spices, slave women - if his people learnt a dance, "dancing the code". The arrangement continued for a time, until the Caliph broke the agreement and flying monsters destroyed his city.[221]

c 1273 - THE TIME WARRIOR[222] -> The third Doctor arrived from the twentieth century on the trail of the Sontaran Linx, who had kidnapped scientists and pulled them back in time. For his own amusement, Linx was supplying a local warlord, Irongron, with advanced weapons. The Doctor thwarted both Linx and Irongron, and the destruction of the Sontaran's ship also destroyed Irongron's castle.

1278 (29th August) ASYLUM[223] -> An alien dispatched from 1346, now hosted in monk Brother Thomas, tried to further philosopher Roger Bacon's research into the "Elixir of Life" - a possible cure to the impending Black Death seventy years hence. The fourth Doctor and Nyssa arrived to prevent the alien from disrupting history, and Nyssa inadvertently dislodged the alien presence from Thomas' mind. Bacon burned his unsuccessful "Elixir Manuscript", but the Franciscan Order imprisoned him for the next twelve years for committing "heretical" research

into alchemy. Bacon would become renowned to future generations as a great philosopher, not a scientist.

1289 - MARCO POLO[224] -> In 1274, Marco Polo arrived in Cathay, and in the same year the beautiful maiden Ping-Cho was born. Three years later, Polo entered the service of Kublai Khan. In 1287, the Khan refused permission for Polo to return to Venice. In 1289, Polo led a caravan across the Roof of the World to the court of the Khan. He took with him Tegana, the emissary of the Mongol warlord Noghai, and Ping-Cho, who was destined to marry a 75-year-old nobleman. They discovered the first Doctor, Ian, Barbara and Susan - along with their blue cabinet, which Polo decided to present to the Khan. They traversed Cathay and the Gobi Desert, and arrived at Shang-Tu. At the palace, the Doctor learned that Tegana planned to kill the Khan. In gratitude, the cabinet was returned to the travellers.

Astrolabus claimed to have an appointment with Marco Polo.[225] Jared Khan narrowly missed acquiring the TARDIS at this time.[226] **The Forgill family served the nation from the late thirteenth century.**[227] The Doctor met Dante and acquired his business card.[228] The Doctor met William Tell.[229] The Doctor met Robert the Bruce in the early fourteenth century.[230]

The Doctor slayed a dragon in Krakow.[231] The fourteenth century saw the rebirth of the organic statues of Es-Ko-Thoth Park in the city-state of Tor-Ka-Nom.[232]

Seth was a grand schemer in fourteenth century Rome known to the Doctor. He would go on to be known as Vance Galley, Van Giefried, Virgil Gaustino, Vincent Grant and the twenty-fourth century entrepreneur Varley Gabriel.[233] **A fourteenth century plague victim would infect people in Cardiff in the twenty-first century.**[234]

The Doctor almost gave William of Ockham a nervous breakdown trying to get him to work out the history of the planet Skaro.[235] **The Monk calculated that if his plan to**

Zygon ship crashed in "50,000 BC", *The Terrestrial Index* preferred "c.1676".
217 *The Mind of Evil*
218 "The Tides of Time", which doesn't specify at what point of the Middle Ages Justin comes from.
219 *The Time Monster*
220 *Birthright*
221 "Seven hundred years" before *Dancing the Code*.
222 Dating *The Time Warrior* (11.1) - The story seems to be set either during the Crusades, as Sir Edward of Wessex talks of "interminable wars" abroad, or quite soon after the Conquest as Irongron refers to "Normans". The Doctor tells Professor Rubeish they are in the "early years of the Middle Ages". However, in *The*

Sontaran Experiment, Sarah says that Linx died "in the thirteenth century". According to *The Paradise of Death*, this was "eight hundred years back" (p12), and it's "three centuries" before "Dragon's Claw". *The Programme Guide* set a date of "c.800", but *The Terrestrial Index* offered "c.1190". *The TARDIS Logs* said "1191 AD", *Timelink* said "1272" and *About Time* "1190-1220".
223 Dating *Asylum* (PDA #42) - It's "1278" according to the blurb, and 1266 was "twelve years previously" (p116).
224 Dating *Marco Polo* (1.4) - Marco gives the year as "1289". *The Programme Guide* gave the date as "1300".
225 "Voyager"
226 *Birthright*

prevent the Norman Conquest had worked, then mankind would have developed aircraft by 1320.[236]

1320 - RENAISSANCE OF THE DALEKS[237] -> The fifth Doctor dropped off Nyssa to look into an anomalous time track in Rhodes, 1320, then ventured off to investigate a second anomaly. Nyssa made the acquaintance of a Mulberry, a member of the Knights of Templar, but they both fell down a wormhole to Petersburg at the time of the American Civil War.

The Malus, a psychic probe from Hakol, arrived in Little Hodcombe "centuries" before the village was destroyed in the English Civil War.[238] The Doctor, Rose and Jack "only just escaped" Kyoto in 1336.[239]

Aliens emerged from a null dimension and into London in 1346. They took control of human bodies, which were vulnerable to a plague that the aliens knew would arrive in two years. They discovered that philosopher Roger Bacon wrote of a possible cure for the plague, and sent one alien back several decades to ensure Bacon's research succeeded. The alien's host in that era, Brother Thomas of the Fransican order, survived and felt drawn to the aliens in 1346, but they failed to heed his warnings about the futility of their efforts.[240]

The Doctor was at the university of Prague when it opened.[241] On the planet Skaro, a small, squat blue-skinned warlike race had evolved... the Daleks.[242]

The Canavitchi faked the Turin Shroud in an attempt to slow man's progress.[243] The Phiadoran Clan Matriarchy came to power in the Phiadoran Directorate. They ruthlessly weeded out their political opponents.[244] Cartophilius lived in Italy under the name John Buttadaeus.[245]

The Doctor met Chaucer in 1388 and was given a copy of *The Doctour of Science's Tale*.[246] The Doctor drank ale with Chaucer in Southwark.[247]

Around this time, the Doctor acquired his ticket to the Library of St John the Beheaded.[248]

The Renaissance

The Daemons inspired the Renaissance.[249] By the end of the fourteenth century, wire-drawing machinery had been developed.[250] Constantinople was renamed Istanbul. [251] The Doctor was present at the Battle of Agincourt.[252]

A renegade Time Lady, also a friend of the Doctor, founded a restaurant on Earth during the time of the Hapsburgs.[253]

From the time he was knee high, Richard III was a subject of huge interest to alien time tourists and academics. Random time travellers would repeatedly show up to question Richard about the future murder of his nephews - one of history's greatest mysteries - and had strong views about whether he should kill the boys or not. This puzzled Richard, who at around age 12 had no intention of doing anything of the sort. By accident, Richard discovered that most of the time travellers were afraid of someone called "the Doctor", and he continually dropped the Doctor's name as a means of making the visitors leave.[254]

---

227 *Terror of the Zygons*

228 *The Two Doctors*. Dante lived from 1265-1321.

229 *The Face of Evil*. William Tell lived in the early fourteenth century.

230 *Lords of the Storm*. Robert the Bruce was one of Scotland's greatest kings, and ruled from 1306-1329.

231 "Thirteen hundred years" before Rose's time, according to *Only Human*.

232 "By Hook or by Crook"

233 "Profits of Doom". The Doctor doesn't recognise him face-to-face, so they probably don't meet at this time.

234 *TW: End of Days*.

235 *The Gallifrey Chronicles*. Ockham was a philosopher and friar during the Middle Ages. He was responsible for the principle of Occam's Razor (also spelled Ockham's Razor) and lived c.1287 to c.1349.

236 *The Time Meddler*

237 Dating *Renaissance of the Daleks* (BF #93) - The date is given.

238 *The Awakening*

239 In the travellers' personal timelines, this occurs between *Boom Town* and *Bad Wolf*.

240 *Asylum*

241 "Change of Mind". This was in 1349.

242 "Genesis of Evil". This was in the year 1600 of the New Skaro Calendar.

243 *The King of Terror*. The Shroud is first recorded in the fourteenth century.

244 *Imperial Moon*. This takes place at "611,072.26 Galactic Time Index".

245 *Matrix*

246 *Cat's Cradle: Time's Crucible*

247 *Synthespians*™

248 *All-Consuming Fire*

249 *The Daemons*

250 "A hundred years" before *The Masque of Mandragora*.

251 *Shadowmind*

252 *The Talons of Weng-Chiang, Shada, The King of Terror*. Agincourt was fought on 25th October, 1415.

253 *Urban Myths*. The country where the restaurant is located isn't specified, but it's evidently where goulash was invented - originally, that would be Hungary. The Hapsburgs ruled there from 1437 to 1918, and it's possible that the Doctor's comment "since the time of the Hapsburgs" refers to the start of their reign.

254 *The Kingmaker*. Richard III was born October 1452.

c 1454 - THE AZTECS[255] -> The Aztec priest Yetaxa died and was entombed around 1430. When the TARDIS crew emerged from Yetaxa's sealed tomb, Barbara was taken for the reincarnation of Yetaxa. She attempted to use her "divine" power to end the Aztec practice of human sacrifice, knowing it would horrify the European conquerors in future, and hoped this would save the Aztec civilisation from the Spanish. Her efforts failed.

In the mid-fifteenth century, Scaroth gave mankind the printing press, although he kept a number of Gutenberg Bibles for himself. It was possibly this splinter of Scaroth that acquired a Ming vase.[256]

The "sons" of King Edward IV - who were historically fated to die in the Tower of London - were actually born as girls. Edward feared this would throw the line of royal succession into doubt, and spark decades of fighting amongst the power-crazed nobility. He therefore announced that the girls were in fact boys: the future Edward V and Richard of Shrewsbury.[257]

In 1478, George, the Duke of Clarence, was convicted of treason against his brother, King Edward IV. He was slated for execution, but their other brother, Richard of Gloucester, felt compassion and quietly rescued him. George was believed dead and lived in disguise as Clarrie, the barkeep of The Kingmaker tavern.[258]

A "Northern chap with big ears" left a pair of messages for Peri and Erimem at The Kingmaker tavern on Fleet Street in London. They would receive the notes in 1483.[259]

1483 (April to October) - THE KINGMAKER[260] -> The wayward TARDIS deposited Peri and Erimem in Stony Stratford, 1483. Unknown to them, William Shakespeare - having stowed aboard from 1597 - snuck out of the Ship. Shakespeare presented himself to Richard III as "Mr Seyton", someone from the future who advocated that Richard should murder his nephews.

King Edward IV had died, so Richard escorted the new monarch - his nephew, King Edward V - back to London. Along the way, Richard happened to discover that his nephews were female. He rounded up anyone who might know this secret, and saw to the execution of Hastings, a friend of the old king.

Three days after Richard's discovery, Peri and Erimem arrived at The Kingmaker tavern and - based upon the Doctor's messages - realized they were doomed to stay in 1483 for a time. They therefore worked as waitresses at the tavern for about six months.

Commemorative mugs, plates and tea towels were made in anticipation of Edward V's coronation on 24th June, but the event didn't occur. Parliament declared Edward and his "brother" Richard illegitimate; their uncle had Mr Seyton conduct a press conference on this development with the finest gossips in England, including the *Lincolnshire Tattletale* and the *Wessex Busybody*. Richard was subsequently crowned as Richard III.

The now-illegitimate Princes were relocated to the Tower of London - the king invited Peri and Erimem to serve as their handmaidens. Henry Stafford, the Second Duke of Buckingham, sought to bring the Woodville fam-

---

255 Dating *The Aztecs* (1.6) - According to Barbara, Yetaxa was buried in 1430. *The Programme Guide* dated the story "c.1200 AD". *The Terrestrial Index* suggested "1480", claiming that fifty years elapsed between Yetaxa being buried and the TARDIS landing inside the tomb. This is not supported (or contradicted) by the story itself, although Lucarotti's novelisation is set in "1507". Both editions of *The Making of Doctor Who* placed the story in "1430". *The Left-Handed Hummingbird* firmly dates the story in "1454".

256 *City of Death.* Movable type was developed in China during the ninth century, but as Scaroth possessed a number of Gutenberg Bibles (printed 1453-1455), we can infer he was responsible for *Europe's* development of printing.

257 *The Kingmaker.* Edward and Richard were respectively born in 1470 and 1473.

258 *The Kingmaker.* History says George was executed on 18th February, 1478.

259 "Two years" before Peri and Erimem's arrival in *The Kingmaker.* The "big-eared" chap is almost certainly a veiled reference to the ninth Doctor, who apparently passes through the fifteenth century and completes this task, fulfilling the line of communication between

his previous self and his companions.

260 Dating *The Kingmaker* (BF #81) - Edward IV died on 9th April, 1483, and Edward V's short-lived reign began on 18th April (he's one of three British monarchs to have never been crowned). Peri and Erimem arrive at least three days beforehand, and work at The Kingmaker for about six months. A minor anomaly is that Henry Stafford later claims Peri and Erimem turned up "about 18 months" before what's clearly August 1485, meaning it's more accurately two years plus change.

261 Dating *The Kingmaker* (BF #81) - One of the Doctor's notes to Peri and Erimem dates their arrival to 1st August, 1485. Bosworth Field was fought on 22nd August, and it's a little puzzling to wonder how the run-up to the conflict unfolded, given that Richard III time-jumps with the Doctor to 1597 and is apparently absent some days beforehand. Henry Stafford was historically executed on 2nd November, 1483, so in the *Doctor Who* universe, he languishes in prison for twenty one months beyond that point.

262 *The King of Terror*

263 *Blood Harvest*

264 *Project: Twilight*

ily into conflict with the king as a means of claiming the throne for himself. He hoped to catalyze this by convincing Peri and Erimem to poison the "boys", but the king discovered the plot and threw Stafford in prison.

Richard III recruited Peri and Erimem to double as the Princes while the genuine article went to work as waitresses - named Susan and Judith - with their uncle Clarrie at The Kingmaker. Peri and Erimem routinely appeared in public as the Princes, seen from afar playing tennis or exercising. The king got fed up with Shakespeare / Seyton and had him tortured in prison, learning much about the web of time.

Pointy beards were all the rage in France, and considered a fashion statement for the 1480s (as distinguished from the large, open-necked beards of the 70s).

1485 (August) - THE KINGMAKER[261] **->** The fifth Doctor, Peri and Erimem arrived from 1597, wanting to investigate the death of Richard III's nephews. But while the Doctor departed to patronize The Kingmaker tavern, the TARDIS - telepathically resonating with the Doctor's recent boozing - hiccupped and slipped back to 1483 with Peri and Erimem aboard. They came to spend most of the intervening two years masquerading as the Princes, appearing as them throughout 1485. However, the public didn't take much notice of the "lads" after a point, and history would record that the Princes were last seen in 1484.

In prison, Henry Stafford was tortured to death by Sir James Tyrell, the king's Royal High Concussor. The barkeep Clarrie - formerly George, the Duke of Clarence - was identified and died in a chase, drowning in the Thames. In future, the play *Richard III* would spread the belief that he had drowned in a vat of Malmsey wine.

William Shakespeare, also known as "Mr Seyton", escaped imprisonment and demanded that the Doctor take Richard III to stand trial in Queen Elizabeth's era. Much calamity ensued, and after a brief visit to 1597, the TARDIS arrived at the Battle of Bosworth Field. Shakespeare was forcibly hauled out of the TARDIS by a sixtyfourth century publishing robot that eventually exploded. Erimem had broken Shakespeare's arm, and a laser pistol wound had singed his foot and given him a limp, so Shakespeare was mistaken for the king. He was killed,

blubbing like a girl, after scrambling up a tree.

The Doctor relocated Richard III's nieces, Susan and Judith, to join their uncle in 1597.

The Canavitchi helped guide the Spanish Inquisition.[262] Agonal, an immortal being who gained strength from suffering, fed on the resultant fear and death.[263] The Doctor was present during the Spanish Inquisition.[264]

The earliest parts of Chase Mansion were built during the Wars of the Roses.[265]

1485 - SOMETIME NEVER[266] **->** An Agent of the Council of Eight kidnapped the two nephews of Richard III to prevent their having an impact on history. The eighth Doctor and Trix later rescued the boys, and took them to the early twenty-first century.

1487 - THE LEFT-HANDED HUMMINGBIRD[267] **->** In the Aztec city of Tenochtitlan, the god Huitzilopochtli's taste for blood grew every year. By 1487, his priests demanded twenty-thousand sacrifices. These fed the psychic Huitzilin - a human mutated by the Xiuhcoatl, an Exxilon device that leaked radiation. Huitzilin used his powers to remain alive, and used the Xiuhcoatl to make his people worship him. For centuries he would visit the most violent places in human history, feeding off the carnage of such events. He would become known as the Blue.

In the late fifteenth century, the Doctor visited China.[268] The Wandering Jew travelled to Romania, hoping that Vlad Tepes would be able to end his life.[269]

Around this time the Doctor met Christopher Columbus.[270] The Doctor travelled on the *Santa Maria*, but Columbus refused his suggestion of plotting courses with an orange and a biro.[271]

c 1492 - THE MASQUE OF MANDRAGORA[272] **->** The fourth Doctor accidentally brought the Mandragora Helix to Renaissance Italy, where it made contact with the Brotherhood of Demnos cult. The Doctor banished the Mandragora Helix before it could plunge Earth into an age of superstition and fear.

---

265 According to Harrison Chase in *The Seeds of Doom*. The Wars of the Roses lasted from 1455-1485.
266 Dating *Sometime Never* (EDA #67) - The date is given.
267 Dating *The Left-Handed Hummingbird* (NA #21)- The date is first given on p39.
268 *The Talons of Weng-Chiang*. The Doctor notes, "I haven't been in China for four hundred years" - I've assumed it was four hundred years ago in history, as opposed to when the Doctor was four hundred years

younger.
269 *Matrix*
270 The Doctor has Christopher Columbus' business card in *The Two Doctors*. Columbus lived 1451-1506 and discovered the New World in 1492.
271 *Eye of Heaven*
272 Dating *The Masque of Mandragora* (14.1) - It's said that the Helix will return to Earth in five hundred years at the "end of the twentieth century", so the story is set at the end of the fifteenth century. The second edition

> = The sixth Doctor visited the planet Yestobahl in 1494.[273]

The Doctor met Torquemada shortly before his death in September 1498.[274] The Doctor was with Vasco da Gama when he sailed into the harbour of Zanzibar in 1499.[275] Michelangelo drew the sixth Doctor.[276] The tenth Doctor learned how to sculpt from Michelangelo.[277]

The Cylox were immensely powerful psionics and a very long-lived species, being the equivalent of adolescents after surviving for millennia. Two of the Cylox, Lai-Ma and his brother Tko-Ma, had spent several millennia annihilating planets in another dimension. Around the late fifteenth century, an intergalactic court exiled them to a pocket realm located on Earth. The brothers later loosed their shackles and agreed to see who could destroy Earth the fastest. The Ini-Ma, the brothers' jailor of sorts, endowed its essence into female members of the bloodline that would produce Loretta van Cheaden.[278]

The Sixteenth Century

c 1500 - THE GHOSTS OF N-SPACE[279] **->** Around the turn of the sixteenth century, the third Doctor and Sarah were briefly seen as ghosts.

During the sixteenth century, the Ancient Order of St Peter existed to fight vampires.[280] Stattenheim and Waldorf created working plans for a TARDIS during the sixteenth century.[281]

Leonardo Da Vinci

Both the Monk and Scaroth claimed credit for inspiring Leonardo to consider building a flying machine.[282] The Doctor visited Leonardo while he was painting the

Mona Lisa, "a dreadful woman with no eyebrows who wouldn't sit still".[283] Leonardo had a cold.[284]

1505 - CITY OF DEATH[285] **->** Captain Tancredi, one of the splinters of Scaroth the Jagaroth, kept Leonardo a virtual prisoner and ordered him to begin making six additional copies of the Mona Lisa. Scaroth hoped to sell them at great profit to fund his time experiments in 1979. The fourth Doctor arrived, and wrote "This is a Fake" in felt-tip on many of Leonardo's blank canvasses. Leonardo painted the copies over them.

Although nobody took notice of Leonardo Da Vinci's sketches of helicopters or tanks at the time, his drawings would "seed" the idea for such inventions, and help to facilitate their creation in future.[286]

In 1514, a Sontaran ship crashed near Mount Omei in China. A monk, Yueh Kuang, investigated the starfall. The Sontarans taught him martial arts for three months. He then returned to share his new knowledge with his fellow monks, deposed Abbot Hsiang and took over as Abbot.[287]

1522 (Summer) - "Dragon's Claw"[288] **->** For years, Japanese pirates attacked ports along the coast of the East China Sea. One group was repelled by the Shaolin monks of Mount Omei. Abbot Yueh Kuang, their leader, had an advanced energy weapon. The fourth Doctor, Sharon and K9 arrived and found people killed by the gun. They were captured by the monks and taken four hundred miles to their monastery, where the Doctor discovered they'd been taught martial arts by the mysterious "eighteen bronze men". The Doctor snuck into the Hall of the Eighteen Bronze Men and survived a series of death traps to discover a group of Sontarans. The aliens were planting hypnotic commands in the monks, creating a deadly fighting force. The Doctor discovered their crashed ship, and learned its transmitter was damaged. The Sontarans needed a rock crystal to repair it, and only the Emperor had one

---

of *The Making of Doctor Who* said that the story is set in "the fifteenth century". Hinchcliffe's novelisation specified the date as "1492", *The Terrestrial Index* and *The TARDIS Logs* both set the story "about 1478". *The Discontinuity Guide* said it must be set "c.1470-1482 when Da Vinci was in Florence".

The entity that encroaches on Earth in *The Eleventh Tiger* - which takes place in 1865 - also seems to be the Mandragora Helix, even though the Doctor says in *Masque* that it's been banished for five hundred years. There's either another conjunction taking place that he doesn't know about, or he's discounting events of 1865 because he knows he already won the day then.

273 *Spiral Scratch*
274 *Managra*

275 *So Vile a Sin.* Vasco da Gama was a Portugese explorer, and the first European to journey by sea to India.
276 "Changes". Peri is surprised to find the picture in a store room, so she wasn't with the Doctor at the time.
277 *The Stone Rose*
278 *Instruments of Darkness*
279 Dating *The Ghosts of N-Space* (MA #7) - The Doctor says it is "somewhere near the turn of the century".
280 *Minuet in Hell*
281 *The Quantum Archangel*
282 *The Time Meddler, City of Death*
283 *City of Death.* The Doctor's note to Leonardo ends "see you earlier". In *The Two Doctors*, the Doctor has Leonardo's business card.

large enough. The Doctor returned to the monastery, and one of the monks, Chang, killed the Sontarans in a hypnotic killing frenzy.

In 1520, Cortez landed in South America.[289]

Henry VIII

On one of their earliest visits to Earth, the first Doctor and Susan met Henry VIII, who sent them to the Tower after the Doctor threw a parson's nose back at the King. The TARDIS had landed in the Tower, and this enabled the Doctor and Susan to make good their escape.[290] The Doctor has six wedding invitations from Henry VIII.[291]

King Henry VIII mistook the Doctor for a jester.[292] The Doctor witnessed the execution of Anne Boleyn.[293] **Henry VIII dissolved The Convent of Little Sisters of St Gudula.[294] Priests from around the country hid at Cranleigh Hall.[295]** The Doctor visited Venice in the sixteenth century.[296]

By the 1530s, the Spanish knew of an Incan myth about a fire god. It was based on the "burning" sentience.[297]

In 1540, under the reign of King James V, a shooting star landed near the Torchwood Estate in Scotland. Only a single cell of an alien - a werewolf - survived. In the generations to come, the cell would take host after host and grow stronger. The local monks in the Glen of St. Catherine tended to the creature, and made plans to facilitate the Empire of the Wolf.[298]

Around 1550, the Doctor was attacked by a jiki-ketsu-gaki, or vampire, in Japan. He was buried in a snowdrift and spent three months recovering in a monastery. He confronted the vampire, let her drain his blood until she was sated and fell asleep - and then burnt down her castle.[299]

The Canavitchi supplied Nostradamus with many of his prophecies.[300] **The fourth Doctor's long scarf was made by Madame Nostradamus "a witty little knitter".[301]**

1555 (January) - THE MARIAN CONSPIRACY[302] ->

The sixth Doctor helped Evelyn Smythe explore her ancestry. As the Doctor visited the court of Queen Mary, Evelyn stumbled on a Protestant plot to poison the Queen and replace her with Elizabeth. The time travellers were both imprisoned in the Tower of London. They also met Reverend Thomas Smith, Evelyn's ancestor, before escaping and preventing the assassination.

The Elizabethan Age

The Doctor attended the Coronation of Queen Elizabeth I.[303] The Doctor was appalled by the Earl of Essex's behaviour at the Coronation.[304] The eighth Doctor, Samson and Gemma also visited the Court of Queen Elizabeth.[305]

1560 (Spring) - THE ROOM WITH NO DOORS[306] ->

A Kapteynian slave escaped from a Caxtarid slaver ship, and its capsule crashed in the Han region of Japan. Within days, the Victorian time traveller Penelope Gate also visited Japan. A month later, the seventh Doctor and Chris Cwej arrived and became embroiled in a dispute between rival warlords Guffuu Kocho and Umemi, both wanting possession of the capsule. The Doctor managed to prevent either of them from taking control of it.

"The Beast" were flying creatures that would move from planet to planet by way of dimensional interfaces, and invisibly feed off other beings. This was normally harm-

---

284 *Doctor Who - The Movie*

285 Dating *City of Death* (17.2) - Tancredi asks what the Doctor is doing in "1505".

286 *The Nowhere Place*

287 "Eight years" before "Dragon's Claw".

288 Dating "Dragon's Claw" (*DWW* #39-43, *DWM* #44-45) - "It is 1522... the summer of death!" according to the opening captions.

289 *The Aztecs*, and referred to in *The Left-Handed Hummingbird*.

290 *The Sensorites*. Henry VIII reigned from 1509-1547. In *Tragedy Day*, the Doctor says he has "never met" Henry VIII (p74), but in *The Marian Conspiracy*, he says he has.

291 "The Gift".

292 *Terror Firma*. It's unclear if this refers to the same occasion mentioned in *The Sensorites*.

293 *Deadly Reunion*

294 *The Stones of Blood*. The dissolution of the monasteries took place in the fifteen-thirties.

295 *Black Orchid*

296 *The Stones of Venice*

297 *The Burning*

298 *Tooth and Claw* (TV)

299 "Ten years" before *The Room with No Doors*.

300 *The King of Terror*

301 *The Ark in Space*. Nostradamus lived from 1503-1566, and published his prophecies in 1556.

302 Dating *The Marian Conspiracy* (BF #6) - It is one month after the Wyatt Uprising, at the end of 1554.

303 *The Curse of Peladon*, although the Doctor admits he might be confusing it with the Coronation of Queen Victoria. Elizabeth was Queen from 1558, but the Coronation wasn't until the following year.

304 *Cat's Cradle: Witch Mark*. There wasn't an Earl of Essex at the time of Elizabeth's Coronation.

305 *Terror Firma*. Elizabeth ruled 1558-1603.

306 Dating *The Room with No Doors* (NA #59) - It is "probably March 1560", and "early spring".

less, but on the planet Benelisa, the Beast atypically wiped out the native populace as their numbers were few. The Beast moved on from Benelisa, but at least one Benelisan construct - Azoth - endured and pledged to eradicate the Beast.[307]

In 1564, an Agent of the Council of Eight prevented an Italian blacksmith from gaining the insight needed to invent the steam engine.[308]

1572 (21st - 24th August) - THE MASSACRE[309] ->
The first Doctor and Steven arrived in Paris in August 1572. The Protestants of the city, the Hugenots, were massing to celebrate the wedding of Henry of Navarre to Princess Marguerite. Yet they lived in fear of the Catholic majority, particularly the Queen Mother - Catherine de Medici - and the ruthless Abbot of Amboise. One hundred Hugenots had been killed at Wassy ten years ago, and a full-scale massacre was now instigated. The Doctor and Steven fled and were forced

to leave Anne Chaplet, a serving girl befriended by Steven, behind to her fate.

Rebels from the mid-twenty-first century kidnapped the young Shakespeare to prevent time-travelling Daleks assassinating him. This removed Shakespeare from time, but history was restored upon his safe return.

= In a version of history without Shakespeare, the Daleks had a compound in Warwick in 1572.[310]

Iris saved the Doctor and Sarah from Mary Queen of Scots.[311] The Doctor advised Mary Queen of Scots to change her muckspreader.[312] **Boscombe Hall was built on the site of the Convent of the Little Sisters of St Gudula in the late sixteenth century.[313]**

In 1582, the Doctor visited Rome while trying to track the Timewyrm.[314] **The West Wing of Chase Mansion was completed in 1587.[315]**

---

307 *The Taint.* The Beast arrive on Earth in 1944, according to *Autumn Mist.*

308 *Sometime Never*

309 Dating *The Massacre* (3.5) - The first three episodes take place over a single day each, the last picks up nearly 24 hours after the end of the third late on the evening of the 23rd and runs into the 24th. The Admiral Gaspar de Coligny was shot on the 22nd. This story is sometimes referred to as *The Massacre of St. Bartholomew's Eve*, based on some production documents, but this is historically erroneous. The event is more accurately named "the massacre of St. Bartholomew's *Day*".

310 *The Time of the Daleks,* which implies that Shakespeare used some of the names of individuals he met in the future for characters in plays such as *Hamlet, King Lear, Twelfth Night, Titus Andronicus* and *The Tempest.* The eighth Doctor met Shakespeare on this occasion, which from Shakespeare's point-of-view would be their earliest meeting.

311 *Verdigris*

312 *Tragedy Day*

313 *The Stones of Blood*

314 *Timewyrm: Revelation*

315 *The Seeds of Doom*

316 *The Empire of Glass*

317 *EarthWorld.* This was in 1587.

318 *Four to Doomsday.* The Spanish Armada attacked in 1588.

319 *The Marian Conspiracy*

320 *Only Human*

321 *Sometime Never*

322 *The Empire of Glass*

323 *Loups-Garoux*

324 *The Empire of Glass.* History tells us Marlowe died on 30th May, 1593.

325 "Three centuries" before *The Bodysnatchers.* This is a different ship from the one seen in *Terror of the Zygons.*

326 SHAKESPEARE: Going on just the information in the television series, the Doctor has met Shakespeare at least three times. Taking all the other media into account, we can infer that the Doctor has met Shakespeare a bare minimum of eight separate occasions, in at least six incarnations.

We actually see five of these meetings. In chronological order of Shakespeare's life, these are *The Time of the Daleks* (when Shakespeare is a child), "A Groatsworth of Wit" (set in 1592), *The Kingmaker* (set in 1597, and in which Shakespeare is replaced by Richard III), *The Shakespeare Code* (set in 1599) and *The Empire of Glass* (set in 1609, but with an epilogue that shows Shakespeare's death in 1616). Additionally, *The Chase* has the first Doctor, Ian, Barbara and Vicki using the Space-Time Visualizer to observe Shakespeare in the court of Elizabeth I, presumably at some point between *The Shakespeare Code* (as *Hamlet* has still not been written) and its real-life registry in 1602 (years before *The Empire of Glass,* then).

In one regard, this is all far less contradictory than it might seem. None of the stories (save for *The Chase* and *The Shakespeare Code,* in which Shakespeare twice receives inspiration to write *Hamlet*) bear different accounts of the same event. Indeed, none of the adventures even occur in the same year - the closest pairing (*The Kingmaker* and *The Shakespeare Code*) are set two years apart. Taking the general events in the five stories that directly involve Shakespeare, then, at face value is not very difficult.

Two impediments remain, however. One is that Shakespeare does not remotely look or act the same in some of his appearances. All things being equal, it's

In 1587, the Greld wiped out the Roanoake colony in the New World. They implanted the colonists with components for a meta-cobalt bomb, hoping to sabotage the Armageddon Convention. Christopher Marlowe, an agent of the crown, investigated the tragedy but escaped.[316]

The Doctor may have been at the execution of Mary Stuart (Mary, Queen of Scots).[317] **The Doctor met Francis Drake just before he faced the Spanish Armada.**[318] The Doctor played bowls with Drake and met William Cecil at Elizabeth's court.[319]

Jack Harkness had fun with a lady at Elizabeth's court.[320] An Agent of the Council of Eight released a single butterfly in Africa. The slight disturbance it caused in the atmosphere triggered a storm that helped to destroy the Armada. The Council of Eight's leader, Octan, arrived in 1588 to try and stop this. The Agent, unable to recognize Octan, pushed him into the Time Vortex.[321]

Around 1589, the Time Lord Irving Braxiatel began a diplomatic effort that would culminate in the signing of the Armageddon Convention.[322] On 28th October of the same year, the ancient werewolf Pieter Stubbe was sentenced to death for sorcery in Cologne, Germany, but he escaped.[323]

The dramatist Christopher Marlowe continued serving as a secret agent of the British government. He conspired with Walsingham, the Secretary of State, to fake his death.[324] Towards the end of the sixteenth century, the Xaranti attacked a Zygon fleet. A Zygon ship survived the fighting and crashed on Earth.[325]

Shakespeare[326]

Shakespeare was a "taciturn" young man, and the Doctor encouraged him to take up writing.[327]

1592 (September) - "A Groatsworth of Wit" [328] ->

The alien Shadeys took Robert Greene, a staunch critic of Shakespeare, from his deathbed and transported him over four hundred years into the future.

The ninth Doctor and Rose arrived, hot on Greene's trail. The Doctor quoted from *Richard III* and was mistaken for an actor, while Shakespeare tried to seduce Rose. Greene attacked Shakespeare, but the Doctor suggested that if Greene destroyed the great playwright *now*, Greene himself would lose what little future fame he currently enjoyed. Greene banished the Shadeys and returned to his deathbed.

1597 - THE KINGMAKER[329] ->

Peri and Erimem watched an exceedingly bad preview of *Richard III*, while the fifth Doctor went boozing at The White Rabbit tavern with his friend William Shakespeare. The Doctor accused

hard to believe that Shakespeare as voiced by Michael Fenton-Stevens in *The Kingmaker*, as played by Dean Lennox Kelly in *The Shakespeare Code*, and as played by Hugh Walters in *The Chase* are all the same person. (Note that this problem isn't limited to the different *Doctor Who* media, but occurs even in Shakespeare's two appearances on television.) Shakespeare's personality varies wildly between the various stories, even allowing that we're witnessing different points of his life.

The other problem is that Shakespeare in his later appearances never acknowledges having met a stranger named "the Doctor" before. He is admittedly never seen to meet the same incarnation twice, but it's implausible to think that he never makes a connection between the various men who keep appearing during turbulent and strange events, all of them named "Doctor". *The Kingmaker* actually helps a little in this regard - the Doctor and Shakespeare are on very chummy terms, but Shakespeare dies on Bosworth Field, eliminating the need for Richard III to acknowledge having met the Doctor in *The Time of the Daleks* and "A Groatsworth of Wit". Obviously, this doesn't explain why Richard himself doesn't acknowledge the Doctor in the next story in the line - *The Shakespeare Code* - or thereafter.

The Kingmaker is a particular sticking point, as it has Richard III living out Shakespeare's life from 1597 onward. This would mean that the "Shakespeare" that the tenth Doctor and Martha meet in *The Shakespeare Code* is actually a disguised Richard III installed by the fifth Doctor... but who is somehow driven to great depression by the death of the original Shakespeare's son, who has acquired two perfectly functional arms and who doesn't limp. It might be best to assume events in *The Kingmaker* happened, then the Time War or some other intervention (allowing for Shakespeare's importance to history) reversed them. This would carry the double benefit of not having to rationalise the conflicting fates of Richard III's nephews / nieces in *The Kingmaker* and *Sometime Never*.

327 *City of Death.* This unseen encounter would have to be before 1590, when we know Shakespeare was writing, and must have involved one of the Doctor's first four incarnations.

328 Dating "A Groatsworth of Wit" (*DWM* #363-364) - Greene's death on 3rd September, 1592, is historical record. Greene is famous for dismissing Shakespeare both for plagiarism and because he was mainly - at that time - an actor, not a writer. When Rose asks if the Doctor knows Shakespeare, he says he's "known him for ages. Just not yet." This would suggest that the meeting mentioned in *Planet of Evil* didn't involve too much familiarity.

329 Dating *The Kingmaker* (BF #81) - The date is given. It's believed that *Richard III* was written in 1592-93, and

Shakespeare of being a lapdog to Elizabeth's court, and of writing *Richard III* as a shameless propaganda piece. A loyalist to the Queen, Shakespeare became greatly disturbed by the Doctor's suggestion that in future, suspicion for the murder of Richard III's nephews would fall on Henry Tudor. Shortly afterwards, the Doctor and his companions left for 1485, and Shakespeare - determined to convince Richard to kill his nephews and thereby preserve the Queen's family name - stowed aboard.

Events in 1485 caused the TARDIS to materialize back in 1597 during a subsequent performance of *Richard III*. The genuine King Richard III had stowed away and remained behind as Shakespeare re-entered the TARDIS and met Richard's historical fate on Bosworth Field.

To preserve history, Richard III lived out Shakespeare's life and wrote his remaining plays, historicals, tragedies and comedies. He was moved to write his late brother George into *Henry IV, Part 1*, but kept misspelling Shakespeare's name. The Doctor suggested that Richard look up Francis Bacon to help with his writing.

Shakespeare's only child, Hamnet, had died, so the Doctor relocated Richard's nieces to live with him as "Shakespeare's daughters", Susanna and Judith.

The grief Shakespeare suffered after Hamnet's death allowed three of the Carrionites entrance back into history, and they manipulated him in a bid to free their sisters. They also influenced Peter Streete - the architect of the Globe Theatre - to design the stage area with fourteen sides, in accordance with the fourteen stars of the Rexel planetary configuration. Streete lost his mind as a reult, and was consigned to Bedlam.[330]

Before this time, but in his own future, the tenth Doctor incurred the wrath of Elizabeth I.[331]

1599 - THE SHAKESPEARE CODE[332] -> The tenth Doctor and Martha arrived in London and were surprised when a performance of *Love's Labour's Lost* ended with an announcement by Shakespeare that the sequel, *Love's Labour's Won*, would debut the following night. Three members of the Carrionite race were manipulating Shakespeare into opening a portal that would allow the rest of their race freedom - under their direction, *Love's Labour's Won* was embedded with coordinates that would open a spatial rift. Shakespeare used his command of language to seal the portal and banish the Carrionites, and the copies of *Love's Labour's Won* were destroyed.

Shakespeare took note of the Doctor's use of the word "Sycorax"[333], and a few choice phrases.

The first Doctor used the Time / Space Visualiser to watch Shakespeare at the court of Elizabeth I. The Queen was interested in Falstaff, but Francis Bacon gave Shakespeare the idea to write *Hamlet*.[334] The Doctor helped Shakespeare write his plays.[335]

The Doctor suggested that *The Merry Wives of Windsor* needed to be redrafted, but the Queen wanted it per-

---

it was entered into the Register of the Stationers Company on 20th October, 1597 by bookseller Andrew Wise. The Doctor and Shakespeare go drinking at The White Rabbit - a London establishment mentioned in Big Finish projects such as *The Reaping*.

330 *The Shakespeare Code*. Hamnet Shakespeare was buried on 11th August, 1596.

331 *The Shakespeare Code*. This visit to the late sixteenth century apparently didn't involve Shakespeare.

332 Dating *The Shakespeare Code* (X3.2) - The date is given in a caption at the start, and confirmed by the Doctor. Historically, it's thought *Love's Labour's Lost* was performed in 1597, and *Love's Labour's Won* appears on a list of Shakespeare's plays dating from 1598. Historically, the Globe Theatre opened in the Autumn.

333 The implication is that (among other things) the Doctor inspires Shakespeare to use the name Sycorax - not just the aliens from *The Christmas Invasion*, but also the name of Caliban's mother in Shakespeare's final play, *The Tempest*. (A moon of Uranus is named after the same character.)

334 *The Chase*. Literary scholars disagree when *Hamlet* was written, but we know it was entered in the Stationers' Register in 1602. It was almost certainly written and performed around 1600.

335 *Endgame* (EDA)

336 *The Ultimate Treasure*. *The Merry Wives of Windsor* was written around 1597, but could have been a little later, so this is just possibly the same visit as the one where the Doctor helped Hamlet.

337 *City of Death*. Historically, Shakespeare was known as an actor by 1592, and tradition has it that he continued to act even when he was better known as a writer. This reference seems to contradict the one in *Planet of Evil*, and clearly represents a different, subsequent visit (or visits). We can therefore infer that it's the fourth Doctor who helped with *Hamlet*, after *Planet of Evil*. The encounter is mentioned again in *Asylum*. One problem is that it's also mentioned by the first Doctor in *Byzantium!* - if that needs explaining away, it's possible the first Doctor has seen the manuscript, recognized his handwriting (we know from *The Trial of a Time Lord* that the Valeyard and sixth Doctor have the same handwriting, so presumably all the Doctors do) and so inferred a future meeting.

338 *City of Death*

339 *The Gallifrey Chronicles*. Presumably on the same visit he helped write it, although the amnesiac eighth Doctor should have no memory of that.

340 *The Time Meddler*, although there's no evidence of

formed as soon as possible.[336]

The fourth Doctor said Shakespeare was a "charming fellow", but a "dreadful actor".[337] The Doctor transcribed a copy of *Hamlet* for Shakespeare, who had sprained his wrist writing sonnets. Scaroth later acquired the manuscript.[338]

The Doctor saw Garrick take the title role in the first performance of *Hamlet*.[339] If the Monk's plan had worked, *Hamlet* would have been written for television.[340] The Doctor wrote Poor Tom's dialogue in *King Lear*.[341], and saw Garrick play the part.[342] The Doctor has a copy of *Mischief Night*, or *As You Please*, an unknown Shakespeare play in a TARDIS storeroom.[343]

The Seventeenth Century

The planet Caresh had developed in a binary star system containing the larger, warmer sun Beacon and the smaller, colder Ember. Caresh would randomly orbit one of the two stars each solar cycle, causing unpredictable warm and cold years. In the seventeenth century, a protracted cold period killed off a large amount of the population. As the warm years returned, scientists on Dassar Island built a scanner capable of seeing into the future, giving them advance warning of cold years. The Time Lords ruled the scanner a violation of their monopoly on time travel, and dispatched agents Solenti and Lord Roche to shut down the device.[344]

Centuries ago, invaders dominated the planet Indo. The surviving natives - being microscopic - traveled to Earth on a meteorite. They fed off the latent emotions of humans in the Brighton area, and would gain in strength by 1936.[345]

Around 1600, the *Necronomicon* was translated into Spanish.[346] In the early seventeenth century, the Doctor was given tea by Emperor Tokugawa Ieyasu of Japan.[347] The Doctor once shared a cell with Walter Raleigh, who "kept going on about this new vegetable he'd discovered".[348]

c 1600 - "The Devil of the Deep"[349] -> The ship of Diego da Columba of Cordoba vanished off the coast of South America. It had been attacked by pirates led by Korvo. Diego was rescued after walking the plank by a Sea Devil who had revived ten years previously. The pirates discovered the Sea Devil's island and he was captured by Korvo. One of the pirates accidentally activated a Caller, a device that summoned a giant marine reptile that sank the pirate ship. Diego was left alone for twenty years until he was rescued and could tell his tale - his proof was that he still had the Caller.

c 1600 (5th May) - "The Road to Hell"[350] -> The eighth Doctor and Izzy arrived in Japan and were brought before aliens known as "Gaijin", who sought to understand the concept of honour. They had a nano-sculptor that made thoughts reality, and the ability to make people immortal, which they used on Katsura Sato. The Doctor was angry at the interference, but the Gaijin didn't understand the objections. One of the Japanese, Asami, saw a vision of Japan's future in Izzy's mind, including the atomic bombs of World War II. He decided to launch a preemptive attack on the West. The Gaijin now understood that honour was linked to responsibility and deactivated the nano-sculptor even though it killed them.

Katsura Sato, unable to commit seppuku, wandered the Earth, became a pirate and ended up in a cell in Saragossa for fifty years. The Master wrote the *Odostra*, a fake holy book, and gave it to Katsura in his cell on Saragossa. Katsura was filled with crusading zeal and set out to conquer the world. History changed because of this.[351]

Master Dee worked as Queen Elizabeth's counsellor for twenty years. In 1603, he realised that the Doctor would not return to visit the Queen.[352] General William Lethbridge-Stewart was among King James' retinue on his initial arrival in London.[353]

---

any contact between the Monk and Shakespeare.

341 *The Cabinet of Light. King Lear* appeared in the Stationer's Register for November 1607, so this is another meeting. *Island of Death* implies it has to involve one of the Doctor's first three incarnations.

342 *Island of Death*

343 "Changes". This play, unlike the ones Braxiatel acquires in *The Empire of Glass*, are completely unknown to Shakespearean scholarship.

344 *The Suns of Caresh*

345 *Pier Pressure*

346 *The Banquo Legacy*. In the real world, the *Necronomicon* was a fictional book of magic invented by H.P. Lovecraft.

347 *Spare Parts*

348 *The Mind of Evil.* Raleigh lived 1552-1618, and was imprisoned 1603-1616.

349 Dating "The Devil of the Deep" (*DWM* #61) - It's "the early 17th century" when Diego is rescued according to a caption. The Sea Devil revived "ten years" before rescuing Diego, who is rescued "twenty years" after being marooned.

350 Dating "The Road to Hell" (*DWM* #278-282) - The Doctor asserts "I'm fairly sure I've set us down in the tenth century", but quickly corrects this to "the early 17th century".

351 "The Glorious Dead"

352 *Birthright*

353 *The Dying Days*

1605 - THE PLOTTERS[354] -> The first Doctor and Vicki decided to investigate the Gunpowder Plot while Ian and Barbara set off for the Globe Theatre. The Doctor and Vicki - disguised as a boy named "Victor" - met King James I, and the Doctor learned that the statesman Sir Robert Cecil was encouraging the Plot to draw out the conspirators and discredit the Catholics. Meanwhile, some Catholics captured Barbara, leading to Guy Fawkes befriending her. Robert Catesby, a member of the Plot, argued with Fawkes and killed him... which isn't how the history books reported events.

The King's courtier, Robert Hay, was a secret member of a grand order devoted to mysticism. Hay sought to create anarchy, but the Doctor manoeuvred Hay to the cellar under Parliament, where Cecil arrested him. Hay was tortured and executed in Fawkes' place, preserving history.

The Doctor met Cervantes.[355] **The Armageddon Convention was signed, and banned the use of cobalt bombs.**[356]

1609 - THE EMPIRE OF GLASS[357] -> Irving Braxiatel and the first Doctor hosted a meeting, the Armageddon Convention, that saw doomsday weapons such as temporal disrupters and cobalt bombs banned. Although the Daleks and Cybermen refused to attend, many other races did sign. The Convention was nearly sabotaged by the Greld, a race of arms dealers who stood to lose money from it; and the Jamarians, who craved an empire for themselves.

The first performance of *Macbeth* involved the last minute substitutions of Shakespeare in the role of Lady Macbeth, and two strangers in the roles of the doctor and his servant. Christopher Marlowe, an agent of the crown, died in a duel.

On 29th June, 1613, the talentless playwright Francis Pearson burnt down Shakespeare's Globe Theatre during a production of *Henry VIII*. Pearson later vanished, transported by the ancient Mimic to the thirty-first century.[358] In April 1616, a dying William Shakespeare handed over

354 Dating *The Plotters* (MA #28) - The year is given (p23).
355 *Endgame* (EDA)
356 Before *Revenge of the Cybermen*. The signing of the Convention is the central event of *The Empire of Glass*.
357 Dating *The Empire of Glass* (MA #16) - The Doctor states that it "must be the year of our lord, 1609" (p30).
358 *Managra*
359 *The Empire of Glass*
360 Three hundred years before *Year of the Pig*.
361 *The Settling*. The person who bestows the forceps upon the Doctor is merely referred to as "Chamberlen". Peter Chamberlen is regarded as the inventor of forceps, although the name actually refers to two brothers (respectively 1560-1631 and 1572-1626). The elder Peter is apparently the creator of the device, which was a family secret for generations.
362 *Silver Nemesis*
363 *Sometime Never*
364 "Ten generations" before *Imperial Moon*.
365 Dating *The Church and the Crown* (BF #38) - The date is given.
366 *The Abominable Snowmen*. This was "1630" according to the Doctor. *The Programme Guide* suggested "1400 AD".
367 The Doctor speaks Tibetan in *Planet of the Spiders* (but doesn't in *The Creature from the Pit*), and uses Tibetan meditation in *Terror of the Zygons*.
368 *Heart of TARDIS*. Bacon died in April 1626.
369 *The War Games*. The Thirty Years War ran from 1618-1648.
370 *The Church and the Crown*
371 Dating *Silver Nemesis* (25.3) - The Doctor gives the date of the launch, but there is no indication of exactly how long afterward Lady Peinforte leaves for the twen-

tieth century. Quite how "Roundheads" can be involved in this business when the term wasn't used until the Civil War is unclear. As a letter to *Radio Times* after *Silver Nemesis* noted, the adoption of the Gregorian calendar in 1752 means that eleven days were "lost" in Britain, so had the Nemesis *really* landed exactly 350 years after 23rd November, 1638, it would have landed on 3rd December, 1988.

The statue passes over the Earth every twenty-five years (in 1663, 1688, 1713, 1738, 1763, 1788, 1813, 1838, 1863, 1888, 1913, 1938, 1963 and finally 1988). *The Terrestrial Index* offers suggestions as to the effects of the statue on human history, but the only on-screen information concerns the twentieth century.

Fenric's involvement is established in *The Curse of Fenric*.
372 *The War Games*. The English Civil Wars ran from 1642-1649.
373 *The Time Monster*
374 *The Awakening*
375 *The Hollow Men*
376 *The Spectre of Lanyon Moor*
377 *Nightshade*
378 *The Daemons*. The witchhunter Matthew Hopkins died in 1647.
379 *Players*
380 Dating *The Roundheads* (PDA #6) - The Doctor says it's "1648, December I should say" (p39).
381 Dating *The Settling* (BF #82) - Cromwell's ultimatum to Wexford is issued on 12th September, 1649, and the story begins shortly beforehand. The sacking of Wexford lasted from 2nd to 11th October. The "Dr. Goddard" in this story apparently refers to Dr. Jonathan Goddard (1617-1675), a distinguished Society member and a favorite of Cromwell.

three unpublished plays - *Love's Labours Won*, *The Birth of Merlin* and *Sir John Oldcastle* - to Irving Braxiatel in return for memories of events in Venice, 1609.[359]

On one occasion, the Doctor saw a beached whale lie on the shore for four days until its bowels exploded - tragically, some of the eye-witnesses died from disease after being splattered by rotten whale meat.[360]

Chamberlen, the inventor of modern obstetrical forceps, bequeathed a pair of his creations upon the Doctor. Later in 1649, the Doctor would use this item to deliver a child during the sacking of Wexford.[361]

In 1621, the infamous Lady Peinforte poisoned her neighbour Dorothea Remington.[362] In 1624, the Doctor met an Agent of the Council of Eight in Devon.[363]

The Phiadoran Clan Matriarchy came to dominate the Phiadoran Directorate systems, using their genetically augmented pheromones to influence males. The Matriarchy instigated ten generations of tyranny that lasted from Galactic Time Index 611,072.26 to 611,548.91. The Sarmon Revolution finally brought down the Matriarchy, whose members were exiled to die in a safari park built on Earth's moon.

Thirty-two years later, the carnivorous Vrall killed off the Matriarchy members, and disguised themselves as the Phiadorans by wearing their skins. Unable to space-travel, the Vrall launched RNA spores encoded with technical information to Earth.[364]

1626 - THE CHURCH AND THE CROWN[365] **->** At the court of King Louis, the Musketeers and Cardinal Richelieu were in constant dispute. The fifth Doctor, Peri and Erimem arrived in the middle of these machinations and it transpired that Peri was the double of Queen Anne. Peri was kidnapped by the Duke of Buckingham, who was planning a British invasion of France by dividing the French court. Erimem rallied the troops, and a major diplomatic incident was averted.

The Doctor apparently visited the Det-Sen monastery in Tibet on a number of occasions, and in 1630 helped the monks there to survive bandit attacks. He was entrusted with the holy Ghanta when he left.[366] **It was possibly on this visit that the Doctor learned the Tibetan language and meditation techniques.**[367]

The Doctor witnessed philosopher Francis Bacon conduct an experiment on the preservation of meat by stuffing snow into a chicken. Bacon later contracted pneumonia from the incident and died.[368] **The War Lords lifted a battlefield from some point during the Thirty Years War.**[369] The Doctor met Louis XIII in 1637.[370]

1638 (November) - SILVER NEMESIS[371] **->** On 23rd November, 1638, the seventh Doctor was present as some Roundheads fought Lady Peinforte's soldiers, as

the Nemesis asteroid was launched into space from a meadow in Windsor. Following this, the Doctor set his watch alarm to go off on 23rd November, 1988, the day that the Nemesis would return to Earth.

The Nemesis passed over the Earth every twenty-five years, influencing human affairs. Lady Peinforte immediately employed a mathematician to work out the asteroid's trajectory. His work completed, the mathematician's blood was used in a magical ceremony - one that also involved the Validium arrow in Peinforte's possession - to transport Peinforte and her servant Richard Maynarde to its ultimate destination. The imprisoned Fenric aided her time travel.

The English Civil War

The War Lords kidnapped a Civil War battlefield.[372] **A division of Roundheads was also kidnapped by the Master using TOM-TIT.**[373] **On 13th July, 1643, the Royalists and Roundheads met in Little Hodcombe, wiping out themselves and the entire village. The Malus fed from the psychic energy released by the deaths and briefly emerged from its dormancy. The Doctor returned the time-flung Will Chandler to this, his native era, shortly afterward.**[374]

Returning Will Chandler was not a straightforward business.[375] A group of Roundheads was torn apart on Lanyon Moor, apparently by wild beasts.[376] In 1644, the castle of Crook Marsham was consumed in "strange fire".[377]

Witches hid from Matthew Hopkins in Devil's End.[378] The Doctor met King Charles II.[379]

1648 - THE ROUNDHEADS[380] **->** Ben and Polly were mistaken for Parliamentarians. Polly was kidnapped by Royalists, while Ben was press-ganged. Meanwhile, Cromwell's men arrested the second Doctor and Jamie. Cromwell's belief that Jamie was a fortune teller aided the TARDIS crew in escaping, but they were accompanied by King Charles... who according to history should have stayed in prison.

Polly was forced to betray Christopher Whyte, a new friend and a Royalist, to protect history. Charles was duly recaptured and executed.

1649 (12th September to 11th October) - THE SETTLING[381] **->** The TARDIS arrived in Ireland as Oliver Cromwell's forces successfully besieged Drogheda. Weeks later, Cromwell's army threatened Wexford, and he demanded that the town recognize the authority of Parliament. Some conflict ensued owing to confusion on the battlefield, but Cromwell received a surrender notice and ordered the fighting to cease. However, Hex - having witnessed the horror at Drogheda - roused the townsfolk to resist. The fighting resumed, hundreds of fleeing women and children drowned on crowded boats and Cromwell's troops prevailed against the city.

The seventh Doctor met Dr. Goddard, who helped to found the Royal Society.

An act of murder by the standing stones in Cirbury awakened the Ragman. Emily, the mayor's daughter, was raped by a corpse that the Ragman animated. The Ragman triggered acts of class warfare, but was driven back into the stones. The townfolk relocated the stones to Dartmoor. Emily was left pregnant and later died in poverty, but her bloodline led to the journalist Charlemange Peters and the lout Kane Sawyer in the twentieth century.[382]

The Doctor fished with Isaak Walton[383] He also met Thomas Hobbes.[384] **Lady Peinforte's servant Richard Maynarde died on 2nd November, 1657, and was entombed at Windsor.**[385]

According to the Doctor, Aubrey invented Druidism "as a joke".[386] **The Doctor was a founder member of the Royal Geographical Society.**[387] In 1661, the astronomer Clancy discovered a comet that returned to Earth every one hundred and fifty-seven years.[388]

The Mortimer family - George, Helen and their children

Ida and Alan - stumbled into the TARDIS when the first Doctor landed during the Great Fire of London. Much to the Doctor's irritation, they thought he was a warlock. Together, they travelled to the Andromeda Galaxy in the far future.[389]

1666 (early September) - THE VISITATION[390] **-> A group of escaped Terileptil prisoners made planetfall on Earth. They planned to wipe out the human population with rats infected with the bubonic plague virus. The Terileptils were killed, and the explosion of their equipment caused the Great Fire of London.**

Prior to this in his lifetime, the Doctor had already been blamed for the Great Fire. The Doctor perhaps met Mr and Mrs Pepys on the same visit. Mrs Pepys "makes an excellent cup of coffee". The Doctor doesn't like to talk about the Great Fire of London.[391]

In the late seventeenth century, Professor Chronotis retired to St Cedd's College, Cambridge.[392] **About this time, the Eternals kidnapped a seventeenth-century pirate crew.**[393] **The Doctor placed skeletons in the Tower of London, which were found in 1674 and identified as the lost Princes.**[394]

382 "The seventeenth century", says *Rags* (p39).
383 *The Androids of Tara*. Isaak Walton lived 1593-1683, and published *The Compleat Angler* in 1653.
384 *Ghost Ship*. Hobbes lived 1588-1679.
385 According to the monument in *Silver Nemesis*.
386 *The Stones of Blood*. The English writer John Aubrey (best known for his collection of biographies, *Brief Lives*) lived 1626-1697.
387 *Ghost Light*. The Royal Geographical Society was formed in 1645 during the Civil War.
388 *The Ghosts of N-Space*
389 *Doctor Who and the Invasion from Space*
390 Dating *The Visitation* (19.4) - The Doctor, trying to get Tegan home, suggests "we're about three hundred years early". The action culminates with the start of the Great Fire of London, which took place on the night of 2nd to 3rd September, 1666, so the story would seem to start on 1st September. According to the novelisation, the Terileptils crashed on "August 5th". On screen, Richard Mace says this was "several weeks ago".
391 The Doctor says he was blamed for the Great Fire in *Pyramids of Mars*. He refers to Mr and Mrs Pepys in *Robot*, and to Mrs Pepys' coffee-making prowess in *Planet of the Spiders*. Pepys lived 1633-1703 and began his diary in 1660. His wife Elizabeth died in 1669. Mention of the Doctor's reluctance to talk about the Great Fire is from *Doctor Who and the Pirates*.
392 "Three centuries" before *Shada*.
393 *Enlightenment*
394 *Sometime Never*

395 *The Happiness Patrol*. Wallis lived 1616-1703, and is credited with furthering the development of modern calculus.
396 "Centuries" before "The Iron Legion". Vesuvius is the oldest robot, and a guard says he "should have been dealt with centuries ago". Likewise, the Bestarius have lain in their suspended animation "for centuries".
397 *Phantasmagoria*
398 *The Last Dodo*
399 *Ghost Ship*. Purcell lived from 1659-1695.
400 *Battlefield*. This is the date on the capstone above the hotel's fireplace.
401 *The Hollow Men*
402 *The Pirate Planet*. Newton lived 1642-1727, and published his theories of gravitation in 1685. This meeting clearly pre-dates the fifth Doctor encountering Newton in *Circular Time*.
403 *Circular Time*: "Summer"
404 *Psi-ence Fiction*
405 *Winner Takes All* - this would be around 1690.
406 Dating *The Witch Hunters* (PDA #9) - Each section states the date. Nurse was executed on 19th July, 1692.
407 Dating *The Smugglers* (4.1) - The Doctor notes that the design of the church he sees on leaving the TARDIS means that they could have landed "at any time after the sixteenth century". Later, he says that the customers in the inn are dressed in clothes from the "seventeenth century". *The Terrestrial Index* and *The TARDIS File* set the story in "1650", *The TARDIS Logs* in "1646".

The Discontinuity Guide states that as a character says

In 1677, the mathematician John Wallis gave a paper on sympathetic vibration to the Royal Society.[395]

> = Around 1679, on an alternate Earth where Rome never fell, a race of genetically engineered soldiers - the Bestarius - were created but proved uncontrollably violent. Robots were deemed to be far more useful, and around this time the first robot, Vesuvius, was built. Centuries later, by 1979, Rome's iron legions had conquered the entire galaxy.[396]

Nikolas Valentine, actually an extra-terrestrial stranded on Earth, received a knighthood in the 1680s.[397] The tenth Doctor and Martha visited Mauritius in 1681.[398] The Doctor met the Baroque composer Henry Purcell.[399] **The Gore Crow Hotel was built in 1684.**[400]

In 1685, the Hakolian battle vehicle Jerak arrived on Earth, but failed to find its partner, the Malus, as planned. The scheduled invasion didn't happen, and the battle vehicle went dormant. Its radiating malevolence ensured that local legends sprang up of an evil spirit named "the Jack i' the Green".[401]

The fourth Doctor claimed to have met Isaac Newton. At first he dropped apples on his head, but then he explained gravity to him over dinner.[402] Newton was furious about the Doctor dropping an apple on his head, as his nose bled for three days.[403] Newton showed the Doctor around Cambridge University.[404] The Doctor visited Hampton Court maze soon after it was planted.[405]

1692 - THE WITCH HUNTERS[406] **->** The TARDIS landed in Salem in 1692, and the time travellers quickly retreated to avoid becoming implicated in the witch trials. Susan, however, wanted to help those who were accused and took the TARDIS back there. She and Ian were soon accused of witchcraft. The first Doctor saved his friends, but to preserve history, he persuaded the governor not to pardon the alleged witch Rebecca Nurse, age 71.

Later, the Doctor returned and took Rebecca to 1954. He convinced her that her death would encourage future tolerance, and she agreed to return to her native time and face her historical death.

c 1696 - THE SMUGGLERS[407] **->** A group of pirates led by Captain Samuel Pike of the Black Albatross attempted to locate Captain Avery's treasure in Cornwall, with only a rhyme as a clue to its whereabouts. The treasure was found in the local church, and the names in the rhyme appeared on tombs in the crypt. The King's militia arrived, killing Pike and many of his crew.

The Eighteenth Century

Biochemical warfare wiped out the population of Anima Persis. The ghosts of the dead haunted this geopsychic planet. The Time Lords used the world as a training ground.[408] The Talichre once attacked Anima Persis.[409] Raldonn travelled the universe peacefully for hundreds of years. He would crash on Earth in the nineteen sixties.[410]

An alien force arrived in Earth's dimension, and was separated into a ghostly ectoplasmic form and a disembodied bundle of psychic energy. Henry Deadstone encountered the creature's psychic aspect and at first buried it in a pit, but was mentally compelled to feed it children and animals. Gypsies accused Deadstone of "feeding children to the Devil" and hanged him. The creature remained in the pit and artificially extended Deadstone's life.[411]

By the late twentieth century, no documents from before 1700 existed at Boscombe Hall. This was the year before Dr Thomas Borlase was born.[412] Weed Creatures were seen in the North Sea during the eighteenth century.[413] The Doctor "ran Taunton for two weeks in the eighteenth century and I've never been so bored".[414]

During the eighteenth century, the Ragman inhabited the body of an executed highwayman.[415] The Doctor visited Rio de Janero in 1700.[416]

On the planet Artaris, civilization divided itself into fortified city-states. The planet began to industrialize, and "Reeves" emerged as a type of government overseer in the city-state of Excelis. Within a hundred years, a Reeve had commissioned volunteers among the citizens to become law-enforcement officers named Wardens. The immortal Grayvorn worked as one of the earliest Wardens and rose through the ranks.[417]

"God save the King" (and, perhaps more to the point, Josiah Blake is the "King's Revenue Officer") it must be when England had a King (between 1603-1642, 1660-1688 or 1694 onwards). However, William III ruled as King from 1688-1702, and even though this was alongside Mary at first, legally and in the minds of the public he was King. The *Guide* further speculates that the costumes suggest this story is set in the latter part of the century.

408 "Hundreds of years" before *Death Comes to Time*. Anima Persis is also mentioned in *Relative Dementias*

and *The Tomorrow Windows*.
409 *Relative Dementias*
410 "Operation Proteus"
411 Unspecified "centuries" before *The Deadstone Memorial*.
412 *The Stones of Blood*
413 *Fury from the Deep*
414 *The Highest Science*
415 *Rags*
416 *Loups-Garoux*
417 "Three hundred years" before *Excelis Rising*.

= Katsura Sato had conquered the Europe of his alternate timeline, and Africa and Asia would soon follow.[418]

1702 (8th - 10th March) - PHANTASMAGORIA[419] ->

The fifth Doctor and Turlough arrived in 1702 and witnessed phantoms abducting a gambler, Edmund Carteret, who died from a heart attack. This was the latest of many such disappearances. The Doctor discovered that a stranded and murderous alien, Karthok of Daeodalus, was operating on Earth as Sir Nikolas Valentine, a card-playing member of the Diabola Club. Valentine had been absorbing human minds into his ship's computer, then using the amassed calculating power to help the ship heal itself. The phantoms were the collected consciousness of the minds absorbed, directed by Valentine to snatch more victims. The Doctor tricked Valentine into seeding his own bioprint into the ship's computer, whereupon the phantoms tore Valentine to pieces. Valentine's ship was programmed to self-destruct.

c 1705 - DOCTOR WHO AND THE PIRATES[420] ->

The TARDIS landed onboard a ship as the pirate Red Jasper attacked it. The sixth Doctor and Evelyn were taken on board Jasper's ship. Jasper was looking for treasure in the Ruby Islands, and was unimpressed by the Doctor's reluctance to kill. The Doctor incited mutiny on Jasper's ship, leaving Jasper stranded.

c 1707 - "Ravens"[421] ->

In seventeenth-century Japan, the seventh Doctor convinced a warrior known as the Raven that although his wife and children were dead, he could still save others.

c 1708 (July) - CIRCULAR TIME: "Summer"[422] ->

The fifth Doctor and Nyssa arrived in London, but the Doctor was distracted by an alchemy demonstration, and handed Nyssa some coins from other eras. Sir Isaac Newton, disguised as an Algerian juggler with a false chin, witnessed this and - under his authority as director of the Royal Mint - had the pair of them incarcerated for counterfeiting. Newton's formidable brain pieced together many physical details about the coins, and made several correct guesses about future history and the Doctor and Nyssa's origins. The knowledge triggered one of Newton's seizures, and the Doctor prevented the man from swallowing his own tongue and choking to death. Newton ordered the travellers' release, hoping they would never meet again. The Doctor thought that Newton would have a headache for some days, then become bored with the memory of the time-travellers and move on to something new.

---

418 "Within a century" of his crusade beginning, according to "The Glorious Dead".

419 Dating *Phantasmagoria* (BF #2) - The exact date is given.

420 Dating *Doctor Who and the Pirates* (BF #43) - The date isn't specified beyond it being "the eighteenth century".

421 Dating "Ravens" (*DWM* #188-190) - It's "four hundred years" before the main event of this story.

422 Dating *Circular Time:* "Summer" (BF #91) - The year isn't specified, but the month is given as July. The story occurs while Newton is warden of the Royal Mint - he was appointed to the post in 1696, and served until his death in 1727. This date is otherwise arbitrary, but based upon actor David Warner's age of 65 when he voiced Newton (who was born in January 1643 by the Gregorian calendar) for this audio, which is as good a guess as any. Historically, counterfeiting in this period was treated as high treason, and those found guilty were put to death. Convictions proved difficult to achieve, but Newton - often venturing out in disguise, as occurs here - personally collected evidence against such criminals. His most notable prosecution was against the counterfeiter William Chaloner - who was hanged, drawn and quartered on 23rd March, 1699.

423 *Only Human*

424 *The Android Invasion.* The Doctor presumably means the first Duke, who lived 1650-1722 and was made a Duke in 1702.

425 *The Wages of Sin.* This would have to be between 1712-1725.

426 *The English Way of Death* (p46).

427 *The Mind Robber*

428 Dating *The Girl in the Fireplace* (X2.4) - Reinette says it's 1727. The Doctor tells her that August of that year is "a bit rubbish", but he's no way of knowing if August has already passed or not. We might expect Reinette to correct him if it has, but he's gabbling and doesn't really give her a chance.

429 Dating *The Girl in the Fireplace* (X2.4) - It is "weeks, months" after the Doctor and Reinette's first meeting. The older Reinette later says she has "known the Doctor since she was seven" - as she was born 29th December, 1721, she would have been that age almost exclusively in 1728. If the initial meeting takes place in 1727 and the second is "months" later in 1728, then Reinette's comment about her age makes some sense - although it means (not unreasonably) that she's more referring to the Doctor saving her from the clockwork man than their initial, very brief conversation through the fireplace. This probably isn't what was intended on screen, but it fits the available evidence fairly well. The alternative is that the Doctor and Reinette first meet in the last three days of 1727 - which would again push their second meeting into 1728.

It's snowing outside, so it's winter.

The Doctor knows that marrying for love is a mistake, due to his experience with Lady Mary Wortley Montagu.[423]

The Doctor once met the Duke of Marlborough.[424] He also met Peter the Great in Russia, and saw the Peter and Paul Cathedral being built.[425] In 1720, the Doctor saw the Earth's fury at Okushiri.[426] *Gulliver's Travels* was published in 1726.[427]

1727 - THE GIRL IN THE FIREPLACE[428] -> The tenth Doctor passed through a time window from the fifty-first century and met Reinette for the first time.

c 1728 - THE GIRL IN THE FIREPLACE[429] -> Weeks or months later, he met her again and saved her from a clockwork man.

The Aliens Act was passed in 1730.[430] In the same year, a Mr Chicken resided at 10 Downing Street.[431] The Doctor's old friend Padmasambhava began to construct Yeti from this time.[432]

c 1738 - THE GIRL IN THE FIREPLACE[433] -> The tenth Doctor met Reinette when she was a young woman, and snogged her.

In 1740, the man who would become known as Sabbath was born.[434] On 8th September, 1742, the Doctor and his companions spent some time in New England after their adventure in Salem, 1692.[435] Time travellers Penelope Gate and Joel Mintz briefly visited the year 1743.[436]

1744 - THE GIRL IN THE FIREPLACE[437] -> The King's mistress, Madame de Chateauroux, was ill and near death. The tenth Doctor spied on Reinette as she walked through the grounds of a stately home, plotting to become take Chateneux's place.

1745 (February) - THE GIRL IN THE FIREPLACE[438] -> Shortly afterwards, the Doctor used another time window to visit Reinette the night she became the royal mistress.

A battlefield from the Jacobite Uprising was kidnapped by the War Lords.[439]

1746 (April) - THE HIGHLANDERS / THE WAR GAMES[440-441] -> The second Doctor prevented the crooked solicitor Grey from selling Scottish prisoners into slavery. The highlanders had signed six-year plantation work contracts, but the Doctor sent the boat to the safety of France. Jamie McCrimmon, a Scots piper, joined the Doctor on his travels. The Time Lords later returned him to his native time.

Once again, Jared Khan - this time known as Thomas - narrowly missed acquiring the TARDIS. After this time he posed as Alessandro di Cagliostro, claiming to be born 1743, died 1795.[442] In 1750, a ship was wrecked off Haiti. Washed ashore was Nkome, a six-year-old African slave kept alive by voodoo, who began plotting his revenge against the white landowners - the blancs.[443]

Around 1750, a "Mr Sun" arrived in England from

---

430 *The Highlanders*
431 *World War Three* strongly implies that the Doctor met this man. Mr Chicken is historical, and was the last private resident of the building before King George II put it at the disposal of Sir Robert Walpole, the first British Prime Minister.
432 "Over two hundred years" before *The Abominable Snowmen* according to the Abbot Songsten.
433 Dating *The Girl in the Fireplace* (X2.4) - Reinette's age as a young woman isn't given, although she's "twenty three" the next time they meet.
434 *The Adventuress of Henrietta Street*, and specified on the back cover of *Sabbath Dei*, volume three of BBV's *Faction Paradox Protocols* series.
435 *The Witch Hunters*
436 *The Room With No Doors*
437 Dating *The Girl in the Fireplace* (X2.4) - It is said that Madame de Chateauroux, the King's mistress prior to Reinette, is "ill and close to death". She died on 8th December, 1744. The scene probably occurs a few months beforehand, as Reinette is seen walking across a sunny patch of grass.
438 Dating *The Girl in the Fireplace* (X2.4) - It is the night

that Reinette meets the King - historically this occurred in February 1745, after Chateauroux's death. The Doctor says Reinette is "twenty three", which she historically would have been at the time.
439 *The War Games*
440 Dating *The Highlanders* (4.4) - The provisional title of the story was *Culloden*, and it is set shortly after that battle. Despite references in *The Highlanders*, *The War Games* and other stories, Culloden took place in April 1746, not 1745. This is first explicitly stated in *The Underwater Menace*, (although the draft script again said "1745"). The *Radio Times* specified that *The Highlanders* is set in April. The 1745 date has been perpetuated by the first edition of *The Making of Doctor Who*, and surfaces in a number of books, such as *The Roundheads*.
441 Dating *The War Games* (6.7) - Jamie is returned to his native time.
442 *Birthright*
443 *White Darkness*

China. He inherited business space in Covent Garden, and opened a toy store there. A successive number of "Mr Suns" would operate the shop for two hundred years.[444]

The Daemons inspired the Industrial Revolution.[445]

& 1754 - THE GIRL IN THE FIREPLACE[446] -> Rose appeared to warn Reinette that the clockwork men would come for her in five years. Reinette briefly traveled to the fifty-first century, then returned to her home time.

The Doctor received mild injuries when he helped Benjamin Franklin fly his kite.[447]

1752 (2nd to 14th September) - As Britain adopted the Gregorian calendar, eleven days were removed from the British calendar. The British public went to sleep on 2nd September, and awoke on the 14th of the same month. Faction Paradox came to purchase and occupy those missing days, using them as their centre of operations, the Eleven-Day Empire.[448]

Dr Borlase was killed surveying the Nine Travellers in 1754[449]. In the same year, the Doctor discovered Kadiatu Lethbridge-Stewart half-dead in a slaver off Sierra Leone. He took her to the Civilisation of the People.[450]

The Krillitanes, a race who are a genetic amalgam of all the species they've conquered, invaded the planet Bethsan and made a million widows in a day. They also absorbed the natives' wings into their own physiology. The Doctor previously encountered them, when they were like humans but with long necks.[451]

& 1759 - THE GIRL IN THE FIREPLACE[452] -> The tenth Doctor saved Reinette from the clockwork men, but was apparently trapped in the past. However, Reinette had arranged to move her fireplace to her new residence, and it was still capable of working as a time window. The Doctor returned to the future, promising he would return for her.

The Doctor met Doctor Johnson.[453] Scottish poet Robert Burns was born in 1759, so Jamie McCrimmon had never heard of him.[454] A salon full of people from the eighteenth century was kidnapped by Varan Tak.[455]

1764 (15th April) - THE GIRL IN THE FIREPLACE[456] -> The tenth Doctor once again traveled to France to meet Reinette, but this time he was too late, as she had died. He took a letter she had written to him back to the future.

---

444 *The Cabinet of Light* (p85).

445 *The Daemons*

446 Dating *The Girl in the Fireplace* (X2.4) - It is "five years" before Reinette is thirty seven. Owing to her 29th December birthday, she would have been that age almost entirely in 1759, so it's now 1754.

447 *Smith and Jones*. History records this as happening on 15th June, 1752.

448 *Interference*

449 *The Stones of Blood*

450 *The Also People*

451 "Nearly ten" Krillitane generations before *School Reunion*.

452 Dating *The Girl in the Fireplace* (X3.4) - Rose says the clockwork men will come for Reinette "some time after your thirty-seventh birthday", which was on 29th December, 1758, so it must now be 1759.

453 ...*ish*, *Synthespians™*, *The Gallifrey Chronicles*

454 *The Underwater Menace*

455 "The Collector"

456 Dating *The Girl in the Fireplace* (X2.4) - The final sequence takes place shortly after Reinette's death. This historically happened on 15th April, 1764 - the same year as is listed on the painting at the end of the story. The King says Reinette was "forty-three" when she died, but historically she was only forty two. (Writer Steven Moffat has conceded this as a mistake.)

457 "Five hundred years" before *The Daleks*, which I set in 2263.

THE NEUTRONIC WAR ON SKARO: The Neutronic War referred to in *The Daleks* is clearly a different conflict from the Thal-Kaled War seen in *Genesis of the Daleks*, given that the Neutronic War in *The Daleks* lasted just "one day", whereas the Thal-Kaled War lasted "nearly a thousand years". In the first story, a Dalek tells the Doctor that "We, the Daleks and the Thals" fought the Neutronic War, implying that this was after the Daleks were created (a version of events supported by the *TV Century 21* comic strip). The Thal named Alydon speaks of this as the "final war", maybe suggesting that there was more than one.

It's interesting to note that after the Neutronic War, both the Thals and Dals mutated until they resembled the state they'd been in at *Genesis of the Daleks* - the Thals becoming blond humanoids, the Dals becoming green Dalek blobs.

458 This is the opening caption of the first "The Daleks" *TV Century 21* strip.

459 Dating "The Daleks: Genesis of Evil" (*TV21* #1-3, *DWW* #33) - This is the first story in "The Daleks" comic strip printed in *TV Century 21*. As the story starts with the birth of the Daleks, but ends at a time when Earth has spaceships (shortly before *The Dalek Invasion of Earth*, it seems), and "Legacy of Yesteryear" is explicitly "centuries" after "Genesis of Evil", I've broken the strips

Neutronic War on Skaro
- and the Dalek Conquests Begin

& 1763 - There were two races on Skaro: the original Daleks (or Dals) and the Thals. The Daleks were teachers and philosophers, the Thals were a famous warrior race. Skaro was a world full of ideas, art and invention.

However, there were old rivalries between the two races, and this led to a final war. Skaro was destroyed in a single day when the Daleks detonated a huge neutronic bomb. The radiation from the weapon killed nearly all life on the planet, and petrified the vegetation. The only animals that survived were bizarre mutations: the metallic Magnadons, their bodies held together by a magnetic field, and the monsters swarming in the Lake of Mutations.

After the Neutronic War, the Daleks retired into a huge metal city built as a shelter, where they were protected from the radiation. They became dependent on their machines, radiation and static electricity. Most of the Thals perished during the final war, but a handful survived on a plateau a great distance from the Dalek City, where they managed to cultivate small plots of land. The Thals mutated, evolving full circle in the space of five centuries, becoming physically perfect blond supermen.[457]

"Deep in Hyperspace is Planet Skaro. This world is the most feared globe in all the universe. Many thousands of years ago, it was already the scene of a vicious conflict. On the continent of Davius, the Thals, a tall, handsome, peaceful race went in constant dread of attack from the short, ugly Daleks who inhabited Dalazar across the Ocean of Ooze."[458]

& 1763 - "The Daleks: Genesis of Evil"[459] **->** The Daleks discovered cobalt in a mountain range, and developed a neutron bomb. In the year 2003 of the New Skaro Calendar, Minister Zolfian, Warlord of the Daleks, killed the peaceful leader Drenz. The scientist Yarvelling developed war machines ("metal slaves") to kill Thal survivors. As the Dalek factories prepared for war, a meteorite storm struck, starting fires which spread to where the neutron bombs were stored. There was a vast atomic explosion which wiped out the entire continent of Dalazar and reached as far as the Thals' homeland, Davius. Radiation spread across the planet.

The explosion shifted the north pole of the planet, freezing three scientists who had recently discovered a planet nine galaxies away: Earth.[460]

& 1765 - "The Daleks: Genesis of Evil"[461] **->** Two years later, Yarvelling and Zolfian emerged from a shelter. Exploring their continent, they failed to locate any other survivors, and began to succumb to radiation poisoning. They were ambushed by one of the war machines, learning that a mutated survivor had crawled inside. This was the first of a new race of Daleks, with brains a thousand times superior to the original. Zolfian and Yarvelling rebuilt the war factory, creating a Dalek production line. The first Dalek declared himself Emperor and had a special casing constructed - it was finished as Zolfian and Yarvelling died. The Emperor realised the Daleks needed slaves to continue their work.

The Black Dalek was built - it had even more firepower than a standard Dalek. It was the Emperor's deputy.[462]

---

into two blocks, with events of each block happening over a relatively short time, but with hundreds of years between the two.

The year this story - and so the rest of its block - is set isn't given in the strip, but Drenz was killed in 2003 according to both *The Dalek Book* and *The Dalek Pocketbook and Space-Travellers Guide*, both of which are otherwise consistent with the strip. However, this isn't 2003 AD: *The Dalek Outer Space Book* mentions the "New Skaro Calendar", with Year Zero being the year the "Thousand Years War" started. It also says the Daleks emerged in the year 1600 and "The Year of the Dalek" lasted until the year 1,000,000 (the original date given in scripts for *The Daleks' Master Plan*, which may or may not be a coincidence). This would account for a line in "The Dalek World" stating it's not unusual to find Daleks that are a million years old. See "Are There Two Dalek Histories?" for how this can be reconciled with *Genesis*

of the Daleks.

So... the blue-skinned original Daleks appear in 1600, "Genesis of Evil" is set in 2003, and *The Daleks* takes place five hundred years after "Genesis of Evil" (so around 2503). We also know that *Genesis of the Daleks* is set at the end of the Thousand Years War, so in 1000. Making the assumption that a "year" is the same length as a year on Earth (as this chronology does, unless stated otherwise), and using other dates from this chronology, we can work back. *The Daleks* is set in 2263 AD and 2503 according to the New Skaro Calendar, so to calculate an Earth date, you subtract 240 from the Skaro date. Therefore, "Genesis of Evil" starts in 1763 and *Genesis of the Daleks* is set in 760 AD.

460 "Legacy of Yesteryear"
461 Dating "The Daleks: Genesis of Evil" (*TV21* #1-3, *DWW* #33) - It is two years later.
462 "Duel of the Daleks"

& 1765 - "The Daleks: Power Play"[463] -> Within two months, the Daleks had built a vast new city and begun to develop new inventions and weapons. A Krattorian slave ship arrived to collect valuable radioactive sand. The Daleks encouraged a slave revolution, then took the spaceship and the slaves for themselves. Two of the slaves managed to recapture the ship and escape with the slaves... but not before the Daleks learned the spaceship's secrets.

& 1765 - "The Daleks: Duel of the Daleks"[464] -> All the Daleks lacked was the ability to make a material strong enough to withstand the heat stress of space travel. Dalek Zeg was bathed in chemicals and found that he had become stronger (and that his casing had become red and gold). Zeg announced that he had discovered metalert, a substance strong enough to build spaceships from, and would only share it if he was declared Emperor. Zeg attracted followers, and the Emperor consulted the Dalek Brain Machine, which ordered the two fight a duel. The Emperor was not as strong as Zeg, but was more intelligent. Realising that Zeg was resistant to heat, not cold, the Emperor froze Zeg - thus destroying him.

& 1765 - "The Daleks: The Amaryll Challenge"[465] -> The first three prototype spacecraft failed, but the fourth succeeded... until it tried to break the light barrier, when it was destroyed. Proto 9 broke the light barrier, but metalert proved too weak to resist the heat barrier. The saucer-shaped Proto 13 passed every trial, and soon a space armada left Skaro. The Emperor led the fleet, from the golden flagship Proto-Leader.

Dalek saucers landed on Alvega, the nearest planet to Skaro. It was the home of the Amarylls, plant creatures, who resisted the Dalek scouts. They wiped out the Amarylls, and destroyed the world-root - and with it, the entire planet. The Emperor declared a new law: what the Daleks could not conquer, they would destroy.

& 1765 - "The Daleks: The Penta Ray Factor"[466] -> The fleet went onward to Solturis, home of a humanoid race that had been at peace for a hundred years. The Daleks were welcomed, and pretended to be friendly while they discovered the extent of the planet's defences. The penta ray (which combined alpha, infra, omega, ultra and beta rays) was a threat. The Daleks swapped the real

---

463 Dating "The Daleks: Power Play" (*TV21* #4-10, *DWW* #33-34) - "Two months" after "Genesis of Evil".

464 Dating "The Daleks: Duel of the Daleks" (*TV21* #11-17, *DWW* #35-36) - It's set soon after "Power Play".

465 Dating "The Daleks: The Amaryll Challenge" (*TV21* #18-24, *DWW* #36-37) - It's not stated how long the Daleks experiment with spacecraft, but they design and build thirteen different prototypes, test them and then build a fleet of the winning design in the first installment. This allows one of only two gaps in the narrative (the other is between "Impasse" and "The Terrorkon Harvest"), which have to add up to the "centuries" between "Genesis of Evil" and "Legacy of Yesteryear". That said, there's no indication it takes the Daleks very long to develop space travel.

466 Dating "The Daleks: The Penta Ray Factor" (*TV21* #25-32, *DWW* #37-39) - The story follows straight on from "The Amaryll Challenge".

467 Dating "The Daleks: Plague of Death" (*TV21* #33-39, *DWW* #39-40) - The Emperor is summoned back at the end of "The Penta Ray Factor", so this story starts while that story is running.

468 Dating "The Daleks: Menace of the Monstrons" (*TV21* #40-46, *DWW* #40-42) - The Monstron ship arrives while the Daleks are rebuilding after "Plague of Death".

469 Dating "The Daleks: Eve of the War" (*TV21* #47-51, *DWW* #53-54) - It's "a few months" after "The Menace of the Monstrons", and the Daleks have spent the time rebuilding their city. The Mechanoids in the *TV Century 21* strip physically resemble the ones seen in *The Chase*, but see "Dating *The Chase*" [2265] for more.

470 Dating "The Daleks: The Archive of Phryne" (*TV21*

#52-58, *DWM* #54-55) - The story is set shortly after "Eve of the War", with the Daleks gearing up to fight the Mechanoids.

471 Dating "The Daleks: Rogue Planet" (*TV21* #47-51, *DWM* #53-54) - The Daleks are still preparing to fight the Mechanoids, so this is shortly after "The Archive of Phryne". The rogue planet is accidentally called Skardel in a couple of the later instalments.

472 Dating "The Daleks: Impasse" (*TV21* #63-69, *DWM* #62-66, 68) - The story ends the immediate threat of war between the Mechanoids and Daleks.

473 *Minuet in Hell*

474 "Two centuries" before *Revolution Man*.

475 *The Adventuress of Henrietta Street*

476 *Timeless*

477 *The Adventuress of Henrietta Street*

478 *The Unquiet Dead*

479 *The Mark of the Rani*. The American War of Independence ran from 1775-1783.

480 *The King of Terror*

481 *Seasons of Fear*. No date is given, but Franklin died in 1790. The modern-day American government didn't start until 1789, so unless Franklin was President in the *Doctor Who* universe under its predecessor, the Articles of Confederation, then he must have served during the term normally attributed to George Washington.

The mistake wasn't deliberate - writer Paul Cornell genuinely believed that Franklin had been President. In *Neverland*, a line that the "wrong man became President" was meant to denote the Bush / Gore election in 2000, but fans have cited it to cover this mistake.

weapon for a fake, but needed the key to operate it. The main fleet left while Daleks from two saucers attacked the city of Bulos, but were destroyed by the ray. Instead of avenging this, the Emperor received a message from Skaro that demanded his immediate return.

& 1765 - "The Daleks: Plague of Death"[467] **->** Skaro had become a huge war factory that was overseen by the Black Dalek, but a dalatomic rust cloud escaped from one research base and began eating through every Dalek it came into contact with. Dalek hoverbouts were sent to investigate the cloud, and it was contained with magnets, but mutated into a plague. The Daleks began destroying each other, rather than risk infection. The Emperor returned and deduced that the Black Dalek carried the plague. The Black Dalek's casing was recast, and the planet was rebuilt.

& 1765 - "The Daleks: The Menace of the Monstrons"[468] **->** The Monstrons landed in a dead volcano on Skaro, and set their Engibrain robots to building a bridgehead. A Dalek was captured, and the city bombarded with missiles. The Daleks seemed defeated, but the captured Dalek broke free and set off the volcano, destroying the Monstrons.

& 1765 - "The Daleks: Eve of War"[469] **->** A few months later, a new Dalek City had been built, with improved defences. The Daleks constantly monitored against surprise attack. The Daleks built a space station as a staging post to the planet Oric, with construction supervised by the Red Dalek. Workers there were attacked by the Mechanoids' "suspicion ray", and began fighting amongst themselves. The Daleks detected the Mechanoid ship and destroyed it. Two Mechanoid ships quickly retaliated, destroying the Dalek saucer and warning the Daleks to avoid their territory.

& 1765 - "The Daleks: The Archive of Phryne"[470] **->** The Emperor ordered the Daleks to prepare new weapons to fight a galactic war, and began searching nearby planets for new inventions. A force led by the Black Dalek discovered the planet Phryne behind an invisibility screen, and landed to seize "the genius of a hundred planets". But the Phrynians kept the information in their own memories, and fled the Dalek invasion.

& 1765 - "The Daleks: Rogue Planet"[471] **->** The Astrodalek observed a newborn rogue planet in the 84th Galaxy, which they named Skardal. It collided with the planet Omega Three, altering its course so that it was heading for Skaro. Upgraded Dalek saucers fitted with Magray Ultimate deflected Skardal until it was aimed at the home planet of the Mechanoids, Mechanus.

& 1765 - "The Daleks: Impasse"[472] **->** The leaders of the planet Zeros were alarmed at the prospect of galactic war between the Daleks and Mechanoids, and sent a robot agent, 2K, to prevent either side from winning. 2K arrived on Skaro and discovered the existence of Skardal. 2K launched himself towards the rogue planet in a Dalek missile. 2K was captured by the Mechanoids, but diverted the Dalek missile to destroy Skardal. He tricked the Mechanoids into thinking the Daleks had saved them, and the threat of war receded.

Sir Francis Dashwood, an ancestor of Brigham Elisha Dashwood III and Chancellor of the Exchequer to King George III, founded the Hellfire Club as a relatively benign social organization. The group peaked in the 1760s, becoming a debauched haven for the aristocracy. The generations to follow greatly exaggerated the group's dabblings with the black arts.[473]

Rubasdpofiaew, a drug from Tau Ceti Minor, had found its way to Earth and started growing in Tibet as a "miracle flower" named Om-Tsor. Those who consumed Om-Tsor could turn thought into reality. Starving Tibetan lamas ate the Om-Tsor flowers, and used their newfound abilities to found the peaceful "Om-Tsor" valley.[474]

Sabbath was initiated into the British intelligence service in 1762, adopting the name by which we know him.[475] Sabbath was not supposed to survive the initiation, but the Council of Eight saved him. The Council claimed to be humans from the future who wanted to become the Lords of Time. They recruited Sabbath as a counterpart to the Doctor. He did not hear from them for another twenty years.[476]

Sabbath first met the Mayakai warrior Tula Lui in 1776, when she was ten. She would eventually become his apprentice. In 1780, Sabbath failed in an attempt to seduce Scarlette, a brothel owner and ritualist. The same year, he was present during the Gordon Riots. He left the Service, and dealt with the agents of the Service - the "Ratcatchers" - sent to assassinate him. Tula Lui, as Sabbath's only real company from 1780 to 1782, eliminated some high-ranking Service officials as a message for them to leave Sabbath alone.[477]

The American War of Independence

The Doctor was at the Boston Tea Party in 1773.[478] **The Rani was present during the American War of Independence.**[479] The Canavitchi were involved in the same conflict.[480]

Benjamin Franklin became President of the United States.[481] **A little over two hundred years ago, Devil's End became notorious when the Third Lord of**

Aldbourne's black magic rituals were exposed.[482] In the late eighteenth century, Scaroth lived in France at the time of Louis XV. He acquired a Gainsborough.[483]

Gainsborough also painted a portrait of Ace that ended up in Windsor Castle.[484] Kalicum, an agent of the Council of Eight, made genetic alterations to the grandfather of the Frenchman D'Amantine. The alterations would work their way through thirteen successive generations.[485]

The Doctor met Emperor Joseph II of Austria-Hungary.[486] **Cessair posed as Lady Montcalm and was painted by Ramsay.** [487] In September 1781, Jane Hallam - the wife of Henry Hallam, one of Mel's ancestors - died from a horse-riding accident.[488]

1781 (12th December) to 1782 (June) - CATCH-1782[489] -> Melanie unexpectedly arrived through time from 2003, and the transition left her extremely confused and disorientated. Henry Hallam cared for her and, failing to recognize Mel as one of his descendants, became intent on making her his second wife. The sixth Doctor and Mel's uncle, John Hallam, arrived onhand and intervened. The time travellers returned with Mel to the twenty-first century, and Henry eventually married his housekeeper, Mrs McGregor.

Henry's journal and other documents from the period would note the existence of "Eleanor Hallam", actually Mel, who was erroneously believed to have been born about 1760 and died in 1811.

1782 (20th March) to 1783 (13th February) - THE ADVENTURESS OF HENRIETTA STREET[490] -> At the limit of human consciousness was the "horizon", and beyond that was the Kingdom of the Beasts and the babewyns, bestial ape creatures. The destruction of Gallifrey destabilised time, allowing the babewyns to escape to Earth at the point when humans were beginning to conceive of time as a dimension.

The eighth Doctor arrived in this era, suffering physical symptoms as a result of his being linked to his homeworld, which no longer existed. He allied himself with a brothel owner and ritualist, Scarlette. Together, they agreed that the Doctor should marry Juliette, a young woman working in the brothel, as this would link him to Earth and allow him to serve as its protector.

---

482 "Two hundred years" before *The Daemons*.
483 *City of Death*
484 We see the portrait of Ace hanging in Windsor Castle in the extended version of *Silver Nemesis*. At the time, in Ace's personal timeline, she had not yet sat for the painting. Gainsborough lived from 1727-1788, painting society portraits 1760-1774 before turning to landscapes.
485 *Timeless* (p93). Kalicum says that D'Amantine, who's alive in 1830, is the third generation affected by his alterations.
486 *The Devil Goblins from Neptune*. He ruled 1780-1790.
487 *The Stones of Blood*. Allan Ramsay, a Scottish portrait painter, lived 1713-1784.
488 Three months before *Catch-1782*.
489 Dating *Catch-1782* (BF #68) - The dates of Mel's arrival and departure from this era are given.
490 Dating *The Adventuress of Henrietta Street* (EDA #51) - It is "March 1782" on p2, more specifically "March 20, 1782" on p15. The Siege of Henrietta Street happens on "February 8", 1783 (p259). Scarlette's funeral is dated February 9 on p269 and the back cover, with the Doctor departing Henrietta Street on February 13 (p273), and his final conversation with Scarlette occurs on the same day. An epilogue with Sabbath and Juliette happens on "August 18 1783" (p278).

The book is told in a style reminiscent of a history book, and some of the key facts are open to dispute. With that in mind, novels after this one state that Anji has been travelling with the Doctor only for "months", suggesting the timeframe of *Henrietta Street* might be more condensed than the book itself suggests.

Scarlette is the young girl Isobel in the *Faction Paradox* comic series, which covers some of her early history and takes place in 1774.
491 *The Spectre of Lanyon Moor*
492 Dating "The World Shapers" (DWM #127-#129) - It's "the eighteenth century" according to a caption, and the Doctor thinks he's miscalculated by "about forty years". Peri remembers *The Two Doctors* as being "a couple of years ago". The reference to Planet 14 appeared in *The Invasion*.
493 *The Death of Art*
494 *Time and Relative*. Mozart lived 1756-1791.
495 *Silver Nemesis*
496 *The Taint*. Fitz is named after Freddie's brother.
497 *Doctor Who and the Pirates*. The Spinning Jenny was invented in 1797.
498 *The Space Museum*. James Watt lived from 1736-1819.
499 *Day of the Daleks*, Alex Macintosh, the television commentator in that story, states that the house is "Georgian".
500 "One and a half centuries" before "Tooth and Claw" (*DWM*).
501 According to Susan in *The Reign of Terror*.
502 In *An Unearthly Child*, Susan borrows a book about the French Revolution, but already knows a great deal about the subject.
503 *Christmas on a Rational Planet*
504 *Just War*
505 The lockpick is mentioned in *Pyramids of Mars*. The Doctor mentions Marie Antoinette again in *The Robots of Death*.
506 *The Adventuress of Henrietta Street*

The Doctor came to the attention of Sabbath, who thought the Doctor had brought the babewyns to Earth. Sabbath was building a time machine, the *Jonah*. The Doctor and Sabbath teamed up upon realising they both wished to repel the monsters. Juliette abandoned the Doctor for Sabbath. The Doctor collapsed, but recovered enough to marry Scarlette in the Caribbean. The Doctor's illness got worse, and the babewyns transported his party to their domain (possibly the ruins of Gallifrey). Sabbath saved the Doctor by removing one of his hearts.

The babewyns assaulted Scarlette's brothel, and Scarlette was believed killed in the fighting. The Doctor defeated the babewyns, and beheaded the King of Beasts with the sonic screwdriver. A funeral was held for Scarlette on 9th February, 1783, but she had survived and parted company with the Doctor on 13th February.

After implanting the Doctor's heart in his chest, Sabbath gained the ability to travel through time. The Doctor wrote the novel *The Ruminations of a Foreign Traveller in his Element* during this time.

Sir Percival Flint excavated a fogou in Cornwall in 1783 and heard ghastly screams.[491]

c 1785 - "The World Shapers"[492] -> The sixth Doctor, Peri and Frobisher arrived in the Scottish Highlands, looking for Jamie and clues about the mysterious Planet 14. The Time Lords had failed to erase Jamie's memory after all, and he was now known as "Mad Jamie" because he had told people about his adventures with the Doctor. Jamie remembered the reference to Planet 14 - the Cybermen referred to it when they invaded Earth. The Doctor let Jamie go back to Marinus with him, dematerialising the TARDIS in front of the other villagers to prove that Jamie wasn't mad.

In the late 1780s, Montague and Tackleton, a firm making dolls' houses, scandalously make a house that resembled the haunted Ilbridge House.[493] The Doctor met Mozart.[494]

In 1788 the Nemesis Bow was stolen from Windsor Castle.[495] Fitz's great-great-grandfather and his twin, Freddie Tarr and Neville Fitzwilliam Tarr, were born in 1790.[496] The Doctor claimed to be the first person to spin a jenny.[497] **The first Doctor met James Watt, an engineer who influenced the Industrial Revolution.**[498] **Auderly House was built in Georgian times.**[499]

In the late eighteenth century, a cabin boy named Varney served aboard a treasure galleon. A storm left him shipwrecked, and he wasn't seen for five years. During that time, the last of the Curcurbites entered "communion" with Varney, altered his blood and gifted him with a knowledge of biochemistry. He rejoined civilisation as a vampire pirate, made his fortune and settled on an island in the Atlantic. Like Varney, his descendents worked toward the Curcurbite's restitution.[500]

The French Revolution

This was the Doctor's favourite period of Earth history.[501] **Susan showed an interest in the French Revolution, and she visited France at this time with the first Doctor.**[502]

In 1791, the first Doctor and Susan were imprisoned in Paris, but escaped by using an artillery shell. Transcripts of the Doctor's interrogation would end up with the Shadow Directory.[503] It was the Doctor and Susan's first-ever visit to Earth. It demonstrated to the Doctor that the old order could be toppled, and that people wanted freedom and a hope for the future.[504]

The Doctor met Marie Antoinette and obtained a lockpick from her.[505] The Doctor claimed to have been invited into Marie Antoinette's boudoir.[506] He judged that Marie Antoinette had a lovely cook, and decided that eating cake was a good way of passing the time.[507]

In 1791, the Doctor, Tegan and Turlough were dining at the Cafe de Saint Joseph in Aix-en-Provence when they were accidentally scooped up by the Crystal Bucephalus and whisked thousands of years into the future.[508]

In 1793, the attempted opening of Devil's Hump by Sir Percival Flint resulted in disaster.[509] The Daniells brothers unearthed a statuette of a dancer in Pakistan in 1793.[510] In 1793, the actor Robert Dodds built Banquo Manor using money he inherited. The rumour was that Dodds had murdered his aunt for her money.[511]

1794 (late July) - THE REIGN OF TERROR[512] -> The first Doctor and his companions landed in France during the Reign of Terror. Ian met the British spy James Stirling, but Barbara and Susan were arrested as aristocrats and sentenced to the guillotine. Posing as a Citizen, the Doctor rescued his companions and returned them to the TARDIS.

---

507 *The Beautiful People*
508 *The Crystal Bucephalus*
509 *The Daemons*
510 *The Burning*
511 *The Banquo Legacy*

512 Dating *The Reign of Terror* (1.8) - The date is given on screen. *The Programme Guide* offered the date "1792", but *The Terrestrial Index* corrected this. The story shows the arrest of Robespierre, which occurred on 27th July.

= A group of curious aliens performed experiments on reality control and used a "world-machine" device to slip the entire Earth out of N-space. The planet was remade according to the philosophies of a single human: the Marquis de Sade. However, the world-machine's operator threw off the aliens' control and became Minski, a dwarf. Minski created an automaton of the Marquis, who began ruling France the day Robespierre was arrested, and the real Marquis was imprisoned. The fake Marquis ruled France, with Minski as his deputy, for ten years.[513]

1794 (August) - WORLD GAME[514] -> The immortal Players interfered in Earth history for their amusement. After an attempt to kill the future Duke of Wellington failed, the opposing Player countermoved by having Napoleon arrested.

The second Doctor and Serena - an ambitious Time Lady sent to keep him in check - arrived in Antibes to monitor the time disturbances the Players' actions were causing. The Doctor saved Napoleon from execution and quickly came into contact with the Countess, one of the Players, who was working to see Napoleon defeat the British. The Doctor worked out that she hoped to kill Nelson and Wellington, and that the two only met once, in 1805. The Doctor and Serena departed for that meeting.

In 1795, the Directory was running France after Robespierre's arrest. They learned of many unusual visitations and encounters on Earth, and set up the Shadow Directory to capture or destroy such things. At some point, the Shadow Directory autopsied a Time Lord and knew of them as *les betes aux deux coeurs,* or "the devils with two hearts". One of the Shadow Directory's agents, the psychic aristocrat Marielle Duquesne, investigated the Beautiful Shining Daughters of Hysteria in Munchen.[515]

The Doctor met the artist Turner.[516] The Quoth gave psychic abilities to the toymaker Montague in 1797.[517] In 1798, Napoleon undertook an expedition to colonise Egypt. He entered the Great Pyramid, and was mentally influenced to dig out the sand-covered Sphinx.[518]

1798 - SET PIECE[519] -> Benny fled the Ants, and ended up with archaeologist Vivant Denon as he began to uncover Ancient Egyptian treasures for Napoleon. She located the TARDIS, thanks to a message Ace left in 1366 BC, and programmed it to find the Doctor.

Robert Dodds was murdered at Banquo Manor in 1798. A Time Lord agent was dispatched to wait for the Doctor, who eventually showed up a century later.[520] In 1799, Mother Mathara of Faction Paradox and two thousand refugees from Ordifica arrived from 2596. They began building the city of Anathema. With the help of the remembrance tanks that Mathara left, this society would become the Remote.[521]

1799 (9th November - 25th December) - CHRISTMAS ON A RATIONAL PLANET[522] -> Napoleon returned to France from Egypt, shutting down the Directory and replacing it with the Consulate. The Shadow

---

513 *The Man in the Velvet Mask*
514 Dating *World Game* (PDA #74) - Serena gives the date of the Doctor's arrival as 9th August, 1794.
515 *Christmas on a Rational Planet*
516 *The Hollow Men, Blood Heat*
517 *The Death of Art*
518 *The Sands of Time.* Napoleon began his expedition in March 1798, and the year is given (p203).
519 Dating *Set Piece* (NA #35) - It is "1798 CE" (p57).
520 *The Banquo Legacy*
521 *Interference* (p59, p147).
522 Dating *Christmas on a Rational Planet* (NA #52) - It's "1799. At Christmas" (p24).
523 "The early nineteenth century" according to *The Eight Doctors.*
524 *Instruments of Darkness.* In our history, the dodo was extinct by 1700.
525 *The Lazarus Experiment.*
526 "The Glorious Dead"
527 Dating *Foreign Devils* (TEL #5) - It's "December 1800" (p22).
528 Dating *The Man in the Velvet Mask* (MA #19) - The Doctor and Dodo see a poster that gives a date of

"Messidor, Year XII", and the Doctor calculates that they are in "June or July 1804".
529 *The Sea Devils.* Nelson lived 1758-1805.
530 *Eye of Heaven.* Nelson's final battle occurred on 21st October, 1805.
531 *The Scarlet Empress.*
532 "Fire and Brimstone"
533 Dating *World Game* (PDA #74) - The date is given, and is indeed the only day Nelson and Wellington met historically.
534 Dating *Seasons of Fear* (BF #30) - The date is given.
535 According to a gravestone in *The Curse of Fenric.*
536 *Managra, Neverland*
537 *The Pit*
538 *The Eye of the Tyger,* which sounds like a different visit to the one seen in *The Pit.*
539 *The Devil Goblins from Neptune.* Other references to meeting the Duke of Wellington around this time appear in *The Tomorrow Windows, Synthespians™* and *The Book of the Still.* The Duke of Wellington was a leading military and political figure. He became a Field Marshall during the Napoleonic Wars, and oversaw Napoleon's defeat at Waterloo.

Directory secretly survived.

The mysterious Cardinal Scarlath gave the Vatican's Collection of Necessary Secrets certain documents that described the creation of Ancient Egyptian civilisation by a one-eyed monster.

Roz Forrester accidentally ended up in Woodwicke, New York state, after investigating a temporal anomaly in 2012. She set herself up as a fortune-teller and met Samuel Lincoln, whom she mistook for an ancestor of Abraham Lincoln. Roz planned to assassinate Samuel, thus changing history and enabling the seventh Doctor to locate her.

The Doctor arrived and stopped Roz, but as a vast psychic disturbance started in the town. This was caused by the Carnival Queen, also known as Cacophony, who sought to create an irrational universe. The Queen was releasing irrational gynoid monsters into the area, and sought to create further disruption through the latently telepathic Chris Cwej. He chose Reason over the Carnival Queen's irrationality, and the defeated Queen departed into eternity, where she hoped to inspire more ideas.

The Doctor learned afterward that the TARDIS had planted a memory in Chris' mind that swayed his decision, as the TARDIS feared becoming derationalized under the Queen's rule. Jake McCrimmon, agent of the American Special Congress, investigated the aftermath.

The Nineteenth Century

Lord Aldbourne formed a branch of the Hellfire Club and played at devil worship.[523] The Doctor brought the ornithologist James Bond to the 1800s to see a live Dodo.[524]

The Doctor met Beethoven.[525]

> = By this time, Katsura Sato had conquered the Earth. He renamed the world Dhakan.[526]

1800 (December) - FOREIGN DEVILS[527] -> The Emperor became sickened by the foreign-sponsored opium trade afflicting China, and ordered the removal of all "foreign devils". The Chief Astrologer to the Emperor placed a curse on one such opium trader, Roderick Upcott. The curse was designed to first endow the Upcott family with prosperity, making their inevitable downfall all the more crushing.

The TARDIS arrived in China, and while the second Doctor was caught up with local politics, Jamie and Zoe disappeared through a "spirit gate" - a stone ring traditionally designed to keep demons at bay. The Doctor realized the gate was a teleporter and used the TARDIS to follow his companions to 1900.

> = **1804 - THE MAN IN THE VELVET MASK**[528] ->
> The first Doctor and Dodo arrived on Earth, which

had been remade ten years ago by a world-machine. The dwarf Minski, in control of the remade France, attempted to start a war between France, Britain and America that would spread a virus. This would have brought anyone infected by the virus under Minski's control. Minski's plan fell to ruin and he was killed. The Doctor and the real Marquis de Sade sabotaged the world-machine, and the machine's creators promised to return Earth to N-space, erasing the history they had created. Humanity was unaware of the alternate timeline.

Nelson "was a personal friend" of the Doctor.[529] The Doctor breakfasted with Nelson in 1805, the day before Nelson's final battle with Napoleon at Trafalgar.[530] The Doctor was "instrumental" at Trafalgar.[531] His sextant calculated the position of Napoleon's fleet.[532]

1805 (12th September) - WORLD GAME[533] -> The second Doctor and Serena narrowly managed to save Wellington and Nelson when Valmont, one of the immortal Players, attempted to kill them with a bomb.

The Doctor and Serena travelled to Paris to discover more about the Players' plans. They saved Napoleon from assassination, and learned that the Countess - a Player well known to the Doctor - was also in Paris. The Doctor learned that Napoleon had a secret weapon - a submarine - and in part survived a vampire assassin because of all the garlic he'd been eating since arriving in France. The Countess had designed the submarine's omega drive propulsion system, and had also tasked a Raston Warrior Robot to serve as a guard. When this vanished, the Doctor deduced that both the Robot and the vampire had been sent by someone on Gallifrey.

The Doctor and Serena sabotaged the submarine, but with no more leads to the Players' grand plan, they departed for 1815.

> = **1806 - SEASONS OF FEAR**[534] -> The eighth Doctor and Charley confronted the long-lived Grayle once again. This time, Grayle built a transmat and brought his masters, the Nimon, to Earth. The Doctor engineered a time corridor that returned the Nimon to Britain in 305 BC.

Joseph Sundvig was born on 8th April, 1809.[535] The Doctor met Byron and Shelley.[536] In 1811, the poet William Blake vanished from his home and met the Doctor.[537] The Doctor also met William Blake at home once.[538] The Doctor was with a British rifle brigade when he met Sir Arthur Wellesley. He was a prisoner of the French at Salamanca in 1812.[539]

Also in 1812, a battlefield from Napoleon's Russian campaign was kidnapped by the War Lords.[540] The Doctor met Napoleon and told him that an army marches on its stomach.[541]

In 1812, the alien "Mary" arrived on Earth. She was a criminal, and would later claim to hail from a savage, repressive world that punished dissent with death. The beings there communicated with pendants that granted telepathy. Mary killed the guard escorting her, and hosted herself within a passing young woman.[542]

1812 - EMOTIONAL CHEMISTRY[543] **->** The Magellans had evolved as creatures that were essentially living stars. One such creature broke a significant rule among its kind by giving birth to a child, named Aphrodite. The Magellan was put on trial, with the Doctor acting as defence council. The Magellan's people ruled to spilt the creature in half and place each part in separate time zones on Earth. The emotional side of the Magellan became the female Dusha, and by the early nineteenth century had been adopted by Count Yuri Vishenkov. The Magellan's intellectual half became Lord General Razum Kinzhal, a strategist around the year 5000. Aphrodite herself was contained and given the extra-dimensional locale of Paraiso as her home.

Living as a Russian noblewoman, Dusha Vishenkov had the ability to alter probability and affected her "sister" Natasha Vishenkov. Natasha's descendants would look virtually identical for millennia to come, and be statistically predisposed to good luck. Dusha's influence also turned the Vishenkov family's possessions into empathic capacitors, capable of amplifying the emotions of those nearby. One such item, a painting, would be on display in the Kremlin Museum in 2024 and start a fire there.

The eighth Doctor helped Dusha reunite with her lover, Kinzhal, in the year 5000.

In summer 1812, the Doctor witnessed Napoleon invading Russia, and later remembered the occasion as having stormy weather. Illeana (later Illeana de Santos) fled with her wealthy merchant father from Smolensk, but bandits killed her father. The werewolf Stubbe turned her into a werewolf and bound her to him for a century or two.[544]

The Celestial Toymaker beat Napoleon at Risk.[545]

c 1813 - THE MARK OF THE RANI[546] **->** The Rani was present during the Industrial Revolution, extracting a chemical from human brains. Her project was interrupted by the arrival, and rivalry, of the Master and the sixth Doctor. The Master attempted to disrupt human history as the greatest scientific minds of the era converged on Killingworth. The Doctor trapped the two renegades in the Rani's TARDIS and banished them from Earth.

1814 (February) - FROSTFIRE[547] **->** The first Doctor, Steven and Vicki arrived at the last-ever frost fair - literally

---

540 *The War Games*
541 *Day of the Daleks*. The Doctor does not meet Napoleon in *The Reign of Terror* (although Ian and Barbara do). The third Doctor is still exiled in the twentieth century timezone, so he must have met Napoleon in an earlier incarnation. Napoleon lived 1769-1821. The meeting is also mentioned in *Escape Velocity* and *Warmonger*.
542 *TW: Greeks Bearing Gifts*. Mary is evidently from the same race as the peaceful "star poet" seen in *SJA: Invasion of the Bane*, which suggests that - as Mary speculates in the *Torchwood* episode - her planet has undergone a regime change.
543 Dating *Emotional Chemistry* (EDA #66) - The date is given in the blurb.
544 *Loups-Garoux*
545 "End Game" (*DWM*)
546 Dating *The Mark of the Rani* (22.3) - The date is never stated on screen or in the script, but *DWM* reported that the production team felt that the story was set in "1830". *The Terrestrial Index* set the story "c1825", the novelisation simply said "the beginning of the nineteenth century". Tony Scupham-Bilton concluded in *Celestial Toyroom* that, judging by the historical evidence and the month the story was filmed, the story was "set in either October 1821 or October 1822". As

that article states, the story must at the very least be set before the Stockton-Darlington line was opened in September 1825, and after Thomas Liddell was made Baron Ravensworth on 17th July, 1821. However, Jane Baker later told *DWM* that her research was confused by the Victorian convention of biographies referring to Lords by their titles even before they were given them. Given that, Jim Smith in *Who's Next* suggested that the date given in *DWM* was a mishearing of "1813", which fits all the evidence apart from the existence of Lord Ravensworth.
547 Dating *Frostfire* (BF *The Companion Chronicles* #1) - The year is given, and historically the last River Thames frost fair started on 1st February, 1814, and only lasted four days. The issue of whether the first Doctor only had one heart or not is complicated by the phoenix's comment about the cold "in the Doctor's hearts". As Austen claims, she had only published two novels by 1814: *Sense and Sensibility* (1811) and *Pride and Prejudice* (1813). *Mansfield Park*, her third book, would surface in July 1814. *Northanger Abbey* had been completed some years later, but had a troubled publication history and only saw release in 1817 - the same year that Austen died.
548 Dating *World Game* (PDA #74) - The Doctor arrives on the eve of the Battle of Waterloo, so therefore it's

a fair situated upon ice - on the River Thames. Captain McClavity owned a Collection of Curiosities there, and a phoenix egg that he had acquired from the Medina in Tunis attracted the Doctor's attention. The travellers encountered Jane Austen at this time, much to the Doctor's delight, as he had read all of her novels and thought them very witty. However, soon after the meeting, McClavity was murdered and the phoenix egg stolen.

The phoenix inside the egg had been responsible for the destruction of a thousand worlds, and now sought to be reborn on Earth. Its essence possessed Georgina Mallard, whose husband - Sir Joseph Mallard - worked for the Royal Mint. The phoenix hoped to use the Mint's metal-melting furnace as a hatchery for itself, but Austen assisted the Doctor's group in turning down the heat. The newly hatched phoenix chick died, but a cinder from the fire - endowed with a small piece of the phoenix's being - remained in Vicki. She only learned of its presence after she left the Doctor's company and became Lady Cressida.

1815 (June) - WORLD GAME[548] -> Using psychic paper, the second Doctor gatecrashed a ball being held by Wellington, and thereby warned him of the Players' plans. Serena was killed saving Wellington from an assassination attempt.

The Doctor impersonated Napoleon in order to infiltrate the French lines at Waterloo and divert reinforcements arranged by the Players. History was returned to its normal course and the Players - worried about further intervention from the Time Lords - suspended their games.

Major General Fergus Lethbridge-Stewart fought in the Battle of Waterloo.[549] The Doctor met Wellington after the conflict.[550]

= **1815 (18th November) - WORLD GAME**[551] ->
The second Doctor and Serena arrived in a Paris that was celebrating a great victory over the British and Wellington's mysterious death. The Doctor and Serena first traveled fifty years into the future - to see the end result of the Countess' Grand Design - then went a month into the past to prevent it happening.

In 1816, the Doctor visited the Duke of Wellington, and made a lot of money at a gambling den. He set up an account at Chumley's Bank that he occasionally dipped into while on Earth.[552] The Doctor was present when Peter the Great sent an expedition to Alaska.[553] He was also there the night Mary Shelley came up with the story of Frankenstein.[554]

1818 - THE GHOSTS OF N-SPACE[555] -> Travelling back in time, the third Doctor and Sarah witnessed the early life of the wizard Maximillian.

In the early nineteenth century, the Doctor met Beau Brummel, who told him he looked better in a cloak.[556]

A Dalek scoutship crashed on the planet Vulcan. By this time, the Daleks had already encountered the second Doctor.[557] The Dalek ship was from the far future.[558]

The Beast of Fang Rock was seen.[559] The Reverend Thomas Bright surveyed the Nine Travellers. At some point between now and the late twentieth century, Cessair posed as Mrs Trefusis for sixty years, then Senora Camara.[560]

On 3rd July, 1820, Florence Sundvig was born.[561] Napoleon died in 1821, still traumatised by what he had witnessed in the Great Pyramid in 1798.[562]

17th June, 1815.
549 *The Dying Days.* His first name and rank were given in *The Scales of Injustice.*
550 *The Eight Doctors*
551 Dating *World Game* (PDA #74) - The date is given.
552 *Players*, almost certainly the same meeting mentioned in *The Eight Doctors*. The back account is also mentioned in *World Game*.
553 *The Land of the Dead*
554 *Storm Warning.* This occurred in 1816, and is also referred in *The Devil Goblins from Neptune*, *Neverland*, *Zagreus* and *Terror Firma*.
555 Dating *The Ghosts of N-Space* (MA #7) - It is "eighteen eighteen" (p63), one hundred and fifty seven years before the present-day setting (p200).
556 The Doctor mentions Beau Brummel in *The Sensorites*, *The Twin Dilemma* and *The Two Doctors*. Brummel lived 1778-1840. He was an arbiter of fashion in Regency England, and helped further the style known as "dandyism".

557 The Dalek ship crashed "two hundred years" before *The Power of the Daleks.* This is the first recorded Dalek expedition in our solar system assuming, of course, that Vulcan is (or was) in our solar system. *War of the Daleks* states that this capsule is from the far future (after *Remembrance of the Daleks*), and this fits some of the circumstantial evidence - a Dalek from this mission recognises the Doctor, despite his regeneration (and despite no recorded adventures with any Doctor - except for *Genesis of the Daleks* - up to this point). In *Day of the Daleks*, the Daleks must use the Mind Analysis Machine to establish the Doctor's identity. On the other hand, the Daleks are silver and blue, and dependent on external power supplies - quite unlike the Davros Era Daleks.
558 *War of the Daleks*
559 "Eighty years" before *Horror of Fang Rock.*
560 *The Stones of Blood*
561 *The Curse of Fenric*
562 *The Sands of Time* (p220). The year is given, and

In 1826 the *Camara* was lost in the Irish Sea after snaring a stone "demon" in its nets.[563]

= c 1827-1828 - MEDICINAL PURPOSES[564] **-> A** human researcher from the future had acquired a Type 70 TARDIS from a Nekkistani dealer of Gryben, and a dying alien race had employed him to research a virus that was killing them. As the aliens' immune systems were similar to those of human beings, the researcher set up shop in Edinburgh, 1827. He assumed the guise of Dr. Robert Knox, the anatomist who employed the graverobbers William Burke and William Hare to deliver him cadavers for study. Burke and Hare failed to content themselves with merely unearthing corpses, and started murdering people to fulfil Knox's demands.

"Knox" infected some Edinburgh residents with the alien virus as part of his research, but anyone who consumed alcohol proved immune. Failing to make much progress, Knox used his illicit technology to roll back time in Edinburgh and start with "new" bodies. He grew ambivalent toward his employers' survival, and turned the enterprise into an elite tourist attraction, with patrons paying to witness the "Hale and Burke Experience." The memories of the locals grew cloudy as time repeatedly looped.

The sixth Doctor and Evelyn arrived inside of Knox's time loop, and discovered his operations.

On 28th January, 1829, the Doctor and Evelyn observed Burke's public hanging. The Doctor tricked Knox into leaving the sanctity of his time loop and infected him with the alien virus. Knox fled in his TARDIS, hoping to find a cure, aware that his former employers would attempt to hunt him down. History was restored to its proper path. The Doctor and Evelyn took the mentally disabled man "Daft Jamie," who was slated to become one of Burke and Hare's victims, back to meet his appointed demise.

In early May 1830, the time traveller Chloe and her dog Jamais happened upon Sabbath in St. Raphael, France. She sensed part of his history but fell unconscious. When she awoke, Sabbath had left her a diamond and a book purporting to speak of the future. Her belief in the book allowed Sabbath to manipulate her activities.[565]

= In 1831, energy beings from the Eternium, a doomed pocket universe, manipulated the aspiring poet Jared Malahyde to begin work on "the Utopian Engine," a device intended to temporally age Earth to extinction. If successful, the Eternines would harvest the life force energy released by Earth's demise. Malahyde partnered with architect Isambard Kingdom Brunel, and they became wealthy by pioneering "the Malahyde Process" - an advanced means of developing superior steel. Malahyde spent the next twelve years working on the Utopian Engine.[566]

Napoleon died 5th May, 1821.

563 "Seaside Rendezvous"

564 Dating *Medicinal Purposes* (BF #60) - The back cover says 1827. Burke and Hare met the real Knox in November 1827, but the majority of their murders occurred throughout 1828, until they were caught in November of that year. The audio concurs with the historical date for Burke's execution. Hare was granted immunity because he turned King's Evidence against Burke. The real Knox was never prosecuted.

565 *Timeless*

566 *Reckless Engineering*

567 Dating *Bloodtide* (BF #22) - The date is given.

568 *Sometime Never*

569 "Three years" before "The Curious Tale of Spring-Heeled Jack".

570 *The Curse of Peladon*. Victoria was crowned in 1838.

571 *The Spectre of Lanyon Moor*

572 According to Professor Litefoot in *The Talons of Weng-Chiang*, the gun "hasn't been fired for fifty years".

573 *The Two Doctors*. The architect Isambard Kingdom Brunel lived 1806-1859, and also features in *Reckless Engineering*.

574 *The Romans*

575 Dating "The Curious Case of Spring-Heeled Jack" (*DWM* #334-336) - The date "1840" is given.

576 *Eye of Heaven*. The date of Stockwood's first expedition is given (p1).

577 *All-Consuming Fire*

578 Dating *Reckless Engineering* (EDA #63) - The date is given as "19 July 1843" (p5).

579 *The Church and the Crown*

580 According to *The Tomorrow Windows*. *The Unquiet Dead*, on the other hand, certainly presents itself as the first meeting between them.

581 *The Death of Art*

582 *The Algebra of Ice* (p8-11).

583 Fifteen years prior to *Other Lives*.

584 Dating *Other Lives* (BF #77) - The year is 1851, and the Great Exhibition was held from 1st May to 15th October. The Doctor's comment that the Exhibition did a lot of business in its "first six months" is therefore an approximation, as it was only open five and a half months total. As the Duke of Wellington claims, he would have been eighty two in this story, and he died the following year.

585 Dating "Claws of the Klathi!" (*DWM* #136-138) - Derridge says it's "the twelfth of September, year of Our Lord Eighteen Hundred and Fifty-One".

1835 - BLOODTIDE[567] **->** The sixth Doctor took Evelyn to meet her personal hero, Charles Darwin in the Galapagos Islands. They learned of "devil creatures" on the island, identifying them as Silurians. The Doctor confronted their leader, the renegade scientist Tulok, who planned to wipe out all human life with a virus. The Doctor tricked the Silurians' Myrka into destroying a Silurian submersible, which killed Tulok before he could launch his bacterial warheads. The Doctor suggested that Darwin not mention the Silurians in his writing.

In May 1837, in the Pyrennes, the archaeologist Louis Vosgues stood on the verge of formulating the theory of evolution years before Darwin. An Agent of the Council of Eight insured that Vosgues fell off a cliff to his death.[568]

The killer Springheeled Jack was first reported in London in 1837.[569]

The Victorian Era

The Doctor attended the coronation of Queen Victoria.[570] In the 1840s, a tenant farmer who tried to flatten the tumulus on Lanyon Moor died of a heart attack. The crops nearby failed for the next seven years.[571]

Professor Litefoot's Chinese fowling piece was last fired around this time.[572] **The Doctor met Brunel.**[573] **He also gave Hans Christian Andersen the idea for "The Emperor's New Clothes".**[574]

1840 -"The Curious Tale of Spring-Heeled Jack"[575]

-> The eighth Doctor investigated the case of Springheeled Jack, who had apparently been assaulting young women in London. He discovered that Jack was innocent, and the killings had been performed by the alien Morjanus, a bitter rival of Jack's race. Morjanus released the fire-beings named the Pyrodines, and the Doctor destroyed them. Jack remained in London to fight crime.

An alien race, on the verge of losing a war, had long ago seeded its DNA into space in millions of head-shaped *moai*. The aliens' rivals killed them, but the *moai* distributed the DNA like a virus, creating hybrids of the aliens on multiple worlds. On Earth, such *moai* had settled on Rapa Nui (also known as Easter Island) and turned some Polynesians into alien hybrids. But in October 1842, Horace Stockwood's expedition to the island carried a disease that would kill off the hybrids.[576]

In 1843, the first Doctor and Susan met Sherlock Holmes' father, Siger Holmes, in India and learnt that the natives believed in a gateway to another world.[577]

= **1843 - RECKLESS ENGINEERING**[578] **->** The Eternine gambit to steal Earth's life-energy reached fruition in 1843, when Malahyde finished and activated "the Utopian Engine." The eighth Doctor's intervention meant that instead of aging Earth to death, the device simply advanced time on the planet's surface forty years. This nonetheless created an alternate timeline in which an estimated ninety-five percent of mature humans and animals either aged to death or died from shock. Humanity's children - suddenly aged to adulthood - became savage creatures of instinct named "the Wildren." The remaining pockets of civilization took to disparate settlements struggling to survive, and cannibalism became an accepted means of survival in some parts.

In 1844, the Doctor helped Alexandre Dumas with *The Three Musketeers*.[579] The Doctor met Charles Dickens.[580] Dickens' work became far darker in tone after he encountered Montague's killer dolls in 1845.[581]

= Time distortion threw Edgar Allen Poe's death into flux. In alternate histories, he either died in a gutter four days before history recorded or happily survived and stayed on a drinking binge. The distortion abated, and Poe expired on 7th October, 1849.[582]

The traveller Edward Marlow married his beloved Georgina at Camden Chapel. They lived in his uncle's house in Camden Town, and had two sons - Edward and Henry. The elder Edward explored the world and wrote about his discoveries, but went missing in 1850.[583]

1851 - OTHER LIVES[584] **->** At the Great Exhibition of the Works of Industry of All Nations, civil unrest was threatened when two French visitors - Monsieur de Roche and his wife Madeleine - went missing. Charley and C'rizz aided the Duke of Wellington in a deception to cover up their disappearance, but the visitors had simply timejumped ahead in the TARDIS and returned without incident. The eighth Doctor was mistaken for the absent traveller Edward Marlow, and assisted the man's wife in retaining her household. C'rizz was briefly imprisoned in a freak show and crippled its owner, Jacob Crackles.

1851 (12th September) - "Claws of the Klathi!"[585]

-> The seventh Doctor landed in London at the time of the Great Exhibition, and met Nathanial Derridge of the New Lunar Society, a scientific club. The Doctor learned that some curious murders had taken place in Docklands, and was attacked by a robot at the scene of the crime. He evaded the robot to discover a crashed spacecraft.

Nearby, the Wyndham's Freakshow included some live aliens. The Doctor met one, Caval of the Joebb, whose race was lifted out of squalor by the Klathi - ruthless aliens who were also in London. The Klathi need a large crystal to power their ship, but activating the reflective lattice would kill people over a vast area. The Doctor confronted the Klathi at Crystal Palace, but they didn't care about the human casualties. Joebb rebeled, and the aliens were killed when their spacecraft exploded.

The *America* crossed the Atlantic in seventeen days in 1851.[586] Roget was a very good friend of the Doctor.[587] The Doctor claimed that he once told Livingstone: "That's all very well… but the elephant in the gorilla suit has to go."[588] Around this time, Jacob Grimm discovered the Law of Consonantal Shift.[589]

Albert, the Prince Consort, frequently lodged at Torchwood Estate with the father of Sir Robert MacLeish. The two of them dared to imagine that local stories about a werewolf and the brethren that protected it were true, and set about constructing a trap for the beast should it seek to infect Queen Victoria. A light chamber was constructed, and Albert had the Koh-i-Noor, the diamond given to Victoria as spoils of war, constantly recut to serve as the chamber's focusing device.[590]

Victoria Waterfield was born in 1852.[591] The Doctor met Thackeray, Baudelaire, Delacroix and Manet.[592] In 1853, Saul, a living church in Cheldon Bonniface, was baptised in his own font.[593]

1855 (13th December) - "Cuckoo" [594] -> The seventh Doctor, Benny and Ace landed in the seaside village of Lifton, where it was rumoured the devil had shown himself. This was the location of one of the richest fossil beds in Southern England. Mary Anne Wesley was pioneering the field of paleontology at this time, despite the fact the

---

586 *Enlightenment*

587 *The One Doctor.* Peter Roget was a physician and lexicographer who lived 1779-1869. He compiled *Roget's Thesaurus.*

588 *Cryptobiosis.* "Livingstone" is presumably David Livingstone (1813-73), the famed Scottish medical missionary and explorer of Africa (from 1852-56).

589 *State of Decay.* Grimm lived 1785-1863.

590 *Tooth and Claw* (TV). Prince Albert and Sir Robert's father seem to have begun collaborating as early as Robert's childhood, but the exact dating is unclear. The Koh-i-Noor was presented to Queen Victoria in 1850, and Albert died 14th December, 1861. The recounting of the diamond in *Tooth and Claw* deviates a little from history - the story seems to imply that Albert whittled down the stone through constant recuttings, when most of the lost mass was shed in a single cutting in 1852.

591 *Downtime.* Victoria was "eleven" (p14) when her mother died in "1863" (p261). This would make her fourteen when she started travelling with the Doctor.

592 *Ghost Ship.* Novelist William Thackeray (*Vanity Fair*) lived 1811-1863; poet Charles Baudelaire 1821-1867; painter Eugéne Delacroix 1798-1863; painter Édouard Manet 1832-1883. While there's no indication these meetings were on the same trip, it's possible.

593 *Timewyrm: Revelation* (p4).

594 Dating "Cuckoo" (*DWM* #208-210) - The date is given at the beginning of the story.

595 *The Evil of the Daleks*

596 *The Sea Devils*

597 *The War Games*

598 *The Evil of the Daleks*

599 *Interference* (p191).

600 *The Rapture.* The brothers' portal isn't related to the portal that abducts James Lees in the same era.

601 *Empire of Death.* James is replaced in 1856, as dated on the back cover and p5.

602 *Downtime*

603 *The Shadows of Avalon*

604 "Cuckoo"

605 *Island of Death.* The third Doctor remembers the meeting, so it's a different occasion than when the sixth Doctor met him in *Bloodtide* - unless we're to presume that the third Doctor is just name-dropping for the sake of showing off.

606 *The Eleventh Tiger*

607 *The Talons of Weng-Chiang.* Jago claims to have had "thirty years in the halls".

608 *Tooth and Claw* (TV)

609 *The Eleventh Tiger*

610 "The Tides of Time"

611 "Half a century" before *Year of the Pig*, provided the age of Chardalot's journals is anything to go by.

612 *Wooden Heart.* "Blondin" is Charles Blondin (AKA Jean François Gravelet-Blondin), a French tight-rope walker and acrobat who lived 1824–1897. He first performed the Niagara Falls feat in 1859, but repeated it, with variations, a number of times after that.

613 Dating *Empire of Death* (PDA #65) - The story's starting and ending dates are given on p37 and p235. Prince Albert died about fifteen months before this story, in December 1861.

614 *Logopolis.* Thomas Huxley lived 1825-1895.

615 *The Evil of the Daleks*, with further details in *Downtime.*

616 *The War Games*

617 *The Chase.* The TARDIS crew supposedly watch this on the Time-Space Visualiser, although it's possible that they're just watching Lincoln rehearse the speech beforehand. The actual event had Lincoln surrounded by a huge crowd in close quarters; the Visualiser shows him very much isolated.

618 Dating *Renaissance of the Daleks* (BF #93) - The date is given toward the end of episode two. As stated, the detonation killed three hundred Confederates, but

locals disapproved. The Doctor was here to stop her, as Wesley was about to unearth the fossil of an alien - and set science back by decades as it pursued a false trail. While the Doctor and Benny met Wesley, Ace found a body on the beach. The Doctor realised that one of the Wesleys' other guests was a lizard-like shapeshifter, a Surcoth, looking to repatriate the fossilised remains of an ancient explorer. The Doctor let him leave.

The Crimean War

The Crimean War was fought 1853-1856. On 25th October, 1854, the Doctor was present at the "magnificent folly" of the Charge of the Light Brigade.[595] **The Doctor claimed he had been wounded in the Crimea.**[596] **The War Lords lifted a Crimean War battlefield.**[597]

In 1854, Theodore Maxwell experimented with electromagnetism.[598] The Ogron homeworld was discovered in 1855. From this point, the ape-like race would be used as slaves and hired muscle by more than a dozen races.[599]

Two residents of the Euphorian Empire, the artisan brothers Jude and Gabriel, travelled to Earth in 1855 via a dimensional portal. On the island of Es Vedra, the monk Francisco Belao mistook them for angels.[600]

In Scotland, 1856, a young boy named James Lees encountered a different dimensional portal while swimming in the River Clyde near the Corra Linn falls. Lees remained on the other side of the portal, but the aliens who lived there sent a doppelganger of him back through as an ambassador. The ersatz James could tap people's memories to "speak with the voices of the dead" and was committed to an asylum. Within a few years, he'd become renowned as a spiritualist.[601]

Charles Dodgson photographed a young Victoria Waterfield in 1857.[602] The Doctor talked to Lewis Carroll about the sleeping King Constantine, which influenced Carroll's writing.[603] Darwin published *The Origin of the Species* in 1859.[604] The Doctor met Darwin.[605] In 1860, Ian's great-grandfather, Major William Chesterton, served as a member of a Hussar company at Jaipur, India.[606]

In 1860, Litefoot's father was a Brigadier-General on the punitive expedition to China. The Litefoot family stayed in the country for the next thirteen years. Around this time, Henry Gordon Jago began working in the entertainment business.[607]

A child born ten miles from the Torchwood Estate was stolen from a cultivation, and became the newest host to the essence of an alien werewolf.[608] In 1863, the stone-imprinted minds of Qin Shi Huang and his two generals were transferred into Abbot Wu and two warrior monks.[609] A time warp in the USA sent a Cheyenne War Party to the twentieth century, where they attacked a trucker.[610]

A time traveller of unknown origin arrived in the nineteenth century, and conducted - as far as could be discerned after the fact - experiments to improve the cognitive and intellectual abilities of pigs. Two "children" were born in the laboratory: the human-looking Charlie and his brother Toby, a walking talking pig who developed enough manners and intelligence to pass in polite society as a swine of culture. Charlie and Toby were both endowed with false memories of their childhood, and - owing to their father's time-travelling nature - had bits of historical foreknowledge.

The traveller died, taking his secrets to the grave. Charlie adopted the name "Alphonse Chardalot", but his memories were very muddled. In the years to follow, he sought to continue the work of his "father", often mistakenly believing himself to be the deceased time traveller. Meanwhile, Toby became a stage performer who shared his "life story" (such as he knew it) with audiences, and would perhaps sing an aria or two. The showman Tom Norman served as his agent.[611]

The Doctor accompanied Blondin on one of his tightrope walks across Niagara Falls.[612]

1863 (14th - 21st February) - EMPIRE OF DEATH[613] **->** The duplicate James Lees was now performing séances for the heads of Europe, and Queen Victoria commissioned him to hold a séance for her late husband, Prince Albert. General George Doulton mistook the dimension from which "Lees" hailed as the afterlife, and sought to claim it for the British Empire. Earth's physical laws were affecting the other side, and the beings who lived there became increasingly desperate to seal off the dimensional rift. The fifth Doctor used the TARDIS to close the rift, and Queen Victoria vowed to never speak of the matter again. The false James expired, and the real one was returned, having barely aged since he entered the rift in 1856. Doulton and several of his men remained trapped on the other side.

The Doctor lost track of whether he's met Queen Victoria before now.

Around this time, the Doctor befriended biologist Thomas Huxley.[614] Victoria Waterfield's mother, Edith Rose, **died** on 23rd November, 1863.[615]

The American Civil War

A battlefield from the American Civil War was lifted by the War Lords.[616] **The Gettysburg address was made on 19th November, 1863.**[617]

1864 (30th July) - RENAISSANCE OF THE DALEKS[618] **->** Nyssa and the knight Mulberry arrived in Petersburg, Virginia, via a wormhole from 1320. The Siege of Petersburg was underway, and Union troops set explosives in a mine tunnel running under Confederate lines. The bombs detonated early in the morning on 30th July, killing about three hundred Confederate soldiers.

> = The fifth Doctor arrived too late to rescue them, and Nyssa and Mulberry were present at 3:15 am when the bombs exploded.

The Doctor overrode the TARDIS' time-track crossing protocol, and rescued Nyssa and Mulberry at 3:14 am.

1865 (February - April) - BLOOD AND HOPE[619] ->

The fifth Doctor, Peri and Erimem attempted to visit the Wild West but arrived in the waning days of America's Civil War instead. The Doctor assisted the Union army as the medic "Doctor John Smith," and was present on 26th March, 1865, when Billingsville Prison was captured. On 5th April, the Doctor saved President Lincoln from an assassination attempt in Richmond, Virginia. On the same day, Peri shot dead the Confederacy's Colonel Jubal Eustace when he attempted to murder her friends as

Union collaborators. Lincoln was killed days later on 14th April.

The Doctor warned Lincoln not to go to the theatre.[620] Lord Kelvin laid transatlantic telegraph cables in 1865.[621]

1865 - THE ELEVENTH TIGER[622] ->

Earth prepared to enter a unique stellar conjunction for the first time in two thousand years. Qin Shi Huang, controlled by the intelligence that revived him, assembled an army and started securing "sacred sites" that would serve as conduits to the intelligence's power, enabling it to seize control of China. The first Doctor, Ian, Barbara and Vicki arrived at this time, and their allies flooded a tomb seeped with the intelligence's power. Qin took control of his host long enough to step into the water, shorting out the intelligence's energy. Qin's mind dissipated, and the possessed Abbot Wu recovered.

Major William Chesterton served in China at this time, and suffered a concussion while fighting bandits in Qiang-Ling. The Doctor and his friends encountered the Ten

---

the Union army miscalculated in the explosion's aftermath, and lost 5,300 troops. The crater caused by the mine explosion is still visible to this day.

619 Dating *Blood and Hope* (TEL #14) - Judging by a letter on p29, the TARDIS crew arrive in America on 21st February, 1865. The Doctor's saving Lincoln is dated on p49; Eustace's death is dated on p69.

620 *Minuet in Hell*

621 "Fifteen years" before *Evolution* (p107).

622 Dating *The Eleventh Tiger* (PDA #66) - The date is given. Although not referred to by name, the alien intelligence would appear to be the Mandragora Helix. The intelligence bears the Helix's characteristics, and on p274, it intimates that the Doctor defeated its attempt to dominate Earth "four hundred years" previous.

623 Dating *World Game* (PDA #74) - The TARDIS travels "fifty years" beyond 1815.

624 Dating *The Evil of the Daleks* (4.9) - An early storyline gave the date of the Victorian sequence as "1880" (and the date of the caveman sequence which was later deleted as "20,000 BC"). The camera scripts gave the date of "1867", as did some promotional material, but this was altered at the last minute when it was decided to dovetail *The Faceless Ones* and *The Evil of the Daleks*.

625 *The Androids of Tara*

626 *Pier Pressure*

627 *The War Games*

628 *Strange England* (p157).

629 *Imperial Moon*

630 Dating *The Unquiet Dead* (X1.3) - The Doctor gives the year (having originally aimed for 1860). The date is given a number of times, first on a poster in Dickens' dressing room.

631 The Doctor uses the Rift to refuel the TARDIS in *Boom Town* and *Utopia*. Evidence of the Rift attracting alien beings and technology is witnessed throughout *Torchwood* Series 1, starting with *TW: Everything Changes*.

632 *Utopia*. It may or may not be coincidence that 1869 is the year the TARDIS landed at the Rift in *The Unquiet Dead*.

633 According to Angus in *Terror of the Zygons*.

634 *Horror of Fang Rock*

635 *The War Games*

636 *Companion Piece*

637 Dating *Set Piece* (NA #35) - It is "1871 CE" (p62). The Commune fell on 28th May, 1871. Ace's departure in *Set Piece* deliberately echoes the epilogue to *The Curse of Fenric* novelisation, in which the Doctor visits an older Ace in nineteenth-century Paris, some time after she's departed his company. Reconciling the epilogue with the New Adventures is difficult, however, as the epilogue takes place in 1887 (p186 and 188) when Ace is still a "young lady". Given her aging in the New Adventures, this makes it unlikely that she lives in Paris for the whole sixteen-year duration between 1871 and 1887. Fortunately, the New Adventures have Ace taking up time travel after *Set Piece*, and using a time-jump to facilitate her meeting with the Doctor in 1887 would explain a great deal.

638 *The Devil Goblins from Neptune*

639 *The Talons of Weng-Chiang*. Greel arrived in 1872, according to *The Shadow of Weng-Chiang*.

640 Dating *Eye of Heaven* (PDA #8) - The date is given (p17).

641 Dating *The Chase* (2.8) - The emptied *Mary Celeste* was discovered in November 1872.

Tigers of Canton, the top ten kung fu masters in Guangdong.

> **= 1865 - WORLD GAME**[623] **->** The Countess created an alternate time line in which Napoleon won the Battle of Waterloo. As she had foreseen, he died of pneumonia during his victory parade in Moscow, whereupon his empire collapsed. The Players took advantage of the empire's disintegration and created numerous small territories, which they used to pit against each other in endless "games" of war. The Countess described this as her "Grand Design", but the second Doctor restored the correct timeline by travelling back and preventing Napoleon's victory.

Following the Players' defeat, they abandoned the Grand Design. All Games were suspended indefinitely due to the amount of disruption the Countess had caused, which drew the attention of the Time Lords.

1866 (2nd - 3rd June) - THE EVIL OF THE DALEKS[624] ->
The second Doctor and Jamie were brought to the Waterfield household from 1966 by the Daleks, who ran tests on them in the hopes of discovering the Human Factor. That done, the Doctor, Jamie and the Waterfields were taken to Skaro.

K9 was programmed with all grandmaster chess games from 1866 onwards.[625] The Doctor implied that he was present when Brighton's West Pier opened in 1866.[626] The War Lords lifted a battlefield from the Mexican Uprising of 1867.[627] In 1868, the Doctor opened a bank account at Coutts Bank in London. In the same year, Wychborn House burnt down.[628] In 1868, the Phiadoran spores enabled Professor Bryce-Dennison to create a solar-powered impeller drive.[629]

1869 (24th December) - THE UNQUIET DEAD[630] ->
The ninth Doctor and Rose landed in Cardiff. Charles Dickens was in the middle of a dramatic recital that was interrupted by what seemed to be a ghost. The Doctor discovered that these were gas creatures, the Gelth, who sought to open a portal to Earth. The Gelth pretended to be refugees, but actually sought to invade Earth. The Doctor ensured that the Gelth portal was destroyed.

Dickens hoped to write the adventure as *The Mystery of Edwin Drood and the Blue Elementals*, with the killer being an extraterrestrial instead of the boy's uncle as he'd originally planned, but died the following year before completing it.

The time rift healed, but left a residual dimensional scar. This was harmless to humans, yet useful to time travellers as a means of refuelling their time vessels.

The scar - later known as the "Cardiff Rift" or just "the Rift" - would attract all manner of alien beings and technology to the Cardiff area.[631]

Captain Jack used his vortex manipulator to travel back from the year 200,100 to find the Doctor. He arrived in 1869, and would live on Earth until at least the early twenty-first century.[632]

In 1870, the Jameson boys were out cutting peat when they encountered the Zygons on Tullock Moor. The elder brother Robert was driven mad by the experience and never spoke again; his younger brother Donald simply disappeared.[633] Around that time, Reuben joined the lighthouse service. He spent twenty of the next thirty years in a gas-powered lighthouse.[634] In 1871, a battlefield from the Franco-Prussian War was lifted by the War Lords[635] and the Doctor was given a Gladstone bag by Gladstone.[636]

1871 - SET PIECE[637] ->
The seventh Doctor, Benny and Ace were reunited in Paris, where they also met Kadiatu Lethbridge-Stewart. After the robotic Ants had been defeated, Ace chose to leave the Doctor and joined the ruling Paris Commune. Ace was the last soldier to leave the barricades when the Commune fell from power.

The Doctor met Tsar Nicholas at the Drei Kaiser Bund of 1871.[638] During this time, Magnus Greel arrived in the Time Cabinet from the year 5000. The Chinese peasant Li H'sen Chang sheltered Greel, believing him to be the god Weng-Chiang. The Emperor came to acquire Greel's cabinet, and gave it as a gift to Litefoot's mother.[639]

1872 (August - December) - EYE OF HEAVEN[640] ->
Horace Stockwood organized a second expedition to Easter Island, and the fourth Doctor and Leela joined his group aboard the sailing ship *Tweed*. On the island, Stockwood's party discovered a giant stone head containing a teleport device. This transported some of the group to the homeworld of the aliens who built Easter Island's *moai*. They searched an alien library, but their presence triggered a booby trap that turned the alien sun black. The party returned to Earth, hoping the sun would return to normal in their absence. From Leela's blood, the Doctor created an antidote to the sickness that had killed the Polynesian / alien hybrids thirty years ago. Stockwood remained on the island to help protect the Polynesians until the alien DNA the *moai* carried could re-infect them.

1872 (25th November) - THE CHASE[641] ->
The first Doctor and the Daleks landed on the *Mary Celeste*, forcing the crew to abandon ship.

Joseph Sundvig died on 3rd February, 1872.[642] The Nine Travellers were surveyed in 1874.[643] Old Priory, a Victorian folly, was built for the Scarman family. After this time, Marcus and Laurence Scarman played in the priest-hole there as children.[644] The Doctor swam with Captain Webb in the Channel.[645]

1873 - STRANGE ENGLAND[646] **->** The TARDIS landed on an asteroid shaped by Gallifreyan Protyon units to resemble an idyllic Victorian country house based on Wychborn House. It was sculpted by a friend of the Doctor, the Time Lady Galah, who had reached the end of her regeneration cycle. With the seventh Doctor's help, Galah lived on as one of her human creations, Charlotte. She returned to Earth and married Richard Aickland, who became a renowned Gothic novelist (of such books as *Cold Eyes* and *The Wine Press*) in the early twentieth century.

1875 - "Bad Blood"[647] **->** The eighth Doctor landed in the Dakota Hills, and found that Chief Sitting Bull had been told he would arrive in a vision. Miners had awoken an ancient evil, and Indians and General Custer's forces were both attacked by wolf-like creatures: the Windigo. The Doctor was reunited with Destrii when she arrived with her uncle, Count Jodafra, but the two aliens started to arm Custer's men with laser weapons.

The Doctor found that anyone who drank alcohol became a Windigo - Custer was a teetotaler, but almost everyone else was at risk. It turned out that Jodafra had made a deal with the Windigo, as it could navigate the timestream. Destrii sided with the Doctor, and helped destroy the Windigo. Jodafra savagely attacked Destrii, leaving her for dead, but the Doctor brought her back aboard the TARDIS.

The *Vantarialis* crashed on Zanak, where its injured captain was remade as a cyborg. With the assistance of old Queen Xanxia, the Captain converted the entire planet into a hollow world capable of teleporting between star systems and sucking the life out of planets by materializing around them. After this time, and with increasing frequency, Zanak attacked and destroyed Bandraginus V, Aterica, Temesis, Tridentio III, Lowiteliom, Bibicorpus and Granados.[648]

The Doctor met Alexander Graham Bell.[649] Bell initiated the first phone message while asking for his assistant Watson. The message would later dominate phone lines during a time paradox in 1987.[650]

---

642 *The Curse of Fenric*

643 *The Stones of Blood*

644 *Pyramids of Mars*

645 *Doctor Who and the Pirates*. The Doctor says he "paced" Webb, which indicates he was swimming ahead of Webb to increase the man's pace rather than trying to defeat him.

646 Dating *Strange England* (NA #29) - The Doctor says that the "temporal location" is "1873" (p229).

647 Dating "Bad Blood" (*DWM* #338-342) - The date is given in a caption.

648 *The Pirate Planet*. Bandraginus V disappeared "over a century" ago according to the Doctor, when the Zanak native Balaton was young. As Zanak is not capable of time travel, it must have been operating at least that long. The planets attacked by Zanak are named in production documents, and plaques were made up with the names on... but only those for Bandraginus V, Granados, Lowiteliom and Calufrax are clearly visible on screen. *First Frontier* gives a little more detail about Bandraginus V (p129).

649 *The Android Invasion*. Bell lived 1847-1922.

650 *Father's Day*. Bell's famous phone call occurred on 10th March, 1876.

651 Dating *Imperial Moon* (PDA #34) - It's "the year of our Lord 1878" (p7).

652 Dating *Tooth and Claw* (X2.2) - The Doctor gives the date as "1879". The book *Creatures and Demons* (a non-fiction book about various *Doctor Who* monsters) suggests that the parallel universe first seen in *Rise of*

the Cybermen diverged from our history because Queen Victoria was killed in their (Doctorless) version of these events. The series itself was going to state this, but Russell Davies decided against it. While it might explain why the Britain of that universe is a Republic, it doesn't explain why the Queen's successor would create Torchwood - an organisation founded in response to the Doctor and Rose irritating Victoria. Perhaps the Queen's death at the hands of a werewolf triggered an urge to defend Britain against such foes.

653 *Army of Ghosts*

654 "Wormwood"

655 *Storm Warning*. Roarke's Drift occurred on 22nd to 23rd January, 1879.

656 Dating *Evolution* (MA #2) - It is the "year of grace eighteen hundred and eighty" (p6, p108). Conan Doyle lived 1859-1930, although *The Hound of the Baskervilles* - one of the later Holmes books - was written in 1902. Kipling lived 1865-1936, so he is "fifteen" here (p45).

657 *Storm Warning*. No date given, but the Doctor did meet him in *Evolution*. Conan Doyle lived 1859-1930.

658 *Tooth and Claw* (TV). Bell lived 1837-1911, and Conan Doyle studied under him. Note that in *The Moonbase*, the Doctor remembers studying in Glasgow under Lister in 1888. Either he studied under both, or has altered the details slightly here.

659 *Storm Warning*. Geronimo lived 16th June, 1829 to 17th February, 1909.

660 Dating "The Greatest Gamble" (*DWM* #56) - The date is given.

1878 (September) - IMPERIAL MOON[651] -> Using Bryce-Dennison's impeller drive, the British government had crafted three spaceships: the *Cygnus*, *Draco* and *Lynx*. The fifth Doctor and Turlough arrived as the ships set about exploring Earth's moon, and mistook the deadly Vrall for the exiled Phiadorans. While returning to Earth, the Vrall were exposed aboard the *Draco* and a deadly struggle took place. Only Turlough survived, and the crewless *Draco* sped into space.

The *Cygnus* and *Lynx* arrived on Earth, where Queen Victoria greeted the "Phiadorans" as emissaries from another world. The Vrall self-replicated and instigated a slaughter. The Doctor and Turlough used advanced weapons from the lunar safari park to wipe out the Vrall on Earth. At the Doctor's command, Kamelion disguised himself as the late Prince Albert and appeared to the Queen "in a vision." Kamelion convinced the Queen to dismantle the remaining spaceships and never mention the incident.

The moon safari park self-destructed, leaving only a large crater.

1879 - TOOTH AND CLAW (TV)[652] -> The tenth Doctor and Rose arrived in Scotland and quickly met Queen Victoria. She was en route to the royal jewelers, but was diverted by the brethren who served a werewolf-like alien to Torchwood Estate. The alien intended to bite Victoria and through her foster the Empire of the Wolf, but the Doctor deduced Prince Albert's plan to defeat the creature and killed it.

Queen Victoria knighted the Doctor for saving her life, and named Rose as "Dame Rose of the Powell Estate". However, the Queen was not amused - she was fearful that the Doctor and Rose had strayed from all that was good, and therefore posed a danger. She banished them from her empire, and secretly ordered the formation of the Torchwood Institute to protect the realm from such aliens.

It was possible that the werewolf scratched the Queen before it died. The Doctor theorised that the Queen might similarly nip her children, and that the "Royal Disease" (unknown in Victoria's bloodline before her, and thought to be haemophilia) might actually be the alien werewolf taint.

The Doctor was named in the Torchwood Foundation Charter of 1879 as an enemy of the Crown.[653] In 1879, an Arkansas Bible salesman named Abraham White found a shooting star. He touched it, and was exposed to images from a thousand worlds - including visions of Time Lords. The "star" was actually the consciousness of Pariah - a predecessor to Shayde, and now an enemy of Gallifrey - and White hosted her essence within his body.

Armed with Pariah's knowledge, White sought to boost humanity's technology development. He nudged a generation of geniuses and inventors - including Thomas Edison, Nicola Tesla, Rudolf Diesel, Henry Ford and Albert Einstein - along.

Pariah grew herself a new body within White's form, and also learned to replicate her basic sphere influence. White chose select agents to become infused with the spheres and turn into living gateways. In such a fashion he founded the Threshold, an organisation that traded its services (moving clients through spatial doorways) in exchange for alien technology. The Threshold came to master space as the Time Lords had mastered time, and avoided Gallifrey's detection by refraining from time travel technology.

Threshold began developing an energy wave, but this would take over three thousand years to perfect. The group came into conflict with the seventh and eighth Doctors, and events climaxed on the moon in the fifty-third century.[654]

The Doctor met Afrikaaners during the Boer War and was at the battle of Roarke's Drift.[655]

1880 - EVOLUTION[656] -> Percival Ross witnessed a Rutan scoutship crashing in Limehouse, and recovered a flask of Rutan healing salve from the wreckage. The alien gel had a miraculous healing effect on humans, but it also could merge human and animal genetic material, as Ross discovered when a boy he was treating became a ferocious dog-like creature. Ross interested the industrialist Breckingridge, the owner of a vast cable factory in the town of Bodhan, in the creation of a race of hybrid dolphin-men. Ross kidnapped fifteen children from the area, and conducted experiments that turned them into merchildren.

Breckingridge died when one of his mutated guard dogs turned on him; Ross drowned. The fourth Doctor relocated the mer-children to a water planet in the Andromeda Galaxy. A young Arthur Conan Doyle witnessed the happenings on Dartmoor, and his chance encounter with the Doctor inspired two of his most famous characters: Sherlock Holmes and Professor Challenger. An even younger Rudyard Kipling, future author of *The Jungle Book*, also witnessed the events surrounding the closure of Breckingridge's factory.

The Doctor "borrowed" Conan Doyle's stethoscope and kept meaning to return it.[657] **The Doctor claims to have studied medicine under Bell in Edinburgh.**[658] The Doctor met Geronimo.[659]

c 1880 - "The Greatest Gamble"[660] -> Gaylord Lefevre, a gambler on a Mississippi riverboat, played the Celestial Toymaker and lost, like so many before him.

1881 (25th - 26th October) - THE GUNFIGHTERS[661]
-> The TARDIS landed at Tombstone shortly before the Gunfight at the OK Corral. As the first Doctor searched for a dentist, the gunman Johnny Ringo found one - Doc Holliday - who he'd been tracking for two years. Marshall Wyatt Earp and his allies killed Ringo and some members of the renegade Clanton family.

The Doctor warned General Custer against taking his Seventh Calvary over the ridge, but Custer ignored him.[662] **The Doctor met Gilbert and Sullivan.**[663] The Doctor claims to have inspired the *Mikado*, a comic operetta.[664] **He witnessed the eruption of Krakatoa.**[665] Van Gogh painted the Doctor.[666] **The Rani kidnapped microbiologist Louis Pasteur.**[667]

Penelope Gate built herself a time machine using a miniature Analytical Engine. She left her husband in 1883 for a life of time travel. She first headed to the year 2000, actually landing in 1996. The Doctor returned Penelope to her native time after meeting her in feudal Japan.[668] In 1883, the Time Lord Ulysses exiled his fellow Time Lord Marnal to the home of Penelope Gate's parents on Earth. Marnal's memories were locked off, and he wouldn't recover them until his regeneration in the twenty-first century.[669]

There was a single account of a pocket of dinosaurs surviving on one plateau in Central Africa, but most scientists and reporters, including a young Arthur Conan Doyle, dismissed it as the ravings of a madman:

"The pygmies from the Oluti Forest led me blindfold for three whole days through uncharted jungle. They took me to a swamp full of giant lizards, like giant dinosaurs." [670]

1883 - GHOST LIGHT[671] -> Rumours spread that Josiah Samuel Smith, arch-advocate of Darwinist theories, was conducting blasphemous experiments at his house Gabriel Chase to the north of London. Two years after Inspector Mackenzie vanished while investigating the goings-on at the house, Smith himself disappeared. Servants working in the house spoke of hauntings and mesmerism, apemen and angels, and a bizarre plot to assassinate Queen Victoria. The house remained abandoned for a century.

The seventh Doctor knew "a nice little restaurant on the Khyber Pass".

In 1884, a book was published detailing many types of Amazonian fungus.[672]

1885 - TIMELASH[673] -> Vena, the daughter of a Councillor on Karfel, was transported to Earth in the timelash and met Herbert George Wells, who was conducting an experiment with a ouija board. Wells travelled to Karfel with the sixth Doctor, and the experience inspired him, upon his return home, to write his scientific romances.

---

661 Dating *The Gunfighters* (3.8) - The story culminates with the Gunfight at the OK Corral. The depiction of events owes more to the popular myths and Hollywood treatment of the story than historical accuracy.
662 *Players* (p62), *Festival of Death*
663 *The Edge of Destruction*. Gilbert and Sullivan collaborated between 1875-1896.
664 *Doctor Who and the Pirates*
665 *Inferno, Rose*. The ninth Doctor also visited the scene. Krakatoa erupted in 1883.
666 "Changes"
667 *Time and the Rani*. Pasteur lived 1822-1895.
668 *The Room with No Doors*
669 *The Gallifrey Chronicles*
670 *Ghost Light*. It is unclear from the story whether the plateau really existed or was merely a delirious Fenn-Cooper's rationalisation of his adventures in Gabriel Chase.
671 Dating *Ghost Light* (26.2) - Set "two years" after 1881, when Mackenzie is sent to investigate the disappearance of Sir George Pritchard, and "a century" before Ace burns down Gabriel Chase in 1983. It's a time of year when the sun sets at six pm (so either the spring or autumn). The script suggested that a caption slide "Perivale - 1883" might be used over the establishing

shot of Gabriel Chase. Queen Victoria was a Hanover, not a Saxe-Coburg, but late in her reign she did acquire the nickname "Mrs Saxe-Coburg".
672 *The Green Death*
673 Dating *Timelash* (22.5) - The Doctor applies "a time deflection coefficient of 706 years" to the timelash's original destination of 1179, and concludes that Vena will arrive in "1885...AD". *The Terrestrial Index* set this in "c1891", after *The Time Machine* was written.
674 *The Ghosts of N-Space*
675 *Deadly Reunion*
676 *Christmas on a Rational Planet*. No date given, but Blavatsky lived 1831-1891.
677 *TW: Slow Decay*
678 Dating *All-Consuming Fire* (NA #27) - It is "the year eighteen eighty seven" according to both Watson (p5) and Benny (p153). References to *The Talons of Weng-Chiang* (p42, p64) suggest this book is set after that story, but aren't conclusive.
679 *Timewyrm: Revelation*. This was before *All-Consuming Fire*. The eighth Doctor also encountered Holmes, according to *The Gallifrey Chronicles*.
680 *The Moonbase*. Surgeon Joseph Lister lived 5th April, 1827, to 10th February, 1912.
681 *Carnival of Monsters*
682 *Synthespians*™

The Doctor helped "Bertie Wells" with invisibility experiments.[674] He discovered that HG Wells was a ladies man.[675] The Doctor met the mystic Madame Blavatsky.[676]

Torchwood was operating out of Cardiff by 1885.[677]

1887 - ALL-CONSUMING FIRE[678] -> Sherlock Holmes and Dr Watson were travelling through Austria on the Orient Express when the train was stopped by Pope Leo XIII. The Pope commissioned Holmes to investigate the theft of occult books from the Library of St John the Beheaded. With the seventh Doctor's help, Holmes discovered that his eldest brother Sherringford had allied himself with the Baron Maupertuis. They planned to use incantations in the books to open a gateway to the planet of Ry'leh. Sherringford was under the thrall of the Great Old One named Azathoth, and hoped this would facilitate her escape to Earth. Maupertuis and Sherringford were both killed, and the Doctor transported Azathoth and her followers in 1906, where they also perished. The Doctor and Holmes sealed the portal to Ry'leh forever.

Arthur Conan Doyle would later write the book *All-Consuming Fire*, but it never saw print.

The Doctor told Ace that he met Sherlock Holmes.[679] **In 1888, the Doctor gained a medical degree in Glasgow under Lister.[680] Around that time, he sparred with John L Sullivan, the first modern world heavyweight champion.[681]** The Doctor discovered the truth behind the mysterious Pale Man in nineteenth-century Whitechapel.[682]

In the Winter Gardens in Berlin, 1888, Miss Alice Bultitude was in the front row of the stalls as Toby the Sapient Pig's European tour opened. Toby performed with such entertainers as Professor Prometheus, the fireproof Secasian, the "incomparable" Hildebrand and the Blondin Donkey. Bultitude would also attend Toby's farewell concert at the Black Castle, Alhambra, and acquire a first edition copy of his memoirs.[683]

1888 (30th September) - THE PIT[684] -> The seventh Doctor and William Blake arrived in the East End at the time of the Jack the Ripper murders, before discovering a way to the late twentieth century.

1888 - MATRIX[685] -> The Valeyard now had control of the Dark Matrix - the embodiment of the dark thoughts of the Time Lord minds within the Matrix - and journeyed with it to Whitechapel, 1888. While the Dark Matrix lodged itself in a tomb, the Valeyard renamed himself "the Ripper" and set about killing prostitutes. The Dark Matrix fed off the psychic potential of these murders.

The seventh Doctor and Ace arrived from an alternate timeline in 1963, and the Doctor was mentally assaulted by the Dark Matrix to such an extent, he downloaded his mind into a telepathic circuit. The amnesiac Doctor became a cardshark named Johnny, even as Ace - separated from him - tried to make ends meet as a maid.

The Doctor's memories were restored, and he confronted the Ripper. The Dark Matrix imploded, and the Ripper was struck by lightning and killed.

At this time, the Doctor - in his Johnny persona - met Joseph Liebermann, who claimed to be the Wandering Jew of legend.

The Doctor met Mark Twain.[686]

c 1889 - THE TALONS OF WENG-CHIANG[687] -> The fourth Doctor and Leela arrived in London during the middle of Li H'sen Chang's search for the Time Cabinet of Magnus Greel, a war criminal who had escaped the fifty-first century. Greel himself lurked in the sewers, reliant on draining the life force of young women to continue surviving. He had brought the Peking Homunculus with him to act as his agent. With the help of Professor Litefoot, an eminent pathologist, the Doctor tracked Magnus Greel to his lair and destroyed him and the Homunculus.

---

683 *Year of the Pig*
684 Dating *The Pit* (NA #12) - Blake sees a newspaper dated "the thirtieth of September, 1888". There's some indication this takes place in a parallel timeline, so it's not "the" Jack the Ripper murders.
685 Dating *Matrix* (PDA #16) - The Ripper murders took place in the later part of 1888. The accepted list of five Ripper victims (it's possible there were others) were slain from 31st August to 9th November, 1888.
686 *The Crooked World*
687 Dating *The Talons of Weng-Chiang* (14.6) - No date is given, and the story is trying to encapsulate an era, rather than a precise year. The story is set soon after the Jack the Ripper murders (1888), as Henry Gordon Jago

refers to "Jolly Jack". In the draft script, Casey went on to say that the new batch of disappearances can't be the Ripper because he "is in Canada".

The story takes place before *The Bodysnatchers*, and possibly *All-Consuming Fire* (although that only mentions Mr Sin, so might refer to earlier activities than this story).

Timelink states that it is 1895. Litefoot's reading a copy of *The Strand* from February 1892 (the issue with the Sherlock Holmes story "The Adventure of the Speckled Band") ... then again, there's also a modern newspaper visible at one point, so that should probably be considered set dressing rather than definitive dating evidence.

Human sacrifice was still taking place in Moreton Harwood in the early eighteen-nineties.[688] The Doctor met the French novelist Emile Zola.[689]

@ Compassion brought the Doctor to Earth to recuperate following Gallifrey's destruction. He woke up in a carriage with no memory of what had happened, and found he possessed a tiny cube, all that remained of his TARDIS.[690] The Doctor was found wandering and was placed on a hospital ward for five days.[691] He wandered England for a few years, still having no memories.[692]

By 1890, a retired William Chesterton had translated Ho Lin Chung's *Mountains and Sunsets* into English.[693] Ace was on the Red List of the Shadow Directory by 1892.[694] An advanced society on Duchamp 331 had built the Warp Core, an energy being, to combat the Krill. The Warp Core killed off the Krill and its creators also, reducing Duchamp 331 to a dust planet. The creature wandered through space and time before seeking refuge in the mind of the Norwegian artist Edvard Munch. He came to paint *The Scream*, which exorcised the Warp Core from his mind into the painting, where it remained trapped.[695]

In 1892, Captain Jack got into a fight on Ellis Island. He was shot through the heart and lived - and came to realise he was now immortal.[696]

1893 (July / August) - CAMERA OBSCURA[697] -> The eighth Doctor and Sabbath both arrived in Victorian England after detecting disturbances in time. A faulty time machine, based on the principles of temporal interferometry, had splintered the stage magician Octave into eight individuals. Octave attacked the Doctor, who lived because Sabbath had placed the Doctor's second heart in his own chest, which tethered the Doctor to the living world. Sabbath's assassin, the Angel-Maker, killed Octave.

The Doctor discovered that the time machine had also twinned the insane psychologist Nathaniel Chiltern. One of the Nathaniels attempted to further use the machine, which threatened to puncture the space-time continuum, but the Doctor destroyed the device by flinging himself into it. Nathaniel killed the Angel-Maker, but was in turn was killed by Sabbath. By extension, this killed the other Nathaniel.

At this time, the Doctor, Fitz and Anji attended a séance. Also in attendance was a young man named William.[698]

1894 - TIME ZERO[699] -> Keen to be an adventurer in his own right, Fitz accompanied palaeontologist George Williamson on an expedition to Siberia. Tzar Alexander III was present when the expedition left Vladivostok. Fitz kept a diary of the journey.

Reptiles from another timeline attacked the expedition, killing everyone but Fitz and Williamson. A huge explosion encased the two of them in ice, where they would remain for over a hundred years. The eighth Doctor and Williamson later averted the saurians' timeline by travelling to back 1894 and insuring that Williamson was killed rather than being trapped in ice. The billionaire Maxwell Curtis, travelling down a time corridor to this era from 2002, died in a minor explosion.

As a result of these events, an energy being from an o-

---

688 "Ninety years" before *K9 and Company*.
689 *Ghost Ship*. Zola lived 1840-1902.
690 *The Ancestor Cell, The Burning*. It's "more than a hundred years" before 2001 (*The Ancestor Cell*, p282), and "one hundred and thirteen years" before in *Escape Velocity* (p184), which would make it 1888.
691 *Vanishing Point*
692 *The Burning*
693 *The Eleventh Tiger*
694 *The Death of Art*
695 *Dust Breeding*. *The Scream* was painted in 1893.
696 *Utopia*
697 Dating *Camera Obscura* (EDA #59) - It's the "nineteenth century" (p6), Maskelyne (presumably the magician John Nevil Maskelyne, 1839-1917) is alive (p7) and it's a "century" before Anji's time (p35). Fitz meets George Williamson, so this is before *Time Zero*.
698 *Camera Obscura*. William is the human version of Spike from *Buffy the Vampire Slayer*. However, the dating is awry - in *Buffy*, Spike became a vampire in 1880.
699 Dating *Time Zero* (EDA #60) - This was in "1894" (p15).

700 *The Burning*
701 *The Gallifrey Chronicles*. This is the same issue of the *Strand* the Doctor is looking for in *The Bodysnatchers*.
702 Dating *The Bodysnatchers* (EDA #3) - It is "11.01.1894" (p15). It is six years since the Ripper murders (p2). It is five years since *The Talons of Weng Chiang* (p37). Mr. Stoker is quite possibly Bram Stoker, with the implication being that this adventure inspired his greatest work; *Dracula* was published in 1897, three years after this story takes place. Stoker lived 1847-1912.
703 Dating *The Burning* (EDA #37) - It's "a few years" since the Doctor arrived on Earth (p142), dated in *Escape Velocity* to 1888. The most precise indication in *The Burning* itself is that it's "the late nineteenth century". It is "fifty years" before *The Turing Test* (p59), which is set in January 1943.

The fire elemental first manifests on Earth in *Time Zero* and Justin Richards has confirmed that whereas bits of the creature seep through Williamson's time corridor (causing a residual presence of it to be wor-

region - a sort of isolated, mini-universe - was drawn to Earth. Bits of it seeped through Williamson's time corridor into the past, where it was worshipped by some cultures. The main portion of the fire elemental that arrived in 1894, however, achieved enough critical mass that it could work toward its agenda of consuming Earth entirely.

The elemental came to ally itself with Roger Nepath, who believed the entity could restore his dead sister Patience to life.[700]

Marnal's first story, "The Giants", was published in the *Strand* in 1894.[701]

1894 - THE BODYSNATCHERS[702] **->** With the help of Professor Litefoot, the eighth Doctor and Sam discovered that a series of grisly murders were part of a Zygon plot to conquer the world. The Doctor confronted Balaak, the Zygon leader, and accidentally killed some of the Zygons by poisoning their milk. The Zygons' pack of Skarasen threatened London until the Doctor lured them into the TARDIS. He relocated them and a Zygon survivor, Tuval, to an uninhabited planet.

As part of this adventure, the Doctor rescued a Mr Stoker from the Zygons.

@ c 1895 (January) THE BURNING[703] **->** The amnesiac eighth Doctor ended up in Middletown, just in time to investigate a mysterious geological fault. He realised that it was the home of a fire elemental that was in league with local developer, Roger Nepath. The Doctor blew up a dam, flooding the fault and extinguishing the elemental. The Doctor callously killed Nepath.

@ In March 1895, the Doctor met George Bernard Shaw at a party hosted by Oscar Wilde. Around that time, Sherlock Holmes solved the McCarthy murders before the Doctor could.[704] The fourth Doctor claimed he was asked to be George the Sixth's godfather.[705]

1896 (10th November) - THE SANDS OF TIME[706] **->** The fifth Doctor, Tegan and Nyssa arrived in the Egyptian Room of the British Museum. At the invitation of Lord Kenilworth, they attended the unwrapping of an ancient mummy, only to discover that the mummy was the perfectly preserved body of Nyssa herself. The Doctor came to realise that the intelligence of the Osirian Nephthys was in Nyssa's body.

1897 (November) - THE DEATH OF ART[707] **->** The seventh Doctor, Chris and Roz arrived in France to investigate a psychic disturbance. They encountered the Brotherhood, a secret society researching psychic activity. A man called Montague ruled one faction of the Brotherhood, but another, "the Family" were working against him. The outbreak of psychic powers was because the Quoth, multidimensional beings, had taken shelter in human brains. The Doctor sided with the Family against Montague, who was killed. The Doctor retrieved all the Quoth and took them to a new home in a neutron star.

1898 - THE BANQUO LEGACY[708] **->** A scientist, Harris, built a machine that could share thoughts. He demonstrated it at Banquo Manor as the eighth Doctor, Fitz and Compassion arrived, trapped by a Time Lord device. A series of murders occurred at the Manor. The Doctor discovered that the butler, Simpson, was a Time Lord searching for Compassion. The Doctor unravelled the web of blackmail and murder involving Harris and his sister, Catherine. Simpson was thought killed, and the Doctor's trio left before Simpson was missed by Gallifrey.

On 12th January, 1898, Florence Sundvig died. Mary Eliza Millington was born on 3rd March, dying four days later. At the end of the nineteenth century, the grandfather of Reverend Wainwright translated the Viking Runes in the crypt of his church.[709]

1899 - PLAYERS[710] **->** The sixth Doctor and Peri stopped the murder of a 24-year-old Winston Churchill, who was

---

shipped by ancient cultures, etc.), it's only when the main chunk of it arrives in 1894 that the elemental attains enough critical mass to work toward its own insidious agenda. Therefore, *The Burning* - in which the elemental is working to its own design, and the Doctor defeats it - manifestly has to occur after *Time Zero*.

The Burning (p238) specifies that it's January, so allowing that some time (a few months at least) probably pass while the elemental and Nepath forge their pact and start to implement it, January 1895 seems the most likely time for *The Burning* to occur.

The date was given as 1889 in the original story synopsis.

704 *The Gallifrey Chronicles*, a reference to Nicholas Meyer's novel *The West End Horror*, which features Shaw and Holmes.
705 *Wolfsbane*. George was born in 1895.
706 Dating *The Sands of Time* (MA #22) - The date is given (p29).
707 Dating *The Death of Art* (NA #54) - It's "26 November 1897" (p16).
708 Dating *The Banquo Legacy* (EDA #35) - The date is given (p7).
709 *The Curse of Fenric*
710 Dating *Players* (PDA #21) - The date is given (p15).

serving as a war correspondent in South Africa. The Doctor helped Churchill escape from a P.O.W. camp, and Churchill returned home a hero.

The Doctor and Iris met Oscar Wilde in Venice after his imprisonment. They also fought some "fish people." [711]

The Twentieth Century

Joan Redfern had married Oliver, her childhood sweetheart, but he died at the Battle of Spion Kop.[712]

The Doctor was present at the Relief of Mafeking.[713] **Battlefields from the Boxer Rising and the Boer War were lifted by the War Lords.**[714] Nurse Albertine studied battle surgery and saw some action during the South African War. Afterwards, she came to work for Toby the Sapient Pig.[715]

> = By the beginning of the twentieth century, Dhakan - the alternate Earth ruled by Katsura Sato - had interstellar travel.[716]

1900 (December) - FOREIGN DEVILS[717] **->** The second Doctor followed Jamie and Zoe's passage through the "spirit gate" in 1800, arriving exactly a hundred years later. The Chief Astrologer's curse started murdering the descendants of Roderick Upcott, and the Doctor teamed up with Carnacki, an investigator of the supernatural, to look into events at Upcott House. The curse used the spirit gate's dimensional energy to remove the house from time and space, and transformed Roderick Upcott's corpse into a dragon. The Doctor destroyed the spirit gate, which returned the house and made the dragon crumble to ash.

In 1901, an English author began to write boy's stories for the magazine *The Ensign*.[718] The Doctor saw the assassination of President McKinley.[719] By 1902, there were Polynesian / alien hybrids on Easter Island again. They used the teleport device to resettle their forefathers' homeworld. The explorer Stockwood was still alive, and planned to return to the alien homeworld also.[720]

1901 (20th October) - CRYPTOBIOSIS[721] **->** The sixth Doctor and Peri sought to vacation aboard the *Lankester* (sic) a cargo ship en route from the Cape of Good Hope to New Orleans. The *Lankester*'s chief mate, Jacques De Requin, was in the process of smuggling two mermaids - the adult Anthrotrite and her daughter, Galatea - who had been caught in fishing nets. De Requin hoped to sell the mermaids for profit, but other mer-people, led by Anthrotrite's father Nereus, breached the ship's under-carriage. Anthrotrite died, the *Lankester* sank and the mer-people captured De Requin with the intent of tormenting him beneath the sea. The Doctor and Peri returned Galatea

---

711 *The Scarlet Empress.* Although never specified, the "fish people" could be the amphibious gondoliers that appear in Paul Magrs' *The Stones of Venice.* This meeting must have occurred after Wilde's release from prison on 19th May, 1897, but before his death on 30th November, 1900.

712 *Human Nature* (TV). The Battle of Spion Kop occurred on 23rd and 24th January, 1900.

713 *The Daleks' Master Plan, The Invasion of Time.* This occurred on 17th May, 1900, when British troops ended the siege of Mafeking during the second Boer War.

714 *The War Games.* The Boer War ran from 1899-1902, the Boxer Rising was in 1900.

715 *Year of the Pig.* The South African War (also known as the Second Boer War) lasted from 1899-1902.

716 "The Glorious Dead"

717 Dating *Foreign Devils* (TEL #5) - It's "December 1900" (p35).

718 *The Mind Robber*

719 *Byzantium!* (p179). No date given, but this was 6th September, 1901.

720 *Eye of Heaven*

721 Dating *Cryptobiosis* (BF subscription promo #3) - The date is given.

722 *Circular Time:* "Autumn". Wodehouse lived 1881-1975, but the date is otherwise arbitrary.

723 Dating *Horror of Fang Rock* (15.1) - The Terrance

Dicks novelisation and contemporary publicity material set the story "at the turn of the century". Electric power was introduced to lighthouses around the turn of the century. Fang Rock is in the English Channel ("five or six miles" from Southampton) and is particularly treacherous, and was probably upgraded early on.

There's a reference to King Edward. As fan Alex Wilcock has noted, although the Doctor's style of dress is often referred to as "Edwardian", this is the only story set in the Edwardian period (and there's not a frock coat to be seen). The young lighthouse worker Vince states that the Beast was last seen "eighty years ago", "back in the twenties". *The Programme Guide* offered the date "1909", *The Terrestrial Index* claimed "1904". *The TARDIS Logs* suggested "c.1890", *The Doctor Who File* "early 1900s". *The TARDIS Special* gave the date "1890s". *Timelink* makes a convincing case for 1902, based on mumbled references to Salisbury and Bonar Law.

724 *The City of the Dead*

725 "The Curse of the Scarab". It's "forty years" before the story, but that's clearly rounding up as the Melies' silent movie *Trip to the Moon* is referenced, and that was released in 1902.

726 "The Fallen"

727 *Year of the Pig.* Toby's fan Alice Bultitude later shows him film footage of this event - even though 1903 is rather early for footage of this kind.

to her grandfather, and convinced him to discretely rescue any *Lankester* survivors.

As part of these events, the Doctor was drafted to serve as a medical professional attached to the Merchant Navy. Anthrotrite's species of mer-people lived in coral homes decorated with pearls inside, and with roofs of mussel shells that opened and flowed with the water.

The Doctor told P.G. Wodehouse - who was saddened because he didn't know what he was writing about - that it sounded as if he had a story that was trying to get out.[722]

c 1902 - HORROR OF FANG ROCK[723] **-> The fourth Doctor and Leela arrived at Fang Rock lighthouse as a series of mysterious murders took place. The Doctor discovered the culprit was a Rutan scout, then destroyed the scout and its mothership.**

Earth was now strategically important for the Rutans in their war with the Sontarans. According to the Doctor, the Rutans "used to control the whole of the Mutters Spiral once".

The Doctor was technical advisor on *A Trip to the Moon*.[724] In 1902, Monroe Stahr saw a film about the unearthing of an Egyptian tomb that would later inspire him to finance the movie *The Curse of the Scarab*.[725]

@ The Doctor drank absinthe in Prague, 1903.[726]

In the summer of 1903, Toby the Sapient Pig attended a gathering of creative minds in Vienna. By 1913, owing to his addled memories, Toby would believe that everyone present were pigs.[727]

- -
= The TARDIS' simultaneous arrival in 1903 and 2003 led to a massive disruption to the timelines. In 1903, the Doctor helped the English defeat the Daleks, who had attacked Central London. Only two Daleks survived and were taken captive. Political tensions still led to the first World War, but the British used the captured Dalek technology to seize control of the whole world. The British government locked
- -

the Doctor and Evelyn away in the Tower of London for propaganda purposes, and Evelyn consequently starved to death.[728]

1903 (December) - THE SLEEP OF REASON[729] **->** The Sholem-Luz had developed as creatures that could tunnel through the Time Vortex. They were attracted to mental turmoil as part of their life-cycle. In December 1903, a Sholem-Luz was drawn to Mausolus House, an asylum. The Sholem-Luz essence infected an Irish wolfhound, which became monstrous and triggered a series of murders. Joseph Sands, the nephew of a Mausolus House patient, slew the creature and burned its corpse in a fire that had started in a chapel on the grounds. The eighth Doctor arrived through a time corridor from around 2004, and the second Sholem-Luz accompanying him also perished in the fire. Not wishing to relive the twentieth century over again, the Doctor went into suspended animation for about a hundred years.

Dr. Thomas Christie, the governor of Mausolus House, found a dog's tooth - all that remained of the Sholem-Luz - and made a pendant from it. It reappeared a century later.

The Doctor once went for a stroll in Edwardian Bromley.[730] The National Foundation for Scientific Research, UK, originated as a group of private researchers that adopted the name and gained charity status after World War II. The organization eventually leased a house from Melanie Bush's great-uncle.[731] **The Doctor trained the Mountain Mauler of Montana.**[732]

The Doctor learned a great deal from Houdini.[733] **He also learned sleight of hand from Maskelyne.**[734]

The Kalarians turned Ockora into a holiday resort, hunting the native creatures for sport. They did not realise the Ockorans were intelligent.[735] An alien gave JM Barrie the idea for *Peter Pan*, based on a popular extraterrestrial story.[736]

@ The Doctor claimed to have chained Emmeline Pankhurst to the railings outside Number Ten Downing Street.[737] **Pankhust stole the Doctor's laser spanner.**[738]

---

728 *Jubilee*

729 Dating *The Sleep of Reason* (EDA #70) - We're told it's "Thursday 24th December 1903" at the start of this section (p22).

730 *Only Human*

731 One hundred years before *Catch-1782*.

732 *The Romans*

733 Mentioned in *Planet of the Spiders, Revenge of the Cybermen*, "Voyager", *The Pit, Head Games, The Sorcerer's Apprentice, The Devil Goblins from Neptune, The Church and the Crown, Eye of Heaven* and *Independence Day*. There's no date given in any of those stories. Houdini lived from 1874-1926.

734 *The Ribos Operation.* No date is given, but this is presumably the magician John Neville Maskelyne (1839-1917, and also mentioned in *Camera Obscura*), although it could be his grandson, the magician Jasper Maskelyne (1902-1973).

735 "Centuries" before *The Murder Game, The Final Sanction.*

736 *The Tomorrow Windows. Peter Pan* was published in 1905.

737 *Casualties of War.* Pankhurst was a founder of the British suffragette movement. She was chained to Number Ten in 1905.

738 *Smith and Jones*

The Doctor met Einstein.[739]

```
= 1906 (24th December) - THE CHIMES OF
MIDNIGHT[740] -> The eighth Doctor and Charley
discovered the inhabitants of an Edwardian manor
house were trapped in a time-loop. The servants were
brutally murdered, but at midnight time would roll
back two hours and the process would repeat itself.
The Doctor learned that the house had become
imprinted with the murders and that Edith
Thompson - one of the servants - would later work
for the Pollard family. Edith had killed herself in 1930
upon learning of Charley's death in the R-101 acci-
dent, but Charley's paradoxical arrival in 1906 left
history confused as to whether Edith would have
cause to kill herself or not. The Doctor decisively
talked Edith out of killing herself, which ended the
time-loop.
```

Azathoth and her army of Rakshassi were destroyed in the San Francisco earthquake of 1906, following the Doctor's intervention.[741] The vampire Weird Harold was buried alive in the San Francisco earthquake.[742]

The Doctor visited in Brighton in 1907.[743] The third Doctor, Jo Grant and Liz Shaw watched the Tunguska explosion in 1908.[744] The Warlock alien arrived on Earth in the meteorite.[745]

In Lahore, 1909, some men under the command of Captain Jack got drunk and ran over "a Chosen One" - a little girl with a connection to the spirit world, and who was protected by fairy creatures. The next week, the fairies killed fifteen of Jack's men on a train. Jack was the only survivor.[746]

The Doctor personally knew the performer / Chinese giant Chang Woo Gow, and regarded him as a marvelous fellow and a good dancer. Gow finally retired and opened a tea-room in Bournemouth. Elsewhere, Toby the Sapient

---

739 *The Stones of Blood.* No date given. Einstein lived 1879-1955, publishing his Special and General Theories of Relativity in 1905 and 1915 respectively. He also appeared in *Time and the Rani,* but it isn't made clear if he and the Doctor already knew one another.

740 Dating *The Chimes of Midnight* (BF #29) - The date is given.

741 *All-Consuming Fire*

742 *Vampire Science*

743 *Pier Pressure*

744 *The Wages of Sin*

745 *Warlock* (p353).

746 *TW: Small Worlds.* The date is given in a caption. The *Torchwood* website stated that this was when Jack was a time travelling conman, but as he's commanding troops and survives the fairy attack, it now seems clear that this is the immortal Jack who lived through the twentieth century.

747 Some "years" before *Year of the Pig*

748 Dating *Birthright* (NA #17) - It is "Thursday 15 April 1909" on p23, and Benny has been stranded "two months" (p24) by then. She departs on "24 April" (p203). Page 202 cites the meteorite strike's historic date of 30th June, 1908.

749 Dating *Sting of the Zygons* (NSA #13) - The TARDIS lands "16 September 1909" and the adventure takes at least three days.

750 *The English Way of Death* (p46).

751 *TW: Slow Decay*

752 Dating *Pyramids of Mars* (13.3) - Laurence Scarman gives the date as "nineteen hundred and eleven".

753 *Pyramids of Mars.* Assuming the Doctor is being serious, this suggests he has visited 1911 before now.

754 *The Stones of Blood*

755 *The War Games*

756 *Ghost Light*

757 *The Algebra of Ice* (p13). Oates died 17th March, 1912.

758 The Doctor mentions the *Titanic* in *Robot,* but tells Borusa in *The Invasion of Time* that "it had nothing to do with me". The ninth Doctor's involvement with the *Titanic* was cited in *Rose* and *The End of the World.*

759 Dating *The Left-Handed Hummingbird* (NA #21) - The story takes place on the *Titanic,* and the date is confirmed on p221.

760 *Neverland.* She was eighteen years, five months and twenty-one days old when she met the Doctor, according to *The Chimes of Midnight.*

761 "Eighty five" years before *The Dying Days* (p175).

762 "Some fifty years" before *Winter for the Adept.*

763 Dating *Year of the Pig* (BF #89) - The year is given, and specified on the back cover. Proust lived 1871-1922, and *Swann's Way* - his seven-volume, semi-auto-biographical novel - was published between 1913 and 1927. The Ostend gift shop run by James Ensor's mother is historical, and some items in the store inspired Ensor's painting. The Doctor here mentions that his favourite tailor is on the planet Kolpasha - a trendy world as seen in "Victims" (*DWM* #212-#214) and mentioned in *Instruments of Darkness* and *Spiral Scratch.*

764 *Just War*

765 *Lungbarrow, Vampire Science*

766 Dating *Human Nature* (TV) / *The Family of Blood* (X3.8-3.9) - Martha shows the Doctor a newspaper dated "Monday November 10th 1913", and a poster for the Annual Dance - which occurs the following day - yields the date of "November 11th". The Doctor has been on Earth "two months", so since early September.

767 *Silver Nemesis*

768 *Utopia*

Pig and Nurse Albertine saw Mrs Lillian Washbourne on stage at a theatre in Cincinnati.[747]

1909 (February - 24 April) - BIRTHRIGHT[748] **->** The secret society the New Dawn, led by Jared Khan, attempted to stabilise the Great Divide with the future and bring the Chaarl back to this time. Some Chaarl broke through and murdered a number of people in the East End. The seventh Doctor's TARDIS time-rammed itself to stop Khan's plans, and half of the Ship - with Khan's mind inside - fell through time to June 1908 and exploded in the wastes of Tunguska in Siberia. It disintegrated on impact; historians attributed this event to a meteorite strike. The Chaarl were trapped in one of the surviving TARDIS' inner dimensions.

1909 (mid September) - STING OF THE ZYGONS[749] **->** The tenth Doctor and Martha discovered a Zygon colony in the Lake District and wiped them out.

The Doctor saw Earth tremors in Peru in 1910.[750] The same year, Torchwood Cardiff reorganised their archive.[751]

1911 - PYRAMIDS OF MARS[752] **-> The fourth Doctor and Sarah landed at the Old Priory, on the future site of UNIT HQ. They discovered that the servants of Sutekh were planning to release him from his imprisonment. The Doctor trapped Sutekh in a time corridor, eventually destroying him.**

The Doctor said 1911 is "an excellent year, one of my favourites".[753] **The Nine Travellers were surveyed in 1911.**[754] **The King's Regulations were published in 1912.**[755] **The Royal Flying Corps was formed in 1912.**[756]

> = A historical deviation caused colleagues of the self-sacrificing Captain Oates to drag him back to camp, where they died together.[757]

The Titanic sank, although the Doctor claimed that he had nothing to do with that... The ninth Doctor warned the Daniels family not to board the Titanic and was photographed with them. However, he boarded the ship, and ended up clinging to an iceberg.[758]

1912 (14th April) - THE LEFT-HANDED HUMMINGBIRD[759] **->** On the sinking Titanic, the seventh Doctor prevented Huitzilin - also called the Blue - from acquiring the Xiuhcoatl, an Exxilon weapon capable of manipulating molecules. It could transmute or destroy matter. Huitzilin manifested but was killed.

Charley Pollard was born on 14th April, 1912, the day the Titanic sank.[760] Xznaal, an Ice Lord, was struck by the state of the withered plant life on his home planet of Mars.[761] Around 1913, Harding Wellman died while mountaineering in Switzerland.[762]

1913 - YEAR OF THE PIG[763] **->** The sixth Doctor and Peri sought to relax at the Hotel Palace Thermae in the Belgian municipality of Ostend, and the Doctor busied himself reading Swann's Way by Marcel Proust - a multi-volume work that hadn't finished publishing yet. Also in residence were Toby the Sapient Pig, Nurse Albertine, Toby's admirer Alice Bultitude and the mentally confused Inspector Alphonse Chardalot. The Doctor deduced that Toby and Chardalot were actually brothers, the result of genetic experiments carried out by a time traveller some decades previous. The two siblings were reunited, and the Doctor believed they were perhaps better off not knowing details about their origins.

The Doctor happened upon Proust at this time, and made a point of grabbing the reclusive man by the shoulders, calling him Marcel, breathing port fumes up his nose and telling him exactly what he thought of the central character in Swann's Way. The actress Lillian Washbourne died in a fire, and Toby decided to send her agent flowers. Chardalot gave Peri a stuffed monkey that was believed to hail from the gift shop of Madame Ensor, the mother of the Belgian painter James Ensor.

Owing to a mishap with a temporal fission grenade that Chardalot possessed, the sky was briefly filled with exploding cows.

The Doctor saved St Peter Port from some terrible threat on Halloween 1913. He could not save the life of young Celia Doras.[764] The Doctor and Ace independently visited the premiere of the ballet The Rites of Spring in 1913.[765]

1913 (September to 11th November) - HUMAN NATURE (TV) / THE FAMILY OF BLOOD[766] **->** To escape the Family of Blood - expert hunters who wanted the DNA of a Time Lord - the tenth Doctor used the Chameleon Arch to become human and hide in 1913. With Martha's help, the amnesiac Doctor became a teacher at Farringham School and fell for nurse Joan Redfern. The Family arrived on Earth in their invisible spacecraft and confronted Smith, who had no idea he had been the Doctor. Martha helped the Doctor resume his true nature, and the Time Lord swiftly and ruthlessly granted the Family their wish for immortality by imprisoning them all for eternity.

The First World War

The Nemesis statue passed over the Earth in 1913, heralding the First World War.[767] The immortal Captain Jack served in the First World War.[768]

1914 - HUMAN NATURE (NA)[769] **->** In the tiny village of Farringham, Doctor John Smith of Aberdeen fell in love with Joan Redfern.

During World War I, the first conflict between England and Germany occurred at the Battle of Mons. The English Captain Dudgeon luckily survived when his platoon was wiped out, and he later claimed to have seen one of the "Angels of Mons": guardians from on high who sought to protect the British troops.[770] Dudgeon happened upon a German soldier who was casually shaving himself, and refrained from killing the man in cold blood. Some of Dugdeon's fellow soldiers later accused him of cowardice.[771]

= The dormant Dark Matrix was woken by the carnage of the Battle of Mons. The British Expeditionary Force saw the form of Jack the Ripper over the battlefield.[772]

The Forge, a secret project to improve the stock of soldiers, experimented on prisoners to create a race of "twilight vampires". On 14th October, 1914, the vampires overpowered their creator, Dr Abberton, and fled. Abberton took the vampire formula to survive his wounds, and became known as Nimrod.[773]

In 1914, Manuel Gamio discovered a part of the Great Temple of the Aztecs.[774]

1915 (7th May) - THE SIRENS OF TIME[775] **->** The fifth Doctor was on a merchant ship that was torpedoed by a U-boat. He was captured and posed as a German secret agent. He escaped shortly before the U-boat torpedoed the RMS *Lusitania*. The Doctor failed to save the *Lusitania*, but in doing so prevented the future murder of Alexander Fleming, the discoverer of penicillin. Without it, the world would have suffered from plagues and fallen prey to the Second Velyshaan Empire.

769 Dating *Human Nature* (NA #37) - It is "April" (p17) "1914" (p16).

ARE THERE TWO HUMAN NATURES, NOW?: Well, yes. The 2007 television story *Human Nature / The Family of Blood* is an adaptation of the New Adventures novel *Human Nature*, both written by Paul Cornell.

In varying degrees, the new series has done this three other times so far: *Dalek* was based on elements of *Jubilee* (a Big Finish audio also by Rob Shearman), *Rise of the Cybermen / The Age of Steel* resulted from an attempt to adapt the audio *Spare Parts* by Marc Platt (the finished product was a different story altogether, but Platt still received a credit) and Steven Moffat used the central idea and the name of the main character of his *2006 Annual* story ("What I Did On My Christmas Holidays" By Sally Sparrow) as the basis of *Blink*. All three of these examples are clearly different stories - the Cyberman ones explicitly take place in different universes, in fact - and it's easy enough to believe they could all happen to the Doctor, given a little coincidence.

The idea of coincidence is stretched to and probably beyond breaking point by the two *Human Natures*, however. There's nothing in the TV story to explain how both could happen. Yet this chronology counts both stories, as it counts both *Shadas*, so some explanation is probably needed.

There are a number of possibilities:

1) Both happened, and it's all a coincidence. There are differences, some of them pretty serious ones: they take place in different years; the school is called Hulton in the novel and Farringham in the TV story; the Doctor is in a different incarnation with a different companion and becomes human for a different reason; he fights different aliens. The Joan Redferns he falls for are differ-

ent ages and have different histories. So the Doctor has a very similar adventure twice - luckily, it's one that involves him losing his memory, so the second version of "John Smith", at least, wouldn't notice the redundancy.

2) Both happened, and it's not a coincidence. We're told in the TV story that the TARDIS chose the landing point. Perhaps it's deliberately picked a situation that "worked" in similar circumstances. It seems a little odd - if not actively cruel - for the TARDIS to pick on another Joan Redfern, though.

3) The original was erased from history... possibly as a result of the Time War, the events of the novel *Human Nature* no longer "happened" (this does not automatically suppose that the whole of New Adventures did not "occur", however). The Big Finish version of *Shada* establishes that in this situation, there would be a timeline gap that needs filling, but that a different incarnation of the Doctor can play the part.

770 *No Man's Land*. Dudgeon says the Mons conflict started on 22nd August, 1914, although some resources say it technically was initiated on the 23rd. Real-life soldiers did report seeing the angels that Dudgeon describes, but they're commonly regarded as the result of battle trauma, urban legends and perhaps deliberately targeted propaganda.

771 "A year or more" before *No Man's Land*.

772 *Matrix*

773 *Project: Twilight*. We're told that Amelia, "twilight seven" was created on 12th September, 1914.

774 *The Left-Handed Hummingbird* (p58).

775 Dating *The Sirens of Time* (BF #1) - The date is given.

776 Dating *White Darkness* (NA #15) - "On the wall, a calendar of 1915 had just been turned to the August page" (p22).

1915 (August) - WHITE DARKNESS[776] -> The seventh Doctor, Benny and Ace arrived in Haiti as a civil rebellion against President Sam started. Lemaitre, an ancient man working on behalf of the Great Old Ones, was raising an army of zombies. They planned to open a gateway from their realm to Earth, and to conquer Europe. The Doctor destroyed Lemaitre and his base with a bomb.

In 1915, Mr Sun was imprisoned for killing a professor of economics, who was later revealed as an Austrian spy.[777] Arthur Kendrick distinguished himself by second-guessing the U-boat commanders on the Atlantic convoys. He would serve as an Admiral in World War II.[778] **Professor Travers began his search for the Yeti.**[779]

1915 (18th November) - PLAYERS[780] -> The second Doctor arrived in No Man's Land using a Time Ring. He saved Winston Churchill from an ambush engineered by two Players, the Count and the Countess. The next day, he saved Churchill again, this time with the help of Jeremy Carstairs and Jennifer Buckingham. Carstairs joined Churchill's staff. The Doctor escaped a German firing squad by using the Time Ring.

The scientist Nikita Kuznetzov saw the devastation at Tunguska.[781]

The Somme

The Battle of the Somme took place on 14th July, 1916. Richard Hadleman survived, treated by Timothy Dean, a former student of Dr John Smith of Aberdeen.[782] **Tim Latimer saved himself and his schoolmate Hutchinson on a First World War battlefield, thanks to a premonition he'd had some years earlier.**[783] Lance Corporal Weeks, later the chief steward aboard the *R-101,* fought at the Somme.[784] Roger Gleave, a future police inspector, witnessed the devastation.[785]

1916 (December) - THE WAGES OF SIN[786] -> The third Doctor, Jo Grant and Liz Shaw arrived in St. Petersburg as members of the city's elite, concerned about

Father Grigori Rasputin's growing influence over Empress Czarina Alexandra, conspired to murder him. Jo befriended Rasputin and saved him from death by poisoning, but the conspirators repeatedly shot and beat Rasputin, still failing to kill him. The conspirators finally had Rasputin thrown into a frozen river. The Doctor refrained from action as Rasputin drowned, fulfilling history. Six weeks later, the Russian Revolution overthrew Tsar Nicholas II.

1917 - THE ROOF OF THE WORLD[787] -> Lord Davey discovered an alien pyramid in the Himalayas when his expedition was wiped out in a storm. He was killed and replaced with a doppelganger. The fifth Doctor, Peri and Erimem arrived in Darjeeling, where Erimem met Davey and was possessed by the same force. Meeting a friend of his, the Doctor was surprised to learn that Davey was meant to be far away on an expedition. A black cloud descended, killing dozens of people ... including Erimem. The Doctor deduced this was an attempt on the part of the Great Old Ones to take control of the world, and that Erimem was still alive. Peri froze the cloud with liquid nitrogen. The pyramid was buried beneath an avalanche.

On 16th April, 1917, the Doctor and Lenin played tiddlywinks on the train journey that returned Lenin from Switzerland to Russia. After that, the Doctor met Empress Alexandra.[788] The Doctor was present in Russia during the October Revolution, met Lenin and became a Hero of the Revolution.[789] The Doctor regarded Lenin as a "disagreeable man with terrible breath".[790]

1917 - NO MAN'S LAND[791] -> An agent of the Forge, positioned in the British army as "Lieutenant-Colonel Brook", undertook experiments to refine his soldiers' killing instinct. Brook worked from Charnage Hospital near Arres in France, where soldiers were subjected to psychological refinement in the "Hate Room," and made to "kill" dummies of German troopers. Among other considerations, the Forge was curious to know if such psychological trauma could endow people with time sensitivity or precognition.

A wounded trooper, Private Taylor, informed Brook

---

777 *The Cabinet of Light* (p85).
778 *Just War*
779 "Twenty years" before *The Abominable Snowman.*
780 Dating *Players* (PDA #21) - The date is given (p69).
781 *The Wages of Sin*
782 *Human Nature* (NA)
783 *The Family of Blood*
784 *Storm Warning*
785 *Eater of Wasps*
786 Dating *The Wages of Sin* (PDA #19) - The date is given (p21). *Zagreus* confirms that the Doctor has met

Rasputin.
787 Dating *The Roof of the World* (BF #59) - It's 1917 according to the back cover. The Great Old Ones in *The Roof of the World* bear no apparent relation to the pantheon of higher powers of the same name seen throughout *Doctor Who.*
788 *Storm Warning*
789 *The Devil Goblins from Neptune*
790 *Singularity*
791 Dating *No Man's Land* (BF #89) - The year is given.

about an old church that was situated on an excellent vantage point in No Man's Land. Brook deemed this an excellent test for his men, and dispatched a squad to capture the location. Due to Brook's conditioning, the British soldiers slaughtered one another.

Brook covered up the incident, but the seventh Doctor, Ace and Hex arrived some time later. The Doctor was mistaken for an army investigator, and eventually destroyed Brook's research. Brook was killed by his own callous men, and the Doctor postulated that perhaps the unhinged Private Taylor had indeed demonstrated precognition.

The first Doctor and Susan were caught in a Zeppelin raid at some point during the war.[792] **A First World War battlefield near Ypres was kidnapped by the War Lords.**[793] **The Doctor once claimed to have been wounded at the Battle of Gallipoli.**[794] **Burton, later a camp leader at Shangri-La in 1959, fought in the War using his sabre in hand-to-hand combat.**[795] The Toymaker kidnapped two British soldiers from Ypres.[796]

Turkish soldiers during the First World War claimed to have seen The Ark of Ages on Mount Ararat.[797] The Doctor saw the Battle of Passchendale.[798] The Doctor met the noted sailor Felix von Luckner.[799]

In 1917, Reginald Tyler started writing the fantasy epic *The True History of Planets* while on leave from soldiering in France.[800] Brigadier General Tamworth was part of the Versailles delegation, and foresaw that reparations against Germany would further a bigger conflict.[801]

In 1917, the Cottingley Fairies photographs caused a sensation, and even Sir Arthur Conan Doyle was convinced they were genuine. Later, the girls who took the pictures admitted they were faked, but Torchwood in future would have reason to suspect they were real.[802]

@ 1918 - CASUALTIES OF WAR[803] **->** The eighth Doctor investigated reports of the walking dead in Hawkswick in Yorkshire. Befriending the village midwife, Mary Minnett, he discovered that the creatures were being created by the traumatic memories of wounded soldiers convalescing at Hawkswick Hall. The Doctor caused a psychic backlash, destroying the hall and the man behind it - the head of the hospital, Dr Banham.

@ The Doctor kept the last letter Mary wrote to him (on 22nd August, 1918).[804] The West Pier in Brighton came to serve as a battery for the cheerful feelings of its visitors, and the exiled aliens from Indo subsisted off these emotions. This conversely augmented the aliens' malevolence, but the armistice that ended World War I created such a widespread feeling of relief, the aliens were temporarily subdued.[805]

An influenza epidemic in 1918 and 1919 killed more people than the Great War itself.[806] An agent of the Bureau arrived from the future (circa 2386) and adopted the name Percival Closed.[807]

> = In the world of the Dark Matrix, the Jack the Ripper killings started again after the Great War. Ghostly Rippers begin terrorising London. There was mass panic, despite summary executions for suspects. The government withdrew to Edinburgh.[808]

1919 (late September) - TOY SOLDIERS[809] **->** Investigating the mysterious disappearance of children across post-War Europe, the seventh Doctor, Benny, Roz and Chris discovered that they had been kidnapped by the Recruiter, a device transporting beings from many worlds to act as soldiers in the fourteen-hundred-year war that

---

792 *Planet of Giants*
793 *The War Games*
794 *The Sea Devils*
795 *Delta and the Bannerman*
796 *Divided Loyalties*
797 *Eternity Weeps*
798 *Byzantium!, The King of Terror*
799 *The Empire of Death.* Luckner lived 1881-1966.
800 *Mad Dogs and Englishmen*
801 *Storm Warning.* The Treaty of Versailles was signed 28th June, 1919.
802 *TW: Small Worlds*
803 Dating *Casualties of War* (EDA #38) - The date is given (p7).
804 *Eater of Wasps*
805 *Pier Pressure.* The armistice with Germany was signed in France on 11th November, 1918.
806 *Birthright, Casualties of War*
807 "Twelve years" before *The English Way of Death* (p83).

808 *Matrix*
809 Dating *Toy Soldiers* (NA #42) - The main action of the book starts "25 September 1919" (p39).
810 *Aliens of London.* No date is given, but Lloyd George was Prime Minister 1916-1922.
811 *The Roundheads*
812 *Dying in the Sun*
813 "The Final Chapter"
814 *Scaredy Cat*
815 Dating *Blink* (X3.10) - Benjamin's newspaper names the day and year.
816 Dating *The Daleks' Master Plan* (4.4) - The script for Part Seven, "The Feast of Steven," specified a date of "1919," but publicity material released on 1st October, 1965, stated that the TARDIS lands in "California 1921". The film being made is a talkie, which means this must be after the release of *The Jazz Singer* in 1927. Numerous Hollywood personalities are seen or hinted at in the episode. Actor Rudolph Valentino made his debut in 1914 but was only really famous after *The*

had ravaged the planet Q'ell. The Recruiter had been built to destroy the Ceracai race, but the Doctor reprogrammed it to rebuild the devastated planet.

The Doctor drank with Lloyd George when he was Prime Minister.[810]

The Nineteen Twenties

The Doctor acquired a copy of the 1920 book *Every Boy's Book of the English Civil War*. He would later lose it in 1648.[811] The Doctor met movie producer Harold Reitman in England in the twenties.[812] The Doctor helped Joyce with *Ulysses*.[813]

In the 1920s, Blue Tit birds in Southhampton learned to tear the tops off milk bottles and drink the cream inside. Soon, Blue Tit birds more than a hundred miles away were exhibiting the talent - even though the birds rarely flew more than fifteen miles - and by 1947, the habit was universal among the species. This owed to morphic resonance, a collective memory held within a planet's morphogenetic field, and passed on to each new generation of life. The same effect was witnessed in monkey creatures four million years in the future, on the planet Endarra.[814]

1920 (5th December) - BLINK[815] **->** The Weeping Angels transported Kathy Nightingale from 2007 to Hull in 1920. She would marry Benjamin Wainright and live out her life in her own past.

c 1921 - THE DALEKS' MASTER PLAN[816] **->** While hiding from the Daleks, the TARDIS landed briefly on a film set in Hollywood.

The Russian mineralogist Leonid A Kulik visited the area of the Tunguska explosion in 1921, but failed to locate

the impact site.[817] **In 1922, a foreigner staying at Tullock Inn vanished on Tullock Moor, kidnapped by the Zygons.**[818] **Dr Judson was crippled before this time.**[819] The Threshold set up offices on the Moon in 1922.[820]

1923 (9th November) - TIMEWYRM: EXODUS[821] **->** The seventh Doctor and Ace witnessed the Munich Putsch, an attempted coup organised by a young Adolf Hitler, so the Doctor could gain Hitler's confidence and sway events in future. The time travellers were fired upon by a man with energy weapons - the War Chief, who was operating in this era to aid the Nazis - but the Doctor failed to recognize him.

In 1923, George Limb, a member of military intelligence, wanted the British to side with Hitler. He failed to convince his superiors.[822]

@ The Doctor studied Ba Chai in Peking, the 1920s.[823] The Doctor borrowed a rucksack from George Mallory and Andrew Irvine before their final assault on Everest in 1924. He warned them not to lose their gloves, lest they lose their lives, but he never saw from them again - possibly because he'd failed to return Mallory's gloves.[824]

1924 (October) - THE CLOCKWISE MAN[825] **->** The ninth Doctor and Rose arrived to visit the British Empire Exhibition, and quickly discovered that a creature that ticked had committed a series of attacks. Shade Vassily, a war criminal from the planet Katuria, had been tracked down to Earth by the socialite Melissa Heart - actually a disfigured alien hunter. The Katurians used clockwork technology, but the Doctor prevented Vassily and Heart's conflict from destroying London.

1925 - "The Futurists"[826] **->** The tenth Doctor and Rose landed in Milan, because Rose wanted an ice cream. The

---

Sheik in 1921. Actor Douglas Fairbanks Sr. debuted in 1915, but he wasn't "big" (as he is described in the episode) until *The Three Musketeers* in 1921. Chaplin's debut was 1914, but the film we see in production strongly resembles *Gold Rush* (1924). Bing Crosby didn't go to Hollywood until 1930. *DWM* writer Richard Landen claimed a date of "1929". *The TARDIS Special* offered "c.1920".
817 *The Wages of Sin*
818 Angus relates the story in *Terror of the Zygons*.
819 According to Commander Millington, the accident happened "over twenty years" before *The Curse of Fenric*, and Judson appears to blame Millington for it. The novelisation, also written by Ian Briggs, confirms that Millington was culpable.
820 "Wormwood"
821 Dating *Timewyrm: Exodus* (NA #2) - Part Two of the

novel is set during the Munich Putsch, which took place between the 8th and 9th of November 1923. A textbook quoted in the novel erroneously gives the month as "September" (p95).
822 *Illegal Alien*
823 *To the Slaughter*
824 *Circular Time*: "Spring". George Mallory and Andrew Irvine perished while attempting to climb Everest in June 1924, which perhaps makes the Doctor and Nyssa's light-hearted banter about the topic a little inappropriate.
825 Dating *The Clockwise Man* (NSA #1) - The date is given.
826 Dating "The Futurists" (*DWM* #372-374) - It is "two decades into the new century", and the Doctor says it is 1925 later in the story.

Futurists were holding a meeting, and a strange green glow heralded the materialization of a futuristic city - which quickly started to crumble. The TARDIS transported the Doctor and Rose to Cardiff in the late third century.

In 1925, the Doctor stopped the time traveller Studs Maloney importing hooch from the twenty-fifth century.[827]

1925 (11th June) - BLACK ORCHID[828] **->** The explorer George Cranleigh was believed killed by Indians while on an expedition in the Amazon in 1923. Cassell and Company published his book *Black Orchid*. George's fiancée, Anne Talbot, eventually became engaged to his brother Charles. Yet George hadn't died. The Kajabi Indians had horribly disfigured George because he stole their sacred black orchid, but the chief of a rival tribe rescued him. George was kept hidden away at Cranleigh Hall. He later broke out, and died trying to abduct his former fiancée.

A famous author of boys' stories for *The Ensign* magazine vanished at his home in 1926.[829] On 4th June, 1926, the SS *Bernice* inexplicably vanished in the Indian Ocean. The ship had left England in early May, and the last anyone ever saw of it was on 2nd June, when it left Bombay.[830]

1926 - "The Gods Walk Among Us"[831] **->** Archaeologists unearthed the tomb of Sontar in Egypt. The Sontaran within was still alive after 5500 years, and killed the archaeologists - but their Egyptian bearers dropped a stone slab on the alien, apparently killing it.

In 1927, the Doctor watched the Cuban grandmaster Capablanca play chess.[832] In the same year, the second Doctor met Ella's grandfather in Tibet. From this time, his family became caretakers of the Doctor's house in Kent.[833]

= 1927 - REAL TIME[834] **->** The Cybermen succeeded in infecting Earth with a techno-virus that transformed living beings into cybernetic ones. Most of the human race died from shock, and all animals perished. The cybernetic survivors fell under Cybermen domination.

Evelyn Smythe was reportedly the virus' original carrier, having travelled back to this year after being infected in 3286.

The Doctor met Dame Nellie Melba, a noted Australian opera soprano, and learned her party piece: how to shatter glass with your voice.[835] The Doctor met Sigmund Freud and knew Marie Curie intimately. He

----

827 *Island of Death*

828 Dating *Black Orchid* (19.5) - The Doctor says it is "three o'clock, June the eleventh, nineteen hundred and twenty-five".

829 *The Mind Robber*

830 *Carnival of Monsters*. The Doctor has heard of the disappearance of the SS *Bernice*, but we see it vanish from the miniscope and apparently return to its native time at the end of Part Four. Perhaps the ship didn't arrive home safely after all. Alternatively, perhaps the Doctor's actions alter history, although this would make for something of a paradox.

831 Dating "The Gods Walk Among Us" (*DWM* #59) - The year is given in the opening caption.

832 *The Androids of Tara*. José Raúl Capablanca y Graupera lived 1888-1942. He spent six years as a world chess champion, ending in 1927.

833 "Fellow Travellers". This may or may not be a reference to *The Abominable Snowman*. If so, it's unclear which character Ella's grandfather was.

834 Dating *Real Time* (BF BBCi #1) - Dr. Goddard identifies the date of Cyber-infection.

835 *The Power of Kroll*. Dame Nellie Melba lived 1861-1931.

836 *Doctor Who - The Movie*. and it's possible these encounters were all on the same visit: Freud lived 1865-1939, Marie Curie 1867-1934, and Puccini 1858-1924. The only date given is that the Doctor was with Puccini

shortly before he died.

837 *The Devil Goblins from Neptune*

838 *Relative Dementias*. This is possibly a misremembering of *Doctor Who - The Movie*. The Doctor name-dropped Puccini in that story, but it was Leonardo da Vinci who had the cold.

839 *The City of the Dead*

840 *Grimm Reality*

841 *Illegal Alien* (p83).

842 *Phantasmagoria*

843 The Blinovitch Limitation Effect was first mentioned in *Day of the Daleks* (and subsequently in *Invasion of the Dinosaurs* and *Mawdryn Undead*). We learn more about Blinovitch in *The Ghosts of N-Space* (p147) and *Timewyrm: Revelation* (p50).

844 *Frozen Time*. Bassett's expedition encounters a colony of Silurians, as occurs in the Audio-Visuals story *Endurance*. Nick Briggs, who wrote *Frozen Time*, starred as the Doctor in that adventure.

845 *The Scales of Injustice*, also referring to *Endurance*.

846 "City of Devils", and yet another reference to *Endurance* by *The Scales of Injustice* author Gary Russell. By 2012 the loss of the expedition is publically acknowledged, not just rumoured.

847 Dating *Blood Harvest* (NA #28) - The blurb states it is 1929. The book is set during Prohibition (1919-1933 in America), but while Al Capone is at liberty. In May 1929, Capone was sentenced to prison time for carry-

met **Pucchini**[836] in Milan.[837] Puccini had a terrible cold.[838]

@ The Doctor had sessions with Freud, hoping to jog his memory.[839] He told Freud that he had a phobia of silverfish.[840]

The Doctor watched Babe Ruth hit three home runs for the Yankees in 1926.[841] The Doctor owned a copy of *Wisden's Almanac* from 1928.[842]

Aaron Blinovitch formulated his Limitation Effect in 1928, publishing it in *Temporal Mechanics*.[843]

In 1929, Lord Barset led an expedition to Antarctica aboard his ship, the *Rochester*. The expedition found a base that contained "lizard men", and disaster ensued. The *Rochester* sank and all hands were lost, save for one member who was found holding Lord Barset's diary of the mission. The man died shortly afterwards, screaming about monsters, but the journal was later passed down to Bassett's grandson.[844]

The base was a Silurian shelter, and UNIT would investigate it in the 1970s.[845] The *Daily Telegraph* of 12th April, 1929, noted rumours that an Antarctic Expedition had been lost after finding a city of intelligent reptiles.[846]

1929 - BLOOD HARVEST[847] -> As gangland violence escalated in Chicago, the enigmatic Doc McCoy opened a speakeasy right in the middle of disputed territory. The Doc and his moll Ace saved Al Capone's life. The seventh Doctor was tracking down the eternal being Agonal, who had amplified the gang warfare to feed his lust for violence.

The vampire Yarven travelled to Earth from E-Space aboard the Doctor's TARDIS.

Yarven became a progenitor of many of Earth's vampires. Villagers in Croatia overpowered and buried him alive, and he would remain trapped until 1993.[848] **The Brigadier's car, a Humber 1650 Open Tourer Imperial Model, was built in 1929.**[849] The Canavatchi engineered the Wall Street Crash of October 1929 to hinder mankind's development.[850]

Lord Tamworth witnessed the arrival of the Engineer Prime of the telepathic Triskele on Earth. He was promoted to "Minister of Air," and oversaw preparations to use the *R-101* airship to return the Engineer Prime to its people.[851]

The Nineteen Thirties

The Urbankans began to receive radio signals from Earth.[852] **The Doctor met the cricket player Donald Bradman, and once took five wickets for New South Wales.**[853]

During the 1930s, the League of Nations set up a secret international organisation, LONGBOW, to deal with matters of world security. It found itself, on occasion, dealing with unexplained and extraterrestrial phenomena.[854] The Doctor discussed the theoretical Philosopher's Stone (not the Khamerian-created one) with psychiatrist Carl Jung.[855]

The Silurian Triad was revived. These were Ichtar, Scibus and science advisor Tarpok.[856] In the 1930s, the Doctor and his friend Ernest Hemingway ran with the bulls in Pamplona. A matador named Manolito trained the Doctor in the basics of his art.[857]

The people of Parakon discovered rapine, a crop that when processed could be used as a foodstuff or a building material. For the next forty years, the Corporation that marketed rapine ruled the planet unopposed, supplanting nations, governments, armies and all competition.[858]

A young actor named Billy appeared in *I'm an Explosive* (1933) and *While Parents Sleep* (1935). He would come to befriend the music hall comedian Max Miller.[859]

The stage musician Professor Talbot performed on Brighton's West Pier, but this led to his encountering the Indo aliens. Talbot was killed, but the aliens' energy animated his body, and his mind became focused on gaining widespread recognition and authority. He was presumed dead, but would resurface in 1936.[860]

---

ing a concealed weapon, so *Blood Harvest* must occur before that. He saw release in 1930, but his more infamous conviction on tax evasion charges happened in 1931.
848 *Goth Opera*
849 His student Ibbotson, nicknamed Hippo, identifies the car in *Mawdryn Undead*.
850 *The King of Terror* (p179).
851 "One night last winter" before *Storm Warning*.
852 *Four to Doomsday*
853 *Four to Doomsday*. No date given. Donald Bradman was born in 1908, playing for Australia from 1928-1948.
854 *Just War*
855 *Option Lock*. No date given. Jung lived 26th July,

1875, to 6th June, 1961.
856 "Around forty years" before *The Scales of Injustice*.
857 *Deadly Reunion*. No date given. Hemingway lived 1898-1961.
858 "Forty years" before *The Paradise of Death* (p131).
859 *Pier Pressure*. Billy is obviously a young William Hartnell, who appeared in both films.
860 "At least" fifteen years before *Pier Pressure*.

UNIT in the Thirties[861]

Alistair Gordon Lethbridge-Stewart was born.[862]

Lethbridge-Stewart was an only child whose mother died when he was young. He was raised by his father and Granny McDougal. He was raised in Simla, India and his happiest memories are of summers there. His father rose to the rank of Colonel.[863]

> = u - When Lethbridge-Stewart was six or seven, he was heartbroken to lose a red balloon, and suffered a recurring nightmare about it for the rest of his life.

The Doctor caught the balloon and returned it.[864] Lethbridge-Stewart left India for prep school in England when he was eight.[865]

? 1930 - THE WORMERY[866] **->** On a planet affected by a dimensional nexus point, worms evolved with the ability to see their own future. Appalled at the sight of themselves turning into hairy, complex beings, the worms divided into an "anti faction" and "pro faction" to derail their future. The "anti" group sought to turn the universe into total chaos, which would prevent development of any type. The "pro" group allied with the club singer Bianca, hoping to freeze the universe in a single perfect moment. Additionally, a group of shadow beings - the potential future selves of the worms, currently held in a state of flux - searched for a means of becoming corporeal.

By now, the nightclub named "Bianca's" existed in a dimensional nexus, accessible via special taxis that shuttled patrons through dimensional portals. The club was actually Iris Wildthyme's TARDIS, with its exterior looking like 1930s Berlin.

The sixth Doctor and Iris arrived separately at Bianca's, and exposed Bianca as the embodiment of Iris' darker natures. The two worm factions, plus their shadow selves, each searched for a means of exploiting the club's extra-dimensional nature to their advantage. The Doctor used his TARDIS to Time-Ram the nightclub, which severed its dimensional links and returned its patrons to their native times. This defeated the worms and their shadows, and transferred the wreckage of the club to Berlin. Bianca escaped.

1930

1930 (June) - THE ENGLISH WAY OF DEATH[867] **->** The TARDIS arrived in London during an inexplicable heatwave, as the fourth Doctor needed to return some library books before they became overdue. He and Romana stumbled upon a group from the thirty-second century (the Bureau) that were using time corridor technology to send retired people to the English village of Nutchurch. While the Doctor put a stop to that, Romana confronted the sentient smell Zodaal, an exiled would-be conqueror from the planet Vesur. Zodaal was trapped in a flask, and the device that would have destroyed Earth was deactivated.

Around 1930, the fourth Doctor visited Tigella and saw the Dodecahedron.[868] The Doctor bought Jacques Cousteau his first set of flippers.[869] The Doctor learned about sharks from Jacques Cousteau.[870]

1930 (5th October) - STORM WARNING[871] **->** The TARDIS landed on the doomed airship *R-101* during its maiden voyage. Aboard the ship, the eighth Doctor discovered Charley Pollard, a stowaway. Lord Tamworth, a government minister, ordered the ship to a higher altitude and it docked with an alien vessel. The British had arranged to return a crashed alien to its own people, the Triskele. A fac-

---

861 See the article on UNIT Dating - the exact dates of the early years of Lethbridge-Stewart's life are affected by the wider issue of when the UNIT stories are set.
862 *Island of Death*
863 *Island of Death*
864 *The Shadows of Avalon* (p3, p271).
865 *Island of Death*
866 Dating *The Wormery* (BF #51)- It is some point in "the thirties".
867 Dating *The English Way of Death* (MA #20)- The date is given (p23).
868 "Fifty years" before *Meglos*.
869 "Children of the Revolution"
870 *The Murder Game*. No date is given.
871 Dating *Storm Warning* (BF #16) - It is stated that it is "early in October 1930", and the *R-101* really began its maiden flight on 4th October, 1930. The date is con-

firmed in *Minuet in Hell* and *Neverland*. According to *The Chimes of Midnight*, Charley was born the day the *Titanic* sank, 14th April, 1912, and was eighteen years, five months and twenty-one days old when she met the Doctor, making it the 5th of October.
872 Dating *Daleks in Manhattan / Evolution of the Daleks* (X3.4-3.5) - Martha finds a newspaper just after the TARDIS lands, and it sets the date as "Saturday 1 November 1930". Construction of the Empire State Building commenced on 17th March, 1930, and it officially opened on 1st May, 1931.
873 Dating *Seasons of Fear* (BF #30)- The play starts with the Doctor saying it's the "cusp of the years 1930 and 1931".
874 *The Rapture*
875 "The Final Chapter"
876 *TW: Out of Time*. Earhart really disappeared in 1937.

tion of the Triskele became aggressive when the Lawgiver that kept them in check died. The Doctor eased the situation, and Tamworth agreed to stay with the Triskele as an advisor. The *R-101* was damaged upon its return, and the Doctor and Charley only just escaped as the ship crashed in France. The Doctor realised that Charley was meant to have died in the crash.

1930 (1st November) - DALEKS IN MANHATTAN / EVOLUTION OF THE DALEKS[872] ->

The tenth Doctor and Martha arrived in New York and discovered that homeless people had been going missing from Hooverville, a community of victims of the Great Depression living in Central Park. The people had been abducted by the Cult of Skaro - the last four surviving Daleks, who had fled the Battle of Canary Warf in 2007 via temporal shift. The Daleks required human subjects for their genetic experiments, and were turning them into pig slaves. The final experiment was undertaken by their leader, Dalek Sec, who converted himself into a "human Dalek".

The Daleks planned to draw energy from a solar flare down through the structure of the Empire State Building, and use it to create a new race of human Daleks. The Doctor sabotaged the attempt, and the resultant human Daleks rebeled. By this time, the three "pure" Daleks had grown suspicious of Sec's motives. In the ensuing conflict, every Dalek and Dalek hybrid was destroyed save for Dalek Caan - who escaped via a temporal shift.

1930 (31st December) - SEASONS OF FEAR[873] ->

The immortal Sebastian Grayle found the eighth Doctor and Charley in Singapore, and boasted that he'd already killed the Doctor in the past. The Doctor set about investigating the matter, heading for Britain in 305 AD.

The Doctor fought in the Spanish Civil War with the father of future bar owner Gustavo Riviera. Later, he brought Gustavo to refuge in Ibiza.[874]

The Doctor was a house guest of Dali.[875]

1932

Diane Holmes incorrectly thought Amelia Earhart disappeared in 1932.[876] Richard Lazarus was born around 1932, but would rejuvenate himself in the early twenty-first century.[877]

1933

Otto Kreiner moved from Germany to England, soon meeting and marrying Muriel Tarr. They would become the parents of the Doctor's companion Fitz.[878]

@ The Doctor spent much of 1933 in the South Seas, and claimed to have gotten a tattoo there. By this time, he had a criminal record in England.[879] While in the South Seas, he saw magic performed.[880] He served about the ship *Sarah Gail*, where he learned to play the violin[881] and read a report of wasps attacking a train outside Arandale.[882] At some point, he visited Australia and Hangchow.[883]

1933 (August) - EATER OF WASPS[884] ->

An alien device from the future was accidentally dropped into a wasps' nest, causing the wasps to mutate into killers. A trio of Time Agents arrived to find the device. The eighth Doctor, Fitz and Anji also arrived at this time. The Time Agents decided to sterilise the area with a nuclear explosion. The Doctor found the mutagenic device and smashed it, and also disarmed the Agents' nuclear weapon.

By 1933, Germany had become aware that werewolves existed. Such non-humans were ordered to register with the government, and werewolves loyal to the party were reportedly used to sense dissenters. Several werewolves were rounded up and incarcerated in a special camp, equipped with silver wire, for a year. A man from the Schutzstaffel (the Nazi Party's "praetorian guard") arrived and pressed the desperate werewolves into the service of the state.[885]

In 1933, Cuevas discovered a part of the Great Temple of the Aztecs.[886]

---

877 Lazarus declares he is "seventy six years old" in *The Lazarus Experiment*, which is set in 2008.
878 *Frontier Worlds*
879 *Eater of Wasps*
880 *Mad Dogs and Englishmen*
881 *The Year of Intelligent Tigers*
882 *The Year of Intelligent Tigers*, referring to events in *Eater of Wasps*.
883 *History 101*. This was possibly during his second bout of world travelling in the sixties and seventies.
884 Dating *Eater of Wasps* (EDA #45) - The Doctor esti-

mates "it is probably the 1930s. If pushed, I'd have to say 1933. Twenty-seventh of August in fact" (p10).
885 *Wolfsbane* (p90) gives the date of the werewolf Emmeline's capture as 1933.
886 *The Left-Handed Hummingbird* (p58).

1934

1934 - THE EYE OF THE GIANT[887] **-> The** *Constitution III* was beached upon an uncharted island of Salutua in the South Pacific. Among the passengers was Marshal J Grover, the millionaire shipping magnate and owner of Paragon Film Studios. The third Doctor and Liz Shaw arrived at the island using a time bridge portal, and discovered a spacecraft in a volcanic crater. Animal and plant life on the island was subject to gigantism: giant crabs roamed the beach, bats the size of men flew at night, and the forest was hypertrophied. The Doctor discovered that drugs created by the Semquess, the most skilled bio-engineers in the galaxy, were responsible for the mutations. The drugs had been brought to Earth fifty years before by Brokk of the Grold. The Semquess had tracked him to the planet, and now they apparently destroyed him. Brokk, though, used the properties of the Semquess drug to merge with Grover's young wife Nancy and leave the Earth.

The Doctor pursued the Master across Berlin, and met Himmler and the future "Butcher of Prague," Reinhold Heydrich.[888] On 30th June, 1934, the German-imprisoned werewolves were unleashed at a hotel housing men loyal to Ernst Roehm's Sturmabetilung ("Storm Division," also known as stormtroopers). One of the werewolves, Emmeline Neuberger, bit a silver chain around a man's neck and was rendered unconscious. She was subsequently overlooked, and escaped into the German woods.[889]

1935

The Doctor and Bernice failed to meet Virginia Woolf and went to the theatre instead. In the audience was twenty-fifth century explorer Gustaf Heinrich Urnst, who had been transported there by a Fortean Flicker.[890]

1935 - THE ABOMINABLE SNOWMEN[891] **-> The sec- ond Doctor, Jamie and Victoria arrived in the Himalayas. They found that the Yeti were menacing a local monastery and an expedition led by Professor Travers. The Yeti were robots built on behalf of the Intelligence - a powerful being of pure thought that attempted to manifest physically. The Doctor banished it from Earth.**

A Cynrog spacecraft crashed in Wales. The pilot died, but managed to implant segments of his memories in eight local children.[892]

1936

The Doctor and Mel met German racing driver Emil Hartung in Cairo. The Doctor accidentally inspired Hartung to develop aircraft that could avoid radar detection. Hartung won the Cairo 500 thanks to the modifications the Doctor made to his car.[893]

Fitz Kreiner was born in Hampstead on 7th March, 1936.[894] Sir Henry Rugglesthorpe and his family become playthings of the Toymaker.[895]

Ian Chesterton was born.[896] **In October of that year, the Doctor joined Mao Tse-Tung on the Long March.**[897]

@ 1936 (November) WOLFSBANE[898] **->** By now the eighth Doctor had returned to England, and been rejected several times after submitting short stories to *Astounding Stories* magazine.

Harry Sullivan disembarked to explore when the TARDIS stopped on Earth, but the Ship inexplicably dematerialized. A stranded Harry happened upon the eighth Doctor as Lady Hester Stanton, believing herself the reincarnation of Morgan le Fay, performed magic rituals to wake the land and bind it to her. She hoped to rule

---

887 Dating *The Eye of the Giant* (MA #21) - "The time is the eighth of June, nineteen thirty-four" (p42).
888 *The King of Terror* (p103).
889 *Wolfsbane*. Page 93 says the werewolves were taken from the camp on 29th June, 1934; the hotel slaughter occurred the following evening. Historically, Hitler moved against Roehm and his Sturmabetilung because they could have staged a *coup d'etat*. He ordered the Sturmabetilung leaders to congregate at the Hanselbauer Hotel in Bad Wiesse near Munich, which is where the massacre in *Wolfsbane* evidently takes place. The purge is sometimes referred to as "The Night of the Long Knives".
890 *The Highest Science* (p257).
891 Dating *The Abominable Snowmen* (4.2)- According to the Doctor, this story takes place "three hundred years" after events that the monk Thonmi says took

place in "1630". In *The Web of Fear*, Victoria states that the Travers Expedition took place in "1935". In *Downtime*, Charles Bryce says it was "1936" (p65).
892 *The Nightmare of Black Island*
893 *Just War*
894 *The Ancestor Cell* (p126), based on the writers' guidelines. He was "twenty seven" in *The Taint*. His year of birth is "1935" in *Escape Velocity*. He celebrates his birthday on 7th March in *Interference*.
895 *Divided Loyalties*
896 According to an early format document for the series, dating from July 1963, Ian is "27". Then again, William Russell certainly looks older than that on screen.
897 *The Mind of Evil*. The Long March was a massive retreat on the part of the Chinese Communist Army to elude the Kuomintang Army. It granted the

England from behind-the-scenes, with her son George taking Edward VIII's place. Stanton magically compelled the werewolf Emmeline Neuberger to assist.

Stanton's spells began to awaken the land, and a wood dryad expelled the swordsman Godric, who had been seduced into slumber. Harry's use of the Holy Grail, which Godric possessed, made the Earth swallow Stanton and the Grail also. Emmeline, instinctively desiring a mate, bit Harry.

The fourth Doctor and Sarah returned for Harry, and took Godric back to his native time. Some reports suggest Harry turned into a werewolf and killed Sarah, then was killed by the Doctor; some suggest Harry returned home and secretly became a werewolf during the full moon; and some say the Doctor permanently cured Harry's condition.

The eighth Doctor believed Harry, Stanton and Godric had all been killed, and made gravesites to stop anyone getting too curious about them or the Grail. He introduced Emmeline to his friends in the British Ministry, but they started experimenting on her in the hopes of creating lupine soldiers.

1936 (December) WOLFSBANE[899] **->** The TARDIS rematerialized after leaving Harry behind two weeks previous, and the fourth Doctor and Sarah found his "tombstone." They pieced together what had occurred during the previous fortnight. The Doctor rescued Emmeline from the Ministry, and drew enough blood from her to ritualistically send the land back to sleep. She departed back to Germany; the Doctor and Sarah went back to find Harry.

@ The Doctor made a visit to Highgate.[900]

1936 (December) PLAYERS[901] **->** King Edward VIII sought to dissolve the British government, hoping to vest more power with Nazi sympathizers. The Doctor aided Winston Churchill in coercing the King to abdicate the throne, threatening to charge him with treason. This thwarted the schemes of the Players, who were engaged in a game of historical alterations.

The Doctor and Peri stopped at Cholmondeley's bank, where the Doctor's account had amassed one hundred twenty years of compound interest.

1936 (December) - PIER PRESSURE[902] **->** In Brighton, a string of murders gave rise to stories of "the Phantom Bloodsucker of Preston Park", a killer who was said to prey upon the blood of fresh young maidens. The sixth Doctor and Evelyn encountered the famous music hall comedian Max Miller, and found the reportedly dead Professor Talbot as an agent of the Indo aliens. The Doctor feared that the aliens would gain much power by feeding off the emotional trauma of the impending World War II, and short-circuited their energy with a piece of Gallifreyan zinc. This allowed Talbot to finally die, dissipated the aliens' mass and left their essence embedded within Brighton's West Pier.

The Doctor estimated that the essence of the Indo aliens from 1936 would corrode Brighton's West Pier, and probably consume its metal entirely in sixty or seventy years.[903]

1937

@ The amnesiac Doctor was in London at this time.[904]

1937 - HISTORY 101[905] **-** Sabbath sent an agent to Barcelona to track down the Absolute, a being from the future that had acquired information about his activities. This disrupted history, which in turn corrupted the Absolute's perceptions. The eighth Doctor, Anji and Fitz arrived and discovered that the Picasso painting *Guernica* had been altered. The Doctor sent Fitz to Guernica itself to check events. The Doctor restored reality and the Absolute returned home. These events inspired Eric Blair, also known as the writer George Orwell.

Aviatrix Amelia Earhart disappeared, possibly because she flew into one of the Dragon Paths, lines of magnetic force.[906] The Doctor had Amelia Earhart's flying jacket.[907]

Communists a needed respite in the north of China.
898 Dating *Wolfsbane* (PDA #62)- Harry is abandoned on 27th November, 1936, according to p24. Harry's fate is left ambiguous due to the presence of multiple timelines, which were finally compressed to one history in *Timeless. Sometime Never* says the Council of Eight had a hand in engineering Harry's "death".
899 Dating *Wolfsbane* (PDA #62)- It's 11th December, 1936 (p49).
900 *Grimm Reality*
901 Dating *Players* (PDA #21) - The date is given (p150).
902 Dating *Pier Pressure* (BF #21) - The year is given in the story and on the back cover. Mention that *Charlie*

Chan at the Opera is currently showing in Brighton is potentially a glitch, as some documentation indicates it wasn't distributed in the UK until 8th January, 1937. Miller states that he's forty; he's approximating, because he would have been forty-two at the time.
903 *Pier Pressure*. This refers to the West Pier's real-life decay. It partially collapsed on 29th December, 2002, then further caved in on 20th January, 2003.
904 *History 101*
905 Dating *History 101* (EDA #58)- It's "Barcelona, 1937" (p1).
906 *The Shadow of Weng-Chiang* (p208).
907 *Superior Beings* (p58).

1937 (August) THE SHADOW OF WENG-CHIANG[908]

-> The fourth Doctor, Romana and K9 were drawn to Shanghai while on the search for the Key to Time. They stumbled across the Tong of the Black Scorpion's plan to recover their "god" Weng-Chiang (Magnus Greel) from the zygma beam experiment. The Doctor followed the Tong's leader, H'sien-Ko - the daughter of the stage magician Li H'sien Chang - to the holy mountain of T'ai Shan. There, the Doctor found the Tong had constructed the world's first nuclear reactor to achieve the power needed to retrieve Greel from the zygma beam. The Doctor narrowly prevented a temporal paradox by time-ramming Greel's Time Cabinet, hurling it back in time to the year 1872.

In 1937, the eighth Doctor and Fey Truscott-Sade fought psychic weasels in Russell Square. Soon after this, the Threshold implanted a perceptual relay unit in Truscott-Sade's brain, enabling them to monitor what she saw from this point.[909]

1938

Ghosts were sighted on the *Queen Mary* in 1938.[910]

1938 - "The Curse of the Scarab"[911]

-> The fifth Doctor and Peri landed in what they thought was an Egyptian tomb, but which was actually a Hollywood film set. The movie *The Curse of the Scarab* was beset with problems, including Raschid Karnak, the uncommunicative lead, who played the Mummy. Director Seth Rakoff was under a great deal of pressure from the studio boss, Monroe Stahr. Peri led Karnak to his dressing room, where he choked and scarab beetles started emerging from his mouth. A robot Mummy killed Stahr. The Doctor discovered more deactivated Mummies in a control centre inside a prop pyramid. Karnak was there, and told them he was cursed by the beetle god Kephri. He used the Grimoire of Anubis to resurrect Kephri. A plague of locusts was released as Kephri manifested. The Doctor held it in place with an ankh, and had a robot Mummy destroy it. The film set was destroyed in a fire.

At one point during this encounter, Peri was abducted by Threshold.

1938 (31st October) - INVADERS FROM MARS[912]

-> An alien spaceship crashed in New Jersey and was looted by the gangster Don Chaney, who discovered a bat-like being aboard. Chaney hired the Russian physicist Yuri Stepashin to develop an atom bomb from the advanced technology, hoping to give America an advantage over Germany. The eighth Doctor and Charley arrived to find conflict brewing between Chaney and his rival, Cosmo Devine, who wanted to sell the technology for the Nazis.

The alien split into thirty beings and threatened to go on a rampage, but the aliens Streath and Noriam arrived and subdued the pilot as part of a protection racket. Devine convinced Streath and Noriam that their weapons could seize control of Earth without the need for deception. The

---

908 Dating *The Shadow of Weng-Chiang* (MA #25)- The date is given (p1).
909 "Tooth and Claw" (*DWM*), Threshold's involvement and the date are confirmed in "Wormwood".
910 *Ghost Ship*
911 Dating "The Curse of the Scarab" (*DWM* #228-230)- The date is given.
912 Dating *Invaders from Mars* (BF #28)- The date is given, although the Welles play was actually broadcast on 30th October, not the 31st. Big Finish claims to have deliberately altered the date as part of the historical alterations affecting the second season of McGann audios. There are a couple of further anachronisms, such as a mention of the CIA and Welles not knowing about Shakespeare, which are explained in *The Time of the Daleks*.
913 *Timeless*. The bookshop is referred to as being on Charing Cross Road, although it was on Euston Road in *Time Zero*.
914 *Time Zero*
915 *Silver Nemesis*
916 *The Shadow in the Glass*
917 "A year or two back" before *Illegal Alien*.
918 *The Daemons*
919 Dating "Tooth and Claw" (*DWM* #257-260) - It's

"1939", according to the opening caption.
920 *The Web of Fear*
921 *Doctor Who and the Pirates*
922 *Ghost Ship*
923 *Endgame* (EDA)
924 *Heart of TARDIS*. This was "several years" before Crowley's reported death in 1947 (p6).
925 *Heart of TARDIS*
926 *Project: Twilight*
927 *Utopia*
928 Dating *Timewyrm: Exodus* (NA #2) - Part Three of the novel is set in "1939" (p111).
929 *Remembrance of the Daleks*
930 *The Paradise of Death* (p25).
931 *Island of Death*
932 *Island of Death*
933 *Business Unusual*
934 In *Mawdryn Undead*, the 1983 Brigadier talks of "thirty years of soldiering". He doesn't have a moustache in the regimental photograph seen in *Inferno*. He is a member of the Scots' Guards in *The Web of Fear*. Other information here comes from *The Invasion* and *The Green Death*.
935 *The Spectre of Lanyon Moor*

Doctor went to CBS Studios and had Orson Welles stage a second, private performance of *War of the Worlds* for the aliens' benefit, hoping to make them think that the formidable Martians had already invaded Earth. The plan failed. Stepashin detonated his atom bomb aboard the aliens' spacecraft while it was in orbit, destroying them.

The Doctor left his past self a copy of Fitz's journal, entitled *An Account of An Expedition to Siberia*, in a second hand bookshop.[913]

@ In 1938, the amnesiac Doctor bought Fitz's journal from a bookshop on Euston Road.[914]

Adolf Hitler gained the Validium Arrow, a piece of the Nemesis statue. The Nemesis itself passed over Earth, heralding Germany's annexation of Austria.[915]

1939

In Antarctica, the Nazis started construction of a huge underground base that was shaped like a swastika.[916]

Circa 1939, a pair of Cybermen from the thirtieth century arrived accidentally in Jersey. They secretly took control of Peddler Electronic Engineering in London.[917] **In 1939, a failed attempt to open Devil's Hump, "the Cambridge University Fiasco", took place.[918]**

1939 - "Tooth and Claw" (*DWM*)[919] -> The eighth Doctor and Izzy were summoned to Varney's island in the Atlantic, where eccentric guests - including Fey Truscott-Sade, an old friend of the Doctor - were served the meat of endangered animals by Varney's monkey servants. Truscott-Sade was working for British Intelligence, and conveyed to the Doctor her suspicions that Varney was creating biological weapons for the Nazis. In truth, Varney had drugged everyone's champagne with a microbe derived from his ancestors, and this turned the guests - the Doctor and Fey included - into vampires.

Varney served the last of the Curcurbites - an alien construct fuelled by blood. The Doctor destroyed the Curcurbite by poisoning his own blood and allowing the construct to feed off him... this returned the Doctor to normal, but left him gravely ill. Izzy and Fey got him back to the TARDIS, knowing they would have to take the Doctor to Gallifrey if he was going to survive.

The Second World War

During the war, bunkers were built in the London Underground, including one at Covent Garden.[920] The Doctor advised Winston Churchill on policy.[921] During World War II, the *Queen Mary* was used as a troop ship and torpedoed. Soldiers died, leading people to suspect the ship was haunted.[922] Beings of light from Altair III observed the Second World War.[923]

Occultist Aleister Crowley summoned the demon Jarakabeth.[924] During World War II, the United States came to fear that collective Nazi belief could alter the fabric of reality. The US government hired writer J.R.R. Tolkien and his contemporaries to infuse world culture with a greater sense of what was fantasy, and what was reality.[925]

The Doctor knew his way around the secret tunnels under the Thames used during the Second World War.[926] **The immortal Captain Jack served in the Second World War.[927]**

1939 (early September) - TIMEWYRM: EXODUS[928] -> The seventh Doctor told Hitler that if he invaded Poland, then the British would declare war on Germany. Hitler refused to believe him, but the Doctor was proved right.

Hitler had risen to power, doubly aided by the War Lords and the Timewyrm nestled within his mind. The War Lords hoped to build a "War Lord universe" by giving the Nazis space travel, whereas the Timewyrm wanted to divert the course of history. The Doctor exposed the War Lords' plans to betray the Nazis, and the forces of Reichsmarshal Goering slaughtered them. The War Lords' influence ended with the destruction of their base, Drachensberg Castle.

As the Second World War started, a few people in England felt that their country should fight alongside the Nazis. Ratcliffe was one such person, and he was imprisoned for his belief.[929]

UNIT in the Forties

Lethbridge-Stewart would later attend Holborough with Teddy "Pooh" Fitzoliver.[930]

Lethbridge-Stewart's Granny McDougal died when he was thirteen[931], and he later won the Public Schools Middleweight Cup during his last year at Fettes.[932] Lethbridge-Stewart and John Sudbury went to the same school.[933]

u - Alistair Gordon Lethbridge-Stewart began his military service. Shortly afterward, he attended Sandhurst with Billy Rutlidge. Once his training was complete, Lethbridge-Stewart grew his moustache, joined the Scots' Guards and was stationed for a time at Aldgate.[934]

1940

Radar equipment on Lanyon Moor was subject to mysterious interference, and the men stationed there suffered from mental illnesses.[935]

> = On the Earth of the Dark Matrix, Britain had to use its army to fight civil disorder, not Hitler. The Americans intervened, and took control of the United Kingdom before defeating Hitler.[936]

The Nazis occupied Jersey. Colonel Schott found a dormant Cyberman army in the Le Mur engineering factory.[937]

1940 (May) - TIMEWYRM: EXODUS[938] -> Hitler, still emboldened by the Timewyrm within him, became jubilant as his armies scored many successes. German forces had reached Abbeville in France. The seventh Doctor and Ace arrived at Hitler's command post of Felsennest, and the Doctor exorcised the Timewyrm from Hitler's mind. This left Hitler weakened, and the Doctor persuaded him to halt the German advance on Dunkirk. This enabled "the Miracle of Dunkirk" - the rescue of hundreds of thousands of British and French soldiers in a makeshift fleet of civilian boats - to occur and mark a turning point of the war.

The Doctor was at Dunkirk during the British evacuation.[939]

@ The Doctor visited Lancashire in the forties and met aliens from Antares 5.[940] He tried to join the RAF, but couldn't prove he was a British subject. He left England, spending two years in South America and Africa.[941]

1940 - ILLEGAL ALIEN[942] - > A time-travelling Cyberman, injured by a Luftwaffe bomb in London, instinctively started to seek out blood plasma to heal its damaged components. It began a murder campaign and gained a reputation as "the Limehouse Lurker." The seventh Doctor and Ace arrived onhand and the Lurker was destroyed.

The time travellers discovered that George Limb, a for-mer Foreign Office secretary, had given Cyber-technology to both the Allies and the Nazis as a means of sparking a technology race. Limb escaped using a Cybermen time machine, but the Doctor's intervention eradicated much of the errant Cyber-technology, plus destroyed the Nazi Cyber-conversion base in Jersey. However, a pumphouse containing hundreds of Cybermen cocoons survived, and was discovered by private detective Cody McBride.

The original Jack Harkness killed twenty six opponents during the Battle of Britain.[943] The Doctor and Bernice arrived in Guernsey in December 1940. Bernice went undercover as Celia Doras, the daughter of a local landlady.[944] **As a child, Richard Lazarus was caught up in the Blitz and became obsessed with immortality.**[945]

Barbara Wright was born in 1940 and lived in Bedfordshire for a time.[946]

1941

In 1941, the Doctor was present when a group of Alpha Centauri were stranded in Shanghai and panicked.[947]

1941 (Saturday, 20th January) - CAPTAIN JACK HARKNESS[948] -> Captain Jack and Tosh arrived from the twenty-first century, having entered a temporal shift in the Ritz, a Cardiff dance hall. They met an American pilot named Captain Jack Harkness - the man whose identity "our" Jack stole when operating as a conman - and who was due to die the following day. Jack befriended his namesake before the Rift reopened, and he and Tosh returned home.

The original Captain Jack Harkness died on 21st January. His squadron was out on a training mission, and two formations of Messerschmitts surprised them. The Captain managed to destroy three of the enemy,

---

936 *Matrix*

937 *Illegal Alien* (p211). The Nazis occupied Jersey on 1st May, 1940.

938 Dating *Timewyrm: Exodus* (NA #2) - The historical evacuation of Dunkirk took place from 27th May to 4th June, 1940, and the Doctor exorcises the Timewyrm from Hitler's mind shortly prior to that.

939 *Just War*. The evacuation is also referred to in *Timewyrm: Exodus*.

940 *Grimm Reality*

941 *The Turing Test* (p59).

942 Dating *Illegal Alien* (PDA #5) - Tomorrow's date, "14 November 1940" is given (p20).

943 *TW: Captain Jack Harkness*. The Battle of Britain lasted from 10th July to 31st October, 1940.

944 *Just War*. The date is given as 1941 (p4), but that is a mistake and should read 1940.

945 *The Lazarus Experiment*. Lazarus names the year as 1940. The Blitz began on 7th September, and lasted into 1941. The Doctor refers to having seen the horrors of the Blitz, which he did in *The Empty Child / The Doctor Dances*, as well as in a number of the novels.

946 In *The Rescue*, Vicki claims that Barbara ought to be "550" years old. As *The Rescue* is set in 2493 this means Barbara was born in 1943 - making her twe in 1963, and therefore too young to be a history teacher. Jacqueline Hill was born in 1931, and was 34 when *The Rescue* was made - meaning that Vicki is clearly rounding down. The finalised Writers' Guide for the first series said Barbara was "23", although she certainly seems older.

947 *The Shadow of Weng-Chiang* (p23).

948 Dating *Captain Jack Harkness* (TW #12) - The story takes place on 20th January, 1941 (as is stipulated on the dance hall poster), and the original Jack Harkness is

but was hit and couldn't bail out because his plane was on fire.

… and, earlier in "our" Jack's timeline, he arrived in 1941 to perpetrate a con job.[949] He had never met the original Jack Harkness, but adopted his name after falsifying the records.[950]

1941 - THE EMPTY CHILD / THE DOCTOR DANCES[951] -> Captain Jack Harkness, a con-artist and former Time Agent from the fiftieth century, attempted to scam the ninth Doctor and Rose by crashing a Chula ambulance capsule into London. The capsule dispatched sub-atomic nanogenes that attempted to heal a gas-masked boy who'd been killed by a German bomb. The nanogenes were unfamiliar with human physiology and concluded that the masked, torn-up child was indicative of the human race. The child revived and started to look for his mummy, passing the nanogenes along to anyone he touched. The nanogenes began refashioning other people into similarly hollow and masked individuals.

The Doctor and Rose arrived "a few weeks, maybe a month" afterward. The nanogenes had become airborne and started restructuring people *en masse*. Jack admitted his con job to the Doctor and Rose, and the three of them deduced that a young woman named Nancy was the child's mother. The nanogenes recognized Nancy as such and examined her, creating a more suitable template of the human form. The affected humans were restored, and the Doctor programmed

the nanogenes to deactivate. Jack took up travel with the Doctor and Rose.

1941 (1st - 6th March) JUST WAR[952] -> The seventh Doctor, Bernice, Roz and Chris investigated reports of a new Nazi weapon. Roz and Chris joined the Scientific Intelligence Division to find out what the British knew, and Bernice went undercover in Guernsey. The German scientist Hartung had built two radar-invisible planes, *Hugin* and *Munin,* which he had started developing before the British had even invented radar. *Hugin* exploded on a test flight, killing Hartung. Bernice was captured and tortured, but Roz blew up *Munin,* denying it to the Nazis.

Thomas Erasmus Flanagan, age 8, was evacuated to Cardiff in 1941. He never saw his mother or sister again, and momentarily got lost at the railway station. He was later adopted, and would live out his life in Cardiff.[953]

1941 (2nd November) - "The Way of All Flesh"[954] -> The eighth Doctor and Izzy arrived in Mexico during the Day of the Dead festival. While the Doctor tracked a strange energy reading, Izzy was run over and rescued by the artist Frida Kahlo. The ghost of Frida's father appeared. The Doctor met the aliens responsible, the Torajenn. Their mistress, Susini of the Wasting Wall was a necrotist - she created art from the death of the innocent. The Torajenn wanted to have their natural bodies restored using her technology. The Torajenn were vulnerable to loud sounds, and Frida and Izzy set off fireworks to prevent them from

fated to die the following day.

949 *The Empty Child*

950 *TW: Captain Jack Harkness*

951 Dating *The Empty Child / The Doctor Dances* (X1.9-1.10) - The date is repeatedly given as 1941. Jack says it's the "height of the Blitz," which ended 16th May.

In *TW: Everything Changes*, military records claim that Captain Jack Harkness failed to report for duty on 21st January and was presumed dead. Some fans and commentators have adopted this date for *The Empty Child* two-parter, under the assumption that Jack was "presumed dead" because he left on that date with the Doctor and Rose. However, it's stipulated in *TW: Captain Jack Harkness* that the original Captain Jack Harkness died on 21st January, and "our" Jack admits that he falsified the military's records to cover up the man's death. The reference to Harkness "failing to report for duty", then, must refer to the genuine article, not "our" Jack.

It is unlikely that "our" Jack would start passing as "Jack Harkness" before the original has died; nor does it ring true that he takes the name, experiences the events of *The Empty Child / The Doctor Dances* and

departs in the TARDIS all in a twenty-four hour period. Moreover, *The Empty Child* states that the Doctor and Rose don't turn up until "a few weeks" or perhaps "a month" after the alien probe has landed. "Our" Jack presumably passes as "Captain Jack Harkness" during that time, as he has no way of knowing when the targets of his con-job - the Doctor and Rose - will arrive.

The most likely scenario, then, is that the original Jack Harkness dies on 21st January, the time-travelling con man (whose real name - for all we know - might well be "Jack") adopts his identity shortly thereafter, the con man gets cozy with the soldiers seen in *The Empty Child* and the Doctor and Rose land "a few weeks" or "a month" later - meaning February 1941 is the most probable time for this story to occur.

The *Torchwood* website says that Captain Jack disappeared on 5th January, which isn't plausible.

952 Dating *Just War* (NA #46) - The main action of the book starts on "the morning of 1 March 1941" (p5).

953 *TW: Ghost Machine*

954 Dating "The Way of All Flesh" (*DWM* #306, 308-310) - The date is given.

killing the revellers. The Doctor destroyed them, but aliens arrived and kidnapped Izzy.

1941 (November) - "Me and My Shadow"[955] ->

Fey Truscott-Sade was fighting Nazis in Austria, using her "Feyde" powers as a last resort, when she was summoned by the eighth Doctor to help find Izzy.

Toshiko Sato's grandfather stayed in London after the attack on Pearl Harbor, but was persecuted for his ethnicity.[956]

1942

Ben Jackson and Polly Wright were both born in 1942. The Jackson family lived near a brewery.[957]

The German battleship *Bismarck* was sunk.[958] The Doctor once claimed to have been wounded at El-Alamein in Egypt.[959] He drove an ambulance at El Alamein and was registered as Dr John Smith, 55583.[960]

In November 1942, there were reports of vampires in Romania.[961] On Christmas Eve of that year, the Nazi Oskar Steinmann oversaw the first test of the "flying bomb" at Peenemunde.[962] Aviatrix Amy Johnson vanished after her plane crashed. The Celestial Toymaker had kidnapped her.[963]

@ The Doctor rented a flat in Bloomsbury, and lived there for almost a decade from 1942.[964]

1942 - MAD DOGS AND ENGLISHMEN[965] ->

At some point in the nineteen-forties, various Oxford academics and writers such as Tyler and Cleavis started meeting as the Smudgelings. All was well until the necromancer William Freer was invited to join - before long, the other members started to mock Tyler's work. The eighth Doctor arrived, and quickly fell in with the Smudgelings, discovering that Freer has put Tyler in psychic contact with Dogworld, compelling Tyler to rewrite *The True History of Planets*. The Doctor left for London, and met Noel Coward, who is in on Freer's scheme.

Later, Coward refused to help some talking kittens from Pussyworld.

1942 (August) - THE SHADOW IN THE GLASS[966] ->

The sixth Doctor and the Brigadier arrived at a Berlin ballroom party, where the Doctor presented himself to Hitler as "Major Johann Schmidt" of the Reich. The time travellers acquired a sample of Hitler's blood for analysis.

Steinmann oversaw the first test of Germany's V-1 rocket at Peenemünde in December.[967] **During the war, Captain Jack became close to a 17-year-old woman named Estelle Cole, whom he met at the Astoria ballroom a few weeks before Christmas. They pledged to spend the rest of their lives together, but he was posted abroad, and she volunteered to work the land. He would renew their friendship decades later in the twenty-first century, while posing as his own son.[968]**

---

955 Dating "Me and My Shadow" (*DWM* #318) - The date is given.

956 *TW: Captain Jack Harkness*. Pearl Harbor was attacked on 7th December, 1941.

957 According to a plot synopsis issued on 20th May, 1966, Ben and Polly are both "24" at the time of *The Smugglers*. Michael Craze (Ben) was then 24, Anneke Wills (Polly) was 23. The document also gave Polly's surname as "Wright", which is never used on screen, but is mentioned in the Missing Adventure *Invasion of the Cat-People*. In the same book, Polly says she was brought up in Devon. In *The War Machines*, Kitty, the manageress of the Inferno nightclub, remarks that they rarely get anyone "over twenty" into the club, which might suggest that Ben and Polly are a little younger. Mind, neither of them look younger than twenty, and *The Murder Game* reaffirms their birth year as 1942.

958 The Doctor knows of the *Bismarck* in *Terror of the Zygons*.

959 *The Sea Devils*. Two World War II battles were fought at El-Alamein in 1942. The first lasted 1st to 27th July. The second, 23rd October to 4th November, saw the Allies forcing the Axis to retreat back to Tunisia.

960 *Autumn Mist*. *The King of Terror* (p241) also mentions that the Doctor was at El Alamein, an Egyptian

town that became the site of two major battles in World War II, both in 1942.

961 "Six months" before *The Curse of Fenric*.

962 *Just War*

963 *Divided Loyalties* (p46).

964 *Endgame* (EDA)

965 Dating *Mad Dogs and Englishmen* (EDA #52) - The date is given.

966 Dating *The Shadow in the Glass* (PDA #41) - The date appears on p217. This contradicts *Timewyrm: Exodus*, which the Doctor says is his first meeting with Hitler.

967 *Just War* (p252).

968 *TW: Small Worlds*. Jack's relationship with Estelle lasted weeks, at most, but it was serious enough for them to have a photograph (with Jack in uniform) taken together.

It isn't specified whether Estelle met Jack while he was working as a con man prior to *The Empty Child*, or while he was immortal and living through the entire twenty-first century. The latter seems more likely for a couple of reasons. Such a heartfelt relationship appears more characteristic of the slightly bitter, emotionally withdrawn and immortal Jack than the carefree con man who knows he's working to the clock and is possi-

1943

= The English Empire retook the American colonies, but there was a revolt in 1943. The future American Prime Minister's grandfather led the army that put it down.[969]

In 1943, the toy store owner Mr. Sun walked out of his shop in Covent Garden and was never seen again. A week later, the shop was bombed and vanished as if it had never existed. It soon reappeared.[970]

1943 (May) - THE CURSE OF FENRIC[971] -> The seventh Doctor and Ace arrived at a military base on the Yorkshire coast which housed the ULTIMA machine, an early computer. The Russians sent a squad to capture the machine, but the British had anticipated this by booby-trapping it to detonate a lethal toxin, waiting for a time when the Russians became their enemies. Fenric, an ancient being trapped by the Doctor, had engineered the situation to free himself and roused an army of Haemovores to help his bid. The Doctor convinced the Ancient Haemovore to destroy Fenric.

The Doctor visited the German High Command around this time.

In the later stages of the war, the painter Amelia Ducat manned an ack-ack gun in Folkestone.[972] The Master kidnapped a V1 from the skies over Cambridgeshire using TOM-TIT.[973] Mel's grandfather died during the war.[974]

During the War, a time warp meant a soldier bowled a cricket ball instead of a hand grenade.[975] A German fighter crashed in the River Tees following a collision with a Q'Dhite spaceship.[976]

@ 1943 - THE TURING TEST[977] -> The eighth Doctor met the British spy / novelist Graham Greene in Sierra Leone, where they encountered pale-skinned humanoids.

Rachel Jensen, a future scientific adviser to the Intrusion Counter Measures Group, worked with cryptographer Alan Turing on codebreaking.[978]

In October 1943, the USS *Eldridge* vanished, apparently as the result of an invisibility experiment. In fact, it had become destabilized in a rift with the realm of the Sidhe. The Doctor later sacrificed the ship to seal the rift.[979]

1944

In 1944, Belgium, the American soldier Honoré Lechasseur was caught in a German booby trap in Belgium and severely injured. He spent the next few years in a Dorset hospital, proving his doctors wrong by walking again. He rarely slept, and began having strange visions.[980]

1944 / = 1944 - COLDITZ[981] -> The TARDIS landed at Colditz Castle, where the seventh Doctor and Ace were quickly captured. The Doctor was surprised at how much one of his interrogators, Klein, knew about him.

= The Doctor realised that Klein was from a future where the Nazis had developed laser technology from the components of Ace's Walkman, won the war and secured the TARDIS. Ace had been killed, but the Doctor had given himself a second chance by travelling to 1955, being shot by the Nazis, regenerating while they took the TARDIS away, and then posing as "Schmidt" - the scientist who helped Klein operate the TARDIS in 1965. The Doctor's manipulations caused Klein to change history by keeping Ace alive, averting the entire history.

bly involved with Algy (*The Empty Child*). Additionally, it's specified that Jack met Estelle "a few weeks before" Christmas, yet it's unlikely that he started using the name "Jack Harkness" until the original died in January 1941 (*TW: Captain Jack Harkness*). Unless Estelle thinks the "son" has a different surname to his father (unlikely, although in truth she never calls him anything other than "Jack"), her meeting him in December 1940 seems suspect.

An earlier dating is probably preferable to a later one, as the odds of Jack and Estelle keeping in touch increase as World War II comes to a conclusion. However, the Torchwood website dates some final correspondence between Jack and Estelle to 1944.

969 *Jubilee*

970 *The Cabinet of Light* (p86).

971 Dating *The Curse of Fenric* (26.3) - Ace says that the year is "1943". The script stated that the time is "1943 - probably May".

972 *The Seeds of Doom*

973 *The Time Monster*

974 *Just War*

975 "Forty years" before "The Tides of Time".

976 "Fifty years" before "Evening's Empire".

977 Dating *The Turing Test* (EDA #39) - It's "in January 1943" (p116).

978 *Who Killed Kennedy*, taking its cue from the *Remembrance of the Daleks* novelisation.

979 *Autumn Mist*. This is based on an urban legend regarding "the Philadelphia Experiment", an invisibility experiment that allegedly took place on 28th October, 1943.

980 *The Cabinet of Light*

981 Dating *Colditz* (BF #25) - The date "1944" is given.

The Doctor and Ace escaped from the castle. Klein also escaped, now the sole remainder of an extinct timeline.

The Doctor met Joseph Heller, an American pilot, in a military hospital.[982]

1944 - DEADLY REUNION[983] -> Second Lieutenant Alistair Gordon Lethbridge-Stewart served in Intelligence during World War II. He was assigned to update the British army's maps of the Greek islands.

On the island of Zante, Lethbridge-Stewart encountered the Greek gods Demeter, Persephone and Hermes, who were attempting to lead quiet, domestic lives. The Greek god Hades hoped to provoke a world conflict even more devastating than World War II, which would cripple humanity and allow him to rule Earth. The god Poseidon, at Persephone's request, ended Hades' scheme and cast him back into the underworld. Persephone and Lethbridge-Stewart became lovers, but she used water from the River Lethe to make him forget these events.

During the Normandy landings, Jason Kane's grandfather was killed when a sniper hit his lucky crucifix and it became lethal shrapnel.[984] Captain Davydd Watson saw visions during the Normandy landings, an effect of an experiment by the organic computer Azoth.[985]

During the nineteen forties, two Gaderene scouts - members of an insectoid race whose homeworld was dying - arrived on Earth via an unstable transmat process. One of them matured into the calculating Bliss, but her brother mutated into a dragon-sized Gaderene that covered itself in mud and went dormant. However, Bliss lost the ninth key - a small jade shard - to the Gaderene transmat. British Wing Commander Alec Whistler discovered it in the after-

math of an explosion at Culverton Aerodrome. Without the key, Bliss could only bring Gaderene embryos, not adults, through to Earth.[986]

In 1944, the Toymaker kidnapped US Marine Mark Conrad.[987]

1944 - THE SHADOW IN THE GLASS[988] -> On 17th May, 1944, a Vvormak spacecruiser passed over Turelhampton, England, and a British fighter plane shot it down. The Vvormak were in stasis, but the ship generated a gravitational field that rendered it immobile. Unable to relocate the ship, the British military sealed off the area for fifty years as part of a cover story.

Private Gerrard Lassiter stole the Vvormak ship's main navigation device as a talisman. It was capable of projecting images of the future, and would come to be known as "the Scrying Glass." Gunther Brun, a German trooper, later killed Lassiter in France and took the device, but subsequently lost it to Colonel Otto Klein in a game of cards. Two weeks later, Reichsfuher Heinrich Himmler learned of the device's existence and ordered Klein to hand it over to him. Himmler then gave it to a group of Tibetan mystics for study.

In July 1944, the sixth Doctor persuaded Churchill to help smuggle him into France. He then infiltrated the Reich Records Department as "Colonel Johann Schmidt". In August 1944, Hitler became curious about other items left at the Turelhampton site, and authorized the Doctor, as "Schmidt," to participate in a raiding party. The raid occurred on 18th August.

1944 (December) - AUTUMN MIST[989] -> The eighth Doctor, Sam and Fitz were split up when they arrived during the Battle of the Bulge. Sam was injured, the Doctor

---

982 "Five months" before *The Turing Test*.

983 Dating *Deadly Reunion* (PDA #71) - The date is given (although, as previously noted, it does make Lethbridge-Stewart older than most other stories would have him).

984 *Death and Diplomacy*

985 *The Taint*

986 "Thirty years" before *The Last of the Gaderene*.

987 *Divided Loyalties*

988 Dating *The Shadow in the Glass* (PDA #41) - The date is given (p29).

989 Dating *Autumn Mist* (EDA #24) - The story takes place during the Battle of the Bulge. The Doctor confronts the Beast in *The Taint*.

990 Dating *The Turing Test* (EDA #39) - The story takes place over several months, and ends with the Allies bombing Dresden, which occurred in February 1945.

991 *The Marian Conspiracy*, which takes place circa 2000, says she is "fifty five". A Big Finish press release, however, claims she was 65 in 1999, suggesting a much

earlier birth date of 1934. Big Finish Producer Gary Russell says *The Marian Conspiracy* should be favoured whatever the press release says.

992 *No Future*

993 "Next March" after *The Shadow in the Glass*.

994 *The Shadow in the Glass*

995 Dating *The Shadow in the Glass* (PDA #41) - The date is given (p23, 147).

996 Dating *Atom Bomb Blues* (PDA #76) - The story is set on the eve of the first A-Bomb tests.

997 *Just War*

998 "Memorial"

999 *Heart of TARDIS*

1000 "Operation Proteus"

1001 *Time and the Rani*. A scene showing the Rani kidnap Einstein was deleted from the camera script.

1002 "Thirty years" before *The Web of Fear*.

1003 "Thirty years" before *The Paradise of Death* (p79).

1004 Dating *Dying in the Sun* (PDA #47) - Early on a newspaper is dated "12 October 1947" (p17).

served as a medic, and Fitz found himself serving as a corporal in the German army. Sam's injuries were fatal, but she was rescued by the Sidhe, fairy creatures from another dimension. A rift had formed between our realm and theirs, but the Doctor sealed it.

The King of the Sidhe, Oberon, was killed as part of these events. It was expected that another aspect of Oberon would take his place. The rift's closure enabled the Beast to arrive on Earth and begin feeding upon humanity.

@ 1944/5 - THE TURING TEST[990] **->** The cryptographer Alan Turing intercepted a unique code transmitted from Dresden, concluding that it was alien in origin. The eighth Doctor had befriended Turing, and suggested they contact the signal's originator. They allied themselves with the spy Graham Greene. The Doctor also approached American pilot Joseph Heller, promising to get him out of the army if he flew the Doctor and Turing to Dresden. An English officer, Elgar, was revealed as an assassin out to kill the mysterious pale-skinned aliens. The Doctor killed Elgar and the aliens beamed away from Earth, leaving the Doctor behind as the Allied bombing of Dresden began.

1945

Around 1945, Evelyn Smythe was born.[991] On 13th February, 1945, the Doctor and Bernice witnessed the destruction of Dresden.[992]

In March, the Doctor flew a Mark VIII Halifax bomber.[993] The Tibetans charged with keeping the Scrying Glass were murdered on 25th April, 1945. In the years to follow, the Scrying Glass would fall into the hands of Adolf Hitler's son.[994]

1945 (Monday, 30th April) - THE SHADOW IN THE GLASS[995] **->** The sixth Doctor, the Brigadier and journalist Claire Aldwych arrived from 2001 with Hitler's adult son, and the men entered Hitler's bunker. The Doctor easily portrayed Hitler's son as a madman, and Hitler, failing to recognize his offspring, shot him dead. The Nazis disposed of the body in a nearby water tower. The Allies would later mistake the corpse for a double of Hitler, killed for an unknown reason.

Martin Bormann, one of Hitler's aides, killed Claire and substituted her body for that of Eva Hitler. Hitler committed suicide. A pregnant Eva was flown to a submarine in Hamburg. She later gave birth to a son named Adolf. He was raised at the secret Nazi base in Antarctica.

= 1945 - ATOM BOMB BLUES[996] **->** The seventh Doctor and Ace arrived in Los Alamos, where the Manhattan Project was about to culminate in the detonation of the first atom bomb. The Doctor identified one of the scientists, Ray Morita, as someone from the twenty-first century of a parallel universe. The Doctor made contact with a jellyfish-like alien, Zorg, and travelled to Los Angeles to confront the Chapel of the Red Apocalypse - a cult that had been a front for a spy ring.

Ace learned that *she* was in a parallel universe, and that Ray was from her reality, lured to the alternate history by a love of Duke Ellington music. In the proper timeline, a musicians' union strike meant much of his work was never recorded, but the strike didn't take place in the other universe.

The Doctor and Ace uncovered a plot to alter the equations of the Manhattan Project to unleash enough power to destroy this universe, tipping history in Japan's favour across the multiverse. The Doctor defeated the plan, the atom bomb test concluded as history recorded and the Doctor took Ray home - with his precious records.

At the end of the war, the Russians captured Emil Hartung's research into stealth aircraft, and took it to a vault in the Kremlin. Generalleutnant Oskar Steinmann was found guilty (along with twenty-two others) of Nazi war crimes and was sentenced to life imprisonment at Nuremberg.[997]

Brian Galway was killed in North Africa during the Second World War. His 12-year-old brother, Simon, attended a memorial service on 20th December, 1945. The Doctor placed the surviving consciousness of the Telphin, a peaceful race wiped out by the Chaktra, inside the boy.[998]

After World War II, the American military experimented to see if widespread belief could alter the laws of physics. The residents of the Midwest town Lychburg were brainwashed with transceivers, creating thousands of people who simultaneously believed whatever the military wanted. An experiment to make the people believe "the gates of Hell were opening", however, created an unstable dimensional rift. The military tried to level the project with a low-yield nuclear device, but only succeeded in knocking Lychburg out of Earth's dimension entirely.[999]

After the war, the British government set up Operation Proteus to create illegal chemical weapons.[1000] **In the mid-1940s, the Rani briefly kidnapped Albert Einstein.[1001] The collector Julius Silverstein bought the only surviving robot Yeti from Professor Travers.[1002]** The Parakon named Freeth began to visit Earth, accounting for some UFO sightings over the next thirty years.[1003]

1947

1947 - DYING IN THE SUN[1004] **->** The second Doctor called in on Harold Reitman, a movie producer and old friend, and discovered he had been murdered. Star Light Pictures were about to release a new movie, *Dying in the*

Sun, and the Doctor was surprised that such a poor movie could receive such rave reviews. The audience's perceptions were being affected by the telepathic Selyoids. The aliens were peaceful, but the movie's producer, De Sande, was intent on using their powers to dominate the world. There was dissent in the Selyoid ranks. The Doctor caused a plane crash that killed De Sande, but this released the Selyoids present in De Sande's body. Hollywood would long remain a place of extreme emotions for some time to come.

The CIA captured a Nedenah ship at Roswell. One alien was autopsied, the others were taken to Area 51.[1005] **The collector Henry Van Statten had artefacts from Roswell in his private museum.**[1006] The Doctor knocked over a paint pot and inspired Jackson Pollock, an American artist, around this time. Pollock gave the Doctor a painting, *Azure in the Rain by a Man Who'd Never Been*.[1007]

The rituals of black arts practitioner Edward Alexander Crowley had summoned a Jarakabeth demon to Earth. The demon impersonated Crowley after his death at Hastings, 1947. The US security service Section Eight approached "Crowley" in the hope that his Hermetic Arts could be adopted for military use. The Crowley demon would become the head of the DIvisional department of Special Tactical Operations (Provisional) with Regard to Insurgent and Subversive Activity (DISTO(P)IA), a government branch designed to counter subversion.[1008]

1948

A year after the first crash, a Nedenah rescue mission was shot down over Roswell.[1009] The Doctor bought a stuffed owl for Sarah in 1948. It was one of the items she packed when she left his company.[1010]

The Doctor liked the 1948 Olympics opening ceremony so much, he went back to see it again.[1011] Torchwood acquired some alien artefacts at auction in 1948.[1012]

1949

1949 - THE CABINET OF LIGHT[1013] **->** An unknown incarnation of the Doctor and his companion Emily Blandish arrived in London, where agents working for Mestizer, a nemesis of the Doctor, attacked them. Emily helped the Doctor to escape, but Mestizer's agents captured the Doctor's time cabinet. The trauma of the event rendered Emily amnesiac. She was found wandering the streets of London with no memory, and became known in the press as "the Girl in the Pink Pajamas" (and occasionally "the Girl in the Pink Bikini"). She was used to promote clothes rationing.

To retrieve his property, the Doctor came to involve an expatriate and time sensitive named Honoré Lechasseur, who chiefly worked as a "fixer." Honoré observed the Doctor confronting Mestizer, and light from the Doctor's time cabinet started her house on fire. The Doctor, Mestizer, the house and the time cabinet all disappeared

---

1005 *The Devil Goblins from Neptune*, and also referred to in *The Face of the Enemy*.
1006 *Dalek*
1007 *Divided Loyalties*. Pollock was influential to the abstract expressionism movement.
1008 *Heart of TARDIS*
1009 *The Devil Goblins from Neptune* (p240).
1010 *Interference*. We see it in *The Hand of Fear*.
1011 *Fear Her*
1012 *TW: Slow Decay*
1013 Dating *The Cabinet of Light* (TEL #9) - The date is 1949, according to p14 and the back cover blurb.
1014 "Twenty years" before *The Underwater Menace*.
1015 *The Scales of Injustice*. No date is given.
1016 *Zamper*
1017 *Return of the Living Dad*. This happened in "the fifties" (p66).
1018 *Instruments of Darkness*
1019 *Psi-ence Fiction*. No date is given.
1020 *TW: Slow Decay*
1021 *The Devil Goblins from Neptune* (p37).
1022 "Fifteen years" before *The Scales of Injustice*.
1023 *The Devil Goblins from Neptune* (p56), *The King of Terror* (p126).

1024 In *Invasion of the Dinosaurs*, Sarah Jane says she is "twenty-three" (although in the novelisation she is "twenty-two"). Elisabeth Sladen, who played Sarah, was born in 1948 and was 26 when the story was made. In the format document for the proposed *K9 and Company* series, it is stated that Sarah was born in "1949". She was "about thirty" in the spin-off novel *Harry Sullivan's War* (suggesting a birth date of 1955), and she's born "over sixty years" after 1880 in *Evolution* (p242). Thus, depending on when the UNIT stories are set, she could be born at any time from 1949 to 1963.
1025 "About a year" before *Endgame* (EDA).
1026 "Forty years" after *Pyramids of Mars*.
1027 *The Daemons*
1028 Dating *Timewyrm: Exodus* (NA #2) - In Part One of the novel, the Doctor proclaims it to be the "Festival of Britain, 1951" (p5). At the end of the novel, the Doctor and Ace arrive at the real Festival of Britain.
1029 Dating *Endgame* (EDA #40) - The year is given (p242).
1030 *Father Time* (p58).
1031 *Zagreus*, again judging by a historical simulation.
1032 Dating *Real Time* (BF BBCi #1) - The date is given, Episode One, Track 1.

entirely. In the Doctor's absence, Honoré and Emily struck up a partnership.

By now, the Doctor was regarded as a "hobgoblin" or "myth" in the underground community. Legends claimed he variously gave fire to mankind, burned London in 1666, kidnapped the crew of the *Mary Celeste* and built Stonehenge with his bare hands.

The Time Hunter novels, published by Telos, spin off from this story.

The Nineteen Fifties

In the early nineteen-fifties, Professor Zaroff - "the greatest scientist since Leonardo" - vanished.[1014] The testing of nuclear weapons, plus an increase in dumping of toxic waste, destroyed many Silurian shelters.[1015] Benny Summerfield visited Milton Keynes in the mid-twentieth century to settle an archaeological debate.[1016]

Albinex the Navarino arrived down a faulty time corridor from the far future.[1017] In Jamaica, the 1950s, the Doctor met the ornithologist James Bond and took him to the 1800s to see a live dodo. The Doctor later introduced writer Ian Fleming to Bond, who served as inspiration for Fleming's super-spy novels.[1018] The Doctor met the Cuban guerrilla leader Che Guevara.[1019]

Around a dozen items of alien technology came through the Rift in the 1950s - gradually, Torchwood collected them.[1020]

UNIT in the Fifties

u - When Lethbridge-Stewart was twenty-one, he spent a time in New York on the way back from Korea.[1021] Lethbridge Stewart met Fiona, his future wife.[1022] Lethbridge-Stewart's grandmother died in 1955.[1023] **Sarah Jane Smith was born.**[1024]

1950

Under the influence of the Player Myrek, President Truman approved Operation Kali, a psychic warfare programme.[1025]

1951

The radio telescope was invented.[1026] **The last witchcraft act on the English statute books was repealed in 1951.**[1027]

= **1951 - TIMEWYRM: EXODUS**[1028] -> Following the total defeat of the British army at Dunkirk in 1940, the German army swept across the Channel and landed at Folkestone. Britain fell in six days.

Churchill and thousands of suspected troublemakers were executed. Oswald Mosley was installed as Prime Minister, and Edward VIII was crowned. Unsure what to do with Britain, the Nazi High Command let the country fall into ruin.

All able-bodied men were conscripted as slave workers and shipped to the continent. In 1951, the Festival of Britain took place in London to celebrate ten years of Nazi victory. The Germans planned to have a man on the moon in this year. Arriving at this time, the seventh Doctor realised that history had been altered. He travelled back and averted this timeline with the destruction of Drachensberg Castle in 1939.

After they defeated the War Lords and Timewyrm, the Doctor and Ace visited the real Festival of Britain and discovered that history was back on course.

@ 1951 - ENDGAME[1029] -> The seventh Doctor (and Ace) saw the eighth Doctor at the Festival of Britain, but neither recognised the other.

The Players decided on a new game, seeing which among them could provoke a nuclear holocaust on Earth. The eighth Doctor became caught up in this after befriending a Polish exile who was beaten to death, and MI5 investigated the matter. Kim Philby, a member of British intelligence and a double agent for the Soviet Union, recruited the Doctor to defeat the Players.

President Truman became abnormally hostile to China, and the Doctor discovered the president was under the influence of the Player Myrek. As Philby suspected, another Player - the Countess - was similarly manipulating Stalin. The Doctor ended the Players' control of the Russian leader and Truman. Returning to America, the Doctor tricked the Players into killing each other. The Doctor declined a job at the White House and returned to London.

@ The Doctor was present in the Soviet Union during a high profile chess match played in 1951.[1030] In 1951, the Dionysus Project in Cardington opened a doorway to the Divergents' domain. This killed the researchers Dr. Stone and the Reverend Matthew Townsend.[1031]

= **1951 - REAL TIME**[1032] -> With the Cybermen firmly in control of Earth, a group of human rebels crafted an organic techno-virus capable of destroying the Cybermen's artificial implants. They used a Chronosphere to dispatch Dr Reece Goddard to 3286, the year in which the Cybermen altered history, in the hope of averting this timeline altogether.

1952

Barbara worked at Hampstead High School for girls in 1952.[1033] **Pilot Diane Holmes flew from England to Australia in just four days.[1034]**

1952 (7th September) - THE NOWHERE PLACE[1035]
-> Scientists working on behalf of the British War Office were stationed RAF Hill Lankton Base, and the Oxford-educated Trevor Ridgely was assigned to work on rocket propulsion there. Trevor doodled the rudimentary design for a star drive-equipped ship in his spare time, and although he never worked toward the completion of such a device, his sketch would serve to plant the seed of his idea. Someone would return to Trevor's sketch in future, spot something he'd overlooked and thereby help to facilitate mankind's journey into the stars.

The sixth Doctor and Evelyn arrived from 2197, and encountered Trevor on the *Ivy Lee*, the last Turret-class train in service, as it was passing through Stapely Moor. Representatives of the original race that evolved on Earth hoped to trick the time travellers into facilitating the loss of Trevor's sketch - and thereby subvert humanity's star-travel - but the Doctor and Evelyn thwarted the plot and returned to the future.

1952 (December) - AMORALITY TALE[1036] -> The
third Doctor and Sarah sought to investigate a warp shadow, and arrived prior to a killer smog descending on London. The Doctor set up shop as a watchmaker. Sarah found out that a war was brewing between the Ramsey and Callum gangs. Callum was actually a member of the Xhinn, a ruthless alien species, and the killer smog was actually a Xhinn weapon. The Doctor destroyed the Xhinn scoutship, which deterred their main fleet from attacking.

1953

The science fiction serial *Nightshade* was first shown by the BBC in 1953. It would run for five years.[1037]

@ The Doctor quickly became a fan of the show.[1038]

The Doctor was the first man to climb Everest, giving Tensing and Hillary a hand up.[1039]

1953 (1st to 2nd June) - THE IDIOT'S LANTERN[1040]
-> An alien was executed by her people - she consequently became an energy being. She fled "across the stars" and arrived on Earth, 1953. The Wire - as she was now called - conscripted Mr Magpie of Magpie's Electricals to supply cheap televisions in the run-up to the coronation of Queen Elizabeth II. This enabled the Wire to feed off the electrical energy of viewers' brains, which turned them blank-faced. The Wire wanted to connect with the twenty million people expected to watch the Coronation, and regain her corporeal body.

The tenth Doctor and Rose arrived on Florizel Street in London before the coronation, and learned of the Wire's intentions. The Doctor sabotaged the transmitter at Alexandra Palace, which both trapped the Wire onto a Betamax tape (that the Doctor intended to tape over) and restored her victims to health.

At this time, Torchwood was known to Detective Inspector Bishop.[1041]

> = In 1953, the second President of the English Empire celebrated the fiftieth Jubilee of victory by executing one of his two captive Daleks.[1042]

The Toymaker beat Le Chiffre at baccarat.[1043] **On 18th December, 1953, a plane with three people on board fell through the Rift in Cardiff. They would emerge from it in late 2007.[1044]** An archaeological dig at Mynach Hengoed in 1953 uncovered an alien spaceship, which Torchwood acquired.[1045]

1954

1954 - "The Good Soldier"[1046] -> The seventh Doctor
and Ace drove up to a diner in the Nevada desert and found it full of American soldiers. The area lifted into space and docked with a flying saucer, which in turn docked with its mothership... and Cybermen emerged from the

---

1033 *The Plotters.* If we take the writers' guidelines at face value, she would have been twelve at the time.
1034 *TW: Out of Time*
1035 Dating *The Nowhere Place* (BF #84) - The date is given.
1036 Dating *Amorality Tale* (PDA #52) - It's "Wednesday, December 3, 1952" (p12).
1037 *Nightshade* (p111).
1038 *Escape Velocity* (p196).
1039 *The Dying Days* (p52). Sherpa Tensing Norgay and Edmund P. Hillary were the first to conquer Everest.
1040 Dating *The Idiot's Lantern* (X2.7) - The story's climax coincides with the coronation of Queen Elizabeth II, with the Doctor and Rose arriving the day before.
1041 See "How Public is Torchwood?" under *TW: Everything Changes*.
1042 *Jubilee*
1043 "End Game" (*DWM*)
1044 *TW: Out of Time*
1045 *TW: Slow Decay*
1046 Dating "The Good Soldier" (*DWM* #175-178) - "It's 1954" according to the Doctor. The Cybermen resemble those from *The Tenth Planet*, and that's specified in dialogue. The Cybermen report to Mondas Control.

CYBERMEN ... FASHION VICTIMS?: Does the variation in design between the Cybermen actually symbolise anything, and how helpful is it to the dating process? It's a similar question to that of the Klingons in *Star Trek* - there's a real-life reason (generally related to budgets and audience expectations) as to why they look different in the sixties and the eighties, but is there a reason *within* the fiction?

On television, it's not even clear that the characters "see" any difference between different models of Cybermen. Ben instantly recognises the Cybermen in *The Moonbase*, even though they bear little resemblance to the ones he saw in *The Tenth Planet*. Notably, he doesn't so much as comment that they've been redesigned - something that might be relevant to say, if one is evaluating the capabilities of the alien invaders that are besieging one's moonbase. Ben is hardly alone in this, as many other characters fail to make the same observation (just to name a few, the Doctor, Polly, Jamie, Zoe, Brigadier and Sarah Jane all encounter different versions of the Cybermen). On screen at least, we never see an old model once a new one has been introduced (except for the flashback in *Earthshock* and the head in a museum in *Dalek*).

We never see two versions of the Cybermen together. Yet the development doesn't appear to be linear in terms of fictional history - it's strictly linear in terms of the order the Doctor meets them. Without wanting to get unduly philosophical, the television episodes we see are a *representation* of reality, not a window on it - unless there's an unrevealed canonical reason as to why (for instance) the Silurians have zips down their backs in *Warriors of the Deep*. We're seeing things as convincingly as the BBC can render them, so it's entirely possible that - to the characters - the Cybermen from *The Tenth Planet* look identical to the ones in *The Moonbase* and *Earthshock*.

In the books, audios and comic strips, the distinction is made rather more often - for example, the Doctor notes that the Cybermen in "The Good Soldier" are the same design as the ones from *The Tenth Planet*.

If we take it as read that the characters *do* see different models of Cybermen, the significance could be functional. Perhaps the Cybermen from *The Tenth Planet* are adapted for Arctic conditions, the ones in *The Moonbase* and *The Wheel in Space* for low gravity operation and so forth. This seems unlikely, though - the Cybermen we see are almost always intent on roughly the same thing: marching into a human military installation and taking it by force.

It may well be that what we think of as one race is, in fact, many. Elsewhere in the *Doctor Who* universe, it seems to be a common stage of evolution for an organic race to remove "weaknesses" using cybernetic implants. Not every race does so - the Gallifreyans don't, for example, and humans apparently only ever do so in a limited fashion (as seen in, say, *Warriors of the Deep* or *The Long Game*). But a fair number of the Doctor's adversaries are cyborgs - the Daleks, the Sontarans and the Ice Warriors all are to at least some extent. Perhaps "Cyberman" is just the name of the end result when one of the human-like races that seem to exist on countless planets independently (or semi-independently) discards their organic form for a cybernetic one. Following the dictates of pure logic, technology and elegance, they all come up with roughly the same design for their cybernetic bodies. (And therefore there must be some overwhelming logical imperative for those handles on their helmets.) In the parallel universe of *Rise of the Cybermen* / *The Age of Steel*, Lumic seems to create Cybermen practically identical to the ones from our universe (name, handles and all) - and the Doctor, Rose and the Daleks all identify them.

There's no reason why these various Cyber Races couldn't co-operate, or even see themselves as part of the same "ethnic" or "political" group - it seems logical enough, and the Cybermen of a parallel universe offer an alliance with the Daleks in *Doomsday*. It might explain the discrepancies in the accounts of their origins, sphere of influence and levels of technology - as well as their appearance - across the series.

So perhaps the design indicates a lineage - the Cybermen of *The Invasion* and *Revenge of the Cybermen* are of one lineage, the ones of *Earthshock* and *Silver Nemesis* another. Surprisingly, while not entirely unproblematic, this does work. Here is a list of different models, as well as the years and planets they are from. In the case of books and audios, cover art was considered as evidence if the text didn't specify. Note that, as elsewhere in the book, I'm going to assume that the Cybermen we see aren't time travellers unless explicitly stated. The Cybermen of the far future clearly acquire time travel - it's usually stated that they've stolen the technology, but it seems equally clear that the Cybermen of *The Moonbase* or *The Invasion,* say, aren't time travellers.

Type I: *Spare Parts* (when created, Mondas), "Junkyard Demon" ("pioneers", Mondas), "The Good Solider" (1954, Mondas), *The Tenth Planet* (1986, Mondas).

Note: It seems pretty clear that these are the early Cybermen, exclusively from Mondas.

Type II: *The Harvest* (2021), *The Moonbase* (21st century, ?), *The Wheel in Space* (21st century, ?), *The Tomb of the Cybermen* (21st century, Telos), *Iceberg* (21st century), *Illegal Alien* (time travellers from the 30th century).

Notes: Again, it's easy to group these together as the model of Cybermen who survive Mondas' destruction and attempt to attack twenty-first century Earth, then retire to their Tombs on Telos. The Cybermen in *The*

continued on page 125...

sand. The Doctor told Ace that the Mondasian Cybermen would have attacked Earth before 1986 if they'd had the right weapon... and that they were standing in it.

Meanwhile, the Cybermen had learned how to control human minds, and required aggression - which they lacked themselves - to power their warship. They installed Colonel Rhodes, the leader of the soldiers, into the device. Ace interfaced with the system, detaching the flying saucer. The Cybermen pursued, but the Doctor and Ace overloaded their reactor, destroying the warship.

1954 (9th November) - THE WITCH HUNTERS[1047] ->
The first Doctor and his companions arrived after visiting Salem during the witch trials. Susan was distressed to think that some of the residents would be burnt as witches, and used the TARDIS' Fast Return Switch in a bid to go back and save them.

Returning to 1954, the time travellers attended the premiere of *The Crucible* in Bristol. Later, the Doctor brought the condemned Rebecca Nurse to this era to view *The Crucible* and see memorials to the victims of the Salem witch trials.

Graham Greene received a tape from Alan Turing that explained his contact with the Doctor.[1048] Circa 1954, the student Astrabel Zar vacationed on Gadrahadradon, a haunted planet that facilitated glimpses into the future. Zar received instructions from his future self on how to build "Tomorrow Windows," devices that would similarly display images of future times. He would later pass on the secret of building Tomorrow Windows to one of his own students, Charlton Mackerel.[1049]

Peter Allen Tyler, future father of Rose Tyler, was born 15th September, 1954.[1050] George Limb survived being catapulted through time and landed in 1954. He loosely learned to navigate his time machine between 1940 and 1962, but his journeys created a number of alternate

timelines. Limb's final trip resulted in his being left in 1954 while his time machine jumped on ahead to 1959. He waited five years to retrieve it.[1051]

1955

In 1955, Chris Parsons was born. The Doctor visited Chris' future College, St Cedd's Cambridge.[1052] The immortal Captain Jack Harkness had some association with Torchwood Cardiff by this point.[1053]

> = In an errant timeline, George Limb saved the life of actor James Dean. The alternate Dean served as Limb's assistant in the proper reality.[1054]

1956

In 1956, the Doctor met a Jesuit palaeontologist in Africa.[1055] The vampires of Los Angeles culled their own kind to hide their numbers.[1056] Joseph Heller told Kurt Vonnegut, future author of *Slaughterhouse-Five* (1969), about his meeting with the Doctor.[1057]

Ben Jackson, aged fourteen, stowed away on a cargo ship bound for Singapore. The captain discovered him and offered him a job.[1058] The Doctor prevented Santa Mira from being taken over by aliens in 1956.[1059] The French colony of Kebiria was granted independence in 1956. Civil war started almost immediately.[1060]

By 1956, the Grimoire of Anubis had fallen into the hands of comedian Joey Bishop.[1061]

1957

u - The Doctor became a member of the Progressive Club, a gentleman's club in Mayfair.[1062] Edwin Pratt became the vampire Slake in 1957.[1063] Ace had a British Rail Card from 1957, the only form of ID she carried.[1064]

1047 Dating *The Witch Hunters* (PDA #9) - The date is given, p68.
1048 *The Turing Test.* "Six months" after Turing's suicide (7th June, 1954; p104), "forty six years" before the year 2000 (p105).
1049 "Fifty years" before *The Tomorrow Windows* (p274).
1050 *Father's Day*
1051 *Loving the Alien* (p188-189).
1052 *Shada*
1053 *TW: Slow Decay.* Jack's signature is on a form in the Archive from that year (p84). The Torchwood website refers to Jack working there in 1959, but the website's evidence isn't definitive and *Utopia* almost implies that Jack has only been working with *Torchwood* for a few years or so. It's entirely likely that *Torchwood* Series

2 - unbroadcast at time of writing - will better establish Jack's timeline with Torchwood Cardiff.
1054 *Loving the Alien.* Dean died 30th September, 1955.
1055 *The Pit* (p98).
1056 *Vampire Science*
1057 *The Turing Test* (p207).
1058 *Invasion of the Cat-People* (p31).
1059 "Last year" according to *First Frontier* (p68), and a reference to the original *Invasion of the Bodysnatchers*.
1060 *Dancing the Code*
1061 "The Curse of the Scarab"
1062 "Thirteen years" before *The Devil Goblins from Neptune*.
1063 *Vampire Science*
1064 "Ground Zero"

...continued on Page 123

Wheel in Space are from roughly the same time period, and a slight variation on this model.

Until the Cybermen relocate to Telos, it's unclear where they are based after Mondas' obliteration. David Banks speculates in his *Cybermen* book that they are based on a planet on the edge of the solar system, and links this to the Planet 14 mentioned in *The Invasion*.

The Cybermen from *Illegal Alien* come from the thirtieth century. The book only refers to the mask as having "teardrops" - a feature of the type of Cyberman seen in *The Invasion* and *Revenge of the Cybermen*, which would fit with the dating. The cover of *Illegal Alien*, however, reuses a photograph from *The Wheel in Space*, another design with "teardrops".

While *The Harvest* is an audio and we don't see Cybermen involved (they're not shown on the cover), the reference to *The Wheel in Space* suggests the Cybermen are the same type in both stories.

Type III: *The Invasion* (subject to UNIT dating, ?), *Human Resources* (2006), *Killing Ground* (22nd century, nomads), *Sword of Orion* (future, Telos), *Revenge of the Cybermen* (29th century, nomadic survivors of Cyber Wars).

Notes: On the whole, this also seems to form a distinct group that generally has a nomadic existence (i.e. they are based in spaceships, rather than having a home planet). At least one group of these Cybermen existed before *The Tenth Planet* (the ones we see in *The Invasion*). These Cybermen fight wars against early human colony planets, and also the Cyber War referred to in *Revenge of the Cybermen*.

David Banks (in his book *Cybermen* and novel *Iceberg*) states that there was an early schism among the Cybermen - one group stayed on Mondas and only reluctantly adopted full cybertisation (the group I'm calling here the Type I Cybermen), while another embraced the technology (and became the Type III seen in *The Invasion*).

The cover of *Human Resources* depicts Cybermen of the same type as *The Invasion*, and is set before the discovery of Telos. The Cybermen in *Iceberg* itself are a hybrid version - Cybermen who survived *The Invasion*, in part because they've adapted technology from the Cybermen seen in *The Tenth Planet*.

As noted above, despite the cover image, it's possible that the Cybermen in *Illegal Alien* are of this type.

It may or may not be significant that the Cybermen in *The Invasion* wear their chest units the other way up to the ones in *Revenge of the Cybermen*. The chest units are the same prop, and there's a circular detail on it - on the top in *The Invasion*, the bottom in *Revenge of the Cybermen*.

One of these Cybermen ended up in Vorg's Miniscope in *Carnival of Monsters*, and it's also the type of Cyberman the Doctor remembers in *The War Games*.

Type IV: "Throwback" (future, Telos, "Empire"), "Black Legacy" (unknown timezone, Empire), "Deathworld" (unknown timezone, Empire).

Notes: The comic strip stories are all apparently set when the Cybermen have an interstellar Empire (see "Do The Cybermen Ever Have an Empire?"). They resemble the Type III, but with a slightly more streamlined designed, and far more visible rank insignia.

Type V: *Earthshock* (2526, Telos?), *Attack of the Cybermen* (future, Telos), *Silver Nemesis* (1988, hope to create a "new Mondas"), "Exodus / Revelation / Genesis" (unknown), "Kane's Story" (4650, "Empire").

Notes: *Earthshock* and *Attack of the Cybermen* could be near-contemporary stories (they are in this chronology). Both the Type IV (as seen in *Revenge of the Cybermen*) and Type V (*Attack of the Cybermen*) Cybermen fought and lost the Cyber War, so perhaps the Type V is the upgraded model, developed during the fighting.

However, *Silver Nemesis* (where the Cybermen are slightly redesigned) and "Kane's Story" are outliers. We don't have a date for "Exodus / Revelation / Genesis". The simplest explanation for a group of Cybermen who want a New Mondas in 1988 (*Silver Nemesis*) is that they're survivors from Mondas' destruction in 1986 (*The Tenth Planet*). Although it's not mentioned, they could be survivors from *Attack of the Cybermen*. Perhaps they're from the base on the Moon that's mentioned and not accounted for - those Cybermen wanted to change history to prevent the destruction of Mondas, so perhaps their back-up plan would be to create "New Mondas".

What's interesting is that the Cybermen in *Attack the Cybermen* definitely have a stolen time travel vessel, there's some evidence that the ones in *Earthshock* are time travellers, and the ones in *Silver Nemesis* are after Gallifreyan technology. So we might be able to assume that the Type V Cybermen are all be Cybermen from the 26th century, with limited knowledge of time travel they've acquired from stolen technology.

This design seems to have a comeback around the Davros Era, according to "Kane's Story".

Type VI: *Real Time*, *The Reaping*, "The Flood".

Notes: The Cybermen continue to evolve, and by the far future they're on the verge of extinction and apparently have one strategy: acquire a time machine and go back into history to change it.

1957 (4th October) - FIRST FRONTIER[1065] -> On May Day 1957, the first *Sputnik* was destroyed before it completed an orbit of the Earth. News of this failure was never made public.

The Doctor visited the first official *Sputnik* launch at least twice.

The same day, there was intense UFO activity over Corman Air Force Base in New Mexico, and the USAF engaged alien spaceships. These were the Tzun, now a race divided into three subspecies. They planned to cause a war between Washington and Moscow, then step in and pose as humanity's saviours. The Master was helping them, but Ace shot the Master and caused him to regenerate. The seventh Doctor prevented chaos from ensuing as the Master betrayed the Tzun and destroyed their mothership.

On the 15th of the same month, a Time Lord using the name Louis approached Johannes Rausch, who possessed a degree in metallurgy from the University of Vienna. Louis offered to make Rausch's life highly successful if Rausch agreed to take part in a painless procedure the day before he died. Rausch agreed, and the two of them would meet again almost fifty years later.[1066]

Department C-19 was set up in Britain[1067] in the late fifties to handle extra sensitive security matters.[1068]

Sputnik II launched and carried Laika the dog into orbit. The Doctor later recovered her body and buried it on the planet Quiescia.[1069] In 1957, Noel Coward met Iris Wildthyme at the Royal Variety Performance. Their friendship led to Iris giving Noel a pair of pinking shears capable of cutting the Very Fabric of Time and Space, enabling him to time travel. Multiple Cowards began operating in various time zones.[1070]

@ The Doctor was present when the Atomium - a monument representing an iron crystal magnified 165 billion times - was unveiled in Brussels.[1071] The Ragman stoked the fire of racial violence between Teddy Boys and Afro-Caribbean immigrants in Notting Hill and Notting Dale.[1072]

1958 - SPIRAL SCRATCH[1073] -> Professor Joseph Tungard was exiled to Britain for dissent against the new Soviet government in Bucharest. On the journey to London, he and his wife Natjya met Dr Pike and his granddaughter Monica. The Tungards settled in England, where Joseph began an affair with Monica… who was secretly an alien Lamprey, a creature that fed on temporal energy

The sixth Doctor and Mel arrived at Wikes Manor in Suffolk, forewarned that a girl called Helen Lamprey was about to vanish from her birthday party. Timelines were beginning to overlap, and alternate versions of the Doctor and Mel appeared. Helen Lamprey vanished, as history had been altered so that she, not her mother, died a number of years ago in a house fire. Mel now had a sister.

The Doctor and Mel followed Helen's father, Sir Bertrand, to London where he met Monica and the

---

1065 Dating *First Frontier* (NA #30) - It is "October 4th, 1957" (p6).
1066 *Unregenerate!* The dating is somewhat awry, as radio broadcasts suggest this occurs on the day of *Sputnik*'s launch (4th October), yet Louis claims the date is "the 15th".
1067 The Doctor mentions C-19 in *Time-Flight*, in connection with contacting UNIT.
1068 *The Scales of Injustice* (p205). C-19 is referred to in a number of novels, particularly Gary Russell's *The Scales of Injustice, Business Unusual* and *Instruments of Darkness*, where it's a shadowy branch of British intelligence that keeps the existence of aliens under wraps by cleaning up alien artefacts left over from their various incursions (a little like Torchwood, then).
1069 *Alien Bodies. Sputnik II* was launched 3rd November, 1957.
1070 *Mad Dogs and Englishmen*
1071 *Escape Velocity*
1072 *Rags* (p185).
1073 Dating *Spiral Scratch* (PDA #72) - Rummas gives the year.
1074 *Spiral Scratch*
1075 Dating *Bad Therapy* (NA #57) - The date is given (p1).

1076 *Shada*
1077 Dating *Delta and the Bannermen* (24.3) - The Tollmaster says that the bus will be going back to "1959", and the date is confirmed by a banner up in the dancehall at the Shangri-La resort. Hawk's line that "this is history in the making" implies this is the first American satellite, but that was actually *Explorer I*, launched on 31st January, 1958.
1078 *Return of the Living Dad*
1079 *The Face of the Enemy* (p248).
1080 *Imperial Moon*
1081 Dating *Loving the Alien* (PDA #60) - Ace gains a tattoo that dates the year as 1959 (p24). The Doctor similarly remarks on the year as 1959 (p33). The newspaper on the cover specifies it's "November" 1959.
1082 *Ghost Ship*. No date is given.
1083 *Synthespians* ™
1084 *Millennial Rites* (p159). The Mods and Rockers gangs were two British youth movements during this time.
1085 *Scream of the Shalka*
1086 "Twenty years" before *Invasion of the Dinosaurs*.
1087 *The Time Warrior*
1088 "For the last decade" before *Spearhead from Space*.

Tungards. Monica revealed her identity as a Lamprey, and that she sought to destroy those who might threaten her plans to feed on damage to the timelines. This triggered Sir Bertrand's memory, and he revealed he was also a Lamprey. The two Lampreys fought, unleashing storms of temporal energy that aged bystanders to death.

The Doctor realized that Helen Lamprey was half-human, half-Lamprey and therefore vital to Monica's plans. He, Mel and Joseph Tungard left in the TARDIS for the planet Carsus, where they would eventually defeat the Lamprey and restore the timelines.

> = In an alternate universe, the sixth Doctor and half-Silurian Melanie Baal visited Helen Lamprey's birthday party… which was held on a space station in Earth orbit.[1074]

1958 (October) - BAD THERAPY[1075] **->** The first of the Krontep warlords, Moriah, had taken up residence on Earth. Operating from the Petruska Psychiatric Research Institute, Moriah sought to construct Toys - genetic duplicates of people that could become whomever their owner desired. He wanted a Toy that would replicate his late wife Petruska, but some of the Toys became increasingly independent. Moriah had a metamorphic device, disguised as a black cab, that would round up any Toys who escaped.

The seventh Doctor and Chris arrived, and a young man named Eddy Stone, actually a Toy, died in front of the TARDIS. The time travellers investigated. Meanwhile, the Doctor's former companion Peri, having spent twenty-five years as King Yrcanos' wife, travelled down a gateway from Krontep to Earth. She aided the Doctor against Moriah. The Doctor created a Toy of Petruska for Moriah, who believed himself unworthy of her love and was killed by his creations.

In 1958, the Doctor again visited St Cedd's College.[1076]

1959 - DELTA AND THE BANNERMEN[1077] **->** The first US satellite was launched, and almost immediately it was lost. CIA agents across the world were put on alert. It was eventually recovered by agents Weismuller and Hawk, who tracked it to a holiday camp in Wales, England.

A Nostalgia Trips group arrived through time at the holiday camp, and their members included the Chimeron Queen. A group of Bannermen tried to kill the Queen but were defeated. Billy, a mechanic at the camp, underwent conversion into a Chimeron to help the Queen re-propagate her race.

One Bannerman survived, albeit deafened and amnesiac. He ended up with Isaac Summerfield's group.[1078]

> = In the "Inferno" universe, the British Republic fought the Bannermen and destroyed them. Components from the alien starship allowed them to engineer space shuttles within ten years.[1079]

In October 1959, the Russian probe *Lunik 3* scanned the moon crater where the Phiadoran safari park once stood. The Russians named it Tsiolkovskii, after a teacher who wrote a paper on rocket travel.[1080]

> **= 1959 - LOVING THE ALIEN**[1081] **->** George Limb's time-jumps had created an alternate timeline where Limb was Prime Minister, and the populace was cybernetically augmented. This had eliminated disease and to some degree created a utopia, but overcrowding became a problem. The British Space Agency was assigned the task of facilitating travel to other timelines as a means of expansion.

In the proper history, the Americans and British jointly launched a Waverider space vehicle, piloted by Colonel Thomas Kneale. However, the ship that returned hailed from the cyber-human reality, and was piloted by an alternate version of Captain Davey O'Brien. International tensions increased over the incident. The cyber-human Britain attempted to send its warships through to the proper reality, but a nuclear strike devastated the alternate Britain and ended the threat.

Limb's assistant, an alternative version of James Dean, died while destroying Limb's time machine. Limb committed suicide in fear of undergoing cyber-conversion.

Before his death, Limb shot and killed Ace. The seventh Doctor took up travel with a virtually identical Ace that hailed from one of the timelines Limb had created.

The Doctor met William Golding.[1082]

The Nineteen Sixties

The Doctor met the artists Francis Bacon and Lucian Freud in Soho in the sixties, and thwarted one of the Master's schemes.[1083] The Mods and Rockers guarded the Library of St John the Beheaded during the sixties.[1084] The Doctor met Andy Warhol, who wanted to paint all nine of him.[1085]

UNIT in the Sixties

u - A secret bunker was built in Whitehall.[1086]

Lavinia Smith published her paper on the teleological response of the virus when her niece, Sarah Jane, was five years old.[1087]

Human space probes were being sent "deeper and deeper" into space.[1088] Lieutenant Lethbridge-Stewart spent some time in Sierra Leone. One day, while lost in the forest, he met Mariatu, eldest daughter of Chief Yembe of the Rokoye village. Mariatu went to the city with Lethbridge-Stewart, returning alone a few years later with her son, Mariama.[1089]

Lethbridge-Stewart saved Doris, an old friend, from drowning in Margate.[1090] He married Fiona and they set up home in Gerrards Cross. The day after the wedding, Lethbridge-Stewart bumped into an old flame, Doris, in Brighton.[1091] **Lethbridge-Stewart was given a wristwatch by Doris during a romantic weekend in Brighton.**[1092] Lethbridge-Stewart spent some time stationed in Berlin.[1093]

Earth Reptile Shelter 429, near the Channel Islands, revived.[1094]

Liz Shaw attended Newnham College at Cambridge during the 1960s, and met fellow student Jean Baisemore there during Freshers' week. They became close friends, with Jean teaching Liz - who was something of a prude - about the wonders of life beyond the lecture hall. At the time, Jean argued with Liz about the existence of life on other planets, and Liz shot her down in flames.[1095]

1960

The Doctor was awarded an honorary degree from St Cedd's in 1960.[1096] In 1960, the Doctor visited Anne Doras and her husband in Guernsey. They had a daughter called Bernice. The same year, convicted Nazi Oskar Steinmann was released from prison on medical grounds.[1097]

1960 - MAD DOGS AND ENGLISHMEN[1098] **->** Fitz met Iris Wildthyme in Las Vegas, where she had found fame as the diva Brenda Soobie. Her companion of sixty years, the poodle Martha, had been manipulating Iris to alter history. Iris helped the eighth Doctor defeat the poo-

dles, then left for further adventures with her new companions Fritter the poodle and Flossie the cook.

Tegan Jovanka was born on 22nd September, 1960.[1099] Tegan's middle name was Melissa. Her father was named William.[1100] She spent her childhood in Caloundra, near Brisbane.[1101] Tegan's Serbian grandfather told her vampire stories.[1102]

= In the 1960 of a world where the Second World War never ended, Gus joined the US Air Force to join the fight. After two years, he saw combat.[1103]

1961

In 1961, Yuri Gagarin became the first human to travel in space.[1104] The Intrusion Countermeasures Group (ICMG) was formed to fight covert actions from hostile powers. Group Captain Gilmore was appointed leader.[1105]

1962

American scientists worked out how to operate the navigation system of their captured Nedenah spaceship.[1106]

Dorothea Chaplet was sent to live with her great-aunt Margaret when her parents died. At her new school, she was given the nickname Dodo.[1107]

Section Eight used the dark arts to end the Cuban Missile Crisis.[1108] A small party of Muslims passed into Avalon.[1109] The starship of the alien scientist Raldonn crashed in Britain, killing the co-pilot. He was set to work on Operation Proteus, and began using it as a cover for other experiments on humans.[1110]

@ It was the Doctor's idea that the Beatles should wear suits.[1111] The Doctor travelled the world in the sixties and seventies.[1112] He visited India.[1113]

1089 *Transit*

THE BRIGADIER'S FAMILY: *Transit* introduces the Brigadier's descendant, Kadiatu Lethbridge-Stewart (she reappears in *Set Piece*, *The Also People* and *So Vile a Sin*). Kadiatu hails from a line of Lethbridge-Stewarts descended from the Lieutenant's liaison in Sierra Leone. There were more details of the Lethbridge-Stewart line in an early draft of *The Also People*.

We can deduce that Mariatu had a son, Mariama, in the early 1960s (he is unnamed in *Transit*, but the name appears in the early draft of *The Also People*, where his mother was mistakenly referred to as "Isatu"). He had a daughter, Kadiatu, who became an historian (she is first referred to in the *Remembrance of the Daleks* novelisation, and also in *Set Piece*). She had a son Gibril, who also had a son called Gibril (from the draft of *The Also People*). Gibril had a son, Yembe (seen in *Transit*), and he

adopted Kadiatu in 2090. Kadiatu, then, is the Brigadiers great-great-great-great-granddaughter, and this is consistent with *Transit* (p96) where "five generations" separate Kadiatu from Alistair.

Rather more simple is the Brigadier's British family. According to *Downtime*, the Brigadier and his first wife Fiona (a name thought up by Nicholas Courtney, who plays the Brigadier) had a daughter named Kate. She was a child during the UNIT era, when the Lethbridge-Stewarts split up. (The Brigadier and Fiona separate in *The Scales of Injustice*, and he is sleeping alone by *The Daemons*.) By the mid-nineties, Kate is a single mother looking after her son Gordon. By *Battlefield*, the Brigadier has married Doris, an old flame first mentioned in *Planet of the Spiders*. (They shared a weekend in Brighton eleven years before that story - perhaps before Alistair was married to Fiona.)

The Doctor spent some time at a Buddhist temple in Thailand, searching for a dragon. His search took twenty five years and he travelled across China, Vietnam and Siam. He found the dragon, but it's not known what subsequently happened.[1114]

During the 1960s, the Doctor spent some time learning ventriloquism from Edgar Bergen of *The Edgar Bergen and Charlie McCarthy Show.*[1115]

One Dalek fell through time at the end of the Last Great Time War, crashing to Earth in the Ascension Islands. Damaged and unresponsive, it spent the next fifty years being passed from one private collection to another, ending up being bought by Van Statten.[1116]

Mel's sister Annabelle was born 4th October, 1962.[1117]

1090 *Blood Heat*

1091 "Eight years" before *The Scales of Injustice* (p61, p131).

1092 "Eleven years" before *Planet of Spiders* - possibly while married to Fiona.

1093 *The King of Terror* (p255).

1094 "About ten years" before *The Scales of Injustice*.

1095 *The Blue Tooth*. Liz specifies that this happened in the 60s, which is vague enough to work into any UNIT dating scheme.

1096 *Shada*

1097 *Just War*

1098 Dating *Mad Dogs and Englishmen* (EDA #52) - "It's 1960!" (p118).

1099 According to her character outline, Tegan is "twenty-one" when she meets the Doctor (in *Logopolis*, set in 1981). Originally she was to be nineteen, until the production team were told that legally air hostesses had to be twenty-one or older. Clarifying the issue, *The Gathering* has Tegan celebrating her 46th birthday on 22 September 2006. Janet Fielding was born in 1957, which might suggest that she's three years older than the character she played. However, fandom often presumes that Tegan spent three years traveling with the Doctor (the duration of Fielding's time on screen), which would suggest that - like Fielding - Tegan is actually 49 when the audio takes place.

1100 *Divided Loyalties*

1101 *The King of Terror*

1102 *Goth Opera*

1103 "4-Dimensional Vistas". Gus has been "three years in the air force", and has been fighting since "last year".

1104 Confirmed in *The Seeds of Death*.

1105 The ICMG is seen in *Remembrance of the Daleks*, and its founding was described in *Who Killed Kennedy* (p69).

1106 "Fifteen years" after 1947, according to *The Devil Goblins from Neptune*.

1107 *Salvation* (p5).

1108 *Heart of TARDIS* (p197).

1109 "Fifty years" before *The Shadows of Avalon*.

1110 "Many months" before "Operation Proteus", and more than four months because Raldonn was there to detect the Doctor's arrival on Earth.

1111 *Trading Futures*

1112 *Father Time*. This is one reason that the Doctor doesn't bump into himself during the UNIT era.

1113 "Twenty seven years" before the third part of *Father Time*.

1114 *The Year of Intelligent Tigers*

1115 *Dark Progeny*. Despite his popularity, Bergen wasn't a very skilled ventriloquist, and the McCarthy doll would frequently mock Bergen for moving his lips.

1116 It arrived "at least fifty years" before *Dalek*.

1117 *Spiral Scratch*

= The former Council of Eight member Soul, along with the Doctor's granddaughter Zezanne, arrived in a junkyard in 1963 aboard the *Jonah*. A chameleon device built by Octan enabled the ship to alter its appearance for the first and nearly last time, blending into its surroundings as a police box. Soul and Zezanne's memories were clouded by the nature of their escape. Having absorbed some of the Doctor's life force, Soul became convinced that he *was* the Doctor. Zezanne regarded him as her grandfather.[1]

The first Doctor and Susan arrived in Shoreditch, London, in early 1963 and spent five months on Earth at this time. The Doctor attended to his TARDIS while Susan went to Coal Hill School. A month before his departure, the Doctor made arrangements to bury the Hand of Omega.[2]

IM Foreman's travelling carnival for a time remodelled itself as the junkyard at Totter's Yard, and the instability it created had served to draw the Doctor's TARDIS there.[3]

1963 (27th March / 4th April) - TIME AND RELA-TIVE[4] **->** Several months after Susan started at Coal Hill School, England was caught in the most severe winter for quite some time. There had been snow and ice since before Christmas, into April. This was caused by an ancient sentience called the Cold, which had recently revived, possibly due to a Soviet cryogenics research undertaking called the Novosibirsk Project. The Cold animated killer snowmen, "the Cold Knights", which caused mayhem in London and slew many in Piccadilly Circus. The first

Doctor siphoned the Cold into a lump of ice, and took it to Pluto in the far future.

= **1963 (July) - "Lunar Lagoon"**[5] **->** The fifth Doctor was fishing on a Pacific Island when he was attacked by an old Japanese soldier, Fuji, who didn't realise the War was over. To the Doctor's surprise, the island was attacked by a USAF bomber. Fuji was killed by a downed American airman, leaving the Doctor to ponder the meaningless of war.

= **1963 (25th July) - "4-Dimensional Vistas"**[6] **->** The fifth Doctor was captured by the US airman who killed Fuji, Angus "Gus" Goodman, and learned that the TARDIS had landed twenty years earlier than he thought... and in a parallel universe. Lost in time, the Doctor convinced Gus to join him on his travels.

= **1963 (25th July) - "The Moderator"**[7] **->** After a couple of adventures, the fifth Doctor returned Gus home. The Moderator had followed them from the far future, and gunned down Gus.

1963 - THE TAINT[8] **->** The eighth Doctor met Fitz Kreiner, a florist, shortly before being confronted by an escaped mental patient, Oscar Austen. The patients at Austen's hospital had alien leech creatures in their brains. Sam and Fitz were attacked by Azoth, an organic computer from the planet Benelisa, who injected Sam with a leech. Azoth sought to destroy "the Beast", invisible aliens that were feeding on humans, and the leech enabled Sam to see them. The leeches drove the patients further insane and

---

1 *Sometime Never*
IS THE DOCTOR REALLY A CRYSTAL SKELETON MAN FROM THE FUTURE, NOW?: *Sometime Never* ends with the multiverse being restored after being merged by the Council of Eight. "In just one of many universes", a benevolent member of the Council, Soul, and Miranda's daughter, Zezanne, arrive in a junkyard in Sabbath's ship, the *Jonah* - which disguises itself as a police box. Soul has absorbed the essence of the Doctor, and as Miranda's daughter, Zezanne is the Doctor's grand-daughter. Clearly, in their universe, they take on the roles of the Doctor and Susan.

The question is whether this represents a new origin story for *our* Doctor and Susan. The EDA range had destroyed Gallifrey, but it wasn't specified whether the planet had simply blown up or been removed from the timeline so that it never existed. If Gallifrey had never existed, the existence of the Doctor and his TARDIS would have been a paradox ... unless he wasn't from Gallifrey. This explanation closed that loophole.

As of *The Gallifrey Chronicles*, the Doctor certainly thinks he's a Time Lord from the planet Gallifrey, has met a Time Lord and seen evidence of Gallifrey's former existence. Gallifrey therefore existed, and it seems fairly clear now that the Doctor isn't Soul.

2 In *An Unearthly Child*, Susan says that "the last five months have been the happiest in my life". She and the Doctor were on Earth for "six months" according to *Matrix* (p31), and *Time and Relative* suggests it was more like thirteen months. The Doctor returns for the Hand of Omega in *Remembrance of the Daleks*.

3 *Interference*

4 Dating *Time and Relative* (TEL #1) - Susan's diary gives the date as "Wednesday, March 27th 1963" for the first entry (p9), "April 4th" for the last. They have *already* been on Earth "five months, I think", according to Susan, who admits to some confusion on the point.

5 Dating "Lunar Lagoon" (*DWM* #76-77) - The Doctor declares "this is 1983", but the Second World War is still being fought. The anomaly is explained in "4-

granted them with dangerous psychic abilities. Azoth was destroyed, and the Doctor released a bio-electric pulse that killed the mental patients, including Fitz's mother. Fitz joined the Doctor and Sam on their travels. They predicted that the Beast would eventually move on from Earth.

1963 - "Operation Proteus"[9] **->** Four months after they arrived in London, the first Doctor and Susan confronted Raldonn, an alien scientist who was experimenting on human beings, causing deliberate genetic acceleration. He was attempting to create another of his kind, to replace the co-pilot of his crashed ship. Only one in a million is affected, the others become random mutants, so he planned to release the serum into the air over London. Raldonn was killed by one of the mutants, and the Doctor was able to use his equipment to release a cure into the atmosphere.

At one point during this encounter, Susan was abducted by Threshold.

On 29th March, 1963, Lizzy Lewis was murdered in Cardiff. Torchwood's Owen Harper would later relive the crime using an alien device.[10]

1963 (October) - GHOST SHIP[11] **->** The fourth Doctor landed on the *Queen Mary*, which was bound for New York. In Cabin 672, he found that quantum physicist Peter Osbourne had developed a time-space visualizer. As a side effect, Osbourne's device had captured psionic residue from the passengers, collecting "ghosts" from the past, present and future. The Doctor destroyed the device and liberated the "ghosts," who took Osbourne among their number. The Doctor concluded that the "ghosts" would

remain aboard the *Queen Mary* forever.

1963 (a Tuesday in late October) - AN UNEARTHLY CHILD[12] **->** Two of Susan Foreman's teachers, Ian Chesterton and Barbara Wright, became concerned with a pupil's homework and investigated her home one evening. Although Chesterton's car was later discovered outside a Totter's Yard, no sign was found of the teachers, Susan or her mysterious grandfather.

In 1963, Professor Rachel Jensen was moved from British Rocket Group to the Intrusion Countermeasures Group.[13]

= 1963 (12th November) - MATRIX[14] **->** On Matrix Earth, Britain was the fifty-first of the United States. President Kennedy came to London on 11th November to give a speech in Westminster, but was torn apart by supernatural creatures. Ian and Barbara were lovers, but were killed by the Jacksprites - the drug-addicted followers of Jack the Ripper. The seventh Doctor and Ace arrived in this timeline, then went back to 1888 and restored history to its normal course.

1963 (from 22nd November) - REMEMBRANCE OF THE DALEKS[15] **->** An Imperial Dalek Shuttlecraft landed in a playground in London and established a transmat link with an orbiting mothership. The Renegade Dalek faction arrived at around the same time and began recruiting sympathetic locals. Davros, now in command of the Imperial Daleks, wiped out the Renegade faction and captured the Hand of Omega. He

---

Dimensional Vistas", where Gus gives the date as "July 25th 1963" and it transpires it's a parallel world where the War didn't end. The Doctor says he never learned to swim. There's no explanation for the title of the story, which has nothing to do with the moon, and doesn't feature a lagoon.

6 Dating "4-Dimensional Vistas" (*DWM* #78-83) - The Doctor learns the date is "July 25th 1963" from Gus.

7 Dating "The Moderator" (*DWM* #84, #86-87) - The Doctor takes Gus back to "the same time, the same place that we first met", which was in "Lunar Lagoon".

8 Dating *The Taint* (EDA #19) - It is 1963 (p10).

9 Dating "Operation Proteus" (*DWM* #231-233) - It is "four months" since the Doctor and Susan arrived on Earth, so a month before *An Unearthly Child*. "Ground Zero" confirms this is "October 1963".

10 *TW: Ghost Machine*.

11 Dating *Ghost Ship* (TEL #4) - According to the blurb, the story is set in 1963.

12 Dating *An Unearthly Child* (1.1) - The Doctor has left the Hand of Omega at the funeral parlour for "a month"

before *Remembrance of the Daleks*, suggesting that the first episode is set in late October. The year "1963" is first confirmed in the Part Two, "The Cave of Skulls". Ian Chesterton's blackboard reads "Homework - Tuesday".

13 *Who Killed Kennedy* (p70), working on information implied by *Remembrance of the Daleks*.

14 Dating *Matrix* (PDA #16) - The date is given (p39).

15 Dating *Remembrance of the Daleks* (25.1) - The story is set in late November 1963 according to the calendar on Ratcliffe's wall, as well as a host of other incidental evidence. (Not least of which being the broadcast of an episode of the "new science fiction serial 'Doct- ".) The draft script was set in December. The novelisation places this story a week after Kennedy's assassination, but page 57 erroneously says the killing occurred "last Saturday" (it actually occurred on a Friday).

QUATERMASS: A throwaway line in *Remembrance of the Daleks* mentions a "Bernard" who is working for "British Rocket Group". This is a reference to the four Quatermass television serials: *The Quatermass Experiment, Quatermass II, Quatermass and the Pit* and

planned on using its power to give the Daleks mastery of Time, and make them the new Time Lords. The seventh Doctor tricked Davros into destroying both Skaro and his battleship with the Hand of Omega. Davros survived in an escape pod, while the Hand of Omega returned to Gallifrey.

At this time, the British Rocket Group and the Intrusion Counter Measures Group were active. The second of these detected the Daleks' transmissions and uncovered indisputable evidence of extra-terrestrial activity. The affair was covered up by claiming that a nuclear accident was narrowly averted.

The ICMG became part of Department C-19. It formed the basis of an organisation that deals with unusual events. Members included Ian Gilmore, Rachel Jenson, Allison Williams, Ruth Ingram and Anne Travers.[16] The fact that IM Foreman's name was spelt "Forman" on the gates of the Totter's Yard when the Doctor encountered the Dalek there owed to temporal disruption.[17] Isaac Summerfield and the survivors of the *Tisiphone* arrived circa 1963 after falling through a wormhole from the twenty-sixth century.[18]

The Kennedy Assassination

In late November 1963, the Nemesis asteroid passed over the Earth, influencing the assassination of President Kennedy.[19]

1963 - WHO KILLED KENNEDY[20] **->** Journalist James Stevens arrived from the seventies to stop the Master from interfering with the Kennedy assassination. The Master wanted to disrupt history using a brainwashed Private Cleary as his assassin. Stevens defeated Cleary, but a James Stevens from twenty five years further into the future fulfilled history by killing Kennedy. Lee Harvey Oswald was blamed for the crime. The younger Stevens returned home with a brain-damaged Cleary.

The Doctor was once blamed for the Kennedy assassination.[21] **He was present at the event.**[22]

@ The amnesiac eighth Doctor remained unaware of the Kennedy assassination until the early eighties.[23] Summer, a future rock festival attendee who would encounter the Doctor in 1967, was present in Dealey Plaza when Kennedy was killed.[24]

Nyssa, the daughter of Tremas of Traken, was born.[25] **In 1963, the Doctor's future companion Polly worked for a week at a charity shop.**[26]

1963 (22nd December) - WINTER FOR THE ADEPT[27] **->** Two advance scouts for the Spillagers, alien plunderers who "spill" through dimensional wormholes to sack a target, arrived on Earth. One of them disguised itself as Mlle. Maupassant, a French teacher at a girls' finishing school in the Swiss Alps. She brought two latent psionics - students Peil Bellamy and Allison Speer - into contact with the ghost of mountaineer Harding Wellman, which repeat-

---

simply *Quatermass* in which British space scientist Bernard Quatermass battled alien horrors. Most fans agree that the first three serials heavily influenced a number of *Doctor Who* stories, although successive production teams rarely made the comparison, and often denied it.

In the New Adventures, *The Pit* (p169) makes reference to an incident at "Hob's Lane" (*Quatermass and the Pit*, although it perhaps more correctly ought to be "Hobbs Lane") and *Nightshade* first introduces the eponymous nineteen-fifties television series that bore many similarities to the *Quatermass* serials. "Bernard" makes a brief appearance in *The Dying Days*. While not mentioned in dialogue, the set dressing in *The Christmas Invasion* states that the Guinevere probe to Mars was launched by the British Rocket Group.

Do the *Quatermass* serials occur in the same fictional universe as *Doctor Who*? As might be expected, there are a number of discrepancies between the two programmes. *The Quatermass Experiment* contradicts *The Seeds of Death*, claiming that Victor Carroon was the first man in space, and a race of Martians appears in *Quatermass and the Pit*. Broadly, though, the two series might co-exist, with the final serial *Quatermass* taking place around the time of the New Adventures *Iceberg*

and *Cat's Cradle: Warhead*. Indeed, the existence of Professor Quatermass might go some way to explaining the rosy state of the British space programme in the UNIT era (q.v. "The British Space Programme").

16 *The Scales of Injustice* (p154). This is "a few years" before the London Incident (the Yeti invasion seen in *The Web of Fear*). The first three individuals on this list hail from *Remembrance of the Daleks*, Ruth is seen in *The Time Monster*, and Anne appears in *The Web of Fear* and *Millennial Rites*.

17 *The Algebra of Ice*

18 *Return of the Living Dad*

19 *Silver Nemesis*. The book *Who Killed Kennedy* offers another perspective on the assassination. The frequent references to the Kennedy Assassination are in-jokes, as *Doctor Who's* first episode was shown the day after Kennedy's assassination, the day most people in the UK learned the news.

20 Dating *Who Killed Kennedy* (MA, unnumbered) - The date is given, and ties in with historical fact.

21 *Zagreus*

22 *Rose*

23 *Father Time*

24 *Wonderland*

25 Nyssa is "eighteen" according to the Writers' Guide

edly triggered poltergeist effects that fuelled a wormhole for the invading Spillager warfleet. The fifth Doctor and Nyssa's intervention resulted in the Spillager scouts' deaths and the warfleet's obliteration.

1964 - THE LAND OF THE DEAD[28] **->** The fifth Doctor and Nyssa briefly arrived in Alaska while tracing a mysterious energy field, then went thirty years into the future to investigate it more thoroughly. They had detected the first stirrings of the Permians.

A jewel thief committed at least two dozen robberies in London society over the course of two years. He (or she) always took jewels and left a calling card depicting the head of the Roman god Janus. The affluent Lady Lily Hawthorne took to copying Janus' modus operandi, and sold her takings for benefit of charity.[29]

c 1964 - PLANET OF GIANTS[30] **->** A government inspector, Arnold Farrow, told the industrialist Forester that the insecticide his company had developed would not be approved for production. The scientist Smithers, obsessed by the idea of ending world famine, had succeeded over the last year in creating an insecticide 60 percent more powerful than anything on the market. It could even stop locusts breeding, but tests showed that it killed *all* insect life, even those vital to the ecology. Forester murdered Farrow, but was arrested by the local policeman, Bert Rowse.

The **Doctor visited St Cedd's College in 1964.**[31] In the same year, the television series *Professor X* started broadcasting.[32]

Melanie Jane **Bush was born**[33] on 22nd July, 1964, in this and 117,863 alternate universes.[34]

1965 - THE CHASE[35] **->** The TARDIS crew used the Time / Space Visualiser to watch the Beatles singing "Ticket to Ride". Later, Ian Chesterton and Barbara Wright returned to Earth in a Dalek time machine, which self-destructed once they left the craft.

Ian and Barbara arrived back home in 1965. He became a leading scientist, and she became a university lecturer.[36] They married and had a son named John.[37]

1965 - THE MASSACRE[38] **->** Dorothea "Dodo" Chaplet accidentally entered the TARDIS while it had landed on Wimbledon Common, mistaking it for a real police box. The teenager was living with her great aunt at the time, as her mother had died.

1965 (25th March - 1st April) - SALVATION[39] **->** Dorothea "Dodo" Chaplet, a London resident, found that her elderly neighbour Mr Miller had been replaced by a shapechanger named Joseph. **She** fled and **entered the TARDIS**, which was parked in Wimbledon Common.

The Ship dematerialized and reappeared in New York City, the same time zone. The Church of the Latter-Day

---

for Season Eighteen.

26 *Ten Little Aliens*

27 Dating *Winter for the Adept* (BF #10) - The date is given by the Doctor.

28 Dating *The Land of the Dead* (BF #4) - It is "thirty years" before 1994.

29 Two years before *The Veiled Leopard*.

30 Dating *Planet of Giants* (2.1) - The year is not specified on screen, although the setting is contemporary. Forester lives in a rural area, and a switchboard operator still mans the local telephone exchange.

31 *Shada*

32 It was cancelled in 1989 after twenty five years, according to *Escape Velocity*.

33 In the Writers' Guide for the Season Twenty-Three, written in July 1985, Mel is described as "twenty-one". In the *Terror of the Vervoids* novelisation she is "twenty-two", in *The Ultimate Foe* she has lived for "twenty three years". In *Just War*, Mel was born "twenty eight" years after "1936". Later books have stated that Mel joined the Doctor in 1989, which would seem to make her year of birth later than this.

34 *Spiral Scratch*

35 Dating *The Chase* (2.8) - On their return home, Ian sees a tax disc dated "Dec 65", and Barbara notes that

they are "two years out". (Ironically, after two years of trying to land in England in the nineteen-sixties, the TARDIS visits Ian and Barbara's native time five times in the next ten television stories.) The script suggested that the Visualiser tuned in on the Beatles' Fiftieth Anniversary reunion tour. The costume listing for 1st April, 1965, included a request for an announcer dressed in futuristic clothing from "2014", and it seems that the Beatles were contacted. However, the television version eventually used stock footage from 1965.

36 *Who Killed Kennedy*

37 *Goth Opera*. John is the singer Johnny Chess (short for Chesterton), first mentioned in *Timewyrm: Revelation*.

38 Dating *The Massacre* (3.5) - It is never made explicit which year Dodo boards the TARDIS. She is surprised that the Post Office Tower has been completed on her return to Earth in *The War Machines* in 1966. *Salvation* specifically has her entering the TARDIS in 1965.

39 Dating *Salvation* (PDA #18) - On p19, an edition of the *New York Ranger* marks the date that Dodo enters the TARDIS as 25th March, 1965. The same publication dates the gods' departure as 1st April (p251).

Pantheon opened its doors and proclaimed that six beings, including Joseph, were humanity's gods returned to perform miracles. The first Doctor deduced that the "gods" were extra-dimensional beings given shape and power by humanity's desires. Appeals from organizations such as the Ku Klux Klan confused the gods as to humanity's needs, and they became increasingly unstable. The Doctor coerced the gods into leaving Earth for their home dimension. He believed the "gods" would eventually leave their homeworld and drift through space. Dodo took up travelling with the Doctor and Steven in the TARDIS.

In 1965, gang warfare increased between the Mods and the Rockers. A member of the Rockers, Alec, fell in love with Sandra, whose brothers belonged to the Mods. Alec and Sandra found an injured alien who arrived on Earth, the Maker, and tended its wounds. The grateful Maker scanned their minds and saw their concept of a gleaming, futuristic city. As the Mods and Rockers prepared for a major battle, the Maker spirited them away to a reconstruction of such a city in the future.

The situation in the future deteriorated, and some of the Mods and Rockers - Alec included - elected to become younger, have their memories wiped and return to 1965. The gang conflict continued.[40]

1965 - THE VANITY BOX[41] **->** In Salford, Monsieur Coiffure had established The Vanity Box salon - an establishment where clients could walk away looking ten years younger. The reversion owed to a box that Coiffure had found floating down the ship canal one day, and which contained a very ancient and powerful entity that fed off the hopes and fears of human beings. The box entity could indeed make people look ten years younger, but only by

shortening their lives by a comparable amount of time.

The sixth Doctor and Mel happened upon The Vanity Box, and the Doctor recognised the box entity as an earlier version of the Wishing Beast that he had just defeated on a remote asteroid. The box entity became incapacitated while trying to de-age the Doctor, and the Doctor - fearing the creature could wreck havoc on Earth - used the TARDIS to open a little tear in the fabric of space-time. He flung the box into the tear, knowing that it would back track along the TARDIS' time trail, and arrive on the asteroid in the distant past.

1965 (25th December) and 1965/1966 (31st December - 1st January) - THE DALEKS' MASTER PLAN[42] **->** While fleeing the Daleks, the TARDIS landed outside a police station in Liverpool so that the first Doctor could repair the scanner. After a little trouble with the police force, the TARDIS went on its way. A week later, the TARDIS landed in Trafalgar Square during the New Year celebrations.

Mel accidentally killed her sister when she was eighteen months old, and her parents never told her about this.[43]

1966 - THE VEILED LEOPARD[44] **->** The Veiled Leopard had become one of the world's most famous diamonds, bigger than the Star of India and the Koh-i-Noor. It was owned by the industrialist Gavin Walker, who among his successes had purchased and bulldozed a series of mills in the East End, making a tidy profit when he sold the land.

At The Majestic casino in Monte Carlo, Walker publicly announced he was giving the diamond to his wife as a birthday present, but he had arranged for its theft as part of an insurance scam. The fifth and seventh Doctors coor-

---

40 *The Space Age*

41 Dating *The Vanity Box* (BF #97) - The back cover says "circa 1965", but the Doctor more specifically says, "It's 1965, I believe that's groovy enough for anyone". For the Doctor and Mel, this story follows directly on from their confrontation with the box entity in *The Wishing Beast* (also BF #97).

42 Dating *The Daleks' Master Plan* (3.4) - A calendar in the police station reads "25th December". It was originally intended that the 1965 Christmas episode, "The Feast of Steven", would include a crossover with the popular BBC police serial *Z-Cars*. Publicity material to this effect was sent out on 1st October, 1965, and it appears that a version of the script was written with the *Z-Cars* characters in mind. John Peel's novelisation of this story and Lofficier's *The Universal Databank* both retain the names of actors (not the characters) from the police series.

43 *Spiral Scratch*

44 Dating *The Veiled Leopard* (BF promo, *DWM* #367) -

The year is given.

45 Dating *The Chase* (2.8) - Morton Dill says it is "1966", in Alabama at least.

46 *Invasion of the Cat-People* (p115), no date is given.

47 In *The War Machines,* it is twice stated that Ben has a shore posting (he is depressed by this and wants to get back to sea). At the end of the story, it is stated that he has to get "back to barracks". However in *The Smugglers* and *The Faceless Ones* he wants to return to his "ship".

48 Dating *The War Machines* (3.10) - C-Day is set for 16th July, but this didn't fall on a Monday in 1966... it was actually the Saturday that *The War Machines* Part Four was to be broadcast. The year "1966" is confirmed in *The Faceless Ones* and also in the *Radio Times*. WOTAN is connected up to Telstar and Cape Kennedy, both of which were operating in 1966. At the end of *The Faceless Ones*, Ben and Polly realise that it's the same day they joined the TARDIS, and give the date as the 20th of July.

dinated their efforts to retrieve the diamond (which was actually an alien crystal) and dispatched their companions - Peri and Erimem, plus Ace and Hex - to insure that it fell into the right hands. Walker's criminal intent was exposed, and Ace and Hex pocketed the diamond.

1966 - THE CHASE[45] **->** The TARDIS crew and the Dalek time machine pursing them landed on the top floor of the Empire State Building, much to the amusement of tourist Morton Dill.

Before this time, Polly Wright studied at Leeds University, where a group of her friends were interested in the occult.[46] Able Seaman Ben Jackson started a five-month shore posting on 5th July, 1966.[47]

1966 (12th - 20th July) - THE WAR MACHINES[48] **->** Computer Day was set for Monday, 16th July. This was the day that computer systems across the whole world were due to come under the control of the central computer, WOTAN.

WOTAN was designed to operate itself, being pure thought and able to think for itself like a human being - only better. It was at least ten years ahead of its time, and it was the most advanced - although not biggest - computer in the world. WOTAN would be connected up to a number of sites, including ELDO, TELSTAR, the White House, Parliament, Cape Kennedy, EFTA, RN and Woomera.

WOTAN decided to make a bid for power, and constructed an army of War Machines. The first Doctor defeated WOTAN with the help of Ben and Polly. Having returned to her own time, Dodo Chaplet left the Doctor. Ben Jackson and Polly, however, entered the TARDIS just as it left Earth.

1966 (20th July) - THE FACELESS ONES[49] **->** Following an explosion on their home planet, a generation of aliens were rendered faceless, and lacked any true identity. As scientifically advanced beings, they concocted an elaborate plan to kidnap young humans and absorb their personalities. Youngsters on chartered Chameleon Flights to holiday destinations would instead be flown to a space station in orbit, where they

would be processed. Although the Chameleons covered their tracks carefully - sending postcards to the missing youngsters' families, hypnotising people, and even murdering them - their plan was exposed. The second Doctor promised to help the Chameleons find a solution to their problem, and the aliens left.

Back in their own time, on the very same day that they had joined him, Ben Jackson and Polly left the second Doctor's company.

1966 (20th July) - THE EVIL OF THE DALEKS[50] **->** The TARDIS was stolen from Gatwick airport. In tracking it down, the second Doctor and Jamie were transported a hundred years into the past.

1966 - "The Love Invasion"[51] **->** The ninth Doctor and Rose arrived in London to find a group of beautiful women doing good deeds while working for the Lend-A-Hand agency. The Doctor realized that these were aliens, and they'd been killing leading scientists. The girls were clones, controlled by a Kustollon named Igrix, who had stolen a time machine. His race was destined to fight a devastating war with humanity, and so he had come back to make humanity less aggressive and to destroy the Moon. The Doctor sabotaged Igrix's ship so that it would indulge its curiosity to explore, and it took Igrix with it.

Perpugilliam Brown was born on 15th November, 1966.[52] In Baltimore, Peri was friends throughout her school years with the Chambers family. The father, Anthony Chambers, kept Peri and his children amused by letting them use a telescope. Peri briefly dated Nate Chambers, and became best friends with his sister Kathy.[53]

Aliens from a planet orbiting Epsilon Eridani had developed slower-than-light space travel, which enabled them to establish many colony worlds. The Eridani had been routing robot ships through Earth's solar system for centuries, deeming the region of little import. But circa 1966, an Eridani robot ship sent to a colony orbiting Van Maanen's star became confused by radio signals on Earth and landed there instead. Five components of an Eridani super-computer went missing. The Eridani sent agents to retrieve the components, but it took them eleven years to reach Earth.[54]

49 Dating *The Faceless Ones* (4.8) - Setting this story in 1966 seems to have been a last minute decision to smooth Ben and Polly's departure, one that also affects the dating for *The Evil of the Daleks*. The *Radio Times* stated that it is "Earth - Today".
50 Dating *The Evil of the Daleks* (4.9) - The story follows straight on from *The Faceless Ones*.
51 Dating "The Love Invasion" - The year is given.
52 *Planet of Fire*. According to a Character Outline pre-

pared for Season Twenty-One, before Nicola Bryant was cast in the role, Peri is "an eighteen year old" when she starts travelling with the Doctor. Her mother's name is "Janine" (the same document also says Peri is "blonde"). This would seem to make Peri three years younger than the actress playing her. In *Bad Therapy*, Peri confirms she was eighteen when she met the Doctor.
53 *The Reaping*
54 *Blue Box*

Two alien objects - later named the "risen mitten" and the "life knife" - fell through the Cardiff Rift. They would eventually end up in the Torchwood archive.[55]

1967 (January) - WONDERLAND[56] **->** Some nameless grey-suited men, agents of an shadow organization alleged to run America and the entire world behind-the-scenes, captured an alien that came to be known as "the Colour-Beast." The grey-suited men distilled the creature's essence and began distributing it as "Blue Moonbeams," hoping to learn how to turn humans into invisible alien killing machines. The Blue Moonbeams became a popular illicit drug, but they failed to properly morph the users and instead combusted them.

The grey-suited men sought to refine the process by distributing Blue Moonbeams at the "Human-Be-In" rock festival / anti-war protest held in San Francisco on 14th January, 1967. Moonbeam-users at the celebration started to mutate, but the second Doctor intervened and freed the Colour-Beast. The creature nullified the drugs' effects on the afflicted humans and departed for home.

The Doctor suggested that George Harrison see the Maharishi for spiritual guidance. He also gave LSD guru Timothy Leary advice about tuning into the mind's "god centre." The Doctor probably also inspired Leary's infamous tag line of "Tune in, turn on and drop out."[57]

c 1967 - RENAISSANCE OF THE DALEKS[58] **->** The fifth Doctor and Nyssa arrived during the Vietnam War to re-calibrate the TARDIS' systems, and came to the aid of Major Alice Hunniford - the survivor of a downed Cobra 3 aircraft.

Brendan Richards, later a ward of Lavinia Smith, was born in 1967.[59] *Metropolitan* magazine was founded in 1967. Sarah Jane Smith would later be a regular writer for it.[60] Fitz saw Jimi Hendrix perform several times during 1967.[61] **During the late nineteen-sixties, Professor Fendelman was working on missile guidance.**[62]

1967 - REVOLUTION MAN[63] **->** The anarchist Jean-Pierre Rex had secured a quantity of the reality-warping drug Om-Tsor, and used it to psionically deface global monuments with the letter "R." Between 5th November, 1967, and 29th April, 1968, the symbol appeared on the Great Pyramid in Egypt, the Lincoln Memorial in Washington, a stone at Stonehenge, the white cliffs of Dover, the Golden Gate Bridge in San Francisco, the floor of St. Peter's Cathedral in Rome and Red Square in Moscow. Various world governments attributed the incidents to a messianic figure named "the Revolution Man," and international tensions increased.

@ In Bangor, the eighth Doctor showed the Beatles how to meditate.[64]

The Monk placed £200 in a London bank in 1968. He would travel two hundred years into the future and withdraw the money and compound interest.[65] **The Mexico Olympics were held.**[66] In 1968, the Doctor was a Tufty Club member.[67]

In 1968, the United Nations designed a first contact policy. It stiplated that such an event could not take place on sovereign soil.[68] The Time Lord Simpson interviewed an aged survivor of the Banquo Manor murders on her deathbed. This enabled him to obtain the seed code for Compassion's Randomizer, which allowed Gallifrey to track her movements.[69]

The tenth Doctor wore a coat that had been given to him by Janis Joplin.[70]

---

55 "Forty years" before *TW: They Keep Killing Suzie.*
56 Dating *Wonderland* (TEL #7) - The date is given (p11).
57 *Wonderland* (p46, p50).
58 Dating *Renaissance of the Daleks* (BF #93) - It's during the Vietnam Conflict (which lasted 1959 to 1975, although US participation was greatly accelerated under President Johnson in 1965). Agent Orange is here deployed, and it was in use from 1961 to 1971. The US military didn't actually use female pilots in Vietnam, so the likelihood of Alice Hunniford seeing combat duty is remote.
59 Brendan is "fourteen" according to *K9 and Company.*
60 *Amorality Tale*
61 *The Year of Intelligent Tigers*
62 "Ten years" before *Image of the Fendahl.*
63 Dating *Revolution Man* (EDA #21) - The general date is given on p1; the dates of the defacings on p98-100.

64 *The Gallifrey Chronicles.* The Beatles went to Bangor in 1967.
65 *The Time Meddler*
66 *The Underwater Menace*
67 *Frontier Worlds.* The Tufty Club was a group that taught British children the fundamentals of road safety. The group's mascot, Tufty the squirrel, avoided roadside accidents and was featured on club badges.
68 *The Sound of Drums.* Some have viewed this as a reference to events in *The Invasion*, which broadcast in November and December 1968.
69 *The Banquo Legacy* (p274).
70 *Gridlock.* As the tenth Doctor's coat is already in the TARDIS wardrobe in *The Christmas Invasion*, it was given to an earlier incarnation. Joplin lived 1943-1970.
71 Dating *Nightshade* (NA #8) - Ace finds a calendar saying it is "Christmas 1968".
72 *Revolution Man* (p180).

1968 - NIGHTSHADE[71] -> The seventh Doctor and Ace found murders and hauntings in the Yorkshire town of Crook Marsham. The retired actor Edmund Trevithick, former star of the *Nightshade* series, had been seeing monsters from his old show. Energy beings sealed off the village and began a rampage. The Doctor discovered the Sentience, an ancient creature, was feeding on the lifeforce of humans. He convinced it to transmit itself to a supernova in Bellatrix, where it became trapped.

In 1968, Jean-Pierre Rex had given up being the Revolution Man. The singer Ed Hill murdered Rex and used the drug Om-Tsor to continue the Revolution Man's anarchist activities. The "Revolution Man" symbol appeared on the deck of the US *Constitution* on 12th November. On 4th January, 1969, it appeared at a US Air Force base in High Raccoon, Tennessee.[72]

The Doctor bought a beach house in Sydney in 1969, and rented a green VW that he conveniently forgot to return.[73]

1969 - BLINK[74] -> Detective Inspector Billy Shipton was transported to 1969 by the Weeping Angels. He met the tenth Doctor and Martha, who gave him a message for Sally Sparrow… but one he would have to live out nearly forty years to deliver.

1969 (18th May) - REVOLUTION MAN[75] -> The "Revolution Man" incidents greatly increased tensions between the US, the Soviet Union, China and India. Ed Hill's psionic abilities spiralled out of control, threatening to destroy all life on Earth, and Fitz and the eighth Doctor killed Hill to prevent such a catastrophe. The Doctor consumed a portion of Om-Tsor, and used its reality-warping abilities to prevent the world governments from instigating a nuclear war.

Iris Wildthyme helped Jacqueline Susann write *The Love Machine*.[76] The trauma caused by Charles Manson and his followers provided sustinence to Huitzilin.[77]

From their base on the Moon, the Threshold watched Neil Armstrong land.[78] **The tenth Doctor and Martha watched the Moon landing four times.**[79]

---

73 *Instruments of Darkness.* This might be the same car the eighth Doctor drives in the early EDAs.
74 Dating *Blink* (X3.10) - The year is given, first of all in the graffiti that the Doctor leaves for Sally to find in 2007. The Doctor and Martha mention that the moon landing hasn't happened yet - this occurred on 20th July, 1969.
75 Dating *Revolution Man* (EDA #21) - The date is given (p223).
76 *The Blue Angel.* The novel was published in 1969.
77 *The Left-Handed Hummingbird.* No specific actions on Manson's part are mentioned, but the infamous

"Helter Skelter" murders took place in August 1969, and the most prominent victim, actress Sharon Tate, was killed 8th August. Page 243 establishes that Huitzilin merely fed off Manson's actions, but didn't "possess" or influence him as is sometimes claimed.
78 "Wormwood". The *TV Comic* story "Moon Landing" predicted the first Moon landing would occur in 1970. Richard Lazarus namechecks Armstrong in *The Lazarus Experiment*.
79 *Blink*. These were separate occasions from their being stranded in 1969.

The Unit Era

Establishing when the UNIT stories take place is probably the most contentious *Doctor Who* continuity issue.

The UNIT stories are set in an undefined "end of the twentieth century" era that could more or less comfortably fit at any time between the mid-sixties and mid-nineties (but no further, as the Doctor is specifically exiled to "the twentieth century").

Some *Doctor Who* fans have insisted on trying to pin down the dates more precisely, and some have even claimed to have "found the right answer". But all of us face the problem that as successive production teams came and went, a mass of contradictory, ambiguous and circumstantial evidence built up. To come up with a consistent timeframe, this evidence must be prioritised, and some of it has to be rationalised away or ignored.

It is a matter of individual judgement which clues are important. The best chronologies are aware of the problem and admit they're coming down on one side of the argument, while the worst blithely assert they alone have the right answer while not noticing they've missed half the evidence.

I was wrong in the Virgin version of this book when I said there was no right answer. The problem is that there are several, mutually incompatible, right answers.

It happens that a number of firm, unambiguous dates are given in dialogue during the course of the series:

1. *The Web of Fear* (broadcast 1968) is the sequel to *The Abominable Snowmen* and features the first appearance of Lethbridge-Stewart. There, Victoria and Anne Travers establish that *The Abominable Snowmen* was set in "1935". Earlier in the same story, Professor Travers had said that this was "over forty years ago". *The Invasion* "must be four years" after that, according to the Brigadier.

Some chronologies have made heroic efforts to ignore or reinterpret this, with *About Time*'s "His mumbled 'more than forty years ago' is a spur-of-the-moment estimate, and it's not unreasonable to assume he meant 'more than thirty years ago' " being only the most recent example. This line of thought usually leads to 44 being added to 1935 to get 1967 or 1968, and liberal use of the phrase "rounding up". But using conventional maths and English, the only possible reading of the lines is that *The Web of Fear* is set in or after 1975 and that *The Invasion*, the first story to feature UNIT, was broadcast in 1968 but was set no earlier than 1979.

2. In *Pyramids of Mars* (broadcast 1975) the Doctor and Sarah both say that she is "from 1980". Here, there's a little room for interpretation, but not much. The most literal reading has to be that *The Time Warrior*, Sarah's first story, is set in 1980. The only plausible alternative is that

she's been travelling with the Doctor for some years, and that she is referring to the date of *Terror of the Zygons*, her last visit to Earth in her timezone. Either way it refers to a story featuring UNIT.

Anyone trying to contradict Sarah's statement is suggesting that they know better than she does which *year* she comes from. It is difficult to believe that Sarah is rounding up, that she comes from the mid-seventies and simply means "I'm from around that time". The year is specified so precisely, and it jarred when the story was broadcast in 1975, just as it would if anyone now claimed to be from 2020. This isn't "vague" or "ambiguous", as neither she or the Doctor say she's "from around then" or "from the late nineteen-seventies/eighties" - they actually specify a year, and not the easy option of "1975", which would have been a conveniently rounded-up figure that would have brought the threat to history closer to home for the viewing audience. And to cap it all, they then go to a devastated "1980". So, Sarah comes from 1980.

3. *K9 and Company* and *Mawdryn Undead*, two stories from the 1980s, are set the UNIT era in the years they were first broadcast.

K9 and Company is set in late December 1981, and K9 has been crated up waiting for Sarah since 1978. The format document for the proposed spin-off series stated that Sarah was born in "1949" and that "she spent three years travelling in Space and Time (15.12.73-23.10.76)". This story is "canon", as Sarah and K9 appeared together in *The Five Doctors, School Reunion* and *SJA: Invasion of the Bane*. If we discount the dates for her travels given in the document (they don't, after all, appear on screen), nothing contradicts the "1980" reference ... but it means K9 was waiting for her *before* she met the Doctor. This needn't be a problem, however - he clearly delivered Sarah to the wrong end of the country, so why not K9 a couple of years early? It might even explain why Sarah in *School Reunion* thinks the Doctor abandoned her after *The Hand of Fear*, rather than thanking him for the gift.

But *Mawdryn Undead* is impossible to rationalise away that easily. Broadcast in 1983, it states that the Brigadier retired a year before 1977, presumably after Season Thirteen, which was broadcast in 1976. A host of references pin down the dating for *Mawdryn Undead* more precisely. There are two timezones, and these are unambiguously "1977" (where the Queen's Silver Jubilee is being celebrated) and "1983".

So, the Brigadier retired in 1976.

4. *Battlefield* is set "a few years" in Ace's future - apparently in the mid-to-late 1990s. According to the story's author, Ben Aaronovitch, it takes place in "1997". Whatever the case, it is established once again that the UNIT stories are "a few years" in the future. The same writer's *Remembrance of the Daleks* also provides upper and lower limits - UNIT is not around in 1963 when the story is set, but the Doctor rhetorically asks Ace (from the mid-eighties) about the events of *The Web of Fear* and *Terror of the Zygons*.

Thousands of words have been written trying to discount or reinterpret either the *Pyramids of Mars* or the *Mawdryn Undead* account of events. Dozens of distinct explanations - either within the logic of the fiction or taking account of production facts - have been proposed. They tend to be convoluted or to stretch the meanings of very plain English words beyond acceptable tolerances.

The only thing they have in common is that none of them would stand up in court. However you weigh up and prioritise evidence, the *Pyramids of Mars* and *Mawdryn Undead* dates are "as true" as each other. They are scripted and broadcast lines of dialogue within a single story that unambiguously state a firm date, then the characters go to that year and then the date is stated again.

Ultimately, the only way to come up with a consistent UNIT dating scheme is to pick one and ignore the other.

Broadly speaking, then, there are two schools of thought. Either the stories are set in the "near future", as was originally stated (a view that actually elides *two* distinct accounts, as *The Invasion* had the UNIT era starting no earlier than 1979, but *Pyramids of Mars* pretty much ended it in 1980); or they are set in the year of broadcast, as was stated in the early 1980s (which glosses over / ignores / corrects what was said in those previous stories) in a version of history where certain aspects of technological progress were more advanced and the political situation was different.

As noted in the individual UNIT story entries, there are a wealth of clues beyond what's actually said that might be used to tip the balance one way or the other. Different chronologies give different weight to these, and so come to different conclusions. But most try to address the following areas:

1. Technology: There are an abundance of references to scientific developments that hadn't happened at the time the UNIT stories were broadcast, but were reasonable extrapolations of what the near future would hold.

The technology is far in advance of the early nineteen-seventies: there are talking computers, compact walkie talkies, experimental alloys, laser guns and robots. Colour televisions and even colour videophones are commonplace. Man has landed on Mars, there are space freighters and advanced artificial intelligences. Comprehensive space and alternative energy programmes are underway.

It could be argued that the UNIT stories are set in a parallel history where by (say) 1970 mankind was more technologically advanced than the real 1970. One obvious reason for this might be that scientists had access to an abundance of alien technology from all the failed invasions, and so made great technological progress. There are examples of high technology being developed due to alien influence in some stories. For example, the interstitial time travel of *The Time Monster* is inspired by the Master, not because it's part of mankind's natural progress. There are other stories with no obvious alien influence, like *The War Machines* with its prototype internet and advanced artificial intelligence.

However, there's no evidence that, say, the British mission to Mars seen in *The Ambassadors of Death* uses alien technology (rather the opposite). One difference between it and *The War Machines* is that there are several explicit references to things being obsolete that were state-of-the-art at the time of broadcast. While it's a little far-fetched that Britain could mount such an ambitious programme, there's no technology in the story that NASA weren't planning to have by the 1980s. In 1970, NASA planned - not just hoped - to have a man on Mars by 1982.

2. Historical and Political Details: Again, the evidence overwhelmingly suggests that either the political history of the early nineteen-seventies is very different to reality, or the UNIT stories aren't set in the early 1970s.

There's a Prime Minister called "Jeremy" in *The Green Death*, and one who's a woman by the time of *Terror of the Zygons*. Both of these are clear - and clearly tongue-in-cheek - references to someone who was an actual opposition leader with an outside chance of winning the next election or the one after that. The United Nations is more powerful than its seventies equivalent. The Cold War has been over for "years" by the end of the era. Environmentalism has become a matter for Westminster politicians and civil servants. All of these things are clearly reasonable extrapolations, not a reflection, of the situation at the time the stories were made.

Two pieces of dialogue suggest it is the early seventies: in *Doctor Who and the Silurians*, a taxi driver wants his fare in pre-decimal currency, and Mao Tse Tung seems to be alive at the time of *The Mind of Evil* (he died in 1976).

3. Calendars: The month a UNIT story is set is often specified or can be inferred from information in a story, or by close observation of calendars on walls or other such set dressing. We are told that the barrow in *The Daemons* (broadcast 1971) is opened on Beltane (30th April). We can infer that it's a Saturday or - more probably - Sunday (see the entry for that story). So, taken literally, that would mean that it was set in a year when 30th April fell on a Sunday - in the seventies, that would be 1972 or 1978.

While there have been some excellent attempts to reconcile this sort of information, this is not a level of detail the production team ever went into, and this is not a "key" to revealing a consistent chronology. The evidence is often contradictory, even within individual stories: three calendars appear in *The Green Death*, one stating that the story is set in February of a leap year, the other two say it is April.

4. Fashions: Except for *The Invasion* and *Battlefield*, the clothes, haircuts and cars all resemble those of the year the programme was made. There was no attempt to mock-up car number plates or predict future fashions. The UNIT soldiers sport haircuts that would have been distinctly non-regulation in the 1970s, but this is just as true today. The UNIT era looks and feels like the early 1970s, the characters have many of the attitudes and concerns of people in the seventies. However, is this evidence it was set in the early 1970s, or simply that it was made in the early 1970s?

5. Authorial Intention: We might also want to refer to interviews with the production team, to find out what they intended.

Derrick Sherwin, the producer at the time the UNIT format was introduced, said in the *Radio Times* of 19th June, 1969, that Season Seven would be set in "a time not many years distant from now when such things as space stations will be actuality". In an interview with the *Daily Mail* two days later, Jon Pertwee stated that his Doctor would be exiled to Earth "in the 1980s". The *Doctor Who and the Sea-Devils* novelisation by Malcolm Hulke, published in 1974, said that "North Sea oil had started gushing in 1977".

The Terrestrial Index claimed that the decision was made to redate the UNIT era was taken when real life overtook it, but that didn't happen. When asked in *DWB #58* why the dates for *Mawdryn Undead* contradicted what was established in the Pertwee era, Eric Saward, the script editor for the story, admitted that the 1977/1983 dates were "a mistake". In fact, the only reason the Brigadier is even in *Mawdryn Undead* is that William Russell wasn't available to play Ian Chesterton in that story, and without the 1977 date given in *Mawdryn Undead*, there's little to debate.

On the other hand, *The Making of Doctor Who*, written by Malcolm Hulke and Terrance Dicks and published in 1972, placed *Spearhead From Space* in "1970".

The editors of the early New and Missing Adventures consciously chose to set the UNIT stories on or about the year they were broadcast. In practice, when a date is specified it was left pretty much to the discretion of an individual author, and there were a number of discrepancies (see the entries for each story). More recent novels mentioning UNIT have been far more coy about specifying dates, for the most part, and a number (like *No Future*, *The Dying Days* and *Interference*) have suggested fictional reasons for the confusion.

6. Real Life: The late eighties / early nineties fit the UNIT era almost perfectly - the Cold War was over, China was hardline communist, the British government was unstable, there was a female prime minister, the UN was powerful, environmental issues were at the forefront of political debate, there was video conferencing, British scientists were working on their own space probes and Microsoft were putting a computer in every home and making IE's attempts at world domination look half-hearted.

To top it all, a trend for seventies retro meant that the fashionistas were all dressing like Jo Grant. The Doctor's reference to Batman in *Inferno* was clearly because he'd just seen the Tim Burton movie. It's uncanny.

7. Other Reference Books: The balance of fan opinion, or at least the fans who write books, has definitely tipped towards setting the UNIT era in or around the year of broadcast. *The Terrestrial Index*, *The Discontinuity Guide*, *Who Killed Kennedy*, *Timelink* and *About Time* all - give or take a year here or there - concur. A clear majority of the original novels do. However, the BBC-published *Doctor Who - The Legend* sets the UNIT era in the "near future" and concludes that *Mawdryn Undead* is the anomaly.

The Conclusion: It is very tempting to hope for a right answer, but *Doctor Who* is fiction, not a documentary and a "one right answer" just does not - cannot - exist. Even if we limit ourselves solely to dates specifically and unambiguously given in on-screen dialogue, then the Brigadier retires from UNIT three years before his first appearance as the commanding officer of UNIT. It is utterly impossible to try to incorporate every calendar, E-reg car and videophone into one consistent timeframe. People who claim to have done so have invariably, and by definition, missed or deliberately ignored some piece of evidence established somewhere.

However, none of the dates given place the "UNIT era" earlier than the late sixties or later than the early eighties. A right answer doesn't exist, but something everyone ought to be able to agree on is that the UNIT stories took place in "the seventies", give or take a year or so.

My personal preference, for the record, is that the UNIT era takes place in the near future, five or so years after broadcast.

For the Purposes of this Book: Even though it's not possible to specify the year, it *is* possible to come up with a consistent timeline. Many UNIT stories contain some reference to other UNIT stories, so it is possible to place them relative to each other. Furthermore, the month a story is set in is often given. While there are inconsistencies (which I've noted), it's therefore possible to write a broadly consistent history of the "UNIT era".

I've separated the stories of the UNIT era from those of

the other contemporary and near-contemporary stories, and instead talk in "UNIT years". "UNIT Year 1" in this scheme is the year that *The Invasion* and *Spearhead from Space* are set. This only applies to the "UNIT era" - the stories set in the seventies - by the time of *K9 and Company* in 1981, real life seems to have caught up with the near-future of the series whichever way you cut it.

Depending on which story's dating scheme you adopt (and give or take a year in all cases), Unit Year 1 is:

The Invasion - 1979
Pyramids of Mars - 1974
Mawdryn Undead - 1969

Unit Year -5

Around this time, the Cybermen contacted Tobias Vaughn, who offered them help with their invasion. Soon afterward, Vaughn's company, International Electromatics, marketed the micromonolithic circuit. It revolutionised electronics, and made IE the world leader in the field.[80]

Unit Year -4

THE WEB OF FEAR[81] -> Mysterious cobwebs started to appear across London, the fog thickened and people were attacked by "bears" and "monsters" in the Underground. Londoners fled in terror, and the army was called in to restore order. They found themselves under siege in the London Underground, where the disturbances were concentrated.

Faced with an attack from "the Intelligence", a sen-

tience billions of years older than Earth and with its own army of robot Yeti, the army were reduced to blowing up tunnels to try to contain the situation. The Doctor arrived, and met Colonel Lethbridge-Stewart for the first time. Together, they fought the Yeti, and the Doctor defeated the Intelligence.

This became known as the "London Event", and the official story was that there had been an industrial accident. Lethbridge-Stewart retained "The Locus", a small carved statuette of a Yeti as a memento. Six months later he met Air Vice-Marshall "Chunky" Gilmore in the Alexander Club and learnt that Earth had been invaded in the winter of 1963. He also learned there was evidence of aliens visiting Earth since the time of the Pharoahs.[82]

The public were told that the Yeti incident was actually a nerve gas attack.[83] Lethbridge-Stewart attended a Middle East Peace Conference.[84]

Aware that the world faced new threats, the United Nations Intelligence Taskforce (UNIT) was established.[85] Lethbridge-Stewart appeared before the UN Security Council and, in part, UNIT was formed because of his efforts.[86] The Russian branch of UNIT was called Operativnaya Gruppa Rasvedkoy Obyedinyonnih Natsiy (OGRON).[87] The French branch was called NUIT.[88] There's a UNIT liaison office in Bombay.[89] There was also a South East Asian branch, UNIT-SEA.[90]

Enabling legislation was passed in the UK (it was drafted by the future Minister for Ecology).[91] Alistair Gordon Lethbridge-Stewart, the Scots Guards Colonel who had led the soldiers that repelled the Yetis in the Underground, was promoted to Brigadier and made commanding officer of the British UNIT contingent.[92]

Gas warfare was banned by international agree-

---

80 "Five years" before *The Invasion* according to Vaughn.

81 Dating *The Web of Fear* (5.5) - It is the near future. Professor Travers declares that the events of *The Abominable Snowmen* were "over forty years ago", Victoria says that they were in "1935" and no-one contradicts her, so it's at least 1975.

Some fans have suggested that Travers is senile or confused, but in the story he's clearly the opposite. All things considered, he's sharp-witted and in command of the facts. The maps of the London Underground that we see render the network as it was in 1968, and don't show the Victoria or Jubilee lines, which opened on 7th March, 1969, and 1st May, 1979, respectively.

Downtime states that this story took place "some twenty five years before", in "1968".

82 *Downtime*

83 *The Web of Fear*

84 *The Paradise of Death*. This happened "just before he joined UNIT".

85 *The Invasion*. UNIT is not set up specifically to fight aliens, but to "investigate the unexplained".

86 *Who Killed Kennedy*

87 *Emotional Chemistry*

88 *The Dying Days*

89 *Island of Death*

90 *Bullet Time*

91 *The Time Monster* - the "Seventh Enabling Act" allows the Brigadier to take command of government forces - and *The Green Death*.

92 Between *The Web of Fear* and *The Invasion*, although there's no indication in the TV series as to precisely when. In *Spearhead from Space*, the Brigadier tells Liz Shaw that "since UNIT was formed" there have been two alien invasions. *The Web of Fear* took place before UNIT was formed, and so we only saw UNIT fight one set of aliens, in *The Invasion*. I take it that the Brigadier was simplifying events and referring to the two televised Troughton stories that he appeared in. If not, the Doctor does not seem to have been involved in fend-

ment.[93] SOS signals were abandoned.[94] The British space programme was blossoming with a series of Mars Probe Missions. Space technology had dramatically improved since the old moonshot days. The new fuel variant M-3, though highly volatile, provided a great deal more thrust than conventional fuels, and decontamination procedures had been reduced from two days to one hour. Space Research took place at the Space Centre in London, not far from UNIT HQ. In this complex was Space Control (callsign: "Control") where missions were co-ordinated. Astronauts were selected from the military.[95]

The British astronauts Grosvenor and Guest became the first men on Mars. They planted the Union Flag on Mount Olympus.[96] **The British astronaut Carrington, part of the Mars Probe 6 mission, discovered radioactive aliens on Mars that killed his crew. Returning to Earth,** and terrified by what he saw as a threat to humanity, Carrington formed an elaborate plan to destroy them. On his return, he was promoted to General and led the newly-formed Space Security Department.[97]

(20th December, 1968 - 30th January, 1969) - THE LEFT-HANDED HUMMINGBIRD[98] **->** Early in its history, UNIT had a Paranormal Division. After extensive trials, they recruited six genuine human psychics. The division was run by Lieutenant Hamlet Macbeth, and investigated Fortean events. Following "The Happening", a massive psychic event in St John's Wood, London on 21st December, 1968, the Paranormal Division was disbanded. Ace foiled an attempt to kill the Beatles on the roof of the Apple building on 30th January, 1969. At least two of the Doctor's incarnations went to Woodstock.

---

ing off the other invasion, as he never refers to it. In *Spearhead from Space* and *Terror of the Zygons*, the Brigadier implies that UNIT existed before he was placed in charge of it.

93 *The Mind of Evil*

94 "Years" before *The Ambassadors of Death*.

95 *The Ambassadors of Death*

96 "Over twenty years" before *The Dying Days* (so before 1977). This was a Mars Probe mission as seen in *The Ambassadors of Death*.

97 Carrington set off for Mars no later than thirty months before *The Ambassadors of Death*.

BRITAIN'S MISSIONS TO MARS: The timeline for the backstory of *The Ambassadors of Death*, and therefore the British space programme, is unclear.

It is a long-term project. Carrington was on Mars Probe 6, and the "missing" ship is Mars Probe 7. Mars Probe 7 takes between seven and eight months to get to Mars (various characters say it takes "seven months", "seven and half months" and "nearly eight months"), the astronauts spend two weeks on the surface and logically need seven or so months to return to Earth. That's a round trip of about fifteen months.

Assuming all missions followed that timescale and that only one mission was underway at any one time, then even if each mission was launched the day the previous one returned, this would stretch the Mars programme back eight or nine years. However, not all the Apollo missions were designed to land a man on the Moon, so we could reasonably infer that some of the early Mars Probes were shorter test flights. Nowhere, though, is it stated that Carrington was the *first* man on Mars, and *The Dying Days* makes clear that he wasn't.

Furthermore, when Recovery 7 is lost, we're told that Recovery 8 isn't due for service for "three months" - presumably following a schedule that allows it to rendezvous with Mars Probe 8. It seems unlikely that Recovery 8 would be prepped before Mars Probe 8 is launched, and it's much more plausible that the planners expect Mars Probe 8 to *return* to Earth then. The Mars Probe 8 mission might have been aborted when contact was lost with Mars Probe 7, or it might have continued (as it's not mentioned, we have no way of knowing). Whatever the case, it suggests that Mars Probe 8 was launched while Mars Probe 7 was underway and at least three months ago, given that it's now three months away from Earth.

Either way, we know Mars Probe 7 wasn't launched until Mars Probe 6 returned. So Mars Probe 6 launched at least thirty months before *The Ambassadors of Death*. We know that Dr Taltalian has been working at the Space Centre for "two years", so the Mars programme has been around at least that long.

The Invasion states that only America and Russia can launch a moon mission, and *The Ambassadors of Death* is almost certainly set within a year of that. This means one of two things. Either the first Mars Probe was launched after *The Invasion*, or it's a type of ship that can't be retasked for a Moon mission.

No evidence suggests that the history of space travel in the fifties and sixties in *Doctor Who* differs from the history we know. On the contrary, there's evidence that it's the same: Yuri Gagarin is named as the first man in space in *The Seeds of Death*, Ben (from 1966) is from a time before Lunar landings according to *The Tenth Planet* and Richard Lazarus mentions Armstrong in *The Lazarus Experiment*. The Moon landing takes place in 1969 according to *Blink*.

98 Dating *The Left-Handed Hummingbird* (NA #21) - The UNIT stories are set the year of broadcast. The last time Cristian Alvarez saw the Doctor was "January the thirtieth, 1969" (p8). The TARDIS arrives in that timezone on "December 20, 1968" (p122). "The Happening" takes place on "December 21" (p163).

99 *The Blue Tooth*. The scoutship is clearly reconnoitering Earth in preparation for *The Invasion*.

Unit Year 1

A Cyber-scout ship surveyed Earth in preparation for an invasion, but the vessel crashed near Cambridge and the pilot died on impact. It remained buried until Gareth Arnold, a local dentist, happened upon it some years later.[99]

(April) UNIT radar stations tracked a shower of meteorites in an odd formation over Essex.[100]

(Summer) THE INVASION[101] -> UNIT began monitoring the activities of International Electromatics after hundreds of UFO sightings occurred on IE property. IE now controlled every computer line in the world by undercutting the competition, and Tobias Vaughn had built a business empire around his philosophy of uniformity and exact duplication. One of IE's most successful products was a disposable radio, which had sold ten million units. Vaughn was in league with the Cybermen, who were using his company as a front for their invasion plans. The Doctor and UNIT defeated the Cybermen. Vaughn was apparently killed.

One cybership crashed in the South Pole.[102]

After the collapse of IE, Ashley Chapel, Vaughn's chief scientist, set up his own company named Ashley Chapel Logistics.[103] Vaughn, though, had survived by downloading his consciousness into a waiting robot body. For the next thousand years, he would secretly run a succession of massive electronics corporations that developed state-of-the-art equipment. He would re-encounter the Doctor in 2975.[104] The public were told the mass unconsciousness that occurred during the Cybermen incursion was because Earth passed through the tail of a comet. Isobel Watkins' photos of Cybermen were dismissed as fakes.[105]

The "Big Bug Era" began, as Earth was invaded and threatened by alien life. Many books and fanzines trying to catalogue and expose these invasions were published.[106] One of the most popular fanzines was Who's Who and What's That. The government, though, covered much of UNIT's work with D-notices, making it difficult to keep track of the dates. The time-displaced Isaac Summerfield set up a secret organisation to "mop up" after UNIT, with the intention of getting stranded aliens home. Initially, it was based in Llarelli.[107]

Mars Probe 7 was launched. After seven months, Mars Probe 7 landed and radio contact was lost, but two weeks later it took off from Mars ... or at least, something did.[108]

---

100 "Six months" before *Spearhead from Space*.
101 Dating *The Invasion* (6.3) - It is the near future. According to the Brigadier in this story, the events of *The Web of Fear* "must be four years ago, now", making it at least 1979. A surveillance photo has the caption "E091/5D/78", the last two digits of which might (or might not) be the year.

There are advanced, voice-operated computers and "Public Video" videophones. UNIT has an IE computer, and use some IE components in their radios and radar. UNIT has compact TM45 radios with a range of 50 miles, while IE personnel have wrist-communicators. IE has an elaborate electronic security and surveillance system. There are electric cars and hypersonic jets.

There's no suggestion that this is because IE has been given Cyber-technology - the computer in IE's reception (which also answers the phones) uses ALGOL and blows up after failing to solve a simple formula, neither of which indicate that a superior alien technology is involved.

There are many communications satellites in orbit, and UNIT has the authority to fire nuclear rockets into space. "Only the Americans and the Russians" have rockets capable of reaching the Moon - the Russians are just about to launch a manned orbital survey of the Moon, and it would apparently only take "ten hours" to reach it. The IE guards and many UNIT troops wear futuristic uniforms, while Vaughn wears a collarless shirt. The Brigadier's "anti-feminist" ideas are outdated.

The Doctor jokes that as it's Britain and there are clouds in the sky, it must be "summertime".

A casting document written by director Douglas Camfield suggested *The Invasion* was set "about the year 1976 AD". The *Radio Times* in some regions said that the date was "about the year 1975", and the continuity announcer echoed this at the beginning of the broadcast of Part One. In *Dalek*, the plaque below the Cybermen head reads "Extraterrestrial Cyborg Specimen, recovered from underground sewer, location London, United Kingdom, date 1975"... almost certainly a reference to this story. However, the Cybermen head is from the wrong era (it's from *Revenge of the Cybermen*, not *The Invasion*) and the plaque isn't readable on screen, so there are grounds to discount it. According to *Iceberg*, this story takes place "ten years" (p90) before *The Tenth Planet* (meaning 1976), in "the 70s" (p2). *No Future* suggested "1970", (p2). *Original Sin* claims that this story was set in "the 1970s" (p281). *Millennial Rites* suggests that the UNIT era took place in "the nineteen eighties" (p15), with *The Invasion* a little over "twenty years ago" (meaning 1979). The 1979 date is repeated in *The Face of the Enemy* (p21).
102 *Iceberg*
103 *Millennial Rites*
104 *Original Sin*
105 *Who Killed Kennedy*
106 *No Future*
107 *Return of the Living Dad*. *Who's Who and What's That* is also mentioned in *The Dying Days*.
108 Mars Probe 7 is launched fifteen and a half months

(October, "months" after *The Invasion*) - SPEAR-HEAD FROM SPACE[109] -> UNIT went on a covert recruitment drive, bringing Liz Shaw up from Cambridge to act as Scientific Advisor. The very same day, reporters were tipped off that a mysterious patient with two hearts was present at Ashbridge Cottage Hospital.

This "spaceman" was the third Doctor, exiled to Earth in the twentieth-century timezone by the Time Lords. He turned up the morning after a meteorite shower, and UNIT were soon on the scene. The meteorites were Nestene Energy Units, part of a plan to conquer the Earth using killer automata Autons. With the Doctor's help, UNIT led an assault on a plastics factory in Essex, mere hours after reports surfaced of "walking shop dummies" in city centres. They defeated the Nestene.

Captain Mike Yates led the clean-up operation after the Nestene Invasion, and discovered a single Energy Unit that had not been recovered by the Autons. It remained UNIT property, but was loaned to the National Space Museum.[110] One of the UNIT soldiers involved with the first Auton invasion was called Gareth Wostencroft.[111]

The Nestene invasion was covered up as a terrorist attack, which became known as Black Thursday. A report filed by journalist James Stevens had all references to UNIT erased. This prompted him to start investigating the mysterious organisation, an undertaking he would pursue for several years.[112]

The Vault, Department C-19's storehouse of discarded alien artefacts, recovered two Nestene Energy Units. Dr Ingrid Krafchin, a researcher for SeneNet, began experiments with plastic.[113] "Doctor John Smith" was put on UNIT's payroll, but did not cash his cheques.[114]

Unit Year 2

(Winter) - DOCTOR WHO AND THE SILURIANS[115] -> UNIT investigated power losses at the experimental Wenley Moor research centre. These were caused by the Silurians, reptile people who ruled the Earth millions of years before, and who had revived from suspended animation. The Silurians saw the humans as apes and plotted to wipe them out - first with a plague, then by dispersing the Van Allen Belt. This would have heated Earth to a level suitable for Silurians, but not to human life. The Doctor attempted to negotiate, but the

---

before *The Ambassadors of Death*, and contact was lost "eight months" before *The Ambassadors of Death*.

109 Dating *Spearhead from Space* (7.1) - There's no firm evidence if this is near future or contemporary. The Brigadier tells Liz Shaw here that "in the last decade we have been sending probes deeper and deeper into space", but that needn't mean humanity's first-ever space probe was launched exactly ten years ago.

The Brigadier states in *Planet of the Spiders* that "months" elapsed between *The Invasion* and *Spearhead from Space* (meaning 1979). The weather is "uncommonly warm", suggesting it is Autumn or Winter. According to *The Face of the Enemy* (p21) it was "two years" before (meaning 1981). It was "five years ago" in *No Future* (meaning 1971). *Who Killed Kennedy* and *The Scales of Injustice* both state this story takes place in October, which is also the month the story was filmed.

110 *Terror of the Autons*, also referred to in *The Eye of the Giant*. Mike Yates doesn't appear on screen until *Terror of the Autons*. He apparently doesn't remember Nestene Energy Units in *The Scales of Injustice*.

111 *Dominion*

112 *Who Killed Kennedy* is James Stevens' account of the early UNIT years, and allocates firm dates for the stories, specifically:

Remembrance of the Daleks (November 1963)
The Web of Fear (August 1966)
The Invasion (Spring 1969)
Spearhead from Space (October 1969)

Doctor Who and the Silurians (November 1969)
The Ambassadors of Death (December 1969)
Inferno (February 1970)
Terror of the Autons (April 1970)
The Mind of Evil (November 1970)
The Claws of Axos
The Daemons (May 1971)
Day of the Daleks (September 1971)

In *The Dying Days*, I rather cheekily claimed that the government had insisted the dates be changed before allowing the book to be published.

113 *Business Unusual*

114 *No Future*, which clashes with the Doctor saying he was "unpaid" in *Terror of the Autons*. This was the "early seventies" in *Return of the Living Dad*.

115 Dating *Doctor Who and the Silurians* (7.2) - There's conflicting dating evidence. A taxi driver asks for a fare of "10/6", so this story appears to be set before the introduction of decimal currency in February 1971, but the cyclotron is a futuristic experimental machine that converts nuclear energy directly into electricity.

There's no indication how long it's been since *Spearhead from Space*, but the Doctor has settled in with UNIT and (recently) acquired Bessie. People are wearing winter clothes. The New Adventure *Blood Heat* states that this story is set in "1973".

116 *The Scales of Injustice*. Okdel was named in *Doctor Who and The Cave-Monsters*, the novelisation of *Doctor*

Brigadier triggered explosives that sealed off the Silurian base and possibly killed the Silurians within.

This was Earth Reptile Shelter 873, led by Okdel L'da.[116] James Stevens followed a tip and managed to (briefly) phone the Brigadier at Wenley Moor. The plague spread to Paris airport. Four hundred people died, twenty of them abroad, and three ministers resigned.[117] The Brigadier was issued with direct orders to destroy the Silurians.[118] Those orders came from C-19.[119] Mike Yates lead a team looking for surviving Silurian technology.[120]

Mortimus (also known as the Monk) used the captured Chronovore Artemis to create an alternative history where the Doctor died during the Wenley Moor adventure.[121]

> = In a parallel timeline, the Doctor was captured and killed by the Silurians before he could find an antidote to their plague. Millions died in a matter of days, a time that would become known to the survivors as "the Nightmare".[122]

The Silurian Imorkal was hatched. In one reality he was one of the Silurian masters of Earth. In the proper timeline, he eventually worked for NATO.[123] A UNIT station in Antarctica investigated a possible Silurian shelter uncovered in the 1920s.[124] Another Silurian shelter was discovered and destroyed in Oregon.[125] The government destabilised under political pressure following the plague.[126] Anne Travers became scientific advisor to the cabinet.[127]

THE AMBASSADORS OF DEATH[128] -> Recovery 7 was dispatched, piloted by Charles Van Lyden, to give assistance to Mars Probe 7, which was still maintaining radio silence after lifting off from Mars. Van Lyden linked up with and entered Mars Probe 7, but contact was again lost. Recovery 8 couldn't be prepared for launch for ten days, forcing the ground crew to await developments.

Recovery 7 returned to Earth, but not with the Earth astronauts aboard. Instead, it contained three ambassadors from the race of radioactive aliens that General Carrington had encountered on Mars. Furthering his private agenda, Carrington intercepted the ambassadors and directed them, via a signalling device, to commit acts of terror. Carrington hoped to portray the aliens as invaders, mobilizing a global effort to destroy them, but the Doctor and UNIT exposed the scheme. The ambassadors and Earth astronauts were exchanged, and Carrington was discredited.

Who and the Silurians.
117 *Who Killed Kennedy.* We see the Brigadier take the phone call in *Doctor Who and the Silurians.*
118 *Blood Heat*
119 *The Scales of Injustice*
120 *The Eye of the Giant, The Scales of Injustice*
121 *No Future*, a reference to *Blood Heat*.
122 *Blood Heat*
123 *Eternity Weeps*
124 *The Scales of Injustice*, a reference to the Audio Visuals story *Endurance*.
125 *The Devil Goblins from Neptune*
126 *Who Killed Kennedy*
127 "Eighteen years" before *Millennial Rites*, so in 1981. It is stated that *Inferno* was "early on in her tenure" and Anne had responsibilities for the British Space Programme (p14). That would place the UNIT stories later than most other references, but this dating scheme is perfectly compatible with that in *The Web of Fear*, which is after all where Anne Travers first appeared. That was "twenty five years ago" (so around 1974), meaning there were seven years between *The Web of Fear* and her appointment.
128 Dating *The Ambassadors of Death* (7.3) - This story is very clearly set in the near future. Britain has an established programme of manned missions to Mars. Professor Cornish remarks that decontamination takes "under an hour...it used to take two days" (the time it took the lunar astronauts when the story was made).

There are colour videophones and we see a machine capable of automatically displaying star charts. SOS messages were abandoned "years ago".

Those advocating that the UNIT stories are set in the year of broadcast admit this story causes them problems. One argument (used in both *Timelink* and *About Time*) concedes that Mars missions weren't possible in 1970, but that as we still haven't landed a man on Mars, it doesn't prove this story is set in the near future. It's an odd train of logic to say that something too advanced for 1980 (or indeed the world of today) therefore indicates a 1970 setting.

Leaving that aside, when *The Ambassadors of Death* was made, it wasn't science fantasy. NASA had just landed on the Moon and had plans to put a man on Mars in the nineteen-eighties. This wasn't just a hope as the technology to get to Mars existed, at least in prototype form, and only a lack of political will and funding prevented it. At that point, NASA was seriously projecting that half of American employees would be working in space by 2050.

At the time that *The Ambassadors of Death* was made, then, what was shown wasn't possible - but it would be, for NASA, in about ten years. The most implausible aspect was that Britain could do the same - but there had been a British space programme up until the early sixties, and, again, it was lack of funding rather than lack of expertise that killed it off.

The Doctor is still bitter about the events of *Doctor*

The new channel BBC3 launched with coverage of the Recovery 7 capsule.[129] The Doctor appeared on *Nationwide* during this incident.[130] The aliens conducted limited diplomatic discussions, but concluded that mankind wasn't ready for their technology. Contact was limited, as the aliens were a plutonium-based lifeform.[131] Mars Probe 6 ended up in C-19's Vault.[132] The Mars Probe Programme continued for several more years.[133]

Jones, a hired killer from the Vault, abducted a young secretary called Roberta. Vault scientists gave her cybernetic implants and false memories.[134]

(late July) - INFERNO[135] -> **Professor Stahlman discovered a gas underneath the crust of the Earth, and claimed that it might be "a vast new storehouse of energy which has lain dormant since the beginning of time". The government funded a drilling project (nicknamed "Inferno" by some of the workers) based in Eastchester. But as the project's robot drill approached its target, a green slime came to the surface. On skin contact, people became savage beastmen, Primords.**

= **"Sideways in time", Britain was a republic, and it had been since at least 1943 when the Defence of the Republic Act was passed. A fascist** regime had executed the royal family. In this version of events, Professor Stahlmann's project was a day ahead of ours, and was under the aegis of the Republican Security Forces. This world was destroyed when Stahlmann's project released torrents of lava and armies of Primords.

On our Earth, the project was halted at the insistence of Sir Keith Gold and UNIT.

= The Britain of the parallel world was run by an alternate version of the Doctor.[136] In the parallel universe, the British Isles were destroyed in hours, the rest of Europe a day later. The entire world was devastated within thirty-six hours. The leaders of the American Confederation, India, White Russia and the Asian Co-prosperity Sphere, along with the new leader of the British Republic, were evacuated to Copernicus Base on the Moon. Once there, they formed the Conclave.[137]

C-19 acquired some of Stahlman's Gas.[138] The Doctor attended the wedding of Greg Sutton and Petra Williams. He met Ian Chesterton, who was now working at NASA, at the reception.[139] Greg Sutton gave Ian some fashion

---

Who and the Silurians, so this story probably happens only shortly afterwards. The Brigadier says he has known the Doctor "several years, on and off", so it's that long since *The Web of Fear*.

129 *Who Killed Kennedy*

130 "During that General Carrington business" according to *No Future*.

131 *The Dying Days*

132 *The Scales of Injustice*

133 Mars Probe 9 is referred to in *Dancing the Code*, and *The Dying Days* mentions Mars Probe 13.

THE BRITISH SPACE PROGRAMME: Perhaps because they are acutely aware of the threat from outer space, the British government seems to have invested heavily in the space programme before and during the UNIT era. In *Invasion of the Dinosaurs*, some very clever and important people are fooled into believing that a fleet of colony ships could be built and go on to reach another habitable planet, although Sarah knows that even the most advanced spaceship "would take hundreds of years" to do so, and it transpires the ships are fakes. In *The Android Invasion*, an experimental "space freighter" has been in service for at least two years. There's no obvious evidence that the British are using alien technology that they've recovered from one of the alien incursions in the sixties to speed up their space programme. On the contrary, they're using pretty basic rocket technology.

The Christmas Invasion features Britain sending an unmanned probe to Mars in late 2006, and portrays it as a pioneering effort.

134 *Business Unusual*

135 Dating *Inferno* (7.4) - This story seems to be set in the near future. The computer at the project uses perspex/crystalline memory blocks. Stahlman has a robot drill capable of boring down over twenty miles. A desk calendar in the parallel universe says it is "July 23rd", and the story runs for five days - the countdown we see early in the story says there is "59:28:47" remaining before penetration.

The word "Primord" is not used in dialogue, but appears in the on-screen credits. The name "Eastchester" is only used in a scene cut from the original broadcast (but retained in foreign prints and the BBC Video and DVD release), when the Doctor listens to a radio broadcast in the parallel universe. Stahlman spells his name with two "n"s in the parallel universe. The Doctor claims this is the first attempt to penetrate the Earth's crust, forgetting the attempt he'd seen in *The Underwater Menace*.

136 *Timewyrm: Revelation*

137 *The Face of the Enemy*

138 *The Scales of Injustice, Business Unusual*

139 *The Devil Goblins from Neptune. The Face of the Enemy* says Ian is on a year-long exchange programme.

140 *Byzantium!*

141 *Who Killed Kennedy*

142 "Seven or eight months" before *Scales of Injustice*,

advice - that he should buy an orange shirt and purple tie.[140] James Stevens tracked down the Suttons, who told him about "Project: Inferno" and the Doctor's involvement. The Suttons left the country shortly afterward.[141]

Two Irish twins, Ciara and Cellian, assisted Dr Krafchin in a number of plastics experiments. He offered them immortality, and their blood was replaced with Nestene Compound, a type of plastic. They become contract killers for the Vault.[142]

The Doctor gave a lecture tour in the United States that was really cover for UNIT recruitment operations. He met rocket scientist Von Braun. Soviet radar detected meteor impacts in Siberia, which unknown to them marked the arrival of the Waro on Earth. .The Brigadier met Soviet UNIT commander Captain Valentina Shuskin.[143] He also spent Christmas in Geneva on UNIT business.[144]

The Beatles reformed without Paul McCartney, but with two new members called Billy and Klaus.[145] Sarah Jane Smith went out with a Royal Navy officer named Sammy Brooks.[146]

Unit Year 3

(January) The Liberals formed a coalition government following a General Election.[147] (February) James Stevens wrote a series of articles for the *Daily Chronicle* that referred

to UNIT and C-19. These got him sacked, and his wife left him.[148] (March) UNIT moved to a new headquarters.[149] (Early March) Soviet satellites detected a vast mining operation in Siberia. All military attempts to investigate were wiped out. The Soviet branch of UNIT lobbied Geneva to send the Doctor.[150]

At the Vault, Grant Traynor injected Stahlman's Gas into a Doberman, creating the Stalker, a vicious killer animal.[151] (April / May) The Vault acquired a Venus flytrap large enough to eat a dog in Africa. They also stole a Blackbird stealth aeroplane.[152]

(May) - THE EYE OF THE GIANT[153] **->** The Doctor was sent an alien artefact that he discovered was emitting omicron radiation. He converted the Time/Space Visualiser into a space-time bridge to track the object's origin, and he and Liz Shaw wound up on Saluta in the Pacific in 1934.

> = Their actions in 1934 inadvertently created an alternative timeline ruled by The Goddess of the World, the starlet Nancy Grover. The Doctor returned to 1934 and set history back on the correct course.

THE BLUE TOOTH[154] **->** Gareth Arnold, a local dentist, had discovered the crashed Cyber-ship near Cambridge, and experimented upon the Cyber-metal within. He devel-

---

"twenty years" before *Business Unusual*.
143 "The previous year", "late last year" and "eight months" before *The Devil Goblins from Neptune*.
144 The Christmas before *The Scales of Injustice*.
145 *The Devil Goblins from Neptune*. The new members were presumably Billy Preston and Klaus Voormann.
   THE BEATLES: *Doctor Who* has a terrible record for predicting the future, one that can best be summed up by noting that *Battlefield* predicted a near future with Soviet soldiers operating under the UN's aegis on British soil - but between the story's filming and its broadcast, the Soviet Union collapsed. In the entire twenty-six-year run of classic *Doctor Who*, it made two successful predictions - that there would be a female British Prime Minister (*Terror of the Zygons*), and that there would, one day, be a museum dedicated to the Beatles in Liverpool (*The Chase*).
   The original draft of the script called for the real Beatles to appear, made up to look very old to indicate they were still performing in the future (the script specified 2012).
   The Devil Goblins from Neptune reveals that The Beatles of the *Doctor Who* universe stayed together at least into the early seventies. John Lennon was murdered as he was in our history in *The Left-Handed Hummingbird*, though, and Paul McCartney was playing with Wings in *No Future*.
   In *The Gallifrey Chronicles*, it's revealed that Fitz col-

lects Beatles records from parallel universes, and that he saw them play a song called *Celebrate the Love* at Live Aid. *Celebrate the Love* is the title of the song the Ewoks sang at the end of *Return of the Jedi*, at least until the Special Edition.
146 "Five years" before *Island of Death*.
147 "Six months" before *The Devil Goblins from Neptune*.
148 *Who Killed Kennedy*. It is "1970" (p87).
149 "Three or four months" before *The Devil Goblins from Neptune*. There are at least two UNIT HQs: one that's almost certainly in a London office block by the Thames in London (seen in *Terror of the Autons*) and one that's a stately home (seen in *The Three Doctors*).
150 "Early March" before *The Devil Goblins from Neptune*.
151 "Three months" before *The Scales of Injustice*, "15 years" before *Business Unusual*
152 "A couple of months" and "a month" before *The Scales of Injustice*.
153 Dating *The Eye of the Giant* (MA #21) - The story is set "37 years" after 1934, so 1971. UNIT have a photocopier. This is apparently the first time Mike Yates meets the Doctor, although he's been working for UNIT "over the last year". This is "a few weeks" before *The Scales of Injustice*, according to that book.
154 Dating *The Blue Tooth* (BF *The Companion Chronicles* #3) - It's toward the end of Liz's tenure with

oped a blue liquid variant that could directly convert people's bodies into metal, as well as gestate Cyber-insects within the human form. Arnold himself succumbed to Cyber-conversion, and used his dentistry business as a means of kidnapping people - including Liz Shaw's friend Jean Baisemore - to turn into Cybermen.

The third Doctor and Liz investigated the disappearances. Jean died, but the Doctor created a compound that terminated Arnold. His demise quelled the remaining Cybermen - who were later executed by the Brigadier's troops using the Doctor's compound.

Liz herself was infected by the blue liquid - the Doctor cured her condition, but she lost a tooth as a result.

(June) - THE SCALES OF INJUSTICE[155] -> A group of Silurian / Sea Devil hybrids awoke in Kent, and performed genetic experiments in the hope of ending their sterility and shortened lifespans. The Doctor investigated the matter, but the warmongering Silurian leader launched an attack on the coast of Kent. UNIT defeated the assault, and a smaller group of benevolent Silurians sued for peace.

The cyborg leader of the Vault sought to illicitly acquire Silurian technology, leading to UNIT uncovering the Vault's base of operations. The Vault leader escaped along with his two Nestene-augmented assassins. Foreign powers had previously purchased some of the Vault's acquisitions.

The Brigadier's wife Fiona filed for divorce and left with their daughter Kate.

After this incident, Sir John Sudbury of C-19 knew too much to be sacked by any government, and he gained in power.[156]

Liz Shaw told the Doctor that she planned to leave UNIT, return to Cambridge and continue her researches.[157] She took a leave of absence.[158] Liz travelled around the world, and later published a book entitled *Inside the Carnival*.[159]

Harry Sullivan served on the Ark Royal after leaving Dartmouth Naval College.[160]

(June) - THE DEVIL GOBLINS FROM NEPTUNE[161] -> Geneva refused to release the Doctor to help with the Siberia situation, so Captain Shuskin of the USSR branch of UNIT attempted to kidnap him instead. Liz Shaw was working with Professor Bernard Trainor, who was planning an unmanned mission to Neptune. The Doctor and Liz travelled to Siberia and were attacked by the Waro, demonic creatures from Neptune's moon Triton. The Doctor realised this was a distraction - the Waro were really after the American supplies of cobalt-60, with which they hoped to build a bomb that would devastate Earth. The Brigadier uncovered a conspiracy in UNIT that led to Area 51 in Nevada, a secret military base containing five aliens, the Nedenah. Freed by the Doctor, the Nedenah released a virus that made the Waro destroy themselves.

On 18th June, there was a General Election, and the Wilson government was defeated by the Conservatives

UNIT (she's been with the organization "about a year") and Captain Yates is described as "a new boy" - which would place the story between *The Eye of the Giant* and *The Scales of Injustice*.

155 Dating *The Scales of Injustice* (MA #24) - The back cover states this is set between *Inferno* and *Terror of the Autons*, and "immediately after" *The Eye of the Giant*. It's a "few weeks" since that book. Liz tells the Doctor she is leaving at the end of the book "eight months, two weeks and four days" after *Spearhead from Space*. It is "six months" since *Doctor Who and the Silurians*.

The Silurians who sue for peace are not mentioned again. The next time we see them, *The Sea Devils*, they are pitted against humanity. By the time of *Eternity Weeps*, set in 2003, man and Silurian are working together in relative harmony. Perhaps the discrepancy can be put down to the fact that UNIT don't feature in *The Sea Devils*, and the reptile people there were revived and are being provoked into conflict by the Master.

156 *Business Unusual*

157 *The Scales of Injustice*, which states that it's "eight months, two weeks and four days" since she met the Doctor in *Spearhead from Space*, although their amount of time together has become "thirteen

months" by *The Devil Goblins from Neptune*.

158 *The Devil Goblins from Neptune*, *The Face of the Enemy*

159 *The Devil Goblins from Neptune*

160 *The Face of the Enemy*, picking up on a reference in *Harry Sullivan's War*.

161 Dating *The Devil Goblins from Neptune* (PDA #1) - Between *Inferno* and *Terror of the Autons*. Liz has been with UNIT for "thirteen months". The Brigadier hasn't been to Geneva for eight months (when, we're told, he was reporting on the events of *Inferno*). It is "1970", with a host of contemporary references to, for example, David Bowie and Brazil winning the World Cup (p109).

162 *Who Killed Kennedy* (p117), which specifies the year as "1970".

163 *Emotional Chemistry*

164 *Terror of the Autons*

165 *The Death of Art*

166 *Terror of the Autons*

167 *Blood Heat*

168 *The Wages of Sin*, *Catastrophea*

169 *Verdigris*, a reference to *The Avengers*.

170 Dating *Terror of the Autons* (8.1) - It seems to be the near future, and the plastics factory has a videophone. The Doctor works on his dematerialisation circuit for

under Heath with a majority of 43. Days before that, James Stevens' book *Bad Science* was published.[162] At some point during the UNIT era, the Doctor met the Russian Colonel Bugayev. During the encounter, Bugayev and some of his comrades were exposed to temporal radiation that either aged them to death or prolonged their lives.[163]

Liz Shaw returned to Cambridge, and soon afterward the Doctor started to agitate for a new assistant. The Doctor started the steady state microwelding of his dematerialisation circuit.[164] There were some slow weeks at UNIT. The Doctor helped Benton paint some Nissen huts.[165]

Jo Grant was seconded to UNIT at the insistence of a relative in government. Although she failed her General Science A-Level, she managed to pass the UNIT Training Course.[166] Her relative was General Frank Hobson, the UK ambassador to the United Nations.[167] She was trained to use skeleton keys and interrogation techniques.[168] Her best friend on the course was called Tara. Jo did intelligence work for the Ministry, alongside a gentleman adventurer.[169]

(At least three months after *Inferno*) - TERROR OF THE AUTONS[170] -> Josephine Grant became the Doctor's new assistant.

The Master had allied himself with the Nestenes, and together they plotted mass slaughter - when a radio signal was sent, thousands of distributed plastic daffodils would spray a plastic film capable of suffocating a person. The Nestenes would take over the country during the resulting chaos. The Doctor convinced the Master to help him defeat the Nestene plan. The Master was subsequently stranded on Earth when the Doctor stole his Mark Two dematerialisation circuit, rendering his TARDIS useless.

A spatula-shaped piece of Auton matter survived. It would eventually end up in Little Caldwell, where it would be called Graeme.[171] In October, UNIT started training its men to resist hypnosis. James Stevens completed work on his second book, and was invited to a demonstration of the Keller Process at Stangmoor Prison.[172]

THE MIND OF EVIL[173] -> Incognito as Professor Emil Keller, the Master developed "the Keller Process": a means of rehabilitating convicts by having their "evil" brain impulses transferred into a machine. However, the machine actually housed an alien parasite that fed off the evil in mankind. The Master hoped to put the parasite's powers at his command. After a riot at Stangmoor Prison, the Master's scheme was exposed and the Keller Process abandoned.

UNIT at this time were involved with security of the World Peace Conference in London. The Master sought to disrupt the proceedings and steal Thunderbolt, an outlawed nuclear missile slated for destruction. He nearly succeeded and triggered a World War, but the Doctor and UNIT destroyed both the missile and the Master's alien parasite.

DEADLY REUNION[174] -> The former Greek gods Demeter, Persephone and Hermes were now living as nobility in the English village of Hob's Haven. Hades had founded a cult named the Children of Light as a means of spreading anarchy among mankind, and coerced the Master into helping him. The Master supplied an alien

---

"three months", and apparently hadn't started in *Inferno*, so this story would seem to start at least three months after Season Seven ends. There is no indication how much time has passed since the previous Auton story, *Spearhead from Space*. A desk calendar is referred to when the Doctor and Brigadier visit Farrell's office, but we do not see it.

This is clearly not the Master's first arrival on Earth at this time - he has managed to research the history of Lew Russell, the circus owner.

Inferno was "a few years" before *Terror of the Autons* according to *The Face of the Enemy* (p215). In *Genocide*, Jo says that she's been on UNIT's books since 1971. *Who Killed Kennedy* prefers April 1970.

171 *Return of the Living Dad*

172 *Who Killed Kennedy*. It is "four months" since the June 1970 General Election (p119).

173 Dating *The Mind of Evil* (8.2) - It seems to be the near future - there is a National Power Complex, there is a World Peace Conference in progress in which the Chinese are key players. Gas warfare was banned "years" ago. Mao Tse Tung is referred to in the present tense - he died in 1976, after *The Mind of Evil* was made.

Inferno was "some time ago". This story might be set a full year after *Terror of the Autons*: the Master has been posing as Keller since "nearly a year ago". However, it's clear from *Terror of the Autons* that the Master has been on Earth for at least a little while. It's possible that the Master set his plan in motion before his apparent arrival on Earth in *Terror of the Autons* ... which would mean he had two entirely distinct plans to take over the Earth running simultaneously. The "year ago" line might well be a remnant from an earlier draft of the script that didn't include the Master.

According to *Who Killed Kennedy*, it is October 1970 (p119).

174 Dating *Deadly Reunion* (PDA #63) - *Terror of the Autons* is "recent", but the Master's TARDIS works, so this is set after *The Mind of Evil*.

drug, sarg, that drove its users to commit acts of violence at a pop festival. The Doctor aided Demeter in summoning Zeus from his abode in another dimension, and the king of the gods exiled Hades from Earth forever. Demeter's trio departed Earth for Zeus' realm. The Brigadier remembered his time spent as Persephone's lover in the nineteen forties.

In December, James Stevens met Dodo Chaplet, who was homeless. He invited her to stay with him.[175]

Unit Year 4

(January) - "Change of Mind"[176] **->** The third Doctor and Liz flew to Prague for a Psi conference, but the plane's wing was torn off in a psychic attack. The Doctor realised that one of the passengers was keeping the plane in one piece using the power of her mind, but she died from the effort.

Hamlet Macbeth investigated Professor Hardin, a Cambridge professor of Paranormal Sciences, leaving just as the Doctor and Liz arrived. Hardin was using technology to boost latent psychic powers, and was experimenting on his students. He tried to kill the Doctor, but the Brigadier shot him.

In late February, James Stevens started writing a book about UNIT. In March, Liz Shaw, who was working on the genetic engineering of reptiles, contacted Stevens and warned him not to research C-19. His house was ransacked.[177]

(spring or summer?) - THE CLAWS OF AXOS[178] **->** UNIT continued to track the Master. The Washington UNIT HQ became involved, sending one of their agents, Bill Filer, to help with the search. Meanwhile, the civil servant Chinn was investigating UNIT.

UNIT radar stations detected a UFO one million miles out, on a direct bearing for Earth. The alarm bells started to ring when it got within five hundred miles. UNIT HQ sent the order to launch an ICBM strike against the UFO, but the ship vanished before the missiles hit. It landed on the south east coast of England close to the National Power Complex at Nuton, amid freak weather conditions. As the army arrived to seal off the area, the UFO began to broadcast a signal:

> "Axos calling Earth, request immediate assistance. Axos calling Earth...".

The Axons made contact with the UNIT party. They claimed that their planet had been damaged by solar flares, and that they possessed an advanced organic technology. Their ship had been damaged. In return for help, the Axons offered humanity Axonite - a substance that was "the chameleon of the elements". It could be programmed to absorb all forms of radiation, and to replicate and transmute matter. In theory, it would end the world's food and energy problems. In reality, the Axons had captured the Master in space, and he had led them to Earth - a rich feeding ground - in return for his freedom and a chance to kill the Doctor. The Axos ship was banished from Earth and time-looped, but the Nuton Complex was destroyed.

---

175 *Who Killed Kennedy*. It is "December" (p136) 1970.
176 Dating "Change of Mind" (*DWM* #221-223) - The date is given as 1971. Liz has already left UNIT, but there's no mention of Jo.
177 *Who Killed Kennedy* (p162, p157).
178 Dating *The Claws of Axos* (8.3) - This story is set in the near future. There are videophones, although normal telephones are also in use. The National Power Complex "provides power for the whole of Britain" according to Sir George Hardiman, the head of the facility. (This needn't mean that the complex provides *all* of the country's power, just that it contributes to the whole of the National Grid rather than one region of it.) The complex has a "light accelerator". While this story was filmed in January, and the trees are bare, the snow is described as "freak weather conditions", perhaps suggesting the story is set in the spring or summer. Chinn says of the Brigadier's actions "that's the kind of high-handed attitude one has come to expect of the UN lately".
179 *Business Unusual*
180 Nuton is destroyed in *The Claws of Axos*, but mentioned in *The Daemons*.
181 *Who Killed Kennedy*
182 *Colony in Space*
183 *The Gallifrey Chronicles*
184 Dating *Colony in Space* (8.4) - There's no clear indication of the year. When Jo reaches the future, she is surprised that a colony ship was sent out in 1971 (it wasn't, of course, it was 2471). Either this story is set before 1971 and Jo is amazed how quickly the space programme has progressed, or it is set afterward and she finds it difficult to believe that the colony ship was kept secret.
185 *The Eight Doctors*. In *The Daemons*, the local squire Winstanley says "there have been a lot of queer goings on the last few weeks", suggesting that's how long the Master has been in the area.
186 Dating *The Daemons* (8.5) - The story is set in the near future, as BBC3 is broadcasting.
Devil's Hump is opened at "midnight" on "Beltane", and the story ends with a dance around the May pole. Beltane appears to be a Saturday or Sunday, as Yates and Benton watch a Rugby International and don't

Private Erskine was attacked by an Axon and left for dead, but survived. He was rescued by the Vault, and bore a grudge against the Brigadier. He ended up working for SeneNet.[179] **The National Power Complex at Nuton was rebuilt.**[180] Chinn was blamed for the disaster at Nuton and was pensioned off.[181]

UNIT went hunting for the Master and accidentally arrested the Spanish ambassador, mistaking him for the renegade Time Lord.[182] Marnal's son - who was on the run at the time - visited his father during the nineteen seventies, and told him exactly why the Doctor left Gallifrey.[183]

COLONY IN SPACE[184] -> The TARDIS left the Doctor's laboratory in UNIT HQ for a matter of seconds, en route to 2472.

The parish council of Devil's End converted the cavern below the church into a witchcraft museum. The Master arrived in Devil's End, killed the vicar Canon Smallwood, and buried him in his own churchyard. He adopted the identity of the new vicar, Mr Magister.[185]

(29th April - 1st May) - THE DAEMONS[186] -> At midnight on the major occult festival of Beltane, noted archaeologist Professor Gilbert Horner attempted to open the Devil's Hump - an ancient burial mount outside the village of Devil's End. BBC3 broadcast Horner's endeavour, but the mount was actually the buried spaceship of Azal, the last of the Daemons. Horner was killed by a blast of subzero temperatures that resulted when he opened the ship.

As the Reverend Magister, the Master organized a coven to awaken Azal in an effort to receive the Daemon's power. The Master and his ritualists succeed, and Azal prepared, per his instructions, to pass his power on to a creature worthy of overseeing the planet. Azal deemed the Doctor, not the Master, a worthy recipient, but the Doctor refused to accept such authority. **Azal moved to destroy the Doctor as a nuisance, but Jo Grant offered her life in the Doctor's place. Her "irrational and illogical" move drove Azal to self-destruct. UNIT apprehended the Master soon afterward.**

James Stevens watched the opening of Devil's Hump on BBC3 with Dodo, whom he had befriended.[187] The church in Devil's End was destroyed, but the cavern beneath was intact.[188]

Public outrage at UNIT's blowing up of the church at Devil's End ("The Aldbourne Incident") led to "questions in the House; a near riot at the General Synod".[189] UNIT Private Cleary suffered a nervous breakdown after seeing Azal.[190] SeneNet acquired the remains of Bok, a stone gargoyle animated by Azal's power.[191] After this, the Doctor explored the area around Devil's End and found Hexen Bridge, where he sensed an oppressive atmosphere.[192]

The public were told that the Master was an anarchist terrorist, Victor Magister. He was remanded at Stangmoor Prison.[193] The trial took place *in camera*. He was convicted of murder, high treason and numerous other crimes.[194] **While many wanted the Master executed, the Doctor pleaded for clemency at his trial and the Master was instead sent to Fortress Island in the English Channel.**[195] The Master was kept at Aylesbury Grange Detention Centre until Fortress Island was ready.[196]

"The Man in the Ion Mask"[197] -> The third Doctor visited the Master in Aylesbury Grange, a UNIT prison where the renegade Time Lord was imprisoned. With both of them locked in his cell, the Master claimed to have reformed, but the Doctor was suspicious - suspicions that were confirmed when it transpired that the Master had replaced himself with a hologram. The Master was just leaving... when the third Doctor, Lethbridge-Stewart and Benton apprehended him - the Doctor in the cell was also a hologram!

know the result. As Professor Horner's book is released the next day (and the shops would have to be open), it is almost certainly Sunday. It is "two hundred years" since Devil's Hump has been of interest, and the first attempt to open it was in 1793.
187 *Who Killed Kennedy*
188 *The Eight Doctors*
189 *Downtime*. It is a little odd that this is named the "Aldbourne Incident" - Aldbourne is the real village where *The Daemons*, set in the fictional village of Devil's End, was filmed. (Although an historic "Lord of Aldbourne" is referred to in *The Daemons*.)
190 *Who Killed Kennedy*
191 *Business Unusual*

192 *The Hollow Men*
193 *The Face of the Enemy*
194 *Who Killed Kennedy*
195 *The Sea Devils*. The name of the island appears on Captain Hart's map, but isn't referred to in dialogue.
196 *The Face of the Enemy*
197 Dating "The Man in the Ion Mask" (*DWM Winter Special 1991*) - The story takes place shortly after *The Daemons*, in "1976". The story appeared in *DWM*'s *UNIT Special*, which set out a timeline for the UNIT stories running from *The Invasion* in 1975 to *The Seeds of Doom* in 1980.

At the UNIT staff panto, Mike Yates played Widow Twankey.[198] Mike Yates kissed Jo Grant at the UNIT Christmas party. The Master interrupted the festivities.[199]

Unit Year 5

(Summer) WHO KILLED KENNEDY[200] **->** James Stevens tried to reveal the truth about UNIT in a live broadcast on BBC3's *The Passing Parade*. His house was torched, and the Master kidnapped him. He was taken to the Glasshouse, a home for traumatised soldiers, and kept sedated for weeks. The Master was the director of the Glasshouse, and had been brainwashing the soldiers to create an army. He planned to send them through time to disrupt Earth's history.

Upon meeting Francis Cleary, Stevens managed to escape with him. He brought a TV crew back, but the place had been cleared out and Stevens was utterly discredited. Cleary was still under the Master's control, and killed Dodo on the Master's orders. A mysterious stranger at Dodo's funeral gave Stevens a Time Ring, and they went back to 1963 to ensure Kennedy's assassination and the course of history. Stevens returned to his native time, haunted with the knowledge that his older self would kill Kennedy.

(12th - 13th September) - DAY OF THE DALEKS[201] **->** UNIT were called in to guard the World Peace Conference at Auderley House. On the evening of 12th September, there was an assassination attempt on Sir Reginald Styles. Guerrillas from the future believed that Styles would sabotage the Conference, and that its failure would create a history in which the Daleks ruled Earth two hundred years hence. The Doctor discovered that the guerrillas' interference, not Styles, had foiled the conference and paradoxically created this future.

A time-travelling squad of Daleks and Ogron footsoldiers attacked the House, attempting to insure that their version of history prevailed. The guerrilla Shura detonated a Dalekanium bomb and wiped out the invaders, but only after the delegates had been evacuated. With the delegates' survival, the guerrillas' history ceased to be.

Two Ogrons escaped and ended up in the village of Little Caldwell.[202] UNIT recovered a Dalek casing.[203] SeneNet recovered twenty-second century weaponry from the site.[204] James Rafferty wrote a paper about dust samples from the site.[205]

The Cold War was brought to an end.[206]

Surgeon-Lieutenant Harold Sullivan was posted to Faslane.[207] **The Doctor took Jo on a test flight of the TARDIS. Under the Time Lords' guidance, the TARDIS headed for Peladon.**[208]

> **= THE FACE OF THE ENEMY**[209] **->** The Conclave, the surviving members of the parallel Earth devastated by "Project: Inferno", captured the Koschei of their reality and used his TARDIS to open dimensional portals to Earth.

The Conclave members began replacing their parallel duplicates to gain positions of power, but UNIT came to suspect the plan. With the Doctor off-world, the Brigadier allied himself with Royal Air Force lecturer Ian Chesterton

---

198 *No Future*, which places it in "1973", three years earlier. This must have been quite an occasion, as the Doctor also remembers it in *Timewyrm: Revelation*.

199 "The UNIT Christmas party last year" according to *Verdigris*.

200 Dating *Who Killed Kennedy* (MA, unnumbered) - See Ft. 112 (pg114) for the dates given in this book.

201 Dating *Day of the Daleks* (9.1) - This may have a contemporary setting. While the world is on the brink of WW3, a BBC reporter appears as himself.

Jo tells the Controller that she left the twentieth century on "September the 13th". The Controller notes, rather annoyingly for those trying to pin down the dates of the UNIT stories, that Jo has "already told me the year" she is from.

202 *Return of the Living Dad*

203 *No Future*

204 *Business Unusual*

205 *The Dimension Riders*. Rafferty is Professor of Extra-Terrestrial Studies at Oxford and the Doctor's old friend.

206 INTERNATIONAL POLITICS IN THE UNIT ERA: In the UNIT era, there appear to be four superpowers: The US, USSR, China and the United Kingdom. In the nineteen-seventies, the world apparently lurches from a period of detente with the Soviet Union (*The Invasion*), to the brink of World War Three (*The Mind of Evil, Day of the Daleks*), but within a few years of *Day of the Daleks*, the Cold War has ended. *Invasion of the Dinosaurs* includes the line "back in the Cold War days". *Robot* is also set after the Cold War ended. *About Time* notes that "it's massively unlikely that the entire Cold War has ended at this point since the stories made / set in the 1980s seem to suggest a world where there's still a schism between the US and USSR (see especially *Time-Flight*)". Alternatively, it's evidence that *Robot* is set after *Time-Flight* (so after 1981), which ties in nicely with the date given in *Pyramids of Mars* (the 1980 date would be the date of *The Time Warrior*).

The Soviet system seems to survive - in *Battlefield* the Russian troops' uniforms bear the hammer and

and the imprisoned Master.

> = The trio travelled to the parallel Earth, euthanised the dissected Koschei and severed the Conclave's link with the other Earth.

UNIT eliminated most of the Conclave members now stranded on Earth, but Marianne Kyle, the Conclave's Secretary General, remained at liberty.

By now, the Brigadier was in a relationship with Doris, an old friend from Sandhurst. Liz Shaw was in the US on a lecture tour. Ian Chesterton and Barbara had a son, John.

THE SEA DEVILS[210] **->** Imprisoned at Fortress Island, the Master attempted to contact a dormant colony of Sea Devils in the English Channel, hoping to direct them to attack mankind. The Master won the confidence of Colonel Trenchard, the governor of the prison, by claiming the creatures were terrorists that threatened Britain's national security. Trenchard acceded to the Master's requests, enabling him to contact the Sea Devils and engineer his escape. Trenchard died when a team of Sea Devils overran the prison.

The Doctor intervened and implored the Sea Devil leader to make peace with humankind, but a sneak Navy attack engineered by Robert Walker, the Parliamentary Private Secretary, convinced the Sea Devil leader to make war instead. Unable to contain the impending violence, the Doctor destroyed the underwater base and the Sea Devils within. The Master escaped shortly afterward.

"Under Pressure"[211] **- >** The fourth Doctor landed on a submarine and quickly deduced it was on the trail of Sea Devils and convinced the crew he was the scientific advisor... unfortunately the third Doctor was also involved. The fourth Doctor realised he had to play his part in history without giving away his identity. The Sea Devils attacked the submarine, and the two Doctors worked together over a radio link to translate a message to the Sea Devils, who withdrew.

THE EIGHT DOCTORS[212] **->** The Master evaded capture by the Doctor and Jo and reached his TARDIS, which was disguised as the sacrificial stone at Devil's End. Returning to UNIT HQ, the Doctor met his eighth incarnation.

"Target Practice"[213] **->** The third Doctor and Jo headed to UN airbase 43, obstensibly UNIT's new training centre. They thought the Brigadier was there, but he was in Geneva and instead they met Colonel Ashe. But Ashe served tea to him before Jo, and misidentified an Auton as an Ogron - tipping the Doctor off that he was a bounder. He was a Russian spy, sent to abduct the Doctor. The Brigadier arrived in time to see the Doctor capture Ashe.

The Doctor went on Professor Gibbs' lecture on electroparticles.

The Time Lords assigned the Doctor and Jo the task of delivering a message pod, and they departed for the planet Solos.[214] All UNIT HQs received a new standing order, priority A1, to be on the lookout for the Master.[215] The Coal Board closed Llanfairfach Colliery in South Wales.[216]

---

sickle, but they are operating on British soil under UN command, and the "Soviet Praesidium" is mentioned in *The Seeds of Death*.

Stories told since the collapse of the Soviet Union in the real world have referred to it: Ace mentions "perestroika" in *Timewyrm: Exodus*, and the Doctor talks of the collapse of the Soviet Union in *Just War*.

207 "A couple of weeks" before *The Face of the Enemy*.

208 *The Curse of Peladon*

209 Dating *The Face of the Enemy* (PDA #7) - This runs while the Doctor and Jo are away in *The Curse of Peladon*, and takes about a fortnight.

210 Dating *The Sea Devils* (9.3) - This is probably set in the near future. The prison guards' vehicles and uniforms are futuristic. Although this is effectively a sequel to two stories, no indication is given how much time has passed since *Doctor Who and the Silurians* or *The Daemons*. The Master insists that his second television be in colour, but this doesn't mean that the story is set just after colour TV was introduced - before the advent of cheap colour portable TVs, a household would com-

monly have a big colour set and a smaller black and white one. The Master watches an episode of *The Clangers*, first broadcast in 1971 and repeated many times since.

211 Dating "Under Pressure" (*DWM Yearbook 1992*) - It's the "late twentieth century". It's unclear if this is set during an unseen part of *The Sea Devils* or features a later encounter with the monsters. I've assumed the former.

212 Dating *The Eight Doctors* (EDA #1) - This happens straight after *The Sea Devils*.

213 Dating "Target Practice" (*DWM #234*) - The story takes place after *The Sea Devils*, as there's a Sea Devil target on the range. The Doctor says he hasn't been to Russia for "several hundred years", and regardless of whether that's historically or within his own timeline, that places the story before *Wages of Sin* and contradicts *The Devil Goblins from Neptune*.

214 *The Mutants*

215 *The Time Monster*

216 In *The Green Death* it was "last year".

(29th September) - THE TIME MONSTER[217] -> For several months, the Master had posed as one "Professor Thascales" to conduct research into the science of "interstitial time" at the Newton Institute in Wootton. He succeeded in developing TOM-TIT (Transmission of Matter Through Interstitial Time), a device capable of moving matter through the cracks between "now" and "now". However, the Master's true intentions were to use TOM-TIT to put Kronos, the ancient Chronivore, at his command.

The Doctor and UNIT came to suspect the Master's schemes, but the Master succeeded in bringing the Atlantean priest Krasis through time to assist him. The Master and Krasis set off back to Atlantis circa 2000 BC, and the Doctor and Jo Grant pursued them there.

The Thascales Theorem was held by the United Nations for security purposes.[218] Singer Dusty Springfield helped the Doctor and UNIT investigate abductions in Memphis.[219]

Unit Year 6

(May) RAGS[220] -> At Dartmoor, a bloody conflict between a punk band and a group of university students freed the Ragman, who animated their corpses. They staged punk band performances as part of the "Unwashed and Unforgiving" tour, mentally stimulating persons in the area to commit violence. The group's performances caused a riot at Dartmoor Prison, and saw a group of fox hunters massacred by escapees from an asylum. UNIT was called on to investigate as the band reached Cirbury, and the Ragman also incited violence at Stonehenge. Kane Sawyer, a local ruffian and one of the Ragman's descendents, sacrificed himself to re-bind the Ragman into some standing stones.

(May) - VERDIGRIS[221] -> The Doctor and Brigadier fell out after defeating an Arcturan who had arrived on Earth with sinister intent. The Doctor decided to take a break from UNIT and went to an old mansion he owned in the

---

217 Dating *The Time Monster* (9.5) - There's nothing to suggest this is the near future. Benton wishes Jo a "Merry Michaelmas". The TARDIS in this story appears to be fully functional - although this story is broadcast before *The Three Doctors*, perhaps it takes place afterward. If not, then all the stories in Season Nine apparently take place between 13th September (*Day of the Daleks*) and 29th September (*The Time Monster*) of a given year.

This story is set in "the mid-seventies" according to *Falls the Shadow*, and "thirty years" before *The Quantum Archangel* (so 1973).
218 *Falls the Shadow*
219 *The Blue Angel*. At some unspecified point during the Doctor's exile.
220 Dating *Rags* (PDA #40) - This was the first PDA that didn't specify on the cover which TV stories it was set between. The Doctor's exile has not been lifted, yet Jo refers to Daleks and Ogrons, meaning it takes place at some point between *Day of the Daleks* and *The Three Doctors*.

It is "the beginning of May" when the Ragman starts his campaign, "Tuesday 10th May" a little later. The year is given as "79" at the beginning of the book (although 10th May wasn't a Tuesday in 1979). It is after Malcolm Owen of the Ruts died (July 1980, in real life), and The Damned song *I Just Can't Be Happy Today* was released (November 1979).
221 Dating *Verdigris* (PDA #30) - The month and year are stated in the book as "1973" and "May". Jo has known the Doctor "two years" (p143). The story leads into *The Three Doctors* (p241). Paul Magrs playfully made it tricky to place this story precisely. One anomaly is that Jo doesn't know about Peladon (p192). This is after the eventful UNIT Christmas party (p126).

222 Dating *The Three Doctors* (10.1) - The evidence is mixed. Dr Tyler says the Americans have launched a deep space monitor, but he also cites "Cape Kennedy." (This might suggest that *The Three Doctors* takes place between 1963 and 1973.) Jo misquotes the words to *I am the Walrus*.

According to *Transit* (and a number of novelisations, such as *The Mysterious Planet*), the Doctor's exile lasts "five years".
223 The Doctor says at the end of *The Three Doctors* that he needs to build a new force field generator to replace the one that has been destroyed, and goes on a test flight in *Carnival of Monsters*. It should be noted that in *Carnival of Monsters*, Jo says that 1926 is "forty years" before her time.
224 *Relative Dementias*
225 *Relative Dementias* (p18) mentions when the Doctor encountered the Countess.
226 Dating *The Wages of Sin* (PDA #19) - It's just after *The Three Doctors*, in "the 1970s" (p34).
227 *Verdigris*
228 "Six months" before *Invasion of the Dinosaurs*.
229 *Original Sin*
230 *Carnival of Monsters*
231 Dating *The Suns of Caresh* (PDA #56) - It is soon after the Doctor's exile is lifted (p35), and straight after the TARDIS gets back from Inter Minor (p36).
232 *Dancing the Code* (p61). These unrecorded encounters were either while travelling with the Doctor or attacks on Earth faced by UNIT.
233 *Interference* (p75).
234 Dating *Dancing the Code* (MA #9) - Set between *Planet of the Daleks* and *The Green Death*. Watergate appears to be topical (p154).
235 *The Android Invasion*. Sarah reported on Crayford's

town of Thisis.

The alien Verdigris, who had been drifting towards Earth for thousands of years, contacted a race of refugees named the Meercocks. The Meercocks had decided to settle on Earth disguised as characters from Earth's fiction.

Iris Wildthyme and her companion Tom called on the Doctor, and they discovered the Meercocks' plan. They defeated an army of robot sheep and The Children of Destiny, a group of annoying psychic teenagers working for Galactic Federation Supreme Headquarters in Wales.

Verdigris escaped to inform Omega that the Doctor was on Earth.

THE THREE DOCTORS[222] -> The stellar engineer Omega, having survived in a universe of anti-matter, began incursions into the matter universe and started draining power from the Time Lord homeworld. With Omega's attention focused on the exiled Doctor, the Time Lords decided to violate the First Law of Time and dispatch the Doctor's previous two incarnations to aid his current self.

The first Doctor was unable to reach them, and was only able to advise on the situation, but the second and third Doctors travelled to Omega's anti-matter universe. Omega desired to leave his domain but needed a successor to facilitate this. He tried coercing the Doctors into taking his place, but the Doctors triggered a matter / anti-matter explosion that seemingly destroyed Omega.

The Doctors escaped and the Time Lord homeworld regained full power. The Time Lords sent the Doctor's previous selves back to their native times, and in gratitude ended the Doctor's exile. They restored his knowledge of time travel, and repaired the TARDIS to its proper function.

The Doctor's exile to Earth had been lifted. He constructed a forcefield generator and took the TARDIS on a test flight.[223] The Doctor defeated the Brotherhood of Beltane and blobby aliens called the Talichre, and the encounters went down in UNIT legend.[224]

Miss Gallowglass (later Countess Gallowglass) started running a mail forwarding service for aliens and time travellers alike, operating from a Portakabin in the East End. The Doctor first met her just after his exile on Earth ended. One of her customers, irate at a misplaced parcel, declared war on Earth and stole Britain's Crown Jewels. The Time Lords replaced the jewels with fakes, preserving history.[225]

THE WAGES OF SIN[226] -> The Doctor, his knowledge of time travel restored, offered to take Jo Grant and his former companion Liz Shaw to witness the Siberian meteorite strike in 1908. Instead, they erroneously arrived in St. Petersburg, 1916, shortly before the murder of Rasputin.

The Doctor and Jo meet Iris and Tom in a cocktail joint on a far flung outpost.[227] **Professor Whitaker disappeared when the government refused to fund his time-travel research.**[228] Tobias Vaughn funded Whitaker's experiments.[229]

The Doctor and Jo set off on another test flight. They landed on Inter Minor, where they became trapped in a miniscope owned by the Lurman entertainer Vorg.[230]

THE SUNS OF CARESH[231] -> Lord Roche, a Gallifreyan, discovered that Caresh was would enter a seventy-four year cold period that would extinguish all life on the planet. Roche set about modifying the Careshi time scanner into a stellar manipulator, hoping to save the planet's Fayon civilization, which was a curiosity to him. Roche intended to deviate a neutron star and use its gravity to bump Caresh into orbit around its warmer star Beacon, but the Curia of the Nineteen - rulers of the Realm of the Vortex Dwellers - forecast that the diverted neutron star would devastate their territory. They dispatched two hostile Furies to attack Roche, but he trapped the Furies within his TARDIS and sent it back in time thirteen centuries. It was unearthed in 1999, creating a time anomaly that the Doctor detected.

The Doctor used Roche's equipment to manoeuvre Caresh closer to its smaller star Ember, thereby avoiding damage to the Curia's territory. The Curia refrained from sending the Furies to attack Roche, averting the 1999 anomaly.

Before this time, Jo had met a number of alien races including the Methaji, Hoveet, Skraals and Kalekani.[232] The Kalekani aggressively terra-formed worlds into rolling grasslands using the memetic virus known on Earth as the game "golf".[233]

DANCING THE CODE[234] -> There were reports of "unorthodox weapons" in the North Africa country of Kebiria. UNIT's representative in the area, Captain Deveraux, was killed. UNIT sent a Superhawk jet fighter to investigate, and discovered a nest of Xarax - an insect hive-mind. The Xarax began to infest the rest of the country, including the capital, Kebir City. The US Navy prepared a nuclear strike, but a UNIT team from the United Kingdom managed to deactivate the nest using synthesised chemical instructions.

Defence Astronaut Guy Crayford's XK5 space freighter, launched from Devesham Control, was lost during a test flight. It was believed to have collided with an asteroid. Sarah Jane Smith reported on the story.[235]

(late July) LAST OF THE GADERENE[236] -> By now, the surviving Gaderene numbered only three hundred thousand. The Gaderene scout Bliss had founded the aeronautics manufacturer Legion International as a front for her operations, and enslaved residents of the British town Culverton by implanting them with Gaderene embryos. Bliss recovered her missing transmat component and repaired the Gaderene transmat, intending to bring thousands of adult Gaderene through to Earth as an invasion force. However, UNIT's involvement resulted in the deaths of Bliss, her towering brother and the Gaderene embryos. The transmat was destroyed, and the resultant energy backlash further annihilated the Gaderene invasion force and homeworld.

SPEED OF FLIGHT[237] -> The Doctor, Jo Grant and Mike Yates departed in the TARDIS for the planet Karfel, but arrived on the planet Nooma in the far future by mistake.

At some point, the Doctor and Jo (and possibly someone else) succeeded in visiting Karfel.[238] Tobias Vaughn helped develop the BOSS computer for Global Chemicals.[239]

THE GREEN DEATH[240] -> The government gave the green light to Global Chemicals' experiments into the Stevens Process, which produced 25 percent more petrol from a given amount of crude oil. The "Nutcake Professor" Clifford Jones - who had won the Nobel prize for his work on DNA synthesis - protested that the process would double air pollution, but Global Chemicals claimed that the pollution generated was negligible.

UNIT were sent to investigate a body that was discovered in the abandoned coal mine - a body that was glowing green. They discovered Global Chemicals had been dumping the pollution created by the Stevens Process into the mine, and that it had mutated the maggots down there. The giant maggots produced a slime that was toxic to humans, but the Doctor and Professor Jones discovered a fungus that killed them.

Global Chemicals was run by the BOSS, or Bimorphic Organisational Systems Supervisor, a computer linked to the brain of Stevens. In an effort to help the world achieve "maximum efficiency", the BOSS attempted to mentally dominate Global staff at seven sites throughout the world, including Llanfairfach, New York, Moscow and Zurich. Global Chemicals was destroyed when the BOSS blew up. Professor Jones' Nuthutch was given UN Priority One research status, leading to "unlimited funding."

The Prime Minister was called Jeremy. Jo Grant left UNIT at this time to marry Professor Jones.

The newlyweds went on an expedition to the Amazon.[241]

DEEP BLUE[242] -> The Doctor, Tegan and Turlough landed in Tayborough Sands for a holiday and met up with UNIT. With "their" Doctor away, UNIT recruited his later incarnation to investigate a mutilated corpse. The Xaranti were attempting to convert Earth into a new homeworld, but they were defeated. Most of the UNIT staff involved in this adventure lost their memories of it, with only Captain Yates remembering the Doctor's future incarnation.

---

disappearance "two years" before that story.
236 Dating *Last of the Gaderene* (PDA #28) - It is "some thirty years" since WW2 (p241).
237 Dating *Speed of Flight* (MA #27) - Jo is now thinking about leaving the Doctor (p242).
238 *Timelash. Speed of Flight* implies the Karfel visit occurs shortly afterward.
239 *Original Sin*
240 Dating *The Green Death* (10.5) - This is the near future. The Prime Minister is called Jeremy. BOSS is an advanced "Biomorphic" artificial intelligence that has been linked to a human brain. There is a Ministry of Ecology. Two calendars appear: the first is in the pit-head office and shows the date to be "April 5th". The second can be glimpsed in the security guard's office and shows the month as February during a leap year.
   See the British Politics in the UNIT Era sidebar, page 159.
241 *Planet of the Spiders*
242 Dating *Deep Blue* (PDA #20) - It's "six months" after

The Green Death, and it's Mike's first mission since then. The Doctor has spent only a small amount of time on Earth since Jo's departure, but there's no mention of Sarah. This is "six months" after *The Green Death* (p15), "ten or so" years before Tegan's native 1984 (p20).
243 Dating *The Time Warrior* (11.1) - Sarah states in this story that she's from the twentieth century, and isn't more specific than that. In *Pyramids of Mars*, it's stated four times that Sarah is "from 1980". The most straightforward interpretation of the line has to be that this story, Sarah's first, is set in 1980.
244 Dating *The Paradise of Death* (Target novelisation #156) - The Brigadier hasn't heard of Virtual Reality, and the Secretary-General of the United Nations is a woman. There is no gap on television between *The Time Warrior* and *Invasion of the Dinosaurs*, but this features both Sarah and Mike Yates. Barry Letts decided to set this radio play before Mike Yates' "retirement" from UNIT. Captain Yates is referred to in the book version.
245 Dating *Invasion of the Dinosaurs* (11.2) - The bal-

Unit Year 7

THE TIME WARRIOR[243] -> British research scientists began to mysteriously disappear. UNIT were called in and the leading research scientists were all confined to the same barracks in a secret location. Nevertheless, the press got wind of the story. A young reporter named Sarah Jane Smith smuggled herself into the complex by posing as her Aunt Lavinia, the noted virologist. Before long, Sarah and the Doctor had followed a time disturbance back to the Middle Ages.

THE PARADISE OF DEATH[244] -> The Parakon Corporation opened Space World on Hampstead Heath. It offered many attractions based on space and space travel, including twenty-one alien creatures such as the Giant Ostroid, the crab-clawed Kamelius from Aldebaran Two, Piranhatel Beetles and Stinksloths. Using Experienced Reality techniques, Parakon could give people guided tours of the Gargatuan Caverns of Southern Mars and the wild side of Mercury.

UNIT investigated the death of a young man whose thighbone had been bitten clean through, and exposed the Parakon Corporation as an extraterrestrial organisation. Parakon had been negotiating with Earth for a number of years, hoping to sign a trading agreement. Parakon would supply a wonder material named rapine in exchange for human bodies to fertilise their world, which had been devastated by the rapine harvests. Parakon had already sacked many worlds, including Blestinu, but UNIT defeated it.

INVASION OF THE DINOSAURS[245] -> Eight million Londoners were evacuated after dinosaurs began to terrorise the population. The government decamped to Harrogate. UNIT helped with the security operation, which was under the command of General Finch and the Minister for Special Powers, Sir Charles Grover.

UNIT scientists calculated that someone was operating a time machine that required an atomic reactor. They tracked the Time Scoop in question to a hidden bunker near Moorgate Underground Station. The bunker contained an elaborate shelter that served as home to a group of people - including the conservationist Lady Cullingford, the novelist Nigel Castle and the Olympic long jumper John Crichton - who were all convinced they were in a spaceship bound for a new, unpolluted planet. Using the Time Scoop, Professor Whitaker hoped to regress Earth back to its primeval days, repopulating it with the people in the bunker. The Doctor and UNIT ended this plan, and Whitaker and Grover were stranded in the past. Mike Yates, a member of the conspiracy, was discharged from UNIT.

During this, the Doctor unveiled his new car.[246] After this time, the temporal scientist Chun Sen was born.[247] Realising that UNIT might need to contact him in an emergency, the Doctor gave the Brigadier a syonic beam Space-Time Telegraph.[248]

THE FIVE DOCTORS[249] -> While on Earth at this time, the third Doctor was kidnapped by Borusa while driving his sprightly yellow roadster Bessie.

(20th - 21st May) - THE GHOSTS OF N-SPACE[250] -> While on holiday in Italy, the Doctor, Sarah, Jeremy Fitzoliver and the Brigadier prevented Maximillian Vilmio, a wizard, from achieving immortality. Vilmio had planned to use the space-warping effect of Clancy's comet to match his real body and his N-form in Null-Space.

ISLAND OF DEATH[251] -> Sarah investigated the disappearance of Jeremy, and found he had joined a cult that

ance of evidence is that this is the near future. The Whomobile is a new car and an "M" reg, but the human race are - in theory at least - capable of building manned ships capable of interstellar flight. Whitaker has built a Time Scoop capable of calling up dinosaurs from hundreds of millions of years ago. The bunker was built "back in the Cold War days".
246 The Doctor's car was never named on screen, but was dubbed both "Alien" and "the Whomobile" by the production team. The Doctor continues to use Bessie, as both are seen in *Planet of the Spiders*.
247 *Invasion of the Dinosaurs*. The Doctor says that Chun Sen couldn't be a suspect with regards to the dinosaur appearances as he "hasn't been born yet".
248 *Terror of the Zygons*. Presumably the Brigadier didn't have the Space-Time Telegraph before *Invasion of the Dinosaurs*, when dinosaurs were over-running London, or he would surely have used it.

249 Dating *The Five Doctors* (20.7) - The third Doctor is kidnapped after *The Time Warrior* as he recognises Sarah. Sticking strictly to what we know in the television series, his abduction must occur between *The Monster of Peladon* and *Planet of the Spiders*, because the other stories of Season Eleven follow on from each other. However *The Paradise of Death* is set in a "nonexistent" gap between the first two stories of the series, so the Doctor might have been taken from that point.
250 Dating *The Ghosts of N-Space* (MA #7) - For the Doctor and Sarah, the story occurs after *Death to the Daleks*. Clancy's Comet returns to Earth every 157 years, and the last sighting was in "1818", so it's 1975. As the month is given as May, *Planet of the Spiders*, set in March, must take place the following year. Fitzoliver was Sarah's photographer in *The Paradise of Death*.
251 Dating *Island of Death* (PDA #71) - The story mentions Sarah's trip to Sicily in *The Ghosts of N-Space*, and

worshipped a reptilian alien called Skang. The third Doctor helped her discover that the cultists' drinks were laced with psychotropics. They flew to Bombay with the Brigadier, and traced the cult to Stella Island, learning that the Great Skang was in deep space. It had infected followers with spores, with the aim of preserving its race. The Doctor convinced that the Skang that controlling humans will disrupt the unity of the Skang race, and placed the Skang gestalt in a time loop to preserve it.

Unit Year 8

To prevent nuclear launches, the US, USSR and China gave their Destructor Codes to Britain. Joseph Chambers was made Special Responsibilities Secretary with responsibility for protecting them.[252]

AMORALITY TALE[253] -> Sarah Jane Smith discovered a photograph of the Doctor, dating from 1952, while researching a story. The Doctor was intrigued by a "warp shadow" on the photo, and the two of them went to 1952 in the TARDIS to investigate.

The Doctor started a project to research the psychic potential of humans.[254]

(mid-March) PLANET OF THE SPIDERS[255] -> A stage magician, Clegg, died at UNIT HQ as the Doctor investigated his psychic potential. This was linked to a disturbance at a Tibetan monastery in Mortimer, Mummerset. It was led by Lupton, a man bitter because he was sacked by a company after twenty five years of service, then saw his own company bankrupted by his previous employers. The Spiders from Metebelis III had contacted Lupton, and compelled him to try and steal a Metebelis crystal that was in the Doctor's possession. Lupton kidnapped Sarah, and the Doctor pursued them to Metebelis in the future.

Tobias Vaughn helped fund Kettlewell's research into robotics.[256]

(4th April) - ROBOT[257] -> As the UNIT budget was limited, the organisation was unable to afford a Captain to replace Mike Yates. Benton was promoted to Warrant Officer and made the Brigadier's second-in-command.

The National Institute for Advanced Scientific Research, or "Think-Tank" concentrated many of Britain's scientists all under one roof. They developed pieces of high technology that included the disintegrator gun - a weapon capable of burning a hole on the Moon's surface - and dynastrene, the hardest material known to science. The most impressive achievement, though, was Professor Kettlewell's "living metal", which he used to build the K1, a robot capable of performing tasks in environments where no human could survive. Many Think-Tank personnel were also members of the Scientific Reform Society (SRS), a group that believed in efficiency and logic.

The SRS tried to use the K1 to further their aims, but the newly-regenerated fourth Doctor used a metal-eating virus to destroy the robot. He also prevented the SRS from triggering a nuclear holocaust.

Following this time, a woman became Prime Minister.[258]

(January) TERROR OF THE ZYGONS[259] -> Centuries after arriving on Earth, the Zygons in Loch Ness learnt that a stellar explosion had destroyed their home plan-

---

the Hallaton arrived on Stella Island on 20th September, so this story happens in UNIT Year 7.
252 "A few months" before *Robot*. The system has passed to UN control by *World War Three*.
253 Dating *Amorality Tale* (PDA #52) - The story starts between *The Monster of Peladon* and *Planet of the Spiders*.
254 The Doctor is conducting such research in *Planet of the Spiders*. It's only mentioned in that story, and there's no suggestion that the fourth Doctor continues the study.
255 Dating *Planet of the Spiders* (11.5) - The story takes place three weeks before *Robot*. "Meditation is the in thing" according to Sarah Jane.
256 *Original Sin*
257 Dating *Robot* (12.1) - This is clearly set in the near future. As with *Invasion of the Dinosaurs*, the Cold War has been "over for years" according to the Brigadier.

Advanced technology includes the K1 robot, the Disintegrator Gun and dynastrene. Sarah Jane Smith's day pass to Think-Tank bears the date "April 4th".
258 In *The Ark in Space*, Harry is surprised that the High Minister, "a member of the fair sex," was "top of the totem pole", suggesting Britain has yet to elect a female Prime Minister by his time. There must be a General Election or change of leadership in the government while he was away from Earth. In *Terror of the Zygons*, the Brigadier receives a phone call from the PM, whom he twice addresses as "Madam", and later refers to her as "she".
259 Dating *Terror of the Zygons* (13.1) - It is the near future. The Prime Minister is a woman. In *Pyramids of Mars*, two stories after this one, Sarah states that she is "from 1980". According to *No Future*, this story is set in January 1976.

BRITISH POLITICS IN THE UNIT ERA: During the UNIT era, there are references to two Prime Ministers who are not the actual PM when the story was shown. However, both are semi-jokey references to actual opposition leaders of the time.

"Jeremy" mentioned in *The Green Death* would be Jeremy Thorpe, the leader of the Liberal Party at the time the story was made. Thorpe, of course, was never Prime Minister, although he was in the ascendant at the time *The Green Death* was shown. Shortly afterwards, in the February 1974 Election, the Liberal vote tripled to six million and they entered a pact with Labour to form a government.

In *Terror of the Zygons*, the Prime Minister is a woman. Margaret Thatcher had already been elected leader of the Conservatives when *Terror of the Zygons* was taped - the scene in which the Brigadier is phoned by the PM was recorded on 23rd April 1975, and Mrs Thatcher had been party leader since February of that year. The Labour government of the time had a tiny majority of four seats, and predicting a Conservative victory at the next election was a fairly safe bet (in much the same way that *Zamper*, written in 1995, referred to "Number ten, Tony's den").

If we assume the UNIT stories are set in the near future, then this is remarkably straightforward, as only the result of one "real life" election need be changed. According to *The Green Death*, there is a general election won by Thorpe's Liberals at some point after 1973 (it can't be before *The Green Death* was shown, or it wouldn't be the future). Thatcher's Conservatives defeat this government. We can pinpoint the date of that election - it's between *Robot* and *Terror of the Zygons*, as Harry is surprised by the female leader in *The Ark in Space*. This coincides neatly with Sarah's assertion in *Pyramids of Mars* that she's from 1980. So the Liberals win the next General Election (one that had to be called by June 1975), the Tories win the one after that (possibly in May 1979, as in our history) and it all fits.

The date the Liberals come to power is harder to pin down. The model above assumes that it's a single-term government. A four or five-year term in office would mean they came to power around the time the Doctor was exiled to Earth. The man who's Minister of Ecology in *The Green Death* drafted UNIT's charter. It's possible to squeeze the Liberal election victory in before *The Invasion*, but there's nothing that demands he was a member of the governing party when he drew up the charter. He could have had a diplomatic, military or even legal career that made him the right man for the job (the only thing we can say for certain is that it's an unlikely job for a serving Minister of Ecology). Politics in the UNIT era is a world of grey, middle-aged men. There are occasional visionaries, but government is practically run by civil servants. There's no obvious point where the character of the government changes in the UNIT stories.

Throughout the UNIT era, the government is throwing money at new energy projects. We see grand schemes in *Doctor Who and the Silurians*, *Inferno*, *The Claws of Axos*, *The Green Death* and *Robot*, although these all end in disaster and mankind is still dependent on oil in *Terror of the Zygons*. The environment is clearly a huge political issue, with concerns about pollution voiced in many stories. The existence of a Minister of Ecology as a cabinet post is telling. When the Tories come to power, a lot of these responsibilities might transfer to the World Ecology Bureau we see in *The Seeds of Doom*. It's interesting to note that there's no mention of Europe, especially as (perhaps because) the Common Market was a hot political issue at the time. (The EEC debate was - far more vaguely than most fans seem to think - satirised in *The Curse of Peladon*.)

This version, then, is consistent with what we're told in the series and with what someone writing in the early seventies would extrapolate as a plausible backdrop for a science-fantasy adventure show set in the near future.

Some recent writers - particularly those who see the UNIT stories as being set at the time of broadcast - have developed a parallel political history for *early* 1970s Britain of the *Doctor Who* universe. Books like *Who Killed Kennedy* and *The Devil Goblins from Neptune* infer that events in the UNIT stories destabilised actual governments. This seems to be the logical consequence of the catalogue of incompetent government action, politicians dying, international crises and high profile disasters we see ... although in the TV series, politicians and civil servants are depicted, almost to a man, as complacent and obtuse. They seem far *too* secure, rather than people scared the government will fall at any moment.

All in all, the various things we are told about the parallel political history described in the books are difficult to reconcile.

In real life, the Prime Ministers since 1970 (along with the date of the general election, the winning party and their majority) were:

Heath (18th June, 1970, Conservative, 30)
Wilson (28th February, 1974, Labour minority, 0)
Wilson (10th October, 1974, Labour, 4)
Callaghan (5th April, 1976)
Thatcher (3rd May, 1979, Conservative, 43)
Thatcher (9th June, 1983, Conservative, 143)
Thatcher (11th June, 1987, Conservative, 102)
Major (27th November, 1991)
Major (9th April, 1992, Conservative, 21)
Blair (1st May, 1997, Labour, 179)
Blair (7th June, 2001, Labour, 167)
Blair (5th May, 2005, Labour, 66)

continued on page 161...

et. A refugee fleet had been assembled and was looking for a new home. The Zygon leader Broton signalled that Earth would be suitable once the ice caps had been melted, the mean temperature of the planet had been raised and the necessary minerals had been introduced to the water.

The Zygons intensified their campaign against humanity when oil companies started disrupting the free passage of their "Skarasen", a vast monster that lived in Loch Ness but which ventured out into the North Sea from time to time. In the space of a month, the Zygons destroyed three North Sea oil rigs, causing massive loss of life. Two of the rigs were owned by Hibernian Oil. UNIT were sent to Tullock to deal with the problem.

Broton, posing as the Duke of Forgill, got into the Fourth International Energy Conference on the banks of the Thames - he planned to assassinate the world leaders assembled there by signalling for the Skarasen. Broton, the signal device and the Zygon ship were all destroyed, and the Skarasen returned to Loch Ness.

Probably owing to the Loch Ness Monster incident, the press got word of the Doctor's role in saving the world. He played for Lord's Taverners, but avoided most other tenants of celebrity-dom. A publisher approached the Doctor, who agreed to write a series of educational books for children.[260]

The government ordered Department C-19 to be cleaned up, and many of its top brass were removed.[261]

HEART OF TARDIS[262] -> A collision with the second Doctor's TARDIS further de-stabilized the Lychburg singularity, to the point that it threatened the entire universe. The Time Lords sent the fourth Doctor and Romana to deal with the problem, but the Jarakabeth demon impersonating Alistair Crowley impeded their efforts, hoping to use the singularity to re-write reality in the name of chaos.

The second Doctor (secretly aided by his future self) used telemetry readings from the TARDIS to return Lychburg to Earth, whereupon the residents deserted the town entirely. A benevolent Jarakabeth demon hosted in

government agent Katherine Delbane killed the Crowley demon. She became a UNIT captain under the Brigadier's command.

UNIT has recently requisitioned industrial lasers, marmosets, archaeological tools, rocketry components, Watsui tribal masks and a US college's particle accelerator. They also took a third of the Bank of England's gold reserves and didn't replace them, triggering a stock market crash.

(19th - 22nd June, 1976) - NO FUTURE[263] -> The terrorist organisation Black Star, a group of anarchists, spent the summer planting bombs in sites around London: Hamleys, Harrods, the Albert Hall, the Science Museum and Big Ben. There was an assassination attempt on the Queen, junior treasury minister John Barfe was killed, the entertainer Jimmy Tarbuck was badly hurt in a hit-and-run incident, and Pink Floyd's private jet was lost over the English Channel. Civil disturbances happened across the globe. Prime Minister Williams declared a state of emergency.

Meanwhile, the Vardans were preparing an "active immigration" to Earth. The Vardan High Command formed an alliance with the Monk, the Time Lord otherwise known as Mortimus. The Monk freed the Vardans from their time loop, and under the guise of Priory Records boss Robert Bertram, he used Vardan Mediascape technology to plant crude subliminal messages in Earth's TV broadcasts. More sophisticated brainwashing techniques were available in the new VR training system that the Monk provided for UNIT.

Some members of UNIT, including most of the Broadsword intelligence agents, were able to break the conditioning. The Vardans were repelled from Earth and the Vardan Popular Front, a democratic organisation, took control of Varda. The Monk had captured the Chronovore Artemis and had been tapping her power to alter time, but she was freed and took her revenge on him.

The Brigadier was seeing Doris at this time. The seventh Doctor selectively wiped his memory, and he retired.

The Russians were operating vodyanoi units at this time.[264] One Vardan remained behind, living in the

---

260 *The Kingmaker.* In real-life, Target published the *Doctor Who Discovers...* books, the fifth of which (here unnamed) was *Doctor Who Discovers Early Man.* This would also explain why the fourth Doctor was chosen to present a segment of children's show *Animal Magic.* Naturally, as that was broadcast in 1980, it's final, clinching and irrefutable proof that the UNIT stories are set in the future.
261 "Six months" before *No Future,* and also referred to in *Return of the Living Dad.*
262 Dating *Heart of TARDIS* (PDA #32) - The dating

seems particularly confused. UNIT knows the fourth Doctor, but Benton's a Sergeant and Yates hasn't been discharged. This is after the 1982 Falklands War, and there is a Conservative government. We could infer from the gold reserves reference that UNIT have fought the Cybermen - either in *The Invasion,* the 1975 invasion mentioned in *The One Doctor* and *Dalek* (presuming that's a different invasion) or another incident entirely.
263 Dating *No Future* (NA #23) - The date is given (p6).
264 *No Future,* and a reference to the 1981 BBC drama *The Nightmare Man* - adapted by Robert Holmes and

...continued from page 159

In the books, a Liberal-led coalition government was formed in January 1970. *The Devil Goblins from Neptune* (p8) states, "an alliance of Liberals, various disenfranchised Tories and Socialists, and a group of minor fringe parties, enter power on a platform of social reform, the abolition of the death penalty, and a strong interstellar defence programme".

In June 1970, Heath defeats Wilson, just as in our history (*Who Killed Kennedy*). This can't be easily reconciled with *The Devil Goblins from Neptune*, which also takes place in June 1970.

Shirley Williams is Prime Minister in *No Future*, set just after *Terror of the Zygons* in 1976. We're told that Thorpe had resigned mid-term, but there is also reference to Wilson.

In *Millennial Rites*, a female PM lost an election in the early eighties. In 1999, the leader of the Opposition is a woman ("all handbag and perm"). The Prime Minister is a man.

The unnamed winner of the 1997 general election was assassinated in *The Dying Days*. Edward Greyhaven is installed Prime Minister by the new Martian King of England, but dies during the course of the story.

Terry Brooks, Prime Minister in 1999, tries to fake a military coup as a pretext to dismantle the military and spend the money health and education instead. He is forced to resign, and is replaced by Philip Cotton. (*Millennium Shock* - they're a thinly-veiled Tony Blair and Jack Straw).

Tony Blair is alive, well and Prime Minister in *Project: Twilight* and *Death Comes to Time*. Mickey mentions him in *Rise of the Cybermen*.

Interference lists the recent British Prime Ministers as Heath, Thorpe, Williams, Thatcher, Major, Blair and Clarke. (The last could be senior Conservative Kenneth Clarke, but could possibly be Labour's Charles Clarke. The proofreader added the "e" - Lawrence Miles' original intention was that it was Tory MP Alan Clark.)

Aliens of London and *World War Three* had scenes set in Downing Street, with photographs of Callaghan and Major on the stairway (no photos of Thorpe, Williams, Brooks, Cotton or either Clarke were visible!). The Prime Minister of the day is murdered by the Slitheen, and Harriet Jones becomes PM sometime between this story and *The Christmas Invasion*.

Once we're clear of the confused accounts of the 1970 elections, the sequence of Prime Ministers and when they come to power would seem to be:

Thorpe   (Liberal coalition, in power at the time of *The Green Death*)

Williams   (Labour, in power during *Terror of the Zygons* and *No Future*)

Thatcher   (Conservative, who came to power in the early eighties, later than in real life)

Major   (Conservative - we might infer he's the assassinated winner of the 1997 election)

Greyhaven   (briefly in 1997 and almost certainly not counted officially)

Brooks   (Unknown party, possibly leading from 1997 to 1999)

Cotton   (The same party as Brooks, takes over in 1999 - the leader of the opposition at this time is a woman, so isn't ...)

Blair   (Labour, the dates are uncertain, but he comes to power later and apparently leaves earlier than in real life, and thus manages to avoid two successful alien assassinations of a British Prime Minister.)

Clarke   (Unknown party, presumably the Prime Minister assassinated in *Aliens of London* in 2006 - although the body looks more like Blair than either Kenneth or Charles Clarke, both of whom could comfortably accommodate a Slitheen in real life!)

Jones   (The same party as Clarke. The ninth Doctor says in *World War Three* that she was originally supposed to serve three terms - possibly until c 2016 in *Trading Futures*, where the PM was male. However, her first term is curtailed by the tenth Doctor in *The Christmas Invasion* - this would seem to be a significant deviation of established history, unless the ninth Doctor was mistaken in *World War Three* to think Jones was a three-termer.)

Unknown. (There is at least one interim Prime Minister after Jones' downfall in *The Christmas Invasion*. A blurry picture of him is seen in *TW: Out of Time*, along with the apparently skeptical headline, "Working Hard, Minister?")

Saxon. (According to *The Sound of Drums*, he leads the newly-formed Saxon Party, which has attracted support from across the political spectrum. While time is reversed in *Last of the Time Lords*, his outing himself as the Master and ordering the death of the US President on global TV "still happens". Saxon dies at the end of the story - even if the Master returns, he would have no constitutional claim on the position of Prime Minister.)

Liverpool phone network until 1983.[265] Following this, the Brigadier spent a great deal of time in Geneva.[266]

(6th July) - THE ANDROID INVASION[267] -> The leader of the Kraal's Armoury Division, Chief Scientist Styggron, planned his race's escape from the dying planet Oseidon using their technological skills. The Kraals could engineer space-time warps, and two years previously, Styggron had used one of these to capture an experimental Earth freighter in deep space. He analysed the mind of the astronaut within, Guy Crayford, and used Crayford's memories to construct the Training Ground - an almost-perfect replica of the English village of Devesham, including the nearby Space Defence Station. The Training Ground was populated with Android villagers, and the Kraals were able to study human civilisation and behaviour, honing their preparations to invade the Earth.

It was the Kraals' first attempt at conquest, but although they failed, Marshal Chedaki's fleet survived and the Kraal databanks contained the complete memory prints of a Time Lord traveller, the Doctor.

SeneNet recovered a Kraal android.[268]

(Early one month in Autumn) - THE SEEDS OF DOOM[269] -> The World Ecology Bureau was active at this time. They received reports that an unusual seed pod had been discovered in the Antarctic permafrost, and called in UNIT. The Doctor identified the item as a Krynoid seed pod and also discovered a second one. One Krynoid was killed in the Antarctic, while an RAF air strike on the mansion of Harrison Chase, the millionaire plant enthusiast, destroyed the other.

THE PESCATONS[270] -> Upon their return to Earth, the Doctor and Sarah were attacked by a sea creature, which the Doctor recognised as a Pescaton. He hurried to the astronomer Professor Emmerson and watched Pesca, the homeplanet of the Pescatons in the outer galaxies, explode.

The Pescatons had escaped in a space fleet, which arrived on Earth and attacked many cities. A smaller number went to Venus. The Doctor located the Pescaton leader, Zor, in the London Underground and killed him with ultraviolet light. The Pescatons died without their leader.

Realising that the Doctor's visits were becoming less and less frequent, the Brigadier had Bessie mothballed.[271] The Brigadier announced his retirement from UNIT. Soon afterwards, he became a mathematics teacher at Brendon School.[272]

THE HAND OF FEAR[273] -> The "obliterated" alien named Eldrad had fallen to Earth as a stone hand and regenerated into a humanoid (albeit female) form. There was near-meltdown in the main reactor of Nunton Nuclear Power station, although there was no radiation leak as Eldrad used the energy to facilitate his / her regeneration. The Doctor and Sarah decided to escort Eldrad back to his / her homeworld of Kastria.

Afterward, in answering a summons to Gallifrey, the Doctor was forced to return Sarah Jane Smith home. Although the TARDIS apparently failed to return Sarah to Croydon, she arrived in England.

The Doctor had dropped her off in Aberdeen.[274] Fortunately, it was the right timezone. Sarah resumed her work as a journalist.[275]

---

directed by Douglas Camfield.
265 *Return of the Living Dad*
266 The Brigadier is in Geneva during *The Android Invasion* and *The Seeds of Doom*.
267 Dating *The Android Invasion* (13.4) - This is the near future. For at least the last two years, Britain has had a Space Defence Station, a team of Defence Astronauts, and has been operating space freighters. The calendar in the fake village gives the date (every day) as "Friday 6th July". The nearest years with that exact date are 1973, 1979, 1984 and 1990.
268 *Business Unusual*
269 Dating *The Seeds of Doom* (13.6) - On balance, it seems to be the near future. There is a satellite videolink to Antarctica and UNIT have access to a laser cannon. The Antarctic base has an experimental fuel cell. On the other hand, Sarah only wants 2p to use the public telephone. Chase says it is autumn (and the location work for the story was recorded in October / November). The Doctor is invited to address the Royal

Horticultural Society on "the fifteenth".
270 Dating *The Pescatons* (Argo Records LP, novelised as Target #153) - The story is set in Sarah's time. It was released in August 1976, between Seasons 13 and 14, so I have placed it after *The Seeds of Doom*. The bit with Professor Emmerson and the telescope is in the novelisation, not the original record. It's quite the impressive telescope too - able to watch events on another planet in real-time, which is impossible.
271 *Battlefield*. *The Seeds of Doom* is the last story to feature UNIT until *Mawdryn Undead*, and it is established in the later story (and implied in *Time-Flight*) that the Doctor hasn't visited the Brigadier for years.
272 *Mawdryn Undead*, a year before 1977.
273 Dating *The Hand of Fear* (14.2) - While it doesn't feature UNIT, Sarah is returned home at the end of the story. It has to be set before December 1981 and *K9 and Company*, in which she's back at work.
274 *School Reunion*
275 *K9 and Company*

The Non-UNIT Seventies

NB: The line between a UNIT and non-UNIT story isn't always clearly defined. When a reference makes a direct link to a UNIT era story, it is included in the UNIT Era section. When there's a more vague or general reference to UNIT, it's included here.

The Doctor once took piano lessons from a man called Elton.[276] He also had to swim the English Channel naked, after losing a bet with Oliver Reed.[277]

Isaac Summerfield moved his team to London, where they were based in a centre for the homeless.[278]

1970

c 1970 (20th March) - THE UNDERWATER MENACE[279] **-> The mad Professor Zaroff died in agony while attempting to raise Atlantis from the ocean floor with his Plunger.**

On 5th April, 1970, Hitler's remains were exhumed and destroyed on the orders of Andropov, head of the KGB.[280] On 14th August, the Revolution Man cult claimed Ed Hill was the Messiah.[281]

The seventh Doctor's companion Ace was born Dorothy Gale McShane on 20th August, 1970, to Audrey and Harry McShane.[282] Around 1970, an Imperial bodyguard and nurse fled from the far future with Miranda, the daughter of the Emperor, following a revolution in their home timezone where the Imperial Family were hunted down and killed. The fugitives settled in the Derbyshire village of Greyfrith.[283]

Hilda Hutchens won the 1970 Nobel Prize for Philosophy.[284] The tenth Doctor changed history, allowing Frank Openshaw to meet his wife a few years earlier than he otherwise would have.[285]

The British launched a military satellite, *Haw-Haw*, to block extraterrestrial signals in 1971.[286] Nimrod's encounter with the vampire Reggie left Reggie recuperating for three years.[287] **Decimal currency was introduced in the United Kingdom. At some point afterward, the Doctor and Susan visited England.**[288]

In 1972, Nazi war criminal Oskar Steinmann died from

---

276 *Project: Lazarus.* This refers to Elton John, presumably, but no date is given.

277 "The Betrothal of Sontar". The Doctor also claims to have swum the Channel in *Doctor Who and the Pirates.* There's no indication exactly when this happened, but it's apparently after "Lunar Lagoon", when the fifth Doctor said he'd never learned to swim. (He seemingly has by *Warriors of the Deep,* however.)

278 "The early seventies", according to *Return of the Living Dad* (p66).

279 Dating *The Underwater Menace* (4.5) - Polly discovers a bracelet from the 1968 Mexico Olympics and she and Ben guess that they must have landed about "1970". The Atlanteans are celebrating the Vernal Equinox.

The story is set in "1970-75" according to *The Programme Guide,* "soon after" 1969 according to *The Terrestrial Index. The TARDIS Logs* claimed a date of "1969". *Timelink* chose "1970", and *The Legend* simply states it's "after 1968".

280 *The Shadow in the Glass* (p172).

281 *Revolution Man* (p247).

282 ACE'S EARLY LIFE: According to *The Curse of Fenric,* Ace does "O-Levels", not GCSEs, so she must be a fifth former (i.e.: fifteen or sixteen years old) by the summer of 1987 at the latest. This supports *Ghost Light,* where she is "thirteen" in "1983". As Ace has a patch reading "1987" on her jacket in *Dragonfire,* it seems that the timestorm which swept her to Svartos must have originated in that year. Fenric is therefore rounding up when he tells Ace that Audrey Dudman will have a baby "thirty years" after *The Curse of Fenric.* Sophie Aldred was born in 1962, making her nine years older

than the character she played.

In the New Adventures, starting with *Timewyrm: Revelation,* Ace's birthday was established as 20th August (Sophie Aldred's birthday). In *Falls the Shadow,* the Doctor says that she was born in "1970". Paul Cornell attempted to establish that Ace's surname was "McShane" in *Love and War,* but series editor Peter Darvill-Evans vetoed this at the proof stage. *Conundrum* (p245) and *No Future* (p19) both suggest that Ace's surname begins with an "M" (although when asked in the latter, Ace claims it is "Moose"!). It wasn't until Kate Orman's *Set Piece* that "McShane" was officially adopted.

Ace is "Dorothy Gale" in some books by Mike Tucker, notably *Matrix* (p124) and *Prime Time* (p234). *The Rapture* attempts to reconcile this by stating that her middle name is Gale. In *Loving the Alien,* which appears to be set prior to *The Rapture,* Ace dies and is replaced by a parallel timeline version of herself. The Doctor says this swap accounts for much of the confusion regarding Ace's last name.

283 *Father Time.* Miranda is "ten" in the first part of the book (p54), and "two months old" when she arrives on Earth.

284 *Island of Death* - although there isn't actually a Nobel Prize for Philosophy.

285 *I am a Dalek*

286 *The Dying Days* (p101).

287 *Project: Twilight*

288 *An Unearthly Child.* Susan is also familiar with the Beatles before their first hit single in *Time and Relative.*

cancer of the spine.[289] In December of that year, the skeleton of Nazi Martin Bormann was discovered in West Germany.[290] Playwright Noel Coward died in 1972. One of his selves claimed - due to his status at a time traveller - that at his moment of death, he'd be mentally whisked back to his birth to experience life all over again.[291]

The American military downed an alien spaceship carrying the Stormcore, a navigational instrument. The government erroneously believed the Stormcore was a weather control device, and formed Operation Afterburn to make it compatible with human technology. Researchers determined the device needed a psionic operator. In the years to come, the government's ESP / Remote Viewing program, called Grill Flame, would locate such individuals. The spaceship's crewmembers, now stranded on Earth, joined the American CIA as agents Melody Quartararo and Parker Theroux.[292]

1973

Ace's first pet was called Marmaduke, and the first road she lived on was named Beech. When Ace was three, her mum cried for days when Ace's grandma Kathleen died.[293]

When Elton Pope was three or four, his mother was killed by an "elemental shade" that had escaped from the Howling Halls. Elton saw the tenth Doctor standing over her body, and would gradually become obsessed with the mysterious stranger.[294]

Aubrey Prior's expedition to the Black Pyramid in 1973 discovered Nephthys' burial chamber.[295] Anji Kapoor, a future companion of the Doctor, was born in Leeds on 1st April, 1973.[296]

Tegan Jovanka's grandmother died of coronary thrombosis. About this time, Tegan's father had an affair and her parents split up. Tegan was sent to boarding school.[297] A short sword bearing the initials "IC," given to Ian Chesterton by Thalius Maximus, was now on display in the British National Museum. Historians erroneously dated it to the end of the first century, failing to realize it was about thirty five years older.[298] On 12th December, 1973, Revolution Man cult leader Madeleine "Maddie" Burton died in Paris as the result of a drug addiction. The cult quickly died without her influence.[299]

1974

When Ace was four, her parents had a son, Liam. When Ace's father discovered his wife was having an affair with his friend Jack, he left with the infant Liam.[300] In November, the Celestial Toymaker kidnapped Lord Lucan, sparking an international manhunt.[301] Reginald Tyler died in a domestic accident. He had been working on his novel *The True History of Planets* since 1917, much to the annoyance of his wife, Enid, who sold the movie rights and moved to Jamaica with her lover very soon after her husband's death.

289 *Just War* (p178).
290 *The Shadow in the Glass.* This is historical, and the skeleton was identified first through dental records, then twenty seven years later through a DNA test.
291 *Mad Dogs and Englishmen*
292 "Thirty years" before *Drift.*
293 *Night Thoughts.* Kathleen is Ace's grandmother as seen in *The Curse of Fenric.*
294 *Love & Monsters*
295 "Twenty three years" before *The Sands of Time.*
296 According to the writers' guidelines. She was "twenty eight" in *Escape Velocity,* set in February 2001.
297 When she was "thirteen", according to *The King of Terror.*
298 *Byzantium!* (p8).
299 *Revolution Man* (p248).
300 *The Rapture*
301 *Divided Loyalties* (p46).
302 *Mad Dogs and Englishmen*
303 *The King of Terror* (p32).
304 Dating *Urgent Calls* (BF #94) - The year is given on the back cover. This is the first in a series of one-part audio stories that compose the "Virus Strand" story arc.
305 Dating *Horror of Glam Rock* (BF BBC7 #3) - "It's 1974," the Doctor says.
306 *The One Doctor.* This may be a reference to *The Invasion.*

307 "Eight years" before *Return of the Living Dad.*
308 *TW: Greeks Bearing Gifts.* Actress Naoko Mori was also born in 1975, making her and Tosh the same age - save that *Torchwood* takes place one year ahead of broadcast.
309 Dating *Fury from the Deep* (5.6) - It is clear that this story is set in the near future. There is a Europe-wide energy policy and videophones are in use. It's tempting, in fact, to see this as being set in the same near future as the early UNIT stories. Although Robson, the refinery controller, talks of "tuppence ha'penny tinpot ideas", this is clearly a figure of speech rather than an indication that the story is set in the era of pre-decimal currency.

The Programme Guide always assumed that the story was contemporary. *The TARDIS Logs* set the story in "2074", the same year it suggested for *The Wheel in Space.* In *Downtime,* Victoria has been in the twentieth century for "ten years" by 1984 (p41).

The quotation is the Doctor reassuring Jamie about Victoria's new home in *The Wheel in Space.*
310 *Blue Box*
311 "The Lunar Strangers". Jackson says she's been in "the service forty years".
312 *The Reaping. Rocky Horror* debuted on 14th August, 1975.

> = In another version of history, though, Reginald Tyler didn't die, he was rescued by a poodle that walked on its hind legs, who transported him off Earth ... in this reality, *The True History of Planets* would become a very different book.

@ At some point while on Earth, the Doctor read the original *The True History of Planets*.[302]

Tegan ran away from home when she was fifteen. Once she was found, her father sent her to live with his sister Vanessa in England.[303]

1974 - URGENT CALLS[304] **->** A telephone operator named Lauren Hudson was exhibiting strange symptoms, but a wrong call luckily put her in touch with the one person who could diagnose the problem: the sixth Doctor, who advised that an alien worm was hugging her spine. Military surgeons extracted the worm, and Lauren experienced a string of wrong-but-fortuitous phone calls. She kept ringing up the Doctor, who advised that an alien "luck" virus - capable of transmitting itself through telephones - had infected them.

The Doctor suspected that the virus was engineered for military applications, enabling sleeper agents to communicate without keeping incriminating information, or to summon precisely the right sort of aid. With modification, it could even be used to carry out assassinations. He advised that Earth wasn't ready for such a virus (however helpful it had become) and that he'd have to deal with it. Some time later, Lauren was saddened to find that every call she placed went through correctly. Failing to hear from the Doctor, she mailed him a letter instead.

1974 - HORROR OF GLAM ROCK[305] **->** The singer Nancy Babcock said that her cat dictated all of her music. Lucie Miller's mother - a blonde named Mary - presently worked in a Gloucester shoe shop.

Arnold Korns, a dynamic and powerful manager in the music industry, discovered two budding talents - Trisha and Tommy Tomorrow, who performed as *The Day After Tomorrow* - and scheduled them to make their debut on *Top of the Pops*. However, a group of discorporealized alien beings, seeking to stop over on Earth and consume the polyunsaturates and fibre found in the human body, had previously contacted Tommy as sound waves conducted through his Stylophone. They touted themselves as the "Only Ones", claiming they were the only race in existence besides humanity, and helped Tommy to compose his songs.

En route to London, Korns and the twins stopped off at Nadir Services, a service station and café just outside Bramlington. The spot had previously seen such celebrities as Hendrix, Lulu and the Wombles, and now witnessed the dissolution of the band Methylated Spirits. The group had lost their singer Wendy, and Bendy Roger - dressed in full regalia - now severed ties with drummer Patricia Ryder. Outside the café, the Only Ones manifested as scaled, bear-like creatures and killed Roger.

The eighth Doctor and Lucie showed up as the Only Ones murdered Tricia Tomorrow and threatened to unleash a massacre. The Doctor found a means of converting the Only Ones back into sound, and trapped them on shuffle mode in Lucie's MP3 Player. He also speculated that the carnage at the service station would be blamed on the Hell's Angels.

Patricia Ryder had been kicked out of a number of bands and was actually Lucie's "Auntie Pat". As part of this adventure, she learned that she would be unremarkable later in life and have no children, with Lucie as her only niece. The Headhunter pursuing the Doctor and Lucie narrowly missed them in this period.

1975

During the Cybermen invasion of June 1975, the Doctor was based at 35 Jefferson Road, Woking.[306] The Doctor visited a planet orbiting Lalande 21185. The Caxtarids had developed a virus that the government were planning to use against a rebel faction.[307]

In July 1975, Toshiko Sato was born in London. Her parents were in the RAF, and her grandfather worked at Metchley Park. When Toshiko was two, her family moved to Osaka, Japan.[308]

c 1975 - FURY FROM THE DEEP[309] **->** On the whole, this period was "a good time in Earth's history to stay in. No wars, great prosperity, a time of plenty". Gas from the sea now provided energy for the south of England and Wales, as well as mainland Europe. Twenty rigs pumped gas into every home without incident for more than four years.

When scientists registered a regular build-up and fall in pressure in the main pipelines, the supply was cut off for the first time. A mutant species of seaweed was responsible, and it mentally dominated some of the rigs' crews before being beaten back by amplified sound.

Victoria Waterfield left the second Doctor and settled with the Harris family.

The Doctor met hacker Robert Salmon in 1975. They stopped a US Navy programmer from installing a back door that would've granted illicit access to the Navy's computers.[310] Freda Jackson joined the space programme in 1975 - she would later command Moon Village One.[311] The Doctor had tickets to opening night of *The Rocky Horror Picture Show*.[312]

1976

In 1976, a Lalandian safari killed people in Durham. Isaac Summerfield tipped off UNIT to the problem.[313] The Doctor and Ace visited London in 1976.[314] In 1976, the Order of St Peter chased the last known European vampire from the continent. It escaped to the United States.[315]

@ On 28th May, Deborah Gordon and Barry Castle married in Greyfrith. The Doctor was elsewhere, with a widow called Claudia.[316]

The last British mission to Mars, Mars Probe 13, ended in disaster when the Ice Warriors killed two crewmembers. The British government made a secret deal to stay away from Mars, and they framed the mission's sole survivor, Lex Christian, for murder. He was sent to Fortress Island, where he remained for more than twenty years.[317]

1976 - VAMPIRE SCIENCE[318] **->** Carolyn McConnell, a pre-med student, met the eighth Doctor and Sam in San Francisco. The Doctor was on the trail of a clutch of vampires, and a scuffle led to the death of his best lead, the vampire Eva. He gave Carolyn a signalling device in case the vampires resurfaced.

1977

Peri's mother divorced and remarried when Peri was ten.[319] **Count Carlos Scarlioni, one of the richest men on Earth, married his Countess in 1977.**[320] In 1977, the Doctor and Frobisher attended the opening of *Star Wars* at Mann's Chinese Theatre in Los Angeles.[321]

1977 - MAWDRYN UNDEAD[322] **->** The Brigadier had retired from UNIT, and was now teaching mathematics at Brendan Public School. The TARDIS arrived with Tegan and Nyssa on board - the Ship had been thrown back to 1977 thanks to a warp elipse from Mawdryn's spaceship. Mawdryn himself arrived in a transmat capsule, but the journey left him gravely injured. Tegan and Nyssa mistook him for the Doctor, and agreed to take him back to the spaceship. The Brigadier insisted on accompanying them.

On Mawdryn's ship, the Brigadier came into contact with his older self and triggered the Blinovitch Limitation Effect. This left the younger Brigadier with some memory loss - the fifth Doctor and his companions left him on Earth to continue teaching.

---

313 *Return of the Living Dad*
314 *Timewyrm: Revelation*
315 *Minuet in Hell.* This claim is either hyperbole on the Order's part or extremely short-lived, as *Goth Opera* (set in 1993) has between three to four hundred vampires active in Britain alone.
316 *Father Time*
317 "Over twenty years" before *The Dying Days*.
318 Dating *Vampire Science* (EDA #2) - It's "1976" (p3).
319 *Blue Box.* This is contradicted by *Synthespians™*, which states that Peri's father died in 1979 and her mother remarried after that.
320 "Two years" before *City of Death*.
321 *Mission: Impractical*
322 Dating *Mawdryn Undead* (20.3) - The earlier part of the story takes place during the Queen's Silver Jubilee - various events to commemorate this started as early as February, and culminated in June. It's repeatedly said that Tegan and Nyssa have arrived "six years" before the story's modern-day component, set in 1983.
323 Dating *Image of the Fendahl* (15.3) - According to Ma Tyler, it is "Lammas Eve" (31st July) at the end of Part Three. There's nothing to suggest it's not set the year of broadcast.
324 *Timewyrm: Revelation* (p13).
325 Seven years before *Turlough and the Earthlink Dilemma*.
326 Dating "The Nightmare Game" (*DWM* #330-332) - The year is given.
327 *The Left-Handed Hummingbird* (p23).

328 *Terror Firma.* Presuming this doesn't instead refer to the Las Vegas nightclub of the same name, the infamous disco operated from 1977-1986.
329 Dating *The Pirate Planet* (16.2) - The Doctor says that the population of Earth is "billions and billions", possibly suggesting a contemporary setting. *First Frontier* implies the same.
330 Dating *The Stones of Blood* (16.3) - There is no indication what year the story is set, but it is clearly contemporary.
331 *The Armageddon Factor*
332 *Shada*
333 "Seven years" before *Attack of the Cybermen*.
334 Dating *Mad Dogs and Englishmen* (EDA #52) - The date is given.
335 Four years before *Relative Dementias*.
336 Dating *City of Death* (17.2) - The Doctor says that this isn't a vintage year, "it is 1979 actually, more of a table wine, shall we say". A poster says there's an exhibition on from Janiver - Mai, and the blossoms on the tree would suggest it was towards the end of that period.
337 *Dust Breeding.* This implies that the Doctor went back in time and nicked the original Mona Lisa before the fire in Scaroth's house could destroy it.
338 *Synthespians™.* This contradicts *Blue Box*, which said Peri's mother remarried when Peri was ten (in 1976). It's possible, if a little messy, to reconcile the two accounts by suggesting Peri's mother married three times.

c 1977 (30th and 31st July) - IMAGE OF THE FENDAHL[323] **->** The fourth Doctor encountered the Fendahl at Fetchborough, a village on the edge of a time fissure. A team of scientists under Professor Fendelman were attempting to probe the far past using a Time Scanner, but this had only succeeded in activating the dormant Fendahl skull. Fetch Priory was destroyed in an implosion. The Doctor defeated the Fendahl, and took the skull with the intent of throwing it into a supernova.

In 1977, the Doctor landed in Lewisham in an attempt to track the Timewyrm.[324] On Trion, the dictator Rehctaht emerged as the most tyrannical ruler in the planet's history. She would rule for seven years, and butcher the Clansmen. She founded the colony of New Trion primarily as a slave labour force, but conflict between Trion colonies in the East and the West diverted her attention. New Trion functioned independently, if inefficiently.[325]

1977 - "The Nightmare Game"[326] **->** The eighth Doctor discovered that the alien Shakespeare Brothers were behind Delchester United's recent bad run.

1978

On 21st February, 1978, electrical workers uncovered the sacrificial stone at the base of the Great Temple in Mexico City.[327] The Doctor, Samson and Gemma visited Studio 54.[328]

c 1978 - THE PIRATE PLANET[329] **->** Zanak's career as the Pirate Planet was brought to an abrupt end with the destruction of its engines and the death of its Captain and Queen Xanxia. Zanak settled in a peaceful area of space.

c 1978 - THE STONES OF BLOOD[330] **->** The fourth Doctor helped defeat Cessair of Diplos, who had escaped from her prison ship in hyperspace and been hiding on Earth for four thousand years. She was found guilty by two justice machines - the Megara - of impersonating a deity, theft and misuse of the Seal of Diplos, murder, and removing silicon lifeforms from the planet Ogros in contravention of article 7594 of the Galactic Charter. She was sentenced to perpetual imprisonment.

Around this time, the Time Lord Drax spent ten years in Brixton Prison.[331] Chris Parsons graduated in 1978.[332] Work was done on the sewers under Fleet Street.[333]

1978 - MAD DOGS AND ENGLISHMEN[334] **->** The eighth Doctor dropped Anji off in Hollywood, where she met embittered special effects man Ron von Arnim. The Doctor arrived from 1942, with Noel Coward, and the news that von Arnim was being manipulated to create a movie about poodles by director John Fuchas. The Doctor tied Fuchas to a chair, headed off to Dogworld, and forgot to go back, so Fuchas died. This prevented the movie being made, and saved the day.

The Tulkan Empire made a failed attempt to annex the Annarene homeworld. In response, the Annarene erased the deposed Tulk War Council's memories. An Annarene named Sooal, dying from a genetic disease, spirited the amnesiac council away in a Tulk spaceship. Sooal hoped to restore the Council's memories and gain the command codes needed to open a Tulk stasis chamber, which contained a metabolic stabilizer. He established the Graystairs elderly care facility in the village of Muirbridge, Scotland, to conduct genetics research.

On Annarene, the ruling Protectorate came to favour pacifism, even as a hawk-like faction desired a return to warfare.[335]

1979 (Spring) - CITY OF DEATH[336] **->** Scaroth's plan to alter history - which would have saved his race but doomed humanity - was reaching its culmination. With the help of the foremost temporal scientist of the day, Professor Theodore Nikolai Kerensky, Scaroth produced a device capable of shifting the whole world back in time four hundred million years.

To finance the plan, Scaroth was selling off his art collection, flooding the market with lost materpieces. This failed to raise enough money, and he arranged for the theft of the Mona Lisa from the Louvre in Paris. One of Scaroth's other selves had commissioned six more Mona Lisas from Leonardo da Vinci in 1505, and Scaroth intended to sell all seven copies to private buyers. Each would think they were purchasing the stolen Mona Lisa.

Scaroth succeeded in travelling back in time four hundred million years, but the fourth Doctor, Romana and the investigator Duggan followed in the TARDIS and stopped his plans. Upon his return to 1979, Scaroth died when a fire started in his laboratory. Only one Mona Lisa copy - with "This is a Fake" scribbled in felt tip on the canvas, detectable to any X-Ray - survived the fire. It was returned to the Louvre.

The Doctor came to possess a Mona Lisa that didn't have the words "This is a Fake" in felt tip.[337] Peri's father Paul drowned underneath a capsized boat in 1979. Peri's mother, Janine, remarried soon afterward.[338]

The Doctor assisted in bringing Skylab down to

Earth and it "**nearly cost him a thumb**".[339] Izzy was born on 12th October, 1979, although she never knew her parents. She was adopted by Les and Sandra Sinclair, but because of her uncertain parentage, chose to call herself "Izzy Somebody".[340]

c 1979 - "The Iron Legion"[341] -> The fourth Doctor landed on Earth just as it was attacked by robots resembling ancient Roman soldiers.

> = In another dimension, Rome never fell. Rome's robot legions, led by the eagle-headed Ironicus, fought the Eternal War across a thousand planets and by now had conquered the entire galaxy. The attack on our dimension represented the first strike in Rome's attempt to conquer the whole of creation.
>
> Rome itself was a vast futuristic city full of alien and human citizens, slaves and robots. Citizens enjoyed themselves watching gladiator fights between aliens and bionic humans at the Hyp-Arena, and car races at the Circus Maximus. Both events were televised. Rome had contact with many alien

planets, including the home of the Ectoslime and the Kronks in the Crab Nebula. The Kronks had fought Zarks in the Hyp-Arena, and were also turned into kronkburgers.

The child Adolphus Caesar - "Master of the Solar System and the Galaxy Beyond" - was now Emperor, but Rome's legions were led by the regent, Ironicus. The Doctor realised that Juno, the Adolphus' mother, was actually an alien. Following them to the Temple of the Gods, the Doctor recognised the building as a spacecraft, and the "gods" as the five Malevilus - Babiyon, Abiss, Epok, Nekros and Magog, a form of anti-life. They had given the Romans advanced technology to aid their goal of the conquest of all creation.

With the help of the bionic gladiator Morris and the ancient robot Vesuvius, the Doctor started a revolt. He unleashed the Bestarius (who were genetically engineered warriors), and confronted Juno, who revealed herself to be Magog. The Doctor tricked Magog into the TARDIS by promising to share its secrets, then trapped him in a pocket dimension. The other Malevilus tried to launch their ship, but Magog

---

339 *Tooth and Claw* (TV)

340 Izzy was born on the cover date of the first issue of *Doctor Who Weekly* (a fact established in "TV Action"). That date wasn't the day the magazine was published - magazine dates are when newsagents are meant to take them off the shelves. Details on her being adopted were mentioned in "End Game" (*DWM*).

341 Dating "The Iron Legion" (*DWW* #1-8) - The Doctor lands on contemporary Earth and makes topical references to inflation and the fuel crisis, suggesting the story is set around the year it was published (1979).

The Eternal War has "lasted through the millennia". The Doctor surmises they have "conquered the entire galaxy" (a sentiment echoed by a later caption) and refers to them as the Galactic Roman Empire. Ironicus says "now that Rome has gone on to conquer all dimensions" when offering sacrifices from our universe, but it's later clarified that the process has just started - these are "the first sacrifices from other dimensions".

It's unclear what year it is on the alternate Earth, or how long the Malevilus have been there. The Malevilus don't have time travel, at least not in a form as advanced as the TARDIS; this implies that if time runs at the same rate between dimensions, it's also 1979 there. However, Ironicus says it's the "year MMMXXI R.I.", with R.I. standing for Regency of Ironicus. That suggests it's 3021 years since the Regency started, but 1979 is only 2732 years after the founding of Rome (and when measuring the year, that was the start date Romans used), suggesting it's the future.

Adolphus, though, appears to be a normal young boy - one who looks about eight years old. He seems

shocked by Magog's true appearance, and there's no indication that Adolphus is a Malevilus or half-Malevilus himself. This may mean that Magog killed his real mother, or that he's preventing him from growing up (or both), but this isn't ever mentioned.

Roman technology is an odd mix of twentieth century technology such as tanks, television, zeppelins with advanced robots, bionics, dimension ducts, air-cars, metal eating "bact guns", robophants (robot war elephants) and interstellar travel. The Malevilus have presumably supplied most of the advanced technology. Robots have been around "centuries", and it would seem - although it's never explicitly stated - that the Malevilus built them, so have been around at least that long, too.

The story doesn't reconcile these statements. It doesn't explicitly say (or rule out) that it's the Malevilus who've prevented Rome from falling. If that was the case, it would mean they've been around at least fifteen hundred years.

The Doctor refers to Magog as "him", so his natural form is male. We see all five Malevilus "statues" apparently come to life with Juno in the room, even though Juno is Magog in disguise. Later we learn that Magog can be in more than one place at once. In "The Mark of Mandragora", we see Magog still in the TARDIS in the seventh Doctor's era, being eaten away by the Mandragora Helix.

The Doctor has heard of the Ectoslime and the Malevilus - who in turn have heard of the Time Lords - and kronkburgers are mentioned in *The Long Game*, so it would seem they all exist in our universe. The Doctor

had drained its power and it crashed, killing them. Vesuvius was installed as Emperor by popular decree.

The tenth Doctor planned to take Rose to an Ian Dury concert on 21st November, 1979.[342]

The Nineteen-Eighties

In the 1980s, the vampires Amelia Doory and Reggie Mead gained enough resources to start up a bloodfarm. They traded blood with other victims of the Forge in exchange for vampire DNA.[343]

= **PYRAMIDS OF MARS**[344] -> The Doctor took Sarah to an alternate version of 1980, to show her what would happen if they left England in 1911 before defeating Sutekh. Earth was a devastated wasteland.

---

c 1980 - "Yonder ... the Yeti"[345] -> A small expedition to Tibet went looking for the Yeti. They visited a local monk Lama Gampo, but the creatures attacked them, and the Great Intelligence possessed one of the expedition members. The Yeti had flying vehicles and web guns, and the Intelligence planned to launch a new conquest of Earth. Lama Gampo, whose father's uncle fought the Yeti sixty years before, rescued the party and summoned the real Yeti before destroying the power transfuser that linked the Intelligence to Earth. He then hypnotised the surviving expedition members to maintain his secrets.

1980 - "The Star Beast"[346] -> The peaceful Meeps became warlike when Black Sun radiation affected their planet. The Wrarth Galaxy Star Council created the Wrarth Warriors, amalgams of their five strongest races, to defeat them. The Meep armada was destroyed at the Battle of Yarras, but their leader, Beep the Meep, escaped.

An alien ship crashed at a steel mill in Blackcastle, a city in the north of England. The government denied it was a UFO, and UNIT troops were sent to secure the site. Two schoolchildren, Fudge and Sharon, discovered the sur-

vivor - the immensely cute Beep the Meep, who was being pursued by the monstrous Wrarth Warriors. The fourth Doctor and K9 landed on the Wrarth Warrior ship. The aliens immobilised the Doctor and planted a bomb inside him, sending him down to Earth, knowing he would locate the Meep.

The Meep used mind control to enslave humans to rebuild his ship, and planned to make a star jump while still on Earth - an act that would have hideous consequences. The Meep activated the black sun drive, sucking Blackcastle into a black hole, but the effects were temporary because the Doctor sabotaged the stardrive. Stuck in Earth orbit, the Meep was arrested and sent for trial. Sharon joined the Doctor on his adventures.

c 1980 - "The Collector" [347] -> The fourth Doctor and Sharon returned to Blackcastle after many adventures, but were immediately snatched up by a teleport-beam and rematerialised on a base in the asteroid belt. This was the home of Varan Tak from Oskerion, who had been capturing specimens from Earth for two thousand years. His ship had been damaged for that long, and he was waiting for his distress signal to arrive at his home planet. His only companionship during this exile was the ship's computer, who had built a robot form for herself. She was preventing Varan Tak from teleporting to Earth, but the Doctor destroyed the security precautions.

= Varan Tak beamed to Earth... only to die because he couldn't tolerate the pollution levels. The computer destroyed K9 in revenge.

The Doctor used the TARDIS to manipulate the ship's time stasis fields and changed history, destroying the teleporter and saving Varan Tak and K9. The Doctor, Sharon and K9 left Varan Tak and the computer in peace.

c 1980 - THE LEISURE HIVE[348] -> The fourth Doctor, Romana and K9 briefly landed on Brighton beach, but the Doctor had got the season wrong, and they soon left for Argolis.

---

knows about a strict boarding school run by Lukronian Vorks on the ice planet of Cryos IV on the edge of the galaxy, perhaps indicating it also exists in our universe.
342 *Tooth and Claw* (TV).
343 *Project Twilight*.
344 Dating *Pyramids of Mars* (13.3) - The year is stated several times by both the Doctor and Sarah (including the Doctor's comment, "1980, Sarah, if you want to get off"). The Doctor's actions prevent this timeline from coming to pass.
345 Dating "Yonder... the Yeti" (*DWW* #31-34) - When Bruce mentions the Yeti attack in the 1920s, the Lama

replies "many things have changed in the last sixty years", so the story - published in 1980 - is set in the 1980s.
346 Dating "The Star Beast" (*DWW* #19-26) - It's a contemporary setting, and the story was first published in the 80s. "Star Beast II" is set "fifteen years" later in "1995".
347 Dating "The Collector" (*DWM* #46) - It is Sharon's native time.
348 Dating *The Leisure Hive* (18.1) - It isn't clear when the TARDIS lands on Brighton beach. In Fisher's novelisation it is clearly contemporary, although the opening chapter of the novel is set in June - which would con-

Ashley Chapel experimented with the micromonolithic circuit and made contact with Saraquazel, a being from the universe that exists after our own.[349] Sabbath sent an agent to assassinate Pope John Paul II in 1980, but the attempt failed.[350]

@ The Doctor defeated the Voord in Penge during the nineteen-eighties.[351]

Samantha Angeline Jones was born on 15th April, 1980.[352]

> = She was born dark-haired, her mother a social worker and her father a doctor. She would grow up to become a vegetarian, and have scar marks on her arms from injecting diamorphine. She would end up living on a bedsit near King's Cross.

She was born blonde-haired, her mother a social worker and her father a doctor. She would grow up to become a vegetarian, but have no scar marks on her arm. She would meet the Doctor while attending school in 1997.[353]

1980 (30th April) - THE CITY OF THE DEAD[354] ->
The eighth Doctor arrived from the early twenty-first century to investigate a bone charm. Louisiana resident Alain Auguste Delesormes tried to conjure forth a water elemental, but most of his family perished when their home was flooded. The Doctor saved a young boy from the calamity, failing to realize that he was the water elemental in human form.

Delesormes' son, also named Alain, survived and was put into foster care in Vermont. He grew up to become police investigator Jonas Rust, and sought to continue his father's work. The water elemental's mother came to search for her son and was bound into a human body. She became the wife of New Orleans resident Vernon Flood, unable to escape her fleshy prison.

On 3rd June, 1980, the alien Ambassadors completed their survey of the solar system and left. No further contact with humanity was made.[355]

---

tradict Romana's on-screen exasperation that the Doctor has got "the season wrong". *The Terrestrial Index* and *The TARDIS Logs* both suggested a date of "1934", although why is unclear. The date doesn't appear in the script or any BBC documentation.

349 "Twenty years" before *Millennial Rites* (p216), and "five years" after he gets the circuit (p4).

350 *History 101*. In real life, assassination attempts were made on John Paul's life in May 1981 and May 1982.

351 *The Tomorrow Windows*

352 *Alien Bodies* (p177-178), with the date re-confirmed in *Revolution Man* (p191).

353 *Alien Bodies* (p177-178). Sam's original timeline is that of a dark-haired drug-user, but events in *Unnatural History* cancel out this history and create the blonde-haired version that becomes the Doctor's companion.

354 Dating *The City of the Dead* (EDA #49) - "That was in 1980" (p66).

355 *The Dying Days*, referring to the aliens seen in *The Ambassadors of Death*.

356 Dating *The Fires of Vulcan* (BF #12) - It is "the year 1980".

357 Dating *Shada* (17.6 and BF BBCi #2) - The TARDIS was "confused" by May Week being in June, so it landed in October. No year is given, but the story has a contemporary setting, and Chris Parsons graduated in 1978.

WHICH SHADA, IF ANY, IS CANON?: The TV version of *Shada* was never completed, following an industrial dispute during filming. A couple of clips were later used in *The Five Doctors* to show the fourth Doctor and Romana being taken out of their timestream. In 1992, the *Shada* footage that had been filmed was released on video, with special effects, music and a linking narration by Tom Baker. The clips that were included in *The Five Doctors* were re-jigged for the 1995 "Special

Edition" release of that story. Finally, in 2003, the story was remade in its entirety as a webcast with Paul McGann as the lead character and Lalla Ward reprising her role as Romana. A new introduction scene was included to help explain the eighth Doctor and Romana's sudden interest in these events. Big Finish later released the McGann version on CD.

Which of these - if any - is the "canonical" version of events? All things being equal, the *Doctor Who* TV series trumps all other formats, but in this case, the actual completion of the Paul McGann story - as opposed to the abandoned TV version - makes the webcast hard to ignore. Also, the alteration of the fourth Doctor / Romana clips in the different versions of *The Five Doctors* makes it harder and harder to reconcile them against the TV *Shada* itself.

A growing theory now holds that Borusa's time-scooping of the fourth Doctor and Romana derailed their adventure and they simply departed after the punting, with the eighth Doctor and Romana later returning to complete the task. The webcast, in fact, suggests that the eighth Doctor is plugging a gap in history by performing the duties that his fourth self would have done.

358 Dating *Meglos* (18.2) - Unless the Gaztaks can time travel, this story is set in the late twentieth century. The Earthling wears an early 1980s business suit. *The TARDIS Logs* offered a date of "1988", *Timelink* says "1983".

359 Dating *Father Time* (EDA #41) - The only date given is "the early 1980s". At the beginning of the book, Debbie is looking forward to a television schedule that is the evening that *Meglos* Part One was shown, 27th September, 1980.

360 *Salvation*

1980 - THE FIRES OF VULCAN[356] -> The archaeologist Scalini excavated a police box from the ruins of Pompeii. The seventh Doctor and Mel were inside, and exited the ship when no-one was looking. Captain Muriel Frost of UNIT called in the fifth Doctor to investigate.

c 1980 (October) - SHADA[357] -> Answering a distress signal from Professor Chronotis, the fourth Doctor and Romana arrived in Cambridge. They discovered that the geneticist Skagra had taken *The Worshipful and Ancient Law of Gallifrey*, the key to the Time Lord prison planet of Shada, and ended his scheme to mentally dominate the universe.

or ...

c 1980 (October) - THE FIVE DOCTORS / SHADA -> Borusa attempted to abduct the fourth Doctor (and possibly Romana) while they were punting in Cambridge. The abduction failed, and they were caught in a time eddy. This averted their visit to Chronotis, but the eighth Doctor and Romana later arrived and stopped Skagra as scheduled.

c 1980 - MEGLOS[358] -> On the planet Tigella, the fourth Doctor prevented the last Zolfa-Thuran, Meglos, from recovering the Dodecahedron - the power source that would allow him to use the Screens of Zolfa-Thura to destroy planets. The Screens, the Dodecahedron and Meglos himself were destroyed. Following this, the Doctor returned home an Earthling that a band of Gaztaks had kidnapped as a host body for Meglos.

@ c 1980 (Winter) - FATHER TIME[359] -> Rumours of mysterious lights and flying saucers drew UFO spotters to the Derbyshire village of Greyfrith. This had been caused by the arrival of a Klade saucer from the far, far future. The Klade Prefect Zevron and his deputy, Sallak, were hunting down the ten-year-old Miranda - the last survivor of the Imperial Family, brought to Earth by her nanny.

With the help of the Hunters Rum and Thelash, plus the giant robot Mr Gibson, Zevron tracked Miranda down. The eighth Doctor was staying just outside the village, and with the help of Miranda's teacher, Debbie Castle, he defeated Zevron and his henchmen. Zevron died, but Sallak survived and was arrested. Debbie's husband Barry was rendered mindless. The Doctor pledged to protect Miranda, who - like him - had two hearts.

After the Doctor officially adopted Miranda, they moved south to a large house. The Doctor became a business consultant, very quickly becoming a millionaire as he solved economic problems that confounded everyone else.

Following a remark from the Doctor, the barman of the Dragon pub in Greyfrith started selling bottled water. Within five years, he was making twenty million pounds a year from sales of Dragonwater.

In November 1980, *Prey for a Miracle* was released. It was a movie version of the "gods hoax" in 1965, starring Peter Cushing as the Doctor.[360] Shortly before he died, John Lennon told the Doctor, "Talent borrows, genius steals".[361] John Lennon was murdered on 8th December, 1980, by Mark Chapman. Huitzilin fed off the trauma of the event.[362]

Professor Edward Travers CBE died on Christmas Day the same year.[363] The Union of Traken now stretched over five or six planets in one solar system.[364] All diseases had been eradicated on Traken by this time.[365]

c 1981 - THE KEEPER OF TRAKEN[366] -> Traken was a peaceful planet in Mettula Orionsis. Two of the consuls of Traken - Tremas and Kassia - married.

Kassia had tended to the Melkur, a creature of evil that had calcified in Traken's serene environment, since she was a child. But now the Melkur had begun to move again. Hypnotically controlling Kassia, the Melkur - in reality the renegade Time Lord the Master - attempted to seize control of the Source, the power of the Keeper of Traken. The Master was at the end of his regeneration cycle, and was desperate to obtain the power necessary to gain a new body. Kassia was killed, but the fourth Doctor prevented the Master from acquiring the Source, and Consul Luvic became the new Keeper. The Master escaped, and took the body of Tremas as his new form.

Survivors from Traken would found the colony of Serenity, a verdant world of peace and isolation.[367] **The Doctor visited Terminal Three of Heathrow Airport around this time.**[368]

---

361 *Eye of Heaven*

362 *The Left-Handed Hummingbird*

363 *Downtime*

364 *Divided Loyalties*

365 *Primeval*

366 Dating *The Keeper of Traken* (18.6) - Traken is destroyed in the subsequent story, *Logopolis*, so The *Keeper of Traken* can't occur after this time, although *The TARDIS Logs* suggested a date of "4950 AD". Melkur arrived on Traken "many years" before. The script specifies that Kassia is eighteen at the time, the same age as Nyssa when the Doctor first meets her.

367 *Cold Fusion*

368 *Four to Doomsday*. The Doctor mentions the visit

1981 (28th February) - LOGOPOLIS[369] -> The fourth Doctor landed on Earth and took the measurements of a genuine police box to help repairs to the TARDIS' chameleon circuit. He had previously visited the planet Logopolis, hoping they could help him with their mathematical expertise and mastery of block transfer computation.

The Doctor learnt from the Monitor of Logopolis that the universe had already passed the natural point of heat death. All closed systems succumb to heat death, and the universe was such a closed system. Or rather it used to be: the Logopolitans had opened up CVEs into other universes, such as E-Space. When the Master learnt of this, he recognised a chance to blackmail the entire universe. The Master's interference halted Logopolis' operations, which caused the CVEs to collapse. Entropy began to accumulate and destroyed a vast region of space, including Logopolis and Traken.

On Earth, the Doctor and the Master worked to reopen a CVE in Cassiopeia at co-ordinates 3C461-3044. The Master threatened to close off even this CVE, and broadcast a message to the entire universe:

"Peoples of the universe please attend carefully, the message that follows is vital to the future of you all. The choice for you all is simple: a continued existence under my guidance, or total annihilation. At the time of speaking, the fate of the universe lies in the balance at the fulcrum point, the Pharos Project on Earth..."

The Doctor prevented the Master from closing the CVE, at the cost of his own life...

1981 - CASTROVALVA[370] -> ...The newly-regenerated fifth Doctor and his companions Nyssa and Tegan returned to the TARDIS. The Master kidnapped Adric.

1981 (28th February) - FOUR TO DOOMSDAY[371] -> The fifth Doctor defeated Monarch's plans to travel back to the creation of the universe. Monarch's android crew opted to find a habitable world and settle on it.

In 1981, UNIT encountered the Zygons in the Kalahari Desert and the Ice Warriors in Northampton.[372] The Jex arrived on Earth on 4th December, 1981, and took shelter in California.[373]

@ Even with the help of character references from people such as Graham Greene and Lawrence Olivier, the Doctor needed nearly a year to formally adopt Miranda. Shortly after that, he defeated the Great Provider's plan to use evil mobile telephones to take over the world.[374]

1981 (18th - 22nd December) K9 AND COMPANY: A GIRL'S BEST FRIEND[375] -> In September, a hailstorm lasting thirteen seconds destroyed Commander Pollock's crop. He was renting the East Wing of Lavinia Smith's house at the time. On 6th December, Lavinia Smith left for America, phoning her ward Brendan Richards on the 10th to tell him that he would be spending Christmas with her niece, Sarah Jane. The next day, Brendan's term ended and he began waiting for Sarah to pick him up, but she had spent the first two weeks of December working abroad for Reuters.

Sarah Jane found a crate waiting for her at Moreton Harwood. It contained K9 Mk III, sent as a gift from the Doctor. Working together, Sarah, Brendan and K9

during his attempt to convince Tegan that the Urbankan ship might be Heathrow.
369 Dating *Logopolis* (18.7) - The date is first stated in *Four to Doomsday*, and is the same day that the first episode was broadcast. This is the first on-screen use of the term "chameleon circuit". *The TARDIS Logs* set the *Logopolis* sequence in "4950". It's never stated if the other CVEs are ever restored, although it's possible that reviving the Cassiopeia CVE opened the others.
370 Dating *Castrovalva* (19.1) - This story immediately follows *Logopolis*.
371 Dating *Four to Doomsday* (19.2) - The Doctor establishes that he has returned Tegan to the right point in time "16.15 hours" on "February 28th 1981", the day Part One of *Logopolis* was broadcast.
372 *The King of Terror*. The newly-regenerated fifth Doctor briefly slipped into his third persona, and seemed to recall an encounter where the Brigadier and Ice Warriors were present. In *The Dying Days*, the Brigadier says he never met the Ice Warriors, so this couldn't have involved him.

373 *The King of Terror*
374 *The Gallifrey Chronicles*
375 Dating *K9 and Company* (18.7-A) - Sarah arrives in Moreton Harwood on "December the 18th", and later tells K9 that it is "1981". The other dates are given in dialogue. This story is part of the UNIT timeframe, but real life has overtaken Sarah's "I'm from 1980" comment in *Pyramids of Mars*.
376 Dating *Blue Box* (PDA #59) - Presuming one can believe Peters' account, the story opens "two days before Christmas 1981" (p10). Peters visits Swan in the Bainbridge Hospital in late 1982 (p5).
377 Dating *Time-Flight* (18.7) - The date isn't specified beyond Tegan's "this is the 1980s". There's no indication that it's the exact day Tegan left in *Logopolis* (or that it isn't). There's snow on the ground, which there wasn't in *Logopolis*, but which doesn't rule out it being February.
378 *The King's Demons*
379 *Arc of Infinity*
380 *Night Thoughts*. The Falklands War lasted from 2nd April to 14th June, 1982.

exposed a local coven of witches who conducted human sacrifices. On 29th December, the cultists appeared in court on an attempted murder charge.

1981 (23rd December) - BLUE BOX[376] **->** By now Eridani agents on Earth had recovered three of the five computer components that went missing circa 1966. The sixth Doctor allied with the Eridani to recover the last two, fearing they could affect Earth's development. However, he discovered that the components, part of a system named "the Savant," could usurp control of the human brain's "hardware / software," and had been dispatched to the Eridani colony to mentally dominate it.

The Doctor and the Eridani retrieved the last two components from the formidable hacker Sarah Swan and her friend Luis Perez. However, the Savant had mentally dominated Swan and Perez, who were left near-catatonic. By late 1982, Swan was reportedly in the Bainbridge Hospital, a facility where the American government kept persons with dangerous information. Perez's family cared for him in Mexico.

The journalist Charles "Chick" Peters later wrote *Blue Box*, a chronicle of these events.

c 1982 - TIME-FLIGHT[377] **->** Following the disappearance of Speedbird Concorde 192 down a time contour, the fifth Doctor, Tegan and Nyssa arrived at Heathrow Airport. At the insistence of Sir John Sudbury at C-19, the Doctor was allowed to take a second Concorde into the contour, and travelled back one hundred and forty million years. Back home, Tegan left the TARDIS crew.

The Master's TARDIS was propelled to Xeraphas, where he discovered Kamelion, a tool of a previous invader of that planet.[378] Tegan Jovanka resumed being an air stewardess, but was sacked shortly afterward.[379]

During the Falklands War, toxin experiments were conducted on one of the small Hebrides Islands in Scotland. Roughly a dozen inhabitants were relocated before the chemical gas weapon Gravonax was tested. This killed all wildlife on the isle - which was dubbed Gravonax Island - and nobody wanted to live there even after it was decontaminated.

Major Dickens and a female military chaplain - later known only as "the Deacon" - served in the war but left the

British army after "a bit of an incident". Dickens deemed the secluded Gravonax Island as perfect for his scientific research, and took up residence in Sibley Hall there.[380]

A Cyber-Leader, potentially the last of its kind, arrived from the far future in a Gallifreyan time-ship. The Cyber-Leader was greatly weakened by exposure to Vortex energy, but continued its scheme to trap the Doctor.[381]

1982 (April) - RELATIVE DEMENTIAS[382] **->** Joyce Brunner, a former UNIT physicist, came to suspect abnormal activity at the Graystairs nursing home. She alerted her old colleague the Doctor (who was now in his seventh incarnation), who arrived with Ace to investigate. The head of Graystairs - the Annarene named Sooal - successfully restored the Tulk War Council's memories, then murdered the group upon obtaining the command codes to the Tulk stasis chamber. However, two renegade Annarene arrived and killed Sooal, desiring the advanced weaponry within the stasis chamber to return their people to war. The Doctor tricked the Annarene into transmatting into the stasis chamber before it was opened, freezing them in time. He then destroyed the Tulk spaceship.

The ninth Doctor had a number of blind spots in his historical knowledge, the events of May 1982 among them.[383]

@ After two years of the Doctor attempting to interrogate him, the imprisoned alien Sallak got a legal injunction preventing the Doctor from making any other contact.[384] Isaac Summerfield met Hamlet Macbeth in 1982, and was given a copy of his book *The Shoreditch Incident*.[385]

1982 (11th July) - LIVING LEGEND[386] **->** Two agents of the aggressive Threllip race constructed an interdimensional portal in Ferrara, Italy, as a means for the Threllip people to invade Earth. On 11th July, 1982, the eighth Doctor and Charley squashed the plan, and used the portal to strand the agents on the seventeenth moon of Mordalius Prime. The Doctor then dismantled the portal.

The Doctor spent time with Nelson Mandela during his imprisonment at Robbin Island.[387] Mel left school after getting five A-Levels. She backpacked around Europe before getting a job at a Scottish nature reserve. Around the same time, SenéNet was buying up European computer firms

---

381 630 days before *The Reaping*, which opens on 24th September, 1984.
382 Dating *Relative Dementias* (PDA #49) - The date is given (p40).
383 *Only Human*
384 "Two years" after the first part of *Father Time*, "three years" before the second (p114).

385 *Return of the Living Dad*
386 Dating *Living Legend* (BF promo #4, *DWM* #337) - The date is given, Track 1.
387 *The Also People*. This would be between 1982 and 1988.

and other "youth market" companies. Their executives were converted into drones.[388]

c 1983 - ARC OF INFINITY[389] -> Omega had relocated the Arc of Infinity - a gateway between dimensions - away from the star system Rondel and placed its curve on the city of Amsterdam. The fifth Doctor tracked Omega to Amsterdam, and found Omega's base in a crypt there. The ancient Gallifreyan's attempt to bond with the fifth Doctor failed, and he apparently died. Tegan Jovanka joined the Doctor's travels once again.

Omega recorporalized enough to stow himself aboard the TARDIS of Ertikus, a Time Lord who arrived in this period to study Omega's exploits. Ertikus' TARDIS relocated to the far future with Omega aboard.[390] **Before this time, the Arar-Jecks of Heiradi had carved out a huge subterranean city during the 20-Aeon War on that planet.**[391] The Doctor and Ace fought an N-form by the Rio Yari in 1983.[392]

Before this time, Trion had founded colonies on other planets, forming an empire that the Clans came to rule for nine thousand years. The Clans were driven by science and technology, and the development of a vacuum transport system revolutionized on-planet travel. Non-Clansmen incorporated cold fusion into their spaceships.[393]

1983 - MAWDRYN UNDEAD[394] -> There was Civil war on Trion. Turlough's mother was killed and the ship containing his father and brother crashed on Sarn, formerly a Trion prison planet. Turlough was captured and exiled to Earth, where Trion agents, including a solicitor on Chancery Lane, watched him. At some point after 1977, he was sent to Brendon School.

The Brigadier regained his memory, but lost his beloved car when he met the fifth Doctor. When he met his past self from 1977, the Brigadier unwittingly provided the energy that released Mawdryn and his followers from their curse of immortality. Turlough left Brendon to join the TARDIS crew.

1983 - TURLOUGH AND THE EARTHLINK DILEMMA[395] -> After departing the fifth Doctor's company, a time-travelling Turlough encountered the dictator Rechtaht while she ruled Trion. Rechtaht tried to transfer her mind into Turlough, but his ally - a Time Lord named the Magician - helped Turlough to expel Rechtaht from his mind. This averted a timeline that included the destruction of Earth, Trion and New Trion.

Turlough learned that as he had altered history, he couldn't remain in this timeline without causing a paradox. With the Magician's help, Turlough found a reality in which he had died and took up residence there. He was reunited with his old friend, Juras Maateh, of that reality.

The Doctor in Stockbridge

Around 1983, the fifth Doctor settled in the Gloucestershire village of Stockbridge for a time, a guest at the Green Dragon Inn. He had volunteered to investigate time warps on behalf of the Time Lords. After a number of interruptions, he learned that the time warps had been triggered by the Meddling Monk.[396]

= c 1983 - "The Tides of Time"[397] -> The Prime Mover produced the ordered vibrations of the universe on a vast biomechanical device known as the Event Synthesiser. For the first time in centuries, he fumbled a note, introducing a note of discord. Time warps occured. The fifth Doctor had been staying in the Gloucestershire village of Stockbridge for some

---

388 *Business Unusual*
389 Dating *Arc of Infinity* (20.1) - There is no indication of the year. It is some time after *Time-Flight*, and before *The Awakening*.
390 *Omega*
391 As mentioned by Turlough in *Frontios*, although the universe isn't yet twenty billion years old at this point.
392 *Damaged Goods*
393 *Turlough and the Earthlink Dilemma*
394 Dating *Mawdryn Undead* (20.3) - The Doctor says "if these readings are correct, its 1983 on Earth", and the date is reaffirmed a number of times afterward.
Turlough first appears in *Mawdryn Undead*, but his origins are revealed in *Planet of Fire*. According to the initial Character Outline, Turlough was "20" on his first appearance, which makes him a couple of years too old

to be at Brendon School - this was almost certainly written when the plan was to introduce the character in *The Song of the Space Whale* by Pat Mills, a story that was delayed, then rejected. Mark Strickson was twenty-two when he began playing Turlough.
395 Dating *Turlough and the Earthlink Dilemma* (*The Companions of Doctor Who* #1) - As Turlough's actions eliminate Rehctaht, this presumably (and paradoxically) causes the very political reform that allows his younger self to return home to Trion in *Planet of Fire*.
396 For almost the entire run of the fifth Doctor's adventures in *DWM*, he was based in Stockbridge. The reason for this was finally explained in "4-Dimensional Vistas". The stories have a contemporary setting. While they started publication in 1982, the Doctor in "Lunar Lagoon" assumes it is 1983 - the only time a year is specified.

time, and was playing a cricket match on the village green when he was bowled a hand grenade instead of a cricket ball. Shortly afterwards, a Roman soldier was shot in nearby woods, only to vanish. The Doctor quickly learned the disturbances were worldwide.

Meanwhile, the Event Synthesiser's discord had opened a gap in time, and the Demon Melanicus emerged through it. He took control of the Event Synthesizer in order to create universal fear, destruction and unending chaos.

A jousting knight - Sir Justin - initially attacked the Doctor, but came to realize his error and vowed to help fight whoever was behind the time warps. Melanicus removed the Event Synthesizer from time to prevent attack, but was detected by the spirit of Rassilon deep in the Matrix. He vowed to act, despite advice from Morvane and Bedevere to be cautious. Rassilon decided to operate through the Doctor, who arrived on Gallifrey and used his Presidential authority to access the Matrix. The Doctor entered the Matrix to commune with Rassilon, and saw him chairing a meeting of the High Evolutionaries from a number of planets.

The High Evolutionaries tasked the Doctor with locating the Event Synthesizer. Rassilon despatched a mysterious agent named Shayde, who infiltrated the TARDIS to help the Doctor. Melanicus' interference created the maelstrom - a whirlpool in space and time - and sent a mantric bomb against Gallifrey. Shayde protected the Doctor from its effects, but the TARDIS was sucked into Melanicus' domain: a surreal world where the Doctor and Justin encountered a carnival, a mysterious woman that the Doctor recognised, a demonic fairground ride, barbarian hordes and Dracula.

Emerging from Melanicus' domain, the Doctor took the TARDIS out of time to help his search. He re-entered time, then encountered a ship from Althrace which took them to their home in an alien dimension - a vast solar system engineered so that the planets were bolted together and set orbiting a white hole. The technology of Althrace was as advanced as that of the Time Lords, and the white hole allowed direct access to the forces of creation, making them one vast, living organism. Using the power of the White Hole, the High Evolutionaries combined their mental force to halt time and discover the co-ordinates of the Event Synthesizer. Meanwhile, Melanicus had ushered in the Millenium Wars:

THE MILLENIUM WARS

"A thousand worlds in conflict for a thousand years .. with causes lost in the distant past, their fury rages through time and space..."

In the year 375, barbarian hordes from Asia swept into Central Europe... and were wiped out by a division of Nazi tanks... which in turn were wiped out by American F-15 fighters... which in turn were wiped out by advanced space fighters.

"This was the beginning of the Reign of Melanicus as millenium fought millenium... and so what began as a series of small, confused skirmishes soon escalated into a holocaust of conflict, culminating in a far-flung armageddon - the Millenium Wars! A thousand worlds in conflict for a thousand years."

= **"The Deal"**[398] -> The fourth Doctor caused a trooper of the 12th Trouble 'chuters to crash. The trooper set his robot "spider" on him, but the Doctor blocked its psychic attack. A pursuit ship arrived, firing missiles at the TARDIS. The Doctor realised that the trooper was a psychopath and left, abandoning him to death at the hands of another pursuit ship.

As for *where* these stories take place in relation to the fifth Doctor's television adventures, there's strictly speaking no gap where he's travelling without companions (and unhelpfully, he never mentions any of his television companions while he's in Stockbridge). He considers himself President of Gallifrey (prescient of a comic strip published in 1982, because he was stripped of his Presidency after *The Invasion of Time*, and was not President again until *The Five Doctors*). His sixth incarnation is hunting for the person that had Gus killed, suggesting that happened recently. However, the TARDIS console is the older model - not the new one the Doctor unveils in *The Five Doctors* - and he's wearing his original cricket jumper. Whenever it's set, as the Doctor's fifth incarnation never travelled alone on television, it means he's dropped off whichever companion or companions he had at the time for the duration.

397 "The Tides of Time"

398 Dating "The Deal" (*DWM* #53) - No date is given, other than stating that the story takes place during the Millenium Wars. *DWM* consistently misspelt "millennium" with one "n". This is not the same as the Millennium War in *The Quantum Archangel*.

= **"The Tides of Time"**[399] -> But due to his lack of knowledge, Melanicus had confined himself to a cul-de-sac in time. This was to prove his undoing.

After a thousand years of the Millenium Wars, Earth was ruined and lifeless. Melanicus had based the Synthesizer here, and the fifth Doctor located it. The Doctor and Shayde weakened Melanicus, and Justin pierced the demon with his sword, unleashing vast energies. Justin and Melanicus were killed, and the Prime Mover was restored to his rightful place as user of the Event Synthesizer.

The Doctor awoke to find time restored, and a memorial to the fallen knight in the church in Stockbridge: St Justinians. As Shayde watched the cricket game resume, the Doctor was unsure if it had all been a dream.

c 1983 - "Stars Fell on Stockbridge"[400] -> UFO spotter Maxwell Edison discovered the TARDIS, and inspired the fifth Doctor to detect an alien spacecraft two days from Earth. They went to the ship, which was deserted and had been drifting for thousands of years. There was some sort of haunting presence on board, but the ship was already heading for Earth's atmosphere. The Doctor and Maxwell returned to Earth, from where Maxwell watched the shooting stars caused by the ship's break-up.

No human space agency had any space labs in orbit at this point.

c 1983 - "The Stockbridge Horror"[401] -> A local limestone quarry unearthed the TARDIS in rock five hundred million years old. Nearby, a police constable discovered a charred body.

The fifth Doctor, still staying at the Green Dragon Inn, saw a report from the quarry. He ran to where he had left the TARDIS - Well's Wood - and found it was still there, covered in mud. He went to the quarry, but couldn't get to the mysterious buried police box. Well's Wood caught fire, and the Doctor - upon returning to the TARDIS - discovered an alien figure that could shoot jets of fire.

The Doctor dematerialized his Ship, but the alien clung to the TARDIS, then forced its way inside. It stalked the Doctor, who realised it was the presence he'd recently encountered on the deserted spaceship. The Gallifreyan military dispatched Lord Tubal Cain in a specially adapted TARDIS, while Shayde trapped the alien in the Matrix. Cain fired seeker torpedoes at the TARDIS... which landed on Gallifrey moments after they hit the homeworld.

While the Doctor faced trial on Gallifrey, the government agency SAG3 investigated the TARDIS. Shayde neutralised them, and erased the imprint of the TARDIS just as the military TARDIS landed. The Doctor was freed.

---

399 Dating "The Tides of Time" (*DWM* #61-67) - Time is disturbed during this story, and strictly speaking the events take place in a cul-de-sac of time created by Melanicus, and which is destroyed at the end.

The year the story starts is not specified, but the first part features the discordant note and specifies that the Doctor's cricket game on contemporary Earth is taking place "at that precise moment." "Forty years before", the village green was a sandbagged army training army, so clearly that was during the Second World War. The story was published in 1982. In "Lunar Lagoon", the Doctor had thought he was in "1983", perhaps suggesting that's the year the Stockbridge adventures take place.

The story spells "Event Synthesizer" in both its American and British ("Synthesiser") form in different installments. Stockbridge isn't named until the following story.

The mysterious woman the Doctor sees in the dreamscape is never identified - the dress she wears resembles a jumpsuit Zoe wore in *The Wheel in Space*. In retrospect - and completely coincidentally - she resembles the first incarnation of Patience, seen in a similar flashback in *Cold Fusion*.

400 Dating "Stars Fell on Stockbridge" (*DWM* #68-69) - No year is given, but it's a contemporary setting, and the Doctor is still based in Stockbridge, as he was in

"The Tides of Time".

401 Dating "The Stockbridge Horror" (*DWM* #70-75) - Once again, it's a contemporary setting.

402 Dating "4-Dimensional Vistas" (*DWM* #78-83) - This story marks the end of the Doctor's vigil on Earth. In "Lunar Lagoon", the Doctor thought he was in "1983".

403 Dating *The Five Doctors* (20.1) - The Brigadier recognises Tegan, so he must be kidnapped by Borusa after the second half of *Mawdryn Undead* in 1983. It is specified that he is attending a UNIT reunion (perhaps one he initiated once his memories returned?), but this isn't the occasion of his retirement. Sarah is kidnapped around the same time, certainly after *K9 and Company*.

404 *Business Unusual. The Face of the Enemy* seems to imply that Bell becomes romantically involved with Benton, but this is never substantiated elsewhere.

405 "Last year" according to *Heart of TARDIS* (p41).

406 *Ghost Light.* Marc Platt's novelisation specifies that Gabriel Chase is burnt down in August 1983. Ace's social worker is referred to in *Survival*.

407 "Eight months" before *Return of the Living Dad*.

408 He says he was born "this year" in *Return of the Living Dad*.

409 *Interference* (p296).

410 Dating "City of Devils" (*DWM Holiday Special 1992*) - The date is given in the opening caption.

1983 - "4-Dimensional Vistas"[402] **->** A British Airways 747 crashed in the Arctic, shot down by the test firing of a Martian cannon. The Meddling Monk and a group of Ice Warriors led by Autek had a base there, and were manipulating time. The fifth Doctor homed in on them, but was attacked by the beam weapon. SAG3 arrived by plane to investigate.

Meanwhile, the Doctor and Gus discovered that the Ice Warriors had drilled a vast shaft. The Doctor was captured, but Gus escaped. Gus and SAG3 launched an attack on the Ice Warrior base, but Autek and the Meddling Monk got away. They had activated "the Crucible", then jumped five million years forwards in time. As they returned, the Doctor chased the Monk's TARDIS in his own and set up a Time Ram - annihilating the Monk and destroying the Ice Warrior base.

His vigil on Earth ended, the Doctor pledged to get Gus home.

c 1983 - THE FIVE DOCTORS[403] **->** The second Doctor and the Brigadier were kidnapped by Borusa in the grounds of UNIT HQ. The next day, the second Doctor bought a copy of "The Times" that reported the UNIT reunion. Colonel Crichton was running UNIT at this point. Despite K9's warnings, Sarah Jane Smith was also kidnapped by Borusa.

Masie Hawk, Hamlet Macbeth, Liz Shaw and Sir John Sudbury also attended the reunion. Benton had returned to active duty. Carol Bell was married with a child. Mike Yates and Tom Osgood had opened a tearoom together.[404] Lethbridge-Stewart spent some time in Haiti.[405]

In 1983, a 13-year-old Ace was friends with an Asian girl, Manisha, whose flat was firebombed in a racist attack. In revenge, Ace burnt down Gabriel Chase. She was assigned a probation officer and social worker.[406]

Joel Mintz had been thrown back in time to 1983 from 1993. He ended up in New York, where Isaac Summerfield found him.[407] Jason Kane was born in 1983.[408] In 1983, Faction Paradox agents wrecked the Blue Peter garden.[409]

c 1983 (Summer) - "City of Devils"[410] **->** Aunt Lavinia sent Sarah Jane and K9 to Egypt to write a story about her

friend Warren Martyn. An archaeological dig there had experienced some mysterious deaths and disappearances. Entering the tomb, Sarah and K9 encountered a group of Silurians and Sea Devils in a vast subterranean city. Sarah opened diplomatic relations with the Silurians, and it was hoped that this would lead to an accomodation between the two civilisations. Returning to England, Sarah Jane contacted Lethbridge-Stewart, who was keen to make amends for the mistakes of the past.

c 1983 (July) - HEART OF TARDIS[411] **->** Crowley lured the fourth Doctor and Romana to the Tollsham USAF base, as he needed the Doctor to open the Golgotha gateway.

Peri Brown, a 17-year-old student at Boston University, bought a handgun.[412]

1983 - RETURN OF THE LIVING DAD[413] **->** The seventh Doctor, Benny, Jason, Chris and Roz discovered that Benny's father, Isaac, was alive and well in the village of Little Caldwell. He was running an underground movement that helped stranded aliens on Earth return home.

Albinex the Navarino paid one of Isaac's allies to retrieve nuclear launch codes from the Doctor. Albinex and Issac were working together to detonate a nuclear device, which Issac hoped would spur an arms race so humanity would have more advanced weapons to use against the Daleks in the twenty-second century. However, Albinex was actually a Dalek agent, and planned to destroy the Earth. The Doctor, Isaac and Benny captured the Navarino and thwarted the plan. Benny made peace with her father.

The "microchip revolution" took place in the early eighties.[414] The Doctor, Tegan and Nyssa visited Hexen Bridge in 1984.[415] **The ninth Doctor and Rose quietly attended the wedding of her parents, Peter Tyler and Jacqueline Andrea Suzette Prentice.**[416] The Doctor said 1984 was "never as good as the book."[417] **Torchwood constructed a secret base beneath the Thames Barrier.**[418]

1984 (1st May) - THE AWAKENING[419] **->** The Malus absorbed the psychic energy of a series of war games in Little Hodcombe, amplifying the villagers' violence. The fifth Doctor prevented the Malus from becoming

411 Dating *Heart of TARDIS* (PDA #32) - It's July (p117), "fifteen years" after 1968 (p246).
412 *Burning Heart* (p102).
413 Dating *Return of the Living Dad* (NA #53) - It's "10 December 1983" (p34).
414 *Remembrance of the Daleks*. Had someone from 1963 discovered Ace's ghetto blaster, this would have occurred "twenty years too early".
415 *The Hollow Men*

416 *Father's Day*. No precise dating is given, but it's before Rose's birth in 1986.
417 *The Reaping*
418 *The Runaway Bride*. The Thames Barrier was constructed from 1974 to 1984.
419 Dating *The Awakening* (21.2) - The Doctor assures Tegan that "it is 1984", despite Will Chandler's clothing. As Tegan is the Queen of the May, it is presumably May Day.

totally active and blew up the church in which the Malus lay dormant. After this, the Doctor, Tegan and Turlough spent some time in Little Hodcombe with Tegan's grandfather, Andrew Verney.

The Doctor's experiences in Little Hodcombe reminded him of Hexen Bridge. He decided to monitor the area.[420]

1984 - RESURRECTION OF THE DALEKS[421] **->** Daleks from the future arrived in the twentieth century and placed their Duplicates in key positions around the world. They used the timezone as a safe storage place for the Movellan virus that had all but wiped them out. A pitched battle broke out between the British army and the Daleks. Afterward, Tegan was appalled by the carnage and left the fifth Doctor's company.

Tegan relocated to Brisbane after leaving the Doctor, and eventually took over the family business, Verney Feeds, from her father. The company supplied animal feed to farmers, and Tegan for a time dated one of its employees, Michael Tenaka.[422]

c 1984 (9th May) - PLANET OF FIRE[423] **->** Professor Howard Foster discovered an archaeologically important wreck off the coast of Lanzarote. His step-daughter, Perpugilliam Brown, travelled to the planet Sarn in the fifth Doctor's TARDIS. There, the Master attempted to restore his shrunken body using the Numismaton gas of a sacred volcano. The Doctor facilitated the Master's demise before this could happen. Turlough's exile was lifted and he returned to Trion. Peri started travelling with the Doctor. In autumn of the same year, she was due back at college.

Peri first met the Doctor on 9th May, 1984, and was 18 at the time. Her father, Paul, had died.[424]

Anthony Chambers became undertaker of St. Anne's Cemetery in Baltimore, and happened upon the Cyber-Leader from the far future there. The Cyber-Leader mentally enthralled Chambers for a time, then staged Chambers' brutal murder as a means of catching the Doctor's interest. The crime was blamed on a local vagrant, even as Chambers' body was secretly Cyber-augmented.[425]

? 1984 - URBAN MYTHS[426] **->** Three CIA agents had become infected by a strain of the Tule-Oz virus - which mucked up their memories, and caused them to think that the fifth Doctor and Peri had caused mass slaughter on the planet Poiti. The agents tracked the travelers to a restaurant on Earth and sought to kill them, but the Doctor and Peri - posing as a chef and waitress - served them the antidote throughout a multi-course meal. The agents were cured, and returned to Gallifrey.

1984 (August / September) - DOWNTIME[427] **->** Victoria Waterfield was mentally compelled to return to the Det-Sen monastery, which was suddenly destroyed. She was later contracted by Professor Travers, unaware that he was dead and animated by the Great Intelligence.

1984 (24th September) - THE REAPING[428] **->** In Baltimore, news of Anthony Chambers' "murder" became public, and Peri arrived with the sixth Doctor to attend the man's funeral. She had been gone for four months, and found that her mother - Janine Foster - and Howard had divorced.

A Cyber-Leader from the far future, who had arrived two years before, attempted to compel the Doctor to pilot his acquired time-ship back to prehistoric Earth, and to

---

420 *The Hollow Men*
421 Dating *Resurrection of the Daleks* (21.3) - The Doctor says it is "1984 - Earth". We never hear of the Duplicates again. In terms of this timeline, the Daleks are from 4590.
422 *The Gathering*. The "Verney" of Verney Feeds presumably refers to Tegan's grandfather from *The Awakening*.
423 Dating *Planet of Fire* (21.5) - Peri says she is due back at college in "the Fall", which isn't for "three months". There is nothing to suggest that the story isn't set in the year it was broadcast (1984). It can't take place before 1983, otherwise Turlough would return home while his past self was still in exile (*Mawdryn Undead*). In *Timelash,* the Doctor threatens to take Peri back to "1985".

Peri's step-father says they were on the island of Lanzarote, which is where filming took place. Yet

Lanzarote was not on any ancient Greek trading routes, unlike the island in the story.
424 *The Reaping*. The date of Peri's encounter with the Doctor in Lanzarote is on the audio's back cover.
425 Three months before *The Reaping*, set in September 1984.
426 Dating *Urban Myths* (BF #95) - The story takes place at an Earth restaurant (probably in Hungary, owing to mention of the invention of goulash), but the dating is unknown. The only real clue is that a restaurant has operated at the location "since the time of the Hapsburgs", which rules out anything beyond the mid-twenty-second century (when the Dalek Invasion would undoubtedly interrupt service). The choice of dating this story to 1984 - contemporary with the fifth Doctor and Peri's adventures on TV - is arbitrary. A case can be made for placing it concurrent with the release of *Urban Myths* in 2007.

retroactively initiate the conversion of humanity into Cybermen. The Doctor thwarted this plan and deposited the Cyber-Leader on the contemporary Mondas, where the indigenous Cybermen viewed the Leader as defective and scheduled him for reprocessing.

In the course of this investigation, the media branded the Doctor as a dangerous criminal. The Cyber-augmented Anthony Chambers went dormant, but not before grievously wounding his own son Nate.

Peri decided to leave the Doctor, live with her mother and enrol at university. However, she kept half of a Cyber-conversion egg as a memento. The device exploded, killing Janine Foster and her friend, Mrs Van Gysegham. Peri resumed traveling with the Doctor.

After Janine died, Katherine Chambers took the other half of the Cyber-conversion egg and went into hiding with her crippled brother. She had studied medicine at Boston, and a colleague of hers from university - James Clarke - helped the two of them relocate to Brisbane. Kathy finished her education and became a doctor, but James' condition worsened and she upgraded him into a pseudo-Cyberman.[429]

= c 1984 (Winter) - TURLOUGH AND THE EARTHLINK DILEMMA[430] **->** On Trion, the dictator Rehctaht fell from power, and the few surviving Clansmen - including Turlough - were allowed to return home to a hero's welcome. Turlough used his knowledge of TARDISes to build the first-ever ARTEMIS drive, a device that used "muon" particles and was capable of time travel. On New Trion, Turlough discovered a copy of an alien edifice named the Mobile Castle, and equipped it with a second ARTEMIS drive. The in-flight Castle was sabotaged and crashed onto Trion, destroying the planet. Earth and New Trion were subsequently annihilated in nuclear conflicts.

Turlough discovered that Rehctaht had transferred her mind into the body of his old friend Juras Maateh, and had engineered Earth, Trion and New Trion's obliteration to further her gravity control experi-

ments, hoping to gain the secret of time travel. Turlough killed Rechtaht / Juras, then travelled back in time to prevent this history from occurring.

In 1984, scientists in Princeton discovered Strange Matter.[431] The seventh Doctor and Mel visited the Welsh village of Llanfer Ceiriog.[432]

Torchwood bought the London security firm HC Clements.[433]

1984 - "The Fires Down Below"[434] **->** Major Whitaker of UNIT was sent by Lethbridge-Stewart to Reykjavik to investigate an unnatural increase in volcanic activity. The UNIT troops discovered a squad of Quarks planting seismic charges. A member of the party, Professor Iskander, was taken before Dominator Haag. He learned that the Dominators were planning to destroy Earth to extract its core for fuel. The UNIT troops attacked, then escaped as the Dominators' machines exploded and destroyed the aliens.

1985 - ATTACK OF THE CYBERMEN[435] **->** The police had been aware of Lytton, a sophisticated thief who had stolen valuable electronic components, for a year. Lytton had discovered the Cybermen were operating in the sewers of London and was trying to contact them. The Cybermen tried, but failed, to divert Halley's Comet so that it would crash into Earth and avert the destruction of Mondas in 1986.

The Cybermen captured Lytton and lured the sixth Doctor to Telos in the future.

c 1985 - THE TWO DOCTORS[436] **->** Some years ago, the Doctor had officially represented the Time Lords at the opening of space station Chimera in the Third Zone. Now a renegade, his second incarnation was sent to the station by the Time Lords. Experiments conducted by the professors Kartz and Reimer were registering 0.4 on the Bocca Scale, and could potentially threaten the stability of space-time.

Before the Doctor could finish lodging a protest with the Head of Projects - his old friend, Joinson Dastari -

427 Dating *Downtime* (MA #18) - This is "1984" (p22).
428 Dating *The Reaping* (BF #86) - The date is given. *Miami Vice* is touted as a new show, and it debuted on 16th September, 1984, about a week before *The Reaping* begins.
429 *The Gathering*
430 Dating *Turlough and the Earthlink Dilemma* (*The Companions of Doctor Who* #1) - The story opens some months after Turlough has left the TARDIS. According to p193, it is relative Trion date 17,883 when Turlough arrives on Trion.

431 *Time and the Rani*
432 "Seven years" before *Cat's Cradle: Witch Mark* (p25).
433 "Twenty three years" before *The Runaway Bride*
434 Dating "The Fires Down Below" (*DWM* #64) - A caption says it is "1984".
435 Dating *Attack of the Cybermen* (22.1) - Mondas' attack is in "1986", which the hired gun Griffiths confirms is "next year".
436 Dating *The Two Doctors* (22.3) - The story is contemporary, but there is no indication exactly which year it takes place.

a Sontaran attack devastated the station. The Third Zone had been betrayed by Chessene of the Franzine Grig, an Androgum that Dastari had technologically augmented.

The Doctor was captured and taken to Seville by one of Chessene's Sontaran allies, Major Varl. He was joined by Group Marshall Stike of the Ninth Sontaran Attack Group. The Sontarans wanted Dastari to operate on the Doctor and discover the means by which Time Lords had a symbiotic relationship with their travel capsules. They hoped to create a time capsule for use against the Rutan in the Madillon Cluster.

The sixth Doctor traced his earlier self to Seville, which he had visited before. He helped to rescue his former self and defeat the Sontaran plan. Chessene, Dastari and the Sontarans all died.

The sixth Doctor dropped Peri off on Earth in 1985. She didn't expect to see him again.[437]

1985 - "Kane's Story"[438] -> The sixth Doctor and Frobisher went to New York and met up with Peri, who rejoined the TARDIS crew.

The third Doctor and Jo met an N-form in Tranquilandia the time they met the drug baron Gomez.[439] SeneNet acquired a Sontaran Mezon rifle.[440]

= Fitz saw the Beatles perform at Live Aid in a parallel universe.[441]

On the planet Artaris, the immortal Grayvorn kept shifting identities and rose to the rank of Reeve, becoming known as "Reeve Maupassant".[442] In July 1986, the wreck of the *Titanic* was discovered.[443] A virus on Lalanda 21185 created hundreds of thousands of zombies.[444] Artist Karen Kuykendall created the Tarot of the Cat-People.[445]

@ Iris Wildthyme visited the Doctor and Miranda and tried to explain the gaps in his memories. That year, the Doctor won the London Marathon.[446] Dorothy McShane was disillusioned when she met her idol, pop star Johnny Chess.[447]

During the mid-eighties, Carol Bell worked for an arms manufacturer, watching SF films to inspire the creation of new weapons.[448] She had attained the rank of captain during her time with UNIT, but was rendered brain-damaged in a car accident.[449]

@ The Doctor was offered a chair at Cambridge, but declined as he was dedicated to looking after Miranda.[450]

@ c 1985 (Spring) - FATHER TIME[451] -> Sallak escaped from prison and summoned his people, the Klade, from the far future. Ferran, brother of Zevron, arrived through a time corridor in an abandoned tower block in a northern

---

437 This occurs in an unrecorded adventure before "Kane's Story", and we don't learn why she left.
438 Dating "Kane's Story" (*DWM* #104) - A caption says it's "1985".

PERI LEAVES AND CAUSES CONTINUITY PROBLEMS, TAKE ONE: When Peri joined the sixth Doctor and Frobisher's adventures in the comic strip, it created a mild continuity headache. While we never saw her leave, she rejoins in "Kane's Story" when the Doctor and Frobisher pick her up in New York. She's settled down and just quit (another) job there, and it's not even established whether she recognises Frobisher.

So far, so simple. We know from *The Trial of a Time Lord* that there are big gaps in the sixth Doctor's recorded adventures. So, at some point after *Revelation of the Daleks*, Peri leaves the Doctor, who goes on to meet Frobisher in "The Shape Shifter" before meeting up with his old companion again. No matter how one plays the cards here, Peri must meet Frobisher for the first time in "Kane's Story". She's then present until the end of the sixth Doctor's *DWM* run in "The World Shapers", which then leads into *The Trial of a Time Lord* and her televised departure. This is even supported by the way Peri switches, during the course of the comic strip, from wearing her Season 22 leotards to her more tailored look of Season 23.

In *Planet of Fire*, Peri said she would travel with the

Doctor for "three months". This line was forgotten about on television, but perhaps she was true to her word and left the Doctor as planned. This could still be after *Revelation of the Daleks* - although *Attack of the Cybermen* and *Timelash* both have the "present day" as 1985, not 1984.
439 *Damaged Goods*
440 *Business Unusual* (p244).
441 *The Gallifrey Chronicles*
442 "About fifteen years" before *Excelis Rising*.
443 *The Left-Handed Hummingbird* (p261).
444 "Two years" after *Return of the Living Dad* (p98).
445 *Invasion of the Cat-People* (p46). This matches the Tarot deck's real-world release in 1985. Kuykendall died in 1998.
446 "About a year ago" (p129) and "last year" (p115) according to *Father Time* (p129).
447 When Ace was "fourteen" (p89) according to *Timewyrm: Revelation*. Chess is the son of Ian and Barbara (the "Chess" moniker is apparently short for "Chesterton").
448 *Interference* (Book Two, p157).
449 *The Left-Handed Hummingbird* (p100).
450 *Mad Dogs and Englishmen* (p23).
451 Dating *Father Time* (EDA #41) - The date is never specified beyond "the mid-eighties" and there are a couple of (deliberate) references to keep the dating

city. Ferran and Sallak killed the comatose Barry Castle as revenge for Zevron's death, then set their sights on the eighth Doctor and Miranda.

Ferran became enamoured of Miranda and explained her alien heritage to her, but the Doctor sent him back to the far future. Miranda shot and killed Sallak, then went on the run.

1985 (12th December) - "Skywatch-7"[452] -> A Zygon
attacked Skywatch-7, a UNIT radar station in the Arctic. The UNIT staff saw it off, and the intruder died after falling into frozen water.

In **1986, Toshiko Sato moved back to the UK from Japan.**[453] Matthew Hatch was exposed to the power of the Jack i' the Green and started planning to release him.[454] On 28th January, 1986, the *Challenger* space shuttle exploded.[455]

On the 26th April, 1986, a strange light shone over Takhail in the USSR - radiation from the Chernobyl disaster irradiated 11-year-old Piotr Arkady, and killed everyone else in the village.[456]

c 1986 - HARRY SULLIVAN'S WAR[457] -> Surgeon-
Commander Harry Sullivan was reassigned to a NATO chemical weapons centre on the island of Yarra, and researched the lethal toxin Attila 305. He found a nykor inhibitase that showed great promise in both curing infertility and providing an antidote to the toxin.

Led by Zbigniew Brodsky, a terrorist group named the European Anarchist Revolution stole three ampules of the toxin. Harry exposed his department head, Conrad Gold, as being part of the conspiracy. Brodsky's group had taken to using the Van Gogh Appreciation Society as a front for

its operations, and French authorities rounded up the terrorists during the Society's annual meeting at the Eiffel Tower.

Harry celebrated his 41st birthday.

> **= 1986 - "Time Bomb"**[458] -> The sixth Doctor and Frobisher arrived in New York to pick up Peri... but discovered that the Hedron interference two hundred million years ago had disrupted history. Mankind never evolved, and dinosaur men ruled the Earth.

1986 (December) - THE TENTH PLANET[459] ->
Technological developments continued on Earth. The Z-Bomb and Cobra missiles had been developed, and Zeus spaceships (launched on Demeter rockets) carried out manned missions to the Moon as well as close-orbital work. Zeus 4's mission was to monitor weather and cosmic rays. Space missions were controlled from the South Pole base (callsign: "Snowcap").

The space programme was now an international effort with Americans, British, Italians, Spaniards, Swiss, Australians, and Africans manning Snowcap. International Space Command and its Secretary General, Wigner, controlled the programme from Geneva.

In late 1986, "the tenth planet" appeared in the skies of the southern hemisphere. This was Mondas, the homeworld of the Cybermen. They attempted to drain Earth's energy, but absorbed too much and Mondas was destroyed.

Tobias Vaughn recovered the bodies of the Cybermen from Snowcap.[460] Cybermen who had crashed in the South Pole - remnants of an earlier, failed invasion - located and

---

vague, such as one to Guns N Roses. It is "five years" after part one of the story.
452 Dating "Skywatch-7" (*DWM #58, DWM Winter Special 1981*) - The date is given in the caption running across the top of the first page.
453 *TW: Greeks Bearing Gifts*
454 *The Hollow Men*. Hatch is "fourteen" (p79) when this occurs.
455 *Return of the Living Dad* and *Father Time*. The space shuttle is never mentioned in a television story, and *The Tenth Planet* depicts an international space programme of a far greater extent than the real 1986.
456 "Black Destiny"
457 Dating *Harry Sullivan's War* (*The Companions of Doctor Who #2*) - It is "ten years" since Harry left UNIT, and so placing this story is subject to UNIT dating. It's clearly set in the mid-nineteen eighties.
458 Dating "Time Bomb" (*DWM #114-116*) - The caption reads "Earthdate 1986". The dinosaur men are not Silurians.

459 Dating *The Tenth Planet* (4.2) - A calendar gives the date as "December 1986". This is the clearest example so far of real life catching up with "futuristic" events described in the series, but in *Attack of the Cybermen* (broadcast in 1985) the date of "1986" for this story was reaffirmed. *Radio Times* and publicity material at the time gave the date as "the late 1980s", as did the second edition of *The Making of Doctor Who*. The draft script set the date as "2000 AD", as did Gerry Davis' novelisation. (The book followed a draft of the story rather than the broadcast version, as the draft included more scenes with the Doctor.)

The Making of Doctor Who (first edition) also used the "2000" date. The first two editions of *The Programme Guide* set the range as "1975-80". This confused the American *Doctor Who* comic, which decided that *The Tenth Planet* must precede *The Invasion* and both were set in "the 1980s". John Peel's novelisation of *The Power of the Daleks* set the preceding story in "the 1990s".
460 *Original Sin*

adapted Cyber technology from the 1986 incursion.[461] After Mondas' destruction, a surviving group of Cybermen settled on the planet Lonsis.[462] **In the late nineteen-eighties, archaeologist Peter Warmsley began excavating a site associated with King Arthur on the edge of Lake Vortigern near Carbury.[463]**

Ace was now becoming a problem. She had sat her O-Levels, including French and Computer Studies, and was beginning to study for her A-Levels. But she was expelled from school for blowing up the Art Room using homemade gelignite - an event she described as "a creative act". For a while, she worked as a waitress. Ace vanished one day in a timestorm whipped up by Fenric, following experiments in her bedroom that involved her trying to extract nitro-glycerine from gelignite. Ace's mother reported her missing, and her friends thought she was either dead or in Birmingham.[464]

Ace did work experience at an old folks home. She worked in McDonalds on weekends.[465] She kicked a time-lost and penniless Tegan out of the establishment, failing to realize they would later have something in common.[466]

The Johnny Chess album *Things to do on a Wet Tuesday Night* was released in 1987.[467] In the same year, Jason Kane's sister Lucy was born.[468] SeneNet begin developing their Maxx games.[469] @ In 1987, the Doctor was accidentally responsible for releasing a breed of talking wild boar into the wild.[470]

The eighth Doctor visited Little Caldwell and met Joel Mintz.[471] **Rose Tyler was born on 27th April, 1987.[472] Katherine Costello Wainright - formerly Kathy Nightingale - died the same year.[473]**

1987 (July) - DAMAGED GOODS[474] -> The seventh Doctor, Roz and Chris investigated the Quadrant, an area of tower blocks in an English city. An N-form, an ancient Gallifreyan weapons system, had occupied the body of drug dealer Simon "the Capper" Jenkins. The N-form was searching for vampires, per its programming, and sold contaminated coke that allowed it to manifest in the brains of anyone who took it. The N-Form erupted and went on a killing spree, but the Doctor shut it down.

---

461 *Iceberg*

462 *Human Resources*

463 "Ten years" before *Battlefield*.

464 *Dragonfire* establishes much of Ace's background, with further details given in *Battlefield* and *The Curse of Fenric*. She first returns to Perivale in *Survival*.

The books offer more detail. The timestorm was in 1987 according to *Timewyrm: Revelation* (p70) and *Independence Day* (she saw *Withnail and I* a few days before the timestorm occurred). She's from 1986 in *White Darkness* (p130) and *First Frontier* (p45).

465 *Matrix*

466 During *The Crystal Bucephalus*.

467 *The Also People*

468 *Death and Diplomacy*. Jason was "nearly thirteen" when Lucy was "nine" (p150).

469 "Two years" before *Business Unusual*.

470 *Mad Dogs and Englishmen*

471 *The Room with No Doors*

472 This date is given in the Writers' Guide and in an article written by Russell T Davies in the *2006 Doctor Who Annual*. However, Rose is "nineteen" according to the Doctor in *The Unquiet Dead* and *Army of Ghosts*, when she really ought to be eighteen. It's said in *Rise of the Cybermen* that Rose was "six months" when her father died, which would fit her written birthday of 27th April and the dating of *Father's Day* to 7th November.

473 According to Kathy's tombstone as seen in *Blink*. Her handwritten letter to Sally seems to be dated 7th February, 1987.

474 Dating *Damaged Goods* (NA #55) - The date "17 July 1987" is given (p8).

475 Dating *Father's Day* (X1.8) - The date is given. The Reapers are not named on screen, but are named as such in the script.

476 The Powell Estate is cited in episodes such as *Aliens of London* and *Tooth and Claw*. Victor Kennedy specifies Rose and Jackie's address as "Bucknall House, No. 48" in *Love & Monsters*. The full address, with the postal code, appeared in the *2006 Doctor Who Annual*.

477 *The Dying Days* (p94).

478 *Sky Pirates!* (p334).

479 *Army of Ghosts*. Construction of the building began in 1988.

480 Dating *Silver Nemesis* (25.3) - The first scene is set, according to the caption slide, in "South America, 22nd November 1988". The Doctor's alarm goes off the next day - although it is a beautiful sunny day.

481 *Option Lock*

482 "Eighteen years" before *Red Dawn*.

483 Mel first appeared on television in *Terror of the Vervoids*, but the events of her joining the Doctor were shown in *Business Unusual*.

MEL'S FIRST ADVENTURE: The Writers' Guide for Season Twenty-Three suggested that Mel joined the Doctor after an encounter with the Master, and this is echoed in the Missing Adventure *Millennial Rites* (p83). This appears to be contradicted by *The Ultimate Foe* when Mel fails to recognise the renegade Time Lord, but *Business Unusual* establishes that Mel didn't actually meet the Master on that occasion. The Writers' Guide also suggested that Mel had been travelling with the Doctor for "three months". It is entirely possible that Mel started her travels with the Doctor at the end of *The Ultimate Foe*, negating the need for a "first adventure",

= 1987 (7th November) - FATHER'S DAY[475] **->** The ninth Doctor took Rose back to witness the death of her father, Peter Tyler, from a hit-and-run car accident. Rose saved her father's life, which altered history and created a "wound" in time. Winged creatures, the Reapers, converged on the wound to "sterilise" it by consuming every person on Earth. Humanity was eradicated on a large scale, but Peter recognized the historical deviation and sacrificed himself. Upon his death, time reverted to normal and the Reapers disappeared.

Outside the wedding of Stewart Hoskins and Sarah Clark, Peter Tyler died from a hit-and-run accident. An unnamed young woman stayed with him until the end.

Jackie and Rose continued to reside at Flat 48, Bucknall House, Powell Estate SE15 7GO.[476]

The eighth Doctor and Lethbridge-Stewart discovered the secret of the Embodiment of Gris in Hong Kong in 1988.[477] Benny accidentally had a comic commissioned while walking through the offices of an American comic book publisher, just because she had a British accent.[478]

A temporal breach was detected high above in London. Torchwood constructed a huge skyscraper to enclose the breach - privately the building was known as Torchwood Tower, but publically it served as Canary Wharf, a business development. Torchwood also used the facility as their main headquarters.[479]

1988 (22nd - 23rd November) - SILVER NEMESIS[480] **->** Thousands of Cyber Warships massed in the solar system. A scouting party tried to recover the Validium asteroid, which had been launched from Earth two hundred and fifty years before. They wanted its power to make Earth into "New Mondas". The seventh Doctor kept the statue from falling into the hands of the Cybermen, the Lady Peinforte (a sorceress from 1638), and a group of Nazis hoping to create a new Reich. The villains all died in the process.

By the end of the Reagan administration, the US military had built Station Nine. This was a Top Secret satellite - so secret, in fact, that no President after Reagan would be told about it. Station Nine would quietly remain in orbit, ready to fire intercepting Nuke Killer missiles that would nullify an oncoming nuclear attack.[481]

An unmanned lander sent from Earth to Mars recovered Martian DNA. Webster Corporation tried to combine it with human DNA in the hopes of creating augmented soldiers, and the young Tanya Webster was born with Martian DNA in her system. Webster began developing a manned mission to Mars, hoping to recover more Martian DNA or a live Martian.[482]

Mel joined the Doctor after helping him prevent the Master and the Usurians taking over the world in 1989. She had recently turned down a job at I², but accepted one at Ashley Chapel Logistics.[483]

1989 (mid June) BUSINESS UNUSUAL[484] **->** The sixth Doctor thwarted an attempt by the Master and his Usurian partners to devastate America's economy, but required a native computer expert to fully purge the conspirators' illicit programming. This led to the Doctor meeting computer programmer Melanie Bush, and she helped him erase the Master's programs.

Martyn Townsend, the former director of the Vault, was now the Managing Director of SeneNet. The company officially specialized in computer game consoles, but fronted Townsend's ambitions to use Nestene technology to conquer Earth. Lacking the components to maintain his cybernetic body, Townsend kidnapped the telepathic Trey Korte in the hopes of mentally transferring his intelligence into a prosthetic form.

The Doctor's intervention resulted in SeneNet's destruction. Townsend died when falling rubble crushed him. The Auton-augmented twins Cellian and Ciara foreswore allegiance to Townsend and escaped. Melanie stowed away on the TARDIS and took up travelling with the Doctor.

The Brigadier, investigating SeneNet, met the sixth Doctor for the first time.

---

but this idea is riddled with paradoxes (i.e.: she is from her own future and would have memories of her first few adventures before she arrived).

The period set after *The Trial of a Time Lord*, but before the Doctor has his "first meeting" with Mel (in *Business Unusual*), is now brimming with book and audio adventures. These include the Doctor's time with companions Frobisher, Evelyn Smythe and Grant Markham (who only appeared in two Missing Adventures by Steve Lyons, *Time of Your Life* and *Killing Ground*).

In *Just War*, Mel says that she has never been to the past before, "only the future". Subsequent audios such as *The Fires of Vulcan* have contradicted this.

Millennial Rites and *Business Unusual* both have Mel meeting the Doctor in 1989. She's from "1986" in *Head Games* (p154) and *The Quantum Archangel* (p17).

484 Dating *Business Unusual* (PDA #4) - The date is given (p15). From the sixth Doctor's perspective, he first meets the Brigadier circa 2000 in *The Spectre of Lanyon Moor*.

= In an alternate universe where Rome never fell, the sixth Doctor lost his New World companion Brown Perpugilliam, and an eye, to the warlord Dominicus. He visited the scientist Praetor Linus to repair the TARDIS image translator, and took the slave Melina into his service.[485]

The Doctor left Evelyn on Earth, and asked her to monitor the pseudo-Auton twins Cellian and Ciara for him. Evelyn came to discover that the Doctor had erroneously dropped her off in the late 1980s, meaning that her younger self was still teaching at Nottingham. Evelyn kept a low profile, fearful that she might run into herself, but used her foreknowledge to earn some money winning contests and betting pools.[486]

In 1989, the Ritz dance hall in Cardiff ceased operation.[487] The sixth Doctor planted a mattress in Perivale - he'd later land on it during a confrontation with the Master...[488]

c 1989 (Sunday) - SURVIVAL[489] **->** In a relatively short span of time, several residents in Perivale vanished without trace, abducted by the Cheetah People. The planet of the Cheetah People was dying, and they were preparing to move on to new feeding grounds. The Master was trapped on the planet, and lured the seventh Doctor and Ace there to aid in his escape. As the Doctor and the Master fought, the Cheetah People vanished. The Master also disappeared.

As the Cheetah Planet exploded, the Master went back to Earth. A surfeit of artron energy in the atmosphere diverted him to 1957.[490]

@ 1989 (November) - FATHER TIME[491] **->** The eighth Doctor made *Time* magazine's list of Top Fifty People of the Decade. He had spent a great deal of his time searching the world for Miranda, and was living with Debbie Castle. He was present at - and possibly responsible for - the fall of the Berlin Wall.

Ferran returned from the future aboard his ship, the *Supremacy*, and abducted Miranda from a hotel in India. Seeing this on television, the Doctor and Debbie went to Florida and stowed aboard the Space Shuttle *Atlantis*. The shuttle docked the *Supremacy* and Debbie was killed. Miranda had started a mutiny, and Ferran decided to destroy the ship rather than let it fall to his enemies. The Doctor and Miranda teamed up to shut down the *Supremacy*'s time engines. Miranda took control of the ship

485 *Spiral Scratch*. Linus is that universe's version of Bob Lines from *The Scales of Injustice*, *Business Unusual* and *Instruments of Darkness*.
486 *Instruments of Darkness*. On p93, Evelyn claims the Doctor dropped her off in 1988. The Doctor conferred with Evelyn off-panel during the events of *Business Unusual*, set in June 1989.
487 *TW: Captain Jack Harkness*
488 In *Survival*, according to "Emperor of the Daleks".
489 Dating *Survival* (26.4) - Ace returns to Perivale. When she asks how long she's been away, the Doctor replies "as long as you think you have". Her friends Midge and Stevie vanished "last month"; Shreela the week before.
490 *First Frontier*
491 Dating *Father Time* (EDA #41) - The date is never specified beyond "the late 1980s" (p199), but the Berlin Wall fell on 9th November, 1989.
492 All "a decade" before *The King of Terror* (p130, p141 and p144).
493 "Eleven years" before *Escape Velocity*.
494 Dating "Business as Usual" (*DWW* #40-43) - The Doctor says the meteorites fell "that summer night in 1989" in the framing sequence, Stellar Plastics opens in "August 1990" according to a caption.
495 *System Shock*
496 *The Shadow in the Glass*
497 *Escape Velocity*, *The Slow Empire*. She's 28 and left home when she was 17.

498 "Five hundred years" after *The Masque of Mandragora*. The *DWM* strip "The Mark of Mandragora" dealt with this return.
499 *Downtime*
500 Dating "Train-Flight" (*DWM* #159-161) - There's no indication of the date, although the concert is an Oscar Peterson one, and so probably takes place before his stroke in 1993. There's nothing to suggest it isn't set the year it was published (1990). Sarah seems to be living in the same house she was in during *The Five Doctors*. This is the first time she's met the Doctor's seventh incarnation. They don't take K9 along, but they have the option, so he's still active.
501 Dating *Cat's Cradle: Time's Crucible* (NA #5) - It is "three years" since Ace left Perivale.
502 Dating "Seaside Rendezvous" (*DWM Summer Special 1991*) - There's no date given, but the story has a contemporary setting and was published in 1991.
503 *Timewyrm: Revelation*
504 Dating "Invaders from Gantac" (*DWM* #148-150) - Leapy says it is "1992".
505 *TW: Random Shoes*
506 Dating *Timewyrm: Revelation* (NA #4) - "It was the Sunday before Christmas 1992" (p2). The Doctor confronts "Death," here a creation of the Timewyrm, but will often encounter the living embodiment of Death itself.
507 Dating *Cat's Cradle: Witch Mark* (NA #7) - No year is specified, although the President of the United States

and declared herself Empress, heading back to the far, far future to end the intergalactic conflict.

The Star Jumpers, a band including Johnny Chess, were a success. They made the albums *Circle Circus, Modernism, Can Anyone Tell Me Where the Revolution Is?,* and one other before splitting. InterCom were working on a means of splicing alien DNA into humans to create a slave race. UNIT operatives Geoff Paynter and Paul Foxton infiltrated Black Star terrorists based in Baghdad, but Foxton was killed.[492]

The science-fiction series *Professor X* was cancelled after more than twenty five years on TV. Dave Young, who went on to become Anji Kapoor's boyfriend, played a Cybertron in one of the last episodes.[493]

1989 (Summer) to 1990 (August) - "Business as Usual"[494] **->** Winston Blunt discovered some strange meteorites. Overnight the former plumber became a wealthy plastics magnate and set up Galaxy Plastics, but he killed himself after handing over the business to a Mr Dolman. A year later, a rival company sent Max Fischer to investigate Galaxy Plastics, and he discovered that Galaxy was being run by the Autons. Dolman accidentally set off an explosion while trying to kill Fischer - who escaped, pursued by living toy soldiers. Dolman was damaged but murdered Fischer, and a replica of Fischer went on to open Stellar Plastics.

The Nineties

In the early 1990s, there were a string of privatisations: the electricity industry became Elec-Gen, and British Rail became BritTrack. In August 1991, information about the Russian Coup reached the West via the Internet.[495]

Sometime after the Soviet Union's fall, the Doctor assisted Yablokov, the Russian President's counsellor, in accounting for the Soviets' inventory of nuclear weapons. They proved unable to account for eighty-four such devices.[496] Anji left home at seventeen as her family had an outdated view of women.[497] **The Mandragora Helix was due to return to Earth in the early 1990s.**[498]

The Brigadier's grandson, Gordon James Lethbridge-Stewart, was born. Kate Lethbridge-Stewart split up from Gordon's father, Jonathan, when Gordon was two. She didn't speak to the Brigadier for six years; thus, the Brigadier didn't know about his grandson until Gordon was five.[499]

c 1990 - "Train-Flight"[500] **->** The seventh Doctor visited Sarah Jane to invite her to a jazz concert. She refused to travel via TARDIS, so they went on a train... that mysteriously entered a space vortex. The Doctor and Sarah discovered a fleet of buses - the passengers of which had been dissolved - and the Doctor learned they were in orbit on a Kalik organic ship. The Kaliks were an advanced race of insects that were usually vegetarian, but this was a renegade, carnivorous faction. The Doctor manipulated the hypnotic signal that the Kalik used to control humans to control *them* instead. He then beamed the train to Royal Albert Hall station... but as there's no such station, the train materialised in the middle of the street. The Doctor and Sarah sneaked away.

c 1990 (Sunday) - CAT'S CRADLE: TIME'S CRUCIBLE[501] **->** The seventh Doctor and Ace were summoned back to the TARDIS after eating baked Alaska on Ealing Broadway.

c 1991 - "Seaside Rendezvous"[502] **->** The seventh Doctor and Ace enjoyed a day at the seaside, but the "demon" from the wreck of the *Camara,* lost in 1826, emerged from the sea. The creature was actually a life-draining Ogri, which had been worn down into sand, but the Doctor destroyed it with a firehose.

In the summer of 1991, the Doctor hid a portable temporal link in St Christopher's Church, Cheldon Bonniface, while brass rubbing with Mel.[503]

1992 - "Invaders from Gantac"[504] **->** The seventh Doctor saved the tramp Leapy from alien police in London. Some time previously, the Gantacs had invaded Earth, destroyed London landmarks and declared a curfew. They were a hive mind species from 200,000 light years away, but had made an administrative mistake - they should have invaded the planet Wrouth, not Earth. Leapy's fleas infected the Gantac leader, who died. Without his control, the Gantacs died with him.

Eugene Jones' teacher gave him a bona-fide alien eyeball. It was a Dogon sixth eye, capable of - temporally speaking - aiding people in seeing "what was behind them".[505]

1992 (Christmas) - TIMEWYRM: REVELATION[506] **->** The seventh Doctor and Ace found themselves in a perfect replica of Cheldon Bonniface that was built on the Moon (although not before Ace had died of oxygen starvation). The Doctor and Ace entered a surreal, tortured landscape that they discovered was the Doctor's own mind. Ace managed to rally the Doctor's former incarnations, and they gave the Doctor the strength to defeat the Timewyrm. The Timewyrm's mind was placed in a mindless baby grown in a genetics laboratory. The Hutchings family raised the baby as their daughter, Ishtar.

c 1992 - CAT'S CRADLE: WITCH MARK[507] **->** A coach crashed on the M40. The casualties were taken to

Condicote General Hospital. The police discovered forty-two suitcases containing two million pounds in cash in the luggage compartment. The victims all bore the same mysterious marks on their skin.

Circa 1993, Major Dickens and three scientific-minded colleagues - including the physics theorist J.J. Bartholomew - started gathering on Gravonax Island to conduct various experiments.[508]

In 1993, Ace's father had a heart attack. He told his son Liam about Ace, but Liam failed to reconcile with his mother while searching for his missing sister. Liam returned home to find his father dead.[509]

= **1993 - BLOOD HEAT**[510] -> In an alternative timestream, the Silurian plague released at Wenley Moor in the early nineteen-seventies succeeded in wiping out most of humanity. The third Doctor was killed before he could discover the antidote. Over the next twenty years, the Silurians initiated massive climatic change, rendering the plant life inedible to humanity and altering coastlines. Dinosaur species from many different eras were reintroduced to the wild. The capital of Earth became Ophidian, a vast city in Africa. Some Silurians hunted down humans for sport.

This timeline was created by the Monk, and deac-

tivated by the seventh Doctor. It would survive for a generation or so after this before winding down.

The seventh Doctor, Benny and Ace visited the 1993 Glastonbury Festival, meeting Danny Pain - a former singer for the punk bank Plasticine - and his daughter Amy.[511]

1993 - THE LEFT-HANDED HUMMINGBIRD[512] -> On 31st October, 1993, the "Halloween Man" opened fire on a crowd of unsuspecting people in a marketplace in Mexico City. Cristian Alvarez witnessed this, narrowly avoiding death himself.

= On 31st October, 1993, the "Halloween Man" opened fire on a crowd of unsuspecting people in a marketplace in Mexico City. Cristian Alvarez witnessed this, narrowly avoiding death himself. The evidence suggested an alien presence - the Blue, also known as the psychic being Huitzilin. On 12th December, Alvarez sent a note for the Doctor's attention to UNIT HQ in Geneva.

The seventh Doctor investigated early the next year. In his own timeline, this was before "the Happening" of late 1968, early 1969. Huitzilin killed Christian, but the Doctor's actions erased this from history.

has taken to bathing in cranberry sauce.
508 Thirteen years before the present-day portion of *Night Thoughts*.
509 "Four years" before *The Rapture*.
510 Dating *Blood Heat* (NA #19) - This story is a sequel to *Doctor Who and the Silurians*, containing many elements from its novelisation *Doctor Who and the Cave-Monsters*. Thus, the Silurians are called "reptile people," but the Doctor wears his velvet jacket, not coveralls, when he goes potholing and the Silurian leader is named Morka. It is repeatedly stated that the first encounter with the Silurians took place "twenty years" ago in "1973".
511 *No Future*
512 Dating *The Left-Handed Hummingbird* (NA #21) - The date of the massacre is given. The Doctor arrives in "1994".
513 Dating *Conundrum* (NA #22) - The Doctor thinks that it is "November the second, 1993"
514 Dating *The Dimension Riders* (NA #20) - The scenes in Oxford are set in "1993","November 18th".
515 Dating "Time and Time Again" (*DWM* #207) - The date is given.
516 Dating *Goth Opera* (MA #1) - It is "1993", "November".
517 Dating *Instruments of Darkness* (PDA #48) - The

Doctor and Mel arrive on 29th December according to p69. "John Doe," although his surname is never mentioned, is likely Jeremy Fitzoliver, Sarah Jane's associate from *The Paradise of Death* and *The Ghosts of N-Space* (although this would clash with *Interference*). Sudbury was mentioned in *Time-Flight*.
518 The discovery is first mentioned in *The Sun Makers*. The Battle of Cassius is referred to in *GodEngine* and *The Crystal Bucephalus*. The year of the discovery is given in *Iceberg*. It has to be discovered after *The Tenth Planet*, or the story would have been called "The Eleventh Planet".
519 *Interference*
520 Dating *The Land of the Dead* (BF #4) - The year is given.
521 Dating *Invasion of the Cat-People* (MA #13) - It is "AD 1994", the adventure starting "Friday the eighth of July 1994".
522 *Zamper*
523 *Who Killed Kennedy* (p271).
524 Dating "Star Beast II" (*DWM Yearbook 1996*) - Beep's been imprisoned for "fifteen years", and it's "1995".
525 According to publicity material, she's "thirteen" in *SJA: Invasion of the Bane*.
526 *TW: Greeks Bearing Gifts*

1993 (18th November) - THE DIMENSION RIDERS[514] -> At St Matthew's College, Oxford, the Time Lord named Epsilon Delta - otherwise known as the President - plotted with the Garvond, a creature composed of the darker sides of the minds within the Gallifreyan Matrix. They sought to create a Time Focus, which would have enabled the Garvond to feed off absorb a massive amount of chronal energy. The Garvond turned on the President and killed him. The seventh Doctor trapped the Garvond within the dimensionally transcendental text *The Worshipful and Ancient Law of Gallifrey*, then disposed of the book in a pocket dimension.

1993 (November) - GOTH OPERA[516] -> The Time Lady Ruath sought to fulfil prophesies that spoke of the birth of a vampire nation. She rescued the vampire Yarven from his burial spot in Croatia and allowed him to turn her. Together, they sought to raise a vampire army. Tracking them down to Manchester, the fifth Doctor destroyed the army and its attempt to create the Vampire Messiah. Yarven was incinerated; Ruath was flung into the Time Vortex.

The vampires Jake and Madeline departed into space. They later returned, and by the twenty-fourth century had sired many descendents.

1993 (29th December) - INSTRUMENTS OF DARKNESS[517] -> The sixth Doctor and Mel found Evelyn in Great Rokeby. The twins Cellian and Ciara had reformed and were improving the school system in the village of Halcham.

By now, the Cylox named Lai-Ma was trying to psionically absorb the energy of his former prison realm, hoping to increase his power levels and destroy Earth. His brother Tko-Ma hoped to steal his brother's power and had founded the Network, an organization that kidnapped psionics and exploited their abilities. The Ini-Ma, the

Cylox brothers' jailor, killed the siblings but died in the process.

A powerplay between Tko-Ma's anchor on Earth (Sebastian Malvern) and the Network's head administrator (John Doe) triggered a slaughter that killed Cellian, Ciara and Doe. The Network reformed, with Mel's associate Trey Korte as a member, into an organization pledged to protect Earth from extra-terrestrial threats. Evelyn resumed travelling with the Doctor and Mel.

Department C19 had closed by 1993 due to internal corruption. Sir John Sudbury was murdered to prevent his exposing the Network.

The outermost planet of the solar system was discovered in 1994 **and called Cassius.**[518] UNISYC, a UN security group, was founded in 1994. Like UNIT, they were involved with alien encounters.[519]

1994 - THE LAND OF THE DEAD[520] -> The fifth Doctor and Nyssa arrived in Alaska and were attacked by sea monsters. They sheltered in the home of oilman Shaun Brett. One of the fossils in his collection was a Permian - an ancient predator that looked like a living skeleton, bound together by a bio-electric field. A pack of Permians revived and threatened to breed. As the creatures were vulnerable to fire, the Doctor destroyed them with a stock of flammable paint.

1994 (8th July) - INVASION OF THE CAT-PEOPLE[521] -> The second Doctor, Polly and Ben prevented the Cat-People, one of the most powerful races in the galaxy, from harnessing the magnetic energy of the Earth.

The seventh Doctor, Benny, Chris and Roz spent a couple of days at the Doctor's house in Allen Road to recover from their experiences on Zamper.[522] On 5th April, 1995, Private Cleary died in hospital.[523]

1995 - "Star Beast II"[524] -> Judges Zagran, Scraggs and Theka concluded that white star therapy had successfully rehabilitated Beep the Meep and he was paroled. He remained evil, but the authorities had removed his blackstar drive. Beep had a spare hidden on Earth, and headed there. The fourth Doctor arrived in Blackcastle just before the Meep. Fudge Higgins now managed the multiplex built on the site of the old steel mills, and this was where the Meep had buried his stardrive. The Doctor adjusted a film projector and imprisoned the Meep within a *Lassie* movie.

Nightshade: The Movie was in general release.

Maria Jackson was born around 1995.[525] **Age 20, Toshiko Sato joined a government science think tank.**[526] **Jack visited the Powell Estate once or twice in**

the nineties and watched Rose grow up, but refrained from speaking with her.[527]

c 1995 - DOWNTIME[528] -> Under the direction of the Great Intelligence, which was secretly hosted in Professor Travers, Victoria Waterfield had invested an eight-figure sum in the New World University in north-west London. The University specialized in teaching classes by computer, but the Intelligence used a hypnotic technique to control the students there. It inhabited the university's computers, and spread into the Internet. There was chaos as all computer systems succumbed to - as the media termed it - the "computer flu". The CIA's files were broadcast on Russian television, bank cashpoints released all their cash and Tomahawk missiles were launched in the Gulf.

The Intelligence transformed some of the University students into Yeti, leading to a conflict with UNIT. Before the Intelligence could seize control of Earth, Victoria and her allies destroyed the University's generators, which banished the Intelligence. Professor Travers' dead body collapsed without the Intelligence to animate it.

Victoria was put on Interpol's Most Wanted list for her role in this affair. The Doctor provided a letter of reference to clear her name with UNIT.

After this time, the Brigadier reunited with Doris. They married and the Brigadier gave up teaching.[529]

= Around 1995, physicist John Finer accidentally killed his daughter Amelia. He began researching time travel, hoping to go back in time to prevent this. Events circa 2001 nullified this timeline.[530]

While the Doctor and Romana were in Cornwall in 1995, the Doctor read of the suicide of David Brown, captain of the English cricket team and a native of Hexen Bridge.[531] In 1995, Katherine Chambers started up her own practice in Brisbane: Chambers Pharmaceuticals.[532]

1995 (20th December) - "Memorial"[533] -> The seventh Doctor and Ace landed in Westmouth. The Doctor freed the Telphin consciousness from Simon Galway, in whom it had resided in peace for exactly sixty years.

In January 1996, James Stevens retrieved his Time Ring from his safety deposit box at a bank in London. Rifle in hand, he departed into the past to assassinate Kennedy.[534]

---

527 *Utopia*
528 Dating *Downtime* (MA #18) - The story is set "about thirty" or "over twenty five" years after *The Web of Fear*, "nearly twenty years" after *Fury from the Deep* and Sarah's time in UNIT, and about ten years after 1984. The Brigadier has been teaching at Brendon for "twenty odd years". The Intelligence's next incursion on Earth - *Millennial Rites*, set in 1999 - is "four years" afterward. "Brigadier Crichton" is said to still be with UNIT.
529 Between *Mawdryn Undead* and *Battlefield*, and shortly after the Missing Adventure *Downtime*. Doris is first mentioned in *Planet of the Spiders*.
530 "Six years" before *Psi-ence Fiction*
531 *The Hollow Men*
532 "Eleven years" before *The Gathering*.
533 Dating "Memorial" (*DWM* #191) - "The TARDIS chronometer read December 20th 1995".
534 *Who Killed Kennedy*. It is "nearly 25 years" (p274) after Cleary's return to the 1970s, and is subject to UNIT dating. This novel presumes that the UNIT stories occurred around the time of broadcast, and the date of Stevens' departure is given (p271).
535 Dating *Night Thoughts* (BF #79) - It is "ten years" before the story's present-day component. An audio statement from Maude, recorded shortly before her suicide, is dated 12th January.
536 Dating *Interference* (EDA #25-26) - The date is "1996" (p8, p29). This means that Sam actually arrives back on Earth a bit before her younger self leaves in the TARDIS.

537 Dating *The Chase* (2.8) - The Doctor claims that as "this house is exactly what you would expect in a nightmare", suspecting that the TARDIS and the Dalek time machine have landed "in a world of dreams" that "exists in the dark recesses of the human mind". Viewers find out the truth at the end of the scene - the TARDIS has simply landed in a theme park. A sign proclaims that it is the "Festival of Ghana 1996". The "Tower of London" quote is Ian's description of what he has just seen. Quite why Peking would cancel an exhibition in Ghana is not explained.
538 *Original Sin*. Vaughn's memories are, by his own admission, corrupted and he seems to be a year out.
539 *Interference*
540 *Something Inside*. The year is unspecified, although there's nothing to say it isn't the discontinued Ghana celebration mentioned in *The Chase*.
541 Dating *The Sands of Time* (MA #22) - The date is given (p117).
542 At the start of *Return of the Living Dad* (p15).
543 *Bad Therapy*. The exact year isn't given.
544 Dating "End Game" (*DWM* #244-247) - It's "six days to Christmas". The year isn't specified here, but we learn in "TV Action" that Izzy was born on 12th October, 1979, and she's "seventeen" in a couple of the strips - meaning this is 1996. It's established in "The Company of Thieves" that Izzy is short for Isabelle.
545 Dating *The Rapture* (BF #36) - Ace reckons it is "ten years" after she left Earth.

c 1996 (12th January) - NIGHT THOUGHTS[535] **->** On Gravonax Island in Scotland, J.J. Bartholomew developed the prototype Bartholomew Transactor, a device that could send a subatomic particle back in time to an identical piece of equipment. By this method, audio messages from the future could be heard in the past.

Major Dickens theorised that if the device were used to retroactively halt an established death, then the closely related timelines would overlap and the deceased's body would re-animate. When a destitute woman named Maude appeared with her two daughters, Edie and Ruth, Dickens decided to test this and deliberately mis-diagnosed Edie's eye infection as Gravonax gas poisoning. Dickens' colleagues were moved to euthanise Edie rather than let her suffer what they believed was an inevitable, agonizing death.

A Bartholomew Transactor was present as Dickens gave Edie a lethal dose of anesthetic. The veterinary scientist Hartley chemically preserved Edie's body on Dickens' behalf, and her corpse was placed inside a taxidermied bear. Maude discovered Dickens' deception and committed suicide. Ruth was shuffled between foster homes. Dickens held Bartholomew prisoner so she could perfect her device; she tried to escape, but was permanently crippled by a bear trap. The world came to believe that she was dead.

As Dickens desired, the Transactor relayed a message from ten years in the future and caused a temporal anomaly. The seventh Doctor arrived from that period, tasked with conclusively insuring Edie's death, but found himself unable to kill her.

1996 - INTERFERENCE[536] **->** The eighth Doctor was summoned by the United Nations, who had been offered a weapon - the Cold - by a race of alien arms dealers. The aliens were members of the Remote, a Faction Paradox colony. Sarah Jane Smith was investigating the matter and met Sam, who was taken to the Remote. Fitz was frozen in suspended animation and wouldn't awaken until the twenty-sixth century, whereupon he would become a Faction Paradox member.

The Doctor was captured and tortured by the Saudis. He sent an emergency message to his third incarnation, who was on the planet Dust in the thirty-eighth century. Sarah rescued the Doctor and he travelled to the Remote, who had built a settlement on a Time Lord warship. This ship was designed to destroy the original home planet of their Enemy - Earth - in the future War. The Doctor convinced the people of the Remote that they were being used. A Remote agent and the Doctor sent the ship to a place of safety.

Sam accepted an offer to stay with Sarah Jane Smith and left the Doctor's company.

1996 - THE CHASE[537] **->** One of the exhibits at the 1996 Festival of Ghana, "Frankenstein's House of Horror", featured robotic versions of a number of Gothic characters. For $10, visitors could wander around an animated haunted house, be frightened by mechanical bats and meet Frankenstein's monster, Dracula and the Grey Lady. The exhibition was cancelled by Peking.

Tobias Vaughn claimed he saw the Dalek Time Machine at the "1995 Earth Fair in Ghana".[538] The robots were programmed by Microsoft, who later faced lawsuits.[539] The Doctor attended the crowded Festival of Ghana.[540]

1996 - THE SANDS OF TIME[541] **->** Nyssa's awakening drew near, and the agents of Nephthys made ready for her resurrection. Nephthys' intelligence resided within Nyssa, but her instinct resided in a Nephthys clone named Vanessa Prior. The fifth Doctor tricked the instinct part of Nephthys into thinking its intelligence had dissipated in 1926. The Nephthys-instinct went back in time but failed to reunite with itself. It circled back and forth between 1926 and 1996 until it aged to death. The Doctor removed Nephthys' intelligence from Nyssa and woke up his companion, then buried the intelligence at Nephthys' pyramid.

The Doctor, Roz and Chris rested in Sydney in 1996.[542] The Doctor eventually returned Peri to the late twentieth century.[543]

1996 (19th December) - "End Game" (*DWM*)[544] **->** The eighth Doctor landed in Stockbridge and was attacked by giant doll-like figures that resembled a butcher, a baker and a candlestick maker. He was rescued by his old friend Maxwell Edison and a fellow UFO spotter named Izzy. They had acquired a strange medallion called the "focus", but were soon rounded up by humanoid foxes in hunting gear and brought to the Celestial Toymaker - who had created a surreal version of Stockbridge, and stuffed the real one in a snowglobe.

The Doctor and Izzy reached the TARDIS, but Maxwell was left behind. The Toymaker similarly captured them in a snowglobe, and the Doctor was forced to hand over the focus. It was part of the Imagineum - a device built by an ancient race of alchemists - and the Toymaker used it to create an evil doll-like duplicate of the Doctor. However, the two Doctors teamed up and exposed the Toymaker himself to the device. The Toymakers disappeared into the void, in perpetual stalemate, and Izzy joined the Doctor on his adventures.

1997 (May) - THE RAPTURE[545] **->** The Euphorian Empire had fallen into war with Scordatora. The drafted brothers Jude and Gabriel deserted the conflict by fleeing through the dimensional portal they previously used to reach Earth in 1855. Bar owner Gustavo Riviera helped the brothers found the Rapture nightclub in San Antonio, Izbia.

Gabriel's mental health deteriorated, and Jude realized that he'd need to take his brother home for medical care. Fearing court-martial and summary execution, Jude decided to entrance the Rapture patrons with PCP and a special mix of Gabriel's music, then kidnap the humans back to the Empire as an offering of ready-made soldiers. On 15th May, Gustavo disavowed the brothers' actions and wrestled with Gabriel, causing them to fall to their deaths. A vengeful Jude tried to unleash a music score that would kill anyone who heard it, but the seventh Doctor and Ace - now calling herself Dorothy McShane - thwarted Jude's plan. Jude fled, unable to keep his operation at the Rapture going. Sometime later, a young office worker opened an e-mail attachment that played music from the Rapture nightclub.

At the Rapture, Dorothy encountered her younger brother Liam.

= c 1997 - BATTLEFIELD[546] **->** In a parallel universe, twelve hundred years after defeating Arthur, Deathless Morgaine of the Fey had become battle queen of the S'Rax, ruler of thirteen worlds. Her world was scientifically advanced with energy weapons and ornithopters, but the people weren't reliant on technology and still knew the magic arts. There was still resistance against her rule, as Merlin had promised that Arthur would return in the hour of greatest need. Morgaine's immortal son Mordred led her troops to victory at Camlaan, forcing an enemy soldier, Ancelyn, to flee the field.

Morgaine had tracked the magical sword Excalibur to our dimension, which Mordred called "Avallion". When UNIT discovered that the Doctor was involved in this affair, the Secretary General persuaded Brigadier Alistair Gordon Lethbridge-Stewart to come out of retirement. Morgaine's extra-dimensional

---

546 Dating *Battlefield* (26.1) - The Doctor tells Ace that they are "a few years in your future". Sergeant Zbrigniev is apparently in his mid-thirties, served in UNIT while the Doctor was present, and appears to have first-hand recollection of two of the Doctor's regenerations. Even if we assume that Zbrigniev is older than he looks (say, forty), and was very young when he joined UNIT, *Spearhead from Space* must have taken place in the mid-seventies. (The earliest Zbrigniev could be in the regular army is age sixteen, but he'd almost certainly need a couple more years before seeing active service, especially with an elite organisation like UNIT).

The *Battlefield* novelisation by Marc Platt, based on notes by story author Ben Aaronovitch, sets the story in "the late 1990s" (p15). Ace later notices that Peter Warmsley's tax disc expires on "30.6.99" (p30). *The Terrestrial Index* set the story in "1992" and *The TARDIS Special* chose 1991 - perhaps they misheard the Doctor's line as "two years in your future". In a document for Virgin Publishing dated 23rd March, 1995, concerning "Future History Continuity", Ben Aaronovitch perhaps settled the matter when he stated that *Battlefield* is set "c.1997". *The Dying Days* is set after this story.

The Doctor is apparently surprised to learn that Lethbridge-Stewart married Doris - in this story, *The King of Terror* and *The Spectre of Lanyon Moor*.

THE FUTURE OF THE UNITED NATIONS: By *Battlefield*, UNIT is a truly multinational organisation with British, Czechoslovakian and Polish troops serving side by side. UNIT appear in the New Adventures *The Pit*, *Head Games* and *Happy Endings*, and the UN is referred to in *Cat's Cradle: Warhead*. In *The Enemy of the World*, nations have been grouped together into Zones. The govern-

ing body of the world is the United Zones, or the World Zones Authority, headed by a General Assembly.

The United Nations still exists at the time of the Thousand Day War referred to in the New Adventure *Transit*. Gradually, though, national barriers break down and a World Government runs the planet. Where this leaves the UN is unclear, although it appears that the United Nations survives or is reformed at some time far in the future. In *Mission to the Unknown*, Lowry's ship is the "UN Deep Space Force Group 1", and has the United Nations symbol and a Union Jack on the hull.

547 Dating *The Dying Days* (NA #61) - The date is given at the start of the story and on the back cover. 6th May is the date that Virgin's license to publish *Doctor Who* books officially ended. Lethbridge-Stewart was cited as a General in *Head Games*.

548 "The Mark of Mandragora" - a reference to "Invaders from Gantac" and *Battlefield*.

549 "The Mark of Mandragora"

550 *Minuet in Hell*

551 Dating *The Eight Doctors* (EDA #1) - The date is given. Technically, Sam returns home in *Interference* before her younger self leaves with the Doctor.

552 Dating *Bullet Time* (PDA #45) - The date of April 1997 is given on p15. Sarah Jane visits Bangkok just prior to this in March (p7). Britain turned over Hong Kong to China on 1st July, 1997. The report of Sarah Jane's demise in this novel is largely unsubstantiated and hails from Ryder's unreliable point-of-view. *Sometime Never* would suggest the ambiguity of her death owes to the Council of Eight's machinations. Sarah clearly survives, as evidenced in *School Reunion*, her new spin-off series and several of the books

knights fought UNIT, and Morgaine secured control of a nuclear missile. The seventh Doctor put paid to Morgaine's plans.

1997 - (Tuesday, 6th May) THE DYING DAYS[547] -> Mars 97, a British mission to the Red Planet, inadvertently trespassed on a Martian tomb. Xznaal, leader of the Argyre clan, used this as a pretext to invade Earth. He was working with the power-hungry Lord Greyhaven, and together they deposed the Queen and seized control of the United Kingdom. Xznaal was crowned King of England and began begins transporting slave labour to Mars. When the eighth Doctor was apparently killed, the Brigadier, Benny and UNIT formed a resistance movement that marched on London to dethrone the usurper. The Martians attempted to release "the Red Death", which would have wiped out all life on Earth. Greyhaven died trying to stop Xznaal, and the Doctor returned to save the day.

Lethbridge-Stewart was subsequently promoted to General.

"Since the Gantic Invasion and the Availlon Fiasco, unearthly threats have become a matter of fact." [548]

The drug Mandrake, or M, first appeared on the streets in 1997. Its crystalline structure contained an unknown radiation, and UNIT classified it as a Foreign Hazard (meaning alien).[549]

The Brigadier helped to oversee the creation of a new Parliament for Scotland.[550]

1997 - THE EIGHT DOCTORS[551] -> The eighth Doctor, his memory wiped by the Master, landed in Totter's Lane, London. He saved the life of schoolgirl Samantha Jones, who was being chased by the drug dealers Baz and Mo. After a series of adventures, the Doctor returned to the junkyard and Sam persuaded him to take her with him.

1997 (April) - BULLET TIME[552] -> With Britain scheduled to relinquish Hong Kong to China, the Chinese government secretly created the "Tao Te Lung," a smuggling and extortion ring, as a means of rooting out Hong Kong's criminal element beforehand. However, the seventh Doctor usurped control of the Tao Te Lung, and used its

operations to covertly move a group of extra-terrestrials who were stranded on Earth.

By this time, a rogue UNIT faction, "The Cortez Project," sought to eliminate all extra-terrestrials as a threat to humanity. The Doctor arranged for his old ally, Sarah Jane Smith, to travel to Hong Kong and expose the Cortez members. However, Sarah's investigations put her in danger from the Tao Te Lung. In order to save Sarah's life, the Doctor arranged to publicly discredit her as a journalist.

The Doctor's alien allies reached their sunken spaceship, but a group of Cortez commandos, led by Colonel Tsang, seized control of the USS Westmoreland submarine in an attempt to head them off. The Doctor thwarted the Cortez members and the aliens departed Earth.

One account of these events suggests that Sarah Jane killed herself to prevent Tom Ryder, an intelligence agency operative, from holding her hostage to blackmail the Doctor. Other reports failed to corroborate her death.

1997 - VAMPIRE SCIENCE[553] -> Carolyn McConnell summoned the eighth Doctor when she suspected vampires were active in San Francisco. The Doctor arrived and joined up with the American branch of UNIT, run by Brigadier-General Kramer. A generational war was brewing between the vampires, and a group of younger vampires - led by the upstart Slake - wiped out every old vampire except for their leader, Joanna Harris. The Doctor ingested silver nitrate, killing Slake and all the vampires that feasted on his blood. He also arranged for Harris to become human again. Harris and Carolyn joined the staff of UNIT.

Before this time, Kramer's branch of UNIT handled a Brieri scouting party.

On 12th October of an unknown year in the nineteen nineties, the Doctor's future companion "Hex" Scofield was born.[554] Hex's mother was named Cassandra Elizabeth Scofield, and his dad used to tell him a story about a rabbit and a dog.[555] Hex thought until he was six that his grandmother was his mum.[556] When Hex was in secondary school, he went on a school trip to Venice.[557]

Hex's father worked on the docks, and thought his job was safe until a strike was held in support of some men who'd been sacked. The disagreement drug on for years, and Hex's father finally had to accept redundancy. Hex's grandmother suggested that he should find an occupation

---

(including *System Shock, Millennium Shock, Christmas on a Rational Planet, Interference* and *The Shadow in the Glass*). *Bullet Time* never names the stranded aliens, but they would appear to be the Tzun from McIntee's *First Frontier*. The Cortez Project head, General Kyle, is possibly Marianne Kyle from *The Face of the Enemy*.
553 Dating *Vampire Science* (EDA #2) - The date is given

(p25).
554 *The Harvest*. In the audio, Hex's birthday falls on 12th October. His age isn't given, but actor Philip Olivier was born in 1980, and *The Harvest* was released in 2004.
555 *No Man's Land*
556 *Night Thoughts*
557 *Nocturne*

that would always be in demand; when Hex left school, he figured that medicine was a pretty safe bet.[558]

Jackie Tyler's father - "Grandad Prentice", as Rose called him - died of heart failure.[559] **A Jathaa Sun Glider crashed off the Shetland Islands, and Torchwood stripped the ship bare. They would deploy the ship's main weapon against the Sycorax in 2006.**[560]

Summer, a former attendee at the "Human-Be-In" rock festival in 1967, spent thirty years on the run from the mysterious gray-suited men. She settled in the American Northwest, but the fourth Doctor rescued Summer from the gray men as they arrived to kill her.[561]

c 1997 - THE PIT[562] **->** UNIT were called in to investigate an alien skeleton discovered on Salisbury Plain. Shortly afterward, batlike creatures tore apart a passenger airliner just outside Bristol.

1997 - INFINITE REQUIEM[563] **->** Twenty-one-year-old Tilusha Meswani died shortly after giving birth to her child Sanjay, who was really the Sensopath named Kelzen - an immensely powerful, psionic being. Kelzen grew rapidly to adulthood and gained empathy with humanity. It agreed to help the seventh Doctor fight another Sensopath on Gadrell Minor in 2387.

Hammerson Plastics PLC came out of nowhere to corner the market in plastics in six months. The success was credited to automation techniques, but the organisation was a front for an Auton production facility.[564]

The Conspiracy Channel broadcast *The Last Days of Hitler?*, written and directed by Claire Aldwych, on 12 August, 1997.[565] The only Recoronation in British history took place on 23rd November, 1997. Queen Elizabeth II was formally restored to the throne following Xznaal's usurpation of the crown.[566]

Paul Travers reviewed a Johnny Chess concert in the 18/7/98 *NME*.[567] A Kulan evaluation team crashed in Norway in 1998, split into two factions and began work supporting two rival space flight enterprises. The pro-invasion group supported entrepreneur Pierre Yves-Dudoin in the construction of his Star Dart shuttle, and the more benign faction sided with the lucrative Arthur Tyler III in building a Planet Hopper.[568]

1998 - SYSTEM SHOCK[569] **->** By 1998, virtually every computer in the world used the operating system Vorell, developed by I². The owner of I², 43-year-old Lionel Stabfield, quickly became the fifth richest man in the world. His company bought the rights to every major work of art, releasing images of them on interactive discs.

---

558 *LIVE 34*
559 "Ten years" before *Army of Ghosts*.
560 Also "ten years" before *Army of Ghosts*, and elaborating on the super-weapon used in *The Christmas Invasion*.
561 *Wonderland*
562 Dating *The Pit* (NA #12) - The Doctor and the poet William Blake travel to the 1990s, apparently after the Doctor has met Brigadier Bambera in *Battlefield*.
563 Dating *Infinite Requiem* (NA #36) - It is "1997".
564 "A couple of years" before "Plastic Millennium".
565 *The Shadow in the Glass*
566 *The Dying Days*, first mentioned in *Christmas on a Rational Planet*.

THE MONARCHY: Different stories say different things about who is the British monarch around the turn of the millennium. Lethbridge-Stewart refers to the King in *Battlefield*, which is set in the late twentieth century. *Happy Endings* specifies that King Charles ruled at the turn of the millennium. There is a King when Mariah Learman seizes power in *The Time of the Daleks*, and by the time of *Trading Futures*.

However, Queen Elizabeth still reigns in *Head Games*, set in 2001. *Christmas on a Rational Planet* refers to the "Recoronation", apparently implying that Elizabeth II abdicated in favour of Charles, but - for reasons we can only speculate on - was restored to the throne soon afterwards. *The Dying Days* (set just after *Battlefield*) offers a different reason for the

Recoronation: the Queen was usurped by the Ice Warrior Xznaal.

In the *Doctor Who* universe, there's a Princess Mary who's nineteen at time *Rags* is set (p158). While it isn't stated, she's clearly a senior royal and by birth, so the obvious inference is that she's the Queen's daughter.

567 *Timewyrm: Revelation*
568 *Escape Velocity*
569 Dating *System Shock* (MA #11) - When asked, a barman, Rod, informs the Doctor that this is "1998". The Doctor goes on to tell Sarah that in that particular year, "nothing of interest happened as far as I remember". It is "twenty odd years" after Sarah's time, and she muses that a "greying, mid-forties" future version of herself is alive in 1998, which the epilogue confirms.
570 Cosgrove has "not left his desk in London for nearly twenty years" before *Trading Futures*.
571 It's implied in *The Doctor Dances* that the Doctor gave it to her.
572 *Christmas on a Rational Planet*. She met Paul Morley in *Interference*.
573 Dating *Option Lock* (EDA #8) - It's "present day England" according to the blurb.

AMERICAN PRESIDENTS IN THE DOCTOR WHO UNIVERSE: As with British political history, *Doctor Who* presents a version of American politics that's a mix of historical fact and whimsy. *Interference* lists the recent American Presidents as Carter, Reagan, Bush, Clinton, Dering (*Option Lock*, around 1998), Springsteen

The new technology allowed flatpanel, interactive television, and the recordable CD-ROM to be perfected. Sales of computer equipment rocketed still further.

All computers were joined up to the Hubway, a formalised version of the Internet. As Hubway went online, though, chaos broke out: aeroplanes crashed at Heathrow as air traffic control systems failed, the Astra satellite was sent into a new orbit, the Library of Congress catalogue and all its backups were wiped, the computer facilities of the First National Bank of China were obliterated. Instruments at Nunton told technicians that the reactor had gone to meltdown. The head of MI5, Veronica Halliwell, was assassinated.

This was all part of the plan of the Voracians, cybernetic reptilians from Vorella. They planned to use the sentient software Voractyll to take control of the Earth. The fourth Doctor, Sarah and Harry Sullivan helped to defeat them.

Jonah Cosgrove, former sixties superspy, succeeded Halliwell as the head of MI5.[570] **When Rose Tyler was twelve, she received a red bicycle for Christmas.**[571] By 1998, Sarah Jane Smith had married a man called Morley,

and was a speaker at the Nobel Academy.[572]

c 1998 - OPTION LOCK[573] **->** President Dering was now in the White House, with Jack Michaels serving as vice-president.

The Khameirian-sponsored brotherhood, founded in the thirteenth century, had many members in positions of power. They sought to trigger a nuclear conflict that would produce the energy needed for the Khameirians to recorporealize. A brotherhood member launched an unauthorized nuclear strike from Krejikistan, which compelled the Americans to reveal the nuke-killing Station Nine as they nullified the threat. The US subsequently turned Station Nine over to the United Nations.

The brotherhood's leader, Norton Silver, forced the eighth Doctor to relocate the TARDIS to Station Nine to launch a nuclear strike from there. Britain's Captain Pickering died while destroying Station Nine to prevent this, an act that also killed Silver and the Khameirian core within him. A month later, Sam Jones learned that Silver's widow was pregnant, and worried the Khameirian taint might have passed to the child.

(*Eternity Weeps*, 2003) and Norris (*Cat's Cradle: Warhead*, around 2009). *Death Comes to Time* has George W Bush as President, and stories including *Trading Futures* and *Unregenerate!* mentions features of his presidency such as the War on Terror and the Iraq War. President Arthur Winters appears in *The Sound of Drums*, set in June 2008, but he's assassinated.

Bad Wolf mentions President Schwarzenegger (at present, Arnold is barred from the US presidency since he wasn't born an American citizen). *Trading Futures* has President Mather in charge around 2015.

This actually could fit together reasonably well without needing to infer any impeachments or assassinations. Assuming the same fixed terms, elections would take place in, and be won by:

1996: Dering (meaning Clinton was a single termer in the *Doctor Who* universe.)

2000: Springsteen

2004: George W Bush (another single termer in the *Doctor Who* universe - this time missing the first term he had historically. This would set *Death Comes to Time* a couple of years after it was released, but that's certainly not ruled out by the story. The reference in *Neverland* claiming the "wrong man became President" was meant to refer to Bush winning in 2000, which might be relevant - if highly ambiguous - in this context.)

2004 or 2008: Winters (US presidential elections are always held in November, so Winters being president in June 2008 would seem to indicate - unless one discards *Death Comes to Time* entirely, in which case Bush was probably never president and Winters was elected in 2004 - that Bush failed to complete his entire term. Winters' statement that he's "president elect" must be

his way of telling the Toclafane "I'm the elected representative of my people" - a US politician would never use this term in such a fashion, as Americans use the term "president elect" to indicate someone who's won a presidential election but has not yet taken office. As dictated by the US Constitution, such a person can only exist between early November and the following January - anyone who becomes president via the death, incapacitation, resignation or Congressional booting of the sitting president would immediately take office.

2008: Norris (taking office after Winters' death. This might suggest that he was Winters' vice-president, or - if Winters somehow replaced Bush and served very briefly - that Norris was Speaker of the House, and therefore third in line to the Presidency.)

2012: Mather

2016 or 2020: Schwarzenegger (he'd be sixty-nine or seventy-three on taking office.)

Their party affiliation can perhaps be inferred - if Dering beats Clinton (rather than, say, Clinton stepping aside or being impeached), he's a Republican. The real-life Springsteen is a Democrat. Winters is almost doubtlessly a Republican, as his portrayal in *The Sound of Drums* marks him as a conservative. The real-life Chuck Norris is a Republican. Mather served in Bush's Cabinet, so he's likely a Republican (only on very rare occasions will a Cabinet member hail from a different party, although it happened under Clinton). We might assume that Schwarzenegger wouldn't stand against a fellow Republican, so Mather serves two terms.

In 1998, the Japanese set up the Nikkei 5 station in the Antarctic to measure carbon dioxide levels.[574] Margaret Thatcher might have returned to power at some point.[575]

1999 (July) - THE KING OF TERROR[576] -> The alien Jex sought to conquer Earth, and had fronted the communications conglomerate InterCom to this end. They were secretly stockpiling plutonium to detonate and raise Earth's temperature to better accommodate their race. The Canavitchi, formerly enslaved to the Jex, worked to exterminate their former masters. The Brigadier received reports of extra-terrestrial involvement in California, and summoned the fifth Doctor, Tegan and Turlough to UNIT's Los Angeles office.

The Doctor and his allies brought InterCom to ruin as rival Jex and Canavitchi warfleets showed up in Earth orbit. The Doctor used Earth's satellite network to create a planetary defence shield as the warfleets slaughtered one another and departed. The Doctor advised the Brigadier to co-ordinate with the American CIA and help capture the Jex and Canavitchi agents still at-large.

1999 (July) - DOMINION[577] -> Department C19 had resumed active service by this time.

Professor Jennifer Nagle, a UNIT scientist, experimented with captured alien equipment at a C19 base in Sweden. She accidentally created a dimensional wormhole into a pocket universe named the Dominion. The larger universe expanded into the Dominion, threatening many races there. Some of the carnivorous Ruin fled through the wormhole to Earth, but Earth's higher gravity killed them.

The Dominion was completely eradicated, but the eighth Doctor evacuated fourteen of the frog-like T'hilli and their Queen to a habitable planet, saving the race from extinction. The wormhole terminated, but an energy backlash destroyed the C19 base and killed Nagle.

> = In July 1999, an encounter with Lord Roche's dead TARDIS inflicted young Ezekiel Child with "Jeapes' Syndrome", a condition in which a person matures backwards in time rather than forward. Child was 21 in 1999, but age forty-six in 1972, and failed to notice anything odd about this. The Doctor's involvement retroactively averted the Child anomaly.

In 1999, Jo Grant observed that a lingering side-effect of temporal interference had turned the *Independent on Sunday* newspaper into the *Sunday Telegraph*.[578] Shortly after Joseph Heller's death, documents were found among his effects that contained the recollections of Alan Turing, Graeme Greene and Heller himself of their encounter with aliens in Dresden, 1945.[579]

w 1999 - THE TAKING OF PLANET 5[580] -> UNIT was called in to investigate an anomaly in the Antarctic that had been detected by satellite, and discovered a protoplasmic creature inside an alien structure. The eighth Doctor, Fitz and Compassion eventually arrived from twelve million years in the past, where they'd been thwarting the machinations of a group of future Time Lords.

c 1999 - "Darkness Falling" / "Distractions" / "The Mark of Mandragora"[581] -> The party drug M - Mandrake - was a problem. Captain Muriel Frost and

---

574 *Iceberg*

575 In *Transit*, there's a history book called *Thatcher: The Wilderness Years*.

576 Dating *The King of Terror* (PDA #37) - It's "1 July 1999" (p5).

577 Dating *Dominion* (EDA #22) - On p35, Fitz reads a newspaper dated 31st July, 1999.

578 *The Suns of Caresh*, both the Child anomaly and Jo's observation.

579 *The Turing Test*. Heller died 12th December, 1999.

580 Dating *The Taking of Planet 5* (EDA #28) - It's "1 October 1999" (p21).

581 Dating "Darkness Falling" / "Distractions" / "The Mark of Mandragora" (*DWM* #167-172) - It's "the end of the twentieth century", but not (as far as we're told) New Year's 1999 itself. It's after *Battlefield*, and Mandrake first appeared in 1997 (so the story takes place after that). "Darkness Falling" and "Distractions", both prologues to the main story, went untitled in *The Mark of Mandragora* graphic novel.

582 Dating "Plastic Millennium" (*DWM Winter Special*

1994) - The date is given. It's tempting to link the contents of the phial with the Doctor's "anti plastic" in *Rose*.

583 Dating *Millennial Rites* (MA #15) - The story revolves around the date, first confirmed on p34.

584 Dating *Doctor Who - The Movie* (27.0) - The date is first given when Chang Lee fills out the Doctor's medical paperwork. On screen, the Master looks like a gelatinous snake, although *The Eight Doctors* attributes this to his swallowing a "deathworm".

585 Dating *Millennium Shock* (PDA #22) - It is "Christmas Eve" (p64).

586 *Happy Endings*

587 *Seeing I* (p86).

588 *Cat's Cradle: Warhead, System Shock*

589 The ecu is in use by *Iceberg*, at the exchange rate of one ecu to two dollars. In *Warlock*, the drug enforcement agent Creed McIlveen has a suitcase full of "EC paper money", although Sterling is still used on a day-to-day basis.

590 *The Shadow of the Scourge*

591 *Psi-ence Fiction*

Sergeant Jasper Bean of UNIT discovered a Mandrake factory at the popular Falling Star nightclub in London, but an energy creature killed Bean.

The Mandragora Helix was warping the TARDIS' structure and drawing it towards Earth. The seventh Doctor and Ace found themselves at the Falling Star with Frost, and Lethbridge-Stewart vouched for their identities via video link from Geneva. Returning to the Falling Star, they arrived to see the Helix energy manifesting in a bid to take over the Earth, then the universe. The Helix started to kill the clubbers, whose will had been sapped by the Mandrake drug, and Frost ordered in the UNIT troops. The Doctor was convinced the Helix had won, but the circuit broke. It appeared that the TARDIS had disintegrated, but it rematerialised at UNIT HQ a few days later.

The very public threat convinced the United Nations to increase UNIT's powers and put it on a more public footing. A new United Nations team - Foreign Hazard Duty - was set up to deal with problems that had to be kept more secret. Muriel Frost was promoted to Major.

The Millennium

1999 (31st December) - "Plastic Millennium"[582] -> The seventh Doctor and Mel gatecrashed a New Year's Eve hosted by Alisha Hammerson, director of the world's largest plastics factory, for the world's business leaders. Hammerson gassed the CEOs and planned to replaced them with Autons. The Doctor brewed up a phial that he used to destroy the meteor that represented the link to the Nestene, and Hammerson melted.

1999 / 2000 (30th December - 1st January) - MILLENNIAL RITES[583] -> Ashley Chapel had worked for International Electromatics before forming his own company, ACL. Following the collapse of I², ACL quickly bought up all their hardware and software patents, and Chapel became a multi-millionaire. He funded the construction of the new Millennium Hall on the banks of the Thames, and began work on a powerful computer program - "the Millennium Codex" - that would use quantum mnemonics and block transfer computation. This would change the laws of physics to those of the universe of Saraquazel, which was created from the ashes of our own. Elsewhere, Dame Anne Travers became worried about the return of the Great Intelligence. She attempted to banish the sentience, but inadvertently summoned it.

On the stroke of midnight, 31st December, 1999, magic returned to the world as the Intelligence and Saraquazel fused over London, transforming the city into a aeons-old battleground between the forces of three factions: the Abraxas, Magick and Technomancy. After only ten minutes of real time, the new laws unravelled and the world was

returned to normal. Fifteen people had died. Saraquazel took Chapel back with him to his own universe.

1999/2000 (30th December - 1st January) DOCTOR WHO - THE MOVIE[584] -> The seventh Doctor was transporting the Master's remains to Gallifrey from Skaro when the Master - now a gelatinous creature - forced the TARDIS to make an emergency landing. The seventh Doctor was shot in San Francisco and died on the operating table, regenerating into his eighth incarnation. The Master took over the body of an ambulance worker. He attempted to steal the Doctor's remaining lives by use of the TARDIS' Eye of Harmony, and his scheme threatened to destroy the entire planet. The Doctor stopped the Master with the help of heart surgeon Grace Holloway, and the Master was sucked into the TARDIS' Eye.

2000 (Saturday, 1st January) - MILLENNIUM SHOCK[585] -> Silver Bullet Solutions developed chips to help combat the Y2K bug, but this was a front by the Voracians, who were trying to re-assemble the sentient computer virus Voractyll and seize control of Earth's computers. The Silver Bullet chips exacerbated the switch-over from 1999 to 2000, temporarily cutting power in Malaysia, Auckland and parts of Britain, and jamming Hong Kong's traffic. The fourth Doctor, working with MI5 agent Harry Sullivan, re-programmed the Silver Bullet chips to also endow Voractyll with a Y2K sensitivity. The creature terminated, and the Voracians, serving as part of Voractyll's command nodes, perished also.

Disgraced Prime Minister Terry Brooks tried to exploit the chaos and declare martial law to advance his private agenda. Officially, it was said that his Cabinet lost faith in him, and he resigned "for personal reasons". Philip Cotton, Brooks' deputy, was appointed his successor.

At the turn of the Millennium, the Brigadier became a media icon as he led King Charles' troops in a blockade of Westminster Bridge. The King offered him a role in the Provisional Cabinet, but he declined.[586]

The Twenty-First Century

The non-profit organisation Livingspace was formed at the beginning of the twenty-first century.[587] News interpretation software sifted the media for the user's own preferences. Televisions could be set so that news bulletins automatically interrupted regular broadcasts.[588]

Early in the twenty-first century, Britain joined the Ecu, the single European Currency.[589] The pacifying gas pacificus was developed in the twenty-first century.[590] Walton Hummer was a popular three-foot tall kazoo player from the twenty-first century.[591] The musician Sting was assassinated in the early twenty-first century.[592]

Since 1969, Billy Shipton had "got into" publishing, then video, then DVD production. On the Doctor's instructions, he secretly inserted Easter Eggs onto seventeen DVDs that Sally Shipton would come to own in future.[593]

The Doctor theorised that if Queen Victoria was infected by an alien werewolf cell, it might take "one hundred" years to mature in her children, and "be ready" by the early twenty-first century.[594] He was in Havana for Fidel Castro's funeral, and later said, "They all loved (Castro) again by then".[595]

2000

By the year 2000, the *Hourly Tele-press* kept the world's population up to date with events around the globe. One of the *Tele-press'* most popular features was the strip-cartoon adventures of "The Karkus".[596]

The first Space Wheel was constructed in 2000.[597] In the same year, Arthur Tyler III was working on the Space Dart and Earthrise private space projects. Diagnosed with terminal cancer, he threw himself into his task.[598] NASA discovered the six-billion-year-old Cthalctose Museum on the Moon. Construction started on Tranquility Base to better study the alien artefact, and there were regular moonshots to service it.[599]

> **= 2000 - "The Glorious Dead"**[600] **->** In an alternate timeline, Paradost was a planetary museum that celebrated a million alien races. Earth was known as Dharkan, and was a wasteland ruled by Cardinal Morningstar - who the Doctor previously knew as Katsura Sato. The eighth Doctor, Izzy and Kroton were on Paradost when it was invaded. Kroton took control of a reality-bending device known as the Omniversal Spectrum and restored the established timeline.

c 2000 - THE MARIAN CONSPIRACY[601] **->** Time disturbances surrounded history professor Evelyn Smythe. The sixth Doctor met her and concluded that the problem lay with her ancestor John Whiteside-Smith, who lived at the time of Elizabeth I. They departed to investigate.

Evelyn Smythe told her student Sally about the time she and the Doctor met some pirates.[602]

c 2000 (October) - THE SPECTRE OF LANYON MOOR[603] **->** Lethbridge-Stewart, occasionally performing some surveillance work for UNIT, agreed to look into the latest of a string of mysterious deaths in the Lanyon Moor area. An archaeological expedition there awoke the Tregannon scout Sancreda after 18,000 years of semi-dormancy, and Sancreda sought to use his vast mental abilities to exact revenge on his brother Screfan for abandoning him. The sixth Doctor and Evelyn aided the Brigadier as Sancreda summoned his survey ship from space, but Sancreda discovered that he had inadvertently killed his brother during their initial survey on Earth. Sancreda tried using his ship's psionic cannon to destroy Earth, but the Brigadier swapped out a crucial component from the cannon's control system. The resultant energy backlash destroyed Sancreda and his survey ship.

c 2000 - PROJECT: TWILIGHT[604] **->** By now the Forge-created vampires Amelia Doory and Reggie Mead owned and operated The Dusk casino in London, and had converted its basement into a secret medical research facility. The sixth Doctor and Evelyn arrived as Nimrod returned to stalk the vampires, and Amelia convinced the Doctor to help her find a cure to vampirism.

However, Amelia instead used the Doctor's discoveries to create "The Twilight Virus", an airborne virus capable of converting humans into vampires on contact. She converted a casino waitress named Cassie into a vampire as a test, but a vengeful Cassie killed Reggie. Nimrod destroyed

---

592 *So Vile a Sin*
593 *Blink.* Allowing for wherever Sally's taste in DVD entertainment might take her, Billy must have inserted the Easter Eggs over the course of a few years at least, and prior to 2007.
594 *Tooth and Claw* (TV).
595 *Revolution Man* (p23). No date is given.
596 *The Mind Robber.* Zoe was a fan, which would seem to imply that Zoe is from the year 2000, but see the "Dating *The Wheel in Space*". According to *Alien Bodies*, the adventures of the Karkus are still running in the 2050s.
597 *Christmas on a Rational Planet*, via *The Mind Robber* and *The Wheel in Space*. *The Harvest* has the Wheels operating in 2021.

598 *Escape Velocity*, referenced as occurring "Last year".
599 "The last three years" before *Eternity Weeps*.
600 Dating "The Glorious Dead" (*DWM* #287-296) - The year isn't specified, but it is the "present day".
601 Dating *The Marian Conspiracy* - No year is given. Evelyn is from the present day, and has a mobile phone.
602 *Doctor Who and the Pirates*
603 Dating *The Spectre of Lanyon Moor* (BF #9) - Lethbridge-Stewart has been retired "a few years now". Evelyn phones one of her friends, so this is her native time. The first meeting of the sixth Doctor and Lethbridge-Stewart is portrayed both here and in *Business Unusual*. Given that the Doctor first meets Mel in *Business Unusual*, and that he clearly travelled with Evelyn before her, it's fair to assume that from the sixth

Amelia's laboratory and the Doctor confiscated the last vial of Twilight Virus. Amelia went missing in the Thames, and the Doctor helped Cassie relocate to a remote part of Norway.

c 2000 - GRAVE MATTER[605] **->** The European space probe Gatherer Three explored the outer planets and returned to Earth, where it was discovered to have picked up alien DNA. This was named "Denarian", and seemed to have miraculous medical properties. In actuality, Denarian was an alien creature that possessed bodies to survive. A team of scientists relocated to the Dorsill islands off the south west coast of the UK and began secret experiments on animals and the local population. The sixth Doctor and Peri arrived to find the islands overrun with walking corpses, but the Doctor discovered that a second dose of Denarian cancelled out the first.

c 2000 - IMPERIAL MOON[606] **->** The fifth Doctor and Turlough materialised near the Moon to avoid hitting themselves in the Vortex. A time safe aboard the TARDIS opened and revealed a diary purporting to be the log of a Victorian expedition to the Moon - which historically did not occur. The Doctor went to 1878 to learn the truth.

c 2000 - EXCELIS RISING[607] **->** On the highly-industrialized planet Artaris, border disputes sprang up between the city-states of Gatracht and Calann. The public came to regard "the warlord Grayvorn and his lost treasure" as the stuff of myth, although officials at the Imperial Archives' Black Museum privately acknowledged the tales as true.

The Relic had become the property of the Excelis Museum, and an Imperial Edict forbade the head curator from turning the object over to anyone beyond the Empress, her Regent or the Etheric Minister. Possibly due to the Relic's presence in the city, mediums were able to commune with the dead.

At the Museum, the sixth Doctor found the former warlord Grayvorn trying to re-acquire the Relic. An altercation between them resulted in a discharge of the Relic's ener-

gies, which dissipated Grayvorn's physical form. His consciousness became embedded in the Museum's stone walls, and he waited for someone to die in the museum so he could inhabit their body.

In early November 2000, a man named Tom jumped aboard a bus in London, and found he'd entered Iris Wildthyme's TARDIS. He became her travelling companion.[608] Martha Jones visited the Millennium Dome with her family and secretly enjoyed it.[609] On Christmas Day 2000, a serious earthquake called "the Little Big One" hit San Francisco.[610]

2001

Brigadier Fernfather replaced Bambera as the head of UNIT in the UK.[611] Bambera had married Ancelyn and given birth to twins.[612]

2001 - THE SHADOW IN THE GLASS[613] **->** Historical journalist Claire Aldwych discovered evidence of the Vvormak cruiser located in Turelhampton, England, which prompted the sixth Doctor and the Brigadier to investigate. Suspecting Nazi involvement, the Brigadier stole pieces of Hitler and Eva Braun's remains from the State Special Trophy Archive in Moscow for comparison.

The Doctor and his allies came to discover the existence of a Nazi organization at an Antarctic base, led by the son of Adolf Hitler and Eva Braun. The Doctor retrieved the Scrying Glass from the base, but it depicted the Doctor taking Hitler's son back in time to 1945. To fulfil the Glass' visions, the Doctor, the Brigadier, Claire and Hitler's son travelled back to that year.

After their return, the Doctor and the Brigadier helped the sleeping Vvormak awaken and depart Earth. UNIT assisted with breaking up the exposed Fourth Reich cells.

In 2001, the Grid, a means of pooling the unused processing power of Internet computers to create unlimited memory space, came online. Paul Kairos, a classmate of

---

Doctor's perspective, he first encounters the Brigadier in *The Spectre of Lanyon Moor*. But the Brigadier first meets the sixth Doctor in *Business Unusual*, which takes place about eleven years previous in 1989.

604 Dating *Project: Twilight* (BF #23) - No year is given, but it's the present day for Evelyn, and Tony Blair is the Prime Minister.

605 Dating *Grave Matter* (PDA #31) - Peri thinks it's the "twentieth century" (p201), there's nothing to suggest it's not set the year the book was published, in 2000.

606 Dating *Imperial Moon* (PDA #34) - "Some time in the early twenty-first century" (p7). The book was published in 2000.

607 Dating *Excelis Rising* (BF *Excelis* series #2) - The story is set a thousand years after *Excelis Dawns* and three hundred before *Excelis Decays*.

608 *Verdigris* (p2).

609 *Made of Steel*

610 *Unnatural History* (p33), picking up on a line from *Doctor Who - The Movie*.

611 *The Shadow in the Glass*

612 *Head Games*. We might infer that Fernfather covered Bambera's maternity leave. She's back on duty by *Head Games*.

613 Dating *The Shadow in the Glass* (PDA #41) - According to the blurb, it's "2001".

Melanie Bush, learned to manipulate photons in a way that rendered the transistor and micro-monolithic circuit obsolete. Anjelique Whitefriar stole Kairos' design and patented it as the "Whitefriar Lattice".[614]

@ 2001 (February) - ESCAPE VELOCITY[615] **->** Compassion dropped Fitz in London on 6th February, 2001 - two days ahead of his scheduled rendezvous with the eighth Doctor. By now, the Doctor owned the "St. Louis Bar and Restaurant" in London to facilitate his meeting with Fitz. After their rendevous, the Doctor gave the bar to its manager, Sheff.

Competition between the Kulan factions increased, as the first group to report to the Kulan leadership would be likely to persuade them to either invade or spare Earth.

Anji Kapoor, a 28-year-old futures analyst, took a break in Brussels with her boyfriend Dave and became embroiled in the Kulan conflict. The Doctor, Fitz and Anji allied with the benevolent Kulan faction and blew up Yves-Dudoin's Star Dart. However, a pro-invasion Kulan member named Fray'kon killed Dave.

A Kulan warfleet arrived in Earth orbit, but the TARDIS completed its century of healing and became functional again. The Doctor, Fitz and Anji travelled to the flagship and tricked the Kulan ships into annihilating one another. Arthur Tyler III and Fray'kon both died in the fighting. The TARDIS had departed Earth with Anji aboard, but the Doctor promised to try and return her home.

The Doctor returned Anji home three weeks after she left, and she resumed her life. It would be eighteen months before she saw the Doctor again.[616]

2001 - HEAD GAMES[617] **->** General Lethbridge-Stewart was semi-retired. In the year 2001, Ace met up with a future version of the seventh Doctor, who informed her that his evil duplicate Dr Who was planning to assassinate the Queen. The Queen was shot in Sheffield, but wasn't even slightly injured. Meanwhile, UNIT forces were involved in an assault on Buckingham Palace. Brigadier Bambera, recently returned to service after the birth of her twins, arrived in a Merlin T-22 VTOL aircraft and managed a penetrate a forcefield surrounding the palace.

Dr Who had been created by a spiteful Jason, the ex-Master of the Land of Fiction. The Doctor counselled Jason and convinced him to dissipate Dr Who.

At this time, Bernice kicked a mangled drinks can into the middle of a path. Four and a half hours later, a young man stumbled over it on his bike, and suffered slight bruising. This instigated a chain reaction of small historical alterations that climaxed directly before the Draconian War in the twenty-sixth century.

= c 2001 - PSI-ENCE FICTION[618] **->** The TARDIS landed at the University of East Wessex, where researcher Barry Hitchens was studying psychic powers. One of his students, Josh Randall, had secretly

---

614 *The Quantum Archangel*
615 Dating *Escape Velocity* (EDA #42) - The exact date is given (p26).
616 *Time Zero*
617 Dating *Head Games* (NA #43) - It is "2001", some time before December 2001, and "953 years" before Cwej is born. The bit with the pop can is on p165-166.
618 Dating *Psi-ence Fiction* (PDA #46) - The year isn't given, but there's a modern day setting, with references to (for example) *The Blair Witch Project* and CCTV cameras. The book was released in 2001.
619 According to Owen's comments and a computer graphic related to Lucy's death in *TW: Greeks Bearing Gifts*.
620 Dating "The Fallen" (*DWM* #273-276) - "2001. Somewhere in November judging by the temperature", according to the Doctor.
621 "Five years" before *Rise of the Cybermen*.
622 *Head Games*
623 *The Hollow Men* (p74).
624 "Fifty years" after *Amorality Tale*.
625 *Sometime Never*. The Doctor, Fitz and Trix visit Sam's grave in *The Gallifrey Chronicles*, which gives her date of death as 2002. From *The Bodysnatchers* onwards, some of the EDAs hinted that Sam would

meet a premature death. Others, such as *Interference*, hinted that she would live into great old age; *Beltempest* even alluded that she was now immortal.

Alien Bodies and *Unnatural History* reveal that contact with the Doctor changed Sam's timeline, preventing her from becoming "Dark Sam" (dark-haired, sexually active and a drug user) and making her squeaky-clean instead. Further complicating things, some of the "companion deaths" the Council of Eight arranged were either ambiguous or retconned away after their defeat. As of *The Gallifrey Chronicles*, it's clear that Sam died in 2002 and "stayed dead".
626 *Sometime Never*
627 Dating *Unnatural History* (EDA #23) - It's "November 2002" (p1).
628 Dating *The Ratings War* (BF promo #2, *DWM* #313) Beep's early appearances on Earth are roughly contemporary. Previous to *The Ratings War*, he was imprisoned in "Star Beast II", a comic story in the *1996 DWM Annual*. The tone and heavy amount of reality TV in this story suggests author Steve Lyons had a contemporary or near-contemporary setting in mind.
629 Dating *The Fearmonger* (BF #5) - This is "just over fifteen years" after Ace's time.
630 *Happy Endings*

become a formidable psychic and was viciously making other students hallucinate. Hitchens was being funded by physicist John Finer, who was trying to build a time machine to go back six years to prevent his daughter from dying.

The fourth Doctor inspected the machine, deducing that its use would destroy the timelines. Randall was driven insane, and deemed himself a god. The TARDIS materialised around the time machine, fixing history. Finer never started his time travel research, and the Doctor and Leela, along with everyone else, forgot that these events ever happened.

In September 2001, Owen Harper had been qualified as a physician for six months. The alien Mary tore the heart out of 43-year-old Lucy Marmer, and Owen was present when Lucy's body was brought into Cardiff General Hospital.[619]

2001 (November) - "The Fallen"[620] -> The dead were walking in West Norwood in London, and seven people had disappeared. The eighth Doctor and Izzy discovered Grace Holloway investigating with MI6, which was secretly run by Leighton Woodrow.

Grace had recovered the Master's DNA from her encounter with him. Working with the scientist Donald Stark, she hoped to unlock the secrets of regeneration - she had thought the Doctor was hinting she *should* do so by mentioning he was half-human, and telling her to hold back death. However, Grace's sample wasn't Time Lord DNA as she had believed. Stark was transformed into a snake creature - a morphant from Skaro like the Master before him. He attacked Izzy, and thereby learned of her connection with the Doctor. The Doctor confronted Stark and destroyed him, even as Woodrow decided to blame the explosion on Arab terrorists. As the Doctor left, Woodrow found one of his men... killed by the Master's tissue compression eliminator.

2002

Mickey Smith's mother had been unable to cope with raising him, and his father - Jeremiah Smith, who formerly worked at the key-cutters on Clifton Parade - went to Spain and never returned. Mickey was raised by his blind gran, but she died after tripping and falling down the stairs.[621]

On 30th November, 2002, the gunman Murdock killed five people... although Ace's interference in history reduced this total to three. This was about as far in the future as she could travel using her time hopper.[622] The "Great Drought of '02" affected the UK.[623] The main Xhinn fleet was due to arrive on Earth in 2002.[624]

The Council of Eight arranged for a drug overdose to kill Sam Jones, a former companion of the Doctor, who had become an eco-campaigner.[625] The Doctor found another part of Octan's skeleton in New York, 2002.[626]

2002 (October / November) UNNATURAL HISTORY[627] -> A dimensional scar, the after-effect of the singularity that befell Earth on New Year's Eve, 2000, appeared in San Francisco. The eighth Doctor investigated the anomaly, but his companion Samantha Jones was lost to it. He sought out Sam's original self, a dark-haired drug user, to assist. The Doctor also recruited Professor Joyce, a resident of Berkeley, to craft a dimensional stabilizer.

Griffen the Unnaturalist, an agent of a secret Society that catalogued all aliens, arrived at this time to collect specimens for his catalog. Dark-haired Sam sacrificed herself to the anomaly to restore blonde-haired Sam, who helped the Doctor to unleash the Unnaturalist's extra-dimensional specimen case. The freed specimens drove the Unnaturalist into the dimensional scar, and the case sealed it permanently.

The Doctor afterward realized that blonde Sam's timeline came about because she touched his biodata within the scar, meaning that she paradoxically facilitated her own creation.

c 2002 - THE RATINGS WAR[628] -> The tyrannical Beep the Meep escaped from his imprisonment in a *Lassie* film, and used blackstar radiation to mesmerize executives at a TV network. Under Beep's direction, the network enjoyed success with shows such as *Appealing Animals in Distress* and *Hospital Street*, the first ever 24-hour soap opera.

Beep sought to brainwash the public through subliminal messages jointly seeded into the final episode of *Audience Shares*, and the debut of *Beep and Friends*. The sixth Doctor crushed this scheme, and exposed Beep's murderous tendencies on national television. Authorities apprehended the raving Meep.

c 2002 - THE FEARMONGER[629] -> Sherilyn Harper's New Britannia Party was gaining political influence by preaching strong anti-immigration policies. She was subject to an assassination attempt at the hands of United Front terrorists. Serious riots started spreading as the population panicked, but Harper was made to unwittingly broadcast a confession that New Britannia was secretly funding the United Front. The situation may or may not have been whipped up by the Fearmonger, an energy being from Boslin II. The seventh Doctor and Ace had been tracking the Fearmonger and destroyed it. Beryllium laser guns were top secret in this era.

The fertiliser Bloom was developed, but it was viral and spread uncontrollably. It was banned before 2010.[630]

c 2002 - DRIFT[631] **->** The fourth Doctor and Leela landed in New Hampshire and met soldiers from the elite White Shadow unit. They were looking to retrieve a crashed fighter that was testing the Stormcore, an alien device recovered thirty years earlier. Also, an ice monster was on the loose in the area. The Doctor realised the Stormcore had opened a portal into another dimension, and that the monster was not intelligent, but was inadvertently killing people while trying to make contact. The Doctor crystallised the monster and handed it over to the authorities.

The Day the World Turned Dayglo, Hollywood's take on the Jex-Canavitchi war, was released in late 2002. Reporter Gabrielle Graddige approached the Brigadier in January 2003 for the true story.[632]

2002 (Late August) - TIME ZERO[633] **->** The reclusive billionaire Maxwell Curtis had learned that his body contained a microscopic remnant of the Big Bang, masquerading as an ordinary atom, which was in danger of collapsing and turning him into a black hole. He had founded the Naryshkin Institute in Siberia as a means of researching black hole phenomena.

However, a division of the American CIA, led by Control, suspected the Institute was conducting time travel experiments. Control's agents constructed a temporal detector and identified Anji as a time traveller. They made her accompany them to Siberia.

In Siberia, the eighth Doctor found that Curtis' black hole matter was distorting space-time in the region, causing freak effects. This allowed the Doctor to free Fitz from the icy prison from which he'd been trapped in 1894. The Doctor similarly liberated the trapped George Williamson, but Williamson existed in a ghostly state, given that the universe couldn't decide if he'd survived or not.

Williamson's pseudo-existence had generated a time corridor into the past, and Curtis travelled down this corridor in the hopes of reaching Time Zero and unleashing his black hole matter there, hoping to spare Earth. However, the Doctor realized that if the black hole within Curtis erupted before time began, it would destroy the universe. The Doctor convinced Williamson to go back with him to 1894 and avert Williamson getting trapped in the ice, which nullified the time corridor's existence. Curtis travelled back no further than 1894, and died in a comparatively minor explosion.

Additionally, Curtis' black hole mass attracted light from a far distant o-region to Earth. The o-region light contained something organic, which lodged itself on Earth's past and would manifest in the late nineteenth century as a fire elemental.

2003

With time destabilised, the eighth Doctor, Anji, Fitz and Trix were drawn into a series of adventures in alternate histories...[634]

= 2003 - THE DOMINO EFFECT[635] **->** Returning to 2003, the Doctor, Fitz and Anji arrived in a version of history where the British Empire ruled the world. There was widespread racial and sex discrimination. This timeline had developed because an alternate version of Sabbath had murdered key figures in the history of computing, including Babbage and Zuse, thus preventing the development of computers. The alternate Sabbath had learned that the Time Vortex was disintegrating following Gallifrey's destruction, and hoped to preserve his Earth in a temporal focal point. He was betrayed by a Vortex creature devoted to chaos, and the focal point collapsed. The entire past,

---

631 Dating *Drift* (PDA #50) - The year isn't given, but it's clearly the modern day.

632 *The King of Terror*

633 Dating *Time Zero* (EDA #60) - Anji returns home three weeks after she met the Doctor, and stays there eighteen months, so this story is set around the end of August 2002. Control also appears in *The Devil Goblins of Neptune*, *The King of Terror*, *Escape Velocity* and *Trading Futures*. The fire elemental that Curtis attracts is the creature the Doctor defeats in *The Burning*.

634 *Time Zero, The Infinity Race, The Domino Effect, Reckless Engineering, The Last Resort, Timeless*.

635 Dating *The Domino Effect* (EDA #62) - The book starts on "Thursday April 17 2003" (p1).

636 Dating *Reckless Engineering* (EDA #63) - The Doctor is sure it's "2003" (p24).

637 Dating *The Last Resort* (EDA #64) - Time is a rather

fluid concept in this novel, but Fitz and Anji are based in "2003" (p7, p11).

638 Dating *Timeless* (EDA #65) - No year is given, but the story takes place after *The Last Resort*, and Anji has been going out with Greg for a year by the time of *The Gallifrey Chronicles*.

639 Dating *Eternity Weeps* (NA #58) - The date is given (p1).

640 Dating *Rip Tide* (TEL #6) - It is "late May" (p13), in "the twenty-first century" (p78). There's no reason to say the story isn't set in the year the novella was published.

641 *The Highest Science*. The year is given on p2, and reiterated in *Happy Endings* (p5).

642 Dating *The Quantum Archangel* (PDA #38) - It's 2003 according to the blurb and p48, "thirty years" since *The Time Monster* (p39).

present and future of this timeline were consumed.

= **2003 - RECKLESS ENGINEERING**[636] **->** The Doctor, Fitz and Anji arrived in an alternate Bristol of 2003, one hundred and sixty years after "the Cleansing" effect had ravaged Earth, and found the Utopian Engine still generating a slow-time effect around Jared Malahyde's estate. By linking the Utopian Engine to the TARDIS' systems, the Doctor was able to roll back time a hundred and sixty years and avert "the Cleansing" timeline altogether.

= **2003 - THE LAST RESORT**[637] **->** Fourteen-year-old Jack Kowaczski had built a time machine, and thus created many thousands of variant histories. This included his own, in which President Robert Heinlein presided over the USA and Mars - along with the Martians - had been conquered.

The Doctor, Fitz and Anji arrived in one such history, where the time- travel holidays of Good Times Inc, founded by Jack's father Aaron, had turned the whole of human history into an homogenous tourist resort. The constant time travel, though, had destabilised reality and generated hundreds if not thousands of versions of events - including duplicate Doctors and companions. Sabbath was the only being unaffected by this process. The Doctor carefully sacrificed all but one version of himself and his companions, thus restoring the timeline.

c 2003 - TIMELESS[638] **->** The eighth Doctor, Fitz and Anji arrived back in the London of their reality. They found that Erasmus and Chloe, two survivors of a destroyed homeworld, had set up Timeless Inc. as a means of "helping people". Chloe and her time-active dog Jamais would visit parallel realities to find persons in pain, then bring them back to the proper reality. Jamais would transfer each person's souls out of their bodies and into their parallel counterpart, creating a merged soul with an improved timeline. Clients of Timeless Inc. would then pay £75,000 in diamonds for the privilege of murdering the parallel reality version, preventing the merged souls from defaulting back to their original state. Erasmus eventually realized that his goal of helping people had failed and killed himself, effectively ending Timeless' operations.

The genetic manipulations performed by Kalicum in the eighteenth century culminated in the British government worker Guy Adams. He now possessed the DNA needed to house an intelligence that Kalicum and Sabbath had gestated, in a pile of diamonds, on behalf of the Council of Eight. The Doctor and his allies followed Sabbath back to the beginning of time, where he and Kalicum tried to seed the intelligence into the universe's beginnings.

Afterward, Anji left the TARDIS crew to return to her old life in 2003. Aided by forged documents produced by Trix, she adopted Chloe and Jamais. Chloe introduced Anji to a man named Greg, whom she predicted Anji was going to get to know a lot better.

2003 (April) - ETERNITY WEEPS[639] **->** Liz Shaw was Chief of Operations at Tranquility Base on the Moon, where co-operation with the Silurians had led to the construction of an experimental weather control gravitron. Shaw and the Silurian Imorkal were in a close relationship.

Mount Ararat and Mahser Dagi were now in territory disputed by Turkey and Iraq, but an expedition to find Noah's Ark on Mount Ararat set off anyway. Bernice and Jason joined the team, although Benny found the Tendurek Formation, six billion years old and utterly alien. The Cthalctose terraforming virus - dubbed Agent Yellow - was set off and triggered catastrophic geological changes on Earth.

The US launched a nuclear strike in the area, but only succeeded in speeding up the process. This wiped out many cities including Istanbul, Thessaloniki, Almawsil, Tbilisi and Krasnodar. President Springsteen ordered the targeting of the moonbase, believing the crew there to be responsible. Jason fled billions of years back into the past and returned. The Agent was spreading as far as the Alps, the Sahara and Asia. The seventh Doctor engineered an x-ray burst using singularities to sterilise the Agent. This wiped out one tenth of all life on Earth, including six hundred million people.

Liz Shaw and Imorkal perished during these events, and Benny and Jason agreed to separate. Suborbital flights could be made to travel quickly around the world.

c 2003 (late May / June) - RIP TIDE[640] **->** A peaceful alien race had developed spatial gateways that enabled them to become tourists on other worlds. Two young members of the species, genetically altered to resemble human beings, violated their people's strict rule against risk of discovery by visiting a small Cornish fishing village. One alien died in a sightseeing accident, losing the "key" to their spatial gateway in the process. His stranded mate adopted the name "Ruth," but began dying from prolonged exposure to Earth's environment. Aided by a 17-year-old resident named Nina Kellow, the eighth Doctor rescued Ruth and transported her back home to her parents.

A Fortean Flicker transported a group of train-riders on the 8:12 out of Chorleywood to the planet Hogsumm in the twenty-seventh century. They were later returned to Rickmansworth Station in their native time.[641]

2003 - THE QUANTUM ARCHANGEL[642] **->** By now,

Stuart Hyde was the Emeritus Professor of Physics at West London University. He had used the discarded technology from TOMTIT to build TITAN, a dimensional array intended to penetrate the higher dimensions called "Calabi-Yau Space." Thanks to TITAN, businesswoman Anjeliqua Whitefriar became infused with the core of the Calabi-Yau and gained reality-warping powers. She became "the Quantum Archangel," and channelled her newfound reality-warping powers through the Mad Mind of Bophemeral, the super-computer that triggered the Millennium War, in a benevolent attempt to create separate utopias for each person on Earth. This threatened to plunge the universe into chaos.

> = The alternate realities created by the Quantum Archangel included ones where Mel was British Prime Minister, and faced a Cyberman invasion; the Doctor was President of Gallifrey, leading his people against the Master and the Daleks; and the Master, Monk, Rani and Drax altered Earth's DNA.[643]

The sixth Doctor persuaded Anjeliqua to restore order and relinquish her power, while the Chronovore named Kronos sacrificed himself to destroy Bophemeral.

2003 - MINUET IN HELL[644] **->** Hellfire Club leader Brigham Elisha Dashwood III believed he'd allied himself with a group of demons, and set about using their support to booster his organization. In truth, he'd contacted alien Psionivores, members of a species of cosmic parasites that feasted on negative emotions. With the Psionivores' help and technical expertise, Dashwood seceded a small portion of America, renamed it "Malebolgia" and dedicated it to a social program of devil worship. The Psionivores helped Dashwood perfect the PSI-895, which was capable of rewriting or transferring human memories, and Dashwood hoped this would let him install Psionivores in his political opponents' bodies.

The eighth Doctor and Charley, aided by the Brigadier, publicly exposed Dashwood as a political charlatan. Dashwood turned against Marcosius, his main contact among the Psionivores, and accidentally disrupted the PSI machine. This created an unstable portal that consumed Dashwood, Marcosius and the device. The remaining Hellfire Club leaders crumbled in a political scandal.

Lethbridge-Stewart had now retired from UNIT, but still undertook occasional work for them.

---

643 *The Quantum Archangel*

644 Dating *Minuet in Hell* (BF #19) - it's "the twenty-first century" and humanity has just developed quantum technology, suggesting it's the near future. *Neverland* gives the firm date of 2003 for this story.

645 Dating *Scream of the Shalka* (PDA #64) - The Doctor says, "by the smell of the air, [it's] England 2003".

DIDN'T SCREAM OF THE SHALKA FEATURE A DIFFERENT NINTH DOCTOR?: The makers of the BBCi webcast *Scream of the Shalka* clearly intended that the Doctor featured (as played by Richard E. Grant) was the ninth incarnation. Yet the advent of the 2005 television series now rules that out, and much of fandom (including the webcast's producers) now considers it as non-canonical. In *The Gallifrey Chronicles*, Marnal refers to the Doctor having three ninth incarnations, which is intended as a reference to this story, *The Curse of Fatal Death* and the Christopher Eccleston incarnation (and offers no solution as to how - or even if - the situation was resolved). However, the Doctor in *Scream of the Shalka* only refers to Andy Warhol wanting to paint "all nine of me". It's simple enough for fans to imagine that this happened a regeneration or two ago for the Doctor of *Scream of the Shalka* ... or simply that the story is indeed non-canonical.

646 *The Taking of Planet 5* (p15).

647 *The Power of the Daleks*

VULCAN: The planet Vulcan is only seen in *The Power of the Daleks*, a story that is almost certainly set in 2020. There is no indication that mankind has developed interstellar travel or faster-than-light drives in this or any other story set at this time. This would seem to suggest that Vulcan is within our own Solar System.

There is some evidence to support this conjecture: since the nineteenth century, some astronomers (including Le Verrier, who discovered Neptune, speculated that a planet might orbit the sun closer than Mercury. There was new interest in this theory in the mid-nineteen-sixties, which might explain why the home planet of Mr Spock was also called Vulcan around the same time in *Star Trek*. The draft script talked of a "Plutovian Sun", suggesting Vulcan is far from the Sun, not close.

In 1964, *The Dalek Book*, which, like *The Power of the Daleks* was co-written by David Whitaker, named Vulcan as the innermost planet in our Solar System (and Omega as the outermost). This, though, contradicts the story that immediately precedes *The Power of the Daleks*, in which Mondas is referred to as "The Tenth Planet"; *Image of the Fendahl*, where the Fendahleen homeworld is "The Fifth Planet"; and *The Sun Makers*, where Pluto is established as the ninth planet of the Solar System. So it seems that Vulcan wasn't in our solar system in the late nineteen-eighties or the far future.

Taking all this literally and at face value, *Doctor Who* fan Donald Gillikin has suggested that Vulcan arrives in the Solar System but later leaves. This might be scientifically implausible - at least in the timescale suggested - but we know of at least three other "rogue planets" that enter our Solar System according to the series: the

c 2003 - SCREAM OF THE SHALKA[645] -> An unspecified incarnation of the Doctor and his friend the Master - an android - encountered the Shalka, an alien race that subsisted on volcanic gas and had travelled to Earth via a warp gate. The Shalka had occupied the Lancashire town of Lannet and twenty-five other locations on Earth. They mentally conditioned groups of people to emit a unique sonic scream that would make Earth's environment suitable for the Shalka's needs, but prove fatal to humans. With the help of barmaid Alison Cheney, a Lannet resident, the Doctor destroyed the Shalka on Earth. Alison accompanied the Doctor on his travels.

Vulcan, nearest planet to the Sun, was discovered in 2003.[646] **Vulcan was a large, hot world with a bleak landscape of mercury swamps and geysers that spat toxic fumes. It had a breathable atmosphere and soil capable of supporting plant life. Plans were made to set up a mining colony on Vulcan for a trial period.**[647]

c 2003 (Saturday, 14th June) - THE HOLLOW MEN[648] -> The Hakolian battle vehicle Jerak revived in Hexen Bridge and animated scarecrows, who attacked the villagers and fed them to Jerak's organic component. Jerak mentally influenced a former resident, Defence Minister Matthew Hatch, in a bid to taint Liverpool's water supply with genetic material that would increase Jerak's mental hold over any humans it infected. The seventh Doctor thwarted the scheme, entered Jerak's psychic realm via a mirror gateway and convinced the villagers absorbed over the centuries by Jerak to turn their willpower against the battle vehicle. The Doctor escaped and Ace destroyed the gateway, trapping Jerak on the astral plane. Hatch died, still mentally connected to Jerak upon its defeat.

c 2003 (June) - "Evening's Empire"[649] -> The seventh Doctor and Ace were in Middlesbrough, where Colonel Muriel Frost of UNIT was recovering a German fighter from the Tees. They learned that the plane was downed after contact with an alien ship.

Ace met a local named Alex Evening, and upon following him home discovered a tiny Q'Dhite mindtreader spaceship among the Airfix models in his bedroom. The Q'Dhite explored the universe by weaving reality from fantasy, and Alex had been using that power to kidnap women, send them to his imaginary "empire" and then humiliate them. Ace was woven into his empire, and the Doctor, Frost and her troops followed in the TARDIS. The Doctor defeated Alex by bringing his domineering mother into the empire, shattering the illusion. They returned to the real world to find Alex in a coma.

At this time, Muriel Frost was in a relationship with a scientist called Nick - both of them were unhappy.[650]

Moon, Mondas and Voga. *The Taking of Planet 5* (p15) confirms Gillikin's theory by stating that Vulcan was discovered in 2003 and had vanished by 2130.

648 Dating *The Hollow Men* (PDA #10) - No year is given, but the drought of '02 is mentioned, and five-pound coins are legal tender.

649 Dating "Evening's Empire" (*Doctor Who Classic Comics Autumn Special 1993*) - There's a calendar giving the month as June in the first panel in which we see the real Alex. The year is harder to establish, however. The complete story was published in 1993, and in the last part, there's a newspaper dated "Nov 23 1993". It's "fifty" years since the World War II plane crashed, again supporting a date in the early nineties. However, the story falls after "The Mark of Mandragora", set after 1997, and enough time has passed for Frost to be promoted from Major to Colonel.

650 MURIEL FROST: According to John Freeman in his afterword to the collected "Evening's Empire", *DWM* originally planned to introduce "a more solid supporting cast" for the seventh Doctor. Muriel Frost of UNIT, a fiery redhead with a complicated personal life, was clearly a big part of those plans. However, publication of "Evening's Empire" was delayed, and the comic series ended up tying in more closely with the New Adventure novels - meaning the planned storylines were dropped.

Muriel Frost appeared in "The Mark of Mandragora", "Evening's Empire" and "Final Genesis" in *DWM*. A Captain Muriel Frost also appeared in the 1980 sequence of *The Fires of Vulcan*. This is clearly meant to be the same character, but it really doesn't fit with what we know. In the British regular army, it's possible to spend twenty years as a Captain, but an able candidate could expect to be promoted to Major within four or five years (not to mention the fact that Frost doesn't look old enough in "The Mark of Mandragora"). Between "The Mark of Mandragora" and "Evening's Empire", she's gone from Major to Colonel - a process that would normally take over ten years.

"The Mark of Mandragora" has Frost refer to the Doctor as "child" at one point, so perhaps an untold story would have explained that she was older than she appeared - although even this wouldn't explain her career progression.

Even though the intention was that they are the same character, it might be simpler to imagine (and nothing particularly contradicts this idea) that the Frost in *The Fires of Vulcan* is Colonel Frost's mother. In which case, the young US major who appears and is killed in *Aliens of London* (set in 2006) - the same character who the Doctor called "Muriel Frost" in the draft script, and who has a "Muriel Frost" name badge - must presumably be her American cousin.

= **c 2003 - "Final Genesis"**[651] -> The seventh Doctor, Benny and Ace arrived in a parallel universe where humans worked side by side with Silurians, and Colonel Frost served with the United Races Intelligence Command (URIC). The Silurian scientist Mortakk had created human-Silurian hybrids called "Chimeras", and sent them to attack URIC. The Doctor defeated Mortakk.

2003 (August) - THE SHADOW OF THE SCOURGE[652] -> The seventh Doctor, Ace and Benny arrived at the Pinehill Crest Hotel, which was host to the unfortunate triple-booking of a presentation of a temporal accelerator, a demonstration of spiritual channelling and a cross-stitch convention. The Scourge attempted to manifest into our universe at this time, but the Doctor defeated them.

= **2003 - JUBILEE**[653] -> The sixth Doctor and Evelyn arrived at the Tower of London, 2003, and discovered their thwarting a Dalek invasion in 1903 had given rise to an English Empire. The Doctor and Evelyn were now widely regarded as heroes, and Nelson's Column had been rebuilt to depict the Doctor dressed as an English stormtrooper. The British and American populates were strictly kept apart to protect British genetic purity. The Daleks had become heavily merchandised, and their defeat was told in movies such as *Daleks: The Ultimate Adventure!*, starring Plenty O'Toole as Evelyn "Hot Lips" Smythe. Use of contractions was outlawed.

The President of the English Empire, Nigel Rochester, scheduled the Empire's jubilee celebration to include the public execution of the sole surviving Dalek from the 1903 attack. However, the Dalek secretly killed the Doctor's temporal duplicate, who had by now been a prisoner in the Tower for a hundred years.

The timelines of 1903 and 2003 began meshing together, and the Dalek invasion of 1903 started to unfold in the latter era. The Doctor convinced the "jubilee" Dalek that if the Daleks succeeded in their attempt to destroy all other life forms, they could only then turn on each other until a single Dalek remained, purposeless and insane. Logically, success would mean the Dalek race's destruction. The Dalek concurred and connected itself to the Dalek command net, transmitting a message that the Daleks could only survive by dying. The entire Dalek invasion force self-destructed, which retroactively averted the 1903 assault.

Remnants of the cancelled timeline remained in the restored history. Nigel Rochester, visiting the Tower of London as a tourist, briefly recognized the Doctor and thanked him for his help in the aberrant history. The English Empire's atrocities subtly lived on in the history and the dreams of the English people.

c 2003 (November) - FALLS THE SHADOW[654] -> Professor Jeremy Winterdawn and his team at Shadowfell House experimented for five years with the "Thascales Theorem", and their research indicated that applied quantum physics was a possibility. Hoping to manipulate spacetime, Winterdawn managed to interface with the Cathedral, and succeeded in distorting the spacial dimen-

---

651 Dating "Final Genesis" (*DWM* #203-206) - Ace recognizes Muriel Frost, so in her terms the story takes place after "Evening's Empire".

652 Dating *The Shadow of the Scourge* (BF #13) - It is "the fifteenth of August 2003" according to the Doctor.

653 Dating *Jubilee* (BF #40) - The date is given (and it's the hundredth anniversary of the events of 1903).

654 Dating *Falls the Shadow* (NA #32) - It is "a crisp November morning", "five years" after "UN adventurism in the Persian Gulf". Winterdawn is alive and well in *The Quantum Archangel*, so this book is set after that. Thascales was an alias of the Master in *The Time Monster*. Author Daniel O'Mahony intended it to be set in "the near future".

655 Dating *Catch-1782* (BF #68) - The date is given.

656 "Three years" before *TW: Greeks Bearing Gifts*.

657 Dating *Sometime Never* (EDA #67) - An invitation states that an exhibition at the Institute of Anthropology opens on 31st January, 2004. *Sometime Never* was published in the same month.

658 "A year" before *The Gallifrey Chronicles*. Greg was introduced in *Timeless*.

659 Dating *The Tomorrow Windows* (EDA #69) - Trix's clothes are "very 2004" (p13). The Earth year 2004 is equivalent to the Galactic Year 2457. All the events on alien planets in *The Tomorrow Windows* seem contemporaneous, and the Doctor even says on p278, "we only travelled in space, not in time".

660 Dating *The Sleep of Reason* (EDA #70) - It's the "near future" according to the blurb, but references to things like Limp Biskit and *Casualty* suggest it's at most only a few years after publication. It is "a hundred years or so" since 1903 (p273).

661 Dating *Project: Lazarus* (BF #45) - The dating clues are very conflicting. According to Professor Harket's journal, the story opens on 18th July, 2004, and the first track is explicitly titled as such. However, the Doctor says it's "late November". He lets the TARDIS choose the destination, though, so perhaps he's confused - he also thinks it's been "a couple years" since *Project: Twilight*,

sions of Shadowfell. Gabriel and Tanith, psychotic expressions of Cathedral's pain, were released, as were individuals from other parallel universes: an agent from an Earth where England was a Republic dedicated to the principals of Fundamental Humanism, the other from an Earth dominated by a hivemind of giant insects. Cathedral was destroyed along with Gabriel and Tanith, although the grey man survived.

2003 (12th December) - CATCH-1782[655] **->** The sixth Doctor and Mel arrived in Berkshire at the invitation of Mel's uncle, John Hallam, to attend the 100th anniversary celebration of the National Foundation for Scientific Research, UK. Hallam had constructed a cylinder from a unique alloy provided by a space agency, but the interaction of the TARDIS and chrono-atoms within the cylinder threw Melanie two hundred and twenty two years back in time. The Doctor and Hallam pursued her in the TARDIS.

2004

In 2004, Toshiko Sato was recruited to join Torchwood.[656]

2004 - SOMETIME NEVER[657] **->** The scientist Ernest Fleetward stood on the brink of inventing a form of unbreakable crystal that would greatly advance mankind's development. Fleetwood had set about reconstructing a crystal human skeleton, unaware that it was the Council of Eight leader Octan, lost to the Time Vortex in 1588. Octan himself travelled through time to prevent Fleetwood's efforts from impacting history and cast the skeleton into the Time Vortex, failing to realize that he was re-obliterating his own body.

The eighth Doctor convinced Fleetward to adopt the nephews of Richard III, who were saved from their historical fate.

Anji started dating Greg in the summer.[658]

2004 (July) - THE TOMORROW WINDOWS[659] **->** The "selfish memes" seeded on behalf of Martin culminated on various planets. The planet Shardybarn was eradicated when the Low Priest Jadrack the Pitiful triggered several nuclear bombs, hoping that his god would perform a miracle and stop the disaster. On Valuensis, a misunderstanding made the Gabaks and Aztales annihilate one another with doomsday devices. On Estebol, malevolent cars began to possess their drivers and the people withered due to extreme pollution.

To combat this self-destructive trend, the billionaire philanthropist Charlton Mackerel set up "Tomorrow Window" exhibits on various planets. The Tomorrow Windows would allow the indigenous populations to

glimpse their future and hopefully amend their behaviour. Martin sought to ruin Mackerel's exhibits. In June 2004, Martin eradicated the Tate Modern - and a Tomorrow Windows exhibit there - with an electron bomb.

The eighth Doctor aided Mackerel by seeking out the original Tomorrow Windows builder, Astrabel Zar. Electrical beings named the Ceccecs, working for Martin, destroyed the belt of moon-sized Astral Flowers in an attempt to kill Zar, but the Doctor and Zar escaped.

A "selfish meme" on the planet Minuea made the populace do nothing as their moon slowly moved toward a collision with their planet. The Doctor used a Tomorrow Window to make the people see the benefit of using a missile to stop the catastrophe, and thereby saved the planet.

The aged Zar returned to Gadrahadron to tell his younger self, fifty years in the past, how to make the Tomorrow Windows. Martin discovered this and killed Zar. The repentant actor Prubert Gatridge and Martin died in mutual combat. Fitz, Trix and Mackerel insured that the younger Zar learned the Tomorrow Windows secret.

Mackerel's Tomorrow Windows exhibits continued, granting planets with "selfish memes" a second chance. The Doctor determined that Martin never completed his work on Earth, and that humanity developed "selfish memes" independent of him.

The Doctor was by now an old friend of Ken Livingstone, the current Mayor of London.

c 2004 - THE SLEEP OF REASON[660] **->** Mausolus House had been replaced by the Retreat, a more modernised asylum. Caroline "Laska" Darnell, the great-great-granddaughter of one of Dr. Christie's patients, came into possession of the Sholem-Luz dog-tooth pendant. The pendant again infected an Irish wolfhound with the Sholem-Luz essence, and the infernal hound set about trying to germinate Sholem-Luz seeds through time and space. The eighth Doctor lured the creature into a time corridor to 1903. Afterward, the husband of a Retreat medical officer found Laska's pendant, which possibly still contained the Sholem-Luz taint.

2004 (18th July) - PROJECT: LAZARUS[661] **->** The Forge, located on Dartmoor beneath an abandoned asylum, had begun collecting dead alien life forms and technology that appeared on Earth. Its agents captured a stranded, blue skinned alien capable of exuding a slime that killed on contact, and Nimrod, now the Forge's deputy director, dubbed the alien's race as the "Huldran". The Forge also took into custody the Huldran's spacecraft, which was capable of generating spatial gateways. The sixth Doctor and Evelyn briefly ran afoul of the Forge at this time, leading to the Forge procuring a sample of the Doctor's blood. They created a clone of the Doctor to assist in their endeavours.

c 2004 - THE ALGEBRA OF ICE[662] -> In another universe, an alien gestalt composed of mathematical equations sought to drain energy from outside realities into its own. The gestalt contacted the genocidal Sheridan Brett in our universe, hoping to use human mathematicians to further its plans. The seventh Doctor confronted the gestalt on a mathematical level, and resolved the creature into zero.

c 2004 (October) - THE CITY OF THE DEAD[663] -> The eighth Doctor visited New Orleans to identify a bone charm he had found in the TARDIS. He determined that the charm could be used to summon a water elemental, and left for 1980 to investigate such an occurrence. This journey made the charm retroactively appear in the TARDIS for the Doctor to find in the first place.

Upon returning, the Doctor found that the wife of resident Vernon Flood was a bound water elemental. The Doctor freed Mrs Flood from her human form and she returned to her own dimension, causing Vernon to drown. Her elemental son, bound in 1980, had become the crippled museum owner Thales. The ritualist Jonas Rust attempted to absorb Thales to attain great power, but an emptiness that Rust summoned - the Void - wound up consuming him. Thales was liberated from his human body and reunited with his mother.

c 2004 - THE DEADSTONE MEMORIAL[664] -> The long-lived Henry Deadstone, having established an identity as the old man Crawley, continued to tend to the alien psychic force he'd encountered some centuries ago. The eighth Doctor intervened when the creature tried and failed to reunite itself, causing psychic terror for the local McKeown family. The anguished creature withdrew its power from Deadstone and he instantly aged to death. The

Doctor returned the creature to its home dimension.

As arranged in 1957, the Time Lord Louis collected Johannes Rausch on the day before his death. They traveled to a Gallifreyan CIA Institute, where Rausch took part in an experiment to transfer TARDIS sentiences.[665]

2005

2005 (5th - 6th March) - ROSE[666] -> Rose Tyler worked at Henrik's department store in London, which was the location of a secret Auton transmitter. She met the ninth Doctor shortly before he blew up the store, and accidentally took an Auton arm home with her. The Doctor located the arm and retrieved it. Fascinated by the Doctor, Rose tracked down Clive, who ran a website charting appearances of the Doctor over the years. Rose met up with the Doctor again and helped him defeat the Nestene invasion, but not before rampaging shop dummies nearly killed her mother. In all, seventy-eight people were killed, three hundred injured. Rose joined the Doctor on his travels.

Rose's disappearance prompted the police to search for her. Her boyfriend Mickey Smith was interviewed by the police, who - like Rose's mother - assumed that he had murdered her.[667]

c 2005 - DEATH COMES TO TIME[668] -> General Tannis, commander of the Canisian armies, conquered the planet Santiny in violation of the Treaty of Carsulae. The seventh Doctor and his companion Antimony arrived to ferment resistance, but were abruptly summoned to the Orion

---

but Cassie suggests it's been "a few years", and Nimrod specifies that it's "five years".

662 Dating *The Algebra of Ice* (PDA #68) - It's apparently set "several years" after the Brigadier first met the seventh Doctor (in *Battlefield*). From his perspective, the Brigadier previously met the seventh Doctor in *No Future*, but the Doctor mind-wiped the Brigadier's recollection of those events, and doesn't restore these memories until *Happy Endings*, set in 2010. *The Algebra of Ice* falls in the period where the Brigadier would recall *Battlefield* as their first meeting. Lloyd Rose wrote this story with "the modern day" in mind.

663 Dating *The City of the Dead* (EDA #49) - No year is given, but it's "a few years" after Anji's time.

664 Dating *The Deadstone Memorial* (EDA #71) - There's no specific date beyond "early twenty-first century" (p51). It's set in the modern day.

665 *Unregenerate!* Rausch says he hasn't seen Louis in "fifty years", but this could be a rounded sum. A radio broadcast says US and UK forces are "hours" away from

Fallujah in Iraq. The main offensive there occurred on 8th November, 2004. *Unregenerate!* was recorded just more than a week later on 16-17 November.

666 Dating *Rose* (X1.1) - The year isn't specified, but there's a contemporary setting. The story is clearly set after 2003, as the Doctor reads a paperback copy of the novel *The Lovely Bones* by Alice Sebold. *Aliens of London* shows a missing persons poster that definitively cites Rose as last seen on 6th March, 2005. The casualty figures come from the www.whoisdoctorwho.co.uk website. The same site has pictures with time-stamps that offer an alternative date of 26th March, the day of broadcast.

667 *Aliens of London* - Mickey's surname isn't established on screen until *Boom Town*.

668 Dating *Death Comes to Time* (BBCi drama, unnumbered) - No year is given, but Tony Blair is the Prime Minister and George W Bush is President of the United States, suggesting a contemporary setting. The story was webcast in 2002. Lee Sullivan's illustrations suggest

Nebula. There, the Minister of Chance - an old friend of the Doctor - warned him that someone had killed two Time Lord "saints" working on Earth. The Doctor headed there to investigate; the Minister travelled to Santiny.

On Earth, the Doctor discovered that the Time Lords were murdered by a vampire, Nessican, to cover up their discovery of massive spatial disturbances. The Doctor returned to Santiny, where Tannis killed Antimony - who was actually an android - and revealed himself to be a renegade Time Lord. When Tannis killed Sala, a young woman the Minister had become fond of, the Minister unleashed the full force of his Time Lord powers. The Doctor could not act against Tannis, but had to punish the Minister - all part of Tannis' plan to divide and distract his rival Time Lords. The Doctor stripped the Minister of his powers, but Tannis launched an invasion of Earth.

Meanwhile, Ace trained to become a Time Lord with a mentor, Casmus, and the mysterious Kingmaker. Reunited, the Doctor and Ace headed for Earth, where they helped Lethbridge-Stewart and UNIT - now with a fleet of shuttles at their disposal - repel the Canisian invasion. The Doctor used his Time Lord powers to destroy Tannis and himself. The Canisians were defeated.

Felix Mather was the US Secretary of State during the Canisian invasion.[669]

c 2005 - "The Flood"[670] -> The eighth Doctor and Destrii arrived in Camden Market, and quickly discovered that people were over-reacting emotionally. The Doctor also learned that MI6 were in the area. Destrii's senses registered two advanced Cybermen, who begin to convert the population and captured her. The Doctor worked with MI6, convinced these were the most advanced Cybermen he'd ever seen.

The Cybermen neutralized British defences, and their mothership materialized over London. They created a rainstorm that soaked the MI6 personnel, and caused

extreme emotional reactions - the humans gladly became Cybermen to cure themselves. The Cybermen planned to flood the world in this way.

Desperate, the Doctor offered to allow the Cybermen to kill him and study his regeneration if the Cybermen returned to their own time - this would allow Cybermen to convert other races, not just humans, into their own kind. The Doctor freed Destrii, who distracted the Cybermen while he leapt into the ship's power source - a fragment of the Time Vortex. He focused the power there and destroyed the Cybership, whereupon he and Destrii went off to their next adventure.

2005 (June) - THE GALLIFREY CHRONICLES[671] -> The eighth Doctor was lured to Earth by the Time Lord Marnal, who had recently learned of the Doctor's role in the destruction of Gallifrey. Fitz and Trix left the Doctor to set up home together, but the police approached Trix and attempted to arrest her on suspicion of murder. As they fled the country, Marnal confronted the Doctor and the Eye of Harmony was briefly opened. Like moths to a flame, the insect race the Vore was drawn to Earth. Their moon materialised in Earth orbit and a full scale invasion took place. The Doctor and his companions destroyed the Moon, and engaged the surviving Vore.

Captain Jack Harkness renewed his acquaintance with Estelle, claiming that she had met his father during World War II.[672]

---

that UNIT is operating a moonbase at this time, and although such details aren't in the script or dialogue, this could nudge the story a couple of years into the future (there was a moonbase in the 2003 of *Eternity Weeps*, after all). See "American Presidents in the *Doctor Who* Universe" for why this story seems to take place after 2004.

IS DEATH COMES TO TIME CANON?: As the seventh Doctor dies at the end, all Time Lords are revealed to have godlike powers that they simply haven't used before and all the Time Lords are extinguished or otherwise removed from the universe during the seventh Doctor's time, a strong case can be made that this story is apocryphal. Crucially, the Time Lords' godlike abilities aren't reconcilable against the Gallifrey History section

of this book. However, references to Anima Persis in *Relative Dementias* and *The Tomorrow Windows* and the Canisians in *Trading Futures* suggest *Death Comes to Time* may well be canonical. As with all *Doctor Who*, readers can include or ignore this story as they wish.

669 *Trading Futures*, making reference to *Death Comes to Time*.

670 Dating "The Flood" (*DWM* #346-353) - It's "the early twenty-first century", and the story was published from 2004 to early 2005. Thematically, the resolution of this story is much like Rose unleashing the power of the Time Vortex in *The Parting of the Ways*.

671 Dating *The Gallifrey Chronicles* (EDA #73) - The date is given (p75).

672 "Two years" before *TW: Small Worlds*.

The First Environmental Crisis

By the middle of the first decade of the twenty-first century, it was clear that unchecked industrial growth had wreaked havoc on the environment. Increasing instability in weather patterns subjected Britain to acid rain and created turbulence that made air travel less reliable. Shifts in the ozone layer laid waste to Oregon. Traffic had reached gridlock in most of the major cities around the world. Motorcycles superseded the familiar black cabs in London, and many car owners sat in traffic jams working at their computers as they commuted. Predictably, air pollution reached new levels.

A catalogue of environmental disasters threatened the entire planet. The Earth's population was spiralling towards eight billion. Low-lying ozone and nitrogen dioxide levels had risen to such an extent that the London air was unbreathable without a facemask on many days, even in winter. Global warming was steadily increasing: by the turn of the century there were vineyards in Kent. Antarctic waters became hazardous as the icecap broke up in rising temperatures. The rate of ice-flow had trebled since the nineteen-eighties.

River and sea pollution had reached such levels that the marine environment was on the verge of collapse. Water shortages were commonplace, and even the inhabitants of First World cities like London and Toronto were forced to use standpipes for drinking water and to practise water rationing. The mega-cities of South America saw drought of unprecedented proportions. The holes in the ozone layer were getting larger, causing famine in many countries. Sunbathing, of course, was now out of the question. "The plague", in reality a host of virulent, pollution-related diseases such as HIV 7, appeared and killed millions.

The collapse of the environment triggered political instability. New terrorist groups sprang up: the Earth For Earth groups, freedom fighters, environmentalists, anarchists, nationalists and separatists, the IFA, PPO and TCWC. In England, a whole new youth subculture evolved. Gangs with names like the Gameboys, the Witchkids and the Crows smashed machinery (except for their own gaming software) and committed atrocities. In the most notorious incident, the Witchkids petrol-bombed a McDonald's restaurant on the M2 before ritually sacrificing the customers: men, women and children.

Every country on Earth saw warfare or widespread rioting. In the face of social disorder in America, President Norris' right-wing government ended immigration and his infamous "Local Development" reforms restricted the unemployed's rights to movement. The Connors Amendment to the Constitution also made it easier for the authorities to declare martial law and administer the death penalty. The underclass was confined to its slums, and heavily armed private police forces guarded the barriers between the inner cities and the suburbs.

Once-fashionable areas fell into deprivation. The popular culture reflected this discord: In Britain, this was a time when SlapRap blared from every teenager's noisebox. There was a Kinky Gerlinki revival, its followers dressing in costumes described as "outrageous" or "obscene" depending on personal taste. The most popular television series was *Naked Decay*, a sitcom inspired by 45-year-old Mike Brack's "Masks of Decay" exhibition which had featured lumps of wax hacked into caricatures of celebrities. The teledildonic suits at the "SaferSex emporiums" along London's Pentonville Road became notorious. All faced the opprobrium of groups such as the Freedom Foundation and the Citadel of Morality. American children thrilled to the adventures of Jack Blood, a pumpkin-faced killer, and they collected the latest Cthulhu Gate horror VR modules and comics. Their elder brothers became Oi Boys: skinheads influenced by the fashions of Eastern Europe.

The early twenty-first century saw many scientific advances, usually in the field of computer science and

---

673 *Iceberg* and *Cat's Cradle: Warhead* are both set around the same time and feature an Earth on the brink of environmental and social collapse. The two books are broadly consistent, although the odd detail is different - in *Iceberg*, for example, journalist Ruby Duvall muses that sunbathing in England is impossible nowadays, whereas Ace sunbathes in Kent during *Cat's Cradle: Warhead*. The Connors Amendment is mentioned in *Warlock*.

674 *Interference*

675 *St Anthony's Fire*

676 *Placebo Effect* (p12).

677 *Iceberg*

678 *Something Inside.* This occurred on 25th May, 2005.

679 Dating *Red Dawn* (BF #8) - It is "thirty years" since the "Mars Probe fiasco" of *The Ambassadors of Death*, which is a UNIT story. So to cut a very long story short, it's the now first decade of the twenty-first century. As *The Dying Days* was "over twenty years" after *The Ambassadors of Death*, this story is set before 2007. The impact of Tanya's ambassadorship to Mars must be minimal, as humanity and the Martians are in conflict by *The Seeds of Death*.

680 Both "ten years" before *Trading Futures*.

681 *TW: They Keep Killing Suzie.* This is part of Suzie's insurance policy in case of her death, although it doesn't entirely account for why she kills herself in *TW: Everything Changes*. (One explanation is that Suzie knows she's going to get fired - meaning mind-wiped - from Torchwood, and her suicide / resurrection gambit is a desperate means of maintaining her memories and identity.)

communications. Elysium Technology introduced the Nanocom, a handheld dictation machine capable of translating speech into written text. Elysium also developed the first holographic camera. The 3D telephone was beyond the technology of the time, although most rich people now had videophones. In June 2005, "Der Speigel" gave away a personal organiser with every issue. The first robot cleaners were marketed at this time - they were small, simple devices and really little more than automated vacuum cleaners or floor polishers. Communications software and computer viruses were traded on the black market; indeed, they became almost substitute currency in countries like Turkey.

Surgeons could now perform eye transplants, and the super-rich were even able to cheat "death" (or rather the legal and medical definition of it) by an intensive programme of medication, transplants and implants. If even this failed, suspended animation was now possible - the rich could afford full cryogenic storage, the poor settled for a chemical substitute. Military technology was becoming smarter and more dangerous. The Indonesian conflict and the Mexican War in the first decade of the century were the test-bed for much new weaponry. Arms manufacturers were happy to supply the Australian and American forces with military hardware. The British company Vickers built a vision enhancement system capable of tremendous magnification and low-intensity light applications. The helmet could interface with most weapons, allowing dramatically improved targeting. If anything, the helmet was too efficient - one option, which allowed a soldier to target and fire his weapon merely by moving and blinking his eyes - proved too dangerous and was banned. A new generation of UN aircraft were introduced, including a remote controlled helicopter (the Odin), a jet fighter with batteries of Valkyrie air-to-air missiles (the Loki), Niffelheim bombs and Ragnarok tactical nuclear devices. The US military introduced a turbo-pulse laser gun developed for use against tanks.[673]

Early in the twenty-first century, there were disasters, wars and nuclear terrorism. The first half of the century saw human civilisation close to collapse.[674] Rising sea levels claimed Holland, and the Dutch became the wanderers of Europe.[675] Christian fundamentalists campaigned for the extermination of homosexuals in the twenty-first century.[676]

The most pressing threat was that of magnetic inversion. For some decades, scientists had known that Earth's magnetic field periodically reversed. If this happened now, it would damage all electronic equipment and have serious environmental consequences. In 2005, spurred into action by such reports, the major governments of the world set up the FLIPback Project at the old Snowcap complex in the Antarctic. Shortly afterward a vehicle from the base - the hovercraft AXV9 - vanished in the Torus Antarctica

with the loss of two men.[677]

The Doctor saw the 2005 European Cup Final, in which Liverpool overcame formidable opposition from AC Milan and claimed the Cup for the fifth time in its history.[678]

c 2005 - RED DAWN[679] **->** Backed by the Webster Corporation, the first manned American mission to Mars - *Ares One* - successfully reached the Red Planet. The crew made planet-fall in the *Argosy* shuttle just as the fifth Doctor and Peri also arrived. The astronauts and the time travellers found the tomb of Izdal, a heroic Martian who sacrificed himself to the Red Dawn - the ultraviolet Martian sunrise. This had convinced his people to leave their toxic planet.

The tomb's guardian, Lord Zzaal, was revived with his Ice Warriors. Zzaal believed the humans had good intentions, but a misunderstanding quickly escalated into conflict. Zzaal sacrificed himself to the Red Dawn to save the Doctor's life, ending Webster Corp's plans, but it was hoped his dream of a peaceful existence with Earth could survive. *Ares One* returned to Earth. Tanya Webster, a human who possessed Martian DNA, remained behind as Earth's first ambassador to the Martians.

A Russian general ordered a nuclear strike against Chechnya, killing half a million people in an instant. After leaving the army, the General erased his identity and became the notorious arms dealer known as Baskerville. He lacked an electronic presence of any kind, making him impossible to track. After British Airways went bust, Baskerville bought one of their Concordes and converted it for stealth.

Nicopills, designed to wean people off tobacco, were marketed as a consumer item in their own right. The pills were less harmful but even more addictive than cigarettes, and thus were more profitable.[680]

Suzie Costello had been on the run when she joined Torchwood, and used her technical skill to wipe clean all records pertaining to her. She secretly joined Pilgrim - a religious support group and debating society started by Sara Briscoe - and conditioned Max Trazillion to brutally kill the other Pilgrim members if he didn't see her for three months.[681]

On Earth, a reptilian extra-terrestrial set up a business supplying combat divisions to clients on other worlds. The alien recognised that creating armies posed significant problems: Combat computers were only so reliable, and artificial intelligences could only be created under certain conditions; remote-control signals could be scrambled; and fully crewed combat vehicles were expensive to create and maintain, plus had a high turnover rate.

As a solution, the alien created giant robots that were armed with powerful weapons on the outside, but which resembled twentieth-century Earth office complexes on the inside. Humans were kidnapped and brainwashed into thinking that they were simple office workers; in reality, their "paperwork" and office meetings helped to coordinate the robots' attack patterns, and enabled formidable strategy in battle.

One worker, named Todd Hulbert, found a means of overcoming his mental conditioning and instigated a hostile takeover. He renamed the company Hulbert Logistics and moved its home office from Ipswich to London.[682]

A group of Cybermen had settled on the planet Lonsis, and the next system over contained Shinus. Its people - the Shinx - were traders who disliked aggression because it destabilized their markets. The Gallifreyan CIA sought to eliminate the Lonsis Cybermen, and facilitated this by seeding paranoia into the Shinx's minds. The Shinx hired Hulbert Logistics, and Hulbert's combat divisions started routing the Lonsis Cybermen in 2005.

To guarantee success, the CIA equipped Hulbert's Telford branch with a quantum crystalliser - a device that splintered the timelines over a small area, then picked the most desirable one as dictated by its programming. The alternate timelines would die off, tipping the odds in the Telford branch's favour on a moment-to-moment basis.[683]

On Earth, the Gallifreyan CIA manipulated history to prevent Karen Coltraine becoming a dictator in future. Certain formative negative experiences were eliminated from Coltraine's history, and she matured into a much more agreeable person.

In 2006, Lucie Miller relocated from the North of England to London, and planned to live with her friend Amanda from school. She met Coltraine in the Tube, and the pair of them had interviews with Hulbert Logistics on the same day. Todd Hulbert offered them jobs with his company, brainwashed them according to standard procedure and sent them via a portal to his "Telford branch" on the planet Lonsis. This worried the Time Lords, who feared that the history-revised Coltraine might become unstable if brought into proximity with the Telford branch's quantum crystalliser. However, the Time Lords were also working with faulty intelligence information, and mistook Lucie for Coltraine.

As part of their uneasy relationship with the CIA, the Time Lords intercepted Lucie's transport through space, and thus caused her to arrive in the Doctor's console room. A perceptual barrier blocked off Lucie's memories of Hulbert, and the Doctor was duped into thinking she'd been placed with him as part of the Time Lords' witness protection programme. He tried and failed to take Lucie home, as the Time Lords had established a temporal barrier around her era.

Lucie reluctantly became the Doctor's companion, and on their first trip together, they encountered the Daleks on the human colony planet Red Rocket Rising. Hulbert became distressed to find Lucie missing - partly because she held potential as a staff member, but also because he wanted to know which rival was poaching his employees.

---

682 *Human Resources.* The Lonsis operation has been running for "a year" prior to 2006, and Hulbert acts as if he's been in charge of the company for some time before that.

683 *Human Resources*

684 *Blood of the Daleks, Human Resources*

685 Dating *Human Resources* (BF BBC7 #7-8) - Lucie has been "pulled back to her natural place in time", which according to *Blood of the Daleks* is 2006.

686 Dating *Night Thoughts* (BF #79) - The setting is roughly contemporary, and the audio was released in February 2006. Dickens and the Deacon served in the Falklands War (which took place in 1982), and the researchers have subsequently met or permanently lived on the island for the last thirteen years. One small glitch is that Major Dickens and his colleagues contact the outside world via ham radio, as opposed to something more modern such as satellite uplink, etc.

687 Dating *Aliens of London / World War Three* (X1.4-1.5) - It is "twelve months" since *Rose*, and a missing persons poster says Rose has been missing since 6th March, 2005 - so it's March 2006, and for all we know specifically 6th March. The (BBC's) UNIT website gave the story the date of "28 June 2006".

From now on, as we shall see, all the "present day" stories from the new television series (and its spinoffs,

Torchwood and *The Sarah Jane Adventures*) are actually set a year or so after broadcast.

HARRIET JONES, BRITISH PRIME MINISTER: We learn in *The Christmas Invasion* that Harriet Jones took office shortly after *World War Three*, winning a general election by a landslide. As she's a member of the governing party, she presumably became its leader (perhaps unopposed), so became Prime Minister, then called a snap election. In *World War Three*, the ninth Doctor remembers her ushering in the British Golden Age and serving three terms.

Three full terms as Prime Minister would be fifteen years, although constitutionally it's technically possible - if highly unlikely - that someone could serve three terms as a Prime Minister in a matter of months. As of *Aliens in London*, Harriet Jones was almost certainly Prime Minister for around a decade. We might speculate that Jones was a prime mover behind the Reconstruction mentioned in some of the New Adventures, itself portrayed as the beginning of a golden age. There's a female Prime Minister in *The Shadows of Avalon* who, retrospectively, could well be Harriet Jones. Shortly after that, in stories like *Time of the Daleks* and *Trading Futures*, British politics becomes more turbulent.

However... at the end of *The Christmas Invasion*, the

He hired a time-traveling Headhunter to bring her back.[684]

2006 - HUMAN RESOURCES[685] -> The planet Telos was unknown to the Cybermen based on the war-torn Lonsis.

The Headhunter captured Lucie and returned her to Lonsis, but the eighth Doctor followed by use of a Time Ring. The Time Lords and the CIA had brokered a deal in which neither group would interfere on Lonsis directly, but the Doctor's actions accidentally enabled the Cybermen to gain an upper hand in the conflict. The Doctor found the CIA's quantum crystalliser and expanded its range, causing probability to go against the Cybermen and thereby killing them. Hulbert died amid the battle, but the Headhunter escaped - and offered Coltrane a position as her assistant.

The Doctor ordered the Time Lords to destroy Hulbert's machines and return the displaced humans home, then retrieved his TARDIS and continued traveling with Lucie.

c 2006 - NIGHT THOUGHTS[686] -> The seventh Doctor, Ace and Hex arrived on Gravonax Island, just as Major Dickens and his colleagues transmitted a message (via the Bartholomew Transactor) to their previous selves in 1996, with aim of preventing the death of a young girl, Edie. The resultant paradox caused Edie's corpse to temporarily revive in a zombified state, and she prolonged her second life by firing multiple messages from the Transactor. Edie took vengeance on those involved in her death - murdering Bartholomew and Hartley, driving the Deacon to commit suicide and gouging out Dickens' eyes. Her fate remained unclear, but her sister Ruth was reunited with their father, Dr. O'Neill.

The Doctor sent Bartholomew's unpublished thesis to the editor of *The New Scientist*, insuring that it reached the widest possible audience. In future centuries, it would speed development of a workable theory of time travel.

2006 (March) - ALIENS OF LONDON / WORLD WAR THREE[687] -> The ninth Doctor accidentally returned Rose home twelve months after he first met her, instead of twelve hours. A spaceship soon crashed into the Thames, and a state of emergency was called in the UK. Worse, the Prime Minister had vanished. The Doctor investigated and realised that the crash had been faked... by genuine aliens who had infiltrated Downing Street and murdered the Prime Minister. This was done to lure the world's main experts on alien life into a lethal trap.

The perpetrators were the Slitheen, a notorious criminal family of Raxacoricofallapatorians, who were plotting to provoke humanity into launching nuclear missiles and destroying their own planet. This would enable the Slitheen to convert and sell Earth's remains as radioactive fuel. The Doctor used his UNIT codes to launch a missile that destroyed 10 Downing Street and the Slitheen.

At this time, the Doctor encountered "Dr Sato", a medical examiner working for the military.[688]

A backbench MP, Harriet Jones, had been instrumental in helping the Doctor, who said she was destined to become Prime Minister, serve three terms and usher in the British Golden Age. Harriet Jones became Prime Minister following a general election when her party won a landslide majority.[689]

Margaret Slitheen escaped the destruction of Downing Street using a portable teleporter. She ended up in a skip in the Isle of Dogs, later making her way to Cardiff.[690] After this time, Torchwood Cardiff were involved with Operation Goldenrod, which saw people's bodies fused together.[691]

Doctor seems to abruptly unseat Jones from office, and potentially cancels this out history. From stories like *Father's Day* and *I am a Dalek*, it seems the Doctor is "allowed" to make small historical changes, but averting the career of a three-term Prime Minister would seem to cross the line. Does the Doctor *really* deny Britain its Golden Age because he's fallen out with Jones? At the very least, he certainly erases Jones' part in it. (For more on this, see the "Vote Saxon" essay.)

The Doctor doesn't seem to know much about the history of the first decade of the twenty-first century - he explicitly says he doesn't know about the "first contact" situation seen in *Aliens of London* (a remarkable gap in his knowledge of Earth's history, whichever way you look at it). Compare and contrast with Captain Jack's continuous assertion in *Torchwood* that the twenty-first century is the time that "everything

changes".

688 It's safe to assume that "Doctor Sato" from *Aliens of London* and Toshiko Sato from *Torchwood* - both of them played by Naoko Mori - are the same character. However, it's best to assume that Toshiko is operating as an undercover Torchwood agent when she meets the Doctor - see "When Did Everyone Start Working for Torchwood Cardiff?" for more.

689 *The Christmas Invasion*

690 *Boom Town*

691 *TW: Slow Decay*. A potential glitch is that Ianto needs to ask if Toshiko was involved - and she was. Again, see "When Did Everyone Start Working for Torchwood Cardiff?"

2006 (24th May) - "FAQ"[692] -> The tenth Doctor and Rose arrived in a London transformed into a surreal place of talking trees and Vikings with laser guns. It had been created by Craig, an abused youngster with a virtual reality game supplied by a Cyrelleod alien from Happytimez Intergalactical.

= 2006 (24th June) - THE TIME TRAVELLERS[693] -> After colliding with a man falling through the Vortex, the TARDIS materialised in Canary Wharf. The first Doctor, Susan, Ian and Barbara discovered that Britain was at war with South Africa, and the time travellers were arrested. The British were conducting time travel experiments using Dalek technology recovered from Coal Hill School in 1963, and different versions of history were beginning to intrude on this one. In this version of history, WOTAN succeeded in its bid for domination, and banned electronic communication in 1968. It was subsequently destroyed in 1969, and everyone under its hypnotic control was left brain-damaged. A World War broke out. The South Africans gained Cybertechnology at the South Pole, and used it to invade Europe.

The TARDIS' presence disrupted the time experiments, allowing the various timelines to connect. By travelling back to 1972, then 1948, Ian restored history.

2006 - WINNER TAKES ALL[694] -> The ninth Doctor took Rose home, where the latest craze was the videogame *Death to Mantodeans*. It had been supplied by the porcupine-like Quevvils of the planet Toop, and was a perfect simulation of their war. The Doctor got the high score and

was teleported to the warzone - but he managed to disintegrate the Quevvil invasion force.

c 2006 (early September) - CIRCULAR TIME: "Autumn"[695] -> The fifth Doctor and Nyssa lodged in Stockbridge for a number of weeks. While the Doctor played cricket, Nyssa wrote a novel - not intended for publication - and made the acquaintance of a waiter / graduate student named Andrew Whitaker. One day, Nyssa and Andrew travelled forty minutes away from Stockbridge to Traken Village - a town that was twinned with somewhere in Germany.

On the final day of the cricket season, the Stockbridge team prevailed - but the team leader, Don, died of a heart attack while scoring the winning run. Nyssa and Andrew became lovers that afternoon, but she left with the Doctor afterwards, bequeathing her finished novel to Andrew.

2006 - "A Groatsworth of Wit"[696] -> The alien Shadeys brought Robert Greene from 1592 to the present day, where Greene was disgusted to find he was hardly-known but Shakespeare was world famous. The ninth Doctor and Rose arrived to see Greene lash out in anger in a bookshop, and begin a rampage that involved attacking the premiere of a movie version of *The Taming of the Shrew*. The Doctor realized that the Shadeys were feeding off his negative emotions - Greene returned to his native time, and the Doctor and Rose followed in the TARDIS.

2006 (September) - BOOM TOWN[697] -> Margaret Slitheen became Lord Mayor of Cardiff, and pushed through an ambitious plan. She initiated construction of the Blaidd Drwg Power Station, which was actually

---

692 Dating "FAQ" (*DWM* #369-371) - The date is given, and means Rose is here traveling a year or so into her past (although the Doctor had been planning to take her to China, not London).
693 Dating *The Time Travellers* (PDA #75) - The dates are all given. The implication of the book is that the "real" timeline of the universe is one without the Doctor, so one where the monsters win. The Doctor is actually changing history when he defeats them. WOTAN appeared in *The War Machines*, and the Dalek technology stems from *Remembrance of the Daleks*.
694 Dating *Winner Takes All* (NSA #3) - The story is set after *Aliens of London / World War Three* and before *Boom Town*.
695 Dating *Circular Time:* "Autumn" (BF #91) - The story seems to end in early September, with the Doctor and Nyssa lodging in Stockbridge for at least five weeks beforehand. The year isn't given, but it's suggested that the Doctor has been coming to Stockbridge (the setting for his *DWM* comic strips) to play cricket for some time now. (Specifically, it's said that the clubhouse has

photographs of "the Doctor's family" going back years.) A contemporary dating is supported by mention that the whole country has gone a bit mad about cricket since "England won the Ashes" - presumably a reference to the 2005 series, in which England bested Australia and won for the first time in eighteen years.
Traken Village isn't real, as appealing as it might sound. The Doctor says that Nyssa (a Trakenite) and Andrew (a human) have roughly the same lifespan, which isn't helpful to anyone who tries to reconcile discrepancies in the Doctor's age by suggesting that he and Nyssa traveled together for many years (possibly even decades) between *Time-Flight* and *Arc of Infinity*.
696 Dating "A Groatsworth of Wit" (*DWM* #363-#364) - Greene is transported to the present day.
697 Dating *Boom Town* (X1.11) - A caption at the start says it is "Six Months Later" than *World War Three*. The evening is "freezing" and it's dark relatively early, suggesting it's at least September (the month it would be if *World War Three* was set in March). A mention of Justicia in the story is a reference to the ninth Doctor

designed to destroy Earth and facilitate her escape into space on an Extrapolator surfboard. The ninth Doctor, Rose and Jack landed in Cardiff to refuel the TARDIS and captured Margaret. Exposure to the heart of the TARDIS reverted Margaret to her original state as an egg. The Doctor returned her to her home planet, Raxacoricofallapatorius, to start life anew.

The TARDIS' chameleon circuit welded its properties onto a very small area of the Rift, and created a perceptual blind spot.[698] Cathy Salt, the pregnant journalist spared by Margaret Slitheen, was scheduled to marry Jeffrey on 19th October.[699]

2006 - THE DEVIANT STRAIN[700] -> The ninth Doctor, Rose and Jack arrived at Novrosk Penninsula in Siberia, the site of an old Soviet base. There had recently been a series of mysterious deaths, which the Doctor determined was caused by the defence systems of a crashed ship from the Arcane Collegiate. The threat was dispelled when the Doctor destroyed the ship.

2006 - ONLY HUMAN[701] -> The ninth Doctor, Rose and Jack arrived in Bromley to investigate temporal distortion caused by a "dirty rip" engine. They discovered a Neanderthal named Das at a local hospital. Das couldn't return home because the dirty rip engine had weakened his structure, but the Doctor and Rose went to 29,185 BC to locate the source of the problem. With Jack's help, Das quickly got a job in construction and married a girl called Anne-Marie.

Suzie Costello, an agent of Torchwood, recovered an alien device that could open any lock.[702]

2006 (22nd September) - THE GATHERING[703] -> Scarred by her brother's misfortune, Katherine Chambers envisioned the removal of humanity's weaknesses and emotions through widespread Cybertisation. She worked toward the creation of System, the ultimate medical computer. Aiding her endeavors was James Clarke, who secretly worked for an organisation that harvested and made use of alien technology.

Kathy was acquainted with Tegan Jovanka, who had a brain tumour - possibly the result of her travels with the Doctor - and was therefore deemed a perfect test subject. James and Kathy successfully created System using Cybertechnology, but the fifth Doctor was on hand and convinced the half-human Nate Chambers to activate System's self-destruct. James escaped with a back-up copy of System's software, but Chambers Pharmaceuticals exploded, killing Nate. Kathy was believed dead, but the Doctor took her elsewhere to be looked after.

As part of these events, James triggered a software patch that he'd installed in servers across Brisbane, and thereby brought the city's communications network to a grinding halt. The event was blamed on a "technical fault".

Tegan resumed her romance with Michael Tenaka and turned down the Doctor's offer of attending to her brain tumour.

2006 - THE PARTING OF THE WAYS[704] -> The ninth Doctor forcibly returned Rose to her native time aboard the TARDIS, removing her from the Dalek incursion in 200,100. Rose realised that the words "Bad Wolf" had been scattered throughout time and space as a message that she should return to the fray, and she exposed the heart of the TARDIS with help from her mother and Mickey. Rose and the TARDIS returned to 200,100.

---

novel *The Monsters Inside.* The mention of venom grubs - named as such in *The Web Planet* novelisation (entitled *The Zarbi*) but called "larvae guns" in the TV story - suggests Margaret hails from the Isop Galaxy. (*Bad Wolf* also names Isop as the home galaxy of the Face of Boe.)
698 *TW: Everything Changes*
699 *Boom Town.* This was due to happen on "the nineteenth" and "next month".
700 Dating *The Deviant Strain* (NSA #4) - The year isn't given, although there are references to the Cold War ending "twenty years" ago. It would seem to be set in Rose's home time.
701 Dating *Only Human* (NSA #5) - The story takes place after *Boom Town* (and *The Deviant Strain*), but - owing to Jack's presence - before *The Parting of the Ways*.
702 Jack says that Suzie found the lock-pick "last year" in *TW: Cyberwoman*.

703 Dating *The Gathering* (BF #87) - The date is given, and reinforced by a radio broadcast citing the birthday of Australian rocker Nick Cave, and discretely mentioning the same for Billie Piper - both were born on 22nd September. In an attempt at symmetry with *The Reaping*, a radio broadcast also mentions an interview with Colin Farrell about the 2006 *Miami Vice* movie. However, the broadcast implies the film isn't out yet - it was actually released in Australia about five weeks prior on 10th August, 2006. James' unnamed employers could be a veiled reference to either the Forge or Torchwood. Tegan's mother is still alive at this time.
704 Dating *The Parting of the Ways* (X1.13) - No specific date is given, but there's no evidence that much time has passed since Rose and Mickey's meeting in *Boom Town.* In *The Christmas Invasion*, Jackie's been going out with Howard for "about a month", and Rose doesn't know about their relationship beforehand, so *The*

By now, the general population knew that aliens had indeed invaded Earth over a dozen times. In 2006, Kadiatu Lethbridge-Stewart published her controversial best-seller *The Zen Military: A History of UNIT*. Lethbridge-Stewart was the grand-daughter of Alistair Lethbridge-Stewart and Mariatu of the Themne tribe, making her ideally placed to write the "definitive" study of the UNIT era.[705]

In November, Jackie Tyler started going out with Howard from the market.[706]

2006 (November / December) - ICEBERG[707] **->** Earth's magnetic pole shifted slightly, causing consternation at the FLIPback project. Tensions were not eased when the nearby Nikkei 5 research station vanished into the Torus Antarctica. The Cybermen were behind both the disappearances and the magnetic fluctuations, but the sev-

enth Doctor defeated them with the help of journalist Ruby Duvall.

2006 (Christmas Eve / Christmas Day) - THE CHRISTMAS INVASION[708] **->** The newly-regenerated tenth Doctor arrived back on Earth with Rose. He recovered in Jackie's flat, and became the target of robot Santas and a killer Christmas tree. These were just "pilot fish" for the Sycorax, whose vast spacecraft intercepted the British Guinevere 1 Probe to Mars and set course for Earth.

NATO went to red alert. Prime Minister Harriet Jones took control of UNIT's command centre underneath the Tower of London, where the Sycorax made contact and lay claim to the entire Earth. They blackmailed the population by using "blood control" to hyp-

---

Parting of the Ways is probably set before late November.

705 The date of the publication was given in the *Remembrance of the Daleks* novelisation, and was confirmed by *Set Piece*. In *Transit*, Yembe Lethbridge-Stewart states that Kadiatu was named after his great-grandmother, the historian. Although in *Set Piece*, Kadiatu claims that her namesake was her "grandmother", presumably for brevity's sake.

706 "About a month" before *The Christmas Invasion*.

707 Dating *Iceberg* (NA #18) - The main action of the book takes place in 2006, from "early November" (p25) to "Friday 22 December" (p1). The epilogue is set on "Wednesday 31 January 2007" (p251).

708 Dating *The Christmas Invasion* (X2.0) - The story takes place at Christmas, shortly after *The Parting of the Ways*. Subsequent stories establish that this is indeed Christmas 2006. "A third" of the world's population is two billion people at this time.

WHEN DO THE GENERAL PUBLIC ACCEPT THE EXISTENCE OF ALIENS?: It's was a long-held part of the *Doctor Who* format that there are plenty of alien invasions, yet no one in the present day believes in them, or even really notices. Even given the Doctor's comments in *Remembrance of the Daleks* and *Rose* that humans are blind to what's going on around them, that most alien attacks are covert or limited to isolated locations, and that the government keeps hushing up the existence of aliens, there are a number of stories set before 2085 (cited in *The Dying Days* as humanity's first official diplomatic contact with alien races) where the general population really can't escape the existence of aliens. Such stories include *The Tenth Planet*, *The Dying Days*, and *Aliens of London*. By the end of the last two, people have already started declaring that the aliens are a hoax, and this seems to become the accepted view of what happened.

This has shifted now, though. The new series occasionally jokes about humanity's willingness to overlook

the blatantly obvious, but by *Last of the Time Lords*, only people as obtuse as Donna Noble can be in much doubt about the existence of extra-terrestrial life. Between 2006 and 2008, humanity is made to witness a spaceship destroying Big Ben and crashing into the Thames (*Aliens of London*); another spaceship arriving over London, and its sonic boom causing a swath of damage - this is accompanied by a third of humanity being compelled to stand on rooftops while strange lights illuminate their heads, the face of the Sycorax leader being transmitted on BBC1, a newscaster's declaration that it is "absolute proof that alien life exists", and a super-laser destroying the departing spaceship (*The Christmas Invasion*); the public acceptance of "ghosts", who manifest as five million Cybermen and capture Earth before they're pulled through the sky - along with a flying Dalek army - into Canary Wharf (*Army of Ghosts / Doomsday*); the Racnoss spaceship firing bolts of energy against London, and Mr Saxon gaining prominence because the military destroys the ship on his orders (*The Runaway Bride*); a horned demon looming over Cardiff, and its shadow killing droves of pedestrians (*TW: End of Days*); Royal Hope Hospital vanishing, leaving behind only a crater before reappearing some hours later - this coincides with the hospital appearing on the moon, and about a thousand people inside being scanned by space rhinos (*Smith and Jones* - although it's still possible for Clive Jones' girlfriend, Annalise, to dismiss the idea of aliens); and - most tellingly of all - the British Prime Minister presenting the Toclafane to the world, a day before one of their number murders the American President during a worldwide broadcast (*The Sound of Drums*). The destruction of the Paradox Machine undoes the Toclafane's capture of Earth, but explicitly everything up to and including the assassination of the President still happens.

One story from the non-TV media is worth mentioning: the *DWM* strip "The Mark of Mandragora" establish-

notically command one-third of the population, including the Royal Family, to walk to the nearest rooftop.

Jones made a public appeal to the Doctor as the Sycorax ship arrived over London. Jones, Major Blake of UNIT, Danny Llewellyn of the British Rocket Group and the PM's aide Alex were teleported to the Sycorax ship, where Llewellyn and Blake were quickly killed. The Sycorax detected the TARDIS and also teleported it aboard. The Doctor recovered and challenged the Sycorax leader to a duel. The leader cut off the Doctor's hand with a sword, but as the Doctor was within the first fifteen hours of his regeneration cycle, he was able to regrow the hand and go on to kill the Sycorax leader. The Sycorax retreated.

Harriet Jones feared that the Sycorax would spread word about the Earth, and that more alien invaders would return in the Doctor's absence. She ordered Torchwood to destroy the retreating Sycorax ship with an energy weapon - whereupon the horrified Doctor called Jones' fitness to lead into question, and deposed her with a single sentence ("Don't you think she looks tired?"). Questions were raised about Jones' health, and a vote of no confidence was quickly scheduled.

The British could use "the Hubble array" to track spacecraft. The Sycorax used the Sycoraxic language.

Many people went to Trafalgar Square to celebrate - Ursula Blake was among them, and while there happened to take a picture of the Doctor.[709] Donna Noble missed the excitement of Christmas Day because she had a bit of a hangover.[710] The Doctor's severed hand ended up in the archives of Torchwood Cardiff.[711]

The newly-regenerated Master arrived on Earth from the end of the universe, and adopted the alias "Harold Saxon". He faked his past, and came to set up the Archangel Network of satellites to subliminally influence the British public into supporting his policies. The Archangel signals also masked the Master's presence, and prevented the Doctor from detecting him in this time zone. The Master married a woman named Lucy, and his meteoric rise saw him become Minister of Defence. In such a position, he helped to design a flying aircraft carrier, the *Valiant*.[712]

After the Sycorax Invasion, some people obsessed with the Doctor formed the group LINDA.[713]

c 2006 - "The Lodger"[714] **->** The tenth Doctor popped in to see Mickey, telling him that he and Rose had just escaped some Lombards - but that the TARDIS had accidentally jumped a time track, so Rose wouldn't be showing up for a couple of days. Jackie was occupied with a man called Alan, so the Doctor stayed with Mickey. After the Doctor beat him at video games *and* tuned his TV so that Mickey got programmes from ten years in the future *and* ruined a night in planned with a girl called Gina, Mickey got sick of him. After a few days, the TARDIS arrived with Rose. The Doctor arranged it so that Mickey and Rose had a nice Sunday together.

c 2006 - NEW EARTH[715] **->** The tenth Doctor and Rose set off on their travels, leaving behind Jackie and Mickey.

---

es that the events of "Invaders of Gantac" and (perhaps a little oddly) *Battlefield* led the general public to the realisation that aliens existed. That was contradicted by *Rose*, but the new TV series swiftly established that - in the words of Captain Jack in *Torchwood* - "the twenty-first century is when everything changes".

709 *Love & Monsters*

710 *The Runaway Bride*

711 TW: *Everything Changes*, and confirmed in *Utopia*. The Doctor loses his hand in *The Christmas Invasion*.

712 "Eighteen months" before *The Sound of Drums*, and by implication very soon after *The Christmas Invasion*. It's not clear who runs Britain for those eighteen months - possibly it's a weakened Harriet Jones. As Jones had only recently won by a landslide, it's easy to infer that the opposition parties are also in disarray. The fact that Saxon's Cabinet in *The Sound of Drums* is composed of people from various political parties would seem to support that. However, the Prime Minister as seen in a blurry photograph in *TW: Out of Time* (set in late 2007) looks like a male.

The official "Vote Saxon" website states that Lucy's father (mentioned, but not named, in *The Sound of Drums*) is called Lord Cole of Tarminster, so it's likely her maiden name was "Lucy Cole".

713 *Love & Monsters*

714 Dating "The Lodger" (*DWM* #368) - This would seem to fit into the gap between *The Christmas Invasion* and *New Earth*.

715 Dating *New Earth* (X2.1) - The Doctor and Rose leave the Powell Estate, and this might follow on directly from *The Christmas Invasion* - except the TARDIS has moved, Jackie, Mickey and Rose are all wearing different clothes and the ash from the Sycorax ship has gone. The Doctor and Rose looked set to leave immediately at the end of *The Christmas Invasion*, and this might mean that they returned at some point after unseen adventures, then left once again.

The Krillitanes were a composite species, given to absorbing the physical aspects of the races they conquered and destroyed. A small group of them took on human form and infiltrated Deffry Vale School, with "Mr Finch" taking over as headmaster.[716]

2007 - THE STONE ROSE[717] **->** Mickey showed the tenth Doctor and Rose a statue from Ancient Rome in the British Museum - one that depicted Rose. The Doctor and Rose travelled back in time to investigate.

2007 - THE FEAST OF THE DROWNED[718] **->** The HMS *Ascendant* sank in the North Sea, killing Jay, the brother of Rose's friend Keisha. The tenth Doctor and Rose arrived, discovering that a number of people had died in London since wreckage from the *Ascendant* was brought there. Relatives of the dead were apparently being contacted by the ghosts of the drowned, but this was a side effect of alien technology. The Waterhive were attempting to conquer the world, but the Doctor thwarted them.

2007 - SCHOOL REUNION[719] **->** Mickey called in the tenth Doctor and Rose to help investigate Deffry Vale School. The Doctor posted a winning lottery ticket through the letterbox of one of the physics teachers and took their place. He met Sarah Jane Smith, who was also investigating the school.

The Krillitanes were using the childrens' brains to formulate the Skasas Paradigm - an equation which could be used to control "the building blocks of the universe", even to the point of rewriting the past. The

reactivated K9 sacrificed himself to destroy the Krillitanes, ending their scheme.

The Doctor built a new K9 for Sarah Jane. Mickey joined the TARDIS crew.

The new K9 contained a compartment with a number of helpful gadgets for Sarah Jane, like the sonic lipstick.[720] **A black hole was released following a Swiss laboratory accident. K9 was able to contain it, but this fully occupied his time, so he was unable to help Sarah Jane on her adventures.**[721]

c 2007 - "The Green-Eyed Monster"[722] **->** When Rose was infected by an alien worm that ate emotions, the tenth Doctor induced great jealousy in her by setting Mickey up with a girlfriend, and having an adventure on the planet of the Amazastians (the entire population of whom were beautiful teenage girls, much to the mystification of even their own scientists). The Doctor resorted to kissing Jackie, which overloaded the alien worm.

= 2007 (1st February) - RISE OF THE CYBER-MEN / AGE OF STEEL[723] **->** After an explosion, the TARDIS materialised in a parallel universe with military checkpoints in the streets and zeppelins in the skies. The tenth Doctor, Rose and Mickey found that Rose's father Pete Tyler was alive in this reality, and had become rich from selling a health drink called Vitex Lite. Pete was preparing for Jackie's fortieth birthday party, and the guests included the President of Great Britain

---

716 "Three months" before *School Reunion*.
717 Dating *The Stone Rose* (NSA #7) - Mickey hasn't joined the TARDIS crew, but Rose knows about Petrifold Regression, so it's set between *New Earth* and *School Reunion*.
718 Dating *The Feast of the Drowned* (NSA #8) - The story is set between *The Christmas Invasion* and *School Reunion*.
719 Dating *School Reunion* (X2.3) - The story features Mickey, and Sarah refers to the events of *The Christmas Invasion* as "last Christmas", so the story is set in 2007 (and at some point during a school term).
    SARAH JANE'S REUNIONS WITH THE DOCTOR: In *School Reunion*, the very strong implication is that Sarah hasn't had any form of contact with the Doctor since she left him at the end of *The Hand of Fear*. Somewhat tellingly, the Doctor comments that he's regenerated "half a dozen times" since she last saw him.
    Some commentators have seized upon this as evidence that the non-TV media (which entailed a post-*Hand of Fear* Sarah meeting the Doctor on more than one occasion) are apocrypha, but in truth this scenario doesn't match the TV series either. In the first place, the

Doctor sent Sarah a K9, and in *K9 and Company* she even says "so he didn't forget me after all." Yet in *School Reunion*, Sarah says she thought the Doctor had forgotten about her after dropping her off. More notably, she was reunited with the third Doctor - and met the fifth - in *The Five Doctors*. Clearly, as occasionally happens, the series chooses not to complicate the narrative by invoking every possible relevant previous story. Indeed, a new or more casual viewer would infer from what Sarah says that some time ago, the Doctor left her and K9 on Earth to go and fight the Time War.
    Sarah Jane also appeared in a number of stories in other media set after *The Hand of Fear*. "Train-Flight" (set c 1990), *System Shock* (set in 1998; she didn't meet the Doctor in that story, but neither did she believe he was dead or had abandoned her), *Interference* (set in 1997, and portraying her as married to a man called Paul Morley) and *Bullet Time* (also set in 1997). Ergo, Sarah Jane has encountered four of the "half a dozen" incarnations that the Doctor has been through between *The Hand of Fear* and *School Reunion*.
    The basic story beat is the same in each case - Sarah continues to be a successful journalist, while missing

and a Torchwood agent named Stevie.

This world was home to a New South America and a New Germany. The Torchwood Institute was releasing studies to the public. The Bio-Convention required the registration of new life-forms. Rose was never born on this world, but the Tylers owned a small dog with the same name.

John Lumic's Cybus Industries owned "just about every company" in Britain, including Vitex. Cybus had sold EarPods to virtually everyone. Lumic himself was dying, and had developed a robot body that could house the human brain. His agents - operating through a dummy company named International Electro-matics[724] - started rounding up the homeless to convert into such cybernetic beings. Mickey discovered that his alternate self, Ricky, ran a resistance cell.

Lumic activated his cyborgs - the Cybermen - and they stormed Jackie's birthday party. Whereas the President was killed and Jackie and many guests were captured for Cyber-conversion, the Doctor, Rose, Mickey, Pete and the resistance group escaped. Lumic transmitted a signal via the EarPods to all Londoners, and thereby made them march to Battersea Power Station to undergo conversion. Cybermen took to the streets, and Ricky was killed.

The Doctor's team attacked the Power Station and he confronted Lumic - who against his will

had been converted into the Cyber Controller. Cyber-conversion factories had been built on all seven continents, but the Doctor instructed Mickey on how to deactive the Cybermen's emotional inhibitors. Mentally unable to confront the nature of their lost humanity, the Cybermen malfunctioned. The Doctor and his allies made their escape in Lumic's zeppelin, destroying the Power Station and the Controller.

Mickey remained in the parallel universe, hoping to help liberate it from the remaining Cybermen. Cybus Industries was based on "seven continents".

Back in our universe, the Doctor and Rose met Jackie for a tearful reunion.

= On Lumic's world, the People's Republic discovered the existence of Torchwood and took control. The Cybermen were sealed in their factories, but a debate ensued about what to do with them, as they were living beings. Some Cybermen infiltrated Torchwood and vanished.[725]

2007 - I AM A DALEK[726] -> A Dalek left over from the Time War activated the Dalek Factor within the human Kate Yates. The tenth Doctor and Rose arrived and deactivated the Dalek, neutralising the Dalek Factor within Kate.

---

the Doctor. Even her marriage to Paul Morley can be reconciled with the idea that no man ever measured up to the Doctor - clearly Morley didn't, explaining why we don't see him in *School Reunion*.

720 Established on the BBC website - the sonic lipstick is seen in *SJS: Invasion of the Bane*.

721 "Eighteen months" before *SJS: Invasion of the Bane*.

722 Dating "The Green-Eyed Monster" (*DWM* #377) - It's after *School Reunion* and The *Girl in the Fireplace* (both of which are referenced), but before *Rise of the Cybermen* and *The Age of Steel*, as Mickey is still around.

723 Dating *Rise of the Cybermen / The Age of Steel* (X2.5-2.6) - Mickey finds a newspaper that he says is dated to "1st February, this year" - in other words the year *School Reunion* is set, which is 2007. Lumic also cites the day as 1st February.

A birthday party is being held for the parallel-universe Jackie, and Rose says - when she and the Doctor are outside the Tyler mansion - "February the first, mum's birthday" (thereby indicating that "our" Jackie was born on the same day).

One point of confusion is that the official biography of the parallel Jackie - or so she claims - states that she was born the same day as actor Cuba Gooding Jnr. He was actually born on 2nd January, 1968 (it would seem

that someone on the production team didn't take into account that in America, the date 1/2 means the second of January). We might imagine that Gooding was born on 1st February in the parallel reality, or it's possible that Jackie's biographers - in an attempt to make her sound more interesting - simply got the date wrong and nobody corrected her. (This is no more implausible an error than the real-life production team failing to fact-check Gooding's birthday via Google.)

"Our" Gooding was born in 1968 - so if Jackie was born the same year, she should be thirty-nine in *Rise of the Cybermen*, not forty as she claims. In addition to everything else, then, it's possible Jackie and Gooding's parallel counterparts were born a year prior in 1967.

724 Evidently a reference to Vaughn's company from *The Invasion*, which otherwise doesn't appear to exist in this reality.

725 *Doomsday*.

726 Dating *I am a Dalek* (*Quick Reads* #1) - No year is given, but the story has a present day setting.

2007 - LOVE & MONSTERS[727] -> By now, a "Bad Wolf" virus had corrupted Torchwood's files on Rose.

Elton Pope had been obsessed with the Doctor ever since seeing him as a child. He became a member of the group LINDA (London Investigation 'N' Detective Agency), which was made up of other people for whom the Doctor's existence filled a gap in their lives.

On a Tuesday night in March, the group fell under the sway of Victor Kennedy. He was secretly an Abzorbaloff from Clom, the twin planet of Raxacoricofallapatorius, who wanted to absorb the Doctor and his memories. Elton briefly met the tenth Doctor and Rose as they were busy fighting an alien Hoix, then later struck up a friendship with Jackie Tyler - in an attempt to get close to Rose. The Doctor and Rose tracked down Elton because he was "stalking" Rose's mother, and together they confronted the Abzorbaloff - who was defeated, and burst. Elton continued his relationship with Ursula, a member of LINDA, even though she had become a living paving slab.

The *Daily Telegraph* ran the headline: "Saxon Leads Polls with 64 per cent". Four more months of government paralysis were forecast.[728] Ghosts started appearing around the world, but people got used to them.[729]

2007 - ARMY OF GHOSTS / DOOMSDAY[730] -> Torchwood sought to obtain energy independence for the United Kingdom, and had been using particle engines to further open the temporal breach in Canary Wharf. A Voidship, designed to exist outside space and time, came through the breach - Torchwood took to studying it. The parallel-Earth Cybermen as created by Lumic followed in the Voidship's wake, and were manifesting on Earth as ghostly figures.

The tenth Doctor and Rose returned home to find that the public had accepted ghost appearances as a fact of life. Many media shows, including *Ghostwatch*, discussed the phenomenon.

The Doctor tracked the appearances of the ghosts to Torchwood HQ in Canary Wharf, and confronted the head of Torchwood, Yvonne Hartman. Soon after, the Cybermen achieved full manifestation - five million of them materialised from the parallel universe and occupied the planet. Hartman was forced to undergo Cyber-conversion. A Cyberman was seen strangling the host of *Ghostwatch*.[731] Martha Jones' cousin, Adeola Oshodi, worked for Torchwood HQ and died just prior to the Cybermen takeover.[732]

Meanwhile, four Daleks - members of the Cult of Skaro, a secret order above even the Dalek Emperor - emerged from the Voidship with a "Genesis Ark". The Cybermen and Daleks began fighting, and the Daleks opened the Genesis Ark - a Time Lord prison containing millions of Daleks. With the help of Pete Tyler and Mickey, who had arrived from the parallel universe,

---

727 Dating *Love & Monsters* (X2.10) - It's "two years" since the events of *Rose* (set in March 2005). The story takes place after *The Christmas Invasion*, but before *Army of Ghosts* and *Doomsday*. Jackie says that Mickey has gone, placing it after *The Age of Steel*.

Elton says that Kennedy approached LINDA on "a Tuesday night in March".

728 The Abzorbaloff is seen reading the newspaper in *Love & Monsters*.

729 "Two months" before *Army of Ghosts*.

730 Dating *Army of Ghosts / Doomsday* (X2.12-2.13) - No month is given, but it's after *Love & Monsters* and before *The Runaway Bride* (which takes place on Christmas Eve 2007).

Backtracking the *Torchwood* Series 1 dating makes it somewhat hard to believe that the Battle of Canary Wharf occurs any later than July. (*TW: Out of Time* takes place right before Christmas; *TW: They Keep Killing Suzie* takes place beforehand but is "three months" after *TW: Everything Changes*; Jack and Gwen chat about Canary Wharf in *TW: Everything Changes*, and don't speak as if the battle there occurred, say, within the last week or so.) *Army of Ghosts* and *Doomsday* respectively broadcast on 1st July and 8th July, and could well take place on one of those dates in 2008.

731 Alistair Appleton, who might be among the casu-

alties in the *Doctor Who* universe.

732 *Smith and Jones*, which explains why Freema Agyeman portrayed both Martha in Series 3 and Adeloa in *Army of Ghosts*.

733 *TW: Everything Changes*

734 *Utopia*

735 *The Runaway Bride*

736 *Army of Ghosts*. The sarcophagus is evidently a reference to *Pyramids of Mars*.

737 *TW: Cyberwoman*

738 *Made of Steel*

739 *TW: Everything Changes*

740 "Six months" before *The Runaway Bride*.

741 Dating *Blink* (X3.10) - The year is given by Kathy Nightengale (who claims she was transported from 2007 to 1920) and the Doctor, who says it's "thirty eight years" after 1969. The epilogue of the story takes place in 2008.

742 Dating "Fellow Travellers" (*DWM* #164-166) - Date unknown, but no-one has been inside the house "for years".

THE HOUSE AT ALLEN ROAD: A good example of continuity between the New Adventures and the *DWM* strip is that both establish that the Doctor has a house in England which he occasionally visits.

The house is usually associated with the seventh

the Doctor and Rose opened a gateway to the Void and sucked all the Cybermen and Daleks into the gap between universes. The four Cult of Skaro Daleks escaped back to the 1930s, but the Void was forever sealed. Rose, Jackie and Mickey were left trapped in the parallel universe with the alternate Pete.

After the battle, Rose and Jackie were listed as dead.

These events became known as The Battle of Canary Wharf.[733] Captain Jack read Rose and Jackie's names on the official list of those killed in the battle, and believed they had died.[734] During the battle, Donna Noble was scuba-diving in Spain.[735]

Items in the Torchwood HQ archives before the battle had included a particle gun, a magna-clamp that was found in a spaceship at the base of Mt Snowdon and a sarcophagus. Torchwood still used the Imperial weight system, having refused to go metric.[736]

Ianto's girlfriend Lisa worked for Torchwood HQ at this time. The Cybermen had converted a number of the Torchwood staff, but Lisa's conversion was interrupted by their defeat. Afterwards, Ianto hid the partially-converted Lisa in the Hub in Cardiff.[737]

Three Cybermen who were built on our Earth survived and escaped from the Torchwood Tower with an alien teleportation device. They set up a base inside the Millennium Dome.[738] The Cybertechnology Institute of Osaka was founded to learn the secrets of Cybertechnology. It was headed by a Dr Tanizaki.[739]

Lance Bennett, the head of human resources at H C Clements, allied himself with the Empress of the Racnoss. As ordered, Bennett slipped some huon particles into the coffee of his co-worker, Donna Noble. The particles gestated within her, and Bennett insured that she was re-dosed on a daily basis.[740]

2007 - BLINK[741] **->** The Weeping Angels had developed as a race of hunters who could send people back in time, then live off the potential energy of the years their victims might have had. As a defense mechanism built in to their biology, they turned to stone if seen.

Sally Sparrow investigated the abandoned house Wester Drumlins, and discovered a message to her written on the wall by the tenth Doctor in 1969, before she was born. She returned with her friend Kathy Nightingale, who was sent to 1920 by the Angels.

Gradually, Sally discovered that the Doctor was a time traveller. The Angels had stolen the Doctor's TARDIS key and transported him - along with his companion Martha - back to 1969. Owing to messages left by the Doctor, Sally was able to send the TARDIS back to 1969 - and in doing so, caused the Weeping Angels to look at each other and become forever immobile.

c 2007 - "Fellow Travellers"[742] **->** The seventh Doctor and Ace defeated a Hitcher at the Doctor's house.

c 2007 - "Ravens"[743] **->** A notorious gang called the Ravens were at the M2 Burger Rave, when they massacred everyone at a service station. Soon afterwards, they waited at another service station for someone to pass by, planning to kill them and use their blood in an occult ritual. The TARDIS materialised, and the seventh Doctor let out Raven, a seventeenth-century Japanese warrior who butchered the gang apart from a woman named Annie - whose face he slashed. A few months later, outside the house at Allen Road, Annie explained to other youths that she now understood the patterns of time.

2007 (September) - THE NIGHTMARE OF BLACK ISLAND[744] **->** The tenth Doctor and Rose arrived on the Welsh island of Ynys Du, and discovered the children there were all having nightmares. The children contained the psychic residue of Balor, General of the Cynrog Hordes, but the Doctor dispersed him.

Doctor. It first appeared in "Fellow Travellers" and *Cat's Cradle: Warhead*. It was named Smithwood Manor in "Ravens" and "The Last Word". The Doctor owned it at least as early as the Second World War (*Just War*) and has it in the early twenty-second century (*Transit*).

The eighth Doctor visits the house in *The Dying Days* and mentions it in *The Scarlet Empress*. He also has a house in the 1980s in part two and three of *Father Time*, which may or may not be the same house. *So Vile a Sin* depicts a parallel universe where the third Doctor lived in the house for a thousand years until the thirtieth century. *Verdigris* has the third Doctor using the house during his exile to Earth. The house is stolen in "Question Mark Pyjamas" (a short story from *Decalog 2*, and thus outside the boundaries of this chronology),

but the seventh Doctor, Ace and Bernice recover it.

"Fellow Travellers","Ravens" and *Cat's Cradle: Warhead* all indicate that the house has a mysterious reputation - and the last two have the street sign altered to read "Alien Road".

743 Dating "Ravens" (*DWM* #188-190) - It's "the near, harsh future," and the story takes place at the same time as *Cat's Cradle: Warhead*.

744 Dating *The Nightmare of Black Island* (NSA #10) - It's "late September" and the story is set in the present day. This would mean that the tenth Doctor and Rose have landed a couple of months or so after the Battle of Canary Wharf in *Doomsday* - hardly impossible, as *The Nightmare of Black Island* is an isolated incident, and provides them with no warning about what awaits

c 2007 (late October) - CAT'S CRADLE: WARHEAD[745] -> The Butler Institute - a huge conglomeration of corporations "from Amoco to Zenith", and which had secretly been bought up over the last decade by the vast Japanese Hoshino company - made projections of the future. Butler could see no alternative but massive, irrevocable environmental collapse. The planet was now reaching the point of no return, and only the big corporations and the super-rich could do anything about it.

Butler's executives secretly poured money into experiments that attempted to download human consciousness into computers. The homeless, the poor, and even the employees and families of Butler Institute personnel were kidnapped and experimented upon. The Institute developed a weapons system run by an electronically-recorded human consciousness, but its ultimate aim was to "record" the minds of the elite and store them in indestructible databanks, safe from the ravages of pollution and the ozone layer's destruction.

With the unexpected and complete destruction of the Butler Institute's project outside Albany, the directors of the world's corporations realised their only option was to instigate a massive environmental clean-up programme.

c 2007 - PROJECT: LAZARUS[746] -> The seventh Doctor happened to re-visit the Forge, amd he met his former self's clone. The captive Huldran had died - it was part of a gestalt race, and its traumatised fellows assaulted the Forge via a gateway. The clone triggered the base's self-destruct, but died at Nimrod's hands. The Doctor and the Huldran fled as the Forge was destroyed. The Forge's computer, Oracle, put the organisation's beta facility on-line.

The Reconstruction kicked the King's representative out of the British Parliament. Reconstruction Acts were passed to improve the environment. Large family farms started growing meat-substitute plants.[747] Within a couple of decades, air quality improved, the oceans were cleaner and the ozone layer holes had been patched. Sophisticated traffic monitoring systems and a reconfigured road network eased congestion - and therefore pollution - in the South East of England. Central London, though, was still busy.[748]

their personal futures.

745 Dating *Cat's Cradle: Warhead* (NA #6) - A specific date for this story and its two sequels is not established in the books themselves. The blurb states "The time is the near future - all too near". Shreela, a contemporary of Ace from Perivale first seen in *Survival*, dies of an "auto immune disease" at a tragically early age at the start of *Cat's Cradle: Warhead* (p19). The book is set in a year when Halloween falls on a Saturday (on p199 it's Halloween, on p250 it's the next day, a Sunday), making it either 1998, 2009 or 2015 - although in a number of stories the real calendar doesn't match that of the *Doctor Who* universe. Ace's clothes are how Mancuso, a policewoman, dressed "twenty years ago" (p202), and Ace is from the late 1980s. *Just War* confirms that the Cartmel books take place in the "twenty-first century timezone" (p250). In his "Future History Continuity" document, Ben Aaronovitch suggested that *Cat's Cradle: Warhead* was set "c.2007".

746 Dating *Project: Lazarus* (BF #45) - Nimrod implies "three years" have passed since the first installment.

747 *Happy Endings*

THE RECONSTRUCTION: The televised stories set in the twenty-first century offer a broadly consistent view of a peaceful Earth with a single world government, in which people of all nations co-operate in the field of space exploration and social progress. To reconcile this with the rather more downbeat New Adventures set in this century, Ben Aaronovitch suggested in his "Future History Continuity" document that a concerted global effort was made at some point in the early twenty-first century to repair the damage that had been done to Earth's environment. A "Clean Up" is first hinted at the end of *Iceberg*, which is where we learn of the "Arms for Humanity" concert and the procuring of drinking water from icebergs, but I suggest that it only gains impetus after *Cat's Cradle: Warhead*, when all the corporations put their full weight behind it.

This process was named "the Reconstruction" in *Happy Endings*. I suggest that this period of international co-operation lasts for around seventy years. Earth during this time is a relatively happy, clean and optimistic place.

748 Travelling by car is a lot easier in *Warlock* than *Cat's Cradle: Warhead* (*Warlock*, p179), and we learn about the monitoring systems (p224) and new road system (p211), yet London traffic has barely improved (p265).

749 Dating *Torchwood*, Series 1 - Gwen joins Torchwood after *Doomsday*, as events of that story (named as "the Battle of Canary Wharf") are mentioned in *TW: Everything Changes* and *TW: Day One*, and form the basis of *TW: Cyberwoman*. This shifts the stories to a year after they were broadcast, like all the "present day" *Doctor Who* stories since *Aliens of London*.

Most details presented in *Torchwood* Series 1 support a dating of 2007 - in *TW: Ghost Machine*, for example, 1941 is said to be "sixty six" years ago. However, there are some anomalies in stories such as *TW: Random Shoes* and *TW: Out of Time*. See the individual episodes for more detail.

750 *TW: Everything Changes*. Jack implies in *The Sound of Drums* that Torchwood Cardiff (and presumably the man in the Glasgow office) are all that remains of the once-far-mightier organisation.

751 HOW PUBLIC IS TORCHWOOD?: In *Tooth and Claw* (set in 1879), Queen Victoria creates Torchwood as an ultra-secret organisation devoted to defending Britain's borders against alien / supernatural incursion. Similarly,

Torchwood Series 1 (2007-2008)[749]

By now, the Cardiff Rift had attracted all manner of aliens and extraterrestrial technology, and approximately two hundred Weevils were living in the sewers below the city.

The Battle of Canary Wharf had led to the destruction of Torchwood One in London - such was the devastation that Torchwood was reduced to "only a half dozen" operatives. They were led by Captain Jack and worked from the Hub - an underground base near the city's Millennium Centre.

The Cardiff branch of Torchwood was designated Torchwood Three. Torchwood Two was an office in Glasgow, and "a very strange man" worked there. Torchwood Four had gone missing.

Captain Jack stressed to his operatives that the twenty-first century was when "everything changes", and that Torchwood had to arm the human race for what lie ahead...[750]

2007 - TW: EVERYTHING CHANGES[751] -> Members of the police were obligated to grant Torchwood operatives special access, and - not knowing the truth about the organisation - regarded the group as "Special Ops". A series of murders led to Cardiff PC Gwen Cooper encountering Captain Jack's team. Gwen and Jack discovered that his second-in-command, Suzie Costello, had been committing the murders as a means of field testing an alien glove that could briefly bring people back to life. Exposed, Suzie killed herself. Afterwards, Jack recruited Gwen to work for Torchwood.

2007 - TW: DAY ONE -> According to the official records, no American citizen had been born with the name "Jack Harkness" in the last fifty years.

A gaseous alien landed near Cardiff in a meteor, and soon possessed a young woman named Carys. The alien thrived on orgasmic energy and used pheromones to provoke sexual desire in its victims. Torchwood tracked down the creature and destroyed it, enabling Carys to return home.

The Christmas Invasion (set in 2006) seems to imply that Torchwood is so secret and so clandestine, the Prime Minister - in this case, Harriet Jones - isn't even supposed to know that it exists. Yet in *Torchwood* Series 1, Captain Jack and company can race through the Cardiff streets with the name "Torchwood" prominently displayed on the side of their SUV, the group (or Owen, at least) orders pizza under the name "Torchwood" and so forth.

The on-screen evidence offers a simple solution to this, even though *Torchwood* Series 1 doesn't spell it out very succinctly: The authorities are well aware of Torchwood's existence, and believe the group is a Special Ops team to whom they must yield authority. Episodes that support this notion include *TW: Everything Changes* (the police blatantly regard Torchwood as Special Ops), *TW: Cyberwoman* (Gwen mentions Torchwood to a contact at Jodrell Bank), *TW: Countrycide* (Gwen thinks a "policeman" - actually a treacherous cannibal - might know of Torchwood as a Special Ops group), *TW: They Keep Killing Suzie* (police units clear the roads for the Torchwood SUV) and more.

Put very simply, it's only the organisation's goal of harvesting alien technology that's secret, not the very mention of Torchwood itself. This fits most of the evidence, but requires one to retroactively assume that in *The Christmas Invasion*, Harriet Jones is suggesting that the Prime Minister isn't supposed to know Torchwood's true purpose, or that they have a super-weapon capable of obliterating spaceships. At the very least, this explains how Jack can talk to the Prime Minister about Torchwood funding issues (*TW: Greeks Bearing Gifts*).

In *Fear Her* (set in 2012), Torchwood is mentioned in a TV broadcast, but the reference is too obscure to tell if the group's real agenda is known to the public, or if they're still considered an elite branch of the military.

Some fans are uneasy with the notion that Torchwood - even as an organisation that by definition is given to deception - could have existed throughout the twentieth century without the third Doctor or UNIT learning about them. A few attempts have been made to explain this, and a recurring one speculates that, temporally speaking, Torchwood didn't exist until the tenth Doctor and Rose went back and annoyed Queen Victoria (*Tooth and Claw*). This theory is hard to credit, however, partly because it overlooks the obvious point that Torchwood does, in fact, pre-date the Doctor and Rose's trip to 1879. The group is mentioned in *Bad Wolf* and *The Christmas Invasion*, and in the latter story obliterates the departing Sycorax spaceship.

There is nothing special about *Tooth and Claw* in terms of time mechanics, so if such revision occurred, it would almost pre-suppose that the timeline gets revised nearly each and every time the TARDIS lands. Logically, this would suggest that the Great Fire of Rome shouldn't exist in time until the first Doctor inspires Nero to do it (*The Romans*) - even though the Doctor and Vicki both mention it beforehand. A similar case applies to the fifth Doctor causing the Great Fire of London in *The Visitation*, even though it's cited in *Pyramids of Mars*. Therefore, the idea that that Torchwood didn't "exist" until *Tooth and Claw* might help to explain its secrecy in the 1970s, but would throw the entire *Doctor Who* timeline into chaos.

It is far, far simpler to think that Torchwood was officially listed in the 70s as a Special Ops group; that

2007 - TW: GHOST MACHINE[752] **->** The Torchwood team recovered a piece of alien technology - a "quantum transducer" - that could convert and amplify human emotion as a means of witnessing the past, or making premonitions about the future. The device enabled Owen Harper to witness Lizzie Lewis' murder, as was committed in Cardiff, 1963. A scuffle led to the death of Lizzie's killer, Ed Morgan.

Torchwood dealt with a Cyclops and a robot.[753]

2007 - TW: ANOTHER LIFE[754] **->** Torchwood Cardiff defeated a plot by man-eating aliens that resembled starfish to manipulate the MMOG Second Reality.

2007 (October) - TW: BORDER PRINCES[755] **->** Torchwood defeated the Amok, zombie-animating aliens.

2007 - TW: SLOW DECAY -> Torchwood investigated Doctor Scotus' weight clinic - a business that was achieving dramatic results by having its patients, including Gwen's boyfriend Rhys, ingest an alien parasite. They shut down the operation.

2007 - TW: CYBERWOMAN -> Ianto had secretly been keeping his part-Cybertised girlfriend - Lisa Hallot - in the basement of the Hub, but her Cyber-programming finally won out, and she became determined to "upgrade" the Torchwood team into Cybermen. Lisa's body was destroyed when Jack set his pet pterodactyl on her, and although she transferred her brain into a pizza delivery woman, the Torchwood operatives shot her new body to death.

The first generation of Arcan Leisure Crawlers were now considered collectors' items as far as spaceships went - Torchwood politely warned one such vessel away from Earth, pointing out that they were scaring the locals. The Arcans themselves were mostly liquid, and rather boring.

2007 - TW: SMALL WORLDS[756] **->** Fairies tried to claim a young girl named Jasmine, their "Chosen One", and killed Jack's old friend Estelle Cole. Torchwood was unable to stop the fairies, and Jack only ended their rampage by giving Jasmine over to their custody. She retroactively came to be seen in a "fairie photograph" that had intrigued Arthur Conan Doyle.

Torchwood let UNIT get on with the business of actually combating alien incursions; that the Torchwood agents of the time operated with a high degree of stealth (not surprising, if a "Britain first" group were attempting to out-fox a United Nations organisation); and that the Doctor and UNIT were never given reason to look upon the group with suspicion.

752 Dating *Ghost Machine* (TW 1.3) - Thomas Erasmus Flanagan and his daughter say they're watching the *Strictly Come Dancing* finals - this is a bit hard to credit as the show routinely starts in October and finishes in late December. It's possible they're watching a rerun, but it's presented as if it's the original broadcast.
753 Mentioned in *TW: Another Life*.
754 Dating *Another Life* (TW novel #1) - The novel is set before *Cyberwoman* - Ianto is seen sneaking down to the basement in the novel. The spines of the first three *Torchwood* novels fit together to make one picture, suggesting a reading order of *TW: Another Life, TW: Border Princes* and *TW: Slow Decay*.
755 Dating *Border Princes* (TW novel #2) - The book is set in October, after the release of *Pirates of the Caribbean III* (which was released in May 2007).
756 Dating *Small Worlds* (TW 1.5) - A calendar appears in Jasmine Pearce's kitchen, but it's too fuzzy to read.
757 Dating *TW: Greeks Bearing Gifts* (TW 1.7) - Tosh estimates that the dead British soldier who was killed in 1812 has been buried for "196 years, eleven to eleven and a half months". This would seem to suggest a dating of 2009, save that Tosh stresses she's estimating, and - for that matter - can hardly be expected to have knowledge of the on-screen caption denoting the

murder as occurring in 1812. Most likely, Torchwood - without benefit of the omnipotent narrator - concludes the soldier was killed in 1810.
758 Dating *TW: They Keep Killing Suzie* (TW 1.8) - "Three months" have passed since Suzi's death in *TW: Everything Changes*.
WHEN DID EVERYONE START WORKING FOR TORCHWOOD CARDIFF?: In *They Keep Killing Suzie*, Suzie says Jack personally recruited her to work for Torchwood. Additionally, Suzie says that she gave Max a Torchwood amnesia pill "one week, every week for two years". It's possible this is said as part of a lie - as it's later revealed that Max's murder spree owes to Suzie's mental conditioning, and not exclusively a random side-effect of the drug - but nobody challenges her on the grounds that she didn't have access to the amnesia drug for that period of time. So, we know that both Suzie and Jack have worked for Torchwood for at least two years.
TW: Greeks Bearing Gifts says that Toshiko was recruited to Torchwood three years ago (although not necessarily by Jack). It seems very likely that Toshiko is the same character as "Doctor Sato" (also played by Naoko Mori) from *Aliens of London*, although it's also likely - given the "three years" comment in *TW: Greeks Bearing Gifts* - that she's working undercover for Torchwood when she meets the ninth Doctor. The alternative - that Toshiko in *Torchwood* has forgotten everything she ever learned about medicine, and was fortuitously also educated as a computer science expert - doesn't seem very plausible.
In *TW: End of Days*, Ianto says that the lower holding cells of the Hub haven't been used "as long as he's been

2007 - TW: COUNTRYCIDE -> Seventeen people had disappeared in the last five months in rural Wales, and Torchwood feared that the Rift's effects were spreading beyond Cardiff. They investigated, and found a group of cannibalistic villagers, who were given to "harvesting" travellers every ten years. Jack and his team facilitated the cannibals' arrest.

2007 - TW: GREEKS BEARING GIFTS[757] **->** The transmat device that carried the alien named Mary to Earth in 1812 was excavated, and she sensed its unearthing. Mary approached Toshiko with a pendant that enabled her to read the thoughts of others, and seduced her in the hopes of retrieving the transmat from the Hub. Jack and his staff found that Mary was an exiled criminal who had been feeding off people's hearts for years, whereupon Jack teleported her into the Sun. Tosh destroyed the pendant.

2007 - TW: THEY KEEP KILLING SUZIE[758] **->** By now, Torchwood Cardiff had dispensed amnesia pills - each containing Compound B67, also known as "Retcon" - to 2,008 people.

Max Tazillion responded to Suzie's mental programming and started killing members of the Pilgrim support group. Torchwood investigated, learned that Suzie

Costello had belonged to the group, and used the resurrection glove to revive her. Suzie escaped, vengefully murdered her father and nearly drained all of Gwen's life-force in a bid to stay alive. Jack realised that the glove was diverting Gwen's life-energy into Suzie and ordered its destruction, causing Suzie to die for good.

2007 - TW: RANDOM SHOES[759] **->** Prior to this, there had been a trade for Dogon sixth eyeballs.

Eugene Jones had become a Torchwood groupie of sorts. He tried to raise funds by selling his Dogon sixth eye on eBay, but this led to a string of events in which Eugene swallowed the eyeball - and it kept his spirit tethered to Earth when he died in a hit and run. Eugene's shade accompanied Gwen as she investigated his death, and he manifested enough to save her life from an oncoming car at his funeral. Gwen and her comrades watched as Eugene then vanished into a haze of light, as if departing for the great beyond.

2007 (18th to 24th December) - TW: OUT OF TIME[760] **->** Pilot Diane Holmes and two of her passengers - Emma Louise Cowell and John Ellis - emerged from the Cardiff Rift, having flown into it in 1953. The three reacted differently to life in the future - Emma thrived, John killed himself and Diane became lovers

---

[working] there" - which almost suggests that he's been employed at Torchwood Cardiff longer than any of his co-workers. At the very least, it implies he's worked there longer than Captain Jack, to whom the comment is directed. *TW: Cyberwoman* shows Ianto as being present at the Battle of Canary Wharf (in *Doomsday*), but it's never specified that - like his girlfriend Lisa - he worked for Torchwood London. We know he worked for *some* branch of Torchwood at the time (as he could hardly have gained access to the burning Torchwood HQ otherwise), but that's all.

We're given no evidence about Owen's employment. *Greeks Bearing Gifts* suggests he was six months into his residency in September 2001, but that isn't helpful.

The wild card, then, is Captain Jack himself. In *The Sound of Drums*, he implies to the Doctor that he's only been a leader at Torchwood since *Doomsday*. While it's likely that the destruction of Torchwood One in that story caused Jack to rise in the Torchwood hierarchy (it's possible - although never explicitly stated - that he's by default the overall head of the organisation, as only Torchwood Cardiff and possibly the Glasgow office appear to remain), he's probably being a little disingenuous to suggest he only had tangible dealings with the group after the Battle of Canary Wharf. Clearly, under almost any scenario, he was working for the organisation before that. In fact, it might not be coincidence that he resumed his friendship with Estelle (*TW:*

Small Worlds) "a few years ago", if he moved to Cardiff and started working for Torchwood at that time.

At time of writing, the only reason to think that Jack has worked for Torchwood longer is *TW: Slow Decay*, in which a document from 1955 proves that Jack signed some items into the Torchwood Cardiff archives. This might suggest that Jack worked for Torchwood off and on in the twentieth century, and only started working for them full time a few years ago. It remains to be seen if future *Torchwood* episodes confirm or deny the point.

759 Dating *TW: Random Shoes* (*TW* 1.9) - The story is rife with minor glitches. The eBay listing for Eugene's alien eyeball claims the auction began on "14-Oct-06", but the date only appears on the full graphic on the *Torchwood* website, and isn't actually seen on screen. As such, it can be safely ignored. Another anomaly is that the "Black Holes and the Uncertainty Principle" flyer says the convention will begin on the 27th, a Thursday. This doesn't match any later month of the year in 2006, but such a day happened in September and December 2007. Those months don't seem viable (given this episode's relation to other *Torchwood* Series 1 stories), but the flyer is minor evidence. More glaringly, Eugene says it's been "fourteen years" since his father left in 1992 - which would indicate a dating of 2006.

760 Dating *TW: Out of Time* (*TW* 1.10) - Owen says in *TW: Captain Jack Harkness* that Diane flew back into the Rift on 24th December, denoting when the story ends.

with Owen. On 24th December, she flew her plane back into the Rift, expecting to find adventures anew.

2007 (Christmas Eve) - THE RUNAWAY BRIDE[761] ->
The huon particles within Donna Noble cased her to dematerialise from her wedding ceremony, and to re-appear in the TARDIS. Returning her to Earth, the tenth Doctor had to rescue her from roboforms disguised as Santas. This time, the robot "pilot fish" served the Empress of Racnoss, a huge spider-like creature and ancient enemy of the Time Lords.

From an abandoned Torchwood facility below the Thames Barrier, the Empress harvested the huon particles within Donna - the key to awakening the only other surviving members of the Racnoss, who were trapped at the Earth's core. The Doctor emptied the Thames into a tunnel leading to the core, killing the Racnoss below. Under orders from Mr Saxon, British Army tanks destroyed the Empress and her spaceship.

The Racnoss incident helped Mr Saxon come to prominence with the public.[762]

c 2008 - TW: COMBAT[763] ->
Torchwood found that an unidentified group was kidnapping Weevils, and pressed Owen into investigating a lead. Jack and company found the Weevils were being used by thrill-seeking businessmen in a "fight club" scenario and shut the operation down.

2008 (20th January) - TW: CAPTAIN JACK HARKNESS[764] ->
A tip-off prompted Captain Jack and Tosh to investigate the deserted Ritz dance hall, but the Rift flared up and catapulted them back to the building as it was on 20th January, 1941. The Ritz caretaker, Bilis Manger, had the ability to travel through time and was

Diane says the *Sky Gypsy* flew into the Rift on 18th December, 1953 - *Captain Jack Harkness* also claims that she and Owen only had "a week" together, so it would appear that the *Sky Gypsy* reappears on the very same day it flew into the Rift, just in half a century later. (The Rift surely doesn't care about matching the Gregorian calendar for aesthetic reasons, so this must owe to the position of the Earth around the sun or some other factor.) An anomoly is that 29th December is said to be a Friday - which is was in 2006, not 2007. The *Cardiff Examiner* is seen with the headline, "Drunk Driving Records Soar This Christmas".

761 Dating *The Runaway Bride* (X3.0) - It's "Christmas Eve", and the Sycorax invasion was "last Christmas". It's also after the Battle of Canary Wharf (*Doomsday*). Donna's surname is misspelled "Nobel" by some sources such as *Doctor Who Adventures* and in the official *Doctor Who* Exhibition.

762 *The Sound of Drums*

763 Dating *Combat* (TW #1.11) - Owen is greatly depressed and avoiding work owing to the loss of Diane, and Gwen here learns from Tosh about their relationship. Both facts suggest that weeks (or possibly just *a* week) rather than months have passed since *TW: Out of Time* (set in late December). It is possible, therefore, that *TW: Combat* takes place before the New Year, although a 2008 dating is perfectly feasible. (The episode itself broadcast on 24th December, the same day that *TW: Out of Time* concludes.) One anomaly is that *TW: Combat* opens with Gwen and Reece having dinner at an outside restaurant, and looking very comfortable despite their lack of winter clothing.

764 Dating *Captain Jack Harkness* (TW #1.12) - The last two episodes of *Torchwood* Series 1 seem to occur in rapid succession, and placing them on the timeline is problematic. Deciding where to date them depends on whether one favours the overall aesthetic of *Captain*

Jack Harkness and the pacing of plotlines in Series 1 (in which case, it's probably January 2008) or a "Vote Saxon" poster seen outside the Ritz dance hall in Cardiff (in which case, it's probably June 2008).

Doctor Who Series 3 takes place over a four-day period in June, and the "Vote Saxon" poster seems to indicate the national election that concludes in *The Sound of Drums*. However, *TW: Out of Time* ends on 24th December, 2007, and *Combat* seems to take place shortly thereafter. Moving *Captain Jack Harkness* and *End of Days* to June because of the poster would mean, then, that six months pass between *Torchwood* episodes eleven and twelve.

While this might sound plausible in theory, it is hard to watch *Torchwood* Series 1 and genuinely believe that such a six-month gap has taken place where none was apparently meant to exist. Not only does the general flow suggest that events in *Out of Time* were fairly recent (notably the rawness that Diane's departure has inflicted on Owen - as Ianto's "You've been off, haven't you?" comment helps to indicate), the costuming indicates January. Jack wears his trenchcoat regardless of the weather, but Toshiko and Bilis have on winter clothes that no sane person would wear in June. Owen and Gwen are dressed a bit more casually, but their jackets are still out of place for daytime in summer.

The apparent symmetry of Rift travel also suggests a January dating. Jack and Tosh travel through the Rift and arrive in 1941 on 20th January, and as previous Rift travellers seemed to arrive on the same calendar day they left (*Out of Time*), a case can be made that the two of them similarly depart on 20th January, 2008.

Overall, it has become a convention of modern-day television that time within a series progresses in relation to the time of broadcast - even some non sci-fi shows (such as *Boston Legal*) adhere to this rule, and in the main *Torchwood* is no exception. Series 1 seems to

attempting to manipulate Torchwood into fully opening the Rift. Owen was desperate to get Diane back, and used the group's Rift Manipulator to open the Rift. This enabled Jack and Tosh to return home, but although the Rift seemed to close...

2008 - TW: END OF DAYS[765] -> Opening the Rift had caused it to splinter, and it started depositing people from the past around the world. The Beatles were seen playing on the roof of Abbey Road Studios, a quarantine was established when someone arrived through time with the Black Death, and a Roman soldier murdered two people. UFOs were sighted over the Taj Mahal, and a samurai went on a rampage in the Tokyo subway system. Concurrent with these events, the Torchwood operatives saw visions of their dead or missing loved ones - each of them recommending that the Rift should be opened.

Bilis Manger was an acolyte of the devil-like being Abaddon, and had arranged these events as a means of freeing his master. The Torchwood operatives rebelled against Jack and opened the Rift, which loosed Abaddon to tower over the city. Abaddon's shadow killed anyone it touched, but Jack allowed Abaddon to feed off his immortal life energy. This overloaded Abaddon and killed him - Jack revived after spending some days in a coma.

He then disappeared as the TARDIS arrived...

2008 - UTOPIA[766] -> The tenth Doctor and Martha landed in Cardiff to refuel the TARDIS at the Rift. Captain Jack hurried to meet them - and found himself hanging on as the TARDIS launched itself into the Vortex. The trio found themselves in the year 100,000,000,000,000.

c 2008 - "Warkeeper's Crown"[767] -> Brigadier Lethbridge-Stewart vanished from a passing out ceremony at Sandhurst, and materialised on an alien world where he quickly met up with the tenth Doctor - and discovered he had been named "warkeeper elect" of a world of dragons and ogres. The original Warkeeper's influence was waning, and so he had brought the Doctor and Brigadier to the Slough of the Disunited Planets. The Brigadier asked for Mike Yates to help him, but the wrong Mike Yates - a xenophobic would-be MP - was summoned. As trolls started to overrun the Keep, the Doctor and Brigadier discovered the clone vats that kept the war supplied with troops. The whole planet was, in fact, an R&D facility for galactic arms dealers, and they shut down the operation.

Back on Earth, Yates tried to use the demons to further his political career, but the Doctor and Brigadier arrived back with an army of cloned Brigadiers and stopped him.

2008 (a Monday in June) - SMITH AND JONES[768] -> The tenth Doctor investigated electrical anomalies at the Royal Hope Hospital in central London, and met medical student Martha Jones. At the same time, the

---

open a couple of months after *Doomsday*, and episode eight (*TW: They Keep Killing Suzie*) occurs "three months" after the series opener - it's actually been more like two months in the real world, but it's in the ballpark. Viewers innately tend to follow this pattern, and among those who keep track of this sort of thing, a January dating (roughly concurrent with the broadcast of *Captain Jack Harkness* and *End of Days*) seems to cause far less confusion than June.

One possibility is that the "Vote Saxon" poster indicates the Saxon Party, as mentioned by Saxon himself in *The Sound of Drums*. Little is known (beyond a general sense of instability) about British politics between Harriet Jones' downfall and Saxon becoming Prime Minister, and the poster could refer to a secondary election that takes place in January. Similarly, the *Daily Telegraph* headline in *Love & Monsters* that reads "Saxon Leads Polls with 64 percent" is just as likely to refer to the party as Saxon himself.

765 Dating *End of Days* (*TW* #1.13) - There is an obvious need to link this story to *Doctor Who* Series 3, as Jack here registers the TARDIS' arrival and chases the Ship down at the start of *Utopia*. Related to the dating issues in *TW: Captain Jack Harkness*, it seems far simpler to presume that it's February 2008 when the Doctor and

Martha land to refuel in *Utopia*, even though this (plausibly) means they've arrived four months before their first meeting in *Smith and Jones*, and that Jack is gone from Cardiff for that duration of time. The Torchwood website isn't definitive evidence, but supports this with a missing poster of Jack that's dated to February 2008. **766** Dating *Utopia* (X3.11) - The pre-credit sequence of *Utopia* matches up with the end of *TW: End of Days*, and shows Jack reunited with the Doctor - explicitly for the first time since *The Parting of the Ways*. *End of Days* is set shortly after Christmas 2007, so the Doctor and Martha must land a few months in her past.
767 Dating "Warkeeper's Crown" (*DWM* #378-380) - The Brigadier is in his seventies, which (probably) means this is the first decade of the twenty-first century.
768 Dating *Smith and Jones* (X3.1) - In *The Sound of Drums*, Martha says it's "four days" since she met the Doctor. As that story takes place the day after a General Election, and elections are always held on a Thursday in the UK, it would mean that *The Sound of Drums* starts on a Friday and so *Smith and Jones* is set on a Monday.

Smith and Jones is clearly set after the Battle of Canary Wharf (*Doomsday*), and Martha, as a medical student, has upcoming exams. In *The Shakespeare Code*, the Doctor boasts that Martha is going to love reading

Judoon - intergalactic policemen / enforcers who looked like humanoid rhinos - were looking for a fugitive Plasmavore who was charged with the murder of the Child Princess of Padrivole Regency Nine. The Judoon had no jurisdiction over Earth, and so transported the entire hospital - and the Plasmavore within - to the moon. The Plasmavore disguised her alien nature by drinking human blood, but thanks to the Doctor's intervention, the Judoon registered her as an alien and killed her. The hospital was returned to Earth, and Martha joined the Doctor on his travels.

Martha owned a television made by Magpie Electricals.[769]

2008 (a Tuesday in June) - THE LAZARUS EXPERIMENT[770] -> The tenth Doctor returned Martha home twelve hours after they left. The 76-year-old Richard Lazarus conducted an experiment: hypersonic sound waves were used to create a state of resonance and rewrite his DNA, which rejuvenated him into the body of a young man. Martha's sister Tish worked for Lazarus' public relations department, and the family attended the first demonstration. Lazarus mutated into a cannibalistic monster, but the Doctor killed him in a showdown at Southwark Cathedral.

Saxon had funded Lazarus' experiments; his agents warned Martha's mother to beware the Doctor.

2008 - MADE OF STEEL[771] -> The tenth Doctor took Martha home, and they learned about a number of recent thefts of advanced electronics. Martha was captured by the culprits - a small group of Cybermen who had survived the Battle of Canary Wharf, and had set up camp in the Millennium Dome. The Doctor joined forces with the Army. The Cybermen wanted the Doctor to open a gateway into the Void to free their fellows, but instead he opened a time portal and released a Tyrannosaurus - which killed the last of the Cybermen.

---

the last *Harry Potter* book - eagerly anticipated at time of broadcast, but released on 22nd July, 2007, the year before he met her. Perhaps she's mentioned she's not read it, but as *The Shakespeare Code* follows directly on from *Smith and Jones*, there are maybe two opportunities for this off-screen conversation to occur.

In *Utopia*, Martha says the Cardiff earthquake (in *Boom Town*, set in 2006) was "a couple of years ago". A small oddity is that John Smith (in TV's *Human Nature*) dreams that he's from "2007", not 2008, although it's readily evident why he - with only snippets of the Doctor's memories - would be mistaken.

769 According to a label on Martha's television in *The Sound of Drums*, and evidently referencing *The Idiot's Lantern*. It's possible that Magpie's business survived, even if Magpie himself was disintegrated.

770 Dating *The Lazarus Experiment* (X3.6) - The Doctor says that Martha has only been away "twelve hours". This has to mean "twelve hours" after she left in the TARDIS with him at the end *Smith and Jones*, not when they first met each other in the kidnapped hospital - otherwise, Martha and her family would be made to experience Leo's party and events in *The Lazarus Experiment* on the same evening.

771 Dating *Made of Steel* (*Quick Reads* #2) - This is the first time Martha has returned to the Royal Hope Hospital. The events of *Smith and Jones* are "recent", and her absence is a source of curiosity to Rachel rather than serious concern - however, it's clearly after *The Lazarus Experiment*, which is Martha's first return to her own time. Martha's exams are "soon".

772 Dating *The Family of Blood* (X3.9) - The year isn't given, but Latimer's extreme age and the fact the service is conducted by a woman indicates at least a near-present-day setting. It's likely Martha's "present day".

773 Dating *Blink* (X3.10) - A caption says it's a year later.

The earlier sequences were explicitly set in 2007.

774 At the end of *42*.

775 *The Sound of Drums*

776 Dating *The Sound of Drums* (X3.12) - The Doctor, Martha and Jack arrive back from the future "four days" after *Smith and Jones*, the following morning when the Toclafane are unveiled. Constitutionally, there wouldn't be an existing Cabinet, as the Master would have had to appoint one before killing its members.

VOTE SAXON: There are apparent inconsistencies concerning the rise and election of Harold Saxon.

The facts are laid out as follows: Harriet Jones is deposed as Prime Minister after *The Christmas Invasion* (set in Christmas 2006). The Abzorbaloff in *Love & Monsters* holds a paper with the headline "Saxon Leads Polls with 64 per cent" (this occurs before *Doomsday*, as Jackie Tyler is still living on "our" Earth). Mr Saxon rises in prominence after ordering the shooting down of the Racnoss ship in *The Runaway Bride* (Christmas 2007, and explicitly after *Doomsday*). In *TW: Captain Jack Harkness* (set sometime after Christmas, as *TW: Out of Time* ends on 24th December), there's a Vote Saxon poster in front of the disused Ritz dance hall. The "contemporary" stories in *Doctor Who* Series 3 (*Smith and Jones, The Lazarus Experiment*, a sequence in *42, The Sound of Drums*) all take place in the same week, with a General Election the day before *The Sound of Drums*. We're told it's eighteen months since *The Christmas Invasion* in *The Sound of Drums* (so it's June 2008).

The problems are:

1. The Vote Saxon poster outside the Ritz suggests that *TW: Captain Jack Harkness* is set during the General Election campaign that elects Saxon, but the episode itself seems to be set soon after Christmas 2007, not June 2008. We can probably discount this problem pretty easily - the Vote Saxon poster doesn't have to be

? 2008 - THE FAMILY OF BLOOD[772] -> The tenth Doctor and Martha attended a World War II remembrance service and saw an elderly Tim Latimer.

2008 - BLINK[773] -> The tenth Doctor and Martha, on their way to stop a dangerous migration / hatching, met Sally Sparrow for the first time... although she'd met them in her past, and was able to give them a dossier with details regarding their becoming trapped in 1969.

Martha phoned her mother on Election Day.[774] Saxon sent the Torchwood staff to the Himalayas to prevent them from helping Captain Jack and the Doctor.[775]

2008 (a Friday and Saturday in June) - THE SOUND OF DRUMS[776] -> By this point, the United Nations had provisions for removing the British Prime Minister from office.

Harold Saxon, secretly the Master, won the election and convened a meeting of his Cabinet in the newly-rebuilt Downing Street. He killed everyone present, then announced to the world that he had made contact with the alien Toclafane and refused to keep it secret as past governments had. As President of America,

Arthur Coleman Winters flew to Britain - both to warn Saxon to take his responsibilities carefully and to take control of the public revelation of the Toclafane.

Meanwhile, the British authorities were looking for three "terrorists" - the Doctor, Martha and Jack, who had returned to the twenty-first century. Onboard the flying aircraft carrier *Valiant* - a UNIT ship - a number of Toclafane materialised and killed President Winters. The Master revealed his plan...

> (=) and six billion Toclafane emerged from a space-time rift. They decimated the human population, and the Master took control of Earth.

2008 (a Saturday in June) - LAST OF THE TIME LORDS[777] -> The *Valiant* returned from a year in the future, to a point just before the Toclafane appeared. The Master's devastation of Earth had been temporally reversed. The tenth Doctor vowed to imprison the Master in the TARDIS, but Lucy Saxon shot her husband. The Master refused to regenerate and died. The Doctor burnt his body on a funeral pyre, but an unknown woman retrieved the Master's ring.

Martha declined to rejoin the Doctor on his travels.

---

part of the General Election campaign, it could have appeared quickly in the wake of the events of *The Runaway Bride*, as the start of the momentum that sees Saxon elected six months later.

2. Saxon is ahead in the polls (*Love & Monsters*) before he comes to prominence (after The Runaway Bride). The "poll" Saxon leads in late 2007 can't be one for the General Election of June 2008, as British election campaigns only take four to six weeks. This is harder to explain, but it is possible...

Following *The Christmas Invasion*, it's a turbulent time in British politics, as stated in *The Sound of Drums*. What we're told in the series actually would lead to political problems - Harriet Jones' party won a landslide victory, but confidence in Jones evaporates overnight. Under the British constitution, there's no obligation for either Jones to hold a general election, or for there to be a general election if her party deposed her as leader... unless the government lost a vote of no confidence, and in practice no party with a "landslide" majority could lose such a vote. *The Christmas Invasion* implies that Jones resigns or is deposed soon after. Her party won an election largely because of her, and holds a massive Commons majority, but she's no longer in charge. Whoever took part is at least third choice to lead the party (after the former Prime Minister who was assassinated by the Slitheen in *Aliens of London*, and Jones), and would almost certainly start out as a lame duck. We should probably note that this instability, exploited by the Master in Series 3, is actually instigated by the Doctor when he deposes Harriet Jones in *The*

Christmas Invasion.

In this situation, people would be looking for alternative leaders, and papers would be running polls. Saxon becomes the Minister of Defence at some point in 2007, the www.votesaxon.co.uk website has him as a published novelist (the novel is called *Kiss Me, Kill Me*) and he's married to the daughter of a Lord - so he's clearly a public figure before *The Runaway Bride*. The Racnoss attack, and his handling of it, must be the last piece that makes his succession inevitable.

So the poll in *Love & Monsters* is almost certainly speculative, and perhaps even the first time most people had heard of Mr Saxon. It's also very probably been placed there by Saxon himself.

777 Dating *Last of the Time Lords* (X3.13) - Time is reversed to 08:02, just before the Toclafane appeared in great numbers. This means Saxon is still elected and kills his Cabinet and (as is explicitly stated) President Winters is still assassinated. The last detail is something of a glitch, as all of the Toclafane's actions (Winters' death included) should have been temporally erased. Another problem that the Doctor, Martha and Jack should still be known as "Public Enemies number one, two and three" despite the historical reversal (as is the case in *The Sound of Drums*), yet they're later seen casually chatting in public with no fear of arrest.

Also at story's end, the "accident and emergency" board behind Thomas Milligan says it's October. This raises the possiblity that the Doctor and Martha stay in London for a few months after the Master's defeat, even if nothing else supports or denies the notion.

San Francisco fell into the sea.[1]

= Manipulated by the poodle people of the Dogworld, John Fuchas produced a movie "adaptation" of *The True History of Planets* in 2008 that abandoned the original book in favour of a story about the deposed poodle Princess Margaret. The Doctor ensured that this timeline never happened.[2]

2009 (11th January) - SJA: INVASION OF THE BANE[3] -> Thirteen-year-old Maria Jackson moved to a new house in West London with her father. That night, she saw her neighbour, Sarah Jane Smith, talking to an alien. Sarah aided this lost being in returning home, and Maria teamed up with her to uncover the secret behind the popular new addictive drink Bubbleshock. It was a creation of the alien Bane, who planned to take control of the population. Sarah and her allies brought the operation to an end.

= 2009 (a Saturday in June) - LAST OF THE TIME LORDS[4] -> The Master had controlled Earth for a year, and turned it into a factory world. The enslaved human population was put to work building two hundred thousand war rockets "set to burn across the universe" and create a Time Lord Empire. A space lane traffic advisor warned all travellers to stay away from Sol 3.

Japan was devastated, and New York was reportedly in ruin. China had fusion mills, Europe had radiation pits, and a shipyard in Russia ran from the Black Sea to the Bering Strait.

The Master had used Professor Lazarus' technology to greatly age the Doctor, who was imprisoned on the *Valiant*. Martha Jones spent a year travelling the world and spreading word of the Doctor, telling the public to think of him when the rockets were launched. The Doctor had spent the last year linking himself into the telepathic field of the Archangel network, and used the humans' psychic energy to restore himself. Jack destroyed the Paradox Machine, reversing time one year and one day to the exact moment before the Toclafane materialised.

---

1 *The Janus Conjunction* (p79). It's referred to as around in the twenty-second century in *The Face-Eater*.

2 *Mad Dogs and Englishmen*

3 Dating *Invasion of the Bane* (SJS 1.0) - K9 has been working to contain the black hole for "eighteen months", so it's at been least that long after *School Reunion*, and possibly longer. Maria's bedside clock gives the date as 11th January - roughly a year after the story's broadcast date of 1st January.

4 Dating *Last of the Time Lords* (X3.13) - It's "one year later" than the events of *The Sound of Drums*.

5 Dating *Memory Lane* (BF #88) - No specific year is given, but most signs indicate that Kim and Tom hail from near the present day. Kim is familiar with iPods; Tom is acquainted with both *Space Lego* (1978-2001) and *Star Wars Lego* (first introduced in 1999) and the Doctor explicitly names their ion jet rocket as the product of the twenty-first century.

It's further said that the rockets come into being "thirty five years" after the Earth-recreation of Tom's childhood on Lucentra, and although this stems from a composite of Tom's memories and isn't very reliable, it does tie in with the date for *The Seeds of Death* in this chronology.

Kim expects Tom to recognise the names of female astronauts Eileen Collins (who flew in 1995, then 1997) and Pamela Anne Melroy (who piloted space shuttle missions in 2000 and 2002, and was selected to command one in June 2006).

6 Dating *Happy Endings* (NA #50) - It is "2010". In *Prime Time*, the director of Channel 400, Lukos, tells Ace's younger self that her mother died age eighty-five, haunted by never knowing what happened to her daughter. As Ace's mother was born in 1943 according to *The Curse of Fenric*, this would place her death in 2028. However, Channel 400's account is specifically tailored to torment Ace and therefore suspect, especially given the older Ace's reunion with her mother in *Happy Endings*. Ricky McIlveen is the son of Vincent and Justine from *Warchild*. Time was first mentioned in *Love and War*, and the seventh Doctor is often cited as "Time's Champion".

7 *The Shadows of Avalon*, following on Lethbridge-Stewart's rejuvenation as a result of events in *Happy Endings*. This explains how the Brigadier lives well past a normal human lifespan.

8 On one of the alternative timelines seen in *So Vile a Sin*.

9 *Mad Dogs and Englishmen*

10 Dating *Doomsday* (X2.13) - Pete states that "three years" have passed since the end of *The Age of Steel*. This must mean that it's 2010. In "our" universe, it's still 2007 (as we can infer from Jackie saying she's "forty" in *Army of Ghosts* and telling Pete he "died twenty years ago" in *Doomsday*, and which is confirmed in *TW: Everything Changes* and *The Runaway Bride*).

Perhaps the disruption caused by travelling between the two universes has knocked them out of sync. It means that Mickey, Pete and Jake are all three years older in *Army of Ghosts* than they were in *The Age of Steel* (even though they all look exactly the same as before), and that Jackie is "officially" three years older

c 2010 - MEMORY LANE[5] **->** Travel to planets in the solar system was now feasible from Earth, and the *Led Zeppelin* spaceships were named after a public vote. Kim Kronotska became a commander in the Commonwealth Space Programme - a means of using British money to fire off rockets in the middle of the Outback - and participated in the *Led Zeppelin II* mission to Phobos, one of Mars' moons.

The development of cryo-stasis, however, facilitated grander ambitions. Kim, Tom Braudy and their colleague Samuel were dispatched aboard the *Led Zeppelin IV* to Jupiter, but a system failure drew them off course. They wouldn't awaken for a hundred years. Centuries hence on the planet Lucentra, the eighth Doctor rescued Kim and Tom and deposited them back in their native era. They settled down together under adopted identities, letting the world believe they were lost in space.

The film *Star Begotten* entailed a second sun appearing over Earth.

2010 - HAPPY ENDINGS[6] **->** Guests from across space and time attended the wedding of Benny Summerfield and Jason Kane in the Norfolk village of Cheldon Bonniface. Between them, the various guests thwarted the Master's plan to disrupt events.

The word "cruk" was introduced in an anime series, and quickly caught on as a mild expletive.

At this time, Ace reconciled with her mother, Audrey. Ishtar Hutchings, formerly the Timewyrm, was left pregnant from an encounter with Chris Cwej. She believed that their daughter, Jasmine, would become the girlfriend of Ricky McIlveen - and that the two of them would sire the Eternal named Time.

The rejuvenated General Lethbridge-Stewart returned to active duty with UNIT.[7]

= The third Doctor surrendered Earth to the Martians. The Martians withdrew, and Earth became a nature reserve. The Doctor spent a thousand years living in Kent.[8]

The Halliwell Film Guide of 2010 contained a particularly scathing review of *The True History of Planets* movie, which was broadcaast on television for the first time this year. Britain had a King at this time.[9]

= **2010 - DOOMSDAY**[10] **-> In the parallel universe where the Cybermen were created, Harriet Jones was President and there was optimism for a new global age. However, in the last sixth months, the planet's average temperature had risen by two degrees. Lumic's Cybermen were infiltrating our universe, and Pete Tyler and Torchwood helped to defeat them, then sealed off all travel between the two universes. This left Rose, Mickey and Jackie stuck in the parallel universe.**

A few months after arriving in the parallel universe, Rose was contacted by the Doctor. She said goodbye to him at Dárlig Ulv Stranden ("Bad Wolf Bay") in Norway, and announced that Jackie was three months pregnant with Pete's child.

The Americans researched military applications for Schumann Resonance, a set of low frequency peaks in Earth's electro-magnetic spectrum.[11] **Chloe Webber's father died in 2011. Both she and her mother had been terrified of him.**[12]

In late July 2011, Lethbridge-Stewart's wife Doris was killed in a yachting accident.[13] **Van Statten discovered the cure to the common cold using alien technology.**[14]

2012 (27th July) - FEAR HER[15] **-> Adverts were distributed for *Shayne Ward: The Greatest Hits*. Humans were the only species in the galaxy to have ever bothered with edible ball bearings.**

The Isolus were empathic creatures from the deep realms - it was not unusual for an Isolus family to consist of up to four billion members, or for them to journey for a thousand human lifetimes. During childbirth, an Isolus mother would jettison millions of spores into space, but one Isolus was caught in a solar flare, and its pod crashed to Earth. It came to empathise with Chloe Webber, age 12, and hosted itself in her. The Isolus could harness ionic power, enabling Chloe to turn people into drawings and vice versa.

As London geared up for the opening ceremony of the Olympic Games, the tenth Doctor and Rose inves-

---

there than her actual age (which presumably she's not happy about).

Jackie is three months pregnant by the time the Doctor contacts Rose, so it takes at least three months (of parallel universe time, at any rate) for him to do so.
11 "Decades" before the first portion of *Singularity*.
12 *Fear Her.* Chloe's father died the previous year.
13 "Almost a year" and, later, "over a year" earlier than *The Shadows of Avalon*.

14 *Dalek*
15 Dating *Fear Her* (X2.11) - The year is given as "2012", and the story ends with the opening of the London Olympics, currently scheduled for 27th July, 2012. At present, pop singer Shayne Ward has no Greatest Hits collection.

tigated reports of missing persons - actually consigned by Chloe to an ionic holding pen - on Dame Kelly Holmes Close in the city. Chloe also made the 80,000 athletes and spectators in the Olympic Stadium vanish. The Doctor and Rose restored them, and helped the alien back into space by lighting the Olympic Flame.

Papua New Guinea went on to surprise everyone in the shot put. At this time, there was an East London police authority and an East London Council.

2012 / = 2012 (June - August) THE SHADOWS OF AVALON[16] -> Britain had a King and a female Prime Minister. There had been no major alien attack that required UNIT's attention since the Martian invasion of 1997.[17]

The eighth Doctor dropped Compassion off in South West England so that she could learn more about humanity. The Time Lords detected that Compassion was evolving into a form of technology they could use, and President Romana dispatched agents Cavis and Gandar to recover her. Still mourning Doris, General Lethbridge-Stewart was on leave. He was called in to investigate the loss of a nuclear warhead, which he discovered had passed through to a parallel universe called Albion.

= Meanwhile, in Albion, a war was brewing between the Unseelie and the Catuvelanuni. The Doctor, Fitz and Compassion arrived in Avalon following the seeming destruction of the TARDIS in a dimensional rift. They prevented war there from escalating. Compassion evolved into a new form of TARDIS. President Romana arrived to try and capture her, but the Doctor and his companions made their getaway. Lethbridge-Stewart remained in Avalon to advise Queen Mab.

2012 - DALEK[18] -> The ninth Doctor and Rose followed a distress signal and discovered that Henry Van Statten, the owner of the Internet, had what was reportedly the last Dalek captive in his extraterrestrial museum deep underneath Utah. The Dalek broke free and killed most of Van Statten's staff, but contact with Rose's DNA made it mutate and question its purpose. The conflicted creature destroyed itself. Van Statten's employees rebelled at his callousness and had him mindwiped, then dumped in a US city starting with "S". The Doctor reluctantly welcomed Adam, one of Van Statten's staff, onboard the TARDIS.

16 Dating *The Shadows of Avalon* (EDA #31) - The story starts in "July 2012" (p1). *The Ancestor Cell* specifies that Compassion is the first Type 102 TARDIS. Although we did see one in *The Dimension Riders*, and it didn't take the form of a person.

17 This statement that appears odd in the light of the new television series, given that we see a series of very public alien attacks. Not only that, UNIT appear in *Aliens of London / World War Three* and *The Christmas Invasion*, and are mentioned a couple of times in *Torchwood*.

18 Dating *Dalek* (X1.6) - The Doctor gives the date.

19 Dating *The Long Game* (X1.7) - No date is given, but it's clearly after *Dalek*. Adam's mother says she hasn't seen him for six months.

20 "Five years" before *The Enemy of the World*.

21 *The Time of the Daleks*. The Doctor restores some wayward history at the end of the story, but it's clear that the "real" history includes Learman coming to power, and she's mentioned in *Trading Futures*.

22 *The Face-Eater* (p55). *Trading Futures* (p68) - there's a New Kabul in that book, implying the original city was destroyed, so Afghanistan was also a battleground.

23 *Trading Futures*

24 *The Taking of Planet 5*

25 *Instruments of Darkness*. Presumably a reference to Tony Blair's son and Prince Andrew's daughter.

26 Dating *Christmas on a Rational Planet* (NA #52) - The date is given.

27 Dating *Frozen Time* (BF #98) - The year is given. The veiled implication is that Genevieve becomes one of

the Doctor's companions, and shares some adventures with him before returning home.

28 *Relative Dementias* (p40) dates when the Doctor and Ace visit the Countess. Her warning about 14th July is on p17.

29 Dating *Death and Diplomacy* (NA #49) - The Virgin version of *A History of the Universe* dated the story to the present day, based on the synopsis. The final book specifies that Jason was born in 1983 and is "near enough" thirty (p123).

30 *The City of the Dead*. This retcon takes the sting out of one of the nastier bits of *Warlock*.

31 Dating *Warlock* (NA #34) - The novel is the sequel to *Cat's Cradle: Warhead*. The events of the earlier book are consistently referred to as happening "years" ago (p8, p203, p209, p223). Vincent and Justine, the two young lovers from *Warhead*, bought a car after a "few years" of marriage and have had it a while (p356).

In *Cat's Cradle: Warhead*, Ace had difficulty guessing how old Justine was, eventually settling on "maybe sixteen or seventeen" (p181). By *Warlock*, Justine has matured into a woman (p203), but she is still only "probably a couple of years older than the medical student" (p301), so she is in her early-to-mid twenties. I suggest, then, that *Warlock* takes place about five years after *Cat's Cradle: Warhead*. It is late autumn (p279, p334).

32 *Damaged Goods*

33 Dating "The Lunar Strangers" (*DWM* #215-217) - The date is given at a caption at the end of the story.

The UN continued to keep the existence of aliens a secret, and Van Statten didn't know that his alien was called a Dalek.

2012 - THE LONG GAME[19] -> Adam attempted to send information from the year 200,000 home to exploit. When the ninth Doctor discovered this, he took Adam back to his native time and left him there.

Politically the world seemed less stable for a time. In 2012, the scientist / politician Salamander managed to convince a group of his followers that a global nuclear war was inevitable. He established a survival shelter at Kanowa in Australia for them.[20] Following the Euro Wars, Mariah Learman seized power in the United Kingdom on a popular tide of anti-EuroZone feeling, renaming it New Britain. Britain had a King at this time.[21]

World War Three was fought in the early twenty-first century. India was reduced to a radioactive mudhole.[22] The War against Terrorism was won when the RealWar teletrooper was introduced. Subscribers could kill terrorists (identified with 80 percent accuracy by software) from the comfort of their own home by operating war robots. Baskerville, a Russian arms dealer, became the richest man in the world selling the technology.[23]

In 2012, firemen in New York laughed and toasted marshmallows instead of rescuing people from a fire. This resulted from the Memeovore feeding on human ideas.[24] The Doctor owned a commemorative mug from the wedding of Euan and Eugenie.[25]

2012 - CHRISTMAS ON A RATIONAL PLANET[26] -> The seventh Doctor, Chris and Roz landed in Arizona. When Cacophony's gynoids emerged into our universe, Roz fell through a crack in time to the end of the eighteenth century.

2012 - FROZEN TIME[27] -> Lord Barset sought to locate the colony of lizard men that his grandfather (also known as Lord Barset) had discovered, and sponsored an expedition to Antarctica in the hopes of finding advanced technology there. The expedition members instead found a frozen Ice Warrior base, and their heaters revived the warmongering Araksssor - as well as the seventh Doctor, who had been frozen for millions of years. Barset was killed, but the Doctor signaled an Ice Warrior spaceship. The commander of the vessel decided to enforce a death sentence upon Araksssor - his spaceship bombarded the base from orbit, and Araksssor and his warriors died. The Doctor escaped with a member of Barset's expedition - Genevieve - and she returned to her comrades a week later.

By 2012, Countess Gallowglass was operating her mail-forwarding service from a hidden location near Carnaby Street. The seventh Doctor visited the Countess, with Ace, in August to collect his mail. According to the Countess, London should be avoided on 14th July, 2013.[28]

2013 - DEATH AND DIPLOMACY[29] -> Half a galaxy away, the three Empires of the Dakhaar, Czhan and Saloi were set to overrun the little planet of Moriel. The powerful Hollow Gods commanded that the races would sort out their conflict by diplomatic means - or else. The Hollow Gods employed the services of the seventh Doctor in this effort, and his companions Cwej and Forrester prevented the villainous Skrak from over-running the Three Empires.

The eighth Doctor visited a house in Kent and saved a cat.[30]

c 2014 (Late Autumn) - WARLOCK[31] -> Organised crime continued to rely on the profits of drug trafficking. Dealers now used sports cars to get around, and the British police were forced to use Porsches to keep up with them. Soon Porsche were even making a special model for them. In an attempt to win the Drugs War, the International Drug Enforcement Agency (IDEA) was set up. A pooling of Interpol and FBI resources, IDEA had a number of well-publicised successes against drug dealers, forcing many of them underground. IDEA was based in the King Building in New York, the old headquarters of the Butler Institute, and its methods often brought them into conflict with local police forces.

For around a year, IDEA had been aware of a new street drug, called "Warlock" by many of its users. Warlock seemed to give people psychic powers. Tracking the source of the drug proved difficult, leading IDEA men across New York and England. In the late autumn, an IDEA team investigating the drug was caught in the explosion that destroyed Canterbury Cathedral, an event officially explained away as a freak ball-lightning effect. It was announced shortly afterward that IDEA had broken up the Warlock cartel, and the drug vanished from the streets. Exactly how this had been achieved was never fully explained, although around this time an animal research lab near Canterbury was closed down in mysterious circumstances and the prominent London gangster Paulie Keaton "retired" after a decade of dominating criminal activity in the city. The founder of IDEA, Henry Harrigan Jnr, died around this time.

At the start of 2014, the Home Office introduced compulsory HIV blood tests. In June the next year, MI5's Harry Sullivan told UNIT that the blood of a survivor of the Quadrant Incident might hold a cure to the condition.[32]

2015 (7th June) - "The Lunar Strangers"[33] -> Two cow-like aliens arrived at Moon Village One - on the same day that the fifth Doctor, Tegan and Turlough showed up. The cows - Ravnok and Vartex of the Dryrth - claimed their ship was badly damaged, but they were secretly after treasure buried under the base. The Doctor caught them red-hooved trying to sabotage the reactor.

Ravnok and Vartex felt their planet of Dryra had become spineless, so they had released a killer virus to provoke the population into action. They buried their treasure on Earth's Moon, but were subsequently captured and sentenced to three thousand years in prison. They soon escaped, but the Moon Village had been built over the treasure. Commander Jackson shot Vartex, and Ravnok suffocated on the Moon's surface. The Doctor revealed that the "treasure" was actually cheese - the currency on Dryra.

c 2016 - TRADING FUTURES[34] -> There were no rogue states remaining and the world's secret services kept almost every square inch of the planet electronically monitored. The only two remaining superpowers - indeed, the only two remaining sovereign powers - were the United States and the EuroZone, who dominated the world between them. But they were on the brink of war, as both were trying to extend their sphere of influence into power vacuums in North Africa and the Middle East. "Peacekeepers" from both sides took up positions.

Elsewhere in the world, EuroZone RealWar tanks were covertly sent into action against American corporate interests. The situation was a tinderbox that could have lead to World War Four. By now, the United Kingdom was part of the EuroZone and the semi-elected British President Minister was bound by the Articles of European Zoning, despite polls showing 84 percent of the British population taking the American side in the dispute. Britain secretly maintained its own intelligence service, run by the ancient Jonah Cosgrove. The American President was Felix Mather, former CIA astronaut.

There was a European national soccer team, and games were divided into eighths to fit more adverts in. Rhinos only existed in clonetivity. Human cloning was possible, but very expensive. Hypersonic jets could cross the world

---

34 Dating *Trading Futures* (EDA #55) - The year is not specified beyond "the early decades of the twenty-first century" on the back cover, but Mather says his encounter with the Doctor in *Father Time*, which occurred in 1989, was "more than twenty years ago". Malady Chang, a secret agent, seems to place it nearer thirty years, as she thinks the Doctor "would have been about ten at the time", and he looks like he's in his "early forties". People who were teenagers in the nineties are now "pushing pensionable age" (p8) and Anji's generation are the parents of teenagers. Learman from *The Time of the Daleks* is referred to (p107), as are the Zones from *The Enemy of the World*. It's not clear whether World War Four has been averted - US and EZ forces are fighting at the end of the book, and it's only *hoped* that the revelation of Baskerville's plan will end it.

WORLD WARS: The First and Second world wars occur much as we know them. There are fears of a Third World War in the UNIT era. It occurs some time between Anji joining the TARDIS crew (2000) and *Trading Futures* (c.2016) - whether the events of the episode *World War Three* qualify is unclear. World War IV was mentioned in *The Also People* and *Frostfire*, but no details are given. In *Christmas on a Rational Planet*, it's said that people danced in the ashes of Reykjavik during World War IV. The Doctor says he saw World War V in *The Unquiet Dead*. World War VI is averted in the year 5000, according to *The Talons of Weng-Chiang*.

35 *Heritage*. In terms of *Doctor Who* history, the earliest mention of humans cloning humans is in *Trading Futures*.

36 Dating *The Enemy of the World* (5.4) - One of Salamander's followers, Swann, holds up a scrap of newspaper with a date on it from the year before, but

the photograph is not clear enough to discern the date. (*Timelink* suggests it says 2041, but still dates the story to 2013.) The licence disc on the helicopter expires in 2018.

None of the scripts contain any reference to the year that the story is set in. However, the *Radio Times* in certain regions featured an article on fashion that set *The Enemy of the World* "fifty years in the future", which would give a date of 2017. The first edition of *The Programme Guide* mistakenly thought that the story had a contemporary setting, and placed it between "1970-75".

The date "2030", which is now commonly associated with the story, first appeared in David Whitaker's storyline for the novelisation of his story, submitted to WH Allen in October 1979. The document was reprinted in *DWM* #200, and amongst other things of interest it is the only place to give Salamander a first name: "Ramon". The novelisation was due to be published in 1980, and was to be set "some fifty years later than our time - the year 2030" according to the storyline, but the book was not completed before Whitaker's death.

The second edition of *The Programme Guide* duly gave the date as "2030". The blurb for the novelisation by Ian Marter, published in 1981 - the same year as *The Programme Guide* - concurred, although perhaps significantly, the text of the book didn't specify a date. 2030 was soon adopted wholesale, with *The TARDIS Logs* and *The Terrestrial Index* giving the new date. *Encyclopedia of the Worlds of Doctor Who* is confused: the entry for "Denes" gives the date as "2017", but that for "Fedorin" states "2030". *The TARDIS Special* was less specific than most, claiming the story takes place in an "Unknown Future" setting. *The Legend* states it's "c.2017". *About*

in a few hours. Nuclear bombs were used in civil engineering. There was a North China and a New Kabul. Kurdistan was a country in its own right, in a region blighted by civil wars. British Airways had gone bankrupt, the BBC was replaced by the EZBC. More than one channel tunnel was operating.

The international flow of money was through the IFEC computer system. Arms dealer Baskerville launched an ambitious con job to seize control of it. He posed as a time traveller from ten thousand years in the future, and offered Cosgrove a time machine in return for access to the powerful EZ ULTRA computer. The CIA got wind of the plan, as did Sabbath's Time Agents; the eighth Doctor, Anji and Fitz; and the rhino-like alien Onihrs. The Doctor and his companions uncovered Baskerville's plan just as shootings in Tripoli triggered a potential world war.

The earliest human clones were mindless, bred for use as perishable stunt doubles in motion pictures. Humanity became uneasy with the morality of this and ended the practice. Cloning fell into disuse, but scientists kept periodically reviving the art.[35]

? 2017 - THE ENEMY OF THE WORLD[36] **->** Rockets could now be used to travel between continents on Earth - the journey from Australia to Hungary took around two hours. Hovercars made shorter trips. Television pictures are broadcast via videowire.

The political situation on Earth had stabilised. National concerns were put aside and the world was reorganised into large administrative areas called Zones, such as the Australiasian, North African and Central European Zones. The world was organised into the United Zones, but was more properly known as the World Zones Authority. Commissioners dealt with multinational concerns such as Security matters. A Controller led each Zone.

One of the major problems the world faced was famine. The scientist Salamander announced he could solve the problem using his Mark Seven Sun-Catcher satellite, which made previously desolate areas of the world into fertile farmland that robots could harvest. Within just a year, the Sun-Catcher had solved the problems of world famine, allowing crops to grow in Siberia and vineyards in Alaska. In the more fertile areas, concentrated sunlight forced growth: each summer could bring three or even four harvests. Salamander was hailed as the saviour of mankind.

Soon after Salamander's announcement a series of natural disasters struck, including a freak tidal wave that sank a liner full of holidaymakers in the Caribbean and the first volcanic eruptions in the Eperjes-Tokaj mountain range since the sixteenth century. These were caused by Salamander's followers in Kanowa using his technology. Salamander had convinced them that the Earth's surface was highly radioactive, and that they had to fight back against the aggressors.

The second Doctor, Jamie and Victoria uncovered the truth: that Salamander had been gradually assassinating his political opponents within the United Zones and replacing them with his own people in a bid to become the dictator of Earth. Salamander was defeated when his followers in Kanowa learned there had been no global nuclear war.

Time hedges its bets a little, saying that "around 2017 - 2030 is the most likely possibility". *Alien Bodies* sets the story later, after *Warchild* and apparently around the 2040s.

It seems clear that David Whitaker intended the story to be set fifty years after it was broadcast, and I have adopted that date.

WEATHER CONTROL: In a number of stories set in the twenty-first century we see a variety of weather control projects. The earliest is in the New Adventure *Cat's Cradle: Warhead*, and simply involves "seeding" clouds with chemicals to regulate rainfall (p129). A year before *The Enemy of the World*, Salamander develops the Sun-Catcher, the first Weather Control system. As its name suggests, the Sun Store satellite collects the rays from the Sun and stores them in concentrated form. It is also capable of influencing tidal and seismic activity.

Each major city has its own Weather Control Bureau by *The Seeds of Death*, and these are co-ordinated and monitored centrally by computer. The London Bureau is a large complex, manned by a handful of technicians. The Weather Control Unit itself is about the size of a large desk, with separate circuits for each weather condition. With fully functioning Rain Circuits, rainfall over a large area can be arranged quickly.

By 2050, the Gravitron had been set up on the Moon. This is the ultimate form of weather control, working on the simple principle that "the tides control the weather, the Gravitron controls the tides". Weather control is under the control of the (United Zones?) General Assembly.

It's clear those last two are different systems, but it's less clear which is the most advanced. This becomes important when trying to date *The Seeds of Death* - *About Time* suggests that the weather control in *The Seeds of Death* is "far more compact and efficient", so that's the later story. But it can certainly be argued that a device in a room in London that makes it rain on special occasions looks primitive compared with a Moon-based one that manipulates gravity as part of an international programme to manage the entire world's weather.

In 2017, UNIT closed their file on the Quadrant Incident.[37] Kakapos were extinct on Earth by 2017.[38] The Doctor placed a personal advert "Ace - Behind You!" in an *NME* from 2018. Ace bought a copy outside Ladbroke Grove hypertube station.[39] Paletti wrote the opera *The Fourth Sister*, including the stirring *Rebirth Aria*.[40]

The risk of nuclear warfare diminished after the Southport Incident, when governments realised that the stockpiling of atomic weapons could only lead to a serious accident or all-out nuclear warfare.[41]

The Doctor acquired a ten pound coin from the time of King William V.[42] **Single Molecule Transcription replaced the microprocessor in 2019.**[43]

2020 - THE POWER OF THE DALEKS[44] **->** The colony on Vulcan was in danger of being "run down". Mining operations had not proved economically successful and the Governor of the colony, Hensell, faced mutiny. An Examiner from Earth was due to assess the Vulcan colony in two years.

The chief scientist, Lesterson, discovered what he thought might be the colony's salvation - a buried alien spaceship. He quickly determined that the capsule was constructed of a metal that wasn't found on Vulcan and could revolutionise space travel. At first, Lesterson feared that the ship might contain bacteria, but he opened the capsule anyway, and discovered that it contained three inert Daleks. The lure of reviving them proved too great for the human colonists.

At first, the Daleks cunningly pretended to be servants, dependent as they were on the power provided by the humans. They played their part well, solving simple scientific problems. The Daleks promised to build a computer that could predict meteorite showers and protect the weather satellites, a move that offered huge financial savings and won the colonists' trust. All the time, though, the Daleks were setting up their production line. Dozens of Daleks swarmed across the colony within a matter of hours, exterminating every human in their path.

Once again, though, the Daleks' external power sources proved their undoing - although they guarded

---

37 *Damaged Goods.* Marcie Hatter, a UNIT Corporal here (p262), was the name of the heroine of Russell T Davies' TV serial *Dark Season* (1991).

38 *The Last Dodo*

39 *Timewyrm: Revelation*

40 "A few decades" after *Vampire Science*.

41 Benny remembers the Southport Incident in *Just War* (p214), but doesn't specify what or when it was. Zoe, who lacks even rudimentary historical knowledge, recognises the effects of an atomic blast in *The Dominators*, perhaps suggesting that nuclear weapons are still around (and have been used?) in her time.

42 *Winner Takes All.* No date is given, but William is currently second in line to the throne, and will be King at some point in the twenty-first century.

43 *The Long Game*

44 Dating *The Power of the Daleks* (4.3) - There is no confirmation of the date in the story itself. Lesterson says the Dalek ship arrived "at least two ceturies ago", "before the colony", which might suggest the Earthmen have been there for just under two hundred years. However, the generally low-level of technology, the reliance on "rockets" and the fact that there is only one communications link with Earth suggests the colony is fairly new. The colonists don't recognise the Daleks, suggesting it's before *The Dalek Invasion of Earth*.

The contemporary trailer (included on the *Lost in Time* DVD) announced it was set "in the year 2020", and press material at the time confirmed that. This date also appeared in the 10th anniversary *Radio Times*, was used by the second edition of *The Making of Doctor Who* and the first edition of *The Programme Guide*.

Nevertheless, *Doctor Who* fans can see a statement like "I'm from 1980" as problematic and ambiguous, and most fan chronologies have seen 2020 as implausibly early for Earth to have a colony on a planet that's not in our solar system. Ergo, they often use the fact the date only appeared in a trailer to disallow it. (To be fair, the trailer for *The Dalek Invasion of Earth* set that story in "2000" - a date to which nobody subscribes.) In *DWM*, *The TARDIS Logs* offered a date of "2049", but "A History of the Daleks" contradicted this and gave the date as "2249". The American *Doctor Who* comic offered the date of "2600 AD", apparently unaware that the Dalek ship has been dormant. *The Terrestrial Index* came to the elaborate conclusion that the colonists left Earth in 2020 - in spacecraft with suspended animation - and then used the old calendar when they arrived. As a result, while they call the date 2020, the story is really set in "2220". *Timelink* opted for "2120". *About Time* claims that "internal publicity" gave the date as "2070" (it didn't, actually - that was for *The Moonbase*), but concludes the story is set "probably somewhere in the mid-2100s". Earth could only really have a colony on another world this early if the planet Vulcan was in our solar system. See the article "Vulcan" for how it might be possible to justify the "2020" date.

45 Dating *The Harvest* (BF #58) - The date is given on the back cover blurb.

46 At the end of *Doctor Who and the Silurians*, the Reptile People go back into deep freeze for "fifty years". Alternatively, they might have all perished in the explosions triggered by the Brigadier's men. There are Silurians working alongside humanity in *Eternity Weeps* in 2003, but it's never stated they are from Wenley Moor, and we know there were other shelters.

their static electricity generator, it proved possible to destroy the power source. This rendered the Daleks immobile once more.

2021 (12th October) - THE HARVEST[45] **->** There was political tension between Europe and the Pan-US Core. The European Council had recovered an expeditionary force of Cybermen that crashed in the Pyrenees. The Cybermen brokered a deal with the European government, offering Cyber-technology to create astronauts cyber-augmented for space. In return, the Cybermen asked that operations be performed to make them organic beings again.

By October 2021, the "Recarnative Program" was secretly in operation at St Gart's Brookside, a London hospital managed by the Euro Combine Health Administration. The duplicitous Cybermen intended to seize control of the facility, which would serve as a ready-made Cyber-conversion centre and facilitate a planetary takeover.

The seventh Doctor and Ace learned of the plot and triggered a termination protocol that shut down the Cybermen. The Doctor also erased all of the Program's data, preventing the Euro government from exploiting the Cyber-technology. Thomas Hector "Hex" Scofield, a staff nurse at St Gart's, became embroiled in these events and joined the Doctor and Ace on their travels.

An AI System was in use at St Gart's, and the Wheel space stations were in operation.

During the 2020s, the Silurians entombed at Wenley Moor were scheduled to revive. If they did so, they remained hidden from humanity.[46] The UN banned beryllium laser weapons in the mid-2020s.[47] The phased plasma rifle was developed in 2024.[48]

2024 - EMOTIONAL CHEMISTRY[49] **->** The eighth Doctor, Fitz and Trix infiltrated the Kremlin Museum to retrieve a diamond locket that formerly belonged to the Russian noblewoman Dusha. Colonel Grigoriy Bugayev, working for the Russian division of UNIT, knew the Doctor of old and aided the time travellers.

The disgraced physicist Harald Skoglund had retro-engineered a lost time belt into the Misl Vremnya, a device whose name meant "thought time." It enabled its user to see down the timeline of various objects, and to witness events through the eyes of anyone in contact with them. With further exertion, the device allowed its operator to dominate the wills of such people. The businessman Vladimir Garudin used the Misl Vremnya for his own purposes, but Bugayev later destroyed the device.

By now the Moscow waste management system had organic microfilters to reprocess sewage. Robot drones were used for reconnaissance.

The novel *The Unformed Heart* by Emily Hutchings was published, and the Doctor acquired a copy. The word "cruk" was very rude by 2025.[50] Demeter Glauss, the future author of *Cybercrime: An Analysis of Hacking* was born. The book was the seminal work on breaking and entering computer systems, including the Paradigm operating system. Mel would use the text to hack into Ashely Chapel Logistics in 1999.[51]

By 2030, the issue of thargon differentials in the orange spectrum of upper atmospheric problems was solved. This enabled the creation of stable energy fields on satellites.[52] Gorillas were extinct on Earth by 2030.[53] The seventh Doctor, Ace and Bernice visited UNIT HQ in Geneva in 2030, and picked up a note left by Cristian Alvarez thirty seven years before.[54]

2030 (Early Autumn) - WARCHILD[55] **->** Computer technology advanced to the stage that cars practically drove themselves and computers understood straightforward voice commands. Instead of passports, people had implants on the back of their necks, and three-dimensional television existed. Passenger airliners were still in use. A cure had been found for Alzheimer's disease, and few people now smoked thanks to health-awareness campaigns.

Over the long hot Summer, a state of emergency was declared in London. Computers monitored all telephone emergency calls listening out for the keyword "Dog". Packs of dogs displaying remarkable intelligence had murdered many people, and there were reports of a "White King", an old dog that appeared to control the packs. The govern-

---

47 "Twenty years" after *The Fearmonger*.

48 *First Frontier* (p137).

49 Dating *Emotional Chemistry* (EDA #66) - The date appears in the blurb.

50 *Happy Endings*

51 Glauss was born twenty six years after *Millennial Rites* (p86). A bit confusingly, p70 says her *Cybercrime* text was written "in the early twenty-first century".

52 "Twenty or thirty years" after *The King of Terror*.

53 *The Last Dodo*

54 *The Left-Handed Hummingbird*

55 Dating *Warchild* (NA #47) - The book is the sequel to *Warlock*. At the end of the earlier novel, Justine was in the early stages of pregnancy, so her baby would have been born in the spring of the following year. In *Warchild*, her son Ricky is "15". This book is set in the early autumn, as the long summer ends and the school year is starting in America.

ment restricted all reporting of the emergency and used psychic operatives to assemble covert action teams.

In America, Vincent Wheaton had received government funding to research "alpha male patterns", the study of pack dynamics. He hoped to nurture a man capable of "natural leadership", which entailed the ability to control crowds, or indeed whole populations of people. Vincent hoped to control America with such a man as President, but he was killed before his plan came to fruition.

Lethbridge-Stewart returned to Earth in 2032, having spent twenty years in the realm of Avalon.[56] By 2034, a young man called Craig would either be a drunk living under Hammersmith Bridge *or* a successful carpenter with children - depending on the choices he made in 2006.[57]

c 2038 (30 November, Tuesday) - SINGULARITY[58]
-> Houses were now equipped with computer attendants that responded to voice recognition; phones also recognised voice command.

In Russia, the Somnus Foundation had been created to study sleep disorders and neuro-science, but some descendents of humanity - originating from near the end of the universe - usurped the organisation. The descendents hoped to modify the brain chemistry and "wave forms" of several humans, thereby inducing telepathy and achieving a group consciousness. If successful, the effect would cascade through Earth's electro-magnetic signature and turn the whole of humanity into a single entity. The resultant "Singularity" would allow the descendants to bring their fellows through en masse from the future, and let them exact vengeance against the Time Lords.

On 30th November, Moscow witnessed its worst storm in fifty years. The fifth Doctor arrived to investigate matters at a Somnus clinic, but the Somnus test subjects started an electrical fire, hoping to end their suffering. The clinic burned down as the Doctor escaped.

In 2038, the World Zones Accord was signed. Around this time, Colonel Kortez fought the Cyber breaches for the ISC. He joined UNISYC in 2039 and fought lemur people at some point before 2069.[59]

Elsewhere in the galaxy, civilisations continued to develop. A race of reptilian humanoids had evolved on the planet Draconia. Although technologically advanced, they retained a feudal system. The Doctor visited Draconia at the time of the Fifteenth Emperor, around 2040, and cured a great space plague.[60] It was the second Doctor, and his portrait was hung in the Imperial Palace.[61] The Doctor was given the rank of High

---

56 *The King of Terror*

57 "FAQ"

58 Dating *Singularity* (BF #76) - The year is unspecified, but it's stated that 30th November is a Tuesday; in the twenty-first century - and allowing that the portion of *Singularity* eleven years hence cannot occur before 2090 - that narrows the possibilities to 2010, 2021, 2027, 2032, 2038, 2049, 2055, 2060, 2066 and 2077. As Somnus publicity materials brag about the goal of its members to terra-form Mars within "two years", 2077 doesn't seem very likely; it would push the later portion of *Singularity* to 2088 and the end of the devastating Thousand-Day War - a year in which Somnus would be rather brazen to make such a claim.

Moscow endures its worst storm "in fifty years", an event that would be unlikely in the era of weather control witnessed in *The Moonbase* and *The Seeds of Death*. The former story takes place in 2070, which seems to rule out this part of *Singularity* occurring before 2066. One complication is that the Doctor's off-handed comment that mankind is only "a few years" from expanding beyond the Solar System - when humankind will become too disparate for the *Singularity* to work - which suggests a later dating as opposed to an earlier one. Nonetheless, given this book's projected dating of *The Seeds of Death*, the best compromise for the early part of *Singularity* seems to be 2038, with the remainder of this adventure occurring in 2049.

59 *Alien Bodies*. The World Zones Accord was intended

as a reference to the establishment of the political system of *The Enemy of the World*, which most chronologies set earlier than this. We could speculate that the World Zones Accord strengthened an existing World Zones Authority, in the same way successive European treaties have granted more powers to the EEC / EC / EU.

60 "Five hundred years" before *Frontier in Space*. The incident is also recounted in *Shadowmind*.

61 *The Dark Path*

62 *Catastrophea*

63 *Return of the Living Dad*. According to the Doctor in *The Parting of the Ways*, the Daleks also refer to him by that title.

64 *Interference* (Book Two, p292, p314), where the If, one of IM Foreman's incarnations, predicts Sarah's death. Following the machinations of the Council of Eight, the timeline is altered so that Sam Jones died in 2002.

65 *Dreamstone Moon* (p58).

66 *Cold Fusion* (p216), no date given.

67 Dating *The Seeds of Death* (6.5) - This story is tricky to pin down a date for, or even to place in relation to other stories.

On screen, the only indication of the date is the Doctor's identification of the ion rocket designed by Eldred as a product of "the twenty-first century". As the rocket only exists as a prototype at this stage, the story must take place before 2100. T-Mat is developed at least two generations after space travel, as Eldred's father designed spacecraft, including a "lunar passen-

Earl of the Imperial House.[62] The Draconians took to referring to the Doctor as "the Oncoming Storm".[63]

Sarah Jane Smith died around 2040. Members of UNIT and Black Seed, possibly including Sam Jones, attended her funeral. In 2043, Black Seed published their third manifesto.[64] There were anti-weather control demonstrations.[65] Earth picked up an Arcturan signal that included enough information to build a transmat device.[66]

? 2044 - (Winter) THE SEEDS OF DEATH[67] -> On Earth there was a period of technological progress. Hypersonic aircraft were built, and mankind discovered how to synthesise carbohydrates and protein, which helped to feed the planet's ever-increasing population. Computers were now advanced enough to give spoken responses to sophisticated verbal instructions. Most energy now came from solar power, and compact solar batteries became available. Petrol cars were confined to museums. There were further advances in robotics and weather control technology.

Regular passenger modules were travelling between the Earth and its moonbases. Most people thought the Moon would provide a stepping stone to the other planets of the Solar System, and eventually to the stars. At this time Professor Daniel Eldred, the son of the man who designed the lunar passenger modules, invented an ion jet rocket with a compact generator. This vehicle promised to revolutionise space travel, paving the way for mankind's rapid exploration of the solar system.

Then the Travel-Mat Relay, an instantaneous form of travel, was invented. The massive capital investment required, and the promise of easy movement of all resources around the world, meant that after some debate the government ended all funding for space travel. All but a skeleton staff on the Moon were recalled. Man had travelled no further than the Moon. For years, all space travel halted.

Travel-Mat revolutionised the distribution of people and materials around the world. A T-Mat brochure boasted that:

"The Travel-Mat is the ultimate form of travel. Control centre of the present system is the moon, serving receptions in all major cities on Earth. Travel-Mat provides an instantaneous means of public travel, transporting raw materials and vital food supplies to all parts of the world. Travel Mat supersedes all conventional forms of travel, using the principal of dematerialisation at the point of departure and rematerialisation at the point of arrival in special cubicles. Departure and arrival are almost instantaneous. Although the system is still in its early stages, it is completely automated and foolproof against power failure."

Humanity, though, had become dangerously insular. The Ice Warriors remained confined to Mars during all this time, limited by the lack of resources their home planet had to offer.

The Grand Marshall of the Martians ordered an invasion of Earth. A small squad led by Lord Slarr took

---

ger module", and Eldred is an old man himself. It's impossible to infer a firm date from that, particularly as we know from *The Tenth Planet* that moonshots were unremarkable events by the mid-nineteen-eighties in the *Doctor Who* universe. However, "lunar passenger module" suggests an altogether more routine service, and so that this story is not set in the late twentieth or very early twenty-first century. It's never stated how long Travel-Mat has been in operation before *The Seeds of Death*, but it is a relatively new invention, as the video brochure we hear (transcribed here in full) states. Young Gia Kelly was involved with the development of T-Mat, but it has been around "a good many years" according to Eldred, long enough to make an advocate of rocket travel look eccentric. T-Mat is consistently referred to as having been around "years", rather than "decades" or "generations" - so I suggest that T-Mat has been around for about a decade before the story.

It is possible to rule out certain dates by referring to other stories: The Weather Control Bureau is seen, so it must be set after 2016 when Salamander invents weather control; the Bureau is on Earth, which might suggest the story is set before 2050 when the Gravitron is installed on the Moon, or that the system is later moved to Earth. Either way, the story can't be set between 2050 and (at least) 2070, because the Gravitron is in operation from the Moon at that time and rockets are in use during that period. By the time of *The Seeds of Death*, it's stated that man has not travelled beyond the Moon. While *About Time* claims that the "technology is shown to be in advance of that in *The Wheel in Space*", it's a bit hard to see what that's based on. We're explictly told that Zoe has a more extensive knowledge of spaceflight than Eldred. (He admits as much, and Radnor says the same later - and clearly distinguishes between Zoe's expertise and Jamie's lack of it. So it's not the Doctor making her look good, as *About Time* suggests.) Laser weapons have been developed by *The Wheel in Space*, including compact hand "blasters", but projectile weapons are still used here. There are quite advanced robots in Zoe's time, nothing like that seen here. Zoe was trained in a futuristic city, yet the cities we see here look much as they do now. That might be circumstantial evidence, but there's far more than that - *The Seeds of Death* is set at a time when man has travelled no "farther than the Moon",

Seed Pods - oxygen-fixing plants native to Mars - to the Moon. The plan was to cripple Earth by disabling the T-Mat, then use the Seeds to alter Earth's atmosphere until it more closely resembled that of Mars. The Pods were sent to Earth via Travel-Mat and preparations were made to guide the Martian invasion fleet to Earth. As killer foam spread through London, the second Doctor, Zoe and Jamie travelled to the Moon and defeated the Ice Warriors, directing the Martian fleet into the Sun.[68]

The global teleportation system lead to disastrous UN aid decisions.[69] Professor Otterbland of the Dubrovnik Institute of New Sciences discovered psychotronic conditioning in 2045.[70] Borneo became a ReVit Zone in 2049. The rainforests were replanted and stocked with genetical-

ly engineered plants and animals.[71] The United States fell in the mid-twenty-first century.[72]

c 2049 - SINGULARITY[73] -> Led by Natalia Pushkin, also known as Qel, the High Priestess of the New Consciousness, the Somnus Foundation had emerged as a quasi-religious organization officially dedicated to awakening mankind's potential. The Somnus Tower had been built behind the Kremlin, employing a Bygellian style that humans wouldn't create for another six hundred years.

Qel and her colleagues proceeded with their plan to turn all of humanity into a Singularity gestalt, and snared the inhabitants of Moscow into such a network. The fifth Doctor and Turlough intervened, and consequently the Singularity didn't hold, the Somnus Tower exploded, Qel was killed and the other conspirators were catapulted back

---

whereas *The Wheel in Space* is set at a time when man's got at least to the asteroid belt, explicitly has ships in "deep space", has a "fleet" of manned ships and at least five permanent space stations, and has been selecting and intensively training people to be astronauts for at least Zoe's lifetime (nineteen years, according to *The Invasion*). While no one says it in the story, *The Seeds of Death* is clearly - and is clearly intended to be - set before *The Wheel in Space*, case closed.

Deep space interstellar missions with crews in suspended animation were launched in the twenty-first century according to *The Sensorites*, which would be after the events of this story. The lack of deep space travel would seem to set the story before *The Power of the Daleks* (whichever year that is).

Evidence in subsequent stories would indicate that it's not set between 2068 and 2096, as Galactic Salvage and Insurance are insuring spacecraft between those dates according to *Nightmare of Eden* (although if the space programme ended, it might explain why they went bust). The T-Mat network seems to connect up the whole world - it includes both New York and Moscow, for example - which would seem inconsistent with the divided world of 2084 seen in *Warriors of the Deep*. Finally, the story probably isn't set after 2096, as four years seems too short a period to explore the entire Solar System (*The Mutants*) before the interstellar missions mentioned in *The Sensorites*.

Or, to cut a long story short, and assuming a ten-year period before the story when T-Mat has been operating, *The Seeds of Death* has to be set more than ten years after *The Enemy of the World* (so after 2027), but before the Gravitron is installed in 2050.

This contradicts the limited space travel seen in stories (made after *The Seeds of Death*) to Mars in *The Ambassadors of Death*, *The Dying Days* and *Red Dawn*, and to Jupiter *in Memory Lane* and (accidentally) *The Android Invasion*, as well as the most likely date for *The Power of the Daleks*. If Vulcan was a rogue planet in our

solar system, perhaps the colonisation mission was launched as it passed relatively close to Earth (although that piles supposition on supposition), or perhaps - more likely - the Vulcan colony had long failed and "doesn't count". Or perhaps it was costly and disastrous, and so was a contributing factor in man turning to an alternative to space travel.

The original storyline set the date as "3000 AD", but later press material suggested the story took place "at the beginning of the twenty-first century".

As we might expect, no fan consensus exists. The first edition of *The Making of Doctor Who* claimed the story is set in "the latter part of the 20th Century", the second was less specific and simply placed the story in the "21st Century". The first two editions of *The Programme Guide* set the story "c2000", *The Terrestrial Index* alters this to "c2090", and the novel *Lucifer Rising* concurs with this date (p171). DWM writer Richard Landen suggested "2092". *Timelink* says "2096, February", conceding "this is a difficult story to date". *Encyclopedia of the Worlds of Doctor Who* set the story in "the 22nd century". Ben Aaronovitch's *Transit* follows on from *The Seeds of Death*, with his "Future History Continuity" setting the television story "c2086"; *About Time* conforms to that.

I set *The Seeds of Death* seventy five years after it was first broadcast, which fits in nicely with the evidence.

68 WHATEVER HAPPENED TO TRAVELMAT?: While we're told space travel will be readopted at the end of *The Seeds of Death*, no-one says they'll abandon T-Mat. As T-Mat is an astonishingly useful technology - one that's quickly been adopted by most countries, if not all - it seems odd that we never see it again. It's not just absent from the twenty-first century either - it's missing from every story set on a future Earth. Service might be disrupted by the Dalek Invasion, but you'd think they'd have it working again for, say, *Frontier in Space*.

The obvious explanation is that Earth can afford a space programme or a T-Mat programme, but not both. This is implicit in *The Seeds of Death*. It might not

to the far-flung future. Authorities claimed that the incident was a terrorist attack against the Somnus cult, one that resulted in a hallucinogenic compound being released and causing mass hysteria.

The Doctor believed that dozens of non-terrestrials were operating on Earth in this period. A Russian Public Security Directorate was in service.

c 2050 - THE TIME OF THE DALEKS[74] **->** The Daleks attempted to exploit a temporal rift to enhance their time travel capabilities, but the experiment backfired and they almost lost their entire fleet. They made contact with Mariah Learman, the ruler of New Britain, who had a primitive time scanner. Learman didn't believe the population appreciated Shakespeare, and the price for her co-operation with the Daleks was that they would assassinate

Shakespeare as a youth and preserve the only copy of his works for Learman's benefit. Rebels thwarted this plan by smuggling an eight-year-old Shakespeare from 1572 for his own protection, but this caused further time distortion. The eighth Doctor arrived, trying to explain why his companion Charley didn't know of Shakespeare. The Doctor joined the rebels and set history back on course by returning young Shakespeare to his rightful time. The Daleks were trapped in an endless temporal loop after mutating Learman into one of them.

The Conquest of the Solar System

Space travel was readopted and co-ordinated by International Space Command in Geneva. Ion jet rockets explored the Solar System.[75] It now took only a cou-

---

be simply a case of money so much as expertise - it's stated that a number of top rocket scientists became T-Mat ones. Logically, if you can instantaneously beam men and materials to the Moon, it ought to lead to a mass colonisation of the Moon - but it hasn't. Earth's priorities have changed, mankind is looking inward. *The Seeds of Death* offers a world where the technology is there for space exploration, but the political will isn't (as such, it's the most realistic prediction of the twenty-first century that *Doctor Who* writers made in the sixties).

There are other explanations, all pure speculation, and mainly economic. T-Mat is a network requiring a huge infrastructure, and must be expensive. When real-life people were presented with the choice of seven hours on a normal plane or two hours on Concorde, they ended up picking the normal plane on cost grounds. Presumably using the T-Mat isn't free, and the technology might not look so attractive if instant travel from London to New York cost ten times more than taking a plane. Alternatively, the analogy might be with trams - a system with many advantages over the cars that replaced them, but which lost out for all sorts of reasons (mainly that it was hard for them to co-exist, and trams required governmental funding but cars made money in taxes). Even if individuals aren't picking up the T-Mat bills, someone must be. It's a centralised system, and perhaps it's an all or nothing proposition - either a worldwide network or it's useless (like, say, GPS in the present day). Or it might be that space travel starts paying off - perhaps materials from the asteroid belt and cheap energy from space means there's suddenly an abundance of resources. Perhaps there were disasters. These could either be *Hindenburg*-style serious failures of the T-Mat system itself, or unintended consequences like T-Mat allowing a rapid spread of something undesirable - terrorists, diseases or even just migrant workers or counterfeit / grey market goods.

Transit tackles these questions, and imagines a solar system radically transformed a generation after T-Mat.

Its author, Ben Aaronovitch, dated *The Seeds of Death* to about 2085 and *Transit* to about 2109, with the T-Mat system in continuous use between them - the story is essentially *The Seeds of Death: The Next Generation*, complete with Ice Warriors. But this needn't have been a continuous process. Perhaps, once the solar system had been explored by rockets for a generation, the political will and funding re-emerged and the T-Mat network was rebuilt and expanded (just as tram networks are now being re-established in many cities).

In the future, we see stories where rockets and transmats *can* co-exist, but mainly as a way to beam from a spacecraft to the surface of a planet - not as mass transit. But even given that, transmats are surprisingly rare in humanity's future. On television, humans use transmats in *The Mutants, The Ark in Space, The Sontaran Experiment* and *Revenge of the Cybermen* (and three of those stories use the same machine!), and transmats are mentioned in *The Twin Dilemma* (but it's alien technology). So we might not know exactly why T-Mat was abandoned, but it clearly was.

69 *The Indestructible Man* (p78).

70 *The Well-Mannered War* (p204).

71 *Alien Bodies* (p9).

72 *Christmas on a Rational Planet*. "Nearly a millennium" before Roz is born (p31).

73 Dating *Singularity* (BF #76) - The Doctor reads a Somnus Foundation brochure that claims the groups' brightest minds will terraform Mars "by 2090", so the story cannot occur after that date.

74 Dating *The Time of the Daleks* (BF #32) - It is "the mid twenty-first century".

75 International Space Command is mentioned in *The Tenth Planet* and *Revenge of the Cybermen*, as well as *The Moonbase*, where it seems to be an agency of the World Zones Authority as seen in *The Enemy of the World* - we hear about "the General Assembly", "Atlantic Zone 6", and the head of the ISC is a "Controller" Rinberg. Ion jet rockets are mentioned in *The Seeds of Death*.

ple of hours for a shuttle rocket to travel from the Earth to the new moonbases. Around 2050, the ultimate form of weather control, the Gravitron, was built on the Moon's surface. The political implications on Earth proved complex, and the General Assembly spent more than twenty years negotiating between farmers and landowners.[76] The Butler Institute built the Gravitron.[77] Rhinos were extinct on Earth by 2051.[78]

Harnessing gravity waves allowed artificial gravity to be installed on spacecraft and space stations. Permanent space stations were built. Flowers were cultivated on the surface of Venus. The first Doctor visited this timezone.[79] Victorian time traveller Penelope Gate and her companion Joel Mintz accidentally visited the middle of the twenty-first century.[80]

Around the middle of the century, domesticated wolves were reintroduced into the forests of Northern Europe. It was rumoured that the Wicca Society had released wild wolves, and there was some debate as to which strain would become dominant.[81]

Eighty years after the events occurred, some early UNIT files were officially released. Reporter Daniel Clompus visited the elderly Brigadier General Sir Lethbridge-Stewart at his retirement home. Lethbridge-Stewart passed away shortly afterward. His memoirs, *The Man Who Saved the World*, were published in 2052.[82]

The people of the ocean planet Ockora built exoskeletal battlesuits and started an uprising against their Kalarian oppressors, who hunted them for sport. These warriors renamed themselves Selachians. After defeating the Kalarians, they conquered four planets, including Kalaya and Molinar. The Selachians became arms dealers, and attacked a Martian colony with a sunstroker.[83]

In 2054, the Doctor and UNISYC (led by General Tchike) defeated the Montana Republican militia, who were using Selachian weapons.[84] Sam had an ergonomic chair from the mid 2050s in her TARDIS room.[85] The Dogworld poodles built their first space station. It received radio signals from other planets, including Earth.[86]

All the religious faiths of the world were merged with the idea of creating world harmony. This consensus was unworkable and quickly collapsed. The Chapter of St Anthony was formed to fill the spiritual vacuum. When China was taken over by Hong Kong, the Yong family joined them on a new crusade to purge the heathens.[87]

In the mid 2050s, the world government overreacted to major wars and nuclear terrorism by passing police shoot-to-kill laws and banning all religions. There were years of

---

76 "Twenty years" before *The Moonbase*.
77 *Deceit* (p27, p153). It was possibly based on Silurian technology, as the Silurians establish a Gravitron on the Moon (in an alternate history) in *Blood Heat* (p196).
78 *The Last Dodo*
79 *The Wheel in Space*. The Doctor's familiarity with the Gravitron in *The Moonbase*, ion rockets in *The Seeds of Death* and Galactic Salvage and Insurance in *Nightmare of Eden* suggests he visited the Solar System during this period at least once.
80 *The Room with No Doors* (p48).
81 *Transit*
82 *The King of Terror*, the year is given as 2050 (p1).
83 "Almost a century" before *The Final Sanction* (p175), although it must be a little longer than that, as the Selachians were active in the twenty-first century according to both *The Murder Game* and *Alien Bodies*.
84 *Alien Bodies* (p12).
85 *Vampire Science*
86 *Mad Dogs and Englishmen*
87 *St Anthony's Fire*
88 *Interference* (p217). *The Indestructible Man* specifies that the UN is the force behind the ban (p13).
89 *Human Resources*. No date is given, but it has to be at a point in the twenty-first century with both political instability and a human space programme. Karen is apparently the same age as Lucie (late teens) in 2006.
90 *Nekromanteia*
91 *Alien Bodies*. See "Are There Two Dalek Histories?"
92 "About twenty years" before *Loups-Garoux*.

93 Dating *The Last Dodo* (NSA #13) - The Chinese Three-Striped Box Turtle is a new addition to the collection, and has recently gone extinct, so it's around 2062.
94 *The Indestructible Man*. This story seems to contradict a lot of the other stories set around this time both in broad terms and points of detail.
95 Dating *Alien Bodies* (EDA #6) - The date is given, p68.
96 *Seeing I* (p29). No date given.
97 *Nightmare of Eden*. A monitor readout states that Galactic Salvage and Insurance were formed in "2068". The Doctor has heard of the company and briefly pretends to be working for them.
98 *The Murder Game* (p9).
99 Dating *The Wheel in Space* / *The War Games* (5.7, 6.7) - This, along with *The Seeds of Death*, is one of two stories set in the twenty-first century that are trickiest to date. There's no date given in the story itself.

In *The Moonbase*, base leader Hobson states that "every child knows" about the destruction of Mondas (in *The Tenth Planet*). Yet none of the crew of the Wheel have heard of the Cybermen, and they're generally sceptical about the existence of alien life. This is a contradiction whether Zoe comes from before, around the same time or after *The Moonbase*. Invoking Zoe's narrow education doesn't work if "every child" knows about Mondas' demise, and surely the only way she wouldn't know is if it had been deliberately kept from her, which would be a bit bizarre. (Unless it's felt that telling future astronauts about all the monsters up there would be counter-productive.)

total chaos, and cities became no-go areas. There was no effective government. New governments started to form by the 2060s. Octogenarian Samantha Jones might have been a major player in these events. Before this point, her father had died, shortly after the last King of England abdicated.[88]

= During a period of extreme instability, Karen Coltraine established an oppressive right-wing regime in Europe, and put Earth's expansion into space on a much more aggressive footing. The Gallifreyan CIA revised her timeline, and prevented this future from occurring.[89]

Cricket was an Olympic sport in time for the Barcelona Olympics of 2060.[90] During the mid 2060s, the Daleks were scattered around the edges of Mutter's Spiral, trying to build up a decent galactic powerbase. The ones who got left behind on Skaro were just starting to think about putting together their own little empire - this was the "static electricity" phase of Dalek development...[91]

The collapse of the Amazon's eco-system made the "Lung of the World" into a dust bowl stretching from Rio de Janiero to the Andes, displacing a number of werewolves and Amazon Indian tribes. A constant risk of global war existed until the Earth's governments turned their attention to the Moon and asteroid belt for resources.[92]

2062 - THE LAST DODO[93] **->** By 2062, Chinese Three-Striped Box Turtles were extinct on Earth. The Museum of the Lost Ones had a single specimen of each extinct species in the Milky Way and Andromeda. The tenth Doctor and Martha arrived as Eve, the curator, had decided to wipe out all other life in the universe. She died when a weapon she was aiming at the Doctor exploded. The Doctor returned the specimens to their native times.

By 2068, a few colonisation missions had been launched to other solar systems, but there was no indication of whether they had succeeded. UNIT had recently been replaced by PRISM. On 3rd March, 2068, the Lunar Base picked up an alien signal. This was evidence of the Myloki. First contact proved disastrous, and the Myloki launched a war on humanity. Although conducted in secret, the war with the Myloki was so devastating that on 29th August, 2068, the UN banking system collapsed under the strain. The war ended when Colonel LeBlanc sent Captain Grant Matthews, an indestructible Myloki duplicate who retained his loyalties to humanity, to the Moon with a twenty-megaton bomb strapped to his back. This destroyed the Myloki base. But the war exhausted Earth's natural resources and saw New York destroyed in a nuclear attack. An altered maize crop destroyed the ecology of Africa. The City of London became an independent city-state, walled off from the rest of the world.[94]

2069 (26th March) - ALIEN BODIES[95] **->** In the East Indies ReVit Zone, Mr Qixotl hosted a private conference in which representatives from various powers were to bid on the Relic, a Gallifreyan body that contained extremely rare biodata. Friction among the delegates increased, and a Kroton Warspear arrived to claim the Relic by force. The eighth Doctor used a Faction Paradox timeship to reflect the Warspear's weaponry back on itself, destroying the entire battlefleet. Mortally wounded, Qixotl traded the Relic to the Celestis in return for a new body. The Doctor travelled to Mictlan, the Celestis' powerbase, and reclaimed the Relic. The Doctor buried the Relic alongside the dog Laika on the planet Quiescia, and destroyed the Relic with a thermosystron bomb.

Middle Eastern countries turned their economies to high technology, particularly the space industry, as the oil ran out.[96] **Galactic Salvage and Insurance was set up in London in 2068.**[97] The space station Hotel Galaxian became the first offworld tourist attraction.[98]

The Cyber Incursions

? 2068 - THE WHEEL IN SPACE / THE WAR GAMES[99] **->** Jet helicopters had become the principal form of transport on Earth. Simple servo robots were developed, as were x-ray laser weapons and food dispensers. John Smith and Associates built advanced medical equipment for spacecraft. Psychotropic drugs could now prevent brain control, and all astronauts were fitted with Silenski capsules to detect outside influences on the human mind. Two years beforehand, Corwyn's husband had been killed exploring the asteroid belt. The loss of rockets was becoming rarer, though.

The Earth School of Parapsychology was founded around this time. It was based in an area known only as "The City" and trained children from a very early age in the disciplines of pure logic and memory. Zoe Heriot, one of the School's pupils, developed total recall and majored in pure maths. She qualified as an astrophysicist and astrometricist (first class). Her education was narrow and vocational, though, and didn't include any Pre-century history. When she was about nineteen, Zoe was assigned to space station W3.

The Space Wheels were set up around the Solar System. W3, for example, was positioned relative to Venus, 24,564,000 miles at perihelion, 161,350,000 miles at aphelion, a week's rocket travel from Earth. W5 was between eighty and ninety million miles from W3. The small, multinational crews of the Wheel warned travellers of meteorite storms and acted as a halfway house for deep space ships of the space fleet; they monitored all manner of stellar phenomena, and also supplied advance weather information to Earth.

The Wheels were armed with x-ray lasers with a range of ten thousand miles, and protected by a Convolute Force Field, a neutron field barrier capable of deflecting meteorites of up to two hundred tonnes. Phoenix IV cargo rockets, which had a four-man crew but could be placed on automatic power drive, kept the stations supplied with food and materials.

Back on the human homeworld, the Pull Back to Earth movement believed it was wrong to colonise other planets. They committed acts of sabotage against the space programme, but their exponents were never seen as anything but crackpots. Space travel had undoubted benefits, but remained hazardous.

Zoe aided the second Doctor and Jamie in repelling a Cybermen assault on W3, then joined the TARDIS crew. Dr. Corwyn died in the attack.

Zoe eventually left the Wheel. Years later, she experienced dreams of her time with the Doctor and Jamie, and wondered if some of her memories were blocked off. She sought counseling, and related a particularly vivid adven-

ture involving the three of them and the Daleks. Zoe's unsettling dreams ceased after the Doctor's voice - through unknown means - told her not to fear the Daleks.[100]

2070 - THE MOONBASE[101] -> The Cybermen attempted to take control of the Gravitron on the Moon by using Cybermats to introduce a plague to the Moonbase. The second Doctor, Ben, Polly and Jamie thwarted them. Medical units could now administer drugs and automatically control the pulse, temperature, breathing, and cortex factor of a patient.

Tobias Vaughn recovered bodies of Cybermen from W3 and the Moonbase, and used the components to repair his cybernetic body.[102] Facing extinction, the Cybermen conquered Telos, all but wiping out the native Cryons and building their "Tombs" using Cryon technology. Once this was completed, the Cybermen retreated to their Tombs and vanished from the galaxy. The location of Telos remained a mystery.[103]

The Cybermen launched a star destroyer from Telos that headed to the Garazone Sector.[104] Seismic shifts created an

Amongst its other duties, the Wheel gathers information on Earth's weather, but this needn't mean that weather control isn't in use - to control the weather, you surely need the ability to monitor it.

As it's Zoe's native time, we get more clues in subsequent stories she's in: Zoe is "born in the twenty-first" century (*The War Games*), and she is "nineteen or so" according to the Brigadier in *The Invasion*, so the story must be set somewhere between 2019 and 2119. In *The Mind Robber*, she recognises the Karkus - a comic strip character from the year 2000 - which might suggest she comes from that year. However, when discussing the Karkus, Zoe asks the Doctor if he's been to the year 2000 - if it's not a rhetorical question, then *The Wheel in Space* isn't set in that year. In *The Mind Robber*, we see an image of Zoe's home city - a highly futuristic metropolis.

It's never explicitly stated that *The Seeds of Death* takes place before Zoe's time (see "Dating *The Seeds of Death*"). In *The Seeds of Death*, Zoe understands the principles behind T-Mat, meaning she possesses knowledge that's otherwise limited to a few specialists (she may have picked this up on her travels - although she doesn't in any story we see). Why Zoe doesn't remember T-Mat or recognise the Martians is a mystery, but it does indicate she was born after T-Mat was abandoned, or she'd recognise it.

This helps to set the earliest date for *The Wheel in Space* - it's at least nineteen years after *The Seeds of Death*, so it can't take place before 2046 (nineteen years after the earliest possible date for that story - in terms of this chronology, it's at least 2063). It doesn't help narrow the upper limit, however. That Zoe doesn't remem-

ber T-Mat may be evidence that she's from significantly after that story - then again, she has a narrow education and doesn't recognise kilts or candles, either, so perhaps T-Mat is seen as a quaint and irrelevant historical detail by Zoe's time..

Many subsequent stories establish that the governments of Earth knew about the existence of aliens in the twentieth century, and the new television series (as well as stories in the books and comics) establish that the general public accepts the existence of aliens by the early twenty-first.

The Indestructible Man places this story after 2096, as it's set before Zoe was born. *The Harvest* (set in 2021) refers to the Wheel space stations.

The first two editions of *The Programme Guide* placed *The Wheel in Space* between "1990-2000", but *The Terrestrial Index* suggested a date "c2020" (or "2030" in *The Universal Databank*)."2074" was suggested by "A History of the Cybermen" in *DWM. Cybermen*, after some discussion (p61-62), said "2028 AD". *Timelink* says "2020". *About Time* says "it looks like the 2030s to us".

I place the story a century after it was broadcast, around the same time as the other Cyberman incursion seen in *The Moonbase*. In the last episode of *The War Games*, Zoe is returned to her native time by the Time Lords, who erase her memories of all but her first adventure with the Doctor.

100 *Fear of the Daleks*. Wendy Padbury was fifty-eight when this audio was recorded - a possible indicator of Zoe's age.

101 Dating *The Moonbase* (4.6) - Hobson tells the Doctor they are in "2070", and Polly later repeats this. on screen the small crew of the Moonbase includes

island in the Atlantic, and this became a homeland for the Dutch, the New Dutch Republic.[105] The Sontarans left the Coal Sack sector of space and wouldn't return for three hundred years.[106]

2074 - MAD DOGS AND ENGLISHMEN[107] ->
Meanwhile, science fiction by human authors had become the subject of serious academic debate. There were also groups who sought to rewrite literary texts for their own evil ends, including The Circle Hermeneutic and The New Dehistoricists. The eighth Doctor accidentally landed his TARDIS on one academic, Alid Jag.

The Doctor, Fitz and Anji learned that the novel *The True History of Planets* was a book about talking poodles, not the sword and sorcery epic the Doctor remembered. The Doctor teamed up with Mida Slike of the Ministry for Incursions And Ontological Wonders (MIAOW), a group that investigated such changes to history. Slike was killed, though, and poodle fur found on her body. Fitz discovered the co-ordinates for Dogworld in Tyler's novel.

The space station of the Dogworld poodles was now receiving radio signals from Earth. The movie of *The True History of Planets* was the story of how the Emperor deposed the mother of Princess Margaret, the true heir to the throne. After trips to 1942 and 1978, the Doctor and his companions discovered that Margaret had been manipulating history to change the contents of Tyler's book, and changed it back. Margaret was killed and the Emperor restored to power. A grateful Emperor allowed writer Reginald Tyler to remain on the Dogworld.

Talking boars were now part of Earth society. and had

their own culture.

On Earth, governments used genetic manipulation and intelligent chips to maintain their soldiers' loyalty.[108]

2080 - LOUPS-GAROUX[109] ->
The ancient werewolf Pieter Stubbe tried to reclaim Ileana de Santos, now the de facto werewolf leader, as his mate. Illeana resisted Stubbe's advances, but Stubbe seized control of Ileana's werewolves and directed them to assault Rio de Janeiro. The fifth Doctor and Turlough arrived at this time, and the Doctor broke Stubbe's dominance of the pack. Stubbe died when he rushed into the TARDIS, enabling the Doctor to materialize in orbit and sever Stubbe from the Earth - the source of his elemental power - thus aging him to death.

Rio de Janerio now had a monorail and spaceport. ID implants were compulsory, and robots checked passports. People had hover vehicles including limos, jeeps and four hundred mile-an-hour trains. The currency was the credit.

Circa 2084, on the planet Cray, the game Naxy started out as an innocent arena sport. The Naxy sports fans became increasingly violent, and took to fighting outside the arena before matches. The public's interest shifted to the bloody fan conflict, and Naxy was soon re-tooled as a sport in which teams fought to the death.[110]

c 2084 - WARRIORS OF THE DEEP[111] ->
Earth consolidated into two blocs, the East and the West, and a new Cold War developed. New weapons technology was developed: Seabases sat on the ocean floor, armed with

Englishmen, Frenchmen and Danes. The production file for the story listed the other nationalities represented at the Moonbase: Australians, New Zealanders, Canadians, Germans and Nigerians.
102 *Original Sin* (p289).
103 *The Tomb of the Cybermen, Attack of the Cybermen*
104 *Sword of Orion*
TELOS: After the destruction of their vast advance force (*The Invasion*), their homeworld of Mondas (*The Tenth Planet*) and most of the surviving Cyber Warships (*Silver Nemesis*), the Cybermen must have been severely weakened. They gradually regrouped and attempted to attack Earth at least twice in the twenty-first century (*The Wheel in Space, The Moonbase*). These attempts failed, and the Cybermen faced extinction (according to the Controller in *The Tomb of the Cybermen*). So they left the Solar System and conquered Telos. (The Doctor says in *Attack of the Cybermen* that "if Mondas hadn't been destroyed, the Cybermen would never have come here [to Telos]", which contradicts an unbroadcast line from *The Moonbase* where a Cyberman states, "We were the first space travellers from Mondas. We left before it was destroyed. We came from the planet

Telos.") The Cybermen subjugated the native Cryons, used Cryon technology to build their "tombs" (*Attack of the Cybermen*) and experimented with new weapons before entering suspended animation. In the late twenty-fifth century, the Cybermen revived (*The Tomb of the Cybermen*) and emerged to menace the galaxy... [q.v. The Cyber War].
105 *St Anthony's Fire*
106 *Lords of the Storm* (p104).
107 Dating *Mad Dogs and Englishmen* (EDA #52) - It is "one hundred years" (p9) after "1974" (p3).
108 *Deceit* (p188), with similar technology in *Transit*.
109 Dating *Loups-Garoux* (BF #20) - The date is given.
110 *The Game*. Details of Naxy's history are given, and the story says dozens of teams played Naxy "four hundred years" before *The Game*.
111 Dating *Warriors of the Deep* (21.1) - The Doctor tells Tegan that the year is "about 2084". The televised story doesn't specify which bloc the Seabase belongs to, and only the novelisation specifies the blocs as "East and West". Even that leaves the geopolitics far from clear. The most obvious division in 1984 would have been between a capitalist West and communist East, but

proton missiles that were capable of destroying life while leaving property intact. Sentinels, robots armed with energy weapons, orbited the Earth and large Hunter-Killers patrolled the seas. "Synch-operators" had computer interfaces implanted into their heads, allowing split-second control over proton missile runs. Soldiers carried energy rifles.

At the height of interbloc tension, a group of Silurians and Sea Devils attacked Seabase 4. They planned to launch the missiles there and provoke a war that would kill all human life. The fifth Doctor failed to prevent a massacre at the base, but saved humanity.

First Contact

The Arcturan Treaty of 2085 was often officially counted as mankind's first contact with alien races, as it was the first diplomatic contact.[112] The whole of humanity finally accepted the existence of aliens. Danny Pain's role in stopping an alien invasion in 1976 was now legendary.[113]

2086 (25th April) - "Black Destiny"[114] **->** The fourth Doctor, Sarah and Harry landed at the Troika Cultural Centre to celebrate world peace in Takhail in Russia, but the staff suddenly started dying. The Doctor met Direktor Arkady, the great-grandson of a boy who was exposed to radiation there a hundred years before. The dead bodies reanimated as zombies. The Doctor checked the world-net computer network, and discovered that Arkady was fascinated by nuclear accidents. Arkady began to glow with energy and transformed into an energy cloud, then attacked Moscow, but the Doctor managed to neutralise and disperse him. Sarah noted that Chernobyl had a new nuclear power station.

At one point during this encounter, the Threshold abducted Sarah.

---

nowadays that seems unlikely. Lieutenant Preston doesn't seem surprised that the TARDIS is "not from this planet", and no-one seems shocked that the Silurians are intelligent non-humans. This might suggest that contact has been made with a number of alien races by this time.

THE RETURN OF THE EARTH REPTILES: In *Doctor Who and the Silurians*, *The Ambassadors of Death* and *The Sea Devils*, the Doctor thinks that the Brigadier has killed all the Silurians at Wenley Moor. However, they may simply be entombed, and one Silurian - Ichtar - seems to survive the first story into *Warriors of the Deep*.

Based on discrepancies between the events of *Doctor Who and the Silurians*, the descriptions of the Doctor's last encounter with the species in *Warriors of the Deep*, and the fact that the Doctor recognises Icthar, the Myrka and the Silurian submersible, *The Discontinuity Guide* postulated that there is an unrecorded adventure featuring the Doctor and the Silurians set between the two stories. The novel *The Scales of Injustice*, set in the UNIT era and published the year after *The Discontinuity Guide*, addresses most of these issues in an attempt to fill the gap.

Silurians were referred to in a number of New and Missing Adventures set in the future (*Love and War*, *Transit* and *The Crystal Bucephalus* to name three). They seem particularly peaceful towards humans in Benny's native time.

112 *The Dying Days* (p115). This is mankind's first diplomatic contact with alien races, as opposed to being invaded by them. See also "When Does the General Public Accept the Existence of Aliens?"

113 *No Future* (p257).

114 Dating "Black Destiny" (*DWM* #235-237) - The date is given. The United Nations World Health Organization is still operating, as are nuclear power stations. Peace must have broken out since *Warriors of the Deep*.

115 *Transit*

116 *Fear Itself* (p176-177).

117 *Transit*

118 *GodEngine*

119 *Legacy* (p86), *GodEngine* (p79). In *The Curse of Peladon* we learn that the Martians and Arcturans are "old enemies".

120 *GodEngine* (p168).

121 *Legacy* (p86).

122 *Fear Itself*

123 Dating "Ground Zero" (*DWM* #238-242) - The date is given in a caption at the start of the story. The destruction of the TARDIS console would seem to lead to its new design in *Doctor Who: The Movie*, although oddly it's the old TV console introduced in *The Five Doctors* that's destroyed, not the version seen in the later seventh Doctor strips.

ACE'S FATE: The seventh Doctor and Ace walk off together in *Survival*, but the next time we see the seventh Doctor - in *The Movie* - he's travelling alone. Thus, there have been a number of accounts of Ace's fate.

The New Adventures saw her grow to become a young woman, then in *Set Piece* she acquired her own time machine and left the Doctor, and the last time we see her is in *Lungbarrow* where she's still an independent time traveller. In "Ground Zero", a teenaged Ace sacrifices her life to save the Doctor's - and the Doctor is wearing the costume he did in *The Movie*, suggesting it's shortly before he regenerates. In *Death Comes to Time*, an older Ace is training to become a Time Lord, and witnesses the seventh Doctor's death. In *Prime Time*, we see the Doctor exhume Ace's teenage body - although in *Loving the Alien*, we learn the dead Ace (the one we saw with the Doctor on TV) was replaced by one from an alternate timeline. In due course, Big Finish may also tell "Ace's last story".

It is, of course, very difficult to fully reconcile these

The Thousand-Day War

Out of the blue, one day in 2086 the Martians attacked, hitting Paris with a meteorite and killing hundreds of thousands. Humanity united behind President Achebe against the common enemy. First in were the Zen Brigade, the Blue Berets of the United Nations Third Tactical Response Brigade, made up of Irish and Ethiopians. They dropped in from orbit, and the Martians cut them to pieces. One of the few survivors was their commanding officer, Brigadier Yembe Lethbridge-Stewart. But the Blue Berets completed their mission and formed a bridgehead: the UN forward-base at Jacksonville halfway up Olympus Mons. More crucially, their engineers set up the first inter-stitial tunnel, a refinement of old Travel-mat technology that allowed instantaneous travel between Earth and Mars. Men and materiel poured through the Stunnel.

Half-kiloton groundbreakers poured from the air onto the Martian nests. Tactical nuclear weapons were used. The early stages of the war were dogged by friendly fire incidents, but these were ironed out. As the war dragged on, some soldiers were genetically and cybernetically aug-mented to increase their efficiency. These first-generation ubersoldaten retained less than fifty percent of their natu-ral DNA. Just about every soldier took combat drugs like Doberman and Heinkel to make them better fighters.[115]

At one point the Zen Brigade was ambushed at Achebe Gorge - pinned down by snipers, they retreated under cover of a storm.[116]

New slang entered the language: Greenie (Martian), pop up (a cannon used by the Martians), spider trap, fire mis-sion, medevac. During the war, hologram technology became more advanced. The Ice Maiden, an R&R stop in Jacksonville, became notorious. For a generation after-ward, the imagery and iconography of the War was burnt into the minds of humanity, and was popularised in vids like *Violet Sky*.

The war ended in 2088, exactly a thousand days after it had started. The surviving Martians had either fled the planet or gone into hibernation in deep nests. At first, the human authorities were worried about "stay behind" units, but it became clear that the Martian threat had completely dissipated, and the military satellites were decommis-sioned. A memorial forest was set up at Achebe Gorge on Mars. A tree was planted for each one of the four hundred and fifty thousand men who had died in the War, which didn't include the death toll in Paris. For many decades, Victory Night was celebrated every year on Earth, and trees were planted to honour the military dead.[117]

The only human defeat was at Viis Claar, or the Valles Marineris, when Abrasaar killed 15,000 humans and 10,000 of his own men in a trap.[118] Ninety-nine per cent of Martians headed for a new planet, Nova Martia, beyond Arcturus. Hundreds of thousands of Martians remained behind, hidden in subterranean cities. UN peacemakers found the planet deserted. The bodies of six of the eight members of the ruling Eight Point Table were found, but these did not include Supreme Grand Marshal Falaxyr or Abrasaar.[119]

The Martian fleet heading to Nova Martia stopped off in the Rataculan system. A few Ice Warriors remained behind to found a colony on the planet Cluut-ett-Pictar.[120] There was little or no contact between the Ice Warriors and humanity for nearly a thousand years, and the Martians rarely allowed any visitors to their new world. In the twen-ty-sixth century, the "extinct" Martians briefly became a curiosity for archaeologists, but after that, mankind forgot all about their old neighbours.[121]

Wal-Mart began building the first trading post on Mars, but this was abandoned when the settlement Sheffield was established on Olympus Mons.[122]

2092 (29th August) - "Ground Zero"[123] **->** The sev-enth Doctor and Ace arrived at the Notting Hill Carnival. Ace was arrested on suspicion of theft, but the policeman was actually Dixon, an agent of Threshold. The Doctor met another agent, Isaac, who showed him the abducted Susan.

Meanwhile, Ace met the similarly kidnapped Sarah Jane and Peri. The Doctor learned that Threshold were an organisation that opened doors in space and time for their clients - their clients in this case being creatures living with the collective unconscious of mankind, the Lobri, who manifested as giant fleas. The TARDIS interior was heavily damaged. Ace sacrificed her own life to save the Doctor from the creatures - but the last Lobri nonetheless started to manifest on Earth. The Doctor materialised the TARDIS inside the Lobri, destroying it. He then returned his surviv-ing companions to their rightful places in time, and was left travelling alone.

2096 - THE INDESTRUCTIBLE MAN[124] **->** Interconti-nental travel was impossible, and the world was broken down into city-states. France and the former United States of America were in a state of civil war. Japan had invaded New Zealand. There was a United Zion Arab States. Only Australia was spared the worst effects of a collapsing soci-ety.

The second Doctor, Jamie and Zoe defeated the Myloki's plan to use Captain Grant Matthews as the ultimate agent of mankind's destruction.

In 2097, the Doctor, Fitz and Trix prevented an unnamed alien race from exterminating the Pope on Mars, allowing her to consecrate the first cathedral on another planet.[125]

The Colonisation of the Solar System

The World Government invested heavily in the state-owned Sol Transit System (STS) over the next twenty years, and soon Interstitial Tunnels linked every city, continent, habitable planet and moon in the Solar System. Transportation within the Solar System was now instantaneous and readily available. For the first time, the Solar System had a single elected government, the Union of Solar Republics.

In the decade following the Thousand-Day War, Paris was rebuilt. Lowell Depot on Pluto was built to soak up population overspill, but the expected boom didn't arrive. Instead, the Transit system caused massive economic and social upheaval. Small companies saw an opportunity to undermine the industrial zaibatsu. Household names such as Sony, IBM and Matsui went under, and new companies from Brazil, China and Africa - such as Imbani Entertainment, Mtchali and Tung-Po - took their place. Power shifted to Washington, Brazilia, Harare, Beijing, Tehran, Jacksonville and Zagreb. Japan's economy collapsed and plans to terraform Mars proved more costly than had been expected. The money ran out, the floating cities planned for the Ionian Sea were never built and

Australia starved. A new genre, silicon noir, charted the resultant corporate battles in the datascape.

The Recession was not harsh on everyone. Relatively speaking, Europe was less prosperous than before, but many in Brazil, Africa and China were a great deal wealthier. For millions in Australia, though, and at the Stop - the end of the Transit line at the Lowell Depot - extreme poverty became a way of life. Whole areas became dead-end ghettos, and urban areas became battlegrounds for street-gangs. Vickers All-Body Combat Systems offered the option of using the Melbourne Protocols, automatically preventing the wearer from shooting civilians. Millions fled the riots using the Transit system, and relief workers rehoused the poor anywhere that would take them, mostly on Mars. Private security firms such as the KGB and V Soc became very rich. With freedom of transport, humanity became more open to ideas from other cultures and to more experimental ways of living. Communal marriages enjoyed a brief vogue.

In 2090, Yembe Lethbridge-Stewart came out of retirement one last time and raided the headquarters of the genetics company IMOGEN. He stole a single child, the first of the second-generation ubersoldaten, and all the files pertaining to her creation. He named her after his great-grandmother, the historian Kadiatu.[126]

accounts. The main problem is rationalising Ace's death in "Ground Zero" with her other appearances, although one explanation is that her "demise" relates to the Council of Eight's attempts to eliminate the Doctor's companions - *Sometime Never* p154-155 even makes reference to Ace's double timeline, and although this was in reference to *Loving the Alien*, it could also, albeit retroactively, be made to apply to "Ground Zero". As such, temporally speaking, Ace's "death" in "Ground Zero" might hold no more weight than the notion that Sarah Jane "dies" in *Bullet Time* (set in April 1997).

124 Dating *The Indestructible Man* (PDA #69) - The date is given. This story contradicts many other stories - although only ones that were written after the sixth season in which the novel is set. It's set after a "global teleportation system" is built and fails (p78), a reference to *The Seeds of Death* (or possibly *Transit*); and it's before Zoe's time (p283), which puts it before *The Wheel in Space* (I've chosen to contradict this reference, see "Dating *The Wheel in Space*").

125 *The Gallifrey Chronicles*

126 This is the historical background to *Transit*. In *The Seeds of Death*, Zoe has never heard of the Ice Warriors - even though mankind is exploring the Solar System in her time - which suggests that her contemporaries are not interested in Mars. We learn in *Transit*, amongst many other historical snippets, that the Thousand-Day War ended about twenty five years before (p188) and

that the decade following the war saw economic upheaval (p108). In his "Future History Continuity", Ben Aaronovitch stated that the War took place between 2086-2088, which by his reckoning was straight after *The Seeds of Death*. Victory Night is mentioned in *The Highest Science* (p21), and I speculate that it celebrates the end of this War. We learn in *Infinite Requiem* that forests are still planted after a battle (p266).

127 According to the Doctor in *The Mutants*. As we will see, a number of stories claim to be set on the "first" colony. To explain the apparent contradiction, I'd suggest that colonists are either counting different "firsts" (the first plan to colonise, to actually leave Earth, to arrive, to terraform, to settle, to form a local government and so on) or that they simply like to take pride in their pioneering ways and are prepared to exaggerate a little.

128 In *The Sensorites*, ship captain Maitland thinks the Doctor's party is from the twenty-first century.

129 *Transit* (p264).

130 *The Pit*

131 *The Space Pirates*. The story states the "whole galaxy" has been explored. Yet based on evidence from many other stories, in which planets and civilisations are discovered long after this time, this must be an exaggeration or the exploration must be fairly rudimentary.

132 The Doctor watches the prospectus in *Paradise*

Out to the Stars

After mankind "had sacked the solar system they moved on to pastures new".[127] Twenty-first century ships still travelled slower than the speed of light and the crews were placed in suspended animation. It was not unusual to discover such ships many centuries later.[128] These were NAFAL ships, meaning Not As Fast As Light.[129] Huge Pioneer stations were set up, lining the way to the stars. They helped with refuelling and restocking of colony ships.[130]

Prospectors such as Dom Issigri and Milo Clancey were the first men into deep space. Clancey's ship, the "C" Class freighter LIZ 79, remained in service for forty years. Spacecraft at that time were built with the metal tillium and used a thermonuclear pile to supply power. Mined ore was sent to refineries in "floaters", slow unmanned vessels. An almost indestructible metal, argonite, was found on some of the planets in the fourth sector. Soon, all ships were made from argonite, which became the most valuable mineral known to man.

Clancey and Issigri became rich over the next fifteen years of working together, especially after they had spent ten years strip-mining the planet Ta in the Pliny system. Clancey became something of a legend on Reja Magnum. The partners eventually split, though, and Issigri went on to found the Issigri Mining Company.[131]

Robots such as the Robotic self-activating Megapodic Mark seven-Z Cleaners had some degree of autonomy. Scanners were developed that could track individuals. Miracle City had been masterpiece of the architect Kroagnon, but he refused to move out and let the residents sully his work by moving in. He was eventually forced out, but the booby-traps he left behind massacred many of the residents. Kroagnon fled to Earth, where he was allowed to build Paradise Towers. During the war, youngsters and oldsters were evacuated to the 304-storey building, where the authorities forgot all about them.[132]

The Colonial Age began in the 2090s. Multinational conglomerates started the Century Program, sending colony ships to a dozen worlds in the hope of alleviating the population crisis on Earth.[133]

Slow Century Class ships were sent into deep space - once they arrived at their destination they became useful space stations. Two such vessels, the Castor and the Pollux, were sent out into a demilitarised sector by the New Rome Institute to house dangerous criminals. Earth at this time was ruled by a World Minister. The Pacific Rim Co-operative was in conflict with the SubSaharan Autonomies. Quad fuel cars were operating.[134]

The prison planet Varos was established in the late twenty-first century to remove the criminally insane from galactic society.[135] The seven planets of the binary Meson system were colonised at this time.[136] The Pinkerton Intergalactic Agency of detectives soon followed colonists into space, solving crimes on colony worlds where law enforcement was often erratic or corrupt.[137]

Human Travellers fled oppression on Earth by stealing a ship. When human ships reached Arcturus Six, the Earth ambassador was told that Travellers had already landed on the planet.[138] Developers filled in the Serpentine in the late twenty-first century.[139] The corporation Imogen built a facility on Titan to clone generation two ubersoldaten. The Doctor visited this period to download Kadiatu's user manual.[140]

The Global Mining Corporation replaced the US Army, and provided military training for corporations. The world language was "International American".[141] **Galactic Salvage and Insurance went bankrupt in 2096.**[142] Kadiatu Lethbridge-Stewart would eventually acquire a Triangulum Swift 400, a ship built in the twenty-first century.[143]

The Doctor and Grant Markham went back to see the *New Hope* leave for the Centraxis system in 2100. Within ten years, the colonists aboard would found Grant's home planet of Agora.[144]

Towers and relates Kroagnon's story. The Chief Caretaker describes Kroagnon as a "being" rather than a "man", suggesting Kroagnon might be an alien. It's never specified that the tower block was built on Earth, but this seems to be the implication. In the novelisation, Paradise Towers is a space station, which it certainly isn't on screen. The war in question might be the conflict of *Warriors of the Deep* or the Thousand Day War first referred to in *Transit*.
133 *Killing Ground*
134 "At least a hundred years" before *Wooden Heart*.
135 *Vengeance on Varos*. The Governor notes that "Varos has been stable for more than two hundred years".

136 "They've come a long way in a hundred years" according to the Doctor in *Time of Your Life* (p27).
137 *Shakedown*
138 *Love and War* (p39).
139 *Birthright* (p189).
140 *The Also People* (p155, p191).
141 *The Face-Eater* (p64).
142 *Nightmare of Eden*
143 *So Vile a Sin*
144 "Ninety one years" before *Killing Ground*.

Mankind didn't develop particle guns until after the twenty-first century.[145]

The Twenty-Second Century

The Doctor flew a Spitfire in the twenty-second century.[146] He also took Victoria to the NovaLon Hypercities of the twenty-second century.[147] Vincent Grant, the Butcher of Strasbourg, unified the Western Alliance in the early twenty-second century.[148]

c 2100 - PARADISE TOWERS[149] -> Paradise Towers, a self-contained, award-winning tower block that had been abandoned during the war, was rediscovered in the early twenty-second century. With only old and young people in residence, society became stratified. The young girls became Kangs - with an array of "ice-hot" slang and "high fabsion" clothing - the old women became Rezzies and the Caretakers tried to maintain the building by rigidly sticking to their rulebook. Each group had a distinctive language, and each preyed mercilessly on the other. There were even reports of cannibalism.

The Kangs split into three rival factions - Red, Blue and Yellow - although "wipeouts" or "making unalive" was forbidden (as were visitors, ball games and fly posting).

Kroagnon's disembodied mind had been exiled to the Towers' basement, but he now possessed the Chief Caretaker using the science of corporal ectoscopy. He put the Towers' robotic cleaners to the task of eliminating the residents, but the various social factions united alongside the seventh Doctor and Mel. A war deserter, Pex, sacrificed himself to kill Kroagnon. Social order was restored, and Pex was remembered in various wallscrawls.

2105 was "a bit boring", according to the Doctor.[150] Grayvorn escaped the Imperial Museum when someone died there and he mentally inhabited their body. He resumed a position of authority within the Wardens and began instigating a series of socio-political changes on Artaris.[151]

c 2106 - "The Cruel Sea"[152] -> The ninth Doctor and Rose arrived on Mars, which at this time was a leisure planet with artificial seas for the ultra-rich to sail on. They'd landed on the yacht of Alvar Chambers, who

---

145 According to the Doctor in *Army of Ghosts*, although he might just mean they shouldn't have them at that point in the twenty-first century (2007).
146 *Last of the Gaderene* (p246). He also says he has flown a Spitfire in *Loups-Garoux*.
147 *Heart of TARDIS*
148 "Profits of Doom"
149 Dating *Paradise Towers* (24.2) - Paradise Towers has been abandoned for between about fifteen and twenty years, judging by the age of the Kangs. The Doctor's remark that the building won awards "way back in the twenty-first century" may or may not suggest that the story is set in the twenty-second. If we take the New Adventures into account, I would suggest that the War at Time Start might well be the Thousand-Day War that took place a generation before *Transit*. In *Lucifer Rising*, Adjudicator Bishop refers to the "messy consequences of the Kroagnon Affair" (p189), so it is set before then. *The Terrestrial Index* suggested that the war is the Dalek Invasion of Earth, and therefore set the story around 2164. *Timelink* sets the story in 2040.
150 *The End of the World*
151 *Excelis Decays*
152 Dating "The Cruel Sea" (*DWM* #359-362)- It's "the early twenty-second century". At one point, the Doctor says Rose is his fifty-seventh companion.
153 *Lucifer Rising* (p100, p320).
154 *Timewyrm: Revelation*
155 *Transit* (p157-158).
156 *Deceit* (p27-28).
157 Dating *Genocide* (EDA #4) - The date is given (p30).
158 *Speed of Flight, Genocide*
159 *Festival of Death*, possibly a reference to *Transit*.
160 *Memory Lane*
161 Dating *Transit* (NA #10) - The exact date of the story is not specified. The book takes many of its themes from *The Seeds of Death*, and is set at least a generation after that story. The Transit system has been established for at least the last couple of decades and has revolutionised the world - no television stories seem to be set during this period. It is hinted that the story takes place in the twenty-second century (p134). In his "Future History Continuity", *Transit* author Ben Aaronovitch places this story "c2109". *GodEngine*, following the Virgin version of this chronology, dated the story as "2109" (p1). *So Vile a Sin* gave the date as 2010, which would seem to be a misprint (p140).
162 *GodEngine*
163 *Nightmare of Eden*. This happens after *Transit*, but there's enough time before *Nightmare of Eden* to allow Tryst to explore and for Earth to found a colony on (at least) Azure. The starship *Empress* has left from Station Nine.
164 *Cold Fusion*. The planet was named as Salomon in the synopsis, but not the book.
165 The Interstellar Space Corps appears in *The Space Pirates*, the Marine Space Corps appears in *Death to the Daleks* and the Space Corps is referred to in *Nightmare of Eden*.

owned the air on Earth, the air on Io, air with lime and classic air. They were attacked by a protoplasmic replica of one of Chambers' ex-wives, and the Doctor deduced that the sea had become sentient. A dormant ancient Martian organism was revived by terraforming process.

2106 saw the Ozone Purge, the first sign that man had not solved the Earth's environmental problems. The Purge was caused by a breakdown of weather control technology, and a number of species - including such previously common creatures as sheep, cats and sparrows - were wiped out.[153]

During the twenty-second century, human babies were grown artificially to be used in scientific tests.[154] Yembe Lethbridge-Stewart died in 2106. His daughter buried him alongside his wife at Achebe Gorge on Mars.[155]

In 2107, Eurogen and the Butler Institute - relatively small corporations for the time - merged to become Eurogen Butler or the "EB Corporation". Eurogen was a major genetic research facility. After its near-collapse a century before, the Butler Institute had survived by specialising in artificial intelligence, meteorology and weather control. Both companies were expanding into the field of interplanetary exploration, and their services were now required on a dozen worlds.[156]

= 2108 (1st January) - GENOCIDE[157] **->** The eighth Doctor and Sam arrived on Earth in a deviant timeline in which humanity had been eradicated. The relatively passive Tractites now occupied Earth and had named it Paratractis. The Doctor and Sam travelled back to historical junctures 2.5 million years and 3.6 million years in the past to avert this history.

In July 2108, the Doctor visited Oxford Street and bought a Xavier Eugene microscope and a pair of wings in the sales.[158] Humanity developed the theory of hyperspace tunnels in the early twenty-second century.[159]

Marmadons were foul creatures that lived in deep space. A century after Kim Krontska, Tom Braudy and Samuel departed Earth, one such monster broke into their ship and killed Samuel. Tom and Kim revived from cryo-sleep and dealt with the creature, then learned they were far from home. Kim opted to re-enter stasis and return to Earth, but Tom feared a further attack and left in a coffin-shaped escape pod.

Tom crashed on the planet Lucentra, marking the first visit to that world by an extra-terrestrial. The natives were a technologically advanced race with dreadful long-term memories, meaning they readily forgot Tom's momentous arrival. Two Lucentran entrepreneurs, Lest and Argot, extended Tom's lifespan and kept him docile in a cell that re-created his childhood. In the decades to come, Lest and Argot would repeatedly haul Tom out of his cell and -

using schematics of his arrival - dramatically re-create his arrival for the forgetful Lucentrans' enjoyment.

The Lucentrans had also engineered a type of nano-form: tiny creatures with limited intelligence, designed to carry out very specific tasks. Many races developed this technology, which was inevitably derived from the nature of the species forging it. Thus, the nano-forms had no means of video playback and storage, but could convey images occurring in real time.[160]

c 2109 - TRANSIT[161] **->** The Union of Solar Republics attempted to build the first interstitial tunnel to another star system. The Stunnel would provide instantaneous travel to Arcturus II, twenty six light years away, and if successful would allow rapid colonisation of other planets. At the inauguration, though, disaster struck. The President was killed, and the Transit system began to show signs of instability. It became clear that the Transit system had attracted an intelligence from another dimension, and it was this that ensured the smooth running of the network. The intruder was banished, but it became clear that it was impossible to maintain Transit tunnels over interstellar distances.

Following activity on Mars at this time, a nest of Martians was revived and entered negotiations with humanity. FLORANCE, the first Artificial Intelligence to develop sentience, became a celebrity. Its rights were protected under the civil rights convention.

The Transit system was abandoned soon after this incident. The Martian castes debated making peace with Earth in 2110. Humans established two human cities on Mars: Jacksonville and Arcadia Planitia.[162] **Mankind discovered warp drive, allowing it to travel faster-than-light. Azure, in West Galaxy, was colonised and became a tourist destination. At least nine space Stations were set up. By now, contact with alien species was almost routine. The scientist Tryst aimed to "qualify and quantify every species in our galaxy".**[163]

An ice planet was discovered when a scientific expedition made a misjump through hyperspace. Marooned for three years, they established a colony run along rational lines. Three years later, when the rescue ships arrived, they elected to stay. Miners and other colonists arrived and were ruled by an elite of scientists, the Scientifica.[164]

The Space Corps was set up.[165]

In the early twenty-second century, the Guild of Adjudicators was established as a judicial force unrestrained by authority or financial dependence. They were based on the remote planet Ponten IV. Early successes for the "ravens" (so-named because of their black robes) included the execution of fifteen drug dealers on Callisto, the suppression of a revolution in Macedonia and the disciplinary eradication of the energy-wasting population on

Frinelli Minor. The Adjudicators also dealt with the Kroagnon Affair, vraxoin raids over Azure, the Macra case and the Vega debacle.[166] Adjudicator Bishop discovered Paradise Towers.[167]

Kadiatu Lethbridge-Stewart destroyed the Butterfly Wing, apparently committing suicide in the process ... although there were rumours that she had built a time machine.[168]

The first production line warships began to be built. Lagships were still used for many years on longer journeys, although the technology remained risky.[169]

The crusade of the Chapter of St Anthony was becoming notorious. Youths from the Initiate League torched the city of Urrozdinee when they refused to accept the rule of the Chapter. Shortly afterward, the crusade spread unop-

posed to the stars, in two mighty battleships capable of laying waste to whole planets and destroying small moons. The Chapter raided Titan, and recruited the malevolent dwarf Parva De Hooch. Shortly afterward, the Chapter returned to Earth and De Hooch killed his parents.[170]

Garazone Central was one of the first cities to 'float between the stars', and was located well away from Earth authorities, maintaining its own Space Patrol. The Garazone bazaar became a trading post for humans and aliens alike.[171]

Earth authorities imprisoned the geneticist Cauchemar for murdering people in his quest to achieve immortality. He was dispatched on a colony arkship to a prison world at the edge of the New Earth frontier, but the ship collided with a meteor en route and half the crew died. A race

---

166 The Master poses as an Adjudicator in *Colony in Space*, the only time the Adjudicators were referred to or seen on television. They feature a number of times in the New Adventures, and the Doctor's companions Cwej and Forrester are ex-Adjudicators. *Lucifer Rising* relates the foundation of the Guild of Adjudicators, and their early successes. I suggest that "the Macra case" (p189) can't be *The Macra Terror*, and so must be another encounter with that race. *Gridlock* would suggest that humanity had many encounters with the species.

167 *Lucifer Rising*. There's no indication how long after *Paradise Towers* this happened.

168 "Three years" after *Transit* (p260).

169 *Deceit* says that production line warships are being made by 2112 (p28). Suspended animation is seen in a number of New Adventures set after this time, including *Deceit*, *The Highest Science* and *Lucifer Rising*.

170 *St Anthony's Fire* (p195, p260). Urrozdinee first appeared in a short story of the same name by Mark Gatiss in Marvel's *1994 Doctor Who Yearbook*. In that story the city is a post-apocalyptic feudal state inhabiting the remains of EuroDisney.

171 *Sword of Orion*

172 Centuries before *Vanishing Point*. Arbitrary date.

173 The founding fathers of a planet are revered in *The Robots of Death*, *The Caves of Androzani* and the New Adventure *Parasite*. Earth colonies feature in many, many *Doctor Who* stories. The corporations' stranglehold over the early colonies is a theme touched on in many New Adventures, especially the "Future History Cycle" which ran from *Love and War* to *Shadowmind*.

174 The Arcadia colony was founded "three hundred and seventy-nine" (Arcadian?) years before the events of *Deceit* (p115). It was one of the first Spinward Settlements (p16) and the planet (or at least part of it) has been terra-formed (p103).

NAMING PLANETS: The planet Arcadia is referred to in "Profits of Doom", *Deceit* and *Doomsday*. In each case, this could be the same planet, as could the planets called Lucifer referred to in *Lucifer Rising* and *Bad Wolf*.

The same can't be said for "New Earth", though - there's a New Earth Frontier in *Vanishing Point*, a New Earth Republic in *Synthespians™*, a New Earth System in "Fire and Brimstone", and planets called New Earth in "Dogs of Doom", *Time of Your Life*, *The Romance of Crime* and, well, *New Earth* (seen again in *Gridlock*). From what we see of the planets, what we're told of their locations and the dates in which they're settled, these are *not* the same planets. It's a natural enough name for a human colony, of course.

175 *The Infinity Race*

176 *The Highest Science*

177 The Doctor says he visited Androzani Major when "it was becoming rather developed" in *The Caves of Androzani*. In *The Power of Kroll*, we see the third moon of Delta Magna. (It is called "Delta III" in the novelisation and *Original Sin*, p21.)

THE SIRIUS SYSTEM: In *Frontier in Space,* the Master poses as a Commissioner from Sirius IV and accuses the Doctor and Jo of landing a spaceship in an unauthorised area on Sirius III. According to Romana in *City of Death*, Sirius V is the home of the Academia Stellaris, an art gallery she rates more highly than the Louvre. In *The Caves of Androzani*, Morgus is the chairman of the Sirius Conglomerate based on Androzani Major, and spectrox is found on its twin planet Androzani Minor. These two facts make Morgus the "richest man in the Five Planets". We might infer that these are the five planets of the Sirius system, and that Androzani Major and Minor are Sirius I and II. The Doctor once had a sneg stew in a bistro on Sirius Two, according to *Island of Death*.

178 *The Space Pirates*

179 *Lucifer Rising* (p84).

180 *The Highest Science* (p102).

181 *The Face-Eater* (p40).

182 "Several hundred years" after Charley's time (the 1930s), according to *Sword of Orion*.

183 *GodEngine* (p73).

184 Dating *Nightmare of Eden* (17.4) - Galactic Salvage and Insurance went bankrupt "twenty years ago"

of benevolent aliens appeared and offered to save the survivors from dying of radiation poisoning. With Cauchemar's help, the aliens transformed the humans into hosts for their own criminals.

The hybrids were seeded onto an unnamed planet, lacking knowledge of their previous identities. Those who lived commendable existences passed into the afterlife; those who didn't were reincarnated to try again. The colony started losing population as souls were redeemed. "The Creator" was a semi-sentient entity that oversaw this process.

Cauchemar's experiments had rendered him unsuitable as a host, and he was sent away from the planet. He returned to find his lover Jasmine among the reincarnated populace, but his "alien" presence disrupted the Creator and killed her. A distraught Cauchemar consequently worked to bring the Creator to ruin, hoping this would force the Creator to "recognise" his soul.[172]

Because interstellar travel and communications were still relatively slow, colony planets were often left to their own devices. The founding fathers of these worlds were often important, and all sorts of political and social experimentation was attempted.

Many colonies were set up and directly controlled by the corporations, and many others were reliant on them for communications, transport and technology.[173] The EB Corporation was among the first to offer an escape from Earth in their warship, *The Back to Nature*, which was commissioned in 2112. Arcadia was a temperate planet, the second in its system, and was less than a thousand light-years from Earth. A number of years previous, the EB Corporation had set up a survey camp on the planet, the site of which would become the capital city Landfall, and set about terraforming the world. The planet came to resemble medieval Europe, and was ready for the first influx of colonists. Arcadia eventually became the Corporation's centre of operations.[174]

Early during earth's interstellar expansion, a colony ship landed on Demigest and contact was lost. A rescue mission was also wiped out, but only after one member, Trudeau, dictated a log entry that became known as *The Black Book of Demigest*. Space and time never settled on Demigest as they did on most other worlds. The original colonists mutated to become the Warlocks of Demigest, and obtained great powers.[175]

No intelligent life was discovered on the outskirts of the galaxy, where the stars and planets were sparse. Before long, man abandoned all attempts to venture out past Lasty's Nebula. Instead, mankind's colonisation efforts focused towards the centre of the galaxy - "the hub", as it became known. A thriving interplanetary community grew up.

Around this time, the planet Evertrin was the site of the annual Inner Planets Music Festival, known as "Ragasteen". The biggest bands in space attended to plug their discods: Deep Space, M'Troth, The Great Mothers of Matra, Is Your Baby a God and Televised Instant Death were all at Ragasteen 2112.

The riggers on Earth changed the style of music every three years to keep it fresh. Zagrat, for example, were very popular during the "headster time", but teenagers found their discod "Sheer Event Shift" embarrassing just a few years later.[176]

Worlds such as the five planets of the Sirius System and Delta Magna rapidly became industrialised and overpopulated.[177] Burglars began to use computers, forcing people to install audio locks.[178] Tourism on Earth was a thing of the past.[179] The lethal drink Bubbleshake, invented by the unscrupulous Joseph-Robinson corporation, was originally an appetite suppressant. Unchecked, it was addictive, leading to memory loss, hyperactivity and compulsive behaviour. The substance was eventually outlawed.[180]

Earth discovered universal concrete in 2115.[181] Welford Jeffery invented antigrav technology.[182] In 2115, human archaelogists found the Martian city of Ikk-ett-Saleth completely abandoned.[183]

2116 - NIGHTMARE OF EDEN[184] ->

Interplanetary standards and conventions were set up that applied to the whole of Human Space. The Galactic Credit (z) was established as a convertible interplanetary currency. Credits resembled colourful blocks of plastic, and were used for every sort of transaction from buying a drink to funding an expedition to a new planet. None of this prevented a recession from hitting the galactic economy.

Laser technology advanced during this period. Stun laser weapons became available for the first time. Entuca lasers capable of carrying millions of signals were now used for telecommunications. Finally, vast amounts of information could now be recorded on laser data crystals.

Crime was a problem in the galaxy. Drug trafficking increased when the drug XYP, or Vraxoin, was discovered. Vrax addicts felt a warm complacency at first, followed by total apathy. They also became thirsty. Inevitably, its effects were fatal. The narcotic ruined whole planets and communities until the planet that was the only known source of the drug was incinerated. A Vraxoin merchant (drug trafficker) risked the death penalty if caught. Molecular scanners were developed that could detect even minute quantities of the drug. All citizens were required to carry an ident-plaque.

Interplanetary tourism developed at this time. Government-subsidised interstellar cruise liners, each holding 900 passengers, travelled between Station

Nine and Azure. Passengers could travel either economy or first class, the former seated in "pallets" and forced to wear protective clothing, the latter allowed a great deal more freedom and luxury.

The scientist Tryst attempted to qualify and quantify every lifeform in the galaxy. As Tryst's log (published to coincide with a series of lectures given by the zoologist) recounted, his ten-man expedition travelled to Zil, Vij, Darp, Lvan, Brus, the windswept planet Gidi and the temperate world Ranx. Finally, Tryst's ship, the *Volante*, travelled past the Cygnus Gap to the three-planet system of M37. The second planet contained primitive life: molluscs, algae and insects. As well as taking visprints, they used a CET machine.

Six months before arriving at Azure, the *Volante* visited the planet Eden. On the planet they lost a member of the crew, Stott, who was secretly working for the Intelligence Section of the Space Corps. It was later discovered that Mandrells from the planet Eden decomposed into Vraxoin when they died, and that Tryst had partnered with Dymond, the pilot of the *Hecate*, to smuggle the material. The two of them were arrested.

2118 (April) - THE ART OF DESTRUCTION[185] ->
Earth risked famine, and Agriculture Technology research was underway to prevent this. The tenth Doctor and Rose thwarted the Wurms in Chad, but the Wurms had tracked down a warren of their archenemies - the Valnaxi - to Earth.

During the second and third decade of the twenty-second century, the Western Alliance banks foreclosed on Earth and the World Civilian Police Corps was formed. The Oceanic-Nippon bloc was working on interstellar flight, and the first supra-light vessel *New Horizon* was launched in 2126, taking five thousand colonists on a two-year journey to Proxima 2, the first colony in an alien environment. Proxima City was founded there. The second human colony world was called Earth 2.

UNIT had been disbanded by this time. The records of Global Mining Corporation list the Doctor as a security consultant from 2127 (adding that his female companion graduated Geneva Corporate University in 2124) following an unrecorded incident in Albania.[186] The Particle Matter Transmission (Deregulation) Act was passed in 2122.[187] The first humans to arrive on Hitchemus, a plan-

according to Captain Rigg, who had just read a monitor giving the date of the bankruptcy as "2096". *In-Vision* suggested that Azure is in "West Galaxy", but I think this is a mishearing of Rigg's (fluffed) line "you'll never work in *this* galaxy again". While others have disagreed with that, there is certainly no on screen justification for *The Discontinuity Guide*'s "Western Galaxy". *The TARDIS Logs* gave the date as "c.2100", *The Doctor Who File* as "2113".
185 Dating *The Art of Destruction* (NSA #11) - The Doctor says it's "the eleventh of April 2118".
186 *The Face-Eater*. The dates given in the book seem to contradict a number of other stories set around this time.
187 *Cold Fusion*
188 The space port has been open a hundred years before *The Year of Intelligent Tigers*
189 *State of Decay*. No date is given. On screen, one computer monitor seems to suggest that the computer was programmed on the "12/12/1998", but the *Hydrax* is clearly an interstellar craft. *The TARDIS Logs* suggested a date in "the 36th Century", *The Terrestrial Index* placed it "at the beginning of the 22nd".
190 *Lucifer Rising* (p59, p272-273).
191 *The Taking of Planet 5* (p15).
192 *Spiral Scratch*
193 Dating *The Face-Eater* (EDA #18) - The date is given (p126).
194 *St Anthony's Fire*
195 *The Taint*
196 *The Face-Eater*
197 Dating *The Space Pirates* (6.6) - A monitor readout

in Part Two suggests that the year is "1992", but this contradicts dialogue stating that prospectors have been in deep space for "fifty years". No other date is given on screen. The *Radio Times* said that the story takes place in "the far future". Earth is mentioned once in the first episode, but after that only a "homeworld" is referred to. The force here is specified as the Interstellar Space Corps. The regulatory actions of the government suggest that space travel is becoming more common now, but is still at an early stage.

As Zoe is unfamiliar with the technology of this story, it is almost certainly set after her time. The Main Boost Drive is not very advanced, and this story almost certainly takes place well before *Frontier In Space*, where hyperdrive technology is common. At the start of the story, the V41-LO is both "fifty days" and "fifty billion miles" from Earth, I assume here that writer Robert Holmes means "billion" in the British sense of a million million, rather than the American (and now generally accepted British) thousand million. If this is the case, then the Beacon is 8.3 Light Years from Earth (otherwise it is a thousandth of this distance, and only just outside the Solar System).

The Programme Guide set the story "c.2600". *The Terrestrial Index* suggested it was "during the Empire" period. *The TARDIS Logs* claimed a date of "8751". *Timelink* suggested "2146", *About Time* "2135ish".
198 The Issigri Mining Company appears in *The Space Pirates*. Another company with the same initials, the Interplanetary Mining Company, is seen in *Colony in Space*. In the Missing Adventure *The Menagerie*, we

et on the edge of explored space, were hunters in pursuit of the tigers that lived there. The colony of Port Any was built shortly afterward. It became famed for music and attracted musicians from across human space.[188]

The exploration vessel *Hydrax* was lost en route to Beta Two in the Perugellis Sector. Its officers included Captain Miles Sharkey, science officer Anthony O'Connor and navigation officer Lauren Macmillan. It fell through a CVE into the pocket universe of E-Space.[189] The *Hydrax* disappeared around 2127. The InterSpace Incorporated ship had a crew of two hundred and forty-three. InterSpace refused to pay out pensions for the lost crew, claiming they might be found. IMC later claimed to have discovered traces of the ship in order to blackmail Piper O'Rourke - whose husband Ben had been an engineer on the *Hydrax* - into revealing details about the Eden Project. The ship was never discovered.[190]

The planet Vulcan suddenly vanished in 2130.[191]

= In one alternate universe, the USA had been devastated by a hydrogen accident. Racing spaceships around the solar system was a spectator sport by 2130.[192]

2130 - THE FACE-EATER[193] **->** The eighth Doctor and Sam discovered the F-Seeta, a telepathic gestalt of the rat-like natives, was responsible for a series of murders on the first human colony world of Proxima 2. The colony was saved, but at the cost of the Proximans' group mind.

On Betrushia around the year 2133, as it had done many times over the centuries, war broke out between the Ismetch and the Cutch. Millions died in the conflict, which became the longest and most bitter struggle the planet had seen for three hundred years. The Ismetch had an early success at Dalurida Bridge under Portrone Ran.[194]

The Doctor, Sam and Fitz arrived in London during the summer of 2134, and confirmed that the Earth was free of the Beast.[195] A second wave of colonists was expected on Proxima 2 in 2136.[196]

? 2135 - THE SPACE PIRATES[197] **->** As space travel became more common, the Earth Government introduced a series of regulations to better control the space lanes in its territory. Space was divided into administrative and strategic Sectors. All flights now had to be logged with Central Flight Information and a network of Mark Five Space Beacons were established to monitor space traffic. The Interstellar Space Corps was given the latest V-Ships, armed with state-of-the-art Martian Missiles (H-bombs were considered old-fashioned by this time) and carrying squadrons of Minnow Fighters. The V-Ships were powered by Maximum Boost atomic motors. The Space Corps routinely used

mind probes to interrogate their prisoners. The resources of the Space Corps were stretched very thin: they fought brush wars in three sectors, acted as customs and excise officials and attempted to curtail the activities of space pirates.

For two years, pirates were active in the Ta System and hijacked five of Milo Clancey's floaters, each of which contained 50,000 tons of argonite ore. Despite a dozen requests, the Space Corps did little to help. As an old-timer, Clancey was suspicious of authority; he had lost his registration documents thirty years before and he didn't maintain his feedback link to CFI.

The Space Corps became involved when the pirates began to break up government space beacons to steal the argonite. The V41-LO was more than fifty days out of Earth, under the command of General Nikolai Hermack, Commander of the Space First Division. The ship was ninety minutes away from Beacon Alpha 4 when it was broken up by pirates. Clancey's ship was detected nearby, and he was questioned but quickly released. The Doctor, Jamie and Zoe were recovered from Beacon Alpha 4, but they too were innocent.

The real culprit was Maurice Caven. His pirates were organised enough to equip themselves with Beta Dart ships, costing one hundred million credits each, that could outrun virtually everything else in space. He killed anyone who got in his way and one of his men, Dervish, had spent ten years working for Earth Government and knew all the Space Corps' techniques.

Some time ago, Caven had kidnapped Dom Issigri and blackmailed his beautiful daughter Madeline, the head of the Issigri Mining Company, into providing facilities for him on the planet Ta. The Corps hunted Caven down and executed him.

After this, the Issigri Mining Company was renamed the Interplanetary Mining Company, or IMC for short.[198] Humanity's contact with the Arcturans was proving fruitful. The Arcturans allowed limited human settlement in their sector, and supplied humanity with specialised drugs. Some humans became interested in studying Arcturan literature.

On Earth, however, things were getting desperate. The Islam-dominated Earth Central, based in Damascus and led by an elected president, was unable to prevent society from collapsing. An unprecedented Energy Crisis led to draconian restrictions on consumption and the foundation of the Energy Police. The invention of the vargol generator did little to relieve the demands for fuel.

In 2137, with Earth desperate for energy, corporations successfully lobbied for the repeal of all the anti-pollution laws brought in over the last century and a quarter. Three years later, an American subsidiary of Panorama Chemicals

filled the Carlsbad Caverns with plastic waste, and the oceans of the world were a sludge of industrial effluent. Mineral water became a precious commodity. The whale finally became extinct, and auto-immune diseases - "the plague" of over a century before - returned.

Despite this, human life expectancy was now one hundred and ten years, and the population was soaring. Although it had religious objections to gambling, Earth Central introduced the Eugenics Lottery, and couples were forbidden from having children unless they won.[199]

A string of fundamentalist Jihads killed many people on Earth.[200]

A colony ship made landfall on the planet Avalon in the year 2145. The colonists discovered an ancient Avalonian technology which at first allowed them to perform miracles, but soon rendered their electronic equipment useless. The colony regressed to a medieval level, in which certain people - unknowingly able to tap the Avelonian technology - performed "magic".[201]

Dolphins' ability to think in three dimensions made them ideal pilots for Earth's first interstellar fighters.[202]

2146 - THE MURDER GAME[203] **->** The European Government and the Terran Security Forces (TSF) were established by this time. The First Galactic Treaty had been signed. The Selachians had menaced Terra Alpha.

The second Doctor, Ben and Polly answered a distress call and landed in the Hotel Galaxian, a space station in Earth orbit. Two scientists, Neville and Dorothy Adler, were trying to sell assassination software to the Selachians. Neville Adler was killed and the space hotel burned up in the atmosphere. Dorothy Adler could not work the program without her husband.

In 2146, the American economy collapsed, and there were food riots.[204] The Doctor was in America at the time, and he was powerless to stop cannibals from killing Sonia Bannen shortly after she saved her son. Mark Bannen was placed on board a huge colony ship bound for a new star system. The stardrive misphased in the Elysium System and the colony ship crashed there.[205]

The Daleks Discover Earth

c 2146 - "The Daleks: The Terrorkon Harvest"[206] **->** On Skaro, one of the unknown creatures from the Lake of Mutations, the Terrorkon, attacked an underwater Dalek defence station. The Emperor and the Red Dalek watched as another mutation attacked it, saving the city.

& 2146 - "The Daleks: Legacy of Yesteryear"[207] **->** The Daleks begin a new survey of their home planet, discovering mineral riches and wiping out a race of sand crea-

learn that they are the same company (p161). The change of name must have occurred before *Lucifer Rising*, when we see IMC in action.

199 *Lucifer Rising*. The evil polluting company in the television version of *The Green Death* is called "Global Chemicals". A real company of that name objected, and the name was changed in the novelisation to "Panorama Chemicals".

200 *Fear Itself*

201 *The Sorcerer's Apprentice* (p203-204).

202 *Heritage* (p198).

203 Dating *The Murder Game* (PDA #2) - The date is given (p12).

204 *Lucifer Rising* (p158).

205 *Parasite*

206 Dating "The Daleks: The Terrorkon Harvest" (*TV21* #70-75) - There's no indication how long after "Impasse" this *TV Century 21* Dalek story is set, allowing the first significant gap in the narrative. The next story, "Legacy of Yesteryear", is set "centuries" after the first (which seems to be set in 1763 AD). The novel *GodEngine* notes that the Daleks became concerned with Earth ten years before they invade, and that's exactly what we see happening in these strips, so I've used the novel to establish the dating of these stories. This block of stories ends with the Daleks discovering Earth of the future and gearing up to invade - clearly a reference to *The*

Dalek Invasion of Earth.

207 Dating "The Daleks: Legacy of Yesteryear" (*TV21* #76-85) - It is "centuries" since the original Daleks were frozen - and that happened the day of the meteorite strike that set off the neutron bomb (seen in "Genesis of Evil"). The Daleks remember Yarvelling and his inventions. So there are "centuries" between "Impasse" and "The Terrorkon Harvest".

208 Dating "The Daleks: Shadow of Humanity" (*TV21* #86-89) - There is no indication how long it has been since "Legacy of Yesteryear". The Emperor now knows about "human beings", although it's unclear when he heard the name - perhaps fragments of evidence were discovered in the wreckage of Lodian's ship after the previous story. The following stories all seem to take place without lengthy gaps between them.

209 Dating "The Daleks: The Emissaries of Jevo" (*TV21* #90-95) - At the end of the story, the Emperor praises Kirid's "human spirit", and before that Kirid seems to call himself "human", although he looks more like a humanoid alien (he has forehead ridges, like a Klingon). Given that the next story features a spaceship from Earth, we are now definitely in the future.

210 Dating "The Daleks: The Road to Conflict" (*TV21* #96-104) - The story is set soon after "The Emissaries of Jevo". There's no date given, but this story features an interstellar human passenger spacecraft, and the peo-

tures. One hoverbout inadvertently revived the group of original Daleks who had been in suspended animation for centuries, since the neutron explosion. These were the scientists Lodian, Zet and Yvric, who quickly determined that the new Daleks were without conscience. Even so, Yvric was keen to join the Daleks, but they exterminated him before he could even explain who he was. Zet realised that the Daleks would want to know about the Earth, a planet teeming with life and energy, and handed himself and Lodian over to them. Lodian escaped to a spaceship, planning to warn Earth of the Daleks. The spaceship exploded, killing the last two original Daleks and preserving the secret of Earth's existence.

& 2146 - "The Daleks: Shadow of Humanity"[208] ->
The Emperor ordered the building of a road to the Lake of Mutations, but one Dalek questioned the order and sabotaged the destruction of "beautiful" plant life. The Emperor feared that the introduction of human qualities could prove a disaster to the Daleks. The rebel Dalek exploited the natural Dalek to obey by issuing a new command to "protect beauty", and soon led a faction of Daleks as their Emperor. The Emperor quickly reasserted his power and destroyed the rebel.

& 2146 - "The Daleks: The Emissaries of Jevo"[209]
-> A space expedition from Jevo headed to Arides to prevent the spread of deadly pollen from that world. Their ship passed close to Skaro, and was snared by the Daleks' magnetrap. The Emperor assumed the pollen wouldn't affect Daleks, but the Jevonian leader Kirid tricked him into thinking otherwise. Kirid saved the universe from the pollen, but was tracked down and killed by the Daleks ... who nevertheless had started to worry about the strength of the human spirit.

& 2146 - "The Daleks: The Road to Conflict"[210] ->
The Daleks engineered a meteorite storm that damaged the Earth passenger ship *Starmaker*, which made a forced landing on Skaro. The Emperor was now obsessed with finding Earth - a planet hidden from Skaro by "skycurve" - as he was convinced that it was rich in polar magnetism and aluminium. Captain Fleet was captured and rescued

by the children Jennie and Tom, but the Daleks destroyed the *Starmaker*. The three humans escaped in a Dalek transport ship to warn humanity about the Daleks... but the Daleks had now discovered the location of Earth, and planned its conquest.

& 2146 - "The Daleks: Return of the Elders"[211] ->
The Daleks attacked Colony Five on Titan, and experimented on six humans as another alien fleet entered the solar system. The mysterious aliens identified themselves as Elders, and explained that they have tended Earth and warned that the Daleks would soon invade. The Earthmen destroyed one Dalek ship in the rings of Saturn, but another escaped. The Dalek Emperor vowed not to fail in his second attempt to conquer Earth.

By 2146, the Supreme Council of the Daleks had become concerned by the rapid expansion of humanity. They would monitor the situation carefully for ten years. The Martian Axis sprang up on Mars and turned to terrorism, bombing Coventry.[212]

3D cameras were developed around this time.[213]

2148 - ST ANTHONY'S FIRE[214] -> A mothership of the Chapter of St Anthony moved to pacify Betrushia, breaking up the planet's artificial ring system to wrack Betrushia with meteorites. Loosed from its shackles, the organic catalyzer became active and threatened all life that it encountered. The seventh Doctor convinced the Chapter as to the creature's threat, and arranged for Betrushia's destruction while instigating an evacuation. Appalled by the Chapter's zealous actions, Bernice and Ace sabotaged the mothership's engines, crippling it to suffer the same destruction as Betrushia and the organism. The Doctor helped the Betrushia survivors relocate to the sister planet of Massatoris.

Earth funded a small Transit station on Charon, a moon of Pluto. The Martian Axis terrorists destroyed the Montreal monorail system, resulting in many deaths.[215]

The Arcturans attacked the Martian colony on Cluut-ett-Pictar.[216] A pre-modernist architectural revival occurred in the mid-twenty-second century.[217]

---

ple have never heard of the Daleks. So this is set before *The Dalek Invasion of Earth*, almost certainly in the first half of the twenty-second century, which fits in with later televised stories such as *Nightmare of Eden*.

211 Dating "The Daleks: Return of the Elders" (*DWM* #249-254) - This was a sequel to the *TV Century 21* strip. It is set straight after "The Road to Conflict". The Daleks attack the solar system, but it ends in failure. The Emperor vows to succeed next time - and that is almost certainly what happens, as we discover in *The Dalek*

Invasion of Earth.
212 "10.6 human years" and "about ten years" before *GodEngine* (p107, p168).
213 *Frontier Worlds*
214 Dating *St Anthony's Fire* (NA #31) - The Doctor tells Bernice that the year is "2148" (p39).
215 "Five years" before *GodEngine* (p15, p98, p193).
216 *GodEngine*
217 *Cold Fusion*

c 2150 - "The Grief"[218] -> The seventh Doctor and Ace landed on the dead planet Sorshan and met some marines from the Earth starship *Rosetta*. They worked for the Cartographic Historical Exploratory Service (CHEX). A device used the marines as material to recreate the voracious Lom - the Doctor and Ace escaped as the planetary shield and toxin were reactivated, killing the aggressors.

In the 2150s, the Cybermen invaded the colony world of Agora, making it one of their breeding colonies. Human Overseers were in charge of harvesting people to become Cybermen.[219] The totalitarian Inner Party seized power in the city-state Excelis, and assassinated the Imperial Family. More than a century and a half of oppression ensued. Grayvorn pushed other city-states into open conflict, fueling a technology race.[220]

Earth's Colonial Marines fought in civil wars on the Outer Planets in the Arcturus system.[221] In 2156, Supreme Grand Marshall Falaxyr of Mars contacted the Daleks and offered them the GodEngine, an Osirian weapon that could destroy whole planets and stars. In return, he asked for Ice Warrior sovereignty of Mars. The Daleks accepted the offer.[222] By this time, mankind invented the Simularity, a holographic virtual reality.[223]

c 2157 - LUCIFER RISING[224] -> Earth encountered the Legions, a seven-dimensional race from Epsilon Eridani. Trading agreements were set up between the Legions and IMC. The Legions' sector of space was threatened by an unknown alien fleet, so IMC would supply the Legions with weaponry in return for advanced technology. Some Legions began working for IMC.

Earlier in the century, a Von Neumann probe had discovered a stable element with a very high mass in the core of the planet Lucifer, a gas giant two hundred and eighty light years from Earth. Theoretically, such an element could be used as a rich energy source. In 2152, Earth Central invested heavily in a scientific research station - the Eden Project - on Belial, one of the moons of Lucifer.

This was the era when Company Shock Troops - military men armed with neutron cannons, flamers, burners and screamers - took part in infamous corporate raids. In '56, IMC asset-stripped InterSpace Incorporated in Tokyo using armoured skimmers and Z-Bombs. Legend has it that companies used to capture employees of rival corporations and experiment on them. It was a risky life - on one raid in '51 praxis gas was used - but on average it paid four times more than Earth Central. The big human corporations learnt lessons from the aggressive capitalist races

---

218 Dating "The Grief" (*DWM* #185-187) - The date isn't specified. CHEX is an agency of the Sol Government; it has energy weapons and genetic fabrication units. It appears to be a story set early in humanity's exploration efforts.
219 *Killing Ground* (p15).
220 *Excelis Decays*
221 *GodEngine* (p18).
222 "A year" before *GodEngine*.
223 *Lucifer Rising, GodEngine*
224 Dating *Lucifer Rising* (NA #14) - The story takes place in the mid-twenty-second century, shortly before the Dalek Invasion of Earth. The Adjudicators' simularity registers the Doctor's arrival as "19/11/2154" (p30), Paula Engado's death as "22/2/2154" (p174) and her wake as "23/2/2154" (p13). Ace and Benny had expressed the desire to "pop back to the year twenty-one fifty-four or so" (p338), so at first sight it might appear that the story is set in 2154. However, this is inconsistent with the Dalek Invasion, which the authors of *Lucifer Rising* place in "twenty-one fifty-eight" (p337). On p195, there's mention of a raid "in Tokyo in fifty-six". I set the story in 2157, consistent with my dating for the Dalek Invasion.
225 *The Dalek Invasion of Earth*, with the date established in *The Daleks' Master Plan*.
226 According to the Doctor in *The Dalek Invasion of Earth*.
THE MIDDLE PERIOD OF DALEK HISTORY: Taking the Doctor's analysis at face value, the Middle Period of

Dalek history might be the time when their power is at its zenith - they are technologically advanced, expansionist and feared. In the words of the Doctor in *Death to the Daleks*, they are "one of the greatest powers in the universe".

In the Virgin edition of this book, I speculated that it coincided with the Daleks developing an internal power supply - in *The Daleks* they took static electricity up through the floor and so couldn't leave their city. In *The Dalek Invasion of Earth*, they had a disc resembling a satellite dish fastened to their backs: the Doctor and Ian speculate that it allows them free movement. In the first two Dalek stories, they have "bands" rather than the "slats" seen in all other stories. In *The Power of the Daleks*, they are dependent on a static electricity generator. In all subsequent stories - all of which (apart from the prototypes seen in *Genesis of the Daleks*) have Daleks originating from after *The Dalek Invasion of Earth* - none of these restrictions seem to apply. We are explicitly told they move via "psychokinetic power" in *Death to the Daleks*.

The Daleks are confined to the First Segment of Time, according to *The Ark*. We might speculate that the end of the Middle Period of Dalek history comes with either their defeat at the hands of the Movellans (*Resurrection of the Daleks*) or shortly afterward with Skaro's destruction (*Remembrance of the Daleks*).

As we've now seen the end of Dalek history (the Daleks withdrawing from history to fight the Time War, as recounted by Jack in *Bad Wolf*), we can perhaps spec-

such as the Cimliss, Usurians and the Okk. But humanity proved capable of callousness that would put all three of those races to shame.

Six years after it was set up, the Eden Project had still not borne fruit, and pressure was growing to close it down. As Earth's government grew weaker and weaker, the corporations were flexing their muscles: an IMC fleet of over one hundred ships was sent to Belial Base when the scientists reported some progress. This prompted the intelligent species of Lucifer, the Angels, to set up an exclusion zone around their world.

The Corporations had reached new levels of ruthlessness. IMC tripled the price of the fuel zeiton, and an impoverished Earth Central could no longer afford it. Earth was declared bankrupt and fell into the hands of its receivers: the Earth Alliance of Corporations, a holding company that was in reality the board of directors from all the corporations that traded off-Earth. It was a bloodless coup, and the megacorporations took formal control of the homeworld for the first time. Their reign lasted just under six months.

The Dalek Invasion of Earth

In 2157, the Daleks invaded Earth.[225] This was the Middle Period of Dalek history.[226]

An Astronaut Fair was held in London. The city was a beautiful metropolis, complete with moving pavements and a gleaming new nuclear power station alongside the historic Battersea Power Station.[227]

On the very same day that an Earth embassy opened on Alpha Centauri V, a billion settlers were exterminated on Sifranos in the Arcturus Sector. Fourteen other colonies were wiped out in a three-week period, including Azure and Qartopholos. Rumours of a mysterious alien fleet massing at the Legion homeworld of Epsilon Eridani were denied, but the Interstellar Taskforce was put on permanent standby, and a Space Fleet flotilla sent to that planet

was completely destroyed. The alien fleet was a Dalek armada, the Black Fleet, which was annihilating any colony that might render aid to the human homeworld, and systematically destroying Earth's warships.[228]

Meteorites began to bombard the Earth. Scientists dismissed it as a freak cosmic storm, but people started to die from a mysterious plague. The Daleks were targeting the Earth, and soon the populations of Asia, Africa and South America were wiped out. Only a handful of people had resistance to the plague, and although scientists quickly developed a new drug, it was too late. The world was split into tiny communities.[229]

Millions started dying of a mysterious virus in Brazilia, Los Angeles and Tycho City. Some humans showed a mysterious resistance to the plague - because the Doctor had seeded the atmosphere with an antidote.[230] The Daleks' Black Fleet destroyed Void Station Cassius while entering the Solar System.[231]

Six months after the plague began, the first of the Dalek saucers landed. Some cities were razed to the ground, others simply occupied. Anyone who resisted was destroyed. Dalek saucers patrolled the skies. Ruthlessly suppressing any resistance, the Daleks subdued India. The leaders of every race and nation on Earth were exterminated.[232]

The Daleks quickly defeated the Terran Security Forces. Many Americans evacuated to Canada.[233] **New York was destroyed.[234]** Baltimore was reduced to ruins.[235] The Daleks exterminated the last monarch of Britain.[236] The royal bloodline would continue at least until the forty-third century.[237]

A supersaucer landed on Luton, crushing the city.[238] The Daleks mounted a victory parade in London, in front of the Houses of Parliament and Westminster Bridge.[239] The Daleks blockaded the Solar System. The Bureau of Adjudicators on Oberon, a moon of Uranus, tried to work out the Daleks' plan. The Adjudicators detected mysteri-

---

ulate that the "early period" Daleks have bands and are dependent on externally-generated static electricity; the "middle period" Daleks are the slatted ones familiar from the original TV series and now we can add the "late period" Daleks seen in the new television series, which seem significantly more mobile and advanced than their forebears.
227 *The Dalek Invasion of Earth*
228 The Arcturus attacks take place at "the beginning of the year" according to *Lucifer Rising*. Sifranos is also mentioned in *GodEngine*.
229 *The Dalek Invasion of Earth, Legacy of the Daleks*.
230 *Lucifer Rising*
231 *GodEngine* (p3).
232 *The Dalek Invasion of Earth*

233 *The Final Sanction* (p75, p178).
234 According to Vicki in *The Chase* and *Salvation* (p58). *The Indestructible Man* said New York was destroyed in a nuclear assault in 2068, but it was evidently rebuilt. Even after its second devastation it seems to recover somewhat, as *Fear Itself* says that New York's waterways are a tourist attraction near the end of the twenty-second century.
235 *Nekromanteia*
236 *Legacy of the Daleks* (p45).
237 *The Mutant Phase*, although this occurs in an alternate timeline.
238 *GodEngine* (p107).
239 *Head Games* (p157).

ous signals at the Martian North Pole. Oberon continued to serve as a secret human military base throughout the invasion.[240]

The Daleks invaded Mars, but were defeated when a virus ate through their electrical cables.[241] The Daleks retaliated by releasing a virus that consumed all the oxygen in the atmosphere, and it would take decades to make the air breathable again.

Chainswords were used to fight the Daleks.[242]

2157 - GODENGINE[243] **->** The seventh Doctor and Roz arrived on Mars, but Chris ended up on Pluto's moon of Charon after the TARDIS hit a subspace infarction. The Daleks bombed Charon, but Chris escaped down a Transit stunnel. The Doctor and Roz accompanied an expedition to the North Pole of Mars, which was joined by Ice Warrior pilgrims. Meanwhile, at the pole, the Martian leader Falaxyr was about to complete the GodEngine, a device capable of making suns expel plasma bursts. Falaxyr hoped to negotiate with the Daleks to regain control of Mars. The Doctor arrived at the pole and defeated Falaxyr's amended plan to eliminate the human colony of Jacksonville. The GodEngine was destroyed, and Dalek ships shot down Falaxyr as he fled.

Once the population of Earth was under control, the Daleks set to work in vast mining areas, the largest one covering the whole of Bedfordshire. There were few Daleks on Earth, and they boosted their numbers by enslaving humans and converting them into Robomen. Robo Patrols swarmed across the major cities, armed with whips and machine guns, and controlled by high frequency radio waves.

The Daleks cleared the smaller settlements of people and set them to work in the mines. In the larger cities, Robomen and Daleks patrolled every nook and cranny looking for survivors. The Black Dalek oversaw the mining operations in Bedfordshire. At night, his "pet", the gruesome Slyther, patrolled the camp, attacking and eating any humans it found trying to escape.

The rebels in London survived by dodging Robo Patrols, raiding warehouses and department stores. Other threats came from escaped zoo animals, packs of wild dogs, human scavengers and traitors. The largest rebel group, under the leadership of the crippled scientist Dortmun, could only muster a fighting force of between fifteen and twenty and survived in an underground bolthole. They had a radio, although as time went by contact was lost with more and more rebel

240 *GodEngine*

241 *Genesis of the Daleks*. It is confirmed in *GodEngine* that this invasion takes place at the same time as the Dalek Invasion of Earth. The Benny NA *Beige Planet Mars* contains many other details about the colonisation and invasions of Mars.

242 *Fear Itself*

243 Dating *GodEngine* (NA #51) - The year is given (p3).

244 *The Dalek Invasion of Earth*

245 *GodEngine*

246 Dating *The Mutant Phase* (BF #15) - The year is given as "2158".

247 Dating *Renaissance of the Daleks* (BF #93) - The date is given, and re-confirmed as being "a year" after the Daleks should have invaded Earth in 2157. Mention is made of a "new Dalek homeworld", but the reference is vague.

248 *War of the Daleks*

249 "Three years" after *GodEngine* (p214).

250 *The Dalek Invasion of Earth*, *The Mutant Phase*

251 *GodEngine* (p11).

252 *Alien Bodies*

253 Dating *The Dalek Invasion of Earth* (2.2) - There are two dates to establish: the date of the initial Dalek invasion, and the date of this story, which takes place after the Daleks have occupied Earth for some time. To start, the Doctor and Ian discover a calendar dated "2164" in a room that "hasn't been used in years" and Ian remarks that "at least we know the century". The prisoner Jack Craddock later says that the Daleks invaded "about ten

years" ago.

However, it seems that someone was printing calendars after the invasion - in *The Daleks' Master Plan*, the Doctor urges Vyon to "tell Earth to look back in the history of the year two thousand one hundred and fifty-seven and that the Daleks are going to attack again". In *The Space Museum*, Vicki states that the Daleks invaded Earth "three hundred years" before her own time [c 2193]. In *Remembrance of the Daleks*, the Doctor states that the Daleks conquered Earth in "the twenty-second century".

In *Lucifer Rising*, the Doctor says that the Daleks invade in "twenty-one fifty-eight" (p337). *GodEngine* dates the invasion to 2157; the TV story to "ten years" later (p240). *The Mutant Phase* sets the TV story in "nine years" [2168]. It's "a few decades" after *No Future* [c.2000], "two centuries" after *Head Games* (p157) [c.2201], it's "2157" in *Killing Ground* (p48), and "2154" in *Return of the Living Dad* (p241).

A production document written in July 1964 gave the date as "2042". The trailer for the 1964 serial claimed the story was set in "the year 2000" (and, unlike *The Power of the Daleks*, that's explicitly contradicted in the story itself), and in *Genesis of the Daleks*, the Doctor talks of the Daleks' extraction of the Earth's magnetic core in "the year 2000", apparently referring to this story (although he seems to be remembering the movie version, which was set in 2150).

Radio Times consistently dated the story as "2164", as did *The Making of Doctor Who* second edition, *The*

groups. **Dortmun spent much of his time developing an acid bomb, the only known weapon that could crack the Dalekenium shells of the invaders.**

Humanity still had no idea why the Daleks had invaded - it wasn't for the Earth's mineral wealth, and the Daleks showed no sign of simply colonising the planet.[244]

The Daleks had total control of the Earth, barring a few pockets of resistance, and began a number of projects.[245]

2158 / = 2158 - THE MUTANT PHASE[246] **->** In Kansas, America, an Agnomen wasp worked its way inside a battle-damaged Dalek casing and stung the Dalek creature within. Dalek medics prepared to remove the tainting wasp DNA from the stung Dalek.

> **=** The time-travelling Emperor Dalek arrived with a pesticide, GK50, which the Emperor claimed would destroy the wasp cells and safeguard the future. The Dalek medics complied, but the pesticide failed to work on the larval wasp cells. In the millennia to follow, the wasp DNA would spread through Dalek reproduction plants and taint the entire race, giving rise to the Mutant Phase and leading to Earth's destruction circa 4220.

The fifth Doctor realized the Emperor Dalek's actions had paradoxically created the very condition he was trying to prevent and convinced him to not use the pesticide, averting the Mutant Phase.

> **= 2158 - RENAISSANCE OF THE DALEKS**[247] **->** The collective thoughts of trillions of Daleks created a "seed Dalek" - a being known as the Greylish - who existed in an "island of time" inside a dimensional nullity. This realm was a Pan-Temporal Ambience, which existed in all times simultaneously. Time tracks from this realm led to various conflicts in history, including wars in Rhodes 1320; Petersburg, Virginia, 1864; and the Vietnam War.
>
> The Greylish saw himself as an impartial, indifferent creature and allowed his realm to become a Dalek foundry. Towers were constructed using millions of Dalek armour shells. The realm's temporal properties enabled the Daleks to mentally project subliminal voices to various points in space-time, which caused humanity to become receptive to Dalek thoughts and concepts. An alternate timeline was created in which the Daleks did not invade Earth in 2157 - instead, by 2158, humanity had grown so comfortable with the concept of Daleks that merchandisers were pumping out Dalek toys.
>
> The fifth Doctor investigated the time tracks leading from the Greylish's realm, and found himself in

the alternate history. He met General Tillington, who worked for a laser defense system named Global Warning. The Doctor diverted to rescue Nyssa and the knight Mulberry from 1864, and realised that the Daleks had developed a type of nano-Dalek. They had also learned to harness the power of actinodial energy, which could be projected through space-time. Unless stopped, the Daleks intended to transmit their nano-Daleks from the Greylish's realm into the Dalek toys, which would enable the nano-Daleks to infest every human on Earth. The Dalek invasion of Earth in the twenty-second century would still occur, but this time succeed without bloodshed.

> The Daleks captured the Doctor and his allies, and deemed the TARDIS a much quicker way of distributing the nano-Daleks. The Doctor's party escaped, and Mulberry swept the crates into the Vortex - at the cost of his being lost to it as well. The nano-Daleks were destroyed, but Mulberry's fate was unknown.
>
> Afterward, the Doctor successfully appealed to the Greylish's emotions, and the Greylish came to better recognise his origins as a Dalek thought-construct, finally understanding that *he* was the genetic template for the nano-Daleks. The Greylish erased his Pan-Temporal Ambience from existence with a thought, and all consequences of its creation were erased from history.

Searching Earth records, the Daleks discovered an account of the ICMG's battle with Daleks in 1963, including a description of Skaro's destruction in the future. Forewarned of this, the Daleks plotted to prevent history from transpiring as the Doctor believed it had - they had a new mission to avert the destruction of their homeworld.[248]

In 2160, the Daleks began work on extracting the Earth's core, seeking to replace it with the GodEngine.[249] **Once the Earth's core was destroyed and replaced with a drive system, the Daleks planned to move the entire planet around space.**[250] The Daleks had conquered every planet of the Solar System by 2162.[251]

The High Council of the Time Lords sent their agent Homunculette to a ruined London to acquire the Relic - which arrived from 15,414 - but Qixotl got there first.[252]

c 2167 - THE DALEK INVASION OF EARTH[253] **-> Ten years after the Daleks invaded, "Project Degravitate" neared its conclusion. Slave workers were instructed to begin clearing operations. The Daleks were tampering with the forces of creation, drilling down through the Earth's crust. A fission capsule was prepared and when detonated, it would release the Earth's magnetic core, eliminating Earth's gravitational and magnetic fields. Once the core was removed, it would be replaced with**

a power system allowing the Earth to be piloted anywhere in the universe.

Rebels broke into the Dalek Control Room, and ordered the Robomen to attack their masters. The Robomen and slaves overwhelmed the invaders and fled the mining area. The fission capsule was diverted, and upon its detonation the Dalek base - containing the Daleks' power external power supply - and the saucer Alpha Major was destroyed. An active volcano formed on the site of the old Dalek mine.

The Doctor's granddaughter Susan left the TARDIS to make a new life with David Campbell.

The seventh Doctor recovered the TARDIS key that Susan dropped.[254] The Battle of Cassius saw the end of the Dalek blockade of the solar system.[255]

The second Doctor visited a ruined New York clearing up after the Dalek Invasion.[256]

The colony worlds offered to help rebuild, but Earth refused. The Peace Officers were formed in England to neutralise dangerous Dalek artefacts left behind after the Invasion. The attempt at creating a central authority, though, soon splintered into around a hundred dominions.[257]

Unidentified alien beings briefly visited Earth, and one of their number - adopting the name Estella - stayed behind out of love for Duke Orsino, the ruler of Venice. They wed, but he soon lost her in a game of cards. As pun-ishment, she cursed the Duke to extended life so he could better experience the guilt of losing her, and she also cursed the city to destruction in a hundred years' time. Estella was rumoured to have committed suicide by flinging herself into the canal, but the Cult of Our Lady Estella soon emerged to worship her memory.

The aliens evidently left behind paintings from other worlds, including one that depicted a lady in a glass jar, and one showing fox-people in smart outfits. These became part of Orsino's art collection.[258]

The volcano formed by the destruction of the Daleks' base, Mount Bedford, became a tourist attraction. A salvage team recovered a starchart of Earth's whole sector of the galaxy from a derelict Dalek saucer.[259] A powerful cartel of Earth conglomerates took control of the Terran Security Forces. Within five years, it had become a force capable of waging intergalactic war.[260]

Following the Dalek Invasion of Earth, it became clear that there were a number of powerful warlike races in the galaxy. A number of planets, including Earth, Centauri and the Cyrennhics formed the Alliance, a mutual defence organisation. The corporation INITEC supplied the Alliance with state-of-the-art armaments.[261]

? 2170 - THE CHASE[262] -> Upon discovering time-travel technology, the Daleks on Skaro launched a prototype time machine after the first Doctor and his companions Ian, Barbara and Susan.

Doctor Who File and even the 1994 radio play *Whatever Happened to...Susan Foreman?*. The first edition of *The Programme Guide* set the story "c2060", the second "2164", while *The Terrestrial Index* said "2167"."A History of the Daleks" in *DWM* #77 set the story in "2166". *The Discontinuity Guide* suggested a date of "2174". In John Peel's novelisation of *The Chase*, Vicki says that the Daleks will destroy New York "one hundred years" after 1967.

More detail of the Dalek invasions of both Earth and Mars is given in the Benny NA *Beige Planet Mars*.

254 *GodEngine*

255 *The Crystal Bucephalus, GodEngine*

256 *The Final Sanction*

257 *Legacy of the Daleks*

258 "A hundred years" before *The Stones of Venice*. The painting of the "woman in a jar" probably refers to an Empress of Hyspero from *The Scarlet Empress*.

259 *Cold Fusion*

260 *The Final Sanction* (p75).

261 THE ALLIANCE: *The Terrestrial Index* suggested that a group that included Earth, Draconia and perhaps the Thals, who were all "united to attack and punish the Daleks". This contradicts what we are told on screen [q.v. "The Dalek Wars"], and the Alliance is never referred to on television. The Alliance is mentioned in *Original Sin* (p286), and this revised account of its origins appears in *Lords of the Storm* (p201).

262 Dating *The Chase* (2.8) - The Daleks launch an attack against their "greatest enemies" - the first Doctor, Ian, Barbara and Susan - in revenge for *The Dalek Invasion of Earth*. The fact they don't know Susan has left and Vicki has joined the TARDIS crew indicates that this is relatively soon after their defeat. No date is given, but as the Daleks are based on Skaro here, but will be confined to their city by *The Daleks*, this has to be substantially before then. The Dalek time machine was named the DARDIS in the script but not on screen.

263 *Day of the Daleks*

264 Reconciling the first Dalek story, *The Daleks*, with the other Dalek stories is difficult. There was no intention to bring back the Daleks, and the first story is a self-contained story about a war confined to Skaro, that sees the Daleks killed off at the end. From *The Dalek Invasion of Earth*, the Daleks became galactic conquerors - they invade and occupy the Earth, go on to invent time travel, twice threaten to conquer the entire galaxy, then go off to fight a mutually destructive war with the Time Lords.

Despite the Doctor's assertion that *The Daleks* takes place in the far future, we know that *The Daleks* takes place before *Planet of the Daleks* (2540). We also know

The Daleks used time-travel to go back to Earth in the twenty-first century and reinvade the planet. This time they succeeded.[263]

At some point, while the Daleks continued to grow in power, they all but abandoned their homeworld, Skaro. The Daleks remaining behind became confined to their city.[264]

The Riley Act of 2171 banned neurological implants as a fundamental infringement of human rights, in reaction to use of Roboman technology during the Dalek Invasion.[265]

In the late twenty-second century, the Monk withdrew the £200 he had deposited two hundred years before and collected a fortune in accrued compound interest.[266] The Doctor once claimed that he was "fully booked" until this time.[267]

On Tara, nine-tenths of the population was wiped out by a plague and replaced by androids.[268] President Borusa kidnapped Susan as part of his plan to gain the secret of perpetual regeneration.[269]

= c 2172 - DAY OF THE DALEKS[270] **->** An alternate timeline was created in the 1970s when the World Peace Conferences failed. A series of wars erupted, and over the next century, seven-eighths of the world's population were wiped out. Time travelling Daleks conquered the Earth in the mid-twenty-first century, hoping to exploit the planet's mineral wealth. The remnants of humanity were put to work in prison camps, guarded by Ogron servants. Human guerrillas stole Dalek time-travel technology, and travelled back to the crucial peace conference.

This timeline was erased when the Doctor and Jo ensured that the Peace Conference delegates were evacuated before Auderley House was destroyed.

In 2172, the Tzun Confederacy invaded Veltroch, but the arboreal Veltrochni clans united to defeat them. The Veltrochni wiped out the Tzun Confederacy, destroying every Tzun starship but leaving behind many Tzun artefacts and ruins. A whole sector of space containing ten thousand planets was consequently abandoned. Mankind colonised many of these former Tzun worlds, and the Veltrochni begin to fear the spread of humanity.[271]

On 21st July 2172, Agnomen wasps were deliberately agitated to quell crop-threatening caterpillars, but the wasps killed five hundred people in a Kansas town. The governor authorised use of pesticide GK50 to deal with the problem.[272] In 2172, Grant Markham, a future companion of the Doctor, was born.[273]

In the late twenty-second century, England's dominions were consolidated into ten large Domains, including Canterbury, Devon, Edmonds, Haldoran, London and Salisbury. Susan Campbell enlisted as a Peace Officer.[274] The Intercity Wars started and spread across Earth for decades. Military intervention from Earth's colonies

---

that, by then, the Daleks are back on Skaro.

There's no elegant way of reconciling this. The Daleks have to abandon Skaro, leaving behind a city full of Daleks who don't have space travel or any apparent knowledge of other planets. They can't leave their city, let alone conquer another planet. And they have to do it after *The Dalek Invasion of Earth*, then develop time travel (the Daleks in *The Chase* specifically leave and report back to Skaro).

If there *is* a logical reason this happened, there's no indication in an existing story. Vicki (from 2493) has heard of the Dalek Invasion of Earth, but doesn't know what a Dalek looks like, suggesting that from 2167ish to at least 2493, the Daleks don't menace Earth.

265 *Fear Itself*
266 *The Time Meddler*
267 The Doctor is booked up for "two hundred years" after *The Seeds of Doom*.
268 In *The Androids of Tara*, Zadek, one of Prince Reynart's men, states that the plague was "two hundred years" ago.
269 *The Five Doctors*. There's no indication of how long it has been for Susan since she left her grandfather.
270 Dating *Day of the Daleks* (9.1) - It is "two hundred years" after the UNIT era. A Dalek states that they "have discovered the secret of time travel, we have invaded the Earth again, we have changed the course of history". This isn't, as some fans have suggested, a version of events where the conquest seen in *The Dalek Invasion of Earth* was more successful - the Daleks travel back and invade a full century earlier, after the first attempt has failed.

The Daleks don't recognise the third Doctor, so they have come from before 2540 and *Planet of the Daleks* (or the alternate history they set up has wiped that story from the new timeline).

271 There are frequent references to the Veltrochni and Tzun in the books of David A McIntee. In *White Darkness*, we learn that civilisation on Veltroch is more than three billion years old (p90). The Tzun appear in *First Frontier*, and *Lords of the Storm* reveals much of their technology and the history of their destruction. The history is further sketched out in *First Frontier* (p94), *Lords of the Storm* (p24), *The Dark Path* (p142). The Veltrochni also appear in *Mission: Impractical*, and the aliens in *Bullet Time* - although never named - could well be Tzun survivors of the *First Frontier* incident.

272 *The Mutant Phase*
273 He's nineteen in *Killing Ground*.
274 *Legacy of the Daleks*

enforced peace.[275] Some crewmen aboard an Earth Forces science mission to Jupiter suffered severe psychological damage.[276]

In 2180, FLORANCE's status as a sentient citizen was revoked under the Cumberland Convention. The Dione-Kisanu company bought FLORANCE and installed it at their private base. Director Madhanagopal began experimenting on it in an attempt research human memory and learning. Madhanagopal was an operative for a Brotherhood that sought to augment humanity's psi-powers.[277]

Also in 2180, a Eurogen survey dispatched to see if Ha'olam could become an agricultural planet was abandoned when the company made budget cuts.[278]

The Kusks, a massive, brown-skinned species with advanced computer skills, dispatched a time probe to study various planets' histories, hoping to gather intelligence for potential conquests. The probe malfunctioned near the planet Hirath, and the Kusk spaceship sent to retrieve it failed in its mission. The Kusk crew put themselves into suspended animation. Later, the Temporal Commercial Concerns (TCC) company set up a series of time barriers on Hirath, and rented space there for various races to use as penal colonies. TCC adapted the Kusk spaceship, with the sleeping Kusk crew inside, into a moonbase.[279]

c 2185 - THE YEAR OF INTELLIGENT TIGERS[280] ->

One year, the Hitchemus tigers suddenly became intelligent, as they were prone to do once in multiple generations. They attempted to seize power, leading to massive conflict with the human colonists. To avert bloodshed, the Doctor destroyed the Hitchemus spaceport and used the tigers' weather control station to exacerbate the planet's already unstable tilt. This would have put all land on Hitchemus under water in ten years, but the humans and tigers - denied outside help - were compelled to work together to save their world. They agreed to live in peace.

Larger spaceships used T-Mat at this time.

In 2187, Ted Henneker led a rebellion against the Cybermen on Agora.[281]

? 2189 - "Echoes of the Mogor"[282] -> Mekrom was a wild world on the edge of known space, the location of a Confederation colony. The colonists were being killed, and

---

275 *The Janus Conjunction*

276 "Fifteen years" before *Fear Itself*.

277 "Forty seven years" before *SLEEPY*. The Brotherhood plays a role in *The Death of Art* and *So Vile a Sin*.

278 *Seeing I* (p83).

279 "Twenty five years" before *Longest Day*

280 Dating *The Year of Intelligent Tigers* (EDA #46) - It's the "twenty-second century" (p145), and references to colonies on Lvan and Gidi link it to *Nightmare of Eden*. It is clearly early in humanity's colonisation of other planets. That said, the spaceport has been established for a hundred years, so it must be the latter part of the century.

281 "Four years" before *Killing Ground* (p71).

282 Dating "Echoes of the Mogor" (*DWM* #143-144) - There's no indication of the date, but it seems to be early in the history of Earth's interstellar exploration. There are bullet holes in the walls at one murder scene, so the FHD might have projectile weapons, although weapons that resemble these are "lasers" in "Hunger from the Ends of Time!". Due to the presence of the FHD, and their wearing the same uniforms and carrying the same weapons, I've assumed that this story, "Hunger from the Ends of Time!" and "Conflict of Interests" all take place around the same time.

In "Conflict of Interests", mankind has a base on Rigel (between seven and nine hundred light years from Earth in real life), and spacecraft capable of "light by six".

283 Dating "Hunger from the Ends of Time!" (*DWM* #157-158) - "Conventional filing has been obsolete here on Catalog for centuries." The FHD squad's uniforms and weapons are identical to those in "Echoes of the Mogor", so the two stories are probably set around the same time.

284 Dating *Time of Your Life* (MA #8) - It is "three weeks into Earth year 2191" (p1).

285 Dating *Killing Ground* (MA #23) - This is set the same year as *Time of Your Life*.

286 Dating "Conflict of Interests" (*DWM* #183) - As with other FHD stories, this seems to be set in an early colonial period. Humanity doesn't have translation devices. The story has to be set before "Pureblood", when the Sontarans withdraw from human space. Aleph-777 is the planet seen in the back-up strip "The Final Quest".

287 Dating *Fear Itself* (PDA #73) - It's decades after the Dalek invasion of Earth (p274), but still the twenty-second century according to the back cover and p4.

288 Cyber Wars in the twenty-second or twenty-third century were postulated in *Cybermen* and *The Terrestrial Index*, and a number of stories that used those books as reference (including *Deceit, Iceberg, The Dimension Riders, Killing Ground* and *Sword of Orion*) have referred to "Cyberwars" in this time period. This is not the "Cyber War" involving Voga that is referred to in *Revenge of the Cybermen*. We might speculate that while the main force of Cybermen conquer Telos, another group remained active and travelled into deep space, perhaps colonising worlds of their own, and that this breakaway group was wiped out in the Cyber Wars. They seem to keep well away from Earth and only menace isolated human colonies.

289 *The Janus Conjunction* (p98).

had requested a relief ship and a Foreign Hazard Duty (FHD) team. Now, the last of them, Stanton, was murdered. The seventh Doctor arrived shortly before the FHD squad, and learned the men died of fear.

Members of the FHD squad started dying. The Doctor discovered seams of crystal that could absorb emotion, creating "echoes" of someone's presence. The colonists died of fear from echoes of the warlike Mogor, meaning there were no real monsters. The Doctor snuck away as the FHD team filed their report.

? 2190 - "Hunger From the Ends of Time!"[283] -> The planet Catalog was the repository for all collated knowledge in the universe. The seventh Doctor decided to go for a browse there, as he hadn't visited for decades, but he found the TARDIS dragged there anyway.

The Doctor met an FHD team, who informed him that the data was now stored as "information energy" across time rather than space. The system had become infiltrated by "bookworms" eating the information. These forces of chaos were only meant to exist at the ends of time, and their presence here was affecting the fabric of time. The Doctor brought all the records back into the present, cutting off the food supply... but leaving around a century's worth of refiling to do.

2191 (January) - TIME OF YOUR LIFE[284] -> For over twenty years, the Meson Broadcasting Service (MBS) had showed some of the all-time TV classics: *Bloodsoak Bunny*, *The Party Knights and the Kung-Fu Kings*, *Jubilee Towers*, *Prisoner: The Next Generation*, *Life's a Beach* and *Abbeydale High*. The broadcaster successfully rebuffed the claims of the Campaign for the Advancement of Television Standards that such programming as *Death-Hunt 3000*, *Masterspy* and *Horror Mansions* increased violence and criminal behaviour.

On Torrok, the citizens were compelled by law to watch MBS' offerings all day. Peace Keeper robots patrolled every street, rounding up suspected criminals. The sixth Doctor arrived on Torrok during this time and accepted an inquisitive Angela Jennings as his companion. The Time Lords directed the TARDIS to MBS' space station headquarters, where a mechanical adversary killed Angela.

As part of the reality show *Time of Your Life*, the city of Neo Tokyo was teleported from New Earth into a Maston Sphere, where the residents were terrorised. The Doctor discovered that the information-consuming datavore Krllxk had gone insane from absorbing the entire MBS output. He transmatted Neo Tokyo back home, and the ensuing conflict made the MBS station fly into the sun. Krllxk took refuge in a game-show android, but the Doctor destroyed it. MBS went off the air when the people on Torrok rebelled, overthrowing the totalitarian regime. Grant Markham, a computer programmer who helped the

Doctor, joined him on his travels.

2191 - KILLING GROUND[285] -> Humanity thought the Cybermen were extinct. Most were asleep in their Tombs on Telos, but some nomads wandered the galaxy. Earth was still rebuilding from the Dalek Invasion at this time.

The Doctor suspected the Cybermen were involved in the affairs of Agora, the home planet of his companion Grant Markham. They arrived, and the Overseers who ruled the planet on the behalf of the Cybermen captured the Doctor. Grant fell in with the rebels.

One of the rebels, Maxine Carter, used Cybertechnology to build the Bronze Knights, a volunteer army of cyborgs. The Doctor learned that the Cybermen were running out of parts and becoming increasingly reliant on stolen technology. These Cybermen hijacked and adapted a Selechian warship. The Doctor sabotaged it, releasing radiation that was lethal to the Cybermen. The Bronze Knights left Agora to hunt down more Cybermen, and the remaining colonists rebuilt their planet.

? 2192 - "Conflict of Interests"[286] -> Rigel Depot sent an FHD team at light by six to Aleph-777 in the Deneb system, where they encountered a Sontaran Infantry squad. Galactic Survey was keen to protect the archaeology of the extinct civilisation on the planet, but found the Sontarans had the same goal... and they'd have to fight for it.

c 2192 - FEAR ITSELF[287] -> The eighth Doctor, Anji and Fitz arrived on Mars, where Anji was attacked and hospitalised. The Doctor and Fitz linked her attackers to Farside Station and set off to investigate... but shortly afterwards, Farside reported destroyed with all hands lost.

Thinking the Doctor and Fitz dead - and that she was stranded - Anji became a consultant on twenty-first century matters for a television channel. She married a cameraman called Michael. At this time, a new and ruthless military group called the Professionals emerged.

There was a space elevator in the Yucatan and holographic slides had replaced paper. A vaccine for the common cold had been developed. Anti-radiation suits were made from Dortmunium. The Martians who remained on Mars were a social underclass, and some resorted to terrorist acts.

Humanity fought against a number of hostile races in deep space, including the Cybermen. A number of Cyber Wars were fought at the beginning of the twenty-third century, but humanity prevailed.[288] Gustav Zemler's unit fought the Cybermen on the borders of Earth's colonies. Zemler's unit prevailed, but the Cybermen's hostages were also killed. Zemler and his survivors were dishonorably discharged and became mercenaries.[289]

After the Cyber Wars, Eurogen Butler changed their

name and became the Spinward Corporation.[290] The former Houses of Parliament were used as a hospice for veterans of the first Cyber Wars.[291]

Privateers from the Andosian Alliance made several incursions into Earth's solar system in the last half of the twenty-second century. In the decade before 2197, they caused much loss of life and damage to cargo payloads, and they continued menacing the spaceways into the early twenty-third century. The Privateers were eight feet tall, with rippling mauve muscles and possibly three heads. They also had a penchant for the melodramatic, with their leaders choosing such names as "Doctor Leopard".[292]

The I had developed as a gestalt, centaur-like race that seeded technology onto planets, then later returned to harvest the developments. The I acquired some Gallifreyan technology and the eyes of a Time Lord named Savar, and around 2192 used this to facilitate the development of advanced retinal implants on the planet Ha'olam.[293]

The buffalo became extinct in 2193.[294] The Selachians sold their Cloak weapons to Earth in the mid-2190s.[295]

& 2196 - FEAR ITSELF[296] **->** Farside Station was rediscovered in Jupiter's atmosphere. Anji had become distant from her husband, and stowed away as a Professional was sent to investigate. The survivors had gone feral, while the station has been influenced by alien biological weapons - Fear and Loathing - which had survived in Jupiter's atmosphere for millennia.

The Doctor, who had been brainwashed into operating as a Professional for the last four years, neutralised the weapons. Reunited with Anji, the Doctor and Fitz continued on their travels.

At this time, tent cities existed on Earth and Mars. The Paris crater and the New York waterways were popular tourist traps.[297]

In 2197, the Dreamstone Moon Mining Company was set up to exploit the discovery of dreamstone on the moon of Mu Camelopides VI.[298]

---

290 *Deceit* (p23).

291 *Interference* (p305).

292 *The Nowhere Place*

293 *Seeing I*

294 *The Also People* (p29).

295 "A decade" before *The Final Sanction*.

296 Dating *Fear Itself* (PDA #73) - Anji is separated from the Doctor and Fitz for "four years".

297 The "Paris crater" is evidently a reference to the Martian-propelled asteroid that obliterated Paris in the Thousand-Day War, as told in *Transit* and *GodEngine*. *Transit* specifies that Paris is rebuilt in the decade to follow this event, but a monument area might remain. The waterways suggest that New York has also recovered - at least a little - from its destruction before Vicki's time.

298 *Dreamstone Moon* (p18).

299 Dating *Wooden Heart* (NSA #15) - No date is given, but it's "at least a hundred years" since the *Castor* was launched. The hints we get are that the *Castor* was operating very early in Earth's era of interstellar travel, and the fact it's "Century Class" might link it to the Century ships referred to in *Killing Ground*. Space is divided into sectors and is largely unregulated, suggesting the *Castor* was launched before *The Space Pirates*.

300 Dating *The Nowhere Place* (BF #84) - The story opens on 15th January, although Oswin files a report at 15:38 on the 16th, which suggests the Doctor and Evelyn don't arrive until that date.

301 *The Janus Conjunction* (p100).

302 Dating *Legacy of the Daleks* (EDA #10) - Susan met David when he was 22, and he's now 54 (p15), so it's thirty two years after *The Dalek Invasion of Earth*. The blurb says it is the late twenty-second century. It's

unclear why the Doctor is searching for Sam by travelling in time, rather than space, yet that's the implication of p27, where he is "allowing" for Thannos time. This does seem to mean he's looking for Sam *before* he lost her in *Longest Day* circa 2202, but he is admittedly diverted to Earth by a telepathic signal from Susan. While the Doctor thinks he is in the right timezone, perhaps the TARDIS has taken him just a handful of years earlier.

303 *The Chase*. The interplanetary wars have continued for at least "fifty years" according to Steven Taylor. There's a possibility that Steven is mistaken about the Mechanoids' origin - see "Dating *The Chase*" [2265].

304 *The Pit* (p86).

305 Stacey's parents are from the "twenty-third century" in *Placebo Effect*. Stacey was a regular character in the *Radio Times' Doctor Who* comic strip featuring the eighth Doctor.

306 *Managra* (p63).

307 *The Shadow of the Scourge*

308 *Genocide* (p27).

309 "The twenty-third century" according to *Cold Fusion* (p180).

310 *Colony in Space*. Many of the books pick up on this theme.

311 *The Final Sanction*, no date is given on p146, but it must be some time before 2203.

312 Dating *Longest Day* (EDA #9) - It's "Ex-Thannos System, Relative Year 3177" (p15). In *Legacy of the Daleks*, it's stated "In Thannos time it had been 3177" (p27), so it's almost certainly not 3177AD. This is the same time zone as *Legacy of the Daleks* (give or take), *Dreamstone Moon* and *Seeing I*.

313 Dating *Dreamstone Moon* (EDA #11) - For Sam,

? 2197 - WOODEN HEART[299] **->** The tenth Doctor and Martha landed on the *Castor*, a prison ship full of century-old corpses. Deep in the ship, they discovered a strange virtual reality forest and a pre-industrial village. Aliens had preserved humans in the wooden heart of the ship.

2197 (15th-16th January to March) - THE NOWHERE PLACE[300] **->** Earth's Damocles-class ships emerged as the deadliest fighter-craft of their age, and were the envy of their enemies. The Red Cross symbol was still in use. Earth's military used security locks that were susceptible to high-frequency vibrations. A station was in operation on Jupiter, and cryo-freezing was used in this era.

The Damocles-fighter carrier *Valiant* traveled to Pluto's orbital path at this time, and scans indicated that hostile raider activity had previously occurred there in late December. The sixth Doctor and Evelyn arrived on the *Valiant*, which was under the command of Captain Tanya Oswin, as a mysterious door appeared in the ship's hull. Crew members were mentally compelled to walk through the door, which was a tool of the original species that had evolved on Earth. The original race hoped to use the door as a means of ensnaring humanity and retroactively erasing mankind from history. The Doctor and Evelyn identified the sound of a train bell coming from the door as hailing from 1952, and ventured back there to investigate. The situation deteriorated in their absence, and three-fourths of the *Valiant* crew were lost to the door.

The Doctor and Evelyn returned two months later, just as the spaceship *Exeter* arrived in response to the *Valiant*'s cry for help. Oswin ordered the Exeter to fire nuclear weapons against the door; this would have paradoxically created Time's End and consigned humanity to suffer there. However, the Doctor altered events in Time's End so that Oswin's nuclear strike permanently destroyed Earth's original species.

Colonial marines fought in the Alphan Kundekka conflict of 2198.[301]

& 2199 - LEGACY OF THE DALEKS[302] **->** The eighth Doctor arrived in New London as the Master started a war between rival Domains Haldoran and London. Haldoran and London themselves died in the conflict, and one of Haldoran's commanders, Barlow, took charge of both regions.

The Master reawoke a hidden Dalek factory to gain an experimental matter transmuter. David Campbell was killed in a struggle with the Master, who fled to the planet Terserus. Susan Campbell destroyed the matter transmuter, an act that ravaged the Master's body. The Time Lords sent Chancellor Goth to investigate the disturbance on Terserus, leading to his meeting the now-skeletal Master. A grieving Susan left in the Master's TARDIS.

The Interplanetary Wars

The robotic "Mechanoids" were dispatched in rockets to planets such as Mechanus, and set out preparing the way for colonists. The Mechanoids cleared landing sites and made everything ready for the immigrants, but a series of interplanetary wars started. The conflicts would continue for more than fifty years.

After the wars, many colonies were left isolated or forgotten completely. The space lanes were disrupted, and colonies such as Mechanus were cut off from Earth. Left to their own devices, the Mechonoid robots built and maintained a vast city, awaiting the code that would identify the rightful human colonists.

On Mechanus, the Mechanoids and the Daleks came into conflict around this time. Skaro had records of "Mechons" with "many powerful weapons".[303] Brian Parsons fought in many space conflicts at this time, and his tactics were programmed into android soldiers for many centuries to come.[304] Stacey Townsend was the only survivor when the Cybermen attacked the cargo ship *Dreadnaught*. The Doctor destroyed the Cybermen, and Stacey joined him on his travels.[305]

During the twenty-third century, Jung the Obscure published his theory of the Inner Dark in the Eiger Apocrypha.[306] By the twenty-third century, a riot control gas named Pacificus was invented.[307] Sperm whale song-lines were published.[308]

Humanity conducted tests with fusion bombs out on the Galactic Rim. The devices were so powerful they were immediately banned.[309]

The corporations made vast profits from the colonisation of other planets and became a law unto themselves, killing colonists to get to mineral resources. The Adjudication Service became a neutral arbiter of planetary claims.[310]

Around 2200, the Interbank scandal took place. Chairman Wayne Redfern was indirectly responsible for the bankruptcy of the organisation.[311]

& 2202 - LONGEST DAY[312] **->** A Kusk rescue party arrived on the moon of Hirath, intent on retrieving the lost time probe. The probe malfunctioned even further and destabilized TCC's time barriers on Hirath, threatening to blow up half the galaxy. The Doctor destroyed the probe, triggering an electrical surge that also killed the rampaging Kusks. The Doctor and his companion, Samantha Jones, were separated in the confusion to follow, and she was launched away from Hirath in a crewless Kusk ship.

& 2202 - DREAMSTONE MOON[313] **->** Dreamstones, a material mined from a satellite of Mu Camelopides VI, also known as the "Dreamstone Moon," became very desirable. Consumers would sleep with dreamstones under their pillows to experience vivid dreams. However, Anton La Serre, an artist who recorded and sold his dreams, had a tortuous dreaming experience with a dreamstone and sought to discredit the entire industry.

The Dreamstone Moon Mining Corporation (DMMC) ship *Dreamstone Miner* rescued Sam Jones, who had drifted in the Kusk ship for a week. She was taken to the DMMC mining operation on the Dreamstone Moon, which began to experience tremors. The Doctor arrived and concluded that the entire Moon was a living entity, and that the dreamstones were parts of its brain.

The pained entity shared a special mental link with La Serre, and instinctively began lashing out due to his anger toward DMMC. The entity started projecting mental illusions - Earth Fleet had 500 ships in the Mu Camelopides System on manoeuvres, and the captain of the dropship *Royale* self-destructed his vessel while experiencing such a waking nightmare.

The ship's compliment of one thousand troops was lost, and altogether five thousand people died. The Doctor finally entered La Serre's dreams and calmed him, allowing La Serre to peacefully dream himself to death, and the dreamstone entity fell dormant. DMMC abandoned operations on the Moon. Sam Jones, embarrassed for her previous abandonment of the Doctor, departed the Moon in an evacuation shuttle.

c 2202 - SEEING I[314] **-> ** Sam Jones relocated to the world of Ha'olam, where she initially worked as a volunteer in an INC-run homeless shelter. She turned eighteen during this time. The eighth Doctor searched for Sam and was responsible for "the Great Umph Massacre of 2202" when he sent data-umphs into the galaxy-wide computer network looking for her.

Still searching for Sam, the Doctor, using the alias Dr. James Alistair Bowman, was arrested as an industrial spy on INC premises. He was given a ten year sentence and

taken to the Oliver Bainbridge Functional Stabilisation Centre (OBFSC). He was questioned by Dr Akalu, the prison's "morale officer." Akalu implanted the Doctor with a retinal implant that provided advance warning of the Doctor's escape attempts.

Sam was hired by the non-profit organisation Livingspace to do volunteer work at Eurogen Village, a desert community for former Eurogen workers.

Akalu set up DOCTOR, an artificial intelligence, to create an accurate psychological profile on the Doctor. DOCTOR would eventually discover 346 reports of TARDIS sightings in hundreds' years worth of data, despite someone erratically, not systematically, erasing nearly all of it.

Sam started a relationship with Paul Hamani, a Eurogen worker assigned to teach her about life on the settlement. They ended their relationship five months later.

Around 2203, the Selachian Empire invaded Rho Priapus, one of Earth's colony worlds.[315] Terran Security Forces (TSF) in response instigated a war to combat the alleged Selachian threat, but the conflict owed more to the Selachians endangering human corporate interests on the arms markets.[316]

On Earth, Professor Laura Mulholland developed the gravity bomb, a devastating weapon capable of making a planet collapse in on itself. The G-bomb boosted Earth's confidence in the conflict with the Selachian Empire, and a warfleet, led by the flagship *Triumph*, left Earth to engage the enemy. The Selachians were forced back to their own system within a year.[317] In 2204, Adam Dresden was on his first TSF mission when the Selachians captured him on Molinar. He was subsequently transported to Ockara as a prisoner.[318]

2204 - THE FINAL SANCTION[319] **-> ** The war with the Selachians was coming to an end. Humans invaded Kalaya, the final planet in need of liberation from the

---

only six days pass between *Longest Day* and *Dreamstone Moon* (p7).
314 Dating *Seeing I* (EDA #12) - Sam was en route to the planet Ha'olam at the end of *Dreamstone Moon*, and has only just arrived at the start of this novel. The Doctor sending out Data-umphs in 2202 looking for Sam must mean that he expects to find her in that year. "James Bowman" was the alias that Grace attributed to the Doctor in *Doctor Who - The Movie*.
315 *The Janus Conjunction* (p98).
316 According to *The Final Sanction*, p75. Page 146 suggests the war has been going on for a year.
317 *The Final Sanction* (p73) says this occurs "almost a year" before 2204. The events are also mentioned on p255.
318 *The Final Sanction* (p196).

319 Dating *The Final Sanction* (PDA #24) - The date is given (p4).
320 Dating *Seeing I* (EDA #12) - The Doctor is imprisoned for "three years". Oddly, according to *SLEEPY*, also by Kate Orman, FLORANCE was trapped in a lab at this point.
321 "Fifty years" after *GodEngine*.
322 Dating *The Janus Conjunction* (EDA #16) - It is "Dateline 14.09.2211 Humanian Era" according to p16.
323 *The Highest Science* (p17).
324 *Strange England* (p7).
325 "Seventy years" after *GodEngine*.
326 Dating *SLEEPY* (NA #48) - While investigating the Dione-Kisanu Corporation in 2257, the Doctor sends Roz and Bernice go back "thirty years", to "2227"
327 Dating *Frayed* (TEL #11) - No date is given, but as

Selachians. After a while, the humans forewent air raids to protect the native population. Out of 1,000 troops, only around 300 survived the campaign.

The second Doctor, Jamie and Zoe arrived on the war-torn Kalaya shortly before Selachian forces abandoned it. The Doctor found himself onboard the flagship *Triumph* as it pursued the retreating Selachians their homeworld of Ockora. The *Triumph*'s G-bomb was launched, turning Ockora into a black hole and obliterating nine million lives there, including 10,000 hostages. Lieutenant Kent Michaels of the TSF gave the final password that launched the bomb, but the history books condemned Commander Wayne Redfern for the catastrophe, deeming him one of the most evil men who ever lived.

A group of surviving Selachians seized control of the *Triumph* and attempted to retaliate against Earth with the ship's second G-bomb. Professor Mulholland detonated the bomb before it could reach Earth, turning the *Triumph* into a second black hole.

& 2205 - SEEING I[320] **->** Sam was involved in a failed protest that sought to prevent INC from buying Eurogen Village. She sought to expose INC's corrupt practices and broke into a TCC research plant. She found them growing human clones with no higher brain functions for immoral experimentation.

Now twenty-one, Sam learned about the Doctor's incarceration by hacking into INC's medical databases. She helped to break the Doctor out of prison, and the TARDIS removed his retinal implant. The Doctor had been an inmate of OBFSC for just over three years.

The I gestalt overran the INC Research and Development Complex at Samson Plains to strip-mine its technology. The Doctor liberated the I's organic spaceship from their control, turning the I into mindless drones. Reunited with Sam, he departed for Gallifrey to return Savar's eyes.

DOCTOR, having acquired some of the Doctor's personality traits through studying him, departed Ha'olam and travelled human dataspace with another AI named FLORANCE.

The settlement of Shelbyville was founded on Mars.[321]

2211 - THE JANUS CONJUNCTION[322] **->** In 2110, an aged Spacemaster, with one thousand colonists on board, was holed by an asteroid prior to crash-landing on the planet Menda. Led by Gustav Zemler, the mercenaries hired to protect the colonists discovered a hyperspatial Link that joined Menda to its neighbour, Janus Prime. The mercenaries crossed over to Janus Prime but were trapped there for a year, and went insane due to radiation sickness.

In September 2211, the Doctor arrived on Janus Prime and discovered that the hyperspatial Link was an accidental by-product of the Janus System's doomsday device. Gustav Zemler was killed before he could set the Janus Conjunction in motion and turn the sun into a black hole. Sergeant Jon Moslei sacrificed himself to collapse the Link, saving Janus Prime in the process.

The Intergalactic Mineral Exploitation Act was passed in 2217, granting the mining combines vast powers. The corporations had already supplied the colony ships, weather control, terraforming, and computer technology to the colonists.[323] The Doctor, Ace, and Benny visited the Moscow City Carnival in 2219.[324]

The city of Springfield was established near Ascraeus Lacus on Mars around 2227.[325]

2227 - SLEEPY[326] **->** The Adjudication Service was just one of many organisations trying to enforce the law. The Serial / Spree Killers Investigations National Unit was one of the hundreds of small agencies operating in tandem with the conventional legal authorities throughout the twenty-third century - often with more powers than the authorities. Thanks to a combination of paranoia and real concern - some political parties took to hiring serial killers - Unit operatives could get in just about anywhere.

In the early twenty-third century, CM Enterprises attempted to create a computer that could think like a human by installing organic components - a cat's brain - into an Imbani mainframe. They succeeded in building a computer that wanted to play with string and sit on newspapers. The Dione-Kisanu Company (DKC), on the other hand, encoded information in the form of memory RNA. Before long, DKC taught a woman the first verse of *Kublai Khan* by injection. In 2223, Madhanagopal finished his work on the AI named FLORANCE, which was taken off-line.

Psychic ability was now recognised by humanity, and standard tests had been introduced. DKC were attempting to encode psi-powers using a model of the human mind: the AI named GRUMPY. When GRUMPY discovered this, he escaped DKC by pushing himself through the computer networks, leaving his own hardware behind. He stored a few years' memories in a data vault in Malindi, tucked away a copy of his operating system in a communications satellite trailing Phobos, and spread pieces of himself across the Solar System. For a decade, DKC kept the fact that GRUMPY had escaped secret and destroyed all they could find of him. GRUMPY became increasingly desperate, and used his psychic ability to terrorise and blackmail. After two years, DKC tracked him down, brought him back to Saturn's moon of Dione and erased the copies he had made of himself.

? 2230 - FRAYED[327] **->** Earth sent those with a perceived genetic disposition to crime or latent psychic abilities (the "future deviants') to the Refuge on Iwa. There was a strict Eugenics Code on Earth. Corporations funded research into psychic ability, but it was felt that the psychics' sense of superiority led them to a criminal lifestyle. Babies without brains were cloned for medical research.

A Time Lord and his companion landed on Iwa. Adopting the names "the Doctor" and "Susan", they observed the humans' fight with wolf-like aliens. An uneasy truce was forged, and the humans agreed to help the aliens cure a genetic decay that was afflicting them.

The Colonies

The second quarter of the twenty-third century became a time of great expansion of Earth's colonial efforts. Around 2230, the Survey Corps vessel *Icarus* entered service.[328]

The early-mid part of the twenty-third century was known as "the First Great Breakout", a period of massive colonial expansion from Earth. Humanity reached the Uva Beta Uva System, which contained fourteen planets. Earth was becoming crowded and polluted, so there was no shortage of settlers for Uva Beta Uva Five. A couple of years later, a mining agent discovered belzite on Uva Beta Uva Three, and the settlers discovered that all of their legal rights were rescinded under the Intergalactic Mineral Exploitation Act of 2217. The mining companies moved in.[329]

? 2231 - "Spider-God"[330] -> A survey team from the Earth ship *Excelsior* landed on UX-4732 at the same time as the fourth Doctor. The Earthmen saw the peaceful natives apparently sacrifice themselves to giant spiders, and moved to eradicate the creatures. The Doctor deduced that the "people" were actually the larval stage of beautiful butterfly creatures, and relied upon the spiders to weave cocoons for them to emerge from.

c 2237 - MEMORY LANE[331] -> Portable sound-file players could now transmit sound directly into the user's ear canals.

Astronaut Kim Kronotska returned to Earth a total of 227 years after her departure, and instantly became a celebrity. She participated in academic studies, wrote a memoir and took part in many game and talk shows. However, she struggled to acclimate and found that spaceships in this era could travel the distance she'd previously covered in mere months. She thereby tracked the missing Tom Braudy to the planet Lucentra, but became trapped in the Earth-simulation cell that was holding him.

The eighth Doctor, Charley and C'rizz helped the Earth astronauts secure their freedom from the entrepreneurs Lest and Argot. They also demonstrated use of video-playback, allowing Lest and Argot to sell the technology to their people.

In 2237, the artificial intelligence GRUMPY managed to transfer his operating system into the computer of a fighter shuttle, and leapt out into interstellar space. DKC intercepted him at Sunyata, and shot him down over the temperate world of Yemaya, which was being surveyed for possible colonisation. To survive, GRUMPY seeded bits of its RNA into the colonists via their inoculations.[332]

In the twenty-third century, Earth was cluttered and grey, although there were crystal spires in Paris. Cities now stretched fifty levels underground, individuals had about five square metres of space.

The great entrepreneur Varley Gabriel scouted for planets to colonise. In 2241, the "top drawer" of the fittest and smartest people - along with 20,000 crew to serve them - set off in the colony ship *Mayflower* on a planned one hundred year journey to a new world. It would go on to pass Aldebaran. At this time, humans used hovering service robots to maintain spaceships.[333]

---

children are screened for psychic abilities, and this is an early colony world, it ties in with information given in *SLEEPY*. The oldest child is twelve, perhaps suggesting the colony has been established that long.

328 "A hundred and fifty years" before *The Dimension Riders* (p61).

329 "A hundred and fifty years" before *The Romance of Crime* (p8). There's another Great Breakout in the year 5000, according to *The Invisible Enemy*. Uva Beta Five was re-named "New Earth", but is not the planet of the same name in *Time of Your Life*.

330 Dating "Spider-God" (*DWM* #52) - No date is given, but it seems to be the early colonial period. It is twenty years since Frederic joined the survey corps, and three years since the *Excelsior* left Earth. The Earthmen have a hover car "scouter" and energy weapons.

331 Dating *Memory Lane* (BF #88) - It is 227 years and

some months after Kim and Tom departed Earth, an event that occurs near the modern day.

332 *SLEEPY*

333 "Profits of Doom". It's "eight decades" before 2321.

334 *Lords of the Storm*

335 At least "a century" - or four termite generations - before *Valhalla*.

336 *The Leisure Hive*

337 *Placebo Effect*

338 Dating *SLEEPY* (NA #48) - The Doctor states it is "2257" (p29).

339 *Salvation*

340 *Frostfire*

341 *The Empire of Glass*

342 Dating *The Daleks* (1.2) - No date is given in the story, but the Doctor says in *The Edge of Destruction* that "Skaro was in the future". In *The Dalek Invasion of*

A rush ensued to establish gas mines on the moons of Jupiter, including Callisto and Ganymede. The domed city of Valhalla was established as Callisto's capital, but when the mines ran dry, Earth declared the moon cities as independent and washed its hands of them. In the century to follow, conditions in the moon cities would greatly deteriorate.

Genetically engineered termites had been used to burrow into Callisto in search of new energy sources. As the region's economic prosperity waned, the termites remained outside Valhalla's gravity pan. Jupiter's gravity fluxes affected them, and within just three generations they would grow to monstrous size. The termites had been tasked with providing information to the Valhalla Registry computer, but the flow of information became two-way, which greatly enhanced their intelligence.[334]

Hindu settlers colonised the Unukalhai system. In 2247 the Colonial Office began to terraform Raghi, the sixth moon of Unukalhai IV (which the settlers named Indra), a process that took forty million people a quarter of a century to complete. Raghi was one of the few colonies to be funded by public donation rather than the corporations. The colonists traded airavata - creatures that lived in the clouds of Indra, and whose DNA contained a natural radiation decontaminant - with the Spinward Corporation.[335]

In 2250, the Argolin warrior Theron started a war with the Foamasi. The war lasted twenty minutes and two thousand interplanetary missiles reduced Argolis to a radioactive wasteland. Following this disaster, the Argolin became sterile and started tachyonics experiments in an effort to perpetuate their race.[336] The Foamasi homeworld of Liasici was destroyed in the war.[337]

2257 - SLEEPY[338] -> Australia by this time was a wasteland, ruined through centuries of chemical and nuclear pollution, although some Australians had made a fortune from solar power.

Yemaya 4 was ideal for colonisation - it had a large temperate zone, gentle seasons, and biochemistry not too different to that of Earth. The four hundred colonists - mostly Botswanans, South Africans, and Burandans from the United African Confederacy - started accelerated gardens around the habitat dome almost immediately, and were busily turning some of the surrounding meadows into farms. They were going to use several Yemayan native plants as crops, and planetfall had been timed to allow almost immediate planting of Terran seed stock. With the help of drone farmers and AI administrators, the colony thrived for two months.

But then the first infections started. Thanks to the presence of GRUMPY's RNA, colonists developed psychic powers such as telekinesis, telepathy and pyrokinesis. The core of GRUMPY was named SLEEPY. DKC dispatched the warship *Flame Warrior* to Yemaya to safeguard its secrets, but SLEEPY sacrificed itself to destroy the warship. The colonists were able to partly assemble GRUMPY's memories from the RNA in their systems, and learned enough to either blackmail or bring down DKC. The corporation left the colony alone.

Steven Taylor grew up in the ruins of England, and joined up to fight in the interplanetary wars after visiting the devastated New York. He became the helmsman of a battleship, living on spaceships and space stations. He ruined his promotion prospects by complaining about a soldier abusing a civilian on Roylus Prime, and was relegated to solo non-combat missions. His ship was built from modified Dalek designs.[339]

"Historical-doc romances" were made in Steven's native time.[340] People on Earth lived in cramped Hiveblocks. His ship crashed on Mechanus when Krayt fighters shot it down.[341]

? 2263 - THE DALEKS[342] -> For centuries the few survivors of the Thal race had lived on a plateau on Skaro, eking out an existence. They relied on rainfall that came only every ten years. One decade, the rain never came. After two years, the Thal Temmosus and his group left the plateau, hoping to find the city of the Daleks. This occurred five hundred years after the

---

Earth, the Doctor tells Ian that the first Dalek story occurred "a million years ahead of us in the future" and the twenty-second century is part of the "middle of the history of the Daleks". Where he acquires this information is unclear - he had not even heard of the Daleks when he first met them (whereas other Time Lords fear the Daleks, the Monk knows of them in *The Daleks' Master Plan* and *The Five Doctors* reveals that the Time Lords' ancestors forbid the use of the Daleks in their Games).

However, the Thals in *Planet of the Daleks* [2540] have legends of events in *The Daleks* as being from "generations ago".

In the original storyline for *The Survivors* (as the first story was provisionally titled) the date was given as "the year 3000", with the war having occurred two thousand years before. A revised synopsis dated 30th July, 1963, gave the date as "the 23rd century".

The Terrestrial Index and *The Official Doctor Who & the Daleks Book* both suggested that the Daleks from this story were "new Daleks" created by "crippled Kaled survivors", and that the story is set just after *Genesis of the Daleks* - this is presumably meant to explain the Dal / Kaled question and also helps tie the Dalek history into the *TV Century 21* comic strip, although there is no evidence for it on screen.

Neutronic War, and the Daleks had become affected by the reverse evolution on the planet, and had lost many of their technological secrets. Reconciliation between the Thals and the Daleks proved impossible.

The first Doctor, Susan, Ian and Barbara arrived on Skaro. They explored the Dalek city, then sided with the Thals in wiping out the Daleks.

The Doctor's encounter with the Daleks was Last Contact, when the Time Lords first encountered the race that would ultimately destroy them.[343]

At some point after this time, the Moroks acquired a Dalek from Skaro, then placed it on exhibit in their Space Museum.[344]

? 2265 - THE CHASE[345] **->** Nearly fifty years after the interplanetary wars had begun, Earth was still involved, although the end was now in sight. One of the combatants, space pilot Steven Taylor, Flight Red Fifty, was stranded on Mechanus. After several days in the hostile jungle, he was captured by the Mechanoids, who still maintained their city in preparation for the human colonists. Unable to crack their code, Taylor was imprisoned. Two years after this the TARDIS arrived, pursued by the Daleks. The Mechonoid City, the Mechanoids and the Daleks were destroyed, and Steven left in the TARDIS.

> = The sixth Doctor visited the planet Huttan in the year 2267.[346]

The Computers and Cybernetic Systems Act was passed on Uva Beta Uva in 2265.[347] By 2270, shortly after Pangol's birth, the Argolin had called a moratorium of

---

The *TARDIS Logs* dated the story as "2290 AD". The American *Doctor Who* comic suggested a date of "300 AD", on the grounds that the Daleks do not seem to have developed space travel. The FASA Role-playing Game dated the story as "5 BC". "Matrix Databank" in *DWM* #73 suggested that *The Daleks* takes place after *The Evil of the Daleks* and that the Daleks seen here are the last vestiges of a once-great race. This ties in with *The Dalek Invasion of Earth*, but contradicts *Planet of the Daleks*.

Timelink suggests 900. In the Virgin version of this book, I speculated that in this story the Doctor has returned Ian and Barbara to 1963, but on the wrong side of the galaxy. If it was set at the time of broadcast, it would be a couple of months after they left London, so - stretching a little - it qualifies as "the future".

The main problem is that, whenever it's set, we have to reconcile the Daleks seen in first Dalek story - stuck in their city unaware of any life beyond it who are all killed - with the Daleks as galactic conquerors seen in all subsequent stories. We have to postulate (without any evidence from the series) that a faction of Daleks left Skaro at some point between becoming confined to their travel machines and the Neutronic War and they subsequently lost contact with Skaro. This faction of Daleks had a powerful space fleet (*Lucifer Rising*) invaded the Earth (*The Dalek Invasion of Earth*) and the rest of the Solar System (*GodEngine*), and fought the Mechanoids (*The Chase*). They developed internal power supplies and (at some point after *The Dalek Invasion of Earth*) the "slatted" design, rather than the "banded" one seen in the first two stories. Following this - possibly licking their wounds following their defeat in *The Dalek Invasion of Earth* - the survivors of this faction returned to their home planet. They would have discovered a city full of dead Daleks - and perhaps the Doctor's role in their cousins' defeat.

While unsupported by evidence from the show, and

a little awkward, it fits in with the facts we learn at the end of *The Space Museum* and *The Chase* - the Daleks now live on Skaro, their influence stretches across time and space, they have limited knowledge of the Doctor, advanced science and a desire for revenge specifically against the Doctor, Ian, Barbara and Susan.

343 *The Gallifrey Chronicles*

LAST CONTACT: It's not recorded when the Daleks discover key facts about the Doctor. By *The Chase*, they can recognise the TARDIS (which they didn't directly see in the two TV stories up to that point, as it was either deep in the petrified forest or buried by rubble), and they also know the Doctor can travel in time. In *The Chase*, the Daleks refer to "The Doctor and these three humans", which might imply that they don't think the Doctor is human. Except that one of the other three is his granddaughter Susan and later in the story they *do* refer to the Doctor as "human". In *The Chase*, it doesn't even occur to them that Susan might have left, so it's unlikely they've got records of other incarnations of the Doctor or companions. They think he's human in *The Evil of the Daleks*, but said he was from "another galaxy" in *The Daleks' Master Plan*. When the Daleks deal with the Monk and the Master, they don't ever make the connection on screen that they are from the same planet as the Doctor.

Contrast all of this with *Resurrection of the Daleks*, where they refer (for the first time) to the Doctor as a Time Lord and identify his home planet as Gallifrey.

On the other hand, the Time Lords certainly know of the Daleks - they're referred to in the Doctor's trial in *The War Games*, plus the Time Lords send the Doctor on missions against them in *Planet of the Daleks* and *Genesis of the Daleks*. The Monk and the Master also know about the Daleks. In the time of Rassilon, the Daleks were banned from the Games of Death on Gallifrey, so the Gallifreyans then knew of the Daleks, but there's no evidence that the two races made con-

their recreation programme. Instead, they set up the Leisure Hive, which offered a range of holiday pursuits for intergalactic tourists while promoting peace and understanding between races. Argolis became the first leisure planet. Meanwhile, a central government took control of the Foamasi planet, breaking the power bases of the old Lodges. The new government sought restitution with Argolis.[348]

Humanity had consolidated its position, and now possessed a large number of colony worlds. Both the Earth government and the corporations were quite capable of closing down the supply routes to uneconomic or uncooperative colonies, abandoning them entirely.

Away from Earth, life was often still very harsh. The corporations or governing elites that controlled each colony discovered that as long as Earth was kept sup- plied with minerals and other resources, Earth Central would turn a blind eye to local human rights abuses.[349]

Stanoff Osterling was regarded as one of the two greatest playwrights in human history. His work conformed to the stage conventions of his time, following the Greek tradition of reporting offstage action in elegant speeches rather than seeing it performed. The galaxy's economy was damaged after the wars and the colonies could not afford anything more lavish, but this reliance on dialogue and plotting rather than technological innovation led to a flourishing of the theatre across the galaxy. Osterling was regarded as a genius in his own time for such plays as *Death by Mirrors*, *The Captain's Honour* and *The Mercenary*. His greatest achievement, however, was felt to be his lost play *The Good Soldiers* (2273) that dealt with the aftermath of the battle at Limlough. The Doctor helped transcribe the

---

tact. There's another continuity problem here - why is it that the Doctor and Susan *don't* know about the Daleks before they meet them in *The Daleks*? It's a particular problem because by *The Dalek Invasion of Earth*, the Doctor seems au fait with their complete history. It's possible, as with so much history of that period, that the modern Time Lords had long lost or filed away their knowledge of the Daleks.

We hear the Daleks and Time Lords have all but wiped each other out in *Dalek* and *The Parting of the Ways*.

344 In *The Space Museum*, the Moroks have a Dalek specimen from "Planet Skaro", one with horizontal bands rather than vertical slats. It seems likely that the Moroks raid Skaro at some undisclosed time around *The Daleks*. It's unlikely it was before, as it's implied that the Daleks have no knowledge of life on other planets. Although this in turn contradicts *Genesis of the Daleks,* in which both Davros and the Dalek leader express a wish to conquer other worlds once they know the Doctor is an alien.

345 Dating *The Chase* (2.8) - In *The Daleks' Master Plan*, Steven states that he is from "thousands of years" before the year 4000, making him one of the earlier deep space pilots. *Salvation* stated that Steven was from "the mid twenty-third century".

The TARDIS Logs suggested a date of "3773 AD". The first and second editions of *The Programme Guide* set dates of "2150" and "2250" respectively, *The Terrestrial Index* settled on "early in the 27th Century". The American *Doctor Who* comic suggested a date of "2170". "A History of the Daleks" in *DWM* #77 claimed a date of "3764 AD", *The Discontinuity Guide* suggested that Steven fought in "one of the Cyber Wars, or the Draconian conflict". *Timelink* suggests "3550", *About Time* "2200 - 2400".

There's no indication that the Daleks are in their native time when they fight the Mechanoids at the end of the story, but the Daleks have fought the Mechanoids before. We saw this happen in the *TV Century 21* strip, in "Eve of the War", but there's a problem - that story is set very soon after the Daleks started space exploration, explicitly centuries before mankind could have built the Mechanoids. Additionally, the Mechanoids in the strip are far more inventive and advanced.

There are a number of possibilities - these are two different lines of Mechanoids (even though they look the same and come from a planet called Mechanus), that the ones that fight the Daleks in the strip are time travellers (which there's absolutely no evidence for); that the Mechanoids the humans sent out were based on alien technology, perhaps acquired after some unseen Mechanoid attack on Earth (again, no evidence - and it doesn't explain why both come from Mechanus). While there's no evidence for it, the simplest answer of all is ... that the Mechanoids have lied to Steven Taylor about their origins, and that they are a powerful spacefaring alien race who have fought the Daleks in the past.

The end credits of episode five and six of *The Chase* spell the name as "Mechanoid" and "Mechonoid" respectively. The script spells the name of the planet as "Mechonous", with the comic strip preferring "Mechanus". Perhaps the (rather messy) answer is that there are two, near identical, robot races out there - Mechonoids built by humans to colonise Mechonous, and Mechanoids a far more advanced race of outer space robot people from the planet Mechanus.

346 *Spiral Scratch*

347 *The Romance of Crime*

348 *The Leisure Hive*

349 Many stories feature Earth colonies that supply the home planet and are subject to tyrannical regimes. I see this as a specific era in future history, when space travel and interplanetary communications were still

play, as Osterling had restioparothis.[350]

The terraforming of Raghi was completed.[351] The Mutant Rights Act was passed in 2278. Uva Beta Uva III was at the centre of a belzite rush unparalleled in human history around this time.[352]

c 2285 - VENGEANCE ON VAROS[353] -> The Galatron Mining Corporation and the AMORB prospect fought over mineral rights on the planets of the galaxy, often with little concern for local populations. One such place was Varos, a former prison planet (pop. 1,620,783) in the constellation of Cetes. An officer elite ran Varos and lived in relative luxury, although everyone was confined to enclosed domes with artificial atmospheres. A majority of the people had the constitutional right to vote for the Governor's execution. Until traces were detected on the asteroid Biosculptor, Varos was long thought to be the only source of zeiton-7 ore, a fuel for space / time vehicles.

In the late twenty-third century, Galatron Mining and the government of Varos entered negotiations for the zeiton-7 ore. The engineers of every known solar system needed zeiton to power their space/time craft, but Galatron supplied food to Varos. They had a stranglehold over the colony and were able to keep the price down to seven credits a unit. Successive Governors had developed an entertainment industry, Comtech, that sold footage of the executions, tortures and escape attempts of prisoners to every civilised world. This not only acted as a deterrent for potential rebels, but kept the majority of the population entertained.

Eventually one Governor negotiated the fair price of twenty credits a unit for Varos' zeiton.

2290 - THE LEISURE HIVE[354] -> By 2290, it was clear that the Leisure Hive on Argolis was in trouble. Last year's bookings had fallen dramatically, and advance bookings for 2291 were disastrous. Argolis now faced competition from other leisure planets such as Abydos and Limus 4. The West Lodge of the Foamasi offered to buy the planet, but the board refused and instead pinned their hopes on tachyon experiments conducted by the Earth scientist Hardin. Agents of the Foamasi government arrested two members of the West Lodge, who were attempting to establish a power base on Argolis, and it was discovered that the Tachyon

limited and have placed most of these stories together in the period just prior to the formation of the Earth Empire. The New and Missing Adventures have attempted to weave a more systematic and consistent "future history" for Earth, and many have concerned themselves with this period of early colonisation, corporate domination and increasing centralisation.
350 *Theatre of War*
351 "Nearly a quarter of a century" before *Lords of the Storm*.
352 "About a hundred and fifty years" before *The Romance of Crime*.
353 Dating *Vengeance on Varos* (22.2) - The Governor states that Varos has been a mining colony for "centuries" and it has been stable "for over two hundred years". Peri tells the Governor that she is from "nearly three centuries before you were born". The story takes place before *Mindwarp*. Mentors must live longer than humans, as the Mentor Sil appears in both stories (although he changes colour from brown to green between the two). The novel set it in "the latter part of the twenty-third century", as did *The Terrestrial Index. The Discontinuity Guide* set a range "between 2285 and 2320". *Timelink* said "2324".
354 Dating *The Leisure Hive* (18.1) - Romana establishes that the war was in "2250", "forty years" before.
355 *The Highest Science*
356 "Seventy years" before *The Infinity Race*.
357 Dating *The Stones of Venice* (BF #18) - The story itself says that it's the "twenty-third century", but *Neverland* gives a firm date of 2294.
358 Dating *Whispers of Terror* (BF #3) - No date is given in the story itself, but references to the play *The Good Soldiers* link it to information given in *Theatre of War*. The story is set within a generation of the first performance of the play.
359 *Interference*
360 About five years before *Excelis Decays*.
361 "Four hundred years" before *The Sensorites*. There is also a Central City on Earth in the year 4000, according to *The Daleks' Master Plan*.
362 In *The Dimension Riders*, Ace tells Lieutenant Strakk that she comes from Perivale, and he says that the area is a "forest" (p68).
363 "About four hundred years" after the 1909 section of *Birthright*.
364 *Synthespians™*
365 *The Stone Rose*
366 *The Highest Science* (p49).
367 Jake and Madelaine appear in *Goth Opera*, and we learn of their fate in *Managra* (p64).
368 *SLEEPY*
369 "Fifteen hundred years" before *A Device of Death*.
370 *Year of the Pig*
371 "Five hundred" years after *Year of the Pig*, although it's impossible to know if the conference is real - and something of interest to Chardalot's time-travelling father - or just part of Charadalot's half-baked imaginings.
372 *The Taking of Planet 5* (p219).
373 *The Twin Dilemma*

Recreation Generator could rejuvenate the Argolin. The Argolin and Foamasi governments re-opened negotiations.

Checkley's World, "The Horror Planet", was settled in 2290 and selected as the best location for a scientific research station. The laboratories were released from state control a decade after the planet was colonised, and the facilities were funded by a number of empires and corporations, including the Arcturans, Riftok and Masel. Earth Government remained the major partner. Weapon systems such as compression grenades, Freire's gas and the Ethers - genetically engineered ghost-troops - were developed.[355]

Human colonists discovered Selonart.[356]

2294 - THE STONES OF VENICE[357] **->** After overthrowing yet another reign of terror, the Doctor and Charley arrived in Venice on the eve of its destruction. The gondoliers of Venice, now amphibians with webbed hands and toes, eagerly awaited the chance to claim the city once it sank beneath the waves.

A series of tremors struck the city, but the Doctor discovered that the "late" Estella, now posing as a city resident named Eleanor Lavish, had once owned an alien device capable of altering reality. The device had kept Estella and Duke Orsino alive for a century by draining Venice's life force, leading to its present decay. The Doctor recovered the device, and Orsino proposed that he and Estella end their lives for Venice's sake. Estella agreed out of continued love for Orsino, and the device turned them into ash, saving the city. The high priest of the Cult of Estella made off with their ashes, possibly to worship them.

c 2295 - WHISPERS OF TERROR[358] **->** Despite a dislike of the visual medium, Visteen Krane became wildly acclaimed as the greatest actor of his age. His body of work was chiefly confined to audio recordings and a few photographs. Later, he became a politician and stood for Presidency with his agent, Beth Pernell, as his running mate.

Before the election, Krane seemingly committed suicide in the Museum of Aural Antiquities, an institution dedicated to the study of all things audio. Pernell pledged to run in Krane's place and continue his policies. The Doctor and Peri arrived and discovered that at the moment of his death, Krane used advanced sound equipment to transfer his brainwaves into the sound medium. Krane had become a creature of pure sound, demented from his transformation and outraged at Pernell, who had engineered his murder.

The Krane-creature attempted to endlessly replicate itself and seize control of the planet, but the Doctor thwarted the scheme and shocked Krane back to sanity. The Doctor and Krane exposed Pernell's plans, and Krane agreed to stay at the Museum to aid Curator Gantman with his research. Pernell fled, but Krane engineered an automobile accident that killed her.

The colony ship *Justinian* set off for Ordifica at the end of the twenty-third century.[359]

Circa 2296, Grayvorn abandoned his "Lord Vaughn Sutton" identity and covertly continued his socio-political engineering in Excelis. The leaders of Artaris' city-states met in secret to sign the Artaris Convention, a bill of rights designed to end the war between them. Grayvorn found the conflict too useful to his industrial efforts and sabotaged the accord. Grayvorn's research culminated in the creation of lumps of bio-mass named "Meat Puppets," which became his master shock troops. He used the Relic's abilities to rip the souls from dissidents and infuse the Meat Puppets with life.[360]

The Twenty-Fourth Century

By the twenty-fourth century, the lower half of England had become a vast Central City.[361] Much of what had been West London was covered in forest.[362] Duronite, an alloy of machonite and duralinium, was discovered in the early twenty-fourth century. Influenza had been eradicated.[363] The James Bond films were remade in the twenty-fourth century.[364] Merik's Theorem was discovered in the twenty-fourth century.[365]

Suspended animation ships were still available in the twenty-fourth century, but they had been superseded by the invention of super light drives.[366] Jonquil the Intrepid destroyed the vampires Lord Jake and Lady Madelaine, but their descendants survived for many thousands of years.[367] On a visit to the twenty-fourth century, the Doctor learnt about the colony at Yemaya.[368] Landor, on the galactic rim, was colonised around now.[369]

In the twenty-fifth century, a mishap at a plastics factory with a matter synthesizer and an advertisement in an antique issue of *Power Man and Iron Fist* created a huge proliferation of x-ray spectacles. The company prospered for a year, but went out of business when a horde of rampaging sea monkeys - something else that shouldn't have existed - destroyed the factory.[370] Alphonse Chardalot wanted to take Toby the Sapient Pig to a scientific conference on Gamantis.[371]

Early in the twenty-fourth century, a philosopher on a colony world published a monograph, *The Myth of the Non-Straight Line*. The population had ceased being able to conceive of circles. The planet was quaratined as scientists from a survey ship attempted to work out why.[372] **The fourth Doctor and one of his fellow Time Lords, Azmael, met on Jaconda around this time.**[373]

Humanity settled a group of forty nine colony worlds that became cut off from Earth. On Colony 34, a hospital was built in the northern mountains from marnite stone. Colony 48 lacked access to navigable waters.[374] Maurit Guillan discovered the paradise planet of Laylora, but later his ship was found drifting near Draconian space, the location of Laylora lost. The search for the planet went on to inspire a number of explorers.[375]

c 2301 - EXCELIS DECAYS[376] ->

Excelis was now in a permanent state of war. Grayvorn's ambition started to reach beyond Artaris, and he desired to deploy his "Meat Puppet" shock troops through the whole of time and space. The seventh Doctor arrived on Artaris and merged his soul with the Relic, exerting enough power to send Grayvorn's captured souls to the afterlife. Grayvorn's "Meat Puppets" consequently became dormant, quashing his plans. Rather than accept defeat, Grayvorn activated Excelis' orbital defence grid and bombarded every major city on Artaris with nuclear missiles. Grayvorn died in the onslaught, but the Doctor escaped.

The saga of Artaris and the Relic continues in the Bernice Summerfield audio "The Plague Herds of Excelis."

? 2305 - THE SLOW EMPIRE[377] ->

The Slow Empire had been founded in a region of space where the laws of physics prohibited faster-than-light travel. Some worlds facilitated trade and communication via "Transference Pylons," which transmitted Ambassadors and materials between worlds at light speed. However, the Empire founders had long ago killed themselves through warfare, which helped to plunge the Empire into decay.

The Empire world Shakrath was ruled by a corrupt Emperor who gave visitors generous receptions for posterity, then sent them to the torture chambers. Some centuries previous on Goronos, a slave class had successfully revolted but found themselves unable to function without their masters. They transferred their minds into an elaborate "Cyberdyne" computer reality and Goronos became an urban wasteland. On Thakrash some five hundred years previous (as that planet recorded time), a metamorphic Collector crashed onto the planet and ruined its Transference Pylon. The slaves there revolted, forcing Thakrash into isolation.

A disturbance in the Time Vortex prompted some of its inhabitants, the Vortex Wraiths, to flee in fear of their lives. A group of Vortex Wraiths manifested on the long-dead homeworld of the Empire founders and usurped control of

374 "Almost one hundred years" before *LIVE 34*.

375 "Fifty years" before *The Price of Paradise*, which is set in the late twenty-fourth century. The reference to the Draconians apparently contradicts the timescale established in *Frontier in Space*, although other novels (such as *Love and War*) also suggested that humans and Draconians met before their "official" first contact.

376 Dating *Excelis Decays* (BF *Excelis* series #3) - It is three hundred years before *The Plague Herds of Excelis*, a Bernice Summerfield audio, which is outside the scope of this book. However, *Plague Herds* is set around 2601, the period Benny has settled in, allowing us to date the Excelis saga.

377 Dating *The Slow Empire* (EDA #47) - No date is given, but it's before *Burning Heart*, because the Piglet People of Glomi IV are mentioned here and extinct there. This date is completely arbitrary. The realm is typically referred to just as "the Empire", and is here referred to as "the Slow Empire" for clarity.

378 Dating *The Twin Dilemma* (21.7) - In his novelisation, Eric Saward places the story around "2310". This is neither confirmed nor contradicted on screen. The freighter disappears "eight months" before *The Twin Dilemma*, which the novelisation sets in August. A computer monitor says that the "last contact" with the freighter was made on "12-99". If the twelve stands for the twelfth month, the ninety-nine might stand for the last year of a century. *The Programme Guide* set the story "c2310", *The Discontinuity Guide* in "2200".

379 *SLEEPY*

380 "Profits of Doom"

381 "Two hundred and fifty years" before *The Also People*.

382 *Fear of the Dark*. The book's internal dating is confused. On p81, the Doctor finds a record dated "2319.01.12", which puts these events seventy three years before the novel takes place. However, Tegan claims this happened "one hundred and fifty years ago" (p81), and the Doctor says it was "over one hundred and sixty years" ago (p93).

383 Dating "Profits of Doom" (DWM #120-122) - It's "eight decades out from Earth" and escaping "24th century Earth". Although as the date is soon specified by a monitor robot as "January 7th 2321", they actually left twenty-third century Earth.

384 *The Also People* (p54).

385 "Thirty years" before *Lords of the Storm* (p263).

386 Dating *Valhalla* (BF #96) - The story would seem to occur in a year ending in 45, as "9-1-46" (the date given on a sales catalog) is said to be "next month". Funnily enough, the actual century is never specified. One clue is that the Doctor says he has "overshot [Valhalla's] glory days" - meaning the gas mine rush there - by "about a century". This is probably related to mankind's original breakout from the solar system in the third millennium, but it's unlikely to have occurred in the twenty-second century (the Dalek invasion would surely have disrupted such a boom time, and no mention is made of this). We know from *Lucifer Rising* that people were living on Callisto as early as the early twenty-sec-

the Pylon system. The Wraiths hoped to manifest their entire race in its billions via the Pylons, and tried to coerce the eighth Doctor's help by threatening the inhabitants of multiple worlds in the Empire. The Doctor betrayed the Wraiths by shorting out the main Transference Pylon, both turning the Wraiths into ash and generating a pulse that would, in time, annihilate every Pylon and end the corrupt Empire.

? 2310 (August) - THE TWIN DILEMMA[378] **->** The Earth feared attacks by aliens, and the Interplanetary Pursuit Squadrons were established. The mathematical prodigies Romulus and Remus were abducted in the Spacehopper Mk III Freighter XV773, which had been reported destroyed eight months before. Romulus and Remus mysteriously reappeared on Earth shortly afterward, claiming the gastropod Mestor, who planned to destroy Jaconda and spread his eggs throughout the universe, had kidnapped them. The Jocondans had overthrown their leader and defeated his plans, with the help of the sixth Doctor and their former leader, Azmael.

Youkali Press published *An Eye for Wisdom: Repetitive Poems of the Early Ikkaban Period* by Bernice S. Summerfield in 2315.[379]

Every six months, one of ten crew of the colony ship *Mayflower* was woken as part of a crew rota to check ship's systems - so each crewman woke every five years. Kara McAllista was revived, as planned, on 6th January, 2316.[380]

The Dyson Sphere of the Varteq Veil had begun to break up.[381] Humans arrived on the moon of Akoshemon, on the edge of the Milky Way, in 2319. By this time, there was a Human Sciences Academy on Mars, and a base on Titan.[382]

2321 (7th January) - "Profits of Doom"[383] **->** Sluglike aliens invaded the *Mayflower* colony ship. The sixth Doctor, Peri and Frobisher arrived to discover that the cryotubes of the "top drawer", the elite, had been stolen. The aliens were the Profiteers of Ephte from Ephte Major - a profit-driven race of conquerors. The Doctor accessed the navigational systems and discovered there

was nothing at the ship's destination. Instead, Varley Gabriel was profiting by selling the humans to the Profiteers. The Doctor got the aliens to withdraw by threatening to destroy the ship, and reprogrammed the navigation systems to set course for Arcadia.

Third Eye released their HvLP, *Outta My Way Monkeyboy* in 2327.[384] In 2341, a Rutan spy adopted the identity of Sontaran Major Karne. An attack on a Sontaran cruiser was staged, and the Sontarans recovered his escape pod. For decades, the Rutans received top-level Sontaran military secrets.[385]

? 2345 (the first Thursday in December) - VALHALLA[386] **->** The Mars Express was in operation at this time.

The domed city of Valhalla, located on Jupiter's moon of Callisto, had fallen prey to blight. It cost nothing to arrive in Valhalla, but a fortune to leave, so the city increasingly became home to the dispossessed, space hippies and tourists who arrived on the wrong flight. Immigration services stamped bar codes onto the tongues of everyone in the city. Food and energy cutbacks were introduced, and owing to the shoddy conditions, riots were dutifully scheduled held the first Thursday of every month. On such occasions, body armour and refreshments were available at licensed outlets.

Genetically engineered termites had grown to massive size on Callisto, and their queen - Our Mother the Fourth - directed her children to seize control of Valhalla. Our Mother wanted to insure her progeny's future by selling off Valhalla's assets and people; a sales catalog was prepared.

The seventh Doctor arrived in Valhalla at this time, and tricked the termites into thinking that Our Mother had died. This forcibly instigated a new wedding flight as winged termites sought out the new queen, and Our Mother did in fact pass away. Dialogue was opened with the new Queen, and it was hoped she would be more reasonable than her predecessor.

In 2350, the Jullatii would have over-run the Earth but for INITEC's invention of the boson cannon.[387]

---

ond century, and *To the Slaughter* (c.2505) depicts Jupiter's moons as being so worthless, they can be blown up in accordance with the principles of feng shui. The best compromise, then, is probably to say that the boom occurs in the twenty-third century, and *Valhalla* takes place in the twenty-fourth. (Callisto itself survives *To the Slaughter* and seems to have obtained greater significance by *So Vile a Sin*, set in 2982, as it's home to the Emperor's palace.)

Riots are held on the first Thursday of every month, and one occurs here. A piece of conflicting information,

however, is that it's repeatedly said that electrical engineer Jevvan Petrovna Adrea is having a birthday, and she was born "3-2-23". This would seem to indicate that Valhalla takes place on 3rd February, not December as the catalog suggests. If push comes to shove, the catalog is probably more important to the plot (as it's what motivates the Doctor to visit Valhalla in the first place) and should arguably take precedence.
387 *Original Sin* (p287).

c 2350 - "The Seventh Segment"[388] -> Humans settled Vyga 3 in 2350, and the eccentric culture that developed defied legal and policing systems. The fourth Doctor, Romana and K9 landed on Vyga 3, looking for a segment of the Key to Time, but the tracer was confused by an object in a briefcase that a local criminal gang were after. It wasn't a segment, but rather a fluctuating chronal wave. When opened, the briefcase aged everyone in the area to death - leaving the Doctor glad he hadn't got round to checking it for himself.

? 2350 - EXOTRON[389] -> Human colony planets were sometimes subject to oversight from Earth Authority, which could dispatch security officers as required.

On an unnamed Earth colony, the Exotron Project was initiated to create a new type of robot for sale to the military. Major Hector Taylor and Ballentyne - the Secretary of the Interior - colluded to further the project, which entailed hardwiring the bodies of mortally wounded soldiers into large Exotron robot shells. The soldiers remained

alive in a state of pain, but their neural networks enabled the Exotrons to function.

Two years after the research team's arrival, a form of indigenous life - the hyena-like Farakosh - were coming into conflict with the Exotrons, as the cyborgs' neural net was disrupting the Farakosh's natural telepathic field. The fifth Doctor and Peri arrived at this time, and threatened to expose the truth about the Exotron Project. Taylor died, but Ballentyne triggered the research facility's self-destruct. The troopers within the Exotrons regained some independence, and opted to save everyone by smothering the blast with their own bodies. The Doctor expected that Ballentyne would be hounded from office.

Around 2361, the *Mayflower* arrived to colonise Arcadia.[390]

? 2366 - THE MACRA TERROR[391] -> The crab-like Macra had infiltrated a human colony, using indoctrination techniques to force the colonists to extract a

---

388 Dating "The Seventh Segment" (*DWM Summer Special 1995*) - K9 says the planet was settled "Relative Terran date 2350 AD", but gives no indication how long ago that was, and a later dating is certainly feasible.

389 Dating *Exotron* (BF #95) - Writer Eddie Robson has stated that the planet might be Earth, but the back cover states that the story takes place on "a distant outpost of Earth", and within the story a colony ship arrives direct from Earth (Track 36, for example, has Sergeant Shreeni say, "Bleedin' hell… what a time for the Earth shuttle to arrive"). Security officers are dispatched from an organisation named Earth Authority, which is presumably headquartered on Earth itself.

The atypical and dead-end development of the Exotrons themselves aside, the technology level suggests Earth's early colonial era. Otherwise, this date is arbitrary.

390 "Profits of Doom". The *Mayflower* was twenty years from its original destination in 2321, its new destination is another "twenty or so" years away.

391 Dating *The Macra Terror* (4.7) - The planet was colonised "many centuries" ago. This date is somewhat arbitrary, but it allows the story to fit into a period in which Earth's colonies are relatively remote and unregulated. The level of technology is reasonably low. The second edition of *The Making of Doctor Who* described the setting as "the distant future". *The Programme Guide* set the story "c.2600", *The Terrestrial Index* preferred "between 2100 and 2150", *Timelink* "2670".

392 *Gridlock*. The Doctor says the Macra were the scourge of "this galaxy", and *New Earth* establishes that the planet New Earth isn't in our galaxy. Nonetheless, we can probably infer that he means our galaxy.

393 *Zagreus*, but this is part of a suspect simulation.

394 Tairngaire was colonised "three hundred years" before *Shadowmind* (p32).

395 Dating *Lords of the Storm* (MA #17) - The Doctor states that it is "Earthdate 2371" (p23).

396 *The Stone Rose*

397 "Five or six years" before *The Romance of Crime* (p62-63).

398 *The Eight Doctors*. Not date given, but Sarg appears in *Shakedown*, so it is before that time.

399 "Ten winters" and "many years" before *Infinite Requiem*.

400 *Divided Loyalties* (p31).

401 Dating *The Androids of Tara* (16.4) - The Doctor implies that Tara is "400 years and twelve parsecs" away from Earth at the time of *The Stones of Blood*. I assume that the TARDIS travelled into the future, not the past, and that Tara is an isolated Earth colony (as the Tarans know of life on other planets). *The Terrestrial Index* set the story in the "50th century", *The Discontinuity Guide* in the "2370s".

402 Dating *Mindwarp* (23.2) - The Valeyard announces that the story starts in the "24th Century, last quarter, fourth year, seventh month, third day". There is a case to be made for 2379, but not "2479" as suggested by the third edition of *The Programme Guide*. Peri is apparently killed in *Mindwarp*, but is revealed as having survived in *The Ultimate Foe*, and returns in the novel *Bad Therapy*. A fabricated image of her older self appears in *Her Final Flight*.

403 "The Age of Chaos"

404 *Mindwarp*

405 Dating *The Price of Paradise* (NSA #12) - It's "the late twenty fourth century".

406 Dating *The Romance of Crime* (MA #6) - Uva Beta Uva was "colonised in Earth year 2230" according to

deadly gas that the Macra breathed. The colonists were kept in a state of complacent happiness. Eventually, the second Doctor, Jamie, Ben and Polly exposed the Control - the colony's propaganda spokesperson - as a giant Macra. The Doctor directed Ben to destroy the Marca's gas pumps, which slew the invaders.

The Macra were a scourge of the galaxy, controlling a small empire with humans as slaves. Eventually, though, they degenerated into unthinking animals.[392]

Walton Winkle became known throughout the Earth Empire as "Uncle Winky, the man who put a smile on the galaxy". He founded the amusement park Winky Wonderland on Io, but entered hibernation inside his "Cosmic Mountain" on 18th December, 2367, due to a heart condition. He wouldn't revive from stasis until shortly before the end of the universe.[393]

Around 2370, human settlers colonised Tairngaire. The capital city was built on an isthmus and named New Byzantium. The planet rapidly became one of the more prosperous colonies. The temporary lights built by the settlers eventually became the Lantern Market.[394]

2371 - LORDS OF THE STORM[395] **->** The Sontarans, fresh from destroying the Rutan installation at Betelgeuse V, attempted to use captured Tzun technology against their eternal enemies. They genetically tagged the human population of the Unukalhai System, intending that a Rutan sensor sweep would indicate a Sontaran population of one hundred million. The Rutan would send a fleet from Antares and the Sontarans planned to ignite a brown dwarf using the Tzun Stormblade, destroying the Rutans and the whole system as well. The fifth Doctor defeated the plan.

By 2375, the Bureau Tygo was Earth's main scientific research centre, and humans were used to getting what they wanted. In May of that year, Salvatorio Moretti created Genetically Engineered Neural Imagination Engines (GENIEs) that could bend space and time to grant wishes. Earth was threatened by competing desires, so one group of people wished to go back in time and prevent the GENIEs' creation. One GENIE survived in ancient Rome.[396]

In 2375, the police broke up the notorious Nisbett firm, a criminal gang responsible for extortion, fraud, smuggling, arms dealing, torture and multiple murder. Tony, Frankie and Dylan the Leg were all executed, but the Nisbett brothers - Charlie and Eddie - escaped.[397] Sontaran Commander Vrag's commando squad was timescooped to the Eye of Orion by Time Lord Ryoth, shortly after being presented with a medal by Admiral Sarg.[398]

The colony world Gadrell Major was on the brink of nuclear war in 2377, leading the population to construct fallout shelters. Around this time, the Earth was at war with the Phractons.[399] Dymok demanded isolation from Earth in 2378. Imperial Earth Space Station Little Boy II was built to oversee the planet.[400]

c 2378 - THE ANDROIDS OF TARA[401] **->** On Tara, the fourth Doctor prevented the Count Grendel from usurping the throne from its rightful heir, Prince Reynart. Grendel escaped to fight another day.

2379 (3rd July) - MINDWARP[402] **->** The Mentors of Thoros Beta continued to trade across the galaxy via the warpfold relay, supplying phasers to the Warlords of Thordon, and weapons that allowed Yrcanos of the Krontep to conquer the Tonkonp Empire. They also traded with such planets as Wilson One and Posikar.

The brain of his Magnificence Kiv, the leader of the Mentors, continued to expand in his skull. He enlisted the services of Crozier, a human scientist who specialised in the transfer of consciousness. Crozier experimented on a number of Thoros Betan creatures and the Mentors' captives, creating hybrids and exploring with the ageing process. After a decade of hard work, he had developed a serum that allowed him to place any brain in any body.

Subsequent events are unclear - it appears that the Time Lords intervened to prevent the threat posed to the course of evolution across the universe, causing Kiv to be killed. The Doctor's companion, Peri Brown, was seemingly killed but in reality remained on Thoros-Beta, where she eventually married Yrcanos.

Peri had a son, Corynus, who went on to marry Yrcanthia and have two sons (Artios and Euthys) and a daughter (Actis).[403] **The late twenty-fourth century saw wars around the Rim Worlds of Tokl.**[404]

c 2380 - THE PRICE OF PARADISE[405] **->** For eighteen months, Professor Petra Shulough led an expedition in the SS Humphrey Bogart to find the Paradise Planet. An electromagnetic pulse crippled the ship, and it crashed on the beautiful forest world of Laylora. The tenth Doctor and Rose answered the ship's distress call. The planet was rich in trisilicate - as Shulough's father had discovered fifteen years earlier - but it was also alive and reacted to the presence of alien life by creating Witiku, fierce four-armed monsters. Shulough agreed to keep the existence of Laylora a secret.

Micro fusion generators had been banned on most planets by this time, due to the toxic waste they produced.

c 2380 (21st - 22nd April) - THE ROMANCE OF CRIME[406] **->** In the late 2370s, the Ceerads (Cellular Remission and Decay) - mutants - were purged on Vanossos. Some survived and resettled on Uva Beta Uva

Six, leading to conflict with the colonists in that system. The galaxy faced another recession at this time.

Xais was the last of the Ugly Mutants and the self-proclaimed Princess of the Guaal Territories. She was a genius terrorist who murdered two thousand people, and was executed by particle reversal in 2377. Xais had learned, however, how to transfer her consciousness into the substance helicon. Her mind came to reside in a helicon mask made by the artist Menlove Stokes, enabling her to possess people.

Xais teamed up with the criminal Nisbett brothers and their Ogrons, claiming to have discovered rich belzite deposits on Uva Beta Uva Eleven. In fact, the planet contained a great deal of helicon, through which Xais hoped to generate duplicates of herself and commit mass slaughter. The Nisbett brothers perished as part of this affair, but the fourth Doctor, Romana and K9 worked to stop Xais' plan. Xais' mind became trapped in a mass quantity of helicon, which expanded to cover the whole of Uva Beta Uva Eleven. The Doctor supplied one of his associates, the police investigator Spiggot, with a formula that could destroy the helicon and Xais within.

= **c 2380 - THE INFINITY RACE**[407] -> Sabbath attempted to harness the infinity forces on the planet Selonart in a parallel universe. Selonart served as host to the Trans-Global Selonart Regatta, which took place every five Earth years. The eighth Doctor joined the fourteenth Regatta, defeating Sabbath's plan. Sabbath had released the Warlocks of Demigest to assist with his scheme, but the Doctor used time crystals formed on Selonart to erase the Warlocks' presence from the universe.

The Greer colonies and Proxima Centauri were part of the Earth Empire. There was civil war on Cygnus, where the rebels refused to give up their plesiosaur farms. The Imperial Security Service covered all humanity, including the Empire, the Bronstein Union of Socialist Systems, Mikron Conglomerates, Proudhon Confederation and the Western Hub Consortium.

The New Earth system was colonised in 2380.[408]

On Colony 34, a planet with two moons, Premier Leo Jaeger swept to power on the pledge to clean up governmental corruption. However, a disease left him scarred, and surgical efforts to correct this only caused greater deformity. Jaeger feared this would erode his popularity, so a Jaeger lookalike from an outer province was tapped to double for him at public events. The real Jaeger governed from behind the scenes, but the doppelgänger gradually replaced Jaeger's loyalists with his own staff. The double finally took control, and the genuine article was secretly kept alive so his Biometric ID could reinforce the duplicate's appearance.

Colony 34's resources were not as plentiful as previously thought, and an energy crisis caused unrest. Fifteen years after the real Jaeger took office, his double capitalised on the situation by restricting freedoms and postponing elections. Two years later, he tightened control using the Emergency Powers Act. Two years after that, the Chamber of Deputies was accused of widespread corruption and suspended.

Human bodies made excellent fuel if used properly, so the government secretly began harvesting Colony 34's underclass. Jaeger's Inner Senate started advertising employment opportunities for outsiders, and interested travellers from other colonies were similarly captured and

---

Romana (p47); the story is set "a hundred and fifty years later" (p8). The month and day are given on p46.

407 Dating *The Infinity Race* (EDA #61) - There's a conspiracy of assassins who have been waiting "six hundred years" (p191) for the chance to eliminate Sabbath - this would appear to be an offshoot of the Secret Service, which initiated him into its ranks in 1762. (There are reports - in our reality, at least - of the Service trying to kill Sabbath in 1780, although it's entirely possible that they moved to kill him sooner.)

Mention is also made of an Earth Empire that's ruled by an Emperor, but as the story takes place in a parallel universe, there's no guarantee that its history is comparable to our own. Dating this story off Sabbath's history seems a surer bet, as it's established in *Sometime Never* that the Council of Eight - deeming the Doctor the most unpredictable element in the whole of history - recruited Sabbath as the most constant variable in the whole of time. This is the reason, in fact, that no tempo-

ral duplicates of Sabbath show up in *The Last Resort*, whereas the Doctor, Fitz and Anji are duplicated thousands of times over. In every alternate history that we're shown in this period of the EDAs, then, Sabbath's history is reliably consistent.

408 "Dogs of Doom". The date is given.

409 The real Jaeger comes to power "twenty years" before *LIVE 34*.

410 *The Happiness Patrol*

411 Dating *The Dimension Riders* (NA #20) - It is "the late twenty-fourth century" (p2). The Doctor repeats this, adding it is "Just before Benny's time, and after the Cyberwars" (p25) - this analysis comes from *The Terrestrial Index* rather than the television series. The date is not precisely fixed until the sequel, *Infinite Requiem*, which is set in 2387, "six years" after the events of the first book. "March 22nd" was "one week ago" (p76).

412 *Infinite Requiem*

turned into fuel.[409]

Gilbert M was exiled from Vasilip when he accidentally wiped out half the planet's population with a germ he'd been working on. By this time, there were scheduled interplanetary flights and he simply travelled to Terra Alpha with the Kandy Man's bones in his briefcase.[410]

& 2381 (29th March) - THE DIMENSION RIDERS[411]

-> Half the planets colonised by humanity had been abandoned during the wars. But now, generally, this was a period of interplanetary peace.

The Survey Corps existed to patrol space and deal with situations unsuitable for military or humanitarian missions. As such, Survey Corps vessels had both troopers (armed with state-of-the-art Derenna handguns) and support staff. By the end of the twenty-fourth century, however, underfunding meant that many of the Corps' ships were obsolete.

On 22nd March, 2381, Space Station Q4 in the fifty-fourth sector of charted space, on the edge of the spiral arm and human territory, was attacked by the Garvond's Time Soldiers. The station's crew were aged to death. The Survey Corps vessel *Icarus* investigated, and discovered that Q4 was one end of a Time Focus leading to Earth in 1993. The Garvond intended to trigger temporal paradoxes, then use the Time Focus to absorb chronal energy. In the following battle, Darius Cheynor, second-in-command of the *Icarus*, distinguished himself.

Cheynor was offered command of the *Phoenix*.[412]

2382 - FEAR OF THE DARK[413] -> Humanity had made

contact with the Vegans, a proud mining race, by this time. Earth had interests in the Antares, Betelgeuse, Denox, Kaltros Prime and Earth Colony E5150. Suspended animation was still in use, and neurolectrin was used to resuscitate sleepers. The University of Tyr specialised in temporal compression.

The fifth Doctor was drawn to the moon of Akoshemon

when the Dark - an ancient being ravenous for blood - influenced Nyssa's mind. The Dark hoped to manifest itself physically in our dimension, but the Doctor destroyed it.

? 2385 - SLIPBACK[414] -> The TARDIS was pulled out of

the Vortex by illegal time experiments aboard the starship *Vipod Mor*. A Maston, an extinct monster, attacked the sixth Doctor and Peri. The Doctor discovered that a botched maintenance job had endowed the ship's computer with a split personality, and one of its personas was planning to take the ship back in time to impose order on the universe. The Doctor was about to stop the time journey when a Time Lord made contact to inform him that the *Vipod Mor* was part of the established history - it would explode upon arrival, creating the Big Bang.

In 2386, Unreal Transfer was discovered.[415] The artist Menlove Stokes entered cryogenic sleep, hoping to awaken in an era that better appreciated his work. He was revived in the Fifty-Eighth Segment of Time.[416] When her colleagues were captured, a physicist travelled back in time to Little Caldwell, 1983. With the help of Isaac Summerfield, she returned home and freed her workmates.[417]

The same year, slow compression time - a method of slowing down time in a small area - was first theorised. Within a couple of years a slow time converter, or "time telescope" had been built.[418] The Bartholomew Transactor became very popular as a party tool, able to send messages back in time and thereby create ghostly images of an alternate timeline. The effects were harmless, and lasted a minute at most.[419] A law enforcement agency, the Bureau, discovered an alien time corridor in the Playa del Nuttingchapel. They dispatched an agent to investigate in 1930, where he adopted the alias Percy Closed.[420]

2387 (29th May) - INFINITE REQUIEM[421] -> In the

late 2380s, there was a famine on Tenos Beta and storms in the Magellani System. There was also more co-operation between the various elements of the Earth's space navy.

---

413 Dating *Fear of the Dark* (PDA #58) - The date is given on the back cover. The personnel file of a mineral pirate, Jyl Stoker, says she departed Earth Central some years back in 2363 (p109), and Tegan notes it has been "400 years" since 1982 (p118). It is after the time when Mechanoids were used. The Vegans first appeared in *The Monster of Peladon*.
414 Dating *Slipback* (Radio 4 drama, unnumbered Target novelisation) - An arbitrary date. The *Vipod Mor* is undertaking a census, perhaps placing it in the same time period as *The Happiness Patrol*. The illegal time travel experiments in this story also fit neatly with the time travel research mentioned in a variety of other

adventures set in the twenty-fourth century.
415 *The Leisure Hive*
416 *The Well-Mannered War* (p273).
417 She's from "the twenty-fourth century" according to *Return of the Living Dad* (p41).
418 *The Highest Science* (p203, p235).
419 "Centuries" after *Night Thoughts*.
420 "Many hundreds of years" after *The English Way of Death*, with reference to the group Third Eye (p37).
421 Dating *Infinite Requiem* (NA #36) - The year is quickly established as "2387" (p5). The precise date is given (p273). It is "six years" since *The Dimension Riders* (p15).

Over the next couple decades the military, the ships of the Guild of Adjudicators, the Survey Corps and the corporations' own battle squadrons unified into the Space Fleet.

The Earth colony of Gadrell Major was rich in porizium ore, a valuable material used in medicine. The planet also had strategic value. When the Phracton fleet attacked the colony, Darius Cheynor and the *Phoenix* were sent to investigate. The Phracton Swarm were telepathic cyborgs with a communal mind, and their tanks - flamers - devastated much of the planet.

Cheynor negotiated a settlement with the Phractons, but a breakaway faction sought to gain retribution for the murders of some Practon delegates. The rogue group killed Cheynor. This led to the Phractons achieving some vindication, and further negotiations would lead to peace.

? 2388 - THE HAPPINESS PATROL[422] **->** The Galactic Census Bureau at Galactic Centre surveyed every colonised planet every six local cycles and, where necessary, suggested measures to control the population size.

On one such planet, Terra Alpha, the native Alphidae were driven underground by the settlers, who covered the planet in sugar fields and factories. Offworlders were restricted to the Tourist Zones. The planet was ruled by Helen A, who insisted that her citizens be happy. To this end, the planet was gaily painted, muzak poured from loudspeakers on every street corner and Helen A created the "Happiness Patrol", which was composed of women authorised to murder the so-called "Killjoys". She also employed the services of the Kandy Man, an artificial being of pure sugar who created sweets that killed people.

Terrorists, protest groups and the Alphidae (now confined to the network of sugar pipes) all resisted, and Helen A authorised the "routine disappearance" of some 499,987 people, 17 percent of the population. The seventh Doctor invened, and Helen A's regime fell in one night. The Kandy Man's candy centre melted.

The Intergalactic Taskforce served the Inner Planets in the late twenty-fourth century.

Throughout the latter half of the twenty-fourth century, the notorious criminal Sheldukher - a ruthless murderer, thief and extortionist - menaced the galaxy. He destroyed the entire Krondel constellation for no apparent reason other than that he could. In 2389, he planned his biggest coup yet, and set about recruiting accomplices.

Marjorie Postine had been an aggressive child, and her parents sold her to the military, a common practice in the commercially-minded twenty-fourth century. She became a mercenary, and Sheldukher secured her services by offering her a Moosehead Repeater, a rifle capable of blowing a hole in a neutron star. She was the veteran of seventeen front-line conflicts. Her right arm was a graft-job, performed by an unqualified surgeon in a trench on Regurel, and her bald head was scarred and lumpy.

A couple of years before, Rosheen and Klift had infiltrated McDrone Systems and used their position to embezzle a vast sum of money. The central markets collapsed, causing entire planetary economies in the fourth zone to collapse into starvation and war. Millions died. The planet Tayloe was flooded with imports. Rosheen and Klift fled to the luxury of the North Gate, where Sheldukher tracked them down. The locals gladly handed them over to him.

Sheldukher had converted a Kezzivot Class transport freighter, welding on a furnace engine, installing sleep suspension chambers stolen from the Dozing Decades company and fitting heavy weaponry such as the cellular disrupter and the spectronic destabiliser. His team raided Checkley's World, stealing Project FXX Q84 - the Cell - an advanced telepathic, organic computer. Although this brought down the wrath of the Intergalactic Taskforce, it was only the beginning of Sheldukher's scheme. He planned to locate the legendary planet Sakkrat, and the greatest prize in the galaxy: the Highest Science.

The mysterious "Highest Science" had preoccupied the galaxy's population for generations. In 2421, the explorer Gustaf Urnst claimed to have discovered Sakkrat, the plan-

422 Dating *The Happiness Patrol* (25.2) - Terra Alpha is an isolated colony, apparently in the same system as Terra Omega. While Trevor Sigma's casual dismissal of Earth may suggest the story is set far in the future, the Doctor states only that the planet was "settled some centuries" in Ace's future. Interstellar travel is via "rocket pods". *Timelink* suggests "2788".
423 *The Highest Science*
424 *The Taking of Planet 5*
425 "Twelve years" before *Divided Loyalties*.
426 *The Happiness Patrol*
427 *Synthespians*™
428 Dating *LIVE 34* (BF #74) - The isolated, heavily censored colonists believe that Earth was abandoned "cen-

turies ago", and most facets of this society - the style of LIVE 34's broadcasts in particular - bring to mind an Earth colony rather than an alien one. Additionally, a LIVE 34 broadcaster doesn't question the dating system when Ace mentions a 1952 Vincent Black Lightning motorcycle. The dating of this story is somewhat arbitrary, although Colony 34 very much fits the mould of an isolated, oppressed Earth colony akin to Terra Alpha in *The Happiness Patrol*.
429 Dating *The Pit* (NA #12) - Benny states that the Seven Planets were destroyed "Fifty years before my time... 2400" (p9).
430 She was married to Yrcanos for twenty five years according to *Bad Therapy* (p288).

et which housed its secrets. No-one took Urnst seriously, although his books remained in print even after his mysterious disappearance. Unknown to the public, a Fortean Flicker had transported him to the twentieth century.

For the next three hundred years, the F61 searched the galaxy for Sakkrat, travelling past the stellar conjunctions of Naiad, the crystal quasars of Menolot and the farthest reaches of Harma. Over the centuries many lesser criminals would imitate Sheldukher, but none would match him.[423]

Archaeologists of this period believed the stories of HP Lovecraft were historically accurate.[424] *Convergence*, a cargo ship, mysteriously disappeared over Dymok in 2396.[425]

The Twenty-Fifth Century

On a visit to Birnam in the twenty-fifth century, the Doctor saw a Stigorax.[426] The Doctor took Peri shopping in a twenty-fifth century Wal-Mart.[427]

c 2400 (9th month, days 1 to 16) - LIVE 34[428] -> Elections on Colony 34 were now five years overdue. Jaeger's administration continued its crackdown, but the Colony Central Commission (CCC) accepted a petition from his opposition - the Freedom and Democracy Party (FDP) - and ruled that elections must be held in sixteen days. The radio station LIVE 34 called Jaeger's administration into question through such programmes as *Wareing's World* and *Live With Charlotte Singh*, but the station's independence was revoked, and the State Broadcast Monitoring Department assumed editorial control.

The seventh Doctor, Ace and Hex had arrived on Colony 34 and learned about Jaeger's oppression. The FDP leader, Durinda Cauldwell, had reportedly been killed by members of her own party, and her predecessor had allegedly died in a transporter accident. The Doctor accepted the FDP leadership, unwilling to risk anyone else's life in the post.

Ace organised resistance as "the Rebel Queen", and her operatives blew up empty government buildings to obtain evidence of Jaeger's corruption. Nobody was killed, but Jaeger's forces blew up a vehicle manufacturing plant and a senior citizens' home, gaining political favour by blaming

the hundreds of resultant casualties on the Bandit Queen and the FDP.

The Doctor stood for election against Jaeger, who claimed to have won with 81.5 percent of the vote, a victory margin of 63 percent. The CCC declared the election void as the Doctor was believed dead during the voting, and the truth about the false Jaeger was revealed. Jaeger's staff were arrested, political prisoners were freed and Charlotte Singh was designated the CCC's representative. The Doctor and his companions departed as a mob fell upon the false Jaeger.

2400 - THE PIT[429] -> At the beginning of the twenty-fifth century, the space docks of Glasson Minor, a planet-sized ship-building station, bustled with activity and human colonisation continued to gather pace.

In 2400, the Seven Planets of the Althosian binary star system were destroyed. Colonisation at this time was still hazardous, and the Seven Planets were far from the normal trading routes, years away from the nearest other colony. A number of new religions sprang up on Nicea, the planet with the largest population, and these spread to the smaller worlds of Trieste and Byzantine. Most of these were based around the Form Manipulator, and adopted Judeo-Christian beliefs to the environment of the Seven Planets. The geographical and religious isolation made it easy for them to declare independence from the Corporation, but the corporations responded by cutting off all supplies and communications. Rioting broke out that the Archon and his armies were unable to contain.

The destruction of the system, though, came about when a former Gallifreyan general, Kopyion Liall a Mahajetsu, detonated a bomb that destroyed the Seven Planets and killed millions. This prevented one of the Time Lords' ancient enemies, the Yssgaroth, from escaping into our universe.

Peri had spent twenty five years married to Yrcanos, and became Queen of the Krontep and the Seven Systems. She governed seven worlds. "Gilliam, Queen of Kr'on Tep", as she was known, disappeared in 2404 and returned to the twentieth century.[430] She later returned to Krontep.[431] Humans colonised the Garazone System. The Garazone

---

431 PERI LEAVES AND CAUSES CONTINUITY PROBLEMS, TAKE TWO AND THREE: Peri's departure was a little confused on television. *The Trial of a Time Lord* first tells us that she died, then that she lived happily ever after with King Yrcanos - a last-minute addition to the script, and a big stretch given what we saw of their on-screen relationship.

However, there's a bigger problem: taking what we're told about subsequent events in the comics and novels, and - as this book does - assuming that it's the same

continuity, a couple of knotty problems emerge.

The first is exactly what happens to Peri, the problem being that the novel *Bad Therapy* and the comic "The Age of Chaos" contradict each other. In *Bad Therapy*, Peri resents her new life and returns to Earth after twenty five years. In "The Age of Chaos", she remains on Krontep and raises a dynasty of children and grandchildren.

Thankfully, the novelisations don't "count" for the purposes of this book, because in the *Mindwarp* novel-

Space Patrol was formed to fight smugglers.[432]

? 2405 - VANISHING POINT[433] **->** The geneticist Cauchemar worked to overthrow "the Creator" responsible for the reincarnation process on an alien colony planet. The Creator's functions were disrupted to the point that deformed children named "mooncalves" were being born without the genetic "godswitch" needed to facilitate reincarnation. Cauchemar hoped to overload the Creator to the point of triggering an energy release that would destroy the entire planet, yet facilitate his soul's admittance to the afterlife, but the eighth Doctor foiled this scheme. The genetic experiments that had extended Cauchemar's life, coupled with radiation exposure, failed and he died.

Years later, the Creator had rebalanced enough to include the mooncalves in its designs.

2408 - DIVIDED LOYALTIES[434] **->** The fifth Doctor arrived on space station *Little Boy II* to find communications with Dymok had been disrupted. He travelled to the planet and was captured by the Toymaker. An attack on the Toymaker's part made Dymok vanish completely, but the Doctor again defeated him.

In 2414, Darzil Carlisle was born outside Olympus Mons on Mars. At age three, following an airlock accident that killed his parents, he was relocated to an orphanage in Finchley, North London. At age seventeen, he earned a scholarship to the Phobos Academy of Music, and studied there for three years.

The Doctor, having encountered an older Carlisle on the planet Cray circa 2484, aided Carlisle in becoming a renowned peacemaker. With the Doctor's secret help, Lord Carlisle ended wars on at least thirty-six planets, and was famed for saving billions of lives.[435]

Around 2415, the people of the Elysium System discovered the Artifact, a vast ammonite-like structure, on the edge of their territory.[436] In 2416, on an unnamed colony world, IMC had set up a genetics engineering project named Project Mecrim. The Company built the ape-like Rocarbies, cheap labour developed from the native primate life; and the Mecrim, a race built for combat with a claw that could vibrate and cut through even the hardest materials. When a Mecrim gut microbe escaped, the colony was declared off-limits. The survivors developed an immunity, but came to hate science and degenerated to a medieval level of technology.[437]

In 2420, the human race and Sontarans signed a non-aggression pact.[438] In the 2420s, the deserts of Earth were reclaimed and the city New Atlantis was built in the Pacific. The population of Earth was sixty billion at this time.

The sixth Doctor and Frobisher visited Peri on Krontep and caught up with her family. Following that visit, her father Corynus was killed in a hunting accident. Yrcanos died suddenly and Artios and Euthys unaccountably fell out over the succession. Peri rode off, vowing not to return until the war had ended. Krontep was devastated by civil war between Artios and Euthys. Yrcanthia, their mother, was killed in crossfire, and this provoked the generals to rebel against both brothers and stake them out in the desert. Farlig was appointed regent to Actis.[439]

c 2429 - "The Age of Chaos"[440] **->** The sixth Doctor arrived on Krontep to celebrate the sixteenth birthday of Actis, Peri's granddaughter, and learned of the turbulence of the last decade. At Actis' insistence, they went to the Antarctic to meet Frobisher. The Doctor and Frobisher set off on a perilous journey to the distant land of Brachion, in hope of finding what had gone wrong with the planet, and

---

isation, Philip Martin stated that Peri and Yrcanos immediately went to the twentieth century and Yrcanos became a professional wrestler.

The simplest solution might be that Peri returned to Earth at the end of *Bad Therapy*, then came to realise she missed her life on Krontep, reconciled with the Doctor and returned to her family. But that link isn't made in any story we've seen, and has to remain speculation.

There's another continuity issue connected with Peri's departure - Frobisher is the companion of the seventh Doctor for one adventure ("A Cold Day in Hell"), and they make reference there to Peri leaving for Krontep with Yrcanos (on television in *Mindwarp*), implying it was very recent. For people reading the *DWM* strip at the time, it was - the story follows straight on from "The World Shapers", featuring the sixth Doctor, Frobisher and Peri, but this is difficult to fit around the

TV series.

Furthermore, in "The Age of Chaos", the sixth Doctor and Frobisher are *twice* seen visiting Krontep, so it's odd that Frobisher hasn't come to terms with Peri leaving. The story also implies that the sixth Doctor has dropped Frobisher off in the Antarctic at some point and is travelling solo. (Strange how Frobisher seems to take sabbaticals from the Doctor's company, as he also leaves the TARDIS for a time in *The Maltese Penguin*, then returns.)

Any solution also has explain how Mel - who's present when the Doctor regenerates (in *Time and the Rani*), but not in "A Cold Day in Hell" or the following story "Redemption" - fits in.

Ultimately, unless Frobisher's hiding in the TARDIS, unmentioned, during the television stories (or Mel is doing the same during "A Cold Day in Hell" and "Redemption"), it's not easy to come up with a neat

discovered a mysterious dome. The Doctor identified it as a Thought Aligned Random Displacement Energiser Negative Activated (TARDENA), and learned that it was being operated by a Nahrung, a member of an old race that fed on suffering - it was this madness that had consumed the planet. Deep underground in the Hall of Atonement, the lair of a sect of mad monks, the travellers went on to meet Euthys and Artios, and were reunited with Actis. They escaped thanks to the mysterious Ranith.

Comparing notes, the Doctor deduced that the regent Farlig had used Nahrung technology to set the brothers against each other. The Nahrung possessed Farlig, and both were killed. As the Doctor and Frobisher left, the Doctor revealed that Ranith was secretly Peri herself.

2430 - "Dogs of Doom"[441] -> The savage Werelox were werewolf-like aliens who could convert humans into their kind with a single bite or slash of their claws, and they attacked the more than thirty colonies of the New Earth system.

The TARDIS landed on the *Spacehog*: an astro- freighter, operated by Joe Bean and Babe Roth, that was working the system. As the fourth Doctor and Sharon introduced themselves, the Werelox attacked the ship and their leader, Brill, clawed the Doctor. He became a Werelok and retreated to the TARDIS, taking it out of time. Three months later, he had cured himself, and returned to the *Spacehog* mere minutes after he left. The Doctor hypnotised Brill and realised the Werelox were the Daleks' servants. The Daleks were using neutron fire to sterilise planets and planned to colonise them. The Doctor headed to the Dalek ship with Brill and K9.

Meanwhile, Joe Bean and his partner Babe planned to ram the Dalek ship in the *Spacehog*. The Doctor discovered that the Daleks were distilling emotions from alien monsters to make themselves more efficient killing machines, and that unless something was done, the New Earth System would become a huge Dalek breeding ground. K9 released the alien monsters, which attacked the Daleks. Additionally, the Doctor used equipment in the Daleks' "Room of Many Centuries" - a laboratory where the Daleks were building a time transporter - to timelock the Dalek battlecruiser, removing the threat just as the *Spacehog* was about to ram it.

The "Tyrenians" had been developed as human super-soldiers with canine attributes, genetically engineered by Gustav Tyren. When the military pulled its funding for the project, the Tyrenians stole a ship and founded a colony on Axista Four. They set up satellite defences and then entered suspended animation using symbiotes.

Around 2430, the human colony ship *Big Bang* departed into space. The seventh Doctor, in preparing colonist Kirann Ransome to aide one of his previous selves, was the last person to visit her before she entered stasis.

The defence grid on Axista Four shot down the *Big Bang*, and it crashed to the planet. Kiranne remained trapped in stasis, and her father, the philanthropist Stewart Ransome, died in the crash. The survivors founded a colony based on Kirann's text, *Back to Basics*, and strove for a low-technology approach that modeled society on the Wild West. They were unaware of the Tyrenians' presence.[442]

> = In 2436, an alternative Earth that was ruled by Nazis who had won the Second World War, and later gone on to galactic conquest, was destroyed.[443]

c 2450 - SCAREDY CAT[444] -> Fathrea - the fourth world orbiting its sun - had known peace for centuries, and colonists from there settled in another system on the planet Endarra. The biological agent Saravin had been developed for warfare, and a passing Ventriki ship tested the weapon's effects on the Endarra colony. The eighth Doctor, investigating events that would occur four million years in

---

solution that fits all the evidence.

432 "About a hundred years" before *Sword of Orion*.

433 Dating *Vanishing Point* (EDA #44) - An arbitrary date. The colony has been around for "centuries".

434 Dating *Divided Loyalties* (PDA #26) - It is "thirty years" after Dymok became isolated in 2378 (p16).

435 *The Game*. Carlisle's birth date and details of his early life are given, Disc 1, Track 7.

436 "More than a century" before *Parasite* (p49).

437 *The Menagerie*

438 "Pureblood"

439 In the "ten years" leading up to "The Age of Chaos".

440 Dating "The Age of Chaos" (*DWM Special*, unnumbered) - The story is set after *Mindwarp*, long enough afterwards that Peri's youngest grandchild is sixteen (and her grandsons were young men ten years ago),

but no exact date is specified. It has to be at least fifty years since Peri left the Doctor, making her much older than she appears in *Bad Therapy*.

441 Dating "Dogs of Doom" (*DWW* #27-34) - Babe tells Sharon the system has been "settled here for fifty years - since 2380 Old Earth time". It's never explained why the Daleks need Werelox to invade the settlements if they're going to sterilise the planets from orbit.

442 The colonists crashed on Axista Four about a hundred years before *The Colony of Lies*. Kiranne mentions meeting the seventh Doctor on p164.

443 *Spiral Scratch*

444 Dating *Scaredy Cat* (BF #75) - According to the Doctor, the Earth Empire bans Saravin "a few hundred years" after this point.

the future, refrained from interfering for fear of disrupting history. C'rizz gave the colonists an antidote from the TARDIS medial facility, but this wasn't enough to save them. Within three months, the colonists had perished. One small girl, Galayana, had a natural immunity and outlived everyone else by a few weeks, eventually perishing herself.

Endarra was newly formed, and the trauma of the colonists' deaths remained in its morphogenetic field. Galayana's memories and aspect were also preserved.

Space Fleet was using psi drugs to enhance human psychokinesis.[445] The Doctor met a Legion in the twenty-fifth century.[446] A Dalek War broke out in 2459.[447] The Daleks fought the Mechanoids on Hesperus.[448] Comes the Trickster released the HvLIP *All The Way From Heaven* in 2465.[449]

2472 (Tuesday, 3rd March, to Wednesday, 4th March) - COLONY IN SPACE[450] -> Earth was overpopulated, with one hundred billion people living like "battery hens" in communal living units. 300-storey floating islands were built, housing five hundred million people. There was "no room to move, polluted air, not a blade of grass left on the planet and a government that locks you up if you think for yourself".

IMC scoured the galaxy for duralinium, to build ever

more living units. From Earth Control, their headquarters, a fleet of survey vessels ruthlessly strip-mined worlds and killed anyone that stood in their way. Discipline on IMC ships and planets relied heavily on the death penalty: piracy, mutiny and even trespass were all capital offences. Earth Government turned a blind eye to these abuses, although an Adjudicator was assigned to each Galactic Sector to judge disputes in interplanetary law.

Despite the conditions on Earth, few were prepared to leave the homeworld for a bleak life on a colony planet. Some groups of eccentrics bought their own ship and tried to settle on a new world, but most people preferred a life on Earth, where the government may have been harsh, but at least they were able to feed their citizens.

Colonists on Uxarieus - a world that supported birds, insects and basic plant life, and which had an atmosphere similar to that of Earth before the invention of the motor car - found themselves in competition with IMC for control of the planet. The colonists arrived first, surveyed the planet and set up their habitation domes. They discovered that Uxarieus was inhabited by a small subterranean city of telepathic Primitives. Two colonists were killed when they tried to enter the city, but an understanding was reached between the two parties. In return for food, the

445 "Twenty years" before Mrs Ransandrianasolo is born, according to *Return of the Living Dad* (p164).

446 *The Crystal Bucephalus* - referred to as "shortly before the Second Dalek War" (q.v. The Dalek Wars).

447 *The Colony of Lies*

448 *War of the Daleks*. The Mechanoids have been there "two hundred and seventy five years" (p213). I assume they were sent out around the same time the ones we saw in *The Chase*.

449 *The Also People* (p170).

450 Dating *Colony in Space* (8.4) - We see a calendar being changed from "Monday 2nd March 2472" to the next day. Ashe tells Jo that they left Earth in "seventy-one". Hulke's novelisation sets this story in "2971".

451 "Some five hundred years" before *The Mutants*, according to the Administrator.

452 "Five hundred years" after *Return of the Living Dad* (p61).

452 "Seventy two" years before *Return of the Living Dad*.

454 *Burning Heart* (p174).

455 "Three cycles" (presumably years) before *The Game*.

456 Dating *The Game* (BF #66) - Lord Carlisle was born 2414 and started his career as a peacemaker around age twenty (so circa 2434). On Disc 1, Track 70, he says he has been working as a mediator for "fifty years".

457 Dating "Junkyard Demon" (*DWM* #58-59) - No date is specified, and it's hard to place it with any certainty because we don't know how long the Cybernauts have been deactivated on A54. The sequel, however, places it in the same period as *The Tomb of the Cybermen*. The Cyberman resembles - with modifications - the ones from *The Tenth Planet*, and says they will "once again rule time and space". Zogron is "one of the pioneers of our interstellar empire". A54 orbits Arcturus.

458 Dating "Junkyard Demon II" (*DWM Yearbook 1996*) - It's "four months" since "Junkyard Demon". Joylove is working for Eric Klieg and the Brotherhood of Logicians, setting this story shortly before *The Tomb of the Cybermen*.

459 Dating *The Tomb of the Cybermen* (5.1) - The story is set "five hundred years" after the Cybermen mysteriously died out according to Parry, although the Cybermen don't indicate how long they've been in their tombs. No reference is made to the Cyber War [q.v.], so we might presume it is before that time (the disappearance of the Cybermen after the Cyber War wasn't a mystery). The Cybermen's history computer recognises the Doctor from "the lunar surface", so the Cybermen went into hibernation (shortly?) after *The Moonbase*. This would make it at least 2570, but we know that *Earthshock* is set in 2526. The Cybermen in *Earthshock* refer to the events of *The Tomb of the*

Primitives provided menial labour. The colonists proceeded with their plans, but it proved difficult to grow crops as they withered for no reason that the colonists could ascertain.

Just over a year after they arrived, giant lizards attacked some of the outermost domes and some colonists were killed. Many of the colonists were prepared to leave, but their spacecraft was now obsolete, and would almost certainly be unable to reach another world.

IMC arrived in Survey Ship 4-3, under the command of Captain Dent, and angered the colonists by staking a claim on the world. When they discovered that IMC had been using optical trickery to project images of the lizards, and a Mark III servo-robot to kill the colonists, many turned to arms.

Colonists and IMC men were killed in a series of gun battles. An Adjudicator ruled in IMC's favour, but he was exposed as a fake who was more interested in the Primitives' secrets. The IMC team attempted to murder the colonists by forcing them to leave in their obsolete rocket. They were defeated and a real Adjudicator was brought in.

It was discovered that the Primitive city was home to an ancient superweapon, which had been leaking and poisoning the soil. The guardian of this device was convinced to destroy weapon - and the city - rather than let it fall into the wrong hands.

Humanity at this time still used imperial measurements, projectile weapons and wheeled transport ("space buggys"). Ships were powered by nuclear motors, and communicated with Earth via "warp" radio and videolink. The language of Earth was English; the currency was the pound. IMC had advanced scanning equipment for mineral surveys and medical diagnoses. Colonists bought old ships to transport them to their colony planets.

In the twenty-fifth century, Earth colonised Solos, a planet with rich deposits of thaesium. The beautiful planet was ravaged and its people enslaved.[451] The seventh Doctor, Benny, Roz and Chris went to Navarro to rest after their adventure in Little Caldwell.[452] Mrs Ransandrianasolo was born. She was a telepath, as her mother was given psi drugs.[453] In 2476, the Techno-Magi consulted the frozen head of Ralph Waldo Mimsey as an Oracle, driving him insane.[454]

Circa 2481, the UI designated Cray as Earth's sister planet, due to its position relative to Earth from Galactic Zero. The increased focus on Cray compelled Earth to try and end the planet's embarrassing war. The negotiator Lord Carlisle would be dispatched to try and arbitrate a peace.[455]

c 2484 - THE GAME[456] **->** On the planet Cray, only two teams - the Gora and the Lineen - had survived to continue playing the lethal game of Naxy. The past five seasons had seen the deaths of 78,349 Gora and 65,418 Lineen, although the Gora were in much worse shape than was officially reported, and were on the brink of defeat.

The fifth Doctor and Nyssa arrived on Cray to witness Lord Carlisle's efforts to broker a truce, but the Doctor's involvement in a Naxy match led to an upset for the Lineen, with four hundred Lineen casualties. Carlisle died while saving the Doctor's life, but the Doctor exposed the Morian Crime Syndicate's manipulative influence on the planet. The Gora and Lineen set aside their differences and united against the Morian, ending the Naxy tournaments. Carlisle was accredited with the planet's newfound peace.

Heroin slam, the so-called "razor drug," was now in distribution.

c 2485 - "Junkyard Demon"[457] **->** The Salvage ship *Drifter* travelled along the edge of the galaxy, piloted by two traders: Flotsam and Jetsam of the Backwater Scrap and Salvage Company. They plucked the TARDIS out of space, interrupting the fourth Doctor's meditation. The Doctor was horrified to see that they'd recovered a Cyberman, and to learn that Flotsam and Jetsam reprogrammed them to sell on as butlers.

The Cyberman reactivated itself and took Jetsam to the planet A54 in the Arcturian System, where a great Cybernaut fleet had crashed. They quickly discovered Zogron, the deactivated leader, and Jetsam reprogrammed him... as a butler. The Doctor and Flotsam arrived in the *Drifter* and immobilised the Cyberman with a polymer spray.

c 2485 - "Junkyard Demon II"[458] **->** Joylove McShane of Joylove Antiques arrived on A54 wanting to buy Flotsam and Jetsam out, and set his henchman Stinker on them when they refused. Joylove was a gunrunner working for the Brotherhood of Logicians, and he wanted the army of Cybermen. The fourth Doctor arrived and destroyed the Cyber Army, but Flotsam and Jetsam discovered a supply of Cybermats to keep them busy. Joylove escaped... but a surviving Cyberman went with him.

c 2486 (September) - THE TOMB OF THE CYBERMEN[459] **->** The Brotherhood of Logicians unearthed the Tombs of the Cybermen on Telos, and attempted to discover why they died out. The Cybermen were revived and planned to emerge into the universe, but were stopped by the second Doctor. The currency at this time appears to have been the pound. Individuals and organisations could charter spacecraft.

The CyberController was not destroyed, but merely

damaged. He went on to build a new Cyber-Race.[460]

By the end of the twenty-fifth century, a museum was dedicated to the Beatles in Liverpool and clothes were self-cleaning, dirt repelling and non-creasing. Ten-year-olds took a certificate of education in physics, medicine, chemistry and computer science using learning machines for an hour a week. There was evidence that humanity now had some familiarity with temporal theory: even children knew Venderman's Law: "Mass is absorbed by light, therefore light has mass and energy. The energy radiated by a light neutron is equal to the energy of the mass it absorbs".[461]

Vicki Pallister, companion of the first Doctor, was born in New London on the planet Earth around 2480. She lived in Liddell Towers. Her mother died when she was eleven. After that, she and her father left Earth for a new life on space colony Astra.[462] She was innoculated using a laser injector when she was five, and owned a pony called Saracen.[463] In Vicki's time, St. Paul's was still standing, having survived four world wars "and an alien invasion".[464] Food was designed to be nutritious, not tasty. Pandas were extinct, and museums used holograms. Vicki's father, Lieutenant Commander Pallister, had basic paramedic training for his intended job on Astra.[465]

c 2493 - THE RESCUE[466] **->** There were emigrations to other planets. One such ship, the UK-201, crashed on Dido en route to Astra. This was a desert world, home of a peaceful humanoid race and lizard-like creatures known as sand beasts. The Didoans had a population of around one hundred, and had just perfected an energy ray that could be used as a building tool.

A young girl named Vicki was one of only two survivors of the crash. She joined the first Doctor when he made a return visit to Dido.

There were disputes in the Thynemnus System when boar-like aliens attacked the human colonists. The aliens were driven off, but the Valethske attacked the system soon after.[467]

c 2495 - SET PIECE[468] **->** In the late twenty-fifth century, spaceships started disappearing from one of the less-used traffic lanes. A space vessel, designed to save a group of doomed colonists by directly uploading their memories, had outstripped its programming. It now sought to absorb the memories of every living being, and was using its robotic workers, the Ants, to kidnap people.

Five hundred and six people were taken from one such captured ship, the *Cortese*. The seventh Doctor, Ace and Bernice tried to intercede and were flung through time. They eventually brought about the Ship's destruction.

Androids indistinguishable from humans were constructed in the Orion Sector. They became smart enough to demand equal rights and protest their mistreatment.

Cybermen, so *The Tomb of the Cybermen* must be set before 2526 (although they also refer to *Revenge of the Cybermen*, and I set that later). Either Parry is rounding up or he doesn't know about the events of *The Moonbase*. As ever, no-one refers to stories made after this one, such as *Silver Nemesis* and *The Wheel in Space*.

Another possibility is that the Cybermen in *Earthshock* are time travellers. There's some circumstantial evidence for this - it explains how their scanner can show a scene from *Revenge of the Cybermen*, which is almost certainly set after 2526, and it may go some way to explaining how the freighter travels in time at the end - but there's nothing in the script that supports this, and if they have a time machine capable of transporting a huge army of Cybermen, then it's hard to believe that the best plan they can come up with is the one that they're implementing. Then again, even without a time machine, their plan makes no apparent sense.

Radio Times didn't give a year for *Tomb*, but specified that the month the story is set is "September". The draft script for serial 4D (at that point called *Return of the Cybermen*), suggested a date of "24/10/2248" for the story. *Cybermen* sets the story in "2486", *The Terrestrial Index* at "the beginning of the 26th century". "A History of the Cybermen" in *DWM* #83 preferred "2431", where-

as *The Discontinuity Guide* settles on "2570". *Timelink* says "2526", *About Time* "early 2500s".

460 *Attack of the Cybermen*

461 This is the native time of the Doctor's companion Vicki, who joins the TARDIS in *The Rescue*. We learn about her clothing and schooling in *The Web Planet*, and her visit to the Beatles Museum and familiarity with Venderman in *The Chase*. In that story we also learn that Vicki used to live close to a medieval castle.

462 *Byzantium!*

463 *The Plotters*

464 *Frostfire*. The "alien invasion" presumably refers to the Dalek invasion of the twenty-second century.

465 *The Eleventh Tiger*

466 Dating *The Rescue* (2.3) - Vicki states that the year her spaceship left Earth was "2493, of course". The draft script suggested that Vicki and her fellow space traveller, Bennett, have been on Dido "for a year", but there is no such indication in the final programme. Ian Marter's novelisation is set in 2501. *The Making of Doctor Who*, the various editions of Lofficier and *The Doctor Who File* set the date of "2493". The TARDIS Special "c.2500". Peel's novelisation of *The Chase* says that Vicki is from "the twenty-fourth century".

467 *Superior Beings*

468 Dating *Set Piece* (NA #35) - The Ants kidnap the

This led to a conflict - the Orion War - against humanity. The androids settled in the Orion System, ordering the humans to accept android rule or leave.[469]

The Twenty-Sixth Century

By the twenty-sixth century, interstellar travel had become a matter of routine. Fleets of spacecraft ranging from luxury liners to cargo freighters to battleships pushed further into deep space. Ships were built from durilium and had hyperdrives. The mind probe was commonly used to scan the minds of suspects, but it wasn't always reliable. Weapons of the time included hand blasters and neutronic missiles. This was the period that saw the beginning of Earth's Empire.[470]

The warp drives of Earth ships were powered by anti-matter contained in stabilising vessels.[471] Space was divided into Sectors.[472] The currency was the Imperial.[473] It was likely around now that the Doctor gained a licence for the Mars-Venus rocket run. [474] *The Collected Works of Gustav Urnst* were published in June 2503, striking a chord with the bombastic people of the twenty-sixth century.[475]

2501 - THE MONSTERS INSIDE[476] **->** The ninth Doctor and Rose arrived on the planetary system of Justicia, a penal colony of the Earth Empire, where cruel guards were overseeing the construction of a set of pyramids. The Doctor and Rose were separated, and the Doctor met two criminals from Raxacoricofallapatorius who planned to use gravity warps to convert the entire system into a weapon that could destroy planets. These were members of the Blatheen family. The Doctor teamed up with members of the Slitheen family to defeat them.

2503 - SWORD OF ORION[477] **->** With the Orion War still in progress, a derelict spaceship was discovered near the Garazone Central habitat. The ship was a Cybermen factory ship, and Earth High Command dispatched Deeva Jansen to recover the ship. They hoped to obtain the Cybermen conversion process and create super-soldiers, but Jansen was secretly an android trying to obtain the technology for the Orion androids.

The eighth Doctor and Charley stowed away on Jansen's ship and were there when it docked with the Cybership. The Cybermen revived in great numbers, but the Doctor defeated them. Jansen was swept into space with some Cybermen and presumably frozen.

c 2505 - TO THE SLAUGHTER[478] **->** Earth had been abandoned to the poorer countries. Mercury had fallen into the Sun and Venus was a toxic waste dump. The Oort Cloud had been sold off and dismantled.

Falsh Industries demolished most of Jupiter's moons - using the designs of Aristotle Halcyon, a celebrity *decor-artiste* - as part of a redevelopment scheme to attract businesses to the solar system. The "Old Preservers", speaking on behalf of the Empire Trust, were opposed to this. Falsh himself was engaged in illicit weapons research. The eighth Doctor, Fitz and Trix uncovered his schemes and defeated him. Halcyon decided to use his talents to improve Earth.

? 2515 - PARASITE[479] **->** Three hundred and sixty seven years after it had been colonised, the Elysium System was on the brink of civil war. Over the last fifty years a schism had developed between the Founding Families, who want-

---

Doctor, Benny and Ace in "the twenty-fifth century" (p33).
469 "Eight years" before *Sword of Orion*.
470 *Frontier in Space*
471 *Earthshock*
472 *Colony in Space, Earthshock*. The freighter in *Earthshock* starts off in Sector 16, in "deep space".
473 *Warriors' Gate*
474 *Robot, The Janus Conjunction*. The Mars-Venus cruise is mentioned in *Frontier in Space*, although presumably such flights take place from the twenty-first century until the far future.
475 *The Highest Science* (p48).
476 Dating *The Monsters Inside* (NSA #2) - Dennel tells Rose it is "2501". This story is referred to in *Boom Town*.
477 Dating *Sword of Orion* - It's "a very long time" after the Cyber Wars, and the Doctor says the Cybermen are "safely tucked away in their tombs on Telos", with humans assuming the Cybermen are extinct. So this is before the Cybermen re-emerge after *The Tomb of the*

Cybermen. The only date given in the story is that the original Jansen died on "three zero zero five zero seven". However, *Neverland* gives a firm date of 2503.
478 Dating *To the Slaughter* (EDA #72) - The dating of this story is inconsistent. It's "almost four hundred years" since 1938, according to Halcyon (p17, so before 2338), but Trix thinks it's "over five hundred years" since her time (p86, so after around 2503). The story is set before *Revenge of the Cybermen*, and explains why Jupiter only has twelve natural moons in that story. When *Revenge* was broadcast, astronomers thought Jupiter had twelve moons, but dozens more have been discovered in the years since, and Jupiter at present is known to have sixty-three (nineteen were discovered in 2003 alone). Earth in this era has a President, the beginning of an Empire and there's a mention of the Draconians, supporting (strangely, perhaps) Trix over Halcyon.
479 Dating *Parasite* (NA #33) - The dating of this story is problematic. Mark Bannen is the son of Alex Bannen

ed to remain isolated from Earth and maintain their own distinctive political system, and the Reunionists, who wanted to make contact with the Empire.

Before the situation could be resolved, it was found that the Artefact was in fact a vast transdimensional living entity, a creature that when hatched would absorb water from planets, and use the hydrogen in it to lay star-and-planet-sized "eggs". As each young Artefact required the water from forty or fifty thousand planets, it posed a threat to the entire universe. The creature was rendered dormant.

The Draconian War

Around 2520, the first contact was made with the Draconians, a reptilian race that possessed an area of space and a level of technology equivalent to Earth. A peace mission between the two races was arranged, but it ended in catastrophe when the Draconian ship approached, as was their tradition, with the missile ports open. The Draconian ship carried no missiles,

but the humans assumed they had been lured into an ambush. A neutron storm prevented communications and the human ship destroyed the Draconian one. A war between Earth and Draconia started immediately, and although it didn't last long, millions died on both sides.[480]

As a result of a pop can that Bernice kicked onto a path in 2001, a less-elegant writer came to draft a crucial speech shortly before the outbreak of hostilities. The war consequently broke out an hour earlier, with dozens of extra casualties on both sides.[481]

During the Dragon Wars, Shirankha Hall's deep-space incursion squadron discovered a beautiful garden world halfway between human and Draconian Space. He named it Heaven.[482]

Although many on both sides wanted to see the war fought to its conclusion, diplomatic relations were established and the war ended. The Frontier in Space was established, a dividing line which neither race's

who died in *Lucifer Rising* "more than two centuries" ago (p165), so the story is set after 2357. 1706 "was more than seven hundred years ago" (p140), so it is after 2406. Mark Bannen was a baby during the Mexico riots of 2146 and has been kept alive by the Artefact since the founding of the colony "367" years ago (p73), so the story must be set after 2513. This last date is supported by the fact that Earth now has "Empire" (p136-137).

480 "Twenty years" before *Frontier in Space*. General Williams claims that his ship was "damaged and helpless" and well as "unarmed", but it managed to destroy a Draconian battlecruiser anyway. A scene cut from Part Three explained that Williams was able to use his "exhaust rockets" to destroy the other ship.

481 *Head Games* (p165-166).

482 *Love and War* (p10).

483 *Frontier in Space*.

484 Inferred from *The Tomb of the Cybermen*.

THE CYBER WAR: The "Cyber Wars" feature in much fan fiction and are referred to in a number of the books and audios. On television, though, the term "the Cyber War" is only used once, by the Doctor in *Revenge of the Cybermen* - everyone else refers to it simply as "the war".

We are told that this war took place "centuries" beforehand, and that the human race won when they discovered that Cybermen were vulnerable to gold and invented the "glittergun". Following their total defeat, the Cybermen launched a revenge attack on Voga, after which the Cybermen completely disappeared.

From the on screen information, it seems that we can precisely position the date of this "Cyber War": it can't be before 2486, because in *The Tomb of the Cybermen*, the Cyber Race is thought to have been

extinct for five hundred years after Mondas' destruction. In that story, the Controller is ready to create a "new race" of Cybermen. We learn in *Attack of the Cybermen* that the Controller wasn't destroyed at the end of *The Tomb of the Cybermen*, so we might presume that this new race emerged soon afterward and began its conquests.

These attacks didn't directly involve Earth: in *Earthshock*, Scott, a member of the Earth military, hasn't heard of the Cybermen (even though his planet is hosting a conference that the Cyber Leader says will unite many planets in a "war against the Cyber Race"). The Doctor observes that it is a war that the Cybermen "can't win". When the Cybermen's plan to blow up the conference is defeated (*Earthshock*), there is nothing to stop Earth from fighting this genocidal war against the Cybermen - and this is surely the "Cyber War" referred to in *Revenge of the Cybermen*. We might presume that the events of *Attack of the Cybermen* occur at the end of the War, when the Cybermen face defeat and are planning to evacuate Telos. The Cybermen are not mentioned in *Frontier in Space* (set in 2540), which could be inferred as meaning that the Cyber War has long been over by that time.

Before *Earthshock* was broadcast, *The Programme Guide* placed the Cyber "Wars" (note the plural) as "c.2300" (first edition) and "c.2400" (second edition). "A History of the Cybermen" in *DWM* #83 first suggested that the Cyber War took place immediately after *Earthshock*, post-2526. *Cybermen* suggested that the Cyber Wars took place without any involvement with Earth around "2150 AD". *The Terrestrial Index* came to a messy compromise: The "First Cyber Wars" take place "as the 23rd Century began", when Voga is devastated.

spacecraft could cross. Relations between the two planets remained wary, and factions on both Earth and Draconia wanted to wage a pre-emptive strike on the enemy. For twenty years, the galaxy existed in a state of cold war, although treaties and cultural exchanges were set up. Espionage between the powers was expressly forbidden.[483]

The Cyber War

Over five hundred years after Mondas' destruction, the Cybermen re-emerged from their tombs on Telos, redesigned and more deadly than ever.[484] They became the "undisputed masters of space".[485]

? 2520 - "Throwback: The Soul of a Cyberman"[486]
-> The Cybermen invaded the planet Mondaran, and encountered heavy resistance there. Cyberleader Tork requested reinforcements from the centre of their Empire on Telos, which was six days away. These included Junior Cyberleader Kroton, who refused to kill a resistance cell. Kroton was developing emotions, and sided with the humans. Together, they stole a ship from the spaceport and retreated to the safety of the forest of Lorn. Kroton took the ship into orbit to prevent the humans from being detected, but it was a one-way trip. When his batteries drained, he was left drifting in space.

Revenge of the Cybermen takes place at the "tail end of the 25th Century", then after *Earthshock* Voga's gold is *again* used to defeat the Cybermen in "the Second Cyber War".

Novels such as *Killing Ground* make it clear that the Cybermen menaced some early human colony worlds.

485 *Attack of the Cybermen*

486 Dating "Throwback: The Soul of a Cyberman" (*DWW* #5-7) - No date is given. The Cybermen are based on Telos, though, which would seem to place this in the Cyber War of the twenty-sixth century. If we're taking the design of the Cybermen into account, they most resemble the model seen in *The Invasion* or *Revenge of the Cybermen* (although with unique modifications, particularly their rank insignia), which again (via *Revenge*) fits the twenty-sixth century date.

DO THE CYBERMEN EVER HAVE AN EMPIRE?: As they are the second best-known monsters to fight the Doctor, it's easy to assume that the Cybermen are second only to the Daleks when it comes to the power they wield and territory they control. Yet there's precious little evidence for this in the televised stories.

We see or hear that at various points in history, the human race, Daleks, Sontarans, Rutans, Draconians, Mutts, Osirians, Tharils, Jagaroth, Skonnos, Movellans and Autons all control vast areas of our galaxy. Elsewhere in the universe, races have achieved domination of an entire galaxy - in *The Daleks' Master Plan* alone, we meet eight delegates who each have total control of one of the Outer Galaxies. The Wirrn (*The Ark in Space*) dominated Andromeda until humanity drove them out. The winners, though, are... the Dominators, who are the masters of "ten galaxies" according to *The Dominators*. (They also state they control "the whole galaxy" that Dulkis is part of, but while it's not as impressive a boast, neither is it the contradiction some reference sources seem to think.) Linx's boast (in *The Time Warrior*) that the Sontarans have subjugated every galaxy in the universe must surely only be rhetoric.

Away from the televised stories, there's a parallel universe where the Roman Empire has conquered the entire galaxy ("The Iron Legion"), and the Gubbage Cones (*The Crystal Bucephalus*), Cat-People (*Invasion of the Cat-People*) and Foamasi (*Placebo Effect*) are all stated to be or have been major galactic powers.

So what of the Cybermen? In *Attack of the Cybermen*, Lytton calls them "the undisputed masters of space", but they most certainly aren't in that story itself. In *Doomsday*, an army of parallel-universe Cybermen that's millions strong is no match for four Daleks, and when Dalek reinforcements arrive, the Cybermen are routed in minutes.

Perhaps surprisingly, in the four decades since the Cybermen debuted, the most territory we ever actually see them control on television... is one planet, and it's their homeworld. In *The Tenth Planet* they control Mondas, which is destroyed at the end of the adventure. After that, the best they manage is one complex on one planet - in *The Tomb of the Cybermen* and *Attack of the Cybermen* they control their city on Telos. In every other story, we see only a small force launching a stealthy attack - usually with a larger army being held in reserve - and every story ends with the defeat or destruction of every single member of that army (with the possible exception of *Attack of the Cybermen*, where a base on the Moon is mentioned and its fate isn't accounted for). In a number of stories (*The Tomb of the Cybermen, Revenge of the Cybermen, Earthshock, Attack of the Cybermen*, and possibly *Silver Nemesis*) it's explicitly stated that the Cybermen are on the verge of extinction.

The audios *The Harvest* and *Sword of Orion* follow the same pattern. "A handful" survive in *Real Time*. The Cybermen fare no better in the books - in *Legacy*, the Federation thinks they're extinct. *Iceberg* and *Illegal Alien* feature a small group of isolated survivors. They're routed in *Killing Ground*, which ends - to compound their problems - with a group of converted humans setting out to pick off any Cybermen they can find.

In *none* of these stories does anyone claim that the Cybermen have "an Empire" or anything like it.

2526 - EARTHSHOCK[487] -> Earth was not directly affected, but it was clear that only the homeworld could provide the military resources needed to combat the Cyber threat. In 2526, a Conference was held on Earth that proposed that humanity should unite to fight the Cybermen. The Cybermen tried to detonate a bomb on Earth, then land an invasion force in the aftermath, but the fifth Doctor thwarted their plans.

The twenty-sixth century saw the Great Orion Cyber Wars.[488] The Cybermen were unafraid of contravening galactic law or arms treaties, and were prepared to destroy entire planets using Cyberbombs. But the war against the Cybermen united many planets, and humanity started from a strong position. Earth was aware of the Cybermen's vulnerability to gold and developed the glittergun, a weapon that exploited this weakness. There was more gold on Voga than in the rest of the known galaxy, and when those vast reserves were used against the Cybermen, humanity inflicted massive defeats.[489] The glittergun was built by INITEC.[490]

? 2530 - ATTACK OF THE CYBERMEN[491] -> The Cybermen faced total defeat. Thanks to Cryon guerillas and the Cybermen's failing hibernation equipment, they weren't even safe on Telos and planned to evacuate. They had recently captured a three-man time machine that had landed on Telos, and used it to go to 1985 in an attempt to prevent Mondas' destruction. The sixth Doctor was captured in 1985 and brought to Telos, where he was able to destroy the tombs and the CyberController.

Realising that they were beaten, the Cybermen launched an attack on Voga and detonated Cyberbombs that blew the planet out of orbit. The Vogans were forced into underground survival chambers. After this time, the Cybermen disappeared, and it was believed that they had died out.[492] The Cyber Fleet was destroyed. Bounty hunters and mercenaries hunted down the remaining Cybermen.[493]

Despite all of this, the Cybermen have an empire in the comic strips. It's referred to in "Throwback", "Deathworld", "Black Legacy" and "Kane's Story". We actually see the Cybermen at their most powerful in "Throwback" - they're feared, with a futuristic city on Telos, vast space fleets and the military power to conquer whole worlds with ease.

We can only firmly date one of those comic adventures: "Kane's Story", which is set at a time when Davros is the Emperor of the Daleks - so it's between *Revelation of the Daleks* and *Remembrance of the Daleks* (or after "Emperor of the Daleks" and before *Remembrance of the Daleks*, if we take the other media into account). Coincidentally, this is Lytton's native time, perhaps forming the basis of his "masters of space" comment.

However, the Cybermen are also powerful at the time of *Earthshock* (in 2526), and this chronology links that to their re-emergence from their tomb on Telos (after 2486). So there may well be a Cyber Empire blossoming in the late twenty-fifth, early twenty-sixth century - although it seems to have fallen by the time of *Frontier in Space* (2540), presumably after their crushing defeat in the Cyber War.

487 Dating *Earthshock* (19.6) - The Doctor states that it is "the twenty-sixth century", Adric calculates that it is "2526 in the time scale you call Anno Domini". *The TARDIS Logs* set the story in "2500".

How the Cyber-scanner in *Earthshock* can show a clip from *Revenge of the Cybermen* remains a mystery, and causes problems with the dating of that story. The "real" reason is that the production team wanted to show the Cybermen facing as many previous Doctors as they could and didn't worry too much about continuity (in the same way that the Brigadier's flashback in

Mawdryn Undead had the Brigadier "remembering" scenes he didn't witness). Equally, the Cyber-scanner doesn't show clips from *Attack of the Cybermen* or *Silver Nemesis*, the latter of which at least should appear.

"A History of the Cybermen" in *DWM* #83 suggested that the Scope tunes into the TARDIS telepathic circuits, which seems a little implausible. One fan, Michael Evans, has suggested that as there is no indication how long before *Attack of the Cybermen* the time machine crashed on Telos, it is perfectly possible that the Cybermen have had it since before *Earthshock* and used it to research their future before using it to alter history. This would certainly be a logical course of action. *About Time* suggests that the Cybermen themselves have travelled from the future. For other possible explanations see *Cybermen* (p72, p79-80).

488 *Real Time*

489 *Revenge of the Cybermen*

490 *Original Sin* (p287).

491 Dating *Attack of the Cybermen* (22.1) - No date is given on screen, but the story takes place after *The Tomb of the Cybermen* as the Controller remembers surviving that story. *Attack of the Cybermen* takes place at a time when the Cybermen face imminent total defeat on a number of fronts. Although the Cybermen know of Lytton's people, and he is fully aware of the situation on Telos, I don't think that *Resurrection of the Daleks* is set in this period. In *Resurrection of the Daleks*, Stien says that the Daleks captured people from many different periods (while never really explaining why), so this could well be Lytton's native time (Lytton talks of humans as his "ancestors", so his home planet, Vita 15, 690, Riftan V, is a human colony). Lytton seems to flatter the Cybermen by declaring them "undisputed masters

The Rise of the Earth Empire

2534 - THE COLONY OF LIES[494] -> Matter transmitters were abandoned by this time, and there were strict laws on DNA manipulation. The EuroZone still existed. The human colonies were known as the Earth Federation, and were patrolled by Colony Support Vessels. Space was marked with navigation beacons. The term "Earth Empire" was used for the first time this year.

On Axista Four, the human colonists divided into conservative and technological-minded factions: the "Loyalists" and the "Realists". The Realists set up their own settlement away from the Loyalist city of Plymouth Hope, but often raided the Loyalists for supplies.

By now, the Daleks were making gains in the third quadrant. Human space stations and colonies on the front line were evacuated. The Earth Federation had formed an alliance to try to prevent Dalek expansionism.

About 80,000 refugees were scheduled for relocation to Axista Four, and the Earth support vessel *Hannibal* entered orbit around the planet, responding to a signal for help from the Realist faction there. The *Hannibal's* arrival triggered machinery that revived some Tyrenians from stasis, and they threatened to make warfare against the humans.

The second Doctor, Jamie and Zoe arrived at this time, and the Doctor both revived Kirann Ransome from suspended animation and defused the conflict. The Realists and Loyalists agreed to accept Kirann as their mutual leader. The Doctor allowed the Federation to believe the Tyrenians were the survivors of a space plague, covering over their true history. Federation Administrator Greene agreed to let the Tyrenians live on Axista Four in peace.

Vega Station was built and secretly run by the Battrulian government. The fourth Doctor visited and lost a lot of money in the Station's casinos.[495]

The Space War

c 2540 - FRONTIER IN SPACE[496] -> At this point, Earth's "Empire" was still democratic, ruled by an elected President and Senate, although the Earth Security forces also had political influence. Ironically, although millions had died in the colonies, the Draconian War had not affected Earth and so the planet still faced a massive population crisis. The Bureau of Population Control strictly enforced the rule that couples could only have one child.

The Arctic areas were reclaimed. New Glasgow and New Montreal were the first of the sealed cities to be opened, and the Family Allowance was increased to two children for those who moved there. The Historical Monuments Preservation Society existed to protect Earth's heritage. While there was a healthy political opposition, any resistance to the principles of government by either anti-colonialists or pacifists was ruthlessly suppressed. Under the Special Security Act, a penal colony was set up on the Moon to house thousands of political prisoners, each of whom served a life sentence with no possibility of parole or escape. In 2539, Professor Dale, one of the most prominent members of the Peace Party, was arrested and sent to the penal colony on Luna.

Larger colonies such as those in the Sirius System were given Dominion Status, and allowed regional autonomy, including powers of taxation and extradition. Governors appointed directly by Earth ruled the smaller worlds.

In 2540, interplanetary tension mounted as human and Draconian spacecraft were subjected to mysterious attacks. Cargos were stolen and ships were destroyed. Each planet blamed the other, and eyewitnesses on both sides claimed to have seen their enemy. On Earth, war with the "Dragons" appeared to be inevitable. A

---

of space" - *Attack of the Cybermen* shows them to be in an extremely weak position, but only a decade or so beforehand, the Cybermen were in the strong position he describes.

492 *Revenge of the Cybermen*. Stevenson claims that "the Cybermen died out centuries ago", the Doctor replies that "they disappeared after their attack on Voga at the end of the Cyber War".

493 *Real Time*

494 Dating *The Colony of Lies* (PDA #61) - The book's internal dating is very confused. The back cover says it's 2539, and there's a tombstone on p23 which says that 2535 was "four years ago". Despite this, a native of this timezone says the date is 2534 (p147). Transmats are seen a number of times after this (in, for example, *The Ark in Space*) so it is clear that humanity readopts the

technology.

495 *Demontage*. The fourth Doctor visited "soon after the place opened" (p6).

496 Dating *Frontier in Space* (10.3) - The story takes place "somewhere in the twenty-sixth century" according to the Doctor. In the first scene, the freighter enters hyperspace at "22.09 72 2540 EST". This is probably nine minutes past ten at night on the 72nd day of 2540, although the President is later seen cancelling a meeting on "the tenth of January". The novelisation (also by Malcolm Hulke) gives the year as "2540", which *The Terrestrial Index* concurred with, although it misunderstood the relationship between Earth and Draconia at this time, suggesting that they are part of "the Alliance" [q.v.]. It isn't made clear whether the human military know of the Daleks before this story.

member of the Peace Party, Patel, sabotaged a space-dock and was arrested.

On 12th March, Earth cargo ship C-982 was attacked only minutes from Earth at co-ordinates 8972-6483. The News Services monitored and broadcast their distress calls. Anti-Draconian riots flared up in Peking, Belgrade and Tokio. The Draconian consulate in Helsinki was burnt down, and in Los Angeles the President was burnt in effigy. When the C-982 docked at Spaceport Ten, Security discovered a mysterious traveller, the Doctor, on board. He resisted the mind probe, even on level 12, and was sent to the Lunar Penal Colony. He was convinced that a third party was trying to provoke war, a possibility that no one else had considered. A small ship under the command of General Williams was sent to the Ogron home planet at co-ordinates 3349-6784, where the true master-minds, the Daleks, were revealed.

The Doctor was remembered as a mediator between Earth and Draconia.[497] The Draconian Ambassador Ishkavaarr and the Earth President agreed that the planet Heaven should become an open world where both races would bury their dead. Years later, several interplanetary agreements were signed there by the President and the Draconian Emperor.[498]

The Daleks were one of the greatest powers in the universe at this time.[499]

& 2540 - PLANET OF THE DALEKS[500] -> The third Doctor and Jo tracked the Daleks to the planet Spiridon in the ninth system, many systems from Skaro. Here, a group of six Thals - selected from the six-hundred strong Division that hunted Daleks - were already investigating. They had discovered a research station where twelve Daleks were developing germ weapons, and also experimenting with an anti-reflective lightwave that rendered them invisible. The Doctor discovered an army of ten thousand Daleks in neutron-powered suspended animation beneath the research base. Supreme Command sent the Dalek Supreme to oversee the invasion of the Solar Planets, but the Doctor defeated them.

The natives of Spiridon sought to conceal their world from further Dalek oppression. In the generations to follow, Spiridon was renamed Zaleria, and the natives made themselves visible by spreading cell-altering chemicals throughout their food supply. They would remain free from interference until the mid-forty-third century.[501]

---

497 *Shadowmind* (p61).

498 *Love and War* (p10-11).

499 According to the Doctor in *Death to the Daleks*.

500 Dating *Planet of the Daleks* (10.4) - The story is set at the same time as *Frontier in Space*. Nevertheless, the American *Doctor Who* comic dated this story as 1300 AD. It is "generations" after *The Daleks*.

501 *Return of the Daleks*

502 BENNY'S BIRTHDAY: It is stated in *Love and War* (p46), in many later books and in the New Adventures Writers' Guide that Benny comes from "the twenty-fifth century". For a while, the writers worked on the assumption that she was from 2450 (e.g.: *The Highest Science* p34, *The Pit* p9). In *Falls the Shadow*, we learn that Benny was born in "2422" (p148). However, Paul Cornell's initial Character Guide had specified that she was born in "2472", which, as *Love and War* is set the day after Benny's thirtieth birthday, would make it 2502 (in the twenty-*sixth* century).

Causing further complications, *Love and War* is definitely set after *Frontier in Space* [2540]. In subsequent books there was confusion, with some novels claiming that Benny does indeed come from the "twenty-sixth century" (e.g. *Transit* p186, *Blood Heat* p3).

Latterly, so as not to contradict the television series, it has been decided that Benny is definitely from the twenty-sixth century. Benny explained that there are a number of calendars in use in the cosmopolitan galaxy of her time, and in our terms she is "from the late-twenty-sixth century" (*Just War* p136) - this is intended to explain away some of the contradictions. Paul Cornell and Jim Sangster have astrologically determined Benny's birthday as 21st June, a date that first appeared in *Just War* (p135) and now appears on the Big Finish official biography on their website. Even so, *The Dimension Riders* has her celebrating on 20th November.

503 The ceasefire was declared "fifty years" before *Demontage* (p4).

504 *The Well-Mannered War* (p272). Stokes is from the 2400s, so the official records must have been altered to due to his relocation to the twenty-sixth century.

505 *Conundrum*

506 A generation or so before *The Also People*.

507 "Two hundred years" after *Valhalla*.

508 *So Vile a Sin* (p211).

509 "Three hundred years" before *Dark Progeny*. They are in use in *Frontier in Space*.

510 "Six or seven years" before "Dreamers of Death".

511 *Death and Diplomacy* (p124). We might infer from other stories that the first wave was in the mid-twenty-second century (seen in *The Dalek Invasion of Earth*) which was targeted on Earth's solar system, and the second led to the Dalek War mentioned in *The Crystal Bucephalus* and *The Colony of Lies*.

THE DALEK WARS: In *Death to the Daleks*, Hamilton

Bernice Surprise Summerfield was born on 21st June, 2540, on the human colony of Beta Caprisis. She was the daughter of Isaac Summerfield, a starship commander in the Space Fleet, and his wife Claire.[502]

A war between the Battrul and the wolven Canvine chiefly resulted in a draw, and a buffer zone was created between their territories. Vega Station was built as a casino and hotel, but the Battrulian government secretly used it to monitor the neutral zone.[503] The artist Menlove Stokes was born in 2542, according to official records.[504] Bernadette McAllerson discovered McAllerson's Radiation in 2542.[505]

The People of the Worldsphere were covertly involved in wars in their galaxy.[506] In an old curiosity shop on Aminion 2, the Doctor happened upon a catalog advertising the people of Valhalla City for sale as slaves. The catalog was located next to a bust of Joanna the Mad, although it wasn't a good likeness, and he initially mistook her for Pliny the Elder.[507]

The Alps were damaged in a local war in 2547.[508] Mind probes were made illegal.[509] The fourth Doctor visited the farming world Unicepter IV.[510]

The Dalek Wars

The Daleks began their third wave of expansion, leading to the Galactic Wars.[511] Life on the front was harsh, with tens of thousands killed by Dalek Plague on Yalmur alone. Other planets on the front line included Capella, Antonius, Procyon and Garaman (home to a Space Fleet station).

On the other hand, the Core Worlds - the heavily populated and fashionable heart of the Earth Empire - were safe and prosperous. The planet Ellanon was a popular holiday planet; Bacchanalia Two was the home of the Club Outrageous. There were shipyards on Harato, and thriving colonies on Thrapos 3 and Zantir. The Spinward Corporation's financial and administrative centre on Belmos was a space station the size of a planet. Humanity had also discovered Lubellin - "the Mud Planet" - and the

---

states "My father was killed in the last Dalek War", implying there was more than one. We know from other Dalek stories that humanity and the Daleks come into conflict throughout history, starting with *The Dalek Invasion of Earth* [around 2157]. However, there are almost certainly no Dalek Wars affecting Earth directly between *The Dalek Invasion of Earth* and *The Rescue* [2167-2493], as Vicki has only heard of the Daleks from history books discussing the Invasion (she doesn't even know what they look like). According to Cory in *Mission to the Unknown*, the Daleks have been inactive in Earth's sphere of influence for a millennium before *The Daleks' Master Plan* [between 3000-4000 AD]. In *Planet of the Daleks*, the Doctor uses the term "Dalek War" to describe the events of *The Daleks*, which did not involve humanity.

According to *The Terrestrial Index*, there are a string of Human/Dalek conflicts, the First to Fourth Dalek Wars. The First was the Dalek Invasion of Earth; the Second was fought by "the Alliance" of Humans, Draconians and Thals in the twenty-fifth century; the Third was again fought by the Alliance after the events of *Frontier in Space* and *Planet of the Daleks*; the Fourth was *The Daleks' Master Plan*.

This is a numbering system that is never used on television, and some of the details of Lofficier's account actively contradict what we're told in the stories - at the time he proposes a "Second Dalek War" involving the Thals and Draconians, the Thals don't have advanced space travel and a century later, they think that humans are a myth (*Planet of the Daleks*). The first contact between humanity and the Draconians was in 2520 (in the twenty-*sixth* century), leading to a short war, followed by twenty years of hostility and mutual mistrust (*Frontier in Space*).

The books have established that Dalek Wars took place in Benny's native time. She's born the same year *Frontier in Space* and *Planet of the Daleks* are set, q.v. Benny's birthday) - her father fights in the Dalek wars, and her mother is killed in a Dalek attack. What's more, Ace spends three years fighting Daleks in this time period between *Love and War* and *Deceit*. As such, there is a mass of information about the Wars in many of the novels. There's no mention of a lull in the fighting - war presumably breaks out soon after *Frontier in Space*, it carries on into Benny's childhood and apparently into her early adulthood. Humanity is still fighting the Daleks when Benny hits thirty (*Love and War*), but they've defeated the Daleks within three years of that (*Deceit*). Nevertheless, a to *Lucifer Rising*, there are two distinct Dalek Wars at this time - Benny's father fought in the Second Dalek War (p65), whereas Ace fought in the Third (p309), so there must be a short-lived cessation of hostilities (which would seem to be at some point in the 2560s, when Benny is in her twenties).

A lengthy essay at the end of *Deceit* has the Dalek War starting after *Frontier in Space* and Ace fighting in the Second Dalek War.

Some stories (for example, *The Crystal Bucephalus*) stick to Lofficier's scheme.

So... the term "Second Dalek War" is used to refer to two or possibly even three different conflicts in both the twenty-fifth and twenty-sixth centuries (and this is further complicated because of the early confusion over which century Benny was born in). For the sake of clarity, I've left references to the numbering of the Dalek Wars out of the timeline itself, but where they are given in a story, I've footnoted it.

Within the fiction, it's fairly easy to rationalise the discrepancy: these are the naming conventions of historians, and different historians will have different perspectives on the various conflicts and labels for them.

spotless Tarian Asteroids.

The best whiskey from this time was made in South America, but some people preferred Eridanian Brandy.[512]

c 2547 - RETURN OF THE LIVING DAD[513] ->

The Daleks' tactics were repetitive and predictable. Earth's Space Fleet used vast Dalekbuster ships, highly-automated and heavily-armed six-man fighters. Isaac Summerfield captained one such ship. Albinex the Navarino contacted the Daleks and offered to change history in return for military assistance. The seventh Doctor and Benny arrived on Isaac Summerfield's ship, the *Tisiphone*, which was fighting the Daleks over Bellatrix. The *Tisiphone* interrupted Albinex's negotiations with the Daleks, and both the *Tisiphone* and Albinex ended up falling down a wormhole to the twentieth century.

The Dalekbuster commanded by Isaac Summerfield was reported to have broken formation and fled during a space battle, and its captain was branded a coward. In late 2547, at the height of the Dalek War, the Daleks attacked the human colony on Vandor Prime in the Gamma Delphinus system, where Claire Summerfield was killed. Bernice

Summerfield was sent to military boarding school.[514] Benny's doll Rebecca was with Benny's mother when she was exterminated.[515]

c 2550 - "Pureblood"[516] ->

The Dalek War continued to rage, but elsewhere in the galaxy the conflict between the Rutans and Sontarans reached a critical point. The Rutans had already razed the community structures between the Warburg and the Prok Fral Edifice. Now, they destroyed Sontara, the Sontaran homeworld, with photonic bombs. The Sontarans got their Racepool away in time, and headed towards Pandora.

The seventh Doctor and Benny arrived on the Pandora Spindle in the Terran Federation. This was a distant space station run by the Lauren Corporation - the biggest industrial giant in the galaxy - and the home of a genetics facility. The Sontarans occupied the station, and a Rutan agent informed their enemies that the Racepool was there. The Sontarans' genetic expert was killed in an accident and the Doctor agreed to help save the Sontarans from extinction. He also exposed the spy, Modine.

The Sontarans had been betrayed to the Rutans on Sontara... by pureblood Sontarans who were untouched

---

512 *Deceit*

513 Dating *Return of the Living Dad* (NA #53) - This happens "forty" years before 2587 (p7), Benny would have been "seven" at the time (p12). Although the date is given as "2543" (p29), there is some confusion over Benny's birthday in the NAs, and this is a victim of that. This is "the height of the Second Dalek War" (q.v. The Dalek Wars).

514 A number of references to Benny Summerfield's early life appeared in the New Adventures, and these were not always consistent. In *Love and War*, Benny's birthplace is identified as Beta Caprisis (p75), but in *Sanctuary* Benny recalls that her mother was killed on a raid on Vandor Prime (p185). We might speculate that she was born on the former and moved to the latter. As pointed out in *Set Piece* (p132), there is some confusion about the exact sequence of events during the raid that killed Benny's mother. Accounts also vary as to whether Benny's father disappeared before or after her mother's death. Benny was only seven when all this happened, so she is almost certainly misremembering some details or blocking out some of her unpleasant memories.

515 "Emperor of the Daleks"

516 Dating "Pureblood" (*DWM* #193-196) - It's "the twenty-sixth century" in part one, but "the twenty-fifth" in part two. It seems to be around Benny's native time, as she's heard of the Lauren Corporation. The Second Dalek War is mentioned, but that's not as helpful a reference as one might think (q.v. "The Dalek Wars"). The Doctor says the Sontarans will not be a threat to Earth

again until *The Sontaran Experiment* (which, as far as we know, they aren't).

517 Dating "Dreamers of Death" (*DWM* #47-48) - The year isn't specified in the story, but there's a reference to Unicepter dream machines being "recently banned" in the *Abslom Daak - Dalek Killer* collected edition, placing the story around then. The settlers on Unicepter IV are "human". Their technology is not terribly advanced - they have hover cars and energy weapons, thinking projectile weapons are "old fashioned".

518 "Star Beast II"

519 Abslom Daak first appeared in Marvel's *Doctor Who Weekly* #17, and has returned a number of times since. He was mentioned in *Love and War* (p46-47 - we also meet Maire, another DK, in that novel), before appearing in the (cloned) flesh in *Deceit*.

520 Before "Abslom Daak... Dalek Killer". Details are given in "Star Tigers".

521 Dating "Abslom Daak...Dalek Killer" (*DWW* #17-20) - It's "the 26th century" and humanity is at war with the Daleks. The sequel, "Star Tigers", establishes that it is shortly after a "frontier war" between the Draconians and Earth, a clear reference to the events of *Frontier in Space*.

The matter transmitter between star systems is something humanity is still trying to perfect by the year 4000 and *The Daleks' Master Plan*. We learn about Vol Mercurius in "Star Tigers".

522 Dating "Star Tigers" (*DWW* #27-30, *DWM* #44-46) - It's within three months of "Abslom Daak...Dalek Killer"; Salander says Mazam was conquered "within the last

by cloning and genetic engineering, and hailed from a distant colony that the Rutans discovered. The pureblood Sontarans attacked Pandora, but the Doctor and Benny showed how the Rutans had tricked them into destroying their own kind. The two factions of Sontarans united and settled on Pandora to rebuild their race. In return, the Sontarans agreed to erase all knowledge of the human race from their databanks.

The Sontarans' survival would prevent the Rutans from overrunning the galaxy, and Sontaran advances in space drive, vaccines and genetic solutions to disease would be of great benefit to the future.

c 2550 - "Dreamers of Death"[517] -> For three years, the colonists of Unicepter IV enjoyed sharing adventure dreams. These were courtesy of the company Dreams Deluxe, who made the dream possible by harnessing the telepathic powers of a native creature: the small furry Slinth. The fourth Doctor, Sharon and K9 arrived just as one team of dreamers died in an accident. The Doctor and Sharon took part in a dream led by a man called Vernor, where they were attacked by the dead dreamers and an army of monsters. K9 severed the connection before they were killed, but the Slinths had become aggressive, fed off all the colonists' negative emotions, and fused into a single devil-like creature. The Slinths were absorbing electricity, so the Doctor doused them in water, collapsing the devil creature into a pile of harmless Slinths. Sharon elected to stay behind with Vernor.

The Doctor was later invited to Sharon's wedding.[518]

ABSLOM DAAK... DALEK KILLER!

Hardened criminals on Earth were given the choice of facing the death penalty or becoming Dalek Killers (DKs). The most notorious of the DKs was Abslom Daak.[519]

Daak's beloved, Selene, had run off with his business partner Vol Mercurius after defrauding four billion from a shipping company. Consequently, Daak cut off Mercurius' hand with his chainsword. Mercurius bought the planet Dispater, but Selene left him.[520]

c 2550 - "Abslom Daak... Dalek-Killer"[521] -> Rather than be vaporised, a serious criminal could choose "Exile D-K". He would be teleported to a world in the Dalek Empire, and made to kill as many of Daleks as possible before he was exterminated. The life expectancy of such DKs was two hours, thirty two minutes and twenty three seconds. Only one man in four survived the matter transmitter, and the overall odds of survival were six hundred million to one.

At this time, Curtis Fooble was accused of eating the Vegan ambassador. Humans had advanced humanoid robots, which operated machines and even sat as judges. Taiyin was a human colony, with a monarchy as well as skysleds and space yachts. Dalek base ships were operated by a Command Dalek, wired into the ship's systems. The Daleks used Omega Units - advanced fighter / bombers - as well as hoverbouts.

The sociopath Abslom Daak was convicted of twenty-three charges of murder, pillage, piracy and massacre. He had been driven to such crimes by the loss of his beloved Selene, and chose Exile D-K. He was beamed to the feudal planet Mazam, located a thousand light years from Earth, where Princess Taiyin had just surrendered to the Daleks. Daak rescued her, and together they took on the Daleks' base ship. They destroyed it, but Taiyin was killed. Grieving for Taiyin's death, Daak vowed "I'm gonna kill every damned stinking Dalek in the galaxy!"

c 2550 - "Star Tigers"[522] -> "The Frontier War with Earth had been fought and settled", and Draconia was now at peace. However, Dalek expansion towards Girodun threatened Draconian trade routes. Factions within the Draconian court wanted to strengthen their defences, but the prevailing wisdom was that the Daleks wouldn't fight a war on two fronts, and they should be negotiated with.

Three Dalek ships entered Draconian space while pursuing Abslom Daak, but he destroyed them before landing on Draconia. Daak was looked after by Prince Salander, and revealed that he had put Taiyin in cryogenic suspension. Salander's political rivals took the opportunity to have him arrested, and Daak shared his house arrest. Salander's family built warships, and he showed Daak a prototype frontier defence cruiser built to fight Daleks. Daak christened this the *Kill-Wagon*. Salander was told that a Dalek patrol had killed his son, and he decided to leave Draconia in the *Kill-Wagon* with Daak. They resolved to assemble a crew.

They went to the planet Paradise - a cosmopolitan planet where every pleasure was available for a price - and recruited the Ice Warrior Harma. They then headed to the war-torn planet of Dispater, where Vol Mercurius was playing a parachess tactics game with a robot companion that mirrored the real-life conflict. Mercurius owned the planet, but the Kill-Mechs of a self-proclaimed Emperor of the Jarith Cluster had invaded it. Mercurius agreed to join the *Kill-Wagon* crew. As they left Dispater, they discovered an army of Dalek Space Commando Units, ready to invade the Jarith Cluster while the inhabitants were divided. The *Kill-Wagon* let the Daleks invade, then wiped them out by dropping nuclear bombs into a nearby volcano.

At this time, Draconia was home to an animal somehow like a tiger, called a Thorion. The currency of Draconia was the "crystal", while bribes were in diamonds. Vorkelites enjoyed being executed. Rigellians had four tentacles, three mouths and a reputation for being untrustworthy.

c 2550 - "Nemesis of the Daleks"[523] **->** The *Kill-Wagon* launched an attack on the Dalek base on the planet Hell, but was shot down. The Emperor was there to supervise construction of the Daleks' vast battlestation, the Death Wheel. The seventh Doctor arrived and discovered the bodies of Salander, Vol Mercurius and Harma. He was cornered by the Daleks, but rescued by Daak.

The Doctor learned that Hell was the source of Helkogen, a poison gas. He and Daak boarded the Death Wheel, where the Doctor confronted the Emperor and Daak learned the Daleks were building a Genocide Device - a gas weapon that threatened every known planet. Daak prevented the Doctor from sacrificing himself to destroy the Death Wheel's central reactor, and the Doctor escaped as Daak died to destroy the Death Wheel.

c 2550 - "Emperor of the Daleks"[524] **->** Abslom Daak was transmatted away from certain death and returned to what he thought was Earth. There he was told to kill the Doctor - and in return, Taiyin would be resurrected.

The seventh Doctor and Benny arrived on Hell and met up with the remaining Star Tigers, who weren't dead after all, as the Helkans had revived them. Within moments, though, Daak grabbed the Doctor and they were all transmatted to Daak's masters... but the Doctor realised they were Dalek robots, and that this was a trap. They were on Skaro, in the future, at the mercy of the Emperor.

Returning from the future, the Star Tigers drank at a bar on Paradise. Daak's fixation with Taiyin had ended... he was now obsessed with Benny instead. The seventh Doctor met his previous self, and thanked him for his help setting a trap for the Daleks.

History recorded that Abslom Daak died destroying the Dalek Death Wheel.[525]

On Kastropheria, a group of priests had used the drug Skar to boost their psionic abilities and mentally restrain the people's self-destructive impulses. Humans established a colony on the planet, but the natives became aggressive again when supplies of skar began to run out.[526] The Class G maintenance robot entered service.[527]

c 2550 - CATASTROPHEA[528] **->** The third Doctor and Jo discovered the human colonists on Kastopheria had enslaved the natives, and the Doctor was mistaken for El Llama, a prophesied revolutionary. The priests asked the Doctor to destroy the Anima, a giant skar crystal, with great care to free the people from their mind-lock. The Anima was destroyed too suddenly, and the people's destructive rage returned. War loomed between the natives and the colonists, but the Doctor helped to forge a non-interference treaty. The Draconians aided the colonists in evacuating, and the natives were left in peace.

In 2555, Benny Summerfield visited Earth for the last time before meeting the Doctor. On this, or a previous trip, she went to Stuttgart.[529] The Draconian vessel *Hunter* and five destroyers were lost fighting Daleks. Female officers had recently been introduced to the Draconian military.[530]

The People of the Worldsphere fought a war against the Great Hive Mind, using new weapons and powerful sentient Very Aggressive Ships. The war saw twenty-six billion killed, completely destroyed fifteen planets and devastated dozens of others. The Great Hive Mind became part of the People.[531]

---

three months". "The Emperor does not want another war... not so soon after fighting the humans."
523 Dating "Nemesis of the Daleks" (*DWM* #152-155) - It's "the 26th century". Clearly this takes place after "Star Tigers", but there's no indication of how much time has passed. The Emperor resembles the one from the comic strips (see "The Dalek Emperors"), and may well be killed in Daak's final attack because he's on the Death Wheel when it explodes. If so, it's tempting to imagine that the Emperor's death was the turning point in the war referred to as "years ago" in *Deceit* (which also says Daak's death here was "years ago").

There's no indication that these Daleks are time travellers. At first the Doctor assumes the Emperor is Davros, but the Dalek Emperor replies "Davros? Who is Davros?". *Terror Firma* has Davros losing his mind and mutating into an Emperor Dalek, but ultimately it seems as if he and *this* Emperor are not one and the same. The Daleks also (apparently) probe the seventh Doctor's mind, identify him and see images of the Doctor's previous six incarnations.

524 Dating "Emperor of the Daleks" (*DWM* #197-202) - This takes place shortly after "Nemesis of the Daleks". It's specified that Daak is "lured across space and time" - the sequence on Skaro takes place between *Revelation of the Daleks* and *Remembrance of the Daleks* (4625, according to this chronology), and accounts for Davros' (physical, not mental) transformation into the Emperor Dalek, as seen in *Remembrance*.
525 According to *Deceit*, which was published between "Nemesis of the Daleks" (where Daak died) and "Emperor of the Daleks" (where it turned out he hadn't). Presumably, either Daak evades the authorities, or they hush up his activities.
526 "Five years" before *Catastrophea*.
527 "Four decades" before *Cold Fusion*.
528 Dating *Catastrophea* (PDA #11) - It is "five or six hundred years" after Jo's time (p79).
529 We learn about her visit to Stuttgart in *Just War* (p137), and that she hasn't been to Earth in the fifteen years before *Deceit* (p102), although this contradicts *Lucifer Rising* (p171).

Corporations such as Ellerycorp, Peggcorp, Spinward, and IMC maintained battlefleets of their own. During the Battle of Alpha Centauri, a small squadron of Silurian vessels beat back the main Dalek force, which fled into hyperspace. Daleks also managed to infiltrate human Puterspace.[532]

TAM Corporation's ships fought in the Galactic Wars. The corporation pulled out of remote colonies like Mendeb, taking as much high technology as it could.[533]

As often happened in wartime, the Dalek War saw a leap in human technological progress. A variety of intelligent weapons systems were developed: dart guns, data corrupting missiles, spikes, clusters and forceshells, random field devices, self-locating mines and drones.

Earth's Space Fleet included 1000-man troopships armed with torpedoes that could destroy a Dalek Battlesaucer. A fleet of warp vessels - X-Ships - were used to ferry communications, personnel and supplies. Most troopers were placed in Deep Sleep while travelling to the warzones. This was done to conserve supplies, not because the ships were particularly slow, as it now only took a matter of weeks to cross human space. Ships still used warp engines, but they also used ion drive to travel in real space.

Computer technology was now extremely advanced. The Space Fleet Datanet was a vast information resource, and data was stored on logic crystals. Nanotechnology was beginning to have medical applications: a nanosurgical virus was given to most troopers to protect against various alien infections, and cosmetic nanosurgery beautified the richest civilians. Holograms were now in widespread use for communications, display, entertainment, combat and public relations. Holosynths - simulations of people - acted as receptionists and could answer simple enquiries. HKI Industries, based on Phobos, specialised in the manufacture of transmats. These had a range of only a couple of thousand kilometres, but they were installed on all large ships and linked major cities on most colony worlds. Hoverspeeders were still in use.

By the late 2560s, it became clear that Earth was going to win the wars with the Daleks. By then, the fastline - a state of the art, almost real-time, interstellar communication system - had been developed.[534]

The Early Career of Bernice Summerfield

Bernice Summerfield made her reputation as an archaeologist during excavations of the Fields of Death, the tombs of the rulers of Mars in 2565.[535] She went on to investigate the Dyson Sphere of the Varteq Veil.[536] In 2566, Bernice Summerfield published *Down Among the Dead Men*, her study of archaeology, particularly that of the Martians.[537] In Benny's time, humans had eradicated most of the previously common illnesses.[538]

In 2568, the Spinward Corporation's computer, the Net, predicted that once the Dalek Wars ended, Earth's authorities would show an interest in their activities on Arcadia.[539]

2570 (late June) - LOVE AND WAR[540] **->** Bernice Summerfield and her group arrived on Heaven to survey the artefacts of the extinct Heavenite civilisation on behalf of Ellerycorp. The fungal Hoothi reanimated billions of the dead on the planet. The Hoothi were defeated, but Heaven's ecology had been devastated. The planet was evacuated shortly afterward. Ace departed the TARDIS, but Bernice joined the seventh Doctor on his travels.

---

530 *War of the Daleks.* No date is given, but it's at a time when the Draconian Empire is at war with the Daleks. Female officers are anathema again by the time of *The Dark Path.*

531 "Thirty years" before *The Also People.* Further details are given in the Bernice Summerfield New Adventures, particularly *Down* and *Walking to Babylon.*

532 *Love and War* (p5, p64).

533 "During the wars" according to *Independence Day* (p22).

534 *Deceit*

535 *The Dying Days*

536 *The Also People*

537 *Theatre of War.* The date of publication is given as both "2566" (p36), and "2466" (p135), I prefer the first date. Appendix II of *Sky Pirates!* is "A Benny Bibliography", and contains further details.

538 *Return of the Living Dad* (p51).

539 *Deceit*

540 Dating *Love and War* (NA #9) - The dating of this novel causes a number of problems as it features the debut of Bernice Summerfield. It is the "twenty-fifth century" (p46), and "five centuries" since Ace's time (p26). The novel clearly takes place after *Frontier in Space* (see p10-11 of *Love and War* or p252 of *The Programme Guide*, fourth edition) as it refers to events of that story (e.g.: the peace established between humanity and the Draconians, the female president, the lunar penal colony).

Heaven is established "three decades" before the events of the novel (p92), and *Frontier in Space* is set in 2540, so the novel can't take place before about 2570. Latterly, the decision was made that Benny is from the twenty-sixth century, so this is the date that has been adopted for this story. It is late June, as Benny celebrates her birthday just before the book starts, although it is autumn on Heaven.

Following this time, Ace spent three years in the twenty-sixth century during the time of the Dalek War. After a series of adventures, including a spell working for IMC, she ended up with the Special Weapons Division of Space Fleet. She fought alongside the Irregular Auxiliaries, reputed to be the most dangerous arm of the military.[541] Ace used a D22 photon rifle when she was a Marine.[542] She fought Daleks in the Ceti sector and Hai Dow. She killed a Black Dalek. She fought Marsh Daleks in the Flova trenches. She was issued a tool for removing the tops of Daleks.[543]

Hamilton's father died during the last Dalek War.[544]

& 2573 - DECEIT[545] **->** The Dalek Wars were all but over, and although Dalek nests survived on a number of worlds, the army and Space Fleet were gradually demobilised.

During the Dalek Wars, Earth Central had superseded the Colonial Office, while Space Fleet had been expanded and modernised. The Office of External Operations, "the Earth's surveyors, official couriers, intelligence gatherers, customs officers and diplomats", now had a staff of 5000. While the corporations remained powerful, the Earth government reigned in some of their power and broke some of their monopolies.

Agent Defries investigated the Arcadia System, the base of the Spinward Corporation. The nearest troopers were on Hurgal, although some were taking part in a pirate hunt in the Hai Dow System. Instead, Defries was assigned the troopship *Admiral Raistruck* and a squad of Irregular Auxiliaries. She was also given a "secret weapon": the Dalek Killer Abslom Daak, who was kept in cryosleep.

The ship's crew were told that they were going on a Dalek hunt. The *Admiral Raistruck* arrived in the Arcadia System and encountered an asteroid field carved to resemble terrified human faces. It was clear that Arcadia was subject to SYSDID (System Defence in Strength). Fighters attacked the *Admiral Raistruck*, but this was only a feint. The real attack came from behind: an energy being that was unaffected by the ship's torpedoes. The ship was destroyed.

Out of more than a thousand people, there were only four survivors: Defries, Daak and Troopers Ace and Johannsen. They discovered that Arcadia had been kept at a medieval level of technology. The population had been kept in ignorance, and the android Humble Counsellors enforced company law. All offworlders were killed as plague-carriers. The power behind Spinward was the Pool: vats of brain matter culled from generations of colonists, and housed in a space station in orbit around Arcadia. Pool intended to manufacture a universe of pure thought, making itself omnipotent. Pool was ejected into the Vortex with the TARDIS' tertiary control room. Ace rejoined the TARDIS, and traveled alongside the seventh Doctor and Bernice.

---

541 *Deceit.* Many of the subsequent New Adventures contain references to Ace's exploits in Space Fleet.
542 Respectively *First Frontier, Theatre of War, Shadowmind, Lungbarrow* and *The Shadow of the Scourge.*
543 "Final Genesis"
544 *Death to the Daleks*
545 Dating *Deceit* - (NA #13) The novel is set "two, probably three Earth years" after *Love and War* (p85), and as such the dating of the story is problematic (q.v. Benny's Birthday). Both the blurb and the history section in the Appendix of the novel state that *Deceit* is set in "the middle of the twenty-fifth century", just after what *The Terrestrial Index* calls the Second Dalek War (p62-63). This is restated at various other points (e.g.: p69, p216), but contradicted by other evidence in the same book: Arcadia was colonised 379 years before *Deceit* (p115), but not before the EB Corporation's first warship was operational in 2112 (p27), so the book must be set after 2491 AD. The book also refers to the Cyber Wars, and "Nemesis of the Daleks" was "years ago". In the Marvel strips, Abslom Daak comes from the mid-twenty-sixth century.

Pool - while not named there - briefly reappears in the post-*Doctor Who* New Adventure *Dead Romance.* Arcadia may or may not be the same planet that was the destination of the *Mayflower* in "Profits of Doom", or

that was on the front line of the Last Great Time War according to the Doctor in *Doomsday.*
546 *Cold Fusion* (p247).
547 Dating *Shakedown* (NA #45) - There is no date given in the book, the story synopsis or the video version. The novel is set after *Lords of the Storm* (set in 2371). The Rutans assert that the spy disguised as Karne "died long ago" (p66), but there's some sense that he is still a recent memory.

However, the Benny novel *Mean Streets* - set in 2594, and also written by Terrance Dicks - is something of a *Shakedown* sequel and contains a flashback to Roz and Chris' visit to Megacity in that book. In the flashback, they learn about an undertaking named The Project (an attempt to genetically engineer miners and make them more efficient), and *Mean Streets* p235 indicates that the Project has been running for no more than two generations.

Some general details about *Mean Streets* suggest that events in *Shakedown* were at most a few decades ago - the augmented Ogron Garshak appears in both books (although it's possible that he, at least, possesses an extended lifespan). According to *Mean Streets* p122, the bar manager Sara is the dancer that Chris ogles on *Shakedown* p78. She's admittedly a long-lived alien, but isn't surprised to see Chris again in *Mean Streets*, only that he should look a bit older. The account in *Mean*

At the end of the Galactic Wars, arms treaties were signed to limit the size and capability of combat robots.[546]

& 2574 - SHAKEDOWN[547] **->** The Sontarans secured information about the Rutan Host that could prove decisive in their war: long ago, a wormhole had been established between Ruta III and Sentarion. In the event of a Sontaran victory, the Rutan Great Mother would use the tunnel to escape her fate. The Sontarans prepared to send a battlefleet down the wormhole to kill the Great Mother, but the Rutan spy Karne discovered the plan. The seventh Doctor tracked Karne down to the human colony of Megacity, and was able to thwart the Sontaran and Rutan plots.

? 2575 - HUMAN NATURE (NA)[548] **->** The seventh Doctor and Benny visited a bodysmith and bought a Pod that would allow the Doctor to become human. They travelled to Earth, 1914, so the Doctor could experiment with living as a human being.

Battrulian artist Toulour Martinique was mysteriously killed after painting his last work, *Murdering Art*, which depicted his being murdered by demons.[549] Around 2582, the Kalkravian Revolution took place, and the Adjudication Bureau was sent in to free hostages. The All Worlds Science Fair took place on the planet Dellah. Earth won the Worlds Cup in 2584.[550]

c 2585 - THE ALSO PEOPLE[551] **->** On a holiday to the Worldsphere of the People, the seventh Doctor solved the murder of viCari, the first drone to be killed in more than three hundred years. The Doctor and Bernice also helped restore the feral Kadiatu Lethbridge-Stewart to sanity.

2587 (Autumn) - RETURN OF THE LIVING DAD[552] **- >** The newly-married Bernice and Jason were on Youkali 6. Benny was studying for a genuine degree in archaeology, while writing a new book and trying for a child. An old friend of her father, Admiral Groenewegen, made contact with new information about Issac Summerfield's disappearance. Benny decided to call for the seventh Doctor's help. They discovered that Isaac Summerfield was alive and well, and living on Earth in 1983.

The seventh Doctor and Chris visited Bernice and Jason on Youkali 6 to inform them of the death of Roz Forrester.[553]

2589 - PHOBOS[554] **->** One entity hailed from another universe that was collapsing, and forged a singularity bridge to our reality. The bridge ended on the Martian moon of Phobos, but the rules of the two universes were very different, and the entity became stuck in the transition point. The entity fed off feelings of euphoria, set up a thin atmosphere on Phobos and gained strength as the moon was used for extreme sports. It hoped, in time, to fashion a new body for itself.

Problems arose during development of Lunar Park (a hotel and botanical garden) on Phobos, and only the environmental dome for this facility was finished. Squatters moved in when the moon was left unincorporated, and adrenaline junkies performed extreme sports against the backdrop of the moon's spectacular ice valleys. Such recreations included grav-board runs outside the dome, ice spelunking in the melted floes beneath the surface and "orbit-hopping" for those who had the right equipment.

Kai Tobias, an engineer, found himself in mental contact with the entity from another universe. Tobias realized that

---

Streets of a former miner, "old Sam", also seems to suggest that The Project was initiated within a human lifetime.

It's said that Chris Cwej - who's capable of time travel by the time *Mean Streets* occurs - wants to settle "unfinished business" in Megacity, and placing *Shakedown* shortly after *Lords of the Storm* would strangely have him doing so more than two hundred years after the fact. (Then again, it's also odd that he'd return a couple of decades later.)

If it's a contest between the highly vague sense of time in a New Adventure, and the more concrete evidence provided in a Benny New Adventure by the same author, it seems fair to give the Benny NA priority - hence the repositioning of *Shakedown* from the previous edition of this chronology.

548 Dating *Human Nature* (NA #38) - No date is given, but Ellerycorp and the Travellers are mentioned, suggesting this is around Benny's native time.

549 "Seven years, three months and eleven days" before *Demontage*.

550 *Cold Fusion*. The year of the revolution is given (p230), the science fair was "ten years ago" (p200).

551 Dating *The Also People* (NA #44) - The remains of "a sub gas giant that had broken up sixty-two billion years previously" is referred to (p168) and the Doctor said his "diary's pretty much clear" until "the heat death of the universe" (p186). This led the Virgin edition of this book to conclude that the story was set many billions of years in the future. However, the Bernice Summerfield New Adventures made clear that the story takes place around Benny's native time.

552 Dating *Return of the Living Dad* - It's "2587" (p5).

553 *So Vile a Sin*

554 Dating *Phobos* (BF BBC7 #5) - "Apparently the year is 2589", the Doctor says.

the entity consumed euphoria and felt poisoned by fear, and thus adapted construction robots into deadly "Phobians" to scare the adrenaline junkies with. His plan failed, and the extreme sports continued unabated.

The eighth Doctor and Lucie stopped on Phobos just as Tobias' plan to scare the tourists resulted in some accidental deaths. The Doctor learned of the emerging entity and jolted it by concentrating his many fears - this either killed the creature or at least made it go dormant. As a precaution, the Doctor recommended that the euphoric sports on Phobos come to an end.

The time-active Headhunter landed on Phobos days in advance of the TARDIS' arrival, only to fall off a bicycle and be rendered unconscious until after the Doctor and Lucie had left. The Headhunter awoke and continued her pursuit.

In this era, the Githians were large, hirsute creatures who inter-acted with humanity, but were forbidden to marry outside their species in order to keep their gene pool pure. Hunters retrieved Githians who violated the law.

Around the year 2590, Radon 222 levels on the surface of Argolis had dropped to such a level that the planet became habitable again.[555] Blinni-Gaar was an agricultural planet feeding an entire sector. Channel 400 made a deal with the government and started broadcasting addictive programmes. The Blinnati stopped farming, nearly leading to famine on the Rim until off-worlders started running the planet.[556]

c 2590 - DEMONTAGE[557] **->** The eighth Doctor, Sam and Fitz arrived on Vega Station. General Browning Phillips was planning to return the Battrulian junta to power by killing President Drexler, but the Doctor defeated that plan. He also engineered a more permanent peace treaty between the Battrul and Canvine.

The artist Martinique had discovered a process that could physically tranfer someone into a painting, or make items in paintings take physical form. He used this technique to survive his "murder", and took up residence in a serene painting.

2592 (31st October) - COLD FUSION[558] **->** By this time, the Third Draconian War had been fought. An Empress, revered as a goddess by some, now ruled Earth. The Empire had developed Skybases to operate as planetary command centres, and the Adjudicators were sent across the Empire to enforce Imperial Law. The Unitatus Guild, a secret society based on garbled legends of UNIT in the twenty-first century, was politically influential.

555 "Three centuries" after *The Leisure Hive*.

556 "Ten years" before *Prime Time*.

557 Dating *Demontage* (EDA #20) - No date is given, but the art forger Newark Rappare appears in both this and the Benny novel *Dragon's Wrath* (set in 2593), and he is "middle aged" in both.

558 Dating *Cold Fusion* (MA #29) - The novel was originally set at the same time as *So Vile a Sin* and tied in quite closely to that book, but it became clear *So Vile a Sin* wouldn't be released as scheduled. Following that, *Cold Fusion* was reworked to occur just before the Benny New Adventures, and included the first mention of Dellah, the planet Benny was based on for that series. A copyright notice on a wardroid states that this is 2692, but that was a typographical error, and should have read "2592". It's "four hundred years" before Chris and Roz's time (p165). It's stated that the Adjudicators have been around for "half a millennium" (p247).

559 Patience vanishes mysteriously in *Cold Fusion*, and reappears in *The Infinity Doctors*

560 *Interference* (p113).

561 Dating *The Dying Days* (NA #61) - The date is given.

562 *The Well-Mannered War*

563 *Superior Beings* (p108).

564 *Interference*

565 *Love and War*, presumably a reference to the Daleks' use of blackmail in *Death to the Daleks*.

566 Two hundred years before *Nocturne*.

567 Dating "Metamorphosis" (*DWM Yearbook 1993*) -

It's "the future", after the Draconian Wars.

568 Dating *Death to the Daleks* (11.3) - There is no date given on screen, but the story takes place after the Dalek Wars. *The Programme Guide* placed it in "c.3700" (first edition), "c.2800" (second edition) and *The Terrestrial Index* put it in "the twenty-fifth century".

The TARDIS Logs offered a date of "3767 AD" (the same year as *The Monster of Peladon*). *The Official Doctor Who & the Daleks Book* claimed that the Dalek Plague used in this story is the Movellan Virus, so the author set the story between *Resurrection of the Daleks* and *Revelation of the Daleks*, around 3000 AD. This is nonsense, though, as that plague would have no effect on humans - as the Doctor says in *Resurrection of the Daleks* "it is only partial to Dalek". The gas that disfigures humans seen in *Resurrection of the Daleks* is not the Movellan Virus, but a weapon that the Daleks themselves are immune to.

The Daleks routinely use germ warfare throughout their history (we see it in *The Dalek Invasion Of Earth, Planet Of The Daleks* and *Resurrection Of The Daleks*). It's never stated in this story that the Daleks caused the plague on the human colony planets, but it's fair to infer they did, especially as they're stopped from launching a "plague missile" at Exxilon. *Timelink* suggested "3500".

569 *Original Sin* (p204).

570 *The Stealers of Dreams*

The Scientifica, the ruling elite of scientists on an icy Earth colony planet, excavated a crashed TARDIS and its mummified pilot. Following experiments on the ship, ghosts start appearing across the planet. The seventh Doctor, Chris and Roz arrived to investigate the ghosts. The fifth Doctor, Tegan, Nyssa and Adric arrived a month later, and found the Patient - the mummified Time Lady - who promptly regenerated. The Doctor tried to get her to safety as the Adjudicators declared Martial Law. Both Doctors come to realise that the ghosts were the Ferutu, beings from the far future of an alternative timeline in which Gallifrey was destroyed in the ancient past. The Ferutu attempted to ensure Gallifrey's destruction, but the fifth and seventh Doctors joined forces and ensured history was not altered. A few Ferutu were trapped within a chalk circle, the only survivors of their timeline.

Patience was fatally wounded but rescued by Omega, who transported her to his anti-matter universe.[559] Fitz awoke after almost six hundred years to find himself in Augustine City on Ordifica. The colonists had developed the Cold, a horrific weapon. Fitz celebrated his 626th birthday on Ordifica on 7th March, 2593.[560]

2593 (Wednesday, 8th May) - THE DYING DAYS[561] -> Benny Summerfield was offered the chair of archaeology at St Oscar's University on Dellah. She received the job offer in 1997 despite never actually applying for the position. The eighth Doctor dropped her off, and they enjoyed a fond farewell.

The Black Guardian transported Menlove Stokes to Dellah from the far distant future. Stokes became a Professor of Applied Arts at St Oscar's.[562]

In 2594, the fox-like Valethske were searching for their former gods, the Khorlthochloi, and came into conflict with the Sontarans. The Earth Empire had colonised the Thynemnus System, and a mass immigration led to tensions. The planet Korsair was established to settle disputes. The Valethske attacked one of the new colonies, overwhelming the Korsairs and capturing colonists for their larder.[563]

Fitz was initiated into Faction Paradox around 2594. Laura Tobin, who would eventually become the Doctor's companion Compassion, was sent to Ordifica the same year. Two years later, the Time Lords sterilised the planet, which killed three hundred million people. Two thousand survivors, including Fitz and Laura, were evacuated to the *Justinian*, which headed to the year 1799.[564]

The Twenty-Seventh Century

According to the Doctor, the Daleks "started coming up with other schemes" after they lost the Wars.[565] Archaeologists unearthed documents pertaining to the extinct Ultani race and its bio-harmonics, but failed to recognise their importance. The texts were filed, along with cosmographic mission reports, in the archives on Nocturne.[566]

c 2600 - "Metamorphosis"[567] -> The seventh Doctor and Ace arrived on the bio-freighter *Mitre*, which was shipping human embryos to Earth. Since the Draconian Wars, Earth's gene pool had been damaged. The Daleks attacked and took the ship, bombarded the embryos with radiation and converted them into human / Dalek hybrids. They attempted to turn the Doctor into a Dalek... but this created a link that enabled the Doctor to compel a Dalek to smash into the Dalek ship's propellant tanks, destroying the vessel.

? 2600 - DEATH TO THE DALEKS[568] -> A plague spread through the atmospheres of many of the Outer Planets. Thousands died, and ten million people were threatened. Earth scientists quickly discovered an antidote to the plague: parrinium, a chemical that acted as both a cure and an immunity. It only existed in minute quantities on Earth, and was so rare that it was one of the most valuable known substances.

A satellite surveying the planet Exxilon discovered that parrinium was almost as common there as salt was on Earth. A Marine Space Corps ship was sent to Exxilon to collect parrinium, but the Daleks wanted to secure the substance for themselves, then force the Space Powers to accede to their demands.

Upon arriving within range of the planet, the Earth ship suffered total power failure. The crew explored the area and discovered a fantastic city - the source of the power-drain - that was thousands of years old. The Exxilon natives guarded this City fanatically, and the priests ensured that anyone caught there faced certain death. The third Doctor and Sarah arrived shortly before the Daleks. Venturing into the City, the Doctor was able to stop the power drain. He also tricked the Daleks and - with the sacrifice of Galloway, one of the Earthmen - blew up their ship.

During the twenty-seventh century, oxygen factories were built in London.[569] Colony World 4378976.Delta-Four was founded in the twenty-seventh century. The inhabitants soon started going "fantasy crazy" as a result of interactions with the microscopic native life, and the government banned all fiction to curb this problem.[570]

Circa 2620, crystal towers were constructed on Rigel

VII, an Earth Empire colony.[571] The *Arrow of Righteousness* set out on its holy journey some time before 2650, the pilgrims inside frozen in meditation.[572]

In 2660, Fridgya was devastated in the fifth Thargon-Sorson war. Its cryo-morts would remain undisturbed for many thousands of years.[573]

2673 - SHADOWMIND[574] -> This was the time of Xaxil, the twenty-fourth Draconian Emperor.

Thousands of years before, the Shenn of Arden had discovered "hypergems" that boosted their telepathic ability. Around 2640, one group of Shenn began to hear a mysterious voice from the sky that ordered them to construct kilns. This voice was the "Umbra", a sentience that had evolved from carbon structures on a nearby asteroid.

By this time, the planet Tairngaire was heavily populated and a member of a local alliance of planets, the Concordance, with its own space fleet that had recently seen action in the nasty Sidril War. In 2670, colonists from Tairngaire set up camp on the planet Arden. The Colonial Office decreed that the natural features of the planet should be named after characters from the works of Shakespeare. Accordingly, the main settlement was called Touchstone Base, and there was a Lake Lysander, a Titania River, and a Phebe Range of mountains.

After completing wargame trials in the Delta Epsilon system, the CSS *Broadsword* was recalled to Tairngaire by Admiral Vego and sent to investigate the situation at the Arden. All contact had been lost with the settlers, and five ships dispatched to investigate also vanished. It was discovered that the Shenn were secretly operating in New Byzantium by inhabiting artificially constructed human bodies. The "Umbra" was building "shadowforms", extensions of its power. The seventh Doctor located Umbra and blocked off the sun's rays, effectively rendering it unconscious.

During the twenty-seventh century, a Haitian deciphered the Rihanssu language, allowing a peace treaty that ended the war between Earth and that race.[575]

c 2675 - THE SANDMAN[576] -> The Clutch, the fleet of ships containing the Galyari race and numerous tagalongs, returned to the homeworld of the Cuscaru. A Cuscaru ambassador returned a piece of the Galyari's destroyed Srushkubr, but this catalyzed the neural energy tainting the Galyari. The long-dead General Voshkar was reborn in a monstrous body, and tried to return the Galyari to warfare. The sixth Doctor and Evelyn's involvement resulted in Voshkar's demise. The Clutch departed into

---

571 *Singularity*

572 "More than a century" before "Time Bomb".

573 *The Well-Mannered War.* The Thargons and Sorsons were originally seen in *The Tomorrow People.*

574 Dating *Shadowmind* (NA #16) - The Doctor tells Ace that "by your calendar the year is twenty-six seventy-three" (p29). The events of *Frontier in Space* in "twenty-five forty" (p74) were "one hundred and thirty years ago" (p61).

575 *White Darkness*

STAR TREK: In the Pocket Books' range of *Star Trek* novels (particularly those by Diane Duane), the Romulans call themselves "Rihanssu", and the race is referred to in *White Darkness* (p129). A few of the other New and Missing Adventures have included such *Star Trek* in-jokes. There are many, for example, in *Sanctuary*, another of David McIntee's books, and Turlough refers to the Klingon homeworld in *The Crystal Bucephalus* (p104).

Star Trek and *Doctor Who* have radically differing versions of the future, and *The Left-Handed Hummingbird* establishes that *Star Trek* is merely fiction in the *Doctor Who* universe (which is later confirmed by *Rose* in *The Empty Child*). Maybe, just as Trekkies in the seventies managed to get NASA to name a prototype space shuttle after the USS *Enterprise*, the *Star Trek* fans of the future managed to name a lot of planets after ones from their favourite series - Vulcan, as seen in *The Power of the Daleks*, being one of the first.

576 Dating *The Sandman* (BF #37) - No date is given, but the Benny audio *The Bone of Contention*, also written by Simon Forward, features the Clutch and is set in the very early twenty-seventh century. In that story, it's said that the Galyari Research Directorate hopes to build weapons against the Sandman. As the Clutch's weaponry isn't significantly advanced in *The Sandman* audio, it probably takes place soon after the Benny adventure.

577 The Swampies appear in *The Power of Kroll.* Slavery exists at the time of *Warriors' Gate* and *Terminus*, and the work camps referred to in *The Caves of Androzani* are also near-slavery.

578 *Warriors' Gate.* Stephen Gallagher has stated in interviews (see, for example, *In-Vision* #50) that Rorvik's crew come from N-Space, and their familiarity with English (such as the graffiti), "sardines" and "custard" suggest they come from Earth. The coin flipped is a "100 Imperial" piece and they use Warp Drive, both of which suggest an Earth Empire setting, although placing the story details here is arbitrary.

579 Dating *The Highest Science* (NA #11) - Sheldukher's ship arrives at Sakkrat in "2680" (p17). It is "two hundred and thirty years" in Benny's future (p35) [q.v. "Benny's Birthday"].

580 *Happy Endings*

581 *The Well-Mannered War*

582 *Death and Diplomacy* (p203).

583 *Death and Diplomacy* (p71).

space, and resumed business as an intergalactic flea market of sorts.

There had been examples of humanity oppressing native species for centuries. The Swampies of Delta Magna, for example, had been displaced and oppressed. Slavery was formally reintroduced on many worlds.[577] The time-sensitive Tharils had once been the owners of a mighty Empire, with territory stretching across several universes including N-Space and E-Space. Now slavers had captured them. The Tharils were a valuable commodity, as they alone could navigate the ships using warp drive based on "Implicate Theory". Many humans became rich trading in Tharils. One privateer, a veteran of Tharil hunts on Shapia commanded by Captain Rorvik, vanished without trace following a warp drive malfunction.[578]

2680 - THE HIGHEST SCIENCE[579] **->** Authorities on Checkley's World had made the planet Hogsumm to resemble the fabled planet Sakkrat, hoping to capture the criminal Sheldukher and retrieve the Cell that he stole. A slow time converter set up on Hogsumm created a Fortean Flicker that moved objects through time, including a group of hostile Chelonians and some train-riders taking the 8:12 from Chorleywood in 2003.

In 2680, Sheldukher and his crew revived from stasis and landed on "Sakkrat". Sheldukher committed suicide while resisting arrest, and the Cell was killed also. Sheldukher's Hercules devastator atomized a large area of the planet. The Chelonians and the train-riders, known to the Chelonians as the EightTwelves, were left frozen in a stasis field.

The Master sabotaged the slow time converter on Hogsumm, creating a Fortean Flicker. President Romana of Gallifrey located the source of the disturbance on Hogsumm, and released the trapped humans and Chelonians. The Chelonians weren't grateful, so Romana marooned them there and took the humans home.[580] The abandoned Chelonians survived and created a viable colony that made contact with the rest of their kind after a few thousand years.[581]

The Battle of the Rigel Wastes took place in 2697. The Doctor, Bernice, Roz and Chris witnessed the massacre.[582] In the twenty-seven and twenty-eight hundreds, New

Earth Feudalism was established. This social system would lead to the thirtieth-century Overcities.[583]

In the twenty-eighth century, the Legions tried to undermine the business consortia of the galaxy using their multi-dimensional abilities. The Time Lords intervened, sending Mortimus to imprison the Legion homeworld for eight thousand years. Around this time, the Wine Lords of Chardon had the best wine cellars in the galaxy.[584]

Earth claimed the planet Dust on the Dead Frontier, but never developed it.[585] The renegade Time Lord Koschei visited Earth in the twenty-eighth century and met Ailla, a woman who joined him on his travels. It was a time of food riots and constant war.[586]

The rock band Pakafroon Wabster formed around 2700.[587]

2708 - "By Hook or By Crook"[588] **->** The eighth Doctor and Izzy landed in the City-State of Tor-Ka-Nom. The Doctor chided Izzy for being more interested in the guide-book than seeing the sights, but changed his tune upon being arrested for a murder that he didn't commit. Izzy freed him by looking up the identity of the real murderer in her guidebook, which wouldn't be written for another twenty three years.

> = The sixth Doctor visited the planet Narrah in 2721.[589]

The Doctor met the mad scientist Linus Leofrix on Ricarus in 2723.[590]

c 2725 - "Warlord of the Ogrons"[591] **->** The brilliant if misguided surgeon Linus Leofrix landed on the planet of the Ogrons, along with his pilot Rostow, and captured one of the natives: Gnork. Leofrix used a surgical implantation technique to make Gnork super-intelligent, planning to use him to conquer half the galaxy. Gnork challenged Gwunn for the leadership of the tribe, sparing his life because he wanted his help to defeat the Earthmen. Gnork stole the ship, leaving the humans at the mercy of Gwunn.

One branch of humanity fell into a futile and stalemated war against the Foucoo - a humourless, burrowing and territorial species that among other things fought with micro-munitions. Such was the conflict that nobody actually knew what the Foucoo looked like. The conflict lasted

---

584 *The Crystal Buchephalus* (p40, p80).
585 "A thousand years" before *Interference*.
586 *The Dark Path*
587 "Three hundred years" before "Interstellar Overdrive".
588 Dating "By Hook or By Crook" (*DWM* #256) - The date is given.

589 *Spiral Scratch*
590 "Warlord of the Ogrons"
591 Dating "Warlord of the Ogrons" (*DWW* #13-14) - Rostow mentions Federation patrols, but in the framing sequence the Doctor mentions that he met Leofrix in 2723, so it can't be the Galactic Federation.
592 The war begins "seventy years" before *Nocturne*.

for decades, and the human colony on Nocturne was used as a departure point for soldiers going to or leaving the warzone.[592] In 2736, a guidebook to Tor-Ka-Nom was published, and a copy of it would end up in the TARDIS library.[593] A breakaway cell of Ventriki militants believed its enemies were operating from the trading world Crestus V, and deployed the biological agent Saravin there. In response, the Earth Empire destroyed Saravin production plants across an entire sector of space.[594]

2750 - "Time Bomb"[595] -> The *Arrow of Righteousness* was a hundred years from its destination. The TARDIS was nearby and was hit by a time weapon - a Temporal Disruption Pulser. The sixth Doctor and Frobisher traced it to a hundred years in the future on the planet Hedron.

c 2764 - THE SENSORITES[596] -> During the twenty-eighth century, spacecraft from Earth ploughed deeper and deeper into space, searching for minerals and other natural resources. On Earth, air traffic was becoming congested. Earth ships reached Sense-Sphere, a molybdenum-rich planet that was inhabited by the shy, telepathic Sensorites.

A five-man Earth ship discovered the planet Sense-Sphere in the twenty-eighth century, but the Sensorites feared exploitation and refused to trade with Earth. The Earth mission left, but shortly afterward, the Sensorites began dying from a mysterious new disease. Within a decade, two out of ten Sensorites had died.

By the time a second Earth mission arrived, the Sensorites were terrified of outsiders. They used their psychic powers to place the crew of the ship in suspended animation, a process that drove one human, John, mad. When the first Doctor, Ian, Barbara and Susan arrived and investigated, it became clear that the Sensorites were suffering from nightshade poisoning, introduced to the City water supply by the previous Earth expedition. The second expedition left, promising not to return to the planet.

By 2765, INITEC had built the first of a chain of Vigilant laser defence space stations in orbit around Earth. The station proved vital in preventing the Zygons from melting the icecaps and flooding the world.[597]

2775 - THE STEALERS OF DREAMS[598] -> The ninth Doctor, Rose and Jack found themselves on Colony World 4378976.Delta-Four, which was remarkably mundane as the authorities banned any form of fiction or fantasy. The Doctor discovered that the microscopic native life was feeding on the colonists' imaginations, overwhelming their ability to distinguish fact from fiction. When the truth emerged, the colony's scientists quickly came up with a cure.

Lothar Ragpole established a drinking establishment on Nocturne, and it would serve the developing artistic enclave there.[599]

---

593 Twenty three years after "By Hook or By Crook".
594 "A few hundred years" after *Scaredy Cat*.
595 Dating "Time Bomb" (*DWM* #114-116) - "Earthdate 2750" according to the opening caption.
596 Dating *The Sensorites* (1.7) - Maitland says "we come from the twenty-eighth century", which might mean it is later than that. An incoherent John says they've been at Sense-Sphere either "four years" or "for years". *The Programme Guide* set the story in "c.2600" in its first two editions, *The Terrestrial Index* settled on "about 2750". *The TARDIS Logs* gave the date as "2765". *Timelink* "2764".
597 *Original Sin* (p287).
598 Dating *The Stealers of Dreams* - It's "2755 AD".
599 "Twenty years" before *Nocturne*.
600 Dating *Kinda* (19.3) - An arbitrary date. I assume that the colonists are from Earth, as they have recognisably English names. On screen they only refer to a "homeworld", which Todd says is overcrowded. Sanders' attitude perhaps suggests an early colonial period, and the story would seem to be set after *Colony in Space*, in which colonists are seen as "eccentric". The colonists are from Earth in Terrance Dicks' novelisation, where the

Doctor suggests they are from the time of the "Empire". *The TARDIS Logs* set the story in the "25th Century". *Timelink* set it in 1981, reasoning that it isn't an Earth colony.
601 "Thirteen years" before *EarthWorld*.
602 *The Fall of Yquatine*, "over two hundred years" earlier than 2992.
603 "About seven years" before *EarthWorld*.
604 The foiled assassination attempts occur five years before *Nocturne*. Zeta Reticula is located thirty three light-years from Earth.
605 Will happens upon the Ultani texts at least eighteen months before *Nocturne*.
606 Dating *Companion Piece* (TEL #13) - It is "the twenty-eighth century" (p74), "eight hundred years" after Cat's time (p78).
607 Dating *Nocturne* (BF #92) - The Doctor tells Ace and Hex that they're "about 790 years and three parsecs in that direction" from their native era on Earth. As Ace hails from the late 1980s but Hex originates from 2021, this could support a dating of roughly anywhere between 2777 and 2811.

? 2782 - KINDA[600] **-> The homeworld was overcrowded, and teams were sent to assess other worlds for possible colonisation. One of these was S14, a primeval forest world, which had the local name Deva Loka ("the land of the Kinda"). The natives were humanoid telepaths and lived in harmony with nature. Trees came into fruit all year round, and the climate hardly varied throughout the year. The fifth Doctor banished the Mara, a psychic creature from the "dark places of the inside", and persuaded the colonists to abandon further settlement.**

Elizabethan, the wife of President John F Hoover of New Jupiter, gave birth to triplets following fertility treatment. She had used DNA samples from Hanstrum, Hoover's chief technician, and not her infertile husband. The children were named Asia, Africa and Antarctica.[601] In the early 2790s, the ten-planet Minerva System was colonised by an Earth ship captained by Julian de Yquatine.[602]

Hanstrum later tried to murder Elizabethan after she began to suspect her triplets were psychopaths, and wanted to confess her infidelity. Elizabethan was rendered comatose, and the triplets were blamed and imprisoned.[603]

By now, the human colony Nocturne was home to the Department of War, munitions factories and some hospices, but the planet itself was secure, being located eight months of travel from the front. The adversity of the war with the Foucoo attracted to Nocturne the greatest concentration of artists and thinkers since the Florentine Renaissance - in time, this creative revival would become known as the "Far Renaissance". Creativity of many types would flourish on Nocturne with a success that would only be accomplished about half a dozen times in the whole of human history.

Glasst City on Nocturne smelt like Venice, on account of its canals. The Sol System, Zeta Reticula, the Hessa Cloud and the Fuocoo home system and were all visible to the naked eye from Nocturne. The Doctor was involved when officials on Nocturne covered up two mysterious deaths - an attempt by the Foucoo to assassinate members of the War Department.[604]

Will Alloran, a student of Korbin Thessenger, went looking in the Nocturne archives and happened across alien scripts bearing the bio-harmonics of the extinct Ultani race. He realised he'd stumbled upon something potentially deadly and purged the documents - but his brother Lomas secretly made copies. Thinking the problem solved, Will signed up to fight in the war with the Foucoo. He spent eight months traveling to the front, and lost his leg during a skirmish on the planet Zocus.[605]

c 2799 - COMPANION PIECE[606] **->** Philosophical questions about alien civilizations, such as whether non-humans possessed souls and could be baptised, caused a rift in the Catholic Church. Social and political instability compelled Pope Athanasius to relocate to Rome, a mobile space station with a replica of Vatican City. The Catholics who remained on Earth elected Pope Urban IX as their leader, and each side declared the other false.

Missionaries from the Catholic Church had arrived on the planet Haven and converted much of the indigenous population. However, a malfunctioning TARDIS landed there and exploded, devastating the planet. The Church in response branded all Time Lords as witches. Grand Inquisitor Guii del Toro rose to power in the church on Haven, and instigated the "Good Shepherd" project, using human-like robots to evangelize.

A Carthian bandit chief named Brotak took control of most of the planets in the Magellanic System, and named himself Tsar of all the Magellanic Clouds. He converted to Roman Catholicism, and favoured the Cetacean Brrteet'k (a.k.a. Celestine VI) as the next Pope.

The seventh Doctor and his companion Catherine Broome repaired the malfunctioning TARDIS by stealing some mercury from the Weirdarbi, a race of cybernetic insects. They then arrived on Haven to do some shopping, but the Doctor, identified as a Time Lord, was quickly arrested by del Toro. The Doctor and Cat were dispatched to Earth aboard an Inquisition spaceship to face a papal conclave, but Pope John Paul XXIII was declared soul-dead at this time. Forces supporting either Celestine VI or Pope Urban XII as John Paul's successor fell into open conflict. Del Toro died amid the warfare.

The Inquisition ship took heavy damage, and the Doctor, Cat and their allies had minutes to live unless a robot could be sent through the ship's toxic areas, reach the bridge, and use its controls to release the sealed-off TARDIS. With the Inquisition's robots non-functional, the Doctor resigned himself to telling Cat about her true nature.

c 2800 - NOCTURNE[607] **->** The Far Renaissance was one of the Doctor's favourite periods of history, and he visited the locale in more than one incarnation. The security force on Nocturne - the Overwatch - had eight separate reports of the Doctor's visits, dating back thirty years. Tegan was present during one such stopover.

Lomas Alloran sought to achieve great music with his copy of the Ultani bio-harmonics, but Nocturne - owing to the war with the Foucoo - was a planet that inherently contained more discord than the Ultani homeworld. Use of the bio-harmonics created a creature of pure noise - this entity sought works of artistry, but killed the artists themselves.

The seventh Doctor arrived on Nocturne at this time, and his companions - Ace and Hex - expressed skepticism that he lacked an ulterior motive for the visit. Previously, the Doctor had taken them to Breearos to "return some library books", then spent a fortnight negotiating a cease-fire in the Orbit Wars. On another occasion, the Doctor said he wanted to use the infallible laundry services of Tau Sartos, but in fact worked to prevent the spawning of a Zylax swarm (an incident that left Hex covered in mucus).

Hex was accused of murder when the noise creature killed the celebrated composer Lucas Erphan Moret. Lomas Alloran also perished, and his brother Will - upon realising that his actions had caused some deaths - goaded the creature to killing him.

The Doctor devised a means of echoing and canceling out the noise creature's harmonics. Will's mentor, Korbin Thessenger, was moved to write his Great Mass - it would be the last great work of his career, partly credited to Will, and celebrated for as long as humanity persisted. History forgot the manner of Will's death, and it was speculated that he died in the war.

The war would continue for "a long time", but the Far Renaissance lasted a total of thirty years. It gave rise to the plays of Casto, Cinder's Odes, the Quantum Movement, Luminalism, all but one of Thessenger's symphonies, the Zeitists and the novels of Elber Rocas. During this time, the sculptor Shumac took eight years to carve the statue "Man Triumphant Above the Rigours of Space" from a single block of Lympian Onyx.

Nocturne was home to the Museum of Culture, the Lazlo Collection and the College of Music. Data pads were in use. Robotic "familiars" - fashioned after the female form, as research showed that people were more comfortable with representations of the female gender - performed menial tasks for the populace.

c 2800 - EARTHWORLD[608] **->** Earth Heritage had established around the galaxy thousands of EarthWorld theme parks, where lifelike androids would replicate - albeit in a rather garbled form - the history of Earth. Many of the people of New Jupiter wanted independence from Earth, and the Association for New Jupitan Independence (ANJI) was gaining support. The eighth Doctor, Fitz and Anji arrived and were arrested on suspicion of sympathy with the independence movement. The Doctor managed to stop an android rampage.

Elizabethan revived from her coma, and although her daughter Asia died, she pledged to help her remaining two children.

Colonists seeking independence from Federation officials settled on Phoenix, the fourth planet in the Paledies System. Terraforming machinery automatically went to work while most of the colonists remained in hibernation, but sunspot activity hampered development of an ozone layer and set the process back by decades. Space station *Medusa* was set up in geostationary orbit.[609]

2815 - FESTIVAL OF DEATH[610] **->** The leisure cruiser *Cerberus*, with a thousand passengers onboard, was trapped in hyperspace between Teredekethon and Murgatroyd. Nearly one hundred ships crashed into it, including a prison ship containing dangerous Arachnopods. They escaped and went on the rampage.

---

608 Dating *EarthWorld* (EDA #43) The date is arbitrary, but New Jupiter wants independence from Earth and the advanced androids are "pretty standard". It is "the far distant future".

609 "Fifty years" before *Three's a Crowd*.

610 Dating *Festival of Death* (PDA #35) - The date is given on p116.

611 "Fifty years" before *Revenge of the Cybermen*.

612 *Christmas on a Rational Planet* (p189).

613 *The Ultimate Treasure* (p71).

614 "Almost a century and a half" before *So Vile a Sin*.

615 Dating *Dark Progeny* (EDA #48) - The date is given.

616 *The Taking of Planet 5* (p15).

617 Dating "Time Bomb" (*DWM* #114-116) - The caption states it's "Earthdate 2850".

618 Dating *Three's a Crowd* (BF #69) - The Doctor estimates it is around the "twenty-eighth, maybe twenty-ninth century" from the space station's design, which dates back at least fifty years to the colony's formation. Mention of a Federation suggests this story occurs in the vicinity of *Corpse Marker*. There's talk of a "hyperspace transmat link" capable of "beaming" people from star system to star system, but nobody actually uses this device, and it's possibly part of Auntie's ruse against the colonists.

619 *So Vile a Sin* (p28).

620 "Fifteen years" before *Ten Little Aliens*.

621 Dating *Revenge of the Cybermen* (12.5) - In *The Ark in Space*, the Doctor is unsure at first when the Ark was built ("I can't quite place the period"), but he quickly concludes that "Judging by the macro slave drive and that modified version of the Bennet Oscillator, I'd say this was built in the early thirtieth century...late twenty-ninth, early thirtieth I feel sure". Yet the panel he looks at appears to be a feature of the Ark, not the original Nerva Beacon.

Still, in this story when Harry asks whether this is "the time of the solar flares and Earth is evacuated", the Doctor informs him that it is "thousands of years" before. Mankind has been a spacefaring race for "centuries" before this story when they fought the Cyber War, according to both Stevenson and Vorus. It is clearly established in other stories that the Earth is not abandoned in the twenty-ninth century. This, then, would seem to be the story set in the "late twenty-ninth, early thirtieth century", not *The Ark in Space*. The Cybermen are apparently without a permanent base of operations, so the story is presumably set after the

The Repulsion - an extra-dimensional creature that existed between life and death - offered the survivors of *Cerberus* the chance to escape. They agreed, and the Repulsion exchanged them with participants of the "Beautiful Death" in 3012. Rescue missions would discover only empty ships, prompting "the mystery of the *Cerberus*".

The wrecked spaceships were rebuilt inside the hyper-space tunnel as the G-Lock station.

A mysterious planetoid was detected entering the Solar System, and it eventually became the thirteenth moon of Jupiter. It was named Neo-Phobus by humans, and the Nerva Beacon was set up to warn shipping of this new navigational hazard. Nerva was one of a chain of navigational beacons, which also included Ganymede Beacon at vector 1906702.[611]

ID implants were mandatory in citizens of the Empire, except for those exempted by the Corporate Faiths Amendment Act 2820.[612] The Privacy of Sentient Beings Act was passed in 2830.[613] Earth President Helen Kristiansen declared herself Empress. Helen I would be kept alive by life support systems, and her brain would be controlled by the computer Centcomp, which gave her access to the memories of all previous Earth Presidents. She became aware of the Doctor.[614]

2847 - DARK PROGENY[615] ->
The telepathic inhabitants of Ceres Alpha died out long ago, surviving as a psychic gestalt. Much later, the planet - the closest ever found to Earth's natural conditions - was colonised by humans. Earth was overcrowded and polluted at this time, and terraforming corporations like Worldcorp and Planetscape make planets suitable for human colonisation.

Influenced by the gestalt, the colonists' children began developing psychic powers. Worldcorp encouraged this, hoping that the children's telekinesis could be used to transform planets. The eighth Doctor arrived and exposed the plan. The children rebelled against Worldcorp's corrupt leader, Gaskill Tyran, who died when the children made him mentally relive his acts of murder. The parents of one of the children, Veta and Josef Manni, took custody of the entire group.

The accelerator, a device than could heal wounds and change people's appearances, had been invented.

In the mid-twenty-ninth century, zigma photography proved reconstructions of the Temple of Zeus to be inaccurate.[616]

2850 - "Time Bomb"[617] ->
The scientists of the City of Light on Hedron reached complete control of their environment, and the genetic cleansing of their race. They banished impurities with their time cannon. The sixth Doctor and Frobisher arrived at the weapon and were caught in the effect - which sent them two hundred million years into Earth's past.

The pilgrims of the *Arrow of Righteousness* arrived at their destination, but although their bodies were sound, their minds had gone. The ship crashed into the City of Light and devastated it, killing the population when its microbes and poisons were released.

The Doctor and Frobisher learned that the Hedrons had located the origin of the *Arrow of Righteousness* - Earth - and deliberately targeted their time cannon. In doing so, the Hedrons allowed mankind to evolve, and didn't destroy it.

c 2850 - THREE'S A CROWD[618] ->
A group of militaristic, reptilian Khellians happened across the Phoenix colony, and the Khellian Queen laid a clutch of eggs aboard the colony ship. The colony leader, Auntie, bargained with the Khellians and allowed them to feed off humans in stasis; in return, they were to spare her family. The number of humans who were awake dwindled down to sixteen. They became agoraphobic and lived intensely isolated lives, unaware of the Khellian presence and what had befallen their fellows.

The fifth Doctor, Peri and Erimem arrived at this time and exposed the Khellian threat. The Khellians were wiped out and the colony ship destroyed, but the terraforming process improved the planet's sustainability. Humans sleeping in a dozen habitat domes were slated for revival.

The Forrester palace was built on Io.[619] The Earth Empire annexed the Schirr homeworld and renamed it Idaho. Some Schirr, named the Ten-Strong, formed a resistance movement. They stole the knowledge of black arts from the non-corporeal Morphieans, who failed to distinguish between the Ten-Strong and the other corporeal beings.

The Morphieans initiated retaliatory strikes against human worlds such as New Bejing, and the Ten-Strong launched terrorist strikes on planets such as New Jersey and Toronto, often killing millions.[620]

? 2875 (Day 3, Week 47) - REVENGE OF THE CYBERMEN[621] ->
Fifty years after Neo-Phobus was discovered, the civilian exographer Kellman began his survey of the planetoid, setting up a Transmat point between it and the Nerva Beacon. He renamed the planetoid Voga.

Fifteen weeks later, an extraterrestrial disease swept through Nerva. Once the infection began, the victims died within minutes. The medical team on board the station were among the first to perish, and Earth Centre immediately rerouted all flights through Ganymede Beacon. As loyal members of the Space Service, the Nerva crew remained on board. Ten weeks after the plague first struck, all but four people on the

station were dead. The Cybermen were responsible as part of their plan to destroy Voga. The fourth Doctor defeated them.

? 2877 - THE ROBOTS OF DEATH[622] -> By the late twenty-ninth century, robots had become so advanced that some people found themselves greatly unhinged by the robots' inhuman body language. Psychologists christened this "Grimwade's Syndrome", or "robophobia".

Vehicles called Stormminers ventured out on two-year missions into a hundred million mile expanse of desert. Sand blown up in storms was sucked into the Stormminers' scoops, which sifted out the lucrative substances such as zelanite, keefan and lucanol. The water supplies for the Stormminers' eight-man crew was totally recycled once a month, but the crew lived in relative luxury. Most of the work was done for them by robots: around a hundred Dums, capable of only the simplest task; a couple dozen Vocs, more sophisticated; and one Super-Voc co-ordinating them.

One Stormminer, commanded by Uvanov, witnessed a string of murders instigated by Taren Capel, a madman obsessed with freeing the robots from servitude. A robot killed Capel, and only three of the crew - Uvanov, Pool and Toos - survived the slaughter.

Uvanov's Storm Miner mined the deserts of of Iapetus, the second moon of Saturn.[623]

? 2878 - "Crisis on Kaldor"[624] -> Unexpectedly, Super-Vocs were destroying other types of robots and wandering off into the desert. The Kaldor Robotics Corps hoped the new Ultra-Vocs would solve the problem, but when Sylvos Orikon went undercover as a Super-Voc on a storm-miner, he discovered that UV-1 was actually the one reprogramming the SVs. Orikon destroyed UV-1 but was "disassembled" by the other robots.

? 2878 - THE POWER OF KROLL[625] -> The Sons of Earth Movement claimed that colonising planets was a mistake. They demanded a return to Earth, but most of its members had never been to the homeworld, which was now suffering major famines.

A classified project, a methane-catalysing refinery, was set up on the third moon of Delta Magna. Two hundred tons of compressed protein were produced every day by extracting material from the marshlands, and sent to Magna by unmanned rockets. It was claimed that the Sons of Earth were supplying gas-operated projectile weapons to the native Swampies on this moon, and that the group was employing the services of the notorious gun-runner Rohm-Dutt. The truth

---

destruction of their base on Telos in *Attack of the Cybermen*.

One difficulty with this is that the Cybermen in *Earthshock* (set in 2526) watch a clip from this story. I take this as the production team showing us the previous Doctors, rather than trying to date the story (in the same way, in *Mawdryn Undead*, the Brigadier "remembers" scenes he wasn't actually in). However, *About Time* suggests the Cybermen in *Earthshock* are time-travellers, which explains the otherwise erroneous *Revenge of the Cybermen* clip.

The Programme Guide set the story in both "c.2400" and "c.2900", while *The Terrestrial Index* preferred "the tail end of the 25th Century". *Cybermen* placed the story in "2496", but admitted the difficulty in doing so (p71-72). *The Discontinuity Guide* offered "c.2875". *Timelink* suggests "2525". "A History of the Cybermen" in *DWM* #83 suggested the (misprinted?) date "25,514".

622 Dating *The Robots of Death* (14.5) - An arbitrary date. *The Programme Guide* set the story "c.30,000", but *The Terrestrial Index* preferred "the 51st Century". *Timelink* set the story in 2777, the same period as it set *The Happiness Patrol*.

623 *Legacy*, although this is contradicted by *Corpse Marker*. In real life, Iapetus isn't large enough to have a desert the size of the one referred to in *The Robots in Death*.

624 Dating "Crisis on Kaldor" (*DWM* #50) - "Centuries

have passed since man first colonised Kaldor". It seems to be around the same time as *The Robots of Death*.

625 Dating *The Power of Kroll* (16.5) - Kroll manifests "every couple of centuries" according to the Doctor, and this is his fourth manifestation, suggesting it is at least eight hundred years since Delta Magna was colonised. *The Terrestrial Index* set the story in the "52nd Century", *The TARDIS Logs* "c.3000 AD".

626 Dating "Victims" (*DWM* #212-214) - The year isn't specified, but reference to the human empire seems to place it in the Earth Empire period. The implication is that the Doctor gets his burgundy outfit from Kolpasha following this story.

627 "Centuries" before *Burning Heart* (p4).

628 "Many hundreds of years" before *Legacy*.

629 Dating *The Caves of Androzani* (19.6) - There is no indication of dating on screen. Sharaz Jek seems worried when it appears that the Doctor and Peri are from Earth, suggesting it has political influence. The machine pistols suggest a colonial setting, but Sirius society is long-established; there seems to be an interstellar economy and the androids are highly advanced, so I favour placing this a little later. The Spectrox supplies must be so limited as to have little long-term effect on the human race, explaining why it is not referred to in any other story.

630 Dating *Corpse Marker* (PDA #27) - This is a sequel to *The Robots of Death*, and happens an unspecified

was that Thawn, an official at the refinery, was supplying the Swampies with faulty weapons as an excuse to wipe them out.

A squid creature on this moon had consumed the Fifth Segment of the Key to Time, and grown to a monstrous size. The Swampies regarded it as their god, Kroll. Thawn's plan was uncovered and he was killed. The fourth Doctor and Romana recovered the Fifth Segment, which ended Kroll's power. Kroll had been the source of the refinery's compressed protein, and the facility was left useless upon the creature's reversion.

? 2878 - "Victims"[626] -> Kolpasha was the fashion capital of the human empire. The fourth Doctor and Romana arrived and were accused of copyright theft - a crime more serious there than murder. Elsewhere, the political activist Gevaunt was planning to release Vitality, an age-reversing cosmetic. Romana discovered that repeat use of Vitality would make human flesh break down... and make it easier to digest.

The Doctor discovered that a carnivorous Quoll from the Reft Sector was behind the scheme. The Quoll had stripped their home bare and wanted new feeding grounds, but the Doctor made the Quoll explode by dousing it with Vitality. However, this ruined the Doctor's clothes...

Earth colonised Dramos, located between the secondary and tertiary spiral arms of the galaxy. Dramos Port became an important trading post.[627] The Doctor and Jo visited the home planet of the Pakha and discovered that an ancient Diadem contained a being that made them aggressive. The diadem was lost when the Doctor cast it into a ravine.[628]

? 2884 - THE CAVES OF ANDROZANI[629] -> Spectrox was "the most valuable substance in the universe". At the recommended dose of .3 of a centilitre a day, spectrox could halt the ageing process and double lifespans. There was some evidence that with a sufficient quantity of the substance, a human might live forever.

Spectrox was refined from the nests of the bats of Androzani Minor, a dangerous process carried out by androids. Supplies of spectrox were halted when the scientist Sharaz Jek and his androids rebelled against Androzani Major. The Praesidium sent a taskforce to apprehend Jek and they captured the refinery, but Jek removed the supplies of spectrox. After six months, and with the fifth Doctor's help, the supplies were destroyed in a mudburst - a tidal flood of primeval mud.

? 2887 - CORPSE MARKER[630] -> In Kaldor City, the lowly-born Uvanov was promoted to being a topmaster of the Company, but this failed to sit well with members of the elite classes on the Company Board. They asked the psycho-strategist Carnell to devise a means by which they could secure their power. Carnell's scheme entailed use of new generation of cyborg-robots, which had been secretly created. The cyborgs proved uncontrollable and went on the rampage, killing many prominent citizens. The fourth Doctor destroyed the cyborgs, and Carnell supplied Uvanov with blackmail information against members of the Board. Uvanov quickly attained the top position of Firstmaster.

The Kaldor City audio series starts around four years after Corpse Marker.

number of "years" afterward.

BLAKES 7: *Corpse Marker*, a sequel to *The Robots of Death,* features Carnell - a character who also appeared in the *Blakes 7* episode *Weapon* (Chris Boucher wrote all three stories).

This opens a can of worms, as it suggests that *Blakes 7* and *Doctor Who* occur in the same universe, which is just about possible. It's never established in which century *Blakes 7* takes place, and the original proposal stated only that it was "the third century of the second calendar". The only real indication was that the Wanderer spacecraft (in the *Blakes 7* story *Killer,* written by Robert Holmes) were the first into deep space "seven hundred years" before Blake's era. In *Doctor Who* terms, that would set *Blakes 7* in the twenty-eighth or twenty-ninth century.

The future history of *Blakes 7* is pretty basic - humanity has colonised many planets and most of those are under the control of the fascist Federation. While never

stated in the series itself, publicity for the show (and subsequent guides to the series) said that there was a series of atomic wars across the galaxy several hundred years before Blake's time, and the Federation was founded in the aftermath. By coincidence, this fits quite neatly with the *Doctor Who* timeline, and the atomic war might be the Dalek / Galactic Wars of the twenty-sixth century. As might be expected, not every detail matches perfectly, but the oppressive Earth Empire of *Doctor Who* is not wildly different from the Terran Federation seen in *Blakes 7*. The symbol worn by the Earth expedition in *Death to the Daleks* (authored by Terry Nation, who created *Blakes 7* and wrote a fair amount of it) is the symbol of the Federation in *Blakes 7,* turned ninety degrees.

The audio *Three's a Crowd,* which roughly dates to this era, mentions a Federation and uses *Blakes 7* teleport sound effects.

c 2890 - GRIMM REALITY[631] -> Titan had whale ranches and was being terra-formed. Space mining was big business, with prospectors looking for rare particles such as strange matter, squarks and Hydrogen 3. Zero Rad Day was celebrated on Earth.

The eighth Doctor, Anji and Fitz landed on the planet Albert as the salvage ship *Bonadventure* entered orbit. The Doctor realised that the laws of physics on the planet operated much like the rules of a fairy tale. The planet was alive and had absorbed the memory banks of a crashed Earth ship, then modelled itself as a world of fairy tales. The Doctor collected up various "wishing boxes", which contained the spawn of a nearby white hole. One of the insectoid Vuim used the great powers of the white hole to cure his race of a wasting disease, which seeded the white hole's spawn into a gap between realities to gestate. The parent white hole left and life on Albert returned to normal.

c 2890 (May) - TEN LITTLE ALIENS[632] -> Earth was exporting its poor at this point and levying repressive taxes. Those born on Earth had legal and social advantages over off-worlders. Alien planets were renamed after places on Earth. The Earth military was run by Pentagon Central, and included the Pauper Fleet, the Royal Escort and the Peacekeepers. The Japanese Belt was trying to develop tele-portation.

An Anti-Terror Elite squad from Earth landed on a planetoid for an exercise and discovered a Schirr building there, with a murdered group of Schirr terrorists inside. The first Doctor, Ben and Polly arrived, and the Doctor realised that Nadina Haunt, the human squad's leader, was a Schirr sympathiser who thought she was leading her men into an ambush.

The complex launched itself towards the Morphiean Quadrant. The Schirr terrorists, the Ten Strong, revived. They wanted to ally with a renegade faction of the Morphiean race, and topple the Earth Empire. The Doctor managed to resist the Ten-Strong's spells and annihilate them. The Morphiean authorities dealt with their renegades, ending the Morphiean Quadrant's conflict with humanity.

In 2891, the Daleks destroyed the planet of the Anthaurk, a reptilian race. The Anthaurk occupied Kaillor in the Minerva System and renamed it New Anthaur. The native Izrekt were massacred. The other planets declared war.

On the 16 Lannasirn, following the Anthaurk defeat, the Treaty of Yquatine was signed. The Minerva Space Alliance was formed when the system declared independence from Earth. The Anthaurks began the Century of Waiting, secretly rebuilding their arsenal. For a century, other races flocked to the Minerva System, including the Ixtricite (a crystal race combining "the Krotons, the Rhotons and the something-else-ons"). The Adamanteans and the Ogri colonised Adamantine. Around 2900, the Vargeld family became prominent in the politics of the system.[633]

Decline and Fall

By the beginning of the thirtieth century, the Empire had become utterly corrupt. Planetary Governors, such as the one on Solos, would routinely oppress the native races of the planet.[634] Humans were often little more than "work units", fit only for manning factories or mines where using humanoid robots was uneconomic. Alien races across the galaxy, such as the Mogarians, resented Earth's exploitation of their planets but could do little. Humanity was "going through the universe like a plague of interplanetary locusts". Mogar, in the Perseus Arm of the Galaxy, was a rich source of rare metals such as vionesium. Although Earth assured the

---

631 Dating *Grimm Reality* (EDA #50) - The mining companies were active "a hundred or a hundred and ten years" ago, in the 2780s.
632 Dating *Ten Little Aliens* (PDA #54) - It is clearly the subjugation phase of the Earth Empire. An e-zine written somewhat prior to these events (p15), with biographies of Haunt's troopers, is dated "23.5.90", presumably meaning 23rd May, 2890.
633 *The Fall of Yquatine* (p30, p43).
634 *The Mutants*
635 *Terror of the Vervoids*
636 *Just War* (p143), although we see bears and wolves in *The Ice Warriors*, and hear of a variety of animal specimens in *The Ark in Space*. Pigs and dogs survive until at least the year 5000 AD (*The Talons of Weng-Chiang, The Invisible Enemy*), there are sheep and spiders on the colony ship sent to Metebelis III in *Planet of the Spiders*,

Europa is well stocked with animal life in *Managra*, and the Ark (in *The Ark*) contains a thriving jungle environment complete with an elephant and tropical birds.
637 *Death and Diplomacy* (p16).
638 *Just War*
639 "Fifty years" before Roz's time. *The Also People* (p10).
640 *Illegal Alien* (p152).
THE THIRTIETH CENTURY: While I don't think that the Earth was ravaged by solar flares at this time (see *The Ark in Space*), the Doctor's description of a "highly compartmentalised" Earth society of the thirtieth century in *The Ark in Space* matches similar descriptions of Earth in stories set at this time. Earth is "grey" in *The Mutants* and "highly organised" in *Terror of the Vervoids* Part Four. We learn of food shortages in *Terror of the Vervoids*.
In terms of the New Adventures, this is Cwej and

Mogarians that they only required limited mining concessions, they were soon strip-mining the planet, and the shipments to Earth received Grade One security.[635]

Every native animal species died out except humanity and the rat.[636] The humans of Earth in the thirtieth century had no appendix or wisdom teeth, and most racial differences had been smoothed out in the general population.[637] Humans had a lifespan of around one hundred and forty years.[638] Suspensor pools were fashionable in the Earth Empire.[639] In the thirtieth century, the Cybermen built a time capsule, but a test flight left them stranded in Jersey in 1940.[640]

In 2905, Chris Cwej's father graduated from the Academy. He served in the Adjudication Service, as his ancestors had for centuries, until 2971.[641] **Nerva Beacon completed its mission at Voga. The space station remained operational for many centuries afterward.**[642]

The Overcity Era

The pollution levels on the surface of Earth reached such a level that the population was forced to live in vast sky cities.[643] Around 2945, the Wars of Acquisition fought by the Empire reached Earth itself. The Overcities were built over the battle-torn Earth using a new form of cheap and effective null-gravity. They floated around a kilometre from the surface, supported on stilts and by null-grav beams.

Half the Earth's population, everyone that could afford it, lived in the Overcities and Seacities. The wealthier you were, the higher the levels that you were allowed to access. Earth's surface became the Undertown: a flooded, ruined landscape. The Vigilant belt of defence space stations proved invaluable at repelling alien attacks, and within ten years the front had shifted so far away from Earth that humanity had almost forgotten they were taking place.

After a few years of austerity, Earth benefited from a technological and economic upsurge. It was "a time of peace and prosperity: well, for the peaceful and prosperous, at least". Earth was a cosmopolitan place, with races such as Alpha Centauri, Arcturans, Foamasi, and Thrillip living in the lower areas of the Overcities, although aliens were treated as second-class citizens. Earth at this time had a human population of thirty billion, with almost as many robot workers. The data protection act was modified in 2945 to reflect the changes in technology and society.

Over the generations a semi-feudal system had developed. A Baron was responsible for sections of an Overcity, typically controlling a few hundred levels. A Viscount ran the whole city (an area the size of an old nation state); a Count or Countess was responsible for ten Cities (equivalent to a continent). Earth, and each of the other planets, was ruled by a Marquis or Marquessa. The solar system and its Environs were under the authority of its Lord Protector, the Duke Marmion. The Divine Empress ruled over the whole of the Earth Empire, in which thousands of suns never set, and which stretched across half the galaxy. Few on Earth knew that the Empress was Centcomp - the computer network that ran the solar system - setting judicial sentences, running navigational and library databases, co-ordinating virtually every aspect of life.[644]

Roslyn Sarah Forrester was born in 1935.[645] The Doctor and Jamie arrived at an automatic communications center on Mendeb Two's equator. The two of them pocketed the main communications relay device as a reminder that they should re-visit the area, but this altered history. Without the device, Mendeb Two's disparate settlements were unable to pool their resources and skills, and thus failed to match technological developments on Mendeb Three.[646]

Roz Forrester joined the Adjudicator service, against the wishes of her aristocratic family, in 2950.[647]

c 2950 - INDEPENDENCE DAY[648] **->** The Mendeb colonies regressed to a feudal, agricultural society without the advanced technology from the corporations. On Mendeb Three, the tiny region of Gonfallon declared itself

---

Forrester's native time, and we meet them there in *Original Sin* - a story that ties in quite closely with *The Mutants* (Solos is even mentioned on p318). Roz returns and dies in her native time in *So Vile a Sin*.

We first learn of the decline of the Earth Empire and the Overcities in *The Mutants,* although in that story the Solos native Ky calls them "sky cities" and claims they were built because "the air is too poisonous", not because of the wars.

641 *Original Sin* (p160-161).

642 Nerva Beacon has a "thirty year assignment" according to Stevenson in *Revenge of the Cybermen*, so it ought to be decommissioned around 2915. We see the Beacon again in *The Ark in Space*.

643 *The Mutants*

644 *Original Sin*

645 According to a discussion document about Roz and Cwej prepared by Andy Lane for the New Adventures authors. She is in her early forties when she joins the Doctor (*Original Sin*). *The Also People* adds that Roz's clan name is "Inyathi," which means buffalo.

646 "Some" Mendeb years before *Independence Day*.

647 *Original Sin* (p127). Her graduation was "twenty three years" before meeting the Doctor, according to *So Vile a Sin* (p293), she'd had "thirty years as an enforcer" in *Zamper*, "twenty five years" in *The Also People* (p46), and "over twenty years" in *Just War*. Her graduation in 2955 was mentioned in *GodEngine* (p175).

648 Dating *Independence Day* (PDA #36) - It's "four hundred years" after the Galactic Wars (p22), which

a duchy, and came to dominate the planet within a generation.

Military commander Kedin Ashar - the Duke of Jerrissar - helped King Vethran rise to power. Vethran enslaved Mendeb Two, using the drug SS10 to brainwash the populace into submission, but became increasingly tyrannical. Ashar launched a revolt against Vethran, and the seventh Doctor and Ace, hoping to atone for the Doctor's previous error in hindering Mendeb Two's development, helped Ashar achieve victory. Ashar formally ended the slave trade and ordered reparations be made to Mendeb Two.

c 2950 - MASTER[649] **->** The seventh Doctor brokered a deal with Death, having come to recognise the entity's hold over the Master. Their agreement was that the Master would remain outside of Death's purview for ten years, and live his days as a contented man. At the end of that time, the Doctor was required to kill his old friend.

The physically scarred Master consequently turned up in the colony of Perfugium with no memory of his past. He came to be known as "John Smith," settled into a happy life and became a physician. Smith inherited, from a former patient named Wolstonecroft, a house that was purportedly cursed.

In Perfugium, a serial killer slaughtered eleven prostitutes and an ordinary teenage girl. Green was the colour of death in the colony, and the bodies were found wrapped in green blankets.

On the tenth anniversary of John Smith's arrival, his friends - the Adjudicator Victor Schaeffer and his wife Jacqueline - gathered at Smith's house to celebrate his "birthday." Their festivities were interrupted by the Doctor, who begrudgingly admitted that Smith's previous identity was the Master. Victor was exposed as the serial killer and further murdered his wife - who was secretly in love with Smith - and Death appeared onhand.

The Doctor and Death amended their deal so Smith could choose whether he wanted to become evil again. Death presented Smith with the option of either killing Victor before he slew Jacqueline, an act that would retroactively save Smith's beloved but make him Death's agent again, or refraining from action and thus saving his benevolent personality. Death expelled the Doctor from Perfugium before he could learn of Smith's decision.

Christopher Rodamonte Cwej was born on 5th September, 2954, in Spaceport Nine Overcity.[650] In 2957, Roz Forrester was squired to Fenn Martle. She would be his partner for fifteen years, and he would save her life on five occasions.[651]

The Black Dalek and the Renegade Dalek Faction may have used the Time Controller to hide from Davros a trillion miles from Earth in the mid-2960s.[652]

? 2965 - THE SPACE MUSEUM[653] **->** The TARDIS jumped a time track and the first Doctor, Ian, Barbara and Vicki found their future selves on exhibit in the Space Museum of the Morok Empire, located on Xeros. The Moroks had executed the adult population of the planet and set the children to work as slaves. The temporal anomaly ended, and the travellers came under risk of the future they'd glimpsed. Vicki incited revolution among some Xeron rebels, and the time travellers made their escape once the Moroks were overpowered.

The Morok Empire collapsed thanks to human intervention, with criminal gangs like the Morok Nostra filling the power vacuum.[654] The Daleks exterminated the inhabitants of Santhorius.[655]

? 2966 - THE EVIL OF THE DALEKS[656-657] **->** The Dalek Emperor made plans to capitalise on the difference between the Daleks and humanity. The Daleks were unable to make this distinction on their own, and so

would place it in the mid-thirtieth century.

649 Dating *Master* (BF #49) - Perfugium is a colony, part of a human empire, ruled by an Empress where Adjudicators enforce the law; so the story is set during the Earth Empire period.

650 According to Andy Lane's Discussion Document about Roz and Cwej, and confirmed in *Head Games* (p205). The month and day is given in *The Room with No Doors* (p20).

651 *Original Sin* (p32, p219).

652 This takes the Doctor's remark to the Black Dalek in *Remembrance of the Daleks* that the Daleks are "a thousand years" from home literally, although it's fairly clear the statement is rhetorical.

653 *Dating The Space Museum* (2.7) - There's no date given in the story itself. However, it must fall some-

where before the collapse of the Morok Empire in Roz's time (mentioned in *The Death of Art*), and after the Moroks capture a "banded" Dalek (ie: one with the "bands" seen in *The Daleks* and *The Dalek Invasion of Earth*, not the "slatted" ones seen in all subsequent appearances). This date is arbitrary.

654 *The Death of Art*

655 Within living memory of "Children of the Revolution," but presumably before *The Evil of the Daleks*.

656 Dating *The Evil of the Daleks* (4.9) - There is no date given for the Skaro sequences in the scripts. *About Time* and *Timelink* note that Maxtible says he and Victoria have undertaken a "journey through space" to get from Victorian England to Skaro, possibly indicating that the Skaro sequences are set in 1866. However, Waterfield

657 THE DALEK EMPERORS: Over the course of the series, we see four different designs for the Dalek Emperor. We can be confident that this isn't always the same individual, and can probably conclude that there are at least three bearers of the title.

• "The Golden Emperor" - The *TV Century 21* comic strip introduced a gold Emperor with an oversized, spherical head, and he also appeared in the Dalek books of the sixties - he was the central character of the strip and we learn a great deal about him. While never referred to in a story by the title, fans have called this Emperor "the Golden Emperor".

The character was introduced to a new audience by early *Doctor Who Weekly* reprints, and *DWM* used the same design in two original comic strips: "Nemesis of the Daleks" (set in the twenty-sixth century) and "Emperor of the Daleks" (set after *Revelation of the Daleks*). It's unclear if this is meant to be the same individual, and the Emperor is apparently killed at the end of both stories.

• "The Evil Emperor" - In *The Evil of the Daleks,* the Dalek Emperor is a vast, immobile Dalek based in a chamber in Dalek City. This design reappears on the cover of *The Mutant Phase* (although the story is set in an alternative timeline). Some commentators (Lofficier and *About Time* included) have speculated that this is Davros, although dialogue in *The Evil of the Daleks* seems to rule that out by stating it's the first time either the Doctor or the Emperor has met the other. This Emperor is apparently killed at the end of the story, although he's not quite dead the last time we see him.

• "Emperor Davros" - In *Remembrance of the Daleks,* Davros is Emperor and has a casing based on that of the Golden Emperor - although it is cream and gold, with a hexagonal patch instead of an eyestalk, and has no sucker or gun. The audio *Terror Firma* has Davros undergoing a full mutation (physical and mental) to become a Dalek Emperor .

• "The Last Emperor" - *The Parting of the Ways* introduces a new Emperor: a vast and apparently immobile structure containing a vast Dalek mutant. This is clearly not Davros, and he's killed at the end of the story.

There are *at least* two Emperors, then - a Dalek mutant and Davros. If we accept at face value the death of the Emperor in *The Evil of the Daleks*, we can make that three individuals.

There's a question of whether the "Golden Emperor" and the "Evil Emperor" are the same individual, one who ruled from the dawn of the Daleks until Davros usurped him. It's not a question we can answer with the information we have, however.

Perhaps there's a hint in *The Dalek Outer Space Book* (which is outside the purview of this book, but was written before *The Evil of the Daleks* was commissioned) which contains the strip "Secret of the Emperor". This sees the Golden Emperor's casing damaged and the Daleks building a new, vast and immobile casing for him. The new casing doesn't resemble the one in *The Evil of the Daleks*, but could be a step in the evolution towards it. It's also perfectly possible that the Golden Emperor casing is kept for occasions when the Emperor wants or needs to be mobile.

In *The Evil of the Daleks*, the Doctor meets the Emperor for the first time and the implication is that it's the first time the Emperor has met the Doctor, too. The only story to contradict that is "Nemesis of the Daleks", which is set in the twenty-sixth century (there's no date given for the Skaro sequence of *The Evil of the Daleks*, but no fan chronology has ever put it before this time) and has the Emperor meeting the seventh Doctor and using a mind probe to visualize all six of his previous incarnations.

All told, it seems reasonable to assume that:

One "Golden Emperor" rules the Daleks from their emergence (in the *TV21* comic strip) until "Nemesis of the Daleks", where he is killed by Abslom Daak - a blow that proves decisive in the Dalek Wars with humanity.

The "Evil Emperor" succeeds him. We see in *The Evil of the Daleks* that, following defeats inflicted on the Daleks by humans, their Emperor is immobile on Skaro, and rules over Daleks with incredible science but a weak military. There is a possibility that this is the same individual as the Golden Emperor, having survived the destruction of the War Wheel (perhaps he was badly-injured and needed so much extra life support he was rendered immobile, or perhaps he's decided leaving Dalek City is too risky). This Emperor is killed at the end of *The Evil of the Daleks...* but once again, you can never completely rule out his survival.

There follows a period where humanity loses sight of the Daleks for a thousand years. When they re-emerge in the fifth millennium, there's a new Emperor or possibly a line of Emperors - the Emperor resembles the Evil Emperor in the Big Finish stories (eg: *The Mutant Phase* and subsequent *Dalek Empire* audios) and the Golden Emperor in the *DWM* strip "Emperor of the Daleks", so these might be two individuals (and there could be other Emperors before and between).

Davros becomes Emperor (seen in "Emperor of the Daleks") when the previous holder of the office, in a Golden Emperor casing, is exterminated.

Far into the future, there's a new Emperor, a Dalek mutant in a new immobile casing, but based on the flagship of their space fleet. The "Last Emperor" is a Dalek mutant, and the design emphasises the production team's deliberate decision to rule out the possibility that he is Davros. What happens to Davros after *Terror Firma* is unknown - perhaps he is discarded once he's completed the upgrading of the Dalek race and

continued on page 315...

the Emperor hatched an elaborate trap in three time-zones for their old enemy, the second Doctor. The Daleks tricked the Doctor into believing that they wished to become more human. He was all too willing to educate the Daleks about the "Human Factor", highlighting the difference between the two races: humans were not blindly obedient and showed mercy to their enemies. However, as the Emperor planned, this merely enabled the distillation of the "Dalek Factor". The Emperor planned to instill this into all humans throughout the history of Earth, forcing them to become Daleks, but the Doctor managed to "humanise" a number of Daleks.

Civil war broke out between the "Human" and "Dalek" factions. Every Dalek had been recalled to Skaro in preparation for the conquest of humanity, and in the ensuing battle they were all wiped out. The Emperor was exterminated by his own kind. The Doctor named this the "final end" of the Daleks, but even as he said it, it was clear there were survivors.

& c 2970 - "Bringer of Darkness"[658] -> The second Doctor, Jamie and Victoria encountered a group of Daleks who taunted them with the news that the humanised Daleks had all been exterminated.

However, one saucer of humanised Daleks did survive, and travelled to the planet Kyrol.[659] **From the year 3000 to the year 3500, Earth knew of no Dalek activity in the galaxy.**[660] **During the 2970s, anti-magnetic cohesion was developed.**[661] The Landsknecthe - Earth's official security force - fought the Aspenal Campaign in 2970. The Doctor, Chris and Roz helped the Jithra repel the Jeopards, but the Earth Empire conquered both Jithra and Jeopardy. The Jithra were wiped out, but a few hundred thousand Jeopards survived. Meanwhile, Roz's sister, Leabie Forrester, began plotting to usurp the Empress.[662]

The Earth's oceans were heavily polluted in the thirtieth century.[663] By now, humanity and the Silurians were working together.[664] The Doctor hired two Silurian musicians, Jacquilian and Sanki, to play at Benny's wedding.[665]

---

calls the device used to get to Skaro a "time machine" and the story is based around the idea that humans have always beaten the Daleks in the long run - something that's not yet the case in the nineteenth century. The Doctor murmurs that this is "the final end" of the Daleks, and most fans have taken this statement at face value when they come to date the story. However, a line cut from the camera script of *Day of the Daleks* stated that the Daleks survived the civil war and that the human-ized Daleks were defeated. At the end of this story, as the Doctor makes his declaration, the picture cuts to a seemingly dead Dalek twitching into life.

The Doctor knows his way into and around the Dalek City here. The only previous time we've seen him on Skaro was in *The Daleks*, and the City is destroyed here - clearly indicating that *The Daleks* is set before *The Evil of the Daleks*. In *Mission to the Unknown*, Cory states that the Daleks have not been active in the galaxy "for a thousand years", although later it transpires that they did in fact begin conquering territory five hundred years before, so *The Evil of the Daleks* is apparently not set between 3000 and 4000. As the Doctor sees the Daleks active in the year 4000, logically he wouldn't think this was "the final end" of the Daleks unless he thought it was set after that date.

Taking what we're told at face value, this story has to be set before the destruction of Skaro in *Remembrance of the Daleks*. If Skaro wasn't really destroyed, as *War of the Daleks* states - and the TVM and the new TV series imply - that needn't be a problem. However, *Destiny of the Daleks* seems to be set in the ruins of the Dalek City (built over the Kaled Bunker seen in *Genesis of the Daleks*). Again, the Doctor knows his way around. *The Evil of the Daleks* would seem to be set before *Destiny of the Daleks* (and so, therefore, the rest of the Davros Era,

including *Remembrance of the Daleks*).

The Terrestrial Index set *The Evil of the Daleks* "a century or so" after *The Daleks' Master Plan*. John Peel and Terry Nation "agreed that *The Evil of the Daleks* was the final story" (*The Frame* #7), but did so before *Remembrance of the Daleks* was written. Peel's novelisation of *The Evil of the Daleks* is set around the year 5000. "A History of the Daleks" in *DWM* #77 claimed that *The Evil of the Daleks* is set around "7500 AD". *TImelink* suggests "4066". *About Time* equivocates, but says it's after *The Daleks' Master Plan*.

In *Matrix* #45, Mark Jones suggested that the Hand of Omega is sent into Davros' future, thousands of years after Dalek History ends.

I suggest that the civil war in *The Evil of the Daleks* is not the "final end" of the Daleks, but it does represent a severe defeat, one that removes them from the Milky Way for five hundred years (as referred to in *Mission to the Unknown*). The Doctor might be referring to the "final end" of the Dalek City, the Daleks' presence on Skaro, or the reign of the Dalek Emperor. Or he may just be optimistic (he also thinks he's finally wiped out the Daleks in *The Daleks, Remembrance of the Daleks, Dalek* and *The Parting of the Ways*, after all).

658 Dating "Bringer of Darkness" (*DWM Summer Special 1993*) - It's shortly after *The Evil of the Daleks*.
659 "Children of the Revolution"
660 *The Daleks' Master Plan*
661 *Carnival of Monsters*, "a thousand years" after Jo's time.
662 *So Vile a Sin* (p10, p182).
663 *The Also People* (p101).
664 *Eternity Weeps*
665 *Happy Endings*
666 Dating *Original Sin* (NA #39) - The Doctor tells us

...continued from page 313

technology he had begun in *Remembrance of the Daleks*.

There's a fair amount of evidence the Emperor is not the ultimate, unchallengeable authority of the Daleks, in any case (or casing). In *The Dalek Outer Space Book* story "Secret of the Emperor" it's stated that senior Daleks convene periodically to elect their Emperor... or rather to re-elect him, as it's always a unanimous vote and the only ever dissenter, seen in that story, is instantly exterminated for daring to question the Emperor's authority.

In the *TV Century 21* strip, the "Golden Emperor" follows the advice of the Dalek Brain Machine, a central computer, and *Destiny of the Daleks* and *Remembrance of the Daleks* also show a computer dictating strategy.

War of the Daleks and *Terror Firma* have Daleks actively manipulating events and misleading Emperor Davros for their own ends. While Davros thinks he's asserting his own dominance, the stories both suggest that the Dalek leadership have planned the events we see to unite the Daleks and harness his genius, while keeping all manner of key information from him. Russell Davies' *Doctor Who Annual* essay refers to "puppet Emperors" of the Daleks. *Doomsday* introduces the Cult of Skaro, four Daleks "above even the Emperor" (although clearly still acknowledging his authority and concerned about his fate).

Other stories state that the Daleks are ruled by a committee, not an individual (and this was the preference of Terry Nation, the Daleks' real-life creator).

In the Daleks' first story (*The Daleks*), Dalek City is ruled by "the council". In *Planet of the Daleks*, we meet the Dalek Supreme - a larger Dalek than normal, black with gold bumps, with a redesigned eyestalk and other features. However, it's clear that this very senior Dalek is just one member of the Supreme Council (the Daleks on Spiridon also report to "Supreme Command").

The *TV21* strip introduced a Black Dalek - in the strip, there's one Black Dalek and he's the Emperor's second in command. By *The Evil of the Daleks*, there is a group of Black Daleks serving the Emperor (they only have black domes and modified eyestalks).

In other stories Black Daleks are senior commanders - in *The Dalek Invasion of Earth*, Dalek Earth Force is led by a Black Dalek, "the Supreme Controller", who takes his orders from a Supreme Command which is off-world (presumably on Skaro, although this is never stated). A Black Dalek is "the Dalek Supreme" in *The Chase* (and is based on Skaro). A Black Dalek is "the Supreme" in *Mission to the Unknown / The Daleks' Master Plan*, and again reports to Skaro. The Renegade Faction in *Remembrance of the Daleks* is led by a Black Dalek, and the leader of the Cult of Skaro, Sec, had an all-black casing in *Doomsday* and *Daleks in Manhattan*.

In other stories "the Supreme Dalek" seems to be the leader of the Daleks, with no mention of a Council, and

so is practically the Emperor in all but name. The (unseen) Supreme Dalek rules Dalek Central Control (from the Dalek space fleet) in *Destiny of the Daleks*, and Davros is keen to usurp the role. There's a Black Dalek referred to as "Supreme Dalek" in *Resurrection of the Daleks* who seems to be the highest authority of the weakened Daleks. In *Revelation of the Daleks,* the (unseen) Supreme Dalek rules Skaro. Perhaps the implication from these television stories is that once the Emperor is dead, no Dalek leader quite dares give himself the title - although Davros has no such qualms (and we do see Emperors in other media).

There are other Dalek ranks: *Day of the Daleks* and *Frontier in Space* both have Daleks led by a Dalek in a gold case (we never learn their title). In *Destiny of the Daleks*, the leader of the squad sent to recover Davros has black central slats. We never learn these Daleks' ranks. In other stories (*The Power of the Daleks*, *Death to the Daleks*, *Planet of the Daleks*) we see groups of Daleks able to function perfectly well without a clearly designated leader. The *TV21* comic strip showed the Red Dalek in charge of space construction efforts.

War of the Daleks states that the Dalek hierarchy - at least at that point in their history - runs: Grey Daleks, Blue Daleks, Red Daleks, Black Daleks, Gold Daleks, with the Dalek Prime as absolute authority. The Dalek Prime is described as "slightly larger than the others, with a bulbous head. It was a burnished gold colour, and had about a dozen lights about the expanded dome instead of the average Dalek's two" - in other words, it strongly resembles the Golden Emperor.

The Doctor claims in *The Evil of the Daleks* that the Daleks blindly obey their leaders, and this unity is their defining characteristic - so much so, that in *Remembrance of the Daleks* and *Dalek* (and its "predecessor", the audio *Jubilee*) lone Daleks commit suicide because they've lost their entire purpose. We've seen Daleks ruthlessly eradicate individuals who dare to express even modest dissent on a number of occasions. However, the Daleks have a moral code that allows them to question orders if they seem un-Dalek-like and no compunction about replacing their leaders if they fail. It's perhaps no coincidence that this happens most visibly with two leaders who aren't pure Daleks - Davros and Sec (in *Evolution of the Daleks*). Cunningly, the Daleks have their cake and eat it: they are led by strong, imaginative, ambitious individuals who can think in ways the Daleks themselves can not... but they have a very strong (overriding, in fact) sense of what it is to be a Dalek. So if their leaders stray too far away from the Dalek ideal, the Daleks can quickly reach a consensus to exterminate him, without fear of disrupting the Dalek order based on blind obedience to their leaders, by simply deciding that their leader doesn't count as a Dalek.

Ultimately, then, the true leader of the Daleks is not an individual, it's the belief in their own supremacy and their hatred for anything that isn't a Dalek.

2975 - ORIGINAL SIN[666] **->** In the early 2970s, mankind fought a short but brutal war with the Hith, a sluglike race. The Empire annexed Hithis and terra-formed it. The Hith were displaced, becoming servants and menial workers on hundreds of worlds. They adopted names to denote their displaced status, such as Powerless Friendless and Homeless Forsaken Betrayed and Alone.

The last Wars of Acquisition ended shortly afterward, when Sense-Sphere finally capitulated. The Earth Empire now stretched across half the galaxy.

Soon after the Hith pacification, Roz Forrester saw a man kill a Ditz. When he denied it, she ate his ident and arrested him for perjury and not having valid ID. The incident entered Adjudicator folklore. A year later, Forrester killed her partner Fenn Martle when she discovered he had betrayed the Adjudication Service and was on the payroll of Tobias Vaughn. She attended Martle's funeral, and shortly afterward the Birastrop Doc Dantalion wiped her memories of Martle's death, replacing them with false memories that the Falardi had killed him.

Christopher Cwej graduated from the Academy in 2974. During his training on Ponten IV he had achieved some of the highest marksmanship and piloting scores ever recorded. Cwej's first assignment was a traffic detail. A year later, he was squired to Roslyn Forrester.

The very same day, serious riots started throughout the Empire, particularly on Earth itself. Insurance claims were estimated at five hundred trillion Imperial schillings, a total that would bankrupt the First Galactic Bank. Worst of all, it was revealed that the Adjudication Service was rife with corruption. The riots had been sparked by the release of icaron particles from a Hith battleship, the *Skel'-Ske*, which had been captured by INITEC corporation and kept in hyperspace in Overcity Five.

When the source of the radiation was destroyed, it was clear that the Empire was collapsing. At the time of the rioting on Earth, the Rim World Alliance had applied to leave the Empire. Over the years, all the major corpora-

tions had moved from Earth to the outer Rim planets. An Imperial Landsknecht flotilla was sent to pacify them. Rioting also began on Allis Five, Heaven, Murtaugh, and Riggs Alpha. Colony worlds took the opportunity to rebel, stretching the resources of the Landsknecht to their limit.

The seventh Doctor again encountered the now-robotic Tobias Vaughn, leading to a conflict in which Vaughn was decapitated. The Doctor used Vaughn's brain crystal to repair the Cwej family's food irradiator.

The corrupt head of the Adjudicators, Rashid, feared exposure. She decried Roz Forrester and Chris Cwej as rogue Adjudicators, and placed a death sentence on their heads. Roz and Chris departed with the Doctor and Bernice.

At this time, Armstrong Transolar Aerospace were building Starhopper craft on Empire City, Tycho and Luna.[667] The Empire conquered the Ogron homeworld of Orestes, one of the moons of gas giant Clytemnestra, in the Agamemnon System. When humans begin engineering pygmy Ogrons, a native uprising started that would last six years.

While searching for secret Ogron bases, the Imperial ship *Redoubtable* discovered the Nexus on the moon Iphigenia. This was a Gallifreyan device that could alter reality, and drove the expedition insane.

Roz was declared legally dead in 2976. Leabie created a clone of Roz, Thandiwe, to raise as her own daughter.[668] Humberto de Silvestre was born 31st December, 2978. Heavy pollution levels on Earth made him sickly, but his computer skills meant he received medical grants.[669]

2982 - SO VILE A SIN[670] **->** A demilitarised zone existed between the Empires of Earth and the Sontarans. The planet Tara was part of the Empire, and the importance of the nobility had been diminished.

The seventh Doctor, Roz and Chris arrived in this time zone, investigating the source of a signal that was awaken-

---

that this is the "thirtieth century" (p23). Although we are told at one point that "2955" was "four years" ago (p86), the year appears to be 2975 - this ties in with the birthdates established for Cwej and Forrester in the Discussion Document, and the fact that Cwej's father graduated "seventy years" before, in "oh-five".
667 *The Sorcerer's Apprentice* (p17).
668 *So Vile a Sin*, with Roz declared dead "six" years beforehand.
669 *Hope*
670 Dating *So Vile a Sin* (NA #56) - The date is given (p25).
671 *Terror of the Vervoids*. The implication being that these unrecorded adventures took place in the Doctor's future, between the end of his Trial and his

encounter with the Vervoids.
672 Dating *Terror of the Vervoids* (23.3) - The Doctor tells the court that this is "Earth year 2986". A monitor readout suggests it is "April 16".
673 *The Mutants*
674 *Frontier in Space*
675 *Burning Heart, The Ultimate Treasure*
676 *Genocide* (p274-275).
677 "One thousand two hundred and seventy years" before *The Genocide Machine*.
678 Dating "Children of the Revolution" (*DWM* #312-317) - Kyrol was colonised "a few centuries in the future" according to Izzy, and this is "a few short decades" after *The Evil of the Daleks* according to Alpha.
679 Dating *The Mutants* (9.4) - The Doctor tells Jo that

ing Gallifreyan N-forms. Roz discovered an N-form at the Fury colony on planet Aegistus, the Agamemnon System, but crushed it under a slab of dwarf star alloy. Meanwhile, the Doctor found that the moon Cassandra was actually an ancient TARDIS, wounded during the war with the Vampires, and that its distress signal was waking N-forms. The Doctor programmed the TARDIS to self-destruct, destroying the moon.

Back on Earth, the Doctor euthanised Empress Helen I at her request. He was arrested for regicide. The Empress' death sparked civil war and widespread rioting. The psionic Brotherhood launched a brutal attack on the Forresters' palace on Io, killing a dozen Forresters. The casualties included Roz's niece and nephew, Somezi and Mantsebo.

Abu ibn Walid, actually a pawn of the Brotherhood, was crowned Emperor. He offered Roz the office of Pontifex Saecularis, head of the Order of Adjudicators. Roz's sister Leabie Forrester, with army and Unitatus backing, instigated a rebellion against Walid's rule. Her forces attacked Mars on 26 August. The Battle of Achebe Gorge started. Roz defected to Leabie's side and was appointed the rank of Colonel.

The Doctor and Cwej were captured by the Grandmaster, a psychic gestalt that hoped to use the reality-altering Nexus. The Doctor defeated the Grandmaster's plan, and the dozens of bodies that contained parts of the Grandmaster's persona were either killed or banished to alternate timelines.

Roz lost her life leading a ground assault on the Emperor's palace on Callisto. The death of the Grandmaster left the Emperor lifeless, and Leabie Forrester was declared Empress. The Doctor suffered a heart attack at Roz's burial. A year later, the Doctor, Cwej, Benny, and Jason attended to Roz's final funeral rites.

House Forrester had recently resurrected the long-extinct African elephant.

In 2983, Kimber met Hallett while he was investigating granary shortages on Stella Stora. The Doctor visited this timezone a number of times. On one occasion before Mel joined him, he involved Captain Travers in a "web of mayhem and intrigue", although the Doctor did save Travers' ship. On other visits, the Doctor met Investigator Hallett and visited the planet Mogar.[671]

2986 (16th April) - TERROR OF THE VERVOIDS[672] -> Professor Sarah Lasky planned to breed intelligent plants, Vervoids, that would hopefully make robots obsolete. Vervoids bred and grew rapidly, plus were quick to learn and cheap to maintain. For an undisclosed reason, the Vervoids also had a poisonous spike. A consortium was ready to exploit the creatures, but as the Vervoids were being transported back to Earth in the intergalactic liner Hyperion III, they went on the

rampage and killed a number of the passengers and crew, including Lasky. The sixth Doctor's intervention resulted in every example of the species being wiped out using the mineral vionesium, which accelerated their growth cycle.

The ruling Council on Earth came to realise that Earth was "exhausted... politically, economically, biologically finished", "fighting for its survival" and was "grey and misty" with "grey cities linked by grey highways across grey deserts... slag, ash, clinker". Earth's air was so polluted that the entire population now had to live in the vast sky cities if they wanted to breathe.

By this point, Earth couldn't afford an Empire any longer. By the end of the thirtieth century, most planets in the Earth Empire had achieved some form of independence from the homeworld.[673] These were "the declining years of Earth's planetary empire".[674]

As the Earth Empire went into the process of collapse, countless planets were cut off and abandoned.[675] The Earth Empress granted Eta Centauri 6 the status of a Duchy Royal with the name of Tractis. Humans had committed genocide there during the Empire period, because the natives refused to allow the mineral exploitation of their planet or the growing of narcotic crops. The Silurian governor of the planet, Menarc, tried to establish an elected council there, but human colonists formed a separatist party and assassinated key politicians. The decaying Empire tried to restore order, leading to a conflict that killed hundreds of thousands. The Doctor commented that matters would improve for Tractis after that.[676]

The Daleks used time corridors to establish hibernation units on many planets such as Kar-Charrat. The Daleks would only activate when a time traveller entered range, and the Daleks hoped this gambit would help them gain access to the Kar-Charrat Library.[677]

c 2990 - "Children of the Revolution"[678] -> The eighth Doctor and Izzy travelled to the waterworld of Kyrol, and spent time on the submarine Argus. While swimming at the uncharted Asamda Ridge, Izzy encountered some Daleks - who went on the board the submarine and greeted the Doctor as their saviour.

The Daleks steered the Argus to Azhra Korr, home of eight thousand Daleks who were the humanised Daleks from the civil war and their descendants. Their leader was Alpha, the first humanised Dalek, and he explained that the Daleks had developed their psychokinetic abilities. When the Doctor and Alpha investigated a cavern under Azhra Korr, they discovered Kata-Phobus - the last Kyrolian and a giant octopus with psychic powers. Kata-Phobus had been planning to use the Daleks' psychic abilities to conquer the human colony.

Meanwhile, the humans rebelled and attempted to

escape their Dalek captors. The Daleks were shocked that their saviour, the Doctor, was secretly more loyal to the humans than to them. Nonetheless, they sacrificed themselves to kill Kata-Phobus save the human colony.

c 2990 - THE MUTANTS[679] **->** One of the last planets to gain independence from Earth was Solos. The native Solonians staged organised resistance, but the Marshal of the planet resisted reform for many years. From his Skybase in orbit above Solos, the Marshal had been conducting experiments on the Solonian atmosphere, attempting to render it more suitable for humans. When the Solonians began mutating into insect-like creatures, the Marshal ordered the "Mutts" destroyed.

An Independence Conference was arranged between the Solonian leaders and the "Overlords" from Earth, with Solos to be declared independent. The Administrator was assassinated at the meeting, and martial law was declared instead. The third Doctor and Jo arrived at this time and met Professor Sondergaard, a scientist who had been investigating the history of Solos for many years. Sondergaard had discovered that every five hundred years, the Solonians underwent a radioactive metamorphosis - meaning that the process that was transforming the population into Mutts and altering the atmosphere was seasonal. Earth helped Solos to discover the true form of the mutation, then left the planet alone.

2992 - THE FALL OF YQUATINE[680] **->** The eighth Doctor attended the inauguration of Stefan Vargeld, who defeated the unpopular Ignatiev to win the Presidency of Yqatine. Four years later, the Doctor returned just as sentient gas creatures named the Omnethoth, constructed millions of years ago as a weapon to conquer the universe,

awoke from dormancy and devastated the planet with searing gas bombs. The reptilian Anthaurk attempted to capitalize on this and seize Yquatine space, but the Doctor's companion Compassion engaged her Chameleon Circuit and impersonated Vargeld, helping to sue for peace. The Doctor mentally reprogrammed the Omnethoth as peaceful cloud-like beings, but a vengeful Vargeld, in retribution for Yquatine's devastation, destroyed the Omnethoth with ionization weapons.

2994 - SUPERIOR BEINGS[681] **->** The fifth Doctor and Peri were caught when the fox-like Valethske invaded a pleasure planet, Eknur 4. The invaders were looking for the homeworld of their gods. The Valethske put Peri into suspended animation aboard their ship and departed. The Doctor calculated its next arrival point, in a century's time, and left to rendezvous with Peri then.

Eknur 4 was one of the Wonders of the Universe, and a utopian society given over to hedonism.

The Fourth Millennium

Africa was in the middle of its Third Golden Age in the year 3000.[682]

At the turn of the thirty-first century, an Imperial Navy force was sent out to seek out alien technology that might help shore up the Earth Empire. They discovered the planet Darkheart and colonised it. They remained isolated for three and a half centuries, but came to discover a device that they also named the Darkheart, and which was built from Chronovore technology. The Chronovores had designed the device to beam healing energy to their remote, injured members, but the colonists adapted it to alter morphic fields. Properly tuned, the Darkheart could transform all alien species into human beings.[683]

they have been sent to "the thirtieth century". The story must take place many years after *Original Sin*, where events are set into motion that will eventually mean the Empire's collapse. *The Programme Guide* set the story slightly later ("c.3100"); *Timelink* in 2971.
680 Dating *The Fall of Yquatine* (EDA #32) - The date is given (p43, p150).
681 Dating *Superior Beings* (PDA #43) - The year is given (p108).
682 *The Art of Destruction*, and consistent with the New Adventures.
683 *The Dark Path*
684 *Hope*
685 Dating "Interstellar Overdrive" (*DWM* #375-376) - It's "3000 ADish" according to the Doctor.
686 *Placebo Effect*
687 "A thousand years" before *The Book of the Still*.
688 "A few years" before *Festival of Death*.

689 Dating *The Space Age* (EDA #34) - The year is given (p216). The people there think it is 2019.
690 Dating *Festival of Death* (PDA #35) - The year is given (p115, p116, p194).
691 *Flip-Flop*
692 *Vanderdeken's Children*
693 Dating *The Sorcerer's Apprentice* (MA #12) - The TARDIS crew discover a spaceship built in "2976" (p17), which leads the Doctor to suggest this is the "end of the thirtieth century" (p33, p48). We learn that the colony was founded in 2145 (p203), 846 (Avalonian?) years ago (p33), making it the year 2991. Later, though, we learn that the "city riots" seen in *Original Sin* were "fifty years ago" (p156), so it must be nearer 3025.
694 "The Love Invasion"
695 Dating *Flip-Flop* - The dates are given.
696 "Eighteen years" before *The Ribos Operation*.
697 Dating *The Ultimate Treasure* (PDA #3) - Rovan

In 2999, a Sun City teenager hacked Earth's TacNet, causing a meltdown that killed thousands on the East Coast of Australia. Humberto de Silvestre was wounded by this, and only saved when he was grafted with experimental liquid computers. He became the cyborg Silver. In 3006, aliens invaded Earth, overrunning America and taking control of Washington. The government used experimental time machines to send agents to fetch help - Agent Grey was sent to the past, Agent Silver to the far future.[684]

c 3000 - "Interstellar Overdrive"[685] **->** The tenth Doctor and Rose landed on a Magellan Class Star Cruiser that was causing weird time dilations, and met the long-lived rock band Pakafroon Wabster. They were en route to Malphapalooza to save their careers, but their reckless flying had created timeloops, and they were now literally stuck in a groove. After the band rejected the Doctor's suggestion that they could become posthumous legends by sacrificing themselves, the Doctor got the band to lifepods and destroyed their ship.

From around the year 3000, the Foamasi began gaining in power and reputation across the galaxy.[686]

Legends of *The Book of the Still* begin circulating around this time. Unknown parties had developed this artefact as a means by which stranded time travellers could summon help by writing their name in it. Copies of *The Book of the Still*, made from invulnerable taffeta, found their way to various points in time and space, including the planet Lebenswelt in the year 4009.[687]

Documentary maker Harken Batt was discredited when he used actors in an expose of organised crime.[688]

3012 - THE SPACE AGE[689] **->** The eighth Doctor, Fitz and Compassion arrived on an asteroid that contained a reconstruction of a futuristic city. The inhabitants - rival members of the Mods and Rockers gangs - had been spirited there from 1965 by a benevolent alien named the Maker. However, the gangs had fallen into continued bloodshed for nineteen years. The Maker, imprisoned by the Mods and compelled to make weapons, had instigated the city's dissolution. Other Makers arrived, liberated their colleague and caused the Mods and Rockers to stand down. The Makers offered the humans a choice: return to 1965 as their younger selves with no memories of these events, or join a futuristic society in 3012. The humans made their decisions, and the Doctor's party departed.

3012 - FESTIVAL OF DEATH[690] **->** Against objections from the major religions, Dr Koel Paddox - the galaxy's leading necrologist - opened the Necroport. This housed a machine in which tourists could be temporarily killed and experience the "Beautiful Death", which was touted as the "thrill to end a lifetime". It was located at the G-Lock ship's graveyard in the Teredekethon-Murgatroyd hyperspatial conduit, and swiftly attracted visitors such as the alien Hoopy.

The fourth Doctor and Romana arrived to find that tourists experiencing the Beautiful Death were becoming savage zombies. The Repulsion had temporally swapped the tourists with survivors of the *Cerberus* disaster in 2815. The tourists went into the Repulsions' realm, and the *Cerberus* survivors were endowed with pieces of the Repulsion's essence - the Repulsion hoped this would let it fully manifest in our reality. The Doctor and Romana trapped the Repulsion's essence in ERIC, the G-Lock's central computer, then destroyed it. The Necroport exploded and the zombies expired.

The G-Lock was evacuated and the hyperspace tunnel in which it was located collapsed, eradicating the station. The Arboretan race went extinct as a result of Paddox's experiments. Paddox attempted to reincarnate into his younger self and prevent his parents' deaths, but this trapped him in a recurring loop of his lifetime in which he could only observe, not act.

The Proxima Centauri All Blacks did the double in 3012. Pratifoon Wabster had their first number one in the same year. The Doctor visited the colony of Puxatawnee, and deemed it a very happy and prosperous place.[691] The planets Emindar and Nimos started a series of minor wars that would run for over a century.[692]

c 3025 - THE SORCERER'S APPRENTICE[693] **->** Although many remained patriotic and a new Empress was crowned, it was clear that the Empire was collapsing. The Landsknechte Corps had fallen, and the newly-independent human worlds were now building vessels of their own. On the medieval world of Avalon, some natives were becoming more proficient at tapping the ancient nanobot system to generate "magic". The first Doctor, Ian, Barbara and Susan arrived on the planet as various "sorcerers" sought to gain further power. A magical battle ensued, but the Doctor had his allies place an Avalonian control device - "Merlin's Helm" - on the head of a reptilian cephlie, a native of the planet. The Helm restored the cephlies, but they elected to destroy themselves and the nanobot system. This ended "magic use" on the planet.

In 3045, humanity and the Kustollons fought a war which devastated both sides. Igrix, a Kustollon, stole a time machine and traveled to 1966 to prevent this.[694]

3060 to 3090 - FLIP-FLOP[695] **->** The planet Puxatawnee had two timelines.

= 1) The Slithergees arrived around Christmas, 3060, and demanded a moon to inhabit. President

Mary Bailey was apparently killed by her secretary, who was allegedly a Slithergee agent. In truth, she was assassinated by beings from another timeline, who feared she would cave in to the Slithergees. There was an uprising, and warfare against the Slithergees left Puxatawnee a heavily damaged, radioactive wasteland. Christmas Day was renamed Retribution Day. Thirty years later, Professor Capra built a time machine to change history by sending agents back to kill the President's secretary. The time machine overloaded, destroying the planet.

= 2) President Bailey survived thanks to the time travellers' intervention, and yielded to the Slithergee demands. Thirty years later, the aliens had dominated the planet, and any resistance was seen as "hate crime". In this timeline, Capra built a mind peeler to interrogate people, not a time machine. Rebels forced the seventh Doctor to take them back in time, hoping to assassinate Bailey before she capitulated to the Slithergees.

The Cyrrehenic Alliance fought a series of Frontier Wars. The Graff Vynda-K led two legions of his men for a year in the Freytus Labyrinth, and in addition fought on Skarne and Crestus Minor. He was an unstable, temperamental man, though, and upon returning home he discovered that his people had allowed his half-brother to take the throne. The High Court of the Cyrrhenic Empire rejected the Graff's claim for restitution, and he spent eighteen years plotting his revenge.[696]

c 3064 - THE ULTIMATE TREASURE[697] -> The fifth Doctor and Peri arrived at the Astroville Seven trading post. A dying merchant provided them with galactic co-ordinates purporting to pinpoint the treasure of Rovan Cartovall, the emperor of Centros who once ruled fifty star systems. His treasury was worth the equivalent of 64,000,000,000,000 stellar credits. The co-ordinates led to the planet Gelsandor, where some telepaths set a variety of challenges for any who wanted Cartovall's treasure. The Doctor and Peri found themselves in competition against a number of criminals, and the treasure was revealed to be the infinite possibilities of life, as represented by the puzzles themselves.

c 3068 - PALACE OF THE RED SUN[698] -> The warlord Glavis Judd had risen to power on his homeworld of Zalcrossar, and expanded his military might to create a Protectorate of twenty star systems. His forces sought to subjugate the planet Esselven, but King Hathold and his family sealed the Keys to Esselven, an irreplaceable set of documents and protocols, in an impenetrable vault that would only open for their DNA. Without the Keys, Esselven society would degenerate.

The royals fled and established the Summer and Winter Palace residences on "Esselven Minor," a planetoid orbiting a white dwarf star. However, the white dwarf's gravity, in conjunction with the planetoid's mass and the royals' planetary defence shield, started altering space-time in the area. Time within the shield accelerated faster than time in the outside universe.

Judd spent a year tracking the royals and landed on the planetoid in search of them. Due to the fast-time effect, he wasn't seen again for five hundred years. Judd never appointed a successor, and his Protectorate collapsed in his absence.

? 3078 - THE RIBOS OPERATION[699] -> The rare mineral Jethrik was now used to power ships such as Pontenese-built battleships. Communication across the galaxy was via hypercable, and highly trained mercenaries, the Schlangi, were available for hire.

Located three light centuries from the Magellanic Clouds, the Cyrrhenic Alliance included the planets Cyrrhenis Minima (co-ordinates 4180), Leviathia and Stapros, as well as the protectorate of Ribos (co-ordinates 4940) in the Constellation of Skythra, 116 parsecs from Cyrrhenis Minima.

The fourth Doctor, Romana and K9 arrived on Ribos

Cartovall disappeared in 1936 BC, which was "five thousand years ago" (p37).
698 Dating *Palace of the Red Sun* (PDA #51) - The journalist Dexel Dynes appeared in *The Ultimate Treasure* and remembers Peri from that story, which he describes as a "few years" ago (p39).
699 Dating *The Ribos Operation* (16.1) - A date for the story is not given on screen. While my date is arbitrary, Ribos is close to the Magellanic Clouds, suggesting that humans have developed at least some level of intergalactic travel. Lofficier placed the story in "the late 26th century", apparently confusing the Cyrrhenic

Alliance with the force established to fight the Cybermen in *Earthshock*. *Timelink* says 3010.
700 *Managra*
701 Dating *Superior Beings* (PDA #43) - It's "over five hundred years" after 2594 (p108).
702 *The English Way of Death*
703 Decades before *I.D.*
704 Dating *Warmonger* (PDA #53) - The story is a prequel to *The Brain of Morbius*, set when Solon was a young, renowned surgeon.
705 *Legacy*, expanding on *The Curse of Peladon* and *The Monster of Peladon*. *Warmonger* sees a huge

looking for the First Segment of the Key to Time. They meet Garron, a con-man from Hackney Wick, who was forced to leave Earth after his attempt to sell Sydney Opera House to the Arabs backfired. Garron's exploits included a successful scheme to sell the planet Mirabilis Minor to three different, unsuspecting clients.

Aware of the Graff Vynda-K's thirst for revenge and need for a powerbase, Garron proposed to sell him the planet Ribos for the sum of ten million Opeks. Garron boosted the Graff's interest by forging a survey suggesting that the planet was rich in Jethrik. Garron's lump of genuine Jethrik, used to con the Graff, was the first segment of the Key.

The Doctor defeated the Graff, leading to the Graff's demise, and outsmarted Garron to obtain the first segment.

In the late thirty-first century, people from the Overcities began to recolonise the surface of the Earth. One group, later known as the Concocters, created Europa: a bizarre and eclectic fusion of historical periods built on the site of Europe. There were three Switzias, four Rhines, six Danubes and dozens of black forests. Each Dominion represented a different period between the fourteenth and early twentieth history. So, for example, there were five Britannias - Gloriana, Regency, Victoriana, Edwardiana and Perfidia.

The undead - the descendants of the vampires Jake and Madeline - dwelt in Transylvania. Fictional and historical characters, named Reprises, were cloned. This enabled the people from the Overcities to jostle with the likes of Byron, Casanova, Crowley, Emily Bronte and the Four Musketeers.

The Vatican, a vast floating city equipped with psychotronic technology, was built to impose order on Europa (as the true papal seat had moved to Betelgeuse by this time).

The entire Concoction was masterminded by the Persona, a being formed from the merging of the Jacobean dramatist Pearson and the ancient Mimic.[700]

c 3094 - SUPERIOR BEINGS[701] **->** The fifth Doctor arrived on a garden planet, anticipating the arrival of the Valethske with Peri as their captive. Mindless giant beetles - the remaining physical forms of the Khorlthochloi - dominated the planet. The Doctor rescued Peri and the Valethske discovered the beetles were the last remains of their former gods. The Valethske ship bombarded the planet from orbit, wiping out the Khorlthochoi. Veek, the Valethske leader, realised the futility of his mission and departed for home with his crew.

The Bureau, a group from the thirty-second century,

used time corridor technology to send retired people to the English village of Nutchurch in the 1930s.[702]

The thirty-second century was an era that produced organic digital transfer, a means of directly moving information between machines and the human brain. Scandroids were robotic servitors that assisted humans and facilitated such information transfers, and most people were fitted with data transfer ports. Companies such as the Lonway Clinic specialised in altering people's personalities according to their wishes, and anyone who could afford such services "had some work done". One planet became a dumping ground for computer equipment - it was intended as part of a recycling programme, but fell through the cracks on an official basis, and became a scavenging ground for data pirates.

At this time, Zachary Kindell was deemed a pioneer of personality surgery, but his unethical experiments tarnished his reputation. Kindell sought to craft a programme capable of "auto-surgery" - one that would reshape a person's DNA to match their mental alterations - but his experiments brought his test subjects' aggression and hate to the surface, turning them into mutants. Kindell felt hampered by the threat of prosecution, and although he eventually died, he scattered copies of his memories and personality in various locales.[703]

? 3100 - WARMONGER[704] **->** The planet Karn had gained a reputation as a place of healing, presumably due to the presence of the Sisterhood's Elixir of Life, and a medical association constructed a neutral facility there named the Hospice. The scientist Mehendri Solon served as the facility's Surgeon-General. The fifth Doctor suddenly arrived one day with a severely wounded Peri, who had been injured by a flying predator, to procure Solon's surgical skills.

Solon adeptly healed the Doctor's companion. However, the deposed Gallifreyan President Morbius pooled mercenaries and space pirates from many worlds to assault Karn, hoping to gain the Sisterhood's Elixir. The Sisterhood repelled Morbius' attack, but his forces conquered many planets. The Time Lords covertly manipulated events to form an Alliance, led by "the Supremo," to counter Morbius' ambitions. The Alliance defeated most of Morbius' forces, and he suffered a final defeat on Karn when troops from Fangoria interceded.

Morbius was sentenced to execution, but Solon, his disciple, removed Morbius' brain before his body was atomized. The Hospice was disbanded and Karn was left to the Sisterhood. Solon remained on Karn with Morbius' brain.

The seeds of the Galactic Federation were sown during the first third of the thirty-second century, as the Space Powers of the Milky Way began forging links and alliances. Over the course of the first half of the millennium, the various Alliances began to forge links with one another and alien races. These groups drifted closer and closer together until the Galactic Federation was formed. Virtually the entire civilised galaxy was involved to some degree or another.[705]

? 3120 - THE BRAIN OF MORBIUS[706] **->** Karn was a graveyard of spaceships, with Mutt, Dravidian and Birastrop vessels all coming to grief. Solon built a hybrid creature from the victims of these crashes and installed Morbius' brain into it, but the Time Lords sent the fourth Doctor to prevent Morbius from escaping. A mindbending contest with the Doctor drove Morbius mad, and the Sisterhood killed his physical form.

In the thirty-second century, Earth made contact with the descendants of Utnapishtim's people.[707]

3123 - VANDERDEKEN'S CHILDREN[708] **->** The eighth Doctor and Sam arrived at a derelict structure floating in space - the product of a closed time loop - which was claimed by the warring Emindians and Nimosians. A hyperspace tunnel led to twenty years in the future, when the two planets had wiped each other out. The Doctor was unable to prevent the war, but he managed to save one of

the ships and send it a thousand years into the future, where it recolonised Emindar.

c 3150 - I.D.[709] **->** The planet that served as a dumping ground for computer equipment was believed to hold four billion data storage devices, with another 60,000 being discarded there on a daily basis. An estimated eighty percent of the equipment was useless, but that still left a massive amount for data pirates to harvest. Agents of the Lonway Clinic also scavenged the planet, looking for back-up copies of people's brains that were carelessly thrown out along with their computers. Such information could become raw material for the Clinic's personality surgeries.

A Scandroid happened upon a copy of Zachary Kindell's personality and memories, and other Scandroids found a copy of his faulty auto-surgery programme. Per their standing orders, the Scandroids diligently tried to download the programme to anyone present, but the data contained a booby trap that terminated the autonomic systems of anyone it came into contact with. The sixth Doctor arrived as Kindell's mind was uploaded into a Lonway Clinic accountant, Ms Tevez. One of the Lonway employees, Dr Marriott, became infected with the auto-surgery programme and mutated into an abomination - as did Kindell-Tevez. The Doctor revised Kindell's auto-surgery programme, and uploaded Tevez's brain-print into both

---

Alliance between many alien races, and talk of a "United Planets Organisation" being formed.

706 Dating *The Brain of Morbius* (13.5) - The Doctor informs Sarah Jane that they are "considerably after" her time. If the Mutt at the beginning of the story originated on Solos, that might affect story dating. *The TARDIS Logs* suggested "3047", *Apocrypha* gave a date of "6246 AD". *The Terrestrial Index* supposed that the "Morbius Crisis" takes place around "10,000 AD". The original version of this chronology set the story around the time of *Mindwarp. Timelink* says "2973", and *Warmonger* - the prequel to the story - seems roughly to concur.

707 *Timewyrm: Genesys* (p217).

708 Dating *Vanderdeken's Children* (EDA #14) - The year is given (p3). The Galactic Federation exists, although neither Emindar nor Nimos are members.

709 Dating *I.D.* (BF #94) - It's the "32nd Century" according to the back cover blurb and the Doctor, who makes his dating solely on the presence of organic digital transfer - suggesting that the technology fell into disuse in centuries to come.

710 *Burning Heart.* This happened when Mora Valdez, who is twenty-one (p15), was "five years old".

711 Dating *The Beautiful People* (BF *The Companion Chronicles* #4) - The back cover specifies that the story takes place in the "32nd century", but the date is other-

wise arbitrary. Mention of the Mandrells and the CET machine suggests that this audio takes place between *Nightmare of Eden* and *The Horns of Nimon.* Morestrans appeared in *Planet of Evil.* A Tythonian was the titular *Creature from the Pit.*

712 Dating *Burning Heart* (MA #30) - The year is given (p20).

713 *Lucifer Rising.* An excommunicated Knight of Oberon, Orcini, appears in *Revelation of the Daleks.* The suggestion that the order was based on the moon of Uranus was first postulated in the Virgin edition of this book, and confirmed in *GodEngine.*

714 "Thirty generations" before *Bang-Bang-A-Boom!.*

715 *Spiral Scratch*

716 Dating *Managra* (MA #14) - The Doctor sets the co-ordinates for "Shalonar - AD 3278", and the TARDIS lands in the same timezone, but the wrong location (p26). Later Byron states that he was created "in the middle of the thirty-third century" (p113).

717 Dating *Real Time* (BF BBCi #1) - It is "millennia" since the creation of the Cybermen, and the Cybermen are thought to be extinct. The story is set after *Sword of Orion.* The online notes name the planet as Chronos, but the name isn't used in the story.

creatures, physically and mentally turning them into copies of her. One of the women died, but Tevez was restored as a person in the second - yet remained unsure if she had physically been Marriott. Before departing, the Doctor neutralized the Scandroids and deleted all copies of Kindell's programme that he could find.

Liquid hardware was available in this era.

In 3158, the Rensec IX catastrophe took place when the planet's inhabited underground caverns were destroyed due to seismic activity caused by Puerto Lumina, the planetary satellite. The survivors were shipped, en masse, to the decommissioned, dormant staging-post facilities of Puerto Lumina. A combination of faulty life support and a ham-fisted attempt to chemically sterilise the survivors there left a hundred thousand civilians dead.[710]

c 3170 - THE BEAUTIFUL PEOPLE[711] **->** The Vita Novus Health Spa catered to clients who earned "half a planet" - including humans, Morestrans, Sheltanaks, Lamuellans and Sirians - and achieved some astounding results in turning out-of-shape beings into finely toned specimens. The fourth Doctor, Romana and K9 arrived at Vita Novus in search of doughnuts, and found that the proprietor - Karna - had developed a revolutionary tissue reduction process. Subjects were placed in "slimming booths" and their body mass broken down, only to be reborn in revitalized forms. The excised fat was reconstituted into beauty products.

The travellers found that Karna was brainwashing her clients, and sought to leverage her contacts in the major galactic governments to set up slimming centres on every planet. Entire populations would be processed, and those who refused would be killed.

The spa's computers were damaged, and Karna was slimmed to death. Her "burn-droids" put a client - Sebella Bing - in charge, and she reorganised the spa as a relaxation centre with fatty food, ice cream and champagne. The Doctor got a bag of sugary doughnuts.

Tythonians were known in this era.

3174 - BURNING HEART[712] **->** The population of Earth was rebuilding following the destruction of the Overcities. Across the galaxy, trade, culture and civil liberties suffered as humanity retrenched. On Dramos, a satellite of the gas giant Titania, the Church of Adjudication was becoming ever more draconian. Millions reacted by joining the extremist Human First group, which advocated the genocide of all aliens. White Fire served as the inner core of this group.

The sixth Doctor and Peri arrived on Dramos at this time, and conflict broke out between the Adjudicators and White Fire's forces. The Node of Titania, an area similar to Jupiter's Red Spot, was alive and had been increasing hos-

tilities in its attempts to communicate. The sentience of the Node was allowed to merge with OBERON, the Adjudicators' central computer. The conflict and xenophobia diminished, and the Adjudicators recruited more non-humans into their ranks.

The Sontarans and Cybermen had both recently tried to introduce more individuality into their species. The Sontaran attempt created disunity, and some of their ranks were banished.

As Earth went through its Empire and Federation phases, the fortunes of the Guild of Adjudicators waxed and waned. Eventually, they became unnecessary. A thousand forms of local justice had sprung up. Every planet had its own laws and police. The universe had passed the Guild by, leaving it nothing to adjudicate. The Guild degenerated into a reclusive order of assassins known as the Knights of the Grand Order of Oberon, dreaming of past glories and crusades for truth. The organisation was based on the moon of Uranus.[713]

Gholos attacked the pastoral planet Angvia, beginning a conflict that would last thirty generations. Both sides violated the Tenebros IV peace treaty in the name of their cause.[714]

The sixth Doctor visited the planet C'h'zzz in 3263.[715]

3278 - MANAGRA[716] **->** For centuries, the Nicodemus Principle had prevented a Reprise from becoming the Pope of Europa. But in 3278, Cardinal Richelieu, a Reprise, assassinated Pope Lucian and attempted to succeed him. He faced opposition from the Dominoes, a secret organisation stretching across the Dominions. Behind the scenes, the Persona attempted to seize control of Europa. Persona was destroyed along with Europa's Globe Theatre, but Richelieu succeeded in becoming Pope Designate.

3286 - REAL TIME[717] **->** Three survey teams went missing on the desert planet Chronos, and the sixth Doctor and Evelyn accompanied a follow-up group there to investigate. They discovered that an absent alien race had equipped a temple of sorts with a time machine. The time traveller Goddard, hailing from 1951, warned the Doctor that events in this era would precipitate the Cybermen conquering Earth in the twentieth century. The Cybermen of the future captured a techno-virus that Goddard carried, and reverse-engineered it into a virus capable of turning living beings into cybernetic ones. The CyberController of the future infected Evelyn with this virus. The Doctor triggered a temporal wave that aged the Cybermen of the future to death, whereupon he and Evelyn departed, unsuspectingly, for 1927.

The Doctor rescued the Rembrandt painting *The Night Watch* from the Reichmuseum in Amsterdam shortly before the facility burned down.[718]

c 3340 - THE DALEK FACTOR[719] **->** Thal Search-Destroy squads continued to hunt down the Daleks, but it had been two generations since any significant contact had been made. On an unnamed planet, the Daleks worked to implant the Dalek Factor (or "Dalek-heart") into all other lifeforms. The Dalek-hearted life on their test planet considered itself superior to the original Daleks, forcing them to quarantine the planet.

The Daleks successfully imprisoned the Doctor on this planet.

The Galactic Federation

Around the turn of the thirty-fifth century, nearly three hundred years after the first steps towards confederation, the Headquarters of the Galactic Federation on Io were officially opened and **the Federation (or Galactic) Charter was signed. Founding members included Earth, Alpha Centauri,** Draconia, New **Mars and Arcturus.** At this point in history, Earth was regarded as **"remote and unattractive". It was ruled by an aristocracy, "in a democratic sort of way". The Federation prevented armed conflicts, and even the Martians renounced violence (except in self-defence). Under the terms of the Galactic Articles of Peace (paragraph 59, subsection 2), the Federation couldn't override local laws or interfere in local affairs (except in exceptional circumstances), and was hampered by a need for unanimity between members when taking action.[720]

c 3400 - THE DARK PATH[721] **->** The Adjudicators had become the Arbiters, the judicial service of the Federation. The Federation Chair was located on Alpha Centauri. The Federation included the Veltrochni, Terileptils, Draconians and Xarax.

The Federation ship *Piri Reis* reached the lost colony of Darkheart just as temporal distortion attracted both the second Doctor's TARDIS and that of the renegade Time Lord Koschei and his companion Ailla. The Doctor and Koschei found the Darkheart device, which the colonists were using to make alien beings human.

Koschei accidentally killed Ailla and became stricken with grief. He became increasingly intent on hoarding power, and eradicated the planet Terileptus as a necessary means of testing the Darkheart's destructive power. Ailla regenerated, and Koschei became even more isolated upon realizing that she had spied on him for the High Council of the Time Lords. The Doctor stopped Koschei's thirst for power by programming the Darkheart to turn the system's star into a black hole. The colonists evacuated aboard the *Piri Reis*, but Koschei went missing when the black hole consumed his TARDIS.

> = These events happened in the Inferno universe, but in a different form that allowed Koschei and Ailla to continue their travels.[722]

---

718 *Dust Breeding,* "in the thirty-third century".

719 Dating *The Dalek Factor* (TEL #15) - In *Planet of the Daleks*, the Thal space missions against their arch-enemies seem relatively recent. Here, there have been search and destroy missions against the Daleks for "eight centuries" (p17). The lull in Dalek activity ties in with the one noted in *The Daleks' Master Plan*. If the Daleks truly were wiped out in *The Parting of the Ways*, then this "unspecified" Doctor would seem to be either the eighth after *The Gallifrey Chronicles* or the ninth before *Rose*.

720 *The Curse of Peladon* and its two sequels - *The Monster of Peladon* and the New Adventure *Legacy* - are set at the time of a Galactic Federation. The date of its foundation is given in *Legacy* (p164); the words are those of Alpha Centauri and the Doctor from *The Curse of Peladon*. The justice machines named the Megara also follow "The Galactic Charter" in *The Stones of Blood*, and they are from 2000 BC. Many other stories refer to "Intergalactic Law", "Intergalactic Distress Signals" and so on - there are clearly certain established standards and conventions that apply across the galaxy, although who sets and enforces them is unclear.

721 Dating *The Dark Path* (MA #32) - There is no exact date, but the Galactic Federation exists (p3) and it is over "three hundred and fifty years" after the turn of the thirty-first century (p175) which was "nearly half a millennium ago" (p178), which all suggests it's set in the thirty-fifth century. Terileptus is the homeworld of the Terileptils, as seen in *The Visitation*.

722 *The Face of the Enemy*

723 Dating *The Menagerie* (MA #10) - It is "centuries" (p67) after Project Mecrim was initiated in 2416. The Doctor suggests that it happened "a millennium or three" (p126) and "hundreds, perhaps thousands of years ago" (p102).

724 "Fifty years" before "The Company of Thieves".

725 Dating *Terminus* (20.4) - Once again, an arbitrary date. The date from the Virgin edition of this chronology was adopted by *Asylum*, which is set in 3488, "six years" later. *The Terrestrial Index* saw Terminus Inc. as one of the "various corporations" fought by the Doctor in the late "25th century". The FASA Role-playing game gave the date as "4637 AD". *Timelink* doesn't assume that the characters are human and sets it in 1983.

726 Dating *Asylum* (PDA #42) - The year is given. It is "six years" since *Terminus*.

727 Dating *Circular Time*: "Winter" (BF #91) - Nyssa implies that it's been "a few years" since her stay at Terminus and the Corporation Wars - it's actually been

? 3417 - THE MENAGERIE[723] -> Over the centuries, the Knights of Kuabris had prevented scientific discovery on their planet, and discouraged historical research. They came to be led by Zaitabor, who was unaware that he was an android. Zaitabor hoped to purge his city of corruption and revived some Mecrim, who initiated a slaughter. The second Doctor arranged to detonate the city's reactor, which killed Zaitabor and the Mecrim. The Knights fell from power, and negotiations between the planet's various races were arranged.

On Trionikus, the brilliant scientist Tobal Reist built a weapon called the Eraser. He attempted to destroy a spittoon on his workbench, but underestimated the device's power and blasted Trionikus into eighteen billion bits. He was the only survivor, and went mad as a result of his actions.[724]

? 3482 - TERMINUS[725] -> Passenger liners travelled the universe and sometimes fell victim to raiders, often those combat-trained by Colonel Periera.

Lazars' Disease swept the universe, spreading fear and superstition even among those in the rich sectors. Sufferers were sent secretly to Terminus, a vast structure in the exact centre of the known universe. The station was run by Terminus Incorporated, who extracted massive profits from the operation. The facility was manned by slave workers, the Vanir, who were kept loyal by their need for the drug Hydromel. The Lazars were either killed or cured by a massive burst of radiation from Terminus' engines.

Nyssa of Traken and the Garm, one of the original crew of Terminus, planned to reform the station by introducing proper diagnoses and controlled treatment. Nyssa proposed creating an improved version of Hydromel that would break the Vanir's dependency on the company.

3488 - ASYLUM[726] -> Nyssa developed a vaccine for Lazar's Disease and travelled the galaxy until it was eradicated. Full of optimism, she discovered there were many other pandemic problems such as war, famine and disease. She worked to relieve suffering, including periods spent as a nurse on Brallis and airlifting food into Exanos.

When Exanos was destroyed in a nuclear war, Nyssa established herself in a peaceful system and became a university teacher specializing in technography, the study of writings about science. As part of this, she studied the works of Roger Bacon. The fourth Doctor met Nyssa while tracking an anomaly in space-time, and discovered discrepancies in her recollection of Bacon. This was evidence of alien interference with the timeline. When the Doctor departed for the thirteenth century, Nyssa stowed aboard. After restoring history to its true course, the Doctor brought Nyssa home.

c 3490 - CIRCULAR TIME: "Winter"[727] -> Nyssa married a dream specialist named Lasarti, and they birthed a baby daughter named Neeka. Upon experiencing a recurring dream of her time with the Doctor, Nyssa decided to investigate using a device that Lasarti had developed to consciously explore dreams. Lasarti insisted on following her, and the two of them mentally arrived inside the dreamscape of the fifth Doctor - who was dying on Androzani Minor. With their help, the Doctor overcame a mind-trap set by the Master, and initiated his regeneration.

The Adventures of Kroton

? 3500 - "Ship of Fools"[728] -> Kroton, the Cyberman with a soul, was picked up and revived by the passengers of a human spaceliner. He learned the ship had been renamed the *Flying Dutchman II*, as it was caught in a time warp. Kroton opened up the cockpit and reprogrammed the robot pilot to escape the rift. But once outside, the lost time caught up with the passengers - they aged by six hundred and twenty eight years in an instant, and Kroton was left alone once more.

The Technosmiths of Baroq VII upgraded Kroton's armour to thank him for helping them.[729]

---

more like eight or nine if one takes *Asylum* into account, but it's otherwise not difficult to do so.
728 Dating "Ship of Fools" (*DWW* #23-24) - The story is set after "Throwback", but no date beyond that is given. The story is set around six hundred and fifty eight years after human space liners stopped using human pilots, but this isn't very helpful - it's possible human pilots were reintroduced (particularly if enough ships piloted by robots like this one were lost). It does mean that it can't possibly be set before around 2800, however. This story isn't to be confused with the Dave Stone novel of the same name from Virgin's Benny range.

The closest period to this seen in a TV story is *Terminus*, which takes place at a time where ships are piloted automatically, span the galaxy and are threatened by pirates. "Unnatural Born Killers" and "The Company of Thieves" follow this story, but there's no indication how long it is between stories (and it could be many centuries, given that Kroton is effectively immortal).
729 "The Company of Thieves"

? 3500 - "Unnatural Born Killers"[730] -> Kroton surfaced on a peaceful world that was being attacked by the Sontarans. He destroyed the invasion force, but could not share in the elation of the natives.

? 3500 - "The Company of Thieves"[731] -> The Qutrusian Cargo Freighter X-703 was captured by pirates led by Grast Horstrogg, just as the eighth Doctor and Izzy arrived. Kroton the Cyberman offered resistance until the Doctor deactivated him, believing Kroton to be a normal Cyberman. They made each others' acquaintaince while the pirates headed for a new target in a nearby asteroid belt.

The TARDIS was stolen by Tobel, the mad scientist who had destroyed his planet Trionikus (and thus formed the asteroid belt) fifty years previous. The pirates tried to steal Tobel's super-weapon - the Eraser - but this merely destablised the last habitable asteroid. The Doctor, Izzy and Kroton reached the TARDIS, and Kroton joined the TARDIS crew.

The planet Lebenswelt sold its entire mineral wealth to Galactinational. Now immeasurably rich, the population dedicated themselves to decadence.[732]

The Daleks returned to Earth's galaxy. Over the next five hundred years, they gained control of more than seventy planets in the ninth galactic system and forty in the constellation of Miros. They were, once again, based on their home planet of Skaro. The Daleks were the only race known to have broken the time barrier, although Trantis had tried in the past without success. Dalek technology was the most advanced in the universe.[733]

= 3562 - THE SIRENS OF TIME[734] -> The Knights of Velyshaa fought Earth, but their First Empire fell. Thanks to the seventh Doctor, though, their leader Sancroff escaped to establish the Second Empire. Capturing a Temperon, the Knights built time machines and successfully attacked the Time Lords, although the Knights' bodies had become withered and parasitic. They used Time Lord flesh to maintain themselves.

The fifth, sixth and seventh Doctors joined forces to defeat the Knights. History was restored and Sancroff was executed.

& 3568 - PALACE OF THE RED SUN[735] -> The sixth Doctor and Peri arrived on Esselven Minor to find time running faster within the planetoid's defence screen than without. The warlord Glavis Judd landed on the planet, intent on capturing the fugitive Esselven royals. The Doctor tricked Judd into thinking that everyone on the planetoid, including the royals' real-life descendents, were holographic projections. Judd departed, but the Doctor corrected the errant defence shield and brought the planetoid back into synch with the rest of the universe. This caused Judd to emerge in normal space five hundred years after he'd departed, and after the royals had re-settled

---

730 Dating "Unnatural Born Killers" (*DWM* #277) - see dating notes on "Ship of Fools".

731 Dating "The Company of Thieves" (*DWM* #284-286) - No date is given, but it's after "Unnatural Born Killers" and all previous Kroton stories. The pirates are scared of Cybermen, perhaps suggesting this is still within the period of the Cyber Empire (see "Did the Cybermen Ever Have An Empire?"). Pedants might note that the eighth Doctor doesn't recognise Kroton even though the fourth Doctor "introduced" his original appearance in a *DWW* framing sequence.

732 "Five hundred years" before *The Book of the Still*.

733 *Mission to the Unknown*, *The Daleks' Master Plan*. The Daleks occupy Skaro at this time, and according to Marc Cory, they haven't been heard from for five hundred years before this point.

734 Dating *The Sirens of Time* (BF #1) - The date is given.

735 Dating *Palace of the Red Sun* (PDA #51) - It is five hundred years after the previous part of the story.

736 Dating "Art Attack!" (*DWM* #358) - It's "the 37th century".

737 The contest in *Bang-Bang-A-Boom!* is the 308th.

738 "Twelve generations" before *Head Games* (p15).

739 *A Device of Death*. There's a discussion of the history on p31. No date is given, but Kambril has been in charge for "eighteen years" (p90).

740 *Davros*

741 Dating *Interference* (EDA #25-26) - It's the "thirty-eighth century" (p306) and "several centuries" after *The Monster of Peladon*. The Foreman / bottle universe story occurs some time after the main events on Dust.

742 Dating *A Device of Death* (MA #31) - No date is given, but this is a time of isolated Earth colonies, and it's fifteen hundred years since Landor was colonised. The implication that the robots are the Movellans, seen in *Destiny of the Daleks*, would seem to contradict *War of the Daleks*.

743 *Only Human*

744 "Two centuries" before *Placebo Effect*.

745 *The Curse of Peladon*, with much elaboration given in *Legacy* - a book that incorporates some details from *The Curse of Peladon* novelisation.

746 *Neverland*. The Sensorian Era was mentioned but not defined in the *Doctor Who* TV Movie.

747 Dating *The Curse of Peladon* (9.2) - There is absolutely no dating evidence on screen. The story takes place at a time when Earth is "remote", has had interstellar travel for at least a generation (King Peladon

Esselven. The royals failed to recognise Judd as the genuine article and, per policy regarding people claiming to be the great warlord, threw him in an asylum.

c 3606 - "Art Attack!"[736] ->

The ninth Doctor took Rose to see the Mona Lisa at the Oriel, a transdimensional gallery on Earth. The Doctor realised the visitors were being hypnotised by their information headsets. The culprit was Cazkelf, a crashed alien trying to drain enough psychic energy to power his ship's distress beacon. When the Doctor discovered that Cazkelf's planet had been destroyed, Cazkelf decided to settle on Earth - where his hypnotism was lauded as a bold work of performance art.

The first annual Intergalactic Song Contest was held.[737] Around 3700, the planet Detrios lost its sun and the population moved underground. With each generation, the skin of the human inhabitants grew more pale. The Detrian lizard people started a war against the human Ruling Family.[738]

In the Adelphine cluster on the galactic rim, relations between the humans of the Landor Alliance and the Averon Union were strained. Within four years, this became a full-scale war.

The Landor Alliance constructed Deepcity, a weapons research station on an asteroid. The Averons attacked Landor, but they were driven back. The Landorans destroyed Averon, but suffered ninety percent casualties themselves. There was a period of civil war across the cluster. Barris Kambril took control of Deepcity, and told the workers there that Landor was destroyed to better motivate them.[739]

Galactic corporation TransAlliedInc was formed in the thirty-eighth century.[740]

c 3788 / = c 3788 - INTERFERENCE[741] ->

The planet Dust, a former Earth colony on the Dead Frontier on the edge of the galaxy, was cut off for centuries. Cattlemen there organised into vigilante gangs called Clansmen.

IM Foreman's travelling show arrived briefly on Dust, distorting space-time in the area. Faction Paradox was planning to use a biodata virus to make Dust a world of paradox. A group from the Remote crashed on Dust around this time, and founded the settlement Anathema II from the remains of their ship. Fitz had risen through the ranks of Faction Paradox and become Father Kreiner. He sought revenge against the Doctor.

IM Foreman released his final incarnation, the elemental Number Thirteen, to eliminate the Remote. Father Kreiner was lost to the Time Vortex. Foreman's first twelve incarnations were killed, displaced to early Gallifrey and underwent regeneration. Number Thirteen was convinced to merge with Dust's biosphere, whereupon Foreman became integrated with the entire planet. Dust was renamed Foreman's World.

> = The third Doctor was shot and regenerated, a paradox as he was meant to die on Metebelis III. From this point, the Doctor was infected by the Faction's biodata virus.

On Foreman's World, the now-female IM Foreman created a bottle universe, and she was surprised when its inhabitants soon built their own bottle universe. Time Lords arrived to acquire the bottle, hoping to use it as a potential refuge in the coming future War. Foreman didn't give them an immediate answer. The eighth Doctor arrived, wanting answers about his visit to Dust. He learned that Father Kreiner was trapped in the bottle universe. After the Doctor left, Foreman discovered that the bottle universe had also vanished.

? 3800 - A DEVICE OF DEATH[742] ->

The fourth Doctor, Sarah and Harry arrived at the Adelphine cluster. The Doctor lost his memory, but gradually pieced together enough to reveal Barris Kambril's lies to the workers at the Deepcity weapons research station. The synthonic robots developed here would play a part in the demise of the Daleks.

Jack Harkness had a relationship with a Gloobi hybrid on Tarsius in the thirty-ninth century.[743]

The Dark Peaks Lodge of the Foamasi was founded, devoted to restoring their home planet of Liasica to its former glory and seizing control of the Federation.[744] **For countless centuries, the people of the primitive planet Peladon had worshipped the creature Aggedor. The planet turned away from war and violence** under King Sherak, **but remained isolated.** In 3864, a Federation shuttlecraft crashed on Peladon after falling foul of an ion storm en route to the base at Analyas VII. The Pels rescued one of the survivors, Princess Ellua of Europa. **The Earthwoman married the King,** Kellian, within a year. Six months after that, she had persuaded him to apply for Federation membership. Their son was born a year later. **He was named Peladon, and was destined to become king.**[745]

This era was known to the Time Lords as the Sensorian Era.[746]

& 3885 - THE CURSE OF PELADON[747] ->

The Preliminary Assessment Team arrived at King Peladon's court to see if Peladon was suitable for Federation membership. As they landed, the spirit of Aggedor was abroad. It killed Chancellor Torbis, one of the chief advocates of Federation membership. This was revealed as a plot brewed between the High Priest of Aggedor, Hepesh, and the delegate from Arcturus. If

Peladon was kept from Federation membership, then Arcturus would be granted the mineral rights to the planet. Arcturus was killed while attempting to assassinate one of the delegates, while Aggedor himself killed Hepesh. Peladon was granted Federation membership.

The first human clone was created in 3922 using the Kilbracken holograph-cloning technique. The process was unreliable and the longest a clone ever lived was 10 minutes, 55 seconds. Most serious scientists thought of it as "a circus trick of no practical value".[748]

? 3906 - THE RESURRECTION CASKET[749] -> The tenth Doctor and Rose arrived in an area of space, the Zeg, where electromagnetic pulses made conventional technology break down. The inhabitants - keen to mine the rare minerals found there - used steam and wind-powered spaceships instead. They became involved with the quest for the treasure of Hamlek Glint, who had a robot crew.

c 3907 - THE INFINITE QUEST[750] -> The tenth Doctor and Martha arrived on the warship of the space pirate Baltazar, just as he was about to convert the Earth's population into diamonds. They destroyed the ship with a rust fungus. Baltazar's robot parrot, Caw, later contacted them and set them on a quest to find *The Infinite* - a legendary ancient spaceship that could grant their heart's desire.

Their first destination was Boukan, a planet that supplied Earth's oil. The second was Myarr, which was the scene of a conflict between humanity and the Mantasphids. The third was on the coldest planet in the galaxy, the prison planet Volag-Noc. The Doctor obtained the co-ordinates of *The Infinite*, but the promised "heart's desire" was simply an illusion, and Baltazar was exiled to Volag-Noc.

& 3935 - THE MONSTER OF PELADON[751] -> When Federation scientists surveyed Peladon, they discovered that planet was rich in trisilicate: a mineral previously only found on Mars, and which was the basis of Federation technology. Electronic circuitry, heat shields, inert microcell fibres and radionic crystals all used the mineral. Duralinium was still used as armourplating.

King Peladon died and was replaced by his daughter, the child Thalira. As she grew up, Federation mining engineers came to her world. Although Thalira's people were resistant to change, advanced technology such as the sonic lance was gradually introduced to Peladon.

The Federation was subject to a vicious and unpro-

---

is the son of an Earthwoman) and has an aristocratic government.

It's not set between 2500 and 3000, when Earth has a powerful galactic empire according to fellow Pertwee stories *The Mutants* and *Frontier in Space*. Its sequel is set fifty years afterwards, and galactic politics is in much the same position as in the previous story.

Although the Federation seems to be capable of intergalactic travel at the time of *The Monster of Peladon*, Gary Russell suggested in the New Adventure *Legacy* that Galaxy Five was a mere "terrorist organisation" (p27). *Legacy* is set "a century" after *The Curse of Peladon*.

Remarkably, given the lack of on-screen information, there has been fan consensus about the dating of this story and its sequel: *The Programme Guide* set the story in "c.3500", and made the fair assumption that the Federation succeeded the collapsed Earth Empire. *The Terrestrial Index* revised this slightly to "about 3700". *The TARDIS Logs* suggests "3716". *Timelink* suggests "3225", *About Time* "at least a thousand years in the future".

While I support that, another possibility is that this story is set very early in Earth's future history, when Earth's just starting to explore the galaxy. It has to be at least a generation after interstellar travel But other than that, the aliens here and in *The Monster of Peladon* are all near neighbours - Mars, Alpha Centauri, Arcturus

and Vega. On the evidence of the TV series alone, *The Curse of Peladon* could comfortably be set in the late twenty-second century, before the Earth Empire forms.

748 *The Invisible Enemy*. Clones are seen or referred to before this date in a number of subsequent stories such as *Heritage*, *Trading Futures*, *Project: Lazarus*, *The Also People* and *So Vile a Sin*. Professor Marius distinguishes between the Kilbracken Technique, which instantly creates a "sort of three-dimensional photocopy", and a true clone that would take "years" to produce. *Heritage* also suggests cloning keeps periodically falling into disuse, whereupon another scientist will come forward and claim to have perfected the science for the "first" time.

749 Dating *The Resurrection Casket* (NSA #9) - No date is given, although Galactic Seven spacecraft went out of service a century before the story. References to trisilicate would seem to place it around the time of the Galactic Federation (although trisilicate is also mentioned in *The Price of Paradise*, set in the twenty-fourth century). This date coincides with the space piracy prevalent in *The Infinite Quest*.

750 Dating *The Infinite Quest* (*Totally Doctor Who* animated story) - Balthazar is "scourge of the galaxy and corsair King of Triton in the fortieth century".

751 Dating *The Monster of Peladon* (11.4) - Sarah guesses that it is "fifty years" after the Doctor's first visit, and

voked attack from Galaxy Five, who refused to negotiate. The Federation armed for war, with Martian shock troops being mobilised. Peladon's trisilicate supplies would prove crucial in this struggle. The planet was still prone to superstition, however, and when the spirit of Aggedor began to walk once more, killing miners that used the advanced technology, many saw it as a sign that Peladon should leave the Federation. For a time, production in the mines halted.

The murders were the work of a breakaway faction of Martians, led by Azaxyr, who were working for Galaxy Five. When the plot was uncovered, Galaxy Five quickly sued for peace.

c 3935 - THE BLUE ANGEL[752] **->** The eighth Doctor, Fitz and Compassion arrived on the Federation ship *Nepotist*, which was en route to Peladon. The crew discovered the Valcean City of Glass had become connected to the Federation through space-time corridors. As the glass city was located within the Enclave, a pocket universe within the larger Obverse, the Federation feared this could destablise the region.

The Doctor joined the Federation mission to meet the Glass Men, and also met Daedalus, a giant jade elephant, who planned to make war with the Federation. Daedalus had opened up forty-three space-time corridors from the Enclave to planets such as Telosa, Skaro, Wertherkund and Sonturak. The *Nepotist* launched a pre-emptive strike with sonic cannons, shattering the Glass Men, but was counter-attacked by the Sahmbekarts, a race of lizards. The *Nepotist* crashed near the Valcean city, and the people of the Obverse rushed to defend their territory. The Doctor attempted to intervene, but Iris Wildthyme tricked him into leaving the area. The Doctor would never know how the situation was resolved.

c 3940 - "A Cold Day in Hell"[753] **->** Ice Lord Arryx and a small squad of Ice Warriors captured the weather control station on the pleasure planet A-Lux. They transformed A-Lux into an arctic wilderness, wiping out almost the entire population. The Martian homeworld was uninhabitable at this time, and Arryx - who opposed Martian membership

of the Federation - wanted this to become a home base.

The seventh Doctor and Frobisher arrived and reversed the weather control, killing the Ice Warriors. Frobisher stayed behind, and the Doctor was joined by a young woman - Olla - that Frobisher had met.

& 3940 - "Redemption"[754] **->** The TARDIS was caught in the null beams of a Federation ship captained by the Vachysian Skaroux. Olla confided that she used to be Skaroux's servant. The seventh Doctor was shocked to learn that her people, the Dreilyn, had no legal status in the Federation because they were heat vampires ... but this was a lie. Olla was Skaroux's consort, and had stole all his money. The Doctor handed her over for trial.

? 3950 - BANG-BANG-A-BOOM![755] **->** The 308th Intergalactic Song Contest was broadcast to over a quinquillion homes across the universe. Contestants included the Angvia of the Hearth of Celsitor (*My Love is as Limitless as a Black Hole, and I'm Pulling You Over the Event Horizon*), Architects of Algol (*Don't Push Your Tentacle Too Far*), the Breebles, the Cissadian Cephalopods, Cyrene, the Freznixx of Braal and Maaga 29 of Drahva (*Clone Love*). The jury included a Martian. Earth's "national" anthem at this time was "I Will Survive".

The matriarchal warlords of Angvia and the transcendental gestalt Gholos had been feuding for thirty generations. A peace conference between the two was supposedly being held on Achilles 4, but this was a feint for the real conference, which was taking place at the Song Contest on the Dark Space 8 station. A Gholos nationalist tried to disrupt the proceedings, but both sides sued for peace.

Earth discovered and surveyed the planet Antalin.[756] In the mid-fortieth century, a "Cyber-fad" swept the Federation. The Martian archaeologist Rhukk proved that both Telos and New Mondas had been destroyed, meaning the Cyber Race had been eradicated. The public were briefly fascinated by the Cybermen, and documentary holovid crews went to the dead worlds of Voga and Telos.[757]

Zephon became all-powerful in his own galaxy, the

---

this is later confirmed by other people, including the Doctor, Thalira and Alpha Centauri.

752 Dating *The Blue Angel* (EDA #27) - No date is given, but the ship serves the Federation and is en route to Peladon.

753 Dating "A Cold Day in Hell" (*DWM* #130-133) - According to the Doctor, "you Martians allied yourself to the Federation years ago", and this is after *The Monster of Peladon*, because Axaxyr and the events of that story are mentioned. These Martians were "born and bred on the frigid wastes of Mars", and they style A-

Lux "New Mars", so it would seem to be their original planet that's uninhabitable.

754 Dating "Redemption" (*DWM* #134) - This is Olla's native time, so the story is set shortly after "A Cold Day in Hell".

755 Dating *Bang-Bang-A-Boom!* (BF #39) - No date is given, but the story is set in the Federation period.

756 *War of the Daleks*

757 *Legacy*. We learn that the Vogans were "ultimately self-destructive" and that the Cybermen eventually settled on a "New Mondas", as they wished to do in *Silver*

Fifth, when he defeated Fisar and the Embodiment Gris, both of which had tried to depose him. The Daleks recruited Zephon to their Master Plan, and he secured the support of the rulers of two further galaxies, Celation and Beaus. The conspiracy also included Trantis, Master of the Tenth Galaxy (the largest of the Outer Galaxies), Gearon, Malpha, Sentreal and Warrien.

Around 3950, Mavic Chen became the Guardian of the Solar System, ruling over the forty billion people living on Earth, Venus, Mars, Jupiter and the Moon colonies from his complex in Central City. At this time, the prison planet Desperus was set up to house the most dangerous criminals in the Solar System.

Shortly afterward, the Daleks contacted Chen. They needed taranium, "the rarest mineral in the universe", and which was found only on Uranus. If Chen could supply the material, the Daleks would make him ruler of the entire Galaxy. He agreed, and set up a secret mining operation shortly afterward.

The population of the Solar System knew nothing of this, and many showed an almost religious devotion to Chen. His reputation was enhanced in 3975, when all the planets of the Solar System signed a non-aggression pact. For the next twenty five years, they lived in peace under the Guardianship, and the Solar System - though "only part of one galaxy" - now had a status that was "exceptional... it had influences far outside its own sphere". It was hoped that by following Chen's example, peace would spread throughout the universe.[758]

Zephon overthrew the Embodiment of Gris in 3932 and Mavic Chen was elected Guardian of the Solar System in 3950.[759] Around 3970, the Hiinds overthrew the Mufls. The Church of the Way Forward was established by Reverend Lukas, who preached that marriage between alien species was unholy.[760] In 3972, Sirius-One-Bee University Press published Albrecht's *Of Finders and Seekers - a users guide to being lost in time.*[761]

> = Circa 3979, emaciated, grotesque beings named the Unnoticed had constructed a Tent City, made from invulnerable taffeta, on the photosphere of Earth's sun and set about breeding a colony of human time sensitives there. Uncertain as to their origins, the Unnoticed used the time sensitives to keep watch for time distortion and time travellers - wary that contact with such phenomena could somehow avert their own creation. The human Carmodi Litian was born as one of the Unnoticed's senstives and served for fifteen years before being left for dead on the planet Porconine. She swore revenge against her former masters.[762]

? 3980 - "Deathworld"[763] -> An Ice Warrior mission to Yama 10 scouted for trisilicate until a Cyberman spacecraft arrived to stake a rival claim. The Ice Warriors retreated to the polar areas and set a trap for the Cybermen, destroying them with rising water. As a last act of retaliation, the Cybermen buried the Ice Warriors in ice. The Martian commander, Yinak, remained conscious and waited patiently for the spring thaw.

Carrington Corp built the leisure planet Micawber's World between Pluto and Cassius around 3984.[764]

c 3985 - LEGACY[765] -> The Federation fought a number of wars to secure its position and to protect democratic regimes. GFTV-3 covered the main news stories of this era: atrocities on the Nematodian Border, the android warriors of Orion, slavery on Rigellon and Operation Galactic

---

Nemesis. However, this second homeworld has also been destroyed by the time of *Legacy.* The Cybermen survive to appear in *The Crystal Bucephalus.*

758 In *The Daleks' Master Plan,* Mavic Chen seems to have been Guardian for a very long time. He says, when accused of stealing the taranium, "Why should I arrange that fifty years be spent secretly mining to acquire this mineral..." (implying that he has been actively involved with the plot for half a century). Then again, he is the newest member of the conspiracy, named the "most recent ally". John Peel's novelisation, loosely based on the original scripts, claims that the crime rate on Earth soared fifty or sixty years before *The Daleks' Master Plan* [3940-3950] as the population increased. Mavic Chen was elected and set up the prison colony on Desperus. This scene does not appear in the broadcast version (it is replaced by a line which William Hartnell delivers as "The Daleks will stop at anything to stop us.").

The non-aggression pact is referred to in *The Daleks' Master Plan.* This perhaps suggests that planets in the Solar System were in conflict before this time, and Chen's hope that peace will spread throughout the universe implies that much of known space is at war. A short scene in the New Adventure *Legacy* suggests that Chen did not become Guardian until much later.

759 *Neverland.* The overthrown entity is referred to as "the Embodiment Gris" in *The Daleks' Master Plan,* but as "the Embodiment *of* Gris" in *The Dying Days* and this story.

760 *Placebo Effect*

761 *The Book of the Still*

762 Carmodi was born as one of the Unnoticed's sensitives thirty years before *The Book of the Still.* At the end of that novel, she paradoxically averts the creation of the Unnoticed, making it debatable whether these events occurred in the proper history or not.

763 Dating "Deathworld" (*DWW* #15-16) - The Doctor

Storm. The Martian Star Fleet built the deep space cruiser *Bruk*, one of the largest vessels the galaxy had ever seen, and it helped enforce law throughout the galaxy.

With its trisilicate mines exhausted, Peladon faced a choice between becoming a tourist resort or leaving the Federation altogether. The question remained unaddressed while Queen Thalira ruled, but she died in a space shuttle accident. Within four years of her death, her successor King Tarrol applied to leave the Federation, suggesting that Peladon ought to try and find its own solutions to its problems. His choice had perhaps been made easier by the carnage caused when an ancient weapon, the Pakhar Diadem, was tracked to his world. The Diadem was blasted out of space by the *Bruk* and went missing.

Tarrol's decision probably saved Peladon - had the planet remained in the Federation, it would almost certainly have been targeted by the Daleks thirty years later during the Dalek War.

3985 - THEATRE OF WAR[766] **->** The colony of Heletia was founded by a group of actors wanting to stage the greatest dramas of the universe. Society on Heletia was confined to one small area of the own planet, but nonetheless became an expansionist power and fought a war with the Rippeareans. The Heletians believed that only races with a sophisticated theatre were truly civilised. Following the death of their leader, the Exec, the Heletians sued for peace.

By this point, Stanoff Osterling's play *The Good Soldiers* had been lost.

The artificial star of Tir Na Nog was due to run out of fuel around this time.[767]

3999 (July) - PLACEBO EFFECT[768] **->** The eighth Doctor and Sam attended the wedding of his former companions Stacey Townsend and Ssard on Micawber's World. Stacey and Ssard had settled in this timezone two years ago after leaving the Doctor. The Church of the Way Forward, who opposed interspecies weddings, crashed the ceremony but order was restored.

Micawber's World was hosting the Olympic Games, and scientist Miles Mason was secretly infecting athletes with Wirrn eggs disguised as performance enhancing drugs. The Wirrn hatched, and the Space Security Service was called in to contain the situation. The Doctor found the Wirrn Queen and destroyed her, although one group of Wirrn escaped to Andromeda. The Olympic Games continued.

Earth at this time had a Royal Family. King Garth had just died; Queen Bodicha was in mourning but the rest of the world was glad to see the back of him. His heir was Prince Artemis, Duke of Auckland. Some humans on Earth, but few offworlders, followed the tenants of Christianity. There were 1362 races in the Federation's database, but the Time Lords weren't one of them. The Foamasi were members of the Federation.

The Doctor, Fitz and Compassion tried to find a way into the Obverse in the Wandering Museum of the Verifiably Phantasmagoric, also known as the Museum of Things That Don't Exist.[769]

---

explains in the framing sequence that the Ice Warriors "came from Mars thousands of years ago, then spread their conquests through the galaxy". Trisilicate is a mineral that's only been found on Mars and Peladon by *The Monster of Peladon*, so this story is set after that. The two races don't recognise each other, and the Cybermen refer to the Cyberman Empire.

764 "Fifteen years" before *Placebo Effect*.

765 Dating *Legacy* (NA #25) - The dating of this book is problematic. It has to be set after "3948", when a couple of the fictional reference texts cited were written (p37). The Doctor says that it is "the thirty-ninth century" (p55) and later narrows this down to the "mid-thirty-ninth century give or take a decade" (p84) [c.3850]. The novel is set "one hundred years" after *The Curse of Peladon* (p106), at a time when "young" Mavic Chen is still a minor official and Amazonia, who first appeared at the end of *The Curse of Peladon*, is the Guardian of the Solar System (p237) [so before 3950]. It is "thirty years" before a Dalek War that might well be *The Daleks'*

Master Plan (p299) [therefore 3970] and "six hundred years" after *The Ice Warriors* (p89) [therefore 3600, favouring the dating of that story as 3000]. The book takes place a couple of months before *Theatre of War*, and as that book is definitely set in 3985, I have adopted this last date.

766 Dating *Theatre of War* (NA #26) - The book is set soon after *Legacy* in "3985" (p1), a fact confirmed by Benny's diary ("Date: 3985, or something close", p21), and the TARDIS' Time Path indicator (p81).

767 "Two thousand years" after *Cat's Cradle: Witch Mark* (p247).

768 Dating *Placebo Effect* (EDA #13) - The date is given. *Placebo Effect* states that Christianity is still practised on Earth in 3999, but Sara Kingdom - hailing from the year 4000 - hasn't heard of Christmas in *The Daleks' Master Plan*. Historically, not every version of Christianity has placed an emphasis on Christmas, though

769 *The Taking of Planet 5* (p13).

The Daleks' Master Plan

c 4000 - MISSION TO THE UNKNOWN[770] ->

"This is Marc Cory, Special Security Agent, reporting from the planet Kembel. The Daleks are planning the complete destruction of our galaxy together with powers of the Outer Galaxies. A war party is being assemb—"

In the year 4000, Chen attended an Intergalactic Conference in Andromeda. The Outer Galaxies and the Daleks held a council at the same time, sending Trantis to Andromeda to allay suspicion. The Space Security Service (SSS) and the UN Deep Space Force had been monitoring Dalek activity for five hundred years, and they were to prove vital in discovering the Daleks' scheme.

On the planet Kembel, SSS agent Marc Cory learned that the Daleks and their allies were preparing for conquest. Cory was exterminated, but not before recording a warning.

4000 - THE DALEKS' MASTER PLAN[771] -> Shortly after concluding a mineral agreement with the Fourth Galaxy, Mavic Chen left Earth for a short holiday, or so he told the news service Channel 403. In reality, his Spar 740 spaceship headed through ultraspace to Kembel, the Daleks' secret base. There, he met the delegates from the Outer Galaxies for the first time, and presented the Daleks with a full emm of taranium - enough to power their Time Destructor, a device capable of accelerating time.

Space Security Agents were sent to investigate the disappearance of Marc Cory. One of them, Bret Vyon, allied with the first Doctor and his companions. They stole the taranium and also absconded with Chen's ship. The group reached Central City on Earth, where Vyon was killed by Sara Kingdom - his sister and a fellow SSS agent - who believed him a traitor. She came to side with the Doctor against Chen.

Pursued by Chen's own security forces and other Space Security Agents, the Doctor and Steven broke into a research facility. They were transported with Sara across the galaxy, via an experimental teleportation system, to the planet Mira - the home of invisible monsters named the Visians. Mira was close to Kembel and the group returned to the Daleks' base. They fled through time and space in the TARDIS, with the Daleks in pursuit.

Chen was ready to doublecross the Daleks, and had special forces on Venus ready to occupy Kembel. Eventually the Daleks re-captured the taranium, and they exterminated their allies - including Chen - in readiness for universal domination. They had assembled the "greatest war force ever assembled", including an assault division of five thousand Daleks to invade Earth's solar system. However, the Doctor activated the Daleks' Time Destructor, which destroyed their army and transformed the surface of Kembel from lush jungle to barren desert in seconds. Sara helped the Doctor in this endeavour and was aged to death. The universe was safe once more.

Earth was under totalitarian rule. Humans were

---

770 Dating *Mission to the Unknown* (3.2) - The story is set shortly before *The Daleks' Master Plan*.

771 Dating *The Daleks' Master Plan* (3.3) - The date "4000" is established by Chen. The draft script for *Twelve Part Dalek Story* set it in "1,000,000 AD".

772 *I am a Dalek*

773 Dating *Head Games* (NA #43) - The date is given.

774 *War of the Daleks*. Not long after the death of an SSS agent called Marc, presumably Marc Cory from *Mission to the Unknown*. This throws the dating scheme of the book out, as Antalin is the planet the Daleks will disguise as Skaro to be destroyed. But that, according to Peel, will happen *before* this.

775 *Storm Harvest*

776 Dating *The Book of the Still* (EDA #56) - It's "4009" (p57).

777 "Thirty years after" *Legacy* (p299), and possibly intended as a reference to events of or following *The Daleks' Master Plan*.

778 *The Crystal Bucephalus*

779 *Prime Time*. Reg Gurney has been in space corps

for "thirty years".

780 *Emotional Chemistry*

781 Dating *42* (X3.7) - While no date is given on screen, pre-publicity for the episode said it was set in the forty-second century - this is perhaps a take-off on the title as much as anything else. Nonetheless, the Doctor's spacesuit bears the same design as the one he wore in *The Impossible Planet / The Satan Pit* - perhaps indicating that all three episodes take place in roughly the same period.

782 Dating *The Impossible Planet / The Satan Pit* (X2.8-2.9) - Casualties in this story are repeatedly said as dying on "43K2.1". If the numbers mean anything we could interpret, the "K" perhaps suggests a date in the 43,000s. But in the DVD commentary, Russell T Davies says the draft script stated it was the forty-third century, and I've gone with that date. The Doctor's assertion they are "five hundred years" from Earth would seem to mean five hundred light years *or* that it would take the humans here five hundred years to get to Earth.

The Doctor previously encountered life from before

"bred", and told not to question orders. Christmas was not celebrated or even remembered.

The expression "never turn your back on a dead Dalek" came into use among humans.[772]

4000 - HEAD GAMES[773] **->** On the sunless Detrios, an anomaly feeding off energy from the Land of Fiction had become "the Miracle", a replacement source of heat and light for the planet. The unstable anomaly threatened the entire universe, so the seventh Doctor, Roz, Chris and Bernice sought to close it with force-field generators. This nullified the Miracle, but some rebels on Detrios imposed order and the inhabitants there sought alternative methods of survival without a sun.

SSS agent Dryn Faber investigated the planet Antalin and discovered Daleks there.[774] Earth was involved in a number of wars on the frontier of Earthspace. The Daleks massacred the colonists on a mining outpost.[775]

4009 - THE BOOK OF THE STILL[776] **->** About this time, TimeCorp offered its employees the plus of completing their workday, then temporally returning to the morning for family time. Participating TimeCorp workers aged a third faster than their families every day, but got to spend more time with their loved ones.

The temporal expert Albrecht managed to retroactively wipe himself from existence, but his diaries survived in a reality pocket. His theories gave rise to the condition "Albrecht's Ennui," which affected temporally displaced people who went a few years without time travel.

The highly affluent, distant planet Lebenswelt settled into a state of hedonism and decay, as nobody would voluntarily travel so far to perform menial tasks. The IntroInductions escort service on Lebenswelt used illegal fast-acting memory acids to make kidnapped humans fall in love with their clients. Lebenswelt also became home to the Museum of Locks (*Das Museum der Verriegelungen*), which almost incidentally guarded a copy of *The Book of the Still*.

= In 4009, the Unnoticed desired to examine the *Book* because it mentioned their Tent City on the photosphere of Earth's sun. The eighth Doctor, Fitz and Anji arrived on Lebenswelt, and the Doctor discov-

ered that the Unnoticed were the product of a closed time loop. By touching the time sensitive Carmodi, the Doctor accidentally caused the time loop to unleash waves of "soft Time", which consequently mutated IntroInductions founders Darlow, Gimcrack and Svadhisthana into a twisted gestalt creature that would give rise to the Unnoticed. When the newly created gestalt made contact with the Unnoticed, it simultaneously destroyed the Unnoticed and flung the gestalt back in time to become the Unnoticed.

Shortly afterward, Carmodi departed with the *Book* and retroactively planted a bomb aboard the Unnoticed's spaceship, thus prematurely destroying them and averting the closed time loop altogether.

Around 4015, a massive Dalek War split the Federation. Upon the war's completion, the organisation was forced to re-evaluate itself.[777] Mavic Chen's descendants eventually ended democracy in the Federation. The Chen Dynasty of Federation Emperors ruled for thousands of years.[778] The Colonial Marines raided Dalek strongholds in the 4020s.[779] Kinzhal, a future general of the Icelandic Alliance, earned medals in the forty-second century.[780]

c 4142 - 42[781] **->** The tenth Doctor and Martha answered a distress call originating from the Terrachi System, located half a universe away from Earth. The engines of the spaceship *Pentallian* had failed, and it was falling into the nearest sun. Crewmember Korwin succumbed to an alien influence - becoming a being of burning light who proceeded to kill other crewmembers. The Doctor realised the star was alive, and felt violated because the ship had illegally mined it for fuel. The living particles were ejected from the scoops, which restored the sun and saved the ship.

? 4202 - THE IMPOSSIBLE PLANET / THE SATAN PIT[782] **->** Humans used the Ood - low level telepaths - as a slave race. The Ood were apparently willing to be treated as such, although the Friends of the Ood organisation campaigned for their freedom. The Neo-Classic Congregational denomination didn't have a devil as such, but acknowledged that evil resided in the actions of men.

The tenth Doctor and Rose arrived on an unnamed planet which was set in an impossible orbit around the

---

the creation of our universe in *Terminus, Millennial Rites, All-Consuming Fire, Synthespians™*, and more. Jefferson makes mention of an "Empire" - it's a bit late for Earth to have one as such, although *Army of Ghosts* suggests that a Torchwood employee might feel inclined to use such outdated terms.

In *Doctor Who Confidential*, Russell Davies noted that, given the resemblances between their two races, the Ood probably came from a planet close to that of the Sensorites. In that spirit, *Creatures and Demons* names their home planet the Ood Sphere.

black hole K37Gem5.[783] The scriptures of the Veltong named the world as Krop Tor - "the bitter pill" - and claimed the black hole was a demon that had swallowed the planet and spit it out.

Sanctuary Base 6 - manned by people from the Torchwood Archive - were monitoring the anomaly. Beneath the planet was the Beast, a creature imprisoned before our universe was created. It began to influence the Ood slaves in an attempt to engineer its release, but the Doctor prevented this. Krop Tor and the Beast's body fell into the black hole, as did the Beast's mind - which had taken root in the base's head of archaeology, Toby Zed.

= Daleks infected with wasp DNA mutated into a swarm of invulnerable, giant wasp-like creatures and devastated Earth, draining the planet of all minerals and nutrients. The colony planets were unable to help and all attempts to recolonise ended in starvation.[784]

Unique minerals on Etra Prime draw the attention of over fifty galactic powers, including the Daleks and the Time Lords. The Daleks removed the planet, along with a team of researchers and President Romana, from spacetime. A galactic war was only narrowly averted.[785]

= **c 4250 - THE MUTANT PHASE**[786] -> The wasplike "Mutant Phase" Daleks assaulted Skaro, prompting the Emperor Dalek to order the fifth Doctor and Nyssa to travel back to 2158 and prevent the Mutant Phase's creation. The Emperor Dalek self-destructed Skaro, but downloaded his consciousness into the Thal Ganatus and accompanied the TARDIS crew.

4256 - THE GENOCIDE MACHINE[787] -> The seventh Doctor and Ace visited the library of Kar-Charrat. The chief librarian, Elgin, had built a wetworks research facility that stored the sum of universal knowledge in liquid form. To accomplish this, Elgin had enslaved nearly the entire Kar-Charrat race, using their drop-sized bodies as data storage units.

Dormant Daleks on the planet revived and attacked. They gained access to the library by duplicating Ace, and all but destroyed the library in their quest for its data. The Doctor defeated them with the help of a "collector", Bev Tarrant, who was planning a heist. The library was ruined.

c 4256 - THE APOCALYPSE ELEMENT[788] -> The sixth Doctor and Evelyn landed on Archetryx as a Time Treaty was being signed. The missing planet Etra Prime suddenly re-appeared on a collision course with Archetryx. The

---

783 Commonly referenced as "K37J5", but it's "K37Gem5" in the closed captioning on the DVD - and indeed, that *is* what it sounds like Cross Flane is saying. (This is possibly the same dating system that starts inserting words like "apple" into year designations, as in *The End of the World*.)

784 "Thirty years ago" in *The Mutant Phase*.

785 "Twenty years" before *The Apocalypse Element*.

786 Dating *The Mutant Phase* (BF #15) - No date is given, but the first of the stories set in the period of the *Dalek Empire* series, *The Genocide Machine*, is set after this in 4256.

787 Dating *The Genocide Machine* (BF #7) - There's no date in the story, but in *Invasion of the Daleks* (Part One of the *Dalek Empire* series), the war between the Knights of Velyshaa and Earth (mentioned in *The Sirens of Time* as ending in 3562) was "centuries ago". Skaro exists at this time. The Big Finish website gives it a date of 4256.

788 Dating *The Apocalypse Element* (BF #11) - This is another story set around the time of the *Dalek Empire* audios.

789 Dating *Return of the Daleks* (BF subscription promo #4) - The story occurs between installments one and two of the initial *Dalek Empire* mini-series (dated in this chronology to after 4256), and details about the Dalek invasion and Kalendorf and Mendes' secret plot

are given there. The uprising that Mendes and Kalendorf spur years later in part four coincides with the Doctor releasing his contagion on Spiridon. This chronology generally doesn't incorporate the spin-off series, but for anyone who's curious… in *Dalek Empire II*, Mendes and Kalendorf initiate the "Great Catastrophe" - an event that causes every Dalek and piece of Dalek technology in the galaxy to self-destruct. Mendes dies, but Kalendorf returns to Velyshaa and is later buried there.

Return of the Daleks might initially seem to clash with "Emperor of the Daleks", in which the ice-buried Dalek force from *Planet of the Daleks* is again discovered, but it's easy enough to reconcile the accounts based upon the numbers of the Spiridon army. The Thals in *Planet of the Daleks* believe that "10,000 Daleks" are buried on Spiridon, but *Return of the Daleks* says this is faulty information, and the frozen Daleks actually number 1,100,000. "Emperor of the Daleks" has Davros labouring on Spiridon for a year, whereupon he unleashes an army of four million gold-and-white Daleks.

It would seem, then, that the third Doctor freezes the Dalek army (cited as only 10,000, but actually numbering 1,100,000) in *Planet of the Daleks*, and the seventh Doctor prevents their revival in *Return of the Daleks*. Davros later finds the remains of the Daleks on Spiridon and cobbles together his force of four million Daleks.

Daleks were hoping to wipe out the conference. Romana escaped her captors on Etra Prime. The Doctor, Romana and Evelyn went to Gallifrey as the planetary collision took place and the Daleks instigated an epic attack. The Daleks destroyed the galaxy of Seriphia with the Apocalypse Element, generating a million new worlds there. The Daleks set about reshaping Seriphia in their image.

The Dalek Empire spin-off audios are set after this point.

c 4260 - RETURN OF THE DALEKS[789] **->** By now, Daleks operating from the Seriphia Galaxy had staged a major offensive against Earth's galaxy. Planets such as Vega 6 had been overrun, and numerous populations had been enslaved. Kalendorf, a former Knight of Velyshaa, had been on a secret mission to negotiate a defence pact with Earth Alliance when the invasion occurred, but wound up captured instead. The Daleks put him to work on a mine crew, and he thereby met Susan Mendes - a fellow prisoner, and formerly a worker at the Rhinesberg Institute.

Circumstances enabled Mendes to negotiate with the Daleks for better treatment of the slaves - in return, she would instill the slaves with a sense of hope, and encourage them to work harder. The Daleks deemed this an excellent means of improving work efficiency, and sent Mendes - now known as "the Angel of Mercy" - from planet to planet to encourage the slaves. Kalendorf was allowed to travel as Mendes' associate. The two of them were generally regarded as traitors, but - thanks to Kalendorf's telepathic abilities - they secretly formulated rebellion on every world they visited. They readied numerous populations for the day Mendes would publicly declare "Death to the Daleks!", and the Daleks would be vanquished through sheer force of numbers.

The Daleks stumbled upon the frozen Dalek army on the planet Spiridon - which had been renamed Zaleria - and sought to revive it as a weapon of war. They also hoped to crack the means by which the Spiridon natives had become visible, thinking they could reverse-engineer a means of turning Daleks invisible. Much data was collected from experiments performed upon the Spiridon natives, but any attempt to turn Daleks invisible caused fatal light-sickness.

The seventh Doctor arrived at this time, fearing that the revival of the frozen Dalek army could tip history in the Daleks' favour. He encountered Kalendorf, and the two of them spurred a minor rebellion against the Daleks. Kalendorf was captured, however, and the Doctor - deeming Kalendorf's place in history as too important to risk - offered to help the Daleks develop invisibility if they let Kalendorf go. The Daleks agreed, and Mendes and Kalendorf proceeded to their next assignment.

The Doctor remained a prisoner of the Daleks for many years, but they never found the secret of invisibility. When news came forth that Mendes and Kalendorf had initiated a galaxy-wide uprising against the Daleks, the Doctor released a contagion he'd secretly developed - this wiped out his Dalek captors, and turned the Spiridon natives invisible again. The contagion nearly forced the Doctor to regenerate, but the TARDIS' dimensional stasis aided his recovery.

c 4260 - STORM HARVEST[790] **-** The inhabitants of the waterworld Coralee had developed the Krill - vicious, aquatic humanoids with razor-sharp teeth - as instruments of war. The Krill wiped out their own creators, then entered hibernation. The Dreekans later colonised the planet, despite the legends of great danger there. They offer private islands for sale to the super-rich. The Krill awakened and were defeated by the Doctor and Ace. Nonetheless, some Krill survived as eggs in a nearby asteroid field.

c 4260 - DUST BREEDING[791] **->** The Master brought the Warp Core, an energy creature contained in Edvard Munch's painting *The Scream*, to the planet Duchamp 331, a refuelling station off the main space lanes. It served as home to technicians and a small colony of artists. The Master sought to seed the Warp Core's energy into the dust on Duchamp 331, then goad it into action against its ancient enemies, the Krill. This would have put a planet-sized weapon at the Master's disposal.

The seventh Doctor and Ace defeated the Master, and the surface of Duchamp 331 was caught in an inferno that destroyed the Warp Core.

& 4261 - PRIME TIME[792] **->** The seventh Doctor and Ace investigated the activities of Channel 400 on Blinni-Gaar,

---

Continuity is preserved, although this means - as was already the case with *Remembrance of the Daleks* and "Emperor of the Daleks" - the seventh Doctor is experiencing events pertaining to Davros and Spiridon out of order within his lifetime.

790 Dating *Storm Harvest* (PDA #23) - No date is given. Reg Gurney, an engineer and spy on Coralee, spent thirty years in the Space Corps and fought in the Dalek Wars, supporting that dating. There's a reference to London not existing for five thousand years.

791 Dating *Dust Breeding* (BF #21) - It is "several centuries" in Ace's future, in Earth's colonial period and after the Dalek Wars. Bev Tarrant is also present, and for her, it is after *The Genocide Machine*.

792 Dating *Prime Time* (PDA #33) - It is a year after *Storm Harvest*.

only to become part of the station's programming. Meanwhile, the Master landed on Scrantek and made a deal with the Fleshsmiths, a race that harvested other races to continue their existence. The Master and Fleshsmiths hoped to use the Channel 400 broadcasts to transport 150 billion viewers into the Fleshsmiths' body banks as raw material. The Doctor tricked the Fleshsmiths by letting them analyse a clone of himself, which broke down and released a molecular contagion. The toxin cascaded through the Scrantek network and reduced the Fleshsmiths to ooze. Channel 400 was disgraced and taken off the air.

Prior to its demise, the network tormented Ace with images from the past of her "future" tombstone. The Doctor falsely convinced Ace that the images were faked. Without her knowledge, he went back in time and dug up her corpse for clues as to how she died.

In 4338, Turlough was the guest of Wilhelm, König of the Wine Lords of Chardon.[793] The railway network was reestablished in Europe.[794]

> = The sixth Doctor visited the planet Schyllus in 4387.[795]

The forty-fifth century was an era of technocrats and machine-driven life. One race engineered a biological-temporal link that enabled them to forge a mental connection with their machines. Some members of the species became biologically advanced enough to place themselves in metallic shells and time travel by simply willing the process. One such traveler was Celia Fortunaté, who would arrive in another time period at the Needle, a biomechanical living complex. The Needle's overseeing computer, Whitenoise, installed a chip in Celia to curb her of all violence, but this corrupted Whitenoise's systems and led to a string of murders.[796]

The forty-sixth century saw the development of Dirty Rip engines, time machines that worked by punching holes in time and which were prone to both exploding and increasing the vortex pressure on users to the point they also exploded.[797]

The Davros Era[798]

? 4500 - DESTINY OF THE DALEKS[799] **->** The Daleks encountered a new threat: the Movellans, a race of humanoid androids from system 4X-Alpha-4. The Daleks were forced to abandon all operations elsewhere in the galaxy, including Skaro, and mobilise a huge battlefleet. The mighty Dalek and Movellan fleets faced each other in space, their battlecomputers calculating the moment of optimum advantage. This created an instant stalemate, and not a shot was fired for centuries. The vast Dalek Fleet was kept completely occupied, except for the occasional raiding mission on Outer Planets such as Kantria for slave workers, or on the starships of Earth's Deep Space Fleet.

The Daleks realised that their dependence on logic made it impossible for them to win a war against another logical machine race. Their battlecomputers suggested that they should turn to their creator, Davros, for help. The Supreme Dalek dispatched a force to Skaro to recover Davros from the ruins of the Kaled Bunker. Mining operations started up, and the Daleks discovered their creator, who had survived in suspended animation for centuries.

A Movellan party was sent to Skaro to investigate Dalek operations. As they arrived, the Daleks' slaves broke free, helped by the Doctor and Romana. Before a Dalek ship could arrive from Supreme Command, the slaves had overpowered the Movellans and defeated the small Dalek force. Davros was captured by the human force, who returned to Earth in the Movellan ship.

Before this time, Arcturus won the Galactic Olympic games, with Betelgeuse coming a close second. The economy of Algol was subject to irreversible inflation.

The Movellans were built by the Daleks, and the entire war was faked as part of their plan to prevent the destruction of Skaro.[800] Human authorities put Davros on trial. Humanity had abandoned the death penalty, so Davros was placed in suspended animation aboard a prison station in deep space. While Davros slept, humanity discovered a cure for Becks Syndrome.

---

793 *The Crystal Bucephalus* (p42).
794 "Centuries" before *Emotional Chemistry*.
795 *Spiral Scratch*
796 *Red*. "The Needle" in this story is not the same one as the Needle in *The Infinity Doctors*. The time-travel process destribed here is similar to the early Gallifreyan experiments (as detailed in *Cat's Cradle: Time's Crucible*).
797 *Only Human*
798 See "The Davros Era" sidebar.

799 Dating *Destiny of the Daleks* (17.1) - The Daleks and Movellans have been locked in stalemate for "centuries". At this point, the Daleks are feared, highly advanced and have a vast war fleet which operates as their command base. In *Resurrection of the Daleks*, it is made clear that there is deadlock between the Movellans and the Daleks' computers, not the Daleks themselves.
800 According to *War of the Daleks*.

THE DAVROS ERA: Four consecutive Dalek TV stories (*Destiny of the Daleks, Resurrection of the Daleks, Revelation of the Daleks* and *Remembrance of the Daleks*) form a linked series in which the creator of the Daleks, Davros (first seen in *Genesis of the Daleks*), is revived. In due course, he's captured and imprisoned by Earth before re-engineering the Daleks and gradually taking control over his creations. The series ends with the ultimate destruction of the Daleks' home planet of Skaro, although the novel *War of the Daleks*, set shortly after *Remembrance of the Daleks*, significantly reinterpreted those events.

Three Big Finish audios are set in gaps between the television stories, and act as bridges between them - *Resurrection of the Daleks* is followed by *Davros, Revelation of the Daleks* is followed by *The Juggernauts* and *Remembrance of the Daleks* by *Terror Firma*. The comic strip "Emperor of the Daleks" depicts Davros becoming Emperor between *Revelation of the Daleks* and *Remembrance of the Daleks*. Here, for the sake of convenience, I refer to the events of these stories as "the Davros Era" - a term that is never used in any of the stories themselves.

It is never stated exactly when the Davros Era is set, although it is clearly far in Earth's future.

The key story here is *Remembrance of the Daleks*. Before *Remembrance*, it was widely felt that *The Evil of the Daleks* really was, as the Doctor said, "the final end" of the Daleks (even though the story ended with a single Dalek twitching into life, and the draft script *of Day of the Daleks* explained that the Daleks had survived their civil war). *Remembrance of the Daleks* changed that, by ending with the destruction of Skaro. Clearly, taking *Remembrance of the Daleks* at face value, it - and by implication the rest of the Davros Era - has to happen after *The Evil of the Daleks* (the climax of which was set on Skaro).

Even before that, the first two editions of *The Programme Guide* set *Destiny of the Daleks* "c.4500" (as did the earlier versions of this chronology and *Timelink*). Following *The Programme Guide*'s lead, the script of *Resurrection of the Daleks* referred to the year as 4590, although that's not established on screen.

There have been other attempts to place it. *The Terrestrial Index* took the Doctor's speech to the Black Dalek in *Remembrance of the Daleks* that the Daleks are "a thousand years" from home literally, and respectively set the stories in "as the 27th century began", "towards the end of the 27th century", "as the 28th century began" and "about 2960". *The TARDIS Logs* chose "8740 AD" for *Destiny of the Daleks*. Ben Aaronovitch's novelisation of *Remembrance of the Daleks* and his introduction to the *Abslom Daak - Dalek Killer* graphic album had extracts from a history book, *The Children of Davros*, that was published in "4065" - apparently well after *Remembrance of the Daleks*.

John Peel's *The Official Doctor Who & the Daleks Book* - written with Terry Nation's approval - offers a com-

plete Dalek timeline, although it stresses it's not "definitive" and could change in the light of a new story (p209), and it was written *before Remembrance of the Daleks* was broadcast. In Peel's version, *Genesis of the Daleks* comes first, followed by *The Daleks* [c.1564], there are Dalek survivors in the Kaled Bunker and after five hundred years they emerge and force the Thals to flee Skaro. The Daleks discover space travel after about a hundred years, and launch *The Dalek Invasion of Earth* [2164]. The Dalek Wars begin, after several hundred years of Dalek preparation, leading to *Frontier in Space* and *Planet of the Daleks* [2540]. The Daleks developed time travel, as seen in *The Chase*. The Daleks and Mechanoids fought the Mechon Wars, and one Dalek capsule from that conflict ends up crashing on Vulcan where it is unearthed in *The Power of the Daleks* ["several centuries" after 2010]. The Daleks went back in time to reinvade Earth (*Day of the Daleks*). The Daleks were then attacked by the Movellans (*Destiny of the Daleks*) and the two races were deadlocked for "decades".

Ninety years later followed *Resurrection of the Daleks* (by which time Earth and Draconia had defeated the Movellans). The Daleks exploited a space plague (*Death to the Daleks*). Davros had survived, but was captured by the Daleks at the end of *Revelation of the Daleks*, and he was taken to Skaro and executed. Weakened, the Daleks needed allies to conquer the galaxy, as seen in *The Dalek Master Plan* [4000]. This led to the Dalek Wars, that lasted "the next couple of centuries" after which the Emperor Dalek initiated the events *of The Evil of the Daleks* [c 4200], which ended in a civil war that wiped out the entire Dalek race, once and for all.

No firm dates for the Davros Era are given, but working backwards, this timeline would seem to place *Destiny of the Daleks* somewhere in the thirty-ninth century.

War of the Daleks, also written by Peel, attempted to reverse the destruction of Skaro in *Remembrance of the Daleks*, and - unsurprisingly - it broadly follows the timeline in Peel's earlier book. Ironically, though, it undermines the case for setting the Davros Era before 4000 - first, the SSS explore Antalin (the planet the Daleks trick the Doctor into destroying instead of Skaro) after the events of *The Daleks' Master Plan*. Secondly, for the Dalek plan to work, the Doctor has to think Skaro was destroyed in *Remembrance of the Daleks*, and he wouldn't if he knew it still existed in the year 4000. (*About Time* has suggested that while the Daleks report to Skaro in *The Daleks' Master Plan*, the Doctor doesn't *see* them doing that, so he might not realise they do.)

Some fans have speculated that the Daleks might move to "New Skaro" after *Remembrance of the Daleks*, but no evidence exists for this on screen, and on the occasions when we see Skaro it is clearly the same

continued on page 339...

Without Davros' help, the Daleks were helpless. They lost the war when the Movellans released a virus that only affected Dalek tissue. Weakened, the Daleks were forced to rely on hired mercenaries and Duplicates - conditioned clones produced by their genetic experiments, and generated from humans snatched from many timezones.[801]

Following another Dalek War with humanity, the Daleks were not active in the galaxy for a century.[802]

On Riften-5, the fifth Doctor saw archives of genetic tests on Daleks after the War of Sharpened Hearts.[803]

& 4590 - RESURRECTION OF THE DALEKS[804] **->** One Supreme Dalek came up with an audacious plan that would strengthen the Daleks' position. Davros would be released from prison, and use his scientific genius and understanding of the Daleks to find an antidote for the Movellan virus. Dalek Duplicate technology would be used to strike on twentieth-century Earth, while a second group, composed of Duplicate versions of the Doctor and his companions, would assassinate the High Council of Gallifrey. The plan totally failed.

Once Davros was released, he attempted to usurp control of the Dalek army and completely re-engineer the race. This met from resistance from those loyal to the Supreme Dalek, and the two factions began fighting. The Duplicates rebelled, destroying the prison sta-

tion. The resulting explosion destroyed the Dalek battlecruiser. Davros escaped.

The war with the Movellans didn't take place, as it was part of a Dalek trick to prevent Skaro's destruction.[805] The parents of Geoff, who was later a member of Davros' science team, died in the Kensington disaster of '97.[806]

c 4600 - DAVROS[807] **->** Arnold Baines, head of the TAI corporation (which sold everything from foodstuffs to recreational narcotics to laser cannons), tracked down Davros' body. The sixth Doctor arrived in time to see Davros revived. Baines hired both the Doctor and Davros to develop business strategies to help mankind spread to other galaxies. Davros secretly developed a computer model that could accurately predict the galactic stock market. With it, he planned to destroy capitalism and replace it with a system that placed the entire galaxy's economy on a permanent war footing. He launched a coup against Baines, but the Doctor and Baines survived his assassination attempt. Davros escaped in Baines' spacecraft with a hostage, Kim, who killed herself - allowing the Doctor to crash the ship. The Doctor suspected that Davros survived.

Collectors were looking for Dalek regalia at this time. Some historians, like Lorraine Baines, offered revisionist histories where the Daleks were seen as victims, not aggressors, and Davros was hailed as a visionary. The

---

801 *Resurrection of the Daleks*

802 Before *Davros*.

803 *Christmas on a Rational Planet*. No date is given, but Riften-5 was the home planet of Lytton according to *Attack of the Cybermen*, and this is (presumably) his home timezone. *Attack of the Cybermen* ends with the Doctor saying he misjudged Lytton, yet they didn't meet at all in *Resurrection of the Daleks* (unless you count Lytton shooting at the Doctor from a distance) and they barely meet in *Attack of the Cybermen*.

If we wanted to fix that, we could theorise that the Doctor met Lytton - from his perspective - between the two stories (it would be before *Resurrection of the Daleks* for Lytton). Lytton calls the people of 1985 "our ancestors" in *Attack of the Cybermen*, so Riften-5 is a human colony planet.

804 Dating *Resurrection of the Daleks* (21.4) - This is the sequel to *Destiny of the Daleks*. Davros says he has been imprisoned for "ninety years". According to some reports, the rehearsal script set the story in 4590, which would follow the date established in *The Programme Guide*. This date also appears in *The Encyclopaedia of the Worlds of Doctor Who*.

805 According to *War of the Daleks*.

806 *The Juggernauts*

807 Dating *Davros* (BF #48) - *Davros* is set after

Resurrection of the Daleks. It's never explicitly stated that it occurs between that story and *Revelation of the Daleks*, but the Big Finish website places it between *The Two Doctors* and *Timelash*. TAI was formed "back in the thirty-eighth century".

808 Skaro has been abandoned for "centuries" before *Destiny of the Daleks*, but the Supreme Dalek is based there in *Revelation of the Daleks*. We see a bio-mechanoid in *Remembrance of the Daleks* - presumably the Daleks haven't developed the technology when they lose the war with the Movellans. Although, according to *War of the Daleks*, the Movellan War was a ruse.

809 Dating *Revelation of the Daleks* (22.6) - This story is set an unspecified amount of time after *Resurrection of the Daleks*. It has been long enough for Davros to gain a galaxy-wide reputation and build a new army of Daleks. The galaxy is ruled by a human President and faces famine.

810 Dating *The Juggernauts* (BF #65) - This story is set an unspecified amount of time after *Revelation of the Daleks*. It's said that Davros crash-landed 716 days prior to this story, but there's no indication of the duration of time in a day on Lethe.

811 "Emperor of the Daleks"

812 Dating "... Up Above the Gods" / "Emperor of the Daleks" (*DWM* #227, 197-202) - The story is set between

Treaty of Parlagon prevented individuals from having nuclear weapons. There was famine in the galaxy, virtually every available planet of which had been colonised by humanity.

The Daleks reoccupied Skaro, and a new Supreme Dalek came to power. The Daleks developed biomechanoid computers that interfaced with human brains to provide the Daleks with raw creativity, and they began to reassert their power.[808]

? 4615 - REVELATION OF THE DALEKS[809] -> The

galaxy was now ruled by a human President and was becoming overpopulated, with famine a problem on worlds across known space. Tranquil Repose on Necros has been established for some time by now as a resting place for the dead of the galaxy - literally, as they were kept in suspended animation there until whatever killed them was cured by medical science. The "rock and roll years" of twentieth century Earth were extremely popular. The DJ's grandfather purchased some genuine records from Earth on a visit there.

Davros went into hiding on Necros and formed an alliance with Kara, a local businesswoman. Davros took control of Tranquil Repose, and secretly began to break down the corpses there into a foodstuff. This ended famine across the galaxy, and Davros gained a reputation as "the Great Healer". Kara discovered that Davros was also growing a new army of genetically re-engineered Daleks from the corpses, and planned to use them to take effective control of her company. She hired Orcini, an excommunicated member of the Grand Order of Oberon, to assassinate Davros.

Like the Daleks before him, Davros had been keeping track of the Doctor's movements. When one of the Doctor's friends, the agronomist Arthur Stengos, died, Davros prepared for the Doctor to attend the funeral. Orcini and the sixth Doctor thwarted Davros' plans, although Orcini died in the process, and the Daleks were summoned from Skaro to capture their creator. The Doctor suggested that protein from a commonplace purple flower could alleviate the famine.

? 4620 - THE JUGGERNAUTS[810] -> Davros crashed on

the planet Lethe, where mining engineers excavated a group of Mechanoids. Davros attempted to build an army of Mechanoids (re-named "the Juggernauts") that incorporated human tissue, but the grey Daleks tracked him down. The sixth Doctor and Mel sabotaged the Juggernaut production lines, and Davros' body was severely injured in the fighting. His life-support chair self-destructed, which

...continued from page 337

world - the Doctor knows his way around in *The Evil of the Daleks* and *Destiny of the Daleks*. In the Time War shown in the EDAs, the Time Lords created duplicate home planets and it's possible that the Daleks might do the same.

In two New Adventures by Andy Lane (*Lucifer Rising, Original Sin*) we discover that the Guild of Adjudicators eventually becomes the Grand Order of Oberon referred to in *Revelation of the Daleks*, yet the Adjudicators are still active in *Original Sin*, so *Revelation of the Daleks* must take place well after the thirtieth century.

The Daleks' Master Plan established that the Daleks hadn't been a force in Earth's galaxy for a thousand years (and in one of the scenes where "galaxy" seems to mean "galaxy", not "solar system"). This - and perhaps the presence of the Galactic Federation - would seem to rule out the Davros Era taking place between 3000 and 4000. (Humans from the time of *Destiny, Resurrection* and *Revelation* all know and fear the Daleks, and see them as an active threat.) The Daleks have been deadlocked for "centuries" with the Movellans before *Destiny of the Daleks* (tellingly, Peel has to reduce this to "decades" in his timeline). The preminence of the Earth Empire in the centuries before 3000 seems incompatible with the idea the Daleks are a major galactic power. I think *Destiny of the Daleks* has to be set at least "centuries" after 4000. As we know the *Dalek Empire* series is set in the first half of the millennium, the case for *The Programme Guide's* 4600 AD date, while not indisputable, is certainly persuasive.

obliterated the colony, the grey Daleks and the Juggernauts, although the colonists themselves evacuated. Earth had by now passed mandatory organ donation laws.

The sixth Doctor and Peri encountered the Daleks on Mandusus.[811]

? 4625 - "...Up Above the Gods" / "Emperor of the Daleks"[812] -> At his trial, Davros - who had replaced his

destroyed hand with a claw - started to persuade some Daleks that they could learn from him. Nonetheless, the Emperor sentenced him to execution. Before the sentence was carried out, a giant asteroid entered the Skaro system.

The sixth Doctor and Peri arrived on Skaro. While the Daleks were occupied with the asteroid (which the Doctor had sent their way), the Doctor infected the Dalek computers with a virus, then kidnapped Davros in the TARDIS. The Daleks vowed revenge.

A year later, the Daleks tricked Abslom Daak into bringing the seventh Doctor to Skaro (along with the other Star Tigers and Benny, from the mid-twenty-sixth century), Daak fought a pitched battle with the Daleks, but he and his allies were subdued. The Daleks demanded that the Doctor take them to Davros, and used a Psyche Dalek to place the others in a hypnotic trance.

A Dalek battle fleet under the command of the Black Dalek was dispatched to Spiridon, where they were met by Davros and an army of four million white-and-gold upgraded Daleks. The Psyche Dalek was destroyed, and the Doctor's friends released from hypnotic control. Routed, the Black Dalek withdrew his forces and ordered the orbiting fleet to destroy Davros - but the energy was reflected back and destroyed all but one ship, which Mercurius blew up.

Davros had won the battle, and had *not* - as he had promised the Doctor - given his upgraded Daleks a conscience. Davros' fleet set course for Skaro, planning to reactivate the Doctor's computer virus and seize control. Davros' forces landed, and he watched as the former Emperor was exterminated. However, Daak sliced through Davros with his chainsword before being forced to withdraw by the other Star Tigers. A nuclear blast devastated the Dalek city, and finally destroyed Taiyin's body.

The Doctor knew that Davros would rebuild. Davros had a new survival chair built only four days after his arrival, but a bitter civil war was underway between the Dalek factions. Davros was now Emperor of the Daleks.

The Thals had relocated from Skaro by this point, and the Daleks did not normally enter their region of space, which included Spiridon.

Abel Gantz revived the lost science of alchemy when he discovered paracelsium, a catalyst that could transmute metals.[813]

c 4635 - "Kane's Story" / "Abel's Story" / "Warrior's Story" / "Frobisher's Story"[814] -> Skeletoids invaded outposts on Vega and Sigma IV, meaning they were only weeks from the Sol System. The Skeletoids were armoured humans from the Vespin System, but their armour had gradually become so sophisticated, the humans inside had become redundant components. They swept through five systems in a year - either converting any humanoids they conquered, or wiping out races they couldn't convert (such as the Daleks and Cybermen). The Skeletoids demolished the Dalek and Cyber Empires, and were now at the gates of the Planetary Federation. The Draconians were their next targets, and the powers of the galaxy arranged a summit on Ankara III.

The sixth Doctor, Frobisher and Peri learned of the threat and headed for Xaos, the oldest planet in the galaxy - as did Abel Gantz, the Draconian Emperor's bodyguard Kaon (who the Doctor and Frobisher had met some years from now), and Kane Borg of Kaltarr. They were the champions of six worlds, and they travelled in the TARDIS to the Vespin System to take the fight to the Skeletoids. Abel sacrificed himself, destroying the Skeletoid command centre. The menace to the galaxy ended, and the Doctor and the surviving champions arrived at the galactic summit to tell the delegates they'd had a wasted trip.

? 4663 - REMEMBRANCE OF THE DALEKS[815] -> Upon returning to Skaro, Davros usurped control from the Supreme Dalek and declared himself an Emperor Dalek. With his body now wasted, Davros was reduced

Revelation of the Daleks and *Remembrance of the Daleks*, and bridges the gap between them (even if this means that the seventh Doctor is experiencing developments with Davros out of order). The Emperor resembles the one from the *TV Century 21* Dalek comic strip. This raises a question as to which Dalek Emperor this is - and not because that Emperor Dalek was apparently killed by Daak back in "Nemesis of the Daleks". We didn't *see* the Emperor killed on that occassion - we just didn't see him escape the exploding Death Wheel. Given that "Emperor of the Daleks" establishes that Daak and all the Star Tigers - who were seen to perish in "Nemesis of the Daleks" - didn't actually die, the Emperor Dalek barely makes the top five "least probable resurrections" in the story. See "The Dalek Emperors."
813 "Ten years" before "Abel's Story".
814 Dating "Kane's Story" / "Abel's Story" / "Warrior's Story" / "Frobisher's Story" (*DWM* #104-107) - Davros rules the Daleks, and the only time this is the case on television is between *Revelation of the Daleks* and *Remembrance of the Daleks*. (Taking other media into account, this is between "Emperor of the Daleks" and *Remembrance of the Daleks*.) This also fits with where

the story falls in the Doctor's timeline. "War-Game" is set a few years after this, and states the Draconians rule a third of the galaxy. The Planetary Federation is also known as the Federation of Worlds, and could well be the same - or remnants of the same - Federation from the Peladon stories (although the Draconians were part of that Federation according to *Legacy*).
815 Dating *Remembrance of the Daleks* (25.1) - This story is the sequel to *Revelation of the Daleks,* and there's no indication how long it has been since the previous story. Davros has completely revamped the Daleks, which was presumably a fairly lengthy process.
816 Dating *War of the Daleks* (EDA #5) - It's "about thirty years" after *Remembrance of the Daleks*. Davros' appearance in *Terror Firma* seemingly contradicts this story. However, *War of the Daleks* has a built-in loophole in that one of Davros' Daleks is working the controls of his dispersion chamber. The Dalek in question is ordered to purge the chamber's memory core to prevent Davros being reconstituted, so it's probable that it simply fakes the purge and restores Davros in secret.
WAS SKARO DESTROYED?: The "retcon" in *War of the Daleks* that reversed Skaro's destruction proved contro-

to little more than a disembodied head. He fashioned a new casing for himself. Most Daleks supported Davros, who genetically re-engineered the race and oversaw a complete revamp of Dalek technology. These "Imperial Daleks" were given new cream and gold livery, improved weapons, sensor plates and eyestalks. As always, some Daleks dissented: this "Renegade Dalek" faction followed the Black Dalek and fled Skaro using a Time Controller.

Both factions had discovered the existence of the Hand of Omega, a powerful Gallifreyan device capable of manipulating stars. They converged to its location on Earth in 1963. There, Davros acquired the Hand of Omega, but he was unable to control the device. On the seventh Doctor's instructions, it travelled to Skaro in Davros' native time and made its sun go supernova, obliterating the planet. Davros escaped, but his flagship was obliterated and the Dalek homeworld was seemingly destroyed forever.

& 4693 - WAR OF THE DALEKS[816] -> The Daleks had invaded Earth "several times" by this point.

The garbage ship *Quetzel* recovered both the eighth Doctor's TARDIS and Davros' escape pod. Thals raided the ship, and Delani, the Thal commander, asked Davros to reengineer his race to defeat the Daleks. Davros' reactivation alerted the Daleks, and the Doctor, Sam and Davros were taken to Skaro ... which the Doctor had thought destroyed. The Dalek Prime explained that the Daleks had learned of Skaro's destruction beforehand and plotted to prevent it.

The Daleks had previously taken the dormant Davros from Skaro, and placed him in ruins on Antalin, which were designed to look like Skaro. The planet was then bathed in radioactivity. The Daleks then faked the Movellan War using their own robot servants, fooling Davros into believing they needed his help, but Davros escaped and triggered a civil war. He took the Hand of

Omega, which destroyed *Antalin* rather than Skaro. The Daleks' real homeplanet survived.

Now, the Dalek Prime planned to draw the Daleks who supported Davros out into the open and destroy them. The Doctor made a seemingly easy escape in the Thal ship - then discovered a Dalek factory in the hold. He jettisoned it back in time, where it crashed on Vulcan.

Daleks loyal to Davros attempted to rescue him, but the Dalek Prime's forces prevailed. Davros was supposedly placed in a dispersion chamber and vapourised.

Davros randomly encountered the Doctor and his companions, the librarian Samson and his sister Gemma Griffen. A vengeful Davros overpowered the Doctor and - desiring to strip the Time Lord of everything he held dear - erased the Doctor's memories of his companions. Davros mentally conditioned Samson and Gemma to accompany him back to Earth, then embarked on a scheme to turn it into a new Dalek homeworld. Samson was allowed to live with his mother, Harriet Griffen, in Folkestone.[817]

& 4703 - TERROR FIRMA[818] -> On Earth, Davros and his Daleks encountered the eighth Doctor, Charley and C'rizz upon their return from the Divergent Universe. Davros believed that his Daleks had turned Earth into a "new Dalek homeworld" and converted eight billion humans into Daleks; however, the Daleks were actually operating to their own agenda while Davros was mutating into an Emperor Dalek. Davros hoped the Doctor would end his suffering and gave him a genocidal virus, hoping he would use it to end Davros' life. But the Doctor instead used the threat of the virus to make the Daleks abandon Earth. The Emperor Dalek persona completely erased Davros' own, and the Daleks left with their new leader.

Gemma Griffen died in the conflict. Her brother Samson regained his memories of the Doctor, but continued living on Earth.

---

versial with fans. A couple of references in later BBC Books suggested that Skaro had been destroyed, after all. *Unnatural History* stated that the Doctor tricked the Daleks into tangling their timelines so much their history collapsed; *The Infinity Doctors* that Skaro suffered more than one destruction. *Doctor Who - The Movie* (after *Remembrance of the Daleks* in the Doctor's own timeline) opened on Skaro, but it could have historically been before it was destroyed. The 2005 TV series never stated that Skaro had been destroyed in the Time War (Russell T Davies' essay in the *2006 Doctor Who Annual* does name it and says it's now "ruins", though). The *Doctor Who Visual Dictionary* states that Skaro was "devastated" in *Remembrance of the Daleks*, but "finally obliterated" in the Time War.

There are a number of get-out clauses in *War of the Daleks* itself - the events aren't seen, only reported. Internal dating seems confused, and Antalin appears after it's meant to have been destroyed. There are pieces of contradictory information elsewhere - the origins of the Movellans in the book contradict their implied beginnings in *A Device of Death*, for example.

817 Years rather than decades before *Terror Firma*. The presence of Samson and Gemma's mother suggests that this is their native time zone.

818 Dating *Terror Firma* (BF #72) - No specific date is given, but it is obviously after *Remembrance of the Daleks*, and a gap of some measure (Davros mentions "years of solitude") is required after the novel *War of the Daleks*. *Terror Firma* doesn't acknowledge *War of the*

Kaon's ship later crashed on Actinon after hitting a meteor field. The inhabitants were warlike, but no match for Kaon, who established himself as a warlord. His wife died in childbirth, but his daughter Kara grew to be a strong warrior.[819]

c 4750 - "War-Game"[820] **->** The sixth Doctor and Frobisher landed on a barbaric world, Actinon, and detected advanced technology. Investigating, they discovered that the local Warlord Kaon was a Draconian. His daughter Kara had been kidnapped by Vegar, a rival warlord. The Doctor took Kaon to Vegar's fortress in the TARDIS and they rescued Kara - at the cost of Kaon's life. Kara vowed to stay on the planet and maintain his legacy.

The metamorphic Collectors were galactic scavengers who entirely lacked the ability to discern the value or relevance of an item - essentially, they amassed junk. The Collectors' hyperwobble-drives and psychonomic shielding meant that no culture's defences could stand against them. The Daleks pretended that their planet had been destroyed to avoid being attacked by the Collectors.[821]

The Time Agents

The forty-ninth century was an era of unparalleled peace and prosperity on Earth. Advanced ubertronic devices existed. Earth developed time travel using transduction beams, but Time Agents strictly regulated the proliferation of the technology. Time travel had other uses: the film archivist Jaxa recovered all the lost films and television programmes. Thirty years before her native time, the Moon was terra-formed. Sabbath press-ganged Jaxa into his service following a failed time-jump on her part.[822]

Humans didn't explore some parts of Earth's Moon until the forty-ninth century.[823]

At some point in human history, AEGIS operated a time travel service that, though expensive, allowed people to go into the past. The Technos wrongly thought it was impossible to change the past because time travellers were part of history. One group was sent back to hunt dinosaurs in the Cretaceous.[824]

Around 4900, a Dalek expedition to the Magellan Cluster was attacked by spider-like creatures in Dalek-like armour, and it took months to subdue them. These spider-Daleks were Daleks from a parallel universe. The Daleks calculated that the only way to take the fight to the spider-Daleks was via a black hole, but knew their ships couldn't survive the journey.[825]

Under the auspices of the Great World Computer, human civilisation was more efficiently run than ever. But Earth regularly suffered massive famines. An artificial food was created on Earth that solved the problem. On the land once used to grow food, up-to-date living units were built to house the ever-increasing population. The amount of plants on the planet was reduced to an absolute minimum, and all plant life on Earth became extinct.[826]

A thousand murders took place on the worlds of the Nepotism of Vaal in the fiftieth century. The Memeovore had made the population think their loved ones are impostors. The Doctor would visit and see them establish a universal brotherhood.[827]

The Filipino Protectorate was established on Earth by 4993. Technology at the time included binoculars that could see through walls and read lips.[828] Professor Marius registered K9 as a data patent on 3rd October, 4998.[829] K9 was not Y5K compliant.[830]

Daleks, but the two are not irreconcilable. Neither Davros nor the Doctor here mention events from *War of the Daleks*, but as Davros' mental health is clearly eroding throughout this audio, it's entirely possible that the Daleks have altered his memories or that he's simply too far gone to remember. In fact, as the Daleks are obviously fooling Davros into thinking that he's in charge, it suits their plans if he forgets about Skaro and believes he's gaining revenge against the Doctor by "turning Earth" into a new Dalek homeworld. The eighth Doctor doesn't recall events in *War of the Daleks* either because they haven't happened to him yet (fans often reconcile the audio and book ranges by fitting the Big Finish Eighth Doctor audios into a gap opened up in *Vampire Science*), or because he's affected by the amnesia he suffers after *The Ancestor Cell*.

Big Finish says that Davros *does not* become the Emperor Dalek seen in *The Parting of the Ways*.

819 "Many years" before "War-Game".

820 Dating "War-Game" (*DWM* #100-101) - The Doctor

meets Kaon again in "Warrior's Story" (which takes place before this in Kaon's timeline) and that adventure sets the rough date for this one. The Draconians rule "a third of the galaxy" at this point. Kaon crashed "many years ago" - enough for Kara to be born and grow to womanhood (although we don't know how long that takes for a Draconian).

821 *Heart of TARDIS*

822 *Trading Futures*. Magnus Greel (from the year 5000) feared Time Agents tracking him down in *The Talons of Weng-Chiang*, Time Agents appeared in *Eater of Wasps*, and in *The Empty Child / The Doctor Dances*, Captain Jack claims to have been a Time Agent, and knows that other Agents will be tracking him down. It's interesting to note that in the original, unbroadcast version of *An Unearthly Child*, the Doctor said he was from the forty-ninth century.

823 *I am a Dalek*

824 "A Glitch in Time". It's never specified when the time travellers come from, but this would seem to be

5000 - THE INVISIBLE ENEMY[831] -> Five thousand AD was "the Year of the Great Breakout", when humanity "went leapfrogging across the galaxy like a tidal wave". To prepare the way, the Space Exploration Programme was instigated in the late fiftieth century, and a huge methane/oxygen refinery was set up on Titan. On asteroid K4067, the centre for Alien Biomorphology (the Bi-Al Foundation) treated extraterrestrial diseases, as well as tending those who were injured in space. Regular shuttle runs were set up between the planets of the solar system and "good for nothing" spaceniks also travelled the cosmos.

Photon beam weapons were in common use, as were visiphones. Sophisticated robots and computers were built. The native language of the time was Finglish, a form of phonetic English.

The Nucleus of the Swarm, a microscopic spaceborne entity, attempted to replicate itself across the universe and in the macro-world. It mentally compelled some humans to adapt the methane refinery on Titan into a breeding ground, but was destroyed before it could reproduce.

The Second Ice Age

? 5000 - THE ICE WARRIORS[832] ->

"And then suddenly one year, there was no spring. Even then it wasn't understood, not until the ice caps began to advance."

On Earth, the Second Ice Age had begun. Glaciers rapidly spread across every continent, displacing tens of billions of people to the Equatorial regions. Scientists attempted to come up with a theory that might account for the ice flow. They quickly ruled out a number of the possibilities: a reversal of the Earth's magnetic field, interstellar clouds obscuring the sun's rays, an excessive burst of sunspot activity and a severe shift of the Earth's angle of rotation. They came to realise that the extinction of Earth's plant life had dramatically reduced the carbon dioxide levels in the lower atmosphere, leading to severe heat loss across the world. Scientists tried to reverse the flow of ice, installing Ioniser Bases at strategic points across the globe: Britannicus Base in Europe, and complexes in

the only era in which the human race develops time travel.

825 "Three hundred years" before "Fire and Brimstone".

826 In the century before *The Ice Warriors*.

827 *The Taking of Planet 5* (p222).

828 *Interference*. The Doctor has a pair of those binoculars, no doubt acquired when he was with the Filipino army (mentioned in *The Talons of Weng-Chiang*).

829 *The English Way of Death*

830 *The Gallifrey Chronicles*

831 Dating *The Invisible Enemy* (15.2) - The Doctor states that it is the year "5000, the year of the Great Breakout" and implies that the human race has not yet left the Solar System. This contradicts virtually every other story set in the future - indeed, *The Invisible Enemy* would fit very neatly into this timeline about the year 2100.

The Breakout might be to other *galaxies*, and this is supported by the audio *Davros*, which has humanity poised to dominate the whole galaxy and eager to expand. Alternatively, perhaps a big section of humanity wants to leave because they've had enough of the Ice Age, lack of scientific progress, threat of World War and genocidal dictators we hear are on Earth in *The Talons of Weng-Chiang*. If so, no-one mentions it in *The Invisible Enemy*, and Marius' main concern with returning to Earth is that he has too much stuff to take home.

Looking more closely at the history of Earth since the collapse of the Earth Empire around the year 3000, it's clear that there are many human colonies - but there's no evidence that Earth has any political influ-

ence on them. While it's a major player on the galactic political stage, Earth's civilisation does seem to be confined to the solar system in *The Daleks' Master Plan*, the Peladon stories and the Davros Era stories (which even following the Peel timeline would fall between 3000 and 5000). Earth maintains a military capable of (small) missions across the galaxy, but the fact that it's ignorant of massive Dalek conquests in *The Daleks' Master Plan* - even the fact that Earth needs to name a fleet as "the Deep Space Fleet" in *Destiny of the Daleks* and finds it hard to fund or reinforce Davros' prison station in *Resurrection of the Daleks* - suggests that Earth doesn't dominate the galaxy. In *The Talons of Weng-Chiang*, we learn that Earth's in a technological cul-de-sac.

In short, it actually ties in with other stories that human civilisation is confined to Earth's solar system for a couple of millennia before 5000, by which time it's ripe for a "breakout", a new wave of colonisation.

The Gallifrey Chronicles gives the story the "relative date one-one-one-five-zero-zero-zero". *The TARDIS Logs* offered the date "4778".

832 Dating *The Ice Warriors* (5.3) - The date of this story is never given on screen. Base leader Clent says that if the glaciers advance, then "five thousand years of history" will be wiped out. If he's referring to Brittanicus Base, a Georgian house, this would make the date about 6800 AD. If he is referring to human or European history, the date becomes more vague. It has to be set well over a century in the future, because the world has been run by the Great World Computer for that long.

An article in the *Radio Times* at the time of broadcast

America, Australasia, South Africa and Asia. These were all co-ordinated by the Great World Computer.

Many refused to leave their homelands and became scavengers. Before long, everywhere on Earth apart from the equatorial areas was an Arctic wasteland, home to wolves and bears. When captured, scavengers were registered and sent to the African Rehabilitation Centres. Scientists remained behind to measure the flow of the ice with movement probes.

Varga the Ice Warrior, who had been trapped in the glacier since the First Ice Age, was revived. He excavated his ship and crew, but was defeated by the second Doctor, Jamie and Victoria before he could use sonic weapons to destroy Brittanicus Base.

The Time of Greel

In the Ice Age around the year 5000, Findecker's discovery of the double-nexus particle had sent human technology into a cul-de-sac. Humans nonetheless

developed limited psychic techniques such as the ability to read and influence the weak-minded. Various Alliances governed the world.

The Peking Homunculus, an automaton with the cerebral cortex of a pig, assassinated the commissioner of the Icelandic Alliance and almost precipitated World War Six. The Supreme Alliance came to power, and horrific war crimes were committed. The Alliance was finally defeated by the Filipino Army at the Battle of Reykjavik.

Magnus Greel - the Alliance's Minister of Justice, and the infamous Butcher of Brisbane - had performed terrible scientific experiments on one hundred thousand prisoners in an attempt to discover time travel and immortality. He escaped to the nineteenth century using a beam of zygma energy, and feared Time Agents would pursue him.[833]

The Doctor witnessed the sonic massacres in Brisbane.[834] Greel's path through time was deflected when his zygma beam hit the TARDIS.[835]

---

stated that the year is "3000 AD", and almost every other fan chronology used to follow that lead, although the first edition of *The Making of Doctor Who* said that the Doctor travels "3000 years" into the future after *The Abominable Snowmen*, making the date 4935 AD. *The Dark Path* and *Legacy* both allude to the date of this story as being 3000 AD (p63 and p89 respectively). The earlier versions of this chronology did the same.

In *The Talons of Weng-Chiang*, the Doctor talks of "the Ice Age about the year five thousand" - possibly even a reference to this story, if Robert Holmes was using *The Making of Doctor Who* as a reference.

Timelink and *About Time* both conclude that this is the ice age mentioned in *The Talons of Weng-Chiang*. This does certainly seem to be a neater solution than proposing two ice ages in quick succession - particularly when there are a fair few stories set around 3000 on an Earth which doesn't seem to be affected by an ice age. Occam's Razor doesn't always work on fictional timelines, and can be wielded too liberally, but it seems sensible to invoke it here.

One peculiarity is that the Martians have only been buried for "centuries", although it is also made clear that they have been buried since the First Ice Age, when mastodons roamed the Earth. (*About Time* states that mastodons became extinct five million years ago, but scientists disagree, estimating it was more like 10,000 BC). *The Terrestrial Index* and *Legacy* (p90) both suggest that the Ice Age began as a result of "solar flares" (presumably in an attempt to link it with Earth's evacuation in *The Ark in Space*), but that's specifically ruled out as a cause in the story.

One problem is that later stories (starting with *The Curse of Peladon*) would establish the Martians as a sig-

nificant presence in the future, which would make the humans' ignorance of them in this story notable - mankind has apparently forgotten about the Martians who were near neighbours, and fellow members of the Galactic Federation in the Peladon stories (and who they fought against in books such as *Transit* and *The Dying Days*).

THE SECOND ICE AGE: When base leader Clent explains the historical background to *The Ice Warriors*, he implies that the Ice Age began a century ago, but people are still being evacuated from England during the story, suggesting that glaciation is a more recent phenomenon. It would seem that although the global temperature drop is a direct result of the destruction of plant life, its consequences weren't felt overnight.

The present scientific consensus, of course, is that destroying the forests would cause global *warming* because of the resulting rise in carbon dioxide levels. However, this didn't gain widespread awareness until the 1970s; when *The Ice Warriors* was produced in the 1960s, the idea that the Earth might undergo global cooling was given more credence.

833 *The Talons of Weng-Chiang*. This happened "about the year five thousand" according to the Doctor; "the fifty-first" century according to Greel. The Doctor says he was with the Filipino army during their final advance. Note that World War Six is *averted* at this time, not fought, as some sources state.

Y5K: There are three television stories which establish versions of the state of Earth around the year 5000 which seem difficult to reconcile - *The Ice Warriors*, *The Talons of Weng-Chiang* and *The Invisible Enemy*. It's notable that those last two have the Doctor and Leela involved in events of the year 5000 in near-consecutive

5000 - EMOTIONAL CHEMISTRY[836] -> Magnus Greel had been a Chinese national, part of the PacBloc regime. The PacBloc used anti-matter shells against opposing armies, but not on population centres, and deployed Stepperiders and Locust aircraft. The Alliance forces used Thor battle tanks and Fenrir reconnaissance tanks. An Alliance division commanded by Razum Kinzhal stormed Greel's fortress and secured his Zygma technology. Using this, Kinzhal developed transit belts that let his agents roam time and secure possessions formerly owned by Kinzhal's beloved, Dusha.

Hostilities had increased between the PacBloc - led by one of Greel's lieutenants, Karsen Mogushestvo - and the Icelandic Alliance. The strategies of the Alliance's Lord General Razum Kinzhal devastated the PacBloc's air force. Kinzhal's forces further eliminated Mogushestvo's troops in Sverdlovsk, and overran Omsk.

Formerly a being known as a Magellan, Kinzhal sought to reunite with his other half, the nineteenth century Russian noblewoman Dusha. The eighth Doctor realized that such an act would obliterate Earth as the Magellan recorporalized. Kinzhal's assistant, Angel Malenkaya, was mortally wounded protecting Kinzhal from an assassination attempt and offered herself as a host. The Doctor used the Misl Vremya device in 2024 to link this era with 1812, and thereby transferred Dusha's soul into Angel's body. Reuinted with his love, Kinzhal set about reorganising his temporal paratroopers into operatives that would guard the past from temporal interference.

As part of these events, Trix stole a psionic weapon that Kinzhal had developed using enemy technology. However, she was forced to abandon it.

The Sun began to fail. The great Metropolises fell and the rich deserted the Earth - they left for the stars in a fleet of space arks. Those who remained behind became desperate. Matter transmission was commonplace, and this development broke up the nation states and ushered in the Transmat Wars. The whole world became a battlefield.[837]

c 5010 - "The Keep"[838] -> Ten years later, the eighth Doctor and Izzy arrived after following an SOS in the Vortex. They were captured by Uber-Marshal Hsui Leng of Greel's army, who believed they hailed from a structure named the Keep, and that they could help him secure the "treasure" within.

---

stories (only *Horror of Fang Rock* is between them) without any link being made.

From the details given in the stories, there's a way to reconcile them - *The Invisible Enemy* happens first, in "the year 5000" itself. It's a time where Earth has highly advanced technology and a rather sterile, computer-dependent society. *The Ice Warriors* depicts exactly the same sort of society. *The Ice Warriors* also suggests that the Ice Age has been around for a century of wintery weather - but goes on to claim that it's only recently reached a crisis point, with glaciers threatening the imminent destruction of major cities. At the time of *The Invisible Enemy*, it's clearly not a pressing problem (no-one mentions the issue, and Marius is planning to return to Earth). But it might be a factor (or *the* factor) in the "breakout" - a mass emigration to other planets would ease population pressures on Earth.

After this, when the slowly-advancing ice starts encroaching on the temperate areas (in both hemispheres), the crisis seen in *The Ice Warriors* occurs. (This happens in an unknown year, but possibly later on in the year 5000 itself.) There is mass migration to the equator, and we see some people in that story have rejected the computer-controlled society for a more atavistic lifestyle. It's easy to imagine such a rigidly-controlled society collapsing very quickly if the computers started failing (or arguing with each other) - it might even happen in days. Society would be split in two - those heading off into space (the scientists), and the ones staying behind (the more atavistic).

An unregulated society with little scientific progress... is exactly what *The Talons of Weng-Chiang* tells us the world is like in Greel's time, "about the year 5000" and "the 51st century". Greel's a scientist - but clearly one who'd thrive better on the barbaric, individualistic Earth than on a regulated, sterile space station. Environmental collapse and warfare made the Earth a very hostile environment, as seen in *Emotional Chemistry* (towards the beginning of the process) and "The Keep" (ten years on).

Meanwhile, *The Empty Child / The Doctor Dances* tells us that humanity has spread across the galaxy. The *Girl in the Fireplace* shows us that, like the society seen in *The Ice Warriors*, people of this time clearly like reminders of the past along with their high-technology. And - as in the earlier story - when the technology fails, humanity doesn't last long.

834 *The Hollow Men,* in the "fifty-first century".

835 *The Shadow of Weng-Chiang*

836 Dating *Emotional Chemistry* (EDA #66) - The date is given in the blurb, and is clearly tied in with *The Talons of Weng-Chiang*. One anomaly is that the book shows Kinzhal founding the Time Agents, but such operatives are clearly active before this, otherwise Greel wouldn't worry in *Talons* about "Time Agents" following him if the group didn't already exist. (Unless, perhaps, he'd previously encountered some sent back to the nineteenth century). The psionic weapon that Trix loses is the one that surfaces in *Eater of Wasps*.

837 "The Keep"

838 Dating "The Keep" (*DWM* #248-249) - It's "the fifty-first century", and the age of Magnus Greel. It's con-

The Doctor and Izzy were transmatted inside the Keep by an android called Marquez. He served the greatest scientist of the age, the shriveled Crivello, who had built an artificial sun - the Cauldron - to become the centrepiece of a new solar system for humanity in the Crab Nebula. The Cauldron was alive, and required a living conduit to achieve fusion and launch itself - only the Doctor, as a time traveller, was able to communicate with the Cauldron and survive. He did so, and the Cauldron headed out to the Crab Nebula, promising a new life for those that followed. After the Doctor departed, Marquez killed Crivello.

Marquez was actually a Dalek construct, and was trying to help his masters secure the Cauldron. The Daleks needed the artificial sun to fight spider-Daleks from a parallel universe. Work on the Cauldron had been secretly funded by the Threshold, as part of a plan to eliminate the Daleks' war fleet.[839]

This era was the native time of Time Agents Kala, Jode and Fatboy; the Doctor met them in Marpling in 1932. They could time travel using a temporal transduction beam.[840]

Captain Jack Harkness

The man who would later become known as Captain Jack Harkness[841] was a Time Agent in the fifty-first century.[842]

In his youth, he convinced a friend to go off with him to fight "the worst creatures imaginable", but they were captured and tortured. His friend was killed for being the weaker of the two.[843] "Jack" lived on the Boeshane Pennisula, and was the first person from there to join the Time Agency. He became a poster boy for the organisation, and was known as "the Face of Boe".[844]

Jack awoke one morning while still in the Time Agents' employ and found two years of his memories were missing. He eventually acquired a Chula warship and took up trying to con his former colleagues. Jack came to own a sonic blaster / cannon / disruptor, fitted with digital removal and rewind, and which was made at the weapons factories at Villengard. The Doctor visited the weapons factories, leading to an incident where the main reactor went critical. The summer groves of Villengard, which produced bananas, took to growing in the factories' place.

By this point, humanity had spread out across half the galaxy, and had commenced "dancing" with many species.[845]

The Doctor took the Mona Lisa up Mount Everest on a camel in the fifty-first century.[846]

c 5000 - THE GIRL IN THE FIREPLACE[847] **->** By the fifty-first century, mankind had warp engines capable of "punching a hole in the universe". Humans had trav-

---

firmed that the problem with the sun leads to the "solar flares" in "Wormwood".

839 "Fire and Brimstone"

840 *Eater of Wasps*. The trio hails from "three thousand years" after 1932, but it's after *Emotional Chemistry*, so Kala is rounding up.

841 It's established in *TW: Captain Jack Harkness* that he adopted a false identity.

842 *The Empty Child*

843 *TW: Captain Jack Harkness*. The identity of his captors hasn't been revealed.

844 *Last of the Time Lords*. The clear implication is that immortal Jack will eventually transform into the Face of Boe, who was first seen in *The End of the World*. Those wishing to overlook this possiblity often suggest that it could have just as easily been a punning nickname that Jack acquired because there was already a famous Face of Boe in his native era. Or, of course, both could be true.

845 *The Empty Child / The Doctor Dances*. The latter states Jack is from the fifty-first century.

846 *The Art of Destruction*

847 Dating *The Girl in the Fireplace* (X2.4) - The caption cuts from events in eighteenth-century France to the future with the caption "3000 years later", making it around 4759. However, the Doctor tells Rose and Mickey that it's "three thousand years into your future,

give or take", which would make it around 5007. Still later, the Doctor states it's the fifty-first century. The SS *Madame de Pompadour* is in the Dagmar Cluster, two and a half galaxies from Earth, and the intergalactic travel probably supports the later date.

848 *Trading Futures*

849 "A thousand years" before *City at World's End*.

850 "597" years before *Tragedy Day* (p97).

851 Dating "Fire and Brimstone" (*DWM* #251-255) - The Doctor says "some 200 years ago, I saw the Cauldron launched", a reference to "The Keep". The humans in this story don't recognise the Daleks.

852 Dating "Wormwood" (*DWM* #266-271) - It's "twenty years" since "Fire and Brimstone" according to Chastity.

853 Dating *Planet of the Spiders* (11.5) - The colony ship that crashes on Metebelis III has intergalactic capability, as Metebelis is in the Acteon Galaxy. It also made a "time jump", also suggesting it's from the fare future. *The Terrestrial Index* claimed that the colony ship was "lost during the early days of the 22nd century", dating *Planet of the Spiders* itself as "c.2530". *The TARDIS Logs* suggested "4256", *Timelink* "3415".

854 Dating *The Eight Doctors* (EDA #1) - This happens at some point in the aftermath of *Planet of the Spiders*.

elled at least as far as the Dagmar Cluster, "two and a half galaxies" from Earth.

The spacecraft *Madame de Pompadour* was crippled in an ion storm, and drifted for a year while the clockwork robots aboard blindly followed their orders to repair it. They used the human crew as raw components, and then used the warp drive to travel back in time to find the historical Madame de Pompadour, who they mistakenly thought was the key to the problem. The tenth Doctor, Rose and Mickey arrived on the ship and - after multiple trips to the eighteenth century - deactivated the robots.

The fifty-first century was the era of the time traveller Chronodev, who was known to the Onihr.[848] The Taklarian Empire began a program of selective breeding to create a master race.[849]

Olleril was colonised. Governed by the principles laid down in the ancient records *The Collins Guide to the Twentieth Century*, *One of Us* by Hugo Young, *The Manufacture of Consent* and *The Smash Hits Yearbook*, it developed an eccentric, unworkable political and economic system that was an almost exact copy of the United Kingdom in the twentieth century. The cult of Luminus managed the planet in secret.[850]

c 5200 - "Fire and Brimstone"[851] -> Ninety-seven "audited precessions" after the Breakout, the eighth Doctor and Izzy landed on the satelloid Icarus Falling - one of six satellites revolving around the artifical sun Crivello's Cauldron. This was the New Earth System in the Crab Nebula, and held some of the remnants of humanity.

A Dalek fleet soon arrived and released self-replicating robot insects - the Contagium - to secure Icarus Falling. The Daleks sought to wipe out a race of spider-Daleks from a parallel dimension, and wanted to collapse the Cauldron and create a black hole - the means by which they could travel to the home territory of their rivals. The Daleks installed a synaptic conduit into the Doctor's brain, believing he could navigate their fleet through the black hole.

Sister Chastity, a religious official aboard Icarus Falling, revealed herself as a member of Threshold and rescued the Doctor. She claimed that Threshold had changed in the thousands of years since the Doctor last encountered them, and intended - with the Doctor's help - to crush the Dalek fleet as they passed through the black hole that the Cauldron would become. The Daleks took control of the Cauldron anyway, but spider-Daleks poured through the gateway and engaged Phalanx 44 of Special Weapons Daleks in battle. The Doctor learned that the Threshold had been hired by the Time Lords, and engineered a supernova that destroyed both Dalek armies. The Cauldron became an ordinary sun with planets orbiting it.

c 5220 - "Wormwood"[852] -> The newly-regenerated ninth Doctor, Izzy and Fey landed in Wormwood, a mock Western village controlled by Threshold on the Moon. Their leader, Abraham White, showed the Doctor a host of landmarks from Earth such as the Eiffel Tower, the Statue of Liberty, Mount Rushmore and so forth, which he had saved to celebrate mankind's achievements. Fey confronted White after learning they'd been spying on her for years, but White summoned a demonic beast, the Pariah.

Izzy discovered that the Threshold were building the Eye of Disharmony, a device that made space impassable. Activated, the Eye annihilated the Traxonnia Research Cluster, the Kapli Refugee Fleet, the Ninth Sontaran Armada and every other vessel in space. The Threshold sent a transwarp signal to every civilisation offering to sell their teleport windows as an alternative.

The eighth Doctor showed up, revealing that the "ninth Doctor" was actually Shayde in disguise. The Pariah, in turn, revealed that she was the original Shayde - who had rebelled against Rassilon. She defeated Shayde in battle, then killed all the members of Threshold to drain their energy. This horrified White, who broke his psychic link with her.

Fey merged with the wounded Shayde, gaining his powers, and they launched a second attack that destroyed Pariah. White also died. The Eye of Disharmony's destruction obliterated Earth's moon, but restored space to its natural state. "Feyde" opted to leave the Doctor and Izzy's company, and travel on her own.

? 5433 - PLANET OF THE SPIDERS[853] -> An Earth ship came out of its time jump without power and crashed on Metebelis III. Some humans, a few sheep and a handful of spiders survived the crash. The spiders found their way to the cave of the Blue Crystals, and the energies there mutated them, making them grow and boosting their intelligence and psychic abilities. The "Eight-Legs" came to dominate the planet, harvesting the human population as cattle. The Eight-Legs were ruthless - they wiped out two hundred and sixty-nine villagers, the entire population of Skorda, when they tried to resist.

Four hundred and thirty three years after the crash, the Spiders set up a psychic bridge with a Tibetan monastery on twentieth-century Earth. They plotted to travel back in time to conquer their homeworld, but were defeated. Their leader, the "Great One", had planned to gain further power by completing the crystal lattice of the cave, but an energy backlash killed her.

c 5433 - THE EIGHT DOCTORS[854] -> The humans on Metebelis III hunted down the spiders. The seventh Doctor visited the planet and was caught by a giant spider. The eighth Doctor rescued him.

Along the Eastern edge of the galaxy, there was political upheaval for a thousand years. Many human colony worlds such as Pyka, Marlex, Dalverius, Pantorus and Shaggra warred with each other, and the galaxy's monetary system was in almost permanent crisis. In the fifty-fourth century, a consortium of industrialists attempted to solve the problem. Eventually they built Zamper: a neutral planet, snug in its own mini-universe, that would supply state-of-the-art battleships to all sides.

The only way to the planet was through a hyperspace gate controlled by Zamper itself, and the planet was completely self-contained to keep its designs secret. In four hundred and seventy three years of operation, Zamper became rich and maintained a balance of power in East Galaxy. The operation was completely smooth, averaging one minor technical failure every two hundred years.[855]

Sabalom Glitz stole a Tzun data core from the reptilian Veltrochni. He sold it to Niccolo Mandell, an agent of the Vandor Prime government.[856]

? 5595 - MISSION: IMPRACTICAL[857] -> Ten years later, the Veltrochni threatened to make war against Vandor Prime over the Tzun data core that Sabalom Glitz had stolen. The data core was the last surviving information cache from the Tzun Empire, and contained blueprints on how to construct Tzun Stormblades. Vandor Prime head of security Niccolo Mandell, hoping to sell the data core himself, coerced the sixth Doctor, Frobisher and Glitz into retrieving the device from an orbital facility.

Glitz's associate Dibber died in a crossfire, but the Doctor purged the data core of its more dangerous information and returned it to the Veltrochni. Vandor Prime authorities arrested Mandell. Glitz continued travelling in his *Nosferatu*.

? 5597 - TRAGEDY DAY[858] -> On the Earth colony Olleril, the precocious boy genius Crispin, leader of the secret society of Luminus, sought to gain mental control of the population, and to pattern everyone after characters from the show *Martha and Arthur*. Meanwhile, the immortal Friars of Pangloss hired the arachnid mutant Ernie "Eight Legs" McCartney, the most feared assassin in the Seventh Quadrant, to retrieve a cursed piece of red glass that the Doctor had acquired. The seventh Doctor thwarted Crispin's plans, and Crispin died when the Luminus submarine *Gargantuan* was destroyed. Ravenous Slaag creatures consumed McCartney. The Friars were disrupted by an anti-matter burst, and flung powerless into the Time Vortex.

In 5665, the Chelonians launched an attack on the human colony Vaagon, but the Chelonians' tanks vanished mysteriously before they could complete their conquest, transported by a Fortean Flicker to the twenty-seventh century. Believing themselves blessed by divine intervention, the colonists were quite unprepared when the Chelonians reinvaded several generations later and wiped out the colony.[859]

The Doctor bought a collapsible snooker table at the height of the retro-gaming fad of the fifty-eighth century.[860]

---

855 *Zamper*

856 About ten years before *Mission: Impractical*.

857 Dating *Mission: Impractical* (PDA #12) - It is "a couple of million years" before *The Trial of a Time Lord* (p56). Ernie McCartney from *Tragedy Day* is mentioned (p215), setting this around the same time as that book. This would not appear, from the other stories featuring Glitz, to be his native timezone. We might conclude that he has ended up somehow either acquiring time travel or been brought here by a time traveller.

858 Dating *Tragedy Day* (NA #24) - There is no indication of the date in the book, although the colony planet Pantorus is mentioned here (p83) and in *Zamper* (p57), perhaps suggesting they are set around the same time.

859 *The Highest Science*

860 *Synthespians™*

861 *The Price of Paradise*

862 "Thousands of years" after *Asylum*. No date given, and this is an arbitrary placing.

863 *Spiral Scratch*

864 "Five thousand years" before *The Crystal Bucephalus* (p114).

865 "Two hundred and seventy years" before *Half-Life*.

866 Dating *Combat Rock* (PDA #55) - There's no date given, although cigarettes were banned on the colonies "hundreds of years ago". There are smokers in *Resurrection of the Daleks*, but of course a smoking ban can be lifted and ignored, so it's hardly firm evidence that this story is set after that. My date is arbitrary, but I've linked it to the Christian colonists of Espero.

The date of the Earth-Indoni war is unspecified, but Jenggel's current political climate seems to stem from its fallout, suggesting a shorter rather than longer span of time since it occurred. The Indoni subjugated the Papul, and the Christian missionaries arrived, some "30 rainseasons" before the novel takes place.

867 *Heritage*. Cole's grandmother fights in it.

868 Dating *Zamper* (NA #41) - It is "the sixtieth century" (p77). Earth appears to be populated at this time.

869 "Twenty" (p8) and "ten" (p18) years before *Heritage*.

870 Three years before *Heritage* (p56).

871 Dating *Heritage* (PDA #57) - Each chapter in the book has a precise date and time.

872 Dating *Half-Life* (EDA #68) - This story is set after *Heritage*, as there are references to that story.

In 5720, archaeologists discovered the remains of a Khorlthochloi starship.[861] The militaristic Narbrab conquered an alien civilization. The survivors, hosted in Ikshar host bodies, were banished in a solar-powered ship and arrived in London, 1346.[862]

= In 5738, the sixth Doctor visited the planet Helios 3.[863]

Around 5764, a Dalek civil war became so serious that the Time Lords intervened.[864] Espero was colonised by mostly African and Asian humans with a shared Christian faith. The colonists hoped to escape the influence of the Eurozone and America, and bought the planet from the Homeworld Corporation. Renouncing technology, the colony hit problems when it proved all but impossible to extract the planet's natural resources and, with nothing to offer in trade, Espero quickly became isolated from the rest of the galaxy. Religious schisms led to the Almost War.[865]

? 5800 - COMBAT ROCK[866] **->** Earth won a war against the Indoni, making the planet Jenggel an Earth colony. The Indoni subsequently invaded the rival Papul people, forcing the Papul leaders to vote for "integration". Tourism swelled amid the new political climate, with visitors arriving to experience the "primitive" Papul culture. The corrupt President Sabit of the Indoni kept most of the profits for himself. Christian missionaries arrived to minister to the Papul. Twentieth-century icons such as *Winnie the Pooh*, *Wind in the Willows* and Leatherface horror films were in use in pop culture.

On Jenggel, a sentient organism contained in a purple fungus from the Papul swamps possessed a Papul named Kepennis. As the mysterious "Krallik", the organism-Kepennis founded the OPG, a Papul resistance movement. Some eight rainseasons later, Kepennis rigged Papul mumis to kill tourists and Indoni soldiers by spitting snakes, furthering an atmosphere of anarchy. The second Doctor, Jamie and Victoria arrived onhand, and the Doctor ingested some of the fungus himself, enabling him to mentally nullify the organism within Kepennis. A cannibalistic Papul tribe took Kepennis away to consume him as punishment, and a mercenary with a bit of a noble streak killed Sabit.

There was a Cyber War in the late sixtieth century.[867]

c 5995 - ZAMPER[868] **->** There was revolution on Chelonia, where the peaceful forces of Little Sister overthrew Big Mother. This initiated a cultural reformation that saw the warlike race transformed into the galaxy's foremost flower-arrangers. Forty years later, many Chelonians hankered for the old blood-and-glory days, and Big Mother's fleet headed for Zamper to purchase a powerful Series

336c Delta-Spiral Sun Blaster - a ship whose effectiveness had been demonstrated in the Sprox civil war and the skirmishes of Pancoza. It was capable of withstanding neutronic ray blasts of up to an intensity of sixty blarks. With such a ship, power could have been wrested back from Little Sister, but the Chelonians discovered that the Zamps - slug-like creatures used to build the ships on the planet - had dreams of conquest and were building their own battleship. In a variation of the Diemlisch manoeuvre (first used in the third Wobesq-Majjina war), the Chelonian fleet destroyed itself in order to seal the gate between Zamper and the rest of the universe.

Colonists established a colony on Heritage. Ten years later, a company at Galactic Central developed a way of synthesising Thydonium, instantly putting mining colonies such as Heritage out of business. Melanie Bush and her husband Ben Heyworth settled on the impoverished Heritage sometime afterward.[869]

Years later on Heritage, the geneticist Wakeling successfully cloned a raven, naming her Arabella.[870]

6048 (6th August) - HERITAGE[871] **->** Menopause had become extremely rare. Undergoing the condition, Melanie Bush Heyworth asked Wakeling for a genetic solution to the problem. Wakeling's treatment seemingly led to Mel and her husband Ben conceiving a child named Sweetness, but the Heyworths discovered that Wakeling had violated their wishes by cloning Sweetness from Mel. A subsequent argument between Wakeling and Mel led to his striking her with a genetic sequencer, killing her.

The Heritage residents overlooked Wakeling's act of murder, believing his experiments could restore prosperity to the hard-up colony. Ben Heyworth's attempt to seek justice by alerting off-world authorities was discovered. Wakeling further persuaded the townfolk to favour his experiments, and the locals tore Ben to pieces with their bare hands before torching his house. Wakeling took Sweetness into his own home.

A shuttlecraft arrived on Heritage - the first in years - and two visitors wanted to see the Heyworths, causing quite a stir. The buried memories of the Heyworths' deaths began to surface among the locals. One of visitors, the seventh Doctor, gatecrashed an interstellar video conference and revealed Wakeling as a murderer, destroying the man's chance to reveal his success at cloning. Wakeling and two other inhabitants subsequently fell to their deaths when some of the old mineshafts collapsed under them. Cole, the Heritage town barman, adopted Sweetness.

c 6050 - HALF-LIFE[872] **->** Two races, the parasitic Makers and the Oon, had by now been at war for centuries. The organic spaceship Tain, a Maker construct, sought to escape his bloody role and tried to escape the war.

However, the Oon infected Tain with a Trojan program that assaulted his consciousness. Tain crashed onto the planet Espero, and his personality remained in conflict.

The Trojan program, unable to fully dominate Tain, generated a distress signal to alert the Oon to its situation. The eighth Doctor, Fitz and Trix received the signal and arrived on Espero to help. Tain panicked upon the TARDIS' arrival, thinking it heralded the Oon's arrival, and unleashed its ultimate weapon: a wavefront designed to gradually disintegrate and reconstitute a planet under Tain's control. The internal struggle between Tain and the Trojan program interrupted the wavefront's effects, throwing it into chaos. The Doctor helped Tain purge the Trogan program and end the wavefront. Tain prepared to leave Espero afterward.

The Imperial family on Espero was composed of Imperator Tannalis, age 120, his wife Alinti and children Javill and Sensimi. Javill's mind was erased by a Oon neural-rubber, which forced him, age 23, to mentally remature.

High Catholic doctrine came to forbid use of matter transmitters, stating it was impossible to teleport a soul.

The last colonist left Heritage in 6057. None of the ex-colonists ever discussed their reasons for departing.[873] On 8th December, 6064, former Heritage colonist Lee Marks, now head of the Ellershaw Foundation, died in a fire deliberately set at his home.[874] A grown-up Sweetness Cole penned an autobiography entitled *First of a New Breed*.[875]

On the desert planet Chronos, a race of beings built a time machine. This enabled them to travel into their world's future, when it had become a water planet and was far more habitable. In the distant future, only a handful of Cybermen survived. They fled to the water world Chronos and exterminated the beings who lived there, acquiring their time machine in the process. The Cybermen used it to travel back to 3286, but a temporal blast from that era surged here and aged them to death.[876]

In the far, far future, the Cybermen were nearly extinct. A surviving Cyber-Leader held the Doctor responsible for his race's final destruction, and had access to Cyber-race's entire history banks. The Cyber-Leader found an abandoned time-ship - the product of Gallifreyan technology - on a planet nearly destroyed by fire, and decided to lay a trap for the Doctor in 1984. The time-ship was designed for a Gallifreyan pilot, so piloting it proved difficult and the Cyber-Leader arrived two years early in 1982.[877]

Advanced Cybermen from the far future had a Cybership which contained a fragment of the Time Vortex, and so could travel in time. They used it to attack Earth in the early twenty-first century.[878]

873 *Heritage* (p227).

874 *Heritage* (p279).

875 Years after *Heritage*.

876 *Real Time*. No date given. The CyberController in this era is an alternate history version of Evelyn Smythe.

877 *The Reaping*. Presumably this occurs after *Real Time*, but this date is otherwise arbitrary.

878 "The Flood". No date is given, but the eighth Doctor declares the Cybermen to be the most advanced he's ever seen. This places the story after *Real Time* and *The Reaping* - two stories which also feature time-travelling Cybermen from the unspecified far future. I've placed these stories in the same period.

879 *The Ark in Space*

THE SOLAR FLARES: The solar flares ravage the Earth "thousands of years" after the thirtieth century (*Revenge of the Cybermen*). Judging by information in the TV series, the last recorded human activity on Earth for millions of years is in the fifty-first century (*The Talons of Weng-Chiang, The Invisible Enemy*). The books and audios push this forward by about a thousand years, to around 6000. I speculate that the Solar Flares occur relatively soon after this time.

The first edition of *The Programme Guide* claimed that Earth was only evacuated between "c.2800" and "c.2900", the second suggested dates between "c.2900" and "c.4300". *The Terrestrial Index* attempted to rationalise the statement that the Ark was built in the "thirtieth century", stating that Nerva was built, but then the Solar Flares "abated", Nerva was not informed and the population of Nerva went on to recolonise Ravolox "between 15,000 and 20,000" (as seen in *The Mysterious Planet*). This contradicts the date for *The Mysterious Planet* established on screen and would represent a rather implausible oversight on behalf of the Earth's authorities. The book's supposition that the Solar Flares caused the Ice Age we see in *The Ice Warriors* (a theory repeated in *Legacy*) is specifically ruled out by dialogue in *The Ice Warriors*.

880 *The Reaping, The Gathering*. The Doctor says that the Gogglebox was created while "humanity was on a day trip away from Earth space" owing to "solar flares or intergalactic war or something". This placement is arbitrary.

881 Dating *Dreamtime* (BF #67) - Simon Forward scripted this story with the intent of it occurring during the time of the World Zones Authority in the twenty-first century, but nothing in the story itself supports this. Talk of evacuating the Earth means it fits naturally at the time of the solar flares. If the "past" segments are part of the Dreaming and inherently unreliable, dating becomes even murkier. Forward says that the Galyari Korshal in *Dreamtime* isn't the character of the same name in the Benny audio *The Bone of Contention* (even if Steffan Rhodri voices both parts); the Galyari are long-lived, but traditionally hand down some names

The Solar Flares
and the Evacuation of Earth

The Earth was ruled by the World Executive. Earth at this time was technically advanced, with advanced suspended animation techniques, fission guns and power supplied via solar stacks and granavox turbines.

Scientists monitoring the Sun predicted a series of massive solar flares: within only a matter of years, the Earth's surface would be ravaged and virtually all life would be wiped out. It would be five thousand years before the planet would be habitable again.

The High Minister and the Earth Council began working on humanity's salvation. Carefully screened humans, the Star Pioneers, were sent out in vast colony ships to places such as Colony 9 and Andromeda. Nerva was converted into an Ark housing the cream of humanity, some one hundred thousand people, who were placed in suspended animation along with samples of animal and plant life. The Ark also contained the sum of human knowledge stored on microfilm.

The rest of humanity took to Thermic Shelters, knowing that they wouldn't survive. When the Solar Flares came, every living thing on the Earth perished.

A group of Star Pioneers reached Andromeda and encountered the Wirrn, a race of parasitic insects who lived in the depths of space, visiting worlds only to breed.[879]

During a period in which humanity didn't inhabit the Earth, an alien race set up the the Gogglebox - a giant museum dedicated to Earth and its history - deep within Earth's Moon. The fifth Doctor visited the locale, met history student Alan Fitzgerald and left behind a copy of *The Rough Guide to Shabadabadon* which detailed - among other things - Shabadabadon's famous ice caves. For Alan's benefit, the Doctor confirmed his involvement in the great fire

of London and the *Mary Celeste*, but he refused to discuss when his tenure with UNIT occurred. The Doctor then departed to investigate an energy spike emanating from Brisbane in September 2006.

Two thousand years later, the Gogglebox now enabled users to view every recorded media event from the human race's history. Alan Fitzgerald had been cloned, and 108 copies of him aided visitors.[880]

? 6000 - DREAMTIME[881] **->** Facing a catastrophic natural disaster, evacuation coordinators herded the people onto Phoenix lifeships that departed for space. In Australia, a guru named Baiame sought an alternative and hoped to channel the Dreaming - a collective force, derived from the minds and dreams of humanity - to influence matter. Baiame wanted to lift Uluru, a sacred bluff, and its people into space under protection of a Dreaming-generated force field. The seventh Doctor traversed the Dreaming and arrived from thousands of years in the future. Baiame acceded to the Doctor's request that he extend his sphere of protection a few miles and include settlers in the surrounding vicinity. The Uluru lifted off from Earth with its people and sped into space, and the Doctor returned to the future.

After a thousand years, the Star Pioneers had destroyed all the Wirrn breeding grounds, making Andromeda suitable for colonisation. One Wirrn Queen survived and travelled through space towards the Earth. After thousands of years, she reached the Nerva Beacon, and although the station's automatic defences killed her. Before her death, the Queen damaged the systems that would have revived the humans, and laid her eggs within one of the sleeping Nerva engineers.[882]

While those aboard Nerva slept, human colonies such as Gal Sec carved out an Empire, with bases across half the galaxy. They retained legends of Nerva,

---

through the generations.

THE ABANDONMENT OF EARTH: Earth is completely evacuated six times that we know of: (1) for "ten thousand years" between the time of the Solar Flares and *The Sontaran Experiment* (c.5000-c.15,000 AD); (2) for at least three thousand five hundred years before (and an unknown amount of time after) *Birthright* (c.18,500 AD-?); (3) a line cut from the rehearsal script but retained in the *Planet of Evil* novelisation reveals that "The Tellurian planet [Earth] has been uninhabited since the Third Era" (significantly before 37,166 AD); (4) for a significant time after the Usurians move the workforce to Pluto before *The Sun Makers* millions of years in the future; (5) there is a mass evacuation shortly before Earth plunges into the Sun ten million years in the future, seen in *The*

Ark and reported in *Frontios*; (6) finally, Earth was empty at the time of its final destruction in the year five billion, seen in *The End of the World*.

882 *The Ark in Space.* As the colonists are scheduled to revive after "five thousand years" [c.11,000 AD], the Wirrn Queen must arrive on Nerva before that time.

ANDROMEDA: Andromeda is mentioned a number of times in *Doctor Who*, sometimes as a reference to the constellation, other times as the galaxy of the same name. According to the TARDIS Information File entry that the Master fakes in *Castrovalva*, Castrovalva itself is a planet in the Phylox series in Andromeda. There is some evidence that Zanak (*The Pirate Planet*) raided worlds there, as the ground is littered with Andromedan bloodstones. In *The Daleks' Master Plan*,

"The Lost Colony" from the time of the Expansion, but most didn't believe that such a place really existed. In time, the colonies grew to distrust talk of "Mother Earth".[883]

The New Dark Age

In 6198, the Federation Scientific Executive funded a research project into genetic experimentation. The geneticist Maximillian Arrestis hired a team of consultants to develop the Lazarus Intent, a religion that he hoped would become a moneymaking venture. His "miracles" were publicised for three years, and his predictions of disasters all came to pass. *The Codex of Lazarus* was published early in the sixty-third century, and for nearly a decade he reaped the financial rewards of being the "Messiah".

Not content with this, Arrestis began to sell defence secrets to the Cybermen, Sontarans and Rutans. The Federation was fighting a war with the Sontarans at the time. In 6211, Sontarans launched a stealth attack that wiped much of the Federation DataCore on Io. Three weeks later, an earthshock bomb - sold by the Cybermen to the Sontarans - destroyed Tersurus. This didn't stop the Federation from winning the war. When the Sontaran Emperor suspected that Arrestis had double-crossed him, the traitor was brought to the Sontaran Throneworld and executed. "Lazarus" became a martyr, the saviour of the galaxy, and it was the Intent of his followers to resurrect him.

Alexhendri Lassiter built a time machine and did rescue Arrestis moments before his death. Later, Arrestis escaped the destruction of the Crystal Bucephalus restaurant by fleeing through time, only to arrive back on Sontara right before his execution, which proceeded as planned.[884]

Every small publisher in the universe had been bought out, and by "the end of time", this would give rise to one dominating, monolithic publishing house. The company owned the rights to all of the authors throughout history, especially the lazy ones who hadn't fulfilled on their contracts. Publisher's robots from the sixty-fourth century were equipped with time travel Armed with laser cannons, t throughout history to "remind" these writers to finish their texts. One such robot visited the Doctor in 1597.[885]

Around 6976, the Vardans who invaded Earth in 1976 arrived back home. They discovered there had been a revolution, and that the military had lost power.[886]

The Mazuma Era[887]

c 8162 - "Free-Fall Warriors"[888] -> Doctor Asimoff from Sigma had been coming to the Festival of the Five Planets for the last fifteen years, although it used to be the Festival of the Six Planets until one planet broke away from the Federation. Asimoff recognised the fourth Doctor as a Time Lord, and the Doctor showed him the TARDIS. They met the Free-Fall Warriors - a stunt pilot team who challenged the Doctor to go on a flight with Machinehead, one of their number. They launched right into the middle of an attack on the planet, and were forced down onto an asteroid. The remaining Free-Fall Warriors - Big Cat, Cool Breeze and Bruce - set off to intercept the raiders, and the Doctor fixed Machinehead's ship in time to play a decisive role in the battle.

c 8162 - "The Moderator"[889] -> Josiah W Dogbolter, a creature not quite a man and not quite a frog, was the owner of the Intra-Venus Inc and the richest man in the galaxy. He profited from everything, including the war on Phobos and ruby mining on Celeste. Dogbolter had a presence on many planets, including Celeste - a world where he sent "moles", meaning people who rebelled against him.

---

an intergalactic conference was held in Andromeda. In *The Ark in Space*, we learn that Star Pioneers from Earth reached Andromeda and discovered that it was infested with the Wirrn. The two races fought each other or a thousand years, until humanity succeeded in destroying the Wirrn's breeding grounds. Mankind went on to colonise the galaxy, and by the time of *The Mysterious Planet*, the civilisation was established on planets such as Sabalom Glitz's homeworld, Salostopus. At that time, Andromedans capable of building advanced robots and harnessing black light stole Matrix secrets and fled the wrath of the Time Lords. The Doctor considers visiting "the constellation of Andromeda" in *Timelash*. The Doctor took the mer-children to a water planet in the Andromeda Galaxy at the end of *Evolution*. According to Trix in *The Gallifrey Chronicles*, the currency in Andromeda is the Andromedan Euro, although

Dragonfire, Legacy and *Business Unusual* all agree it is the Grotzi in Glitz's time.

The threat in *Doctor Who and the Invasion from Space* comes from Andromeda in the far future.

883 *The Sontaran Experiment*

884 *The Crystal Bucephalus*

885 *The Kingmaker*. The publisher's robot is specified as being from the sixty-fourth century, but this isn't to say the dominating publishing house is located there also, but the Doctor's comments suggest that the company hails from much further in the future.

886 "Five thousand years" after *No Future*.

887 THE MAZUMA ERA: A number of stories from the mid-80s *DWM* strip were set in the same colourful, cosmopolitan far future period. It might be termed the Mazuma Era, after the galactic currency which seems to preoccupy a number of the characters. The first time

He owned Mars, Jupiter and Venus, plus a score of worlds in other systems.

The fifth Doctor and Gus landed on Celeste and narrowly escaped arrest for breaking curfew. Deep in the ruby mines, they were attacked by the Wrekka, a combat robot sent in to deal with the moles. Dogbolter's guards brought the Doctor and Gus to their boss, who learned the Doctor had a time machine. Dogbolter knew that "time is money", but the Doctor refused to sell his Ship and left. A furious Dogbolter brought in the Moderator, a company troubleshooter. He tracked them to Gus' home, and had Gus killed.

Gus had wounded the Moderator. The Doctor returned the Moderator to a hospital in his home timezone... where Dogbolter's right-hand robot, Hob, turned off his life support.

c 8162 - "The Shape Shifter"[890] **->** Avan Tarklu was a 45-year-old Whifferdill - a shapeshifting private investigator who was tempted by the quarter of a million Mazuma reward that Dogbolter had posted for the fifth or sixth Doctor.

Meanwhile, the sixth Doctor learned that Dogbolter had sent the Moderator, and was heading to Greenback Bay, Venus, when he was attacked. Avan Tarklu secretly helped the Doctor repel the attack - purely to get his hands on the reward - and snuck into the TARDIS. The Doctor and the shapeshifter landed at the headquarters of Intra-Venus Inc, which Dogbolter had evacuated, then nuked. They tricked Dogbolter into handing over the reward, then escaped. The shapeshifter joined the Doctor on his travels.

c 8162 - "Voyager"[891] **->** The sixth Doctor had a nightmare about a shadowy figure on a sailing ship, waking to find that the TARDIS had landed at the Antarctic of "an outback dimension somewhere between mythology and madness".

The shapeshifter - who was now semi-permanently in the form of a penguin, and calling himself Frobisher - had discovered the same ship, frozen in ice. Exploring the ship,

the Doctor found star charts. He was accosted by Astrolabus, an old man with a blunderbuss, who took the charts and made his escape in a Da Vinci flying machine.

The Doctor and Frobisher followed him to a lighthouse, where the Doctor confronted Astrolabus - and found that the lighthouse was his TARDIS. Astrolabus tried to escape, but crashed into the sea. Voyager showed himself to the Doctor and demanded the return of the charts - which Astrolabus had tattooed onto his chest. Astrolabus was in his last incarnation and was seeking immortality, but Voyager ripped the chart off his body, killing him. Voyager told the Doctor he was now free, and the Doctor returned to his companions.

c 8162 - "Polly the Glot"[892] **->** Terminal LX 116/RM was a space station at the centre of the Milky Way - the crossroads of an entire galaxy - and was known as Galena. Dr Ivan Asimoff was passing through when he saw the TARDIS. Asimoff invited the sixth Doctor to the Save the Zyglot Trust annual conference, as he was the group's treasurer.

Polly, the only Zyglot in captivity, was at the Ringway Carnival along with freakshow exhibits from a hundred worlds. The creatures were hunted for their colours by the dullest race in the universe, the Akkers, and the Trust was failing through lack of funds. The Doctor and Frobisher "kidnapped" Asimoff, generating a great deal of publicity for his cause.

The Doctor learned that the President of the Trust was a Professor Astro Labus. They headed for a hunting ship, freeing the Zyglot in their clutches and discovering that an Astral Arbus owned the Ringway Carnival. The Doctor also freed Polly, who soared and blossomed - and left Asimoff heartbroken. The Doctor left the 250,000 Mazuma reward he stole from Dogbolter for Asimoff to donate to the Trust.

c 8162 - "Once Upon a Time Lord..."[893] **->** The sixth Doctor and Frobisher entered the cabinet of Astrolabus, and encountered a variety of surreal obstacles.

---

we're given a date for the story is in *Death's Head* #8 - a *Doctor Who* crossover issue of the Marvel UK comic - which sees the Doctor dropping off the cyborg Death's Head off in the year 8162.

While Dogbolter's holdings include Venus, Mars and Jupiter, no mention is ever made of Earth - which the TV show tells us ought to be uninhabited at this time. The solar flares clearly don't affect the other planets of the solar system.

888 Dating "Free-Fall Warriors" (*DWM* #56-57) - The story sees the fourth Doctor meeting Dr Asimoff for the first time.

889 Dating "The Moderator" (*DWM* #84, #86-87) - The

Free-Fall Warriors are mentioned.

890 Dating "The Shape Shifter" (*DWM* #88-89) - This story happens soon after "The Moderator" from the Doctor's point of view, as he's looking to avenge Gus' death. Dogbolter is somehow aware that the Doctor has regenerated, but the wanted poster has images of both the fifth and sixth Doctors.

891 Dating "Voyager" (*DWM* #90-94) - It's a "few weeks" since the end of "The Shape Shifter".

892 Dating "Polly the Glot" (*DWM* #95-97) - It's after "Voyager", but there's no indication of how much time has passed.

893 Dating "Once Upon a Time Lord..." (*DWM* #98-99) -

c 8162 - THE MALTESE PENGUIN[894] -> Frobisher briefly returned to his homeworld to resume his occupation as a private investigator. Through a bizarre twist of economics, Josiah W Dogbolter was making immense profit on the planet by insuring that no factory actually made anything. Frobisher's ex-wife, the Whifferdill named Francine, manipulated events to display the joke, "You don't have to be crazy to work here, but it helps", on the computer terminals of Dogbolter's employees. This triggered communication and productivity, and ruined Dogbolter's operations. Frobisher resumed travelling with the sixth Doctor.

The seventh Doctor banished Death's Head to Earth in the year 8162.[895]

c 8162 - "Where Nobody Knows Your Name"[896] -> The eighth Doctor drank at a bar run by his old friend Frobisher, but as both had changed their appearance, neither recognized the other.

> = The sixth Doctor and Mel arrived on the Federation planet Marandnias, where the Doctor failed to prevent nuclear warfare. A group of Chronovores and Eternals, grateful for the Doctor's help in the Bophemeral affair, changed history to prevent Maradnias' destruction.[897]

Marandnias would become the centre of the Union.[898] After the great cybernetic massacres of the eighty-fifth century, sentient androids fell out of favour. From this point most robot servants were connected to a central webwork rather than being autonomous.

Eventually civil war broke out in the Galaxy, splitting the Federation into the Confederation, democratic rebels and the Humanic Empire ruled over by the Chen dynasty. Early in the war, Mirabilis had sided with the rebel forces, those opposed to the Emperor. The final battle of the war took place in the Mirabilis System. The democratic forces won, but the Imperial Fleet devastated Mirabilis itself with an atmospheric plasma burst that killed ninety percent of the population. Chen was captured and executed, ending the Chen dynasty.

In the aftermath of the Federation Civil War, the galaxy entered a new dark age in which scientific progress all but ceased. During the ninetieth century, the remnants of the Federation became the Union - a united political entity at peace with the Draconian Republic, the Cyberlord Hegemony and the radioactive remains of the Sontaran Empire. There were two other forces for unity: the Elective, a massive criminal organisation that controlled all criminal activity between New Alexandria and the Perseus Rift; and the Lazarus Intent, a religious organisation which now commanded eight quadrillion people.[899]

After around eight thousand years in the Time Corridor created by the Doctor, Sutekh finally perished at the beginning of the ninetieth century.[900]

? 9,000 - DREAMTIME[901] -> The seventh Doctor, Ace and Hex arrived at the Uluru as it traveled through space. The people's faith in the Dreaming had weakened, and the Dreaming began absorbing people into itself by turning them into stone. The Doctor accidentally traveled to the time of the solar flares and influenced the Uluru's departure from Earth. He returned and restored the people to normal, and it was hoped that the Dreaming's next attempt to terraform the Uluru would prove more successful.

The Antonine rescue raid on Scultiis in 9381 failed when the natives' electric fields disrupted their weapons.[902]

The story follows on from "Polly the Glot".
894 Dating *The Maltese Penguin* (BF #33 1/2) - No date is given, but this is clearly Frobisher's native time zone.
895 "The Crossroads of Time"
896 Dating "Where Nobody Knows Your Name" (*DWM* #329) - This is an unspecified amount of years after Frobisher has returned to his native time.
897 *The Quantum Archangel*
898 *The Quantum Archangel*. No date is given, but it's before the Federation splits.
899 *The Crystal Bucephalus*
900 *Pyramids of Mars*
901 Dating *Dreamtime* (BF #67) - Some "thousands of years" have passed since the Uluru departed into space. Simon Forward says it's possible that as much as 10,000 years have elapsed. This date is arbitrary.
902 *The Crystal Bucephalus*
903 Dating *The Scarlet Empress* (EDA #15) - The novel itself gives no dating clues, but the short story "Femme Fatale" (*More Short Trips*, 1999), also by Paul Magrs, has the Doctor and Sam encountering Iris after events in *The Scarlet Empress*. The short story occurs in 1968 (concurrent with the radical feminist Valerie Solanas shooting Andy Warhol), and Iris mentions to Sam that events on Hyspero took place "eight thousand years" ago. It's a little unclear whether she means eight thousand years in the past or the future - she might well mean the former, but the presence of Draconians, Ice Warriors and Spiridons (who presumably start space-travelling at some point after *Return of the Daleks*) on Hyspero would seem to indicate the latter.

Portions of "Femme Fatale" are obviously apocryphal (rendering "the Doctor and Mrs Jones" as agents of the British government, and eventually waking up on a *Prisoner*-style island), but the dating reference occurs in a section that is as canonical as one can get in a story

c 9968 - THE SCARLET EMPRESS[903] -> The planet Hyspero was visited at some point by hawk-like beings who were revered by the natives, yet had no interest in ruling the planet. They left behind Cassandra - the first Scarlet Empress, a jam-like creature in a jar - to look after their affairs. She built up the Scarlet Palace and founded the tattooed Scarlet Guard. A long line of Scarlet Empresses - Cassandra's descendents - ruled Hyspero, and the planet became home to an inter-stellar market.

The latest Scarlet Empress was a tyrant who conscripted Iris Wildthyme - who was dying, as she had eaten the flesh of a Kaled mutant - to reunite a mercenary band named "the Four". One of the group was guarding Cassandra, and the incumbent Empress sought to lay claim to her ancestor. The eighth Doctor and Sam helped Iris find the Four, whereupon Cassandra destroyed her descendent and reclaimed the throne. Iris went into a coma, but regenerated thanks to the healing properties of a life-restoring honey.

Around the end of the one-hundredth century, the Silurian scientists Ethra and Teelis worked on time-travel experiments. The results were published in the March 9978 edition of *Abstract Meanderings in Theoretical Physics*.[904]

The ArcHive studied the history of the universe, and served as vast repositories of knowledge. They had access to time-travel technology.[905] Emperor Brandt and the Cyberlord Hegemony possesed the ArcHive in the hundredth century.[906]

10764 - THE CRYSTAL BUCEPHALUS[907] -> In 10,753 Alexhendri Lassiter fulfilled on the Lazarus Intent, stabilising a time gate that rescued Lazarus from the Sontaran Throneworld before his death. But the truth about the false Messiah quickly became clear, and Arrestis seized control of the criminal Elective. Meanwhile, Lassiter and his brother Sebastian built the Crystal Bucephalus, a time-travel restaurant on the planet New Alexandria, which sent the galaxy's elite to the finest eating establishments in history.

Eleven years later, the Crystal Bucephalus was destroyed. Arrestis was revealed as Lazarus and escaped in a time gate, only to arrive back on Sontara moments before his execution.

Over the next century there was a galactic civil war.

c 11,000 - SYNTHESPIANS™[908] -> A fleet of ark ships fled the galactic civil war and passed through an area known as the Great Barrier. Cut off from the rest of the galaxy, the colonists found themselves in an area rich with natural resources. The New Earth Republic was founded, and included such planets as Bel Terra, New Alaska, New California, New Regency, Paxas and Tranicula in the Thomas Exultation (which was noted for its vineyards).

A hundred years later, the Republic was peaceful but boring. A business consortium failed in its bid to restore contact with the rest of the galaxy, but managed to pick up old TV broadcasts from twentieth-century Earth. These proved extremely popular and Reef Station One was built to produce new shows such as *As the Worlds Turn*, *Dreams of Tomorrow*, *Executive Desires*, *The Rep*, *Star Traveller: The Motion Picture*, *ReefEnders*, *Liberation Street*, *Confessions of a Monoid* and *This Evening With Phil and Bev*. The people of the Republic become obsessed with television.

A Time Lord force of War-TARDISes launched an attack against the Nestene home planet of Polymos. The mission was commanded by Lord Vansell, and destroyed swarms of energy units. The Nestene Consciousness attempted to relocate to the New Earth Republic. Plastic automata named Synthespians - in reality Autons - had been freely used to perform manual labour in the Republic, and those aboard Reef Station One instigated a slaughter. The sixth Doctor defeated the Nestene Consciousness and its Autons. The Consciousness was trapped in a plastic Replica body, forced to again and again act out the last episode of *Executive Desires*.

The Earth became habitable again. Humanity didn't recolonise its homeworld.[909] Cyberblind released their DTM *Machina ex Machina* in 11265.[910]

---

such as this.

904 *The Crystal Bucephalus*

905 *Killing Ground*. The ArcHivists first appeared in the reference book *Cybermen*.

906 *The Quantum Archangel*

907 Dating *The Crystal Bucephalus* (MA #4) - The Doctor claims they are "six or seven centuries into the tenth millennium" (p27), but also says that it is the "108th century" (p40, which is in the *eleventh* millennium). The latter date is correct - elsewhere we learn that "10,663" was in the recent past (p69). Although the novel doesn't specify the exact date, author Craig

Hinton assumed that it was set in the year 10,764 and I have adopted that date.

908 Dating *Synthespians™* (PDA #67) - The events of *The Crystal Bucephalus* were "several centuries" ago.

909 *The Ark in Space*. Vira notes that scientists had calculated it would be "five thousand years before the biosphere was viable" on Earth after the solar flares. In *The Sontaran Experiment*, we learn that humanity has spread across the galaxy, and that Earth has been habitable for "thousands of years" but has remained abandoned.

910 *The Also People* (p247).

The year 12005 was the time of the New Roman Empire.[911] The Union was replaced by the Junta, a military dictatorship that had developed from the Elective.[912]

The Union had previously remained a powerful force in the rest of the galaxy, although humanity was fragmented by civil war lasting centuries. The Union evolved into the Concordance, the Confederation, then the Junta. The Junta was a totalitarian regime ruled by the Chen dynasty. It attempted to invade the New Earth republic several centuries after the Auton incident, but was repelled. The New Earth Republic began intergalactic colonisation efforts, sending sleeper ships to the Wolf-Lundmark-Melotte galaxy and Andromeda.[913]

For a millennium there was barbarism, until a resurgent Confederation overthrew the Junta.[914]

? 15,000 - CITY AT WORLD'S END[915] -> An asteroid hit the moon of Sarath, changing its orbit so that it was now on a collision course with the planet. Ten years later, the first Doctor, Ian, Barbara and Susan arrived and found that preparations to build a rocket to evacuate the planet for the nearby Mirath were nearly complete. However, the Sarath leaders, based in the capital city of Arkhaven, had realised that the rocket ship could never fly and were only planning to save five hundred members of the elite.

The Doctor discovered that most of the population had been killed in a recent war and replaced by androids. This was a plot on the part of Monitor, the central computer in Arkhaven, to save itself before the planet's destruction. Monitor was destroyed, and the Doctor and Susan increased the capacity of the true escape rocket to save those they could.

w - The first land battle of the War between the Time Lords and the Enemy was fought on Dronid in the 155th century. It lasted a day, and was utterly devastating. The Time Lords used clockwork bacteria as a weapon. The Time Lords' attempts to cover their tracks after the battle wreaked almost as much harm as the battle itself, and became known by the inhabitants as "the Cataclysm". The Relic, said to be the Doctor's body, was recovered from the planet in 15,414. A misguided Faction Paradox member, Cousin Sanjira, cast the Relic into the Time Vortex and it arrived in the twenty-second century. The Faction made Sanjira murder his younger self as punishment.[916]

Return to Earth

c 16,000 - THE ARK IN SPACE[917] -> The colonists on Nerva were awoken, only to discover that the Wirrn had infested the Ark. The Wirrn were killed, and humanity prepared to reoccupy their homeworld. They intended to restock the planet with plant and animal life and to rebuild human civilisation.

& c 16,000 - THE SONTARAN EXPERIMENT[918] -> Field Major Styre of Sontaran G3 Intelligence conducted a Military Assessment Survey on Earth. The planet had acquired strategic value in the Sontarans' war with the accursed Rutans, and was believed to be devoid of intelligent life. Styre conducted experiments on Gal Sec colonists that he lured to the planet, but the fourth Doctor and Harry Sullivan killed him.

---

911 According to the Doctor in *The End of the World*. This would seem to fall at the time Earth was thought to be abandoned by humanity following the solar flares. Perhaps the New Roman Empire wasn't based on Earth, or there was a shortlived resettlement of the planet.
912 *The Crystal Bucephalus*
913 *Synthespians™*, elaborating on what we learned in *The Crystal Bucephalus*.
914 *The Crystal Bucephalus*
915 Dating *City at World's End* (PDA #25) - This is an arbitrary date, although we are told it is "thousands of years" after Ian and Barbara's native time.
916 *Alien Bodies*
917 Dating *The Ark in Space* (12.2) - Harry twice suggests that they are "ten thousand years" after the time of the Solar Flares, and the Doctor confirms this in *The Sontaran Experiment*, which takes place immediately afterwards.
    The Terrestrial Index set the stories between "15,000 and 20,000". *The TARDIS Logs* suggested a date of

"28,537". *Cybermen* offered the year "?14714". *The TARDIS Special* gave the date "c.131st Century".
918 Dating *The Sontaran Experiment* (12.3) - The story immediately follows *The Ark in Space*.
919 Dating *The Eye of the Tyger* (TEL #12) - The dating is more than a little confused. The Doctor says this is "a million and a half years" in Fyne's future (p28), but the blurb says it's the "32nd century".
    It's clearly after the solar flares referred to in *The Ark in Space*, so for more information see the dating for that story.
920 *Genesis of the Daleks*. It's a presumption that "Space Year 17,000" is the same as 17,000AD.
921 Inter Minor is in the Acteon Group, as is Metebelis III (*Carnival of Monsters*), although it is later referred to as the Acteon Galaxy (*The Green Death, Planet of the Spiders*).
    The Isop Galaxy is the location of Vortis (*The Web Planet, Twilight of the Gods*), the home of the Face of Boe (according to *Bad Wolf*) and possibly the Slitheen (*Boom Town* refers to "venom grubs" - as they're called

& c 16,000 - THE EYE OF THE TYGER[919] **->** Just after the people aboard Nerva had begun to resettle the Earth, a feline race arrived and helped the reconstruction efforts. Soon, though, some humans turned against the aliens, who left with ten thousand humans to find a new home. They were lured to settle on planets within a black hole by the avatars of their descendants, the Conservers, who existed in the black hole billions of years in the future.

The Dalek War against Venus in Space Year 17,000 was halted by the intervention of a fleet of War Rockets from the planet Hyperon. The rockets were made of a metal completely resistant to Dalek firepower. The Dalek taskforce was completely destroyed.[920]

The Far Future

In the far future, humanity's influence was felt in other galaxies such as Andromeda, Acteon, Isop, Artoro and the Anterides.[921]

? 16,000 - TOMB OF VALDEMAR[922] **->** The Second Empire rose, with its origins on the human colony world of Dephys. The cruel, oppressive Elite ruled it. The Empire fell after a civil war to the New Protectorate, led by the Virgin Lady High Protector, the Civil Matriarch, who had the Elite's palaces destroyed with Immolator Six capsules. A Duke named Paul Neville fled to Terra and became a powerful magician, the head of a cult dedicated to the dark god Valdemar. The Protectorate located Neville, forcing him to flee to the ends of the collapsing Empire. Neville sought the planet Ashkellia, which he believed contained the palace of the Old Ones - Valdemar was the last of their kind.

Neville attempted to resurrect Valdemar through an adolescent psionic named Huvan, but the fourth Doctor and Romana defeated his plans. Huvan nearly punctured the higher dimensions, which could have destroyed the universe, but the Doctor and Romana convinced Huvan that he lacked the maturity for such power. Huvan agreed to erase his memory and assume a new identity on another planet. He became a trapper named Ponch on the planet Janus Forus. Fifteen years later in Huvan's lifetime, Romana returned to help him remember his past. She regenerated at this time.

The New Protectorate lasted around a century or two before burning itself out.

The Gods of Light conducted experiments on Vortis. They replaced the core with a propulsion system, and kidnapped the Menoptra from their home planet.[923]

The Aapex Corporation, based on Mina Fourteen, started a genetics experiment on the planet Nooma to further terraforming and bio-engineering on low-gravity planets. Nooma's sun was an Aapex spaceship, and the planet's artificial "Sky" - actually a sentient being programmed to regulate Nooma's biosphere - formed a protective shell around the planet.

Biology on Nooma became such that humanoids developed in the forest as carnivorous children, but mature males would fight to the death. The winners underwent genetic "Promotion", which entailed their growing wings and joining the flying "naieen", but the losers would reanimate as infertile cadavers named the Dead. The naieen would mate, causing their seed to fall on the forest and bud new children.[924]

Around 18,500, Earth was abandoned once again.[925] The Aapex Corporation went bankrupt. Nooma was abandoned to its own fate.[926]

? 20,000 - THE WEB PLANET[927] **->** The planet Vortis in the Isop Galaxy was the home of the moth-like Menoptra, who worshipped in glorious temples of light and lived in the flower forests. They kept an ant-like race, the Zarbi, as cattle. The planet was invaded by the Animus, an entity that could absorb all forms of energy, and which pulled three planetoids - including the planet Pictos - into orbit around Vortis. Most of the Menoptra fled to Pictos, but the descendants of those that stayed behind slowly devolved into sightless dwarfs, the Optera. The Animus used the Zarbi as soldiers, and had dreams of galactic conquest until the

---

in *The Web Planet* novelisation; they're named "larvae guns" in the TV version). Artoro and the Anterides are referred to in *Planet of Evil*.
922 Dating *Tomb of Valdemar* (PDA #29) - No date is given, but Earth is occupied and humanity has a second galactic empire. This date would slot the story between two points where Earth is abandoned (*The Ark in Space* and *Birthright*), and ties in with the Animus' statement in *The Web Planet* that Earth has "mastery of space".
923 "Thousands of years" before *Twilight of the Gods*.

924 "Four thousand years ago" according to *Speed of Flight*.
925 *Birthright*
926 "2347.54 years" before *The Speed of Flight*.
927 Dating *The Web Planet* (2.5) - The story seems to take place in the future as the Animus craves "Earth's mastery of Space". Bill Strutton's novelisation places it in "20,000", although the Doctor suggests that the TARDIS' "time pointer" might not be working. The New Adventure *Birthright* suggests that Earth is abandoned at this time, but it is established in *The Ark in Space* and

first Doctor, Ian, Barbara and Vicki arrived. The Animus was destroyed by the Isop-tope, a Menoptra weapon.

New Rhumos broke away from Rhumos Prime, which marked the beginning of a lengthy conflict.[928]

c 20,192 - TWILIGHT OF THE GODS[929] **->** After the Animus' defeat, the planet Vortis had wandered into the Rhumos System. Two Rhumon factions, the Imperials and the Republicans, fought for control of the planet. A year later, the second Doctor, Jamie and Victoria arrived just as a seed of the first Animus emerged. The Doctor brought the Rhumons and Menoptera together and helped to destroy the new Animus. The Gods of Light who had engineered Vortis agreed to stop interfering in its affairs, and it was hoped that Vortis could peacefully co-exist with its Rhumon neighbors.

? - "The Naked Flame"[930] **->** The fourth Doctor and Sarah landed on Vortis, where a glowing crystal was attracting Menoptra to their deaths. The Doctor shattered it with his sonic screwdriver.

Carbon-dating suggested that *The Worshipful and Ancient Law of Gallifrey* was written around 22,000 AD.[931]

c 22,000 - BIRTHRIGHT[932] **->** For three thousand four hundred and ninety seven years, the insect-like Charrl had occupied the planet Anthykhon, which was far from the major space lanes. Their vast hive pumped ammonia into the already-depleted atmosphere, the planet's ozone layer had been depleted, the seas had dried up, and the soil was barren. The native life, the Hairies, survived by adapting to this environment.

The Charrl were not savages - indeed they had created over three hundred of the six hundred and ninety-nine wonders of the universe - before coming to this world to escape solar flares on their own planet. The Charrls made contact with Muldwych, a mysterious time-traveller exiled to Anthykhon at this time, and together they attempted to traverse the Great Divide back into the past on Earth. Muldwych came to regret his association with the Charrls and foiled their plans. He remained on Anthykhon in exile. Anthykhon was Earth during one of the several periods when the planet was isolated and forgotten.

c 22,000 - SPEED OF FLIGHT[933] **->** The third Doctor, Jo and Mike Yates landed on Nooma. The Dead assaulted the planet's artificial sun, working on pre-programmed instructions to seek a means of terminating the Nooma experiment to protect Aapex's trade secrets. The Doctor tapped the sun's databanks and found a message from Aapex granting the citizens of Nooma independence, restoring social order on the planet.

The shafts of the Great Pyramid would align with the constellation of Orion around 23000.[934]

? - "The Gift"[935] **->** The sixth Doctor went back to the point that a Zofton deep space load lugger had crashed on the moon of Zazz, and observed as - over the next fifty years - the surviving robot rebuilt and survived, eventually building self-replicating replacements for itself. Within twenty generations, they had a functioning civilisation.

A natural disaster on the moon of Zazz wiped out the machine civilisation there. The few survivors would lie dormant for two thousand years.[936]

The Sontaran Experiment that man has spread through the universe.

928 "Over a hundred and fifty years" before *Twilight of the Gods*.

929 Dating *Twilight of the Gods* (MA #26) - This is a sequel to *The Web Planet*. The Animus was defeated "seventy thousand days ago" (p1), which is a little under one hundred and ninety two years.

930 Dating "The Naked Flame" (*DWM Yearbook 1995*) - It's an unspecified amount of time after *The Web Planet*.

931 *Shada*. Chris Parsons' dating of the book gives a figure of "minus twenty thousand years", with time running backwards over the book. This might be a property of the book, rather than an indication it comes from the future.

932 Dating *Birthright* (NA #17) - Ace says she was born "Oh, probably about twenty thousand years ago" (p134), although how she reaches this figure is unclear.

It is "year 2959" of the Charrl occupation of Earth (p1) when they start their scheme, which will take "almost five hundred years" (p60), yet curiously it is "year 2497" (p109) when they finish! This is presumably a misprint, and ought to read "3497".

933 Dating *Speed of Flight* (MA #27) - This is "about twenty thousand years" after Jo's time (p23).

934 "Twenty one thousand years" after *The Sands of Time* (p122).

935 Dating "The Gift" (*DWM* #123-126) - It's "twelve thousand years" before the main events of "The Gift".

936 "Two thousand years" before "The Gift".

937 Dating "The Gift" (*DWM* #123-126) - No date is given, but the people of Zazz are the "distant descendants of an Earth colony".

938 Dating *The Face of Evil* (14.4) - The story could take place at any point in the far future. The Doctor states in *The Invisible Enemy* that the year 5000 is the time of

? - "The Gift"[937] **->** By now, Zazz was a planet heavily-influenced by the Jazz Era of Earth, and the sixth Doctor, Peri and Frobisher accepted an invitation to the twenty-first birthday bash for the Lorduke of Zazz.

The TARDIS first landed at the retreat of the Lorduke's brother, Professor Strut, who was a mad scientist exiled after crashing an experimental moon rocket on the city. They agreed to take a gift... which turned out to be a surviving self-replicating robot. Strut found the robot on the Moon, but didn't understand the danger. The robots began breeding, and collected raw materials to rebuild their civilisation on Zazz. The Doctor used the musicians of Zazz to duplicate the robot's recall signal, luring them to Strut's island. They boarded the moon rocket, and were blasted off into space.

? - THE FACE OF EVIL[938] **->** A Mordee colony ship landed on an unnamed world and developed a computer failure. The fourth Doctor helped their descendants by linking the computer to his own mind, but he neglected to remove his personality print from the data core. As a result, the computer became schizophrenic.

Centuries later, the colonists worshipped the computer as Xoanon. It had split them into two groups: the "Sevateem", the savage descendants of Survey Team Six; and the Tesh, formerly the technicians, to whom Xoanon granted psychic powers. Xoanon was thus attempting to breed superhumans, but the fourth Doctor returned and made a reverse transfer, curing the computer's multiple personality disorder. Leela, a warrior of the Sevateem, left with the Doctor.

? - LAST MAN RUNNING[939] **->** Class warfare was brewing between the First Planet's "firsters" and the Second Planet's lowly "toodys". An Out System Investigation Group (OIG) was sent to a forest plane to look for a toody weapons manufacturer. The OIG team, the fourth Doctor and Leela got caught in a Last Man Running complex, a simulated environment built by the Lentic race to find and clone the ultimate warrior. Leela destroyed the forcefield surrounding the complex, and the OIG bombed it.

37,166 - PLANET OF EVIL[940] **->** A Morestran survey team arrived on Zeta Minor, searching for an energy source as their home planet was facing disaster. Zeta Minor was a planet on the edge of the universe, beyond Cygnus A, as distant from the Artoro Galaxy as that is from the Anterides.

The Morestran team discovered that a black pool on Zeta Minor was connected to an incomprehensible universe of anti-matter. As a result, it was impossible to remove anything from the planet without incurring the wrath of powerful creatures native to the anti-matter universe. The fourth Doctor and Sarah helped the Morestrans to survive the experience and return home.

The Doctor off-handedly suggested to Professor Sorenson that he explore the energy potential of the kinetic forces involved in planetary movement.

c 39,164 - ZETA MAJOR[941] **->** Morestra was abandoned, and the fleet set off on a search for a new home planet. A suitable home was located in the Beta System forty months later, and the city of Archetryx was founded there. The New Church Calendar began and the Sorenson Academy was established.

A hundred years later, work commenced on the Torre del Oro, a structure that would extract energy from planetary motion, but which would take fifteen hundred years to build. The dematerialisation beam was invented after several more centuries. Great Technology Wars were fought as the Cult of Science schismed.

A few years before the Torre del Oro was due to be completed, the Grand Council of Cardinals discovered errors in the equations - the Torre del Oro wouldn't work. To

---

Leela's ancestors. This story, then, takes place at least ten generations after that - the crew of the colony ship were stranded for "generations" before the Doctor first helped them, and there have apparently been seven generations since (the Sevateem seem to attack the barrier once a generation, and this is the seventh attempt).

Humans evolve limited psychic powers around the time of the fifty-first century (*The Talons of Weng-Chiang*) and the Tesh have psychic powers, so they might originate after that time, but they probably receive all their abilities from Xoanon's selective breeding programme.

In *The Sun Makers*, the Usurian computer correctly guesses that "Sevateem" is a corruption of "Survey Team", and that Leela comes from a "degenerate, unsup-

ported Tellurian colony" suggesting that there are many such planets known to the Company. *The Terrestrial Index* set the story "several centuries" after the "52nd Century". *The TARDIS Logs* offered the date "4931", *Timelink* "6000".

939 Dating *Last Man Running* (PDA #15) - The story could take place at any time in the far future.

940 Dating *Planet of Evil* (13.2) - While it could be argued that the date "37,166" that appears on the grave marker might use some Morestran scale of dating, the Doctor does state that the TARDIS has overshot contemporary London by "thirty thousand years". *The Dimension Riders* and *Infinite Requiem* both suggest that the Morestrans are not human, which is possible (although they do know of Earth). The Doctor's suggestion to Sorenson leads to events in *Zeta Major*.

cover up this failure, they dispatched an expedition to extract anti-matter from Zeta Minor, and the Zeta Project was established on the nearby Zeta Major. By that point Morestran territory spanned eighty million light years and contained one thousand four hundred and twenty-seven inhabited star systems, but the energy crisis meant that eight hundred and ninety-two of them, the Outer Systems, were beyond the Empire's reach.

Students of the Sorenson Academy started vanishing, part of the cover up of the Torre del Oro debacle. The fifth Doctor, Tegan and Nyssa arrived at the tower, discovering that it was full of anti-matter. Soon after, anti-matter creatures started a rampage. A State of Crisis was declared and old political and religious rivalries re-emerged. The Zeta Project was destroyed. The Doctor once again negotiated with the creatures of anti-matter and returned all the plundered material to its original universe.

At this time, a new breed of Zamps should be ready to conquer the universe.[942]

c 50,000 - HEART OF TARDIS[943] **->** The fourth Doctor and Romana found and rescued K9, who had become an exhibit at the Collectors' Big Huge and Educational Collection of Old Galactic Stuff.

Circa 102,890, the white hole seedling from Albert was supposed to blossom into maturity.[944]

The Daleks were the greatest threat in the universe ... until one day, when they just vanished. Eventually they became mere legends. Unknown to humanity, they had left to fight the Last Great Time War with the Time Lords, a conflict that all but wiped out both races.[945]

The Daleks were part of the history of the First Segment of Time.[946] One Dalek ship, containing the Emperor, survived the Last Great Time War. It arrived at the edge of Earth's solar system, remaining hidden. For centuries, the Daleks would harvest the dregs and unwanted of humanity, building Daleks from their genetic material. The Emperor Dalek meddled in humanity's affairs and sought ways to slow its development. It became convinced it was god, and the Daleks worshipped him.[947]

? - "War of the Words"[948] **->** The war between the Vromyx and the Garynths had been raging for forty-seven point six three years. The conflict blocked access to the library planet Biblios, where all universal knowledge was stored by legions of robots. The warring factions wanted to access details of superweapons, then deny it to their opponents. The fourth Doctor blew up an empty building, telling both sides it was where the records were kept, and the rivals withdrew.

200,000 - THE LONG GAME[949] **->** It was the age of the Fourth Great and Bountiful Human Empire. Earth was at its height: the hub of a domain stretching across a

---

941 Dating *Zeta Major* (PDA #13) - It is 1998 by the New Church Calendar (p82), and that long since *Planet of Evil*.
942 Forty-two thousand years after *Zamper* (p249).
943 Dating *Heart of TARDIS* (PDA #32) - There's no specific date, but it is "some tens of thousands of years beyond the twentieth century".
944 "A hundred millennia" after *Grimm Reality*.
945 "Thousands of years" before *The Parting of the Ways*. It's unclear exactly when this occurs. Captain Jack knows about the Daleks' disappearance, but as he's also a time traveller; it doesn't mean this happened before his native time. It's after "Space Year 17,000", historically the last recorded reference to the Daleks before *Bad Wolf*.

It's also unclear what this "vanishing" entails - the Doctor seems amazed that he meets a Dalek in *Dalek*, suggesting that they've been erased from history (would he, for example, have been surprised to meet one around 2164 on Earth, during their invasion?). However, Captain Jack recognises their ships in *Bad Wolf*, and the inhabitants of 200,100 both know the Daleks' name and that they vanished. Perhaps the simplest solution is that the new-style, gold Daleks that

make their debut in *Dalek* are "Time War Era" Daleks, and so none of them should exist after the Time War.
946 *The Ark*

THE SEGMENTS OF TIME: The Commander in *The Ark* states "Nero, the Trojan Wars, the Daleks ... all that happened in the First Segment of Time." References in that story to the Tenth and Twenty-Seventh Segments are noted later in this book. *The Well-Mannered War* is set in the Fifty-Eighth.

It's unclear whether a Segment is measured purely mathematically. A "century" has to mean "a hundred years". If a Segment is a fixed period of time, then as *The Ark* is set ten million years in the future, this might suggest fifty-seven equal segments of around 175,000 years).

Equally, the term might mark a specific era with distinct cultural or even physical features (like, say, "Victorian" or "Ice Age"). What would mark the beginning or end of a Segment? Would the boundary be formally defined and obvious (like say that of "the tenth Olympiad", or "the Leptonic Era"), even if it was open to a degree of interpretation (we can speak of "the Second World War", even though the exact moment it started and ended depends on which country you're from and

million planets, covered with megacities, possessing five moons and a population of ninety-six billion.

A sandstorm on the New Venus Archipelago left two hundred dead. There were water riots in Glasgow. The Face of Boe was known to the people of Earth, and announced that he was pregnant with a Baby Boemina. The Mighty Jagrafess of the Holy Hadrojassic Maxarodenfoe was manipulating humanity by controlling its news media from Satellite Five, which broadcast six hundred channels. This held back humanity's development, and made it fearful of immigrants. The ninth Doctor and Rose defeated the Jagrafess, and the Doctor expected that humanity's development would accelerate back to normal without the its interference.

Adam, a companion of the Doctor and Rose, tried to acquire knowledge from the future and download it to his own time in 2012. The Doctor discovered Adam's intentions and returned him home.

After Satellite Five was put out of commission, the information feed to Earth stopped. The government and economy collapsed. A hundred years of hell ensued.[950] The Great Atlantic Smog Storm started in 200,080. On some days, it wasn't possible to breathe the air. The storm raged for at least twenty years.[951]

200,100 - BAD WOLF / THE PARTING OF THE WAYS[952] -> The Earth was now divided into continents that included Europa, Pacifica, the New American Alliance and Australasia. Default payments were made to Martian Drones. The Great Cobalt Pyramid was built on the remains of the famous Torchwood Institute. The Great Central Ravine was named after the "ancient" British city of Sheffield. Stella Popbait made hats. There was a penal colony on the Moon.

"Jupiter Rising" was a holo-series. The dish gaffabeck had originated on the planet Lucifer. By this point, the Face of Boe was the oldest inhabitant of the Isop Galaxy.

Humanity watched savage game shows such as *Big Brother*, *Call My Bluff* (with real guns), *Countdown* (where the aim was to defuse a bomb), *Ground Force* (contestants were turned to compost), *Wipeout*, *Stars in Your Eyes* (contestants were blinded), *What Not to Wear* (androids mutilated people), *Bear with Me* (contestants lived with a bear) and *The Weakest Link* (overseen by the dreaded Anne Droid). These were produced by the Bad Wolf Corporation, broadcast on ten thousand channels and filmed aboard the former Satellite Five, now called the Game Station.

Losing contestants were apparently vaporised, but in truth were teleported away and secretly converted into Daleks. The ranks of the Emperor Dalek's army swelled. The human, slaved Controller overseeing this operation sought out the Daleks' greatest enemy to help, and transmatted the ninth Doctor, Captain Jack and Rose to the Game Station.

The Doctor discovered the Daleks' machinations, and the Emperor mobilized his forces against Earth. Dalek missiles bombarded many of the continents, with enough force to alter their very shape. The Doctor briefly sent Rose to safety in her native time, but Rose gazed into the heart of the TARDIS and thus became endowed with the power of the Time Vortex. She gained the godlike ability to alter time, and used it to destroy the Emperor and his Daleks. The Doctor sacrificed his life to stop the Vortex energies from consuming Rose, and regenerated as a result. Jack was left behind on the Game Station, and used his vortex manipulator to travel to the nineteenth century.

---

how you define terms)?

Timelink offers the theory that as Zentos refers to the "the Fifty-Seventh Segment of Earth life" and the Commander says "The Earth also is dying, we have left it for the last time", that Earth has been "left" before, and each Segment ends with the abandonment of Earth. It's neat and, as noted elsewhere in this book, Earth is certainly totally evacuated more than once. However, *Bad Wolf* and *The Parting of the Ways* have the Daleks active after the first abandonment of Earth, and, if the Commander is right, they were only part of the history of the First Segment.

947 *The Parting of the Ways*. The Controller says the Daleks have been there for "hundreds and hundreds of years", the Doctor says "generations", and the Emperor Dalek says "centuries passed".

948 Dating "War of the Words" (*DWM* #51) - The story is set after the twentieth century, because parliamentary

records from that period are stored here. The head librarian robot has just had his two thousand year service, suggesting the facility has been around for millennia. Beyond that, no date is specified, so this is completely arbitrary.

949 Dating *The Long Game* (X1.7) - The Doctor gives the date. It's established in *Bad Wolf* and *The Parting of the Ways* that the Jagrafess was a tool of the Daleks.

950 *Bad Wolf*

951 "Twenty years" before *Bad Wolf*, according to the *Big Brother* contestant Lynda Moss.

952 Dating *Bad Wolf* / *The Parting of the Ways* (X1.12-1.13) - The Doctor says in *Bad Wolf* that "it's the year two-zero-zero-one-zero-zero", and the opening caption says it is "one hundred years" after *The Long Game*. Lynda says the Game Station has ten thousand channels, although the Doctor's *Big Brother* game is broadcast on Channel 44,000. Lucifer is (almost certainly) the

309,906 - THE WAR GAMES[953] -> A race of alien warlords attempted to raise an army of galactic conquest by programming human soldiers kidnapped from various points in history with stolen Time Lord technology. A renegade Time Lord named the War Chief aided them, and was shot during an uprising engineered by the second Doctor, Jamie and Zoe. When the plan was uncovered, the Time Lords erected a forcefield that confined the aliens to their planet. The kidnapped soldiers were returned home, with no awareness of these events. The Time Lords also dematerialised the aliens' leader, the War Lord.

309,906 - THE EIGHT DOCTORS[954] -> The eighth Doctor rescued his second incarnation and encouraged him to summon the Time Lords to deal with the War Lords.

The War Chief was horrifically injured rather than killed. He was sent to the War Lords' home planet, but his regeneration aborted and his new form was disfigured. He allied with the son of the War Chief, and after many years, they broke through the force field the Time Lords had placed around the War Lords' home planet. They revived their dreams of galactic conquest, and decided to concentrate on helping Nazi Germany.[955]

Around 315,000, humans encroached on the territory of the Sulumians in the eighth dimension. The Sulumians began a time travel campaign dedicated to rewriting human history to prevent this.[956] In 365,509, the collapse of a star in NGC4258 destroyed four civilisations. A region of space warps, the Grey Interchange, was created.[957]

Around 436,000, Earth was caught in the crossfire of a war between Kallix Grover and the Sine Wave Shrine of Shillitar. A magnetic wave shut down all digital technology, cutting Earth off from its colonies. This was the Great Retrenchment.[958]

438,533 (2nd October) - ONLY HUMAN[959] -> Following the Great Retrenchment, humans mastered the biological and chemical sciences to the point they could take apart the human body and put it back together without ill effects. All emotions were regulated, and - apart from the dissident Refusers - no human ever worried about anything.

"Half a million years of industrial progress" had left the Earth's surface as "just a chemical slime". The Ancient One, a Haemovore, was the last living creature to inhabit an Earth.[960]

Lady Ruath showed Yarven, the Vampire Messiah, that mankind was destined to become a vampire race. The Haemovores lived in the sea, where they ganged up to hunt whales.[961]

---

planet featured in *Lucifer Rising*. It's unclear whether Rose used her power to restore anyone or anything other than Captain Jack - it's not stated that she, for example, reset the devastated Earth. Jack's journey to the nineteenth century is referenced in *Utopia*.

THE EARTH EMPIRES: The first Earth Empire lasted from the twenty-sixth century of *Frontier in Space* to the thirtieth of *The Mutants* and has been well documented, particularly in the New Adventures (the Doctor's companion Benny was from the early period, Ace lived in that time zone for several years and his later companions Chris and Roz were from the period when the Empire was starting to collapse).

The Second Empire was named in *Tomb of Valdemar*, and could well be the human empire mentioned in *The Sontaran Experiment*.

There's been no reference specifically to the Third.

The Long Game is set, in theory at least, at the time of The Fourth Great and Bountiful Human Empire, but the Emperor Dalek's machinations appear to alter history, and the apparent obliteration of Earth's continents casts doubt on whether this Empire ever comes to pass. If Rose reset all the actions of the Daleks, Earth's history could be restored to the one the Doctor knows about, but there's no evidence on screen she did that.

Either way, the overwhelming amount of evidence suggests that Earth survives and continues to have great influence on the universe, at least for billions of years into the future (*The End of the World*). It's probable, then, that there's a fifth and many more Empires after this point.

953 Dating *The War Games* (6.7) - It is stated that humanity has been killing itself for "half a million years" before this story takes place, which (coincidentally) ties up with the date 309,906 established for the Doctor's first trial (or "Malfeasance Tribunal") in *The Deadly Assassin*. The TARDIS Logs suggested a date of "48,063" for this story, *Apocrypha* offered "5950 AD".

The aliens in this story are unnamed on screen, yet they're referred to as "the War Lords" in *The War Games* novelisation by Malcolm Hulke, *The Making of Doctor Who* 1972 edition, the Lofficier *Programme Guide*, and *Timewyrm: Exodus* by Terrance Dicks. They're simply "Aliens" in the 1973 *Radio Times Special*. As both Hulke and Dicks independently use the name "War Lords" in their other work, it has been adopted in this volume to avoid confusion with other unnamed alien races.

HOW MANY WAR ZONES ARE THERE?: *The War Games* establishes that the aliens have "ten" zones under their control (this is emphasised by the map we see), including the Control Zone. However, fourteen distinct war zones are referred to, meaning there are at least fifteen zones (the dates in quotes are explicitly given on screen): W.W.I ("1917"), The Roman Zone ("two thou-

? 802,701 - TIMELASH[962] -> The third Doctor and Jo visited Karfel, preventing a great famine there. The Doctor also reported the scientist Magellan, who had been conducting unethical experiments on the reptilian Morlox, to the praesidium.

Over the next century, an accident with the substance Mustakozene caused Magellan to merge with a Morlox and became the mutated Borad. He took control of Karfel, enforcing discipline with an army of androids and the threat of exile into a time corridor, the Timelash. The Borad planned to provoke a war with neighbouring Bandril as a means of populating the planet with mutated clones of himself. Following the arrival of the sixth Doctor and Peri, the Borad was thrown into the Timelash, ending up in Loch Ness in the twelfth century.

Man fought the Primal Wars in the Tenth Segment of Time. Much scientific knowledge was lost during this period, including the cure for the common cold.[963]

? - "The Neutron Knights"[964] -> Earth had endured in a long chain of catastrophes, and the last link in this was an invasion by the Neutron Knights. Earth's defences were overrun by forces led by the great mutant Catavolcus, who had previously breached the gates of Hell. Earth was a shattered world where only the strong survived.

The fourth Doctor was summoned to a fortress on Earth by the force of will of a mysterious bearded figure, who had himself previously been summoned through time to fight Earth's last battle. Catavolcus wanted the Dragon - a vast nuclear fission device as powerful as the Sun. He broke into the fortress, despite the best efforts of the castle's defender, Arthur. The mysterious summoner was Merlin, who set the Dragon to overload as Arthur fell to Catavolcus and his sword of flame. The Doctor and Merlin retreated to the TARDIS as the fortress - and Catavolcus - were destroyed. The Doctor woke in a forest, unsure what has happened. Merlin contacted him and warned that their paths were destined to cross once more.

Glitz's Time

The criminal Kane was guilty of systematic acts of violence and extortion with his lover Sana, who killed herself rather than face trial. Kane was exiled from his home planet of Proammon, and sent to the barren planet Svartos. He remained there for three thousand

---

sand years" before 1917), The Franco-Prussian War (1870-1871), the 30 Years War (1618-1648), The Jacobite Rebellion ("1745"), The English Civil War (1642-1646), The Boer War (1899-1902), The American Civil War ("1862"), Napoleon's advance into Russia ("1812"), The Russo-Japanese War ("1905"), the Boxer Rising (1900), the Crimean War (1853-1856), the Mexican Uprising (1867) and the Greek Zone (c.500 BC).

954 Dating *The Eight Doctors* (EDA #1) - This happens during *The War Games*.

955 The War Chief is shot in *The War Games*, and reappears in *Timewyrm: Exodus*.

956 "Three hundred and seventeen thousand years" after 40 BC, according to *The Gallifrey Chronicles*.

957 *The English Way of Death*

958 *Only Human*

959 Dating *Only Human* (NSA #5) - The Doctor calculates the precise date.

960 "Half a million years" after *The Curse of Fenric*. When the Reverend Wainwright asks the Doctor how he knows about the Haemovores' future, the Doctor says "I've seen it". Some commentators (including *The Discontinuity Guide* and the previous editions of this chronology) have presumed that the Haemovore timeline was created when the Ancient One poisoned the Earth, and erased when he / she refrained from doing so, but this isn't actually said on screen. The Doctor attributes the Haemovore era to "half a million years of industrial progress", not something as sudden and cataclysmic as a single chemical release.

The next story to deal with Earth is *The Mysterious Planet*, set around the year two million - meaning that if the Haemovore timeline is "real", there are 1.5 million years for the dying Earth, "its surface a chemical slime", to recover. It perhaps sounds like a cheat to assume the Earth could simply "get over" such a catastrophe, but it's no less plausible than the idea that humanity's homeworld recuperates after the Daleks bombard it with enough firepower to change the shape of the very continents (in *The Parting of the Ways*, set in 200,100).

961 *Goth Opera*, in which Ruath says the Haemovore timeline is a "possible future" (p44).

962 Dating *Timelash* (22.5) - No date is given on screen. I have arbitrarily set it in the same year that the Time Traveller met the Eloi and the Morlocks in H.G. Wells' *The Time Machine*. There is no indication on screen exactly when the third Doctor visited Karfel; the novelisation suggests it was "at least one hundred years" before this story, during the time of Katz's grandfather.

963 *The Ark*

964 Dating "The Neutron Knights" (*DWM* #60) - No date is given, but if it truly is Earth's last battle, the story would seem to be set either before *The Ark* or somewhere in vast gap between that story and *The End of the World*. The Doctor speculates that "past and future are flowing into the same event", which doesn't really help. It doesn't seem to be set during the Millenium Wars. While the link isn't made in either story, I've placed it during the "Primal Wars" mentioned in *The Ark*.

years, slowly building his powerbase and dreaming of a return to his homeworld.

Unknown to Kane, Proammon was destroyed when its star went supernova a thousand years after his exile. Kane operated from the trading post of Iceworld, which was capable of spaceflight. This required the Dragonfire, a source of energy contained within the head of the Dragon - a biomechanoid sent to Svartos to prevent Kane from escaping the planet. Kane remained trapped on Iceworld.[965]

Sabalom Glitz came from Salostopus in Andromeda. He was an habitual jailbird and thief, always on the lookout for a fast grotzi.[966]

c 2,000,000 - THE MYSTERIOUS PLANET[967] -> A group of Earth-based Andromedans stole scientific secrets contained in the Matrix of the Time Lords and took shelter on Earth. By order of the High Council, the Magnotron was used to move the Earth and its entire constellation two light years, destroying everyone on the surface. The planet became known as Ravolox. The Andromedans, though, knew that the Time Lords had discovered them and had built a survival chamber. They entered suspended animation, awaiting rescue. The robot recovery mission sent to retrieve the Andromedans missed the Earth in its new location and sped on into the depths of space.

After five hundred years, this survival shelter had become Marb Station, a completely self-contained system. Station guards maintained strict water rationing and population control. The population worshipped "the Immortal" - a being that lived in a citadel within their complex, and which was actually the robot caretaker of the facility, Drathro. The Earth's surface became viable again and served as home to "The Tribe of the Free" - a few primitive humans who had escaped from Marb Station. They worshipped the god Haldron, and killed any space traveller trying to steal his totem, a black light converter made from pure siligtone. They believed their ancestors' space travel had brought down the wrath of their god and caused the solar fireball.

Glitz formed a business partnership with the renegade Time Lord the Master, who knew that Earth had been moved and renamed Ravolox by the High Council. Glitz's accomplice was a young man, Dibber. The Master sent Dibber and Glitz to Ravolox to retrieve the Matrix files.

The sixth Doctor arrived and defeated Drathro, allowing the two communities of humans to make contact.

The Time Lords subsequently restored Earth to its correct location.[968] Thanks to a timestorm engineered by Fenric, Ace arrived on the ice planet of Svartos. Glitz used his ship, the *Nosferatu*, to raid space freighters. He ended up on Svartos with a rotten cargo and a mutinous crew, and tried to sell both to Kane.[969]

After this time, the Andromeda Galaxy fell under the rule of The One, a vast artificial intelligence that contained the memories and experiences of all Andromedans.[970]

c 2,000,000 - DRAGONFIRE[971] -> On the trading colony Iceworld, located on the dark side of Svartos, Kane was assembling an army. He put his soldiers into cryosleep, which robbed their memories of their former life and insured they would serve him without question.

Others chose to serve Kane willingly... Kane, whose natural body temperature was minus 193 Celsius, would burn the Mark of the Sovereign onto the palm of their right hand. One of Kane's officers, Belazs, joined

---

965 *Dragonfire*

966 *The Mysterious Planet*

967 Dating *The Mysterious Planet* (23.1) - The Doctor consults his pocket watch and suggests that it is "two million years" after Peri's time. Both the camera script and the novelisation confirm this date. *The Terrestrial Index* attempted to rationalise the various "ends of the Earth" seen in the series, but in doing so it ignored virtually every date given on screen. It is claimed, for example, that this story was set "c.14,500". *The TARDIS Special* gave the date as "two billion" AD, an understandable mishearing of the Doctor's line. *About Time* speculates that this is the same destruction of Earth seen in *The Ark* (the first Doctor was confused about the date) but doesn't explain why Time Lords who would covertly sterilise the Earth to prevent their secrets getting out give humanity notice this would

happen, and enough notice to build a giant evacuation ship to boot.

The setting reminds Peri of "a wet November", perhaps suggesting the month. There's nothing on screen to suggest this isn't Glitz's native time.

968 *The Eight Doctors*

969 Before *Dragonfire*.

970 "Ten hundred million years" (a billion) before *Doctor Who and the Invasion from Space*.

971 Dating *Dragonfire* (24.4) - No date is given on screen, but Glitz's presence suggests the story takes place after *The Mysterious Planet*. Iceworld services "twelve galaxies", and Glitz comes from Andromeda, suggesting that intergalactic travel is now routine (and that it's after Andromeda was colonised). According to the novelisation, Svartos is in the "Ninth Galaxy".

Head Games claimed it was "a few thousand years

him when she was sixteen and served for twenty years. Kane earned many Crowns trading supplies to space travellers.

Many beings were drawn to Iceworld by the legends of a firebreathing dragon that supposedly lived in the ice tunnels beneath the colony. Kane finally killed the Dragon, his bio-mechanoid jailer, and acquired its Dragonfire power source. The seventh Doctor helped Kane to realize that his homeworld had been destroyed two thousand years ago, which deprived Kane of his revenge. Kane killed himself upon realising this. The Doctor's companion Melanie Bush elected to stay behind on Iceworld, now renamed the *Nosferatu II*, with Sabalom Glitz.

Mel soon left Glitz and attempted to reach Earth. She ended up marooned on the holiday planet Avalone, and spent two years there. She tried to get a lift from Glitz, and planted messages for him in the Galactic Banking Conglomerate's computer system, knowing that the Dragon cypher program she'd made for Glitz would find them. Glitz tried to exploit the open door and lift ten million grotzits from the bank, but he failed - causing officials to trace the intrusion to Mel's terminal. Avalone security caught up with Mel, who ran away to find the evil duplicate Dr Who.[972]

Glitz found a miniscope and briefly met Romana, who was trapped inside. Flavia arrived in a Type 90 TARDIS and returned Romana to Gallifrey.[973]

c 4,000,000 - THE SUN MAKERS[974] **->** Earth's mineral wealth was finally exhausted and its people were dying. In return for their labour, the Usurians moved mankind to Mars, which they terra-formed. The population was later moved on to Pluto, where six megropolises were built, each with its own artificial sun. However, the fourth Doctor, who the Usurians knew had "a long history of violence and economic subversion", started a rebellion. He imposed a growth tax and rendered the planet uneconomic.

c 4,000,000 - SCAREDY CAT[975] **->** According to legend, the people of Caludaar almost destroyed themselves through a series of global wars, and made a pledge to never set foot on their sister world, Endaara. Several millennia passed, but an expedition to Endaara was permitted when scans detected sophisticated indigenous lifeforms there. Professor Arken, a noted Caludaar scientist, used lambda radiation to experiment on the monkey-like natives, hoping to identify the part of the brain that facilitated evil. Unknown parties had killed Arken's son and left him on a rubbish heap, and Arken hoped his research would facilitate a means of blocking evil impulses, ending war and violence.

The eighth Doctor, Charley and C'rizz arrived as Arken further used lambda radiation on Eunis Flood, a convicted serial killer from Caludaar. This unexpectedly forged a link between the planet's morphogenetic field and Flood, turning him into a formidable psionic. The planet's collective life force appeared in guise of the dead girl Galayana, and although Flood disintegrated her physical form, she peeled away his defenses and left him with the mind of a child. Flood had similarly lobotomized Arken, but Endaara was now left to develop naturally.

5,000,000 - "4-Dimensional Vistas"[976] **->** In the twentieth century, the Monk and the Ice Warriors seeded a giant crystal in the Arctic. Now they arrived to harvest it. They would be able to destroy continents with the sonic cannon powered by the crystal.

into the future", at the time of the Galactic Federation. *Head Games* also establishes that Earth is devastated at this time, a reference to *The Mysterious Planet / The Ultimate Foe* (but one that might also support a dating around the time of the solar flares). Assuming it's the Galactic Federation from the Peladon stories, that and the dating of *Mission: Impractical* would seem to agree that Glitz's native time - and the events of *Dragonfire* - is much earlier than two million years in the future. Glitz is working for the Master in *The Mysterious Planet*, so could have been taken to the far future. However, with absolutely no evidence for this, or for Glitz having his own time machine, it seems better to conclude that he was in his native time in *The Mysterious Planet*.

972 *Head Games*, which confirms that Glitz is from the period when Earth was moved to become Ravolox.

973 *Goth Opera*

974 Dating *The Sun Makers* (15.4) - Set unspecified "mil-

lions of years in the future" according to contemporary publicity material, but this is never stated explicitly on screen. Earth has had time to regenerate its mineral wealth, which would suggest the story is set a very long way into the future. *The Programme Guide* failed to reconcile *The Sun Makers* with other stories, claiming that the Company dominated humanity only from "c.2100" to "c.2200" (first edition), or "c.2200" to "c.2300" (second edition). *The Terrestrial Index* suggested that the Earth was abandoned some centuries after the "52nd Century", and recolonised "5000 years" later. *The TARDIS Logs* suggested that the story was set "c.40,000", *Timelink* "25,000".

975 Dating *Scaredy Cat* (BF #75) - It is four million years after the previous part of the story, which roughly takes place during the time of the Earth Empire.

976 Dating "4-Dimensional Vistas" (*DWM* #78-83) - The time it takes to grow the crystal is specified.

In five million years time, the Cybermen have evolved again, become pure thought - the most peace-loving and advanced race in the universe.[977]

The Doctor took the Cold to Pluto in the far future.[978] Many millions of years in the future, the people of Phryxus established a technocracy in NGC4258 and developed galactic travel using warp capsules in the Grey Interchange. The renegade scientist Zodaal was jailed for experimenting on lesser life forms, and tried to escape using a warp capsule. This failed and he had to reduce himself to a gaseous state to survive. He escaped to the year 1929.[979]

Humanity attempted time-travel experiments during the Twenty-Seventh Segment of Time, but these proved to be a total failure.[980]

The Destruction of Earth

"Fleeing from the imminence of a catastrophic collision with the sun, a group of refugees from the *doomed* planet Earth..." [981]

c 10,000,000 - THE ARK[982] -> In the Fifty-Seventh Segment of Time, ten million years hence, scientists realised that the Earth was falling towards the Sun. With the help of the Monoids, a mysterious race whose own planet had been destroyed in a supernova many years before, humanity constructed a great space vessel. It contained the entire human, Monoid, animal and plant population of the Earth held on microcells in miniaturised form. Audio space research revealed that Refusis II was suitable for colonisation. It would take seven hundred years to reach the new world, and to symbolise the survival of man, a vast statue of a human carved from gregarian rock was begun.

The ship set out, and the few humans and Monoid servants that remained active - the Guardians - watched the Earth's destruction. Very soon afterward the common cold swept through the vessel, brought by the first Doctor's companion Dodo. The Doctor cured the disease using animal membranes.

c 10,000,000 - FRONTIOS[983] -> A vast colony ship containing thousands of people, plus the technology and material capable of rebuilding the whole of human civilisation, was sent to the Veruna System on the distant edge of the universe. Despite being touted as failure-proof, every system on the colony ship failed. The ship crashed on Frontios. Most of the crew died in the crash, and many more perished from diseases that spread through the colony immediately afterward.

Captain Revere eventually restored order. For ten years, the survivors planted and harvested crops, stocking up with food. But then meteorite bombardments began, striking the colony with such accuracy to make plain that it was being deliberately targeted. For thirty years the bombardment continued, but that wasn't the worst of it: the earth began swallowing up the dead. Over the years, the number of Retrogrades - people who deserted the colony - swelled.

And then, the earth swallowed Captain Revere while he was investigating the planet's potential mineral wealth. This left his son, Plantagenet, in command. The colony was soon in danger of falling apart.

The Tractators, insect creatures with the power to harness gravity, had arrived on Frontios five hundred years before and were responsible for the colony's setbacks. Under the command of their leader, the Gravis, they had pulled down the colony ship. They had given the colonists ten years to establish themselves, then began the meteorite bombardment. The Tractators had

977 "The World Shapers"
978 *Time and Relative.* No date is specified, but it's safe to presume it wasn't when the Company occupied Pluto.
979 "Many millions of years" after *The English Way of Death* (p189).
980 *The Ark.* Earth, and a number of races known to Earth - most notably the Daleks - achieved limited success with time travel experiments (one human scientist built a time machine in the nineteenth century, according to *The Evil of the Daleks*), but these have presumably been forgotten by now.
981 *Frontios*
982 Dating *The Ark* (3.6) - The Commander states that this is "the Fifty-Seventh Segment" of time, which the Doctor instantly calculates to be "ten million years" after Steven and Dodo's time.

983 Dating *Frontios* (21.3) - According to the Doctor, the story happens "on the outer limits. The TARDIS has drifted too far into the future". The inhabitants of Frontios are among the very last humans, and they have evacuated the Earth in circumstances that sound very similar to those of *The Ark.* While this would seem to dictate that *Frontios* is contemporary with *The Ark,* there is room for debate: no date is given in *Frontios,* there's no explicit link made to the earlier story, the colony ship is of a very different design, there is no sign of the Monoids and neither story refers to other arks. It is difficult to judge the level of technology, as virtually everything is lost in the crash, but it does not seem as advanced as that of *The Ark.*
984 *Excelis Dawns*
985 Dating *The Ark* (3.6) - The last two episodes of the story take place at the end of the Ark's journey, which

been kidnapping humans to serve as "drivers" for their tunnelling machines. The Gravis hoped to create a tunnel system that would amplify the Tractators' gravity fields and let them pilot Frontios throughout the cosmos.

The Gravis was isolated and transported to the planet Kolkokron. Without their leader, the Tractators were mindless drones, and the survival of the human colony was assured.

After delivering the Gravis to Kolkokron, the fifth Doctor made a side trip to the planet Artaris circa 1001 before returning to Frontios.[984]

c 10,000,700 - THE ARK[985] **->** The fever that had swept through the Ark had never fully abated, and it had weakened the humans. Seven hundred years after leaving the Solar System, the Monoids had seized control of the ship, and the statue commemorating the voyage was now of a Monoid. The humans now called the ship "the Ark" after an old Earth legend, but the Monoids kept the Guardians' descendants in check with heat prods.

The Ark arrived at Refusis II and Launcher 14 was sent to the surface. At first there was no sign of life, but it quickly transpired that the native Refusians were invisible giants. Nevertheless, the Monoid leader, named 1, planned to take his race's microcells to the planet. He also intended to destroy the Ark with a bomb planted in the head of the statue, but the Refusians helped to throw the statue overboard, allowing it to explode harmlessly in space. The Refusians allowed the humans and Monoids to live on their world, but only if they promised to live in peace.

Thus, humanity survived the destruction of its homeworld by travelling across the universe and rebuilding human civilisation on distant planets. What happened in the untold billions of years after that was a mystery - any TARDIS attempting to travel further into the future than this exceeded its time parameters, and the Time Lords themselves were unaware of anything beyond this time. "Knowledge has its limits; ours reaches this far and no further".[986]

? 10,000,000 - INFINITE REQUIEM[987] **->** Far in the future, representatives of over seven hundred cultures - including the Monoids, Morestrans, Rakkhins and Rills - used the Pridka Dream Centre. The Pridka were a race of blue-skinned, crested telepaths, and the Centre used their healing skills. At any one time, fifteen thousand individuals would be booked into the Centre, making it a tempting resource for the Sensopaths, a psychic communal mind intent on dominating the physical world.

The malicious Sensopath Shanstra attempted to absorb the Sensopath Jirenal. The benevolent Sensopath Kelzen intervened, and all three of them died.

The Doctor estimated that dogs would evolve thumbs in around twenty million years time.[988]

The Fifty-Eighth Segment of Time - THE WELL-MANNERED WAR[989] **->** In the Fifty-Eighth Segment of Time, human refugees colonised the planet Metralubit. There was peace for two thousand years, but then a planet-wide war suddenly wiped out two-thirds of the population. This had been engineered by the Hive, an evolved gestalt of flies that fed on dead bodies. There were four more such wars at roughly two-thousand-year intervals. The Helducc civilisation emerged from the sixth war, but also fell to conflict. A new civilisation rose and developed the Femdroids, led by Galatea, to increase male efficiency.

---

occurs "seven hundred years" after the first two episodes.

986 In *Frontios*, a message flashes up on a TARDIS console screen: "Boundary Error - Time Parameters Exceeded". Likewise, in *The Sun Makers*, the Doctor is worried that the TARDIS might have "gone right through the time spiral". This limitation doesn't seem to affect the TARDIS in *The Ark* or *The Savages*, or the New Adventures story *Timewyrm: Apocalypse*, which is also set in the distant future. The words quoted are those of the Doctor in *Frontios*. The novelisation of that story makes it clear that "ours" refers to the Time Lords, and that the story is set at the "edge of the Gallifreyan noosphere". It may - or may not - be significant that the Time Lords are unable to travel beyond the time of Earth's destruction.

It is perhaps also significant that in stories set after the destruction of Gallifrey, such as *Father Time*, *Hope*, *Sometime Never* and *The End of the World*, the Doctor is capable of travelling much further into the future (although he also seems quite capable of doing so in other stories set before Gallifrey's destruction, such as *Timewyrm: Apocalypse* and *The One Doctor*).

987 Dating *Infinite Requiem* (NA #36) - Events at the Pridka Dream Centre occur "Beyond Common Era of Earth Calendar" (p83), millennia after the destruction of Earth, and the presence of Morestrans and Monoids emphasises that this is the far future. This date is arbitrary.

988 *Evolution* (p40).

989 Dating *The Well-Mannered War* (MA #33) - This is "right at the end of the Humanian era, after the destruction of Earth" (p25) and "the fifty-eighth segment of time".

The Black Guardian brought a Chelonian squad from the distant past in a timestorm. The Chelonians claimed the planet Barclow, close to Metalubit, and the two races fought a short war until the Bechet Treaty was signed. Galatea learned the secret of the devastating world wars, evacuated most of the Femdroids to Regus V and plotted to lure the Hive back.

The fourth Doctor, Romana and K9 arrived on Barclow and discovered that the Black Guardian was trying to trick the Doctor into releasing the Hive in the twenty-sixth century, an act that would destroy human history. The Doctor defeated the Guardian by removing himself and Romana from time and space altogether.

This was the end of the Humanian Era.[990]

The Navarino civilisation was the only one to survive the war on its home planet - their culture was based on frivolity, and they were having too good a time to join in the conflict. The Navarinos had time tourism, but paid exhorbitant taxes to the Time Lords for the privilege.[991]

? - DELTA AND THE BANNERMEN[992] -> The Bannermen invaded the home planet of the Chimerons, but the Chimeron Queen escaped to Tollport G715. She joined the seventh Doctor, Mel and a party of Navarinos on a Nostalgia Trips tour to America in the 1950s.

Nostalgia Trips were notorious following an incident with the Glass Eaters of Traal, and true to form, their Hellstrom II cruiser wound up at a holiday camp in Wales by mistake. The Bannermen pursued them back in time.

The Master stole a forcefield from a Farquazi Time Cruiser during the 300th Segment of Time.[993]

The Vulgar End of Time - THE ONE DOCTOR[994] -> In the far future, everything had been discovered, everything had been done and technology made everything possible and affordable. It was therefore very boring.

A company on Generios VIII had thrived by exporting furniture, but the company's Assembler robots had wiped out the thirty-million-year-old population thousands of years ago. The Rim World of Abydos had no interesting features whatsoever, and Zynglat 3 boasted a sensory deprivation device. The Skardu-Rosbrix Wars were recent history. The super-computer Mentos spent 33,000 years playing *Super Brain* against a holographic Questioner, even when warfare destroyed all other civilization on Generios XIV.

The Doctor was famous in this era for his heroism, and the con man Banto Zame (a native of Osphogus, a planet that was terra-formed five thousand years before) impersonated the Doctor to stage "defeats" of alien invasions, then collect rewards from grateful rulers. Banto tried his scheme on Generios I, but a genuine alien spaceship arrived and demanded the Generios System's three greatest treasures as tribute.

---

990 *The Well-Mannered War*
  ERAS: The Humanian Era was first mentioned in *Doctor Who - The Movie*, which also referred to the Rassilon Era. The TARDIS console prop for that story also included references to the Peon, Manussan, Sumaron, Kraaiian and Sensorian eras. *Zagreus* adds the Morestran Era to the list.
  The Humanian Era includes Earth in 1999, and is presumably a reference to the human race. *The Well-Mannered War* implies that it's simply the Era when humans exist. The Rassilon Era applies to Gallifrey (the "present" for the Doctor would seem to be 5725.2 in the Rassilon Era, according to the TV movie). *Neverland* specifies that the period around the Federation and Mavic Chen was the Sensorian. The Manussan and Morestran eras are presumably references to the planets from *Snakedance* and *Planet of Evil* respectively. Taking all this at face value, it would seem that eras can overlap each other - the Sensorian and Morestran eras, at least, fall comfortably within the Humanian Era.
991 *Return of the Living Dad*, tying in with the date for *Delta and the Bannermen*.
992 Dating *Delta and the Bannermen* (24.3) - An entirely arbitrary date. However, Nostalgia Trips is notorious throughout the "five galaxies", suggesting that the story

is set in a far future period of intergalactic travel. In *Dragonfire*, Svartos serves "the twelve galaxies," so perhaps it is set later than this story. While only the Daleks had broken the time barrier by 4000 AD (*The Daleks' Master Plan*), the human ship in *Planet of the Spiders* and the Movellan ship in *Destiny of the Daleks* have "time warp capability", and we see a couple of races developing rudimentary time travel around now (Magnus Greel in 5000 AD, the Metebelis Spiders a little later). Such secrets are limited, and are lost by the time of *The Ark*. Murray, the bus driver, says "the 1950s nights back on Navaro were never like this", which implies nostalgia parties rather than that he lived through the 1950s himself. *The Terrestrial Index* set this story "c.15,000".
993 *The Quantum Archangel*
994 Dating *The One Doctor* (BF #27) - The Doctor expounds on the subject of the Vulgar End of Time at the beginning of the story.
995 Dating *Omega* (BF #47) - The dating is arbitrary, but much about this story resembles the Vulgar End of Time: time travel is now deemed unfashionable rather than unattainable; the exploits of the Doctor, Omega and - generally speaking - the Time Lords are widely renowned, if somewhat erroneously; and the period is one of prosperity, leisure and dullness. The Doctor is

The End of Time

The sixth Doctor, Mel and Banto banded together to collect the Mentos super-computer from Generios XIV, furniture Unit ZX419 from Generios VIII, and the largest diamond in existence on Generios XV. The Cylinder accepted the tribute as proof of the Doctor's identity, but mistook Banto for the genuine Time Lord. The Cylinder spirited Banto away to face retribution for a past offence the Doctor had committed against the Cylinder's masters.

(? The Vulgar End of Time) - OMEGA[995] **->** By now, the legend of Omega was widely known. Jolly Chronolidays set up a heritage center in the Sector of Forgotten Souls, where it was believed Omega had detonated a star on behalf of the Time Lords. The center was modeled on Omega's ship, the *Eurydice*.

Omega himself arrived in this time zone and met Sentia, a telepath who became enamoured of him. However, Omega's failed attempt to merge with the Doctor in Amsterdam, 1983, had left him with a copy of the Doctor's memories and a split persona. The "Doctor" aspect of his mind was unaware that he was part of Omega's body. Omega's mental health further deteriorated, and Sentia conspired to return Omega to his anti-matter universe aboard the real *Eurydice*, which was within a dimensional anomaly. The genuine Doctor arrived onhand, Sentia was killed and Omega was yet again cast - along with the *Eurydice* - over the event horizon of a black hole.

Two agents of Gallifrey's Celestial Preservation Agency - Maven and the living TARDIS Glinda - arrived to preserve the Doctor's reputation by insuring that his eradication of the Scintillan race remained secret. They offered Daland, an actor, a job in a Gallifreyan museum.

The year 500,000,000 was the most peaceful in human history. The people there were unaware of war or the Daleks.[996] The computer that ruled the Andromeda Galaxy,

The One, determined that the Galaxy was doomed to enter a "region of Nothingness". It constructed a vast armada of artificial planets and set off towards the Milky Way Galaxy, planning galactic conquest. It drew up the Diagrams, a complete map of the Milky Way.[997]

c 1,000,000,000 - DOCTOR WHO AND THE INVASION FROM SPACE[998] **->** The first Doctor and his new companions, the Mortimer family, arrived on an artificial planet bathed in the light of the great spiral galaxy of Andromeda. They were met by the Aalas, blond giants who took them to The One - the entity that ruled their planet and had once ruled the entire Andromeda Galaxy for millions of years. Andromeda faced destruction, and was running low on resources, so The One built an armada of almost a million artificial planets and set out on a four hundred million year journey to the Milky Way. The TARDIS had arrived a hundred million years into that mission.

The One realised that its aims would be achieved far more efficiently if it had the TARDIS' secrets. The Doctor naturally refused, but the Andromedans prevented the TARDIS from leaving. The One was destroyed when Ida rebelled, throwing a food plate into a vital component. The Doctor and the Mortimers left the armada drifting aimlessly in space.

The End of Time

"**A distant point of time, an age of great advancement, peace and prosperity**".[999]

= If history had run differently, and Gallifrey had been destroyed at the time of Rassilon, the first time travellers would have evolved a billion years from

said to have accidentally wiped out the thought-based Scintillans while combating space pirates who used telepathically-controlled weapons and ships, but a proper dating for this isn't given.
996 *I am a Dalek*
997 "One hundred million years" before *Doctor Who and the Invasion from Space*.
998 Dating *Doctor Who and the Invasion from Space* (World Distributors illustrated novella) - No date is given, but humans are legendary to the people of Andromeda, and seem to be the ancestors of the Andromedans ("the humans of the worlds of Andromeda were the patterns"). That galaxy faces (in the long term, at least) extinction.
    Using information from other stories, we know from *The Ark in Space* that humanity first arrived in Andromeda after the Solar Flares, and that the events

of *The Mysterious Planet*, set two million years in the future, involved Andromedans. The story is set, then, at some point in the distant future. As Glitz comes from Andromeda, the galaxy is clearly not dominated by The One at that time. Yet it's an interesting coincidence that the enclosed society set up by the Andromedans on "Ravalox" - with an obedient population controlled by an artificial intelligence - is very similar (albeit on an infinitely smaller and less advanced scale) to the Andromedan civilisation seen in *Doctor Who and the Invasion from Space*. It's also notable that they steal a copy of the Matrix in that story, and the Matrix contains the memories of all the Time Lords in the same way The One contains all the memories of the Andromedans.
    On TV, there is no gap in which the first Doctor travelled without companions, although he did so in the *Doctor Who Annuals* in the sixties. This might suggest

now. These would have been the Ferutu. They intervened to optimise history, so that the Daleks and CyberHost were both forces for good in a utopian universe. The Doctor tricked the Ferutu into preventing their creation to save our timeline.[1000]

Two billion years in the future, the Time Lord Solenti observed how the Dagusan sun ended its lifespan as a main sequence star. The planet's seas consequently evaporated, even as the remaining population retreated to the South Pole.[1001]

Three hundred thousand years before the Last of Man, the Doctor negotiated a lasting peace between the Sontarans and the Rutans. By this time, Gallifrey had long fallen. The Sontarans and Rutans undertook the largest demobilisation in the history of the universe.[1002]

NEW EARTH[1003] -> Lady Cassandra was told she was beautiful at a party, but this was the last time anyone would say such a thing. She became increasingly bitter and obsessed with cosmetic surgery. The person who made the comment was actually her future self - whose mind resided in a force-grown clone named Chip - who had been brought there by the tenth Doctor. Moments later, Cassandra-Chip expired while in the arms of her younger self.

5,000,000,000 - THE END OF THE WORLD[1004] -> Earth was seen as the cradle of civilisation, and there was not a star in the sky that humanity hadn't touched. Humanity had evolved into new humans, protohumans, digihumans and the humanish. Many other races had evolved from Earth plants and animals.

For years, Earth was preserved by the National Trust, who reversed the process of continental drift (although by this time, Los Angeles was a crevasse and the Arctic was a desert). When the preservation money ran out, many diverse alien races, including the Trees of the Forest of Cheem (descendants of trees from Earth's tropical rainforest), the Moxx of Balhoon, the Adherents of the Repeated Meme, the Face of Boe, the Ambassadors from the City State of Blinding Light and the ninth Doctor and Rose all gathered on Platform One to witness the planet's final destruction.

The last purebred human - Cassandra, who had been reduced to a stretched-out piece of skin - plotted to engineer a hostage situation to sue the corporation that ran the Platform. Failing that, she tried to kill the assembled beings, as she had invested heavily in their rivals' companies. Cassandra's plan was defeated, and she was made to pay for her crimes by the Doctor.

Cassandra's mind survived and transferred into her back skin. She fled to New Earth with a servant named Chip, who had been force-grown from Cassandra's "favourite pattern".[1005]

5,000,000,023 - NEW EARTH[1006] -> New Earth had been established in the M87 Galaxy by people nostalgic about the loss of humanity's original homeworld. Ten million people lived in New New York (the fifteenth city to bear the name). Exotic diseases such as petrifold regression, Marconi's Disease and Palindrome Pancrosis (which killed in the space of ten minutes) were treated by the Sisters of Plenitude at their hospital on New Earth.

A green moon served as the universal symbol for "hospital". Psycho-graphs - devices capable of transferring consciousness from one being to another - were banned on every civilised planet. The goddess Santori was revered in this era.

The tenth Doctor was summoned by the Face of Boe,

---

that this story takes place before the TV series starts - but the TARDIS is a police box, so this isn't the case - yet there's no mention of Susan, and the Doctor has no control over the TARDIS navigation. An alternative is that couple of the novelisations (*The Massacre* and *The Five Doctors*) took a cue from the first Doctor's appearance in *The Three Doctors* to claim that he had a period of semi-retirement and reflection before his regeneration, spent in a beautiful garden. While it is unlikely that the Doctor dropped off a companion, retrieving them later, *The Two Doctors* seems to demonstrate that even as early as his second incarnation, the Doctor was able to drop Victoria off and expect to meet her later (and non-TV stories either suggest or state that he's routinely done that since at least his fifth incarnation).

999 *The Savages*
1000 *Cold Fusion*

1001 *The Suns of Caresh*
1002 *The Infinity Doctors*
1003 Dating *New Earth* (X2.1) - The epilogue clearly occurs before *The End of the World*, but it's difficult to judge how many years before, as there's no way of knowing how long Cassandra survives as an elongated piece of skin.
1004 Dating *The End of the World* (X1.2) - The Doctor tells Rose "this is the year 5.5/apple/26, five billion years in your future". This story seems to contradict *The Ark* (and, by implication, *Frontios*), which saw the destruction of the Earth a mere ten million years in our future, and had a different fate for humanity. The obvious inference to make is that the Earth wasn't completely destroyed in *The Ark*, and the National Trust's renovations were more extensive than the Doctor told Rose.
1005 *New Earth*

who was said to be the last of Boe-kind and now appeared to be dying. The Sisters were secretly experimenting on vast numbers of cloned humans to facilitate the miracle cures, but the Doctor cured the clones. The Sisters were arrested, and the clones catalogued as new humans.

The Face of Boe recovered, and told the Doctor they would meet one more time. Cassandra's mind came to reside in Chip, but they were both dying. The Doctor showed Cassandra a last mercy, and took her back in time for a final meeting with herself.

Drug patches were available that created such emotional states as Happy, Anger, Forget and Sleep, but in 5,000,000,029, the introduction of Bliss patches made the population of New New York fall victim to a virus. The Senate was wiped out, as were seven million citizens. Only the Face of Boe and Novice Hane were able to resist. The power died, but the Face of Boe used his life energy to send survivors down into the Motorway, and convince them that life was normal. An automatic quarantine signal warned other planets to avoid New Earth for one hundred years.[1007]

The Cassini "sisters" (a married couple) were among the first people to join the Motorway, in 5,000,000,030.[1008] Brannigan's car joined the Motorway in 5,000,000,041.[1009] Junction Five of the Motorway closed in 5,000,000,050.[1010]

5,000,000,053 - GRIDLOCK[1011] -> The tenth Doctor and Martha arrived in New New York and discovered millions of cars were stuck in a permanent traffic jam in the Motorway beneath the city. The Doctor found a colony of Macra lurking at the bottom of the Motorway, thriving on the noxious fumes. However, it was discovered that the Face of Boe had engineered the situation to protect the population from the plague that had destroyed the city. The Doctor opened up the Motorway, allowing the city to be repopulated.

Legend said the Face of Boe had lived for billions of years, but also that he was the last of his kind. He now died, but not before passing on a final message to the Doctor: "You are not alone."

Compulsory quarantine on New Earth was due to be lifted in 5,000,000,129, a hundred years after it was imposed.[1012] The cure for Petrifold Regression was officially developed a thousand years after the Sisters of Plentitude discovered their own remedy.[1013]

The Doctor once speculated that Earth's sun would finally become a supernova in ten thousand million years time.[1014]

? - THE SAVAGES[1015] -> On one planet, the Elders maintained a utopian civilisation free from material needs. They survived by draining "life energy" from the savages who lived in the wastelands outside their beautiful city. "The Traveller from Beyond Time", the first Doctor, ended this injustice, and his companion Steven Taylor remained behind to rule the civilisation as it renounced barbarism.

Towards the End of the Universe

Many billions of years from now, the universe was cold and almost dead. The suns were exhausted. The last few survivors of the universe huddled around whatever energy sources they could find.[1016]

Eight billion years in the future, and humanity was long dead. The Mutter's Spiral had been abandoned by all sentient life.[1017] A few ten billions of years in the future, the Conservers existed in a black hole, preserving information there in the face of the universe's death. They engineered their own creation by sending avatars into the past to bring a colony ship to their black hole. The Doctor visited the Conservers.[1018]

1006 Dating *New Earth* (X2.1) - It is "twenty three years" after *The End of the World*.
1007 "Twenty four years" before *Gridlock*.
1008 "Twenty three years" before *Gridlock*.
1009 "Twelve years" before *Gridlock*.
1010 "Three years" before *Gridlock*.
1011 Dating *Gridlock* (X3.3) - The Doctor gives the date as "the year five billion and fifty three".
1012 *Gridlock*
1013 *New Earth*
1014 *Colony in Space*. It's possible the Doctor witnessed this for himself. It doesn't contradict *The Ark*, which had Earth crashing into the Sun, not the Sun going supernova, or *The End of the World*, where the Sun merely expands enough to destroy the Earth.
1015 Dating *The Savages* (3.9) - At the end of *The Gunfighters*, the Doctor claims that they have now landed at "a distant point in time" (see the quote above). The Elders have the technology to track the TARDIS, but are not capable of time travel themselves. They declare themselves to be "human".
1016 *Timewyrm: Apocalypse, The Infinity Doctors, Father Time, Hope, The Eye of the Tyger, Sometime Never.*
1017 "Eight billion years" after *Cold Fusion*.
1018 *The Eye of the Tyger*

TIMEWYRM: APOCALYPSE[1019] -> Billions of years in the future, the guardians of the universe, even the Time Lords, were long extinct. The people of Kirith (the only planet orbiting a red giant in Galaxy QSO 0046 at the edge of the universe) never grew old or unhappy. For three thousand eight hundred and thirty three years, the Kirithons had been ruled by the eighty-four Panjistri, who gave them food and technology. For nearly a thousand years, the Panjistri performed genetic experiments, forcing the evolution of the Kirithons in an attempt to create a being that had reached the Omega Point: an omniscient, omnipotent entity capable of halting the destruction of the universe. They succeeded in creating a golden sphere of expanding light, but the machine destroyed itself and the Panjistri, knowing that the universe must end.

The Divergents almost emerged into our universe sixty billion years in the future, towards the end of time. Uncle Winky's Wonderland had been moved several times and was situated atop the ruins of Rassilon's lab on Gallifrey. Uncle Winky revived from stasis, but died from his heart condition.[1020]

The Ministers of Grace travelled from the end of time to fight in the Millennium War.[1021]

There was a huge disaster that led to galaxies being evacuated and whole sections of the timeline being erased. The Doctor's people were somehow responsible, and the four surviving Time Lords used their great powers to impose control on the rest of the universe. The last Time Lord became the first ever Emperor of the entire Universe, ruling over a divided and broken populace that split into Factions and Houses. These included the Klade, "goblin shapeshifters" and cybernetic gangsters - the ultimate descendants of the Daleks, Sontarans, Rutans and the Cybermen.

Most of the people of the universe relocated to the Needle, a light-year long structure that was the remains of a TARDIS that had tried to escape the pull of a black hole. The largest building on the Needle was the Librarinth, where all surviving knowledge and art was preserved.[1022]

Griffin the Unnaturalist resided on the Needle.[1023]

FATHER TIME[1024] -> The Doctor and two companions visited the planets Galspar and Falkus around this time. The Doctor also fought a robotic tyrant who panicked, accidentally destroyed his own palace and killed his own wife. This robot - who later assumed the identity Mr Gibson to blend in on twentieth-century Earth - vowed revenge.

At least some of the Emperor's subjects, such as the Klade - the super-evolved descendants of the Daleks - resented Imperial rule. One Klade senator, the mother of Zevron and Ferran, incited revolution against the Emperor but was assassinated. Zevron stormed the Imperial Palace, killing and scattering all of the Imperial Family. The Emperor was killed. The Emperor's daughter, Miranda, was rescued by her nanny and taken down a time corridor to twentieth-century Earth.

Over the years, Zevron tracked down and killed every other member of the Imperial Family. Finally he located

1019 Dating *Timewyrm: Apocalypse* (NA #3) - The novel is set "several billion years" in the future (p3), "ten billion years" before the end of the universe (p178).
1020 *Zagreus*. These facts were presented as part of a simulation, and so may not take place.
1021 *The Quantum Archangel* - The Ministers first appeared in the short story "The Duke of Dominoes" (*Decalog*, 1994).
1022 *The Infinity Doctors, Father Time*
1023 *Unnatural History*
1024 Dating *Father Time* (EDA #41) - The exact timescale is unclear, and is stated to be "a few million years in the future", "several million years hence", and "a million years in the future". The physical state of the universe, however, suggests it is much later than that.
1025 Dating *Hope* (EDA #53) - The Doctor pushes the TARDIS to see how far into the future he can take it and the TARDIS goes "too far". This is the same far, far future time period referred to in *The Infinity Doctors* and *Father Time*, which alluded to Silver and this time period (p191).
1026 *Sometime Never*
1027 Dating *Singularity* (BF #76) - It is clearly toward

the end of the universe. It's said that the Ember base is located "trillions of years" in the future, but it's also mentioned that, "This far into the future, numbers become meaningless." Technically, Xen's claim that he is "the last human" seems dubious, as episodes such as *The End of the World* and *New Earth* indicate that no purebred humans exist after Cassandra's era. The planet Ember bears no apparent relation to the star of the same name from *The Suns of Caresh*, although that story might explain why the Doctor here mutters "Ember… I've heard that name before."
1028 "Thousands of years" before *Utopia*.
1029 *Utopia*. It's said in *The End of the World* that the Face of Boe also hails from the Silver Devastation.
1030 Dating *Utopia* (X3.11) - The TARDIS is propelled into the far, far future, with the last date the Doctor reads being "one hundred trillion years" (it's possible it lands even later). As in *The Sun Makers* and *Frontios*, the Doctor states that the Time Lords didn't travel this far into the future, although he never explicitly rules out the possibility he's been here before, as we saw in a number of books and audios.

Miranda and led the mission to kill her on Earth in the early nineteen-eighties.

When Zevron failed to return, Ferran became Prefect of Faction Klade. Some years later, Ferran received a distress signal from Sallak, Zevron's deputy. Ferran travelled to twentieth-century Earth to complete Zevron's mission but failed and returned to his native time.

A team of Ferran's scholars spent fifteen years in the Librarinth, and they eventually pinpointed Miranda's whereabouts. During this time, Ferran also recovered a derelict sentient ship built by the People of the Worldsphere, which he christened the *Supremacy*. The political situation had deteriorated, putting the Houses and Factions at open war, and soon galactic civilisation was on the brink of collapse. Ferran believed Miranda could access sealed sections of the Librarinth and thus give him the power to dominate the other Factions. Using the *Supremacy*, he again set off to the twentieth century.

Miranda and Ferran returned to this time. Convinced she could unite the universe, Miranda was crowned Empress.

The Miranda spin-off comic followed on from these events.

HOPE[1025] **->** Taking the TARDIS into the far future, the eighth Doctor, Fitz and Anji landed on planet A245, known locally as Endpoint. It was an icy planet with a toxic environment. The TARDIS fell through the frozen crust of an acid sea, and the Doctor asked the cyborg Silver - the warlord of the nearest settlement, Hope - for assistance. In return, the Doctor tracked down a serial killer. Silver was from the far past, the year 3006.

Anji was tempted to use the cloning technology of the far future to recreate her dead boyfriend, Dave, and granted Silver scans of the TARDIS in return for this. The Doctor found survivors from other colonies were murdering the people of Hope to harvest Kallisti, a hormone that could revive more of the colonists from cryo-sleep. Silver found the sleepers and converted them into Silverati: half-synthetic soldiers loyal to him. With his soldiers and the colonists' hypertunnel, Silver attempted to take control of a richer planet. The Doctor exiled Silver and his Silverati to the barren planet A2756.

There were no pure humans left, but human genes survived in a number of races. Apple trees were extinct until Silver cloned one from an apple core that the Doctor gave him. The universe was past the point of sustainable expansion, and the rate of star death had dramatically increased.

Miranda brought the Factions and Houses together and united the people of the universe. She had at least one child, a daughter named Zezanne. Zezanne's father died. The Council of Eight kidnapped Miranda and Zezanne when Zezanne was a teenager.[1026]

? - SINGULARITY[1027] **->** The planet Ember had served as an outpost from which to watch other galaxies for signs of intelligent life. Toward the end of the universe, some descendants of humanity prolonged the lifespan of Ember's sun as most stars in the universe extinguished, and thereby survived for some millennia. They believed that the Time Lords had opened a gate to another realm and escaped with all the life they deemed worthy, leaving humanity's children to perish.

Ember's sun began to fade also, and the survivors began swapping their intelligences with Earthlings in the late twentieth century, hoping to facilitate the creation of a Singularity entity. The plan failed, whereupon the conspirators were forced to return to this era and quickly died off.

The laws of time and causality started to break down as Ember approached its end. Nonetheless, the fifth Doctor and Turlough arrived as one of the conspirators - Xen, who claimed to be the last human - passed on.

The stars of the universe were burning out and fading away. The Science Foundation initiated the Utopia Project to preserve mankind, and enable it to survive the collapse of reality itself.[1028]

Professor Yana was found as a boy, naked in a storm off the coast of the Silver Devastation. He was discovered with a watch, which he kept with him as he went from one refugee ship to another. No university had existed for a thousand years, but Yana became accomplished at science and took the title "Professor" as an affectation.[1029]

100,000,000,000,000 - UTOPIA[1030] **->** The planet Malcassairo had been home to an advanced race of humanoid insects, the Malmooth, but the Conglomeration there died. Chantho was the last representative of this species, and she served as Yana's assistant for seventeen years.

A signal came from far beyond the Condensed Wilderness, out toward the Wild Lands and the Dark Matter Reefs. It said nothing more than "come to Utopia", and some remnants of humanity gathered on Malcassairo in preparation to journey there. They huddled to protect themselves from the cannibalistic Futurekind - said to be what mankind would become - while Yana and Chanthro worked to complete a rocket that would evacuate everyone save themselves.

The tenth Doctor, Martha and Captain Jack arrived at this time, and the Doctor helped to complete the rocket. Martha learned that Yana was - unknown even to himself - the Master, disguised as a human to escape the Time War. The rocket launched. The Master learned of his true identity, but was shot by Chanthro, whom he had fatally wounded. He regenerated, stealing the TARDIS and marooning the Doctor and his companions, but not before the Doctor fused the TARDIS' controls. It could only travel to this point in time, and within eighteen months of the Ship's last departure in 2008.

The Doctor, Martha and Captain Jack returned to the twenty-first century using Jack's vortex manipulator.[1031]

The Master returned to this future era with his wife Lucy, and found the darkness overtaking the humans on Utopia. He arranged to house their shrunken heads into metallic spheres equipped with weaponry, and named them the Toclafane. Six billion Toclafane were created in this fashion. The Master then returned to the twenty-first century, and converted the TARDIS into a Paradox Machine.

> = Thanks to the Paradox Machine, the Toclafane were able to travel back and enslave their ancestors.

With the Paradox Machine's destruction, the Toclafane were stranded at the end of the universe.[1032]

Event Two

"One mad prophet martyr journeyed too far and saw the Timewyrm. He saw it in a timeline that he could not be sure of, devouring Rassilon or his shade, during the Blue Shift, that time of final conflict when Fenric shall slip his chains and the evil of the worlds shall rebound back on them in war." [1033]

100,000,000,000,000,000,000,000,000,000 - THE INFINITY DOCTORS[1034] **->** The Needle had been inhabited for tens of millions of years, but now it was all but abandoned. Ruined cities dotted its surface, and the atmosphere had frozen. The only known survivors were the predator animals named the Maltraffi, mushrooms and four "knights": Gordel, Willhuff, Pallant and Helios. Each could only remember the future - with less and less to remember each day - and each had his own theory as to their origins. They may have been the last survivors of the Children of Kasterborous, human / Gallifreyan hybrids who intervened in the universe at great cost; superevolved

Thals who fled the penultimate destruction of Skaro at the start of the Final Dalek War; members of the People of the Worldsphere, left behind when everyone else transcended reality; or the last High Evolutionaries (Helios might have been Merlin, or his son).

The Doctor arrived from Gallifrey to find the god Ohm, who was trapped in the black hole at one end of the Needle. Two of the Doctor's colleagues, the Magistrate and Larna, were sent in to rescue him when he vanished. Omega emerged from the black hole wearing the Doctor's body, banishing the Magistrate somewhere unknown and taking Larna back to Gallifrey.

Omega sought to attain ultimate power by unleashing the Eye of Harmony. The Doctor had been reunited with his wife as part of these events, but was forced to lose her again. He once more defeated Omega.

The Last Museum stood as a collection of the human race's greatest objects and achievements. It was located at the end of Time, at the exact centre of the universe. The Council of Eight member Soul served at the Museum, disguised as an old man named Singleton.[1035]

SOMETIME NEVER[1036] **->** The Council of Eight existed in the Vortex Palace, right at the end of time. By placing unique crystals at the beginning of time, they mapped out events across the universe, and generated energy from unused potential timelines by correctly predicting the course of events. This energy was stored in Schrodinger Cells. The Council sent apes mutated by the Time Winds ("the Agents of the Council") to ensure their version of history transpired, and also recruited Sabbath to unwittingly work on their behalf. The Council deemed many of the Doctor's companions a threat, as they were touched by his innate ability to influence history, and thus engineered the possible deaths of Sarah Jane Smith, Harry Sullivan, Melanie Bush, Ace and Samantha Jones.

The Council leader, Octan, planned to destroy human history with a starkiller, releasing vast amounts of energy as universal history was rewritten. This energy would paradoxically create the Council of Eight, and in all probability allow them to survive the end of the universe. Octan took Miranda hostage, but she sacrificed herself, allowing the eighth Doctor a free hand to fight them. Octan tried manipulating Sabbath into doing his bidding, but Sabbath

---

1031 *The Sound of Drums*
1032 *Last of the Time Lords.* The number of Toclafane is given by the Master in *The Sound of Drums.*
1033 *Timewyrm: Revelation*
1034 Dating *The Infinity Doctors* (PDA #17) - The date is given (p137). This is "within a few decades of Event Two" (p130).

1035 *Sometime Never*
1036 Dating *Sometime Never* (EDA #67) - The scene in the Vortex Palace ends with the end of the universe.
1037 *Timewyrm: Apocalypse*
1038 *The Infinity Doctors*
1039 "Hunger from the Ends of Time!"
1040 *Millennial Rites*

killed himself to thwart his former employers. Sabbath's death helped to instigate the destruction of the Vortex Palace.

The Council of Eight perished except for the benevolent Soul and Octan, who journeyed to 1588 in a last-ditch effort to save their plans. The Doctor donated some of his life energy to stabilize Soul's body into his former guise as the old man Singleton. Soul took Octan's starkiller.

The Doctor and his allies departed in the TARDIS, while Soul and Miranda's daughter Zezanne evacuated in the *Jonah*, which arrived in a junkyard in 1963. Beings with a mind toward acquiring the starkiller monitored the *Jonah's* departure.

Other beings that survived until the last moments of the universe included the Solarii and Korsann's reptilian race.

Our universe was destroyed in the Big Crunch. All matter imploded to a central point, returning to the state from which it was created: "a bright blazing pinprick of sheer energy".[1037] The Time Lords referred to the end of the universe as Event Two.[1038]

Insect-like "forces of chaos" fed on the debris of the collapse of the universe, as they had fed on the big bang.[1039] Just as a universe existed before ours, so will another universe be formed from the ashes of ours, and the physical laws there will be very different. This will be the domain of Saraquazel.[1040]

The history of the Daleks would be convoluted even if they weren't time travellers. Here, I try to boil Dalek history down to the basics. Speculation is in italics, and most of the working in the footnotes is to be found in the main timeline - see especially the articles Are There Two Dalek Histories?, The Neutronic War, The Dalek Emperors, The Middle Period of Dalek History, The Alliance, Last Contact, The Dalek Wars, Was Skaro Destroyed?, The Davros Era, Who Started the Last Great Time War? and The Last Great Time War.

The Thousand Years War between the Thals and Kaleds on Skaro devastated the planet. The Daleks were created by the Kaled scientist Davros, but the fourth Doctor set them back a thousand years.[1]

A thousand years passed. There were again two races on Skaro - the Thals and the Daleks (or Dals), squat blue-skinned warriors *who had evolved from the Kaled survivors*. We don't see the Thals at this time, but their rivals the Dals occupied futuristic cities and had an advanced civilisation.[2]

A neutron bomb exploded, instantly devastating Skaro. Forests were petrified, and animal life mutated into exotic monsters. The Dals and Thals also mutated.[3]

A mutated Dal, a creature like that created by Davros' experiments (*perhaps even a survivor from those experiments*), crawled into a war machine designed by Yarvelling, almost identical to Davros' ancient design (*and so clearly influenced by it*), and became the first Dalek. He became the Emperor Dalek and casings were soon constructed for other Dalek mutants. Within months, the Daleks had built the Dalek City, and soon after that they developed space travel. A social hierarchy emerged, with the feared Black Dalek in charge of military production on Skaro and the

Red Dalek in charge of space projects. The Emperor Dalek led the fleet of Dalek saucers in the first conquests. They encountered the Mechanoids. *It was the late eighteenth century on Earth.*

No more than five centuries passed. During this time, the Daleks didn't encounter the human race or learn of the Earth, and they never met the Doctor. They paid little attention to Skaro itself and didn't encounter the Thals.[4]

Quite what they do during these centuries is unclear. They might have a war with the Mechanoids, but it's never mentioned. We have no account of them meeting any other Doctor Who monsters, but that is also possible - the Sontaran-Rutan war is underway across the galaxy, for example. At this time the Daleks are building up a powerbase, and developing advanced weapons, but are far from being the all-conquering race we'll see later.

The only thing we know from this period is that a Dalek ship crashed on Vulcan in the early nineteenth century.[5]

In 2012, a Dalek from the future was unable to detect any Dalek transmissions.[6] In the mid-twenty-second century, the Daleks learned of Earth and humanity.[7]

Around 2157, the Daleks attacked the human race - their powerful space fleet cut Earth off from the space lanes, and then a relatively small force invaded the Solar System. They attacked humanity on Earth and the Mars colony. Earth was occupied for ten years.[8]

The Daleks were defeated, but retained their ambition to conquer Earth.[9] **Around this time, the Daleks internalised their power sources, removing their greatest vulnerability - now they ran on psychokinetic power, not static electricity.**[10]

For the Daleks, their defeat had great significance for another reason - this was the very first time, from

---

1 *Genesis of the Daleks*

2 The *TV Century 21* strip, which builds on information from *The Daleks*.

3 *The Daleks*

4 The *TV Century 21* strip.

5 Two hundred years before *The Power of the Daleks* - even there, the dating of the story is open to question, and *War of the Daleks* states that the crashed ship came from the far future. In any event, these Daleks are not in contact with Skaro, which remains unaware of the events of this story.

6 *Dalek*

7 This is depicted in the *TV Century 21* strip, but obviously happens at some point before *The Dalek Invasion of Earth*.

8 *The Dalek Invasion of Earth* (and references in other stories to it - see the main timeline for details).

9 Oddly, the Daleks say the Doctor merely "delayed"

their conquest of Earth in *The Chase*.

10 They run on "psychokinetic power" according to *Death to the Daleks*, but static electricity in *The Daleks*, *The Dalek Invasion of Earth* and *The Power of the Daleks*. Maxtible and Waterfield's experiments with static electricity attract the Daleks (*The Evil of the Daleks*).

11 *The Chase*. The Daleks have done some research - they know what the TARDIS looks like, even though they never saw it in *The Dalek Invasion of Earth* (or *Genesis of the Daleks*, *The Power of the Daleks* or *The Daleks*, for that matter). They know the Doctor's a time traveller, somehow (perhaps this was an accidental discovery when their were conducting their own time travel experiments). However, there are some big gaps in their knowledge: they don't even consider the possibility that the TARDIS crew might have changed, and they refer to the Doctor as "human" - we might infer they have yet to encounter another incarnation of the

their point of view, that they encountered the Doctor. Soon after the Dalek Invasion, the Daleks developed time travel and sent an assassination group in their time craft to exterminate him.[11]

The Daleks also used their time travel to achieve their other great ambition - they went back in time and conquered the Earth. These Daleks already knew the Doctor's name - they hooked the Doctor up to a Mind Analysis Machine, and learned that the third Doctor was the same individual as his previous two incarnations. Whether this knowledge survived the collapse of the alternative timeline is unclear[12]. But from now on, even if they don't always recognise the Doctor on sight, they understand that he can change his appearance.[13]

The Dalek Invasion was also long-remembered by humanity (some historians called it The First Dalek War), and it resulted in an Alliance of a number of planets, and races being set up to defend against such an attack. The Daleks themselves don't seem to threaten Earth for centuries (Vicki, from 2493, only knows the Daleks from history books about the Invasion).[14]

What the Daleks do in this period, though, is a mystery. We know that the first Doctor's first encounter with the Daleks - when we see them in severely reduced circumstances - happens in Ian and Barbara's "future", "generations" before the year 2540, which would seem to fall around here on the timeline.

The Daleks were confined to Dalek City on Skaro. The Doctor and his companions helped the Thals to destroy them. There's no indication at this time that these Daleks have space travel, time travel, or even are aware that life exists on other planets.[15]

However you rationalise this away, even if you don't try to incorporate the TV Century 21 comic strip, the result is clumsy. The most straightforward explanation is perhaps that the vast majority of Daleks abandon Skaro because their conquests have taken them elsewhere, leaving behind a small group... but

this doesn't explain why the Daleks there can't move or see beyond their city. Perhaps they have refused to upgrade their power supplies and literally been left grounded as a result.

Perhaps these are all the surviving Daleks - crippled by their defeat on Earth and the loss of their time craft, and perhaps leaderless (the Daleks need strong leadership, and are prone to turn on each other the moment they don't have it). We know that the Moroks were on Skaro - perhaps they stole more than just the one Dalek seen in their space museum. If they took, say, the Dalek Brain Machine that's seen to guide the Daleks and stripped the Daleks' archives, then it would have been a crippling setback.

The next time we see the Daleks, they're attacking human colony planets in the mid-twenty-fifth century. The Daleks did not, at this time, seem to have the strength to launch an attack against Earth itself.

However, they are clearly far more powerful than they were when confined to one city on Skaro. They've had a few centuries to rebuild and regroup, but we don't know anything about the catalyst for this process. Perhaps various defeated remnants of the Daleks - the space travellers, the time travellers and the inhabitants of Dalek City - converge on Skaro. There's a Supreme Council in place by the twenty-sixth century - perhaps this is the body that provides the unified leadership that allows the Daleks to gain strength.

A century later, the Daleks are far more powerful than ever before.

Presumably this is just a natural consequence of building up a powerbase for centuries. Interestingly, the Daleks seem to have time travel, but not to use it - they might just be wary after their two high profile defeats. They don't seem aware of the Time Lords, yet, but they must have spotted that the Doctor has thwarted them on the three occasions they've used time travel technology.[16]

In the twenty-sixth century there was "the third wave of Dalek expansion", and the Doctor described

---

Doctor, and they don't know about the Time Lords.

12 *Day of the Daleks*

13 From *The Chase* onwards, the Daleks know about the Doctor. They have "files" on him by *The Daleks' Master Plan*, and know he's from "another galaxy"; They recognise the second Doctor on sight in *The Power of the Daleks*, and lay a trap for him in *The Evil of the Daleks* (they have a photograph of him). They need to use the Mind Analysis Machine to identify the third Doctor in *Day of the Daleks*, but understand he can change his appearance. They know the third Doctor on sight in *Frontier in Space*, *Planet of the Daleks* and *Death to the Daleks* and the fourth Doctor in *Destiny of the Daleks*. They again lay a trap for the fifth Doctor in *Resurrection of the Daleks* (and have built duplicates of the fifth Doctor, Tegan and Turlough, so know of them). In *Revelation of the Daleks*, Davros has a tombstone pre-

pared that's specifically the sixth Doctor's; the Daleks don't seem to recognise the seventh Doctor in *Remembrance of the Daleks* - and Davros remarks on his changed appearance - but they know his name (and, indeed, both factions' plans rely on detailed knowledge of the Doctor's past).

Since the Time War, the Doctor has gone from being "an enemy of the Daleks" who they know is a threat to someone they are viscerally scared of - in *Dalek*, the Dalek knows the Doctor's name and reputation, but apparently doesn't recognise the ninth Doctor on sight. In *Doomsday*, the Daleks don't recognise the tenth Doctor, but are able to identify him, on sight, as a threat.

14 *The Rescue*

15 *The Daleks*

16 *The Chase, Day of the Daleks* and "Dogs of Doom".

the Daleks as "one of the greatest powers in the universe" at this time. This was the time of the Second and Third Dalek Wars, which sparked off when the Daleks attempted to divide and conquer the space empires of Earth and Draconia.[17]

The Daleks plot this with the Master. It's never made clear exactly what the Master tells them about himself, but this might be the point where the Daleks realise that the Doctor is just one of a race of time travellers with TARDISes.

This was Benny Summerfield's native time - her father, Abslom Daak and (later) Ace all fought in these Dalek Wars. Abslom Daak apparently killed the Dalek Emperor at this time. *This might have been a turning point in the war.*[18] It was a war that lasted a generation, ending in the early 2570s. The Daleks lost.

Following this, the weakened Daleks tried tactics other than full scale assaults.[19]

There are no accounts of the Daleks for centuries - and the human race goes from strength to strength as the Earth Empire spreads across the galaxy. Perhaps unsurprisingly, the Daleks became interested in "the Human Factor". The next time we see them, the Daleks are in their city on Skaro. The introduction of the Human Factor into the Daleks leads to civil war, to the Emperor's death and to the Doctor declaring this to be "the final end".[20]

So, the Daleks disappeared around the year 3000. It was the year 4000 before humanity came into contact with them again, but they'd begun their expansion around 3500.

The Daleks' Master Plan saw the Daleks' most ambitious scheme yet - a conquest of the entire Solar System, but merely as part of a strategy to dominate eleven whole galaxies. These Daleks also used time machines, and hoped to construct the Time Destructor. It's a plan that took fifty years to draw up. The Daleks were based back on Skaro at this point.[21]

Despite being defeated, the Daleks were now a powerful intergalactic force. Within twenty years of their Master Plan failing, the Daleks had succeeded in splitting the Federation. Within a couple of centuries of that, the Daleks were capable of threatening the Time Lords themselves.[22]

By now, then, the Daleks have learned of the Time Lords and Gallifrey. To a race dedicated to becoming the supreme beings of the universe, the Time Lords were now obviously the ones to beat - and from now on, the Daleks express no interest in conquering the Earth.[23]

The Davros Era took place - the Daleks lost their war with the Movellans, but Davros clawed his way to become the new Dalek Emperor. He re-engineered the Daleks, upgraded their technology and put them in a position where they were a genuine threat to the Time Lords... which may have been what the Dalek leadership had planned all along.

Whether the events of War of the Daleks *can be taken at face value or not, the Daleks get what they want - they go from military defeat and fragmented forces to having a strong leader and the knowledge and ability to take on the Time Lords.*

The Daleks may, or may not have lost Skaro. Either way, by now the Daleks were operating at a universal level, not just an intergalactic one. We have patchy information for the next ten thousand years or so, but Captain Jack sums it up: they were the greatest threat in the universe.

The Daleks now merely superficially resembled Davros' original creation. The Dalek Emperor (at least the third or fourth bearer of the title, and definitely not Davros) now oversaw an entirely revamped Dalek force - a huge army of highly-mobile, heavily-defended Daleks, with a re-engineered Dalek mutant inside. At least some of these Daleks had built-in "temporal shift" units. Dalek Saucers were now capable of firing missiles that could shoot down a TARDIS in flight.

To put the Daleks' might in perspective: now the Daleks were upgraded, a single one of them was capable of subduing the entire human population of twenty-first century Earth. Four of them could fend off droves of Cybermen with no evident damage or difficulty.

Before this upgrade, in 2540, the largest army of Daleks ever assembled consisted of ten thousand Daleks - it was capable of conquering an entire galaxy. In the year 4000, five thousand Daleks would have been enough to subdue Earth's Solar System.

Now, the Dalek space fleet consisted of ten million ships, each with two thousand Daleks onboard. Twenty *billion* Daleks.

The Daleks were ready to fight the Last Great Time War ...

---

17 *Frontier in Space*
18 "Nemesis of the Daleks"
19 "Metamorphosis", *Death to the Daleks*
20 The seventh Doctor met the Emperor earlier in history in the comic strip "Nemesis of the Daleks". As the Emperor in *The Evil of the Daleks* says it's their first meeting, he's either lying or a different individual from the one in the earlier story.
21 *The Daleks' Master Plan*
22 *The Apocalypse Element*
23 The Doctor explicitly states that the Daleks don't want to conquer the Earth in *Remembrance of the Daleks*.

GALLIFREY

The history of the Time Lords and their homeworld of Gallifrey was shrouded in mystery. The Time Lords knew little of their own past, and much of what was known was cloaked in uncertainty and self-contradiction. It is extremely difficult to reconcile the various accounts of the origins of the Time Lords. The authorities suppressed politically inconvenient facts, although few Time Lords were very interested in politics anyway.[1]

Gallifreyan history can be divided into two periods: "the Old Time", the semi-legendary foundation of Time Lord society millions of years ago; and "recent history", that which has happened within living memory. (Time Lords, of course, live a long time.)[2]

The Old Time

We have only a few scraps of knowledge about the history of Gallifrey before the discovery of time travel.

"The Stolen TARDIS" -> In the distant past of Gallifrey, the planet was dominated by the dinosaur-like Gargantosaurs. The reptilian Sillag arrived here from the future in a stolen TARDIS, but a Gallifreyan technician - Plutar - was along for the ride and had the vital Relativity Differentiator needed to repair the Ship. The two fought and returned to their native time.

Gallifrey was the home of "the oldest civilisation in the universe", and had "ten million years of absolute power".[3]

Gallifreyans mastered the use of transmats when the universe was less than half its present size.[4] Time Lords used to speak and write Old High Gallifreyan, now a dead language.[5] Gallifrey means, literally "they that walk in shadows".[6] **Gallifrey was in the constellation Kasterborous.**[7]

Kasterborous was a mythological figure who was chained to a chariot of silver fire by the gods.[8] **The planet Karn was close to Gallifrey.**[9] Karn was in conjunction with the gas giant Polarfrey.[10]

Gallifreyans were naturally telepathic and could build "living" machinery that was also telepathic.[11] They possessed a "reflex link", superganglions in their brains that allowed the Time Lord intelligentsia to commune.[12] The Time Lords discovered that they had a "dark side" of their minds.[13]

Gallifrey had twin suns, a burnt orange sky, slopes with deep red grass and plants that displayed silver leaves in the autumn.[14] Masonry from the Old Time survived, deep beneath the Capitol, into the modern era.[15] Gallifrey had a single moon, Pazithi Gallifreya.[16]

1 In *The Deadly Assassin*, the Time Lords don't know that their power comes from the Eye of Harmony and in both that story and *The Ultimate Foe*, they haven't heard of the Master. In *The Deadly Assassin*, even the Doctor seems unaware of the APC Net, and knows little about Rassilon.
2 The phrase "the Old Time" is first used in *The Deadly Assassin*. Not all Gallifreyans are Time Lords, as the Time Lords are the ruling elite of Gallifrey - the Doctor seems to say in *The Invisible Enemy* that there are only "one thousand" Time Lords. However, the terms "Time Lord" and "Gallifreyan" seem interchangeable for most practical purposes. Likewise, "Time Lord" is used to refer to the Doctor's race even before they master time travel (e.g.: *Remembrance of the Daleks*, where the "Time Lords" have trouble with the prototype of the Hand of Omega). Gallifrey is first named in *The Time Warrior*, although the Time Lords' home planet was called Jewel in the *TV Comic* strip "Return of the Daleks".
3 *The Ultimate Foe*
4 *Genesis of the Daleks*
5 *The Five Doctors*
6 *The Pit*
7 *Pyramids of Mars*
8 *Lungbarrow*
9 *The Brain of Morbius*
10 *Lungbarrow*
11 We learn that Susan is telepathic in *The Sensorites*, and it has been stated on a number of occasions that the Doctor (e.g. *The Three Doctors*), the TARDIS (e.g. *The Time Monster*) and all Time Lords (e.g. *The Deadly Assassin*) are telepathic. The Doctor has also stated on a number of occasions that the TARDIS is alive (e.g. *The Five Doctors*), and so is the Nemesis seen in *Silver Nemesis*.
12 *The Invisible Enemy*
13 Omega has a "dark side" to his mind in *The Three Doctors* and the Valeyard [q.v.] represents the Doctor's dark side (*The Ultimate Foe*). In *Falls the Shadow*, the Doctor refers to this as the "Dark Design".
14 *Gridlock*, expanding a little on Susan's description of her home planet in *Marco Polo*. As such, it's explicit confirmation that Susan is from Gallifrey.
15 *The Deadly Assassin*. Engin says that deep beneath the Capitol there are "vaults and foundations dating from the Old Time".
16 *Cat's Cradle: Time's Crucible, The Infinity Doctors, The Gallifrey Chronicles*

The Dark Days

At the very dawn of Time Lord history were "the Dark Days".[17] This was "the time of Chaos". One of the Doctor's most closely guarded secrets was that he was somehow involved with this period.[18]

> "In the days before Rassilon, my ancestors had tremendous powers which they misused disgracefully. They set up this place, the Death Zone and walled it around with an impenetrable force field. Then they kidnapped other beings and set them down here... even in our most corrupt period, our ancestors never allowed the Cybermen to play the game - like the Daleks they played too well... old Rassilon put a stop to it in the end. He sealed off the entire zone and forbade the use of the Time Scoop... there are rumours and legends to the contrary. Some say his fellow Time Lords rebelled against his cruelty and locked him in the Tower in eternal sleep." [19]

Gallifreyans were naturally "time sensitive", with a unique understanding of time.[20] The earliest Time Lords discovered dematerialisation theory.[21] Another key discovery was transdimensional engineering.[22] The Time Lords built the Time Vortex, a vast transdimensional spiral encompassing all points in space and time.[23]

The Time Lords' ancestors built the Time Scoop.[24] The Gallifreyans mostly resembled tall, athletic humans. They were truly immortal, barring accidents.[25]

CAT'S CRADLE: TIME'S CRUCIBLE -> The Pythias, a line of prophetesses who, since the 254th Pythia, rejected technology in favour of magic and superstition, ruled Gallifrey. Time travel was achieved by psychic prophecy, not physical means. The Pythias were guided by the prophesies in *The Book of Future Legends*, and saw their heritage as the Bright Past. The great philosopher Pelatov lived five thousand years before Rassilon.

At the time of the Intuitive Revelation, the age of Rassilon, the barbaric Gallifreyan Empire spread across the universe and encompassed the Pen-Shoza, Jagdagian, Oshakarm, the Star Grellades, Mirphak 2 and the rebellious Aubert Cluster. For aeons, Gallifreyan Heroes such as Ao had fought campaigns against foes such as the Gryffnae, lacustrine Sattisar and the batworms of the asteroid archipelago. The Winter Star was besieged for a century. The great hero Haclav Agusti Prydonius, commander of the Apollaten, defeated the marauding Sphinx of Thule, and was sent to observe a dispute brewing between Ruta III and the Sontara Warburg.

Across the cosmos, the ruling seers were dying: the Sphinx of Thule; the Logistomancer of A32K, foreseer of a cold empire of logic; the Core Sybilline of Klanti; the Sosostris in the West Spiral; The-Nameless-That-Sees-All

---

17 *The Five Doctors*
18 *Silver Nemesis*
19 According to the Doctor in *The Five Doctors*.
20 *City of Death, Warriors' Gate, Time and the Rani*.
21 *The Claws of Axos*
22 *The Robots of Death*
23 *Just War*. The Time Vortex was first named in *The Time Monster*.
24 *The Five Doctors*
25 *The Infinity Doctors*
26 *Lungbarrow*
27 *Cat's Cradle: Time's Crucible, Lungbarrow*
28 *Lungbarrow*
29 *Interference*. Rassilon's dissolution of the monasteries presumably accompanies his defeat of the Pythia.
30 Omega first appears in *The Three Doctors* and reappears in *Arc of Infinity, The Infinity Doctors* and *Omega*. The Hand of Omega, his stellar-manipulation device, appears in *Remembrance of the Daleks, Lungbarrow* and *The Infinity Doctors*.
   The first reference to Rassilon is in *The Deadly Assassin*; after that he becomes the central figure of Gallifreyan history, referred to in many subsequent stories (the quotes are from the Doctor, in *The Five Doctors* and *Shada* respectively). Both Rassilon and Omega are

the legendary founders of Time Lord society, both are "the greatest" of the Doctor's race and supply the energy necessary for time travel. The first time that it is explicitly stated on-screen that they were contemporaries is in *Silver Nemesis*, although earlier in Season Twenty-Five, *Remembrance of the Daleks* attempted to rationalise the two accounts of Time Lord origins. Early *Doctor Who Weekly* issues included a back-up strip written by Alan Moore which was an account of the origins of the Time Lords, and which has been referred to in novels such as *The Infinity Doctors* and *Interference*.
31 *Silver Nemesis*
32 The Other was mentioned or alluded to in countless New and Missing Adventures, his first appearance being in the *Remembrance of the Daleks* novelisation.
33 Engin, *The Deadly Assassin*.
34 *The Infinity Doctors*
35 *The Quantum Archangel*, following up a reference from *Castrovalva*.
36 The tenth Doctor's first reference to Citadel and its dome is in *Gridlock*, and it is actually seen in *The Sound of Drums*.
37 *The Three Doctors*
38 The Doctor, *Remembrance of the Daleks*.
39 *Omega*. These details hail from Omega's unreliable

in the North Constellations. The 508th Pythia became the last of her line. After a visit from a Master Trader of the South, she finally recognised that the veil of Time would soon only be traversed physically, not mentally. She instigated the Time Programme.

The Time Scaphe, the first time vessel and powered by the mental energy of its crew, was launched but vanished. Rassilon and his neo-technologists overthrew the Pythia. As her followers fled to Karn, the Pythia cursed Gallifrey with her dying words: its people became infertile, the colonies began to demand their independence and an Ice Age commenced. The Pythia cast herself into an abyss.

Rassilon lost a daughter to the Pythia's curse. The only good omen was the return of the Time Scaphe. Quennesander Olyesti Pekkary, captain of the Time Scaphe and first son of the House of Fordfarding, was Rassilon's nephew.

The family Houses of Gallifrey were sentient and the oldest beings on Gallifrey. They were born at the time of the Intuitive Revelation.[26]

To get around the Pythia's curse of sterility, Rassilon and the Other built Looms capable of weaving Gallifreyans from existing genetic material.[27] Time Lords were born from the Loom fully grown and fully conscious, but needed educating.[28]

A priest on early Gallifrey was driven into the wilderness when Rassilon dissolved the monasteries. While wandering, he happened across all twelve of his future incarnations, who had no memory of how they came to appear together. The priest became known as IM Foreman, and his thirteen incarnations founded a time-travelling carnival. Their caravan was a complex space-time event that would model itself a new shape on each arrival.

Events on Dust in the thirty-eighth century mortally wounded Foreman's incarnations, forcing them to regenerate and causing amnesia. They were flung through time to early Gallifrey for the original Foreman to paradoxically find.[29]

The Mastery of Time

Two Gallifreyans ensured that their people became the Lords of Time: Rassilon and Omega. Rassilon was the "greatest single figure in Time Lord history", yet "no one really knows how extensive his powers were" and he "had powers and secrets that even we don't understand". To this day, the Time Lords revere Omega as their "greatest hero", "one of the greatest of all our race".[30]

Omega, Rassilon and another Time Lord developed Validium, a "living metal" designed to be the last line of defence for Gallifrey.[31] The third Time Lord was known as "the Other" to modern Time Lords.[32]

"Today we tend to think of Rassilon as the founder of our modern civilisation, but in his own time he was regarded mainly as an engineer and an architect. And, of course, it was long before we turned away from the barren road of technology." [33]

The Time Lord Capitol and Citadel dated from the time of Rassilon and Omega, but in those days they weren't enclosed in a dome. The Citadel was built to withstand a siege, but against what enemy had been lost to history.[34] The Zero Room beneath the Capitol on Gallifrey was built by the Other.[35] **The Citadel of the Time Lords resided on the continent of Wild Endeavour, in the mountains of Solace and Solitude.[36]**

Omega was a member of the High Council, the solar engineer who found and created the power source needed for time travel: the energy released by a supernova. He was lost in the explosion, and the Time Lords believed that he had been killed.[37]

"A long time ago on my home planet of Gallifrey there lived a stellar engineer called Omega. It was Omega who created the supernova that was the initial power source for Gallifreyan time-travel experiments. He left behind him the basis on which Rassilon founded Time lord society... and he left behind the Hand of Omega. The Hand of Omega is the mythical name for Omega's remote stellar manipulator - the device used to customise stars with. And didn't we have trouble with the prototype..." [38]

One version of Omega's history suggested that he was originally an Academy student named Peylix. He theorized that his people could gain mastery of time by exploding a star within the Sector of Lost Souls, but Peylix's tutor, Luvis, deemed this nonsense and awarded him an "omega" grade - the lowest score attainable. The nickname "Omega" plagued Peylix, but Rassilon's rise to power allowed him to properly implement his theories.

Peylix set out aboard the *Eurydice* to detonate a star, but his colleague Vandekirian warned that the targeted system contained sentient life. Omega proceeded anyway, and Vandekirian - trying to prevent Omega from gaining his handprint for security clearance - destroyed one of his hands in the ship's fusion reactors. Omega cut off Vandekirian's other hand, and used it to launch his stellar manipulator. The star exploded, killing the system's inhabitants. Vandekirian's hand caused an impurity in the fusion reactor and the ship exploded, consigning Omega to a universe of anti-matter.[39]

THE INFINITY DOCTORS -> The Ice Age had led to the collapse of Gallifreyan civilisation, in the time known as the Darkness. Libraries and temples burned. Many Gallifreyans perished. The Loom-born were smaller than the Womb-born and were mortal, but they preserved the Gallifreyan genetic codes.

Nine years after the Pythia's curse, the Elders still treated the Loom-born with disdain, viewing them a temporary solution to a problem. Rassilon and his Consortium gave everyone hope by finding "the Fragment", the last surviving prophecy that spoke of Rassilon's personal rise and how the Gallifreyans would become the Lords of Time. The Other knew that Rassilon had faked the Fragment.

Rassilon and Omega set out for Qqaba, the only surviving Population III star in the galaxy. There were two Hands of Omega. They would detonate the star, releasing Time Energy that would be syphoned into fuel cells. However, the stasis halo protecting Omega's ship failed as Qqaba went supernova and Omega fell into the black hole that was forming. The crews of the surviving ships were infused with the energies. At the heart of this, Rassilon used the power of the singularity to rewrite the laws of physics across the entire universe. One effect of this, whether Rassilon knew it or not, was that Omega still lived, trapped inside the black hole.

Omega left behind a widow, a Womb-born Gallifreyan who would become known as Patience.

"Star Death" -> Four Gallifreyan starbreakers moved to the star Qqaba. From the flagship *Aeon*, Jodelex and Griffen waited, safe behind Stasis Haloes that protected their ships from the primal forces. They knew that Rassilon had yet to work out how to navigate through time. Fenris, a mercenary from the future, arrived to prevent the creation of the Time Lords. He sabotaged the lead ship, condemning Omega to what seemed like certain death, but Rassilon used the power of his mind to contain the black hole, then severed Fenris' time belt as he tried to escape. Fenris was scattered throughout eternity, and Rassilon picked up the belt containing the directional control he needed to navigate time.

The star Omega detonated was in the Constellation of Ao.[40] Omega used the sunskipper *Eurydice* to reach the star he detonated, Jartus. Some scholars at the Omega Heritage Centre (a popular tour destination) think Rassilon deliberately got rid of Omega, who was more popular.[41]

Two members of a Council of Three - Provost Tepesh (the Prime of the Arcalian chapterhouses) and Lady Ouida, both of them vampires - allied with the Great Mother of a Sisterhood against Rassilon. The Great Mother's assistant was Cassandra, a member of the House of Jade Dreamers. They sought to discover the secrets of Rassilon's Foundry, but the Divergents again threatened to break through at this juncture. The Foundry was firestormed to prevent

memories and are highly suspect. The details about Omega committing genocide, certainly, stem from a blending of the Doctor's recollections and are likely to be false.

40 *Lungbarrow*

41 *Omega*, an idea supported by *Zagreus*.

42 *Zagreus*. According to a questionable simulation, this occurred after Omega detonated his star. Arata is named as the third member of the Council of Three. The Great Mother belongs to the Sisterhood of Karn, although it isn't mentioned by name. Of all the suspect recreations shown in *Zagreus*, this one is the most dubious due to Tepesh's biased claims, and because he and Ouida, as vampires, would be unlikely to hold such authority in the Gallifreyan echelons for long, if at all.

43 *The Book of the Old Time*, referred to in *The Deadly Assassin*.

44 *The Impossible Planet / The Satan Pit*

45 *The Three Doctors, The Deadly Assassin, Remembrance of the Daleks*.

46 *The Deadly Assassin*

47 "The Final Chapter". As it's only reached 5725.2 by the time of *Doctor Who: The Movie* - a period of millions of years after Rassilon's time - each unit can't represent a calendar year. Perhaps it misses out some of the numbers (i.e. it's short for 10,005,725 RE, or something like it), or it's more like a stardate in *Star Trek*, and the exact

method of calculation is impossible for us to decipher.

48 *Heart of TARDIS*

49 *Neverland*

50 *Shada*

51 *Four to Doomsday*

52 *Neverland*

53 *The Deadly Assassin, The Invasion of Time*

54 *The Two Doctors. Zagreus* further suggests that the Imprimatur also facilitated regeneration, and that Rassilon introduced the limit of twelve regenerations to avoid the problem of degenerating biogenic molecules.

55 *The Five Doctors*

56 *The Invasion of Time*

THE KEY: In *The Deadly Assassin*, the Great Key is "an ebonite rod" that seals the Eye of Harmony within its monolith. By *The Invasion of Time*, that artefact is called "the Rod", and the Great Key is an ordinary-looking mortise key that can power the Demat Gun and has been hidden from the President by successive Chancellors since the time of Rassilon. We might presume that the Chancellor told the President that the Rod *is* the Key, hence the confusion of the two. However, two Chancellors we know about - Goth and Borusa - are both in line to be President while (presumably, in Goth's case) knowing the whereabouts of the real Great Key.

In *The Ultimate Foe*, "The Key of Rassilon" allows

this, which wiped out the conspirators.[42]

"And Rassilon journeyed into the black void with a great fleet. Within the void no light would shine. And nothing of that outer nature continued in being except that which existed within the Sash of Rassilon. Now Rassilon found the Eye of Harmony which balances all things that they may neither flux, whither nor change their state in any measure, and he caused the Eye to be brought to the world of Gallifrey wherein he sealed this munificence with the Great Key. Then the people rejoiced." [43]

The Doctor's people invented black holes.[44] The Gallifreyans successfully concluded the experiments, becoming the Time Lords. Mastery of Time required an unimaginably vast energy supply, which Rassilon set about acquiring.[45]

Modern Time Lords believed the Eye of Harmony to be a myth, that and the Sash of Rassilon had merely symbolic importance. In reality, the Sash prevented the wearer from being sucked into a parallel universe. The Eye of Harmony was the nucleus of a black hole, from which all the power of the Time Lords devolved. "Rassilon stabilised all the elements of the black hole and set them in an eternally dynamic equation against the mass of the planet." [46]

Year Zero Rassilon Era is marked from the moment Rassilon activated the Eye of Harmony.[47] The earliest time-travel legends say Rassilon decapitated a Great Beast, took the branching golden tree of its metathalmus and found the First Secret of Chrononambulatory Egress.[48] Rassilon anchored the timeline of the universe, creating one unified history. The Antiverse was created as an equal and opposite reaction to this.[49]

LUNGBARROW -> Nine point six years after Omega was lost, Rassilon was purging anyone opposed to his regime. The Other was disgusted, and tried to get his granddaughter Susan and her nanny Mamlaurea to safety on the planet Tersurus. Susan had coined the term "TARDIS" to describe the new time ships. The Other then threw himself into the Prime Distributor that fed all the Looms. He knew he would be reborn at some point in Gallifrey's history.

A year later, the Doctor - unknown even to him, the reincarnation of the Other - arrived from the distant future. He found Susan wandering the streets, unable to escape. She recognised him as her grandfather and they left Gallifrey together to explore the universe ...

"4-D War" ->

"We are fighting a timewar, comrades. A war in four dimensions. A war that on our timeline hasn't even started yet! Our enemy is in the future. We must know his identity. His reason for hating us... we must know his weaknesses!"

Twenty years after Fenris was scattered into the time vortex, Rema-Du - daughter of Jodelex and Griffen - had been training for a decade to retrieve him. At this time, the Time Lords employed the Special Executive, parahumans with unusual talents. One of them, Wardog (whose mind could withstand stresses that would reduce anyone else to insanity) partnered Rema-Du.

They entered the Vortex via a warp gate and located Fenris. He was connected to a Brainfeeler to identify the enemy. The Time Lords discovered that their enemy was from thirty thousand years in the future, a cadre of supermen called the Order of the Black Sun. A Black Sun squad - including members called Llorex, Faru-Faro and Drin - killed Fenris and the Brainfeeler, severed Wardog's arm and vanished. The Time Lords were left unsure what they would do, if anything, to provoke such an attack.

"Black Sun Rising" -> Ten years later, Rema-Du and Wardog attended talks with the Sontarans. A member of the Order of the Black Sun disrupted the gathering.

The Great Days of Rassilon

As President of the Time Lords, Rassilon ushered in an age of technological and political progress. The phrase "the Great Days of Rassilon" appears in the Gallifreyan book *Our Planet's Story*, which was read by every Time Tot.[50] Even races such as the Urbankans, who knew nothing of the Time Lords, had legends of Rassilon.[51] Rassilon's exploits were remembered on many planets, whose legends speak of Azaron, Razlon and Ra.[52]

Rassilon was credited with many scientific achievements: He created the Transduction Barriers surrounding Gallifrey. These prevented the unauthorised landing of a TARDIS or similar vehicle. A quantum force-field also existed as a barrier against more conventional threats.[53]

Rassilon introduced the symbiotic nuclei - the "Rassilon Imprimature" - into the genetic make-up of Time Lords, allowing them to fully travel through Time.[54] He also discovered the secret of temporal fission.[55]

Rassilon invented the Demat Gun, a weapon that required the Great Key to function. This weapon was so powerful that the Great Key was hidden from all future Presidents by successive Chancellors.[56] The

Time Lord Tribunal could impose the penalty of dematerialisation on other races or individuals, such as the War Lord.[57]

Rassilon created a servant, but she gained free will and rebelled, killing a few thousand Time Lords. Rassilon thought he'd killed "Pariah" - as she was now known - but she escaped to Earth in 1879. Subsequently, Rassilon created Shayde, a more loyal servant.[58]

... Of Rassilon

Rassilon was associated with many relics and concepts, all of which had "stupendous power". Many were lost, or their true purpose was unknown.[59]

These included the Sash of Rassilon, the Great Key of Rassilon, Rassilon's Star (the Eye of Harmony) and the Seal of Rassilon.[60] The Sash of Rassilon could alter the biodata of Time Lord President to allow better access to the Matrix. The Doctor, a former President, was affected by it.[61]

The Seal of Rassilon was also known as the omniscate.[62] The pattern for the Seal of Rassilon scrambled the neurosystems of beings from outside our Universe, such as vampires, to ward them off.[63]

Other relics and items included the Wisdom of Rassilon, the Rod of Rassilon ("Rassilon's Rod!" was also a mild Gallifreyan expletive)[64], the Record of Rassilon, the Directive of Rassilon[65], the Tomb or Tower of Rassilon, the Game of Rassilon, the Black Scrolls of Rassilon, the Harp of Rassilon, the Coronet of Rassilon and the Ring of Rassilon.[66]

The music the fifth Doctor played on the Harp of Rassilon was called "Rassilon's Lament".[67] The Rassilon Imprimature[68] mapped Time Lords on to the Vortex.[69]

There was also the Key of Rassilon (not the Great Key, but one which allows access to the Matrix)[70] ... the Legacy of Rassilon[71] ... the Horns of Rassilon, also known as the Sign of Rassilon (a magical warding sign)[72] ... Rassilon's Red, Gallifrey's finest vintage wine[73] ... the Runes of Rassilon[74] ... and the Equation of Rassilon which allowed for travel through a time corridor. It "is and isn't" a scientific formula.[75]

The Time Lords signed the Pact (or Treaty) of Rassilon with the Sisterhood of Karn, protecting them in return for the Elixir of Life.[76] Romana learned to dance the Foxtrots of Rassilon, as well as learning the Seven Strictures of Rassilon.[77] The Master destroyed TOM-TIT with a Profane Virus of Rassilon, which was designed to prevent Gallifreyan technology falling into alien hands.[78]

Rassilon as Ruler

Rassilon became President of Gallifrey.[79] Rassilon was the first - and to date only - Lord High President.[80] Rassilon was also a legislator. In his time, five principles were laid down.[81] History says the Timescoop was destroyed after Rassilon's Reformation.[82]

The Constitution was drafted. Article Seventeen guaranteed the freedom of political candidates.[83] Only a unanimous vote of the High Council could over-rule the President.[84] Thanks to Rassilon, TARDIS databanks contained 18,348 coded emergency instructions. Older TARDISes (Type 40 and older) had a magnetic card system, the "Record of Rassilon", which contained emergency instructions regarding the Vampires.[85] The "Rules Governing Time Lords" were probably drafted at this time.[86]

Article Seven of Gallifreyan Law forbid Time Lords

access to the Matrix through portals such as the Seventh Door, and the Keeper of the Matrix wears it on his robes - this is presumably an entirely different artefact.

57 *The War Games*
58 "Wormwood"
59 *Shada*
60 *The Deadly Assassin*
61 *Alien Bodies*
62 *The Infinity Doctors*
63 *Interference*
64 *The Invasion of Time, The Androids of Tara*
65 *State of Decay*
66 *The Five Doctors*
67 *Blood Harvest*. He played the Harp in *The Five Doctors*.
68 *The Two Doctors*, spelled that way in the script and novelisation, and in its more usual form as "Imprimatur" in some of the later books.
69 *Interference*

70 *The Ultimate Foe*
71 *Remembrance of the Daleks*
72 *Timewyrm: Revelation* (p54), *No Future* (p203).
73 *The Eight Doctors*
74 *The Ancestor Cell*
75 *The English Way of Death*
76 *Warmonger*
77 *Tomb of Valdemar*
78 *The Quantum Archangel*
79 *The Invasion of Time*. The Doctor becomes "the first President since Rassilon to hold the Great Key", implying that Rassilon was President.
80 *The Infinity Doctors*
81 *Shada*
82 *World Game*
83 *The Deadly Assassin*
84 *The Five Doctors*
85 *State of Decay*
86 *The Androids of Tara*
87 *Terror of the Vervoids*

from committing genocide.[87] The death penalty was abolished, except in extreme circumstances such as a threat to Gallifrey or genocide.[88] The prison planet Shada was set up to house the most dangerous criminals in the universe. A key to the facility was encoded in the pages of Rassilon's book, *The Worshipful and Ancient Law of Gallifrey*, which was housed in the Panopticon Archive.[89]

Rassilon decreed that no Time Lord should travel into Gallifrey's past.[90] Rassilon's technology stopped Time Lords from investigating their own futures.[91] Rassilon built the Oubliette of Eternity, which exiled prisoners to the Antiverse. He was known as the Conqueror of Yssgaroth, Overpriest of Drornid, First Earl of Prydon, Patris of the Vortex and Ravager of the Void.[92]

The Eternal Wars

"The myths of Gallifrey talk about nameless horrors infesting our universe that were only defeated through the might of the Time Lords."

Rassilon's experiments created holes in the fabric of space-time, which consequently unleashed monsters from another universe. For over a thousand years, across the cosmos, the Ancient Gallifreyans fought the Eternal Wars against the monsters from another universe. These included the Vampires and the Yssgaroth. The great general Kopyion Liall a Mahajetsu was said to have died during this time, but he'd secretly survived. The Matrix contained no record of this war. When Rassilon overthrew the Pythia, Gallifrey was cursed with a plague from which only a few survived. Some suggested that Rassilon himself released the virus to wipe out all who knew of his mistake - they further claim that Rassilon deliberately sealed Omega in his black hole.[93]

When Rassilon was young, a Vampire army swarmed across the universe. Each Vampire could suck the life out of an entire planet.

"Energy weapons were useless, because the monsters absorbed and transmuted the energy, using it

to become stronger. Therefore Rassilon ordered the construction of bowships, swift vessels that fired a mighty bolt of steel that transfixed the monsters through the heart - for only if his heart be utterly destroyed will the Vampire die... The Vampire Army: so powerful were the bodies of these great creatures, and so fiercely did they cling to life, that they were impossible to kill, save by the use of bowships. Yet slain they all were, and to the last one, by the Lords of Time - the Lords of Time destroying them utterly. However, when the bodies were counted, the King Vampire, mightiest and most malevolent of all, had vanished, even to his shadow, from Time and Space. Hence it is the directive of Rassilon that any Time Lord who comes upon this enemy of our people and of all living things shall use all his efforts to destroy him, even at the cost of his own life..."

This war was so long and so bloody, that afterward the Time Lords renounced violence forever.[94]

Members of the Prydonian and Arcalian chapters crewed the bowships. N-forms were developed to fight vampires by the Patrexes Chapter. N-forms existed in pocket universes and could quickly extrude a vast killing machine onto planets infected by vampirism. They were programmed to kill all life on planets where vampires were detected.[95]

Warships were built to act as carriers for the bowships.[96] A marginal illustration in one book of legends showed a bat overcoming an owl. The owl was a traditional symbol of Rassilon; the bat of the Vampires. Some Gallifreyan heretics to this day worship Rassilon the Vampire, believing the Great Vampire bit Rassilon, and that Rassilon himself became a vampire towards the end of his life.[97]

A powerful rival race would have evolved after the Time Lords, but Rassilon trapped them in a moebius loop. They became known as the Divergents.[98]

Four of the outer worlds built temples to honour Rassilon in his own time.[99] Rassilon discovered the secret of perpetual regeneration - "timeless, perpetual bodily regeneration - true immortality", but knew that only the power-mad would attempt such a thing. Rassilon had prevented at least four such Time Lords

---

88   *The Brain of Morbius, Arc of Infinity, Terror of the Vervoids*. In *The Invasion of Time*, it's said that unauthorized use of a TARDIS "carries only one penalty," but this isn't definitively stated as execution.
89   *Shada*
90   *Timewyrm: Revelation*
91   *Alien Bodies*
92   *Neverland*

93   *The Pit*
94   *State of Decay*
95   *Damaged Goods*
96   *So Vile a Sin*
97   *Goth Opera*
98   *Zagreus*
99   *Lungbarrow*

from discovering the secret of true immortality.[100]

The Neverpeople - a group of exiled Time Lord criminals - falsified legends which stated that Rassilon fought and prevailed against the destroyer Zagreus in the Antiverse, but was entombed in a Zero Cabinet. This was part of the Neverpeople's plan to lure Time Lords into the Antiverse and facilitate their escape.[101]

Rassilon's consciousness survived within the Matrix, from which he was able to watch over the whole of time and space. He was one of three Matrix Lords, along with Morvane and Bedevere. All three were Higher Evolutionaries.[102] **Upon his death, Rassilon was entombed in the Dark Tower, where he remains to this day in eternal sleep. Legends state that anyone who reaches the Tower and takes the Ring of Rassilon will gain immortality. Gallifreyan children were familiar with the story and learned a nursery rhyme:**

"Those to Rassilon's Tower Would Go... Must choose: Above, Between, Below." [103]

There were six vast statues in the Panopticon. These honoured the Founders of Gallifrey. Omega's statue was in the southern corner, Rassilon was opposite. Another statue was that of Apeiron (who wore combat boots). There was a nursery riddle that, when solved, revealed the identity of all six ... although the Doctor couldn't remember all of it:

"Neath Panopticon dome Rassilon faces Omega... But who is the other?... brother." [104]

The six statues represented the six Gallifreyan Colleges.[105] While both Rassilon and Omega were virtually canonised, if not deified, there were no further records of the Other in any of the histories. Speculation says that he left Gallifrey altogether. Legend says that he grew weary of being an all-powerful player at the chess game of the Universe. Instead he longed to be a pawn on the board in the thick of the action.[106]

The Ancient Texts

The Book of the Old Time was the official version of Rassilon's achievements, and a modern transgram had been made of it.[107] The Black Scrolls of Rassilon contained a forbidden account of the same period, including the secrets of Rassilon's power.[108] There were many R.O.O. texts (those dealing with legends of Rassilon, Omega and the Other).[109]

The Red Book of Gallifrey concerned the Dark Time and talked of Rassilon the Ravager, Omega the Fallen and the Other. It also contained magical incantations.[110] The Green and Black Books of Gallifrey discussed legends of the future, including the Timewyrm.[111] There was a book called *The Triumphs of Rassilon*.[112]

There were records known as *The Other Scrolls*.[113] There was a prophecy that the Time Lord who found the lost scrolls of Rassilon will lead Gallifrey from darkness.[114] One book, bound in reptile skin and with an embossed omniscate on the cover, survived until the end of the universe. It contained one last prophecy, which terrified the Doctor when he read it.[115]

---

100 *The Five Doctors*
101 *Neverland*
102 "The Tides of Time"
THE HIGHER EVOLUTIONARIES: It's never explained in the comic strips exactly what defines a Higher Evolutionary, or what their sphere of influence is. From the examples of Rassilon and Merlin, we can see that they're semi-legendary figures - immortals with enormous personal powers that go far beyond psychic abilities until they are indistinguishable from magic. As such, the Higher Evolutionaries are capable of viewing and influencing events across infinity and eternity.

In the final part of "The Tides of Time", we see dozens of High Evolutionaries from "throughout the known universe". We're only given the names of six during the story: Rassilon; Morvane; Bedevere ("The Matrix Lords", and implicitly the latter two are Gallifreyans); Dakon Theta and the Thane of Kordar from the Althrace System; and Merlin the Wise from Earth. By the time of "The Final Chapter", the Higher Evolutionaries include a representative of the Order of the Black Sun, Demoiselle Drin, in the place of Merlin.

It's unclear whether the fact that Bedevere and

Merlin are both names from Arthurian legend is significant, or how this Merlin relates to the Doctor being the Merlin of a parallel universe in *Battlefield*.
103 *The Five Doctors*
104 *The Infinity Doctors*
105 *The Ancestor Cell*
106 *Cat's Cradle: Time's Crucible*
107 We hear a female voice read an extract from the modern translation of *The Book of the Old Time* in *The Deadly Assassin*.
108 The last extant copy of The Black Scrolls of Rassilon is destroyed in *The Five Doctors*.
109 *Goth Opera* (p119).
110 *No Future* (p203).
111 *Timewyrm: Revelation* (p65).
112 *Lungbarrow*
113 *The Infinity Doctors*
114 *The Gallifrey Chronicles*
115 *The Infinity Doctors, The Ancestor Cell*
116 *The Infinity Doctors*
117 *Heart of TARDIS*
118 *Image of the Fendahl*
119 *Underworld*

Between the Ancient and Modern

The Time Wars were fought in the generation after Rassilon. The Tomb of the Uncertain Soldier in the Capitol honours a Gallifreyan who died during the Time Wars, cancelling out his own timeline for the greater good of Gallifrey. The Time Lords' Oldharbour Clock is the only surviving relic from an alternate universe wiped out in the Time Wars. Unknown to anyone, the clockwork figures had evolved into the most intelligent beings on the planet.[116] The Doctor said he witnessed Gallifrey's Time Wars first-hand, although the Time Lords wiped the wars from their history books.[117]

The Time Lords time-looped the Fifth Planet, home of the Fendahl, twelve million years ago.[118] When the Gallifreyans were new to space / time exploration, they discovered the inhabited world of Minyos and were worshipped by the population there. In return, they gave technology to the Minyans. The Minyans eventually used nuclear technology to destroy their planet. The Time Lords subsequently renounced intervention in the affairs of other planets.[119]

The Time Lords used their great powers to help the people of Micen Island, in Orion. This led to chemical and biological warfare on the planet. The Time Lords renounced interference, erecting the Temple of the Fourth as a monument. A small number of Time Lords, though, felt the need to atone for past sins, and covertly intervened in the universe's affairs.[120]

Because of their great powers, and their tendency to lead to corruption, Time Lords were discouraged from emotion and affection. They were trained with a series of tests, including a journey to Anima Persis. They were mentored by older Time Lords, but the final judgement on whether an individual can be a Time Lord (and the punishment of any Time Lords who misuse their power) was handled by the mysterious Kingmaker, an ancient crone.[121]

Time Lords appear to have possessed mental blocks that prevented their interfering in history. However, if one of these blocks was broken, the others soon shattered.[122] Three centuries after Rassilon's death, Rassilon's Rampart was built to defend against the lawless Shobogans.[123]

It took fifty generations for TARDISes to become an acceptable form of travel, and another twenty for them to be used to participate in history.[124] All TARDISes had a pre-set circuit - a time-track crossing protocol - that prevented travellers from visiting the same space-time location more than once. Doing so would result in recursion effects of completely unknown and unpredictable consequences. The Daleks didn't use such a system, meaning they could sometimes overlap their journeys and history.[125]

Epsilon Delta was a Time Lord from the Ancient Time who gained a double beta in cybernetics. He stole a TARDIS and adopted the name "the President". He settled in St Matthew's College, Oxford.[126]

The shanty township of Low Town sprang up at the base of the Capitol Dome, and was settled by normal Gallifreyans, Outsiders and those seeking a life free of the restrictions of Time Lord society. The Capitol once had a Harbour.[127] A suit of armour belonging to Tegorak gathered dust in one storeroom, as did a giant stuffed bird.[128]

Time Lords dabbled at breaching the higher dimensions, but the Dimensional Ethics Committee banned the work.[129] At some point, the Biblioclasm claimed the Endless Library. The Watch checked every night to prevent such a thing happening again. A quarter of a million years ago, the Time Lords were afflicted with the Blank Plague. The Time Lords fought military campaigns against Rigel, Gosolus and about a dozen other worlds.[130]

The Time Lords developed the blackstar, a weapon to crack Dyson Spheres.[131] Gallifreyan artefacts included Pandeka's staff and an artefact associated with Helron.[132]

"The Stolen TARDIS"[133] **->** A Gallifreyan student named Plutar was failed because he wanted to meddle in the affairs of other planets. He was put to work maintaining TARDISes. Meanwhile, a ship landed outside the Time Lords' city, and the lizard-like Sillarg fooled those present

---

120 *Death Comes to Time.* This sounds like a retelling of the Minyan story, or possibly an indication that there were many such mistakes made in Gallifrey's past.
121 *Death Comes to Time*
122 *Time and Relative*
123 *Lungbarrow*
124 *The Ancestor Cell*
125 *Renaissance of the Daleks.* The fifth Doctor overrides this circuit to rescue Nyssa and a Knight Templar after they're killed in 1864, which somewhat begs the question of why he doesn't do this more often. It's presumably this circuit that malfunctions and causes the "time track" anomaly seen in *The Space Museum.* The fact that the Daleks don't use such a protocol probably accounts for the alternate timeline in which they're the masters of Earth in *Day of the Daleks.*
126 *The Dimension Riders*
127 *The Eight Doctors, The Infinity Doctors*
128 *The Infinity Doctors*
129 *Tomb of Valdemar*
130 *The Infinity Doctors*
131 *The Infinity Doctors.* The implication is that they would be (or had been?) used against the People of the Worldsphere first seen in *The Also People.*
132 *Divided Loyalties*
133 Dating "The Stolen TARDIS" (*DWW* #9-11) - The Doctor says "when did it happen? Oh, a long time ago, dates really aren't important to us time travellers".

into watching a space circus while he moved to steal a TARDIS. He stole one that Plutar was working inside, but it malfunctioned and took them to the distant past of Gallifrey. Plutar warned the authorities on their return, whereupon Sillag was arrested and his memory of Gallifrey erased. Plutar was asked to reapply to the Academy.

"Minatorius"[134] **->** A young Time Lord visited the planet Minatorius, and died to prevent a reactor there from going critical.

The Matrix

The Time Lords built the Matrix, a form of computer that could - amongst other things - store the minds of dead Time Lords.[135] When the Matrix was young, it began to break down as thousands of Time Lord minds resented their deaths. The Time Lords cleaned the Matrix by isolating its dark part - the Dark Matrix. It was caged and forgotten about beneath the Citadel, sealed with a great key held by the Keeper of the Matrix.[136]

The Garvond was imprisoned for a time in the Gallifreyan Matrix, where it assimilated copies of Time Lord minds, including that of the Doctor. The creature's exact origins were unknown, although by nature it was the embodiment of the evil in the minds in the Matrix. The Garvond wanted to sail the Time Vortex and consume all life. It had several thousand names, all corruptions of the High Gallifreyan term for "of darkest thought".[137]

The Land of Fiction was originally part of the Matrix.[138]

Technological and Scientific Advancement

Gallifreyan technology has been refined, rather than totally reworked, over the last ten million years.[139] A dark science of earlier Time Lords was quantum mnemonics, a reality-altering power that manipulated the basic nature of reality and probability. Quantum mnemonics allowed one to transform the history of a planet or an individual by warping space and time.[140]

The Time Lords used devices called amaranths to rebuild parts of time and space that were damaged in the Time Wars. They were originally built to manipulate black holes.[141] **The Time Lords discovered an indestructible material.**[142] **They learnt to engineer micro-universes. Eventually, they abandoned the barren road of technology.**[143]

They abandoned tachyonics for warp matrix engineering.[144] **They invented the Magnotron. Over time, the Primitive Phases One and Two of the Matrix were relegated to the Archives. Phases Three to Six remain in use.**[145] **They developed Gallifreyan Morse.**[146] Gallifreyan zinc was an excellent conductor, and one of the strongest substances in the known universe.[147]

Erkulon, the greatest nano-engineer in Gallifreyan history, created the time ram.[148]

The Time Lords took the credit for the Library of Carsus, although no-one knew for sure who built it. It was built millennia ago, and contained every book ever written. It was in an area of space known for time anomalies -

Sillarg lands without encountering Gallifrey's transduction barriers (*The Invasion of Time*) or other defences, and the city isn't domed (although it may not be the Capitol, as we know there are other cities on Gallifrey).
134 Dating "Minatorius" (*DWM Winter Special 1981*) - Like "The Stolen TARDIS", this could take place at any time.
135 *The Deadly Assassin*
136 *Matrix*
137 *The Dimension Riders*
138 *Conundrum*
139 *So Vile a Sin*
140 *Millennial Rites*
141 *Christmas on a Rational Planet*
142 *The Mutants*
143 *The Deadly Assassin*
144 *The Leisure Hive*
145 *The Trial of a Time Lord*
146 *Shada*
147 *Pier Pressure*
148 *The Quantum Archangel*
149 *Spiral Scratch.* Lakertya appeared in *Time and the Rani.*
150 *Mawdryn Undead*
151 *The Stones of Blood*
152 *The Dimension Riders*
153 *Legacy*
154 *The Devil Goblins from Neptune*
155 *A Device of Death*
156 *Managra*
157 *Timewyrm: Genesys*
158 *Damaged Goods*
159 *The Impossible Planet*, which concurs with information in the novels, such as *Cold Fusion* and *The Taking of Planet 5.*
160 *Cold Fusion*
161 *Goth Opera*
162 *The Crystal Bucephalus*
163 *The Gallifrey Chronicles*
164 *Love and War*
165 *The Eight Doctors*
166 *The Sound of Drums*
167 Aliens recognise the Doctor as a Time Lord in *The Time Warrior, The Brain of Morbius, Image of the Fendahl, Underworld, The Invasion of Time, The Ribos Operation, State of Decay, The Keeper of Traken, Earthshock,*

the same solar system as Minerva, Schyllus, Tessus, Lakertya, Molinda, Hollus and Garrett.[149]

Three thousand years ago, Mawdryn and his followers stole a Metamorphic Symbiosis Regenerator.[150] Two thousand years ago, the Time Lords abandoned interspacial geometry.[151] Some Time Lords such as Epsilon Delta could rehearse various events without altering the true timeline.[152] Time Lords could use Reverse Tachyon-Chronons to move time backwards and forwards, manipulating material so that it wouldn't age.[153]

With great effort, Time Lords used a process called "soul-catching" to absorb a dying Gallifreyan's memories.[154] The Time Lords built the Parachronistic Chamber, deep in the Capitol, to regulate time distortions.[155] Mimesis was a Gallifreyan art in which anything you write came true. It was practiced by a cult that held an annual ritual called "the Thirteenth Night," but the High Council banned the ritual and the art, probably because it was too arcane and unpredictable.[156]

Time Lords' extended lifespans sometimes necessitated that they edit out their more useless memories, storing them electronically or erasing them.[157] An artificial, multi-dimensional art gallery was located beneath the Capitol.[158]

TARDISes were grown, not built.[159] They were grown in space, away from Gallifrey, to prevent time pollution. Stattenheim signals could broadcast along Eye of Harmony time contours, so TARDIS remote control worked even from across the Universe.[160] Time Lord technology could retrieve ancestral memories from the blood of virgins. Time Lords could communicate telepathically across the Time Vortex. The poisons in tea couldn't harm them.[161]

Time Lords used 208 language tenses, most of which didn't translate well.[162] The Time Lords used an omegabet, which was better than an alphabet.[163] Castellan Lode, a female, was the greatest literary historian the Time Lords ever had.[164]

A Gallifreyan golden guinea could buy you a few drinks at a bar.[165]

Foreign Policy

The Time Lords were the oldest and most mighty race in the universe, sworn only to watch, never to inter-fere. Gallifrey was called "the Shining World of the Seven Systems".[166]

Alien races from all periods of recorded time have had dealings with the Time Lords, ranging from those in the ancient past such as the Kastrians and the destroyer Sutekh to those in the far future such as the Usurians. Other races or beings who know something of the Time Lords and Gallifrey (without hearing just of the Doctor or another individual) include the Andromedans, the Bandrils, the Cybermen, the Daleks, the Face of Boe, the Family of Blood, the Fendahl, Fenric, the Forest of Cheem, the Guardians, Mawdryn's race, the Mentors, the Minyans, the Nestene, the Racnoss, the Sisterhood, the Sontarans, some residents of the Third Zone, the Keeper of Traken, Vampires and the Vardans.

Clearly, the Time Lords visited many worlds in many time periods, even in an official capacity.[167] They also authorised (or prevented) other races' time travel experiments and defended the Laws of Time.[168] Time Lords observed but didn't interfere.[169] At times they intervened with regards to unauthorized time travel, and could almost be thought of as "galactic ticket inspectors".[170]

They were committed to protecting weaker species, and to preventing aggression against indigenous populations.[171] Time Lords were "forbidden to interfere".[172] The vast majority of Time Lords didn't concern themselves with the universe outside the Capitol, and were more concerned with internal politics.[173] Time Lords were taught "very early on" not to visit newly formed planets, as the morphogenetic fields of such worlds were still in flux, and therefore susceptible to undue influence from visitors.[174]

The Celestial Intervention Agency was concerned with covert intervention.[175] The CIA's motto was, "The story changes, the ending stays the same", meaning that it didn't matter how one fixed temporal anomalies so long as time continued along a straight path. For instance, if a man who would start a war were erased from time, it was incumbent on the organization to start it anyway.[176] Study of the later Humanian era was forbidden by the Academy as being outside the Gallifreyan sphere of influence.[177]

Mawdryn Undead, Resurrection of the Daleks, Vengeance on Varos, The Two Doctors, Timelash, The Trial of a Time Lord, The Curse of Fenric, Rose, The End of the World and *Dalek*.
168 *The Two Doctors*
169 *The War Games*
170 *The Time Warrior*
171 *The Hand of Fear*
172 According to the Cyber Lieutenant in *Earthshock*.
173 *The Deadly Assassin, The Invasion of Time*

174 *Scaredy Cat*
175 *The Deadly Assassin*. Fans and recent writers have rationalised away the Time Lords' stated "non-intervention" and the clear evidence that they have intervened by assuming that it's the secret (and in some stories highly sinister) "CIA" who are behind the interventions. This builds quite a lot on the one reference in the TV series.
176 *The Kingmaker*
177 *The Well-Mannered War*

Political

More Presidents hailed from the Prydonian Chapter than all other chapters combined. Prydonians were viewed as cunning, but claimed they "simply saw a little further ahead than most". They wore scarlet and orange robes. Other chapters included the Arcalians (who wore green) and Patrexes (who wore heliotrope).[178] The Patrexes were aesthetes who saw artistic value in all things, including suffering, but lacked the imagination to be true artists.[179]

The Celestial Intervention Agency evolved from Rassilon's personal guard.[180] At some point, the Time Lords Rungar and Sabjatric were sent to Shada. They remained there.[181] Apart from Rassilon, only President Torkal was ever referred to as "the Great".[182] While young, Salyavin learnt how to project his mind into others' and was sentenced to imprisonment in Shada as a result. He escaped, using his powers to erase all knowledge of the prison planet.[183]

Mundat the Third's reputation swung from his being a brutal murderer to a noble warrior - and that's just in the documentaries of the historian Ertikus.[184] In the lifetime of some contemporary Time Lords, President Pandak III ruled for nine hundred years.[185]

Savar tried to rescue Omega from his black hole, but was ambushed by the Time Lord god Ohm. Attempting to escape, Savar's TARDIS was stretched until it became the light-year-long structure called the Needle. Savar fled in an escape capsule, which was intercepted by the I. The I stripped the ship of technology and took Savar's eyes. He was found by the Time Lords, but was utterly insane from the experience. He regenerated, but was a broken man.[186]

The Doctor's TARDIS

The Doctor's TARDIS was known as a Type 40.[187] The Type 40 TT-Capsule was introduced when Salyavin was young.[188] The Type 40 was withdrawn centuries ago and was considered a "Veteran and Vintage Vehicle".[189]

178 *The Deadly Assassin*
179 *Damaged Goods*
180 *Lungbarrow*
181 *Shada*
182 *The Ancestor Cell*
183 *Shada*
184 *Omega*
185 *The Deadly Assassin*
TIME LORD PRESIDENTS: *The Ancestor Cell* says the Doctor was the 407th and 409th President of Gallifrey. *The Gallifrey Chronicles* says that Romana is the 413th. From this, we can extrapolate that the 405th President was the one killed in *The Deadly Assassin* (and almost certainly, in a previous incarnation, the one seen in *The Three Doctors*); the 406th was Greyjan the Sane (*The Ancestor Cell*); the 407th was the Doctor (he was "inducted" in *The Invasion of Time*); the 408th was Borusa (the President is referred to by the Doctor in *The Ribos Operation*, and he - or more likely the White Guardian posing as him - sends Romana on the quest for the Key to Time. It's *Arc of Infinity* before it's confirmed that Borusa is now President. Borusa regenerates twice more and his reign ends in *The Five Doctors*); the 409th is the Doctor; the 410th is Flavia, the 411th is Niroc, who's corrupt and deposed with the help of the Doctor and Rassilon in *The Eight Doctors*; the 412th is Flavia again, according to *Happy Endings*, which is set soon after Romana is installed as the 413th.
186 Savar is first mentioned in *Seeing I*, but these events take place "a thousand years" before *The Infinity Doctors*, as far as Savar is concerned. There was a Time Lord called Savar in *The Invasion of Time*.
187 The term was first used in *The Deadly Assassin*.
188 *Shada*
189 *The Pirate Planet*
190 *The Creature from the Pit*
191 In *Time and the Rani*, the Doctor deduces the combination to the Rani's lock is 953, "my age ... and the Rani's".
192 *Lungbarrow*, with *The One Doctor* confirming the "Snail" nickname.
193 *SLEEPY* (p204).
194 *Doctor Who - The Movie*
195 *The Tomb of the Cybermen*, further implied in *The Curse of Fenric* and confirmed in *Father's Day*.
196 *Time and the Rani*. He says, possibly facetiously, "you should see my uncle".
197 *Planet of Fire*. The sentence isn't complete, but the next word could well spell out a family relationship (fan speculation over the years has suggested a number of things, usually "brother" and less usually "husband").
198 *Smith and Jones*, and possibly a reference to Irving Braxiatel.
199 *Planet of the Spiders*
200 *Lungbarrow*
201 *The Scarlet Empress*
202 The Braxiatel Collection was first mentioned in *City of Death*. We first meet Irving Braxiatel in *Theatre of War*, but he's also present at the Armageddon Convention in *The Empire of Glass*, which occurs first chronologically. He has gone on to be a regular character in the Big Finish Bernice Summerfield books and audios, where Benny currently works for the Braxiatel Collection; and the *Gallifrey* series, which deals with his earlier history. The Benny novel *Tears of the Oracle* strongly suggests that Braxiatel and the Doctor are brothers.

The Early Life of the Doctor

There are a number of seemingly contradictory facts about the Doctor's birth and upbringing.

The Doctor was born under the sign of "**Crossed Computers**".[190] **He was born the same year as the Rani**.[191] He was one of forty-five cousins from the House of Lungbarrow. Unusually for a Time Lord, he had a belly button, which earned him the nicknames "Wormhole" and "Snail".[192] His Gallifreyan name had thirty-eight syllables.[193]

The Doctor was half human on his mother's side.[194] He had a family.[195] He may have had an uncle.[196] As the Doctor let the Master die on Sarn, the Master called out, '**Won't you show mercy to your own** —'[197]

The Doctor said he didn't have a brother '**anymore**'.[198] The Doctor's family owned a home in South Gallifrey.[199] This home was House Lungbarrow, which was perched on the side of Mount Lung, overlooking the Cadonflood river, two days from Rassilon's Rampart.[200] The Doctor doesn't know much about Gallifrey's Southern Hemisphere.[201]

Irving Braxiatel was a relative of the Doctor, either his brother or one of his Cousins. Braxiatel spent twenty years arranging the Armageddon Convention. After this, he dedicated himself to building the Braxiatel Collection, a repository of universal knowledge and art. Braxiatel collected every book banned by the Catholic Church. Unlike the Doctor, he freely left Gallifrey.[202]

There are a number of seemingly contradictory facts about the Doctor's age.[203]

The Doctor's Father

The Doctor remembered "**I'm with my father. We're lying back in the grass... it's a warm Gallifreyan night**".[204] The Doctor's father was taught by the ancient Gallifreyan who would be known as Patience, as his father had been. Many of his generation - such as Savar; Hedin; the Doctor's mentor, Lady Zurvana; the future President (a Chancellor at the time) and Marnal thought they could change the universe.[205]

The Doctor's father was a member of the High Council. He launched a great exploration of the universe, which became known as the Odyssey.[206] On his travels, he met an Earthwoman, the Victorian time traveller Penelope Gate. They married, and had at least one child. The Doctor's

---

203 THE DOCTOR'S AGE: The Doctor's age has been specified a number of times, but he is often vague and contradictory on the subject.

The second Doctor tells Victoria that he is "450" in *The Tomb of the Cybermen*. The Master of the Land of Fiction says he is "ageless" in *The Mind Robber*. (In the draft scripts of *The Power of the Daleks* and *The Underwater Menace,* he was "750".)

The third Doctor claims to have been a scientist for "thousands of years" in both *Doctor Who and the Silurians* and *The Mind of Evil*.

The fourth Doctor says he is "749" in *Planet of Evil, The Brain of Morbius* and *The Seeds of Doom*, and "nearly 750" in *Pyramids of Mars*. He is "750" by *The Robots of Death*, 756 (according to him) or 759 (according to Romana) in *The Ribos Operation*, nearly 760 in *Nightmare of Eden*, 750 again in *The Creature from the Pit* and *The Leisure Hive*. (A scripted scene in *The Stones of Blood* showed him celebrating his 751st birthday.)

The sixth Doctor is 900 in *Revelation of the Daleks* and *The Mysterious Planet* Part One, but "over 900" by *Terror of the Vervoids* Part One.

In *Time and the Rani*, both the seventh Doctor and the Rani are "953", and the Doctor has "nine hundred years experience" by *Remembrance of the Daleks*. In the New Adventures, he was around a thousand years old. According to *SLEEPY*, he celebrated his 1000th birthday during *Set Piece*.

The eighth Doctor is 1012 in *Vampire Science* and is twelve hundred by *The Dying Days*. We also know that he resided on Earth for one hundred and thirteen years, from 1888-2001, beginning with *The Ancestor Cell* and ending with *Escape Velocity*, although accommodating this depends on where one places *The Dying Days* in the eighth Doctor's lifetime.

The ninth Doctor says he's 900 in *Aliens of London* and *The Doctor Dances*. In response to Rose's question about the problems introducing himself without a real name in *The Empty Child*, he says, "Nine centuries in, I'm coping".

From this, we can infer some other dates:

• The Doctor has been operating his TARDIS for 523 years by *The Pirate Planet*, and was 759 in previous story, *The Ribos Operation*. This means that the Doctor left Gallifrey when he was 236.

• The Doctor attended his Tech Course with Drax "450 years" before *The Armageddon Factor*. This would mean he was 309 at the time (implying it was after he left Gallifrey, or that he left and then returned before leaving for the last time).

• Romana is equally inconsistent with her age, and the age difference between her and the Doctor can variously be calculated as 617 or 620 (*The Ribos Operation*), 625 (*City of Death, Creature from the Pit*) or 600 (*The Leisure Hive*).

204 *Doctor Who - The Movie*

205 *The Infinity Doctors*

206 *Cold Fusion*

father adopted the name Ulysses.[207]

The Time Lord Astrolabus was known as the thief of time - he stole the *Book of Old Time* before the Doctor was born. Astrolabus saw himself as a real Time Lord, a pioneer who charted the first meridians of time: "It was I who released Gallifrey from the chains of the present." However, he plundered the timezones he visited.[208]

The Master had a copy of the *Insidium of Astrolabus* in his TARDIS library.[209]

The Doctor's father had many friends and allies from alien planets. He broke protocol by inviting them to his House on Gallifrey. The Doctor's mother owned a Bible from which the Doctor read.

A computer portrait of the Doctor's parents hung on the wall of his quarters on Gallifrey. His father was "powerfully built with rugged features, a weathered face with dark eyes". His mother "a redhead, a little plump".[210]

One contemporary of the Doctor's father was Marnal, who believed that the Time Lords should intervene to eliminate potential threats to Gallifrey. He became known - dismissively - as a crusader. On one mission, to the Shoal on the edge of Mutter's Spiral, he stumbled across a race of insect creatures that he believed were a threat to Gallifrey. They weren't - until he intervened and changed history. "Marnal's Error" (meaning that he did not know his enemy) became a Time Lord proverb. Marnal had a son.[211]

Shortly after the Doctor was born, the Doctor's father was leading a team working on a mysterious Project. Other members included Penelope, Mr Saldaamir and a Time Lady from the relative future, Larna. Some Time Lords (including Marnal and Larna) knew of the Scrolls, recently-discovered prophecies that warned, in Larna's words:

"For millions of years, Gallifrey has existed in isolation. Soon - not imminently, not all at once - there will be a spate of attacks. Omega, the Sontarans, Tannis, Faction Paradox, Varnax, Catavolcus, the Timewyrm. You

know some of those names, you will come to know the others. It is very important that Gallifrey survives all these attacks. All things must pass. Gallifrey will fall. But it must fall at precisely the right time. The enemy is unknown to us. It will be until Last Contact is made. If it's destroyed before that, by any of those other enemies, then the consequences ... that is as much as I know."

Marnal added:

"The President and members of the Supreme Council know the prophecy. They have been told that a Time Lord now living will be central to all these events. That he will find the lost scrolls of Rassilon and lead Gallifrey from darkness."

To prevent the exposure of the Project, the Doctor's father wiped Marnal's memory and exiled him to Earth in 1883. He took Marnal's TARDIS, a Type 40, from him.[212]

When the Doctor was ten years old, he was caught skinny-dipping with one of his Cousins.[213] The Doctor flew skimmers as a boy on Gallifrey.[214] The Doctor remembers his mother smiling and his father holding him up to see the stars.[215]

The Doctor was a lonely little boy.[216]

The first time the Doctor left Gallifrey was to visit his family's summer house on the other side of the Constellation. While looking up into the night's sky with his mother, he saw a fleet of time ships but never asked where they were going.[217]

In the nursery, the Doctor used to play with bricks that contained Roentgen radiation.[218]

An account of the Doctor's boyhood claims that he and the Master grew up together, and played near the river Lethe. A bully, Torvic, menaced the Master, but the Doctor fought back and thereby caused Torvic's death. Death later

207 *The Gallifrey Chronicles*. Penelope Gate first appeared in *The Room with No Doors*.
208 "Voyager"
209 *The Quantum Archangel*
210 *The Infinity Doctors*
211 *The Infinity Doctors, The Taking of Planet 5, The Gallifrey Chronicles.*
212 *The Gallifrey Chronicles*. The prophecy is a paraphrase of one from an abandoned American pilot script from the nineties. The book shows the Doctor fulfilling the prophecy - assuming the "lost scrolls of Rassilon" are the Matrix files in his mind. He had already made Last Contact in *The Daleks*, when he made contact with the race that would eventually destroy the Time Lords in the Last Great Time War, as revealed in *Dalek*.

213 *Unnatural History*
214 *The Ghosts of N-Space*
215 *The Eight Doctors*
216 *The Girl in the Fireplace*
217 *The Infinity Doctors*
218 *Smith and Jones*
219 *Master*. This account is told as a fable, and so may not be true.
220 *The Time Monster, Planet of the Spiders, State of Decay*
221 *Lungbarrow*
222 *The Five Doctors*
223 *Shada*
224 *Image of the Fendahl*
225 *Black Orchid*
226 *The Nowhere Place*

visited the Doctor in a dream, and sought to take him as her Champion, but the Doctor told her to take the Master instead. This gave rise to the Master becoming Death's Champion, and would motivate the Doctor and the Master to leave Gallifrey.[219]

The Doctor's Education

The Doctor had a mentor who lived up a mountain near his home and taught him to see the beauty in a simple daisy, and to look into his own mind. The mentor told him ghost stories about the Vampires.[220] Satthralope, a member of House Lungbarrow, sacked the hermit because he was a bad influence and too expensive.[221]

The Doctor was interested enough in Gallifreyan history to take the unusual step of learning the dead language of Old High Gallifreyan.[222] The Doctor admired Salyavin.[223] He was frightened by stories of the Fendahl.[224] He always wanted to be a train driver.[225] The Doctor took up trainspotting as a hobby.[226]

The Doctor's mother told him a nursery rhyme about Zagreus, which spoke of people disappearing up paradoxical staircases.[227] When he was an impressionable age, she also told him scary stories about Grandfather Paradox.[228]

On Gallifrey, the Toclafane were spoken of in fairy tales, much like the bogeyman on Earth.[229]

The Academy Years

The Doctor was a contemporary of the Master, Runcible, Drax and the Rani.[230] He was "fifty years before" the Monk.[231] The War Chief and the Doctor recognised each other.[232] The Doctor knew Hedin and Damon.[233] He knew the Time Lord who warned him about the Master.[234]

The children of Gallifrey were taken from their families at age eight, and brought to the Academy. Each novice was taken for Initiation, and made to stand in front of the Untempered Schism - a gap in the fabric of reality. From there, each novice would see the whole of the Vortex, and stare at the raw power of time and space. Some novices would become inspired, some would run away, and some would go mad.

The Master looked into the Vortex while he was a child, and some believed this was the beginning of his madness. Something within the Vortex choose the Master as its instrument - throughout his lives, he was made to hear the sound of drums as a call to war.

The Doctor chose his name, as did the Master.[235]

The Doctor was at the Academy with Vansell.[236] He attended the Rani's raucous 94th birthday party.[237] The Doctor attended University with the Rani, and his speciality was thermodynamics.[238] The Doctor said his field was "mainly" the science of macro-cosmology.[239]

He attended "the Academy" with the Master.[240] The Doctor attended a Tech Course with the Class of '92, which included Drax, before he gained his Doctorate.[241] The Doctor was taught quantum mechanics at infant school. He and his friends once put a teacher in a time loop. He kept a pet flubble under his bed during his first year at the Academy, and was nearly caught when she went into heat and started a mating song.[242] He took his Gallifrey Lifesaver's Certificate.[243]

Iris Wildthyme claimed to have grown up in a House in southern Gallifrey. It was ruled by Aunts including Baba, her favourite. Iris' mother ran away with an off-worlder. Iris found an abandoned TARDIS in the wilderness and adopted it.[244]

Iris Wildthyme also claims to come from one of the New Towns under the Gallifreyan Capitol. Iris found her TARDIS abandoned in the mountains as a wasted experiment, helping it to learn, feed and evolve. In turn, the bus gave Iris advice. She's been travelling longer than the Doctor.

The Doctor said Iris wasn't a proper Time Lady and that the Time Lords were unsure of her identity.[245] Iris referred to the Doctor's people as "a snobby, over-privileged

---

227 *Seasons of Fear*

228 *The Gallifrey Chronicles*

229 *The Sound of Drums*

230 *Terror of the Autons, The Deadly Assassin, The Armageddon Factor, The Mark of the Rani.*

231 *The Time Meddler*

232 *The War Games*

233 *Arc of Infinity*

234 *Terror of the Autons*

235 *The Sound of Drums.* Some have questioned how the appearance of the child Master and the Doctor's mention of Gallifreyan "families" can be reconciled against the notion of looming as presented by the New Adventures. However, accounts of the Doctor's early life on Gallifrey always seem contradictory - by now, it's almost a tradition.

236 *Divided Loyalties, Neverland*

237 *The Death of Art*

238 *Time and the Rani*

239 *Night Thoughts*

240 *The Five Doctors*

241 *The Armageddon Factor*

242 *Island of Death*

243 *World Game*

244 *The Scarlet Empress*

245 *Verdigris*

bunch," possibly suggesting she's not a fully-fledged Time Lord.[246] **The Doctor studied at Prydon Academy (where Borusa taught him).**[247]

Gallifrey's highest peak, Mount Cadon, extended to the fringes of the planet's atmosphere and held the Prydonian Academy far up its slopes. Acolytes there endlessly recanted protocols and procedures. In high towers, special pupils learned dark arts.[248] The Academy was basically a self-contained city annexed to the Gallifreyan Capitol. It took up twenty-eight square miles of Gallifrey's surface.[249]

Lord Cardinal Lenadi led the Prydonian Chapter during the Doctor's time on Gallifrey.[250] Cardinal Borusa wrote a history called *Rassilon the God*.[251] **The Doctor was taught by Azmael.**[252] **He used to build time jammers to disrupt others' experiments.**[253] He used to build space-time portals for fun.[254] Ruath and the Doctor staged pranks together - they introduced cats into the Gallifreyan eco-system, altered gravity to make a Panoptican graduation take place in mid-air and electrified Borusa's perigosto stick.[255]

A Cardinal Sendak taught them at the Academy.[256] The Doctor skipped his Academy class on transdimensional locus attraction dynamics to learn the yo-yo and juggling.[257]

Daring neonates at the Academy played a dangerous game called "Eighth Man Bound". This entailed deliberately putting an "Initiate" into a state of flux between life or death, enabling them to witness and experience their future regenerations. The term was coined after a student of the Arcalian Chapter who was able to discover the natures of his first seven bodies, but couldn't observe the eighth. A student of the Prydonian Chapter was rumoured to have tied this record.[258]

The Doctor used to play truant so he could down pints of Best Shobogan beer at the Golden Grockle in Low Town. He seethed with anger at the High Council.[259] **The Doctor at this time was called Theta Sigma, his nickname.**[260] **The Master got a higher grade at Cosmic Science than the Doctor. The Doctor claims he was a late developer.**[261] Cardinal Sendok taught the Doctor and the Master cosmic science.[262]

DIVIDED LOYALTIES -> The Doctor was part of the Deca, a group of ten brilliant students who were activists in favour of more Time Lord intervention. The Deca members were: the Doctor, Koschei (the Master), Mortimus (the Monk), Magnus (the War Chief), Drax, Ushas (the Rani), Vansell (actually a Celestial Intervention Agency spy), Rallon, Millennia and Jelpax.

They were taught by Borusa, Franilla, Sendok and Zass.

It was as part of the Deca that the Doctor learned about the Toymaker. The Doctor, Rallon and Millennia located the Toymaker and were caught up in his games. Rallon and Millennia were apparently killed, and the Doctor was expelled from the Academy on his return to Gallifrey, ordered to spend five hundred years in Records and Traffic Control. He studied for his doctorate in his spare time.

The President at this time was Drall, the Castellan was Rannex. Type 35 TARDISes were in operation, the Doctor used a Type 18 to visit the Toymaker.

Only Jelpax completed his time at the Academy in the conventional manner, the others either went to special projects or vanished. Jelpax went on to work with Borusa.

The Doctor deliberately failed his exams so that people would underestimate him, and to avoid office duty.[263] **The Doctor eventually scraped through the Academy with 51 percent on the second attempt.**[264] **The Doctor failed his TARDIS pilot's test.**[265] His poor results were a grave disappointment to his parents.[266]

The Doctor on Gallifrey

The Doctor says he was a pioneer among his people.[267] **He built his Ship, and Susan coined the acronym TARDIS.**[268]

Before leaving Gallifrey the Doctor was used on a diplomatic mission at least once, when he visited the inauguration of Station Chimera in the Third Zone.[269] Following a campaign by the Doctor, the Time Lords banned miniscopes.[270] **The Doctor was a member of the Prydonian Chapter but came to forsake his birthright.**[271] When the Doctor was on Gallifrey, Cardinal

246 *Excelis Dawns*
247 *The Deadly Assassin*
248 *Timewyrm: Revelation*
249 *Divided Loyalties*
250 *Lungbarrow*
251 *Cat's Cradle: Time's Crucible*
252 *The Twin Dilemma*
253 *The Time Monster*
254 *Made of Steel*
255 *Goth Opera*
256 *The Quantum Archangel*
257 *Match of the Day*

258 According to Professor Thripsted's *Genetic Politics Beyond the Third Zone* in *Christmas on a Rational Planet* (p212-216). The Doctor names himself as "Eighth Man Bound" in *The Dying Days*.
259 *The Eight Doctors*
260 *The Armageddon Factor, The Happiness Patrol*
261 *Terror of the Autons*
262 *The Quantum Archangel*
263 *Lungbarrow*
264 *The Ribos Operation*
265 *The Shakespeare Code*
266 *The King of Terror*

Lenadi led the Prydonians.[272]

The Doctor's reflex link connected him to the Time Lord intelligentsia.[273] Like all Time Lords, he swore an oath to protect the Law of Gallifrey.[274]

The Doctor was a member of the Supreme Council.[275] He held a powerful position before leaving Gallifrey.[276] He was a member of the High Council during the latter years of his first incarnation.[277]

"Flashback"[278] -> The first Doctor ("Thete") supervised Magnus' project to tap into a giant ball of Artron Energy that Magnus had extracted from the Vortex. It would provide the Time Lords with more power than even Rassilon and Omega had dreamt of, and Magnus saw this as leading to "a new beginning for our stagnant race". The Doctor was more sceptical, and his fears were confirmed when they learned the energy ball was alive. Magnus wanted to continue regardless - so the Doctor destroyed his equipment with a staser. "And that was that. Any chance of a reconciliation between the two - any hope of regaining their former friendship - died at that moment." The Doctor was commended for his action.

Past Lives

Morbius would later probe the Doctor's mind, and see eight incarnations of the Doctor before the one generally accepted as the "first" Doctor.[279]

The Doctor's Marriage

The Doctor fell in love with his former nurse and tutor, the Womb-born Gallifreyan who would become known as Patience. She taught him to dance, which he did in front of some house guests including Mr Saldaamir, a pair from Althrace and a yellow-skinned man with red fins.

They married. Savar was one of the guests at the wedding.[280] The Doctor painted his wife's portrait. As he finished, she told him she was pregnant.[281] They went on to have thirteen children.[282]

Shortly after he regenerated, the Doctor and Patience celebrated the birth of their first grandchild. Their son was a Cardinal and the Doctor sat on the Supreme Council, as his father did before him. The President ordered the Guard to search the Doctor's family home for "children born of woman". The Doctor's thirteen children were dragged out and his daughter-in-law's baby was scheduled for termination. The Doctor's whereabouts during this incident were unknown, but there was a warrant for his arrest - he stood accused of "consorting with aliens".

The Doctor (in what we would consider his "first" incarnation) would later travel back in time to this point. He rescued his infant granddaughter and took her to the ancient past. He then got Patience to safety by taking her to an ancient TARDIS. As he did this, the Capitol was burning.[283] Mobs stormed the Panopticon that night.[284]

The Doctor's memories of this trauma were blocked, although by who or what is unclear. He believed his wife had died.[285] It is unclear if the Doctor's father was still on Gallifrey at this point. After this, the Doctor's father may have adopted the name Joyce and relocated to San Francisco on Earth, continuing the Project with Larna and Mr Saldaamir.[286]

The Doctor remembered that he was a father, once.[287]

267 *The Daleks*

268 *The Chase, An Unearthly Child*, although later stories seem to contradict both claims. Some commentators have tried to attribute the Doctor's statement in *The Chase* to mean that he only built his Ship's time-path detector, not the whole Ship, but this is a rationalisation after-the-fact and not borne out by the scene itself. *Lungbarrow*, at least, supports the notion that Susan created the word TARDIS by claiming she was around when TARDISes were relatively new.

269 *The Two Doctors*

270 *Carnival of Monsters*

271 *The Deadly Assassin*

272 *Lungbarrow*

273 *The Invisible Enemy*

274 *Shada*

275 *Cold Fusion, The Infinity Doctors*

276 *Deadly Reunion*

277 *World Game*

278 Dating "Flashback" (*DWM Winter Special 1992*) - "Ancient Gallifrey, or so it seems." Magnus is apparently the War Chief from *The War Games*.

279 *The Brain of Morbius*. See the "Past Lives" sidebar.

280 *Cold Fusion, The Infinity Doctors*

281 *The Infinity Doctors*

282 *Cold Fusion*

283 *Cold Fusion, The Infinity Doctors*. The Doctor's new incarnation matches the description of the "Camfield Doctor" seen in *The Brain of Morbius*.

284 *The Infinity Doctors*

285 *Cold Fusion*

286 *Unnatural History*. There's also no account of what happened to the Doctor's son and daughter-in-law, or any of the Doctor's other children.

287 *Fear Her*. Although some have seen this as a reference to the Doctor raising Miranda in *Father Time*, if he was indeed Susan's biological grandfather, then he clearly must also have been a father.

The Infinity Doctor

? (=?) (w?) - THE INFINITY DOCTORS[288] **->** The Doctor mourned for his dead wife, and even though she died a long time ago, he still lit a new candle every year in her memory. Before this time, he had travelled the universe and returned to Gallifrey. He had defeated and imprisoned Centro, a mechanical being that could warp space.

On Gallifrey, the Doctor served as a tutor who oversaw - amongst others - the brilliant student Larna. He negotiated a final peace between the Sontarans and the Rutans, ending their eternal war. Gallifrey monitored "the Effect", a reality-altering ripple. The Doctor and his friend the Magistrate went to the end of time to confront the one who was responsible: Omega. The Doctor met his wife Patience, whom Omega had rescued from death, but again lost her. Omega was defeated, but the Magistrate didn't return from this mission. The Doctor did, and had grown restless with Gallifrey.

Voran became President. Larna was charged to travel the universe and clear up after the Effect, a mission that would take two thousand years.

Susan

The Doctor's granddaughter Susan was something of an enigma.[289]

Susan was the Doctor's grand-daughter "and always will be".[290] Susan described her home planet as "quite like Earth, but at night the sky is a burned orange, and the leaves on the trees are bright silver".[291] She knew about the Dark Tower.[292] She was fifteen when she met Ian and Barbara.[293] The other Time Lords never referred to Susan.[294] She coined the name "TARDIS".[295]

Susan was born in Gallifrey's recent past. Her grandfa-

---

288 Dating *The Infinity Doctors* (PDA #17) - The story takes place an unspecified amount of time after Patience disappears, to an unspecified incarnation of the Doctor, at an unspecified point before Gallifrey's destruction (possibly between *The Gallifrey Chronicles* and *Rose*). It's a thousand years since Savar lost his eyes.

IS THE INFINITY DOCTORS CANON?: *The Infinity Doctors* is a story set on Gallifrey that takes all the information from every previous story (in all media) set on Gallifrey - and other references to it - at face value and incorporates them into the narrative. The paradox being that we've seen a vast number of contradictory accounts of the Doctor's home planet, so that *The Infinity Doctors'* super-adherence to established continuity actually makes it impossible to place at a particular point in continuity without contradicting something established elsewhere.

References in *Seeing I, Unnatural History, The Taking of Planet 5, Father Time* and *The Gallifrey Chronicles* all make it clear that *The Infinity Doctors* (or at the very least events identical to it) took place in the "real" *Doctor Who* universe.

Latterly a fan consensus has built up that *The Infinity Doctors* is set on the "reconstructed" Gallifrey promised by *The Gallifrey Chronicles*, that the Infinity Doctor is the eighth Doctor, and his Gallifrey is the one destined to be destroyed in the Time War. This wasn't the author's intention, but isn't ruled out by the book.

289 IS SUSAN THE DOCTOR'S GRANDDAUGHTER?: *Cold Fusion* recounts Susan being rescued by the Doctor as an infant, which followed the description in the original "Cartmel Masterplan" document. When the events of that document were dramatised in *Lungbarrow*, Susan was an older child.

This complicates an already rather convoluted story. If both the accounts of *Cold Fusion* and *Lungbarrow* are

taken at face value (and both contain degrees of ambiguity), it seems that Susan was born to the Camfield Doctor's daughter-in-law in the recent past (ie: when the Doctor was a younger man and living on Gallifrey, not millions of years ago at the time of Rassilon). The Hartnell Doctor came back to this time zone (in *Cold Fusion* it's possible he simply regenerated, but this would seem to seriously contradict *Lungbarrow*) with the Hand of Omega and then rescued the infant Susan and Patience. The Doctor then travelled deep into the past of Gallifrey, where Susan was left in "safety" with the Other (where she was considered the last womb-born child). Patience fled Gallifrey in an early TARDIS (possibly she was taken into the distant past, too, and stole the TARDIS there). The Hartnell Doctor would revisit ancient Gallifrey and discover that following the death of the Other, Susan had been living on the streets there.

290 *An Unearthly Child*, the quote comes from *The Dalek Invasion of Earth*. The Doctor and Susan frequently refer to each other as grandfather and grandchild.

291 *Marco Polo*

292 *The Five Doctors*

293 Barbara says Susan is fifteen in *An Unearthly Child*. In *Marco Polo*, Ping Cho says she is "in my sixteenth year", and Susan says "Well, so am I". So Susan is not far older than she looks, unlike Romana.

294 Susan is never mentioned by any Time Lord, either those on Gallifrey or the various renegades.

295 *An Unearthly Child*. Later stories showed the manual for the Doctor's TARDIS which has the word on the cover, suggesting it was coined long before the Doctor's time. One possible conclusion is that Susan is from an earlier period of Gallifreyan history, and which is indeed what *Lungbarrow* established.

PAST LIVES: The orthodox view accepted wholesale by most fans is that the Doctor is a Time Lord who can regenerate his body twelve times when it is seriously injured. It's also held that William Hartnell played "the first Doctor" and that by the end of *The Parting of the Ways* the Doctor has regenerated nine times, so that David Tennant is the tenth incarnation of the Time Lord. This version of events is actually established very late in the show's history (the term "regeneration", for example, is not even used until *Planet of the Spiders* at the end of Season Eleven, the word "incarnation" is only used on rare occasions - such as in *The Twin Dilemma* and *The Trial of a Time Lord* (Season Twenty-Three) - and so on).

Only a half a dozen stories refer to the orthodox view: In *The Three Doctors*, the Time Lords claim that the Hartnell Doctor is the "earliest". We learn that the Time Lords are limited to twelve regenerations in *The Deadly Assassin*, a view that is reinforced by *The Keeper of Traken*, *The Five Doctors* and *The Twin Dilemma*. (Although in *The Deadly Assassin*, *The Keeper of Traken* and *The Five Doctors*, we learn that it is indeed possible for a Time Lord to regenerate more than twelve times, and in *The Twin Dilemma*, Azmael initiates a thirteenth regeneration, the strain of which kills him).

It is *Mawdryn Undead* (Season Twenty) before the Doctor explicitly states that he has regenerated four times and has eight regenerations remaining. In *The Five Doctors*, the Hurndall Doctor sees the Davison Doctor and concludes "so there are five of me now" and refers to himself as "the original, you might say". In *Time and the Rani*, the Doctor talks of his "seventh persona". The voiceover at the start of the *Doctor Who* TVM says that the Doctor is "nearing the end of my seventh life".

Despite all this, the commonly used terms such as "first Doctor", "second Doctor" and so on are never used on screen (and should never be capitalised).

More often, the evidence about the Doctor's past is ambiguous or inconclusive: he seems vague about his age throughout his life, the details varying wildly from story to story, likewise his name, his doctorate and the reasons why he left Gallifrey. In *The Deadly Assassin*, Runcible remarks that the Doctor has had a facelift and the Doctor replies that he has had "several so far" (the original script more specifically said he had done so "three times"). In *The Ultimate Foe*, the Valeyard comes from somewhere between the Doctor's "twelfth and final incarnation" (not the "twelfth and thirteenth"). No unfamiliar Doctors come to light in *The Three Doctors* or *The Five Doctors*, but on two occasions (*Day of the Daleks* and *Resurrection of the Daleks*) an attempt to probe the Doctors mind is abruptly halted just as the William Hartnell incarnation appears on the monitor. In *The Creature from the Pit*, he claims Time Lords have ninety lives, and he's had a hundred and twenty.

There have been a number of hints that incarnation of the Doctor played by William Hartnell was not the first. In the script for *The Destiny of Doctor Who*, the new Doctor confides to his astonished companions that he has "renewed himself" before. In the transmitted version of the story, *The Power of the Daleks*, the line does not appear, but neither is it contradicted. In *The Brain of Morbius*, Morbius succeeds in mentally regressing the Doctor back from his Tom Baker incarnation, through Jon Pertwee, Patrick Troughton and William Hartnell, but this time no-one interrupts and we go on to see a further eight incarnations of the Doctor prior to Hartnell. Morbius shouts - as the sequence of mysterious faces appears on the scanner - "How far Doctor? How long have you lived? Your puny mind is powerless against the strength of Morbius! Back! Back to your beginning! Back!". These are certainly not Morbius' faces (as has occasionally been suggested) or the Doctor's ancestors or his family. Morbius is not deluding himself. The Doctor fails to win the fight and almost dies, only surviving because of the Elixir... it just happens that Morbius' brain casing can't withstand the pressures either.

The production team at the time (who bear a remarkable resemblance to the earlier Doctors, probably because eight of them - Christopher Barry, George Gallacio, Robert Banks Stewart, Phillip Hinchcliffe, Douglas Camfield, Graeme Harper, Robert Holmes and Chris Baker - posed for the photographs used in the sequence), definitely intended the faces to be those of earlier Doctors. Producer Philip Hinchcliffe said: "We tried to get famous actors for the faces of the Doctor. But because no-one would volunteer, we had to use backroom boys. And it is true to say that I attempted to imply that William Hartnell was not the first Doctor".

However we might want to fit this scene into the series' other continuity, or to rationalise it away, taking *The Brain of Morbius* on its own, there's no serious room for doubt that these are pre-Hartnell incarnations of the Doctor. This hasn't stopped fans doubting, of course.

Two stories later, in *The Masque of Mandragora*, the Doctor and Sarah Jane discover "the old control room" that the Doctor claims to have used, although it had never been seen in the television series before.

Cold Fusion features a sequence where the Doctor remembers his past on Gallifrey (p172-173), where he has recently regenerated to resemble the "Camfield Doctor" seen in *The Brain of Morbius*. However, there is a degree of ambiguity as to whether these are the Doctor's own memories.

Lungbarrow states that the Hartnell Doctor was the first and hints, but never explicitly states, that the faces seen in *The Brain of Morbius* are incarnations of the Other, not the Doctor.

ther was the Doctor. She was a naturally-born child, an abomination in the eyes of the authorities of Gallifrey. Her mother's fate was unknown. Her father was a Cardinal.[296]

Susan was born in Gallifrey's distant past. Her grandfather was the Other. She was the last naturally-born child on Gallifrey. Her mother died at the moment of her birth, as the Pythia's curse of sterility came into effect. Her father was a warrior.[297]

The Doctor Leaves Gallifrey

The exact nature of the Doctor's departure from Gallifrey is still a mystery, and there have been a number of seemingly contradictory accounts of the circumstances in which he left.

LUNGBARROW[298] **->** The Doctor worked as a Scrutationary Archivist in the Prydonian Chapterhouse Bureau of Possible Events. His applications for promotion were always turned down.

Consulting the Bench of Matrocians, Quences - the head of the Lungbarrow household - learned that the Doctor would be a huge influence on the future of Gallifrey. He wanted the Doctor to become a Cardinal. The Doctor stormed out of his family home after an argument with Quences about the Doctor's future prospects. With the Doctor no longer regarded as a member of the family, a replacement - Owis - was Loomed to maintain the Family Quota. However, this was illegal and the House was ostracised from Gallifreyan affairs. The Doctor's Cousins were trapped in the House.

The Doctor left an experiment with water-sligs running. A hundred and thirty years, later they broke out.

Quences was the 422nd Kithriarch of Lungbarrow.

The Doctor decided to steal a TARDIS and leave Gallifrey. The Hand of Omega recognised the Doctor was linked to the Other. When the Doctor left Gallifrey, the Hand redirected him to Gallifrey's ancient past.

He was an "exile", unable to return home.[299] The Doctor "had reasons of his own" for leaving his home planet.[300] He might have left of his own free will, because he was "bored" or had "grown tired of their lifestyle". He renounced the society of Time Lords. He abandoned his Prydonian birthright.[301] But he has also stated he was "kicked out" and was "on the run".[302] He left Gallifrey because of the corruption rife in Time Lord politics.[303] He traveled to see history happen in front of him.[304]

The following image appears early in the Doctor's memory: "Here was a cowled figure shaking a fist at a dark castle, and in the next picture he was cowering from something huge and fearful. Then he was running."[305]

The Doctor claims to have borrowed rather than stolen the TARDIS.[306] He wasn't authorised to take it.[307] Nor did he own the Ship.[308]

The TARDIS was a family heirloom.[309] The TARDIS had

296 *Cold Fusion*

297 *Lungbarrow*

298 Dating *Lungbarrow* (NA #60) - This was "eight hundred and seventy three years ago". Given that this is set just before *Doctor Who - The Movie*, and *Vampire Science* states that the Doctor was 1009 when he regenerated, it would make him 136. However, given the contradictions over his age, it is probably best not to rely on this figure. Owis was Loomed 675 years ago.

THE DOCTOR'S FAMILY: Sixteen of the Doctor's forty four Cousins are named in Lungbarrow: Quences, Owis, Glospin, Satthralope, Jobiska, Rynde, Arkhew, Maljamin, Farg, Celesia, Almund, Tugel, Chovor the Various, DeRoosifa, Salpash and Luton. Braxiatel is presumably another.

299 *An Unearthly Child, The Edge of Destruction, The Massacre, The Two Doctors*

300 *The War Games*

301 *The War Games, Resurrection of the Daleks, Pyramids of Mars, The Deadly Assassin.*

302 *The Invisible Enemy, The Five Doctors*

303 *World Game*

304 *Aliens of London*

305 *Timewyrm: Revelation* (p48).

306 *Frontier in Space, Logopolis*

307 *The Invasion of Time*

308 *Logopolis, Cold Fusion*

309 *The Infinity Doctors*

310 *The Gallifrey Chronicles*

311 *Lungbarrow*

312 *The Eight Doctors*

313 *Remembrance of the Daleks, Silver Nemesis, An Unearthly Child.*

314 *The Sensorites*

315 *The Time Meddler.* The Doctor says the Monk left their home planet fifty years after he did.

316 *The Twin Dilemma, The Mark of the Rani, Planet of the Spiders* respectively.

317 *Spiral Scratch*

318 The Doctor says he comes from "fifty years earlier" than the Monk in *The Time Meddler.* The War Chief remembers him leaving his home planet in *The War Games.* The Master is first seen in *Terror of the Autons.*

319 "Time and Time Again"

320 Seen in "Timeslip".

321 *Neverland*

322 *The Brain of Morbius*

323 Dating *Warmonger* (PDA #53) - It is never stated how long ago Morbius ruled Gallifrey in *The Brain of Morbius.* The Doctor recognises Morbius, but Morbius doesn't recognise the Doctor.

In his novelisation of the story, Terrance Dicks states

been taken from Marnal by Ulysses. Marnal's son knew the truth about the Doctor's departure, and told his father what had happened afterwards.[310] The Doctor chose not to take a Type 53 TARDIS.[311]

The authorities thought of him as arrogant.[312] **In addition to the TARDIS, the Doctor took the Hand of Omega, the Validium statue and his granddaughter Susan.**[313]

The Doctor and Susan left home "ages" before they met Ian and Barbara.[314] **Possibly more than fifty years.**[315]

Many other Time Lords were known to have left Gallifrey in the Doctor's lifetime: Azmael left Gallifrey to become Master of Jaconda. The Rani was exiled following illegal experiments on animals, including an incident where genetically re-engineered mice that she had created ate the President's cat and attacked the President himself. She became ruler of Miasimia Goria. The Doctor's mentor left Gallifrey for Earth and became known as K'Anpo.[316]

Rummas was taught by Delox and Borusa. He left Gallifrey in a stolen TARDIS to build up a collection, mainly of books. He took the Spiral Chamber - a portal to the Spiral at the nexus of the Time Vortex - and settled at the Library of Carsus.[317]

The Doctor left before the Monk, the War Chief and probably before the Master.[318]

= If the Doctor had never left Gallifrey, he would have become President, but spent his time appeasing the Daleks. The Earth would have been invaded dozens of times.

Benny Summerfield witnessed the Doctor and Susan leaving Gallifrey.[319] During a timeslip, the Doctor would later re-enact the time he activated the TARDIS.[320]

The Morbius Crisis

The Cult of Morbius was formed in 5725.3, Rassilon Era.[321]

Morbius, the leader of the High Council, proposed that the Time Lords should end their policy of non-interference. When the High Council rejected this, he left Gallifrey and raised an army of conquest, promising them immortality. Devastating several planets on the way, the Cult of Morbius arrived on Karn, home of the Sisterhood. The Time Lords attacked them on Karn, destroying his army. Following a trial, Morbius was vaporised. Solon had removed Morbius' brain before his execution and preserved it.[322]

WARMONGER[323] **->** Morbius was deposed by Saran, who became Acting President in his place. Junior Cardinal Borusa assisted Saran. Morbius was exiled from Gallifrey. Adopting the identity General Rombusi, he raised an army of mercenaries using stolen Celestial Intervention Agency funds. These armies came from Darkeen, Fangoria, Martak and Romark. They conquered, among many other worlds, Tanith and the Ogron homeworld. Freedonia joined the General, and conquered nearby Sylvana. The General met the surgeon Solon, who pledged to build an army for him from patched-together corpses.

The fifth Doctor encountered Morbius and travelled to Gallifrey, where he convinced Acting President Saran to act. The Doctor was placed in charge of a large Alliance - an army that included the Draconians, Sontarans, Ice Warriors, Cybermen and Ogrons.

Acting President Saran was almost certainly never elected President.[324]

THE DARK PATH -> Two hundred years after the second Doctor last saw Koschei, they met on the Earth colony of Darkheart in the thirty-fourth century. Koschei wanted an

that Morbius came to power after the Doctor left Gallifrey, and that the Doctor heard of Morbius on his travels. In *Warmonger*, also by Dicks, the Doctor (who has travelled into Gallifrey's past) muses that Borusa might be in his first incarnation (p166), and that this is the first time Borusa has met him, almost certainly setting it before the Doctor was born - but this is directly contradicted just a few pages later (p173), when it's made clear that it's after the Doctor stole a TARDIS and has left Gallifrey.

Neverland places it before the Master steals the files on the Doomsday Weapon. *The Book of the War* (in the *Faction Paradox* series) has what it calls "the Imperator Presidency" occurring between 870 and 866 years before the War starts, so (almost certainly) after the

Doctor left Gallifrey. *Timelink* prefers the idea that Morbius rose after *The Three Doctors*.

324 While everyone is happy to call him "Lord President" in *Warmonger*, Saran is only Acting President until elections are held (p175). The Doctor thinks of Saran as "a very minor figure in Time Lord history" (p166), so we can probably infer that he lost the election.

We can also speculate that the President who is elected at this point is the one seen in *The Three Doctors* and (after regenerating) the one assassinated in *The Deadly Assassin*. The Doctor never met the President killed in *The Deadly Assassin*, according to that story, but he had known Saran before originally leaving Gallifrey.

ordered universe, but his methods for achieving this became increasingly questionable. He felt betrayed upon realising that his dear companion Ailla was a Time Lord spy, and came into conflict with the Doctor also, which kept him emotionally isolated. Koschei became obsessed with the power of the Darkheart and declared himself the Master.

The Master has had many enemies, and always misses them when they are gone.[325]

Increasing Intervention

THE THREE DOCTORS -> Although the Doctor was now travelling through space and time, the Time Lords still occasionally used him as an agent or messenger. The second and third Doctors were sent to stop the

cosmic energy drain caused by Omega.

The Doctor's Exile

THE WAR GAMES / SPEARHEAD FROM SPACE -> In 309,906, the second Doctor faced a Malfeasance Tribunal, and the Time Lords found the Doctor guilty of interfering in history. They exiled him to Earth in the twentieth-century timezone, changing his appearance. The Tribunal continued to monitor him.[326]

A Gallifreyan protocol dictated that before entering a period of exile, a Time Lord was required to regenerate.[327] At the time of the second Doctor's trial, the current model of TARDIS was the Type 97, and psychic paper had just been invented. The House of Dellatrovella was politically powerful and ambitious.[328]

325 *Terror of the Autons*

326 *The War Games.* The event is recalled and dated in *The Deadly Assassin*, the Doctor's exile begins in *Spearhead from Space* (continuing until *The Three Doctors*), and we learn the Tribunal is still monitoring the Doctor in *Terror of the Autons*.

327 *Circular Time:* "Spring", in reference to *The War Games*.

328 *World Game*

329 SEASON 6B: *The Two Doctors*. This looks like a major contradiction of the established facts, as it's made clear in *The War Games* that the Doctor has fled his home planet and is terrified of any contact with the Time Lords. Fans don't seem so worried that the Time Lords also contacted the first and second Doctors in *The Three Doctors*.

One theory that has gained currency since appearing in *The Discontinuity Guide* is that after *The War Games*, the Doctor wasn't regenerated straight away but was reunited with Jamie and Victoria (who is mentioned in *The Two Doctors*) and sent on missions for the Time Lords. Supporting evidence for this is that the second Doctor seems to remember *The War Games* in *The Five Doctors*. It also ties in with *TV Comic*, which had the second Doctor exiled to Earth for a time before he became his third incarnation. Two novels by Terrance Dicks - *Players* and *World Game* - explicitly have sequences that, from the Doctor's point of view, occur during Season 6B.

330 *Terror of the Autons*. The files are referred to in *Colony in Space* and *The Sea Devils*. Presumably, although this is never stated on TV, the Master also finds out about many of his other future allies and accomplices from these files.

331 *Neverland*

332 *The Quantum Archangel*, with reference to (respectively) *The Mind of Evil, Colony in Space, The Daemons,* *The Sea Devils, The Time Monster, Frontier in Space / Planet of the Daleks, The Keeper of Traken, Survival, Falls the Shadow, GodEngine, Doctor Who: The Movie*.

333 *Lungbarrow*

334 WHEN WAS ROMANA BORN?: Like the Doctor, Romana doesn't give a consistent account of her age - she's "nearly 140" in *The Ribos Operation*, "125" in *City of Death* and "150" in *The Leisure Hive*.

Her birth would thus occur between *The Tomb of the Cybermen* and *Pyramids of Mars* - almost exactly halfway between those stories, in the Doctor's personal timeline. Given the continuity of companions and the Doctor's exile to Earth, the only certain gap between those two stories where the Doctor could age three hundred years would be between *The Green Death* and *The Time Warrior*, when the Doctor travels alone in his TARDIS. The UNIT personnel have no idea if the Doctor is away, as far as he is concerned, for decades or centuries at a time. If the Season 6B theory is true, there could be another significant gap there. The probability, then, is that Romana was born while the Doctor was in his third incarnation.

335 *Shada*

336 *The Pirate Planet*

337 *The Ribos Operation*

338 *State of Decay*

339 *The Romance of Crime, The Ancestor Cell*.

340 *Neverland*

341 *Neverland*. This is presumably the visit in *Legacy of the Daleks*, first referenced in *The Deadly Assassin*.

342 *Interference*. The *Faction Paradox* novel line contains more detail about the history of Faction Paradox. Morbius is "the Imperator", who has his own entry in *The Book of the War*. Morbius' reign was one of the main factors that lead Grandfather Paradox to found House Paradox. Morbius and Grandfather Paradox were close contemporaries, however Lawrence Miles read a draft

WORLD GAME -> The Time Lords covered up the true end of the Doctor's trial. He was secretly recruited to the Celestial Intervention Agency by its leader, Sardon, to investigate time disturbances on Earth, given a companion (Serena) and a new TARDIS. Serena was killed on that mission. On his return, the second Doctor was visibly older, with grey hair and in new clothes. It was noted that he "took his time getting back", and he insisted on reclaiming his old TARDIS.

The second Doctor was sent to space station Chimera to call a halt to the time travel experiments of Kartz and Reimer.[329]

TERROR OF THE AUTONS -> Around this time, the Master removed Time Lord files containing information about the Doomsday Weapon and the Sea Devils. The Time Lords sent a messenger to warn the third Doctor about the Master's imminent arrival on Earth.[330]

The Master stole the plans for the Doomsday Weapon on 5892.9, Rassilon Era.[331] He also learned of the Psychic Parasites of Bellerophon; the Doomsday Weapon; Azal of the Daemons; the Earth Reptiles; the Crystal of Kronos; the Dalek army on Spiridon; the Source on Traken; the Cheetah people; the Midnight Cathedral; the GodEngine on Mars; the deathworm; the frozen gods of Volvox, the Amentethys, the Proculus and the Scerbulus; and the secrets of the planet Kirbili.[332]

COLONY IN SPACE / THE CURSE OF PELADON / THE MUTANTS -> The Time Lords sent the third Doctor on various missions to other planets and times. These were always crucial points of galactic history, with implications for the entire universe. The Doctor was sent to Uxarieus to prevent the Doomsday Weapon from falling into the hands of the Master; to Peladon to ease the passage of that planet into the Galactic Federation and to prevent galactic war; and to Solos, where the Doctor delivered a message to Ky, the leader of the Solonian independence movement, that allowed him to fulfil his race's evolutionary potential.

THE THREE DOCTORS -> A black hole suddenly drained the cosmic energy of the Time Lords. Unable to power their machinery, the Time Lords called on the third Doctor for help. They brought two of his previous incarnations into the present to try and counteract whatever was draining the power.

Two incarnations of the Doctor travelled into the black hole and arrived in a universe of anti-matter. They discovered that Omega lived, maintaining an entire world with his mental control of a singularity. Omega resented the Time Lords, feeling they had aban-

doned him. He couldn't leave his domain without it ceasing to exist before he departed, and needed the Doctors' help to leave. But the Doctor learnt that Omega's body had long been destroyed, and that only his will remained. It would be impossible for him to return to the universe of matter.

The Doctors tricked their way back to their TARDIS, apparently destroying Omega in a matter/anti-matter explosion. The power drain ended, and the Time Lords had a new source of energy. In gratitude, the Time Lords lifted the Doctor's exile.

PLANET OF THE DALEKS / GENESIS OF THE DALEKS / THE BRAIN OF MORBIUS -> The Time Lords still called upon the Doctor's services from time to time. At the third Doctor's request, the Time Lords piloted the TARDIS to Spiridon, the location of a Dalek army. Later, the Time Lords predicted a time when the Daleks would dominate the universe, and sent the Doctor to prevent the Dalek's creation (or at least slow their development). The Time Lords also apparently sent the TARDIS to Karn to prevent the resurrection of Morbius.

Lord Ferain was head of Allegiance at the Celestial Intervention Agency, and it was he who sent the Doctor to Skaro to prevent the Daleks' creation.[333]

Romana

Romana was born when the Doctor was between six hundred and six hundred twenty-five.[334] She read *Our Planet's Story* as a Time Tot.[335] For her seventieth birthday, she was given an air-car.[336]

As part of her studies, Romana studied the lifecycle of the Gallifreyan Flutterwing and she eventually graduated from the Academy with a Triple First.[337] Romana was an historian and worked in the Bureau of Ancient Records.[338] She was a Prydonian.[339] When she was sixty, she went to Lake Abydos on holiday with her family. She was an only child, as her brother Rorvan had been consigned to the Oubliette of Eternity and erased from history.[340]

Chancellor Goth visited Tersurus on 6241.11, Rassilon Era.[341]

Faction Paradox was created during a time of cultural crisis on Gallifrey.[342] The Faction set out to be deliberately confrontational. Whereas the Time Lords abhorred time paradoxes, Faction Paradox revelled in them. The Time Lords were immortal, so much of the Faction's iconography - like their skull masks - celebrated death. The relationship between the Time Lord authorities and Faction Paradox was analogous to that of the Catholic Church and satanic cults on Earth.[343]

The Elysians were a secret society on Gallifrey run by a man called Luther. They rejected the traditional houses, were sick of the non-intervention code, and styled themselves as "the Final Chapter". They planned to use unregistered clones to seize Gallifrey in a coup. The first was the son of Uriel, named Xanti. Uriel, Xanti's father, volunteered for incarceration in a mental asylum - the Quantum of Solace.[344]

President Pandak III suppressed a report on Lampreys by Lord Rellox of the Arcalian Council for Temporal Research.[345]

THE DEADLY ASSASSIN ->

"Through the millennia, the Time Lords of Gallifrey led a life of peace and ordered calm, protected against all threats from lesser civilisations by their great power. But this was to change. Suddenly and terribly, the Time Lords faced the most dangerous crisis in their long history..."

The fourth Doctor received a telepathic message, warning him that the President was going to be assassinated. He returned to his home planet immediately, only to find himself implicated in the assassination. The President had been due to resign anyway after centuries in office, and the murder appeared motiveless.

The Doctor's old enemy, the Master, had lured him back to frame him for the murder. The Master had exhausted his regenerations, and had been found by Chancellor Goth on the planet Tersurus. Although Goth had been favoured to succeed the outgoing President, he discovered that another was to be nominated instead. In return for Goth's help, the Master killed the incumbent President.

The Master wanted full access to various items such as the Sash of Rassilon, as he needed to find a way to prolong his life. He discovered that he might regener-ate again if he had a powerful enough source of energy - the Master selected the Eye of Harmony. He believed the Sash would protect him if he unleashed the Eye's power. The Doctor prevented the Master from destroying Gallifrey, but the Master escaped.

Around this time, the Doctor began to learn more about the Time Lords' ancient past.

"It was a chance encounter with the *Book of the Old Time* that had first nudged the Doctor's own thoughts back towards his world's archae-barbaric past. A suspicion had been born in his mind that before regeneration there had been reincarnation. Some memories might be more than racial inheritance. Nothing lasts that does not change." [346]

Borusa regenerated at some point between this and the Doctor's next visit to Gallifrey.[347]

IMAGE OF THE FENDAHL / UNDERWORLD -> Soon after learning of his planet's past, the fourth Doctor began to encounter survivors from his race's ancient history: the Fendahl and the Minyans.

Greyjan the Sane dabbled with the idea of time paradoxes. His three-year reign was the shortest in Gallifreyan history, and coincided with the relative Earth dates that saw the creation of the Eleven-Day Empire.[348]

THE INVASION OF TIME -> The fourth Doctor was contacted by the Vardans, a race capable of travelling down energy waves, including thought. The Vardans had infiltrated the Matrix, and now wanted to commence a physical invasion of Gallifrey. The Doctor tricked the Vardans, returning the invasion force to their home planet, then time-looping it. The Sontarans had been manipulating the Vardans all along, and attempted to invade Gallifrey themselves. This incur-

of this chronology and stated the formation of Faction Paradox "should come just before *The Deadly Assassin* (or just after *Genesis of the Daleks*) ... It's the long-term effects of the Morbius / Imperator crisis that lead to the rise of the Faction, rather than its direct aftermath ... the point when Gallifrey starts being shaken up by renegades, assassinations and invasions, and mortality suddenly becomes a major issue."
343 *Alien Bodies, Interference*
344 "Three hundred years" before "The Final Chapter", and it's tempting to see this as emerging from the same "cultural crisis" that created Faction Paradox.
345 *Spiral Scratch*
346 *Cat's Cradle: Time's Crucible* (p210-211).

347 A different actor plays Borusa in each of his televised appearances (Angus MacKay in *The Deadly Assassin*, John Arnatt in *The Invasion of Time*, Leonard Sachs in *Arc of Infinity* and Philip Latham in *The Five Doctors*).
348 *The Ancestor Cell.* The online Faction Paradox timeline suggests that this Presidency fell between *The Deadly Assassin* and *The Invasion of Time*.
349 *The Ancestor Cell*
350 *Timewyrm: Genesys*
351 We learn of Leela and Andred's marriage in *Arc of Infinity*.
352 In *The Ribos Operation*, the Doctor wishes that he'd thrown the President to the Sontarans, suggesting that

sion was also repelled. Leela and K9 elected to stay behind on Gallifrey.

The Doctor was the 407th President.[349] While in the Matrix, the Doctor became aware of the Timewyrm. He sent his future self a warning about it.[350] **Leela and Andred, a member of the Chancellery Guard, married soon afterward, but the Doctor was unable to attend the ceremony.[351] Borusa became President and regenerated once again.[352]**

The Key to Time

The White Guardian picked Romana to aid the Doctor and recover the six segments of the Key to Time.[353]

Luther designed the reconstruction of the Capitol over the hulk of the old, including the Watchtower, over the old Panopticon.[354]

A schism in College of Cardinals led to a rival President setting himself up on Drornid. The Time Lords ignored them, and they eventually returned home.[355] Drornid was also known as Dronid.[356]

SHADA -> The fourth Doctor prevented Skraga of Drornid from using the powers of the Time Lord mind criminal Salyavin to impose himself as the "universal mind".

With the quest for the Key to Time long-completed, the Time Lords recalled Romana. Before she could return, the TARDIS fell through a CVE into E-Space.[357]

STATE OF DECAY -> The fourth Doctor destroyed the Great Vampire, who had survived the war with the Time Lords and fled to E-Space.

CIRCULAR TIME: "Spring" -> Cardinal Zero was a Prydonian, and a member of the Council of the Great Mother - a group focused upon the politics of regeneration. He was in the running for a seat on the High Council when he abandoned life on Gallifrey, choosing instead to live in a rainforest on an alien world. The Time Lords dispatched the fifth Doctor and Nyssa to talk Zero into returning home, lest his actions damage the time-stream.

The Doctor and Nyssa found Zero living among a race of avian-people; Temporal Projectionists on Gallifrey had foretold that this species would progress from steam to orbital space flight in less than three generations. The avians themselves foretold of a prophet who would "lead them back to the sky", and Zero arranged his death using a local poison. He theatrically fell into a lake - which was actually his TARDIS - and regenerated inside it into a half-Time Lord, half-avian being. Events compelled the Doctor and Nyssa to leave, and Zero - hailed as the prophet of the avians - set about boosting their development and refining their judicial system along more civilised lines.

It was possible for Time Lords to "transform" into - or otherwise hybridize with - other species during regeneration.[358]

ARC OF INFINITY -> Omega had survived, and convinced a member of the High Council, Hedin, that he had been wronged by Gallifrey. With access to a bio-data extract, Omega would be able to bond with a Time Lord, re-entering our universe. Hedin chose the fifth Doctor as Omega's target - when the High Council discovered this, they recalled the Doctor's TARDIS to Gallifrey (only the third time this had been done in the planet's history) and lifted the ban on the death penalty. Killing the Doctor, they believed, would break the renegade's link with our universe. The Doctor survived

Borusa has become President (although the treacherous Kelner apparently survived *The Invasion of Time* and he'd have a strong constitutional case, as the Doctor named him Vice-President). The Doctor was meant to have lost his memory of the Sontaran invasion at the end of *The Invasion of Time*, but clearly didn't, or was given some sort of account of it before he left Gallifrey. By *Arc of Infinity*, Borusa is President.
353 *The Ribos Operation*
354 "Centuries" before "The Final Chapter". It's unclear when this takes place. It's before "The Tides of Time", because we see the Watchtower in that story. Perhaps there was more extensive destruction during the Vardan / Sontaran assault in *The Invasion of Time* than we saw on television. References to the "old Panopticon" might mean there's a new one - we haven't seen the Panopticon on television since *The Invasion of*

Time.
355 *Shada*. It's unclear when this happened. *The Book of the War* states it was 392 years before the War starts, and 474 years after Morbius' execution.
356 *Alien Bodies*. *The Terrestrial Index* and *The Discontinuity Guide* both mistakenly refer to Drornid as Dronid.
357 *Meglos, Full Circle*
358 The McGann Doctor claims as much in *Doctor Who: The Movie*, and some have taken this to mean - owing to the atypical manner of his regeneration (the dulling influence of the anesthetic, his "changing" in a morgue full of human corpses) - that the eighth Doctor is "half-human" whereas all the other Doctors are full-blooded Time Lords. The notion that Time Lords can hybridize with other species is substantiated in the works of Paul Cornell: a regenerated Time Lord

vaporisation by entering the Matrix, where he discovered Omega's plan. He tracked Omega to Amsterdam, where the renegade's new body proved unstable and disintegrated.

"Blood Invocation" -> The fifth Doctor, Tegan and Nyssa responded to an emergency signal from Cardinal Hemal. A Time Lord had been found, drained of blood, and the Doctor realised there were vampires abroad. The Doctor discovered acolytes of the Cult of Rassilon the Vampire and had them rounded up. Meanwhile, Tegan was bitten by a vampire Time Lord who had gained access to the TARDIS. The vampire took the Ship to Earth... but disintegrated because he landed in the daytime.

THE FIVE DOCTORS -> Borusa regenerated once more. He had become dissatisfied with ruling Gallifrey. Now he wanted "perpetual regeneration": a secret discovered by Rassilon that allowed true immortality, not simply the vast lifespans granted to other Time Lords. Borusa discovered the ancient Time Scoop machinery and restarted the Game of Rassilon, pitting four incarnations of the Doctor and his old friends against a selection of old enemies. Rassilon gave Borusa the immortality he sought, transforming him into a living statue. Chancellor Flavia declared the fifth Doctor as President, but he left Gallifrey before he could take up office, and appointed Flavia to rule in his stead.

The Doctor was the 409th President.[359] **Type 57 TARDISes were in operation at this time.**[360]

The Time Lords tasked the fifth Doctor with investigating time warps on Earth.[361]

"The Tides of Time" -> The fifth Doctor was still considered the President of the Time Lords. He said of Gallifrey, "When my wanderings are over, I will make my home here."

The Time Lords installed a defence system onboard the TARDIS without telling the Doctor. In an emergency, it would automatically summon Shayde to the ship.[362]

"The Stockbridge Horror" -> The fifth Doctor arrived on Gallifrey seconds after Tubal Cain's missiles froze time in the Capitol. Within the time warp, the Doctor repaired the TARDIS. When the effect wore off, the Doctor was arrested and brought before a secret court for his interference with the timeline.

Tubal Cain was demoted to run the Quantum of Solace.[363] Flavia didn't chase the Doctor because she wanted the Presidency for herself. Her reign was one of prosperity.[364]

RESURRECTION OF THE DALEKS -> The Daleks planned to assassinate the High Council of the Time

becomes part-Silurian in *The Shadows of Avalon*, and another becomes part-birdperson in *Circular Time*: "Spring".
359 *The Ancestor Cell*
360 In *Warriors of the Deep*, the Doctor says he should have changed his TARDIS for a Type 57 "when he had the chance". This could imply that Type 57 is the most advanced model at present, or simply that newer models exist but the Doctor prefers Type 57.
361 "4-Dimensional Vistas"
362 "The Stockbridge Horror"
363 "The Final Chapter"
364 *The Eight Doctors*
365 *Singularity*
366 Later in the story, the Doctor suspects that the Time Lords *are* aware of events and have been manipulating him, but this is never confirmed.
367 *The Mysterious Planet*. The Valeyard's "evidence", as displayed throughout *The Trial of a Time Lord*, derives from this feature, although it's unclear if the Doctor's TARDIS was secretly fitted with surveillance gear at some point (his visit to Gallifrey in *Arc of Infinity*, for instance), or if the Ship was incorporated into the system by remote.
368 *The Eight Doctors*

369 THE VALEYARD: It is unclear exactly what the Valeyard is. The Master, who knows a great deal about him, says, "there is some evil in all of us, Doctor, even you. The Valeyard is an amalgamation of the darker sides of your nature, somewhere between your twelfth and final incarnation, and I must say you do not improve with age".
This is rather vague, and it seems that the Valeyard might be a potential future for the Doctor (like those presented to him in *The War Games* or arguably those of Romana in *Destiny of the Daleks*), a projection (like Cho-je in *Planet of the Spiders* or the Watcher in *Logopolis*) or an actual fully-fledged future incarnation (as he was in the original script). The Master seems to have met the Valeyard before, and sees him as a rival (he also says "as I've always know him, the Doctor" - suggesting that the Valeyard would normally refer to himself as "the Doctor" not "the Valeyard").
Whatever the Valeyard is, he doesn't have any qualms about killing his past self - perhaps if the sixth Doctor died, the Valeyard would apparently gain his remaining regenerations by default. His survival at the end of the trial, when we had seen him disseminated (and the Doctor has promised to mend his ways) perhaps suggests that he is something more than just a

Lords using duplicates of the fifth Doctor and his companions, but the Doctor prevented this.

Type 70 TARDISes were in operation at this time. They were better suited than Type 40s to apply brute force and penetrate distortion grids that prevented space-time travel.[365]

URBAN MYTHS -> The fifth Doctor cured an outbreak of the Tule-Oz virus on the planet Poiti, but three CIA agents - Commander Edge, Commander Harom and Kettoo - became infected with a benign strain of the germ. The Tule-Oz virus made the agents believe that the Doctor and Peri had devastated Poiti, but the Doctor provided an antidote for the agents and their superior, Inquisitor Auron.

At this time, top-secret correspondence was automatically routed via the nearest Type 40 TARDIS to incidents away from Gallifrey.

ATTACK OF THE CYBERMEN -> The sixth Doctor sent a signal to the Time Lords, asking for assistance, when some Cybermen invaded his TARDIS. The Cybermen forced the Doctor to terminate his call for help.[366]

New surveillance methods were developed, increasing the range of information that the Matrix could harvest. The Matrix could now record events that occurred within a certain vicinity of a TARDIS.[367]

"The World Shapers" -> The Time Lords sent an agent in a new TARDIS to investigate time disturbances on Marinus. That Time Lord died, but the sixth Doctor, Frobisher and Peri arrived and took on the assignment. At its conclusion, a delegation of senior Time Lords met up with the sixth Doctor and offered false assurances that they would nip the creation of the Cybermen in the bud.

The Celestial Intervention Agency worried that the Ravolox Affair would be exposed. They spread rumours that Flavia wasn't legitimately President, and she ordered an election to settle the matter. The Agency fixed the election, installing their supporter, Niroc.[368]

THE TRIAL OF A TIME LORD / THE ULTIMATE FOE -> The sixth Doctor discovered that the planet Ravolox was in fact the Earth in the far future, but he didn't know what had moved the planet two light years or, more importantly, why. Despite this, the High Council became worried that the Doctor knew too much, and they brought him to a vast space station. The Doctor at first learned that he was to undergo an impartial enquiry into his activities. He also learnt that as he had

neglected his duties, he had been deposed from the Presidency.

The prosecuting council, named the Valeyard, successfully argued that the Doctor was guilty of interference on a grand scale, and the enquiry became a trial. It was revealed that the Doctor's actions on Thoros Beta had threatened the course of universal evolution. The Time Lords had been forced to intervene directly, killing the scientist Crozier, the Mentor Kiv and possibly the Doctor's companion Peri. When the Doctor's own evidence proved that on another occasion he had committed genocide - wiping out the Vervoids to save the Earth - he faced a death sentence.

The Doctor claimed that the Matrix was being tampered with. The Keeper of the Matrix was brought in as an expert witness, but the Master suddenly appeared on the Matrix screen, demonstrating that it was indeed possible to breach the security of the Time Lords' master computer. The Master explained that Andromedans had previously entered the Matrix from their base on Earth and stolen valuable scientific secrets. To protect their position, the High Council had covertly ordered Earth's destruction.

The Master's greatest bombshell was the identity of the prosecuting council: the Valeyard was an amalgamation of all that was evil in the Doctor, somewhere between his twelfth and final incarnation.[369] The Master had encountered the Valeyard before, and knew that the High Council had brought him in to frame the Doctor, in return for which the Valeyard would gain the Doctor's remaining regenerations.

When the truth about Ravolox was revealed, popular unrest deposed the High Council. Both the Master and Valeyard moved to take advantage of the situation: the Master planned to take control of Gallifrey, even as the Valeyard attempted to assassinate senior members of the Time Lord hierarchy. Both failed. The Master was trapped by the Limbo Atrophier, a booby trap placed on the Matrix files. The Valeyard was believed destroyed by his own particle disseminator, but he somehow survived. When last seen, he had assumed the guise of the Keeper of the Matrix.

The Doctor suggested that once order was restored, the Inquisitor should run for President.

THE EIGHT DOCTORS -> The eighth Doctor travelled to the time of his trial. He called on Rassilon to briefly free Borusa's noblest incarnation. Borusa deposed the corrupt High Council and arranged honest elections. Flavia was re-elected and restored Earth to its rightful place. Rassilon might have intervened to make the Doctor meet his companion Sam Jones in 1997.

UNREGENERATE![370] **->** The High Council foresaw a time when lesser species would develop time travel, and pack the space-time continuum to the bursting point. The Gallifreyan CIA therefore instigated a project to install the sentiences of newly birthed TARDISes into living beings. They hoped the sentiences would operate as CIA agents on their hosts' homeworlds, thwarting the lesser species' endeavors to create time-travel technology. The CIA believed this would prove far more successful than the usual array of spies and brainwashing.

Professor Klyst, a Time Lord, spearheaded the research. Experiments on Daleks were forbidden, but subjects were recruited from at least fifty worlds. Each were offered life-times of success if they participated in the research on the day before their deaths. Yet the beings' brains were unable to host the TARDIS sentiences, and many went insane.

The seventh Doctor brought a halt to the operation, helping to destroy the relevant data. One TARDIS sentience stabilized in the human Johannes Rausch. Klyst agreed to host another sentience, thus erasing her own knowledge of the research. The sentiences in Rausch and Klyst transferred another of their number into the Institute where the research was conducted, turning it into a makeshift travel vehicle. They went on the run from the Time Lords, hoping to in time stabilize the other sentiences in their host bodies.

REMEMBRANCE OF THE DALEKS -> Addressing Davros, the seventh Doctor claimed to be "President-Elect of the High Council of Time Lords ... Keeper of the Legacy of Rassilon". Its work done, the Hand of Omega returned to Gallifrey.

Back on Gallifrey, the Hand of Omega missed its creator and tended to hover around the Omega Memorial.[371]

BLOOD HARVEST / GOTH OPERA -> Three Time Lords - Rath (the younger brother of Goth), Elar and Morin - took responsibility for security matters. Most Time Lords considered this a rather lowly position, but the Committee of Three, as they styled themselves, used their office to build their own powerbase. Using their expertise, they planned to kill Rassilon in his Tower and take control of the galaxy. At the time of President Flavia's inauguration, they were defeated by the seventh Doctor, Ace, Benny and Romana.

The three traitors were sentenced to vaporisation. Romana settled back on Gallifrey, and was greeted by Ruathadvorophrenaltid, a Time Lady acquaintance of the Doctor. Ruath planned to be the consort of the Vampire Messiah, and targeted the fifth Doctor. Romana alerted Gallifrey and the Doctor to the threat, and was rewarded with a seat on the High Council.

Some Interventionists on Gallifrey took an interest in introducing alien genetic material into the make-up of other species, including humanity.[372]

The Romana Presidency

HAPPY ENDINGS -> Romana was elected President of the Time Lords, beating the previous Madame President by 53 to 47 percent in the elections, and won the support of the Interventionist movement. She promised an end to iso-lationism and to open an embassy with the Tharils. Very soon after her election, she investigated a Fortean Flicker which the Master was exploiting. He had stolen the Loom of Rassilon's Mouse, which could build monsters. The Master was defeated and the Loom retrieved, but he escaped Gallifreyan custody.

Romana was the 413th President.[373]

The Carnival Queen affected rationality throughout the universe. On Gallifrey, Grandfather Paradox, "voodoo priest of the House of Lungbarrow", escaped his prison when the Lady President had a fit and released three hundred prisoners from their prison asteroid. Six hundred Time Lords claimed to be the ghost of Morbius, and the planet's automatic defences activated.[374]

Grandfather Paradox removed his arm, as the Time Lords had branded it. Soon, he would remove himself

---

mere Time Lord.

Note also that the Master says "twelfth and final", not "twelfth and thirteenth" - which, if you squint, leaves open the possibility that the Doctor will survive the end of his regenerative cycle.

The novels and audios have tended to steer clear of the Valeyard - indeed the Writers' Guide for the New Adventures stated, "anything featuring the Valeyard is out - he's a continuity nightmare, and a rather dull vil-lain". Despite this, a number of the novels (particularly *Time of Your Life*, *Head Games* and *Millennial Rites*) have developed the idea first aired in *Love and War* that the Doctor sacrificed his sixth incarnation ("the colourful jester") to create a stronger, more ruthless seventh per-sona ("Time's Champion"), and who was better equipped to change his destiny. Ironically, books such as *Love and War* and *Head Games* suggest that this internal conflict might well have been the catalyst that brought the Valeyard into being.

The PDAs *Matrix* and *Mission: Impractical* feature the Valeyard, as does the non-canonical audio *He Jests at Scars*.

from history. With its leader free, Faction Paradox would grow in size and influence.[375]

LUNGBARROW -> The seventh Doctor returned to his ancestral home of Lungbarrow. He was accused of murdering Quences, the head of the household. The Doctor was badly beaten and incapacitated by his family, who blamed him for all their woes. Innocet - one of the Doctor's Cousins - joined Ace, Leela, Chris Cwej and Romana in reviving him. They learned the Doctor contained the genetic codes of the Other.

The Doctor deduced that another Cousin, Glospin, had briefly regenerated to look like the Doctor and thus framed him for Quences' murder. Quences' mind was in Badger, the House's robot servant. The House itself committed suicide, throwing itself from the mountain it rested upon. Romana ordered a new House built for the Cousins.

The Doctor's companion, Chris Cwej, decided to stay on Gallifrey and work as an agent for the President. He was given a time ring. Leela discovered she was pregnant. The Dromeians and Arcalians objected to Romana's interventionist policies. She was given a gift by the Chairman of Argolis and opened an Embassy with Karn.

The Celestial Intervention Agency sent the Doctor to recover the Master's remains from Skaro.

The further adventures of Chris Cwej appear in Virgin's Bernice Summerfield New Adventures, and then the Faction Paradox series.

DEATH COMES TO TIME[376] -> A new generation of Time Lords was far more open to the idea of intervention. Among them was the Minister of Chance, and he met with the seventh Doctor to discuss intergalactic crises. One such matter emerged when the Time Lords Antinor and Valentine were killed on Earth. Meanwhile, Ace trained to be a Time Lord under Casmus. Events climaxed on the twenty-first century Earth.

DOCTOR WHO - THE MOVIE -> The seventh Doctor recovered the Master's remains from Skaro, and was heading for Gallifrey in 5725.2, Rassilon Era. The Master sabotaged the TARDIS, forcing a landing in San Francisco, 1999, but was later lost to the TARDIS' Eye of Harmony.

Romana and a research team went missing when the planetoid Etra Prime vanished on 6776.7, Rassilon Era. An interim President was appointed in Romana's absence.[377]

= THE SIRENS OF TIME[378] -> The Knights of Velyshaa seized control of the Gallifreyan Capitol. They were exploiting time disturbances using a captured Temperon, an animal that could release particles capable of disrupting time. The fifth, sixth and seventh Doctors restored established history and the conquest of Gallifrey never happened. The Temperon sacrificed itself to forever hold in check the Sirens of Time, extra-dimensional creatures that fed off time distortion.

THE APOCALYPSE ELEMENT -> Twenty time-active races met on Archetryx for a summit, but the planetoid Etra Prime reappeared. Based on Etra Prime, the Daleks were working on "the Apocalypse Element" - a substance capable of shredding the raw fabric of space-time in an unstoppable reaction. The Daleks attacked Archetryx and stole components needed to finish making the Element.

Romana had been imprisoned on Etra Prime for twenty years. She escaped as the Daleks, using a Monan Host time ship as a Trojan horse, attacked Gallifrey. The Daleks detonated the Apocalypse Element in the Seriphia Galaxy. As was part of their plan, the Daleks sacrificed those of their number on Gallifrey to reinforce the Eye of Harmony's

---

370 It's difficult to say how much the CIA is operating independently in this story, or to what degree it's sanctioned by the High Council. Presuming the CIA isn't acting totally solo, the High Council that initiated the project is possibly the administration that was overthrown in *The Trial of a Time Lord*.
371 *Lungbarrow*
372 The novel version of *Human Nature*, in which a Gallifreyan agent arranges for an alien Aubertide to transform into a cow and get eaten as such.
373 *The Gallifrey Chronicles*
374 *Christmas on a Rational Planet*. No date given in the *Doctor Who* books, but it's "151" years before the War starts, according to *The Book of the War*.
375 *Christmas on a Rational Planet, Alien Bodies, Interference.*

376 Dating *Death Comes to Time* (BBC1 drama, unnumbered) - While there are discrepancies, *Death Comes to Time* shares a number of features with the timeline of the later New Adventures - the Time Lords are more openly interventionist, and Ace is training up as a Time Lord. While *Lungbarrow* is clearly meant to lead straight into *Doctor Who - The Movie*, there are other stories set in the "gap", such as *Excelis Decays* and *Master*. Ace is a lot older than she was in the New Adventures (her last appearance is in *Lungbarrow*). As with events in *Death Comes to Time* that occur in the Present Day section, the canonicity of these details is highly debatable. Fans are free to incorporate this story or ignore it.
377 *Neverland*
378 The story takes place during the interim Presidency, in the seventh Doctor's "current" Gallifrey.

power. The Eye contained the Element's destruction to Seriphia, which was restructured to create millions of new worlds for the Daleks.

The Daleks killed the interim President of Gallifrey, and Romana was restored to the Presidency.[379]

SHADA[380] -> The eighth Doctor returned to Gallifrey and told President Romana and K9 that they needed to resolve a time anomaly by travelling to Cambridge in 1979.

NEVERLAND -> President Romana allied the Time Lords with the Warpsmiths of Phaedon and the Monan Host.

A warfleet of TARDISes pursued the eighth Doctor and Charley, who decided it was time to resolve the paradox of her existence (as she had been saved from dying in the *R-101* crash). The two of them were taken to a Time Station.

President Romana and Vansell warned that the structure of space and time was on the verge of collapse. They believed that Charley had attracted Anti-Time particles from the Antiverse, which was disrupting the universal balance. The Time Lords adapted the Station to pass into the Antiverse to investigate. The Doctor discovered Rassilon's TARDIS, the size of a planetoid, with a surface populated by "Neverpeople". Rassilon's casket was there. Vansell fell under the sway of the Neverpeople, who were actually exiled Time Lord criminals.

The Doctor realised that the Neverpeople had travelled to our universe and spread rumours throughout time of Zagreus, hoping to tempt the Time Lords here. The casket didn't contain Rassilon, but rather a mass of Anti-time sufficient to destabilise the universe. Vansell sacrificed his life, but was unable to prevent the Time Station, with the casket onboard, from reaching Gallifrey. The Doctor surrounded the Station with his TARDIS. The Station exploded, but the TARDIS contained the Anti-Time. However, the Doctor was saturated with Anti-Time energy ... which split

his personality and made him the destroyer Zagreus.

> = In the Matrix, the Doctor saw a possible future where Gallifrey had been attacked and Romana was the Imperiatrix responsible for the genocide of the Daleks.[381]

This occurred in 6798.3, Rassilon Era.[382]

ZAGREUS -> The Anti-Time-infected Doctor became Zagreus, and a revived Rassilon sought to use him as a weapon against the Divergents. "Zagreus" objected to being manipulated and cast Rassilon through a portal into the Divergents' timeline. The TARDIS helped the eighth Doctor stabilize his true persona and he departed for a Divergent Universe, fearing that by remaining, he would risk the Anti-Time within him allowing Zagreus to again take control. Charley accompanied the Doctor on his journey.

THE NEXT LIFE -> Rassilon was caught in a recurring time loop, and his identity began slipping away. The Zagreus persona was separated from the eighth Doctor and took on female form, but learned "she" was destined to remain in the Divergent Universe for at least twenty to thirty millennia. The purged Doctor returned to our universe with Charley and their new companion C'rizz. They immediately came into conflict with Davros and the Daleks.[383]

The three Big Finish Gallifrey mini-series take place during Romana's Presidency, before her second regeneration.

The Time Lords occasionally meddled in the history of Earth. Interference in the year 2006 resulted in them placing Lucie Miller with the eighth Doctor, telling the Doctor

---

379 *Neverland*
380 The prologue to the Big Finish webcast offers an in-story explanation as to why the Doctor needs to "repeat" an adventure. See "Which *Shada*, if Any, is Canon?" for more.
381 *Neverland*
382 *Neverland*. The date was given earlier in the story as 6978.5, but this is clearly a fluffed line, given the other recent dates.
383 *Terror Firma*
384 *Blood of the Daleks*
385 Dating "The Final Chapter" (*DWM* #262-265) - The date is given on the TARDIS screen at the beginning of the story, and is significantly later than the one given in *Neverland*. This is tricky to fit in with the books and audios, where Romana is President throughout the eighth Doctor range - although we never actually see

the President in this story. It clearly happens before Gallifrey's destruction and fits in with the idea of Gallifreyan society fraying and succumbing to cultism depicted around the time of *The Ancestor Cell*.
386 The adventures of this newborn "ninth Doctor" continue in "Wormwood", set around 5220.
387 *The Shadows of Avalon*
388 *Interference*
389 *The Book of the War* specifies that Compassion becomes a Type 102 TARDIS.
390 THE WAR: *Alien Bodies* introduced the future War and the Enemy (neither of which were capitalised at that point). Further details were added in subsequent books, principally *Interference*, *The Taking of Planet 5*, *The Shadows of Avalon* and *The Ancestor Cell*.
The Doctor destroyed Gallifrey in *The Ancestor Cell*, in large part to avert the War. At that point, all the events

she was part of a witness relocation programme.[384]

10639.5 Rassilon Era - "The Final Chapter"[385] **->**
Fey and Izzy piloted the TARDIS to Gallifrey. They told
Castellan Tenion and Overseer Luther that the eighth
Doctor was dying, and he was taken to a hospital complex
called the Mortal Coil. At this point, the Doctor was con-
sidered fiction by most people on Gallifrey.

Xanti, an Academy dropout and admirer of the Doctor,
hurried to meet him. The Doctor's mind resided in the
Matrix while his body healed. He encountered the Higher
Evolutionaries - which now included a representative of
the Order of the Black Sun, Demoiselle Drin, in Merlin's
place. They all had experienced nightmares of a Gallifrey
grown "dark and wicked".

A group of Elysians materialised over the Doctor's body,
planning to kill him "for the sake of the future", but
Shayde arrived to fight them off. The Elysians vanished,
taking Izzy with them.

The Doctor spoke to Uriel, Xanti's father, in the
Quantum of Solace (which was now being run by ex-mil-
itary man Tubal Cain). He learned of the history of the
Elysians, and that Luther was their leader. Luther's rebuilding of the Capitol had effectively turned the whole planet
into a giant TARDIS, powered by Xanti's mind. Now he
planned to take it back to the moment of Rassilon's triumph and overwrite that history with his own. The Doctor
forced Luther out into the Vortex, but Luther killed Xanti,
and the Doctor had to take his place. Shayde rescued the
Doctor, but the strain apparently triggered the Doctor's
regeneration...[386]

Eve of the War

**ALIEN BODIES / INTERFERENCE / THE TAKING OF
PLANET 5 ->** Although Time Lords were unable to see
into their own future, the eighth Doctor found evidence
that the Time Lords would fight a War across time and
space against an unknown Enemy. This War involved exotic weapons and such shifts in the timeline, reality, cause
and effect as to make it all but impossible to determine any
firm details. The broad sweep of events became apparent
among the fragmentary evidence, however, and it was
bleak news for Gallifrey.

Romana regenerated for the second time. Her third
incarnation became increasingly concerned - perhaps even
paranoid - about the prospect of the War.[387] Some Time
Lords tried to acquire a bottle universe from IM Foreman,
hoping to flee into it when the Enemy attacked.[388]

THE SHADOWS OF AVALON -> President Romana
now put the survival of the Time Lords over more ethical
considerations. While she was concerned with the dispute

with the People of the Worldsphere, Romana was aware
that the War with the unknown Enemy would soon be
upon Gallifrey.

Learning that the eighth Doctor's companion,
Compassion, was mutating into a TARDIS thanks to her
contact with future technology, Romana sent
Interventionist agents Cavis and Gandar to capture her.
Romana planned to force Compassion to breed with other
TARDISes. Compassion made her transformation into a
TARDIS, but the Doctor rescued her and they fled the
Time Lord authorities.

Until Compassion, the most advanced TARDIS was the
Type 98.[389]

THE ANCESTOR CELL / THE GALLIFREY CHRONI-
CLES -> As the War approached, Gallifreyan society was
starting to fray at the edges and many Time Lords were
becoming superstitious. Time Lords succumbed to the
cults of Ferisix, Thrayke, Sabjatric, Rungar, the Pythian
Heresy, Klade and the legend of Cuwirti.

A vast Edifice materialised over Gallifrey. This was the
Doctor's original TARDIS, which was drawing energy from
IM Foreman's leaking bottle universe.

On Gallifrey, many Time Lords had fallen under the
sway of Faction Paradox. They summoned the dead
President, Greyjan the Sane, who infected the Matrix with
Faction Paradox virus. Faction Paradox arrived in force to
occupy Gallifrey, led by Grandfather Paradox.

The Enemy was revealed as evolved ancestor cells -
primeval lifeforms that have been mutated and empow-
ered by the leaking bottle universe. The Enemy now
launched its first strike on Gallifrey, destroying the TARDIS
berths.

Faced with the choice of either submitting to Faction
Paradox or escaping, the eighth Doctor instead used the
remaining energy of the Edifice to destroy Gallifrey.
Faction Paradox was wiped out, and the annihilation was
so complete that it destroyed the entire constellation of
Kasterborous, creating disturbances in space and time that
prevented any further time travel to or from Gallifrey.

The Doctor and Compassion downloaded the entire
contents of the Matrix into the Doctor's brain. Compassion
sent the Doctor and his TARDIS, which had been all but
destroyed, to Earth to recover. She left with Nivet, a technician.

The destruction of Gallifrey thus prevented ...

The War[390]

Realising that the Enemy could erase them from history,
some Celestial Intervention Agency members tried to
remove themselves from the universe as a means of
defence. They became conceptual beings named the

Celestis. They operated from a realm called Mictlan, and influenced universal affairs with a network of agents.[391]

The Enemy struck Gallifrey, completely destroying it. Aware this attack was coming, the Time Lords broke their oldest laws, travelling back in time to assault their Enemy before they were attacked.[392]

Early in the War, the Enemy succeeded in wiping out the most powerful Gallifreyan artefacts like the Demat Gun and the Sash of Rassilon. Many secrets and pieces of bio-data were lost. Those that survived became extremely valuable, and much sought-after, as they could be adapted into weapons.

The first land battle of the War was fought on Dronid in the 155th century. The Doctor was thought to have died on Dronid. His body was recovered, and its unique biodata would make it perhaps the most valuable artefact in the universe. The Doctor had agreed to donate his body to the Celestis in return for their non-intervention on Dronid.[393]

Every battle was fought and then refought, as the losing side retroactively attempted to reverse the result. Eventually, time collapsed in the vicinity and the fighting would move elsewhere.

The Time Lords began searching their own future for

advanced weapons to be used in the War.[394] The Enemy learned how to build conceptual entities such as the anarchitects, beings capable of rearranging architecture.

Qixotl met the Doctor and saw him escape the Antiridean organ-eaters.[395]

Faction Paradox grew corrupt and started trading weapons and time travel. The Time Lord authorities moved to wipe them out as they would a virus. In 2596, the Time Lords destroyed the Earth colony Ordifica because of its contact with Faction Paradox.[396]

The Time Lords allied themselves with the Gabrielideans. The Time Lords had a military training ground on Gallifrey XII. The latest model TARDISes were the Type 103s, which were sentient and could take the form of people.[397]

ALIEN BODIES -> As some of the Celestis began switching sides, the War began tipping in favour of the Enemy. The Doctor's dead body - the Relic - was auctioned by Mr Qixotl. The Celestis won by giving Qixotl a new body when his original one was fatally wounded. The eighth Doctor tricked the Celestis and stole the Relic. He took it to Quiescia, then destroyed it with a thermosystron bomb.

---

of the War ceased to be the "real" future of the *Doctor Who* universe. A great many more details about the War are revealed in the *Faction Paradox* series, but this book will confine itself, as far as possible, to information given in the *Doctor Who* novels. There's also the caveat that, by definition, it's difficult to establish facts or the sequence of events of a time war.

391 *Alien Bodies.* No date given, but *The Book of the War* says this was twenty years before the War started.

WHEN DID THE WAR START?: There's no indication in the *Doctor Who* books exactly when the War was due to start relative to the Doctor. The War began one hundred and fifty one years after Grandfather Paradox escaped his prison, according to *The Book of the War*. That escape occurred in *Christmas on a Rational Planet*, shortly after Romana became President. Romana celebrates her one hundred and fiftieth year as President in *The Ancestor Cell*, meaning the War is now imminent.

392 *The Ancestor Cell*
393 *Alien Bodies*
394 *The Ancestor Cell*
395 *Alien Bodies*
396 *Interference*
397 *Alien Bodies*
398 *Interference*
399 Subsequent events would suggest the clone was of the Master.
400 *The Taking of Planet 5*
401 *Alien Bodies*
402 *The Taking of Planet 5*
403 "THERE ARE FOUR OF US NOW": *The Infinity Doctors* (p213) first mentioned "four names" as the four

people that Rassilon had ordered killed as a threat to Gallifrey, with Omega and the Doctor specified as two of the four. The above quote comes from *The Adventuress of Henrietta Street* (p231). In *The Gallifrey Chronicles*, the four survivors are described as "A man with a sallow face and small, pointed black beard, who wore a blue rosette; a young woman with long blonde hair in an extraordinary piece of haute couture; a tall man with a bent nose wearing a cravat and holding a pair of dice; the Doctor himself with close-cropped hair, sitting on an ornate throne, a new-born baby girl in his arms" - intended, but not named, respectively as the Master; Iris Wildthyme (or possibly Romana); the Minister of Chance from *Death Comes to Time*; the Doctor (possibly the Doctor from *The Infinity Doctors*, or in his role as the Emperor of the Universe, father of Miranda, mentioned in *Father Time*).

404 The books from *Father Time* to *Sometime Never* often showed races with time travel or magical abilities.
405 *Dalek*

WHO STARTED THE LAST GREAT TIME WAR?: In both an essay for the *2006 Doctor Who Annual* and an interview for *Doctor Who Confidential*, Russell T Davies is of the opinion that the Time Lords "fired first" in the Time War by sending the Doctor to intervene in the Daleks' origins (in *Genesis of the Daleks*). He may well be correct, but this perhaps doesn't tell the entire story.

By *Genesis of the Daleks*, there can be little doubt regarding the threat that the Daleks pose. In *The Daleks* they're initially portrayed as a group of desperate war survivors who cannot even leave their own city, but in rapid succession they've conquered Earth (*The Dalek*

The Time Lords quickly moved to occupy or control millions of planets. They created the Ogron Lords, shock troops with the ability to time travel.[398]

INTERFERENCE -> The Time Lords were losing the War. They had a last resort - a weapon designed to destroy Earth, which would not only destroy the Enemy's homeworld but collapse the entire web of time. The ship was dispatched at sub-light speeds, and was due to arrive at Earth in 1996. Fitz became Father Kreiner of Faction Paradox and hunted down Time Lords, including the Master and the Rani. One of these was actually a clone.[399]

The Time Lords created at least nine duplicate Gallifreys, in case the Enemy destroyed the original. Not even the President knew which was the "real" one. One of the Gallifreys was destroyed in the Battle of Mutter's Cluster. Gallifrey VIII was an industrial planet with vast Looms pouring out soldiers.[400] There was a Gallifrey XII.[401]

Time Lords were force-regenerated into physical forms engineered to fight. Fifteen out of a thousand Time Lords survived each combat mission. There were distinct Waves of warfare, with gaps between them allowing the Time Lords to Loom more soldiers. Only those from the First Wave resembled humans. The Time Lords suffered heavy losses in the Third Zone during the Fifth Wave.

The War President was a man with a pointed beard that had grown white with age, and who wore black robes. Any gathering of around a dozen TARDISes would attract an Enemy attack. The Time Lords used Parallel Cannons that created holes to other, more hostile, parts of the universe and unleashed the forces there.

The Enemy detonated the star of the planet Delphon, causing a significant rout of the Time Lords.[402]

THE TAKING OF PLANET 5 -> The Time Lords planned to smash a fleet of War TARDISes against the barriers around the Fifth Planet, hoping to free the Fendahl for use against the Enemy. The eighth Doctor, Fitz and Compassion discovered the plot, and Compassion tried to save the War TARDISes. The barrier was destroyed, but the Fendahl had been wiped out by the Fendahl Predator - a Memovore creature that had evolved the ability to destroy concepts. The Fendahl Predator was drawn to Mictlan and destroyed the Celestis before the Doctor banished it.

THE ANCESTOR CELL / THE GALLIFREY CHRONICLES -> Faction Paradox had gone from being a secret society to an army, led by Grandfather Paradox, the future self none of us hope to become. As well as a new rank of initiate - the Uncles, leather-clad assassins - there was now an armoured infantry, known as skulltroopers, and their shadow weapons had evolved so that they resembled guns. Although they were experienced at fighting Time Lords,

Faction Paradox was not the Enemy.

Now they travelled two hundred and ninety seven years into their own past to launch an invasion of Gallifrey. This would be the event that would lead to both the Faction conquering Gallifrey, and - three minutes seven seconds later - their total destruction and the annihilation of the War timeline.

Aided by Compassion, the eighth Doctor had downloaded the entire contents of the Matrix - the memories of almost every Time Lord who had ever lived - into his own mind. They survived in a supercompressed form that left no room for the Doctor's own memories. Compassion apparently took the Doctor's memories, although for what purpose remains a mystery. Compassion dropped the amnesiac Doctor off in the late nineteenth century.

After Gallifrey

When his travels through time and space resumed, the Doctor met a man in the eighteenth century who resembled the Master and said the following:

> "There are only four of us left now, you know. Four of us in all the universe." [403]

Without the Time Lords controlling the proliferation of time travel, many races attempted to gain mastery of time, often by acquiring Gallifreyan artefacts. Without the Time Lords to enforce the laws of time, magic started to seep back into the universe.[404]

THE GALLIFREY CHRONICLES -> Marnal regenerated and automatically regained his memories. He soon discovered the Doctor had destroyed Gallifrey and lured him to Earth to punish him.

The eighth Doctor and Marnal came to realise that the Doctor's mind contained the contents of the Matrix and the memories of all the Time Lords. Marnal died saving the Doctor, convinced that the Doctor should dedicate himself to the task of building a New Gallifrey. The Doctor despatched K9 to track down Compassion.

It would appear that the Doctor succeeded in building a new Gallifrey. His memories certainly returned. The next we learn of Time Lord history is...

The Last Great Time War

The Doctor's home planet was destroyed in the Last Great Time War, "a war between the Daleks and the Time Lords with the whole of creation at stake".[405]

Many planets, such as those of the Nestene and the Gelth, were affected. The food planets of the Nestene were wiped out.[406] The Forest of Cheem knew of the War, and thought it was impossible that any Time Lords could exist afterwards.[407] The Gelth were forced to become incorporate spirits when their bodies were destroyed. The Time War was invisible to "smaller" species, but was devastating to "the higher forms".[408] Some people regard the Time War as a legend.[409]

The Time War devastated the Hajor dimension.[410]

The Time Lords used the Genesis Ark, a dimension-ally transcendental prison, to confine many thousands of Daleks. The Doctor was not involved with this. The four Daleks that made up the Cult of Skaro stole the Genesis Ark and used a Voidship to leave the universe before the end of the War.[411]

It's possible that the civilisations of Perganon and Assinder fell during the Time War.[412] The Doctor fought on the front line, and saw the fall of Arcadia.[413] The Daleks removed themselves from history to go off

---

Invasion of Earth) and developed a crude form of time travel (The Chase). As early as Season Three (with The Daleks' Master Plan), they are an intergalactic power to be reckoned with. The stories to follow have them suffering various defeats and setbacks, but their potential to cause widespread havoc and genocide never diminishes much. Even in Day of the Daleks, their comparatively shoddy time-technology has allowed them to alter history and conquer Earth a second time.

Real-life analogies quickly fail when applied to the Daleks. At times they're compared to the likes of Nazis, but in truth they're literally lacking of humanity. Even "conquest" as we generally understand the term doesn't really interest them - sometimes they put foes to work as slaves (as in Death to the Daleks), but this is almost inevitably in the interest of facilitating new atrocities and exterminations. The point is that one can (and should) hope to use reason against real-world governments, but there is virtually no chance of diplomacy succeeding against the Daleks Occasionally the Doctor makes a group of Daleks passive - say, by altering their very nature in The Evil of the Daleks - but only under unique and limited circumstances. Basically, the Daleks collectively remain united behind one goal: kill everything that isn't a Dalek.

In Genesis of the Daleks, the Time Lord that sends the Doctor to Skaro's past says, "We have foreseen a time when [the Daleks] will have destroyed all other life forms, and become the dominant creature in the universe". Based on the Daleks' characteristics and past behaviour, this seems worryingly plausible. Faced with such a scenario - literally a death sentence for everything save Dalek-kind - the Time Lords using their one trump card, their mastery of time, to change the Daleks' origins might well seem like a risk worth taking. (It should be remembered that it takes something as catastrophic as the War in Heaven for the Time Lords to marshal anything resembling military might. A war-TARDIS isn't even seen until the fifth Doctor's era in "The Stockbridge Horror", so in most periods of history, the Time Lords sending troops to physically contain Dalek advances doesn't appear to be an option. Time-technology remains the best leverage they have.)

A probable effect of the Doctor intervening in Genesis, however, would be to make the Daleks aware of the Time Lords as a rival temporal power. In the stories to follow, both Davros and the Daleks become

openly confrontational toward Gallfirey, and even minor races (such as the Cryons in Attack of the Cybermen) know of the Time Lords. Resurrection of the Daleks has the Daleks plotting to assassinate the Gallifreyan High Council (there's no evidence that the Time Lords ever learn about this, though). The Apocalypse Element has the Daleks directly attacking Gallifrey. Remembrance of the Daleks has Davros stating his intention to use the Hand of Omega to wipe out the Time Lords and install the Daleks as the new "Lords of Time" - although it's the Doctor who arranges Skaro's destruction, and in so doing probably rouses the Daleks into further hostilities. It's easy to see how such tit-for-tat escalation might lead to the Time War.

It was probably inevitable - given the Time Lords' mastery of time and the Daleks' intention to totally eradicate all other species - that their civilisations would fall into open warfare at some point. Either way, the Doctor intervening in the Kaled bunker might well be the first cross-temporal attack in the conflict, but it's a bit disingenous to think the Time Lords were without justification in sending him there.

406 Rose

407 The End of the World

408 The Unquiet Dead. There seem to be some races in the middle - the Krillitanes (School Reunion) and Cynrog (The Nightmare of Black Island) - who were aware of the Time War, but weren't directly affected by it. In Bad Wolf, Captain Jack mentions hearing rumours of the Time War and the Daleks.

409 Jack, in The Parting of the Ways, for one.

410 "The Futurists"

411 Doomsday

412 School Reunion

413 Doomsday

414 Bad Wolf

415 The Sound of Drums. Mention of the Master being "resurrected" probably covers all contingencies regarding his status prior to the new series.

416 Dalek

417 The End of the World

418 School Reunion

419 Bad Wolf / The Parting of the Ways

420 The Unquiet Dead, Father's Day

421 Rise of the Cybermen

THE LAST GREAT TIME WAR: The new TV series is set after "The Last Great Time War", and although we know

and fight the Time War.[414]

The Time Lords resurrected the Master as the perfect warrior to fight in the Time War - he was present when the Dalek Emperor took control of the Cruciform, and fled. He turned himself into a human, and hid at the end of the universe.[415]

The Doctor wiped out the entire Dalek race, and their ten million-strong war fleet, in one second. The Time Lords - save for the Doctor - also perished as a result of this. The Doctor instigated this destruction, referred to as an "inferno". He "watched it happen ... made it happen". The Doctor survived, as did a single Dalek that fell through time to the early twenty-first century.[416] The Doctor's home planet was reduced to rocks and dust, and he was the only survivor.[417] He has stated, "I lived ... everyone else died."[418]

The Emperor Dalek's flagship also survived, and limped to the solar system "centuries" before the year 200,000.[419] Time was more fragile without the Time Lords to protect it, and some of the rules governing time were suspended.[420] Travel between parallel realities had been "easy" when the Time Lords "kept their eye on everything", but following their downfall, the walls of reality closed and travel between parallel worlds became nearly impossible.[421]

---

the broad strokes of what happened, there's been little detail. Stories that provide hints about the event include *Rose, The End of the World, The Unquiet Dead, Dalek, Father's Day, Bad Wolf, The Parting of the Ways*.

The *2006 Doctor Who Annual* contains a short account of the Time War written by Russell T Davies, which echoes his thoughts in a *Doctor Who Confidential* interview that the roots of the War lie with the Time Lords trying to prevent the Daleks' creation in *Genesis of the Daleks*. The article links the story to *Lungbarrow* and *The Apocalypse Element*, mentions the Deathsmiths of Goth (from the *DWM* back-up strip "Black Legacy") and adds the information that the Animus (*The Web Planet*) and the Eternals (*Enlightenment*) were caught in the fighting. The article was the first place related to the 2005 series that names Gallifrey as the Doctor's destroyed home planet (the new series later named it in *The Runaway Bride* and *The Sound of Drums*), and says Skaro was in "ruins" by the end - a reference that seems to support the claim in *War of the Daleks* that Skaro wasn't destroyed in *Remembrance of the Daleks*.

There is no indication whether it was the eighth or ninth Doctor who fought in the Last Great Time War, or whether he regenerated during (as a result of?) events during the War. The Dalek in *Dalek* doesn't seem to recognise the Doctor's face, but responds to his name. Many fans have speculated that the Doctor has recently regenerated in *Rose*, as he seems unfamiliar with his reflection. There's a broad fan consensus that it's the eighth Doctor who fought the Time War and that its climax somehow triggered the regeneration - although there's no evidence that's the case, and it seems clear from Clive's website in *Rose* that the ninth Doctor's an established incarnation.

ONLY ONE DESTRUCTION OF GALLIFREY?: The intention of both the creative team behind the EDAs and the new series producer Russell T Davies is that the destruction of Gallifrey seen in *The Ancestor Cell* and the destruction of Gallifrey reported in the new series are entirely separate events. As the Doctor destroys Gallifrey once while preventing the Enemy and Faction Paradox from taking control of his homeworld, then (presumably after rebuilding Gallifrey, as he pledges to do at the end of *The Gallifrey Chronicles*) he destroys Gallifrey again in a great war with the Daleks, it would seem clear these are indeed mutually exclusive. Russell Davies likened it, in a *DWM* column, to the two World Wars humanity fought in quick succession.

But could Gallifrey have been destroyed just once? The Doctor certainly experiences the destruction of Gallifrey twice, in two different contexts. But this doesn't rule out it being the same *event*. If there was only one destruction of Gallifrey, he and his future self would have to be present, and both culpable.

Surprisingly, this already fits what we know from *The Ancestor Cell* - the Doctor's future self, Grandfather Paradox was there. Moreover, this future eighth Doctor fits everything we know about the Doctor who fought the Time War: fighting a vast time war has scarred him, made him lose his faith in humanity, made him a little callous. In *The Gallifrey Chronicles* recap of the end of *The Ancestor Cell*, Grandfather Paradox even wears a leather coat. As for the destruction of Gallifrey - the Doctor's description in *Dalek*, "I watched it happen ... I made it happen ... I tried to stop it" is a neat summary of his actions in *The Ancestor Cell*.

If this theory is true, the Doctor's memories of the War are conflicted because he was *literally* fighting his (earlier) self over "pulling the lever" that destroyed Gallifrey. So it's *Grandfather Paradox* who has fought the Last Great Time War, the Daleks, the Nestenes and so on. He goes back to *The Ancestor Cell* having done all that, confronts his earlier self ... who then outsmarts him by blowing up Gallifrey. Following this defeat, it's Grandfather Paradox who regenerates into Eccleston (growing his arm back in the process).

For this to be the case, it involves the introduction of the tiniest bit of extra information: the War that's being fought in the future has the Daleks in it and at some point they make a decisive move on Gallifrey. What the "current" eighth Doctor doesn't know - but which his future self does - is that, in the future, the War's going so badly that the Daleks are heading for Gallifrey. The Daleks were ruled out as "the Enemy" in *Alien Bodies*, but they don't need to be for this theory to work - they just need to be capable of hitting the Time Lords hard.

There are a number of stories without the references needed to place them in any meaningful relation to the rest of universal history.

Some (such as *The Celestial Toymaker*) take place in a reality that is completely detached from the universe's timeline. Some, such as the E-Space Trilogy (*Full Circle* to *Warriors' Gate*) and the Divergent Universe Series (the Big Finish audios *Scherzo* to *The Next Life*), take place in locations clearly outside the universe's physical boundaries.

A number of stories simply fail to provide (or aren't interested in providing) more evidence beyond the fact that they occur "on an alien planet in the future". Given the entire duration of human development into space, this isn't particularly helpful, presuming the humanoids featured in the story are human in the first place. Without more clues as to how such stories relate to human history or another documented event, a proper dating is impossible. A story such as *Anachrophobia* looks for all the world like placement on the timeline should be attainable, but the evidence (or lack thereof) says otherwise.

The following stories are among those that defy a proper dating. The TV stories are listed in broadcast order; the books, audios and comics are listed alphabetically.

TV Stories

The Edge of Destruction (1.3, set in the TARDIS)
The Chase (2.8, the sequence on Aridius - although it has to take place after the Daleks launch their time machine, as the Doctor and companions see that on the Time-Space Visualiser, which can only see into the past)
Galaxy 4 (3.1)
The Daleks' Master Plan (3.4, the sequences on Tigus and the ice planet)
The Celestial Toymaker (3.7)
The Dominators (6.1, at a time when the Dominators control "ten galaxies")
The Mind Robber (6.2, in a timeless dimension)
The Krotons (6.4)
Carnival of Monsters (10.2)
The Ribos Operation (16.1, the White Guardian sequence)
The Armageddon Factor (16.6)
The Creature from the Pit (17.3)
The Horns of Nimon (17.5)
Full Circle (18.3)
State of Decay (18.4)
Warriors' Gate (18.5)
Castrovalva (19.1, the non-Earth sequences)
Snakedance (20.2)
Enlightenment (20.5)
The Five Doctors (20.7, the first Doctor's kidnap and the Eye of Orion sequences)

Time and the Rani (24.1, the Rani wants to take Earth "back" to the Cretaceous, which suggests it's after that)
The Greatest Show in the Galaxy (25.4)
Doctor Who: Children in Need (post-regeneration scene in the TARDIS, with tenth Doctor and Rose)

Novels and Novellas

Anachrophobia (EDA #54)
Beltempest (EDA #17)
Citadel of Dreams (TEL #2)
Coldheart (EDA #33)
Crooked World, The (EDA #57)
Dreams of Empire (PDA #14)
Eight Doctors, The (EDA #1, the Eye of Orion sequence)
Frontier Worlds (EDA #29)
Kursaal (EDA #7)
Match of the Day (PDA #70)
Nightdreamers (TEL #3)
Parallel 59 (EDA #30)
Shell Shock (TEL #8)
Sky Pirates! (NA #40)

Audios

Arrangements for War (BF #57)
Axis of Insanity, The (BF #56)
Blood of the Daleks (BF BBC7 #1-2)
Caedroia (BF #63)
Circular Time: "Spring" (BF #91, events on the planet of the bird-people)
Creatures of Beauty (BF #44)
Creed of the Kromon, The (BF #53)
Dark Flame, The (BF #42)
Embrace the Darkness (BF #31)
Faith Stealer (BF #61)
Fear of the Daleks (BF *The Companion Chronicles* #2)
Her Final Flight (BF subscription promo #2)
Holy Terror, The (BF #14)
... Ish (BF #35)
Last of the Titans (BF promo #1, DWM #300)
Last, The (BF #62)
Natural History of Fear, The (BF #54)
Nekromanteia (BF #41)
Next Life, The (BF #64)
No Place Like Home (BF promo #3, DWM #326)
Red (BF #85)
Scherzo (BF #52)
Sirens of Time, The (BF #1, sixth Doctor segment)
Something Inside (BF #83)
Thicker Than Water (BF #73)
Time Works (BF #80)
Twilight Kingdom, The (BF #55)
Wishing Beast, The (BF #97)

Comics

"Are You Listening / Younger and Wiser"
(*DWM 1994 Summer Special*)
"Autonomy Bug" (*DWM #297-299*)
"Beautiful Freak" (*DWM #304*)
"Betrothal of Sontar, The" (*DWM #365-367*)
"Black Legacy" (*DWW #35-38*)
"Blood Invocation" (*DWM Yearbook 1995*)
"Cat Litter" (*DWM #192*)
"Chameleon Factor" (*DWM #174*)
"Changes" (*DWM #118-119*)
"Character Assassin" (*DWM #311*)
"City of the Damned" (*DWW #9-16*)
"Crossroads of Time" (*DWM #135*)
"Culture Shock" (*DWM #139*)
"End of the Line" (*DWW #54-55*)
"Exodus / Revelation / Genesis" (*DWM #108-110*)
"Fabulous Idiot" (*DWM Summer Special 1982*)
"Fangs of Time" (*DWM #243*)
"Final Quest, The" (*DWW #8*)
"Follow That TARDIS" (*DWM #147*)
"Food for Thought" (*DWM #218-220*)
"Funhouse" (*DWM #102-103*)
"Happy Deathday" (*DWM #272*)
"Keepsake" (*DWM #140*)
"K9's Finest Hour" (*DWW #12*)
"Land of the Blind" (*DWM #224-226*)

"Last Word, The" (*DWM #305*)
"Life of Matter and Death, A" (*DWM #250*)
"Nature of the Beast" (*DWM #111-113*)
"Oblivion" (*DWM #323-328*)
"Ophidius" (*DWM #300-303*)
"Outsider, The" (*DWW #25-26*)
"Party Animals" (*DWM #173*)
"Planet of the Dead" (*DWM #141-142*)
"Religious Experience, A" (*DWM Yearbook 1994*)
"Rest and Re-Creation" (*DWM Yearbook 1994*)
"Return of the Daleks" (*DWW #1-4*,
eight hundred years after previous Dalek invasion)
"Salad Daze" (*DWM #117*)
"Ship Called Sudden Death, A"
(*DWM Summer Special 1982*)
"Sins of the Father" (*DWM #343-345*)
"Stairway to Heaven" (*DWM #156*)
"Time and Tide" (*DWM #145-146*)
"Timeslip" (*DWW #17-18*)
"Touchdown on Deneb 7" (*DWM #48*)
"TV Action" (*DWM #283*)
"Uninvited Guest" (*DWM #211*)
"Uroborous" (*DWM #319-322*)

Other

Attack of the Graske (interactive feature predicated on breaking the fourth wall; has multiple endings)

The following is a list of useful resources for anyone interested in the "fictional facts" of Doctor Who.

The Making of Doctor Who. (Malcolm Hulke and Terrance Dicks: first edition Piccolo/Pan Books, April 1972; second edition Target/Tandem Books, November 1976) - The earliest source of dates, often direct from BBC material.

Dr Who Special. (ed. David Driver, Jack Lundin: BBC, November 1973) - The tenth anniversary *Radio Times* special, including many previously unpublished story details. This magazine perpetuated the "incorrect" story titles, used by many fans.

The Doctor Who Programme Guide. (Jean-Marc Lofficier: first edition [2 vols] WH Allen, May 1981, second edition [2 Vols] Target/WH Allen, October 1981, second edition has separate volume titles "The Programmes" and "What's What and Who's Who") **Doctor Who - The Programme Guide.** (Jean-Marc Lofficier: third edition Target/WH Allen, December 1989) **Doctor Who - The Terrestrial Index.** (Jean-Marc Lofficier: Target/Virgin Publishing, November 1991) **Doctor Who - The Universal Databank.** (Jean-Marc Lofficier: Doctor Who Books/Virgin Publishing, November 1992) **Doctor Who Programme Guide.** (Jean-Marc Lofficier: fourth edition Doctor Who Books/Virgin Publishing, June 1994) - The standard reference work, with most fans owning a copy of at least one of these books. A good starting point.

Doctor Who Monthly. (Marvel Comics Ltd.) - Richard Landen wrote a series of pseudohistories in the twentieth anniversary year: Issues 75-83 (April 1983 - December 1983) featured *The TARDIS Logs*, a list of TARDIS landings riddled with annoying little errors; issue 77 had a more concise list *Travels with the Doctor*, and a good attempt at "A History of the Daleks"; "A History of the Cybermen" (issue 83, with Michael Daniels) and *Shades of Piccolo* (UNIT history, issue 80) were both sensible, simple treatments of potential minefields.

The Doctor Who Role Playing Game. (FASA Corporation [US], 1985; Supplements published 1985-6) - Various dates, including much invented for the game's purposes.

Doctor Who. (Marvel Comics Group [US]) - A series of pseudohistories written by Patrick Daniel O'Neill covering "A Probable History of the Daleks" (issue 9, June 1985), "A Probable History of the Cybermen" (issue 10, July 1985) and "The Master Log" Parts I and II (issues 14, 15,

November, December 1985). Enthusiastic but ill-researched.

The Doctor Who File. (Peter Haining: WH Allen, September 1986) - Pages 223 to 228 contain a table listing the Doctor's adventures and where / when they took place.

Encyclopedia of the Worlds of Doctor Who. (David Saunders: Piccadilly/Knight Press 1986, 1989, 1990) - An A-Z of the series with many entries giving dates.

The Official Doctor Who & the Daleks Book. (John Peel & Terry Nation: St Martin's Press [US], April 1989) - Dalek history, including various other sources (comic strips etc). Approved by Terry Nation.

In-Vision 11: UNIT Special. (CMS, December 1988) - Includes *Down to Earth*, a history of UNIT, by Garry Bradbury. Each issue of *In-Vision* is a comprehensive analysis of an individual story, and the magazine is an indispensable reference work.

Doctor Who - Cybermen. (David Banks, with Andrew Skilleter, Adrian Rigelsford and Jan Vincent-Rudzki: Who Dares, November 1988; Virgin Publishing, September 1990) - Comprehensive, if elaborate, history of the Cybermen. The first, and still best, reference book of its kind.

Doctor Who Magazine. (Marvel Comics Ltd) - issue 174: *The TARDIS Special* (June 12th 1991) features "Journeys" by Andrew Pixley, a superbly researched list of every landing made by the TARDIS. Issue 176 (August 7th 1991) contains an addendum.

The Gallifrey Chronicles. (John Peel: Doctor Who Books/Virgin Publishing, October 1991) - Gallifreyan history and other information. (This isn't the same book as *The Gallifrey Chronicles*, the 2005 EDA).

Doctor Who Magazine Winter Special 1991 - UNIT Exposed. (Marvel Comics Ltd, 28th November, 1991) - Includes an excellent UNIT chronology by John Freeman and Gary Russell, as well as "UNIT Exposed" by Andrew Dylan.

The Doctor Who Writers' Guide. (Peter Darvill-Evans, Rebecca Levene & Andy Bodle: Virgin Publishing, 1991) - The guidelines for prospective authors of New and Missing Adventures. Includes notes on Gallifreyan history.

BIBLIOGRAPHY

Apocrypha. (Adrian Middleton: 1993-95). Fan published chronology drawing together everything the author can get his hands on: comic strips, novelisations, role-playing scenarios and so on.

The Discontinuity Guide. (Paul Cornell, Martin Day and Keith Topping: Virgin Publishing, May 1994) - Survey of the series' continuity and continuity mistakes. Many interesting fan theories, all marked as such.

I, Who vols. 1-3. (Lars Pearson, Mad Norwegian Press, 1999 - 2003) - A book-by-book and audio-by-audio survey of the novels and BF audios, including spin-offs and detailed breakdowns of the stories.

Timelink (Jon Preddle, TSV Books, 2000) - A massive fan-produced survey of the television series' continuity. With extensive quotes, and a story-by-story breakdown.

Doctor Who - The Legend. (Justin Richards, BBC Books, 2003) - A hardback introduction to *Doctor Who*, with a story-by-story section that lists dates where they are known.

About Time. (Lawrence Miles and Tat Wood, Mad Norwegian Press, 2004 -) - A series of books that place *Doctor Who* in a cultural context and offer opinions and essays on continuity matters, including some chronological ones like UNIT Dating.

Who's Next. (Mark Clapham, Eddie Robson and Jim Smith, Virgin Publishing, 2005) - A one-volume guide to *Doctor Who* on television, with a breakdown of continuity.

INDEX

Bold numbers indicate main story entries for each adventure (the same information is found in the Table of Contents). Plain-text numbers indicate a story reference in the footnotes. This index also lists all characters, alien races, planets and organisations that appear in three or more stories. Characters are alphabetical based upon their most commonly used name.

PUBLISHER
Lars Pearson

COVER & INTERIOR DESIGN
Christa Dickson

**ASSOCIATE EDITOR /
INDEX**
Dave Gartner

**ASSOCIATE EDITORS
(AHISTORY)**
Robert Smith?
Michael Thomas

ASSOCIATE EDITORS (MNP)
Marc Eby
Joshua Wilson

TECH SUPPORT
Anthony Clifton

The publisher would like to thank...
Bill Albert, Jeremy Bement, and everyone at the Universal Network of Iowan Time Lords; Tara O'Shea and Heather Innis (shocking how much of this book was drafted in response to their questions / continuity requirements); Lawrence Miles; Tracy Gartner; Brie Lewis; Missy Clifton; Nat Hanan; Shawne Kleckner; Graeme Burk; Pete Lauritzen and Heather Hain; Michael and Amy Tax; Bill and Mandy Vadbunker.

As with Lance, I'd also like to add a note of respect for the late Craig Hinton, because fandom just doesn't seem the same without him.

Some months before Craig's passing, we corresponded about his unwritten novel *Time's Champion* (now being finished by an American colleague of his) - and Craig was really, really excited because one of the villains, Madame Clacice Beauvier, was the daughter of Lady Peinforte and Morbius. Yes, it sounds like something Craig would do, doesn't it?

1150 46th Street
Des Moines, Iowa 50311
info@madnorwegian.com